THE MIDDLE AGES
David / Simpson

THE SIXTEENTH CENTURY
Logan / Greenblatt

THE EARLY SEVENTEENTH CENTURY
Lewalski / Maus

THE RESTORATION AND THE EIGHTEENTH CENTURY
Lipking / Noggle

THE ROMANTIC PERIOD
Stillinger / Lynch

THE VICTORIAN AGE
Christ / Robson

THE TWENTIETH CENTURY AND AFTER
Stallworthy / Ramazani

The Norton Anthology
of English Literature

EIGHTH EDITION
VOLUME F
The Twentieth Century and After

The Norton Anthology of English Literature

EIGHTH EDITION

Stephen Greenblatt, *General Editor*
COGAN UNIVERSITY PROFESSOR OF THE HUMANITIES, HARVARD UNIVERSITY

M. H. Abrams, *Founding Editor Emeritus*
CLASS OF 1916 PROFESSOR OF ENGLISH EMERITUS, CORNELL UNIVERSITY

VOLUME F
THE TWENTIETH CENTURY AND AFTER

Jon Stallworthy   Jahan Ramazani

W • W • NORTON & COMPANY • *New York • London*

W. W. Norton & Company has been independent since its founding in 1923, when William Warder Norton and Mary D. Herter Norton first published lectures delivered at the People's Institute, the adult education division of New York City's Cooper Union. The Nortons soon expanded their program beyond the Institute, publishing books by celebrated academics from America and abroad. By mid-century, the two major pillars of Norton's publishing program—trade books and college texts—were firmly established. In the 1950s, the Norton family transferred control of the company to its employees, and today—with a staff of four hundred and a comparable number of trade, college, and professional titles published each year—W. W. Norton & Company stands as the largest and oldest publishing house owned wholly by its employees.

Editor: Julia Reidhead
Managing Editor, College: Marian Johnson
Developmental Editor: Kurt Wildermuth
Electronic Media Editor: Eileen Connell
Production Manager: Diane O'Connor
Associate Editor: Erin Granville
Copy Editors: Alice Falk, Katharine Ings, Candace Levy, Alan Shaw, Ann Tappert
Permissions Managers: Nancy Rodwan, Katrina Washington
Text Design: Antonina Krass
Art Research: Neil Ryder Hoos

Composition by Binghamton Valley Composition
Manufacturing by RR Donnelley

Copyright © 2006, 2000, 1993, 1990, 1986, 1979, 1974, 1968, 1962
by W. W. Norton & Company, Inc.

Since this page cannot legibly accommodate all the copyright notices,
Permissions Acknowledgments constitutes an extension of the copyright page.

The Library of Congress has cataloged another edition as follows:

The Norton anthology of English literature / Stephen Greenblatt, general editor ; M.H. Abrams, founding editor emeritus.—8th ed.
p. cm.
Includes bibliographical references and indexes.

ISBN 0-393-92713-X (v. 1) — ISBN 0-393-92531-5 (v. 1: pbk.)
ISBN 0-393-92715-6 (v. 2) — ISBN 0-393-92532-3 (v. 2: pbk.)

1. English literature. 2. Great Britain—Literary collections. I. Greenblatt, Stephen, 1943– II. Abrams, M. H. (Meyer Howard), 1912–
PR1109.N6   2005
820.8—dc22
2005052313

The Twentieth Century and After: ISBN 0-393-92722-9 (pbk.)

W. W. Norton & Company, Inc., 500 Fifth Avenue, New York, N.Y. 10110
www.wwnorton.com

W. W. Norton & Company Ltd., Castle House, 75/76 Wells Street, London WIT 3QT

9 0

Contents

Preface to the Eighth Edition

The outpouring of English literature overflows all boundaries, including the capacious boundaries of *The Norton Anthology of English Literature*. But these pages manage to contain many of the most remarkable works written in English during centuries of restless creative effort. We have included epic poems and short lyrics; love songs and satires; tragedies and comedies written for performance on the commercial stage, and private meditations meant to be perused in silence; prayers, popular ballads, prophecies, ecstatic visions, erotic fantasies, sermons, short stories, letters in verse and prose, critical essays, polemical tracts, several entire novels, and a great deal more. Such works generally form the core of courses that are designed to introduce students to English literature, with its history not only of gradual development, continuity, and dense internal echoes, but also of sudden change and startling innovation.

One of the joys of literature in English is its spectacular abundance. Even within the geographical confines of England, Scotland, Wales, and Ireland, where the majority of texts brought together in this collection originated, one can find more than enough distinguished and exciting works to fill the pages of this anthology many times over. The abundance is all the greater if one takes, as the editors of these volumes do, a broad understanding of the term *literature*. In the course of several centuries, the meaning of the term has shifted from the whole body of writing produced in a particular language to a subset of that writing consisting of works that claim special attention because of their unusual formal beauty or expressive power. Certain literary works, arousing enduring admiration, have achieved sufficient prominence to serve as widespread models for other writers and thus to constitute something approximating a canon. But just as in English-speaking countries there have never been academies empowered to regulate the use of language, so too there have never been firmly settled guidelines for canonizing particular texts. Any individual text's claim to attention is subject to constant debate and revision; established texts are jostled both by new arrivals and by previously neglected claimants; and the boundaries between the literary and whatever is thought to be "nonliterary" are constantly challenged and redrawn. The heart of this collection consists of poems, plays, and prose fiction, but, like the language in which they are written, these categories are themselves products of ongoing historical transformations, and we have included many texts that call into question any conception of literature as only a limited set of particular kinds of writing. English literature as a field arouses not a sense of order but what Yeats calls "the emotion of multitude."

Following the lead of most college courses, we have separated off, on pragmatic grounds, English literature from American literature, but, in keeping with the multinational, multicultural, and hugely expansive character of the language, we have incorporated, particularly for the modern period, a substantial number of texts by authors from other countries. This border-crossing is not a phenomenon of modernity only. It is fitting that among the first works here is *Beowulf*, a powerful epic written in the Germanic language known as Old English about a singularly restless Scandinavian hero. *Beowulf*'s remarkable translator in *The Norton Anthology of English Literature*, Seamus Heaney, is one of the great contemporary masters of English literature——he was awarded the Nobel Prize for Literature in 1995—but it would be potentially misleading to call him an "English poet" for he was born in Northern Ireland and is not in fact English. It would be still more misleading to call him a "British poet," as if the British Empire were the most salient fact about the language he speaks and writes in or the culture by which he was shaped. What matters is that the language in which Heaney writes is English, and this fact links him powerfully with the authors assembled in these volumes, a linguistic community that stubbornly refuses to fit comfortably within any firm geographical or ethnic or national boundaries. So too, to glance at other authors and writings in the anthology, in the sixteenth century William Tyndale, in exile in the Low Countries and inspired by German religious reformers, translated the New Testament from Greek and thereby changed the course of the English language; in the seventeenth century Aphra Behn deeply touched her readers with a story that moves from Africa, where its hero is born, to South America, where Behn herself may have witnessed some of the tragic events she describes; and early in the twentieth century Joseph Conrad, born in Ukraine of Polish parents, wrote in eloquent English a celebrated novella whose vision of European empire was trenchantly challenged at the century's end by the Nigerian-born writer in English, Chinua Achebe.

A vital literary culture is always on the move. This principle was the watchword of M. H. Abrams, the distinguished literary critic who first conceived *The Norton Anthology of English Literature*, brought together the original team of editors, and, with characteristic insight, diplomacy, and humor, oversaw seven editions and graciously offered counsel on this eighth edition. Abrams wisely understood that the dense continuities that underlie literary performance are perpetually challenged and revitalized by innovation. He understood too that new scholarly discoveries and the shifting interests of readers constantly alter the landscape of literary history. Hence from the start he foresaw that, if the anthology were to be successful, it would have to undergo a process of periodic revision and reselection, an ambitious enterprise that would draw upon the energy and ideas of new editors brought in to work with the seasoned team.

The Eighth Edition of *The Norton Anthology of English Literature* represents the most thoroughgoing instance in its long publishing history of this generational renewal. Across the whole chronological breadth of the volumes, new editors joined forces with the existing editors in a spirit of close collaboration. The revitalized team has considered afresh each of the selections and rethought all the other myriad aspects of the anthology. In doing so, we have, as in past years, profited from a remarkable flow of voluntary corrections and suggestions proposed by teachers, as well as students, who view the anthology with a loyal but critical eye. Moreover, we have again solicited and received detailed information on the works actually assigned, proposals for deletions and additions, and suggestions for improving the editorial matter, from over two hundred reviewers from around the world, almost all of them teachers who use the book in a course. The active participation of an engaged and dedicated community of readers has been crucial as the editors of the *Norton Anthology* grapple with the task of retaining (and indeed strengthening) the selection of more traditional texts even while adding many texts that reflect the transformation and expansion of the field of English studies. The great challenge (and therefore the interest) of the task is linked to the space constraints that even these hefty volumes must observe. The virtually limitless resources of the anthology's Web site make at least some of the difficult choices less vexing, but the editorial team kept clearly in view the central importance in the classroom of the printed pages. The final decisions on what to include were made by the editors, but we were immeasurably assisted by our ongoing collaboration with teachers and students.

With each edition, *The Norton Anthology of English Literature* has offered a broadened canon without sacrificing major writers and a selection of complete longer texts in which readers can immerse themselves. Perhaps the most emblematic of these longer texts are the two great epics *Beowulf* and *Paradise Lost*. To the extensive list of such complete works, the Eighth Edition has added many others, including Sir Thomas More's *Utopia*, Samuel Johnson's *Rasselas* (restored to its entirety), Eliza Haywood's *Fantomina*, Robert Louis Stevenson's *The Strange Case of Dr. Jekyll and Mr. Hyde*, Tom Stoppard's *Arcadia*, and Brian Friel's *Translations*.

Though this latest edition of *The Norton Anthology of English Literature* has retained the works that have traditionally been identified and taught as the principal glories of English literature, many of the newer selections reflect the fact that the *national* conception of literary history, the conception by which English Literature meant the literature of England or at most of Great Britain, has begun to give way to something else. Writers like William Butler Yeats (born in Dublin), Hugh MacDiarmid (born in Dumfriesshire, Scotland), Virginia Woolf (born in London), and Dylan Thomas (born in Swansea, Wales) are now being taught, and are here anthologized, alongside such writers as Nadine Gordimer (born in the Transvaal, South Africa), Alice Munro (born in Wingham, Ontario), Derek Walcott (born on Saint Lucia in the West Indies), V. S. Naipaul (born in Trinidad), and Salman Rushdie (born in Bombay, India). English literature, like so many other collective enterprises in our century, has ceased to be principally about the identity of a single nation; it is a global phenomenon.

We have in this edition continued to expand the selection of writing by women in all of the historical periods. The sustained work of scholars in recent years has recovered dozens of significant authors who had been marginalized or neglected by a male-dominated literary tradition and has deepened our understanding of those women writers who had managed, against considerable odds, to claim a place in that tradition. The First Edition of the *Norton Anthology* included 6 women writers; this Eighth Edition includes 67, of whom 16 are newly added and 15 are reselected or expanded. Poets and dramatists whose names were scarcely mentioned even in the specialized literary histories of earlier generations—Aemilia Lanyer, Lady Mary Wroth, Elizabeth Cary, Margaret Cavendish, Mary Leapor, Anna Letitia Barbauld, Charlotte Smith, Letitia Elizabeth Landon, and many others—now appear in the company of their male contemporaries. There are in addition four complete long prose works by women—Aphra Behn's *Oroonoko*, Eliza Haywood's *Fantomina*, Jane

Austen's *Love and Friendship,* and Virginia Woolf's *A Room of One's Own*—along with new selections from such celebrated fiction writers as Maria Edgeworth, Jean Rhys, Katherine Mansfield, and Doris Lessing.

The novel is, of course, a stumbling block for an anthology. The length of many great novels defies their incorporation in any volume that hopes to include a broad spectrum of literature. At the same time it is difficult to excerpt representative passages from narratives whose power often depends upon amplitude or upon the slow development of character or upon the onrushing urgency of the story. Therefore, better to represent the achievements of novelists, the publisher is making available the full list of Norton Critical Editions—more than 180 titles—including the most frequently assigned novels: Jane Austen's *Pride and Prejudice,* Mary Shelley's *Frankenstein,* Charles Dickens's *Hard Times,* Charlotte Brontë's *Jane Eyre,* and Emily Brontë's *Wuthering Heights.* A free Norton Critical Edition may be packaged with Volume 1 or 2 clothbound, paperbound, or three-volume package.

Building on an innovation introduced in the Seventh Edition, the editors have included for each of the periods several clusters that gather together short texts illuminating the cultural, historical, intellectual, and literary concerns of the age. In the Eighth Edition we have rethought, streamlined, and more closely coordinated these clusters with three aims: to make them easier to teach in the space of a class meeting or two, to make them more lively and accessible, and to heighten their relevance to the surrounding works of literature. Hence, for example, a new cluster for the Middle Ages, "Christ's Humanity," broaches one of the broadest and most explosive cultural and literary movements of the period, a movement that brought forth new kinds of readers and writers and a highly contested cultural politics of the visual. Similarly, a new cluster for the eighteenth century, "Liberty," goes to the heart of a central and momentous contradiction: on the one hand, the period's passionate celebration of liberty as the core British value, and, on the other hand, its extensive and profitable engagement in the slave trade. The implications of this contradiction, as the conjoined texts demonstrate, ripple out through English philosophy, law, and literature. Another new cluster, to take a final example, focuses on the fraught relationship between nation and language in the twentieth and twenty-first centuries. Through the vast extent of the former British Empire and, more recently, through American economic and political power, the English language has displaced or commingled with indigenous languages in many parts of the world. In consequence, imaginative writers from India to Africa, from the Caribbean to Hong Kong, have grappled with the kind of vexed questions about linguistic and national identity that have been confronted by generations of Welsh, Scottish, and Irish writers. The political, psychological, and cultural complexity of these questions is evident in the array of texts brought together in the "Nation and Language" cluster, while their rich literary potential is fully apparent in Brian Friel's powerful play *Translations.* We supplement the topical clusters for each period by several more extensive topical selections of texts, with illustrations, on the anthology Web site.

Now, as in the past, cultures define themselves by the songs they sing and the stories they love to tell. But the central importance of visual media in contemporary culture has heightened our awareness of the ways in which songs and stories have always been closely linked to the images that societies have fashioned. The Eighth Edition of *The Norton Anthology of English Literature* features sixty pages of color plates (in seven new color inserts).

In addition, black-and-white engravings and illustrations by Hogarth, Blake, and Dante Gabriel Rossetti provide compelling examples of the hybrid art of the "visual narrative." In selecting visual material—from the Sutton Hoo treasure of the seventh century to Anish Kapoor's immense *Marsyas* in the twenty-first century—the editors sought to provide images that conjure up, whether directly or indirectly, the individual writers in each section; that relate specifically to individual works in the anthology; and that shape and illuminate the culture of a particular literary period. We have tried to choose visually striking images that will interest students and provoke discussion, and our captions draw attention to important details and cross-reference related texts in the anthology.

Period-by-Period Revisions

The scope of the extensive revisions we have undertaken can be conveyed more fully by a list of some of the principal texts and features that have been added to the Eighth Edition.

The Middle Ages. The period, edited by Alfred David and James Simpson, is divided into three sections: Anglo-Saxon Literature, Anglo-Norman Literature, and Middle English Literature of the Fourteenth and Fifteenth Centuries. The heart of the Anglo-Saxon section is the great epic *Beowulf,* in an acclaimed translation, specially commissioned for *The Norton Anthology of English Literature,* by Seamus Heaney. The selection of Anglo-Saxon texts has been newly augmented with the alliterative poem *Judith* and with King Alfred's preface to the *Pastoral Care.* The Anglo-Norman section—a key bridge between the Anglo-Saxon period and the time of Chaucer—includes two clusters of texts: "Legendary Histories of Britain" traces the origins of Arthurian romance in the accounts of Geoffrey of Monmouth, Wace, and Layamon. "Celtic Contexts" explores the complex multilingual situation of the period, represented by the Old Irish "Exile of the Sons of Uisliu"; newly added, the conclusion of Thomas of England's *Le Roman de Tristan,* which comes from Irish, Welsh, and Breton sources and was written down in Old French; and Marie de France's magnificent Breton lay *Lanval,* one of the period's principal texts, as well as her *Chevrefoil,* in a new verse translation by Alfred David. A tale from the *Confessio Amantis* of John Gower, a new author, complements the generous selections from Chaucer's *Canterbury Tales.* We have added new selections from the remarkable Margery Kempe and from Langland's *Piers Plowman* and an important new topical cluster, "Christ's Humanity." Our representation of medieval drama has been strengthened by the addition of the powerful *York Play of the Crucifixion.*

The Sixteenth Century. For the first time with this edition, the anthology includes the whole of Thomas More's *Utopia,* the visionary masterpiece that helped to shape the modern world. Edited by George Logan and Stephen Greenblatt, this period includes five other complete longer texts: Book 1 of Spenser's *Faerie Queene,* Marlowe's *Hero and Leander* and *Doctor Faustus,* and Shakespeare's *Twelfth Night* and *King Lear.* The selection of poems offers new works by Wyatt, five additional sonnets by Sidney, five additional sonnets by Shakespeare, and two sonnets by a poet introduced here for the first time, Richard Barnfield. In addition we provide modern prose translations of several of Petrarch's *rime* in order to show their close relationship with sonnets by Wyatt, Sidney, and Ralegh. The cluster on the period's bitter religious controversies, "Faith in Conflict," has been redesigned in order to better represent the Catholic as well as the Protestant position. A new cluster, "Women in Power," greatly expands the selections from Queen Elizabeth and sets her writings alongside those of three compelling new figures: Mary Tudor ("Bloody Mary"), Lady Jane Grey, the tragic queen for nine days, and Mary, Queen of Scots, Elizabeth's cousin and prisoner. The topic as a whole provides insight into the strange position of female rulers attempting to shape their public performances in a society that ordinarily allowed little scope for women's shaping power.

The Early Seventeenth Century. At the heart of this section, edited by Barbara Lewalski and Katharine Eisaman Maus, is John Milton's *Paradise Lost,* presented in its entirety. Other complete longer works include John Donne's soul-searching *Satire 3,* Aemilia Lanyer's country-house poem "The Description of Cookham," three major works by Ben Jonson (*The Masque of Blackness, Volpone* [freshly edited by Katharine Eisaman Maus], and the Cary-Morison ode), John Webster's tragedy *The Duchess of Malfi,* and Milton's *Lycidas.* Significant additions have been made to the works of Donne, Jonson, Bacon, Carew, and Hobbes. Three newly conceived topical clusters will help teachers organize the rich profusion of seventeenth-century texts. "The Gender Wars" offers the stark contrast between Joseph Swetnam's misogynistic diatribe and Rachel Speght's vigorous response. "Forms of Inquiry" represents the vital intellectual currents of the period by bringing together reselected texts by Bacon, Burton, Browne, and Hobbes. And introducing riveting reports on the trial and execution of Charles I, political writings by the conservative Filmer and the revolutionaries Milton and Winstanley, and searching memoirs by Lucy Hutchinson, Edward Hyde, Earl of Clarendon, Lady Anne Halkett, and Dorothy Waugh, "Crisis of Authority" shows how new literary forms arose out of the trauma of political conflict.

The Restoration and the Eighteenth Century. In response to widespread demand and our own sense of its literary merit, the editors, Lawrence Lipking and James Noggle, include the complete text of Samuel Johnson's philosophical fable *Rasselas.* We introduce as well *Fantomina,* a novella of sexual role-playing by an author new to the anthology, Eliza Haywood. Other complete longer texts in this section include Dryden's satires *Absolom and Achitophel* and *MacFlecknoe,* Aphra Behn's novel *Oroonoko,* Congreve's comedy *The Way of the World,* Pope's *Essay on Criticism, The Rape of the Lock,* and *Epistle to Dr. Abuthnot,* Gay's *Beggar's Opera,* Hogarth's graphic satire "Marriage A-la-Mode," Johnson's *Vanity of Human Wishes,* Gray's "Elegy Written in a Country Churchyard," and Goldsmith's "The Deserted Village." Additions have been made to the works of John Wilmot, Second Earl of Rochester, and Mary Leapor, and the selection from Joseph Addison and Sir Richard Steele has been recast. "Liberty," a new thematic cluster on freedom and slavery, brings together texts by John Locke, Mary Astell, Anthony Ashley Cooper, Third Earl of Shaftesbury, David Hume, Edmund Burke, and others.

The Romantic Period. The principal changes introduced by the editors, Jack Stillinger and Deidre Shauna Lynch, center on significantly increased attention to women writers of both poetry and prose. There are more poems by Anna Letitia Barbauld, Charlotte Smith (including the great long work *Beachy Head* and a substantial selection from *The Emigrants*), Mary Robinson, Joanna Baillie, and Felicia Hemans. Mary Wollstonecraft and Dorothy Wordsworth are now joined by two new woman authors, Maria Edgeworth and Jane Austen. Mary Shelley is represented by two works, her introduction to *The Last Man* and her story "The Mortal Immortal" (*Frankenstein*, formerly in the anthology, is now available in a Norton Critical Edition). There are additional poems by Robert Burns, William Wordsworth, Percy Bysshe Shelley, and John Keats and new prose pieces by Sir Walter Scott, Charles Lamb, and John Clare. A new topic, "The Gothic and the Development of a Mass Readership," focuses on the controversial history of a genre that continues to shape popular fiction and films. Writings by Horace Walpole, William Beckford, Ann Radcliff, and "Monk" Lewis, together with commentaries and reviews by contemporaries such as Anna Barbauld and Samuel Taylor Coleridge, illuminate the promise and menace that this period saw in a mode of writing that opened up a realm of nightmarish terror to literary exploration.

The Victorian Age. Among the major additions to this section, edited by Carol Christ and Catherine Robson, are Robert Louis Stevenson's *The Strange Case of Doctor Jekyll and Mr. Hyde*; two new long poems—Elizabeth Barrett Browning's poem *The Runaway Slave at Pilgrim's Point* and Dante Gabriel Rossetti's *Jenny*; a new complete text of FitzGerald's *The Rubáiyát of Omar Kayyam*; and Rudyard Kipling's *The White Man's Burden* and *If*. Kipling's novella *The Man Who Would Be King* and Oscar Wilde's comedy *The Importance of Being Earnest* continue to be featured, as does the poetry of Tennyson, Robert Browning, Elizabeth Barrett Browning, Dante Gabriel Rossetti, Christina Rossetti, and others. Along with the widely assigned "Victorian Issues" clusters (Evolution, Industrialism, and the "Woman Question"), we present the topic "Empire and National Identity." This is an innovative and highly teachable sequence of paired texts, grappling with fiercely contentious issues that repeatedly arose across the empire's vast extent.

The Twentieth Century and After. A host of new writers and topics mark this major revision by the editors, Jon Stallworthy and Jahan Ramazani. The section now features two brilliant plays, Brian Friel's *Translations* and Tom Stoppard's *Arcadia*, both of which have vital connections to literary and cultural issues that extend throughout these volumes. The many writers introduced to the anthology for the first time include the Indian poet A. K. Ramanujan, the Canadian poet Anne Carson, and the English poet Carol Ann Duffy. There are new stories by E. M. Forster and Jean Rhys, a new selection from J. M. Coetzee's *Waiting for the Barbarians*, and new poems by W. B. Yeats, W. H. Auden, Derek Walcott, and Ted Hughes. There is, as before, a remarkable array of complete longer texts, including Hardy's "On the Western Circuit," Conrad's *Heart of Darkness*, Woolf's *A Room of One's Own*, Eliot's *The Waste Land*, Mansfield's "The Garden Party" and "The Daughters of the Late Colonel," Beckett's *Endgame*, Lessing's "To Room Nineteen," Pinter's *The Dumb Waiter*, Achebe's *Things Fall Apart*, and Naipaul's *One Out of Many*. And two new, highly innovative topics will enable teachers to introduce students to major aspects of the period's cultural scene. The first, "Modernist Manifestos," brings together the radical experiments of T. E. Hulme, Ezra Pound, H. D., Wyndham Lewis, and Mina Loy. The second, "Nation and Language," gets to the heart of the questions that face colonial and postcolonial writers who must grapple with the power, at once estranging and liberating, of the English language. The voices in this cluster, Claude McKay, Hugh MacDiarmid, Louise Bennett, Brian Friel, Kamau Brathwaite, Wole Soyinka, Tony Harrison, Ngũgĩ wa Thiong'o, Salman Rushdie, and John Agard, bear eloquent witness to the global diffusion of English, the urgency of unresolved issues of nation and identity, and the rich complexity of literary history. That history is not a straightforward sequence. Seamus Heaney's works, to which two new poems have been added, provide the occasion to look back again to Heaney's translation of *Beowulf* at the beginning of the anthology. This translation is a reminder that the most recent works can double back upon the distant past, and that words set down by men and women who have crumbled into dust can speak to us with astonishing directness.

Editorial Procedures

The Eighth Edition adheres to the core principles that have always characterized *The Norton Anthology of English Literature*. Period introductions, headnotes, and annotation are designed to enhance students' reading and, without imposing an interpretation, to give students the information they need to understand each text. The aim of these editorial materials is to make the anthology self-sufficient, so that it can be read anywhere—in a coffee bar, on a bus, or under a tree. Above all, we have tried always to keep in mind the actual classroom situation. Teachability is central to every aspect of these volumes.

Our fidelity to a trusted and well-tried format may make it difficult for long-time users to take in, at first glance, how thoroughgoing and extensive the revisions to the Eighth Edition actually are. The editorial team undertook to rethink and update virtually everything in these pages, from the endpaper maps, scrutinized for accuracy by Catherine Robson and redrawn by cartographer Adrian Kitzinger, to the appendix on English money, which, thanks to James Noggle's clever chart, now provides, at a glance, answers to the perennial question, But what was money actually worth? Similarly, "Religions in England," rewritten by Katharine Maus, and "Geographic Nomenclature," revised by Jahan Ramazani, quickly and elegantly illuminate what students have often found obscure. Each volume of the anthology includes a "Poems in Process" section, revised and expanded by Deidre Lynch with the help of Alfred David and James Simpson, which reproduces from manuscripts and printed texts the genesis and evolution of a number of poems whose final form is printed in that volume. And, thanks to the thoroughgoing work of James Simpson, we now have a freshly conceived and thoroughly rewritten "Literary Terminology" appendix, recast as a quick-reference alphabetical glossary with examples from works in *The Norton Anthology of English Literature*.

Drawing upon the latest scholarship and upon classroom experience, the editors have substantially rewritten the period introductions and headnotes. We have updated as well the bibliographies and have carefully revised the timelines. And we have provided in-text references to the *Norton Literature Online* Web site. With all aspects of the anthology's apparatus our intention is to facilitate direct and informed access to the extraordinary works of literature assembled here.

The Norton Anthology of English Literature prides itself on both the scholarly accuracy and the readability of its texts. To ease students' encounter with some works, we have normalized spelling and capitalization in texts up to and including the Romantic period—for the most part they now follow the conventions of modern English; we leave unaltered, however, texts in which such modernizing would change semantic or metrical qualities. From the Victorian period onward, we have restored the original spelling and punctuation to selections retained from the previous edition.

We continue other editorial procedures that have proved useful in the past. After each work, we cite the date of first publication on the right; in some instances, this date is followed by the date of a revised edition for which the author was responsible. Dates of composition, when they differ from those of publication and when they are known, are provided on the left. We have used square brackets to indicate titles supplied by the editors for the convenience of readers. Whenever a portion of a text has been omitted, we have indicated that omission with three asterisks. If the omitted portion is important for following the plot or argument, we have provided a brief summary within the text or in a footnote. Finally, we have reconsidered annotations throughout and increased the number of marginal glosses for archaic, dialect, or unfamiliar words.

Additional Resources

With the Eighth Edition of *The Norton Anthology of English Literature*, the publisher is proud to launch an extensive new resource—Norton Literature Online (*wwnorton.com/literature*)—the gateway to all of the outstanding online literature resources available from Norton. Students who activate the password included in each new copy of the anthology will find at Norton Literature Online a deep and broad array of general resources, among them a glossary of literary terms, advice on writing about literature and using MLA documentation style, study aids and quizzes, a portrait gallery featuring 380 authors, more than 100 maps, and over 90 minutes of recorded readings and musical selections. To encourage students to explore Norton Literature Online, cross-references in the anthology draw attention to relevant materials, notably to the 27 topical clusters (augmenting the 17 in-text topics) in the much-praised Norton Topics Online site. Prepared by the anthology editors, each topic includes an introduction, a gathering of annotated texts and images, and study questions and research links. For use with the Eighth Edition, three entirely new Twentieth Century topics—"Imagining Ireland," "Modernist Experiment," and "Representing the Great War"—and a recast Romantic topic, "The Satanic and Byronic Hero," have been added, among other updates and improvements. Norton Literature Online is also the portal to the Online Archive (*wwnorton.com/nael/noa*), which offers more than 150 downloadable texts from the Middle Ages through the early Victorian period, as well as some 80 audio files. An ongoing project, the Online Archive is being expanded with all public-domain texts trimmed from *The Norton Anthology of English Literature* over six editions. A new feature of the archive, a Publication Chronology, lists over 1,000 texts and the edition of the anthology in which each was introduced, dropped, and sometimes reintroduced. As such, the table, and the archive of texts now being assembled (a massive project of a few years' duration) are a unique window on changing interests in the teaching of English literature over four decades.

Teaching with The Norton Anthology of English Literature: *A Guide for Instructors* has been reconceived for ease of use and substantially rewritten by Sondra Archimedes, University of California, Santa Cruz, Elizabeth Fowler, University of Virginia, Laura Runge, University of South Florida, and Philip Schwyzer, University of Exeter. The Guide offers extensive help with teaching a course, from planning, to developing a syllabus and course objectives, to preparing exams. For authors and works, the Guide entries provide a "hook" to start class discussion; a "Quick Read" section to help instructors review essential information about a text or author; teaching suggestions that call out interesting textual or contextual features; teaching clusters of suggested groups or pairs of texts; and discussion questions. Built into the *Guide for Instructors* is a freestanding Media Guide, by Philip Schwyzer, which offers specific suggestions for integrating the anthology's rich multimedia resources with the text and for incorporating them into traditional or distance-learning courses. Finally, the Norton Resource Library (*wwnorton.com/nrl*), also by Philip Schwyzer, offers instructors brief period introductions and "class sessions" to facilitate close reading, art galleries and literary links, enhanced period timelines, essay assignments, sample syllabi, and instructions for customizing the material. These materials are compatible with WebCT and other course management systems.

The editors are deeply grateful to the hundreds of teachers worldwide who have helped us to improve *The Norton Anthology of English Literature*. A list of the advisors who prepared in-depth reviews and of the instructors who replied to a detailed questionnaire follows on a separate page, under Acknowledgments. The editors would like to express appreciation for their assistance to Elizabeth Anker (University of Virginia), Sandie Byrne (Oxford University), Timothy Campbell (Indiana University), Sarita Cargas (Oxford University), Jason Coats (University of Virginia), Joseph W. Childers (University of California, Riverside), Daniel Cook (University of California, Davis), Linda David, Christopher Fanning (Queens University), William Flesch (Brandeis University), Robert Folkenflik (University of California, Irvine), Robert D. Fulk (Indiana University), Omaar Hena (University of Virginia), Tom Keirstead (Indiana University), Shayna Kessel (University of Southern California), Joanna Lipking (Northwestern University), Ian Little (Liverpool University), Tricia Lootens (University of Georgia), Erin Minear (Harvard University), Elaine Musgrave (University of California, Davis), J. Morgan Myers (University of Virginia), Kate Nash (University of Virginia), Ruth Perry (M.I.T.), Emily Peterson (Harvard University), Kate Pilson (Harvard University), Jane Potter (Oxford Brookes University), Leah Price (Harvard University), Angelique Richardson (Exeter University), Philip Schwyzer (Exeter University), and Ramie Targoff (Brandeis University). We especially thank John W. Sider (Westmont College) for his meticulous review of standing annotations and myriad suggestions for improvements. We also thank the many people at Norton who contributed to the Eighth Edition: Julia Reidhead, who served not only as the inhouse supervisor but also as an unfailingly wise and effective collaborator in every aspect of planning and accomplishing this Eighth Edition; Marian Johnson, managing editor for college books, who kept the project moving forward with a remarkable blend of focused energy, intelligence, and common sense; Kurt Wildermuth, developmental and project editor; Alice Falk, Katharine Ings, Candace Levy, Alan Shaw, and Ann Tappert, manuscript editors; Eileen Connell, electronic media editor; Diane O'Connor, production manager; Nancy Rodwan and Katrina Washington, permissions managers; Toni Krass, designer; Neil Ryder Hoos, art researcher; Erin Granville, associate editor; and Catherine Spencer, editorial assistant. All these friends provided the editors with indispensable help in meeting the challenge of representing the unparalleled range and variety of English literature.

We dedicate this Eighth Edition of *The Norton Anthology of English Literature* to our friend, mentor, and inspiring guide M. H. Abrams. His shaping power over these volumes and the profession it serves will long endure.

Acknowledgments

Among our many critics, advisors, and friends, the following were of especial help toward the preparation of the Eighth Edition, either by offering advice or by providing critiques of particular periods of the anthology: Daniel Albright (University of Rochester), David L. Anderson (Butler County Community College), Judith H. Anderson (Indiana University), David Barnard (University of Regina), Ian Baucom (Duke University), Dr. Richard Beadle (St John's College, Cambridge University), Elleke Boehmer (Nottingham Trent University), Scott Boltwood (Emory and Henry College), Joseph Bristow (University of California, Los Angeles), James Chandler (University of Chicago), William Cohen (University of Maryland, College Park), Helen Cooper (Oxford University), Valentine Cunningham (Oxford University), Timothy Drake (Queen's University), Ian Duncan (University of California), Elizabeth Hanson (Queen's University), Brean Hammond (University of Nottingham), Claudia Johnson (Princeton University), Emrys Jones (Oxford University), Suzanne Keen, Shanya Kessel (University of Southern California), Bruce King, Rebecca Krug (University of Minnesota), David Kuijt (University of Maryland), John Leonard (University of Western Ontario), Peter Lindenbaum (Indiana University), Jesse Matz (Kenyon College), Brian May (Northern Illinois University), Father Germain Marc'hadour (Angers, France), Vincent Gillespie (Oxford University), Leah S. Marcus (Vanderbilt University), Paula McDowell (Rutgers University), Clarence H. Miller (St. Louis University), Tyrus Miller (University of California, Santa Cruz), Michael Moses (Duke University), Barbara Newman (Northwestern University), Michael North (University of California, Los Angeles), Stephen Orgel, (Stanford University), Ruth Perry (Massachusetts Institute of Technology), Adela Pinch (University of Michigan), David Porter (University of Michigan), Laura Quinney (Brandeis University), Alan Richardson (Boston College), Phillip Rogers (Queen's University), Mary Beth Rose (University of Illinois at Chicago), Elizabeth Scala (University of Texas), Nigel Smith (Princeton University), Janet Sorensen (Indiana University), Michele Stanco (Università degli Studi di Napoli "Frederico"), Marta Straznicky (Queen's University), Helen Thompson (Northwestern University), Blakey Vermeule (Northwestern University), Richard Wendorf (Boston Athenæum), Johnny Wink (Ouachita Baptist University), David Wyatt (University of Maryland), Steven Zwicker (Washington University, St. Louis).

The editors would like to express appreciation and thanks to the hundreds of teachers who provided reviews: Laila Abdalla (Central Washington University), Avis Adams (Green River Community College), Kimberly VanEsveld Adams (Elizabethtown College), Thomas Amarose (Seattle Pacific University), Mark Addison Amos (Southern Illinois University, Carbondale), M. G. Aune (North Dakota State College), E. Baldwin (University of Victoria), Jackson Barry (University of Maryland, College Park), Elisa E. Beshero-Bondar (The

Pennsylvania State University), Thomas Bestul (University of Illinois at Chicago), J. Christopher Bittenbender (Eastern University), Dr. K Blumerich (Grand Valley State University), Karl Boehler (University of Wisconsin, Osh Kosh), Bruce Brandt (South Dakota State University), Caroline Breashears (St. Lawrence University), Dr. Chris Brooks (Wichita State University), M. Brown (SUNY, Morrisville), Jennifer Bryan (Oberlin College), Kristin Bryant (Portland Community College), Stephen Buhler (University of Nebraska-Lincoln), Michel Camp (Jackson State Community College), Joseph Candido (University of Arkansas, Fayetteville), Tim Carens (College of Charleston), Cynthia Caywood (University of San Diego), Merlin Cheney (Weber State University), William Christmas (San Francisco State University), Caroline Cherry (Eastern University), Joyce Coleman (University of North Dakota), Brian Connery (Oakland University), Kevin L. Cope (Louisiana State University, Baton Rouge), J. Cortelloni (Lincoln College), Richard Cox (Abilene Christian University), Joanne Craig (Bishop's University), S. B. Darrell (Southern Indiana University), J. A. Dane (University of South California), M. V. Davidson (University of Wisconsin, La Crosse), William Dawson (University of Missouri), Danette DiMarco (Slippery Rock University), Michael Doerrer (University of Maryland, College Park), Alfred J. Drake (California State University, Fullerton), George Drake (Central Washington University), Ende Duffy (University of California, Santa Barbara), Judy Elsley (Weber State University), Dan Embree (Mississippi State University), Audrey Fisch (New Jersey City University), Annette Federico (James Madison University), Robert Forman (St. John's University), Thomas Frosch (City University of New York, Queens), Dr. Donald Fucci (Ramapo College), Mark Fulk (Buffalo State College), Kevin Gardner (Baylor University), Robert Geary (James Madison University), Marc Geisler (Western Washington University), Jason Gieger (California State University, Sacramento), Cynthia Gilliatt (James Madison University), Julia Giordano (Nassau Community College), Stephen Glosecki (University of Alabama at Birmingham), William Gracie (Miami University of Ohio), Kenneth Graham (University of Waterloo), Loren C. Gruber (Missouri Valley College), Leigh Harbin (Angelo State University), H. George Hahn (Towson University), Douglas Hayes (Winona State University), Aeron Haynie (University of Wisconsin, Green Bay), Regina Hewitt (University of South Florida), Matthew Hill (University of Maryland, College Park), Jim Hoogenakker (Washburn University), Robert Hoskins (James Madison University), Kathy Houff (University of Georgia), Claudia House (Nashville State Tech Community College), Darren Howard (University of California, Los Angeles), Rebecca Kajs (Anne Arundel Community College), Bridget Keegan (Creighton University), Erin Kelly (University of Maryland), Julie Kim (Northeastern Illinois University), Pamela King (University of Bristol), Jackie Kogan (California State University, Northridge), Neal Kramer (Brigham Young University), Deborah Knuth (Colgate University), E. Carole Knuth (Buffalo State College), Wai-Leung Kwok (San Francisco State University), Elizabeth Lambert (Gettysburg College), Mary Lenard (University of Wisconsin, Parkside), George Evans Light (Mississippi State University), Henry Limouze (Wright State University), Sherry Little (San Diego State), Debbie Lopez (University of Texas, San Antonio), Susan Lorsch (Hofstra University), Thomas Lyons (University of Colorado, Boulder), Susan Maher (University of Nebraska, Omaha), Phoebe Mainster (Wayne State University), W. J. Martin (Niagara University), Nicholas Mason (Brigham Young University), Ian McAdam (University of Lethbridge), Ruth McAdams (Tarrant County College), John McCombe (University of Dayton), Kristen McDermott (Central Michigan University), Joseph McGowan (University of San Diego), Christian Michener (St. Mary's University, Minnesota), D. Keith Mikolavich (Diablo Valley College), Nicholas Moschovakis (George Washington University), Gwendolyn Morgan (Montana State University), Daniel Mosser (Virginia Polytechnic Institute), K. D. Neill (University of Victoria, British Columbia), Douglas Nordfor (James Madison University), Michael North (University of California, Los Angeles), Bernie O'Donnell (University of Florida). Michael Olmert (University of Maryland, College Park), C. R. Orchard (Indiana University of Pennsylvania), Jennifer Panek (University of Ottawa), Cynthia Patton (Emporia State University), James Persoon (Grand Valley State University), Sara Pfaffenroth (County College of Morris), John Pfordreshen (Georgetown University), Jennifer Phegley (University of Missouri, Kansas City), Trey Philpotts (Arkansas Technical University), Brenda Powell (University of St. Thomas, St. Paul), Tison Pugh (University of Central Florida), Katherine Quinsey (University of Windsor), Eric Reimer (University of Montana), Kathryn Rummel (California Polytechnic State University), Harbindar Sanghara (University of Victoria, Canada), William Scheuede (University of South Florida), Michael Schoenfeldt (University of Michigan), R. M. Schuler (University of Victoria, British Columbia), D. Schwartz (Cal Poly, Saint Louis Obispo), Michael Schwartz (California State University, Chico), Richard Sha (American University), George Shuffelton (Carleton College), Brandie Sigfried (Brigham Young University), Elizabeth Signorotti (Binghamton University), Dawn Simmons (Ohio State University), Erik Simpson (Grinnell College), Sarah Singer (Delaware County Community College), Dr. Mary-Antoinette Smith (Seattle University), Jonathan Smith (University of Michigan, Dearborn), Nigel Smith (Princeton University), Malinda Snow (Georgia State University), Jean Sorenson (Grayson County College), C. Spinks (Trinity College), Donald Stone (City University of New York, Queens), Kevin Swafford (Bradley University), Andrew Taylor (University of Ottawa), Rebecca Totaro (Florida Gulf Coast University), Bente Videbaek (State University New York, Stony Brook), Joseph Viscome (University of North Carolina, Chapel Hill), Jennie Wakefield (Clemson University), David Ward (University of Pittsburgh), Tracy Ware (Queen's University), Alexander Weiss (Radford University), Lachlan Whalen (Marshall University), Christopher Wheatley (Catholic University of America), C. Williams (Mississippi State University), Jodi Wyett (Xavier University, Cincinnati), Jiyeon Yoo (University of California, Los Angeles), Richard Zeikowitz (University of South Alabama).

The Norton Anthology of English Literature

EIGHTH EDITION

VOLUME F

THE TWENTIETH CENTURY AND AFTER

The Twentieth Century and After

1914–18: World War I
1922:   James Joyce's *Ulysses*; T. S. Eliot's *The Waste Land*
1929:   Stock market crash; Great Depression begins
1939–45: World War II
1947:   India and Pakistan become independent nations
1953:   Premiere of Samuel Beckett's *Waiting for Godot*
1957–62: Ghana, Nigeria, Uganda, Jamaica, and Trinidad and Tobago become independent nations
1958:   Chinua Achebe's *Things Fall Apart*
1991:   Collapse of the Soviet Union
2001:   Attacks destroy World Trade Center

HISTORICAL BACKGROUND

The roots of modern literature are in the late nineteenth century. The aesthetic movement, with its insistence on "art for art's sake," assaulted middle-class assumptions about the nature and function of art. Rejecting Victorian notions of the artist's moral and educational duties, aestheticism helped widen the breach between writers and the general public, resulting in the "alienation" of the modern artist from society. This alienation is evident in the lives and work of the French symbolists and other late-nineteenth-century bohemians who repudiated conventional notions of respectability, and it underlies key works of modern literature, such as James Joyce's *Portrait of the Artist as a Young Man* and T. S. Eliot's *Waste Land*.

The growth of public education in England as a result of the Education Act of 1870, which finally made elementary schooling compulsory and universal, led to the rapid emergence of a mass literate population, at whom a new mass-produced popular literature and new cheap journalism (the "yellow press") were directed. The audience for literature split up into "highbrows," "middle-brows," and "lowbrows," and the segmentation of the reading public, developing with unprecedented speed and to an unprecedented degree, helped widen the gap between popular art and art esteemed only by the sophisticated and the expert. This breach yawned ever wider with the twentieth-century emergence of modernist iconoclasm and avant-garde experiment in literature, music, and the visual arts.

Queen Victoria's contemporaries felt her Jubilee in 1887 and, even more, her Diamond Jubilee in 1897 marked the end of an era. The reaction against middle-class Victorian attitudes that is central to modernism was already under way in the two decades before the queen's death in 1901. Samuel Butler savagely attacked the Victorian conceptions of the family, education, and religion in his novel *The Way of All Flesh* (completed in 1884, posthumously published in 1903), the bitterest indictment in English literature of the Victorian way of life. And the high tide of anti-Victorianism was marked by the publication in 1918 of a classic of ironic debunking, Lytton Strachey's collection of biographical essays *Eminent Victorians*.

A pivotal figure between Victorianism and modernism, Thomas Hardy marked the end of the Victorian period and the dawn of the new age in "The Darkling Thrush," a poem originally titled "By the Century's Deathbed" and postdated December 31, 1900, the last day of the nineteenth century. The poem marks the demise of a century of relative conviction and optimism, and it intimates the beginnings of a new era in its skeptical irresolution, its bleak sense of the modern world as "hard and dry"—favorite adjectives of later writers such as Ezra Pound and T. E. Hulme:

> The land's sharp features seemed to be
> The Century's corpse outleant,
> His crypt the cloudy canopy,
> The wind his death-lament.
> The ancient pulse of germ and birth
> Was shrunken hard and dry,
> And every spirit upon earth
> Seemed fervourless as I.

This poem and other works by Hardy, A. E. Housman, and Joseph Conrad exemplify the pessimism of imaginative writing in the last decade of the nineteenth century and the first decade of the twentieth. Stoicism—a stiff-upper-lip determination to endure whatever fate may bring—also characterizes the literature written in the transitional period between the Victorian era and modernism, including the work of minor authors such as Robert Louis Stevenson and Rudyard Kipling.

By the dawn of the twentieth century, traditional stabilities of society, religion, and culture seemed to have weakened, the pace of change to be accelerating. The unsettling force of modernity profoundly challenged traditional ways of structuring and making sense of human experience. Because of the rapid pace of social and technological change, because of the mass dislocation of populations by war, empire, and economic migration, because of the mixing in close quarters of cultures and classes in rapidly expanding cities, modernity disrupted the old order, upended ethical and social codes, cast into doubt previously stable assumptions about self, community, the world, and the divine.

Early-twentieth-century writers were keenly aware that powerful concepts and vocabularies were emerging in anthropology, psychology, philosophy, and the visual arts that reimagined human identity in radically new ways. Sigmund Freud's seminal *Interpretation of Dreams* was published in 1900, and soon psychoanalysis was changing how people saw and described rationality, the self, and personal development. In his prose and poetry D. H. Lawrence adapted the Oedipus complex to interpret and present his relationships with his parents, though rejecting Freud's negative definition of the unconscious. By the time of his death in 1939, Freud had become, as W. H. Auden wrote in an elegy for him, "a whole climate of opinion / / under whom we conduct our different lives." Also in the early twentieth century, Sir James Frazer's

Golden Bough (1890–1915) and other works of anthropology were altering basic conceptions of culture, religion, and myth. Eliot observed that Frazer's work "influenced our generation profoundly," and the critic Lionel Trilling suggested that "perhaps no book has had so decisive an effect upon modern literature as Frazer's." For both anthropologists and modern writers, Western religion was now decentered by being placed in a comparative context as one of numerous related mythologies, with Jesus Christ linked to "primitive" fertility gods thought to die and revive in concert with the seasons. Furthering this challenge to religious doctrine were the writings of Friedrich Nietzsche, the nineteenth-century German philosopher who declared the death of God, repudiated Christianity, and offered instead a harshly tragic conception of life: people look "deeply into the true nature of things" and realize "that no action of theirs can work any change," but they nevertheless laugh and stoically affirm their fate. W. B. Yeats, who remarks in a 1902 letter that his eyes are exhausted from reading "that strong enchanter," greets death and destruction in a Nietzschean spirit of tragic exultation.

These profound changes in modern intellectual history coincided with changes of a more mundane sort, for everyday life was also undergoing rapid transformation during the first years of the twentieth century. Electricity was spreading, cinema and radio were proliferating, and new pharmaceuticals such as aspirin were being developed. As labor was increasingly managed and rationalized, as more and more people crowded into cities, as communications and transportation globalized space and accelerated time, literature could not stand still, and modern writers sought to create new forms that could register these profound alterations in human experience. This was a period of scientific revolution, as exemplified in German physics by Max Planck's quantum theory (1900) and Albert Einstein's theory of relativity (1905), and T. S. Eliot reflects the increasing dominance of science when he argues that the poet surrenders to tradition and thus extinguishes rather than expresses personality: "It is in this depersonalization that art may be said to approach the condition of science," he claims, adding that "the mind of the poet is the shred of platinum" that catalyzes change but itself remains "inert, neutral, and unchanged" ("Tradition and the Individual Talent").

The early twentieth century also brought countless advances in technology: the first wireless communication across the Atlantic occurred in 1901, the Wright Brothers flew the first airplane in 1903, and Henry Ford introduced the first mass-produced car, the Model T or "Tin Lizzie," in 1913. Not that modern writers univocally embraced such changes. Although some were more sanguine, many modern writers were paradoxically repulsed by aspects of modernization. Mass-produced appliances and products, such as the "gramophone" and canned goods ("tins"), are objects of revulsion in Eliot's *Waste Land*, for example. Because scientific materialism and positivism, according to which empirical explanations could be found for everything, were weakening the influence of organized religion, many writers looked to literature as an alternative. His "simple-minded" Protestantism spoiled by science, Yeats says in his autobiography, he "made a new religion, almost an infallible church of poetic tradition." Whether or not they welcomed the demise of tradition, habit, and certitude in favor of the new, modern writers articulated the effects of modernity's relentless change, loss, and destabilization. "Things fall apart," Yeats wrote, "the centre cannot hold." Eliot describes in *Four Quartets* his quest for the "still point of the turning world." The modernist drive to "make it new"—in

Ezra Pound's famous slogan—thus arises in part out of an often ambivalent consciousness of the relentless mutations brought by modernization.

The position of women, too, was rapidly changing during this period. The Married Woman's Property Act of 1882 allowed married women to own property in their own right, and women were admitted to universities at different times during the latter part of the century. Since the days of Mary Wollstonecraft, women in Great Britain had been arguing and lobbying for the right to vote, but in the first decades of the twentieth century, Emmeline Pankhurst and her daughter Christabel encouraged suffragettes, as they were known, to take a more militant approach, which included boycotts, bombings, and hunger strikes. The long fight for women's suffrage was finally won in 1918 for women thirty and over, and in 1928 for women twenty-one and over. These shifts in attitudes toward women, in the roles women played in the national life, and in the relations between the sexes are reflected in a variety of ways in the literature of the period.

Britain's modern political history begins with the Anglo-Boer War (1899–1902), fought by the British to establish political and economic control over the Boer republics (self-governing states) of South Africa. It was an imperial war against which many British intellectuals protested and one that the British in the end were slightly ashamed of having won. The war spanned the reign of Queen Victoria, who died in 1901, and Edward VII, who held the throne from 1901 to 1910. This latter decade is known as the Edwardian period, and the king stamped his extrovert and self-indulgent character upon it. The wealthy made it a vulgar age of conspicuous enjoyment, but most writers and artists kept well away from involvement in high society: in general this period had no equivalent to Queen Victoria's friendship with Tennyson. The alienation of artists and intellectuals from political rulers and middle-class society was proceeding apace. From 1910 (when George V came to the throne) until World War I broke out in August 1914, Britain achieved a temporary equilibrium between Victorian earnestness and Edwardian flashiness; in retrospect the Georgian period seems peculiarly golden, the last phase of assurance and stability before the old order throughout Europe broke up in violence. Yet even then, under the surface, there was restlessness and experimentation. The age of Rupert Brooke's idyllic sonnets on the English countryside was also the age of T. S. Eliot's first experiments in a radically new kind of poetry, James Joyce's and Virginia Woolf's in radically new forms of fiction.

Edwardian as a term applied to English cultural history suggests a period in which the social and economic stabilities of the Victorian age—country houses with numerous servants, a flourishing and confident middle class, a strict hierarchy of social classes—remained unimpaired, though on the level of ideas a sense of change and liberation existed. *Georgian* refers largely to the lull before the storm of World War I. That war, as the bitterly skeptical and antiheroic work of Wilfred Owen, Siegfried Sassoon, Isaac Rosenberg, and other war poets makes clear, produced major shifts in attitude toward Western myths of progress and civilization. The postwar disillusion of the 1920s resulted, in part, from the sense of utter social and political collapse during a war in which unprecedented millions were killed.

By the beginning of World War I, nearly a quarter of the earth's surface and more than a quarter of the world's population were under British dominion, including the vast African territories acquired in the preceding hundred years. Some of the colonies in the empire were settler nations with large European populations, such as Canada, Australia, and New Zealand, and in 1907 the empire granted them the new status of dominions, recognizing their relative control over internal affairs. Over time these largely independent nations came to be known as the British Commonwealth, an association of self-governing countries. The twentieth century witnessed the emergence of internationally acclaimed literary voices from these dominions, from the early-century New Zealander Katherine Mansfield to the late-century Australian Les Murray and Canadians Alice Munro and Anne Carson. The rest of the colonies in the British Empire consisted primarily of indigenous populations that had little or no political power, but nationalist movements were gaining strength in the early years of the century—as when, in 1906, the Congress movement in India first demanded *swaraj* ("self-rule") soon to become the mantra of Indian nationalism. In Britain imperialist and anti-imperialist sentiments often met head on in Parliament and the press, the debate involving writers as far apart as Rudyard Kipling and E. M. Forster.

A steadily rising Irish nationalism resulted in increasingly violent protests against the cultural, economic, and political subordination of Ireland to the British Crown and government. During the Easter Rising of 1916, Irish rebels in Dublin staged a revolt against British rule, and by executing fifteen Irish leaders, the British inadvertently intensified the drive for independence, finally achieved in 1921–22 when the southern counties were declared the Irish Free State. (The six counties of Northern Ireland remained, however, part of Great Britain.) No one can fully understand Yeats or Joyce without some awareness of the Irish struggle for independence, and the way in which the Irish literary revival of the late nineteenth and early twentieth centuries (with Yeats at the forefront) reflected a determination to achieve a vigorous national life cultur- ally even if the road seemed blocked politically.

Depression and unemployment in the early 1930s, followed by the rise of Hitler and the shadow of Fascism and Nazism over Europe, with its threat of another war, deeply affected the emerging poets and novelists of the time. While Eliot, Lawrence, Wyndham Lewis, Yeats, Pound, and others of the older generation turned to the political right, the impotence of capitalist govern- ments in the face of Fascism combined with economic dislocation to turn the majority of young intellectuals (and not only intellectuals) in the 1930s to the political left. The 1930s were the so-called red decade, because only the left seemed to offer any solution in various forms of socialism, communism, and left liberalism. The early poetry of W. H. Auden and his contemporaries cried out for "the death of the old gang" (in Auden's phrase) and a clean sweep politically and economically, while the right-wing army's rebellion against the left-wing republican government in Spain, which started in the summer of 1936 and soon led to full-scale civil war, was regarded as a rehearsal for an inevitable second world war and thus further emphasized the inadequacy of politicians. Yet though the younger writers of the period expressed the up-to- date, radical political views of the left, they were less technically inventive than the first-generation modernists, such as Eliot, Joyce, and Woolf. The outbreak of World War II in September 1939—following shortly on Hitler's pact with the Soviet Union, which so shocked and disillusioned many of the young left-wing writers that they subsequently moved politically to the cen- ter—marked the sudden end of the red decade. What was from the beginning expected to be a long and costly war brought inevitable exhaustion. The dim- inution of British political power, its secondary status in relation to the United

States as a player in the Cold War, brought about a painful reappraisal of Britain's place in the world, even as countries that had lost the war—West Germany and Japan—were, in economic terms, winning the peace that followed.

In winning a war, Great Britain lost an empire. The largest, most powerful, best organized of the modern European empires, it had expropriated enormous quantities of land, raw materials, and labor from its widely scattered overseas territories. India, long the jewel in the imperial Crown, won its independence in 1947, along with the newly formed Muslim state of Pakistan. The postwar wave of decolonization that began in South Asia spread to Africa and the Caribbean: in 1957 Ghana was the first nation in sub-Saharan Africa to become independent, unleashing an unstoppable wave of liberation from British rule that freed Nigeria in 1960, Sierra Leone in 1961, Uganda in 1962, Kenya in 1963; in the Caribbean, Jamaica and Trinidad and Tobago in 1962, Barbados and Guyana in 1966, and Saint Lucia in 1979. India and Pakistan elected to remain within a newly expanded and reconceived British Commonwealth, but other former colonies did not. The Irish Republic withdrew from the Commonwealth in 1949; the Republic of South Africa, in 1961. Postwar decolonization coincided with and encouraged the efflorescence of postcolonial writing that would bring about the most dramatic geographic shift in literature in English since its inception. Writers from Britain's former colonies published influential and innovative novels, plays, and poems, hybridizing their local traditions and varieties of English with those of the empire. The names of the Nobel Prize winners Wole Soyinka, Nadine Gordimer, Derek Walcott, V. S. Naipaul, and J. M. Coetzee were added to the annals of literature in English.

While Britain was decolonizing its empire, the former empire was colonizing Britain, as Louise Bennett wryly suggests in her poem "Colonization in Reverse." Encouraged by the postwar labor shortage in England and the scarcity of work at home, waves of Caribbean migrants journeyed to and settled in "the motherland," the first group on the *Empire Windrush* that sailed from Jamaica to Tilbury Docks in 1948. Migrants followed from India, Pakistan, Bangladesh, Africa, and other regions of the "New Commonwealth." Even as immigration laws became more restrictive in the 1960s, relatives of earlier migrants and refugees from these and other nations continued to arrive, transforming Britain into an increasingly multiracial society and infusing energy into British arts and literature. But people of Caribbean, African, and South Asian origin, who brought distinctive vernaculars and cultural traditions with them, painfully discovered that their official status as British subjects often did not translate into their being welcomed as full-fledged members of British society. The friction between color-blind and ethnically specific notions of Englishness prompted a large-scale and ongoing rethinking of national identity in Britain. Among the arrivals in England were many who journeyed there to study in the late 1940s and 1950s and eventually became prominent writers, such as Bennett, Soyinka, Kamau (then Edward) Brathwaite, and Chinua Achebe. In the 1970s and 1980s a younger generation of black and Asian British writers emerged—some born in the U.K., some in the ex-empire—including Salman Rushdie, Hanif Kureishi, John Agard, and Caryl Phillips, and in the 1990s and the first decade of the new millennium, still younger writers including Jackie Kay and Zadie Smith.

London, as the capital of the empire, had long dominated the culture as well as the politics and the economy of the British Isles. London spoke for Britain in the impeccable southern English intonations of the radio announcers of the state-owned British Broadcasting Corporation (known as the BBC), but from the end of World War II this changed. Regional dialects and multicultural accents were admitted to the airwaves. Regional radio and television stations sprang up. In the 1940s and 1950s the BBC produced a weekly program called "Caribbean Voices," which proved an important stimulus to anglophone writing in the West Indies. The Arts Council, which had subsidized the nation's drama, literature, music, painting, and plastic arts from London, delegated much of its grant-giving responsibility to regional arts councils. This gave a new confidence to writers and artists outside London—the Beatles were launched from Liverpool—and has since contributed to a notable renaissance of regional literature.

From the 1960s London ceased to be essentially the sole cultural stage of the United Kingdom, and though its Parliament remained the sole political stage until 1999, successive governments came under increasing pressure from the regions and the wider world. After decades of predominantly Labour governments, Margaret Thatcher led the Conservatives to power in the general election of 1979, becoming thereby the country's first woman to hold the office of prime minister, an office she was to hold for an unprecedented twelve years. Pursuing a vision of a "new," more productive Britain, she curbed the power of the unions and began to dismantle the "welfare state," privatizing nationalized industries and utilities in the interests of an aggressive free-market economy. Initially her policies seemed to have a bracing effect on a nation still sunk in postwar, postimperial torpor, but writers such as Ian McEwan and Caryl Churchill and filmmakers such as Derek Jarman protested that Conservative reforms widened the gap between rich and poor, black and white, north and south, and between the constituent parts of the United Kingdom.

Thatcher was deposed by her own party in 1990, and the Conservatives were routed in the election of 1997. The electorate's message was clear, and Tony Blair, the new Labour prime minister, moved to restore the rundown Health Service and system of state education. Honoring other of his campaign pledges, he offered Scotland its own parliament and Wales its own assembly, each with tax-raising powers and a substantial budget for the operation of its social services, and each holding its first elections in 1999. Though a commanding figure in British politics, Blair faced increasing skepticism over his justification for joining forces with the U.S.-led invasion and occupation of Iraq in 2003.

Meanwhile the Labour government made significant progress toward solving the bitter and bloody problems of Northern Ireland, where, since the late 1960s, the Irish Republican Army (IRA) had waged a violent campaign for a united Ireland and against British rule, met by violent suppression by the British Army and reprisals by Protestant Unionists, who sought to keep Northern Ireland a part of the United Kingdom. In the 1990s politics finally took precedence over armed struggle in the Republican movement. In 1998 the Good Friday Agreement, also known as the Belfast Agreement, led to elections to a Northern Ireland Assembly, which met for the first time in 1999, and the leaders of the main Roman Catholic and Protestant parties were jointly awarded the Nobel Peace Prize. Although hope persisted that peaceful coexistence and substantial self-governance in Ulster could continue, disagreements between the parties over IRA weapons and alleged spying led to the suspension of the Northern Ireland Assembly and Executive Committee in 2002.

POETRY

The years leading up to World War I saw the start of a poetic revolution. The imagist movement, influenced by the philosopher poet T. E. Hulme's insistence on hard, clear, precise images, arose in reaction to what it saw as Romantic fuzziness and facile emotionalism in poetry. (Like other modernists, the imagists somewhat oversimplified the nineteenth-century aesthetic against which they defined their own artistic ideal, while scanting underlying continuities.) The movement developed initially in London, where the modernist American poet Ezra Pound was living, and quickly migrated across the Atlantic, and its early members included Hulme, Pound, H. D. (Hilda Doolittle), Amy Lowell, Richard Aldington, John Gould Fletcher, and F. S. Flint. As Flint explained in an article in March 1913, partly dictated by Pound, imagists insisted on "direct treatment of the 'thing,' whether subjective or objective," on the avoidance of all words "that did not contribute to the presentation," and on a freer metrical movement than a strict adherence to the "sequence of a metronome" could allow. Inveighing in manifestos against Victorian discursiveness, the imagists wrote short, sharply etched, descriptive lyrics, but they lacked a technique for the production of longer and more complex poems.

Other new ideas about poetry helped provide this technique, many of them associated with another American in London, T. S. Eliot. Sir Herbert Grierson's 1912 edition of John Donne's poems both reflected and encouraged a new enthusiasm for seventeenth-century Metaphysical poetry. The revived interest in Metaphysical "wit" brought with it a desire on the part of pioneering poets to introduce into their work a much higher degree of intellectual complexity than had been found among the Victorians or the Georgians. The full subtlety of French symbolist poetry also now came to be appreciated; it had been admired in the 1890s, but more for its dreamy suggestiveness than for its imagistic precision and complexity. At the same time modernist writers wanted to bring poetic language and rhythms closer to those of conversation, or at least to spice the formalities of poetic utterance with echoes of the colloquial and even the slangy. Irony, which made possible several levels of discourse simultaneously, and wit, with the use of puns (banished from serious poetry for more than two hundred years), helped achieve that union of thought and passion that Eliot, in his review of Grierson's anthology of Metaphysical poetry (1921), saw as characteristic of the Metaphysicals and wished to bring back into poetry. A new critical movement and a new creative movement in poetry went hand in hand, with Eliot the high priest of both. He extended the scope of imagism by bringing the English Metaphysicals and the French symbolists (as well as the English Jacobean dramatists) to the rescue, thus adding new criteria of complexity and allusiveness to the criteria of concreteness and precision stressed by the imagists. Eliot also introduced into modern English and American poetry the kind of irony achieved by shifting suddenly from the formal to the colloquial, or by oblique allusions to objects or ideas that contrasted sharply with the surface meaning of the poem. Nor were Eliot and the imagists alone in their efforts to reinvent poetry. From 1912 D. H. Lawrence began writing poems freer in form and emotion, wanting to unshackle verse from the constraints of the "gem-like" lyric and approach even the "insurgent naked throb of the instant moment." Thus between, say, 1911 (the first year covered by Edward Marsh's anthologies of Georgian poetry) and 1922 (the year of the publication of *The Waste Land*), a major revolution occurred in English—and for that matter American—poetic theory and practice, one that determined the way in which many poets now think about their art.

This modernist revolution was by no means an isolated literary phenomenon. Writers on both sides of the English Channel were influenced by the French impressionist, postimpressionist, and cubist painters' radical reexamination of the nature of reality. The influence of Italian futurism was likewise strong on the painter and writer Wyndham Lewis, whose short-lived journal *Blast* was meant to be as shocking in its visual design as in its violent rhetoric. The poet Mina Loy shared the futurist fascination with modernity and speed, while repudiating its misogyny and jingoism, as evidenced by her "Feminist Manifesto." Pound wrote books about the French sculptor Henri Gaudier-Brzeska and the American composer George Antheil, and indeed the jagged rhythms and wrenching dissonances of modern music influenced a range of writers. Wilfred Owen wrote in 1918: "I suppose I am doing in poetry what the advanced composers are doing in music"; and Eliot, while writing *The Waste Land* three years later, was so impressed by a performance of the composer Igor Stravinsky's *Le Sacre du Printemps* (*The Rite of Spring*) that he stood up at the end and cheered.

The posthumous 1918 publication by Robert Bridges of Gerard Manley Hopkins's poetry encouraged experimentation in language and rhythms, as evidenced by the verse's influence on Eliot, Auden, and the Welshman Dylan Thomas. Hopkins combined precision of the individual image with a complex ordering of images and a new kind of metrical patterning he named "sprung rhythm," in which the stresses of a line could be more freely distributed.

Meanwhile Yeats's remarkable oeuvre, stretching across the whole modern period, reflected varying developments of the age yet maintained an unmistakably individual accent. Beginning with the ideas of the aesthetes, turning to a tougher and sparer ironic language without losing its characteristic verbal magic, working out its author's idiosyncratic notions of symbolism, developing in its full maturity into a rich symbolic and Metaphysical poetry with its own curiously haunting cadences and with imagery both shockingly realistic and movingly suggestive, Yeats's work encapsulates a history of English poetry between 1890 and 1939.

In his poem "Remembering the 'Thirties," Donald Davie declared: "A neutral tone is nowadays preferred." That tone—Auden's coolly clinical tone—dominated the poetry of the decade. The young poets of the early 1930s—Auden, Stephen Spender, C. Day Lewis, Louis MacNeice—were the first generation to grow up in the shadow of the first-generation modern poets. Hopkins's attention to sonorities, Hardy's experiments in stanzaic patterns, Yeats's ambivalent meditations on public themes, Eliot's satiric treatment of a mechanized and urbanized world, and Owen's pararhymed enactments of pity influenced Auden and the other poets in his circle. But these younger poets also had to distinguish themselves from the still-living eminences in poetry, and they did so by writing poems more low-pitched and ironic than Yeats's, for example, or more individually responsive to and active in the social world than Eliot's.

As World War II began, the neutral tone gave way to, as in Auden's work, an increasingly direct and humane voice and to the vehemence of what came to be known as the New Apocalypse. The poets of this movement, most notably Dylan Thomas, owed something of their imagistic audacity and rhetorical violence to the French surrealists, whose poetry was introduced to English readers in translations and in *A Short Survey of Surrealism* (1936) by David Gascoyne, one of the New Apocalypse poets. Many of the surrealists, such as Salvador Dalí and André Breton, were both poets and painters, and in their verbal as well as their visual art they sought to express, often by free association, the operation of the unconscious mind.

With the coming of the 1950s, however, the pendulum swung back. A new generation of poets, including Donald Davie, Thom Gunn, and Philip Larkin, reacted against what seemed to them the verbal excesses and extravagances of Dylan Thomas and Edith Sitwell, as well as the arcane myths and knotty allusiveness of Yeats, Eliot, and Pound. "The Movement," as this new group came to be called, aimed once again for a neutral tone, a purity of diction, in which to render an unpretentious fidelity to mundane experience. Larkin, its most notable exponent, rejected the intimidating gestures of an imported modernism in favor of a more civil and accessible "native" tradition that went back to Hardy, Housman, and the Georgian pastoralists of the 1910s.

Not everyone in England followed the lead of Larkin and the Movement, some rejecting the Movement's notion of a limited, rationalist, polished poetics. In the late 1950s and the 1960s Ted Hughes began to write poems in which predators and victims in the natural world suggest the violence and irrationality of modern history, including the carnage of World War I, in which his father had fought. Geoffrey Hill also saw a rationalist humanism as inadequate to the ethical and religious challenges of twentieth-century war, genocide, and atrocity, which he evoked in a strenuous language built on the traditions of high modernism and Metaphysical poetry.

Since the 1980s the spectrum of Britain's poets has become more diverse in class, ethnicity, gender, and region than ever before, bringing new voices into the English literary tradition. Born in the northern industrial city of Leeds, Tony Harrison brings the local vernacular, the oral energy and resonance of Yorkshire idiom and rhythms, into contact with traditional English and classical verse. Born in Scotland to an Irish mother in a left-wing, working-class Catholic family, Carol Ann Duffy grew up amid Irish, Scottish, and Standard varieties of English, and this youthful experience helped equip her to speak in different voices in her feminist monologues.

Post–World War II Ireland—both North and South—was among the most productive spaces for poetry in the second half of the twentieth century. Born just two and a half weeks after Yeats died, Seamus Heaney, his most celebrated successor, responds to the horrors of sectarian bloodshed in Northern Ireland with subtlety and acute ethical sensitivity in poems that draw on both Irish genres and sonorities and the English literary tradition of Wordsworth, Hopkins, and Ted Hughes. Paul Muldoon, one of Heaney's former students in Belfast, also writes about the Troubles in Northern Ireland but through eerily distorted fixed forms and multiple screens of irony, combining experimental zaniness with formal reserve. Born in the Irish Republic, Eavan Boland has made a space within the largely male tradition of Irish verse—with its standard, mythical emblems of femininity—for Irish women's historical experiences of suffering and survival.

The massive postwar change in the geographical contours of poetry written in English involved, in part, the emergence of new voices and styles from the "Old Commonwealth," or dominions, such as Canada and Australia. Self-conscious about being at the margins of the former empire, Les Murray fashions a brash, playful, overbrimming poetry that mines the British and classical traditions while remaking them in what he styles his "redneck" Australian manner. Anne Carson continues Canadian poetry's dialogue with its British literary origins, imaginatively transporting, for example, the Victorian writers Charlotte and Emily Brontë into a Canadian landscape, but she also illustrates a heightened interest in U.S. poetry and popular culture, bringing into the literary mix influences that range from ancient Greek poetry to Ezra Pound and Sylvia Plath, television and video.

From the former colonies of the British Empire in the so-called Third World came some of the most important innovations in the language and thematic reach of poetry in English. Born under British rule, students of colonial educations that repressed or denigrated native languages and traditions, these postcolonial poets grew up with an acute awareness of the riches of their own cultural inheritances, as well as a deep knowledge of the British literary canon. They expanded the range of possibilities in English-language poetry by hybridizing traditions of the British Isles with their indigenous images and speech rhythms, creoles and genres. Some of these writers, such as the Nobel laureate Derek Walcott, the most eminent West Indian poet, have drawn largely on British, American, and classical European models, though Walcott creolizes the rhythms, diction, and sensibility of English-language poetry. "I have Dutch, nigger, and English in me," declares the mulatto hero of "The Schooner *Flight*, "and either I'm nobody, or I'm a nation." Other poets have emphasized even more strongly Afro-Caribbean inheritances in speech and culture. When colonial prejudices still branded West Indian English, or Creole, a backward language, a "corruption" of English, the Afro-Jamaican poets Claude McKay and Louise Bennett claimed its wit, vibrancy, and proverbial richness for poetry. In the late 1960s the Barbadian Kamau (then Edward) Brathwaite revalued the linguistic, musical, and mythic survivals of Africa in the Caribbean—resources long repressed because of colonial attitudes. In poetry as well as fiction, Nigeria was the most prolific anglophone African nation around the time of independence, said to be the "golden age" of letters in sub-Saharan Africa. Wole Soyinka, later the first black African to win the Nobel Prize, stretched English syntax and figurative language in poems dense with Yoruba-inspired wordplay and myth. At the same time poets from India were bringing its great variety of indigenous cultures into English-language poetry. A. K. Ramanujan's sharply etched poems interfuse Anglo-modernist principles with the south Indian legacies of Tamil and Kannada poetry. All of these poets respond with emotional ambivalence and linguistic versatility to the experience of living after colonialism, between non-Western traditions and modernity, in a period of explosive change in the relation between Western and "native" cultures.

A century that began with a springtime of poetic innovation drew to its close with the full flowering of older poets such as Walcott, Hill, and Heaney, and the twenty-first century opened with welcome signs of fresh growth in English-language poetry, including new books by Paul Muldoon, Anne Carson, and Carol Ann Duffy.

FICTION

Novels—"loose baggy monsters," in Henry James's phrase—can be, can do, can include anything at all. The form defies prescriptions and limits. Yet its variety converges on persistent issues such as the construction of the self within society, the reproduction of the real world, and the temporality of human experience and of narrative. The novel's flexibility and porousness, its omnivorousness and multivoicedness have enabled writers to take advantage of modernity's global dislocation and mixture of peoples, while meeting the challenges to the imagination of mass death and world war, of the relentless and rapid mutations in modern cultures and societies, in evolving knowledge and belief.

The twentieth century's novels may be divided roughly into three main subperiods: high modernism through the 1920s, celebrating personal and textual inwardness, complexity, and difficulty; the reaction against modernism, involving a return to social realism, moralism, and assorted documentary endeavors, in the 1930s, 1940s, and 1950s; and the period after the collapse of the British Empire (especially from the time of the countercultural revolution of the 1960s), in which the fictional claims of various realisms—urban, proletarian, provincial English (e.g., northern), regional (e.g., Scottish and Irish), immigrant, postcolonial, feminist, gay—are asserted alongside, but also through, a continuing self-consciousness about language and form and meaning that is, in effect, the enduring legacy of modernism. By the end of the century, modernism had given way to the striking pluralism of postmodernism and postcolonialism. Yet the roots of the late-century panoramic mix of voices and styles lay in the early part of the century, when writers on the margins of "Englishness"—a Pole, Joseph Conrad; an Irishman, James Joyce; an American, Henry James; an Englishwoman, Virginia Woolf; and a working-class Englishman, D. H. Lawrence—were the most instrumental inventors of the modernist "English" novel.

The high modernists wrote in the wake of the shattering of confidence in the old certainties about the deity and the Christian faith, about the person, knowledge, materialism, history, the old grand narratives, which had, more or less, sustained the Western novel through the nineteenth century. They boldly ventured into this general shaking of belief in the novel's founding assumptions—that the world, things, and selves were knowable, that language was a reliably revelatory instrument, that the author's story gave history meaning and moral shape, that narratives should fall into ethically instructive beginnings, middles, and endings. Trying to be true to the new skepticisms and hesitations, the modernists also attempted to construct credible new alternatives to the old belief systems.

The once-prevailing nineteenth-century notions of ordinary reality came under serious attack. In her famous 1919 essay "Modern Fiction," Virginia Woolf explicitly assaulted the "materialism" of the realistic Edwardian heirs of Victorian naturalist confidence, Arnold Bennett, H. G. Wells, and John Galsworthy. For Woolf, as for other modernists, what was knowable, and thus representable, was not out there as some given, fixed, transcribable essence. Reality existed, rather, only as it was perceived. Hence the introduction of the impressionistic, flawed, even utterly unreliable narrator—a substitute for the classic nineteenth-century authoritative narrating voice, usually the voice of the author or some close substitute. Even a relatively reliable narrator, such as Conrad's Marlow, the main narrating voice of *Heart of Darkness,* as of *Lord Jim,* dramatized the struggle to know, penetrate, and interpret reality, with his large rhetoric of the invisible, inaudible, impossible, unintelligible, and so unsayable. The real was offered, thus, as refracted and reflected in the novel's representative consciousness. "Look within," Woolf urged the novelist. Reality and its truth had gone inward.

Woolf's subject would be "an ordinary mind on an ordinary day." The life that mattered most would now be mental life. And so the modernist novel turned resolutely inward, its concern being now with consciousness—a flow of reflections, momentary impressions, disjunctive bits of recall and half-memory, simultaneously revealing both the past and the way the past is repressed. Psychoanalysis partly enabled this concentration: to narrate the reality of persons as the life of the mind in all its complexity and inner tumult—consciousness, unconsciousness, id, libido, and so on. And the apparent truths of this inward life were, of course, utterly tricky, scattered, fragmentary, spotty, now illuminated, now twilit, now quite occluded. For Woolf, Joyce's *Ulysses* was a prime expression of this desired impressionistic agenda: "he is concerned at all costs to reveal the flickerings of that innermost flame which flashes its messages through the brain."

The characters of Joyce and Woolf are caught, then, as they are immersed in the so-called stream of consciousness; and some version of an interior flow of thought becomes the main modernist access to "character." The reader overhears the characters speaking, so to say, from within their particular consciousnesses, but not always directly. The modernists felt free also to enter their characters' minds, to speak as it were on their behalf, in the technique known as "free indirect style" (*style indirect libre* in French).

A marked feature of the new fictional selfhood was a fraught condition of existential loneliness. Conrad's Lord Jim, Joyce's Leopold Bloom and Stephen Dedalus, Lawrence's Paul Morel and Birkin, and Woolf's Mrs. Dalloway were people on their own, individuals bereft of the old props, Church, Bible, ideological consensus, and so doomed to make their own puzzled way through life's labyrinths without much confidence in belief, in the knowable solidity of the world, above all in language as a tool of knowledge about self and other. Jacob of Woolf's *Jacob's Room* remains stubbornly unknowable to his closest friends and loved ones, above all to his novelist. The walls and cupboards of Rhoda's room in *The Waves,* also by Woolf, bend disconcertingly around her bed; she tries in vain to restore her sense of the solidity of things by touching the bottom bed rail with her toes; her mind "pours" out of her; the very boundaries of her self soften, slip, dissolve. The old conclusive plots—everything resolved on the novel's last page, on the model of the detective story—gave place to irresolute open endings: the unending vista of the last paragraph in Lawrence's *Sons and Lovers;* the circularity by which the last sentence of Joyce's *Finnegans Wake* hooks back to be completed in the novel's first word, so that reading simply starts over.

Novelists built modern myths on the dry bones of the old Christian ones. In his review of *Ulysses* ("*Ulysses,* Order, and Myth," 1923), T. S. Eliot famously praised the novel for replacing the old "narrative method" by a new "mythical method": Joyce's Irish Jew, Bloom, is mythicized as a modern Ulysses, his day's odyssey often ironically reviving episodes in Homer's *Odyssey.* This manipulation of "a continuous parallel between contemporaneity and antiquity" was, Eliot thought, "a step toward making the modern world possible for art," much in keeping with the new anthropology and psychology as well as with what Yeats was doing in verse. Such private myth-making could, of course, take worrying turns. The "religion of the blood" that D. H. Lawrence celebrated led directly to the fascist sympathies of his *Aaron's Rod* and the revived Aztec blood cult of *The Plumed Serpent*.

Language and textuality, reading and writing were now central to these highly metafictional novels, which are often about writers and artists, and surrogates for artists, such as Woolf's Mrs. Ramsay with her dinners and Mrs. Dalloway with her party, producers of what Woolf called the "unpublished works of women." But this self-reflexivity was not necessarily consoling—Mrs. Flanders's vision blurs and an inkblot spreads across the postcard we find her writing in the opening page of *Jacob's Room*. Perhaps the greatest modernist example of language gone rampant, *Finnegans Wake* taxes even its most dedicated readers and verges on unreadability for others.

The skeptical modernist linguistic turn, the rejection of materialist externality and of the Victorians' realist project, left ineradicable traces on later fiction, but modernism's revolutions were not absolute or permanent. *Ulysses* and *Finnegans Wake* were influential but unrepeatable. And even within the greatest modernist fictions the worldly and the material, political and moral questions never dried up. Woolf and Joyce, for example, celebrate the perplexities of urban life in London and Dublin, and, indeed, modernist fiction is largely an art of the great city. Lawrence was preoccupied with the condition of England, industrialism, provincial life. Satire was one of modernism's recurrent notes. So it was not odd for the right-wing novelists who came through in the 1920s, such as Wyndham Lewis and Evelyn Waugh, to resort to the social subject and the satiric stance, nor for their left-leaning contemporaries—who came to be seen as even more characteristic of the red decade of the 1930s—such as Graham Greene and George Orwell, to engage with the human condition in ways that Dickens or Balzac, let alone Bennett-Wells-Galsworthy, would have recognized as not all that distant from their own spirit.

Despite the turn to documentary realism in the 1930s, the modernist emphasis on linguistic self-consciousness did not disappear. Instead the new writers politicized the modern novel's linguistic self-consciousness: they deployed the discourse of the unemployed or of the West Midlands' proletariat, for example, for political ends. The comically chaotic meeting of English and German languages in Christopher Isherwood's Berlin stories is central to the fiction's dire warning about Anglo-German politics; Newspeak in George Orwell's *Nineteen-Eighty-Four* is the culmination of the author's nearly two decades of politically motivated engagement with the ways of English speakers at home and abroad. In this politicized aftermath of the modernist experiment, novelists such as Aldous Huxley in *Brave New World* satirically engage the socio-politico-moral matter of the 1930s in part through reflections on the corruptions of language.

Where World War I was a great engine of modernism, endorsing the chaos of shattered belief, the fragility of language and of the human subject, the Spanish Civil War and then World War II confirmed the English novel in its return to registering the social scene and the historical event. World War II provoked whole series of more or less realist fictions, including Evelyn Waugh's *Sword of Honour* trilogy, as well as powerful singletons such as Graham Greene's *Ministry of Fear* and Waugh's *Brideshead Revisited*. The new fictions of the post–World War II period speak with the satirical energies of the young demobilized officer class (Kingsley Amis's *Lucky Jim* set the disgruntled tone), and of the ordinary provincial citizen finding a fictional voice yet again in the new Welfare State atmosphere of the 1950s, as in Alan Sillitoe's proletarian Nottingham novel *Saturday Night and Sunday Morning*.

Questing for new moral bases for the post-Holocaust nuclear age, William Golding published the first of many intense post-Christian moral fables with *The Lord of the Flies*, and Iris Murdoch the first of many novels of moral philosophy with *Under the Net*, both in 1954. Murdoch espoused the "sovereignty of good" and the importance of the novel's loving devotion to "the otherness of the other person." Murdoch and Golding were consciously retrospective (as were the contemporary Roman Catholic novelists Greene, Waugh, and Muriel Spark) in their investment in moral form. But even such firmly grounded determinations could not calm the anxieties of belatedness. As the century drew on, British fiction struggled with a disconcertingly pervasive sense of posteriority—postwar flatness, postimperial diminutions of power and influence, and the sense of the grand narratives now losing their force as never before.

Some younger novelists, such as Ian McEwan and Martin Amis (son of Kingsley), became obsessed with Germany (the now accusingly prosperous old foe), and with the still haunting ghosts of the *Hitlerzeit*—and not least after 1989, when the Berlin Wall came down and wartime European horrors stirred into vivid focus. The dereliction of the once-grand imperial center, London, became a main topic for McEwan and for Amis, as well as for the later Kingsley Amis and the ex-Rhodesian Doris Lessing. Whereas Conrad, E. M. Forster (*A Passage to India*), and Jean Rhys (*Wide Sargasso Sea*) had been harshly accusatory about Britain's overseas behavior, now nostalgia for old imperial days shrouded the pages of Lawrence Durrell's *Alexandria Quartet* and Paul Scott's *Raj Quartet* and *Staying On*. Observers of English fiction worried that the only tasks left for it were to ruminate over past history and rehash old stories. The modernist Joycean strategy of resurrecting ancient narratives to revitalize present consciousness had given way to a fear that the postmodern novelist was condemned to a disabled career of parroting old stuff. *On est parlé*, "one is spoken," rather than speaking for oneself, thinks the main character of Julian Barnes's *Flaubert's Parrot*, reflecting in some dismay on this dilemma. Ventriloquial reproduction of old voices became Peter Ackroyd's trademark. Worries about being merely possessed by the past came to seem central to late-twentieth-century English fiction, as in A. S. Byatt's *Possession*, which is about the magnetism of past (Victorian) writers and writings.

Yet this was also a time for the spectacular emergence of many robust new voices, particularly from assorted margins—writers for whom the enervation at the English center represented an opportunity for telling their untold stories. After a sensational trial in 1960, the ban on D. H. Lawrence's erotically explicit *Lady Chatterley's Lover* was finally lifted, ensuring greater freedom in the narrative exploration of sexuality. Relaxing views on gender roles, the influx of women into the workplace, and the collapse of the grand patriarchal narratives also gave impetus to feminist revisionary narratives of history, and the remaking of narrative technique as more fluid and free. In the 1980s and 1990s prominent and inventive women's voices included those of Jeanette Winterson, celebrator of women's arts and bodiliness, and Angela Carter, feminist neomythographer, reviser of fairy tales, rewriter of the Marquis de Sade, espouser of raucous and rebellious heroines. Among the chorus of voices seeking to express with new intimacy and vividness experiences once held taboo were those of uncloseted gay writers, such as Alan Hollinghurst, pioneer of the openly male-homosexual literary novel of the post–World War II period, and Adam Mars-Jones, short-story chronicler of the HIV/AIDS crisis. The literary counterpart for political decolonization and devolution within the British Isles was the emergence of a multitude of regional and national voices outside the south of England, many deploying a vigorously local idiom, such as the Scottish novelist Irvine Welsh and the Irish writer Roddy Doyle, who reached mass international audiences through 1990s film versions of their novels *Trainspotting* (Welsh) and *The Commitments* (Doyle).

While postimperial anxieties and exhaustion seemed to beset many postwar English writers, postcolonial novelists were energetically claiming for literature in English untold histories, hybrid identities, and vibrantly creolized vocabularies. A major phase in the huge geographic shift in the center of gravity of English-language fiction occurred during the postwar decolonization of much of South Asia, Africa, and the Caribbean, when Chinua Achebe's *Things Fall Apart* (1958) was published, just two years before Nigerian independence. Retelling the story of colonial incursion from an indigenous viewpoint, Achebe's influential novel intricately represents an African community before and after the arrival of whites, in a language made up of English and Igbo words, encompassed by a narrative that enmeshes African proverbs and oral tales with English realism and modernist reflexivity. A few years later and on the eve of his natal island's independence, the Trinidad-born writer V. S. Naipaul published his first major novel, *A House for Mr. Biswas* (1961), one of many works that brilliantly develop the potential of a translucent realist fiction to explore issues such as migrant identities, cross-cultural mimicry, and the spaces of colonialism. The Indian-born Salman Rushdie, more restive than Naipaul in relation to Englishness and English literary traditions, has exuberantly championed hybrid narrative forms made out of the fresh convergence of modern European fiction and "Third World" orality, magical realism, and polyglossia, his novels, such as *Midnight's Children* (1981) and *The Satanic Verses* (1988), wryly offering a "chutnification of history" in South Asia and in an Asianized England. The colonies where English literature had once been used to impose imperial models of "civilization" now gave rise to novelists who, ironically, outstripped in imaginative freshness, cultural energy, and narrative inventiveness their counterparts from the seat of the empire.

White fiction writers from the colonies and dominions, many of them women, and many of them resident in England, such as Katherine Mansfield, Doris Lessing, and Jean Rhys, had long brought fresh perspectives to the novel from the outposts of empire, each of these eminent writers sharply etching a feminist critique of women's lives diminished by subordination to the colonial order. South Africa, not least because of its fraught racial and political history, can count among its progeny some of the most celebrated fiction writers of the late twentieth century. Nadine Gordimer has extended the potential of an ethical narrative realism to probe the fierce moral challenges of apartheid and its aftermath, whereas J. M. Coetzee has used self-reflexively postmodern and allegorical forms to inquire into the tangled complexities and vexed complicities of white South African experience.

Late-twentieth-century and early-twenty-first-century "English" fiction would have looked startlingly thin and poverty-stricken were it not for the large presence in Britain of writers of non-European origin. Like the first modern novelists, many of the novelists who have most enriched English-language fiction in recent decades are migrants, émigrés, and expatriates, such as Naipaul and Rushdie, and such as the delicately ironic realist Kazuo Ishiguro, from Japan, and the postsurreal fabulist Wilson Harris, from Guyana. Still others are the sons and daughters of non-European immigrants to Britain, such as two of the most visible exemplars of the often comically cross-cultural fiction of a new multiracial England, Hanif Kureishi and Zadie Smith, both born on the peripheries of London, Kureishi to a Pakistani father and English mother, Smith to a Jamaican mother and English father. These and other "British" novelists of color, giving voice to new and emergent experiences of immigration, hybridization, and cross-racial encounter, take advantage of the novel's fecund polymorphousness with little anxiety about belatedness, no fright over parroting, and no neomodernist worries about attempting realistic encounters with the world.

DRAMA

Late Victorians from one perspective, Oscar Wilde and Bernard Shaw can also be seen as early moderns, forerunners of the twentieth century's renovators of dramatic form. The wit of Wilde's drawing-room comedies is combative and generative of paradoxes, but beneath the glitter of his verbal play are serious—if heavily coded—reflections on social, political, and feminist issues. Shaw brought still another kind of wit into drama—not Wilde's lighthearted sparkle but the provocative paradox that was meant to tease and disturb, to challenge the complacency of the audience. Over time the desire to unsettle, to shock, even to alienate the audience became one hallmark of modern drama.

Wilde and Shaw were both born in Ireland, and it was in Dublin that the century's first major theatrical movement originated. To nourish Irish poetic drama and foster the Irish literary renaissance, Yeats and Lady Augusta Gregory founded the Irish Literary Theatre in 1899, with Yeats's early nationalist play The Countess Cathleen as its first production. In 1902 the Irish Literary Theatre was able to maintain a permanent all-Irish company and changed its name to the Irish National Theatre, which moved in 1904 to the Abbey Theatre, by which name it has been known ever since. J. M. Synge brought the speech and imagination of Irish country people into theater, but the Abbey's 1907 staging of his play The Playboy of the Western World so offended orthodox religious and nationalist sentiment that the audience rioted. While defending Synge and other pioneers of Irish drama, Yeats also continued to write his own plays, which drew themes from old Irish legend and which, after 1913, stylized and ritualized theatrical performance on the model of Japanese Noh drama. In the 1920s Sean O'Casey brought new vitality to the Abbey Theatre, using the Easter Rising and Irish civil war as a background for controversial plays (one of which again sparked riots) that combined tragic melodrama, humor of character, and irony of circumstance. In England T. S. Eliot attempted with considerable success to revive a ritual poetic drama with his Murder in the Cathedral (1935), though his later attempts to combine religious symbolism with the chatter of entertaining society comedy, as in The Cocktail Party (1950), were uneven.

Despite the achievements of Yeats, Synge, O'Casey, and Eliot, it cannot be said of Irish and British drama, as it can of poetry and fiction in the first half of the century, that a technical revolution changed the whole course of literary history. The major innovations in the first half of the twentieth century were on the Continent. German expressionist drama developed out of the dark, psychological focus of the later plays of the Swedish dramatist August Strindberg (1849–1912). Another worldwide influence was the "epic" drama of the leftist German dramatist Bertolt Brecht (1898–1956): to foster ideological awareness, he rejected the idea that the audience should identify with a play's characters and become engrossed in its plot; the playwright should break the illusion of reality through the alienation effect (*Verfremdungseffekt*) and foreground the play's theatrical constructedness and historical specificity. The French dramatist Antonin Artaud (1896–1948) also defied realism and rationalism, but unlike Brecht, his theory of the theater of cruelty sought a transformative, mystical communion with the audience through incantations and sounds, physical gestures and strange scenery. Another French dramatist, the Romanian-born Eugène Ionesco (1909–1994), helped inaugurate the theater of the absurd just after World War II, in plays that enact people's hopeless efforts to communicate and that comically intimate a tragic vision of life devoid of meaning or purpose. In such Continental drama the influences of symbolism (on the later Strindberg), Marxism (on Brecht), and surrealism (on Artaud and Ionesco) contributed to the shattering of naturalistic convention in drama, making the theater a space where linear plot gave way to fractured scenes and circular action, transparent conversation was displaced by misunderstanding and verbal opacity, a predictable and knowable universe was unsettled by eruptions of the irrational and the absurd.

In Britain the impact of these Continental innovations was delayed by a conservative theater establishment until the late 1950s and 1960s, when they converged with the countercultural revolution to transform the nature of English-language theater. Meanwhile the person who played the most significant role in the anglophone absorption of modernist experiment was the Irishman Samuel Beckett. He changed the history of drama with his first produced play, written in French in 1948 and translated by the author as *Waiting for Godot* (premiered in Paris in 1953, in London in 1955). The play astonishingly did away with plot ("Nothing happens—twice," as one critic put it), as did *Endgame* (1958) and Beckett's later plays, such as *Not I* (1973) and *That Time* (1976). In the shadow of the mass death of World War II, the plotlessness, the minimal characterization and setting, the absurdist intimation of an existential darkness without redemption, the tragicomic melding of anxiety, circular wordplay, and slapstick action in Beckett's plays gave impetus to a seismic shift in British writing for the theater.

The epicenter of the new developments in British drama was the Royal Court Theatre, symbolically located a little away from London's West End "theater land" (the rough equivalent of Broadway in New York). From 1956 the Royal Court was the home of the English Stage Company. Together they provided a venue and a vision that provoked and enabled a new wave of writers. John Osborne's *Look Back in Anger* (1956), the hit of the ESC's first season (significantly helped by the play's television broadcast), offered the audience "lessons in feeling" through a searing depiction of class-based indignation, emotional cruelty, and directionless angst, all in a surprisingly nonmetropolitan setting. At the Royal Court the working-class naturalism of the so-called "kitchen sink" dramatists and other "angry young men" of the 1950s, such as Arnold Wesker, author of the trilogy *Chicken Soup with Barley* (1958), also broke with the genteel proprieties and narrowly upper-class set designs that, in one unadventurous drawing-room comedy after another, had dominated the British stage for decades. The political consciousness of the new theater was still more evident in John Arden's plays produced for the Royal Court, such as *Sergeant Musgrave's Dance* (1959), which explores colonial oppression, communal guilt for wartime atrocities, and pacifism in the stylized setting of an isolated mining town. By the later 1960s the influence of the counterculture on British theater was unavoidable. Joe Orton challenged bourgeois sentiment in a series of classically precise, blackly comic, and sexually ambiguous parodies, such as his farce *What the Butler Saw* (1969).

While plays of social and political critique were one response to the postwar period, Beckett and the theater of the absurd inspired another group of Royal Court writers to refocus theater on language, symbolism, and existential realities. Informed by kitchen-sink naturalism and absurdism, Harold Pinter's "comedies of menace" map out a social trajectory from his early study of working-class stress and inarticulate anxiety, *The Room* (1957), through the film-noirish black farce of *The Dumb Waiter* (1960) and the emotional power plays of *The Caretaker* (1960), to the savagely comic study of middle-class escape from working-class mores in *The Homecoming* (1965). Later plays reflect on patrician suspicion and betrayal, though in the 1980s his work acquired a more overtly political voice. Though less bleak than Pinter, Tom Stoppard is no less indebted to Beckett's wordplay, skewed conversations, and theatrical technique, as evidenced by *Rosencrantz and Guildenstern Are Dead* (1967) and other plays, many of which embed within themselves earlier literary works (such as *Godot* and *Hamlet*) and thus offer virtuoso postmodernist reflections on art, language, and performance. This enjoyment and exploitation of self-conscious theatricality arises partly out of the desire to show theater as different from film and television and is also apparent in the 1970s productions of another playwright: the liturgical stylization of Peter Shaffer's *Equus* (1973) and the bleak mental landscape of his Antonio Salieri in *Amadeus* (1979) emphasize the stage as battleground and site of struggle (an effect lost in their naturalistic film versions). Stoppard's time shifts and memory lapses in *Travesties* (1974) allow a nonnaturalistic study of the role of memory and imagination in the creative process, a theme he returns to in *Arcadia* (1993), a stunning double-exposure account of a Romantic poet and his modern critical commentators occupying the same physical space but never reaching intellectual common ground.

Legal reform intensified the postwar ferment in British theater. Since the Theatres Act of 1843, writers for the public stage had been required to submit their playscripts to the Lord Chamberlain's office for state censorship, but in 1968 a new Theatres Act abolished that office. With this new freedom from conservative mores and taste, Howard Brenton, Howard Barker, Edward Bond, and David Hare were able to write challenging studies of violence, social deprivation, and political and sexual aggression, often using mythical settings and epic stories to construct austere tableaux of power and oppression. Bond's *Lear* (1971) typifies his ambitious combination of soaring lyrical language and alienatingly realistic violence. Directors such as Peter Brook took advantage of the new freedom in plays that emphasized, as had Artaud's theater of cruelty, physical gesture, bodily movement, and ritualized spectacle. The post-1968 liberalization also encouraged the emergence of new theater groups addressing specific political agendas, many of them inspired by Brecht's "epic" theater's distancing, discontinuous, and socially critical style. Companies such as Monstrous Regiment, Gay Sweatshop, Joint Stock, and John McGrath's 7: 84 worked collaboratively with dramatists who were invited to help devise and develop shows. Increasingly in the 1970s published plays were either transcriptions of the first production or "blueprints for the alchemy of live performance" (Micheline Wandor). In Ireland the founding of the Field Day Theatre Company in 1980 by the well-established playwright Brian Friel and actor Stephen Rea had similar motives of collaborative cultural catalysis. Their first production, Friel's *Translations* (1980), exploring linguistic colonialism and the fragility of cultural identity in nineteenth-century Ireland, achieved huge international success.

This ethos of collaboration and group development helped foster the first major cohort of women dramatists to break through onto mainstream stages. Working with Joint Stock and Monstrous Regiment in the late 1970s on plays such as the gender-bending anticolonial *Cloud Nine* (1979), Caryl Churchill developed plays out of workshops exploring gender, class, and colonialism. She carefully transcribes and overlaps the speech of her characters to create a seamlessly interlocking web of discourse, a streamlined version of the ebb and flow of normal speech. In *Top Girls* (1982) and *Serious Money* (1987), plays that anatomize the market-driven ethos of the 1980s, she explores modern society with the wit and detachment of Restoration comedy. Pam Gems studies the social and sexual politics of misogyny and feminism in her campy theatrical explorations of strong women—*Queen Cristina* (1977), *Piaf* (1978), *Camille* (1984)—while Sarah Daniels reinterprets the naturalism of kitchen-sink drama by adding to it the linguistic stylization of Churchill.

Massive strides in the diversification of English-language theater occurred during the era of decolonization, when two eminent poets, Derek Walcott and Wole Soyinka, helped breathe new life into anglophone drama. As early as the 1950s Derek Walcott was writing and directing plays about Caribbean history and experience, re-creating in his drama a West Indian "oral culture, of chants, jokes, folk-songs, and fables," at a time when theater in the Caribbean tended to imitate European themes and styles. After moving to Trinidad in 1958, he founded what came to be known as the Trinidad Theatre Workshop, and for much of the next twenty years devoted himself to directing and writing plays that included *Dream on Monkey Mountain*, first produced in 1967, in which Eurocentric and Afrocentric visions of Caribbean identity collide. Since then, a notable breakthrough in Caribbean theater has been the collaborative work of the Sistren Theatre Collective in Jamaica, which, following the lead of Louise Bennett and other West Indian poets, draws on women's personal histories in dramatic performances that make vivid use of Jamaican speech, expression, and rhythm. Meanwhile in Africa, Wole Soyinka, who had been involved with the Royal Court Theatre in the late 1950s when Brecht's influence was first being absorbed, returned to Nigeria in the year of its independence to write and direct plays that fused Euromodernist dramatic techniques with conventions from Yoruba popular and traditional drama. His play *Death and the King's Horseman*, premiered in Nigeria in 1976, represents a tragic confrontation between colonial officials and the guardians of Yoruba rituals and beliefs. While Soyinka has been a towering presence in sub-Saharan Africa, other playwrights, such as the fellow Nigerian Femi Osofisan and the South African Athol Fugard, have used the stage to probe issues of class, race, and the often violent legacy of colonialism. In England playwrights of Caribbean, African, and Asian origin or descent, such as Mustapha Matura, Caryl

Phillips, and Hanif Kureishi, the latter of whom is best-known internationally for his screenplays for *My Beautiful Laundrette* (1985), *Sammy and Rosie Get Laid* (1988), *My Son the Fanatic* (1998), and *The Mother* (2004), have revitalized British drama with a host of new vocabularies, new techniques, new visions of identity in an increasingly cross-ethnic and transnational world. The century that began with its first great dramatic movement in Ireland was followed by a century that began with English-language drama more diverse in its accents and styles, more international in its bearings and vision than ever before.

———————

Additional information about the Twentieth Century and After, including primary texts and images, is available at Norton Literature Online (www .wwnorton.literature). Online topics are

- Representing the Great War
- Modernist Experiment
- Imagining Ireland

TEXTS	CONTEXTS
1899, 1902 Joseph Conrad, *Heart of Darkness*	
	1900 Max Planck, quantum theory
	1901 First wireless communication across the Atlantic
	1901–10 Reign of Edward VII
	1902 End of the Anglo-Boer War
	1903 Henry Ford introduces the first mass-produced car. Wright Brothers make the first successful airplane flight
	1905 Albert Einstein, theory of special relativity. Impressionist exhibition, London
1910 Bernard Shaw, *Pygmalion*	**1910** Postimpressionist exhibition, London
	1910–36 Reign of George V
1913 Ezra Pound, "A Few Don'ts by an Imagiste"	
1914 James Joyce, *Dubliners*. Thomas Hardy, *Satires of Circumstance*	**1914–18** World War I
1914–15 *Blast*	
1916 Joyce, *A Portrait of the Artist as a Young Man*	**1916** Easter Rising in Dublin
1917 T. S. Eliot, "The Love Song of J. Alfred Prufrock"	
1918 Gerard Manley Hopkins, *Poems*	**1918** Armistice. Franchise Act grants vote to women thirty and over
1920 D. H. Lawrence, *Women in Love*. Wilfred Owen, *Poems*	**1920** Treaty of Versailles. League of Nations formed
1921 William Butler Yeats, *Michael Robartes and the Dancer*	**1921–22** Formation of Irish Free State with Northern Ireland (Ulster) remaining part of Great Britain
1922 Katherine Mansfield, *The Garden Party and Other Stories*. Joyce, *Ulysses*. Eliot, *The Waste Land.*	
1924 Forster, *A Passage to India*	
1927 Virginia Woolf, *To the Lighthouse*	
1928 Yeats, *The Tower*	**1928** Women twenty-one and over granted voting rights
1929 Woolf, *A Room of One's Own*. Robert Graves, *Goodbye to All That*	**1929** Stock market crash; Great Depression begins
	1933 Hitler comes to power in Germany
1935 Eliot, *Murder in the Cathedral*	

TEXTS	CONTEXTS
	1936–39 Spanish Civil War
	1936 Edward VIII succeeds George V, but abdicates in favor of his brother, crowned as George VI
1937 David Jones, *In Parenthesis*	
1939 Joyce, *Finnegans Wake*. Yeats, *Last Poems and Two Plays*	1939–45 World War II
1940 W. H. Auden, *Another Time*	1940 Fall of France. Battle of Britain
	1941–45 The Holocaust
1943 Eliot, *Four Quartets*	
1945 Auden, *Collected Poems*. George Orwell, *Animal Farm*	1945 First atomic bombs dropped, on Japan
1946 Dylan Thomas, *Deaths and Entrances*	
	1947 India and Pakistan become independent nations
	1948 *Empire Windrush* brings West Indians to U.K.
1949 Orwell, *Nineteen-Eighty-Four*	
	1950 Apartheid laws passed in South Africa
1953 Premiere of Samuel Beckett's *Waiting for Godot*	
	1956 Suez Crisis
	1957 Ghana becomes independent
1958 Chinua Achebe, *Things Fall Apart*	
	1960 Nigeria becomes independent
	1961 Berlin Wall erected
1962 Doris Lessing, *The Golden Notebook*	1962 Cuban missile crisis. Uganda, Jamaica, Trinidad and Tobago become independent
1964 Philip Larkin, *The Whitsun Weddings*	
	1965 U.S. troops land in South Vietnam
1966 Nadine Gordimer, *The Late Bourgeois World*. Tom Stoppard, *Rosencrantz and Guildenstern Are Dead*. Jean Rhys, *Wide Sargasso Sea*	1966 Barbados and Guyana become independent
	1969 Apollo moon landing
1971 V. S. Naipaul, *In a Free State*	1971 Indo-Pakistan War, leading to creation of Bangladesh
	1972 Britain enters European Common Market
	1973 U.S. troops leave Vietnam
1975 Seamus Heaney, *North*	

TEXTS	CONTEXTS
1979 Caryl Churchill, *Cloud 9*	1979 Islamic Revolution in Iran; the Shah flees. Soviets invade Afghanistan
	1979–90 Margaret Thatcher is British prime minister
1980 J. M. Coetzee, *Waiting for the Barbarians*	1980–88 Iran-Iraq War
1981 Salman Rushdie, *Midnight's Children*. Brian Friel, *Translations*	
	1982 Falklands War
1985 Production of Hanif Kureishi's *My Beautiful Laundrette*	
1988 Rushdie, *The Satanic Verses*	
1989 Kazuo Ishiguro, *The Remains of the Day*	1989 Fall of the Berlin Wall. Tiananmen Square, Beijing, demonstration and massacre
1990 Derek Walcott, *Omeros*	
	1991 Collapse of the Soviet Union
1992 Thom Gunn, *The Man with Night Sweats*	
1993 Tom Stoppard, *Arcadia*	
	1994 Democracy comes to South Africa
1997 Arundhati Roy, *The God of Small Things*	1997 Labour Party victory in the U.K. ends eighteen years of Conservative government
	1998 British handover of Hong Kong to China. Northern Ireland Assembly established
1999 Carol Ann Duffy, *The World's Wife*	
2000 Zadie Smith, *White Teeth*	
	2001 September 11 attacks destroy World Trade Center
2002 Paul Muldoon, *Moy Sand and Gravel*	2002 Euro becomes sole currency in most of European Union
	2003 Invasion of Iraq led by U.S. and U.K.

THOMAS HARDY
1840–1928

Thomas Hardy was born near Dorchester, in that area of southwest England that he was to make the "Wessex" of his novels. He attended local schools until the age of fifteen, when he was apprenticed to a Dorchester architect with whom he worked for six years. In 1861 he went to London to continue his studies and to practice as an architect. Meanwhile he was completing his general education informally through his own erratic reading and was becoming more and more interested in both fiction and poetry. After some early attempts at writing both short stories and poems, he decided to concentrate on fiction. His first novel was rejected by the publishers in 1868 on the recommendation of George Meredith, who nevertheless advised Hardy to write another. The result was *Desperate Remedies,* published anonymously in 1871, followed the next year by his first real success (also published anonymously), *Under the Greenwood Tree.* His career as a novelist was now well launched; Hardy gave up his architectural work and produced a series of novels that ended with *Jude the Obscure* in 1895. The hostile reception of this novel—lambasted as *Jude the Obscene*—sent him back to poetry. Straddling the Victorian and modern periods, he published all his novels in the nineteenth century, all but the first of his poetry collections, *Wessex and Other Verses* (1898), in the twentieth. His remarkable epic-drama of the Napoleonic Wars, *The Dynasts,* came out in three parts between 1903 and 1908; after this he wrote mostly lyric poetry.

Hardy's novels, set in a predominantly rural "Wessex," show the forces of nature outside and inside individuals combining to shape human destiny. Against a background of immemorial agricultural labor, with ancient monuments such as Stonehenge or an old Roman amphitheater reminding us of the human past, he presents characters at the mercy of their own passions or finding temporary salvation in the age-old rhythms of rural work or rural recreation. Men and women in Hardy's fiction are not masters of their fates; they are at the mercy of the indifferent forces that manipulate their behavior and their relations with others, but they can achieve dignity through endurance, heroism, or simple strength of character. The characteristic Victorian novelist—e.g., Dickens or Thackeray—was concerned with the behavior and problems of people in a given social milieu, which were described in detail; Hardy preferred to go directly for the elemental in human behavior with a minimum of contemporary social detail. Most of his novels are tragic, exploring the bitter ironies of life with an almost malevolent staging of coincidence to emphasize the disparity between human desire and ambition on the one hand and what fate has in store for the characters on the other. But fate is not a wholly external force. Men and women are driven by the demands of their own nature as much as by anything outside them. Perhaps the darkest of Hardy's novels, *Tess of the D'Urbervilles* (1891) is the story of an intelligent and sensitive young woman, daughter of a poor family, driven to murder and so to death by hanging, by a painfully ironic concatenation of events and circumstances. Published in the same year as *Tess,* the story anthologized here, "On the Western Circuit," similarly has at its center a young country woman seduced by a sophisticated city man; her "ruin" (see also Hardy's poem "The Ruined Maid") leads—contrary to the good intentions of the three protagonists, and again as the result of bitter irony—to *his* ruin and a lifetime of misery for all concerned.

Hardy denied that he was a pessimist, calling himself a "meliorist"—that is, one who believes that the world can be made better by human effort. But there is little sign of meliorism in either his most important novels or his lyric poetry. A number of his poems, such as the one he wrote about the *Titanic* disaster, "The Convergence of the Twain," illustrate the perversity of fate, the disastrous or ironic coincidence. Other poems go beyond this mood to present with quiet gravity and a carefully controlled elegiac feeling some aspect of human sorrow or loss or frustration or regret, always grounded in a particular, fully realized situation. "Hap" shows Hardy in the characteristic mood of complaining about the irony of human destiny in a universe ruled by chance, but a poem such as "The Walk" (one of a group of poems written after the death of his first wife in 1912) gives, with remarkable power, concrete embodiment to a sense of loss.

Hardy's poetry, like his prose, often has a self-taught air about it; both can seem, on first reading, roughly hewn. He said he wanted to avoid "the jewelled line," and like many modern and contemporary poets, he sought instead what he called "dissonances, and other irregularities" in his art, because these convey more authenticity and spontaneity. "Art is a disproportioning . . . of realities," he declared. Though he adheres to the metered line, Hardy roughens prosody and contorts syntax, and he creates irregular and complex stanza forms. His diction includes archaisms and deliberately awkward coinages (e.g., "Powerfuller" and "unblooms" in "Hap"). He distorts many conventions of traditional genres such as the sonnet, the love poem, the war poem, and the elegy. Though rooted in the Victorian period, Hardy thus looks ahead to the dislocations of poetic form carried out by subsequent poets of the twentieth century.

The sadness in Hardy—his inability to believe in the government of the world by a benevolent God, his sense of the waste and frustration involved in human life, his insistent irony when faced with moral or metaphysical questions—is part of the late-Victorian mood, found also, say, in A. E. Housman's poetry and, earlier, in Edward FitzGerald's *Rubáiyát of Omar Khayyám,* published when Hardy was nineteen. What has been termed "the disappearance of God" affected him more deeply than it did many of his contemporaries, because until he was twenty-five he seriously considered becoming an Anglican priest. Yet his characteristic themes and attitudes cannot be related simply to the reaction to new scientific and philosophical ideas (Darwin's theory of evolution, for example) that we see in many forms in late-nineteenth-century literature. The favorite poetic mood of both Tennyson and Arnold was also an elegiac one (e.g., in Tennyson's "Break, Break, Break" and Arnold's "Dover Beach"), but the mood of Hardy's poetry differs from Victorian sorrow; it is sterner, more skeptical, as though braced by a long look at the worst. It is this sternness, this ruggedness of his poetry, together with its verbal and emotional integrity, its formal variety and tonal complexity, its quietly searching individual accent, that helped bring about the steady rise in Hardy's reputation as a poet. Ezra Pound remarked in a 1934 letter: "Nobody has taught me anything about writing since Thomas Hardy died." W. H. Auden begins an essay with this testament to the effect of Hardy's verse: "I cannot write objectively about Thomas Hardy because I was once in love with him." And Hardy appears as the major figure—with more poems than either Yeats or Eliot—in Philip Larkin's influential *Oxford Book of Twentieth-Century English Verse* (1973).

On the Western Circuit[1]

I

The man who played the disturbing part in the two quiet feminine lives hereunder depicted—no great man, in any sense, by the way—first had knowledge of them on an October evening, in the city of Melchester. He had been standing in the Close,[2] vainly endeavouring to gain amid the darkness a

---

1. When first published in magazine form in England and America in 1891, "On the Western Circuit" was altered to minimize its illicit sexuality. References to Anna's seduction and pregnancy were eliminated, and Mrs. Harnham was made a widow rather than a wife. When Hardy published the story in his collection *Life's Little Ironies*

(1894), he restored it to its original form. The Western Circuit was the subdivision of England's High Court of Justice with jurisdiction over the southwestern counties. In Hardy's literary landscape Melchester is Salisbury, which has a particularly beautiful cathedral.

2. Closed yard surrounding a church.

glimpse of the most homogeneous pile of mediæval architecture in England, which towered and tapered from the damp and level sward[3] in front of him. While he stood the presence of the Cathedral walls was revealed rather by the ear than by the eyes; he could not see them, but they reflected sharply a roar of sound which entered the Close by a street leading from the city square, and, falling upon the building, was flung back upon him.

He postponed till the morrow his attempt to examine the deserted edifice, and turned his attention to the noise. It was compounded of steam barrel-organs, the clanging of gongs, the ringing of hand-bells, the clack of rattles, and the undistinguishable shouts of men. A lurid light hung in the air in the direction of the tumult. Thitherward he went, passing under the arched gate-way, along a straight street, and into the square.

He might have searched Europe over for a greater contrast between juxta-posed scenes. The spectacle was that of the eighth chasm of the Inferno as to colour and flame, and, as to mirth, a development of the Homeric heaven. A smoky glare, of the complexion of brass-filings, ascended from the fiery tongues of innumerable naphtha lamps affixed to booths, stalls, and other temporary erections which crowded the spacious market-square. In front of this irradiation scores of human figures, more or less in profile, were darting athwart and across, up, down, and around, like gnats against a sunset.

Their motions were so rhythmical that they seemed to be moved by machin-ery. And it presently appeared that they were moved by machinery indeed; the figures being those of the patrons of swings, see-saws, flying-leaps, above all of the three steam roundabouts[4] which occupied the centre of the position. It was from the latter that the din of steam-organs came.

Throbbing humanity in full light was, on second thoughts, better than archi-tecture in the dark. The young man, lighting a short pipe, and putting his hat on one side and one hand in his pocket, to throw himself into harmony with his new environment, drew near to the largest and most patronized of the steam circuses, as the roundabouts were called by their owners. This was one of brilliant finish, and it was now in full revolution. The musical instrument around which and to whose tones the riders revolved, directed its trumpet-mouths of brass upon the young man, and the long plate-glass mirrors set at angles, which revolved with the machine, flashed the gyrating personages and hobby-horses kaleidoscopically into his eyes.

It could now be seen that he was unlike the majority of the crowd. A gen-tlemanly young fellow, one of the species found in large towns only, and Lon-don particularly, built on delicate lines, well, though not fashionably dressed, he appeared to belong to the professional class; he had nothing square or practical about his look, much that was curvilinear and sensuous. Indeed, some would have called him a man not altogether typical of the middle-class male of a century wherein sordid ambition is the master-passion that seems to be taking the time-honoured place of love.

The revolving figures passed before his eyes with an unexpected and quiet grace in a throng whose natural movements did not suggest gracefulness or quietude as a rule. By some contrivance there was imparted to each of the hobby-horses a motion which was really the triumph and perfection of round-about inventiveness—a galloping rise and fall, so timed that, of each pair of steeds, one was on the spring while the other was on the pitch. The riders were quite fascinated by these equine undulations in this most delightful

---

3. Grassy surface of ground.   4. Carousels.

holiday-game of our times. There were riders as young as six, and as old as sixty years, with every age between. At first it was difficult to catch a personality, but by and by the observer's eyes centred on the prettiest girl out of the several pretty ones revolving.

It was not that one with the light frock and light hat whom he had been at first attracted by; no, it was the one with the black cape, grey skirt, light gloves and—no, not even she, but the one behind her; she with the crimson skirt, dark jacket, brown hat and brown gloves. Unmistakably that was the prettiest girl.

Having finally selected her, this idle spectator studied her as well as he was able during each of her brief transits across his visual field. She was absolutely unconscious of everything save the act of riding: her features were rapt in an ecstatic dreaminess; for the moment she did not know her age or her history or her lineaments, much less her troubles. He himself was full of vague latter-day glooms and popular melancholies, and it was a refreshing sensation to behold this young thing then and there, absolutely as happy as if she were in a Paradise.

Dreading the moment when the inexorable stoker, grimily lurking behind the glittering rococo-work,[5] should decide that this set of riders had had their pennyworth, and bring the whole concern of steam-engine, horses, mirrors, trumpets, drums, cymbals, and such-like to pause and silence, he waited for her every reappearance, glancing indifferently over the intervening forms, including the two plainer girls, the old woman and child, the two youngsters, the newly-married couple, the old man with a clay pipe, the sparkish youth with a ring, the young ladies in the chariot, the pair of journeyman[6]-carpenters, and others, till his select country beauty followed on again in her place. He had never seen a fairer product of nature, and at each round she made a deeper mark in his sentiments. The stoppage then came, and the sighs of the riders were audible.

He moved round to the place at which he reckoned she would alight; but she retained her seat. The empty saddles began to refill, and she plainly was deciding to have another turn. The young man drew up to the side of her steed, and pleasantly asked her if she had enjoyed her ride.

'O yes!' she said, with dancing eyes. 'It has been quite unlike anything I have ever felt in my life before!'

It was not difficult to fall into conversation with her. Unreserved—too unreserved—by nature, she was not experienced enough to be reserved by art, and after a little coaxing she answered his remarks readily. She had come to live in Melchester from a village on the Great Plain,[7] and this was the first time that she had ever seen a steam-circus; she could not understand how such wonderful machines were made. She had come to the city on the invitation of Mrs Harnham, who had taken her into her household to train her as a servant, if she showed any aptitude. Mrs Harnham was a young lady who before she married had been Miss Edith White, living in the country near the speaker's cottage; she was now very kind to her through knowing her in childhood so well. She was even taking the trouble to educate her. Mrs Harnham was the only friend she had in the world, and being without children had wished to

5. Florid ornamentation. "Stoker": man who stokes the furnace powering the "steam circus."
6. Craftsman who has completed an apprenticeship but not yet attained mastership of his craft or guild.
7. In Hardy's Wessex the Salisbury Plain, a large plateau on which stands Stonehenge.

have her near her in preference to anybody else, though she had only lately come; allowed her to do almost as she liked, and to have a holiday whenever she asked for it. The husband of this kind young lady was a rich wine-merchant of the town, but Mrs Harnham did not care much about him. In the daytime you could see the house from where they were talking. She, the speaker, liked Melchester better than the lonely country, and she was going to have a new hat for next Sunday that was to cost fifteen and ninepence.[8]

Then she inquired of her acquaintance where he lived, and he told her in London, that ancient and smoky city, where everybody lived who lived at all, and died because they could not live there. He came into Wessex two or three times a year for professional reasons; he had arrived from Wintoncester yesterday, and was going on into the next county in a day or two. For one thing he did like the country better than the town, and it was because it contained such girls as herself.

Then the pleasure-machine started again, and, to the light-hearted girl, the figure of the handsome young man, the market-square with its lights and crowd, the houses beyond, and the world at large, began moving round as before, countermoving in the revolving mirrors on her right hand, she being as it were the fixed point in an undulating, dazzling, lurid universe, in which loomed forward most prominently of all the form of her late interlocutor. Each time that she approached the half of her orbit that lay nearest him they gazed at each other with smiles, and with that unmistakable expression which means so little at the moment, yet so often leads up to passion, heart-ache, union, disunion, devotion, overpopulation, drudgery, content, resignation, despair.

When the horses slowed anew he stepped to her side and proposed another heat. 'Hang the expense for once,' he said. 'I'll pay!'

She laughed till the tears came.

'Why do you laugh, dear?' said he.

'Because—you are so genteel that you must have plenty of money, and only say that for fun!' she returned.

'Ha-ha!' laughed the young man in unison, and gallantly producing his money she was enabled to whirl on again.

As he stood smiling there in the motley crowd, with his pipe in his hand, and clad in the rough pea-jacket and wideawake[9] that he had put on for his stroll, who would have supposed him to be Charles Bradford Raye, Esquire, stuff-gownsman,[1] educated at Wintoncester, called to the Bar at Lincoln's-Inn,[2] now going the Western Circuit, merely detained in Melchester by a small arbitration after his brethren had moved on to the next county-town?

II

The square was overlooked from its remoter corner by the house of which the young girl had spoken, a dignified residence of considerable size, having several windows on each floor. Inside one of these, on the first floor, the apartment being a large drawing-room, sat a lady, in appearance from twenty-

---

8. Approximately one dollar.
9. Soft felt hat.
1. A junior counsel, who wears a gown of "stuff" rather than silk; qualified to plead cases in court but not appointed to a senior position.
2. One of the four London Inns of Court, at which lawyers must be trained to qualify for the bar and to which they afterward must belong to practice law. "Wintoncester": Winchester College, the oldest English public school (the equivalent in the American system of an elite private secondary boarding school).

eight to thirty years of age. The blinds were still undrawn, and the lady was absently surveying the weird scene without, her cheek resting on her hand. The room was unlit from within, but enough of the glare from the market-place entered it to reveal the lady's face. She was what is called an interesting creature rather than a handsome woman; dark-eyed, thoughtful, and with sensitive lips.

A man sauntered into the room from behind and came forward.

'O, Edith, I didn't see you,' he said. 'Why are you sitting here in the dark?'

'I am looking at the fair,' replied the lady in a languid voice.

'Oh? Horrid nuisance every year! I wish it could be put a stop to.'

'I like it.'

'H'm. There's no accounting for taste.'

For a moment he gazed from the window with her, for politeness sake, and then went out again.

In a few minutes she rang.

'Hasn't Anna come in?' asked Mrs Harnham.

'No m'm.'

'She ought to be in by this time. I meant her to go for ten minutes only.'

'Shall I go and look for her, m'm?' said the house-maid alertly.

'No. It is not necessary: she is a good girl and will come soon.'

However, when the servant had gone Mrs Harnham arose, went up to her room, cloaked and bonneted herself, and proceeded downstairs, where she found her husband.

'I want to see the fair,' she said; 'and I am going to look for Anna. I have made myself responsible for her, and must see she comes to no harm. She ought to be indoors. Will you come with me?'

'Oh, she's all right. I saw her on one of those whirligig things, talking to her young man as I came in. But I'll go if you wish, though I'd rather go a hundred miles the other way.'

'Then please do so. I shall come to no harm alone.'

She left the house and entered the crowd which thronged the market-place, where she soon discovered Anna, seated on the revolving horse. As soon as it stopped Mrs Harnham advanced and said severely, 'Anna, how can you be such a wild girl? You were only to be out for ten minutes.'

Anna looked blank, and the young man, who had dropped into the background, came to help her alight.

'Please don't blame her,' he said politely. 'It is my fault that she has stayed. She looked so graceful on the horse that I induced her to go round again. I assure you that she has been quite safe.'

'In that case I'll leave her in your hands,' said Mrs Harnham, turning to retrace her steps.

But this for the moment it was not so easy to do. Something had attracted the crowd to a spot in their rear, and the wine-merchant's wife, caught by its sway, found herself pressed against Anna's acquaintance without power to move away. Their faces were within a few inches of each other, his breath fanned her cheek as well as Anna's. They could do no other than smile at the accident; but neither spoke, and each waited passively. Mrs Harnham then felt a man's hand clasping her fingers, and from the look of consciousness on the young fellow's face she knew the hand to be his: she also knew that from the position of the girl he had no other thought than that the imprisoned hand was Anna's. What prompted her to refrain from undeceiving him she could hardly tell. Not content with holding the hand, he playfully slipped two of his fingers inside her glove, against her palm. Thus matters continued till the pressure lessened; but several minutes passed before the crowd thinned sufficiently to allow Mrs Harnham to withdraw.

'How did they get to know each other, I wonder?' she mused as she retreated. 'Anna is really very forward—and he very wicked and nice.'

She was so gently stirred with the stranger's manner and voice, with the tenderness of his idle touch, that instead of re-entering the house she turned back again and observed the pair from a screened nook. Really she argued (being little less impulsive than Anna herself) it was very excusable in Anna to encourage him, however she might have contrived to make his acquaintance; he was so gentlemanly, so fascinating, had such beautiful eyes. The thought that he was several years her junior produced a reasonless sigh.

At length the couple turned from the roundabout towards the door of Mrs Harnham's house, and the young man could be heard saying that he would accompany her home. Anna, then, had found a lover, apparently a very devoted one. Mrs Harnham was quite interested in him. When they drew near the door of the wine-merchant's house, a comparatively deserted spot by this time, they stood invisible for a little while in the shadow of a wall, where they separated, Anna going on to the entrance, and her acquaintance returning across the square.

'Anna,' said Mrs Harnham, coming up. 'I've been looking at you! That young man kissed you at parting, I am almost sure.'

'Well,' stammered Anna; 'he said, if I didn't mind—it would do me no harm, and, and, him a great deal of good!'

'Ah, I thought so! And he was a stranger till tonight?'

'Yes ma'am.'

'Yet I warrant you told him your name and everything about yourself?'

'He asked me.'

'But he didn't tell you his?'

'Yes ma'am, he did!' cried Anna victoriously. 'It is Charles Bradford, of London.'

'Well, if he's respectable, of course I've nothing to say against your knowing him,' remarked her mistress, prepossessed, in spite of general principles, in the young man's favour. 'But I must reconsider all that, if he attempts to renew your acquaintance. A country-bred girl like you, who has never lived in Melchester till this month, who had hardly ever seen a black-coated man till you came here, to be so sharp as to capture a young Londoner like him!'

'I didn't capture him. I didn't do anything,' said Anna, in confusion.

When she was indoors and alone Mrs Harnham thought what a well-bred and chivalrous young man Anna's companion had seemed. There had been a magic in his wooing touch of her hand; and she wondered how he had come to be attracted by the girl.

The next morning the emotional Edith Harnham went to the usual week-day service in Melchester cathedral. In crossing the Close through the fog she again perceived him who had interested her the previous evening, gazing up thoughtfully at the high-piled architecture of the nave: and as soon as she had taken her seat he entered and sat down in a stall opposite hers.

He did not particularly heed her; but Mrs Harnham was continually occupying her eyes with him, and wondered more than ever what had attracted him in her unfledged maid-servant. The mistress was almost as unaccustomed as the maiden herself to the end-of-the-age young man, or she might have wondered less. Raye, having looked about him awhile, left abruptly, without regard to the service that was proceeding; and Mrs Harnham—lonely, impressionable creature that she was—took no further interest in praising the Lord. She wished she had married a London man who knew the subtleties of love-making as they were evidently known to him who had mistakenly caressed her hand.

III

The calendar at Melchester had been light, occupying the court only a few hours; and the assizes[3] at Casterbridge, the next county-town on the Western Circuit, having no business for Raye, he had not gone thither. At the next town after that they did not open till the following Monday, trials to begin on Tuesday morning. In the natural order of things Raye would have arrived at the latter place on Monday afternoon; but it was not till the middle of Wednesday that his gown and grey wig, curled in tiers, in the best fashion of Assyrian bas-reliefs, were seen blowing and bobbing behind him as he hastily walked up the High Street from his lodgings. But though he entered the assize building there was nothing for him to do, and sitting at the blue baize table in the well of the court, he mended pens with a mind far away from the case in progress. Thoughts of unpremeditated conduct, of which a week earlier he would not have believed himself capable, threw him into a mood of dissatisfied depression.

He had contrived to see again the pretty rural maiden Anna, the day after the fair, had walked out of the city with her to the earthworks[4] of Old Melchester, and feeling a violent fancy for her, had remained in Melchester all Sunday, Monday, and Tuesday; by persuasion obtaining walks and meetings with the girl six or seven times during the interval; had in brief won her, body and soul.

He supposed it must have been owing to the seclusion in which he had lived of late in town that he had given way so unrestrainedly to a passion for an artless creature whose inexperience had, from the first, led her to place herself unreservedly in his hands. Much he deplored trifling with her feelings for the sake of a passing desire; and he could only hope that she might not live to suffer on his account.

She had begged him to come to her again; entreated him; wept. He had promised that he would do so, and he meant to carry out that promise. He could not desert her now. Awkward as such unintentional connections were, the interspace of a hundred miles—which to a girl of her limited capabilities was like a thousand—would effectually hinder this summer fancy from greatly encumbering his life; while thought of her simple love might do him the negative good of keeping him from idle pleasures in town when he wished to work hard. His circuit journeys would take him to Melchester three or four times a year; and then he could always see her.

The pseudonym, or rather partial name, that he had given her as his before knowing how far the acquaintance was going to carry him, had been spoken

3. Sessions of the superior court. "Calendar": list of cases to be tried.   4. Banks of earth constructed as fortifications in ancient times.

on the spur of the moment, without any ulterior intention whatever. He had not afterwards disturbed Anna's error, but on leaving her he had felt bound to give her an address at a stationer's not far from his chambers, at which she might write to him under the initials 'C. B'.

In due time Raye returned to his London abode, having called at Melchester on his way and spent a few additional hours with his fascinating child of nature. In town he lived monotonously every day. Often he and his rooms were enclosed by a tawny fog from all the world besides, and when he lighted the gas to read or write by, his situation seemed so unnatural that he would look into the fire and think of that trusting girl at Melchester again and again. Often, oppressed by absurd fondness for her, he would enter the dim religious nave of the Law Courts by the north door, elbow other juniors habited like himself, and like him unretained; edge himself into this or that crowded court where a sensational case was going on, just as if he were in it, though the police officers at the door knew as well as he knew himself that he had no more concern with the business in hand than the patient idlers at the gallery-door outside, who had waited to enter since eight in the morning because, like him, they belonged to the classes that live on expectation. But he would do these things to no purpose, and think how greatly the characters in such scenes contrasted with the pink and breezy Anna.

An unexpected feature in that peasant maiden's conduct was that she had not as yet written to him, though he had told her she might do so if she wished. Surely a young creature had never before been so reticent in such circumstances. At length he sent her a brief line, positively requesting her to write. There was no answer by the return post, but the day after a letter in a neat feminine hand, and bearing the Melchester post-mark, was handed to him by the stationer.

The fact alone of its arrival was sufficient to satisfy his imaginative sentiment. He was not anxious to open the epistle, and in truth did not begin to read it for nearly half-an-hour, anticipating readily its terms of passionate retrospect and tender adjuration. When at last he turned his feet to the fireplace and unfolded the sheet, he was surprised and pleased to find that neither extravagance nor vulgarity was there. It was the most charming little missive he had ever received from woman. To be sure the language was simple and the ideas were slight; but it was so self-possessed; so purely that of a young girl who felt her womanhood to be enough for her dignity that he read it through twice. Four sides were filled, and a few lines written across, after the fashion of former days; the paper, too, was common, and not of the latest shade and surface. But what of those things? He had received letters from women who were fairly called ladies, but never so sensible, so human a letter as this. He could not single out any one sentence and say it was at all remarkable or clever; the *ensemble* of the letter it was which won him; and beyond the one request that he would write or come to her again soon there was nothing to show her sense of a claim upon him.

To write again and develop a correspondence was the last thing Raye would have preconceived as his conduct in such a situation; yet he did send a short, encouraging line or two, signed with his pseudonym, in which he asked for another letter, and cheeringly promised that he would try to see her again on some near day, and would never forget how much they had been to each other during their short acquaintance.

IV

To return now to the moment at which Anna, at Melchester, had received Raye's letter.

It had been put into her own hand by the postman on his morning rounds. She flushed down to her neck on receipt of it, and turned it over and over. 'It is mine?' she said.

'Why, yes, can't you see it is?' said the postman, smiling as he guessed the nature of the document and the cause of the confusion.

'O yes, of course!' replied Anna, looking at the letter, forcedly tittering, and blushing still more.

Her look of embarrassment did not leave her with the postman's departure. She opened the envelope, kissed its contents, put away the letter in her pocket, and remained musing till her eyes filled with tears.

A few minutes later she carried up a cup of tea to Mrs Harnham in her bed-chamber. Anna's mistress looked at her, and said: 'How dismal you seem this morning, Anna. What's the matter?'

'I'm not dismal, I'm glad; only I—' She stopped to stifle a sob.

'Well?'

'I've got a letter—and what good is it to me, if I can't read a word in it!'

'Why, I'll read it, child, if necessary.'

'But this is from somebody—I don't want anybody to read it but myself!' Anna murmured.

'I shall not tell anybody. Is it from that young man?'

'I think so.' Anna slowly produced the letter, saying: 'Then will you read it to me, ma'am?'

This was the secret of Anna's embarrassment and flutterings. She could neither read nor write. She had grown up under the care of an aunt by marriage, at one of the lonely hamlets on the Great Mid-Wessex Plain where, even in days of national education, there had been no school within a distance of two miles. Her aunt was an ignorant woman; there had been nobody to investigate Anna's circumstances, nobody to care about her learning the rudiments; though, as often in such cases, she had been well fed and clothed and not unkindly treated. Since she had come to live at Melchester with Mrs Harnham, the latter, who took a kindly interest in the girl, had taught her to speak correctly, in which accomplishment Anna showed considerable readiness, as is not unusual with the illiterate; and soon became quite fluent in the use of her mistress's phraseology. Mrs Harnham also insisted upon her getting a spelling and copy book, and beginning to practise in these. Anna was slower in this branch of her education, and meanwhile here was the letter.

Edith Harnham's large dark eyes expressed some interest in the contents, though, in her character of mere interpreter, she threw into her tone as much as she could of mechanical passiveness. She read the short epistle on to its concluding sentence, which idly requested Anna to send him a tender answer.

'Now—you'll do it for me, won't you, dear mistress?' said Anna eagerly. 'And you'll do it as well as ever you can, please? Because I couldn't bear him to think I am not able to do it myself. I should sink into the earth with shame if he knew that!'

From some words in the letter Mrs Harnham was led to ask questions, and the answers she received confirmed her suspicions. Deep concern filled Edith's heart at perceiving how the girl had committed her happiness to the issue of this new-sprung attachment. She blamed herself for not interfering in a flirtation which had resulted so seriously for the poor little creature in her charge; though at the time of seeing the pair together she had a feeling that it was hardly within her province to nip young affection in the bud. However, what was done could not be undone, and it behoved her now, as Anna's only protector, to help her as much as she could. To Anna's eager request that she, Mrs Harnham, should compose and write the answer to this young London man's letter, she felt bound to accede, to keep alive his attachment to the girl if possible; though in other circumstances she might have suggested the cook as an amanuensis.[5]

A tender reply was thereupon concocted, and set down in Edith Harnham's hand. This letter it had been which Raye had received and delighted in. Written in the presence of Anna it certainly was, and on Anna's humble note-paper, and in a measure indited by the young girl; but the life, the spirit, the individuality, were Edith Harnham's.

'Won't you at least put your name yourself?' she said. 'You can manage to write that by this time?'

'No, no,' said Anna, shrinking back. 'I should do it so bad. He'd be ashamed of me, and never see me again!'

The note, so prettily requesting another from him, had, as we have seen, power enough in its pages to bring one. He declared it to be such a pleasure to hear from her that she must write every week. The same process of manufacture was accordingly repeated by Anna and her mistress, and continued for several weeks in succession; each letter being penned and suggested by Edith, the girl standing by; the answer read and commented on by Edith, Anna standing by and listening again.

Late on a winter evening, after the dispatch of the sixth letter, Mrs Harnham was sitting alone by the remains of her fire. Her husband had retired to bed, and she had fallen into that fixity of musing which takes no count of hour or temperature. The state of mind had been brought about in Edith by a strange thing which she had done that day. For the first time since Raye's visit Anna had gone to stay over a night or two with her cottage friends on the Plain, and in her absence had arrived, out of its time, a letter from Raye. To this Edith had replied on her own responsibility, from the depths of her own heart, without waiting for her maid's collaboration. The luxury of writing to him what would be known to no consciousness but his was great, and she had indulged herself therein.

Why was it a luxury?

Edith Harnham led a lonely life. Influenced by the belief of the British parent that a bad marriage with its aversions is better than free womanhood with its interests, dignity, and leisure, she had consented to marry the elderly wine-merchant as a *pis aller*,[6] at the age of seven-and-twenty—some three years before this date—to find afterwards that she had made a mistake. That contract had left her still a woman whose deeper nature had never been stirred.

She was now clearly realising that she had become possessed to the bottom of her soul with the image of a man to whom she was hardly so much as a name. From the first he had attracted her by his looks and voice; by his tender touch; and, with these as generators, the writing of letter after letter and the reading of their soft answers had insensibly developed on her side an emotion

5. Secretary.   6. Last resort (French).

which fanned his; till there had resulted a magnetic reciprocity between the correspondents, notwithstanding that one of them wrote in a character not her own. That he had been able to seduce another woman in two days was his crowning though unrecognised fascination for her as the she-animal.

They were her own impassioned and pent-up ideas—lowered to monosyllabic phraseology in order to keep up the disguise—that Edith put into letters signed with another name, much to the shallow Anna's delight, who, unassisted, could not for the world have conceived such pretty fancies for winning him, even had she been able to write them. Edith found that it was these, her own foisted-in sentiments, to which the young barrister mainly responded. The few sentences occasionally added from Anna's own lips made apparently no impression upon him.

The letter-writing in her absence Anna never discovered; but on her return the next morning she declared she wished to see her lover about something at once, and begged Mrs Harnham to ask him to come.

There was a strange anxiety in her manner which did not escape Mrs Harnham, and ultimately resolved itself into a flood of tears. Sinking down at Edith's knees, she made confession that the result of her relations with her lover it would soon become necessary to disclose.

Edith Harnham was generous enough to be very far from inclined to cast Anna adrift at this conjuncture. No true woman ever is so inclined from her own personal point of view, however prompt she may be in taking such steps to safeguard those dear to her. Although she had written to Raye so short a time previously, she instantly penned another Anna-note hinting clearly though delicately the state of affairs.

Raye replied by a hasty line to say how much he was concerned at her news: he felt that he must run down to see her almost immediately.

But a week later the girl came to her mistress's room with another note, which on being read informed her that after all he could not find time for the journey. Anna was broken with grief; but by Mrs Harnham's counsel strictly refrained from hurling at him the reproaches and bitterness customary from young women so situated. One thing was imperative: to keep the young man's romantic interest in her alive. Rather therefore did Edith, in the name of her protégée, request him on no account to be distressed about the looming event, and not to inconvenience himself to hasten down. She desired above everything to be no weight upon him in his career, no clog upon his high activities. She had wished him to know what had befallen: he was to dismiss it again from his mind. Only he must write tenderly as ever, and when he should come again on the spring circuit it would be soon enough to discuss what had better be done.

It may well be supposed that Anna's own feelings had not been quite in accord with these generous expressions; but the mistress's judgment had ruled, and Anna had acquiesced. 'All I want is that niceness you can so well put into your letters, my dear, dear mistress, and that I can't for the life o' me make up out of my own head; though I mean the same thing and feel it exactly when you've written it down!'

When the letter had been sent off, and Edith Harnham was left alone, she bowed herself on the back of her chair and wept.

'I wish his child was mine—I wish it was!' she murmured. 'Yet how can I say such a wicked thing!'

V

The letter moved Raye considerably when it reached him. The intelligence itself had affected him less than her unexpected manner of treating him in relation to it. The absence of any word of reproach, the devotion to his interests, the self-sacrifice apparent in every line, all made up a nobility of character that he had never dreamt of finding in womankind.

'God forgive me!' he said tremulously. 'I have been a wicked wretch. I did not know she was such a treasure as this!'

He reassured her instantly; declaring that he would not of course desert her, that he would provide a home for her somewhere. Meanwhile she was to stay where she was as long as her mistress would allow her.

But a misfortune supervened in this direction. Whether an inkling of Anna's circumstances reached the knowledge of Mrs Harnham's husband or not cannot be said, but the girl was compelled, in spite of Edith's entreaties, to leave the house. By her own choice she decided to go back for a while to the cottage on the Plain. This arrangement led to a consultation as to how the correspondence should be carried on; and in the girl's inability to continue personally what had been begun in her name, and in the difficulty of their acting in concert as heretofore, she requested Mrs Harnham—the only well-to-do friend she had in the world—to receive the letters and reply to them off-hand, sending them on afterwards to herself on the Plain, where she might at least get some neighbour to read them to her, if a trustworthy one could be met with. Anna and her box then departed for the Plain.

Thus it befell that Edith Harnham found herself in the strange position of having to correspond, under no supervision by the real woman, with a man not her husband, in terms which were virtually those of a wife, concerning a corporeal condition that was not Edith's at all; the man being one for whom, mainly through the sympathies involved in playing this part, she secretly cherished a predilection, subtle and imaginative truly, but strong and absorbing. She opened each letter, read it as if intended for herself, and replied from the promptings of her own heart and no other.

Throughout this correspondence, carried on in the girl's absence, the highstrung Edith Harnham lived in the ecstasy of fancy; the vicarious intimacy engendered such a flow of passionateness as was never exceeded. For conscience' sake Edith at first sent on each of his letters to Anna, and even rough copies of her replies; but later on these so-called copies were much abridged, and many letters on both sides were not sent on at all.

Though sensuous, and, superficially at least, infested with the self-indulgent vices of artificial society, there was a substratum of honesty and fairness in Raye's character. He had really a tender regard for the country girl, and it grew more tender than ever when he found her apparently capable of expressing the deepest sensibilities in the simplest words. He meditated, he wavered; and finally resolved to consult his sister, a maiden lady much older than himself, of lively sympathies and good intent. In making this confidence he showed her some of the letters.

'She seems fairly educated,' Miss Raye observed. 'And bright in ideas. She expresses herself with a taste that must be innate.'

'Yes. She writes very prettily, doesn't she, thanks to these elementary schools?'

'One is drawn out towards her, in spite of one's self, poor thing.'

The upshot of the discussion was that though he had not been directly advised to do it, Raye wrote, in his real name, what he would never have decided to write on his own responsibility; namely that he could not live without her, and would come down in the spring and shelve her looming difficulty by marrying her.

This bold acceptance of the situation was made known to Anna by Mrs Harnham driving out immediately to the cottage on the Plain. Anna jumped for joy like a little child. And poor, crude directions for answering appropriately were given to Edith Harnham, who on her return to the city carried them out with warm intensifications.

'O!' she groaned, as she threw down the pen. 'Anna—poor good little fool—hasn't intelligence enough to appreciate him! How should she? While I—don't bear his child!'

It was now February. The correspondence had continued altogether for four months; and the next letter from Raye contained incidentally a statement of his position and prospects. He said that in offering to wed her he had, at first, contemplated the step of retiring from a profession which hitherto had brought him very slight emolument, and which, to speak plainly, he had thought might be difficult of practice after his union with her. But the unexpected mines of brightness and warmth that her letters had disclosed to be lurking in her sweet nature had led him to abandon that somewhat sad prospect. He felt sure that, with her powers of development, after a little private training in the social forms of London under his supervision, and a little help from a governess if necessary, she would make as good a professional man's wife as could be desired, even if he should rise to the woolsack.[7] Many a Lord Chancellor's wife had been less intuitively a lady than she had shown herself to be in her lines to him.

'O—poor fellow, poor fellow!' mourned Edith Harnham.

Her distress now raged as high as her infatuation. It was she who had wrought him to this pitch—to a marriage which meant his ruin; yet she could not, in mercy to her maid, do anything to hinder his plan. Anna was coming to Melchester that week, but she could hardly show the girl this last reply from the young man; it told too much of the second individuality that had usurped the place of the first.

Anna came, and her mistress took her into her own room for privacy. Anna began by saying with some anxiety that she was glad the wedding was so near.

'O Anna!' replied Mrs Harnham. 'I think we must tell him all—that I have been doing your writing for you?—lest he should not know it till after you become his wife, and it might lead to dissension and recriminations—'

'O mis'ess, dear mis'ess—please don't tell him now!' cried Anna in distress. 'If you were to do it, perhaps he would not marry me; and what should I do then? It would be terrible what would come to me! And I am getting on with my writing, too. I have brought with me the copybook you were so good as to give me, and I practise every day, and though it is so, so hard, I shall do it well at last, I believe, if I keep on trying.'

Edith looked at the copybook. The copies had been set by herself, and such progress as the girl had made was in the way of grotesque facsimile of her

---

7. Seat of the Lord Chancellor in the House of Lords, formerly made of a sack of wool.

mistress's hand. But even if Edith's flowing calligraphy were reproduced the inspiration would be another thing.

'You do it so beautifully,' continued Anna, 'and say all that I want to say so much better than I could say it, that I do hope you won't leave me in the lurch just now!'

'Very well,' replied the other. 'But I—but I thought I ought not to go on!'

'Why?'

Her strong desire to confide her sentiments led Edith to answer truly:

'Because of its effect upon me.'

'But it *can't* have any!'

'Why, child?'

'Because you are married already!' said Anna with lucid simplicity.

'Of course it can't,' said her mistress hastily; yet glad, despite her conscience, that two or three out-pourings still remained to her. 'But you must concentrate your attention on writing your name as I write it here.'

VI

Soon Raye wrote about the wedding. Having decided to make the best of what he feared was a piece of romantic folly, he had acquired more zest for the grand experiment. He wished the ceremony to be in London, for greater privacy. Edith Harnham would have preferred it at Melchester; Anna was passive. His reasoning prevailed, and Mrs Harnham threw herself with mournful zeal into the preparations for Anna's departure. In a last desperate feeling that she must at every hazard be in at the death of her dream, and see once again the man who by a species of telepathy had exercised such an influence on her, she offered to go up with Anna and be with her through the ceremony—'to see the end of her,' as her mistress put it with forced gaiety; an offer which the girl gratefully accepted; for she had no other friend capable of playing the part of companion and witness, in the presence of a gentlemanly bridegroom, in such a way as not to hasten an opinion that he had made an irremediable social blunder.

It was a muddy morning in March when Raye alighted from a four-wheel cab at the door of a registry-office in the S.W. district of London, and carefully handed down Anna and her companion Mrs Harnham. Anna looked attractive in the somewhat fashionable clothes which Mrs Harnham had helped her to buy, though not quite so attractive as, an innocent child, she had appeared in her country gown on the back of the wooden horse at Melchester Fair.

Mrs Harnham had come up this morning by an early train, and a young man—a friend of Raye's—having met them at the door, all four entered the registry-office together. Till an hour before this time Raye had never known the wine-merchant's wife, except at that first casual encounter, and in the flutter of the performance before them he had little opportunity for more than a brief acquaintance. The contract of marriage at a registry is soon got through; but somehow, during its progress, Raye discovered a strange and secret gravitation between himself and Anna's friend.

The formalities of the wedding—or rather ratification of a previous union—being concluded, the four went in one cab to Raye's lodgings, newly taken in a new suburb in preference to a house, the rent of which he could ill afford just then. Here Anna cut the little cake which Raye had bought at a pastry-cook's on his way home from Lincoln's Inn the night before. But she did not do much besides. Raye's friend was obliged to depart almost immediately, and when he had left the only ones virtually present were Edith and Raye, who exchanged ideas with much animation. The conversation was indeed theirs only, Anna being as a domestic animal who humbly heard but understood not. Raye seemed startled in awakening to this fact, and began to feel dissatisfied with her inadequacy.

At last, more disappointed than he cared to own, he said, 'Mrs Harnham, my darling is so flurried that she doesn't know what she is doing or saying. I see that after this event a little quietude will be necessary before she gives tongue to that tender philosophy which she used to treat me to in her letters.'

They had planned to start early that afternoon for Knollsea, to spend the few opening days of their married life there, and as the hour for departure was drawing near Raye asked his wife if she would go to the writing-desk in the next room and scribble a little note to his sister, who had been unable to attend through indisposition, informing her that the ceremony was over, thanking her for her little present, and hoping to know her well now that she was the writer's sister as well as Charles's.

'Say it in the pretty poetical way you know so well how to adopt,' he added, 'for I want you particularly to win her, and both of you to be dear friends.'

Anna looked uneasy, but departed to her task, Raye remaining to talk to their guest. Anna was a long while absent, and her husband suddenly rose and went to her.

He found her still bending over the writing-table, with tears brimming up in her eyes; and he looked down upon the sheet of note-paper with some interest, to discover with what tact she had expressed her good-will in the delicate circumstances. To his surprise she had progressed but a few lines, in the characters and spelling of a child of eight, and with the ideas of a goose.

'Anna,' he said, staring; 'what's this?'

'It only means—that I can't do it any better!' she answered, through her tears.

'Eh? Nonsense!'

'I can't!' she insisted, with miserable, sobbing hardihood. 'I—I—didn't write those letters, Charles! I only told *her* what to write! And not always that! But I am learning, O so fast, my dear, dear husband! And you'll forgive me, won't you, for not telling you before?' She slid to her knees, abjectly clasped his waist and laid her face against him.

He stood a few moments, raised her, abruptly turned, and shut the door upon her, rejoining Edith in the drawing-room. She saw that something untoward had been discovered, and their eyes remained fixed on each other.

'Do I guess rightly?' he asked, with wan quietude. '*You* were her scribe through all this?'

'It was necessary,' said Edith.

'Did she dictate every word you ever wrote to me?'

'Not every word.'

'In fact, very little?'

'Very little.'

'You wrote a great part of those pages every week from your own conceptions, though in her name!'

'Yes.'

'Perhaps you wrote many of the letters when you were alone, without communication with her?'

'I did.'

He turned to the bookcase, and leant with his hand over his face; and Edith, seeing his distress, became white as a sheet.

'You have deceived me—ruined me!' he murmured.

'O, don't say it!' she cried in her anguish, jumping up and putting her hand on his shoulder. 'I can't bear that!'

'Delighting me deceptively! Why did you do it—*why* did you!'

'I began doing it in kindness to her! How could I do otherwise than try to save such a simple girl from misery? But I admit that I continued it for pleasure to myself.'

Raye looked up. 'Why did it give you pleasure?' he asked.

'I must not tell,' said she.

He continued to regard her, and saw that her lips suddenly began to quiver under his scrutiny, and her eyes to fill and droop. She started aside, and said that she must go to the station to catch the return train: could a cab be called immediately?

But Raye went up to her, and took her unresisting hand. 'Well, to think of such a thing as this!' he said. 'Why, you and I are friends—lovers—devoted lovers—by correspondence!'

'Yes; I suppose.'

'More.'

'More?'

'Plainly more. It is no use blinking that. Legally I have married her—God help us both!—in soul and spirit I have married you, and no other woman in the world!'

'Hush!'

'But I will not hush! Why should you try to disguise the full truth, when you have already owned half of it? Yes, it is between you and me that the bond is—not between me and her! Now I'll say no more. But, O my cruel one, I think I have one claim upon you!'

She did not say what, and he drew her towards him, and bent over her. 'If it was all pure invention in those letters,' he said emphatically, 'give me your cheek only. If you meant what you said, let it be lips. It is for the first and last time, remember!'

She put up her mouth, and he kissed her long. 'You forgive me?' she said, crying.

'Yes.'

'But you are ruined!'

'What matter!' he said, shrugging his shoulders. 'It serves me right!'

She withdrew, wiped her eyes, entered and bade good-bye to Anna, who had not expected her to go so soon, and was still wrestling with the letter. Raye followed Edith downstairs, and in three minutes she was in a hansom driving to the Waterloo station.

He went back to his wife. 'Never mind the letter, Anna, to-day,' he said gently. 'Put on your things. We, too, must be off shortly.'

The simple girl, upheld by the sense that she was indeed married, showed her delight at finding that he was as kind as ever after the disclosure. She did not know that before his eyes he beheld as it were a galley, in which he, the fastidious urban, was chained to work for the remainder of his life, with her, the unlettered peasant, chained to his side.

Edith travelled back to Melchester that day with a face that showed the very stupor of grief, her lips still tingling from the desperate pressure of his kiss. The end of her impassioned dream had come. When at dusk she reached the Melchester station her husband was there to meet her, but in his perfunctoriness and her preoccupation they did not see each other, and she went out of the station alone.

She walked mechanically homewards without calling a fly.[8] Entering, she could not bear the silence of the house, and went up in the dark to where Anna had slept, where she remained thinking awhile. She then returned to the drawing-room, and not knowing what she did, crouched down upon the floor.

'I have ruined him!' she kept repeating. 'I have ruined him; because I would not deal treacherously towards her!'

In the course of half an hour a figure opened the door of the apartment.

'Ah—who's that?' she said, starting up, for it was dark.

'Your husband—who should it be?' said the worthy merchant.

'Ah—my husband!—I forgot I had a husband!' she whispered to herself.

'I missed you at the station,' he continued. 'Did you see Anna safely tied up? I hope so, for 'twas time.'

'Yes—Anna is married.'

Simultaneously with Edith's journey home Anna and her husband were sitting at the opposite windows of a second-class carriage which sped along to Knollsea. In his hand was a pocket-book full of creased sheets closely written over. Unfolding them one after another he read them in silence, and sighed.

'What are you doing, dear Charles?' she said timidly from the other window, and drew nearer to him as if he were a god.

'Reading over all those sweet letters to me signed "Anna," ' he replied with dreary resignation.

1891

Hap[1]

<blockquote>

If but some vengeful god would call to me
From up the sky, and laugh: 'Thou suffering thing,
Know that thy sorrow is my ecstasy,
That thy love's loss is my hate's profiting!'

5   Then would I bear it, clench myself, and die,
Steeled by the sense of ire° unmerited;   *anger*
Half-eased in that a Powerfuller than I
Had willed and meted° me the tears I shed.   *allotted, given*

But not so. How arrives it joy lies slain,
10   And why unblooms the best hope ever sown?
—Crass Casualty obstructs the sun and rain,

</blockquote>

---

8. Carriage.   1. I.e., chance (as also "Casualty," line 11).

And dicing Time for gladness casts a moan. . . .
These purblind Doomsters[2] had as readily strown
Blisses about my pilgrimage as pain.

1866   1898

Neutral Tones

We stood by a pond that winter day,
And the sun was white, as though chidden of° God,   *rebuked by*
And a few leaves lay on the starving sod;°   *turf*
    —They had fallen from an ash, and were gray.

5   Your eyes on me were as eyes that rove
Over tedious riddles of years ago;
And some words played between us to and fro
    On which lost the more by our love.

The smile on your mouth was the deadest thing
10   Alive enough to have strength to die;
And a grin of bitterness swept thereby
    Like an ominous bird a-wing . . .

Since then, keen lessons that love deceives,
And wrings with wrong, have shaped to me
15   Your face, and the God-curst sun, and a tree,
    And a pond edged with grayish leaves.

1867   1898

I Look into My Glass[1]

I look into my glass,
And view my wasting skin,
And say, 'Would God it came to pass
My heart had shrunk as thin!'

5   For then, I, undistrest
By hearts grown cold to me,
Could lonely wait my endless rest
With equanimity.

But Time, to make me grieve,
10   Part steals, lets part abide;
And shakes this fragile frame at eve
With throbbings of noontide.

1898

2. Half-blind judges.   1. Mirror.

A Broken Appointment

You did not come.
And marching Time drew on, and wore me numb.—
Yet less for loss of your dear presence there
Than that I thus found lacking in your make
5   That high compassion which can overbear
Reluctance for pure lovingkindness' sake
Grieved I, when, as the hope-hour stroked its sum,
    You did not come.

    You love not me,
10 And love alone can lend you loyalty;
—I know and knew it. But, unto the store
Of human deeds divine in all but name,
Was it not worth a little hour or more
To add yet this: Once you, a woman, came
15 To soothe a time-torn man; even though it be
    You love not me?

1901

Drummer Hodge

1

They throw in Drummer Hodge, to rest
    Uncoffined—just as found:
His landmark is a kopje-crest
    That breaks the veldt[1] around;
5 And foreign constellations[2] west°   *set*
    Each night above his mound.

2

Young Hodge the Drummer never knew—
    Fresh from his Wessex home—
The meaning of the broad Karoo,[3]
10   The Bush,[4] the dusty loam,
And why uprose to nightly view
    Strange stars amid the gloam.

3

Yet portion of that unknown plain
    Will Hodge for ever be;
15 His homely Northern breast and brain

1. South African Dutch (Afrikaans) word for a plain or prairie. "Kopje-crest": Afrikaans for a small hill. The poem is a lament for an English soldier killed in the Anglo-Boer War (1899–1902).
2. Those visible only in the Southern Hemisphere.
3. A dry tableland region in South Africa (usually spelled "Karroo").
4. British colonial word for an uncleared area of land.

Grow to some Southern tree,
And strange-eyed constellations reign
His stars eternally.

1899, 1901

The Darkling[1] Thrush

I leant upon a coppice gate[2]
    When Frost was spectre-gray,
And Winter's dregs made desolate
    The weakening eye of day.
5 The tangled bine-stems[3] scored the sky
    Like strings of broken lyres,
And all mankind that haunted nigh°   *near*
    Had sought their household fires.

The land's sharp features seemed to be
10   The Century's corpse outleant,[4]
His crypt the cloudy canopy,
    The wind his death-lament.
The ancient pulse of germ and birth
    Was shrunken hard and dry,
15 And every spirit upon earth
    Seemed fervourless as I.

At once a voice arose among
    The bleak twigs overhead
In a full-hearted evensong
20   Of joy illimited;
An aged thrush, frail, gaunt, and small,
    In blast-beruffled plume,
Had chosen thus to fling his soul
    Upon the growing gloom.

25 So little cause for carolings
    Of such ecstatic sound
Was written on terrestrial things
    Afar or nigh around,
That I could think there trembled through
30   His happy good-night air
Some blessed Hope, whereof he knew
    And I was unaware.

1900, 1901

---

1. In the dark.
2. Gate leading to a small wood or thicket.
3. Twining stems of shrubs.

4. Leaning out (of its coffin); i.e., the 19th century was dead. This poem was dated December 31, 1900.

The Ruined Maid

'O 'Melia,[1] my dear, this does everything crown!
Who could have supposed I should meet you in Town?
And whence such fair garments, such prosperi-ty?'—
'O didn't you know I'd been ruined?' said she.

5 —'You left us in tatters, without shoes or socks,
Tired of digging potatoes, and spudding up docks;[2]
And now you've gay bracelets and bright feathers three!'—
'Yes: that's how we dress when we're ruined,' said she.

—'At home in the barton° you said "thee" and "thou",   *farmyard*
10 And "thik oon", and "theäs oon", and "t'other"; but now
Your talking quite fits 'ee for high compa-ny!'—
'Some polish is gained with one's ruin,' said she.

—'Your hands were like paws then, your face blue and bleak
But now I'm bewitched by your delicate cheek,
15 And your little gloves fit as on any la-dy!'—
'We never do work when we're ruined,' said she.

—'You used to call home-life a hag-ridden dream,
And you'd sigh, and you'd sock;° but at present you seem   *sigh*
To know not of megrims° or melancho-ly!'—   *low spirits*
20 'True. One's pretty lively when ruined,' said she.

—'I wish I had feathers, a fine sweeping gown,
And a delicate face, and could strut about Town!'—
'My dear—a raw country girl, such as you be,
Cannot quite expect that. You ain't ruined,' said she.

1866   1901

A Trampwoman's Tragedy

(182–)

I

From Wynyard's Gap[1] the livelong day,
        The livelong day,
We beat afoot the northward way
        We had travelled times before.
5   The sun-blaze burning on our backs,
        Our shoulders sticking to our packs,

---

1. Diminutive form of Amelia.
2. Digging up a species of thick-rooted weed.
1. The places named are in Somerset, in south-west England on the northern edge of the area that
Hardy called "Wessex" and of which his native Dorset, the county south and southwest of Somerset, reaching to the English Channel, was the major part.

By fosseway,[2] fields, and turnpike tracks
    We skirted sad Sedge-Moor.[3]

2

Full twenty miles we jaunted on,
10   We jaunted on,—
My fancy-man, and jeering John,
    And Mother Lee, and I.
And, as the sun drew down to west,
We climbed the toilsome Poldon crest,
15 And saw, of landskip° sights the best,   *landscape*
    The inn that beamed thereby.

3

For months we had padded side by side,
    Ay, side by side
Through the Great Forest, Blackmoor wide,
20   And where the Parret ran,
We'd faced the gusts on Mendip ridge,
Had crossed the Yeo unhelped by bridge,
Been stung by every Marshwood midge,
    I and my fancy-man.

4

25 Lone inns we loved, my man and I,
      My man and I;
'King's Stag', 'Windwhistle'[4] high and dry,
    'The Horse' on Hintock Green,
The cozy house at Wynyard's Gap,
30 'The Hut' renowned on Bredy Knap,
And many another wayside tap°   *taproom, inn*
    Where folk might sit unseen.

5

Now as we trudged—O deadly day,
    O deadly day!—
35 I teased my fancy-man in play
    And wanton idleness.
I walked alongside jeering John,
I laid his hand my waist upon;
I would not bend my glances on
40   My lover's dark distress.

6

Thus Poldon top at last we won,
    At last we won,

---

2. Path running along a ditch.
3. Sad because of the Battle of Sedgemoor (1685), when the rebellion of the duke of Monmouth against James II was crushed with excessive cruelty.
4. The highness and dryness of Windwhistle Inn was impressed upon the writer two or three years ago, when, after climbing on a hot afternoon to the beautiful spot near which it stands and entering the inn for tea, he was informed by the landlady that none could be had, unless he would fetch water from a valley half a mile off, the house containing not a drop, owing to its situation. However, a tantalizing row of full barrels behind her back testified to a wetness of a certain sort, which was not at that time desired [Hardy's note].

And gained the inn at sink of sun
Far-famed as 'Marshal's Elm'.[5]
45 Beneath us figured tor and lea,[6]
From Mendip to the western sea—
I doubt if finer sight there be
Within this royal realm.

7

Inside the settle all a-row—
50   All four a-row
We sat, I next to John, to show
That he had wooed and won.
And then he took me on his knee,
And swore it was his turn to be
55 My favoured mate, and Mother Lee
Passed to my former one.

8

Then in a voice I had never heard,
    I had never heard,
My only Love to me: 'One word,
60   My lady, if you please!
Whose is the child you are like to bear?—
His? After all my months o' care?'
God knows 'twas not! But, O despair!
I nodded—still to tease.

9

65 Then up he sprung, and with his knife—
    And with his knife
He let out jeering Johnny's life,
    Yes; there, at set of sun.
The slant ray through the window nigh
70 Gilded John's blood and glazing eye,
Ere scarcely Mother Lee and I
    Knew that the deed was done.

10

The taverns tell the gloomy tale,
    The gloomy tale,
75 How that at Ivel-chester jail
    My Love, my sweetheart swung;
Though stained till now by no misdeed
Save one horse ta'en in time o' need;
(Blue Jimmy stole right many a steed
80   Ere his last fling he flung).[7]

11

Thereaft I walked the world alone,
    Alone, alone!

5. "Marshal's Elm," so picturesquely situated, is no longer an inn, though the house, or part of it, still remains. It used to exhibit a fine old swinging sign [Hardy's note].
6. Rocky hill and tract of open ground.

7. "Blue Jimmy" was a notorious horse stealer of Wessex in those days, who appropriated more than a hundred horses before he was caught, among others one belonging to a neighbor of the writer's grandfather. He was hanged at the now demol-

On his death-day I gave my groan
    And dropt his dead-born child.
85 'Twas nigh° the jail, beneath a tree,   *near*
None tending me; for Mother Lee
Had died at Glaston, leaving me
    Unfriended on the wild.

12

And in the night as I lay weak,
90   As I lay weak,
The leaves a-falling on my cheek,
    The red moon low declined—
The ghost of him I'd die to kiss
Rose up and said: 'Ah, tell me this!
95 Was the child mine, or was it his?
    Speak, that I rest may find!'

13

O doubt not but I told him then,
    I told him then,
That I had kept me from all men
100   Since we joined lips and swore.
Whereat he smiled, and thinned away
As the wind stirred to call up day . . .
—'Tis past! And here alone I stray
    Haunting the Western Moor.

Apr. 1902   1909

One We Knew

(M. H.[1] 1772–1857)

She told how they used to form for the country dances—
    'The Triumph,' 'The New-rigged Ship'—
To the light of the guttering wax in the panelled manses,
    And in cots to the blink of a dip.[2]

5 She spoke of the wild 'poussetting' and 'allemanding'[3]
    On carpet, on oak, and on sod;°   *turf*
And the two long rows of ladies and gentlemen standing,
    And the figures the couples trod.

She showed us the spot where the maypole was yearly planted,
10   And where the bandsmen stood
While breeched and kerchiefed partners whirled, and panted
    To choose each other for good.[4]

---

ished Ivel-chester or Ilchester jail above mentioned—that building formerly of so many sinister associations in the minds of the local peasantry, and the continual haunt of fever, which at last led to its condemnation. Its site is now an innocent-looking green meadow [Hardy's note].
1. Hardy's grandmother.
2. I.e., in cottages by the light of a candle.

3. Allemande is the name of a dance originating in Germany. To pousette is to dance round with hands joined.
4. A tall pole, gaily painted and decorated with flowers and ribbons ("the maypole"), was danced around on May 1 by men (wearing "breeches," or trousers) and women (wearing "kerchiefs," or headscarves).

She told of that far-back day when they learnt astounded
    Of the death of the King of France:
15 Of the Terror; and then of Bonaparte's unbounded
    Ambition and arrogance.

Of how his threats woke warlike preparations
    Along the southern strand,
And how each night brought tremors and trepidations
20   Lest morning should see him land.

She said she had often heard the gibbet creaking
    As it swayed in the lightning flash,
Had caught from the neighbouring town a small child's shrieking
    At the cart-tail under the lash. . . .

25 With cap-framed face and long gaze into the embers—
    We seated around her knees—
She would dwell on such dead themes, not as one who remembers,
    But rather as one who sees.

She seemed one left behind of a band gone distant
30   So far that no tongue could hail:
Past things retold were to her as things existent,
    Things present but as a tale.

May 20, 1902   1909

She Hears the Storm

There was a time in former years—
    While my roof-tree was his—
When I should have been distressed by fears
    At such a night as this.

5 I should have murmured anxiously,
    'The pricking rain strikes cold;
His road is bare of hedge or tree,
    And he is getting old.'

But now the fitful chimney-roar,
10   The drone of Thorncombe trees,
The Froom in flood upon the moor,
    The mud of Mellstock Leaze,[1]

The candle slanting sooty wick'd,
    The thuds upon the thatch,
15 The eaves-drops on the window flicked,
    The clacking garden-hatch,°   *gate*

1. The place-names in Hardy's fictional "Wessex" were often invented ("Thorncombe," "Mellstock Leaze"), but he also used the names of real loca-tions, as in "A Trampwoman's Tragedy." "The Froom" is presumably the river Frome, flowing through Dorset and Somerset.

And what they mean to wayfarers,
    I scarcely heed or mind;
He has won that storm-tight roof of hers
20   Which Earth grants all her kind.

1909

Channel Firing[1]

That night your great guns, unawares,
Shook all our coffins as we lay,
And broke the chancel[2] window-squares,
We thought it was the Judgement-day

5 And sat upright. While drearisome
Arose the howl of wakened hounds:
The mouse let fall the altar-crumb,
The worms drew back into the mounds,

The glebe cow[3] drooled. Till God called, 'No;
10 It's gunnery practise out at sea
Just as before you went below;
The world is as it used to be:

'All nations striving strong to make
Red war yet redder. Mad as hatters[4]
15 They do no more for Christès[5] sake
Than you who are helpless in such matters.

'That this is not the judgement-hour
For some of them's a blessed thing,
For if it were they'd have to scour
20 Hell's floor for so much threatening. . . .

'Ha, ha. It will be warmer when
I blow the trumpet (if indeed
I ever do; for you are men,
And rest eternal sorely need).'

25 So down we lay again. 'I wonder,
Will the world ever saner be,'
Said one, 'than when He sent us under
In our indifferent century!'

And many a skeleton shook his head.
30 'Instead of preaching forty year,'

---

1. Written in April 1914, when Anglo-German naval rivalry was growing steadily more acute; the title refers to gunnery practice in the English Channel. Four months later (August 4), World War I broke out.
2. Part of church nearest to the altar.
3. I.e., cow on a small plot of land belonging to a church (a "glebe" is a small field).
4. Cf. the Mad Hatter in Lewis Carroll's *Alice's Adventures in Wonderland* (1865).
5. The archaic spelling and pronunciation suggest a ballad note of doom.

My neighbour Parson Thirdly said,
'I wish I had stuck to pipes and beer.'

Again the guns disturbed the hour,
Roaring their readiness to avenge,
35   As far inland as Stourton Tower,
And Camelot, and starlit Stonehenge.[6]

1914   1914

The Convergence of the Twain

(*Lines on the loss of the* Titanic)[1]

I

In a solitude of the sea
Deep from human vanity,
And the Pride of Life that planned her, stilly couches she.

2

Steel chambers, late the pyres
5   Of her salamandrine[2] fires,
Cold currents thrid,[3] and turn to rhythmic tidal lyres.

3

Over the mirrors meant
To glass the opulent
The sea-worm crawls—grotesque, slimed, dumb, indifferent.

4

10   Jewels in joy designed
To ravish the sensuous mind
Lie lightless, all their sparkles bleared and black and blind.

5

Dim moon-eyed fishes near
Gaze at the gilded gear
15   And query: 'What does this vaingloriousness down here?' . . .

6

Well: while was fashioning
This creature of cleaving wing,
The Immanent Will[4] that stirs and urges everything

6. The sound of guns preparing for war across the Channel reaches Alfred's ("Stourton") Tower (near Stourton in Dorset), commemorating King Alfred's defeat of a Danish invasion in 878; also the site of King Arthur's court at Camelot (supposedly near Glastonbury) and the famous prehistoric stone circle of Stonehenge on Salisbury Plain.
1. The *Titanic* was the largest and most luxurious ocean liner of the day. Considered unsinkable, it sank with great loss of life on April 15, 1912, on the ship's maiden voyage, from Southampton to the United States, after colliding with an iceberg. "Twain": two.
2. I.e., destructive. The salamander was supposed to be able to survive fire.
3. A variant form of the verb *thread*.
4. The force (blind, but slowly gaining consciousness throughout history) that drives the world, according to Hardy's philosophy.

7

Prepared a sinister mate
20   For her—so gaily great—
A Shape of Ice, for the time far and dissociate.

8

And as the smart ship grew
In stature, grace, and hue,
In shadowy silent distance grew the Iceberg too.

9

25 Alien they seemed to be:
    No mortal eye could see
The intimate welding of their later history,

10

Or sign that they were bent
    By paths coincident
30 On being anon° twin halves of one august° event,   *soon / important*

11

Till the Spinner of the Years
    Said 'Now!' And each one hears,
And consummation comes, and jars two hemispheres.

1912   1912, 1914

Ah, Are You Digging on My Grave?

'Ah, are you digging on my grave
    My loved one?—planting rue?'[1]
—'No: yesterday he went to wed
One of the brightest wealth has bred.
5 'It cannot hurt her now,' he said,
    "That I should not be true." '

'Then who is digging on my grave?
    My nearest dearest kin?'
—'Ah, no; they sit and think, "What use!
10 What good will planting flowers produce?
No tendance of her mound can loose
    Her spirit from Death's gin." '°   *trap*

'But some one digs upon my grave?
    My enemy?—prodding sly?'
15 —'Nay: when she heard you had passed the Gate
That shuts on all flesh soon or late,
She thought you no more worth her hate,
    And cares not where you lie.'

1. A yellow-flowered herb, traditionally an emblem of sorrow (*rue* is also an archaic word for "sorrow").

'Then, who is digging on my grave?
20   Say—since I have not guessed!'
—'O it is I, my mistress dear,
Your little dog, who still lives near,
And much I hope my movements here
    Have not disturbed your rest?'

25 'Ah, yes! *You* dig upon my grave . . .
    Why flashed it not on me
That one true heart was left behind!
What feeling do we ever find
To equal among human kind
30   A dog's fidelity!'

'Mistress, I dug upon your grave
    To bury a bone, in case
I should be hungry near this spot
When passing on my daily trot.
35 I am sorry, but I quite forgot
    It was your resting-place.'

1914

Under the Waterfall

'Whenever I plunge my arm, like this,
In a basin of water, I never miss
The sweet sharp sense of a fugitive day
Fetched back from its thickening shroud of gray.
5   Hence the only prime
    And real love-rhyme
    That I know by heart,
    And that leaves no smart,
Is the purl° of a little valley fall   *rippling flow*
10 About three spans wide and two spans tall
Over a table of solid rock,
And into a scoop of the self-same block;
The purl of a runlet that never ceases
In stir of kingdoms, in wars, in peaces;
15 With a hollow boiling voice it speaks
And has spoken since hills were turfless peaks.'

'And why gives this the only prime
Idea to you of a real love-rhyme?
And why does plunging your arm in a bowl
20 Full of spring water, bring throbs to your soul?'

'Well, under the fall, in a crease of the stone,
Though where precisely none ever has known,
Jammed darkly, nothing to show how prized,
And by now with its smoothness opalized,
25   Is a drinking-glass:

        For, down that pass
        My lover and I
        Walked under a sky
Of blue with a leaf-wove awning of green,
30   In the burn of August, to paint the scene,
And we placed our basket of fruit and wine
By the runlet's rim, where we sat to dine;
And when we had drunk from the glass together,
Arched by the oak-copse from the weather,
35   I held the vessel to rinse in the fall,
Where it slipped, and sank, and was past recall,
Though we stooped and plumbed the little abyss
With long bared arms. There the glass still is.
And, as said, if I thrust my arm below
40   Cold water in basin or bowl, a throe°   *violent pang*
From the past awakens a sense of that time,
And the glass we used, and the cascade's rhyme.
The basin seems the pool, and its edge
The hard smooth face of the brook-side ledge,
45   And the leafy pattern of china-ware
The hanging plants that were bathing there.

'By night, by day, when it shines or lours,
There lies intact that chalice of ours,
And its presence adds to the rhyme of love
50   Persistently sung by the fall above.
No lip has touched it since his and mine
In turns therefrom sipped lovers' wine.'

                                                         1914

The Walk

        You did not walk with me
        Of late to the hill-top tree
           By the gated ways,
           As in earlier days;
5   You were weak and lame,
           So you never came,
And I went alone, and I did not mind,
Not thinking of you as left behind.

        I walked up there to-day
10   Just in the former way:
           Surveyed around
           The familiar ground
           By myself again:
           What difference, then?
15   Only that underlying sense
Of the look of a room on returning thence.

1912–13   1914

The Voice

Woman much missed, how you call to me, call to me,
Saying that now you are not as you were
When you had changed from the one who was all to me,
But as at first, when our day was fair.

5   Can it be you that I hear? Let me view you, then,
Standing as when I drew near to the town
Where you would wait for me: yes, as I knew you then,
Even to the original air-blue gown!

Or is it only the breeze, in its listlessness
10   Travelling across the wet mead° to me here,   *meadow*
You being ever dissolved to wan wistlessness,°   *inattention*
Heard no more again far or near?

Thus I; faltering forward,
Leaves around me falling,
15   Wind oozing thin through the thorn from norward,°   *northward*
And the woman calling.

Dec. 1912   1914

The Workbox

'See, here's the workbox, little wife,
That I made of polished oak.'
He was a joiner,° of village life;   *carpenter*
She came of borough folk.°   *townspeople*

5   He holds the present up to her
As with a smile she nears
And answers to the profferer,
' 'Twill last all my sewing years!'

'I warrant it will. And longer too.
10   'Tis a scantling° that I got   *small piece of wood*
Off poor John Wayward's coffin, who
Died of they knew not what.

'The shingled pattern that seems to cease
Against your box's rim
15   Continues right on in the piece
That's underground with him.

'And while I worked it made me think
Of timber's varied doom;
One inch where people eat and drink,
20   The next inch in a tomb.

'But why do you look so white, my dear,
    And turn aside your face?
You knew not that good lad, I fear,
    Though he came from your native place?'

25 'How could I know that good young man,
    Though he came from my native town,
When he must have left far earlier than
    I was a woman grown?'

'Ah, no. I should have understood!
30   It shocked you that I gave
To you one end of a piece of wood
    Whose other is in a grave?'

'Don't, dear, despise my intellect,
    Mere accidental things
35 Of that sort never have effect
    On my imaginings.'

Yet still her lips were limp and wan,
    Her face still held aside,
As if she had known not only John,
40   But known of what he died.

1914

During Wind and Rain

They sing their dearest songs—
He, she, all of them—yea,
Treble and tenor and bass,
    And one to play;
5   With the candles mooning° each face. . . .   *lighting*
      Ah, no; the years O!
How the sick leaves reel down in throngs!

They clear the creeping moss—
Elders and juniors—aye,
10 Making the pathways neat
    And the garden gay;
And they build a shady seat. . . .
      Ah, no; the years, the years;
See, the white storm-birds wing across.

15   They are blithely breakfasting all—
Men and maidens—yea,
Under the summer tree,
    With a glimpse of the bay,
While pet fowl come to the knee. . . .

20   Ah, no; the years O!
     And the rotten rose is ript from the wall.

         They change to a high new house,
         He, she, all of them—aye,
         Clocks and carpets and chairs
25   On the lawn all day,
         And brightest things that are theirs. . . .
            Ah, no; the years, the years;
     Down their carved names the rain-drop ploughs.

                                                    1917

In Time of 'The Breaking of Nations'[1]

                        1
         Only a man harrowing clods
            In a slow silent walk
         With an old horse that stumbles and nods
            Half asleep as they stalk.

                        2
5   Only thin smoke without flame
            From the heaps of couch-grass;
         Yet this will go onward the same
            Though Dynasties pass.

                        3
         Yonder a maid and her wight°   man
10   Come whispering by:
         War's annals will cloud into night
            Ere their story die.

1915   1916, 1917

He Never Expected Much

                      [or]
              A CONSIDERATION
     (*A reflection*) On my Eighty-Sixth Birthday

     Well, World, you have kept faith with me,
            Kept faith with me;
     Upon the whole you have proved to be
            Much as you said you were.
5   Since as a child I used to lie
     Upon the leaze° and watch the sky,   pasture
     Never, I own, expected I
            That life would all be fair.

---

1. Cf. "Thou art my battle axe and weapon of war: for with thee will I break in pieces the nations" (Jeremiah 51.20). The poem was written during World War I.

'Twas then you said, and since have said,
10   Times since have said,
In that mysterious voice you shed
       From clouds and hills around:
'Many have loved me desperately,
Many with smooth serenity,
15 While some have shown contempt of me
       Till they dropped underground.

'I do not promise overmuch,
       Child; overmuch;
Just neutral-tinted haps° and such,'   *happenings*
20   You said to minds like mine.
Wise warning for your credit's sake!
Which I for one failed not to take,
And hence could stem such strain and ache
       As each year might assign.

1926   1928

JOSEPH CONRAD
1857–1924

Joseph Conrad was born Józef Teodor Konrad Korzeniowski in Poland (then under Russian rule), son of a Polish patriot who suffered exile in Russia for his Polish nationalist activities and died in 1869, leaving Conrad to be brought up by a maternal uncle. At the age of fifteen he amazed his family and friends by announcing his passionate desire to go to sea; he was eventually allowed to go to Marseilles, France, in 1874, and from there he made a number of voyages on French merchant ships to Martinique and other islands in the Caribbean. In 1878 he signed on an English ship that brought him to the east coast English port of Lowestoft, where (still as an ordinary seaman) he joined the crew of a small coasting vessel plying between Lowestoft and Newcastle. In six voyages between these two ports he learned English. Thus launched on a career in the British merchant service, Conrad sailed on a variety of British ships to East Asia, Australia, India, South America, and Africa, eventually gaining his master's certificate in 1886, the year he became a naturalized British subject. He received his first command in 1888, and in 1890 took a steamboat up the Congo River in nightmarish circumstances (described in *Heart of Darkness*, 1899) that permanently afflicted his health and his imagination.

In the early 1890s he was already thinking of turning some of his Malayan experiences into English fiction, and in 1892–93, when serving as first mate on the *Torrens* sailing from London to Adelaide, he revealed to a sympathetic passenger that he had begun a novel (*Almayer's Folly*), while on the return journey he impressed the young novelist John Galsworthy, who was on board, with his conversation. Conrad found it difficult to obtain a command, and this difficulty, together with the interest aroused by *Almayer's Folly* when it was published in 1895, helped turn him away from the sea to a career as a writer. He settled in London and in 1896 married an Englishwoman. This son of a Polish patriot turned merchant seaman turned writer was henceforth—after twenty years at sea—an English novelist.

In his travels through Asian, African, and Caribbean landscapes that eventually made their way into his fiction, Conrad witnessed at close range the workings of

European empires, including the British, French, Belgian, Dutch, and German, that at the time controlled most of the earth's surface and were extracting from it vast quantities of raw materials and profiting from forced or cheap labor. In the essay "Geography and Some Explorers," Conrad describes the imperial exploitation he observed in Africa as "the vilest scramble for loot that ever disfigured the history of human conscience and geographical exploration." What he saw of the uses and abuses of imperial power helped make him deeply skeptical. Marlow, the intermediate narrator of *Heart of Darkness,* reflects: "The conquest of the earth, which mostly means the taking it away from those who have a different complexion or slightly flatter noses than ourselves, is not a pretty thing when you look into it too much. What redeems it is the idea only. An idea at the back of it. . . ." And yet in this novella, the ideas at the back of colonialism's ruthless greed and violence are hardly shown to redeem anything at all.

Conrad's questioning of the ethics of empire, perhaps harkening back to his childhood experience as a Pole under Russian occupation, is part of his many-faceted exploration of the ethical ambiguities in human experience. In his great novel *Lord Jim* (1900), which like *Heart of Darkness* uses the device of an intermediate narrator, he probes the meaning of a gross failure of duty on the part of a romantic and idealistic young sailor, and by presenting the hero's history from a series of different points of view sustains the ethical questioning to the end. By deploying intermediate narrators and multiple points of view in his fiction, he suggests the complexity of experience and the difficulty of judging human actions.

Although Conrad's plots and exotic settings recall imperial romance and Victorian tales of adventure, he helped develop modern narrative strategies—frame narration, fragmented perspective, flashbacks and flash-forwards, psychologically laden symbolism—that disrupt chronology, render meaning indeterminate, reveal unconscious drives, blur boundaries between civilization and barbarism, and radically cast in doubt epistemological and ethical certainties. Another indication of Conrad's modernist proclivities is the alienation of his characters. Many of his works expose the difficulty of true communion, while also paradoxically exposing how communion is sometimes unexpectedly forced on us, often with someone who may be on the surface our moral opposite, so that we are compelled into a mysterious recognition of our opposite as our true self. Other stories and novels—and Conrad wrote prolifically despite his late start—explore the ways in which the codes we live by are tested in moments of crisis, revealing either their inadequacy or our own. Imagination can corrupt (as with Lord Jim) or save (as in *The Shadow-Line,* 1917), and a total lack of it can either see a person through (Captain MacWhirr in *Typhoon,* 1902) or render a person comically ridiculous (Captain Mitchell in *Nostromo,* 1904). Set in an imaginary Latin American republic, *Nostromo* subtly studies the corrupting effects of politics and "material interests" on personal relationships. Conrad wrote two other political novels—*The Secret Agent* (1906) and *Under Western Eyes* (1911). The latter is a story of Dostoyevskian power about a Russian student who becomes involuntarily associated with anti-government violence in czarist Russia and is maneuvered by circumstances into a position where, although a government spy, he has to pretend to be a revolutionary among revolutionaries. Having to pretend consistently to be the opposite of what he is, this character, like others in Conrad's fiction, is alienated, trapped, unable to communicate. Conrad was as much a pessimist as Hardy, but Conrad aesthetically embodied his pessimism in subtler ways.

He was also a great master of English prose, an astonishing fact given that English was his third language after Polish and French, that he was twenty-one before he learned English, and that to the end of his life he spoke English with a strong foreign accent. He approached English's linguistic and literary conventions aslant, but the seeming handicap of his foreignness helped him bring to the English novel a fresh geopolitical understanding, a formal seriousness, and a psychological depth, all of which opened up new possibilities for imaginative literature in English, as indicated by his profound, if vexed, influence on later writers as different from himself as the Nigerian Chinua Achebe and the Anglo-Trinidadian V. S. Naipaul.

Preface to *The Nigger of the "Narcissus"*[1]

[THE TASK OF THE ARTIST]

A work that aspires, however humbly, to the condition of art should carry its justification in every line. And art itself may be defined as a single-minded attempt to render the highest kind of justice to the visible universe, by bringing to light the truth, manifold and one, underlying its every aspect. It is an attempt to find in its forms, in its colours, in its light, in its shadows, in the aspects of matter and in the facts of life what of each is fundamental, what is enduring and essential—their one illuminating and convincing quality—the very truth of their existence. The artist, then, like the thinker or the scientist, seeks the truth and makes his appeal. Impressed by the aspect of the world the thinker plunges into ideas, the scientist into facts—whence, presently, emerging they make their appeal to those qualities of our being that fit us best for the hazardous enterprise of living. They speak authoritatively to our common-sense, to our intelligence, to our desire of peace or to our desire of unrest; not seldom to our prejudices, sometimes to our fears, often to our egoism—but always to our credulity. And their words are heard with reverence, for their concern is with weighty matters: with the cultivation of our minds and the proper care of our bodies, with the attainment of our ambitions, with the perfection of the means and the glorification of our precious aims.

It is otherwise with the artist.

Confronted by the same enigmatical spectacle the artist descends within himself, and in that lonely region of stress and strife, if he be deserving and fortunate, he finds the terms of his appeal. His appeal is made to our less obvious capacities: to that part of our nature which, because of the warlike conditions of existence, is necessarily kept out of sight within the more resisting and hard qualities—like the vulnerable body within a steel armour. His appeal is less loud, more profound, less distinct, more stirring—and sooner forgotten. Yet its effect endures forever. The changing wisdom of successive generations discards ideas, questions facts, demolishes theories. But the artist appeals to that part of our being which is not dependent on wisdom; to that in us which is a gift and not an acquisition—and, therefore, more permanently enduring. He speaks to our capacity for delight and wonder, to the sense of mystery surrounding our lives; to our sense of pity, and beauty, and pain; to the latent feeling of fellowship with all creation—and to the subtle but invincible conviction of solidarity that knits together the loneliness of innumerable hearts, to the solidarity in dreams, in joy, in sorrow, in aspirations, in illusions, in hope, in fear, which binds men to each other, which binds together all humanity—the dead to the living and the living to the unborn.

---

1. Conrad wrote *The Nigger of the "Narcissus"* in 1896–97, shortly after his marriage; it was published first in *The New Review*, August–December 1897, and then in book form in 1898. Conrad took particular pleasure in writing the novel and later called it "the story by which, as a creative artist, I stand or fall." A few months after finishing it, feeling that he was now wholly dedicated to writing and had "done with the sea," he wrote this preface, which first appeared in the 1898 edition.

It is only some such train of thought, or rather of feeling, that can in a measure explain the aim of the attempt, made in the tale which follows,[2] to present an unrestful episode in the obscure lives of a few individuals out of all the disregarded multitude of the bewildered, the simple and the voiceless. For, if any part of truth dwells in the belief confessed above, it becomes evident that there is not a place of splendour or a dark corner of the earth that does not deserve, if only a passing glance of wonder and pity. The motive then, may be held to justify the matter of the work; but this preface, which is simply an avowal of endeavour, cannot end here—for the avowal is not yet complete.

Fiction—if it at all aspires to be art—appeals to temperament. And in truth it must be, like painting, like music, like all art, the appeal of one temperament to all the other innumerable temperaments whose subtle and resistless power endows passing events with their true meaning, and creates the moral, the emotional atmosphere of the place and time. Such an appeal to be effective must be an impression conveyed through the senses; and, in fact, it cannot be made in any other way, because temperament, whether individual or collective, is not amenable to persuasion. All art, therefore, appeals primarily to the senses, and the artistic aim when expressing itself in written words must also make its appeal through the senses, if its high desire is to reach the secret spring of responsive emotions. It must strenuously aspire to the plasticity of sculpture, to the colour of painting, and to the magic suggestiveness of music—which is the art of arts. And it is only through complete, unswerving devotion to the perfect blending of form and substance; it is only through an unremitting never-discouraged care for the shape and ring of sentences that an approach can be made to plasticity, to colour, and that the light of magic suggestiveness may be brought to play for an evanescent instant over the commonplace surface of words: of the old, old words, worn thin, defaced by ages of careless usage.

The sincere endeavour to accomplish that creative task, to go as far on that road as his strength will carry him, to go undeterred by faltering, weariness or reproach, is the only valid justification for the worker in prose. And if his conscience is clear, his answer to those who in the fulness of a wisdom which looks for immediate profit, demand specifically to be edified, consoled, amused; who demand to be promptly improved, or encouraged, or frightened, or shocked, or charmed, must run thus:—My task which I am trying to achieve is, by the power of the written word to make you hear, to make you feel—it is, before all, to make you *see*. That—and no more, and it is everything. If I succeed, you shall find there according to your deserts: encouragement, consolation, fear, charm—all you demand—and, perhaps, also that glimpse of truth for which you have forgotten to ask.

To snatch in a moment of courage, from the remorseless rush of time, a passing phase of life, is only the beginning of the task. The task approached in tenderness and faith is to hold up unquestioningly, without choice and without fear, the rescued fragment before all eyes in the light of a sincere mood. It is to show its vibration, its colour, its form; and through its movement, its form, and its colour, reveal the substance of its truth—disclose its inspiring secret: the stress and passion within the core of each convincing moment. In a single-minded attempt of that kind, if one be deserving and fortunate, one may perchance attain to such clearness of sincerity that at last the presented vision of regret or pity, of terror or mirth, shall awaken in the hearts of the

2. *The Nigger of the "Narcissus."*

beholders that feeling of unavoidable solidarity; of the solidarity in mysterious origin, in toil, in joy, in hope, in uncertain fate, which binds men to each other and all mankind to the visible world.

It is evident that he who, rightly or wrongly, holds by the convictions expressed above cannot be faithful to any one of the temporary formulas of his craft. The enduring part of them—the truth which each only imperfectly veils—should abide with him as the most precious of his possessions, but they all: Realism, Romanticism, Naturalism, even the unofficial sentimentalism (which like the poor, is exceedingly difficult to get rid of),[3] all these gods must, after a short period of fellowship, abandon him—even on the very threshold of the temple—to the stammerings of his conscience and to the outspoken consciousness of the difficulties of his work. In that uneasy solitude the supreme cry of Art for Art itself, loses the exciting ring of its apparent immorality. It sounds far off. It has ceased to be a cry, and is heard only as a whisper, often incomprehensible, but at times and faintly encouraging.

Sometimes, stretched at ease in the shade of a roadside tree, we watch the motions of a labourer in a distant field, and after a time, begin to wonder languidly as to what the fellow may be at. We watch the movements of his body, the waving of his arms, we see him bend down, stand up, hesitate, begin again. It may add to the charm of an idle hour to be told the purpose of his exertions. If we know he is trying to lift a stone, to dig a ditch, to uproot a stump, we look with a more real interest at his efforts; we are disposed to condone the jar of his agitation upon the restfulness of the landscape; and even, if in a brotherly frame of mind, we may bring ourselves to forgive his failure. We understood his object, and, after all, the fellow has tried, and perhaps he had not the strength—and perhaps he had not the knowledge. We forgive, go on our way—and forget.

And so it is with the workman of art. Art is long and life is short,[4] and success is very far off. And thus, doubtful of strength to travel so far, we talk a little about the aim—the aim of art, which, like life itself, is inspiring, difficult— obscured by mists. It is not in the clear logic of a triumphant conclusion; it is not in the unveiling of one of those heartless secrets which are called the Laws of Nature. It is not less great, but only more difficult.

To arrest, for the space of a breath, the hands busy about the work of the earth, and compel men entranced by the sight of distant goals to glance for a moment at the surrounding vision of form and colour, of sunshine and shadows; to make them pause for a look, for a sigh, for a smile—such is the aim, difficult and evanescent, and reserved only for a very few to achieve. But sometimes, by the deserving and the fortunate, even that task is accomplished. And when it is accomplished—behold!—all the truth of life is there: a moment of vision, a sigh, a smile—and the return to an eternal rest.

1897   1898

---

3. "For the poor always ye have with you" (John 12.8).

4. *Ars longa, vita brevis:* a Latin proverb, deriving from a dictum of the Greek physician Hippocrates.

Heart of Darkness

This story is derived from Conrad's experience in the Congo in 1890. Like Marlow, the narrator of the story, Conrad had as a child determined one day to visit the heart of Africa. "It was in 1868, when nine years old or thereabouts, that while looking at a map of Africa at the time and putting my finger on the blank space then representing the unsolved mystery of that continent, I said to myself with absolute assurance and an amazing audacity which are no longer in my character now: 'When I grow up I shall go *there'* " (*A Personal Record,* 1912).

Conrad was promised a job as a Congo River pilot through the influence of his distant cousin Marguerite Poradowska, who lived in Brussels and knew important officials of the Belgian company that exploited the Congo. At this time the Congo, although nominally an independent state, the Congo Free State (État Indépendent du Congo), was virtually the personal property of Leopold II, king of Belgium, who made a fortune out of it. Later, the appalling abuses involved in the naked colonial exploitation that went on in the Congo were exposed to public view, and international criticism compelled the setting up of a committee of inquiry in 1904. From 1885 to 1908 masses of Congolese men were worked to death, women were raped, hands were cut off, villages were looted and burned. What Conrad saw in 1890 shocked him profoundly and shook his view of the moral basis of colonialism, of exploration and trade in newly discovered countries, indeed of civilization in general. "*Heart of Darkness* is experience, too," Conrad wrote in his 1917 "Author's Note," "but it is experience pushed a little (and only very little) beyond the actual facts of the case for the perfectly legitimate, I believe, purpose of bringing it home to the minds and bosoms of the readers." And later he told Edward Garnett: "Before the Congo I was just a mere animal."

Conrad arrived in Africa in May 1890 and made his way up the Congo River very much as described in *Heart of Darkness.* At Kinshasa (which Conrad spells Kinchassa) on Stanley Pool, which he reached after an exhausting two-hundred-mile trek from Matadi, near the mouth of the river, Conrad was taken aback to learn that the steamer of which he was to be captain had been damaged and was undergoing repairs. He was sent as supernumerary on another steamer to learn the river. This steamer was sent to Stanley Falls to collect and bring back to Kinshasa one Georges Antoine Klein, an agent of the company who had fallen so gravely ill that he died on board. Conrad then fell seriously ill and eventually returned to London in January 1891 without ever having served as a Congo River pilot. The Congo experience permanently impaired his health; it also permanently haunted his imagination. The nightmare atmosphere of *Heart of Darkness* is an accurate reflection of Conrad's response to his traumatic experience.

The theme of the story is partly the "choice of nightmares" facing whites in the Congo—either to become like the commercially minded manager, who sees Africa, its people, and its resources solely as instruments of financial gain, or to become like Kurtz, the self-tortured and corrupted idealist (inspired by Klein). The manager is a "hollow man" (T. S. Eliot used a quotation from this story as one epigraph for his poem "The Hollow Men"); his only objections to Kurtz are commercial, not moral: Kurtz's methods are "unsound" and would therefore lose the company money. At the last Kurtz seems to recognize the moral horror of his having succumbed to the dark temptations that African life posed for the European. "He had summed up—he had judged." But the story also has other levels of meaning, and the counterpointing of Western civilization in Europe with what that civilization has done in Africa (see the concluding interview between Marlow and Kurtz's "intended"—based on an interview between Conrad and the dead Klein's fiancée) throws out several of these. The story first appeared in *Blackwood's Magazine* in 1899 and was revised for book publication in 1902 as part of *Youth: A Narrative, and Two Other Stories.* See also the extract from Chinua Achebe's essay "An Image of Africa: Racism in Conrad's *Heart of Darkness*" (p. 2709).

Heart of Darkness

1

The *Nellie*, a cruising yawl,[1] swung to her anchor without a flutter of the sails, and was at rest. The flood had made, the wind was nearly calm, and being bound down the river, the only thing for it was to come to and wait for the turn of the tide.

The sea-reach of the Thames stretched before us like the beginning of an interminable waterway. In the offing the sea and the sky were welded together without a joint, and in the luminous space the tanned sails of the barges drifting up with the tide seemed to stand still in red clusters of canvas sharply peaked, with gleams of varnished sprits. A haze rested on the low shores that ran out to sea in vanishing flatness. The air was dark above Gravesend,[2] and farther back still seemed condensed into a mournful gloom, brooding motionless over the biggest, and the greatest, town on earth.

The Director of Companies was our captain and our host. We four affectionately watched his back as he stood in the bows looking to seaward. On the whole river there was nothing that looked half so nautical. He resembled a pilot, which to a seaman is trustworthiness personified. It was difficult to realise his work was not out there in the luminous estuary, but behind him, within the brooding gloom.

Between us there was, as I have already said somewhere, the bond of the sea. Besides holding our hearts together through long periods of separation, it had the effect of making us tolerant of each other's yarns—and even convictions. The Lawyer—the best of old fellows—had, because of his many years and many virtues, the only cushion on deck, and was lying on the only rug. The Accountant had brought out already a box of dominoes, and was toying architecturally with the bones. Marlow sat cross-legged right aft, leaning against the mizzenmast. He had sunken cheeks, a yellow complexion, a straight back, an ascetic aspect, and, with his arms dropped, the palms of hands outwards, resembled an idol. The Director, satisfied the anchor had good hold, made his way aft and sat down amongst us. We exchanged a few words lazily. Afterwards there was silence on board the yacht. For some reason or other we did not begin that game of dominoes. We felt meditative, and fit for nothing but placid staring. The day was ending in a serenity of still and exquisite brilliance. The water shone pacifically; the sky, without a speck, was a benign immensity of unstained light; the very mist on the Essex marshes was like a gauzy and radiant fabric, hung from the wooded rises inland, and draping the low shores in diaphanous folds. Only the gloom to the west, brooding over the upper reaches, became more sombre every minute, as if angered by the approach of the sun.

And at last, in its curved and imperceptible fall, the sun sank low, and from glowing white changed to a dull red without rays and without heat, as if about to go out suddenly, stricken to death by the touch of that gloom brooding over a crowd of men.

Forthwith a change came over the waters, and the serenity became less brilliant but more profound. The old river in its broad reach rested unruffled

---

1. Two-masted boat.
2. River port on the south bank of the Thames twenty-four miles east (downriver) of London.

at the decline of day, after ages of good service done to the race that peopled
its banks, spread out in the tranquil dignity of a waterway leading to the uttermost ends of the earth. We looked at the venerable stream not in the vivid
flush of a short day that comes and departs for ever, but in the august light of
abiding memories. And indeed nothing is easier for a man who has, as the
phrase goes, "followed the sea" with reverence and affection, than to evoke
the great spirit of the past upon the lower reaches of the Thames. The tidal
current runs to and fro in its unceasing service, crowded with memories of
men and ships it has borne to the rest of home or to the battles of the sea. It
had known and served all the men of whom the nation is proud, from Sir
Francis Drake to Sir John Franklin,[3] knights all, titled and untitled—the great
knights-errant of the sea. It had borne all the ships whose names are like jewels
flashing in the night of time, from the *Golden Hind* returning with her round
flanks full of treasure, to be visited by the Queen's Highness and thus pass
out of the gigantic tale, to the *Erebus* and *Terror*, bound on other conquests—
and that never returned. It had known the ships and the men. They had sailed
from Deptford, from Greenwich, from Erith—the adventurers and the settlers;
kings' ships and the ships of men on 'Change; captains, admirals, the dark
"interlopers"[4] of the Eastern trade, and the commissioned "generals" of East
India fleets. Hunters for gold or pursuers of fame, they all had gone out on
that stream, bearing the sword, and often the torch, messengers of the might
within the land, bearers of a spark from the sacred fire. What greatness had
not floated on the ebb of that river into the mystery of an unknown earth! . . .
The dreams of men, the seed of commonwealths, the germs of empires.

The sun set; the dusk fell on the stream, and lights began to appear along
the shore. The Chapman lighthouse, a three-legged thing erect on a mud-flat,
shone strongly. Lights of ships moved in the fairway[5]—a great stir of lights
going up and going down. And farther west on the upper reaches the place of
the monstrous town was still marked ominously on the sky, a brooding gloom
in sunshine, a lurid glare under the stars.

"And this also," said Marlow suddenly, "has been one of the dark places of
the earth."

He was the only man of us who still "followed the sea." The worst that could
be said of him was that he did not represent his class. He was a seaman, but
he was a wanderer too, while most seamen lead, if one may so express it, a
sedentary life. Their minds are of the stay-at-home order, and their home is
always with them—the ship; and so is their country—the sea. One ship is very
much like another, and the sea is always the same. In the immutability of their
surroundings the foreign shores, the foreign faces, the changing immensity of
life, glide past, veiled not by a sense of mystery but by a slightly disdainful
ignorance; for there is nothing mysterious to a seaman unless it be the sea
itself, which is the mistress of his existence and as inscrutable as Destiny. For

---

3. Sir John Franklin (1786–1847), Arctic explorer
who in 1845 commanded an expedition consisting
of the ships *Erebus* and *Terror* in search of the
Northwest Passage. The ships never returned. Sir
Francis Drake (ca. 1540–1596), Elizabethan naval
hero and explorer, sailed around the world on his
ship *The Golden Hind*. Queen Elizabeth knighted
Drake aboard his ship, loaded with captured Spanish treasure, on his return.
4. Private ships muscling in on the monopoly of
the East India Company, which was founded in
1600, lost its trading monopoly in 1813, and transferred its governmental functions to the Crown in
1858. Deptford, on the south bank of the Thames,
on the eastern edge of London, was once an important dockyard. Greenwich is on the south bank of
the Thames immediately east of Deptford. Erith is
eight miles farther east. " 'Change": the Stock
Exchange.
5. Navigable part of a river, through which ships
enter and depart.

the rest, after his hours of work, a casual stroll or a casual spree on shore suffices to unfold for him the secret of a whole continent, and generally he finds the secret not worth knowing. The yarns of seamen have a direct simplicity, the whole meaning of which lies within the shell of a cracked nut. But Marlow was not typical (if his propensity to spin yarns be excepted), and to him the meaning of an episode was not inside like a kernel but outside, enveloping the tale which brought it out only as a glow brings out a haze, in the likeness of one of these misty halos that sometimes are made visible by the spectral illumination of moonshine.

His remark did not seem at all surprising. It was just like Marlow. It was accepted in silence. No one took the trouble to grunt even; and presently he said, very slow:

"I was thinking of very old times, when the Romans first came here, nineteen hundred years ago—the other day. . . . Light came out of this river since—you say Knights? Yes; but it is like a running blaze on a plain, like a flash of lightning in the clouds. We live in the flicker—may it last as long as the old earth keeps rolling! But darkness was here yesterday. Imagine the feelings of a commander of a fine—what d'ye call 'em?—trireme[6] in the Mediterranean, ordered suddenly to the north; run overland across the Gauls in a hurry; put in charge of one of these craft the legionaries—a wonderful lot of handy men they must have been too—used to build, apparently by the hundred, in a month or two, if we may believe what we read. Imagine him here—the very end of the world, a sea the colour of lead, a sky the colour of smoke, a kind of ship about as rigid as a concertina—and going up this river with stores, or orders, or what you like. Sandbanks, marshes, forests, savages—precious little to eat fit for a civilised man, nothing but Thames water to drink. No Falernian wine[7] here, no going ashore. Here and there a military camp lost in a wilderness, like a needle in a bundle of hay—cold, fog, tempests, disease, exile, and death—death skulking in the air, in the water, in the bush. They must have been dying like flies here. Oh yes—he did it. Did it very well, too, no doubt, and without thinking much about it either, except afterwards to brag of what he had gone through in his time, perhaps. They were men enough to face the darkness. And perhaps he was cheered by keeping his eye on a chance of promotion to the fleet at Ravenna[8] by and by, if he had good friends in Rome and survived the awful climate. Or think of a decent young citizen in a toga—perhaps too much dice, you know—coming out here in the train of some prefect, or tax-gatherer, or trader, even, to mend his fortunes. Land in a swamp, march through the woods, and in some inland post feel the savagery, the utter savagery, had closed round him—all that mysterious life of the wilderness that stirs in the forest, in the jungles, in the hearts of wild men. There's no initiation either into such mysteries. He has to live in the midst of the incomprehensible, which is also detestable. And it has a fascination, too, that goes to work upon him. The fascination of the abomination—you know. Imagine the growing regrets, the longing to escape, the powerless disgust, the surrender, the hate."

He paused.

"Mind," he began again, lifting one arm from the elbow, the palm of the

6. Ancient Greek and Roman galley with three ranks of oars.
7. Wine from a famed wine-making district in Campania (Italy).

8. A city in northern Italy once directly on the Adriatic Sea and an important naval station in Roman times. It is now about six miles from the sea, connected with it by a canal.

hand outwards, so that, with his legs folded before him, he had the pose of a Buddha preaching in European clothes and without a lotus-flower—"Mind, none of us would feel exactly like this. What saves us is efficiency—the devotion to efficiency. But these chaps were not much account, really. They were no colonists; their administration was merely a squeeze, and nothing more, I suspect. They were conquerors, and for that you want only brute force—nothing to boast of, when you have it, since your strength is just an accident arising from the weakness of others. They grabbed what they could get for the sake of what was to be got. It was just robbery with violence, aggravated murder on a great scale, and men going at it blind—as is very proper for those who tackle a darkness. The conquest of the earth, which mostly means the taking it away from those who have a different complexion or slightly flatter noses than ourselves, is not a pretty thing when you look into it too much. What redeems it is the idea only. An idea at the back of it; not a sentimental pretence but an idea; and an unselfish belief in the idea—something you can set up, and bow down before, and offer a sacrifice to. . . ."

He broke off. Flames glided in the river, small green flames, red flames, white flames, pursuing, overtaking, joining, crossing each other—then separating slowly or hastily. The traffic of the great city went on in the deepening night upon the sleepless river. We looked on, waiting patiently—there was nothing else to do till the end of the flood; but it was only after a long silence, when he said, in a hesitating voice, "I suppose you fellows remember I did once turn fresh-water sailor for a bit," that we knew we were fated, before the ebb began to run, to hear about one of Marlow's inconclusive experiences.

"I don't want to bother you much with what happened to me personally," he began, showing in this remark the weakness of many tellers of tales who seem so often unaware of what their audience would best like to hear; "yet to understand the effect of it on me you ought to know how I got out there, what I saw, how I went up that river to the place where I first met the poor chap. It was the farthest point of navigation and the culminating point of my experience. It seemed somehow to throw a kind of light on everything about me—and into my thoughts. It was sombre enough too—and pitiful—not extraordinary in any way—not very clear either. No, not very clear. And yet it seemed to throw a kind of light.

"I had then, as you remember, just returned to London after a lot of Indian Ocean, Pacific, China Seas—a regular dose of the East—six years or so, and I was loafing about, hindering you fellows in your work and invading your homes, just as though I had got a heavenly mission to civilise you. It was very fine for a time, but after a bit I did get tired of resting. Then I began to look for a ship—I should think the hardest work on earth. But the ships wouldn't even look at me. And I got tired of that game too.

"Now when I was a little chap I had a passion for maps. I would look for hours at South America, or Africa, or Australia, and lose myself in all the glories of exploration. At that time there were many blank spaces on the earth, and when I saw one that looked particularly inviting on a map (but they all look that) I would put my finger on it and say, When I grow up I will go there. The North Pole was one of these places, I remember. Well, I haven't been there yet, and shall not try now. The glamour's off. Other places were scattered about the Equator, and in every sort of latitude all over the two hemispheres. I have been in some of them, and . . . well, we won't talk about that. But there was one yet—the biggest, the most blank, so to speak—that I had a hankering after.

"True, by this time it was not a blank space any more. It had got filled since my boyhood with rivers and lakes and names. It had ceased to be a blank space of delightful mystery—a white patch for a boy to dream gloriously over. It had become a place of darkness. But there was in it one river especially, a mighty big river, that you could see on the map, resembling an immense snake uncoiled, with its head in the sea, its body at rest curving afar over a vast country, and its tail lost in the depths of the land. And as I looked at the map of it in a shop-window, it fascinated me as a snake would a bird—a silly little bird. Then I remembered there was a big concern, a Company for trade on that river. Dash it all! I thought to myself, they can't trade without using some kind of craft on that lot of fresh water—steamboats! Why shouldn't I try to get charge of one? I went on along Fleet Street,[9] but could not shake off the idea. The snake had charmed me.

"You understand it was a Continental concern, that Trading Society; but I have a lot of relations living on the Continent, because it's cheap and not so nasty as it looks, they say.

"I am sorry to own I began to worry them. This was already a fresh departure for me. I was not used to get things that way, you know. I always went my own road and on my own legs where I had a mind to go. I wouldn't have believed it of myself; but, then—you see—I felt somehow I must get there by hook or by crook. So I worried them. The men said, 'My dear fellow,' and did nothing. Then—would you believe it?—I tried the women. I, Charlie Marlow, set the women to work—to get a job. Heavens! Well, you see, the notion drove me. I had an aunt, a dear enthusiastic soul. She wrote: 'It will be delightful. I am ready to do anything, anything for you. It is a glorious idea. I know the wife of a very high personage in the Administration, and also a man who has lots of influence with,' etc. etc. She was determined to make no end of fuss to get me appointed skipper of a river steamboat, if such was my fancy.

"I got my appointment—of course; and I got it very quick. It appears the Company had received news that one of their captains had been killed in a scuffle with the natives. This was my chance, and it made me the more anxious to go. It was only months and months afterwards, when I made the attempt to recover what was left of the body, that I heard the original quarrel arose from a misunderstanding about some hens. Yes, two black hens. Fresleven—that was the fellow's name, a Dane—thought himself wronged somehow in the bargain, so he went ashore and started to hammer the chief of the village with a stick. Oh, it didn't surprise me in the least to hear this, and at the same time to be told that Fresleven was the gentlest, quietest creature that ever walked on two legs. No doubt he was; but he had been a couple of years already out there engaged in the noble cause, you know, and he probably felt the need at last of asserting his self-respect in some way. Therefore he whacked the old nigger mercilessly, while a big crowd of his people watched him, thunder-struck, till some man—I was told the chief's son—in desperation at hearing the old chap yell, made a tentative jab with a spear at the white man—and of course it went quite easy between the shoulder-blades. Then the whole population cleared into the forest, expecting all kinds of calamities to happen, while, on the other hand, the steamer Fresleven commanded left also in a bad panic, in charge of the engineer, I believe. Afterwards nobody seemed to trouble much about Fresleven's remains, till I got out and stepped into his shoes. I couldn't let it rest, though; but when an opportunity offered at last to meet

9. Street in central London.

my predecessor, the grass growing through his ribs was tall enough to hide his bones. They were all there. The supernatural being had not been touched after he fell. And the village was deserted, the huts gaped black, rotting, all askew within the fallen enclosures. A calamity had come to it, sure enough. The people had vanished. Mad terror had scattered them, men, women, and children, through the bush, and they had never returned. What became of the hens I don't know either. I should think the cause of progress got them, anyhow. However, through this glorious affair I got my appointment, before I had fairly begun to hope for it.

"I flew around like mad to get ready, and before forty-eight hours I was crossing the Channel to show myself to my employers, and sign the contract. In a very few hours I arrived in a city that always makes me think of a whited sepulchre. Prejudice no doubt. I had no difficulty in finding the Company's offices. It was the biggest thing in the town, and everybody I met was full of it. They were going to run an over-sea empire, and make no end of coin by trade.

"A narrow and deserted street in deep shadow, high houses, innumerable windows with venetian blinds, a dead silence, grass sprouting between the stones, imposing carriage archways right and left, immense double doors standing ponderously ajar. I slipped through one of these cracks, went up a swept and ungarnished staircase, as arid as a desert, and opened the first door I came to. Two women, one fat and the other slim, sat on straw-bottomed chairs, knitting black wool. The slim one got up and walked straight at me— still knitting with downcast eyes—and only just as I began to think of getting out of her way, as you would for a somnambulist, stood still, and looked up. Her dress was as plain as an umbrella-cover, and she turned round without a word and preceded me into a waiting-room. I gave my name, and looked about. Deal table in the middle, plain chairs all round the walls, on one end a large shining map, marked with all the colours of a rainbow. There was a vast amount of red—good to see at any time, because one knows that some real work is done in there, a deuce of a lot of blue, a little green, smears of orange, and, on the East Coast, a purple patch, to show where the jolly pioneers of progress drink the jolly lager-beer. However, I wasn't going into any of these. I was going into the yellow. Dead in the centre. And the river was there— fascinating—deadly—like a snake. Ough! A door opened, a white-haired secretarial head, but wearing a compassionate expression, appeared, and a skinny forefinger beckoned me into the sanctuary. Its light was dim, and a heavy writing desk squatted in the middle. From behind that structure came out an impression of pale plumpness in a frockcoat. The great man himself. He was five feet six, I should judge, and had his grip on the handle-end of ever so many millions. He shook hands, I fancy, murmured vaguely, was satisfied with my French. *Bon voyage*.

"In about forty-five seconds I found myself again in the waiting-room with the compassionate secretary, who, full of desolation and sympathy, made me sign some document. I believe I undertook amongst other things not to disclose any trade secrets. Well, I am not going to.

"I began to feel slightly uneasy. You know I am not used to such ceremonies, and there was something ominous in the atmosphere. It was just as though I had been let into some conspiracy—I don't know—something not quite right; and I was glad to get out. In the outer room the two women knitted black wool feverishly. People were arriving, and the younger one was walking back and forth introducing them. The old one sat on her chair. Her flat cloth slippers were propped up on a foot-warmer, and a cat reposed on her lap. She wore a starched white affair on her head, had a wart on one cheek, and silver-rimmed spectacles hung on the tip of her nose. She glanced at me above the glasses. The swift and indifferent placidity of that look troubled me. Two youths with foolish and cheery countenances were being piloted over, and she threw at them the same quick glance of unconcerned wisdom. She seemed to know all about them and about me too. An eerie feeling came over me. She seemed uncanny and fateful. Often far away there I thought of these two, guarding the door of Darkness, knitting black wool as for a warm pall, one introducing, introducing continuously to the unknown, the other scrutinising the cheery and foolish faces with unconcerned old eyes. *Ave!* Old knitter of black wool. *Morituri te salutant.*[1] Not many of those she looked at ever saw her again— not half, by a long way.

"There was yet a visit to the doctor. 'A simple formality,' assured me the secretary, with an air of taking an immense part in all my sorrows. Accordingly a young chap wearing his hat over the left eyebrow, some clerk I suppose— there must have been clerks in the business, though the house was as still as a house in a city of the dead—came from somewhere upstairs, and led me forth. He was shabby and careless, with ink-stains on the sleeves of his jacket, and his cravat was large and billowy, under a chin shaped like the toe of an old boot. It was a little too early for the doctor, so I proposed a drink, and thereupon he developed a vein of joviality. As we sat over our vermuths he glorified the Company's business, and by and by I expressed casually my surprise at him not going out there. He became very cool and collected all at once. 'I am not such a fool as I look, quoth Plato to his disciples,' he said sententiously, emptied his glass with great resolution, and we rose.

"The old doctor felt my pulse, evidently thinking of something else the while. 'Good, good for there,' he mumbled, and then with a certain eagerness asked me whether I would let him measure my head. Rather surprised, I said Yes, when he produced a thing like callipers and got the dimensions back and front and every way, taking notes carefully. He was an unshaven little man in a threadbare coat like a gaberdine, with his feet in slippers, and I thought him a harmless fool. 'I always ask leave, in the interests of science, to measure the crania of those going out there,' he said. 'And when they come back too?' I asked. 'Oh, I never see them,' he remarked; 'and, moreover, the changes take place inside, you know.' He smiled, as if at some quiet joke. 'So you are going out there. Famous. Interesting too.' He gave me a searching glance, and made another note. 'Ever any madness in your family?' he asked, in a matter-of-fact tone. I felt very annoyed. 'Is that question in the interests of science too?' 'It would be,' he said, without taking notice of my irritation, 'interesting for science to watch the mental changes of individuals, on the spot, but . . .' 'Are you an alienist?'[2] I interrupted. 'Every doctor should be—a little,' answered that original[3] imperturbably. 'I have a little theory which you Messieurs who go out there must help me to prove. This is my share in the advantages my country shall reap from the possession of such a magnificent dependency. The mere wealth I leave to others. Pardon my questions, but you are the first

1. "Hail! . . . Those who are about to die salute you" (Latin). The Roman gladiators' salute to the emperor on entering the arena.

2. Doctor who treats mental diseases. (The term has now been replaced by *psychiatrist*.)
3. Eccentric person.

Englishman coming under my observation . . .' I hastened to assure him I was not in the least typical. 'If I were,' said I, 'I wouldn't be talking like this with you.' 'What you say is rather profound, and probably erroneous,' he said, with a laugh. 'Avoid irritation more than exposure to the sun. Adieu. How do you English say, eh? Good-bye. Ah! Good-bye. Adieu. In the tropics one must before everything keep calm.' . . . He lifted a warning forefinger. . . . 'Du calme, du calme. Adieu.'

"One thing more remained to do—say good-bye to my excellent aunt. I found her triumphant. I had a cup of tea—the last decent cup of tea for many days—and in a room that most soothingly looked just as you would expect a lady's drawing-room to look, we had a long quiet chat by the fireside. In the course of these confidences it became quite plain to me I had been represented to the wife of the high dignitary, and goodness knows to how many more people besides, as an exceptional and gifted creature—a piece of good fortune for the Company—a man you don't get hold of every day. Good heavens! and I was going to take charge of a two-penny-halfpenny river-steamboat with a penny whistle attached! It appeared, however, I was also one of the Workers, with a capital—you know. Something like an emissary of light, something like a lower sort of apostle. There had been a lot of such rot let loose in print and talk just about that time, and the excellent woman, living right in the rush of all that humbug, got carried off her feet. She talked about 'weaning those ignorant millions from their horrid ways,' till, upon my word, she made me quite uncomfortable. I ventured to hint that the Company was run for profit.

" 'You forget, dear Charlie, that the labourer is worthy of his hire,' she said brightly. It's queer how out of touch with truth women are. They live in a world of their own, and there had never been anything like it, and never can be. It is too beautiful altogether, and if they were to set it up it would go to pieces before the first sunset. Some confounded fact we men have been living contentedly with ever since the day of creation would start up and knock the whole thing over.

"After this I got embraced, told to wear flannel, be sure to write often, and so on—and I left. In the street—I don't know why—a queer feeling came to me that I was an impostor. Odd thing that I, who used to clear out for any part of the world at twenty-four hours' notice, with less thought than most men give to the crossing of a street, had a moment—I won't say of hesitation, but of startled pause, before this commonplace affair. The best way I can explain it to you is by saying that, for a second or two, I felt as though, instead of going to the centre of a continent, I were about to set off for the centre of the earth.

"I left in a French steamer, and she called in every blamed port they have out there, for, as far as I could see, the sole purpose of landing soldiers and custom-house officers. I watched the coast. Watching a coast as it slips by the ship is like thinking about an enigma. There it is before you—smiling, frowning, inviting, grand, mean, insipid, or savage, and always mute with an air of whispering, Come and find out. This one was almost featureless, as if still in the making, with an aspect of monotonous grimness. The edge of a colossal jungle, so dark green as to be almost black, fringed with white surf, ran straight, like a ruled line, far, far away along a blue sea whose glitter was blurred by a creeping mist. The sun was fierce, the land seemed to glisten and drip with steam. Here and there greyish-whitish specks showed up clustered inside the white surf, with a flag flying above them perhaps—settlements some centuries old, and still no bigger than pin-heads on the untouched expanse of their background. We pounded along, stopped, landed soldiers; went on, landed custom-house clerks to levy toll in what looked like a God-forsaken wilderness, with a tin shed and a flag-pole lost in it; landed more soldiers—to take care of the custom-house clerks presumably. Some, I heard, got drowned in the surf; but whether they did or not, nobody seemed particularly to care. They were just flung out there, and on we went. Every day the coast looked the same, as though we had not moved; but we passed various places—trading places—with names like Gran' Bassam, Little Popo; names that seemed to belong to some sordid farce acted in front of a sinister back-cloth. The idleness of a passenger, my isolation amongst all these men with whom I had no point of contact, the oily and languid sea, the uniform sombreness of the coast, seemed to keep me away from the truth of things, within the toil of a mournful and senseless delusion. The voice of the surf heard now and then was a positive pleasure, like the speech of a brother. It was something natural, that had its reason, that had a meaning. Now and then a boat from the shore gave one a momentary contact with reality. It was paddled by black fellows. You could see from afar the white of their eyeballs glistening. They shouted, sang; their bodies streamed with perspiration; they had faces like grotesque masks—these chaps; but they had bone, muscle, a wild vitality, an intense energy of movement, that was as natural and true as the surf along their coast. They wanted no excuse for being there. They were a great comfort to look at. For a time I would feel I belonged still to a world of straightforward facts; but the feeling would not last long. Something would turn up to scare it away. Once, I remember, we came upon a man-of-war anchored off the coast. There wasn't even a shed there, and she was shelling the bush. It appears the French had one of their wars going on thereabouts. Her ensign dropped limp like a rag; the muzzles of the long six-inch guns stuck out all over the low hull; the greasy, slimy swell swung her up lazily and let her down, swaying her thin masts. In the empty immensity of earth, sky, and water, there she was, incomprehensible, firing into a continent. Pop, would go one of the six-inch guns; a small flame would dart and vanish, a little white smoke would disappear, a tiny projectile would give a feeble screech—and nothing happened. Nothing could happen. There was a touch of insanity in the proceeding, a sense of lugubrious drollery in the sight; and it was not dissipated by somebody on board assuring me earnestly there was a camp of natives—he called them enemies!—hidden out of sight somewhere.

"We gave her her letters (I heard the men in that lonely ship were dying of fever at the rate of three a day) and went on. We called at some more places with farcical names, where the merry dance of death and trade goes on in a still and earthy atmosphere as of an overheated catacomb; all along the formless coast bordered by dangerous surf, as if Nature herself had tried to ward off intruders; in and out of rivers, streams of death in life, whose banks were rotting into mud, whose waters, thickened into slime, invaded the contorted mangroves,[4] that seemed to writhe at us in the extremity of an impotent despair. Nowhere did we stop long enough to get a particularised impression, but the general sense of vague and oppressive wonder grew upon me. It was like a weary pilgrimage amongst hints for nightmares.

"It was upward of thirty days before I saw the mouth of the big river. We

4. Tropical evergreen trees or shrubs with roots and stems forming dense thickets.

anchored off the seat of the government. But my work would not begin till some two hundred miles farther on. So as soon as I could I made a start for a place thirty miles higher up.

"I had my passage on a little sea-going steamer. Her captain was a Swede, and knowing me for a seaman, invited me on the bridge. He was a young man, lean, fair, and morose, with lanky hair and a shuffling gait. As we left the miserable little wharf, he tossed his head contemptuously at the shore. 'Been living there?' he asked. I said, 'Yes.' 'Fine lot these government chaps—are they not?' he went on, speaking English with great precision and considerable bitterness. 'It is funny what some people will do for a few francs a month. I wonder what becomes of that kind when it goes up country?' I said to him I expected to see that soon. 'So-o-o!' he exclaimed. He shuffled athwart, keeping one eye ahead vigilantly. 'Don't be too sure,' he continued. 'The other day I took up a man who hanged himself on the road. He was a Swede, too.' 'Hanged himself! Why, in God's name?' I cried. He kept on looking out watchfully. 'Who knows? The sun too much for him, or the country perhaps.'

"At last we opened a reach. A rocky cliff appeared, mounds of turned-up earth by the shore, houses on a hill, others with iron roofs, amongst a waste of excavations, or hanging to the declivity. A continuous noise of the rapids above hovered over this scene of inhabited devastation. A lot of people, mostly black and naked, moved about like ants. A jetty[5] projected into the river. A blinding sunlight drowned all this at times in a sudden recrudescence of glare. 'There's your Company's station,' said the Swede, pointing to three wooden barrack-like structures on the rocky slope. 'I will send your things up. Four boxes did you say? So. Farewell.'

"I came upon a boiler wallowing in the grass, then found a path leading up the hill. It turned aside for the boulders, and also for an undersized railway truck lying there on its back with its wheels in the air. One was off. The thing looked as dead as the carcass of some animal. I came upon more pieces of decaying machinery, a stack of rusty nails. To the left a clump of trees made a shady spot, where dark things seemed to stir feebly. I blinked, the path was steep. A horn tooted to the right, and I saw the black people run. A heavy and dull detonation shook the ground, a puff of smoke came out of the cliff, and that was all. No change appeared on the face of the rock. They were building a railway. The cliff was not in the way or anything; but this objectless blasting was all the work going on.

"A slight clinking behind me made me turn my head. Six black men advanced in a file, toiling up the path. They walked erect and slow, balancing small baskets full of earth on their heads, and the clink kept time with their footsteps. Black rags were wound round their loins, and the short ends behind waggled to and fro like tails. I could see every rib, the joints of their limbs were like knots in a rope; each had an iron collar on his neck, and all were connected together with a chain whose bights swung between them, rhythmically clinking. Another report from the cliff made me think suddenly of that ship of war I had seen firing into a continent. It was the same kind of ominous voice; but these men could by no stretch of imagination be called enemies. They were called criminals, and the outraged law, like the bursting shells, had come to them, an insoluble mystery from the sea. All their meagre breasts panted together, the violently dilated nostrils quivered, the eyes stared stonily uphill.

5. Wharf or pier.

They passed me within six inches, without a glance, with that complete, death-like indifference of unhappy savages. Behind this raw matter one of the reclaimed, the product of the new forces at work, strolled despondently, carrying a rifle by its middle. He had a uniform jacket with one button off, and seeing a white man on the path, hoisted his weapon to his shoulder with alacrity. This was simple prudence, white men being so much alike at a distance that he could not tell who I might be. He was speedily reassured, and with a large, white, rascally grin, and a glance at his charge, seemed to take me into partnership in his exalted trust. After all, I also was a part of the great cause of these high and just proceedings.

"Instead of going up, I turned and descended to the left. My idea was to let that chain-gang get out of sight before I climbed the hill. You know I am not particularly tender; I've had to strike and to fend off. I've had to resist and to attack sometimes—that's only one way of resisting—without counting the exact cost, according to the demands of such sort of life as I had blundered into. I've seen the devil of violence, and the devil of greed, and the devil of hot desire; but, by all the stars! these were strong, lusty, red-eyed devils, that swayed and drove men—men, I tell you. But as I stood on this hillside, I foresaw that in the blinding sunshine of that land I would become acquainted with a flabby, pretending, weak-eyed devil of a rapacious and pitiless folly. How insidious he could be, too, I was only to find out several months later and a thousand miles farther. For a moment I stood appalled, as though by a warning. Finally I descended the hill, obliquely, towards the trees I had seen.

"I avoided a vast artificial hole somebody had been digging on the slope, the purpose of which I found it impossible to divine. It wasn't a quarry or a sandpit, anyhow. It was just a hole. It might have been connected with the philanthropic desire of giving the criminals something to do. I don't know. Then I nearly fell into a very narrow ravine, almost no more than a scar in the hillside. I discovered that a lot of imported drainage-pipes for the settlement had been tumbled in there. There wasn't one that was not broken. It was a wanton smash-up. At last I got under the trees. My purpose was to stroll into the shade for a moment; but no sooner within than it seemed to me I had stepped into the gloomy circle of some Inferno. The rapids were near, and an uninterrupted, uniform, headlong, rushing noise filled the mournful stillness of the grove, where not a breath stirred, not a leaf moved, with a mysterious sound—as though the tearing pace of the launched earth had suddenly become audible.

"Black shapes crouched, lay, sat between the trees, leaning against the trunks, clinging to the earth, half coming out, half effaced within the dim light, in all the attitudes of pain, abandonment, and despair. Another mine on the cliff went off, followed by a slight shudder of the soil under my feet. The work was going on. The work! And this was the place where some of the helpers had withdrawn to die.

"They were dying slowly—it was very clear. They were not enemies, they were not criminals, they were nothing earthly now—nothing but black shadows of disease and starvation, lying confusedly in the greenish gloom. Brought from all the recesses of the coast in all the legality of time contracts, lost in uncongenial surroundings, fed on unfamiliar food, they sickened, became inefficient, and were then allowed to crawl away and rest. These moribund shapes were free as air—and nearly as thin. I began to distinguish the gleam of eyes under the trees. Then, glancing down, I saw a face near my hand. The black bones reclined at full length with one shoulder against the tree, and slowly the eyelids rose and the sunken eyes looked up at me, enormous and vacant, a kind of blind, white flicker in the depths of the orbs, which died out slowly. The man seemed young—almost a boy—but you know with them it's hard to tell. I found nothing else to do but to offer him one of my good Swede's ship's biscuits I had in my pocket. The fingers closed slowly on it and held—there was no other movement and no other glance. He had tied a bit of white worsted[6] round his neck—Why? Where did he get it? Was it a badge—an ornament—a charm—a propitiatory act? Was there any idea at all connected with it? It looked startling round his black neck, this bit of white thread from beyond the seas.

"Near the same tree two more bundles of acute angles sat with their legs drawn up. One, with his chin propped on his knees, stared at nothing, in an intolerable and appalling manner: his brother phantom rested its forehead, as if overcome with a great weariness; and all about others were scattered in every pose of contorted collapse, as in some picture of a massacre or a pestilence. While I stood horror-struck, one of these creatures rose to his hands and knees, and went off on all-fours towards the river to drink. He lapped out of his hand, then sat up in the sunlight, crossing his shins in front of him, and after a time let his woolly head fall on his breastbone.

"I didn't want any more loitering in the shade, and I made haste towards the station. When near the buildings I met a white man, in such an unexpected elegance of get-up that in the first moment I took him for a sort of vision. I saw a high starched collar, white cuffs, a light alpaca[7] jacket, snowy trousers, a clear necktie, and varnished boots. No hat. Hair parted, brushed, oiled, under a green-lined parasol held in a big white hand. He was amazing, and had a penholder behind his ear.

"I shook hands with this miracle, and I learned he was the Company's chief accountant, and that all the book-keeping was done at this station. He had come out for a moment, he said, 'to get a breath of fresh air.' The expression sounded wonderfully odd, with its suggestion of sedentary desk-life. I wouldn't have mentioned the fellow to you at all, only it was from his lips that I first heard the name of the man who is so indissolubly connected with the memories of that time. Moreover, I respected the fellow. Yes; I respected his collars, his vast cuffs, his brushed hair. His appearance was certainly that of a hairdresser's dummy; but in the great demoralisation of the land he kept up his appearance. That's backbone. His starched collars and got-up shirt-fronts were achievements of character. He had been out nearly three years; and, later, I could not help asking him how he managed to sport such linen. He had just the faintest blush, and said modestly, 'I've been teaching one of the native women about the station. It was difficult. She had a distaste for the work.' Thus this man had verily accomplished something. And he was devoted to his books, which were in apple-pie order.

"Everything else in the station was in a muddle,—heads, things, buildings. Strings of dusty niggers with splay feet arrived and departed; a stream of manufactured goods, rubbishy cottons, beads, and brass-wire sent into the depths of darkness, and in return came a precious trickle of ivory.

"I had to wait in the station for ten days—an eternity. I lived in a hut in the

6. Fine wool fabric.
7. Made from the wool of a South American animal by that name.

yard, but to be out of the chaos I would sometimes get into the accountant's office. It was built of horizontal planks, and so badly put together that, as he bent over his high desk, he was barred from neck to heels with narrow strips of sunlight. There was no need to open the big shutter to see. It was hot there too; big flies buzzed fiendishly, and did not sting, but stabbed. I sat generally on the floor, while, of faultless appearance (and even slightly scented), perching on a high stool, he wrote, he wrote. Sometimes he stood up for exercise. When a truckle-bed with a sick man (some invalided agent from up country) was put in there, he exhibited a gentle annoyance. 'The groans of this sick person' he said, 'distract my attention. And without that it is extremely difficult to guard against clerical errors in this climate.'

"One day he remarked, without lifting his head, 'In the interior you will no doubt meet Mr Kurtz.' On my asking who Mr Kurtz was, he said he was a first-class agent; and seeing my disappointment at this information, he added slowly, laying down his pen, 'He is a very remarkable person.' Further questions elicited from him that Mr Kurtz was at present in charge of a trading-post, a very important one, in the true ivory-country, at 'the very bottom of there. Sends in as much ivory as all the others put together . . . ' He began to write again. The sick man was too ill to groan. The flies buzzed in a great peace.

"Suddenly there was a growing murmur of voices and a great tramping of feet. A caravan had come in. A violent babble of uncouth sounds burst out on the other side of the planks. All the carriers were speaking together, and in the midst of the uproar the lamentable voice of the chief agent was heard 'giving it up' tearfully for the twentieth time that day. . . . He rose slowly. 'What a frightful row,' he said. He crossed the room gently to look at the sick man, and returning, said to me, 'He does not hear.' 'What! Dead?' I asked, startled. 'No, not yet,' he answered, with great composure. Then, alluding with a toss of the head to the tumult in the station-yard, 'When one has got to make correct entries, one comes to hate those savages—hate them to the death.' He remained thoughtful for a moment. 'When you see Mr Kurtz,' he went on, 'tell him from me that everything here'—he glanced at the desk—'is very satisfactory. I don't like to write to him—with those messengers of ours you never know who may get hold of your letter—at that Central Station.' He stared at me for a moment with his mild, bulging eyes. 'Oh, he will go far, very far,' he began again. 'He will be a somebody in the Administration before long. They, above—the Council in Europe, you know—mean him to be.'

"He turned to his work. The noise outside had ceased, and presently in going out I stopped at the door. In the steady buzz of flies the homeward-bound agent was lying flushed and insensible; the other, bent over his books, was making correct entries of perfectly correct transactions; and fifty feet below the doorstep I could see the still tree-tops of the grove of death.

"Next day I left that station at last, with a caravan of sixty men, for a two-hundred-mile tramp.

"No use telling you much about that. Paths, paths, everywhere; a stamped-in network of paths spreading over the empty land, through long grass, through burnt grass, through thickets, down and up chilly ravines, up and down stony hills ablaze with heat; and a solitude, a solitude, nobody, not a hut. The population had cleared out a long time ago. Well, if a lot of mysterious niggers armed with all kinds of fearful weapons suddenly took to travelling on the road between Deal and Gravesend, catching the yokels right and left to carry heavy loads for them, I fancy every farm and cottage thereabouts would get empty very soon. Only here the dwellings were gone too. Still, I passed through several abandoned villages. There's something pathetically childish in the ruins of grass walls. Day after day, with the stamp and shuffle of sixty pair of bare feet behind me, each pair under a 60-lb. load. Camp, cook, sleep, strike camp, march. Now and then a carrier dead in harness, at rest in the long grass near the path, with an empty water-gourd and his long staff lying by his side. A great silence around and above. Perhaps on some quiet night the tremor of far-off drums, sinking, swelling, a tremor vast, faint; a sound weird, appealing, suggestive, and wild—and perhaps with as profound a meaning as the sound of bells in a Christian country. Once a white man in an unbuttoned uniform, camping on the path with an armed escort of lank Zanzibaris,[8] very hospitable and festive—not to say drunk. Was looking after the upkeep of the road, he declared. Can't say I saw any road or any upkeep, unless the body of a middle-aged negro, with a bullet-hole in the forehead, upon which I absolutely stumbled three miles farther on, may be considered as a permanent improvement. I had a white companion too, not a bad chap, but rather too fleshy and with the exasperating habit of fainting on the hot hillsides, miles away from the least bit of shade and water. Annoying, you know, to hold your own coat like a parasol over a man's head while he is coming-to. I couldn't help asking him once what he meant by coming there at all. 'To make money, of course. What do you think?' he said scornfully. Then he got fever, and had to be carried in a hammock slung under a pole. As he weighed sixteen stone[9] I had no end of rows with the carriers. They jibbed, ran away, sneaked off with their loads in the night—quite a mutiny. So, one evening, I made a speech in English with gestures, not one of which was lost to the sixty pairs of eyes before me, and the next morning I started the hammock off in front all right. An hour afterwards I came upon the whole concern wrecked in a bush—man, hammock, groans, blankets, horrors. The heavy pole had skinned his poor nose. He was very anxious for me to kill somebody, but there wasn't the shadow of a carrier near. I remembered the old doctor—'It would be interesting for science to watch the mental changes of individuals, on the spot.' I felt I was becoming scientifically interesting. However, all that is to no purpose. On the fifteenth day I came in sight of the big river again, and hobbled into the Central Station. It was on a back water surrounded by scrub and forest, with a pretty border of smelly mud on one side, and on the three others enclosed by a crazy fence of rushes. A neglected gap was all the gate it had, and the first glance at the place was enough to let you see the flabby devil was running that show. White men with long staves in their hands appeared languidly from amongst the buildings, strolling up to take a look at me, and then retired out of sight somewhere. One of them, a stout, excitable chap with black moustaches, informed me with great volubility and many digressions, as soon as I told him who I was, that my steamer was at the bottom of the river. I was thunderstruck. What, how, why? Oh, it was 'all right.' The 'manager himself' was there. All quite correct. 'Everybody had behaved splendidly! splendidly!'—'You must,' he said in agitation, 'go and see the general manager at once. He is waiting!'

"I did not see the real significance of that wreck at once. I fancy I see it

8. Natives of Zanzibar, an island off the east coast of Africa, once part of the sultanate of Zanzibar and a British protectorate, now part of the independent state of Tanzania. Zanzibaris were used as mercenaries throughout Africa.
9. One stone equals 14 pounds. The man weighed 224 pounds.

now, but I am not sure—not at all. Certainly the affair was too stupid—when I think of it—to be altogether natural. Still . . . But at the moment it presented itself simply as a confounded nuisance. The steamer was sunk. They had started two days before in a sudden hurry up the river with the manager on board, in charge of some volunteer skipper, and before they had been out three hours they tore the bottom out of her on stones, and she sank near the south bank. I asked myself what I was to do there, now my boat was lost. As a matter of fact, I had plenty to do in fishing my command out of the river. I had to set about it the very next day. That, and the repairs when I brought the pieces to the station, took some months.

"My first interview with the manager was curious. He did not ask me to sit down after my twenty-mile walk that morning. He was commonplace in complexion, in feature, in manners, and in voice. He was of middle size and of ordinary build. His eyes, of the usual blue, were perhaps remarkably cold, and he certainly could make his glance fall on one as trenchant and heavy as an axe. But even at these times the rest of his person seemed to disclaim the intention. Otherwise there was only an indefinable, faint expression of his lips, something stealthy—a smile—not a smile—I remember it, but I can't explain. It was unconscious, this smile was, though just after he had said something it got intensified for an instant. It came at the end of his speeches like a seal applied on the words to make the meaning of the commonest phrase appear absolutely inscrutable. He was a common trader, from his youth up employed in these parts—nothing more. He was obeyed, yet he inspired neither love nor fear, nor even respect. He inspired uneasiness. That was it! Uneasiness. Not a definite mistrust—just uneasiness—nothing more. You have no idea how effective such a . . . a . . . faculty can be. He had no genius for organising, for initiative, or for order even. That was evident in such things as the deplorable state of the station. He had no learning, and no intelligence. His position had come to him—why? Perhaps because he was never ill . . . He had served three terms of three years out there . . . Because triumphant health in the general rout of constitutions is a kind of power in itself. When he went home on leave he rioted on a large scale—pompously. Jack ashore—with a difference—in externals only. This one could gather from his casual talk. He originated nothing, he could keep the routine going—that's all. But he was great. He was great by this little thing that it was impossible to tell what could control such a man. He never gave that secret away. Perhaps there was nothing within him. Such a suspicion made one pause—for out there there were no external checks. Once when various tropical diseases had laid low almost every 'agent' in the station, he was heard to say, 'Men who come out here should have no entrails.' He sealed the utterance with that smile of his, as though it had been a door opening into a darkness he had in his keeping. You fancied you had seen things—but the seal was on. When annoyed at meal-times by the constant quarrels of the white men about precedence, he ordered an immense round table to be made, for which a special house had to be built. This was the station's mess-room. Where he sat was the first place—the rest were nowhere. One felt this to be his unalterable conviction. He was neither civil nor uncivil. He was quiet. He allowed his 'boy'—an overfed young negro from the coast—to treat the white men, under his very eyes, with provoking insolence.

"He began to speak as soon as he saw me. I had been very long on the road. He could not wait. Had to start without me. The up-river stations had to be relieved. There had been so many delays already that he did not know who was dead and who was alive, and how they got on—and so on, and so on. He paid no attention to my explanations, and, playing with a stick of sealing-wax, repeated several times that the situation was 'very grave, very grave.' There were rumours that a very important station was in jeopardy, and its chief, Mr Kurtz, was ill. Hoped it was not true. Mr Kurtz was . . . I felt weary and irritable. Hang Kurtz, I thought. I interrupted him by saying I had heard of Mr Kurtz on the coast. 'Ah! So they talk of him down there,' he murmured to himself. Then he began again, assuring me Mr Kurtz was the best agent he had, an exceptional man, of the greatest importance to the Company; therefore I could understand his anxiety. He was, he said, 'very, very uneasy.' Certainly he fidgeted on his chair a good deal, exclaimed, 'Ah, Mr Kurtz!' broke the stick of sealing-wax and seemed dumbfounded by the accident. Next thing he wanted to know 'how long it would take to' . . . I interrupted him again. Being hungry, you know, and kept on my feet too, I was getting savage. 'How can I tell?' I said, 'I haven't even seen the wreck yet—some months, no doubt.' All this talk seemed to me so futile. 'Some months,' he said. 'Well, let us say three months before we can make a start. Yes. That ought to do the affair.' I flung out of his hut (he lived all alone in a clay hut with a sort of verandah) muttering to myself my opinion of him. He was a chattering idiot. Afterwards I took it back when it was borne in upon me startlingly with what extreme nicety he had estimated the time requisite for the 'affair.'

"I went to work the next day, turning, so to speak, my back on that station. In that way only it seemed to me I could keep my hold on the redeeming facts of life. Still, one must look about sometimes; and then I saw this station, these men strolling aimlessly about in the sunshine of the yard. I asked myself sometimes what it all meant. They wandered here and there with their absurd long staves in their hands, like a lot of faithless pilgrims bewitched inside a rotten fence. The word 'ivory' rang in the air, was whispered, was sighed. You would think they were praying to it. A taint of imbecile rapacity blew through it all, like a whiff from some corpse. By Jove! I've never seen anything so unreal in my life. And outside, the silent wilderness surrounding this cleared speck on the earth struck me as something great and invincible, like evil or truth, waiting patiently for the passing away of this fantastic invasion.

"Oh, these months! Well, never mind. Various things happened. One evening a grass shed full of calico, cotton prints, beads, and I don't know what else, burst into a blaze so suddenly that you would have thought the earth had opened to let an avenging fire consume all that trash. I was smoking my pipe quietly by my dismantled steamer, and saw them all cutting capers in the light, with their arms lifted high, when the stout man with moustaches came tearing down to the river, a tin pail in his hand, assured me that everybody was 'behaving splendidly, splendidly,' dipped about a quart of water and tore back again. I noticed there was a hole in the bottom of his pail.

"I strolled up. There was no hurry. You see the thing had gone off like a box of matches. It had been hopeless from the very first. The flame had leaped high, driven everybody back, lighted up everything—and collapsed. The shed was already a heap of embers glowing fiercely. A nigger was being beaten near by. They said he had caused the fire in some way; be that as it may, he was screeching most horribly. I saw him, later, for several days, sitting in a bit of shade looking very sick and trying to recover himself: afterwards he arose and went out—and the wilderness without a sound took him into its bosom again.

As I approached the glow from the dark I found myself at the back of two men, talking. I heard the name of Kurtz pronounced, then the words, 'take advantage of this unfortunate accident.' One of the men was the manager. I wished him a good evening. 'Did you ever see anything like it—eh? it is incredible,' he said, and walked off. The other man remained. He was a first-class agent, young, gentlemanly, a bit reserved, with a forked little beard and a hooked nose. He was standoffish with the other agents, and they on their side said he was the manager's spy upon them. As to me, I had hardly ever spoken to him before. We got into talk, and by and by we strolled away from the hissing ruins. Then he asked me to his room, which was in the main building of the station. He struck a match, and I perceived that this young aristocrat had not only a silver-mounted dressing-case but also a whole candle all to himself. Just at that time the manager was the only man supposed to have any right to candles. Native mats covered the clay walls; a collection of spears, assegais,[1] shields, knives, was hung up in trophies. The business entrusted to this fellow was the making of bricks—so I had been informed; but there wasn't a fragment of a brick anywhere in the station, and he had been there more than a year—waiting. It seems he could not make bricks without something, I don't know what—straw maybe. Anyway, it could not be found there, and as it was not likely to be sent from Europe, it did not appear clear to me what he was waiting for. An act of special creation perhaps. However, they were all waiting—all the sixteen or twenty pilgrims of them—for something; and upon my word it did not seem an uncongenial occupation, from the way they took it, though the only thing that ever came to them was disease—as far as I could see. They beguiled the time by backbiting and intriguing against each other in a foolish kind of way. There was an air of plotting about that station, but nothing came of it, of course. It was as unreal as everything else—as the philanthropic pretence of the whole concern, as their talk, as their government, as their show of work. The only real feeling was a desire to get appointed to a trading-post where ivory was to be had, so that they could earn percentages. They intrigued and slandered and hated each other only on that account—but as to effectually lifting a little finger—oh no. By heavens! there is something after all in the world allowing one man to steal a horse while another must not look at a halter. Steal a horse straight out. Very well. He has done it. Perhaps he can ride. But there is a way of looking at a halter that would provoke the most charitable of saints into a kick.

"I had no idea why he wanted to be sociable, but as we chatted in there it suddenly occurred to me the fellow was trying to get at something—in fact, pumping me. He alluded constantly to Europe, to the people I was supposed to know there—putting leading questions as to my acquaintances in the sepulchral city, and so on. His little eyes glittered like mica[2] discs—with curiosity—though he tried to keep up a bit of superciliousness. At first I was astonished, but very soon I became awfully curious to see what he would find out from me. I couldn't possibly imagine what I had in me to make it worth his while. It was very pretty to see how he baffled himself, for in truth my body was full only of chills, and my head had nothing in it but that wretched steamboat business. It was evident he took me for a perfectly shameless prevaricator. At last he got angry, and, to conceal a movement of furious annoyance, he yawned. I rose. Then I noticed a small sketch in oils, on a panel, representing

1. Slender iron-tipped spears.   2. Glassy mineral.

a woman, draped and blindfolded, carrying a lighted torch. The background was sombre—almost black. The movement of the woman was stately, and the effect of the torchlight on the face was sinister.

"It arrested me, and he stood by civilly, holding an empty half-pint champagne bottle (medical comforts) with the candle stuck in it. To my question he said Mr Kurtz had painted this—in this very station more than a year ago—while waiting for means to go to his trading-post. 'Tell me, pray,' said I, 'who is this Mr Kurtz?'

" 'The chief of the Inner Station,' he answered in a short tone, looking away. 'Much obliged,' I said, laughing. 'And you are the brickmaker of the Central Station. Every one knows that.' He was silent for a while. 'He is a prodigy,' he said at last. 'He is an emissary of pity, and science, and progress, and devil knows what else. We want,' he began to declaim suddenly, 'for the guidance of the cause entrusted to us by Europe, so to speak, higher intelligence, wide sympathies, a singleness of purpose.' 'Who says that?' I asked. 'Lots of them,' he replied. 'Some even write that; and so *he* comes here, a special being, as you ought to know.' 'Why ought I to know?' I interrupted, really surprised. He paid no attention. 'Yes. To-day he is chief of the best station, next year he will be assistant-manager, two years more and . . . but I daresay you know what he will be in two years' time. You are of the new gang—the gang of virtue. The same people who sent him specially also recommended you. Oh, don't say no. I've my own eyes to trust.' Light dawned upon me. My dear aunt's influential acquaintances were producing an unexpected effect upon that young man. I nearly burst into a laugh. 'Do you read the Company's confidential correspondence?' I asked. He hadn't a word to say. It was great fun. 'When Mr Kurtz,' I continued severely, 'is General Manager, you won't have the opportunity.'

"He blew the candle out suddenly, and we went outside. The moon had risen. Black figures strolled about listlessly, pouring water on the glow, whence proceeded a sound of hissing; steam ascended in the moonlight; the beaten nigger groaned somewhere. 'What a row the brute makes!' said the indefatigable man with the moustaches, appearing near us. 'Serve him right. Transgression—punishment—bang! Pitiless, pitiless. That's the only way. This will prevent all conflagrations for the future. I was just telling the manager . . .' He noticed my companion, and became crestfallen all at once. 'Not in bed yet,' he said, with a kind of servile heartiness; 'it's so natural. Ha! Danger—agitation.' He vanished. I went on to the river-side, and the other followed me. I heard a scathing murmur at my ear, 'Heap of muffs—go to.' The pilgrims could be seen in knots gesticulating, discussing. Several had still their staves in their hands. I verily believe they took these sticks to bed with them. Beyond the fence the forest stood up spectrally in the moonlight, and through the dim stir, through the faint sounds of that lamentable courtyard, the silence of the land went home to one's very heart—its mystery, its greatness, the amazing reality of its concealed life. The hurt nigger moaned feebly somewhere near by, and then fetched a deep sigh that made me mend my pace away from there. I felt a hand introducing itself under my arm. 'My dear sir,' said the fellow, 'I don't want to be misunderstood, and especially by you, who will see Mr Kurtz long before I can have that pleasure. I wouldn't like him to get a false idea of my disposition. . . .'

"I let him run on, this papier-mâché Mephistopheles, and it seemed to me that if I tried I could poke my forefinger through him, and would find nothing inside but a little loose dirt, maybe. He, don't you see, had been planning to be assistant-manager by and by under the present man, and I could see that the coming of that Kurtz had upset them both not a little. He talked precipitately, and I did not try to stop him. I had my shoulders against the wreck of my steamer, hauled up on the slope like a carcass of some big river animal. The smell of mud, of primeval mud, by Jove! was in my nostrils, the high stillness of primeval forest was before my eyes; there were shiny patches on the black creek. The moon had spread over everything a thin layer of silver—over the rank grass, over the mud, upon the wall of matted vegetation standing higher than the wall of a temple, over the great river I could see through a sombre gap glittering, glittering, as it flowed broadly by without a murmur. All this was great, expectant, mute, while the man jabbered about himself. I wondered whether the stillness on the face of the immensity looking at us two were meant as an appeal or as a menace. What were we who had strayed in here? Could we handle that dumb thing, or would it handle us? I felt how big, how confoundedly big, was that thing that couldn't talk and perhaps was deaf as well. What was in there? I could see a little ivory coming out from there, and I had heard Mr Kurtz was in there. I had heard enough about it too—God knows! Yet somehow it didn't bring any image with it—no more than if I had been told an angel or a fiend was in there. I believed it in the same way one of you might believe there are inhabitants in the planet Mars. I knew once a Scotch sailmaker who was certain, dead sure, there were people in Mars. If you asked him for some idea how they looked and behaved, he would get shy and mutter something about 'walking on all-fours.' If you as much as smiled, he would—though a man of sixty—offer to fight you. I would not have gone so far as to fight for Kurtz, but I went for him near enough to a lie. You know I hate, detest, and can't bear a lie, not because I am straighter than the rest of us, but simply because it appals me. There is a taint of death, a flavour of mortality in lies—which is exactly what I hate and detest in the world—what I want to forget. It makes me miserable and sick, like biting something rotten would do. Temperament, I suppose. Well, I went near enough to it by letting the young fool there believe anything he liked to imagine as to my influence in Europe. I became in an instant as much of a pretence as the rest of the bewitched pilgrims. This simply because I had a notion it somehow would be of help to that Kurtz whom at the time I did not see—you understand. He was just a word for me. I did not see the man in the name any more than you do. Do you see him? Do you see the story? Do you see anything? It seems to me I am trying to tell you a dream—making a vain attempt, because no relation of a dream can convey the dream-sensation, that commingling of absurdity, surprise, and bewilderment in a tremor of struggling revolt, that notion of being captured by the incredible which is of the very essence of dreams. . . ."

He was silent for a while.

". . . No, it is impossible; it is impossible to convey the life-sensation of any given epoch of one's existence—that which makes its truth, its meaning—its subtle and penetrating essence. It is impossible. We live, as we dream—alone. . . ."

He paused again as if reflecting, then added:

"Of course in this you fellows see more than I could then. You see me, whom you know. . . ."

It had become so pitch dark that we listeners could hardly see one another. For a long time already he, sitting apart, had been no more to us than a voice. There was not a word from anybody. The others might have been asleep, but

I was awake. I listened, I listened on the watch for the sentence, for the word, that would give me the clue to the faint uneasiness inspired by this narrative that seemed to shape itself without human lips in the heavy night-air of the river.

". . . Yes—I let him run on," Marlow began again, "and think what he pleased about the powers that were behind me. I did! And there was nothing behind me! There was nothing but that wretched, old, mangled steamboat I was leaning against, while he talked fluently about 'the necessity for every man to get on.' 'And when one comes out here, you conceive, it is not to gaze at the moon.' Mr Kurtz was a 'universal genius,' but even a genius would find it easier to work with 'adequate tools—intelligent men.' He did not make bricks—why, there was a physical impossibility in the way—as I was well aware; and if he did secretarial work for the manager, it was because 'no sensible man rejects wantonly the confidence of his superiors.' Did I see it? I saw it. What more did I want? What I really wanted was rivets, by heaven! Rivets. To get on with the work—to stop the hole. Rivets I wanted. There were cases of them down at the coast—cases—piled up—burst—split! You kicked a loose rivet at every second step in that station yard on the hillside. Rivets had rolled into the grove of death. You could fill your pockets with rivets for the trouble of stooping down—and there wasn't one rivet to be found where it was wanted. We had plates that would do, but nothing to fasten them with. And every week the messenger, a lone negro, letter-bag on shoulder and staff in hand, left our station for the coast. And several times a week a coast caravan came in with trade goods—ghastly glazed calico that made you shudder only to look at it, glass beads value about a penny a quart, confounded spotted cotton handkerchiefs. And no rivets. Three carriers could have brought all that was wanted to set that steamboat afloat.

"He was becoming confidential now, but I fancy my unresponsive attitude must have exasperated him at last, for he judged it necessary to inform me he feared neither God nor devil, let alone any mere man. I said I could see that very well, but what I wanted was a certain quantity of rivets—and rivets were what really Mr Kurtz wanted, if he had only known it. Now letters went to the coast every week. . . . 'My dear sir,' he cried, 'I write from dictation.' I demanded rivets. There was a way—for an intelligent man. He changed his manner; became very cold, and suddenly began to talk about a hippopotamus; wondered whether sleeping on board the steamer (I stuck to my salvage night and day) I wasn't disturbed. There was an old hippo that had the bad habit of getting out on the bank and roaming at night over the station grounds. The pilgrims used to turn out in a body and empty every rifle they could lay hands on at him. Some even had sat up o' nights for him. All this energy was wasted, though. 'That animal has a charmed life,' he said; 'but you can say this only of brutes in this country. No man—you apprehend me?—no man here bears a charmed life.' He stood there for a moment in the moonlight with his delicate hooked nose set a little askew, and his mica eyes glittering without a wink, then, with a curt Good-night, he strode off. I could see he was disturbed and considerably puzzled, which made me feel more hopeful than I had been for days. It was a great comfort to turn from that chap to my influential friend, the battered, twisted, ruined, tinpot steamboat. I clambered on board. She rang under my feet like an empty Huntley & Palmer biscuit-tin kicked along a gutter; she was nothing so solid in make, and rather less pretty in shape, but I had expended enough hard work on her to make me love her. No influential friend would have served me better. She had given me a chance to come out a bit—to find out what I could do. No, I don't like work. I had rather laze about and think of all the fine things that can be done. I don't like work—no man does—but I like what is in the work—the chance to find yourself. Your own reality—for yourself, not for others—what no other man can ever know. They can only see the mere show, and never can tell what it really means.

"I was not surprised to see somebody sitting aft, on the deck, with his legs dangling over the mud. You see I rather chummed with the few mechanics there were in that station, whom the other pilgrims naturally despised—on account of their imperfect manners, I suppose. This was the foreman—a boiler-maker by trade—a good worker. He was a lank, bony, yellow-faced man, with big intense eyes. His aspect was worried, and his head was as bald as the palm of my hand; but his hair in falling seemed to have stuck to his chin, and had prospered in the new locality, for his beard hung down to his waist. He was a widower with six young children (he had left them in charge of a sister of his to come out there), and the passion of his life was pigeon-flying. He was an enthusiast and a connoisseur. He would rave about pigeons. After work hours he used sometimes to come over from his hut for a talk about his children and his pigeons; at work, when he had to crawl in the mud under the bottom of the steamboat, he would tie up that beard of his in a kind of white serviette[3] he brought for the purpose. It had loops to go over his ears. In the evening he could be seen squatted on the bank rinsing that wrapper in the creek with great care, then spreading it solemnly on a bush to dry.

"I slapped him on the back and shouted 'We shall have rivets!' He scrambled to his feet exclaiming 'No! Rivets!' as though he couldn't believe his ears. Then in a low voice, 'You . . . eh?' I don't know why we behaved like lunatics. I put my finger to the side of my nose and nodded mysteriously. 'Good for you!' he cried, snapped his fingers above his head, lifting one foot. I tried a jig. We capered on the iron deck. A frightful clatter came out of that hulk, and the virgin forest on the other bank of the creek sent it back in a thundering roll upon the sleeping station. It must have made some of the pilgrims sit up in their hovels. A dark figure obscured the lighted doorway of the manager's hut, vanished, then, a second or so after, the doorway itself vanished too. We stopped, and the silence driven away by the stamping of our feet flowed back again from the recesses of the land. The great wall of vegetation, an exuberant and entangled mass of trunks, branches, leaves, boughs, festoons, motionless in the moonlight, was like a rioting invasion of soundless life, a rolling wave of plants, piled up, crested, ready to topple over the creek, to sweep every little man of us out of his little existence. And it moved not. A deadened burst of mighty splashes and snorts reached us from afar, as though an ichthyosaurus[4] had been taking a bath of glitter in the great river. 'After all,' said the boiler-maker in a reasonable tone, 'why shouldn't we get the rivets?' Why not, indeed! I did not know of any reason why we shouldn't. 'They'll come in three weeks,' I said confidently.

"But they didn't. Instead of rivets there came an invasion, an infliction, a visitation. It came in sections during the next three weeks, each section headed by a donkey carrying a white man in new clothes and tan shoes, bowing from that elevation right and left to the impressed pilgrims. A quarrelsome band of footsore sulky niggers trod on the heels of the donkey; a lot of tents, camp-

---

3. Table napkin.   4. Large prehistoric marine creature.

stools, tin boxes, white cases, brown bales would be shot down in the court-yard, and the air of mystery would deepen a little over the muddle of the station. Five such instalments came, with their absurd air of disorderly flight with the loot of innumerable outfit shops and provision stores, that, one would think, they were lugging, after a raid, into the wilderness for equitable division. It was an inextricable mess of things decent in themselves but that human folly made look like the spoils of thieving.

"This devoted band called itself the Eldorado⁵ Exploring Expedition, and I believe they were sworn to secrecy. Their talk, however, was the talk of sordid buccaneers: it was reckless without hardihood, greedy without audacity, and cruel without courage; there was not an atom of foresight or of serious inten-tion in the whole batch of them, and they did not seem aware these things are wanted for the work of the world. To tear treasure out of the bowels of the land was their desire, with no more moral purpose at the back of it than there is in burglars breaking into a safe. Who paid the expenses of the noble enter-prise I don't know; but the uncle of our manager was leader of that lot.

"In exterior he resembled a butcher in a poor neighbourhood, and his eyes had a look of sleepy cunning. He carried his fat paunch with ostentation on his short legs, and during the time his gang infested the station spoke to no one but his nephew. You could see these two roaming about all day long with their heads close together in an everlasting confab.⁶

"I had given up worrying myself about the rivets. One's capacity for that kind of folly is more limited than you would suppose. I said Hang!—and let things slide. I had plenty of time for meditation, and now and then I would give some thought to Kurtz. I wasn't very interested in him. No. Still, I was curious to see whether this man, who had come out equipped with moral ideas of some sort, would climb to the top after all, and how he would set about his work when there."

2

"One evening as I was lying flat on the deck of my steamboat, I heard voices approaching—and there were the nephew and the uncle strolling along the bank. I laid my head on my arm again, and had nearly lost myself in a doze, when somebody said in my ear, as it were: 'I am as harmless as a little child, but I don't like to be dictated to. Am I the manager—or am I not? I was ordered to send him there. It's incredible.' . . . I became aware that the two were stand-ing on the shore alongside the forepart of the steamboat, just below my head. I did not move; it did not occur to me to move: I was sleepy. 'It *is* unpleasant,' grunted the uncle. 'He has asked the Administration to be sent there,' said the other, 'with the idea of showing what he could do; and I was instructed accord-ingly. Look at the influence that man must have. Is it not frightful?' They both agreed it was frightful, then made several bizarre remarks: 'Make rain and fine weather—one man—the Council—by the nose'—bits of absurd sentences that got the better of my drowsiness, so that I had pretty near the whole of my wits about me when the uncle said, 'The climate may do away with this difficulty for you. Is he alone there?' 'Yes,' answered the manager; 'he sent his assistant down the river with a note to me in these terms: "Clear this poor devil out of

5. Fabled land of gold (*el dorado*, Spanish for "the gilded") imagined by the Spanish conquistadors to exist in South America.
6. Confabulation, talk.

the country, and don't bother sending more of that sort. I had rather be alone than have the kind of men you can dispose of with me." It was more than a year ago. Can you imagine such impudence?' 'Anything since then?' asked the other hoarsely. 'Ivory,' jerked the nephew; 'lots of it—prime sort—lots—most annoying, from him.' 'And with that?' questioned the heavy rumble. 'Invoice,' was the reply fired out, so to speak. Then silence. They had been talking about Kurtz.

"I was broad awake by this time, but, lying perfectly at ease, remained still, having no inducement to change my position. 'How did that ivory come all this way?' growled the elder man, who seemed very vexed. The other explained that it had come with a fleet of canoes in charge of an English half-caste clerk Kurtz had with him; that Kurtz had apparently intended to return himself, the station being by that time bare of goods and stores, but after coming three hundred miles, had suddenly decided to go back, which he started to do alone in a small dugout with four paddlers, leaving the half-caste to continue down the river with the ivory. The two fellows there seemed astounded at anybody attempting such a thing. They were at a loss for an adequate motive. As for me, I seemed to see Kurtz for the first time. It was a distinct glimpse: the dugout, four paddling savages, and the lone white man turning his back suddenly on the headquarters, on relief, on thoughts of home—perhaps; setting his face towards the depths of the wilderness, towards his empty and desolate station. I did not know the motive. Perhaps he was just simply a fine fellow who stuck to his work for its own sake. His name, you understand, had not been pronounced once. He was 'that man.' The half-caste, who, as far as I could see, had conducted a difficult trip with great prudence and pluck, was invariably alluded to as 'that scoundrel.' The 'scoundrel' had reported that the 'man' had been very ill—had recovered imperfectly. . . . The two below me moved away then a few paces, and strolled back and forth at some little distance. I heard: 'Military post—doctor—two hundred miles—quite alone now—unavoidable delays—nine months—no news—strange rumours.' They approached again, just as the manager was saying, 'No one, as far as I know, unless a species of wandering trader—a pestilential fellow, snapping ivory from the natives.' Who was it they were talking about now? I gathered in snatches that this was some man supposed to be in Kurtz's district, and of whom the manager did not approve. 'We will not be free from unfair competition till one of these fellows is hanged for an example,' he said. 'Certainly,' grunted the other; 'get him hanged! Why not? Anything—anything can be done in this country. That's what I say; nobody here, you understand, here, can endanger your position. And why? You stand the climate—you outlast them all. The danger is in Europe; but there before I left I took care to—' They moved off and whispered, then their voices rose again. 'The extraordinary series of delays is not my fault. I did my possible.'[7] The fat man sighed, 'Very sad.' 'And the pestiferous absurdity of his talk,' continued the other; 'he bothered me enough when he was here. "Each station should be like a beacon on the road towards better things, a centre for trade of course, but also for humanising, improving, instructing." Conceive you—that ass! And he wants to be manager! No, it's—' Here he got choked by excessive indignation, and I lifted

7. Literal rendering of the French *J'ai fait mon possible* (I have done all I could). Conrad sprinkles the conversation of his Belgian characters with Gallicisms to remind us that their words, though reported in English, were spoken in French. Other examples are "a species of wandering trader" (above), "Conceive you" (below), "I would be desolated" (p. 1921).

my head the least bit. I was surprised to see how near they were—right under me. I could have spat upon their hats. They were looking on the ground, absorbed in thought. The manager was switching his leg with a slender twig: his sagacious relative lifted his head. 'You have been well since you came out this time?' he asked. The other gave a start. 'Who? I? Oh! Like a charm—like a charm. But the rest—oh, my goodness! All sick. They die so quick, too, that I haven't the time to send them out of the country—it's incredible!' 'H'm. Just so,' grunted the uncle. 'Ah! my boy, trust to this—I say, trust to this.' I saw him extend his short flipper of an arm for a gesture that took in the forest, the creek, the mud, the river—seemed to beckon with a dishonouring flourish before the sunlit face of the land a treacherous appeal to the lurking death, to the hidden evil, to the profound darkness of its heart. It was so startling that I leaped to my feet and looked back at the edge of the forest, as though I had expected an answer of some sort to that black display of confidence. You know the foolish notions that come to one sometimes. The high stillness confronted these two figures with its ominous patience, waiting for the passing away of a fantastic invasion.

"They swore aloud together—out of sheer fright, I believe—then, pretending not to know anything of my existence, turned back to the station. The sun was low; and leaning forward side by side, they seemed to be tugging painfully uphill their two ridiculous shadows of unequal length, that trailed behind them slowly over the tall grass without bending a single blade.

"In a few days the Eldorado Expedition went into the patient wilderness, that closed upon it as the sea closes over a diver. Long afterwards the news came that all the donkeys were dead. I know nothing as to the fate of the less valuable animals. They, no doubt, like the rest of us, found what they deserved. I did not inquire. I was then rather excited at the prospect of meeting Kurtz very soon. When I say very soon I mean it comparatively. It was just two months from the day we left the creek when we came to the bank below Kurtz's station.

"Going up that river was like travelling back to the earliest beginnings of the world, when vegetation rioted on the earth and the big trees were kings. An empty stream, a great silence, an impenetrable forest. The air was warm, thick, heavy, sluggish. There was no joy in the brilliance of sunshine. The long stretches of the waterway ran on, deserted, into the gloom of overshadowed distances. On silvery sandbanks hippos and alligators sunned themselves side by side. The broadening waters flowed through a mob of wooded islands; you lost your way on that river as you would in a desert, and butted all day long against shoals, trying to find the channel, till you thought yourself bewitched and cut off for ever from everything you had known once—somewhere—far away—in another existence perhaps. There were moments when one's past came back to one, as it will sometimes when you have not a moment to spare to yourself; but it came in the shape of an unrestful and noisy dream, remembered with wonder amongst the overwhelming realities of this strange world of plants, and water, and silence. And this stillness of life did not in the least resemble a peace. It was the stillness of an implacable force brooding over an inscrutable intention. It looked at you with a vengeful aspect. I got used to it afterwards; I did not see it any more; I had no time. I had to keep guessing at the channel; I had to discern, mostly by inspiration, the signs of hidden banks; I watched for sunken stones; I was learning to clap my teeth smartly before my heart flew out, when I shaved by a fluke some infernal sly old snag that would have ripped the life out of the tin-pot steamboat and drowned all the pilgrims; I had to keep a look-out for the signs of dead wood we could cut up in the night for next day's steaming. When you have to attend to things of that sort, to the mere incidents of the surface, the reality—the reality, I tell you—fades. The inner truth is hidden—luckily, luckily. But I felt it all the same; I felt often its mysterious stillness watching me at my monkey tricks, just as it watches you fellows performing on your respective tight-ropes for—what is it? half a crown a tumble—"

"Try to be civil, Marlow," growled a voice, and I knew there was at least one listener awake besides myself.

"I beg your pardon. I forgot the heartache which makes up the rest of the price. And indeed what does the price matter, if the trick be well done? You do your tricks very well. And I didn't do badly either, since I managed not to sink that steamboat on my first trip. It's a wonder to me yet. Imagine a blind-folded man set to drive a van over a bad road. I sweated and shivered over that business considerably, I can tell you. After all, for a seaman, to scrape the bottom of the thing that's supposed to float all the time under his care is the unpardonable sin. No one may know of it, but you never forget the thump—eh? A blow on the very heart. You remember it, you dream of it, you wake up at night and think of it—years after—and go hot and cold all over. I don't pretend to say that steamboat floated all the time. More than once she had to wade for a bit, with twenty cannibals splashing around and pushing. We had enlisted some of these chaps on the way for a crew. Fine fellows—cannibals—in their place. They were men one could work with, and I am grateful to them. And, after all, they did not eat each other before my face: they had brought along a provision of hippo-meat which went rotten, and made the mystery of the wilderness stink in my nostrils. Phoo! I can sniff it now. I had the manager on board and three or four pilgrims with their staves—all complete. Sometimes we came upon a station close by the bank, clinging to the skirts of the unknown, and the white men rushing out of a tumble-down hovel, with great gestures of joy and surprise and welcome, seemed very strange—had the appearance of being held there captive by a spell. The word 'ivory' would ring in the air for a while—and on we went again into the silence, along empty reaches, round the still bends, between the high walls of our winding way, reverberating in hollow claps the ponderous beat of the stern-wheel. Trees, trees, millions of trees, massive, immense, running up high; and at their foot, hugging the bank against the stream, crept the little begrimed steamboat, like a sluggish beetle crawling on the floor of a lofty portico. It made you feel very small, very lost, and yet it was not altogether depressing, that feeling. After all, if you were small, the grimy beetle crawled on—which was just what you wanted it to do. Where the pilgrims imagined it crawled to I don't know. To some place where they expected to get something, I bet! For me it crawled towards Kurtz—exclusively; but when the steam-pipes started leaking we crawled very slow. The reaches opened before us and closed behind, as if the forest had stepped leisurely across the water to bar the way for our return. We penetrated deeper and deeper into the heart of darkness. It was very quiet there. At night sometimes the roll of drums behind the curtain of trees would run up the river and remain sustained faintly, as if hovering in the air high over our heads, till the first break of day. Whether it meant war, peace, or prayer we could not tell. The dawns were heralded by the descent of a chill stillness; the woodcutters slept, their fires burned low; the snapping of a twig would make you start. We were wanderers on a prehistoric earth, on an earth that wore the aspect of an unknown planet. We could have fancied ourselves the first of men taking possession of an accursed inheritance, to be subdued at the cost of profound anguish and of excessive toil. But suddenly, as we struggled round a bend, there would be a glimpse of rush walls, of peaked grass-roofs, a burst of yells, a whirl of black limbs, a mass of hands clapping, of feet stamping, of bodies swaying, of eyes rolling, under the droop of heavy and motionless foliage. The steamer toiled along slowly on the edge of a black and incomprehensible frenzy. The prehistoric man was cursing us, praying to us, welcoming us—who could tell? We were cut off from the comprehension of our surroundings; we glided past like phantoms, wondering and secretly appalled, as sane men would be before an enthusiastic outbreak in a madhouse. We could not understand because we were too far and could not remember, because we were travelling in the night of first ages, of those ages that are gone, leaving hardly a sign—and no memories.

"The earth seemed unearthly. We are accustomed to look upon the shackled form of a conquered monster, but there—there you could look at a thing monstrous and free. It was unearthly, and the men were—No, they were not inhuman. Well, you know, that was the worst of it—this suspicion of their not being inhuman. It would come slowly to one. They howled and leaped, and spun, and made horrid faces; but what thrilled you was just the thought of their humanity—like yours—the thought of your remote kinship with this wild and passionate uproar. Ugly. Yes, it was ugly enough; but if you were man enough you would admit to yourself that there was in you just the faintest trace of a response to the terrible frankness of that noise, a dim suspicion of there being a meaning in it which you—you so remote from the night of first ages—could comprehend. And why not? The mind of man is capable of anything—because everything is in it, all the past as well as all the future. What was there after all? Joy, fear, sorrow, devotion, valour, rage—who can tell?— but truth—truth stripped of its cloak of time. Let the fool gape and shudder— the man knows, and can look on without a wink. But he must at least be as much of a man as these on the shore. He must meet that truth with his own true stuff—with his own inborn strength. Principles? Principles won't do. Acquisitions, clothes, pretty rags—rags that would fly off at the first good shake. No; you want a deliberate belief. An appeal to me in this fiendish row— is there? Very well; I hear; I admit, but I have a voice too, and for good or evil mine is the speech that cannot be silenced. Of course, a fool, what with sheer fright and fine sentiments, is always safe. Who's that grunting? You wonder I didn't go ashore for a howl and a dance? Well, no—I didn't. Fine sentiments, you say? Fine sentiments be hanged! I had no time. I had to mess about with white-lead and strips of woollen blanket helping to put bandages on those leaky steam-pipes—I tell you. I had to watch the steering, and circumvent those snags, and get the tin-pot along by hook or by crook. There was surface-truth enough in these things to save a wiser man. And between whiles I had to look after the savage who was fireman. He was an improved specimen; he could fire up a vertical boiler. He was there below me, and, upon my word, to look at him was as edifying as seeing a dog in a parody of breeches and a feather hat, walking on his hind legs. A few months of training had done for that really fine chap. He squinted at the steam-gauge and at the water-gauge with an evident effort of intrepidity—and he had filed teeth too, the poor devil, and the wool of his pate shaved into queer patterns, and three ornamental scars on each of his cheeks. He ought to have been clapping his hands and stamping his feet on the bank, instead of which he was hard at work, a thrall to strange witchcraft, full of improving knowledge. He was useful because he had been instructed; and what he knew was this—that should the water in that transparent thing disappear, the evil spirit inside the boiler would get angry through the greatness of his thirst, and take a terrible vengeance. So he sweated and fired up and watched the glass fearfully (with an impromptu charm, made of rags, tied to his arm, and a piece of polished bone, as big as a watch, stuck flatways through his lower lip), while the wooded banks slipped past us slowly, the short noise was left behind, the interminable miles of silence—and we crept on, towards Kurtz. But the snags were thick, the water was treacherous and shallow, the boiler seemed indeed to have a sulky devil in it, and thus neither that fireman nor I had any time to peer into our creepy thoughts.

"Some fifty miles below the Inner Station we came upon a hut of reeds, an inclined and melancholy pole, with the unrecognisable tatters of what had been a flag of some sort flying from it, and a neatly stacked wood-pile. This was unexpected. We came to the bank, and on the stack of firewood found a flat piece of board with some faded pencil-writing on it. When deciphered it said: 'Wood for you. Hurry up. Approach cautiously.' There was a signature, but it was illegible—not Kurtz—a much longer word. Hurry up. Where? Up the river? 'Approach cautiously.' We had not done so. But the warning could not have been meant for the place where it could be only found after approach. Something was wrong above. But what—and how much? That was the question. We commented adversely upon the imbecility of that telegraphic style. The bush around said nothing, and would not let us look very far, either. A torn curtain of red twill hung in the doorway of the hut, and flapped sadly in our faces. The dwelling was dismantled; but we could see a white man had lived there not very long ago. There remained a rude table—a plank on two posts; a heap of rubbish reposed in a dark corner, and by the door I picked up a book. It had lost its covers, and the pages had been thumbed into a state of extremely dirty softness; but the back had been lovingly stitched afresh with white cotton thread, which looked clean yet. It was an extraordinary find. Its title was, *An Inquiry into some Points of Seamanship*, by a man Towser, Towson—some such name—Master in His Majesty's Navy. The matter looked dreary reading enough, with illustrative diagrams and repulsive tables of figures, and the copy was sixty years old. I handled this amazing antiquity with the greatest possible tenderness, lest it should dissolve in my hands. Within, Towson or Towser was inquiring earnestly into the breaking strain of ships' chains and tackle, and other such matters. Not a very enthralling book; but at the first glance you could see there a singleness of intention, an honest concern for the right way of going to work, which made these humble pages, thought out so many years ago, luminous with another than a professional light. The simple old sailor, with his talk of chains and purchases, made me forget the jungle and the pilgrims in a delicious sensation of having come upon something unmistakably real. Such a book being there was wonderful enough; but still more astounding were the notes pencilled in the margin, and plainly referring to the text. I couldn't believe my eyes! They were in cipher! Yes, it looked like cipher. Fancy a man lugging with him a book of that description into this nowhere and studying it—and making notes—in cipher at that! It was an extravagant mystery.

"I had been dimly aware for some time of a worrying noise, and when I lifted my eyes I saw the wood-pile was gone, and the manager, aided by all the pilgrims, was shouting at me from the river-side. I slipped the book into my pocket. I assure you to leave off reading was like tearing myself away from the shelter of an old and solid friendship.

"I started the lame engine ahead. 'It must be this miserable trader—this intruder,' exclaimed the manager, looking back malevolently at the place we had left. 'He must be English,' I said. 'It will not save him from getting into trouble if he is not careful,' muttered the manager darkly. I observed with assumed innocence that no man was safe from trouble in this world.

"The current was more rapid now, the steamer seemed at her last gasp, the stern-wheel flopped languidly, and I caught myself listening on tiptoe for the next beat of the float,[8] for in sober truth I expected the wretched thing to give up every moment. It was like watching the last flickers of a life. But still we crawled. Sometimes I would pick out a tree a little way ahead to measure our progress towards Kurtz by, but I lost it invariably before we got abreast. To keep the eyes so long on one thing was too much for human patience. The manager displayed a beautiful resignation. I fretted and fumed and took to arguing with myself whether or no I would talk openly with Kurtz; but before I could come to any conclusion it occurred to me that my speech or my silence, indeed any action of mine, would be a mere futility. What did it matter what any one knew or ignored? What did it matter who was manager? One gets sometimes such a flash of insight. The essentials of this affair lay deep under the surface, beyond my reach, and beyond my power of meddling.

"Towards the evening of the second day we judged ourselves about eight miles from Kurtz's station. I wanted to push on; but the manager looked grave, and told me the navigation up there was so dangerous that it would be advisable, the sun being very low already, to wait where we were till next morning. Moreover, he pointed out that if the warning to approach cautiously were to be followed, we must approach in daylight—not at dusk, or in the dark. This was sensible enough. Eight miles meant nearly three hours' steaming for us, and I could also see suspicious ripples at the upper end of the reach. Nevertheless, I was annoyed beyond expression at the delay, and most unreasonably too, since one night more could not matter much after so many months. As we had plenty of wood, and caution was the word, I brought up in the middle of the stream. The reach was narrow, straight, with high sides like a railway cutting. The dusk came gliding into it long before the sun had set. The current ran smooth and swift, but a dumb immobility sat on the banks. The living trees, lashed together by the creepers and every living bush of the undergrowth, might have been changed into stone, even to the slenderest twig, to the lightest leaf. It was not sleep—it seemed unnatural, like a state of trance. Not the faintest sound of any kind could be heard. You looked on amazed, and began to suspect yourself of being deaf—then the night came suddenly, and struck you blind as well. About three in the morning some large fish leaped, and the loud splash made me jump as though a gun had been fired. When the sun rose there was a white fog, very warm and clammy, and more blinding than the night. It did not shift or drive; it was just there, standing all round you like something solid. At eight or nine, perhaps, it lifted as a shutter lifts. We had a glimpse of the towering multitude of trees, of the immense

8. Automatic water-level regulator opening and closing a water-supply valve.

matted jungle, with the blazing little ball of the sun hanging over it—all perfectly still—and then the white shutter came down again, smoothly, as if sliding in greased grooves. I ordered the chain, which we had begun to heave in, to be paid out again. Before it stopped running with a muffled rattle, a cry, a very loud cry, as of infinite desolation, soared slowly in the opaque air. It ceased. A complaining clamour, modulated in savage discords, filled our ears. The sheer unexpectedness of it made my hair stir under my cap. I don't know how it struck the others: to me it seemed as though the mist itself had screamed, so suddenly, and apparently from all sides at once, did this tumultuous and mournful uproar arise. It culminated in a hurried outbreak of almost intolerably excessive shrieking, which stopped short, leaving us stiffened in a variety of silly attitudes, and obstinately listening to the nearly as appalling and excessive silence. 'Good God! What is the meaning—?' stammered at my elbow one of the pilgrims—a little fat man, with sandy hair and red whiskers, who wore side-spring boots, and pink pyjamas tucked into his socks. Two others remained open-mouthed a whole minute, then dashed into the little cabin, to rush out incontinently and stand darting scared glances, with Winchesters at 'ready' in their hands. What we could see was just the steamer we were on, her outlines blurred as though she had been on the point of dissolving, and a misty strip of water, perhaps two feet broad, around her—and that was all. The rest of the world was nowhere, as far as our eyes and ears were concerned. Just nowhere. Gone, disappeared; swept off without leaving a whisper or a shadow behind.

"I went forward, and ordered the chain to be hauled in short, so as to be ready to trip the anchor and move the steamboat at once if necessary. 'Will they attack?' whispered an awed voice. 'We will all be butchered in this fog,' murmured another. The faces twitched with the strain, the hands trembled slightly, the eyes forgot to wink. It was very curious to see the contrast of expressions of the white men and of the black fellows of our crew, who were as much strangers to that part of the river as we, though their homes were only eight hundred miles away. The whites, of course greatly discomposed, had besides a curious look of being painfully shocked by such an outrageous row. The others had an alert, naturally interested expression; but their faces were essentially quiet, even those of the one or two who grinned as they hauled at the chain. Several exchanged short, grunting phrases, which seemed to settle the matter to their satisfaction. Their headman, a young, broad-chested black, severely draped in dark-blue fringed cloths, with fierce nostrils and his hair all done up artfully in oily ringlets, stood near me. 'Aha!' I said, just for good fellowship's sake. 'Catch 'im,' he snapped, with a bloodshot widening of his eyes and a flash of sharp teeth—'catch 'im. Give 'im to us.' 'To you, eh?' I asked; 'what would you do with them?' 'Eat 'im!' he said curtly, and, leaning his elbow on the rail, looked out into the fog in a dignified and profoundly pensive attitude. I would no doubt have been properly horrified, had it not occurred to me that he and his chaps must be very hungry: that they must have been growing increasingly hungry for at least this month past. They had been engaged for six months (I don't think a single one of them had any clear idea of time, as we at the end of countless ages have. They still belonged to the beginnings of time—had no inherited experience to teach them, as it were), and of course, as long as there was a piece of paper written over in accordance with some farcical law or other made down the river, it didn't enter anybody's head to trouble how they would live. Certainly they had brought with them some rotten hippo-meat, which couldn't have lasted very long, any-way, even if the pilgrims hadn't, in the midst of a shocking hullabaloo, thrown a considerable quantity of it overboard. It looked like a high-handed proceed-ing; but it was really a case of legitimate self-defence. You can't breathe dead hippo waking, sleeping, and eating, and at the same time keep your precarious grip on existence. Besides that, they had given them every week three pieces of brass wire, each about nine inches long; and the theory was they were to buy their provisions with that currency in river-side villages. You can see how *that* worked. There were either no villages, or the people were hostile, or the director, who like the rest of us fed out of tins, with an occasional old he-goat thrown in, didn't want to stop the steamer for some more or less recondite reasons. So, unless they swallowed the wire itself, or made loops of it to snare the fishes with, I don't see what good their extravagant salary could be to them. I must say it was paid with a regularity worthy of a large and honourable trading company. For the rest, the only thing to eat—though it didn't look eatable in the least—I saw in their possession was a few lumps of some stuff like half-cooked dough, of a dirty lavender colour, they kept wrapped in leaves, and now and then swallowed a piece of, but so small that it seemed done more for the look of the thing than for any serious purpose of sustenance. Why in the name of all the gnawing devils of hunger they didn't go for us—they were thirty to five—and have a good tuck-in for once, amazes me now when I think of it. They were big powerful men, with not much capacity to weigh the con-sequences, with courage, with strength, even yet, though their skins were no longer glossy and their muscles no longer hard. And I saw that something restraining, one of those human secrets that baffle probability, had come into play there. I looked at them with a swift quickening of interest—not because it occurred to me I might be eaten by them before very long, though I own to you that just then I perceived—in a new light, as it were—how unwholesome the pilgrims looked, and I hoped, yes, I positively hoped, that my aspect was not so—what shall I say?—so—unappetising: a touch of fantastic vanity which fitted well with the dream-sensation that pervaded all my days at that time. Perhaps I had a little fever too. One can't live with one's finger everlastingly on one's pulse. I had often 'a little fever,' or a little touch of other things—the playful paw-strokes of the wilderness, the preliminary trifling before the more serious onslaught which came in due course. Yes; I looked at them as you would on any human being, with a curiosity of their impulses, motives, capac-ities, weaknesses, when brought to the test of an inexorable physical necessity. Restraint! What possible restraint? Was it superstition, disgust, patience, fear—or some kind of primitive honour? No fear can stand up to hunger, no patience can wear it out, disgust simply does not exist where hunger is; and as to superstition, beliefs, and what you may call principles, they are less than chaff in a breeze. Don't you know the devilry of lingering starvation, its exas-perating torment, its black thoughts, its sombre and brooding ferocity? Well, I do. It takes a man all his inborn strength to fight hunger properly. It's really easier to face bereavement, dishonour, and the perdition of one's soul—than this kind of prolonged hunger. Sad, but true. And these chaps too had no earthly reason for any kind of scruple. Restraint! I would just as soon have expected restraint from a hyena prowling amongst the corpses of a battlefield. But there was the fact facing me—the fact dazzling, to be seen, like the foam on the depths of the sea, like a ripple on an unfathomable enigma, a mystery greater—when I thought of it—than the curious, inexplicable note of desperate grief in this savage clamour that had swept by us on the river-bank, behind the blind whiteness of the fog.

"Two pilgrims were quarrelling in hurried whispers as to which bank. 'Left.' 'No, no; how can you? Right, right, of course.' 'It is very serious,' said the manager's voice behind me; 'I would be desolated if anything should happen to Mr Kurtz before we came up.' I looked at him, and had not the slightest doubt he was sincere. He was just the kind of man who would wish to preserve appearances. That was his restraint. But when he muttered something about going on at once, I did not even take the trouble to answer him. I knew, and he knew, that it was impossible. Were we to let go our hold of the bottom, we would be absolutely in the air—in space. We wouldn't be able to tell where we were going to—whether up or down stream, or across—till we fetched against one bank or the other—and then we wouldn't know at first which it was. Of course I made no move. I had no mind for a smash-up. You couldn't imagine a more deadly place for a shipwreck. Whether drowned at once or not, we were sure to perish speedily in one way or another. 'I authorise you to take all the risks,' he said, after a short silence. 'I refuse to take any,' I said shortly; which was just the answer he expected, though its tone might have surprised him. 'Well, I must defer to your judgment. You are captain,' he said, with marked civility. I turned my shoulder to him in sign of my appreciation, and looked into the fog. How long would it last? It was the most hopeless look-out. The approach to this Kurtz grubbing for ivory in the wretched bush was beset by as many dangers as though he had been an enchanted princess sleeping in a fabulous castle. 'Will they attack, do you think?' asked the manager, in a confidential tone.

"I did not think they would attack, for several obvious reasons. The thick fog was one. If they left the bank in their canoes they would get lost in it, as we would be if we attempted to move. Still, I had also judged the jungle of both banks quite impenetrable—and yet eyes were in it, eyes that had seen us. The river-side bushes were certainly very thick; but the undergrowth behind was evidently penetrable. However, during the short lift I had seen no canoes anywhere in the reach—certainly not abreast of the steamer. But what made the idea of attack inconceivable to me was the nature of the noise—of the cries we had heard. They had not the fierce character boding of immediate hostile intention. Unexpected, wild, and violent as they had been, they had given me an irresistible impression of sorrow. The glimpse of the steamboat had for some reason filled those savages with unrestrained grief. The danger, if any, I expounded, was from our proximity to a great human passion let loose. Even extreme grief may ultimately vent itself in violence—but more generally takes the form of apathy. . . .

"You should have seen the pilgrims stare! They had no heart to grin, or even to revile me; but I believe they thought me gone mad—with fright, maybe. I delivered a regular lecture. My dear boys, it was no good bothering. Keep a look-out? Well, you may guess I watched the fog for the signs of lifting as a cat watches a mouse; but for anything else our eyes were of no more use to us than if we had been buried miles deep in a heap of cotton-wool. It felt like it too—choking, warm, stifling. Besides, all I said, though it sounded extravagant, was absolutely true to fact. What we afterwards alluded to as an attack was really an attempt at repulse. The action was very far from being aggressive—it was not even defensive, in the usual sense: it was undertaken under the stress of desperation, and in its essence was purely protective.

"It developed itself, I should say, two hours after the fog lifted, and its commencement was at a spot, roughly speaking, about a mile and a half below Kurtz's station. We had just floundered and flopped round a bend, when I saw an islet, a mere grassy hummock of bright green, in the middle of the stream. It was the only thing of the kind; but as we opened the reach more, I perceived it was the head of a long sandbank, or rather of a chain of shallow patches stretching down the middle of the river. They were discoloured, just awash, and the whole lot was seen just under the water, exactly as a man's backbone is seen running down the middle of his back under the skin. Now, as far as I did see, I could go to the right or to the left of this. I didn't know either channel, of course. The banks looked pretty well alike, the depth appeared the same; but as I had been informed the station was on the west side, I naturally headed for the western passage.

"No sooner had we fairly entered it than I became aware it was much narrower than I had supposed. To the left of us there was the long uninterrupted shoal,[9] and to the right a high steep bank heavily overgrown with bushes. Above the bush the trees stood in serried ranks. The twigs overhung the current thickly, and from distance to distance a large limb of some tree projected rigidly over the stream. It was then well on in the afternoon, the face of the forest was gloomy, and a broad strip of shadow had already fallen on the water. In this shadow we steamed up—very slowly, as you may imagine. I sheered her well inshore—the water being deepest near the bank, as the sounding-pole informed me.

"One of my hungry and forbearing friends was sounding in the bows just below me. This steamboat was exactly like a decked scow. On the deck there were two little teak-wood houses, with doors and windows. The boiler was in the fore-end, and the machinery right astern. Over the whole there was a light roof, supported on stanchions. The funnel projected through that roof, and in front of the funnel a small cabin built of light planks served for a pilot-house. It contained a couch, two camp-stools, a loaded Martini-Henry[1] leaning in one corner, a tiny table, and the steering-wheel. It had a wide door in front and a broad shutter at each side. All these were always thrown open, of course. I spent my days perched up there on the extreme fore-end of that roof, before the door. At night I slept, or tried to, on the couch. An athletic black belonging to some coast tribe, and educated by my poor predecessor, was the helmsman. He sported a pair of brass earrings, wore a blue cloth wrapper from the waist to the ankles, and thought all the world of himself. He was the most unstable kind of fool I had ever seen. He steered with no end of a swagger while you were by; but if he lost sight of you, he became instantly the prey of an abject funk, and would let that cripple of a steamboat get the upper hand of him in a minute.

"I was looking down at the sounding-pole, and feeling much annoyed to see at each try a little more of it stick out of that river, when I saw my poleman give up the business suddenly, and stretch himself flat on the deck, without even taking the trouble to haul his pole in. He kept hold on it though, and it trailed in the water. At the same time the fireman, whom I could also see below me, sat down abruptly before his furnace and ducked his head. I was

9. Sandbank.
1. Rifle combining the seven-grooved barrel of the Scottish gun maker A. Henry with the block-action breech mechanism introduced by the Swiss inventor F. Martini.

amazed. Then I had to look at the river mighty quick, because there was a snag in the fairway. Sticks, little sticks, were flying about—thick; they were whizzing before my nose, dropping below me, striking behind me against my pilot-house. All this time the river, the shore, the woods, were very quiet— perfectly quiet. I could only hear the heavy splashing thump of the stern-wheel and the patter of these things. We cleared the snag clumsily. Arrows, by Jove! We were being shot at! I stepped in quickly to close the shutter on the land-side. That fool-helmsman, his hands on the spokes, was lifting his knees high, stamping his feet, champing his mouth, like a reined-in horse. Confound him! And we were staggering within ten feet of the bank. I had to lean right out to swing the heavy shutter, and I saw a face amongst the leaves on the level with my own, looking at me very fierce and steady; and then suddenly, as though a veil had been removed from my eyes, I made out, deep in the tangled gloom, naked breasts, arms, legs, glaring eyes—the bush was swarming with human limbs in movement, glistening, of bronze colour. The twigs shook, swayed, and rustled, the arrows flew out of them, and then the shutter came to. 'Steer her straight,' I said to the helmsman. He held his head rigid, face forward; but his eyes rolled, he kept on lifting and setting down his feet gently, his mouth foamed a little. 'Keep quiet!' I said in a fury. I might just as well have ordered a tree not to sway in the wind. I darted out. Below me there was a great scuffle of feet on the iron deck; confused exclamations; a voice screamed, 'Can you turn back?' I caught sight of a V-shaped ripple on the water ahead. What? Another snag! A fusillade burst out under my feet. The pilgrims had opened with their Winchesters, and were simply squirting lead into that bush. A deuce of a lot of smoke came up and drove slowly forward. I swore at it. Now I couldn't see the ripple or the snag either. I stood in the doorway, peering, and the arrows came in swarms. They might have been poisoned, but they looked as though they wouldn't kill a cat. The bush began to howl. Our wood-cutters raised a warlike whoop; the report of a rifle just at my back deafened me. I glanced over my shoulder, and the pilot-house was yet full of noise and smoke when I made a dash at the wheel. The fool-nigger had dropped everything, to throw the shutter open and let off that Martini-Henry. He stood before the wide opening, glaring, and I yelled at him to come back, while I straightened the sudden twist out of that steamboat. There was no room to turn even if I had wanted to, the snag was somewhere very near ahead in that confounded smoke, there was no time to lose, so I just crowded her into the bank—right into the bank, where I knew the water was deep.

"We tore slowly along the overhanging bushes in a whirl of broken twigs and flying leaves. The fusillade below stopped short, as I had foreseen it would when the squirts got empty. I threw my head back to a glinting whizz that traversed the pilot-house, in at one shutter-hole and out at the other. Looking past that mad helmsman, who was shaking the empty rifle and yelling at the shore, I saw vague forms of men running bent double, leaping, gliding, dis-tinct, incomplete, evanescent. Something big appeared in the air before the shutter, the rifle went overboard, and the man stepped back swiftly, looked at me over his shoulder in an extraordinary, profound, familiar manner, and fell upon my feet. The side of his head hit the wheel twice, and the end of what appeared a long cane clattered round and knocked over a little camp-stool. It looked as though after wrenching that thing from somebody ashore he had lost his balance in the effort. The thin smoke had blown away, we were clear of the snag, and looking ahead I could see that in another hundred yards or so I would be free to sheer off, away from the bank; but my feet felt so very warm and wet that I had to look down. The man had rolled on his back and stared straight up at me; both his hands clutched that cane. It was the shaft of a spear that, either thrown or lunged through the opening, had caught him in the side just below the ribs; the blade had gone in out of sight, after making a frightful gash; my shoes were full; a pool of blood lay very still, gleaming dark-red under the wheel; his eyes shone with an amazing lustre. The fusillade burst out again. He looked at me anxiously, gripping the spear like something precious, with an air of being afraid I would try to take it away from him. I had to make an effort to free my eyes from his gaze and attend to the steering. With one hand I felt above my head for the line of the steam whistle, and jerked out screech after screech hurriedly. The tumult of angry and warlike yells was checked instantly, and then from the depths of the woods went out such a tremulous and prolonged wail of mournful fear and utter despair as may be imagined to follow the flight of the last hope from the earth. There was a great commotion in the bush; the shower of arrows stopped, a few dropping shots rang out sharply—then silence, in which the languid beat of the stern-wheel came plainly to my ears. I put the helm hard a-starboard at the moment when the pilgrim in pink pyjamas, very hot and agitated, appeared in the doorway. 'The manager sends me—' he began in an official tone, and stopped short. 'Good God!' he said, glaring at the wounded man.

"We two whites stood over him, and his lustrous and inquiring glance enveloped us both. I declare it looked as though he would presently put to us some question in an understandable language; but he died without uttering a sound, without moving a limb, without twitching a muscle. Only in the very last moment, as though in response to some sign we could not see, to some whisper we could not hear, he frowned heavily, and that frown gave to his black death-mask an inconceivably sombre, brooding, and menacing expression. The lustre of inquiring glance faded swiftly into vacant glassiness. 'Can you steer?' I asked the agent eagerly. He looked very dubious; but I made a grab at his arm, and he understood at once I meant him to steer whether or no. To tell you the truth, I was morbidly anxious to change my shoes and socks. 'He is dead,' murmured the fellow, immensely impressed. 'No doubt about it,' said I, tugging like mad at the shoe-laces. 'And by the way, I suppose Mr Kurtz is dead as well by this time.'

"For the moment that was the dominant thought. There was a sense of extreme disappointment, as though I had found out I had been striving after something altogether without a substance. I couldn't have been more disgusted if I had travelled all this way for the sole purpose of talking with Mr Kurtz. Talking with . . . I flung one shoe overboard, and became aware that that was exactly what I had been looking forward to—a talk with Kurtz. I made the strange discovery that I had never imagined him as doing, you know, but as discoursing. I didn't say to myself, 'Now I will never see him,' or 'Now I will never shake him by the hand,' but, 'Now I will never hear him.' The man presented himself as a voice. Not of course that I did not connect him with some sort of action. Hadn't I been told in all the tones of jealousy and admiration that he had collected, bartered, swindled, or stolen more ivory than all the other agents together? That was not the point. The point was in his being a gifted creature, and that of all his gifts the one that stood out pre-eminently, that carried with it a sense of real presence, was his ability to talk, his words—the gift of expression, the bewildering, the illuminating, the most exalted and the most contemptible, the pulsating stream of light, or the deceitful flow from the heart of an impenetrable darkness.

"The other shoe went flying unto the devil-god of that river. I thought, By Jove! it's all over. We are too late; he has vanished—the gift has vanished, by means of some spear, arrow, or club. I will never hear that chap speak after all—and my sorrow had a startling extravagance of emotion, even such as I had noticed in the howling sorrow of these savages in the bush. I couldn't have felt more of lonely desolation somehow, had I been robbed of a belief or had missed my destiny in life. . . . Why do you sigh in this beastly way, somebody? Absurd? Well, absurd. Good Lord! mustn't a man ever— Here, give me some tobacco." . . .

There was a pause of profound stillness, then a match flared, and Marlow's lean face appeared, worn, hollow, with downward folds and dropped eyelids, with an aspect of concentrated attention; and as he took vigorous draws at his pipe, it seemed to retreat and advance out of the night in the regular flicker of the tiny flame. The match went out.

"Absurd!" he cried. "This is the worst of trying to tell . . . Here you all are, each moored with two good addresses, like a hulk with two anchors, a butcher round one corner, a policeman round another, excellent appetites, and temperature normal—you hear—normal from year's end to year's end. And you say, Absurd! Absurd be—exploded! Absurd! My dear boys, what can you expect from a man who out of sheer nervousness had just flung overboard a pair of new shoes? Now I think of it, it is amazing I did not shed tears. I am, upon the whole, proud of my fortitude. I was cut to the quick at the idea of having lost the inestimable privilege of listening to the gifted Kurtz. Of course I was wrong. The privilege was waiting for me. Oh yes, I heard more than enough. And I was right, too. A voice. He was very little more than a voice. And I heard—him—it—this voice—other voices—all of them were so little more than voices—and the memory of that time itself lingers around me, impalpable, like a dying vibration of one immense jabber, silly, atrocious, sordid, savage, or simply mean, without any kind of sense. Voices, voices—even the girl herself—now—"

He was silent for a long time.

"I laid the ghost of his gifts at last with a lie," he began suddenly. "Girl! What? Did I mention a girl? Oh, she is out of it—completely. They—the women I mean—are out of it—should be out of it. We must help them to stay in that beautiful world of their own, lest ours gets worse. Oh, she had to be out of it. You should have heard the disinterred body of Mr Kurtz saying, 'My Intended.' You would have perceived directly then how completely she was out of it. And the lofty frontal bone of Mr Kurtz! They say the hair goes on growing sometimes, but this—ah—specimen was impressively bald. The wilderness had patted him on the head, and, behold, it was like a ball—an ivory ball; it had caressed him, and—lo!—he had withered; it had taken him, loved him, embraced him, got into his veins, consumed his flesh, and sealed his soul to its own by the inconceivable ceremonies of some devilish initiation. He was its spoiled and pampered favourite. Ivory? I should think so. Heaps of it, stacks of it. The old mud shanty was bursting with it. You would think there was not a single tusk left either above or below the ground in the whole country. 'Mostly fossil,' the manager had remarked disparagingly. It was no more fossil than I am; but they call it fossil when it is dug up. It appears these niggers do bury the tusks sometimes—but evidently they couldn't bury this parcel deep enough to save the gifted Mr Kurtz from his fate. We filled the steamboat with it, and had to pile a lot on the deck. Thus he could see and enjoy as long as he could see, because the appreciation of this favour had remained with him to the last. You should have heard him say, 'My ivory.' Oh yes, I heard him. 'My Intended, my ivory, my station, my river, my—' everything belonged to him. It made me hold my breath in expectation of hearing the wilderness burst into a prodigious peal of laughter that would shake the fixed stars in their places. Everything belonged to him—but that was a trifle. The thing was to know what he belonged to, how many powers of darkness claimed him for their own. That was the reflection that made you creepy all over. It was impossible—it was not good for one either—trying to imagine. He had taken a high seat amongst the devils of the land—I mean literally. You can't understand. How could you?—with solid pavement under your feet, surrounded by kind neighbours ready to cheer you or to fall on you, stepping delicately between the butcher and the policeman, in the holy terror of scandal and gallows and lunatic asylums—how can you imagine what particular region of the first ages a man's untrammelled feet may take him into by the way of solitude—utter solitude without a policeman—by the way of silence—utter silence, where no warning voice of a kind neighbour can be heard whispering of public opinion? These little things make all the great difference. When they are gone you must fall back upon your own innate strength, upon your own capacity for faithfulness. Of course you may be too much of a fool to go wrong—too dull even to know you are being assaulted by the powers of darkness. I take it, no fool ever made a bargain for his soul with the devil: the fool is too much of a fool, or the devil too much of a devil—I don't know which. Or you may be such a thunderingly exalted creature as to be altogether deaf and blind to anything but heavenly sights and sounds. Then the earth for you is only a standing place—and whether to be like this is your loss or your gain I won't pretend to say. But most of us are neither one nor the other. The earth for us is a place to live in, where we must put up with sights, with sounds, with smells, too, by Jove!—breathe dead hippo, so to speak, and not be contaminated. And there, don't you see? your strength comes in, the faith in your ability for the digging of unostentatious holes to bury the stuff in—your power of devotion, not to yourself, but to an obscure, back-breaking business. And that's difficult enough. Mind, I am not trying to excuse or even explain—I am trying to account to myself for—for—Mr Kurtz—for the shade of Mr Kurtz. This initiated wraith from the back of Nowhere honoured me with its amazing confidence before it vanished altogether. This was because it could speak English to me. The original Kurtz had been educated partly in England, and—as he was good enough to say himself—his sympathies were in the right place. His mother was half-English, his father was half-French. All Europe contributed to the making of Kurtz; and by and by I learned that, most appropriately, the International Society for the Suppression of Savage Customs had entrusted him with the making of a report, for its future guidance. And he had written it too. I've seen it. I've read it. It was eloquent, vibrating with eloquence, but too high-strung, I think. Seventeen pages of close writing he had found time for! But this must have been before his—let us say—nerves went wrong, and caused him to preside at certain midnight dances ending with unspeakable rites, which—as far as I reluctantly gathered from what I heard at various times—were offered up to him—do you understand?—to Mr Kurtz himself. But it was a beautiful piece of writing. The opening paragraph, however, in the light of later information, strikes me now as ominous. He began with the argument that we whites, from the point of development we had arrived at, 'must necessarily appear to them [savages] in the nature of supernatural beings—we approach them with the might as of a deity,' and so on, and so on. 'By the simple exercise of our will we can exert a power for good practically unbounded,' etc. etc. From that point he soared and took me with him. The peroration was magnificent, though difficult to remember, you know. It gave me the notion of an exotic Immensity ruled by an august Benevolence. It made me tingle with enthusiasm. This was the unbounded power of eloquence—of words—of burning noble words. There were no practical hints to interrupt the magic current of phrases, unless a kind of note at the foot of the last page, scrawled evidently much later, in an unsteady hand, may be regarded as the exposition of a method. It was very simple, and at the end of that moving appeal to every altruistic sentiment it blazed at you, luminous and terrifying, like a flash of lightning in a serene sky: 'Exterminate all the brutes!' The curious part was that he had apparently forgotten all about that valuable postscriptum, because, later on, when he in a sense came to himself, he repeatedly entreated me to take good care of 'my pamphlet' (he called it), as it was sure to have in the future a good influence upon his career. I had full information about all these things, and, besides, as it turned out, I was to have the care of his memory. I've done enough for it to give me the indisputable right to lay it, if I choose, for an everlasting rest in the dust-bin of progress, amongst all the sweepings and, figuratively speaking, all the dead cats of civilisation. But then, you see, I can't choose. He won't be forgotten. Whatever he was, he was not common. He had the power to charm or frighten rudimentary souls into an aggravated witchdance in his honour; he could also fill the small souls of the pilgrims with bitter misgivings: he had one devoted friend at least, and he had conquered one soul in the world that was neither rudimentary nor tainted with self-seeking. No; I can't forget him, though I am not prepared to affirm the fellow was exactly worth the life we lost in getting to him. I missed my late helmsman awfully—I missed him even while his body was still lying in the pilot-house. Perhaps you will think it passing strange this regret for a savage who was no more account than a grain of sand in a black Sahara. Well, don't you see, he had done something, he had steered; for months I had him at my back—a help—an instrument. It was a kind of partnership. He steered for me—I had to look after him, I worried about his deficiencies, and thus a subtle bond had been created, of which I only became aware when it was suddenly broken. And the intimate profundity of that look he gave me when he received his hurt remains to this day in my memory—like a claim of distant kinship affirmed in a supreme moment.

"Poor fool! If he had only left that shutter alone. He had no restraint, no restraint—just like Kurtz—a tree swayed by the wind. As soon as I had put on a dry pair of slippers, I dragged him out, after first jerking the spear out of his side, which operation I confess I performed with my eyes shut tight. His heels leaped together over the little doorstep; his shoulders were pressed to my breast; I hugged him from behind desperately. Oh! he was heavy, heavy; heavier than any man on earth, I should imagine. Then without more ado I tipped him overboard. The current snatched him as though he had been a wisp of grass, and I saw the body roll over twice before I lost sight of it for ever. All the pilgrims and the manager were then congregated on the awning-deck about the pilot-house, chattering at each other like a flock of excited magpies, and there was a scandalised murmur at my heartless promptitude. What they wanted to keep that body hanging about for I can't guess. Embalm it, maybe. But I had also heard another, and a very ominous, murmur on the deck below. My friends the wood-cutters were likewise scandalised, and with a better show of reason—though I admit that the reason itself was quite inadmissible. Oh, quite! I had made up my mind that if my late helmsman was to be eaten, the fishes alone should have him. He had been a very second-rate helmsman while alive, but now he was dead he might have become a first-class temptation, and possibly cause some startling trouble. Besides, I was anxious to take the wheel, the man in pink pyjamas showing himself a hopeless duffer at the business.

"This I did directly the simple funeral was over. We were going half-speed, keeping right in the middle of the stream, and I listened to the talk about me. They had given up Kurtz, they had given up the station; Kurtz was dead, and the station had been burnt—and so on—and so on. The red-haired pilgrim was beside himself with the thought that at least this poor Kurtz had been properly revenged. 'Say! We must have made a glorious slaughter of them in the bush. Eh? What do you think? Say?' He positively danced, the bloodthirsty little gingery beggar.[2] And he had nearly fainted when he saw the wounded man! I could not help saying, 'You made a glorious lot of smoke, anyhow.' I had seen, from the way the tops of the bushes rustled and flew, that almost all the shots had gone too high. You can't hit anything unless you take aim and fire from the shoulder; but these chaps fired from the hip with their eyes shut. The retreat, I maintained—and I was right—was caused by the screeching of the steam-whistle. Upon this they forgot Kurtz, and began to howl at me with indignant protests.

"The manager stood by the wheel murmuring confidentially about the necessity of getting well away down the river before dark at all events, when I saw in the distance a clearing on the river-side and the outlines of some sort of building. 'What's this?' I asked. He clapped his hands in wonder. 'The station!' he cried. I edged in at once, still going half-speed.

"Through my glasses I saw the slope of a hill interspersed with rare trees and perfectly free from undergrowth. A long decaying building on the summit was half buried in the high grass; the large holes in the peaked roof gaped black from afar; the jungle and the woods made a background. There was no enclosure or fence of any kind; but there had been one apparently, for near the house half a dozen slim posts remained in a row, roughly trimmed, and with their upper ends ornamented with round carved balls. The rails, or whatever there had been between, had disappeared. Of course the forest surrounded all that. The river-bank was clear, and on the water side I saw a white man under a hat like a cart-wheel beckoning persistently with his whole arm. Examining the edge of the forest above and below, I was almost certain I could see movements—human forms gliding here and there. I steamed past prudently, then stopped the engines and let her drift down. The man on the shore began to shout, urging us to land. 'We have been attacked,' screamed the manager. 'I know—I know. It's all right,' yelled back the other, as cheerful as you please. 'Come along. It's all right. I am glad.'

"His aspect reminded me of something I had seen—something funny I had seen somewhere. As I manœuvred to get alongside, I was asking myself, 'What

2. Little redheaded rascal.

does this fellow look like?' Suddenly I got it. He looked like a harlequin.[3] His clothes had been made of some stuff that was brown holland[4] probably, but it was covered with patches all over, with bright patches, blue, red, and yellow—patches on the back, patches on the front, patches on elbows, on knees; coloured binding round his jacket, scarlet edging at the bottom of his trousers; and the sunshine made him look extremely gay and wonderfully neat withal, because you could see how beautifully all this patching had been done. A beardless, boyish face, very fair, no features to speak of, nose peeling, little blue eyes, smiles and frowns chasing each other over that open countenance like sunshine and shadow on a wind-swept plain. 'Look out, captain!' he cried; 'there's a snag lodged in here last night.' What! Another snag? I confess I swore shamefully. I had nearly holed my cripple, to finish off that charming trip. The harlequin on the bank turned his little pug nose up to me. 'You English?' he asked, all smiles. 'Are you?' I shouted from the wheel. The smiles vanished, and he shook his head as if sorry for my disappointment. Then he brightened up. 'Never mind!' he cried encouragingly. 'Are we in time?' I asked. 'He is up there,' he replied, with a toss of the head up the hill, and becoming gloomy all of a sudden. His face was like the autumn sky, overcast one moment and bright the next.

"When the manager, escorted by the pilgrims, all of them armed to the teeth, had gone to the house, this chap came on board. 'I say, I don't like this. These natives are in the bush,' I said. He assured me earnestly it was all right. 'They are simple people,' he added; 'well, I am glad you came. It took me all my time to keep them off.' 'But you said it was all right,' I cried. 'Oh, they meant no harm,' he said; and as I stared he corrected himself, 'Not exactly.' Then vivaciously, 'My faith, your pilot-house wants a clean up!' In the next breath he advised me to keep enough steam on the boiler to blow the whistle in case of any trouble. 'One good screech will do more for you than all your rifles. They are simple people,' he repeated. He rattled away at such a rate he quite overwhelmed me. He seemed to be trying to make up for lots of silence, and actually hinted, laughing, that such was the case. 'Don't you talk with Mr Kurtz?' I said. 'You don't talk with that man—you listen to him,' he exclaimed with severe exaltation. 'But now—' He waved his arm, and in the twinkling of an eye was in the uttermost depths of despondency. In a moment he came up again with a jump, possessed himself of both my hands, shook them continuously, while he gabbled: 'Brother sailor . . . honour . . . pleasure . . . delight . . . introduce myself . . . Russian . . . son of an arch-priest . . . Government of Tambov . . . What? Tobacco! English tobacco; the excellent English tobacco! Now, that's brotherly. Smoke? Where's a sailor that does not smoke?'

"The pipe soothed him, and gradually I made out he had run away from school, had gone to sea in a Russian ship; ran away again; served some time in English ships; was now reconciled with the arch-priest. He made a point of that. 'But when one is young one must see things, gather experience, ideas; enlarge the mind.' 'Here!' I interrupted. 'You can never tell! Here I met Mr Kurtz,' he said, youthfully solemn and reproachful. I held my tongue after that. It appears he had persuaded a Dutch trading-house on the coast to fit him out with stores and goods, and had started for the interior with a light heart, and no more idea of what would happen to him than a baby. He had

3. Character from Italian comedy traditionally dressed in multicolored clothes. 4. Coarse linen fabric.

been wandering about that river for nearly two years alone, cut off from everybody and everything. 'I am not so young as I look. I am twenty-five,' he said. 'At first old Van Shuyten would tell me to go to the devil,' he narrated with keen enjoyment; 'but I stuck to him, and talked and talked, till at last he got afraid I would talk the hind-leg off his favourite dog, so he gave me some cheap things and a few guns, and told me he hoped he would never see my face again. Good old Dutchman, Van Shuyten. I sent him one small lot of ivory a year ago, so that he can't call me a little thief when I get back. I hope he got it. And for the rest I don't care. I had some wood stacked for you. That was my old house. Did you see?'

"I gave him Towson's book. He made as though he would kiss me, but restrained himself. 'The only book I had left, and I thought I had lost it,' he said, looking at it ecstatically. 'So many accidents happen to a man going about alone, you know. Canoes get upset sometimes—and sometimes you've got to clear out so quick when the people get angry.' He thumbed the pages. 'You made notes in Russian?' I asked. He nodded. 'I thought they were written in cipher,' I said. He laughed, then became serious. 'I had lots of trouble to keep these people off,' he said. 'Did they want to kill you?' I asked. 'Oh no!' he cried, and checked himself. 'Why did they attack us?' I pursued. He hesitated, then said shamefacedly, 'They don't want him to go.' 'Don't they?' I said curiously. He nodded a nod full of mystery and wisdom. 'I tell you,' he cried, 'this man has enlarged my mind.' He opened his arms wide, staring at me with his little blue eyes that were perfectly round."

3

"I looked at him, lost in astonishment. There he was before me, in motley, as though he had absconded from a troupe of mimes, enthusiastic, fabulous. His very existence was improbable, inexplicable, and altogether bewildering. He was an insoluble problem. It was inconceivable how he had existed, how he had succeeded in getting so far, how he had managed to remain—why he did not instantly disappear. 'I went a little farther,' he said, 'then still a little farther—till I had gone so far that I don't know how I'll ever get back. Never mind. Plenty time. I can manage. You take Kurtz away quick—quick—I tell you.' The glamour of youth enveloped his particoloured rags, his destitution, his loneliness, the essential desolation of his futile wanderings. For months— for years—his life hadn't been worth a day's purchase; and there he was gallantly, thoughtlessly alive, to all appearance indestructible solely by the virtue of his few years and of his unreflecting audacity. I was seduced into something like admiration—like envy. Glamour urged him on, glamour kept him unscathed. He surely wanted nothing from the wilderness but space to breathe in and to push on through. His need was to exist, and to move onwards at the greatest possible risk, and with a maximum of privation. If the absolutely pure, uncalculating, unpractical spirit of adventure had ever ruled a human being, it ruled this be-patched youth. I almost envied him the possession of this modest and clear flame. It seemed to have consumed all thought of self so completely, that, even while he was talking to you, you forgot that it was he— the man before your eyes—who had gone through these things. I did not envy him his devotion to Kurtz, though. He had not meditated over it. It came to him, and he accepted it with a sort of eager fatalism. I must say that to me it appeared about the most dangerous thing in every way he had come upon so far.

"They had come together unavoidably, like two ships becalmed near each other, and lay rubbing sides at last. I suppose Kurtz wanted an audience, because on a certain occasion, when encamped in the forest, they had talked all night, or more probably Kurtz had talked. 'We talked of everything,' he said, quite transported at the recollection. 'I forgot there was such a thing as sleep. The night did not seem to last an hour. Everything! Everything! . . . Of love too.' 'Ah, he talked to you of love!' I said, much amused. 'It isn't what you think,' he cried, almost passionately. 'It was in general. He made me see things—things.'

"He threw his arms up. We were on deck at the time, and the head-man of my wood-cutters, lounging near by, turned upon him his heavy and glittering eyes. I looked around, and I don't know why, but I assure you that never, never before, did this land, this river, this jungle, the very arch of this blazing sky, appear to me so hopeless and so dark, so impenetrable to human thought, so pitiless to human weakness. 'And, ever since, you have been with him, of course?' I said.

"On the contrary. It appears their intercourse had been very much broken by various causes. He had, as he informed me proudly, managed to nurse Kurtz through two illnesses (he alluded to it as you would to some risky feat), but as a rule Kurtz wandered alone, far in the depths of the forest. 'Very often coming to this station, I had to wait days and days before he would turn up,' he said. 'Ah, it was worth waiting for!—sometimes.' 'What was he doing? exploring or what?' I asked. 'Oh yes, of course'; he had discovered lots of villages, a lake too—he did not know exactly in what direction; it was danger-ous to inquire too much—but mostly his expeditions had been for ivory. 'But he had no goods to trade with by that time,' I objected. 'There's a good lot of cartridges left even yet,' he answered, looking away. 'To speak plainly, he raided the country,' I said. He nodded. 'Not alone, surely!' He muttered some-thing about the villages round that lake. 'Kurtz got the tribe to follow him, did he?' I suggested. He fidgeted a little. 'They adored him,' he said. The tone of these words was so extraordinary that I looked at him searchingly. It was curi-ous to see his mingled eagerness and reluctance to speak of Kurtz. The man filled his life, occupied his thoughts, swayed his emotions. 'What can you expect?' he burst out; 'he came to them with thunder and lightning, you know—and they had never seen anything like it—and very terrible. He could be very terrible. You can't judge Mr Kurtz as you would an ordinary man. No, no, no! Now—just to give you an idea—I don't mind telling you, he wanted to shoot me too one day—but I don't judge him.' 'Shoot you!' I cried. 'What for?' 'Well, I had a small lot of ivory the chief of that village near my house gave me. You see I used to shoot game for them. Well, he wanted it, and wouldn't hear reason. He declared he would shoot me unless I gave him the ivory and then cleared out of the country, because he could do so, and had a fancy for it, and there was nothing on earth to prevent him killing whom he jolly well pleased. And it was true too. I gave him the ivory. What did I care! But I didn't clear out. No, no. I couldn't leave him. I had to be careful, of course, till we got friendly again for a time. He had his second illness then. Afterwards I had to keep out of the way; but I didn't mind. He was living for the most part in those villages on the lake. When he came down to the river, sometimes he would take to me, and sometimes it was better for me to be careful. This man suffered too much. He hated all this, and somehow he couldn't get away. When I had a chance I begged him to try and leave while there was time; I offered to go back with him. And he would say yes, and then he would remain; go off on another ivory hunt; disappear for weeks; forget himself amongst these people—forget himself—you know.' 'Why! he's mad,' I said. He protested indignantly. Mr Kurtz couldn't be mad. If I had heard him talk, only two days ago, I wouldn't dare hint at such a thing. . . . I had taken up my binoculars while we talked, and was looking at the shore, sweeping the limit of the forest at each side and at the back of the house. The consciousness of there being people in that bush, so silent, so quiet—as silent and quiet as the ruined house on the hill—made me uneasy. There was no sign on the face of nature of this amazing tale that was not so much told as suggested to me in desolate exclamations, completed by shrugs, in interrupted phrases, in hints ending in deep sighs. The woods were unmoved, like a mask—heavy, like the closed door of a prison—they looked with their air of hidden knowledge, of patient expectation, of unapproachable silence. The Russian was explaining to me that it was only lately that Mr Kurtz had come down to the river, bringing along with him all the fighting men of that lake tribe. He had been absent for several months—getting himself adored, I suppose—and had come down unexpectedly, with the intention to all appearance of making a raid either across the river or down stream. Evidently the appetite for more ivory had got the better of the—what shall I say?—less material aspirations. However, he had got much worse suddenly. 'I heard he was lying helpless, and so I came up—took my chance,' said the Russian. 'Oh, he is bad, very bad.' I directed my glass to the house. There were no signs of life, but there was the ruined roof, the long mud wall peeping above the grass, with three little square window-holes, no two of the same size; all this brought within reach of my hand, as it were. And then I made a brusque movement, and one of the remaining posts of that vanished fence leaped up in the field of my glass. You remember I told you I had been struck at the distance by certain attempts at ornamentation, rather remarkable in the ruinous aspect of the place. Now I had suddenly a nearer view, and its first result was to make me throw my head back as if before a blow. Then I went carefully from post to post with my glass, and I saw my mistake. These round knobs were not ornamental but symbolic; they were expressive and puzzling, striking and disturbing—food for thought and also for the vultures if there had been any looking down from the sky; but at all events for such ants as were industrious enough to ascend the pole. They would have been even more impressive, those heads on the stakes, if their faces had not been turned to the house. Only one, the first I had made out, was facing my way. I was not so shocked as you may think. The start back I had given was really nothing but a movement of surprise. I had expected to see a knob of wood there, you know. I returned deliberately to the first I had seen—and there it was, black, dried, sunken, with closed eyelids—a head that seemed to sleep at the top of that pole, and, with the shrunken dry lips showing a narrow white line of the teeth, was smiling too, smiling continuously at some endless and jocose dream of that eternal slumber.

"I am not disclosing any trade secrets. In fact the manager said afterwards that Mr Kurtz's methods had ruined the district. I have no opinion on that point, but I want you clearly to understand that there was nothing exactly profitable in these heads being there. They only show that Mr Kurtz lacked restraint in the gratification of his various lusts, that there was something wanting in him—some small matter which, when the pressing need arose, could not be found under his magnificent eloquence. Whether he knew of this deficiency himself I can't say. I think the knowledge came to him at last—

only at the very last. But the wilderness had found him out early, and had taken on him a terrible vengeance for the fantastic invasion. I think it had whispered to him things about himself which he did not know, things of which he had no conception till he took counsel with this great solitude—and the whisper had proved irresistibly fascinating. It echoed loudly within him because he was hollow at the core. . . . I put down the glass, and the head that had appeared near enough to be spoken to seemed at once to have leaped away from me into inaccessible distance.

"The admirer of Mr Kurtz was a bit crestfallen. In a hurried, indistinct voice he began to assure me he had not dared to take these—say, symbols—down. He was not afraid of the natives; they would not stir till Mr Kurtz gave the word. His ascendancy was extraordinary. The camps of these people surrounded the place, and the chiefs came every day to see him. They would crawl . . . 'I don't want to know anything of the ceremonies used when approaching Mr Kurtz,' I shouted. Curious, this feeling that came over me that such details would be more intolerable than those heads drying on the stakes under Mr Kurtz's windows. After all, that was only a savage sight, while I seemed at one bound to have been transported into some lightless region of subtle horrors, where pure, uncomplicated savagery was a positive relief, being something that had a right to exist—obviously—in the sunshine. The young man looked at me with surprise. I suppose it did not occur to him that Mr Kurtz was no idol of mine. He forgot I hadn't heard any of these splendid monologues on, what was it? on love, justice, conduct of life—or what not. If it had come to crawling before Mr Kurtz, he crawled as much as the veriest savage of them all. I had no idea of the conditions, he said: these heads were the heads of rebels. I shocked him excessively by laughing. Rebels! What would be the next definition I was to hear? There had been enemies, criminals, workers—and these were rebels. Those rebellious heads looked very subdued to me on their sticks. 'You don't know how such a life tries a man like Kurtz,' cried Kurtz's last disciple. 'Well, and you?' I said. 'I! I! I am a simple man. I have no great thoughts. I want nothing from anybody. How can you compare me to . . . ?' His feelings were too much for speech, and suddenly he broke down. 'I don't understand,' he groaned. 'I've been doing my best to keep him alive, and that's enough. I had no hand in all this. I have no abilities. There hasn't been a drop of medicine or a mouthful of invalid food for months here. He was shamefully abandoned. A man like this, with such ideas. Shamefully! Shamefully! I—I—haven't slept for the last ten nights. . . . '

"His voice lost itself in the calm of the evening. The long shadows of the forest had slipped down hill while we talked, had gone far beyond the ruined hovel, beyond the symbolic row of stakes. All this was in the gloom, while we down there were yet in the sunshine, and the stretch of the river abreast of the clearing glittered in a still and dazzling splendour, with a murky and overshadowed bend above and below. Not a living soul was seen on the shore. The bushes did not rustle.

"Suddenly round the corner of the house a group of men appeared, as though they had come up from the ground. They waded waist-deep in the grass, in a compact body, bearing an improvised stretcher in their midst. Instantly, in the emptiness of the landscape, a cry arose whose shrillness pierced the still air like a sharp arrow flying straight to the very heart of the land; and, as if by enchantment, streams of human beings—of naked human beings—with spears in their hands, with bows, with shields, with wild glances and savage movements, were poured into the clearing by the dark-faced and pensive forest. The bushes shook, the grass swayed for a time, and then everything stood still in attentive immobility.

" 'Now, if he does not say the right thing to them we are all done for,' said the Russian at my elbow. The knot of men with the stretcher had stopped too, half-way to the steamer, as if petrified. I saw the man on the stretcher sit up, lank and with an uplifted arm, above the shoulders of the bearers. 'Let us hope that the man who can talk so well of love in general will find some particular reason to spare us this time,' I said. I resented bitterly the absurd danger of our situation, as if to be at the mercy of that atrocious phantom had been a dishonouring necessity. I could not hear a sound, but through my glasses I saw the thin arm extended commandingly, the lower jaw moving, the eyes of that apparition shining darkly far in its bony head that nodded with grotesque jerks. Kurtz—Kurtz—that means 'short' in German—don't it? Well, the name was as true as everything else in his life—and death. He looked at least seven feet long. His covering had fallen off, and his body emerged from it pitiful and appalling as from a winding-sheet. I could see the cage of his ribs all astir, the bones of his arm waving. It was as though an animated image of death carved out of old ivory had been shaking its hand with menaces at a motionless crowd of men made of dark and glittering bronze. I saw him open his mouth wide—it gave him a weirdly voracious aspect, as though he had wanted to swallow all the air, all the earth, all the men before him. A deep voice reached me faintly. He must have been shouting. He fell back suddenly. The stretcher shook as the bearers staggered forward again, and almost at the same time I noticed that the crowd of savages was vanishing without any perceptible movement of retreat, as if the forest that had ejected these beings so suddenly had drawn them in again as the breath is drawn in a long aspiration.

"Some of the pilgrims behind the stretcher carried his arms—two shot-guns, a heavy rifle, and a light revolver-carbine—the thunderbolts of that pitiful Jupiter. The manager bent over him murmuring as he walked beside his head. They laid him down in one of the little cabins—just a room for a bedplace and a camp-stool or two, you know. We had brought his belated correspondence, and a lot of torn envelopes and open letters littered his bed. His hand roamed feebly amongst these papers. I was struck by the fire of his eyes and the composed languor of his expression. It was not so much the exhaustion of disease. He did not seem in pain. This shadow looked satiated and calm, as though for the moment it had had its fill of all the emotions.

"He rustled one of the letters, and looking straight in my face said, 'I am glad.' Somebody had been writing to him about me. These special recommendations were turning up again. The volume of tone he emitted without effort, almost without the trouble of moving his lips, amazed me. A voice! a voice! It was grave, profound, vibrating, while the man did not seem capable of a whisper. However, he had enough strength in him—factitious no doubt—to very nearly make an end of us, as you shall hear directly.

"The manager appeared silently in the doorway; I stepped out at once and he drew the curtain after me. The Russian, eyed curiously by the pilgrims, was staring at the shore. I followed the direction of his glance.

"Dark human shapes could be made out in the distance, flitting indistinctly against the gloomy border of the forest, and near the river two bronze figures, leaning on tall spears, stood in the sunlight under fantastic head-dresses of spotted skins, warlike and still in statuesque repose. And from right to left along the lighted shore moved a wild and gorgeous apparition of a woman.

"She walked with measured steps, draped in striped and fringed cloths, treading the earth proudly, with a slight jingle and flash of barbarous ornaments. She carried her head high; her hair was done in the shape of a helmet; she had brass leggings to the knee, brass wire gauntlets to the elbow, a crimson spot on her tawny cheek, innumerable necklaces of glass beads on her neck; bizarre things, charms, gifts of witch-men, that hung about her, glittered and trembled at every step. She must have had the value of several elephant tusks upon her. She was savage and superb, wild-eyed and magnificent; there was something ominous and stately in her deliberate progress. And in the hush that had fallen suddenly upon the whole sorrowful land, the immense wilderness, the colossal body of the fecund and mysterious life seemed to look at her, pensive, as though it had been looking at the image of its own tenebrous and passionate soul.

"She came abreast of the steamer, stood still, and faced us. Her long shadow fell to the water's edge. Her face had a tragic and fierce aspect of wild sorrow and of dumb pain mingled with the fear of some struggling, half-shaped resolve. She stood looking at us without a stir, and like the wilderness itself, with an air of brooding over an inscrutable purpose. A whole minute passed, and then she made a step forward. There was a low jingle, a glint of yellow metal, a sway of fringed draperies, and she stopped as if her heart had failed her. The young fellow by my side growled. The pilgrims murmured at my back. She looked at us all as if her life had depended upon the unswerving steadiness of her glance. Suddenly she opened her bared arms and threw them up rigid above her head, as though in an uncontrollable desire to touch the sky, and at the same time the swift shadows darted out on the earth, swept around on the river, gathering the steamer into a shadowy embrace. A formidable silence hung over the scene.

"She turned away slowly, walked on, following the bank, and passed into the bushes to the left. Once only her eyes gleamed back at us in the dusk of the thickets before she disappeared.

" 'If she had offered to come aboard I really think I would have tried to shoot her,' said the man of patches nervously. 'I had been risking my life every day for the last fortnight to keep her out of the house. She got in one day and kicked up a row about those miserable rags I picked up in the storeroom to mend my clothes with. I wasn't decent. At least it must have been that, for she talked like a fury to Kurtz for an hour, pointing at me now and then. I don't understand the dialect of this tribe. Luckily for me, I fancy Kurtz felt too ill that day to care, or there would have been mischief. I don't understand. . . . No—it's too much for me. Ah, well, it's all over now.'

"At this moment I heard Kurtz's deep voice behind the curtain: 'Save me!— save the ivory, you mean. Don't tell me. Save *me*! Why, I've had to save you. You are interrupting my plans now. Sick! Sick! Not so sick as you would like to believe. Never mind. I'll carry my ideas out yet—I will return. I'll show you what can be done. You with your little peddling notions—you are interfering with me. I will return. I . . .'

"The manager came out. He did me the honour to take me under the arm and lead me aside. 'He is very low, very low,' he said. He considered it necessary to sigh, but neglected to be consistently sorrowful. 'We have done all we could for him—haven't we? But there is no disguising the fact, Mr Kurtz has done more harm than good to the Company. He did not see the time was not ripe for vigorous action. Cautiously, cautiously—that's my principle. We must be cautious yet. The district is closed to us for a time. Deplorable! Upon the whole, the trade will suffer. I don't deny there is a remarkable quantity of ivory—mostly fossil. We must save it, at all events—but look how precarious the position is—and why? Because the method is unsound.' 'Do you,' said I, looking at the shore, 'call it "unsound method"?' 'Without doubt,' he exclaimed hotly, 'Don't you?' . . . 'No method at all,' I murmured after a while. 'Exactly,' he exulted. 'I anticipated this. Shows a complete want of judgment. It is my duty to point it out in the proper quarter.' 'Oh,' said I, 'that fellow—what's his name?—the brickmaker, will make a readable report for you.' He appeared confounded for a moment. It seemed to me I had never breathed an atmosphere so vile, and I turned mentally to Kurtz for relief—positively for relief. 'Nevertheless, I think Mr Kurtz is a remarkable man,' I said with emphasis. He started, dropped on me a cold heavy glance, said very quietly, 'He *was*,' and turned his back on me. My hour of favour was over; I found myself lumped along with Kurtz as a partisan of methods for which the time was not ripe: I was unsound! Ah! but it was something to have at least a choice of nightmares.

"I had turned to the wilderness really, not to Mr Kurtz, who, I was ready to admit, was as good as buried. And for a moment it seemed to me as if I also were buried in a vast grave full of unspeakable secrets. I felt an intolerable weight oppressing my breast, the smell of the damp earth, the unseen presence of victorious corruption, the darkness of an impenetrable night. . . . The Russian tapped me on the shoulder. I heard him mumbling and stammering something about 'brother seaman—couldn't conceal—knowledge of matters that would affect Mr Kurtz's reputation.' I waited. For him evidently Mr Kurtz was not in his grave; I suspect that for him Mr Kurtz was one of the immortals. 'Well!' said I at last, 'speak out. As it happens, I am Mr Kurtz's friend—in a way.'

"He stated with a good deal of formality that had we not been 'of the same profession,' he would have kept the matter to himself without regard to consequences. He suspected 'there was an active ill-will towards him on the part of these white men that—' 'You are right,' I said, remembering a certain conversation I had overheard. 'The manager thinks you ought to be hanged.' He showed a concern at this intelligence which amused me at first. 'I had better get out of the way quietly,' he said earnestly. 'I can do no more for Kurtz now, and they would soon find some excuse. What's to stop them? There's a military post three hundred miles from here.' 'Well, upon my word,' said I, 'perhaps you had better go if you have any friends amongst the savages near by.' 'Plenty,' he said. 'They are simple people—and I want nothing, you know.' He stood biting his lip, then: 'I don't want any harm to happen to these whites here, but of course I was thinking of Mr Kurtz's reputation—but you are a brother seaman and—' 'All right,' said I, after a time. 'Mr Kurtz's reputation is safe with me.' I did not know how truly I spoke.

"He informed me, lowering his voice, that it was Kurtz who had ordered the attack to be made on the steamer. 'He hated sometimes the idea of being taken away—and then again . . . But I don't understand these matters. I am a simple man. He thought it would scare you away—that you would give it up, thinking him dead. I could not stop him. Oh, I had an awful time of it this last month.' 'Very well,' I said. 'He is all right now.' 'Ye-e-es,' he muttered, not very convinced apparently. 'Thanks,' said I; 'I shall keep my eyes open.' 'But quiet—eh?' he urged anxiously. 'It would be awful for his reputation if anybody here—' I promised a complete discretion with great gravity. 'I have a canoe and three black fellows waiting not very far. I am off. Could you give me a few Martini-Henry cartridges?' I could, and did, with proper secrecy. He helped himself, with a wink at me, to a handful of my tobacco. 'Between sailors—you know—good English tobacco.' At the door of the pilot-house he turned round—'I say, haven't you a pair of shoes you could spare?' He raised one leg. 'Look.' The soles were tied with knotted strings sandal-wise under his bare feet. I rooted out an old pair, at which he looked with admiration before tucking it under his left arm. One of his pockets (bright red) was bulging with cartridges, from the other (dark blue) peeped 'Towson's Inquiry,' etc. etc. He seemed to think himself excellently well equipped for a renewed encounter with the wilderness. 'Ah! I'll never, never meet such a man again. You ought to have heard him recite poetry—his own too it was, he told me. Poetry!' He rolled his eyes at the recollection of these delights. 'Oh, he enlarged my mind!' 'Good-bye,' said I. He shook hands and vanished in the night. Sometimes I ask myself whether I had ever really seen him—whether it was possible to meet such a phenomenon! . . .

"When I woke up shortly after midnight his warning came to my mind with its hint of danger that seemed, in the starred darkness, real enough to make me get up for the purpose of having a look round. On the hill a big fire burned, illuminating fitfully a crooked corner of the station-house. One of the agents with a picket of a few of our blacks, armed for the purpose, was keeping guard over the ivory; but deep within the forest, red gleams that wavered, that seemed to sink and rise from the ground amongst confused columnar shapes of intense blackness, showed the exact position of the camp where Mr Kurtz's adorers were keeping their uneasy vigil. The monotonous beating of a big drum filled the air with muffled shocks and a lingering vibration. A steady droning sound of many men chanting each to himself some weird incantation came out from the black, flat wall of the woods as the humming of bees comes out of a hive, and had a strange narcotic effect upon my half-awake senses. I believe I dozed off leaning over the rail, till an abrupt burst of yells, an overwhelming outbreak of a pent-up and mysterious frenzy, woke me up in a bewildered wonder. It was cut short all at once, and the low droning went on with an effect of audible and soothing silence. I glanced casually into the little cabin. A light was burning within, but Mr Kurtz was not there.

"I think I would have raised an outcry if I had believed my eyes. But I didn't believe them at first—the thing seemed so impossible. The fact is I was completely unnerved by a sheer blank fright, pure abstract terror, unconnected with any distinct shape of physical danger. What made this emotion so overpowering was—how shall I define it?—the moral shock I received, as if something altogether monstrous, intolerable to thought and odious to the soul, had been thrust upon me unexpectedly. This lasted of course the merest fraction of a second, and then the usual sense of commonplace, deadly danger, the possibility of a sudden onslaught and massacre, or something of the kind, which I saw impending, was positively welcome and composing. It pacified me, in fact, so much that I did not raise an alarm.

"There was an agent buttoned up inside an ulster[5] and sleeping on a chair on deck within three feet of me. The yells had not awakened him; he snored very slightly; I left him to his slumbers and leaped ashore. I did not betray Mr

5. Long overcoat.

Kurtz—it was ordered I should never betray him—it was written I should be loyal to the nightmare of my choice. I was anxious to deal with this shadow by myself alone—and to this day I don't know why I was so jealous of sharing with any one the peculiar blackness of that experience.

"As soon as I got on the bank I saw a trail—a broad trail through the grass. I remember the exultation with which I said to myself, 'He can't walk—he is crawling on all-fours—I've got him.' The grass was wet with dew. I strode rapidly with clenched fists. I fancy I had some vague notion of falling upon him and giving him a drubbing. I don't know. I had some imbecile thoughts. The knitting old woman with the cat obtruded herself upon my memory as a most improper person to be sitting at the other end of such an affair. I saw a row of pilgrims squirting lead in the air out of Winchesters held to the hip. I thought I would never get back to the steamer, and imagined myself living alone and unarmed in the woods to an advanced age. Such silly things—you know. And I remember I confounded the beat of the drum with the beating of my heart, and was pleased at its calm regularity.

"I kept to the track though—then stopped to listen. The night was very clear; a dark blue space, sparkling with dew and starlight, in which black things stood very still. I thought I could see a kind of motion ahead of me. I was strangely cocksure of everything that night. I actually left the track and ran in a wide semicircle (I verily believe chuckling to myself) so as to get in front of that stir, of that motion I had seen—if indeed I had seen anything. I was circumventing Kurtz as though it had been a boyish game.

"I came upon him, and, if he had not heard me coming, I would have fallen over him too, but he got up in time. He rose, unsteady, long, pale, indistinct, like a vapour exhaled by the earth, and swayed slightly, misty and silent before me; while at my back the fires loomed between the trees, and the murmur of many voices issued from the forest. I had cut him off cleverly; but when actually confronting him I seemed to come to my senses, I saw the danger in its right proportion. It was by no means over yet. Suppose he began to shout? Though he could hardly stand, there was still plenty of vigour in his voice. 'Go away—hide yourself,' he said, in that profound tone. It was very awful. I glanced back. We were within thirty yards of the nearest fire. A black figure stood up, strode on long black legs, waving long black arms, across the glow. It had horns—antelope horns, I think—on its head. Some sorcerer, some witch-man no doubt: it looked fiend-like enough. 'Do you know what you are doing?' I whispered. 'Perfectly,' he answered, raising his voice for that single word: it sounded to me far off and yet loud, like a hail through a speaking-trumpet. If he makes a row we are lost, I thought to myself. This clearly was not a case for fisticuffs, even apart from the very natural aversion I had to beat that Shadow—this wandering and tormented thing. 'You will be lost,' I said—'utterly lost.' One gets sometimes such a flash of inspiration, you know. I did say the right thing, though indeed he could not have been more irretrievably lost than he was at this very moment, when the foundations of our intimacy were being laid—to endure—to endure—even to the end—even beyond.

" 'I had immense plans,' he muttered irresolutely. 'Yes,' said I; 'but if you try to shout I'll smash your head with—' There was not a stick or a stone near. 'I will throttle you for good,' I corrected myself. 'I was on the threshold of great things,' he pleaded, in a voice of longing, with a wistfulness of tone that made my blood run cold. 'And now for this stupid scoundrel—' 'Your success in Europe is assured in any case,' I affirmed steadily. I did not want to have the throttling of him, you understand—and indeed it would have been very little use for any practical purpose. I tried to break the spell—the heavy, mute spell of the wilderness—that seemed to draw him to its pitiless breast by the awakening of forgotten and brutal instincts, by the memory of gratified and monstrous passions. This alone, I was convinced, had driven him out to the edge of the forest, to the bush, towards the gleam of fires, the throb of drums, the drone of weird incantations; this alone had beguiled his unlawful soul beyond the bounds of permitted aspirations. And, don't you see, the terror of the position was not in being knocked on the head—though I had a very lively sense of that danger too—but in this, that I had to deal with a being to whom I could not appeal in the name of anything high or low. I had, even like the niggers, to invoke him—himself—his own exalted and incredible degradation. There was nothing either above or below him, and I knew it. He had kicked himself loose of the earth. Confound the man! he had kicked the very earth to pieces. He was alone, and I before him did not know whether I stood on the ground or floated in the air. I've been telling you what we said—repeating the phrases we pronounced—but what's the good? They were common everyday words—the familiar, vague sounds exchanged on every waking day of life. But what of that? They had behind them, to my mind, the terrific suggestiveness of words heard in dreams, of phrases spoken in nightmares. Soul! If anybody had ever struggled with a soul, I am the man. And I wasn't arguing with a lunatic either. Believe me or not, his intelligence was perfectly clear—concentrated, it is true, upon himself with horrible intensity, yet clear; and therein was my only chance—barring, of course, the killing him there and then, which wasn't so good, on account of unavoidable noise. But his soul was mad. Being alone in the wilderness, it had looked within itself, and, by heavens! I tell you, it had gone mad. I had—for my sins, I suppose, to go through the ordeal of looking into it myself. No eloquence could have been so withering to one's belief in mankind as his final burst of sincerity. He struggled with himself too. I saw it—I heard it. I saw the inconceivable mystery of a soul that knew no restraint, no faith, and no fear, yet struggling blindly with itself. I kept my head pretty well; but when I had him at last stretched on the couch, I wiped my forehead, while my legs shook under me as though I had carried half a ton on my back down that hill. And yet I had only supported him, his bony arm clasped round my neck—and he was not much heavier than a child.

"When next day we left at noon, the crowd, of whose presence behind the curtain of trees I had been acutely conscious all the time, flowed out of the woods again, filled the clearing, covered the slope with a mass of naked, breathing, quivering, bronze bodies. I steamed up a bit, then swung downstream, and two thousand eyes followed the evolutions of the splashing, thumping, fierce river-demon beating the water with its terrible tail and breathing black smoke into the air. In front of the first rank, along the river, three men, plastered with bright red earth from head to foot, strutted to and fro restlessly. When we came abreast again, they faced the river, stamped their feet, nodded their horned heads, swayed their scarlet bodies; they shook towards the fierce river-demon a bunch of black feathers, a mangy skin with a pendent tail—something that looked like a dried gourd; they shouted periodically together strings of amazing words that resembled no sounds of human language; and the deep murmurs of the crowd, interrupted suddenly, were like the responses of some satanic litany.

"We had carried Kurtz into the pilot-house: there was more air there. Lying on the couch, he stared through the open shutter. There was an eddy in the mass of human bodies, and the woman with helmeted head and tawny cheeks rushed out to the very brink of the stream. She put out her hands, shouted something, and all that wild mob took up the shout in a roaring chorus of articulated, rapid, breathless utterance.

" 'Do you understand this?' I asked.

"He kept on looking out past me with fiery, longing eyes, with a mingled expression of wistfulness and hate. He made no answer, but I saw a smile, a smile of indefinable meaning, appear on his colourless lips that a moment after twitched convulsively. 'Do I not?' he said slowly, gasping, as if the words had been torn out of him by a supernatural power.

"I pulled the string of the whistle, and I did this because I saw the pilgrims on deck getting out their rifles with an air of anticipating a jolly lark. At the sudden screech there was a movement of abject terror through that wedged mass of bodies. 'Don't! don't you frighten them away,' cried some one on deck disconsolately. I pulled the string time after time. They broke and ran, they leaped, they crouched, they swerved, they dodged the flying terror of the sound. The three red chaps had fallen flat, face down on the shore, as though they had been shot dead. Only the barbarous and superb woman did not so much as flinch, and stretched tragically her bare arms after us over the sombre and glittering river.

"And then that imbecile crowd down on the deck started their little fun, and I could see nothing more for smoke.

"The brown current ran swiftly out of the heart of darkness, bearing us down towards the sea with twice the speed of our upward progress; and Kurtz's life was running swiftly too, ebbing, ebbing out of his heart into the sea of inexorable time. The manager was very placid, he had no vital anxieties now, he took us both in with a comprehensive and satisfied glance: the 'affair' had come off as well as could be wished. I saw the time approaching when I would be left alone of the party of 'unsound method.' The pilgrims looked upon me with disfavour. I was, so to speak, numbered with the dead. It is strange how I accepted this unforeseen partnership, this choice of nightmares forced upon me in the tenebrous land invaded by these mean and greedy phantoms.

"Kurtz discoursed. A voice! a voice! It rang deep to the very last. It survived his strength to hide in the magnificent folds of eloquence the barren darkness of his heart. Oh, he struggled! he struggled! The wastes of his weary brain were haunted by shadowy images now—images of wealth and fame revolving obsequiously round his unextinguishable gift of noble and lofty expression. My Intended, my station, my career, my ideas—these were the subjects for the occasional utterances of elevated sentiments. The shade of the original Kurtz frequented the bedside of the hollow sham, whose fate it was to be buried presently in the mould of primeval earth. But both the diabolic love and the unearthly hate of the mysteries it had penetrated fought for the possession of that soul satiated with primitive emotions, avid of lying fame, of sham distinction, of all the appearances of success and power.

"Sometimes he was contemptibly childish. He desired to have kings meet him at railway stations on his return from some ghastly Nowhere, where he intended to accomplish great things. 'You show them you have in you something that is really profitable, and then there will be no limits to the recognition of your ability,' he would say. 'Of course you must take care of the motives— right motives—always.' The long reaches that were like one and the same reach, monotonous bends that were exactly alike, slipped past the steamer with their multitude of secular[6] trees looking patiently after this grimy fragment of another world, the forerunner of change, of conquest, of trade, of massacres, of blessings. I looked ahead—piloting. 'Close the shutter,' said Kurtz suddenly one day; 'I can't bear to look at this.' I did so. There was a silence. 'Oh, but I will wring your heart yet!' he cried at the invisible wilderness.

"We broke down—as I had expected—and had to lie up for repairs at the head of an island. This delay was the first thing that shook Kurtz's confidence. One morning he gave me a packet of papers and a photograph—the lot tied together with a shoe-string. 'Keep this for me,' he said. 'This noxious fool' (meaning the manager) 'is capable of prying into my boxes when I am not looking.' In the afternoon I saw him. He was lying on his back with closed eyes, and I withdrew quietly, but I heard him mutter, 'Live rightly, die, die . . .' I listened. There was nothing more. Was he rehearsing some speech in his sleep, or was it a fragment of a phrase from some newspaper article? He had been writing for the papers and meant to do so again, 'for the furthering of my ideas. It's a duty.'

"His was an impenetrable darkness. I looked at him as you peer down at a man who is lying at the bottom of a precipice where the sun never shines. But I had not much time to give him, because I was helping the engine-driver to take to pieces the leaky cylinders, to straighten a bent connecting-rod, and in other such matters. I lived in an infernal mess of rust, filings, nuts, bolts, spanners, hammers, ratchet-drills—things I abominate, because I don't get on with them. I tended the little forge we fortunately had aboard; I toiled wearily in a wretched scrap-heap—unless I had the shakes too bad to stand.

"One evening coming in with a candle I was startled to hear him say a little tremulously, 'I am lying here in the dark waiting for death.' The light was within a foot of his eyes. I forced myself to murmur, 'Oh, nonsense!' and stood over him as if transfixed.

"Anything approaching the change that came over his features I have never seen before, and hope never to see again. Oh, I wasn't touched. I was fascinated. It was as though a veil had been rent. I saw on that ivory face the expression of sombre pride, of ruthless power, of craven terror—of an intense and hopeless despair. Did he live his life again in every detail of desire, temptation, and surrender during that supreme moment of complete knowledge? He cried in a whisper at some image, at some vision—he cried out twice, a cry that was no more than a breath:

" 'The horror! The horror!'

"I blew the candle out and left the cabin. The pilgrims were dining in the mess-room, and I took my place opposite the manager, who lifted his eyes to give me a questioning glance, which I successfully ignored. He leaned back, serene, with that peculiar smile of his sealing the unexpressed depths of his meanness. A continuous shower of small flies streamed upon the lamp, upon the cloth, upon our hands and faces. Suddenly the manager's boy put his insolent black head in the doorway, and said in a tone of scathing contempt:

" 'Mistah Kurtz—he dead.'

"All the pilgrims rushed out to see. I remained, and went on with my dinner. I believe I was considered brutally callous. However, I did not eat much. There was a lamp in there—light, don't you know—and outside it was so beastly,

6. Centuries old.

beastly dark. I went no more near the remarkable man who had pronounced a judgement upon the adventures of his soul on this earth. The voice was gone. What else had been there? But I am of course aware that next day the pilgrims buried something in a muddy hole.

"And then they very nearly buried me.

"However, as you see, I did not go to join Kurtz there and then. I did not. I remained to dream the nightmare out to the end, and to show my loyalty to Kurtz once more. Destiny. My destiny! Droll thing life is—that mysterious arrangement of merciless logic for a futile purpose. The most you can hope from it is some knowledge of yourself—that comes too late—a crop of unextinguishable regrets. I have wrestled with death. It is the most unexciting contest you can imagine. It takes place in an impalpable greyness, with nothing underfoot, with nothing around, without spectators, without clamour, without glory, without the great desire of victory, without the great fear of defeat, in a sickly atmosphere of tepid scepticism, without much belief in your own right, and still less in that of your adversary. If such is the form of ultimate wisdom, then life is a greater riddle than some of us think it to be. I was within a hair's-breadth of the last opportunity for pronouncement, and I found with humiliation that probably I would have nothing to say. This is the reason why I affirm that Kurtz was a remarkable man. He had something to say. He said it. Since I had peeped over the edge myself, I understand better the meaning of his stare, that could not see the flame of the candle, but was wide enough to embrace the whole universe, piercing enough to penetrate all the hearts that beat in the darkness. He had summed up—he had judged. 'The horror!' He was a remarkable man. After all, this was the expression of some sort of belief; it had candour, it had conviction, it had a vibrating note of revolt in its whisper, it had the appalling face of a glimpsed truth—the strange commingling of desire and hate. And it is not my own extremity I remember best—a vision of greyness without form filled with physical pain, and a careless contempt for the evanescence of all things—even of this pain itself. No! It is his extremity that I seem to have lived through. True, he had made that last stride, he had stepped over the edge, while I had been permitted to draw back my hesitating foot. And perhaps in this is the whole difference; perhaps all the wisdom, and all truth, and all sincerity, are just compressed into that inappreciable moment of time in which we step over the threshold of the invisible. Perhaps! I like to think my summing-up would not have been a word of careless contempt. Better his cry—much better. It was an affirmation, a moral victory paid for by innumerable defeats, by abominable terrors, by abominable satisfactions. But it was a victory! That is why I have remained loyal to Kurtz to the last, and even beyond, when a long time after I heard once more, not his own voice, but the echo of his magnificent eloquence thrown to me from a soul as translucently pure as a cliff of crystal.

"No, they did not bury me, though there is a period of time which I remember mistily, with a shuddering wonder, like a passage through some inconceivable world that had no hope in it and no desire. I found myself back in the sepulchral city resenting the sight of people hurrying through the streets to filch a little money from each other, to devour their infamous cookery, to gulp their unwholesome beer, to dream their insignificant and silly dreams. They trespassed upon my thoughts. They were intruders whose knowledge of life was to me an irritating pretence, because I felt so sure they could not possibly know the things I knew. Their bearing, which was simply the bearing of commonplace individuals going about their business in the assurance of perfect safety, was offensive to me like the outrageous flauntings of folly in the face of a danger it is unable to comprehend. I had no particular desire to enlighten them, but I had some difficulty in restraining myself from laughing in their faces, so full of stupid importance. I daresay I was not very well at that time. I tottered about the streets—there were various affairs to settle—grinning bitterly at perfectly respectable persons. I admit my behaviour was inexcusable, but then my temperature was seldom normal in these days. My dear aunt's endeavours to 'nurse up my strength' seemed altogether beside the mark. It was not my strength that wanted nursing, it was my imagination that wanted soothing. I kept the bundle of papers given me by Kurtz, not knowing exactly what to do with it. His mother had died lately, watched over, as I was told, by his Intended. A clean-shaven man, with an official manner and wearing gold-rimmed spectacles, called on me one day and made inquiries, at first circuitous, afterwards suavely pressing, about what he was pleased to denominate certain 'documents.' I was not surprised, because I had had two rows with the manager on the subject out there. I had refused to give up the smallest scrap out of that package, and I took the same attitude with the spectacled man. He became darkly menacing at last, and with much heat argued that the Company had the right to every bit of information about its 'territories.' And, said he, 'Mr Kurtz's knowledge of unexplored regions must have been necessarily extensive and peculiar—owing to his great abilities and to the deplorable circumstances in which he had been placed: therefore—' I assured him Mr Kurtz's knowledge, however extensive, did not bear upon the problems of commerce or administration. He invoked then the name of science. 'It would be an incalculable loss if,' etc. etc. I offered him the report on the 'Suppression of Savage Customs,' with the postscriptum torn off. He took it up eagerly, but ended by sniffing at it with an air of contempt. 'This is not what we had a right to expect,' he remarked. 'Expect nothing else,' I said. 'There are only private letters.' He withdrew upon some threat of legal proceedings, and I saw him no more; but another fellow, calling himself Kurtz's cousin, appeared two days later, and was anxious to hear all the details about his dear relative's last moments. Incidentally he gave me to understand that Kurtz had been essentially a great musician. 'There was the making of an immense success,' said the man, who was an organist, I believe, with lank grey hair flowing over a greasy coat-collar. I had no reason to doubt his statement; and to this day I am unable to say what was Kurtz's profession, whether he ever had any—which was the greatest of his talents. I had taken him for a painter who wrote for the papers, or else for a journalist who could paint—but even the cousin (who took snuff during the interview) could not tell me what he had been—exactly. He was a universal genius—on that point I agreed with the old chap, who thereupon blew his nose noisily into a large cotton handkerchief and withdrew in senile agitation, bearing off some family letters and memoranda without importance. Ultimately a journalist anxious to know something of the fate of his 'dear colleague' turned up. This visitor informed me Kurtz's proper sphere ought to have been politics 'on the popular side.' He had furry straight eyebrows, bristly hair cropped short, an eyeglass on a broad ribbon, and, becoming expansive, confessed his opinion that Kurtz really couldn't write a bit—'but heavens! how that man could talk! He electrified large meetings. He had faith—don't you see?—he had the faith. He could get himself to believe anything—anything. He would have been a splendid leader of an extreme party.' 'What party?' I asked. 'Any party,' answered the other. 'He was an—an—extremist.' Did I not think so? I assented. Did I know, he asked, with a sudden flash of curiosity, 'what it was that had induced him to go out there?' 'Yes,' said I, and forthwith handed him the famous Report for publication, if he thought fit. He glanced through it hurriedly, mumbling all the time, judged 'it would do,' and took himself off with this plunder.

"Thus I was left at last with a slim packet of letters and the girl's portrait. She struck me as beautiful—I mean she had a beautiful expression. I know that the sunlight can be made to lie too, yet one felt that no manipulation of light and pose could have conveyed the delicate shade of truthfulness upon those features. She seemed ready to listen without mental reservation, without suspicion, without a thought for herself. I concluded I would go and give her back her portrait and those letters myself. Curiosity? Yes; and also some other feeling perhaps. All that had been Kurtz's had passed out of my hands: his soul, his body, his station, his plans, his ivory, his career. There remained only his memory and his Intended—and I wanted to give that up too to the past, in a way—to surrender personally all that remained of him with me to that oblivion which is the last word of our common fate. I don't defend myself. I had no clear perception of what it was I really wanted. Perhaps it was an impulse of unconscious loyalty, or the fulfilment of one of those ironic necessities that lurk in the facts of human existence. I don't know. I can't tell. But I went.

"I thought his memory was like the other memories of the dead that accumulate in every man's life—a vague impress on the brain of shadows that had fallen on it in their swift and final passage; but before the high and ponderous door, between the tall houses of a street as still and decorous as a well-kept alley in a cemetery, I had a vision of him on the stretcher, opening his mouth voraciously, as if to devour all the earth with all its mankind. He lived then before me; he lived as much as he had ever lived—a shadow insatiable of splendid appearances, of frightful realities; a shadow darker than the shadow of the night, and draped nobly in the folds of a gorgeous eloquence. The vision seemed to enter the house with me—the stretcher, the phantom-bearers, the wild crowd of obedient worshippers, the gloom of the forests, the glitter of the reach between the murky bends, the beat of the drum, regular and muffled like the beating of a heart—the heart of a conquering darkness. It was a moment of triumph for the wilderness, an invading and vengeful rush which, it seemed to me, I would have to keep back alone for the salvation of another soul. And the memory of what I had heard him say afar there, with the horned shapes stirring at my back, in the glow of fires, within the patient woods, those broken phrases came back to me, were heard again in their ominous and terrifying simplicity. I remembered his abject pleading, his abject threats, the colossal scale of his vile desires, the meanness, the torment, the tempestuous anguish of his soul. And later on I seemed to see his collected languid manner, when he said one day, 'This lot of ivory now is really mine. The Company did not pay for it. I collected it myself at a very great personal risk. I am afraid they will try to claim it as theirs though. H'm. It is a difficult case. What do you think I ought to do—resist? Eh? I want no more than justice.' . . . He wanted no more than justice—no more than justice. I rang the bell before a mahogany door on the first floor, and while I waited he seemed to stare at me out of the glossy panel—stare with that wide and immense stare embracing, condemning, loathing all the universe. I seemed to hear the whispered cry, 'The horror! The horror!'

"The dusk was falling. I had to wait in a lofty drawing-room with three long windows from floor to ceiling that were like three luminous and bedraped columns. The bent gilt legs and backs of the furniture shone in indistinct curves. The tall marble fireplace had a cold and monumental whiteness. A grand piano stood massively in a corner; with dark gleams on the flat surfaces like a sombre and polished sarcophagus. A high door opened—closed. I rose.

"She came forward, all in black, with a pale head, floating towards me in the dusk. She was in mourning. It was more than a year since his death, more than a year since the news came; she seemed as though she would remember and mourn for ever. She took both my hands in hers and murmured, 'I had heard you were coming.' I noticed she was not very young—I mean not girlish. She had a mature capacity for fidelity, for belief, for suffering. The room seemed to have grown darker, as if all the sad light of the cloudy evening had taken refuge on her forehead. This fair hair, this pale visage, this pure brow, seemed surrounded by an ashy halo from which the dark eyes looked out at me. Their glance was guileless, profound, confident, and trustful. She carried her sorrowful head as though she were proud of that sorrow, as though she would say, I—I alone know how to mourn for him as he deserves. But while we were still shaking hands, such a look of awful desolation came upon her face that I perceived she was one of those creatures that are not the playthings of Time. For her he had died only yesterday. And, by Jove! the impression was so powerful that for me too he seemed to have died only yesterday—nay, this very minute. I saw her and him in the same instant of time—his death and her sorrow—I saw her sorrow in the very moment of his death. Do you understand? I saw them together—I heard them together. She had said, with a deep catch of the breath, 'I have survived'; while my strained ears seemed to hear distinctly, mingled with her tone of despairing regret, the summing-up whisper of his eternal condemnation. I asked myself what I was doing there, with a sensation of panic in my heart as though I had blundered into a place of cruel and absurd mysteries not fit for a human being to behold. She motioned me to a chair. We sat down. I laid the packet gently on the little table, and she put her hand over it. . . . 'You knew him well,' she murmured, after a moment of mourning silence.

" 'Intimacy grows quickly out there,' I said. 'I knew him as well as it is possible for one man to know another.'

" 'And you admired him,' she said. 'It was impossible to know him and not to admire him. Was it?'

" 'He was a remarkable man,' I said unsteadily. Then before the appealing fixity of her gaze, that seemed to watch for more words on my lips, I went on, 'It was impossible not to—'

" 'Love him,' she finished eagerly, silencing me into an appalled dumbness. 'How true! how true! But when you think that no one knew him so well as I! I had all his noble confidence. I knew him best.'

" 'You knew him best,' I repeated. And perhaps she did. But with every word spoken the room was growing darker, and only her forehead, smooth and white, remained illumined by the unextinguishable light of belief and love.

" 'You were his friend,' she went on. 'His friend,' she repeated, a little louder. 'You must have been, if he had given you this, and sent you to me. I feel I can speak to you—and oh! I must speak. I want you—you who have heard his last words—to know I have been worthy of him. . . . It is not pride. . . . Yes! I am proud to know I understood him better than any one on earth—he told me so himself. And since his mother died I have had no one—no one—to—to—'

"I listened. The darkness deepened. I was not even sure whether he had given me the right bundle. I rather suspect he wanted me to take care of another batch of his papers which, after his death, I saw the manager examining under the lamp. And the girl talked, easing her pain in the certitude of my sympathy; she talked as thirsty men drink. I had heard that her engagement with Kurtz had been disapproved by her people. He wasn't rich enough or something. And indeed I don't know whether he had not been a pauper all his life. He had given me some reason to infer that it was his impatience of comparative poverty that drove him out there.

" ' . . . Who was not his friend who had heard him speak once?' she was saying. 'He drew men towards him by what was best in them.' She looked at me with intensity. 'It is the gift of the great,' she went on, and the sound of her low voice seemed to have the accompaniment of all the other sounds, full of mystery, desolation, and sorrow, I had ever heard—the ripple of the river, the soughing of the trees swayed by the wind, the murmurs of the crowds, the faint ring of incomprehensible words cried from afar, the whisper of a voice speaking from beyond the threshold of an eternal darkness. 'But you have heard him! You know!' she cried.

" 'Yes, I know,' I said with something like despair in my heart, but bowing my head before the faith that was in her, before that great and saving illusion that shone with an unearthly glow in the darkness, in the triumphant darkness from which I could not have defended her—from which I could not even defend myself.

" 'What a loss to me—to us!'—she corrected herself with beautiful generosity; then added in a murmur, 'To the world.' By the last gleams of twilight I could see the glitter of her eyes, full of tears—of tears that would not fall.

" 'I have been very happy—very fortunate—very proud,' she went on. 'Too fortunate. Too happy for a little while. And now I am unhappy for—for life.'

"She stood up; her fair hair seemed to catch all the remaining light in a glimmer of gold. I rose too.

" 'And of all this,' she went on mournfully, 'of all his promise, and of all his greatness, of his generous mind, of his noble heart, nothing remains—nothing but a memory. You and I—'

" 'We shall always remember him,' I said hastily.

" 'No!' she cried. 'It is impossible that all this should be lost—that such a life should be sacrificed to leave nothing—but sorrow. You know what vast plans he had. I knew of them too—I could not perhaps understand—but others knew of them. Something must remain. His words, at least, have not died.'

" 'His words will remain,' I said.

" 'And his example,' she whispered to herself. 'Men looked up to him—his goodness shone in every act. His example—'

" 'True,' I said; 'his example too. Yes, his example. I forgot that.'

" 'But I do not. I cannot—I cannot believe—not yet. I cannot believe that I shall never see him again, that nobody will see him again, never, never, never.'

"She put out her arms as if after a retreating figure, stretching them black and with clasped pale hands across the fading and narrow sheen of the window. Never see him! I saw him clearly enough then. I shall see this eloquent phantom as long as I live, and I shall see her too, a tragic and familiar Shade, resembling in this gesture another one, tragic also, and bedecked with powerless charms, stretching bare brown arms over the glitter of the infernal stream, the stream of darkness. She said suddenly very low, 'He died as he lived.'

" 'His end,' said I, with dull anger stirring in me, 'was in every way worthy of his life.'

" 'And I was not with him,' she murmured. My anger subsided before a feeling of infinite pity.

" 'Everything that could be done—' I mumbled.

" 'Ah, but I believed in him more than any one on earth—more than his own mother, more than—himself. He needed me! Me! I would have treasured every sigh, every word, every sign, every glance.'

"I felt like a chill grip on my chest. 'Don't,' I said, in a muffled voice.

" 'Forgive me. I—I—have mourned so long in silence—in silence. . . . You were with him—to the last? I think of his loneliness. Nobody near to understand him as I would have understood. Perhaps no one to hear. . . .'

" 'To the very end,' I said shakily. 'I heard his very last words. . . .' I stopped in a fright.

" 'Repeat them,' she murmured in a heart-broken tone. 'I want—I want—something—something—to—to live with.'

"I was on the point of crying at her, 'Don't you hear them?' The dusk was repeating them in a persistent whisper all around us, in a whisper that seemed to swell menacingly like the first whisper of a rising wind. 'The horror! The horror!'

" 'His last word—to live with,' she insisted. 'Don't you understand I loved him—I loved him—I loved him!'

"I pulled myself together and spoke slowly.

" 'The last word he pronounced was—your name.'

"I heard a light sigh and then my heart stood still, stopped dead short by an exulting and terrible cry, by the cry of inconceivable triumph and of unspeakable pain. 'I knew it—I was sure!' . . . She knew. She was sure. I heard her weeping; she had hidden her face in her hands. It seemed to me that the house would collapse before I could escape, that the heavens would fall upon my head. But nothing happened. The heavens do not fall for such a trifle. Would they have fallen, I wonder, if I had rendered Kurtz that justice which was his due? Hadn't he said he wanted only justice? But I couldn't. I could not tell her. It would have been too dark—too dark altogether. . . ."[7]

Marlow ceased, and sat apart, indistinct and silent, in the pose of a meditating Buddha. Nobody moved for a time. "We have lost the first of the ebb," said the Director suddenly. I raised my head. The offing was barred by a black bank of clouds, and the tranquil waterway leading to the uttermost ends of the earth flowed sombre under an overcast sky—seemed to lead into the heart of an immense darkness.

1898–99   1899, 1902

---

7. Writing to William Blackwood (editor of *Blackwood's Magazine*, where the story first appeared) in May 1902, Conrad referred to "the last pages of Heart of Darkness where the interview of the man and the girl locks in—as it were—the whole 30,000 words of narrative description into one suggestive view of a whole phase of life, and makes of that story something quite on another plane than an anecdote of a man who went mad in the Centre of Africa" (Joseph Conrad, *Letters to William Blackwood and David S. Meldrum*, ed. William Blackburn, 1958).

A. E. HOUSMAN
1859–1936

Alfred Edward Housman was born in Fockbury, Worcestershire (close to the Shropshire border), and attended school at the nearby town of Bromsgrove. He studied classics and philosophy at Oxford and in 1881 shocked his friends and teachers by failing his final examinations (he was at the time in a state of psychological turmoil resulting from his suppressed homosexual love for a fellow student). He obtained a civil service job and pursued his classical studies alone, gradually building up a reputation as a great textual critic of Latin literature. In 1892 he was appointed to the chair of Latin at University College, London, and from 1911 until his death he was professor of Latin at Cambridge.

Housman's classical studies consisted of meticulous, impersonal textual investigations; both his scholarship and his life were reserved and solitary. Yet his feeling for literature ran strong and deep, and in his lecture "The Name and Nature of Poetry" (1933) he says that poetry should be "more physical than intellectual," having a skin-bristling, spine-shivering effect on the reader. His own poetry was limited both in quantity and in range, but—stark, lucid, elegant—it exemplifies the "superior terseness" he prized in verse. Two "slim volumes"—*A Shropshire Lad* (1896) and *Last Poems* (1922)—were all that appeared during his lifetime, and after his death his brother Laurence brought out another small book, *More Poems* (1936).

As a poet Housman aimed not to expand or develop the resources of English poetry but by limitation and concentration to achieve an utterance both compact and moving. He was influenced by Greek and Latin lyric poetry, by the traditional ballad, and by the lyrics of the early-nineteenth-century German poet Heinrich Heine. His favorite theme is that of the doomed youth acting out the tragedy of his brief life; the context is agricultural activity in England, with the land bearing visual reminders of humanity's long history. Nature is beautiful but indifferent and is to be enjoyed while we are still able to enjoy it. Love, friendship, and conviviality cannot last and may well result in betrayal or death, but are likewise to be relished while there is time. Wryly ironic in tone, stoic in temperament, Housman sounds a note of resigned wisdom with quiet poignancy. He avoids self-pity by projecting emotion through an imagined character, notably the "Shropshire lad," so that even the first-person poems seem to be distanced in some degree. At the same time the poems are distinguished from the "gather ye rosebuds" (or carpe diem) tradition by the undertones of fatalism and even doom.

Loveliest of Trees

> Loveliest of trees, the cherry now
> Is hung with bloom along the bough,
> And stands about the woodland ride
> Wearing white for Eastertide.
>
> 5 Now, of my threescore years and ten,
> Twenty will not come again,
> And take from seventy springs a score,
> It only leaves me fifty more.

And since to look at things in bloom
10 Fifty springs are little room,
About the woodlands I will go
To see the cherry hung with snow.

1896

When I Was One-and-Twenty

When I was one-and-twenty
   I heard a wise man say,
"Give crowns and pounds and guineas
   But not your heart away;
5 Give pearls away and rubies
   But keep your fancy free."
But I was one-and-twenty,
   No use to talk to me.

When I was one-and-twenty
10   I heard him say again,
"The heart out of the bosom
   Was never given in vain;
'Tis paid with sighs a plenty
   And sold for endless rue."°   *repentance*
15 And I am two-and-twenty,
   And oh, 'tis true, 'tis true.

1896

To an Athlete Dying Young

The time you won your town the race
We chaired you through the market-place;
Man and boy stood cheering by,
And home we brought you shoulder-high.

5 Today, the road all runners come,
Shoulder-high we bring you home,
And set you at your threshold down,
Townsman of a stiller town.

Smart lad, to slip betimes away
10 From fields where glory does not stay,
And early though the laurel[1] grows
It withers quicker than the rose.

Eyes the shady night has shut
Cannot see the record cut,°   *broken*

1. In ancient Greece and Rome victorious athletes were crowned with laurel wreaths.

15 And silence sounds no worse than cheers
   After earth has stopped the ears:

Now you will not swell the rout°   *crowd*
Of lads that wore their honours out,
Runners whom renown outran
20 And the name died before the man.

So set, before its echoes fade,
The fleet foot on the sill of shade,
And hold to the low lintel up
The still-defended challenge-cup.

25 And round that early laurelled head
Will flock to gaze the strengthless dead
And find unwithered on its curls
The garland briefer than a girl's.

1896

Terence,[1] This Is Stupid Stuff

"Terence, this is stupid stuff:
You eat your victuals fast enough;
There can't be much amiss, 'tis clear,
To see the rate you drink your beer.
5 But oh, good Lord, the verse you make,
It gives a chap the belly-ache.
The cow, the old cow, she is dead;
It sleeps well, the hornèd head:
We poor lads, 'tis our turn now
10 To hear such tunes as killed the cow.
Pretty friendship 'tis to rhyme
Your friends to death before their time
Moping melancholy mad:
Come, pipe a tune to dance to, lad."

15 Why, if 'tis dancing you would be,
There's brisker pipes than poetry.
Say, for what were hop-yards meant,
Or why was Burton built on Trent?[2]
Oh many a peer[3] of England brews
20 Livelier liquor than the Muse,
And malt does more than Milton can
To justify God's ways to man.[4]
Ale, man, ale's the stuff to drink
For fellows whom it hurts to think:

---

1. *The Poems of Terence Hearsay* was Housman's intended title for *The Shropshire Lad*.
2. Burton-on-Trent is the most famous of all English brewing towns.

3. A reference to the "beer barons," brewery magnates raised to the peerage (i.e., made nobles).
4. Cf. Milton's promise in *Paradise Lost* (1.17–26) to "justify the ways of God to men."

25 Look into the pewter pot
To see the world as the world's not.
And faith, 'tis pleasant till 'tis past:
The mischief is that 'twill not last.
Oh I have been to Ludlow⁵ fair
30 And left my necktie God knows where,
And carried half-way home, or near,
Pints and quarts of Ludlow beer:
Then the world seemed none so bad,
And I myself a sterling lad;
35 And down in lovely muck I've lain,
Happy till I woke again.
Then I saw the morning sky:
Heigho, the tale was all a lie;
The world, it was the old world yet,
40 I was I, my things were wet,
And nothing now remained to do
But begin the game anew.

　　Therefore, since the world has still
Much good, but much less good than ill,
45 And while the sun and moon endure
Luck's a chance, but trouble's sure,
I'd face it as a wise man would,
And train for ill and not for good.
'Tis true the stuff I bring for sale
50 Is not so brisk a brew as ale:
Out of a stem that scored° the hand　　　　　　　　*cut*
I wrung it in a weary land.
But take it: if the smack is sour,
The better for the embittered hour;
55 It should do good to heart and head
When your soul is in my soul's stead;
And I will friend you, if I may,
In the dark and cloudy day.

　　There was a king reigned in the East:
60 There, when kings will sit to feast,
They get their fill before they think
With poisoned meat and poisoned drink.
He gathered all that springs to birth
From the many-venomed earth;
65 First a little, thence to more,
He sampled all her killing store;
And easy, smiling, seasoned sound,
Sate the king when healths went round.
They put arsenic in his meat
70 And stared aghast to watch him eat;
They poured strychnine in his cup
And shook to see him drink it up:
They shook, they stared as white's their shirt:

5. A market town in Shropshire.

Them it was their poison hurt.
75 —I tell the tale that I heard told.
Mithridates, he died old.[6]

1896

The Chestnut Casts His Flambeaux[1]

The chestnut casts his flambeaux, and the flowers
    Stream from the hawthorn in the wind away,
The doors clap to, the pane is blind with showers.
    Pass me the can,° lad; there's an end of May.   *tankard*

5 There's one spoilt spring to scant our mortal lot,
    One season ruined of our little store.
May will be fine next year as like as not:
    Oh ay, but then we shall be twenty-four.

We for a certainty are not the first
10   Have sat in taverns while the tempest hurled
Their hopeful plans to emptiness, and cursed
    Whatever brute and blackguard made the world.

It is in truth iniquity on high
    To cheat our sentenced souls of aught they crave,
15 And mar the merriment as you and I
    Fare on our long fool's-errand to the grave.

Iniquity it is; but pass the can.
    My lad, no pair of kings our mothers bore;
Our only portion is the estate of man:
20   We want the moon, but we shall get no more.

If here today the cloud of thunder lours°   *looks threatening*
    Tomorrow it will hie° on far behests;°   *go quickly / commands*
The flesh will grieve on other bones than ours
    Soon, and the soul will mourn in other breasts.

25 The troubles of our proud and angry dust
    Are from eternity, and shall not fail.
Bear them we can, and if we can we must.
    Shoulder the sky, my lad, and drink your ale.

1922

---

6. The story of Mithridates, king of Pontus, who made himself immune to poison by taking small doses daily, is told in Pliny's *Natural History*.

1. Literally, torches. Housman here refers to the erect flower clusters (white, dashed with red and yellow) of the horse chestnut tree.

Epitaph on an Army of Mercenaries[1]

These, in the day when heaven was falling,
  The hour when earth's foundations fled,
Followed their mercenary calling
  And took their wages and are dead.

5 Their shoulders held the sky suspended;
  They stood, and earth's foundations stay;
What God abandoned, these defended,
  And saved the sum of things for pay.

1922

---

1. To honor the heroism of the professional soldiers of the British Regular Army in the First Battle
of Ypres (1914), Housman published this poem in
The Times on the third anniversary of the turning
point of that battle, October 31, 1917. See Hugh
MacDiarmid's angry response, "Another Epitaph
on an Army of Mercenaries" (p. 2468).

'Epitaph on an Army of Mercenaries'

Voices from World War I

The original spark that set off what proved to be the bloodiest and most widespread war that had yet been fought was the murder of the Archduke Ferdinand of Austria in the Balkan state of Serbia on June 28, 1914. Austria, supported by Germany, used the murder as a reason for declaring war on Serbia, which in turn was supported by its fellow-Slav country Russia. Because Russia was bound by a treaty obligation to both France and Britain, Russia and France were soon at war with Germany and Austria. The most effective way for Germany to attack France was to go through Belgium, though all the powers had guaranteed Belgian neutrality. The attack on Belgium impelled Britain to declare war on Germany on August 4, but rival imperialisms, an international armaments race, France's desire to regain Alsace-Lorraine, which it had lost to Germany in 1870, and German and Austrian ambitions in the Balkans were some of the many other factors that brought about the four-year struggle, a struggle that shook the world. Turkey sided with Germany and Austria in October 1914, and Bulgaria allied itself with them the following year. Britain and France were joined by Japan late in August 1914, by Italy (although Italy had in 1882 joined the "Triple Alliance" with Germany and Austria directed against France and Russia) in May 1915, and by the United States in April 1917.

Before the collapse of Germany followed by the armistice of November 11, 1918, some 8,700,000 lives had been lost (including 780,000 British—virtually a whole generation of young men) and the prolonged horrors of trench warfare had seared themselves into the minds of the survivors. For three years the battle line, "the Western Front," was stabilized between northwest France and Switzerland, with both sides dug in and making repeated, costly, and generally useless attempts to advance. The German use of poison gas at the Second Battle of Ypres in 1915, the massive German attack at Verdun in 1916, and the British introduction of tanks on the Somme in the same year failed to produce the breakthrough each side desired. Desolate, war-scarred landscapes with blasted trees and mud everywhere, trenches half-filled with water and infested with rats, miles of protective barbed wire requiring individual "volunteers" to crawl through machine-gun fire and cut it so an advance could begin, long-continued massive bombardments by heavy artillery, and a sense of stalemate that suggested to the soldiers involved that this living hell could go on forever—all this was long kept from the knowledge of the civilians at home, who continued to use the old patriotic slogans and write in old-fashioned romantic terms about glorious cavalry charges and the noble pursuit of heroic ideals. But those poets who were involved on the front, however romantically they may have felt about the cause when they first joined up, soon realized the full horror of war, and this realization affected both their imaginations and their poetic techniques. They had to find a way of expressing the terrible truths they had experienced, and even when they did not express them directly, the underlying knowledge affected the way they wrote.

The poetry that was in vogue when war broke out, and that some poets continued to write for some years afterward, was named "Georgian" in honor of King George V, who had succeeded Edward VII in 1910. The term was first used of poets when Edward Marsh brought out in 1912 the first of a series of five anthologies called *Georgian Poetry*. The work therein represented an attempt to wall in the garden of English poetry against the disruptive forces of modern civilization. Cultured meditations of the English countryside ("I love the mossy quietness / That grows upon the great stone flags") alternated with self-conscious exercises in the exotic ("When I was but thirteen or so / I went into a golden land, / Chimporazo, Cotopaxi / Took me by the hand"). Sometimes the magical note was authentic, as in many of Walter de la Mare's poems, and sometimes the meditative strain was original and impressive, as in Edward Thomas's poetry. But as World War I went on, with more and more poets killed and the survivors increasingly disillusioned, the whole world on which the Georgian imagination rested came to appear unreal. A patriotic poem such as Rupert Brooke's "The Soldier" became a ridiculous anachronism in the face of the realities of trench warfare, and the even more blatantly patriotic note sounded by other Georgian poems (as in John Freeman's "Happy Is England Now," which claimed that "there's not a nobleness of heart, hand, brain / But shines the purer; happiest is England now / In those that fight") seemed obscene. The savage ironies of Siegfried Sassoon's war poems and the combination of pity and irony in Wilfred Owen's work portrayed a world undreamed of in the golden years from 1910 to 1914.

World War I left throughout Europe a sense that the bases of civilization had been destroyed, that all traditional values had been wiped out. We see this sense reflected in the years immediately after the war in different ways in, for example, T. S. Eliot's *Waste Land* and Aldous Huxley's early fiction. But the poets who wrote during the war most directly reflected the impact of the war experience.

For more documents, images, and contexts related to this subject, see "Representing the Great War" at Norton Literature Online.

RUPERT BROOKE
1887–1915

Rupert Brooke was educated at Rugby School and at King's College, Cambridge. When World War I began he was commissioned as an officer into the Royal Naval Division and took part in its brief and abortive expedition to Antwerp. On leave in December 1914 he wrote the "war sonnets" that were to make him famous; five months later he died of dysentery and blood poisoning on a troopship destined for Gallipoli.

Brooke was the most popular of the Georgians, pastoral poets who infused nature with nationalist feeling. His early death symbolized the death of a whole generation of patriotic Englishmen. Shortly before then the dean of St. Paul's read "The Soldier" in a sermon from the Cathedral pulpit, and in a 1915 valediction in the London *Times,* Winston Churchill sounded a note that swelled over the following months and years: "Joyous, fearless, versatile, deeply instructed, with classic symmetry of mind and body, he was all that one would wish England's noblest sons to be in days when no sacrifice but the most precious is acceptable, and the most precious is that which is most freely proffered." Brooke's *1914 and Other Poems* was published in June 1915, and during the next decade this and his *Collected Poems* sold three hundred thousand copies.

The Soldier

If I should die, think only this of me:
    That there's some corner of a foreign field
That is forever England. There shall be
    In that rich earth a richer dust concealed;

5 A dust whom England bore, shaped, made aware,
    Gave, once, her flowers to love, her ways to roam,
A body of England's, breathing English air,
    Washed by the rivers, blest by suns of home.

    And think, this heart, all evil shed away,
10   A pulse in the Eternal mind, no less
      Gives somewhere back the thoughts by England given,
Her sights and sounds; dreams happy as her day;
And laughter, learnt of friends; and gentleness,
    In hearts at peace, under an English heaven.

1914   1915

EDWARD THOMAS
1878–1917

Edward Thomas was born of Welsh parents in London and was educated there and at Lincoln College, Oxford, which he left with a wife, a baby, and high literary ambitions. Despite his chronic depression, which became more marked over the difficult years that followed, he reviewed up to fifteen books a week, published thirty books between 1897 and 1917, and during those twenty years edited sixteen anthologies and editions. His great gifts as a literary critic appeared to best advantage in his reviewing of poetry, and he was the first to salute new stars in the literary firmament such as Robert Frost and Ezra Pound.

Although he had long been conscientiously reviewing poetry, which he regarded as the highest form of literature, he apparently made no serious attempt to write poems until the autumn of 1914. Then, under the stress of deciding whether or not to enlist, poems began to pour out of him: five between December 3 and 7, and ten more before the end of the month. His friend Frost offered to find him work in the United States, but feelings of patriotism, and the attraction of a salary that would support his growing family, led him to enlist in July 1915. His awareness of the natural world, its richness and beauty, was then intensified by a sense of impending loss and the certainty of death—his own and others'. In the long sentences that make up his verse, he ruminates with great delicacy on beauty and nature, but he also demonstrates an unsentimental toughness. In "Rain," for example, he compares the dead to "Myriads of broken reeds all still and stiff." As violence to the natural order of things, war indirectly but persistently shadows Thomas's poems. In January 1917 he was sent to the Western Front and, on Easter Monday, was killed by a shell blast.

Adlestrop[1]

Yes, I remember Adlestrop—
The name, because one afternoon
Of heat the express-train drew up there
Unwontedly. It was late June.

---

1. A village in Gloucestershire.

5 The steam hissed. Someone cleared his throat.
No one left and no one came
On the bare platform. What I saw
Was Adlestrop—only the name

And willows, willow-herb, and grass,
10 And meadowsweet, and haycocks dry,
No whit less still and lonely fair
Than the high cloudlets in the sky.

And for that minute a blackbird sang
Close by, and round him, mistier,
15 Farther and farther, all the birds
Of Oxfordshire and Gloucestershire.

Jan. 1915   1917

Tears

It seems I have no tears left. They should have fallen—
Their ghosts, if tears have ghosts, did fall—that day
When twenty hounds streamed by me, not yet combed out
But still all equals in their rage of gladness
5 Upon the scent, made one, like a great dragon
In Blooming Meadow that bends towards the sun
And once bore hops: and on that other day
When I stepped out from the double-shadowed Tower
Into an April morning, stirring and sweet
10 And warm. Strange solitude was there and silence.
A mightier charm than any in the Tower
Possessed the courtyard. They were changing guard,
Soldiers in line, young English countrymen,
Fair-haired and ruddy, in white tunics. Drums
15 And fifes were playing "The British Grenadiers."[1]
The men, the music piercing that solitude
And silence, told me truths I had not dreamed,
And have forgotten since their beauty passed.

Jan. 1915   1917

The Owl

Downhill I came, hungry, and yet not starved;
Cold, yet had heat within me that was proof
Against the North wind; tired, yet so that rest
Had seemed the sweetest thing under a roof.

---

1. Famous British marching song about the Brigade of Guards, an elite infantry unit.

5   Then at the inn I had food, fire, and rest,
     Knowing how hungry, cold, and tired was I.
     All of the night was quite barred out except
     An owl's cry, a most melancholy cry

     Shaken out long and clear upon the hill,
10   No merry note, nor cause of merriment,
     But one telling me plain what I escaped
     And others could not, that night, as in I went.

     And salted° was my food, and my repose,   *flavored (as with salt)*
     Salted and sobered, too, by the bird's voice
15   Speaking for all who lay under the stars,
     Soldiers and poor, unable to rejoice.

Feb. 1915   1917

Rain[1]

     Rain, midnight rain, nothing but the wild rain
     On this bleak hut, and solitude, and me
     Remembering again that I shall die
     And neither hear the rain nor give it thanks
5   For washing me cleaner than I have been
     Since I was born into this solitude.
     Blessed are the dead that the rain rains upon:
     But here I pray that none whom once I loved
     Is dying tonight or lying still awake
10   Solitary, listening to the rain,
     Either in pain or thus in sympathy
     Helpless among the living and the dead,
     Like a cold water among broken reeds,
     Myriads of broken reeds all still and stiff,
15   Like me who have no love which this wild rain
     Has not dissolved except the love of death,
     If love it be towards what is perfect and
     Cannot, the tempest tells me, disappoint.

Jan. 1916   1917

The Cherry Trees

     The cherry trees bend over and are shedding
     On the old road where all that passed are dead,

1. Cf. Thomas's account of an English walking tour, *The Icknield Way* (1913): "In the heavy, black rain falling straight from invisible, dark sky to invisible, dark earth the heat of summer is annihilated, the splendour is dead, the summer is gone. The midnight rain buries it away where it has buried all sound but its own. I am alone in the dark still night, and my ear listens to the rain piping in the gutters and roaring softly in the trees of the world. Even so will the rain fall darkly upon the grass over the grave when my ears can hear it no more. . . . Black and monotonously sounding is the midnight and solitude of the rain. In a little while or in an age—for it is all one—I shall know the full truth of the words I used to love, I knew not why, in my days of nature, in the days before the rain: 'Blessed are the dead that the rain rains on.' "

Their petals, strewing the grass as for a wedding
This early May morn when there is none to wed.

May 1916   1917

As the Team's Head Brass[1]

    As the team's head brass flashed out on the turn
The lovers disappeared into the wood.
I sat among the boughs of the fallen elm
That strewed an angle of the fallow,[2] and
5 Watched the plough narrowing a yellow square
Of charlock.° Every time the horses turned   *wild mustard*
Instead of treading me down, the ploughman leaned
Upon the handles to say or ask a word,
About the weather, next about the war.
10 Scraping the share he faced towards the wood,
And screwed along the furrow till the brass flashed
Once more.
          The blizzard felled the elm whose crest
I sat in, by a woodpecker's round hole,
The ploughman said. "When will they take it away?"
15 "When the war's over." So the talk began—
One minute and an interval of ten,
A minute more and the same interval.
"Have you been out?" "No." "And don't want to, perhaps?"
"If I could only come back again, I should.
20 I could spare an arm. I shouldn't want to lose
A leg. If I should lose my head, why, so,
I should want nothing more. . . . Have many gone
From here?" "Yes." "Many lost?" "Yes, a good few.
Only two teams work on the farm this year.
25 One of my mates is dead. The second day
In France they killed him. It was back in March,
The very night of the blizzard, too. Now if
He had stayed here we should have moved the tree."
"And I should not have sat here. Everything
30 Would have been different. For it would have been
Another world." "Ay, and a better, though
If we could see all all might seem good." Then
The lovers came out of the wood again:
The horses started and for the last time
35 I watched the clods crumble and topple over
After the ploughshare and the stumbling team.

May 1916   1917

---

1. Also known as horse brass: a decorative brass
medallion or emblem attached to a horse's harness.

2. Ground plowed and harrowed but left uncrop-
ped for a year or more.

SIEGFRIED SASSOON
1886–1967

Siegfried Sassoon was educated at Marlborough College and Clare College, Cambridge (which he left without taking a degree). His father came from a prosperous family of Sephardic Jews, his mother from Anglican English gentry. As a young man he divided his time between literary London and the life of a country gentleman. These worlds and the brutally different one of the trenches, in which he found himself in 1914, are memorably described in his classic *Memoirs of a Fox-Hunting Man* (1928) and its sequel, *Memoirs of an Infantry Officer* (1930).

He fought at Mametz Wood and in the Somme Offensive of July 1916 with such conspicuous courage that he acquired the Military Cross and the nickname Mad Jack. After a sniper's bullet went through his chest, however, he was sent back to England at the beginning of April 1917, and he began to take a different view of the war. Eventually, with courage equal to any he had shown in action, he made public a letter he sent to his commanding officer: "I am making this statement as an act of wilful defiance of military authority, because I believe that the war is being deliberately prolonged by those who have the power to end it." Sassoon continued: "I am a soldier, convinced that I am acting on behalf of soldiers. I believe that this war, upon which I entered as a war of defence and liberation, has now become a war of aggression and conquest." (For the full text, see "Representing the Great War" at Norton Literature Online.) The military authorities, rather than make a martyr of him, announced that he was suffering from shell shock and sent him to a hospital near Edinburgh, where he met and befriended Wilfred Owen.

Sassoon's public protest may have been smothered, but his poems, with their shock tactics, bitter irony, and masterly use of direct speech (learned from Thomas Hardy), continued to attack the old men of the army, Church, and government, whom he held responsible for the miseries and murder of the young. His poems satirically play on contrasts between the romanticization of war and the grim realities. They angrily flaunt the grisly effects of violence: in "The Rear-Guard" a corpse is "a soft unanswering heap" whose "fists of fingers clutched a blackening wound."

Sassoon returned to the Western Front in 1918, was wounded again, and was again sent home. An increasingly reclusive country gentleman, he continued to write poetry, but his style never regained the satiric pungency of the war poems that made him famous. His 1933 marriage failed because of his homosexuality; and after he became a Roman Catholic in 1957, he wrote mainly devotional poems.

'They'

    The Bishop tells us: "When the boys come back
    They will not be the same; for they'll have fought
    In a just cause: they lead the last attack
    On Anti-Christ; their comrades' blood has bought
5   New right to breed an honourable race,
    They have challenged Death and dared him face to face.'

    'We're none of us the same!' the boys reply.
    'For George lost both his legs; and Bill's stone blind;
    Poor Jim's shot through the lungs and like to die;
10 And Bert's gone syphilitic: you'll not find

A chap who's served that hasn't found *some* change.'
And the Bishop said: 'The ways of God are strange!'

Oct. 31, 1916   1917

The Rear-Guard

(Hindenburg Line, April 1917)[1]

    Groping along the tunnel, step by step,
He winked his prying torch with patching glare
From side to side, and sniffed the unwholesome air.
Tins, boxes, bottles, shapes too vague to know;
5   A mirror smashed, the mattress from a bed;
And he, exploring fifty feet below
The rosy gloom of battle overhead.

    Tripping, he grabbed the wall; saw some one lie
Humped at his feet, half-hidden by a rug,
10 And stooped to give the sleeper's arm a tug.
'I'm looking for headquarters.' No reply.
'God blast your neck!' (For days he'd had no sleep)
'Get up and guide me through this stinking place.'
Savage, he kicked a soft unanswering heap,
15 And flashed his beam across the livid face
Terribly glaring up, whose eyes yet wore
Agony dying hard ten days before;
And fists of fingers clutched a blackening wound.

    Alone he staggered on until he found
20 Dawn's ghost that filtered down a shafted stair
To the dazed, muttering creatures underground
Who hear the boom of shells in muffled sound.
At last, with sweat of horror in his hair,
He climbed through darkness to the twilight air,
25 Unloading hell behind him step by step.

Apr. 22, 1917   1918

The General

    'Good-morning; good-morning!' the General said
When we met him last week on our way to the line.
Now the soldiers he smiled at are most of 'em dead,
And we're cursing his staff for incompetent swine.

---

1. In 1916 Field Marshal Paul von Hindenburg
(1847–1934) became commander in chief of the
German armies and, for a time, blocked the Allied
advance in western France with the massive defensive "line" named after him. Its barbed-wire entanglements, deep trenches, and gun emplacements
ran from Lens to Rheims.

⁵ 'He's a cheery old card,' grunted Harry to Jack
As they slogged up to Arras¹ with rifle and pack.

. . .

But he did for them both by his plan of attack.

Apr. 1917   1918

Glory of Women

You love us when we're heroes, home on leave,
Or wounded in a mentionable place.
You worship decorations; you believe
That chivalry redeems the war's disgrace.
⁵ You make us shells.¹ You listen with delight,
By tales of dirt and danger fondly thrilled.
You crown our distant ardours while we fight,
And mourn our laurelled² memories when we're killed.
You can't believe that British troops 'retire'
¹⁰ When hell's last horror breaks them, and they run,
Trampling the terrible corpses—blind with blood.
     O German mother dreaming by the fire,
While you are knitting socks to send your son
His face is trodden deeper in the mud.

1917   1918

Everyone Sang

Everyone suddenly burst out singing;
And I was filled with such delight
As prisoned birds must find in freedom,
Winging wildly across the white
⁵ Orchards and dark-green fields; on—on—and out of sight.

Everyone's voice was suddenly lifted;
And beauty came like the setting sun:
My heart was shaken with tears; and horror
Drifted away . . . O, but Everyone
¹⁰ Was a bird; and the song was wordless; the singing will never be done.

Apr. 1919   1919

---

1. A city in northern France, in the front line through much of the war. The British assault on the Western Front that began on April 9, 1917, was known as the Battle of Arras.

1. Many women were recruited into munitions factories during the war.
2. In ancient Greece and Rome, victorious generals were crowned with laurel wreaths.

On Passing the New Menin Gate[1]

Who will remember, passing through this Gate,
The unheroic Dead who fed the guns?
Who shall absolve the foulness of their fate,—
Those doomed, conscripted, unvictorious ones?
5   Crudely renewed, the Salient[2] holds its own.
Paid are its dim defenders by this pomp;
Paid, with a pile of peace-complacent stone,
The armies who endured that sullen swamp.

Here was the world's worst wound. And here with pride
10   'Their name liveth for ever,' the Gateway claims.
Was ever an immolation so belied
As these intolerably nameless names?
Well might the Dead who struggled in the slime
Rise and deride this sepulchre° of crime.   *tomb*

1927–28   1928

From Memoirs of an Infantry Officer

[THE OPENING OF THE BATTLE OF THE SOMME]

On July [1916] the first the weather, after an early morning mist, was of the kind commonly called heavenly. Down in our frowsty cellar we breakfasted at six, unwashed and apprehensive. Our table, appropriately enough, was an empty ammunition box. At six-forty-five the final bombardment began, and there was nothing for us to do except sit round our candle until the tornado ended. For more than forty minutes the air vibrated and the earth rocked and shuddered. Through the sustained uproar the tap and rattle of machine-guns could be identified; but except for the whistle of bullets no retaliation came our way until a few 5.9[1] shells shook the roof of our dug-out. Barton and I sat speechless, deafened and stupefied by the seismic state of affairs, and when he lit a cigarette the match flame staggered crazily. Afterwards I asked him what he had been thinking about. His reply was 'Carpet slippers and Kettle-holders'. My own mind had been working in much the same style, for during that cannonading cataclysm the following refrain was running in my head:

> *They come as a boon and a blessing to men,*
> *The Something, the Owl, and the Waverley Pen.*

For the life of me I couldn't remember what the first one was called. Was it the Shakespeare? Was it the Dickens? Anyhow it was an advertisement which I'd often seen in smoky railway stations. Then the bombardment lifted and lessened, our vertigo abated, and we looked at one another in dazed relief. Two Brigades of our Division were now going over the top on our right. Our

---

1. The names of 54,889 men are engraved on this war memorial outside Brussels.
2. Protruding part of fortifications or, as here, line of defensive trenches. Salients are particularly vul-

nerable, being exposed to enemy fire from the front and both sides.
1. I.e., 5.9-caliber.

Brigade was to attack 'when the main assault had reached its final objective'. In our fortunate rôle of privileged spectators Barton and I went up the stairs to see what we could from Kingston Road Trench. We left Jenkins crouching in a corner, where he remained most of the day. His haggard blinking face haunts my memory. He was an example of the paralysing effect which such an experience could produce on a nervous system sensitive to noise, for he was a good officer both before and afterwards. I felt no sympathy for him at the time, but I do now. From the support-trench, which Barton called 'our opera box', I observed as much of the battle as the formation of the country allowed, the rising ground on the right making it impossible to see anything of the attack towards Mametz. A small shiny black note-book contains my pencilled particulars, and nothing will be gained by embroidering them with afterthoughts. I cannot turn my field-glasses on to the past.[2]

7.45. The barrage is now working to the right of Fricourt and beyond. I can see the 21st Division advancing about three-quarters of a mile away on the left and a few Germans coming to meet them, apparently surrendering. Our men in small parties (not extended in line) go steadily on to the German front-line. Brilliant sunshine and a haze of smoke drifting along the landscape. Some Yorkshires[3] a little way below on the left, watching the show and cheering as if at a football match. The noise almost as bad as ever.

9.30. Came back to dug-out and had a shave. 21st Division still going across the open, apparently without casualties. The sunlight flashes on bayonets as the tiny figures move quietly forward and disappear beyond mounds of trench debris. A few runners come back and ammunition parties go across. Trench-mortars are knocking hell out of Sunken Road trench and the ground where the Manchesters[4] will attack soon. Noise not so bad now and very little retaliation.

9.50. Fricourt half-hidden by clouds of drifting smoke, blue, pinkish and grey. Shrapnel bursting in small bluish-white puffs with tiny flashes. The birds seem bewildered; a lark begins to go up and then flies feebly along, thinking better of it. Others flutter above the trench with querulous cries, weak on the wing. I can see seven of our balloons,[5] on the right. On the left our men still filing across in twenties and thirties. Another huge explosion in Fricourt and a cloud of brown-pink smoke. Some bursts are yellowish.

10.5. I can see the Manchesters down in New Trench, getting ready to go over. Figures filing down the trench. Two of them have gone out to look at our wire gaps![6] Have just eaten my last orange. . . . I am staring at a sunlit picture of Hell, and still the breeze shakes the yellow weeds, and the poppies glow under Crawley Ridge where some shells fell a few minutes ago. Manchesters are sending forward some scouts. A bayonet glitters. A runner comes back across the open to their Battalion Headquarters, close here on the right. 21st Division still trotting along the sky line toward La Boisselle. Barrage going strong to the right of Contalmaison Ridge. Heavy shelling toward Mametz.

1916   1930

---

2. The extracts that follow are edited versions of the actual entries in Sassoon's diary. (See *Siegfried Sassoon: Diaries 1915–1918*, ed. Rupert Hart-Davis, 1983, pp. 82–83.)
3. Men of a Yorkshire regiment.
4. Men of the Manchester regiment.
5. Long cables, tethering such balloons, prevented attacks by low-flying aircraft.
6. Holes, made by shell fire, in the long coils of barbed wire protecting the trenches.

IVOR GURNEY
1890–1937

Ivor Bertie Gurney was born in Gloucester and showed an early aptitude for music. After five years at the King's School, Gloucester, he won a scholarship to the Royal College of Music. He first acquired a modest reputation as a composer. After war broke out in August 1914, he enlisted; his battalion was sent to France the following year, and Gurney experienced the horrors of the Western Front. He was wounded in April 1917, and when in the hospital in Rouen, he sent some of his poems to friends in London. The resultant volume, *Severn and Somme,* was published that year. (The Severn is the English river at the head of whose estuary Gloucester is situated; it appears often in his poetry. The Somme is the northern French river that was the scene of some of the most murderous fighting in the war.) Gurney was returned to the front in time to take part in the grim Paschendale offensive of the summer of 1917. He suffered the effects of a poison-gas attack on August 22 and was sent home, where he moved from hospital to hospital. He returned to the Royal College of Music to study under the composer Ralph Vaughan Williams (1872–1958) and continued also to write poetry. His second book of poems, *War's Embers,* appeared in 1919. Gurney, now believed to have been schizophrenic, spent the last fifteen years of his life in mental asylums.

Gurney was a mere private in the war, unlike officers such as Wilfred Owen and Siegfried Sassoon, and his poems recapture with immediacy particular scenes and moments in the trenches. He was influenced by the poetry of Edward Thomas, with whom he shares a limpid directness, and Gerard Manley Hopkins, whose "terrible" sonnets are racked by despair. Though ruminating on traditional subjects such as landscape, nature, and mortality, Gurney dislocates these Georgian conventions through the compression, disharmony, and unredemptive language of his poetry. His "modern" techniques include syntactic contortions, colloquial diction, shifting rhythms and rhymes, and enjambments that accentuate the jarring experience of war (a body described as "that red wet / Thing" in "To His Love").

To His Love

He's gone, and all our plans
   Are useless indeed.
We'll walk no more on Cotswold[1]
   Where the sheep feed
5   Quietly and take no heed.

His body that was so quick
   Is not as you
Knew it, on Severn river°   *a British river*
   Under the blue
10   Driving our small boat through.

You would not know him now . . .
   But still he died
Nobly, so cover him over
   With violets of pride
15   Purple from Severn side.

---

1. Range of hills in Gloucestershire, in western England.

Cover him, cover him soon!
And with thick-set
Masses of memoried flowers—
Hide that red wet
20   Thing I must somehow forget.

1919

The Silent One

Who died on the wires,[1] and hung there, one of two—
Who for his hours of life had chattered through
Infinite lovely chatter of Bucks[2] accent:
Yet faced unbroken wires; stepped over, and went
5   A noble fool, faithful to his stripes—and ended.
But I weak, hungry, and willing only for the chance
Of line—to fight in the line, lay down under unbroken
Wires, and saw the flashes and kept unshaken,
Till the politest voice—a finicking accent, said:
10   "Do you think you might crawl through there: there's a hole."
Darkness, shot at: I smiled, as politely replied—
"I'm afraid not, Sir." There was no hole no way to be seen
Nothing but chance of death, after tearing of clothes.
Kept flat, and watched the darkness, hearing bullets whizzing—
15   And thought of music—and swore deep heart's deep oaths
(Polite to God) and retreated and came on again,
Again retreated—and a second time faced the screen.

1954

1. The barbed wire protecting the front from   2. Buckinghamshire, in southern England.
infantry attack.

ISAAC ROSENBERG
1890–1918

Isaac Rosenberg was born in Bristol to a poor Jewish family that moved to London in 1897. There, at Stepney, he attended elementary schools until the age of fourteen, when he became apprenticed as an engraver in a firm of art publishers and attended evening classes at the Art School of Birkbeck College. His first ambition was to be a painter, and in 1911, when his apprenticeship was over, a group of three Jewish women provided the means for his studying at the Slade School of Art. His interest in writing poetry steadily developed, and with his sister's encouragement he circulated copies of his poems among members of London's literary set and gained a certain reputation, though neither his poetry nor his painting won him any material success. In 1912 he published *Night and Day*, the first of three pamphlets of poetry at his own expense. The other two were *Youth* (1915) and *Moses, A Play* (1916).

In 1915 Rosenberg enlisted in the army, and he was killed in action on April 1,

1918. After his death his reputation steadily grew as an unusually interesting and original poet, who, though he did not live to maturity, nevertheless broke new ground in imagery, rhythms, and the handling of dramatic effects. His poetry strangely amalgamates acerbic irony (the sardonic grin of a rat in "Break of Day in the Trenches") with lush, resonant, even biblical diction and imagery ("shrieking iron and flame / Hurled through still heavens"). The fierce apprehension of the physical reality of war, the exclamatory directness of the language, and the vivid sense of involvement distinguish his poems. Perhaps Rosenberg's working-class background had something to do with this vividness: like Ivor Gurney and David Jones, he served in the ranks.

Break of Day in the Trenches

The darkness crumbles away.
It is the same old druid[1] Time as ever,
Only a live thing leaps my hand,
A queer sardonic rat,
5   As I pull the parapet's[2] poppy
To stick behind my ear.
Droll rat, they would shoot you if they knew
Your cosmopolitan sympathies.
Now you have touched this English hand
10   You will do the same to a German
Soon, no doubt, if it be your pleasure
To cross the sleeping green between.
It seems you inwardly grin as you pass
Strong eyes, fine limbs, haughty athletes,
15   Less chanced than you for life,
Bonds to the whims of murder,
Sprawled in the bowels of the earth,
The torn fields of France.
What do you see in our eyes
20   At the shrieking iron and flame
Hurled through still heavens?
What quaver—what heart aghast?
Poppies whose roots are in man's veins
Drop, and are ever dropping;
25   But mine in my ear is safe—
Just a little white with the dust.

June 1916   1922

Louse Hunting

Nudes—stark and glistening,
Yelling in lurid glee. Grinning faces
And raging limbs
Whirl over the floor one fire.
5   For a shirt verminously busy

---

1. Ancient Celtic priest.   2. Wall protecting a trench.

Yon soldier tore from his throat, with oaths
Godhead might shrink at, but not the lice.
And soon the shirt was aflare
Over the candle he'd lit while we lay.

10   Then we all sprang up and stript
To hunt the verminous brood.
Soon like a demons' pantomime
The place was raging.
See the silhouettes agape,
15   See the gibbering shadows
Mixed with the battled arms on the wall.
See gargantuan hooked fingers
Pluck in supreme flesh
To smutch° supreme littleness.   blacken, besmirch
20   See the merry limbs in hot Highland fling[1]
Because some wizard vermin
Charmed from the quiet this revel
When our ears were half lulled
By the dark music
25   Blown from Sleep's trumpet.

1917   1922

Returning, We Hear the Larks

Sombre the night is.
And though we have our lives, we know
What sinister threat lurks there.

Dragging these anguished limbs, we only know
5   This poison-blasted track opens on our camp—
On a little safe sleep.

But hark! joy—joy—strange joy.
Lo! heights of night ringing with unseen larks.
Music showering on our upturned list'ning faces.

10   Death could drop from the dark
As easily as song—
But song only dropped,
Like a blind man's dreams on the sand
By dangerous tides,
15   Like a girl's dark hair for she dreams no ruin lies there,
Or her kisses where a serpent hides.

1917   1922

1. In wild Scottish dance.

Dead Man's Dump

The plunging limbers[1] over the shattered track
Racketed with their rusty freight,
Stuck out like many crowns of thorns,
And the rusty stakes like sceptres old
5   To stay the flood of brutish men
Upon our brothers dear.

The wheels lurched over sprawled dead
But pained them not, though their bones crunched,
Their shut mouths made no moan.
10   They lie there huddled, friend and foeman,
Man born of man, and born of woman,
And shells go crying over them
From night till night and now.

Earth has waited for them,
15   All the time of their growth
Fretting for their decay:
Now she has them at last!
In the strength of their strength
Suspended—stopped and held.

20   What fierce imaginings their dark souls lit?
Earth! have they gone into you?
Somewhere they must have gone,
And flung on your hard back
Is their soul's sack,
25   Emptied of God-ancestralled essences.
Who hurled them out? Who hurled?

None saw their spirits' shadow shake the grass,
Or stood aside for the half-used life to pass
Out of those doomed nostrils and the doomed mouth,
30   When the swift iron burning bee
Drained the wild honey of their youth.

What of us who, flung on the shrieking pyre,
Walk, our usual thoughts untouched,
Our lucky limbs as on ichor[2] fed,
35   Immortal seeming ever?
Perhaps when the flames beat loud on us,
A fear may choke in our veins
And the startled blood may stop.

---

1. Two-wheeled carts, here carrying barbed wire.
2. In Greek mythology the ethereal fluid that flowed in the veins of the gods.

The air is loud with death,
40 The dark air spurts with fire,
The explosions ceaseless are.
Timelessly now, some minutes past,
These dead strode time with vigorous life,
Till the shrapnel called "An end!"
45 But not to all. In bleeding pangs
Some borne on stretchers dreamed of home,
Dear things, war-blotted from their hearts.

A man's brains splattered on
A stretcher-bearer's face;
50 His shook shoulders slipped their load,
But when they bent to look again
The drowning soul was sunk too deep
For human tenderness.

They left this dead with the older dead,
55 Stretched at the crossroads.

Burnt black by strange decay
Their sinister faces lie;
The lid over each eye,
The grass and coloured clay
60 More motion have than they,
Joined to the great sunk silences.

Here is one not long dead;
His dark hearing caught our far wheels,
And the choked soul stretched weak hands
65 To reach the living word the far wheels said,
The blood-dazed intelligence beating for light,
Crying through the suspense of the far torturing wheels
Swift for the end to break,
Or the wheels to break,
70 Cried as the tide of the world broke over his sight.

Will they come? Will they ever come?
Even as the mixed hoofs of the mules,
The quivering-bellied mules,
And the rushing wheels all mixed
75 With his tortured upturned sight.
So we crashed round the bend,
We heard his weak scream,
We heard his very last sound,
And our wheels grazed his dead face.

1917   1922

WILFRED OWEN
1893–1918

Wilfred Owen was brought up in the backstreets of Birkenhead and Shrewsbury, and on leaving school he took up a post as lay assistant to a country vicar. Removed from the influence of a devout mother, he became increasingly critical of the Church's role in society. His letters and poems of this period show an emerging awareness of the poor's sufferings and the first stirrings of the compassion that was to characterize his later poems about the Western Front. In 1913 he broke with the vicar and went to teach English in France.

For more than a year after the outbreak of war, Owen could not decide whether he ought to enlist. Finally he did, and from January to May 1917 he fought as an officer in the Battle of the Somme. Then, suffering from shell shock, he was sent to a hospital near Edinburgh, where he had the good fortune to meet Siegfried Sassoon, whose first fiercely realistic war poems had just appeared. The influence of Sassoon's satiric realism was a useful tonic to Owen's lush, Keatsian Romanticism. Throughout his months in the hospital, Owen suffered from the horrendous nightmares symptomatic of shell shock. The experience of battle, banished from his waking mind, erupted into his dreams and then into poems haunted with obsessive images of blinded eyes ("Dulce et Decorum Est") and the mouth of hell ("Miners" and "Strange Meeting"). The distinctive music of such later poems owes much of its power to Owen's mastery of alliteration, onomatopoeia, assonance, half-rhyme, and the para-rhyme that he pioneered. This last technique, the rhyming of two words with identical or similar consonants but differing, stressed vowels (such as *groined / groaned, killed / cold, hall / hell*), of which the second is usually the lower in pitch, produces effects of dissonance, failure, and unfulfillment that subtly reinforce his themes.

Echoing Dante, Shakespeare, Shelley, Keats, and the Bible, Owen puts literary and religious language into jarring new relationships with the absurdities of modern war experience. He recuperates but distorts the conventions of pastoral elegy, relocating them to scenes of terror, extreme pain, and irredeemable mass death.

In the year of life left to him after leaving the hospital in November 1917, Owen matured rapidly. Success as a soldier, marked by the award of the Military Cross, and as a poet, which had won him the recognition of his peers, gave him a new confidence. He wrote eloquently of the tragedy of young men killed in battle. In his later elegies a disciplined sensuality and a passionate intelligence find their fullest, most moving, and most memorable expression.

Owen was killed in action a week before the war ended.

Anthem for Doomed Youth

What passing-bells for these who die as cattle?
　—Only the monstrous anger of the guns.
　Only the stuttering rifles' rapid rattle
Can patter out their hasty orisons.°   *prayers*
5 　No mockeries now for them; no prayers nor bells;
　　Nor any voice of mourning save the choirs,—
　The shrill, demented choirs of wailing shells;
　　And bugles calling for them from sad shires.°   *counties*

What candles may be held to speed them all?
10 　Not in the hands of boys but in their eyes

Shall shine the holy glimmers of goodbyes.
     The pallor of girls' brows shall be their pall;
Their flowers the tenderness of patient minds,
And each slow dusk a drawing-down of blinds.

Sept.–Oct. 1917   1920

Apologia Pro Poemate Meo[1]

I, too, saw God through mud,—
     The mud that cracked on cheeks when wretches smiled.
War brought more glory to their eyes than blood,
And gave their laughs more glee than shakes a child.

5   Merry it was to laugh there—
     Where death becomes absurd and life absurder.
For power was on us as we slashed bones bare
Not to feel sickness or remorse of murder.

     I, too, have dropped off Fear—
10   Behind the barrage, dead as my platoon,
And sailed my spirit surging light and clear
Past the entanglement where hopes lay strewn;

And witnessed exultation—[2]
     Faces that used to curse me, scowl for scowl,
15   Shine and lift up with passion of oblation,[3]
     Seraphic° for an hour; though they were foul.   ecstatic

I have made fellowships—
     Untold of happy lovers in old song.
For love is not the binding of fair lips
20   With the soft silk of eyes that look and long,

By Joy, whose ribbon slips,—
     But wound with war's hard wire whose stakes are strong;
Bound with the bandage of the arm that drips;
Knit in the webbing of the rifle-thong.

25   I have perceived much beauty
     In the hoarse oaths that kept our courage straight;
Heard music in the silentness of duty;
Found peace where shell-storms spouted reddest spate.

     Nevertheless, except you share
30   With them in hell the sorrowful dark of hell,

1. This Latin title, meaning "Apology for My Poem," may have been prompted by that of Cardinal Newman's *Apologia Pro Vita Sua*, "Apology for His Life." Here an apology is a written vindication rather than a remorseful account.
2. Cf. Shelley, *A Defence of Poetry*: "Poetry is a mirror which makes beautiful that which is distorted. . . . It exalts the beauty of that which is most beautiful, and it adds beauty to that which is most deformed; it marries exultation and horror."
3. Sacrifice offered to God.

Whose world is but the trembling of a flare
And heaven but as the highway for a shell,

You shall not hear their mirth:
    You shall not come to think them well content
35   By any jest of mine. These men are worth
    Your tears. You are not worth their merriment.

Nov.–Dec. 1917   1920

Miners[1]

There was a whispering in my hearth,
    A sigh of the coal,
Grown wistful of a former earth
    It might recall.

5   I listened for a tale of leaves
    And smothered ferns,
Frond-forests, and the low sly lives
    Before the fauns.

My fire might show steam-phantoms simmer
10   From Time's old cauldron,
Before the birds made nests in summer,
    Or men had children.

But the coals were murmuring of their mine,
    And moans down there
15   Of boys that slept wry sleep, and men
    Writhing for air.

And I saw white bones in the cinder-shard,
    Bones without number.
Many the muscled bodies charred,
20   And few remember.

I thought of all that worked dark pits
    Of war,[2] and died
Digging the rock where Death reputes
    Peace lies indeed.

25   Comforted years will sit soft-chaired,
    In rooms of amber;
The years will stretch their hands, well-cheered
    By our life's ember;

1. Wrote a poem on the Colliery Disaster [of Jan. 12, 1918, at Halmerend]: but I get mixed up with the War at the end. It is short, but oh! sour [Owen's Jan. 14 letter to his mother]. The explosion killed about 150 miners.
2. Miners who dug tunnels under no-man's-land in which to detonate mines beneath the enemy trenches.

The centuries will burn rich loads
30   With which we groaned,
Whose warmth shall lull their dreaming lids,
    While songs are crooned;
But they will not dream of us poor lads,
    Left in the ground.

Jan. 1918   1931

Dulce Et Decorum Est[1]

Bent double, like old beggars under sacks,
Knock-kneed, coughing like hags, we cursed through sludge,
Till on the haunting flares we turned our backs
And towards our distant rest began to trudge.
5   Men marched asleep. Many had lost their boots
But limped on, blood-shod. All went lame; all blind;
Drunk with fatigue; deaf even to the hoots
Of tired, outstripped Five-Nines[2] that dropped behind.

Gas! GAS! Quick, boys!—An ecstasy of fumbling,
10   Fitting the clumsy helmets just in time;
But someone still was yelling out and stumbling,
And flound'ring like a man in fire or lime . . .
Dim, through the misty panes[3] and thick green light,
As under a green sea, I saw him drowning.

15   In all my dreams, before my helpless sight,
He plunges at me, guttering, choking, drowning.

If in some smothering dreams you too could pace
Behind the wagon that we flung him in,
And watch the white eyes writhing in his face,
20   His hanging face, like a devil's sick of sin;
If you could hear, at every jolt, the blood
Come gargling from the froth-corrupted lungs,
Obscene as cancer, bitter as the cud
Of vile, incurable sores on innocent tongues,—
25   My friend,[4] you would not tell with such high zest
To children ardent for some desperate glory,
The old Lie: Dulce et decorum est
Pro patria mori.

Oct. 1917–Mar. 1918   1920

1. The famous Latin tag [from Horace, *Odes* 3.2.13] means, of course, *It is sweet and meet to die for one's country. Sweet!* And *decorous!* [Owen's Oct. 16, 1917, letter to his mother].
2. I.e., 5.9-caliber shells.
3. Of the gas mask's celluloid window.

4. Jessie Pope, to whom the poem was originally to have been dedicated, published jingoistic war poems urging young men to enlist. See her poems in "Representing the Great War" at Norton Literature Online.

Strange Meeting[1]

It seemed that out of battle I escaped
Down some profound dull tunnel,[2] long since scooped
Through granites which titanic wars had groined.°   grooved

    Yet also there encumbered sleepers groaned,
5   Too fast in thought or death to be bestirred.
Then, as I probed them, one sprang up, and stared
With piteous recognition in fixed eyes,
Lifting distressful hands, as if to bless.
And by his smile, I knew that sullen hall,—
10 By his dead smile I knew we stood in Hell.

    With a thousand pains that vision's face was grained;
Yet no blood reached there from the upper ground,
And no guns thumped, or down the flues made moan.
"Strange friend," I said, "here is no cause to mourn."
15 "None," said that other, "save the undone years,
The hopelessness. Whatever hope is yours,
Was my life also; I went hunting wild
After the wildest beauty in the world,
Which lies not calm in eyes, or braided hair,
20 But mocks the steady running of the hour,
And if it grieves, grieves richlier than here.
For by my glee might many men have laughed,
And of my weeping something had been left,
Which must die now. I mean the truth untold,
25 The pity of war, the pity war distilled.[3]
Now men will go content with what we spoiled,
Or, discontent, boil bloody, and be spilled.
They will be swift with swiftness of the tigress.
None will break ranks, through nations trek from progress.
30 Courage was mine, and I had mystery,
Wisdom was mine, and I had mastery:
To miss the march of this retreating world
Into vain citadels that are not walled.
Then, when much blood had clogged their chariot-wheels,
35 I would go up and wash them from sweet wells,
Even with truths that lie too deep for taint.[4]
I would have poured my spirit without stint
But not through wounds; not on the cess[5] of war.
Foreheads of men have bled where no wounds were.

1. Cf. Shelley, *The Revolt of Islam*, lines 1828–32:

  And one whose spear had pierced me, leaned
    beside,
  With quivering lips and humid eyes;—and all
  Seemed like some brothers on a journey wide
    Gone forth, whom now strange meeting did
    befall
  In a strange land.

The speaker of Owen's poem imagines his victim a
poet like himself.

2. Cf. Sassoon's "The Rear-Guard" (p. 1961).
3. My subject is War, and the pity of War. The
Poetry is in the pity [Owen's draft preface to his
poems].
4. Cf. "Thoughts that do often lie too deep for
tears," line 203 of William Wordsworth's "Ode:
Intimations of Immortality" (1807).
5. Luck, as in the phrase *bad cess to you* (may evil
befall you), and muck or excrement, as in the word
cesspool.

40   "I am the enemy you killed, my friend.
I knew you in this dark: for so you frowned
Yesterday through me as you jabbed and killed.
I parried; but my hands were loath and cold.
Let us sleep now. . . ."

May [?] 1918   1920

Futility

Move him into the sun—
Gently its touch awoke him once,
At home, whispering of fields half-sown.
Always it woke him, even in France,
5   Until this morning and this snow.
If anything might rouse him now
The kind old sun will know.

Think how it wakes the seeds—
Woke once the clays of a cold star.
10   Are limbs, so dear achieved, are sides
Full-nerved, still warm, too hard to stir?
Was it for this the clay grew tall?
—O what made fatuous sunbeams toil
To break earth's sleep at all?

May 1918   1920

S.I.W.[1]

I will to the King,
And offer him consolation in his trouble,
For that man there has set his teeth to die,
And being one that hates obedience,
Discipline, and orderliness of life,
I cannot mourn him.

W. B. YEATS[2]

I. The Prologue

Patting goodbye, doubtless they told the lad
He'd always show the Hun[3] a brave man's face;
Father would sooner him dead than in disgrace,—
Was proud to see him going, aye, and glad.
5   Perhaps his mother whimpered how she'd fret
Until he got a nice safe wound to nurse.
Sisters would wish girls too could shoot, charge, curse . . .

---

1. Military abbreviation for self-inflicted wound.
2. Irish poet and playwright (1865–1939). The passage from the play *The King's Threshold* (1906)

describes the poet Seanchan's heroic resolve to die.
3. German soldier; in the fourth century a nomadic people feared for their military prowess.

Brothers—would send his favourite cigarette.
Each week, month after month, they wrote the same,
10   Thinking him sheltered in some Y.M. Hut,[4]
Because he said so, writing on his butt°   *rifle's stock*
Where once an hour a bullet missed its aim.
And misses teased the hunger of his brain.
His eyes grew old with wincing, and his hand
15   Reckless with ague.° Courage leaked, as sand   *fever*
From the best sandbags after years of rain.
But never leave, wound, fever, trench-foot, shock,
Untrapped the wretch. And death seemed still withheld
For torture of lying machinally shelled,
20   At the pleasure of this world's Powers who'd run amok.

He'd seen men shoot their hands, on night patrol.
Their people never knew. Yet they were vile.
'Death sooner than dishonour, that's the style!'
So Father said.

II. The Action

One dawn, our wire patrol
25   Carried him. This time, Death had not missed.
We could do nothing but wipe his bleeding cough.
Could it be accident?—Rifles go off . . .
Not sniped? No. (Later they found the English ball.)

III. The Poem

It was the reasoned crisis of his soul
30   Against more days of inescapable thrall,
Against infrangibly° wired and blind trench wall   *unbreakably*
Curtained with fire, roofed in with creeping fire,
Slow grazing fire, that would not burn him whole
But kept him for death's promises and scoff,
35   And life's half-promising, and both their riling.

IV. The Epilogue

With him they buried the muzzle his teeth had kissed,
And truthfully wrote the mother, 'Tim died smiling.'

Sept. 1917, May 1918   1920

Disabled

He sat in a wheeled chair, waiting for dark,
And shivered in his ghastly suit of grey,
Legless, sewn short at elbow. Through the park

---

4. Hostel of the Young Men's Christian Association.

Voices of boys rang saddening like a hymn,
5   Voices of play and pleasure after day,
Till gathering sleep had mothered them from him.

* * *

About this time Town used to swing so gay
When glow-lamps budded in the light blue trees,
And girls glanced lovelier as the air grew dim,—
10   In the old times, before he threw away his knees.
Now he will never feel again how slim
Girls' waists are, or how warm their subtle hands.
All of them touch him like some queer disease.

* * *

There was an artist silly for his face,
15   For it was younger than his youth, last year.
Now, he is old; his back will never brace;
He's lost his colour very far from here,
Poured it down shell-holes till the veins ran dry,
And half his lifetime lapsed in the hot race
20   And leap of purple spurted from his thigh.

* * *

One time he liked a blood-smear down his leg,
After the matches, carried shoulder-high.[1]
It was after football, when he'd drunk a peg,[2]
He thought he'd better join.—He wonders why.
25   Someone had said he'd look a god in kilts,
That's why; and maybe, too, to please his Meg,
Aye, that was it, to please the giddy jilts[3]
He asked to join. He didn't have to beg;
Smiling they wrote his lie: aged nineteen years.[4]
30   Germans he scarcely thought of; all their guilt,
And Austria's, did not move him. And no fears
Of Fear came yet. He thought of jewelled hilts
For daggers in plaid socks;[5] of smart salutes;
And care of arms; and leave; and pay arrears;
35   Esprit de corps;[6] and hints for young recruits.
And soon, he was drafted out with drums and cheers.

* * *

Some cheered him home, but not as crowds cheer Goal.
Only a solemn man who brought him fruits
Thanked him; and then enquired about his soul.

* * *

40   Now, he will spend a few sick years in institutes,
And do what things the rules consider wise,

---

1. Cf. Housman's "To an Athlete Dying Young" (p. 1949, lines 1–4).
2. Slang for a drink, usually brandy and soda.
3. Capricious women.
4. The recruiting officers entered on his enlistment form his lie that he was nineteen years old and, therefore, above the minimum age for military service.
5. Kilted Scottish Highlanders used to carry a small ornamental dagger in the top of a stocking.
6. Regard for the honor and interests of an organization or, as here, a military unit. "Pay arrears": back pay.

> And take whatever pity they may dole.
> Tonight he noticed how the women's eyes
> Passed from him to the strong men that were whole.
> 45 How cold and late it is! Why don't they come
> And put him into bed? Why don't they come?

Oct. 1917–July 1918   1920

From Owen's Letters to His Mother

16 January 1917

* * *

I can see no excuse for deceiving you about these last 4 days. I have suffered seventh hell.

I have not been at the front.

I have been in front of it.

I held an advanced post, that is, a 'dug-out' in the middle of No Man's Land.

We had a march of 3 miles over shelled road then nearly 3 along a flooded trench. After that we came to where the trenches had been blown flat out and had to go over the top. It was of course dark, too dark, and the ground was not mud, not sloppy mud, but an octopus of sucking clay, 3, 4, and 5 feet deep, relieved only by craters full of water. Men have been known to drown in them. Many stuck in the mud & only got on by leaving their waders, equipment, and in some cases their clothes.

High explosives were dropping all around out, and machine guns spluttered every few minutes. But it was so dark that even the German flares did not reveal us.

Three quarters dead, I mean each of us ¾ dead, we reached the dug-out, and relieved the wretches therein. I then had to go forth and find another dug-out for a still more advanced post where I left 18 bombers. I was responsible for other posts on the left but there was a junior officer in charge.

My dug-out held 25 men tight packed. Water filled it to a depth of 1 or 2 feet, leaving say 4 feet of air.

One entrance had been blown in & blocked.

So far, the other remained.

The Germans knew we were staying there and decided we shouldn't.

Those fifty hours were the agony of my happy life.

Every ten minutes on Sunday afternoon seemed an hour.

I nearly broke down and let myself drown in the water that was now slowly rising over my knees.

Towards 6 o'clock, when, I suppose, you would be going to church, the shelling grew less intense and less accurate: so that I was mercifully helped to do my duty and crawl, wade, climb and flounder over No Man's Land to visit my other post. It took me half an hour to move about 150 yards.

I was chiefly annoyed by our own machine guns from behind. The seeng-seeng-seeng of the bullets reminded me of Mary's canary. On the whole I can support[1] the canary better.

---

1. Tolerate. Mary: Owen's sister.

In the Platoon on my left the sentries over the dug-out were blown to nothing. One of these poor fellows was my first servant whom I rejected. If I had kept him he would have lived, for servants don't do Sentry Duty. I kept my own sentries half way down the stairs during the more terrific bombardment. In spite of this one lad was blown down and, I am afraid, blinded.[2]

31 December 1917

Last year, at this time, (it is just midnight, and now is the intolerable instant of the Change) last year I lay awake in a windy tent in the middle of a vast, dreadful encampment. It seemed neither France nor England, but a kind of paddock where the beasts are kept a few days before the shambles. I heard the revelling of the Scotch troops, who are now dead, and who knew they would be dead. I thought of this present night, and whether I should indeed—whether we should indeed—whether you would indeed—but I thought neither long nor deeply, for I am a master of elision.

But chiefly I thought of the very strange look on all faces in that camp; an incomprehensible look, which a man will never see in England, though wars should be in England; nor can it be seen in any battle. But only in Étaples.[3]

It was not despair, or terror, it was more terrible than terror, for it was a blindfold look, and without expression, like a dead rabbit's.

It will never be painted, and no actor will ever seize it. And to describe it, I think I must go back and be with them.

Preface[1]

This book is not about heroes. English poetry is not yet fit to speak of them.

Nor is it about deeds, or lands, nor anything about glory, honour, might, majesty, dominion, or power, except War.

Above all I am not concerned with Poetry.

My subject is War, and the pity of War.[2]

The Poetry is in the pity.

Yet these elegies are to this generation in no sense consolatory. They may be to the next. All a poet can do today is warn. That is why the true Poets must be truthful.

(If I thought the letter of this book would last, I might have used proper names; but if the spirit of it survives—survives Prussia[3]—my ambition and those names will have achieved fresher fields than Flanders.[4] . . .)

1918   1920

2. This incident prompted Owen's poem "The Sentry."
3. Until 1914, a fishing port of 5,800 inhabitants, Étaples and its surrounding hills housed 100,000 soldiers on their way to and from the front in 1917.
1. In May 1918 Wilfred Owen was posted in Ripon, North Yorkshire, England, and was preparing a book of his war poems. Around this time he drafted this unfinished preface, which was published posthumously, along with most of his poems, in *Poems* (1920), edited by his friend the poet Siegfried Sassoon. The text is reprinted from

The Poems of Wilfred Owen (1985), ed. Jon Stallworthy.
2. Cf. Jude 1.25: "To the only wise God our Saviour, be glory and majesty, dominion and power, both now and ever."
3. Dominant region of the German Empire until the end of World War I.
4. In western Belgium, site of the front line. The Canadian poet John McCrae (1872–1918) memorialized one devastating 1915 battle in his famous poem "In Flanders Fields."

MAY WEDDERBURN CANNAN
1893–1973

Born and educated in Oxford, May Wedderburn Cannan was the daughter of the secretary to the delegates (or chief executive) of the Oxford University Press. At eighteen, she joined the Red Cross Voluntary Aid Detachment, and when England entered the war three years later, she was active in the Red Cross mobilization, setting up a hospital in a local school. During the early part of the war, she worked at Oxford University Press, continued her volunteer nursing, and spent a month as a volunteer worker in a soldiers' canteen in Rouen, France. In 1918 she joined the War Office in Paris to work in intelligence. Her fiancé, Bevil Quiller-Couch, survived the devastating Battle of the Somme and the remainder of the war, only to die of pneumonia several months after the armistice. Canaan later worked at King's College, London, and at the Athenaeum Club as assistant librarian. She wrote three books of poems— In War Time (1917), The Splendid Days (1919), and The House of Hope (1923)— and a novel, The Lonely Generation (1934). Her unfinished autobiography, Grey Ghosts and Voices, was published posthumously in 1976.

"Rouen," with its echoes of G. K. Chesterton's incantatory "Tarantella" (beginning "Do you remember an Inn, / Miranda?"), voices emotions closer to those of Rupert Brooke's "The Soldier" than to any given expression by the other soldier poets in this section. In 1917, however, Cannan and Brooke spoke for what was then the majority. As she wrote in her autobiography: "Siegfried Sassoon wrote to the Press from France saying that the war was now a war of conquest and without justification, and declared himself to be a conscientious objector. . . . A saying went round, 'Went to the war with Rupert Brooke and came home with Siegfried Sassoon.' " Her own poems pose an alternative to protest and despair: "I had much admired some of Sassoon's verse but I was not coming home with him. Someone must go on writing for those who were still convinced of the right of the cause for which they had taken up arms."

Rouen

26 April–25 May 1915

Early morning over Rouen, hopeful, high, courageous morning,
And the laughter of adventure and the steepness of the stair,
And the dawn across the river, and the wind across the bridges,
And the empty littered station and the tired people there.

5 Can you recall those mornings and the hurry of awakening,
And the long-forgotten wonder if we should miss the way,
And the unfamiliar faces, and the coming of provisions,
And the freshness and the glory of the labour of the day?

Hot noontide over Rouen, and the sun upon the city,
10 Sun and dust unceasing, and the glare of cloudless skies,
And the voices of the Indians and the endless stream of soldiers,
And the clicking of the tatties,[1] and the buzzing of the flies.

Can you recall those noontides and the reek of steam and coffee,
Heavy-laden noontides with the evening's peace to win,

---

1. Screens or mats hung in a doorway and kept wet to cool and freshen the air.

15　And the little piles of Woodbines,[2] and the sticky soda bottles,
　　And the crushes[3] in the "Parlour," and the letters coming in?

　　Quiet night-time over Rouen, and the station full of soldiers,
　　All the youth and pride of England from the ends of all the earth;
　　And the rifles piled together, and the creaking of the sword-belts,
20　And the faces bent above them, and the gay, heart-breaking mirth.

　　Can I forget the passage from the cool white-bedded Aid Post
　　Past the long sun-blistered coaches of the khaki Red Cross train
　　To the truck train full of wounded, and the weariness and laughter,
　　And "Good-bye, and thank-you, Sister,"[4] and the empty yards again?

25　Can you recall the parcels that we made them for the railroad,
　　Crammed and bulging parcels held together by their string,
　　And the voices of the sergeants who called the Drafts[5] together,
　　And the agony and splendour when they stood to save the King?[6]

　　Can you forget their passing, the cheering and the waving,
30　The little group of people at the doorway of the shed,
　　The sudden awful silence when the last train swung to darkness,
　　And the lonely desolation, and the mocking stars o'erhead?

　　Can you recall the midnights, and the footsteps of night watchers,
　　Men who came from darkness and went back to dark again,
35　And the shadows on the rail-lines and the all-inglorious labour,
　　And the promise of the daylight firing blue the window-pane?

　　Can you recall the passing through the kitchen door to morning,
　　Morning very still and solemn breaking slowly on the town,
　　And the early coastways engines that had met the ships at daybreak,
40　And the Drafts just out from England, and the day shift coming down?

　　Can you forget returning slowly, stumbling on the cobbles,
　　And the white-decked Red Cross barges dropping seawards for the tide,
　　And the search for English papers, and the blessed cool of water,
　　And the peace of half-closed shutters that shut out the world outside?

45　Can I forget the evenings and the sunsets on the island,
　　And the tall black ships at anchor far below our balcony,
　　And the distant call of bugles, and the white wine in the glasses,
　　And the long line of the street lamps, stretching Eastwards to the sea?

　　. . . When the world slips slow to darkness, when the office fire burns lower,
50　My heart goes out to Rouen, Rouen all the world away;
　　When other men remember I remember our Adventure
　　And the trains that go from Rouen at the ending of the day.

　　　　　　　　　　　　　　　　　　　　　　　　　　　　　　　1916

---

2. Popular brand of cheap cigarette.　　　　　5. Groups of soldiers.
3. Crowded social gatherings.　　　　　　　　6. I.e., to sing the British National Anthem, "God
4. Nurse.　　　　　　　　　　　　　　　　　Save the King."

From Grey Ghosts and Voices

I suppose it is difficult for anyone to realise now what "France" meant to us. In the second war I met a young man of the Left who assured me that Rupert Brooke's verse was of no account, phoney, because it was "impossible that anyone should have thought like that." I turned and rent him, saying that he was entitled to his own opinion of Rupert Brooke's verse, but *not* entitled to say that no one could have thought like that. How could he know how we had thought?—All our hopes and all our loves, and God knew, all our fears, were in France; to get to France, if only to stand on her soil, was something; to share, in however small a way, in what was done there was Heart's Desire.

I asked my Father[1] could I take all my holidays in one and go for four weeks to France—I did not want holidays, I said, but I did want France. It was dark and we were walking home through the confines of Little Clarendon Street; my voice, I knew, shook; he took his pipe out of his mouth, halted his step for a moment and looked down at me. "Ah! France," he said, "France, yes I think you should go. We'll manage." I stammered thanks and we walked home in silence, understanding each other.

The Canteen was started at Rouen because Lord Brassey's yacht, *The Sunbeam*, had made two or three journeys there during the shortage of hospital ships bringing wounded home. Lady Mabelle Egerton, his daughter, looking round the desolate railway yards beyond the quays asked the R[ail]. T[ransport]. O[fficer]. if there was anything that could be done for the troops; drafts going up the line to Railhead, who had to spend a long day there, and sometimes a long night.

He said that the men brought their rations, including tea, but that there was no means of making hot water. (It was long before the days of another war when motorised infantry "brewed up" with their petrol cans)—Could she find some philanthropic person to take on the job? She could find no one—and decided to do it herself, and so the canteen, later known affectionately to thousands of the B[ritish]. E[xpeditionary]. F[orce]. and the New Armies, as "the Coffee Shop" was born.

I had a passport. I packed. Left as little urgent work behind me as I could, and met Lucie, who I adored, in London. We travelled to Southampton and Hilary, who after sick leave had been posted to a home battalion of his regiment in Hampshire, came to dinner and we sat far into the night talking. He had been in France; I was going, and generously he treated me as if I was one of the fraternity. . . .

I had done nothing about a berth, and there was none to be had so I spent the night curled up, blissfully happy, on a coil of rope in the bow where no one noticed me, and woke in the early morning as we came into Le Havre. There were English soldiers in the streets, and in the cold spring sunshine a battery clattered by. We went up by train to Rouen. Someone had got us a couple of rooms in a small hotel with a restaurant below that overlooked the quays; those same broad quays where Bevil had disembarked. I fell into bed too happy to worry or to dream and went on duty after breakfast next morning.

Along the length of railway line ran a row of sheds with huge sliding doors.

---

1. Chief executive of the Oxford University Press, for which his daughter then worked.

In the first, and smaller one, was established a boiler room where enormous vats of hot water forever boiled. * * *

When the big trains were due in we opened the sliding doors of the sheds, the train doors banged and banged down the long line of the corridors and some 2,000 men would surge in. Barricaded behind our heavy table, and thankful for it when the pressure was heavy or a draft[2] had somehow got hold of some drink, we handed out bowls of coffee and sandwiches, washed dirty bowls till the water in the tall vats was chocolate brown, and served again.

Someone would play the piano; Annie Laurie; Loch Lomond.[3] Blurred lanterns lit the scene as best they might when it rained and our candles in the tills under the tables guttered in the wind. One was hot or horrid cold, harried, dirty, and one's feet ached with the stone floors. When the smaller drafts came one could distinguish faces, and regimental badges; have a word or two. * * *

When the whistle blew they stood to save the King[4] and the roof came off the sheds. Two thousand men, maybe, singing—it was the most moving thing I knew. Then there'd be the thunder of seats pushed back, the stamp of army boots on the pavé, and as the train went out they sang Tipperary.[5]

1976

2. Group of soldiers.
3. Two Scottish songs.
4. I.e., to sing the British National Anthem, "God

Save the King."
5. The Irish song "It's a Long Way to Tipperary."

ROBERT GRAVES
1895–1985

Robert von Ranke Graves was born in London of partly Anglo-Irish and partly German descent—his great-uncle was the distinguished German historian Leopold von Ranke. He left Charterhouse School to go immediately into the army, serving in World War I until he was invalided out in 1917. After the war he went to Oxford, took a B.Litt. degree, and in 1929 published *Goodbye to All That,* a vivid account of his experiences in the war, including his almost dying from severe chest wounds. His autobiography, as he put it, "paid my debts and enabled me to set up in Majorca as a writer." He lived on that Spanish island with the American poet Laura Riding—his muse and mentor—until in 1936 the outbreak of the Spanish Civil War forced them to leave. Their relationship soon ended, and after World War II he returned to Majorca, where he remained for the rest of his life.

Graves began as a Georgian poet, but he was a Georgian with a difference. The mingling of the colloquial and the visionary in his vocabulary, the accent of conversation underlying the regular rhythms of his stanzas, the tension between a Romantic indulgence in emotion and a cool appraisal of its significance—these are qualities found even in his early poetry. His best work combines the ironic and the imaginative in a highly individual manner, and he is also capable of a down-to-earth poetry, often mocking in tone and dealing with simple domestic facts or even the more annoying of personal relationships. He admired Thomas Hardy but chided Yeats, Pound, and Eliot for their obscurity and slovenliness, preferring that poetry be lucid, orderly, and civil.

Graves made his living by his prose, which is extensive and varied and includes, in addition to *Goodbye to All That*, a number of historical novels in which characters and events from the classical or biblical past are reconstructed in a modern idiom: the most notable of his historical novels are *I, Claudius* (1934), *Claudius the God* (1934), and *King Jesus* (1946). In *The White Goddess* (1948), a study of mythology drawn from a great variety of sources and devoted to what he considered the great female inspirational principle, Graves argued that only a return to goddess worship and an abandonment of patriarchal for matriarchal society could help modern poetry recover its lost force, clarity, and mythic wisdom.

From Goodbye to All That

[THE ATTACK ON HIGH WOOD]

Next evening, July 19th, we were relieved and told that we would be attacking High Wood,[1] which could be seen a thousand yards away to the right at the top of a slope. High Wood, which the French called 'Raven Wood', formed part of the main German battle-line that ran along the ridge, with Delville Wood not far off on the German left. Two British brigades had already attempted it; in both cases a counter-attack drove them out again. The Royal Welch[2] were now reduced by casualties to about four hundred strong, including transport, stretcher-bearers, cooks and other non-combatants. I took command of 'B' Company.

The German batteries were handing out heavy stuff, six- and eight-inch, and so much of it that we decided to move back fifty yards at a rush. As we did so, an eight-inch shell burst three paces behind me. I heard the explosion, and felt as though I had been punched rather hard between the shoulder-blades, but without any pain. I took the punch merely for the shock of the explosion; but blood trickled into my eye and, turning faint, I called to Moodie: 'I've been hit.' Then I fell. A minute or two before I had got two very small wounds on my left hand; and in exactly the same position as the two that drew blood from my right hand during the preliminary bombardment at Loos.[3] This I took as a lucky sign, and for further security repeated to myself a line of Nietzsche's, in French translation:

Non, tu ne me peus pas tuer![4]

One piece of shell went through my left thigh, high up, near the groin; I must have been at the full stretch of my stride to escape emasculation. The wound over the eye was made by a little chip of marble, possibly from one of the Bazentin[5] cemetery headstones. [Later, I had it cut out, but a smaller piece has since risen to the surface under my right eyebrow, where I keep it for a souvenir.] This, and a finger-wound which split the bone, probably came from another shell bursting in front of me. But a piece of shell had also gone in two inches below the point of my right shoulder-blade and came out through my chest two inches above the right nipple.

---

1. The battle for High Wood, one of the bloodiest fights of the Somme Offensive, began on July 14, 1916, and was won by the British on September 15, 1916.
2. Royal Welch Fusiliers.

3. The Battle of Loos, September 1915.
4. No, you cannot kill me. Friedrich Nietzsche (1844–1900), German philosopher.
5. The Battle of Bazentin Ridge, July 14–17, 1916, part of the Somme Offensive.

My memory of what happened then is vague. Apparently Dr Dunn came up through the barrage with a stretcher-party, dressed my wound, and got me down to the old German dressing-station at the north end of Mametz Wood.[6] I remember being put on the stretcher, and winking at the stretcher-bearer sergeant who had just said: 'Old Gravy's got it, all right!' They laid my stretcher in a corner of the dressing-station, where I remained unconscious for more than twenty-four hours.

Late that night, Colonel Crawshay came back from High Wood and visited the dressing-station; he saw me lying in the corner, and they told him I was done for. The next morning, July 21st, clearing away the dead, they found me still breathing and put me on an ambulance for Heilly, the nearest field hospital. The pain of being jolted down the Happy Valley, with a shell hole at every three or four yards of the road, woke me up. I remember screaming. But back on the better roads I became unconscious again. That morning, Crawshay wrote the usual formal letters of condolence to the next-of-kin of the six or seven officers who had been killed. This was his letter to my mother:

22.7.16

Dear Mrs Graves,

I very much regret to have to write and tell you your son has died of wounds. He was very gallant, and was doing so well and is a great loss.

He was hit by a shell and very badly wounded, and died on the way down to the base I believe. He was not in bad pain, and our doctor managed to get across and attend to him at once.

We have had a very hard time, and our casualties have been large. Believe me you have all our sympathy in your loss, and we have lost a very gallant soldier.

Please write to me if I can tell you or do anything.

Yours sincerely,
C. Crawshay, Lt.-Col.

Then he made out the official casualty list—a long one, because only eighty men were left in the battalion—and reported me 'died of wounds'. Heilly lay on the railway; close to the station stood the hospital tents with the red cross prominently painted on the roofs, to discourage air-bombing. Fine July weather made the tents insufferably hot. I was semi-conscious now, and aware of my lung-wound through a shortness of breath. It amused me to watch the little bubbles of blood, like scarlet soap-bubbles, which my breath made in escaping through the opening of the wound. The doctor came over to my bed. I felt sorry for him; he looked as though he had not slept for days.

I asked him: 'Can I have a drink?'

'Would you like some tea?'

I whispered: 'Not with condensed milk.'

He said, most apologetically: 'I'm afraid there's no fresh milk.'

Tears of disappointment pricked my eyes; I expected better of a hospital behind the lines.

'Will you have some water?'

---

6. Recently captured by the British.

'Not if it's boiled.'

'It is boiled. And I'm afraid I can't give you anything alcoholic in your present condition.'

'Some fruit then?'

'I have seen no fruit for days.'

Yet a few minutes later he returned with two rather unripe greengages.[7] In whispers I promised him a whole orchard when I recovered.

The nights of the 22nd and 23rd were horrible. Early on the morning of the 24th, when the doctor came round the ward, I said: 'You must send me away from here. This heat will kill me.' It was beating on my head through the canvas.

'Stick it out. Your best chance is to lie here and not to be moved. You'd not reach the Base alive.'

'Let me risk the move. I'll be all right, you'll see.'

Half an hour later he returned. 'Well, you're having it your way. I've just got orders to evacuate every case in the hospital. Apparently the Guards have been in it up at Delville Wood, and they'll all be coming down tonight.' I did not fear that I would die, now—it was enough to be honourably wounded and bound for home.

A brigade-major, wounded in the leg, who lay in the next bed, gave me news of the battalion. He looked at my label and said: 'I see you're in the Second Royal Welch. I watched your High Wood show through field-glasses. The way your battalion shook out into artillery formation, company by company—with each section of four or five men in file at fifty yards interval and distance—going down into the hollow and up the slope through the barrage, was the most beautiful bit of parade-ground drill I've ever seen. Your company officers must have been superb.' Yet one company at least had started without a single officer. When I asked whether they had held the wood, he told me: 'They hung on to the near end. I believe what happened was that the Public Schools Battalion came away at dark; and so did most of the Scotsmen. Your chaps were left there more or less alone for some time. They steadied themselves by singing. Afterwards the chaplain—R. C.[8] of course—Father McCabe, brought the Scotsmen back. Being Glasgow Catholics, they would follow a priest where they wouldn't follow an officer. The centre of the wood was impossible for either the Germans or your fellows to hold—a terrific concentration of artillery on it. The trees were splintered to matchwood. Late that night a brigade of the Seventh Division relieved the survivors; it included your First Battalion.'

1929, 1957

The Dead Fox Hunter

(In memory of Captain A. L. Samson, 2nd Battalion Royal Welch Fusiliers, killed near Cuinchy,[1] Sept. 25th, 1915)

> We found the little captain at the head;
> His men lay well-aligned.
> We touched his hand—stone cold—and he was dead,

7. Type of plum.
8. Roman Catholic.

1. Village in northern France.

And they, all dead behind,
5 Had never reached their goal, but they died well;
They charged in line, and in the same line fell.

The well-known rosy colours of his face
    Were almost lost in grey.
We saw that, dying and in hopeless case,
10   For others' sake that day
He'd smothered all rebellious groans: in death
His fingers were tight clenched between his teeth.

For those who live uprightly and die true
    Heaven has no bars or locks,
15 And serves all taste . . . or what's for him to do
    Up there, but hunt the fox?
Angelic choirs? No, Justice must provide
For one who rode straight and in hunting died.

So if Heaven had no Hunt before he came,
20   Why, it must find one now:
If any shirk and doubt they know the game,
    There's one to teach them how:
And the whole host of Seraphim° complete   *angels*
Must jog in scarlet to his opening Meet.

1916

Recalling War

Entrance and exit wounds are silvered clean,
The track aches only when the rain reminds.
The one-legged man forgets his leg of wood,
The one-armed man his jointed wooden arm.
5 The blinded man sees with his ears and hands
As much or more than once with both his eyes.
Their war was fought these twenty years ago
And now assumes the nature-look of time,
As when the morning traveller turns and views
10 His wild night-stumbling carved into a hill.

What, then, was war? No mere discord of flags
But an infection of the common sky
That sagged ominously upon the earth
Even when the season was the airiest May.
15 Down pressed the sky, and we, oppressed, thrust out
Boastful tongue, clenched fist and valiant yard.
Natural infirmities were out of mode,
For Death was young again: patron alone
Of healthy dying, premature fate-spasm.

20 Fear made fine bed-fellows. Sick with delight
  At life's discovered transitoriness,
  Our youth became all-flesh and waived the mind.
  Never was such antiqueness of romance,
  Such tasty honey oozing from the heart.
25 And old importances came swimming back—
  Wine, meat, log-fires, a roof over the head,
  A weapon at the thigh, surgeons at call.
  Even there was a use again for God—
  A word of rage in lack of meat, wine, fire,
30 In ache of wounds beyond all surgeoning.

  War was return of earth to ugly earth,
  War was foundering° of sublimities,   *collapsing*
  Extinction of each happy art and faith
  By which the world had still kept head in air,
35 Protesting logic or protesting love,
  Until the unendurable moment struck—
  The inward scream, the duty to run mad.

  And we recall the merry ways of guns—
  Nibbling the walls of factory and church
40 Like a child, piecrust; felling groves of trees
  Like a child, dandelions with a switch.
  Machine-guns rattle toy-like from a hill,
  Down in a row the brave tin-soldiers fall:
  A sight to be recalled in elder days
45 When learnedly the future we devote
  To yet more boastful visions of despair.

1935   1938

DAVID JONES
1895–1974

David Jones was born in Brockley, Kent, son of a Welsh father and an English mother, and studied at the Camberwell School of Art before joining the army in January 1915 to serve as a private soldier until the end of World War I—service that provided the material for his modern epic of war, *In Parenthesis*. He attended Westminster Art School after the war and subsequently made a name for himself as an illustrator, engraver, and watercolorist. In 1921 he joined the Roman Catholic Church and a few months later began working with the Catholic stone carver and engraver Eric Gill. Jones's Welsh and English origins, his visual sensitivity as an artist, and his interest in Catholic liturgy and ritual can be seen in his literary work, which includes the obscure but powerful long religious poem *The Anathémata* (1952) and *The Sleeping Lord and Other Fragments* (1973).

 In Parenthesis, Jones's first literary work, was published in 1937 and won the Hawthornden Prize. Its seven parts, combining prose and poetry, evoke the activities of a

British infantry unit from its training in England to its participation in the Somme Offensive of July 1916. The work proceeds chronologically, beginning with a battalion parade in England before embarkation for France, moving to the preparation for the offensive, and concluding when the protagonist Private John Ball's platoon is destroyed. Far from a straightforward narrative, since every contemporary detail is associated with the heroic past, the poem echoes in carefully patterned moments Shakespeare's history plays, Malory's accounts of Arthurian quests, Welsh epics of heroic and futile battles, the Bible, and Catholic liturgy. Even so, *In Parenthesis* avoids the traditional epic concentration on high-ranking heroes and builds its narrative around ordinary characters, both English and Welsh. Identified with historical or mythological figures, they—Mr. Jenkins, Sergeant Snell, Corporal Quilter, Lance-Corporal Lewis, and John Ball, who is wounded in the leg, as Jones was at the First Battle of the Somme—are presented in vivid silhouettes and sudden stabs of personal memory.

Begun a decade after the armistice, *In Parenthesis* could not have been written when Wilfred Owen and Siegfried Sassoon wrote their war poems. Jones profits from the ways in which James Joyce's *Ulysses* and T. S. Eliot's *Waste Land* drew on mythology and ritual and thus gained depth and scope. He has combined the pity for and irony of the soldier that we see in Owen with the distanced, more elaborately illustrated, less immediately personal style of Eliot's long poem. And like Eliot, he introduces notes to help the reader follow the mythological and literary references. Unique among the soldier poets, Jones combines the immediacy of war poetry with high modernism's strategies of formal discontinuity and rich allusiveness. The poem conveys the texture of war experience through comic or sardonic references to popular soldiers' songs, to follies and vices and vanities and every kind of trivial behavior. At the same time the poem is multilayered and densely textured, its complex allusions to history, ritual, and heroic myth infusing the characters and the war with mysterious meaning.

The extracts printed here are, first, from Jones's preface, in which he explains his intention and method, and, second, from part 7, describing events during and after the attack. At the beginning of the last section quoted, Ball is wounded and crawling toward the rear through the mingled bodies of British and German soldiers. In his fevered imagination he sees the Queen of the Woods distributing flowers to the dead. He wonders whether he can continue carrying his rifle, which he finally leaves under an oak tree. (At the end of the medieval French epic *Chanson de Roland* [*Song of Roland*], the dying Roland tries in vain to shatter his sword, Durendal, to prevent its being taken as a trophy by the Saracens; he finally puts it under his body.) In the end Ball lies still under the oak beside a dead German and a dead Englishman, hearing the reserves coming forward to continue the battle.

FROM IN PARENTHESIS

From Preface

This writing has to do with some things I saw, felt, & was part of. The period covered begins early in December 1915 and ends early in July 1916. The first date corresponds to my going to France. The latter roughly marks a change in the character of our lives in the Infantry on the West Front. From then onward things hardened into a more relentless, mechanical affair, took on a more sinister aspect. The wholesale slaughter of the later years, the conscripted levies filling the gaps in every file of four, knocked the bottom out of the intimate, continuing, domestic life of small contingents of men, within whose structure Roland could find, and, for a reasonable while, enjoy, his Oliver.[1] In the earlier months there was a certain attractive amateurishness, and elbow-room for idiosyncrasy that connected one with a less exacting past. The period of the individual rifle-man, of the "old sweat" of the Boer campaign, the "Bairns-father"[2] war, seemed to terminate with the Somme battle. There were, of course, glimpses of it long after—all through in fact—but it seemed never quite the same. * * *

My companions in the war were mostly Londoners with an admixture of Welshmen, so that the mind and folk-life of those two differing racial groups are an essential ingredient to my theme. Nothing could be more representative. These came from London. Those from Wales. Together they bore in their bodies the genuine tradition of the Island of Britain, from Bendigeid Vran to Jingle and Marie Lloyd. These were the children of Doll Tearsheet. Those are before Caractacus[3] was. Both speak in parables, the wit of both is quick, both are natural poets; yet no two groups could well be more dissimilar. It was curious to know them harnessed together, and together caught in the toils of "good order and military discipline"; to see them shape together to the remains of an antique regimental tradition, to see them react to the few things that united us—the same jargon, the same prejudice against "other arms" and against the Staff, the same discomforts, the same grievances, the same maims, the same deep fears, the same pathetic jokes; to watch them, oneself part of them, respond to the war landscape; for I think the day by day in the Waste Land, the sudden violences and the long stillnesses, the sharp contours and unformed voids of that mysterious existence, profoundly affected the imaginations of those who suffered it. It was a place of enchantment. It is perhaps best described in Malory,[4] book iv, chapter 15—that landscape spoke "with a grimly voice."

I suppose at no time did one so much live with a consciousness of the past, the very remote, and the more immediate and trivial past, both superficially and more subtly. No one, I suppose, however much not given to association, could see infantry in tin-hats, with ground-sheets over their shoulders, with sharpened pine-stakes in their hands, and not recall

> . . . or may we cram,
> Within this wooden O . . .[5]

But there were deeper complexities of sight and sound to make ever present

the pibble pabble in Pompey's camp.[6]

Every man's speech and habit of mind were a perpetual showing: now of Napier's expedition, now of the Legions at the Wall, now of "train-band captain," now of Jack Cade, of John Ball, of the commons in arms. Now of *High*

---

1. Roland's close friend and companion-at-arms in the medieval French epic *Chanson de Roland* (*Song of Roland*).
2. Bruce Bairnsfather (1888–1959), English cartoonist and journalist, best-known for his sketches of life in the trenches during World War I.
3. Caractacus or Caradoc, king of the Silures in the west of Britain during the reign of Roman emperor Claudius. He was taken to Rome as a prisoner in 51 C.E., but was pardoned by Claudius,

who was impressed by his nobility of spirit. Bendigeid Vran, hero in Welsh heroic legend. Alfred Jingle, character in Dickens's *Pickwick Papers*. Marie Lloyd (real name Matilda Alice Victoria Wood), English music-hall comedienne. Doll Tearsheet, prostitute in Shakespeare's *2 Henry IV*.
4. Sir Thomas Malory, author of *Morte Darthur*.
5. Shakespeare's *Henry V*, prologue, lines 12–13. The "wooden O" is the stage of the theater.
6. Cf. *Henry V* 4.1.71.

Germany, of *Dolly Gray,* of Bullcalf, Wart and Poins; of Jingo largenesses, of things as small as the Kingdom of Elmet; of Wellington's raw shire recruits, of ancient border antipathies, of our contemporary, less intimate, larger unities, of *John Barleycorn,* of "sweet Sally Frampton." Now of Coel Hên—of the Celtic cycle that lies, a subterranean influence as a deep water troubling, under every tump[7] in this Island, like Merlin[8] complaining under his big rock.[9] * * *

* * *

This writing is called *In Parenthesis* because I have written it in a kind of space between—I don't know between quite what—but as you turn aside to do something; and because for us amateur soldiers (and especially for the writer, who was not only amateur, but grotesquely incompetent, a knocker-over of piles, a parade's despair) the war itself was a parenthesis—how glad we thought we were to step outside its brackets at the end of '18—and also because our curious type of existence here is altogether in parenthesis.

D. J.

From Part 7: The Five Unmistakeable Marks[1]

Gododdin I demand thy support.
It is our duty to sing: a meeting
place has been found.[2]

* * *

The gentle slopes are green to remind you
of South English places, only far wider and flatter spread and grooved and
harrowed criss-cross whitely and the disturbed subsoil heaped up albescent.[3]

Across upon this undulated board of verdure[4] chequered bright
when you look to left and right
small, drab, bundled pawns severally make effort
moved in tenuous line
and if you looked behind—the next wave came slowly, as successive surfs creep
in to dissipate on flat shore;
and to your front, stretched long laterally,

7. Mound or tumulus.
8. The powerful enchanter of the Arthurian legends.
9. The mass of references here provide a wide area of historical and literary association, beginning with *Henry V* and going on to refer to Sir William Napier, who fought in the Peninsular War and later wrote a famous history of that campaign; to the Roman legions who manned the Great Wall built by the Romans in Britain; to Jack Cade, who led an unsuccessful popular revolt against the misrule of Henry VI in 1450, and John Ball, a leader of the Peasants' Revolt of 1381; to a number of English ballads and popular songs and to characters in *Henry IV*; to the ancient British kingdom of Elmet in southwest Yorkshire, finally overthrown by Anglo-Saxon invaders early in the 7th century; to Wellington's "raw shire recruits," who helped win the Battle of Waterloo; and concluding with a reference to the old Celtic British myths that lie

beneath everything.
1. Carroll's *Hunting of the Snark,* Fit the 2nd verse 15 [Jones's note]. Lewis Carroll's mock-heroic nonsense poem concerns the hunting of the elusive animal Snark, which may be known by "five unmistakable marks." A reference to the five wounds of the crucified Christ may also be intended.
2. From *Y Gododdin,* early Welsh epical poem attributed to Aneirin (6th century); commemorates raid of 300 Welsh of Gododdin (the territory of the Otadini located near the Firth of Forth) into English kingdom of Deira. Describes the ruin of this 300 in battle at Catraeth (perhaps Catterick in Yorkshire). Three men alone escaped death, including the poet, who laments his friends [Jones's note].
3. Becoming white.
4. Green vegetation.

and receded deeply,
the dark wood.

And now the gradient runs more flatly toward the separate scarred saplings,
where they make fringe for the interior thicket and you take notice.
    There between the thinning uprights
at the margin
straggle tangled oak and flayed sheeny beech-bole, and fragile birch
   whose silver queenery is draggled and ungraced
and June shoots lopt
and fresh stalks bled
            runs the Jerry[5] trench.
And cork-screw stapled trip-wire
to snare among the briars
and iron warp with bramble weft[6]
with meadow-sweet and lady-smock
for a fair camouflage.

Mr Jenkins half inclined his head to them—he walked just barely in advance
of his platoon and immediately to the left of Private Ball.
    He makes the conventional sign
and there is the deeply inward effort of spent men who would make response
for him,
and take it at the double.
He sinks on one knee
and now on the other,
his upper body tilts in rigid inclination
this way and back;
weighted lanyard[7] runs out to full tether,
          swings like a pendulum
          and the clock run down.
Lurched over, jerked iron saucer over tilted brow,
clampt unkindly over lip and chin
nor no ventaille[8] to this darkening
    and masked face lifts to grope the air
and so disconsolate;
enfeebled fingering at a paltry strap—
buckle holds,
holds him blind against the morning.
    Then stretch still where weeds pattern the chalk predella[9]—
where it rises to his wire[1]—and Sergeant T. Quilter takes over.

                     *   *   *

It's difficult with the weight of the rifle.
Leave it—under the oak.
Leave it for a salvage-bloke[2]
let it lie bruised for a monument

---

5. British army slang for "German" in both world
wars.
6. Warp and weft are the horizontal and vertical
threads of woven cloth.
7. Short cord (here "weighted" by a whistle).

8. Hinged visor of a helmet.
9. A platform or shelf below or behind an altar.
1. The approach to the German trenches here
rose slightly, in low chalk ridges [Jones's note].
2. Man (slang).

dispense the authenticated fragments to the faithful.
It's the thunder-besom for us
it's the bright bough borne
it's the tensioned yew for a Genoese jammed arbalest[3] and a scarlet square for
a mounted *mareschal*,[4] it's that county-mob back to back.[5] Majuba mountain
and Mons Cherubim[6] and spreaded mats for Sydney Street East,[7] and come
to Bisley for a Silver Dish.[8] It's R.S.M. O'Grady[9] says, it's the soldier's best
friend if you care for the working parts and let us be 'aving those springs
released smartly in Company billets on wet forenoons and clickerty-click and
one up the spout and you men must really cultivate the habit of treating this
weapon with the very greatest care and there should be a healthy rivalry among
you—it should be a matter of very proper pride and
    Marry it man! Marry it!
Cherish her, she's your very own.
    Coax it man coax it—it's delicately and ingeniously made—it's an instru-
ment of precision—it costs us tax-payers, money—I want you men to remember that.
    Fondle it like a granny—talk to it—consider it as you would a friend—
and when you ground these arms she's not a rooky's gas-pipe for greenhorns
to tarnish.[1]
You've known her hot and cold.
You would choose her from among many.
You know her by her bias, and by her exact error at 300, and by the deep scar
at the small, by the fair flaw in the grain, above the lower sling-swivel—
but leave it under the oak.

                    *   *   *

The secret princes between the leaning trees have diadems given them.
    Life the leveller hugs her impudent equality—she may proceed at once
to less discriminating zones.

The Queen of the Woods has cut bright boughs of various flowering.
    These knew her influential eyes. Her awarding hands can pluck for each
their fragile prize.
    She speaks to them according to precedence. She knows what's due to
this elect society. She can choose twelve gentle-men. She knows who is most
lord between the high trees and on the open down.
    Some she gives white berries
        some she gives brown

3. A powerful medieval crossbow.
4. Marshal (French).
5. The Gloucestershire Regiment, during an
action near Alexandria, in 1801, about-turned
their rear rank and engaged the enemy back to
back [Jones's note].
6. The British were defeated by the Boers on
Majuba Hill on February 27, 1881. The "Angels of
Mons" were angels (varying in number from two to
a platoon) widely believed to have helped the British repel an attack at Mons by superior German
forces on August 23, 1914.
7. In what became known as the Siege or Battle
of Sydney Street, Winston Churchill, when he was
home secretary in 1911, directed military operations in London against a group of anarchists. "It

is said that in 'The Battle of Sydney Street' under
Mr. Churchill's Home Secretaryship mats were
spread on the pavement for troops firing from the
prone position" [Jones's note].
8. At Bisley marksmen compete annually in rifle
shooting for trophies such as "a Silver Dish."
9. "R.S.M.": regimental sergeant major. "R.S.M.
O'Grady," according to Jones's note, "refers to
mythological personage figuring in Army exercises,
the precise describing of which would be tedious.
Anyway these exercises were supposed to foster
alertness in dull minds—and were a curious blend
of the parlour game and military drill."
1. I have employed here only such ideas as were
common to the form of speech affected by Instructors in Musketry [Jones's note].

Emil has a curious crown it's
    made of golden saxifrage.
Fatty wears sweet-briar,
he will reign with her for a thousand years.
For Balder she reaches high to fetch his.
Ulrich smiles for his myrtle wand.
That swine Lillywhite has daisies to his chain—you'd hardly credit it.
    She plaits torques[2] of equal splendour for Mr Jenkins and Billy Crower.
    Hansel with Gronwy share dog-violets for a palm, where they lie in serious embrace beneath the twisted tripod.
    Siôn gets St John's Wort—that's fair enough.
    Dai Great-coat,[3] she can't find him anywhere—she calls both high and low, she had a very special one for him.
    Among this July noblesse she is mindful of December wood—when the trees of the forest beat against each other because of him.
    She carries to Aneirin-in-the-nullah[4] a rowan[5] sprig, or the glory of Guenedota.[6] You couldn't hear what she said to him, because she was careful for the Disciplines of the Wars.

At the gate of the wood you try a last adjustment, but slung so, it's an impediment, it's of detriment to your hopes, you had best be rid of it—the sagging webbing and all and what's left of your two fifty[7]—but it were wise to hold on to your mask.

You're clumsy in your feebleness, you implicate your tin-hat rim with the slack sling of it.
    Let it lie for the dews to rust it, or ought you to decently cover the working parts.
    Its dark barrel, where you leave it under the oak, reflects the solemn star that rises urgently from Cliff Trench.
    It's a beautiful doll for us
it's the Last Reputable Arm.
    But leave it—under the oak.
leave it for a Cook's tourist to the Devastated Areas and crawl as far
    as you can and wait for the bearers.[8]

1937

2. Collars, like those of gold worn by warriors of *Y Gododdin.*
3. Character whose first name is the familiar Welsh form of David, alluding to a figure in Malory's *Morte Darthur.*
4. A river, stream, or riverbed.
5. Also called mountain ash, a tree with magical properties in Celtic folklore.
6. The northwest parts of Wales. The last king of Wales, Llywelyn, was killed there in 1282. Jones refers to his death in another note on this part of Wales. He adds: "His [Llywelyn's] contemporary, Gruffydd ap yr Ynad Côch, sang of his death: 'The voice of lamentation is heard in every place . . . the

course of nature is changed . . . the trees of the forest furiously rush against each other.' "
7. Two hundred and fifty rounds of ammunition.
8. This may appear to be an anachronism, but I remember in 1917 discussing with a friend the possibilities of tourist activity if peace ever came. I remember we went into details and wondered if the unexploded projectile lying near us would go up under a holiday-maker, and how people would stand up to be photographed on our parapets. I recall feeling very angry about this, as you do if you think of strangers ever occupying a house you live in, and which has, for you, particular associations [Jones's note].

Modernist Manifestos

At the beginning of the twentieth century, traditions and boundaries of many kinds were under assault across the Western world. Rapid developments in science and technology were transforming the texture of everyday life and conceptions of the universe; psychology, anthropology, and philosophy were challenging old ways of conceiving the human mind and religion; empire, migration, and city life were forcing together peoples of diverse origins. This dizzying pace of change, this break with tradition, this eruption of modernity can also be seen in the cutting-edge art and literature of the time. Avant-garde modernism caught fire in Europe in the decade before World War I. The Spanish expatriate artist Pablo Picasso's landmark cubist painting of 1907, *Les Demoiselles d'Avignon* (see the color insert), shattered centuries of artistic convention. Two years later the Italian poet F. T. Marinetti published his first futurist manifesto in the French journal *Le Figaro*, blasting the dead weight of "museums, libraries, and academies," glorifying "the beauty of speed." Written from 1911 to 1913, the Russian-born composer Igor Stravinsky's ballet *Le Sacre du Printemps* (*The Rite of Spring*) marked such a daring departure from harmonic and rhythmic traditions in Western classical music that its first performance, in Paris, sparked a riot. Like Picasso, Marinetti, and Stravinsky, other avant-garde modernists—advocates of radical newness in the arts—exploded conventions in music, painting, fiction, poetry, and other genres, opening up new formal and thematic possibilities for the twentieth century.

In just a few years the rebellious energies and convention-defying activities of avant-garde modernism swept through the major European cities, from Moscow and Milan to Munich, Paris, and London. Some of the leading figures of avant-garde modernism published manifestos, public declarations explaining, justifying, and promoting their ambitions and revolutionary views. The modernists were not the first artists to adapt the manifesto from the political sphere, but they used manifestos widely and vociferously, trumpeting iconoclastic ideas in terms that were meant not only to rally but also, in some cases, to shock. These documents were so influential that they have become an integral part of the history of modernism.

London, where the startling impact of cubism and futurism was felt almost immediately, became a central site in the formation of anglophone modernism. London's publishing opportunities and literary ferment attracted an array of visiting and expatriate writers. The American poet Ezra Pound arrived there in 1908, at twenty-three, and soon ignited London's literary avant-garde, his apartment in Kensington a magnet for like-minded innovators. He befriended the English philosopher poet T. E. Hulme, who led an avant-garde literary group. Like the cubists and futurists, these modernists advocated a radical break with artistic convention. In lectures Hulme influentially denounced Romanticism as so much moaning and whining and proposed a "hard, dry" literature in its stead—a notion Pound echoed in his call for "harder and saner" verse, "like granite." After T. S. Eliot came to England in 1914, astonishing Pound by his having "modernized himself *on his own*," he also composed essays marked by Hulme's influence. Aggressively asserting new form and subject matter while holding up the standard of classic texts, the modernists repudiated what they saw as the slushy, self-indulgent literature of the nineteenth century—"blurry, messy," and "sentimentalistic," in Pound's words. This desire to break decisively with Romanticism and Victorianism—often realized more in theory than in practice—became a recurrent feature in their public declarations. The 1914 manifesto of the journal *Blast* thunders, "**BLAST** / years **1837** to **1900**": like other avant-garde manifestos, this one damns the middle class for perpetuating Victorian taste and conventional mores.

The agitations, declarations, and poetic experiments of Hulme, Pound, and others resulted in the formation of imagism. Leaders of this London-born movement advocated clear and immediate images, exact and efficient diction, inventive and musical rhythms. The imagist poem was to be brief and stripped down, presenting an image in as few words as possible without commenting on it. In his lecture "Romanticism and Classicism" Hulme said the poet must render "the exact curve of what he sees whether it be an object or an idea in the mind." Having arranged for the nascent movement to be announced by the English poet and critic F. S. Flint in a brief article/interview entitled "Imagisme" (spelled in the French manner), Pound demanded, through Flint's introductory synopsis of imagism's precepts, "Direct treatment of the 'thing,' whether subjective or objective." The principles of imagism and Pound's further recommendations in "A Few Don'ts by an Imagiste" had a profound transatlantic influence long after the movement had petered out.

The American poet H. D. (then called Hilda Doolittle) arrived in London in 1911, just in time to become a major figure in the imagist movement. Her poems, written under the influence of ancient Greek lyrical fragments, so impressed Pound that he sent them, signed "H. D. Imagiste" at his insistence, to Harriet Monroe, the founding editor of *Poetry,* a Chicago clearinghouse for modern verse. He told Monroe that H. D.'s poems were "modern" and "laconic," though classical in subject: "Objective— no slither; direct—no excessive use of adjectives, no metaphors that won't permit examination. It's straight talk, straight as the Greek!" Eventually H. D. and Pound wrote ambitious long poems that broke the mold of the imagist lyric, but even in their more capacious work, imagist compression, immediacy, and juxtaposition remained generative principles.

As early as 1914 Pound was tiring of imagism as too static and insufficiently rigorous. Together with the London-based English painter and writer Wyndham Lewis, he helped found a new modernist movement in the arts, vorticism, which emphasized dynamism of content. Pound conceived the vortex—an image of whirling, intensifying, encompassing energy—as the movement's emblem. Like imagism, vorticism lasted for only a few years. Its most raucous embodiment was the 1914 vorticist manifesto in Wyndham Lewis's journal *Blast,* and its main aesthetic achievements were Lewis's paintings and the London-based French artist Henri Gaudier-Brzeska's sculptures.

The *Blast* manifesto is clearly influenced by continental modernism, most visibly Italian futurism in the experimental layout and the fire-breathing rhetoric of destruction: the vorticists blast conventions, dull people, and middle-class attitudes. The English-born poet Mina Loy became closely involved with the leaders of the futurist movement, including Marinetti, while in Florence from 1906 to 1916. She was excited by futurism's embrace of modernity and its violent rebuke of tradition, but her typographically experimental "Feminist Manifesto" also marks a break with the movement's misogyny and jingoism. Marinetti, Pound, and Lewis—despite their progressive prewar views on many social and artistic matters—later embraced fascism, believing it would help advance their cultural ideals.

Modernist manifestos take on a variety of different forms. Some are individual statements, such as Hulme's lecture "Romanticism and Classicism." Others are meant to be declarations on behalf of an emergent group or movement, such as "A Few Don'ts by an Imagiste" or the *Blast* manifesto. Occasionally, and paradoxically, a manifesto is a nonpublic declaration, unpublished in the author's lifetime, as in the case of Loy's "Feminist Manifesto." Although the manifesto is not an art form in the same sense as a poem or painting is, manifestos became an important literary genre in the modernist era, and some are more than mere declarations of doctrine. The vorticist manifesto and Loy's "Feminist Manifesto," for example, cross poetry with poster art, creatively manipulating words on the page for maximum effect. In their jagged typography, wild energy, and radical individualism turned to a collective purpose, these modernist manifestos helped advance and now exemplify elements of innovative art through the twentieth century.

For more documents, images, and contexts related to this subject, see "Modernist Experiment" at Norton Literature Online.

T. E. HULME

Although he published only six poems during his brief life, T. E. Hulme (1883–1917), English poet, philosopher, and critic, was one of the strongest intellectual forces behind the development of modernism. In this essay, probably composed in either 1911 or 1912 and probably delivered as a lecture in 1912, Hulme prophesies a "dry, hard, classical verse" that exhibits precision, clarity, and freshness. He sharply repudiates the "spilt religion" of Romanticism, responsible for vagueness in the arts. Hulme sees human beings as limited and capable of improvement only through the influence of tradition. These ideas were an important influence on the thought and poetry of T. S. Eliot. Hulme's views of conventional language, the visual image, and verbal exactitude also shaped the imagism and vorticism of Ezra Pound and others.

Hulme was born in Staffordshire, England, and attended St. John's College, Cambridge, from which he was expelled for rebellious behavior in 1904 without finishing his degree. He lived mainly in London, where, befriending Pound and other poets and artists, he became a central figure of the prewar avant-garde. A critic of pacifism, Hulme enlisted as a private in the army when World War I broke out in 1914, and was killed in battle in 1917. First published posthumously in *Speculations* (1924), this essay is excerpted from *The Collected Writings of T. E. Hulme* (1994), ed. Karen Csengeri.

From Romanticism and Classicism

I want to maintain that after a hundred years of romanticism, we are in for a classical revival, and that the particular weapon of this new classical spirit, when it works in verse, will be fancy. * * *

I know that in using the words 'classic' and 'romantic' I am doing a dangerous thing. They represent five or six different kinds of antitheses, and while I may be using them in one sense you may be interpreting them in another. In this present connection I am using them in a perfectly precise and limited sense. I ought really to have coined a couple of new words, but I prefer to use the ones I have used, as I then conform to the practice of the group of polemical writers who make most use of them at the present day, and have almost succeeded in making them political catchwords. I mean Maurras, Lasserre and all the group connected with *L'Action Française*.[1]

At the present time this is the particular group with which the distinction is most vital. Because it has become a party symbol. If you asked a man of a

---

1. Charles Maurras (1868–1952) and Pierre Lasserre (1867–1930) were intellectuals associated with *l'Action Française*, a reactionary political movement that denigrated Romanticism and sup- ported the Catholic Church as a force for order. (T. S. Eliot also fell under the movement's influence.)

certain set whether he preferred the classics or the romantics, you could deduce from that what his politics were.

The best way of gliding into a proper definition of my terms would be to start with a set of people who are prepared to fight about it—for in them you will have no vagueness. (Other people take the infamous attitude of the person with catholic tastes who says he likes both.)

About a year ago, a man whose name I think was Fauchois gave a lecture at the Odéon on Racine,[2] in the course of which he made some disparaging remarks about his dullness, lack of invention and the rest of it. This caused an immediate riot: fights took place all over the house; several people were arrested and imprisoned, and the rest of the series of lectures took place with hundreds of gendarmes[3] and detectives scattered all over the place. These people interrupted because the classical ideal is a living thing to them and Racine is the great classic. That is what I call a real vital interest in literature. They regard romanticism as an awful disease from which France had just recovered.

The thing is complicated in their case by the fact that it was romanticism that made the revolution.[4] They hate the revolution, so they hate romanticism.

I make no apology for dragging in politics here; romanticism both in England and France is associated with certain political views, and it is in taking a concrete example of the working out of a principle in action that you can get its best definition.

What was the positive principle behind all the other principles of '89? I am talking here of the revolution in as far as it was an idea; I leave out material causes—they only produce the forces. The barriers which could easily have resisted or guided these forces had been previously rotted away by ideas. This always seems to be the case in successful changes; the privileged class is beaten only when it has lost faith in itself, when it has itself been penetrated with the ideas which are working against it.

It was not the rights of man—that was a good solid practical war-cry. The thing which created enthusiasm, which made the revolution practically a new religion, was something more positive than that. People of all classes, people who stood to lose by it, were in a positive ferment about the idea of liberty. There must have been some idea which enabled them to think that something positive could come out of so essentially negative a thing. There was, and here I get my definition of romanticism. They had been taught by Rousseau[5] that man was by nature good, that it was only bad laws and customs that had suppressed him. Remove all these and the infinite possibilities of man would have a chance. This is what made them think that something positive could come out of disorder, this is what created the religious enthusiasm. Here is the root of all romanticism: that man, the individual, is an infinite reservoir of possibilities; and if you can so rearrange society by the destruction of oppressive order then these possibilities will have a chance and you will get Progress.

One can define the classical quite clearly as the exact opposite to this. Man is an extraordinarily fixed and limited animal whose nature is absolutely con-

2. Jean Racine (1639–1699), French tragic playwright associated with classicism. The riot occurred at a lecture delivered by French playwright René Fauchois (1882–1962) at the Odéon Theater, Paris, on November 3, 1910.
3. Police officers (French).

4. The French Revolution (1789–99).
5. Jean-Jacques Rousseau (1712–1778), Swiss-born French writer and philosopher whose ideas greatly influenced the leaders of the French Revolution and the development of Romanticism.

stant. It is only by tradition and organisation that anything decent can be got out of him.

* * *

Put shortly, these are the two views, then. One, that man is intrinsically good, spoilt by circumstance; and the other that he is intrinsically limited, but disciplined by order and tradition to something fairly decent. To the one party man's nature is like a well, to the other like a bucket. The view which regards man as a well, a reservoir full of possibilities, I call the romantic; the one which regards him as a very finite and fixed creature, I call the classical.

One may note here that the Church has always taken the classical view since the defeat of the Pelagian heresy[6] and the adoption of the sane classical dogma of original sin.

It would be a mistake to identify the classical view with that of materialism. On the contrary it is absolutely identical with the normal religious attitude. I should put it in this way: That part of the fixed nature of man is the belief in the Deity. This should be as fixed and true for every man as belief in the existence of matter and in the objective world. It is parallel to appetite, the instinct of sex, and all the other fixed qualities. Now at certain times, by the use of either force or rhetoric, these instincts have been suppressed—in Florence under Savonarola, in Geneva under Calvin, and here under the Roundheads.[7] The inevitable result of such a process is that the repressed instinct bursts out in some abnormal direction. So with religion. By the perverted rhetoric of Rationalism, your natural instincts are suppressed and you are converted into an agnostic. Just as in the case of the other instincts, Nature has her revenge. The instincts that find their right and proper outlet in religion must come out in some other way. You don't believe in a God, so you begin to believe that man is a god. You don't believe in Heaven, so you begin to believe in a heaven on earth. In other words, you get romanticism. The concepts that are right and proper in their own sphere are spread over, and so mess up, falsify and blur the clear outlines of human experience. It is like pouring a pot of treacle[8] over the dinner table. Romanticism then, and this is the best definition I can give of it, is spilt religion.

I must now shirk the difficulty of saying exactly what I mean by romantic and classical in verse. I can only say that it means the result of these two attitudes towards the cosmos, towards man, in so far as it gets reflected in verse. The romantic, because he thinks man infinite, must always be talking about the infinite; and as there is always the bitter contrast between what you think you ought to be able to do and what man actually can, it always tends, in its later stages at any rate, to be gloomy. I really can't go any further than to say it is the reflection of these two temperaments, and point out examples of the different spirits. On the one hand I would take such diverse people as Horace, most of the Elizabethans and the writers of the Augustan age, and on the other side Lamartine, Hugo, parts of Keats, Coleridge, Byron, Shelley and Swinburne.[9]

6. Controversial Church doctrine denying the transmission of original sin, named after the theologian Pelagius (ca. 354–after 418).
7. Puritan members of the Parliamentary Party during the English Civil War (1642–51), named for their short haircuts. Girolamo Savonarola (1452–1498), Dominican monk who denounced the extravagance of the Renaissance. John Calvin (1509–1564), Protestant theologian who stressed the predestination and the depravity of humankind.
8. Molasses (British).
9. Horace (65–8 B.C.E.), Roman poet. "The Elizabethans": English poets and playwrights (such as Shakespeare) writing during the reign of Queen Elizabeth I (1558–1603). "The Augustan age": the

What I mean by classical in verse, then, is this. That even in the most imaginative flights there is always a holding back, a reservation. The classical poet never forgets this finiteness, this limit of man. He remembers always that he is mixed up with earth. He may jump, but he always returns back; he never flies away into the circumambient gas.

You might say if you wished that the whole of the romantic attitude seems to crystallise in verse round metaphors of flight. Hugo is always flying, flying over abysses, flying up into the eternal gases. The word infinite in every other line.

In the classical attitude you never seem to swing right along to the infinite nothing. If you say an extravagant thing which does exceed the limits inside which you know man to be fastened, yet there is always conveyed in some way at the end an impression of yourself standing outside it, and not quite believing it, or consciously putting it forward as a flourish. You never go blindly into an atmosphere more than the truth, an atmosphere too rarefied for man to breathe for long. You are always faithful to the conception of a limit. It is a question of pitch; in romantic verse you move at a certain pitch of rhetoric which you know, man being what he is, to be a little high-falutin. The kind of thing you get in Hugo or Swinburne. In the coming classical reaction that will feel just wrong. * * *

*　　*　　*

I object even to the best of the romantics. I object still more to the receptive attitude.[1] I object to the sloppiness which doesn't consider that a poem is a poem unless it is moaning or whining about something or other. I always think in this connection of the last line of a poem of John Webster's which ends with a request I cordially endorse:

'End your moan and come away.'[2]

The thing has got so bad now that a poem which is all dry and hard, a properly classical poem, would not be considered poetry at all. How many people now can lay their hands on their hearts and say they like either Horace or Pope? They feel a kind of chill when they read them.

The dry hardness which you get in the classics is absolutely repugnant to them. Poetry that isn't damp isn't poetry at all. They cannot see that accurate description is a legitimate object of verse. Verse to them always means a bringing in of some of the emotions that are grouped round the word infinite.

The essence of poetry to most people is that it must lead them to a beyond of some kind. Verse strictly confined to the earthly and the definite (Keats is full of it) might seem to them to be excellent writing, excellent craftsmanship, but not poetry. So much has romanticism debauched us, that, without some form of vagueness, we deny the highest.

In the classic it is always the light of ordinary day, never the light that never

---

late seventeenth and early eighteenth centuries, when English writers such as John Dryden (1631–1700) and Alexander Pope (1688–1744) embraced a classicism likened to the Augustan Age of Rome. Alphonse Lamartine (1790–1869), French poet and politician. Victor Hugo (1802–1885), French poet and novelist. John Keats (1795–1821), Samuel Taylor Coleridge (1772–1834), George Gordon (Lord) Byron (1788–1824), Percy Bysshe Shelley (1792–1822), Algernon Charles Swinburne (1837–1909), English poets.

1. Elsewhere in the essay, Hulme claims that every sort of verse has an accompanying receptive attitude by which readers come to expect certain qualities from poetry. These receptive attitudes, he explains, sometimes outlast the poetry from which they develop.

2. From *The Duchess of Malfi* (1623) 4.2, by the English dramatist John Webster (ca. 1580–ca. 1625).

was on land or sea. It is always perfectly human and never exaggerated: man is always man and never a god.

But the awful result of romanticism is that, accustomed to this strange light, you can never live without it. Its effect on you is that of a drug.

* * *

* * * It is essential to prove that beauty may be in small, dry things.

The great aim is accurate, precise and definite description. The first thing is to recognise how extraordinarily difficult this is. It is no mere matter of carefulness; you have to use language, and language is by its very nature a communal thing; that is, it expresses never the exact thing but a compromise— that which is common to you, me and everybody. But each man sees a little differently, and to get out clearly and exactly what he does see, he must have a terrific struggle with language, whether it be with words or the technique of other arts. Language has its own special nature, its own conventions and communal ideas. It is only by a concentrated effort of the mind that you can hold it fixed to your own purpose. I always think that the fundamental process at the back of all the arts might be represented by the following metaphor. You know what I call architect's curves—flat pieces of wood with all different kinds of curvature. By a suitable selection from these you can draw approximately any curve you like. The artist I take to be the man who simply can't bear the idea of that 'approximately'. He will get the exact curve of what he sees whether it be an object or an idea in the mind. I shall here have to change my metaphor a little to get the process in his mind. Suppose that instead of your curved pieces of wood you have a springy piece of steel of the same types of curvature as the wood. Now the state of tension or concentration of mind, if he is doing anything really good in this struggle against the ingrained habit of the technique, may be represented by a man employing all his fingers to bend the steel out of its own curve and into the exact curve which you want. Something different to what it would assume naturally.

* * *

This is the point I aim at, then, in my argument. I prophesy that a period of dry, hard, classical verse is coming. I have met the preliminary objection founded on the bad romantic æsthetic that in such verse, from which the infinite is excluded, you cannot have the essence of poetry at all.

* * *

* * * Poetry * * * is a compromise for a language of intuition which would hand over sensations bodily. It always endeavours to arrest you, and to make you continuously see a physical thing, to prevent you gliding through an abstract process. It chooses fresh epithets and fresh metaphors, not so much because they are new, and we are tired of the old, but because the old cease to convey a physical thing and become abstract counters. A poet says a ship 'coursed the seas' to get a physical image, instead of the counter word 'sailed'. Visual meanings can only be transferred by the new bowl of metaphor; prose is an old pot that lets them leak out. Images in verse are not mere decoration, but the very essence of an intuitive language. Verse is a pedestrian taking you over the ground, prose—a train which delivers you at a destination.

* * *

* * * The point is that exactly the same activity is at work as in the highest verse. That is the avoidance of conventional language in order to get the exact curve of the thing.

* * *

* * * A powerfully imaginative mind seizes and combines at the same instant all the important ideas of its poem or picture, and while it works with one of them, it is at the same instant working with and modifying all in their relation to it and never losing sight of their bearings on each other—as the motion of a snake's body goes through all parts at once and its volition acts at the same instant in coils which go contrary ways.

A romantic movement must have an end of the very nature of the thing. It may be deplored, but it can't be helped—wonder must cease to be wonder.

I guard myself here from all the consequences of the analogy, but it expresses at any rate the inevitableness of the process. A literature of wonder must have an end as inevitably as a strange land loses its strangeness when one lives in it. Think of the lost ecstasy of the Elizabethans. 'Oh my America, my new found land,'[3] think of what it meant to them and of what it means to us. Wonder can only be the attitude of a man passing from one stage to another, it can never be a permanently fixed thing.

1911–12   1924

3. Line 27 of John Donne's "To His Mistress Going to Bed."

F. S. FLINT AND EZRA POUND

In the March 1913 issue of *Poetry* magazine, the English poet and translator F. S. Flint published an article summarizing an interview with an unidentified "imagiste"— surely Ezra Pound. The article, partly dictated and rewritten by Pound, famously states the three principles of imagism—directness, economy, musical rhythm—which Pound later said he and the poets H. D. and Richard Aldington had agreed on in 1912. Flint's prefatory piece was followed in the same issue by Pound's manifesto, "A Few Don'ts by an Imagiste." There Pound defines the image and issues injunctions and admonitions to help poets strip their verse of unnecessary rhetoric and abstraction. Poets, he argues, should write direct, musically cadenced, image-grounded verse.

Born in London, F. S. Flint (1885–1960) worked in the British civil service, translated poetry (mostly French), and eventually published volumes of his own imagist poetry. Ezra Pound (1885–1972) was born in Hailey, Idaho, and was educated at the University of Pennsylvania and Hamilton College. During his twelve years in London, from 1908 to 1920, where he became closely associated with W. B. Yeats and T. E. Hulme, he was the most vigorous entrepreneur of literary modernism, helping James Joyce, T. S. Eliot, and other writers launch their careers. In London he also began working on material for his major work, the massive poem *The Cantos*. Living briefly in Paris and then for twenty years in Italy as an ardent supporter of the Fascist regime, he was arrested for treason in 1945, having made Rome Radio broadcasts against the U.S. war effort. He spent twelve years, from 1946 to 1958, in a Washington, D.C., asylum for the criminally insane before returning to Italy, where he fell into an almost complete silence until the end of his life.

Imagisme[1]

Some curiosity has been aroused concerning *Imagisme*, and as I was unable to find anything definite about it in print, I sought out an *imagiste*, with intent to discover whether the group itself knew anything about the "movement." I gleaned these facts.

The *imagistes* admitted that they were contemporaries of the Post Impressionists and the Futurists; but they had nothing in common with these schools. They had not published a manifesto. They were not a revolutionary school; their only endeavor was to write in accordance with the best tradition, as they found it in the best writers of all time,—in Sappho, Catullus, Villon.[2] They seemed to be absolutely intolerant of all poetry that was not written in such endeavor, ignorance of the best tradition forming no excuse. They had a few rules, drawn up for their own satisfaction only, and they had not published them. They were:

1. Direct treatment of the "thing," whether subjective or objective.
2. To use absolutely no word that did not contribute to the presentation.
3. As regarding rhythm: to compose in sequence of the musical phrase, not in sequence of a metronome.

By these standards they judged all poetry, and found most of it wanting. They held also a certain 'Doctrine of the Image,' which they had not committed to writing; they said that it did not concern the public, and would provoke useless discussion.

The devices whereby they persuaded approaching poetasters to attend their instruction were:

1. They showed him his own thought already splendidly expressed in some classic (and the school musters altogether a most formidable erudition).
2. They re-wrote his verses before his eyes, using about ten words to his fifty.

Even their opponents admit of them—ruefully—"At least they do keep bad poets from writing!"

I found among them an earnestness that is amazing to one accustomed to the usual London air of poetic dilettantism. They consider that Art is all science, all religion, philosophy and metaphysic. It is true that *snobisme* may be urged against them; but it is at least *snobisme* in its most dynamic form, with a great deal of sound sense and energy behind it; and they are stricter with themselves than with any outsider.

F. S. Flint

A Few Don'ts by an Imagiste

An "Image" is that which presents an intellectual and emotional complex in an instant of time. I use the term "complex" rather in the technical sense

---

1. In response to many requests for information regarding *Imagism* and the *Imagistes*, we publish this note by Mr. Flint, supplementing it with further exemplification by Mr. Pound. It will be seen from these that *Imagism* is not necessarily associated with Hellenic subjects, or with *vers libre* as a prescribed form ["Editor's Note" from original].
"*Vers libre*": free verse (French).
2. François Villon (1431–after 1463), French poet. Sappho (fl. ca. 610–ca. 580 B.C.E.), Greek poet. Catullus (ca. 84–ca. 54 B.C.E.), Roman poet.

employed by the newer psychologists, such as Hart,[1] though we might not agree absolutely in our application.

It is the presentation of such a "complex" instantaneously which gives that sense of sudden liberation; that sense of freedom from time limits and space limits; that sense of sudden growth, which we experience in the presence of the greatest works of art.

It is better to present one Image in a lifetime than to produce voluminous works.

All this, however, some may consider open to debate. The immediate necessity is to tabulate A LIST OF DONT's for those beginning to write verses. But I can not put all of them into Mosaic negative.[2]

To begin with, consider the three rules recorded by Mr. Flint, not as dogma—never consider anything as dogma—but as the result of long contemplation, which, even if it is some one else's contemplation, may be worth consideration.

Pay no attention to the criticism of men who have never themselves written a notable work. Consider the discrepancies between the actual writing of the Greek poets and dramatists, and the theories of the Graeco-Roman grammarians, concocted to explain their metres.

Language

Use no superflous word, no adjective, which does not reveal something.

Don't use such an expression as "dim lands of *peace*." It dulls the image. It mixes an abstraction with the concrete. It comes from the writer's not realizing that the natural object is always the *adequate* symbol.

Go in fear of abstractions. Don't retell in mediocre verse what has already been done in good prose. Don't think any intelligent person is going to be deceived when you try to shirk all the difficulties of the unspeakably difficult art of good prose by chopping your composition into line lengths.

What the expert is tired of today the public will be tired of tomorrow.

Don't imagine that the art of poetry is any simpler than the art of music, or that you can please the expert before you have spent at least as much effort on the art of verse as the average piano teacher spends on the art of music.

Be influenced by as many great artists as you can, but have the decency either to acknowledge the debt outright, or to try to conceal it.

Don't allow "influence" to mean merely that you mop up the particular decorative vocabulary of some one or two poets whom you happen to admire. A Turkish war correspondent was recently caught red-handed babbling in his dispatches of "dove-gray" hills, or else it was "pearl-pale," I can not remember.

Use either no ornament or good ornament.

Rhythm and Rhyme

Let the candidate fill his mind with the finest cadences he can discover, preferably in a foreign language so that the meaning of the words may be less likely to divert his attention from the movement; e.g., Saxon charms, Hebri-

---

1. British psychologist Bernard Hart (1879–1966) discusses "the complex" in *The Psychology of Insanity* (1912), a book that helped popularize psycho-

analysis.
2. Reference to the Ten Commandments delivered to Moses (Exodus 20).

dean Folk Songs, the verse of Dante, and the lyrics of Shakespeare—if he can dissociate the vocabulary from the cadence. Let him dissect the lyrics of Goethe[3] coldly into their component sound values, syllables long and short, stressed and unstressed, into vowels and consonants.

It is not necessary that a poem should rely on its music, but if it does rely on its music that music must be such as will delight the expert.

Let the neophyte know assonance and alliteration, rhyme immediate and delayed, simple and polyphonic, as a musician would expect to know harmony and counterpoint and all the minutiae of his craft. No time is too great to give to these matters or to any one of them, even if the artist seldom have need of them.

Don't imagine that a thing will "go" in verse just because it's too dull to go in prose.

Don't be "viewy"—leave that to the writers of pretty little philosophic essays. Don't be descriptive; remember that the painter can describe a landscape much better than you can, and that he has to know a deal more about it.

When Shakespeare talks of the "Dawn in russet mantle clad"[4] he presents something which the painter does not present. There is in this line of his nothing that one can call description; he presents.

Consider the way of the scientists rather than the way of an advertising agent for a new soap.

The scientist does not expect to be acclaimed as a great scientist until he has *discovered* something. He begins by learning what has been discovered already. He goes from that point onward. He does not bank on being a charming fellow personally. He does not expect his friends to applaud the results of his freshman class work. Freshmen in poetry are unfortunately not confined to a definite and recognizable class room. They are "all over the shop." Is it any wonder "the public is indifferent to poetry?"

Don't chop your stuff into separate *iambs*. Don't make each line stop dead at the end, and then begin every next line with a heave. Let the beginning of the next line catch the rise of the rhythm wave, unless you want a definite longish pause.

In short, behave as a musician, a good musician, when dealing with that phase of your art which has exact parallels in music. The same laws govern, and you are bound by no others.

Naturally, your rhythmic structure should not destroy the shape of your words, or their natural sound, or their meaning. It is improbable that, at the start, you will be able to get a rhythm-structure strong enough to affect them very much, though you may fall a victim to all sorts of false stopping due to line ends and caesurae.

The musician can rely on pitch and the volume of the orchestra. You can not. The term harmony is misapplied to poetry; it refers to simultaneous sounds of different pitch. There is, however, in the best verse a sort of residue of sound which remains in the ear of the hearer and acts more or less as an organ-base. A rhyme must have in it some slight element of surprise if it is to give pleasure; it need not be bizarre or curious, but it must be well used if used at all.

---

3. Johann Wolfgang von Goethe (1749–1832), German Romantic poet, playwright, and novelist.
4. From Horatio's speech in the opening scene of Shakespeare's *Hamlet*: "But look, the morn in russet mantle clad / Walks o'er the dew of yon high eastern hill" (1.1.147–48).

Vide further Vildrac and Duhamel's notes on rhyme in "*Technique Poetique*."[5]

That part of your poetry which strikes upon the imaginative *eye* of the reader will lose nothing by translation into a foreign tongue; that which appeals to the ear can reach only those who take it in the original.

Consider the definiteness of Dante's presentation, as compared with Milton's rhetoric. Read as much of Wordsworth[6] as does not seem too unutterably dull.

If you want the gist of the matter go to Sappho, Catullus, Villon, Heine when he is in the vein, Gautier when he is not too frigid; or, if you have not the tongues, seek out the leisurely Chaucer.[7] Good prose will do you no harm, and there is good discipline to be had by trying to write it.

Translation is likewise good training, if you find that your original matter "wobbles" when you try to rewrite it. The meaning of the poem to be translated can not "wobble."

If you are using a symmetrical form, don't put in what you want to say and then fill up the remaining vacuums with slush.

Don't mess up the perception of one sense by trying to define it in terms of another. This is usually only the result of being too lazy to find the exact word. To this clause there are possibly exceptions.

The first three simple proscriptions[8] will throw out nine-tenths of all the bad poetry now accepted as standard and classic; and will prevent you from many a crime of production.

"... *Mais d'abord il faut etre un poete*,"[9] as MM. Duhamel and Vildrac have said at the end of their little book, "*Notes sur la Technique Poetique*"; but in an American one takes that at least for granted, otherwise why does one get born upon that august continent!

Ezra Pound

5. Charles Vildrac (1882–1971), French poet, playwright, and critic, and Georges Duhamel (1884–1966), French novelist and critic, cowrote *Notes sur la Technique Poétique* (1910). "*Vide*": consider.
6. John Milton (1608–1674) and William Words-worth (1770–1850), English poets.
7. Geoffrey Chaucer (ca. 1342–1400), English poet. Heinrich Heine (1797–1856), German poet. Théophile Gautier (1811–1872), French poet.
8. Noted by Mr. Flint [Pound's note].
9. But first it is necessary to be a poet (French).

AN IMAGIST CLUSTER:
T. E. HULME, EZRA POUND, H. D.

At the inception of imagism in London, the key imagists included the English poet philosopher T. E. Hulme and the expatriate American poets Ezra Pound and H. D. The paths of these three writers were densely interconnected at this juncture. In his poetry volume *Ripostes* (1912), Pound published an appendix of five poems, "The Complete Poetical Works of T. E. Hulme," prefaced by a note that printed the term *imagistes* for the first time. That year, in a London teashop, Pound had announced to the English poet Richard Aldington and the American poet H. D. that they were "imagistes," and two years later he included their and his work in the first imagist anthology, *Des Imagistes*. Although imagism began in London, with a French-styled name, the American poet Amy Lowell (1874–1925), derided by Pound for watering down imagism's principles, helped disseminate its ideas in the United States, where she publicized and promoted imagism in anthologies, lectures, and readings.

In spare, hard-edged poems the imagists sought to turn verse away from what they saw as the slack sentimentality and fuzzy abstraction, the explanatory excess and metrical predictability of Victorian poetry. Imagism owed a debt to the symbolism of Yeats and nineteenth-century French poets, but it shifted the emphasis from the musical to the visual, the mysterious to the actual, the ambiguously suggestive symbol to the clear-cut natural image. The imagists looked to models from East Asia (haiku for Pound's "In a Station in the Metro") and classical Europe (Greek verse for H. D.'s "Oread"). Their poetry is compressed, achieving a maximum effect with a minimum of words. It is often centered in a single figurative juxtaposition, conjoining tenor and vehicle without explanation. And it typically relies not on strict meters but on informal rhythms or cadences.

H. D. (1886–1961) was born Hilda Doolittle in Bethlehem, Pennsylvania, and educated at Bryn Mawr College. In 1911 she went to Europe for what she thought would be a brief visit but became a lifelong stay, mainly in England and in Switzerland. After her initial imagist phase she wrote more expansive works, including the three long, meditative poems that make up *Trilogy* (1973), precipitated by the experience of the London bombings in World War II.

T. E. HULME: Autumn

A touch of cold in the Autumn night—
I walked abroad,
And saw the ruddy moon lean over a hedge
Like a red-faced farmer.
5   I did not stop to speak, but nodded,
And round about were the wistful stars
With white faces like town children.

                                          1912

EZRA POUND: In a Station of the Metro

The apparition of these faces in the crowd;
Petals on a wet, black bough.[1]

                                          1913, 1916

1. Pound describes this poem's genesis in *Gaudier-Brzeska* (1916): "Three years ago in Paris I got out of a 'metro' train at La Concorde, and saw suddenly a beautiful face, and then another and another, and then a beautiful child's face, and then another beautiful woman, and I tried all that day to find words for what this had meant to me, and I could not find any words that seemed to me worthy, or as lovely as that sudden emotion. And that evening . . . I was still trying and I found, suddenly, the expression. I do not mean that I found words, but there came an equation . . . not in speech, but in little splotches of colour. . . . The 'one-image poem' is a form of super-position, that is to say, it is one idea getting out of the impasse in which I had been left by my metro emotion. I wrote a thirty-line poem, and destroyed it. . . . Six months later I made a poem half that length; a year later I made the following *hokku*-like sentence." "*Hokku*": another term for haiku.

H. D.: Oread[1]

Whirl up, sea—
Whirl your pointed pines,
Splash your great pines
On our rocks,
5   Hurl your green over us,
Cover us with your pools of fir.

1914

H. D.: Sea Rose

Rose, harsh rose,
marred and with stint of petals,
meagre flower, thin,
sparse of leaf,

5   more precious
than a wet rose,
single on a stem—
you are caught in the drift.

Stunted, with small leaf,
10   you are flung on the sands,
you are lifted
in the crisp sand
that drives in the wind.

Can the spice-rose
15   drip such acrid fragrance
hardened in a leaf?

1916

1. Greek nymph of the mountains.

BLAST

The journal *Blast* was published only twice—on June 20, 1914, though released on July 2, one month before Great Britain entered World War I, and a year later, during the war that would bring its short life to an end. But its initial preface and two-part manifesto, printed in the first pages of the first number and excerpted below, are among the most important documents in the history of modernism. They rhetorically and typographically embody the violent iconoclasm of vorticism, an avant-garde movement in the literary and visual arts centered in London. The English writer and painter Wyndham Lewis founded and edited *Blast,* whose title he said, "means the blowing away of dead ideas and worn-out notions" (it also suggests *fire, explosion,* and *damn!*). He drafted much of the vorticist manifesto and fashioned its shocking visual design, likening *Blast* to a "battering ram." Ezra Pound became a vorticist after abandoning imagism, because he felt that the *vortex,* "the point of maximum energy," offered a more dynamic model for art than the static image of the imagists. The French sculptor Henri Gaudier-Brzeska (1891–1915), killed in World War I and memorialized both in the "War Number" of *Blast* and in Pound's book named for him, was another key vorticist leader. In the pages of *Blast* 1 and 2, artworks by Lewis, Gaudier-Brzeska, and other visual artists appeared alongside writings by Lewis, Pound, T. S. Eliot, and other avant-gardists.

The vorticist manifesto, signed by Lewis, Pound, and Gaudier-Brzeska, among others, reflects the London modernists' competitive anxiety about European avant-gardes such as cubism and especially futurism. Under the charismatic leadership of F. T. Marinetti, the futurists celebrated speed, modernization, and the machine, while calling for the destruction of the museums, the libraries, all such bastions of the past. The vorticists—in lists of things and people to "**BLAST**" and "**BLESS**" compiled at group meetings—similarly blast convention, standardization, the middle class, even the "years **1837** to **1900**." And yet despite their cosmopolitan enthusiasms, the vorticists also assert their independence, repeatedly criticizing the futurists. For all their antipathy toward England, they also "**BLESS**" it, revaluing, for example, English mobility (via the sea) and inventiveness (as the engine of the Industrial Revolution).

Wyndham Lewis (1882–1957) studied for several years at London's Slade School of Art before exploring the avant-garde visual arts in Paris. On returning to London in 1909, he began to write fiction and exhibit his paintings. During World War I he served as an artillery officer and then as a war artist, and afterward he continued to paint and publish essays, poetry, and fiction, including his first novel, *Tarr* (1918). Like Ezra Pound, he alienated many friends because of his subsequent support of fascism.

The excerpts below are taken from *Blast: Review of the Great English Vortex,* No. 1 (1914). For the complete two-part *Blast* manifesto and more on futurism and cubism, see "Modernist Experiment" at Norton Literature Online.

Long Live the Vortex!

Long live the great art vortex sprung up in the centre of this town![1]

We stand for the Reality of the Present—not for the sentimental Future, or the sacripant[2] Past.

We want to leave Nature and Men alone.

We do not want to make people wear Futurist Patches, or fuss men to take to pink and sky-blue trousers.[3]

---

1. London
2. Boastful of valor.
3. The futurists celebrated the technology, power, and dynamism of the modern age and sought to break with the past and traditional forms.

We are not their wives or tailors.

The only way Humanity can help artists is to remain independent and work unconsciously.

WE NEED THE UNCONSCIOUSNESS OF HUMANITY—their stupidity, animalism and dreams.

We believe in no perfectibility except our own.

Intrinsic beauty is in the Interpreter and Seer, not in the object or content.

We do not want to change the appearance of the world, because we are not Naturalists, Impressionists or Futurists (the latest form of Impressionism),[4] and do not depend on the appearance of the world for our art.

WE ONLY WANT THE WORLD TO LIVE, and to feel it's crude energy flowing through us.

It may be said that great artists in England are always revolutionary, just as in France any really great artist had a strong traditional vein.

Blast sets out to be an avenue for all those vivid and violent ideas that could reach the Public in no other way.

Blast will be popular, essentially. It will not appeal to any particular class, but to the fundamental and popular instincts in every class and description of people, TO THE INDIVIDUAL. The moment a man feels or realizes himself as an artist, he ceases to belong to any milieu or time. Blast is created for this timeless, fundamental Artist that exists in everybody.

The Man in the Street and the Gentleman are equally ignored.

Popular art does not mean the art of the poor people, as it is usually supposed to. It means the art of the individuals.

Education (art education and general education) tends to destroy the creative instinct. Therefore it is in times when education has been non-existant that art chiefly flourished.

But it is nothing to do with "the People."

It is a mere accident that that is the most favourable time for the individual to appear.

To make the rich of the community shed their education skin, to destroy polite-ness, standardization and academic, that is civilized, vision, is the task we have set ourselves.

We want to make in England not a popular art, not a revival of lost folk art, or a romantic fostering of such unactual conditions, but to make individuals, wherever found.

We will convert the King[5] if possible.

A VORTICIST KING! WHY NOT?

DO YOU THINK LLOYD GEORGE[6] HAS THE VORTEX IN HIM?

MAY WE HOPE FOR ART FROM LADY MOND?[7]

4. Naturalism, a late-nineteenth-century school of realism, claimed all human life was governed by natural laws. Impressionism emphasized the sub-jectivity of perspective over any inherent quality in a represented object.

5. George V ascended the British throne in 1910 and remained the king until 1936.

6. David Lloyd George (1863–1945), British pol-itician, prime minister 1916–22.

7. Wife of wealthy industrialist Sir Robert Mond, and a prominent member of fashionable London society.

We are against the glorification of "the People," as we are against snobbery. It is not necessary to be an outcast bohemian, to be unkempt or poor, any more than it is necessary to be rich or handsome, to be an artist. Art is nothing to do with the coat you wear. A top-hat can well hold the Sixtine. A cheap cap could hide the image of Kephren.[8]

AUTOMOBILISM (Marinetteism)[9] bores us. We don't want to go about making a hullo-bulloo about motor cars, anymore than about knives and forks, elephants or gas-pipes.

Elephants are VERY BIG.   Motor cars go quickly.

Wilde gushed twenty years ago about the beauty of machinery. Gissing,[1] in his romantic delight with modern lodging houses was futurist in this sense.

The futurist is a sensational and sentimental mixture of the aesthete of 1890 and the realist of 1870.

The "Poor" are detestable animals! They are only picturesque and amusing for the sentimentalist or the romantic! The "Rich" are bores without a single exception, *en tant que riches!*[2]

We want those simple and great people found everywhere.

Blast presents an art of Individuals.

BLAST
years 1837 to 1900[1]
Curse abysmal inexcusable middle-class
(also Aristocracy and Proletariat).

BLAST
pasty shadow cast by gigantic Boehm[2]
(Imagined at introduction of BOURGEOIS VICTORIAN VISTAS).

8. Ancient Egyptian pharaoh buried in one of the great pyramids at Giza. "The Sixtine": the Sistine Chapel, in the Vatican.
9. Filippo Tommaso Marinetti (1876–1944), Italian writer and founder of Futurism, glorified war and technology and invented a "drama of objects" in which human actors play no parts.
1. George Gissing (1837–1903), naturalist English novelist. Oscar Wilde (1854–1900), Irish writer and critic; in his 1891 essay "The Soul of Man under Socialism," he writes: "All unintellectual

labour, all monotonous, dull labour, all labour that deals with dreadful things, and involves unpleasant conditions, must be done by machinery. . . . At *present machinery competes against man. Under proper conditions machinery will serve man.*"
2. Insofar as they are rich (French).
1. Queen Victoria reigned from 1837 to 1901. This sixth list of items in the "BLAST" section comes last, before the "BLESS" section.
2. Joseph Edgar Boehm (1834–1890) sculpted a colossal marble statue of Queen Victoria.

WRING THE NECK OF all sick inventions born in that progressive white wake.

BLAST their weeping whiskers—hirsute[3]
RHETORIC of EUNUCH and STYLIST—
SENTIMENTAL HYGIENICS
ROUSSEAUISMS[4] (wild Nature cranks)
FRATERNIZING WITH MONKEYS
DIABOLICS—raptures and roses
of the erotic bookshelves culminating in
PURGATORY OF PUTNEY.[5]

CHAOS OF ENOCH ARDENS

> laughing Jennys
> Ladies with Pains
> good-for-nothing Guineveres.[6]

SNOBBISH BORROVIAN running after
GIPSY KINGS and ESPADAS[7]

> bowing the knee to
> wild Mother Nature,
> her feminine contours,
> Unimaginative insult to
> MAN.

DAMN

all those to-day who have taken on that Rotten Menagerie, and still crack their whips and tumble in Piccadilly Circus, as though London were a provincial town.

3. Hairy.
4. Jean-Jacques Rousseau (1712–1778), French philosopher who argued that humans are good and noble in their natural state, before society and civilization corrupt them.
5. A middle-class London suburb.
6. In late-medieval romance, King Arthur's queen in Camelot; also, the title character in two narrative poems by the English poet Alfred, Lord Ten-nyson (1809–1892). "Enoch Arden" (1864) is another narrative poem by Tennyson, rejected here for its sentimentalism. Jenny is the title character of another sentimental poem (1870), by the English poet Dante Gabriel Rossetti (1828–1882).
7. Swords (Spanish). "Borrovian": from George Henry Borrow (1803–1881), English writer of popular gypsy romances, such as *The Zincali: An Account of the Gypsies of Spain* (1843).

WE WHISPER IN YOUR EAR A GREAT SECRET.

LONDON IS <u>NOT</u> A PROVINCIAL TOWN.

We will allow Wonder Zoos. But we do not want the

GLOOMY VICTORIAN CIRCUS[8] in Piccadilly Circus.

IT IS PICCADILLY'S CIRCUS!

NOT MEANT FOR MENAGERIES trundling

out of Sixties **DICKENSIAN CLOWNS, CORELLI LADY RIDERS,[9] TROUPS OF PERFORMING GIPSIES** (who complain besides that 1/6 a night does not pay fare back to Clapham).[1]

BLAST[2]

The Post Office	**Frank Brangwyn**	**Robertson Nicol**
Rev. Pennyfeather		**Galloway Kyle**
(Bells)		**(Cluster of Grapes)**

Bishop of London and all his posterity

Galsworthy	**Dean Inge**	**Croce**	**Matthews**
	Rev Meyer	**Seymour Hicks**	

---

8. "Circus": here traveling entertainment act with animals and acrobats; also British traffic circle. "Wonder Zoos": traveling exhibition of exotic animals.

9. Marie Corelli, pseudonym of Mary Mackay (1855–1924), best-selling (and royal favorite) English writer of romances and religious novels in which she aimed to reform social ills. "Dickensian clowns": from the novels of English writer Charles Dickens (1812–1870).

1. Suburban district of London. "1/6": 18d, or a shilling and sixpence, then equivalent to about thirty-five cents.

2. Those blasted here range from individuals, such as Charles Burgess Fry, England's star cricket player and a tireless self-promoter, to things blasted seemingly for the thrill of doing so, such as codliver oil. Blasted, too, are institutions or members of the national, literary, or cultural establishment (e.g., the post office, a much-lauded model of Victorian efficiency, and the British Academy, established in 1902 by Royal Charter as the

Lionel Cust   C. B. Fry   Bergson   Abdul Bahai

Hawtrey   Edward Elgar   Sardlea

Filson Young   Marie Corelli   Geddes

Codliver Oil   St. Loe Strachey   Lyceum Club

Rhabindraneth Tagore   Lord Glenconner of Glen

Weiniger   Norman Angel   Ad. Mahon

Mr. and Mrs. Dearmer   Beecham   Ella

A. C. Benson   (Pills, Opera, Thomas)   Sydney Webb

British Academy   Messrs. Chapell

Countess of Warwick   George Edwards

Willie Ferraro   Captain Cook   R. J. Campbell

Clan Thesiger   Martin Harvey   William Archer

George Grossmith   R. H. Benson

Annie Besant   Chenil   Clan Meynell

Father Vaughan   Joseph Holbrooke   Clan Strachey

1914

national academy for humanities and social sciences), including various clergy and public leaders (e.g., Bishop of London; William Ralph Inge, dean of St. Paul's Cathedral; the Reverends Pennyfeather and Meyer; R. J. Campbell, English Congregationalist minister in the City Temple of London, and a Pantheist; Cardinal Herbert Vaughan, archbishop of Westminster and superior of the Catholic Missionary Society; Norman Angell, pacifist British economist; Arthur Christopher Benson, schoolmaster at Eton College, author of Edward VII's coronation ode). Critics unfriendly to the avant-garde are also included (e.g., William Archer, drama critic for the Nation; Sir William Robertson Nicoll, biblical editor and sometime literary critic; Lionel Cust, director of the National Portrait Gallery and contributor to the Dictionary of National Biography, etc.). Also blasted are artists and writers whom the Vorticists believed were meager talents in spite of their popularity (e.g., painter Frank Brangwyn, poet Ella Wheeler Wilcox, actors George Grossmith and Seymour Hicks, composers Joseph Holbrooke and Edward Elgar, etc.), as well as those associated with fads (e.g., Sir Abdul Baha Bahai, leader of the Bahai faith) or idealistic social reform (e.g., author Marie Corelli; Sidney Webb, a leader of the Fabian Socialist organization; Annie Besant, theosophist and suffragist). Some names (e.g., Indian poet Rabindranath Tagore) are misspelled. For a detailed discussion of the cursing and blessing in Blast, see William C. Wees, Vorticism and the English Avant-Garde (1972).

MINA LOY

Mina Loy (1882–1966) was born in London to a Protestant mother and a Jewish father. She began her artistic career in the visual arts, but she later became an experimental poet, writing lyrics and long poems that created a stir because of their poetic, linguistic, and sexual iconoclasm. From 1899 to 1916 she lived and worked mostly in Munich, Paris, and especially Florence. She moved to New York in 1916 and to Paris in 1923, then settled in the United States in 1936.

Loy composed this manifesto, which she considered a rough draft and never published, in November 1914 and sent it to her friend Mabel Dodge (1879–1962), American author and celebrated patron of the arts. In the decade before she wrote it, feminist activism had intensified in England, particularly the militant civil disobedience of Christabel Pankhurst and other suffragettes in the Women's Social and Political Union. Loy's piece, which bears fruitful comparison with the masculine *Blast* manifesto published a few months earlier, was partly the result of Loy's quarrels with the Italian futurists, with whom she was closely associated despite the movement's misogyny. In the manifesto Loy tries to harness for feminism the radicalism and individualism of the avant-garde, calling for a complete revolution of gender relations. She abandons the suffragette movement's central issue of equality and insists instead on an adversarial model of gender, claiming that women should not look to men for a standard of value but should find it within themselves. First published in *The Last Lunar Baedeker* (1982), the manifesto is reprinted from *The Lost Lunar Baedeker* (1996); both volumes were edited by Roger L. Conover.

For a sample of Loy's poetry, see "Modernist Experiment" at Norton Literature Online.

Feminist Manifesto

The feminist movement as at present instituted is

Inadequate

Women if you want to realise yourselves—you are on the eve of a devastating psychological upheaval—all your pet illusions must be unmasked—the lies of centuries have got to go— are you prepared for the **Wrench**—? There is no half- measure—NO scratching on the surface of the rubbish heap of tradition, will bring about **Reform**, the only method is

Absolute Demolition

Cease to place your confidence in economic legislation, vice- crusades & uniform education—you are glossing over

Reality.

Professional & commercial careers are opening up for you—

Is that all you want ?

And if you honestly desire to find your level without prejudice—be **Brave** & deny at the outset—that pathetic clap-trap war cry **Woman is the
equal of man**—

She is **NOT!**   for

The man who lives a life in which his activities conform to a
social code which is a protectorate of the feminine element—
——is no longer **masculine**
The women who adapt themselves to a theoretical valuation of
their sex as a **relative impersonality** , are not yet
Feminine
Leave off looking to men to find out what you are **not** —seek
within yourselves to find out what you **are**
As conditions are at present constituted—you have the choice
between **Parasitism, & Prostitu-
tion** —or **Negation**

Men & women are enemies, with the enmity of the exploited
for the parasite, the parasite for the exploited—at present they
are at the mercy of the advantage that each can take of the
others sexual dependence—. The only point at which the
interests of the sexes merge—is the sexual embrace.

The first illusion it is to your interest to demolish is the
division of women into two classes   **the mistress,
& the mother** every well-balanced & developed woman
knows that is not true, Nature has endowed the complete
woman with a faculty for expressing herself through all her
functions—there are **no restrictions** the woman who is
so incompletely evolved as to be un-self-conscious in sex, will
prove a restrictive influence on the temperamental expansion
of the next generation; the woman who is a poor mistress will
be an incompetent mother—an inferior mentality—& will
enjoy an inadequate apprehension of **Life** .

To obtain results you must make sacrifices & the first &
greatest sacrifice you have to make is of your "virtue"
The fictitious value of woman as identified with her physical
purity—is too easy a stand-by——rendering her lethargic in
the acquisition of intrinsic merits of character by which she
could obtain a concrete value— therefore, the first self-
enforced law for the female sex, as a protection against the
man made bogey of virtue—which is the principle instrument
of her subjection, would be the unconditional surgical
destruction of virginity through-out the female population at
puberty—.

The value of man is assessed entirely according to his use or
interest to the community, the value of woman, depends
entirely on chance, her success or insuccess in manoeuvering
a man into taking the life-long responsibility of her—
The advantages of marriage of too ridiculously ample—
compared to all other trades—for under modern conditions a
woman can accept preposterously luxurious support from a
man (with-out return of any sort—even offspring)—as a thank
offering for her virginity
The woman who has not succeeded in striking that
advantageous bargain—is prohibited from any but
surreptitious re-action to Life-stimuli— **& entirely**
debarred maternity.
Every woman has a right to maternity—
Every woman of superior intelligence should realize her race-
responsibility, in producing children in adequate proportion to
the unfit or degenerate members of her sex—

Each child of a superior woman should be the result of a
definite period of psychic development in her life—& not
necessarily of a possibly irksome & outworn continuance of an
alliance—spontaneously adapted for vital creation in the
beginning but not necessarily harmoniously balanced as the
parties to it—follow their individual lines of personal
evolution—

For the harmony of the race, each individual should be the
expression of an easy & ample interpenetration of the male &
female temperaments—free of stress
Woman must become more responsible for the child than
man—
Women must destroy in themselves, the desire to be loved—

The feeling that it is a personal insult when a man transfers
his attentions from her to another woman
The desire for comfortable protection instead of an intelligent
curiosity & courage in meeting & resisting the pressure of life
sex or so called love must be reduced to its initial element,
honour, grief, sentimentality, pride & consequently jealousy
must be detached from it.
Woman for her happiness must retain her deceptive fragility of
appearance, combined with indomitable will, irreducible
courage, & abundant health the outcome of sound nerves—
Another great illusion that woman must use all her
introspective clear-sightedness & unbiassed bravery to
destroy—for the sake of her self respect is the impurity of sex
the realisation in defiance of superstition that there is nothing
impure in sex—except in the mental attitude to it—will
constitute an incalculable & wider social regeneration than it
is possible for our generation to imagine.

1914   1982

WILLIAM BUTLER YEATS
1865–1939

William Butler Yeats was born to an Anglo-Irish family in Dublin. His father, J. B.
Yeats, had abandoned law to take up painting, at which he made a somewhat precarious living. His mother came from the Pollexfen family that lived near Sligo, in the
west of Ireland, where Yeats spent much of his childhood. The Yeatses moved to
London in 1874, then returned to Dublin in 1880. Yeats attended first high school
and then art school, which he soon left to concentrate on poetry.

Yeats's father was a religious skeptic, but he believed in the "religion of art." Yeats,
religious by temperament but unable to believe in Christian orthodoxy, sought all his
life to compensate for his lost religion. This search led him to various kinds of mysticism, to folklore, theosophy, spiritualism, and neoplatonism. He said he "made a
new religion, almost an infallible church of poetic tradition."

Yeats's childhood and young manhood were spent between Dublin, London, and Sligo, and each of these places contributed something to his poetic development. In London in the 1890s he met the important poets of the day, founded the Irish Literary Society, and acquired late-Romantic, Pre-Raphaelite ideas of poetry: he believed, in this early stage of his career, that a poet's language should be dreamy, evocative, and ethereal. From the countryside around Sligo he gained a knowledge of the life of the peasantry and of their folklore. In Dublin, where he founded the National Literary Society, he was influenced by Irish nationalism and, although often disagreeing with those who wished to use literature for political ends, he nevertheless came to see his poetry as contributing to the rejuvenation of Irish culture.

Yeats's poetry began in the tradition of self-conscious Romanticism, strongly influenced by the English poets Edmund Spenser, Percy Shelley, and, a little later, William Blake, whose works he edited. About the same time he was writing poems (e.g., "The Stolen Child") deriving from his Sligo experience, with quietly precise nature imagery, Irish place-names, and themes from Irish folklore. A little later he drew on the great stories of the heroic age of Irish history and translations of Gaelic poetry into "that dialect which gets from Gaelic its syntax and keeps its still partly Tudor vocabulary." The heroic legends of ancient Ireland and the folk traditions of the modern Irish countryside helped brace his early dreamlike imagery. "The Lake Isle of Innisfree"— "my first lyric with anything in its rhythm of my own music," said Yeats—is both a Romantic evocation of escape into dream, art, and the imagination, and a specifically Irish reverie on freedom and self-reliance.

Yeats vigorously hybridizes Irish and English traditions, and eventually draws into this potent intercultural mix East and South Asian cultural resources, including Japanese Noh theater and Indian meditative practices. Resolutely Irish, he imaginatively reclaims a land colonized by the British; imposes Irish rhythms, images, genres, and syntax on English-language poetry; and revives native myths, place-names, and consciousness. Yet he is also cosmopolitan, insisting on the transnationalism of the collective storehouse of images he calls "Spiritus Mundi" or "Anima Mundi," spending much of his life in England, and cross-pollinating forms, ideas, and images from Ireland and England, Europe and Asia.

Irish nationalism first sent Yeats in search of a consistently simpler and more popular style, to express the elemental facts about Irish life and aspirations. This led him to the concrete image, as did translations from Gaelic folk songs, in which "nothing . . . was abstract, nothing worn-out." But other forces were also working on him. In 1902 a friend gave him the works of the German philosopher Friedrich Nietzsche, to which he responded with great excitement, and it would seem that, in persuading the passive love-poet to get off his knees, Nietzsche's books intensified his search for a more active stance, a more vigorous style. At the start of the twentieth century, Yeats wearied of his early languid aesthetic, declaring his intentions, in a 1901 letter, to make "everything hard and clear" and, in another of 1904, to leave behind "sentiment and sentimental sadness." He wished for poems not of disembodied beauty but that could "carry the normal, passionate, reasoning self, the personality as a whole." In poems of his middle period, such as "Adam's Curse" and "A Coat," Yeats combines the colloquial with the formal, enacting in his more austere diction, casual rhythms, and passionate syntax his will to leave behind the poetic "embroideries" of his youth and walk "naked." The American poet Ezra Pound, who spent winters from 1913 to 1916 with Yeats in a stone cottage in Sussex, strengthened Yeats's resolve to develop a less mannered, more stripped down style.

In 1889 Yeats had met the beautiful actor and Irish nationalist Maud Gonne, with whom he was desperately in love for many years, but who persistently refused to marry him. She became the subject of many of his early love poems, and in later poems, such as "No Second Troy" and "A Prayer for My Daughter," he expresses anger over her self-sacrifice to political activism. He had also met Lady Gregory, Anglo-Irish writer and promoter of Irish literature, in 1896, and Yeats spent many holidays at her aristocratic country house, Coole Park. Disliking the moneygrubbing and prudery of the middle classes, as indicated in "September 1913," he looked for his ideal characters either below them, to peasants and beggars, or above them, to the aristocracy, for each of these had their own traditions and lived according to them. Under Lady Gregory's influence Yeats began to organize the Irish dramatic movement in 1899 and, with her help, founded the Abbey Theater in 1904. His active participation in theatrical production—confronting political censorship, economic problems of paying carpenters and actors, and other aspects of "theatre business, management of men"—also helped toughen his style, as he demonstrates in "The Fascination of What's Difficult." Yeats's long-cherished hope had been to "bring the halves together"—Protestant and Catholic—through a literature infused with Ireland's ancient myths and cultural riches before the divisions between rival Christianities. But in a string of national controversies, he ran afoul of both the Roman Catholic middle class and the Anglo-Irish Protestant ascendancy, and at last, bitterly turning his back on Ireland, moved to England.

Then came the Easter Rising of 1916, led by men and women he had long known, some of whom were executed or imprisoned by the British. Persuaded by Gonne (whose estranged husband was one of the executed leaders) that "tragic dignity had returned to Ireland," Yeats returned. His culturally nationalist work had helped inspire the poet revolutionaries, and so he asked himself, as he put it in the late poem "Man and the Echo," did his work "send out / Certain men the English shot?" Yeats's nationalism and antinationalism, his divided loyalties to Ireland and to England, find powerfully ambivalent expression in "Easter, 1916" and other poems. Throughout his poetry he brilliantly mediates between contending aspects of himself—late-Romantic visionary and astringent modern skeptic, Irish patriot and irreverent antinationalist, shrewd man of action and esoteric dreamer. As he said: "We make out of the quarrel with others, rhetoric, but of the quarrel with ourselves, poetry." Conceiving consciousness as conflict, he fashioned a kind of poetry that could embody the contradictory feelings and ideas of his endless inner debate.

To mark his recommitment to Ireland, Yeats refurbished and renamed Thoor (Castle) Ballylee, the Norman tower on Lady Gregory's land, in which he lived off and on, and which became, along with its inner winding stair, a central symbol in his later poetry. In 1922 he was appointed a senator of the recently established Irish Free State, and he served until 1928, playing an active part not only in promoting the arts but also in general political affairs, in which he supported the views of the minority Protestant landed class. At the same time he was continuing his esoteric studies. He married Georgie (changed by Yeats to George) Hyde Lees in 1917, when he was fifty-two, and she proved so sympathetic to his imaginative needs that the automatic writing she produced for several years (believed by Yeats to have been dictated by spirits) gave him the elements of a symbolic system that he later worked out in his book *A Vision* (1925, 1937). The system was a theory of the movements of history and of the different types of personality, each movement and type being related to a different phase of the moon. At the center of the symbolic system were the interpenetrating cones, or "gyres," that represented the movement through major cycles of history and across antitheses of human personality.

He compressed and embodied his personal mythology in visionary poems of great scope, linguistic force, and incantatory power, such as "The Second Coming" and "Leda and the Swan." In poems of the 1920s and 1930s, winding stairs, spinning tops, "gyres," spirals of all kinds, are important symbols, serving as a means of resolving some of the contraries that had arrested him from the beginning—paradoxes of time and eternity, change and continuity, spirit and the body, life and art. If his earliest poetry was sometimes static, a beautifully stitched tapestry laden with symbols of inner states, his late poetry became more dynamic, its propulsive syntax and muscular rhythms more suited to his themes of lust, rage, and the body. He had once screened these out of his verse as unpoetic, along with war, violence, "the mire of human veins." Now he embraced the mortal world intensely. In "A Dialogue of Self and Soul," the self defies the soul's injunction to leave the world behind: "I am content to live it all again / And yet again, if it be life to pitch / Into the frog-spawn of a blind man's ditch." Yeats no longer sought transcendence of the human, but instead aimed for the active interpenetration of the corporeal and the visionary. In his Nietzsche-inspired poems of "tragic joy," such as "Lapis Lazuli," he affirmed ruin and destruction as necessary to imaginative creation.

One key to Yeats's greatness is that there are many different Yeatses: a hard-nosed skeptic and an esoteric idealist, a nativist and a cosmopolitan, an Irish nationalist and an ironic antinationalist, a Romantic brooding on loss and unrequited desire and a modernist mocking idealism, nostalgia, and contemporary society. Similarly, in his poetic innovations and consolidations, he is both a conservative and a radical. That is, he is a literary traditionalist, working within such inherited genres as love poetry, the elegy, the self-elegy, the sonnet, and the occasional poem on public themes. But he is also a restless innovator who disrupts generic conventions, breaking up the coherence of the sonnet, de-idealizing the dead mourned in elegies, and bringing into public poems an intense personal ambivalence. In matters of form, too, he rhymes but often in off-rhyme, uses standard meters but bunches or scatters their stresses, employs an elegant syntax that nevertheless has the passionate urgency of colloquial speech; his diction, tone, enjambments, and stanzas intermix ceremony with contortion, controlled artifice with wayward unpredictability. A difficulty in reading Yeats— but also one of the great rewards—is comprehending his manysidedness.

Like Pound, T. S. Eliot, and Windham Lewis, Yeats was attracted to right-wing politics, and in the 1930s he was briefly drawn to fascism. His late interest in authoritarian politics arose in part from his desire for a feudal, aristocratic society that, unlike middle-class culture, in his view, might allow the imagination to flourish, and in part from his anticolonialism, since he thought a fascist Spain, for example, would "weaken the British Empire." But eventually he was appalled by all political ideologies, and the grim prophecy of "The Second Coming" seemed to him increasingly apt.

Written in a rugged, colloquial, and concrete language, Yeats's last poems have a controlled yet startling wildness. His return to life, to "the foul rag-and-bone shop of the heart," is one of the most impressive final phases of any poet's career. In one of his last letters he wrote: "When I try to put all into a phrase I say, 'Man can embody truth but he cannot know it.' . . . The abstract is not life and everywhere draws out its contradictions. You can refute Hegel but not the Saint or the Song of Sixpence." He died in southern France just before the beginning of World War II. His grave is, as his poem directed, near Sligo, "under Ben Bulben." He left behind a body of verse that, in variety and power, has been an enduring influence for English-language poets around the globe, from W. H. Auden and Seamus Heaney to Derek Walcott and A. K. Ramanujan.

The Stolen Child[1]

Where dips the rocky highland
Of Sleuth Wood[2] in the lake,
There lies a leafy island
Where flapping herons wake
5   The drowsy water-rats;
There we've hid our faery vats,

---

1. I.e., a child stolen by fairies to be their companion, as in Irish folklore.
2. This and other places mentioned in the poem are in County Sligo, in the west of Ireland, where Yeats spent much of his childhood.

Full of berries
And of reddest stolen cherries.
Come away, O human child!
10 *To the waters and the wild*
With a faery, hand in hand,
For the world's more full of weeping than you can understand.

Where the wave of moonlight glosses
The dim grey sands with light,
15 Far off by furthest Rosses
We foot it all the night,
Weaving olden dances,
Mingling hands and mingling glances
Till the moon has taken flight;
20 To and fro we leap
And chase the frothy bubbles,
While the world is full of troubles
And is anxious in its sleep.
Come away, O human child!
25 *To the waters and the wild*
With a faery, hand in hand,
For the world's more full of weeping than you can understand.

Where the wandering water gushes
From the hills above Glen-Car,
30 In pools among the rushes
That scarce could bathe a star,
We seek for slumbering trout
And whispering in their ears
Give them unquiet dreams;
35 Leaning softly out
From ferns that drop their tears
Over the young streams.
Come away, O human child!
To the waters and the wild
40 *With a faery, hand in hand,*
For the world's more full of weeping than you can understand.

Away with us he's going,
The solemn-eyed:
He'll hear no more the lowing
45 Of the calves on the warm hillside
Or the kettle on the hob
Sing peace into his breast,
Or see the brown mice bob
Round and round the oatmeal-chest.
50 *For he comes, the human child,*
To the waters and the wild
With a faery, hand in hand,
From a world more full of weeping than he can understand.

1886, 1889

Down by the Salley Gardens[1]

Down by the salley gardens my love and I did meet;
She passed the salley gardens with little snow-white feet.
She bid me take love easy, as the leaves grow on the tree;
But I, being young and foolish, with her would not agree.

5   In a field by the river my love and I did stand,
And on my leaning shoulder she laid her snow-white hand.
She bid me take life easy, as the grass grows on the weirs;°   *dams*
But I was young and foolish, and now am full of tears.

                                                                    1889

The Rose of the World[1]

Who dreamed that beauty passes like a dream?
For these red lips, with all their mournful pride,
Mournful that no new wonder may betide,
Troy[2] passed away in one high funeral gleam,
5   And Usna's children died.[3]

We and the labouring world are passing by:
Amid men's souls, that waver and give place
Like the pale waters in their wintry race,
Under the passing stars, foam of the sky,
10   Lives on this lonely face.

Bow down, archangels, in your dim abode:
Before you were, or any hearts to beat,
Weary and kind one lingered by His seat;
He made the world to be a grassy road
15   Before her wandering feet.

                                                                    1892, 1895

---

1. Originally titled "An Old Song Resung," with Yeats's footnote: "This is an attempt to reconstruct an old song from three lines imperfectly remembered by an old peasant woman in the village of Ballysodare, Sligo, who often sings them to herself." "Salley": a variant of *sallow*, a species of willow tree.
1. The Platonic idea of eternal beauty. "I notice upon reading these poems for the first time for several years that the quality symbolized as The Rose differs from the Intellectual Beauty of Shelley and of Spenser in that I have imagined it as suffering with man and not as something pursued and seen

from afar" [Yeats, in 1925]. Yeats wrote this poem to Maud Gonne.
2. Ancient city destroyed by the Greeks, according to legend, after the abduction of the beautiful Helen.
3. In Old Irish legend the Ulster warrior Naiose, son of Usna or Usnach (pronounced *Úskna*) carried off the beautiful Deirdre, whom King Conchubar of Ulster had intended to marry, and with his two brothers took her to Scotland. Eventually Conchubar lured the four of them back to Ireland and killed the three brothers.

The Lake Isle of Innisfree[1]

I will arise and go now, and go to Innisfree,
And a small cabin build there, of clay and wattles[2] made:
Nine bean-rows will I have there, a hive for the honey-bee,
And live alone in the bee-loud glade.

5   And I shall have some peace there, for peace comes dropping slow,
Dropping from the veils of the morning to where the cricket sings;
There midnight's all a glimmer, and noon a purple glow,
And evening full of the linnet's wings.

I will arise and go now, for always night and day
10 I hear lake water lapping with low sounds by the shore;
While I stand on the roadway, or on the pavements grey,
I hear it in the deep heart's core.

1890   1890, 1892

The Sorrow of Love[1]

The brawling of a sparrow in the eaves,
The brilliant moon and all the milky sky,
And all that famous harmony of leaves,
Had blotted out man's image and his cry.

5   A girl arose that had red mournful lips
And seemed the greatness of the world in tears,
Doomed like Odysseus and the labouring ships
And proud as Priam murdered with his peers;[2]

Arose, and on the instant clamorous eaves,
10 A climbing moon upon an empty sky,
And all that lamentation of the leaves,
Could but compose man's image and his cry.

1891   1892, 1925

---

1. Inis Fraoigh (Heather Island) is a small island in Lough Gill, near Sligo, in the west of Ireland. In his autobiography Yeats writes: "I had still the ambition, formed in Sligo in my teens, of living in imitation of Thoreau on Innisfree . . . and when walking through Fleet Street [in London] very homesick I heard a little tinkle of water and saw a fountain in a shop-window which balanced a little ball upon its jet, and began to remember lake water. From the sudden remembrance came my poem Innisfree, my first lyric with anything in its rhythm of my own music."
2. Stakes interwoven with twigs or branches.
1. For earlier versions of this poem, see "Poems in Process," in the appendices to this volume.
2. Odysseus (whom the Romans called Ulysses) is the hero of Homer's Odyssey, which describes how, after having fought in the siege of Troy, he wandered for ten years before reaching his home, the Greek island of Ithaca. Priam was king of Troy at the time of the siege and was killed when the Greeks captured the city.

When You Are Old[1]

When you are old and grey and full of sleep,
And nodding by the fire, take down this book,
And slowly read, and dream of the soft look
Your eyes had once, and of their shadows deep;

5   How many loved your moments of glad grace,
And loved your beauty with love false or true,
But one man loved the pilgrim soul in you,
And loved the sorrows of your changing face;

And bending down beside the glowing bars,[2]
10   Murmur, a little sadly, how Love fled
And paced upon the mountains overhead
And hid his face amid a crowd of stars.

1891   1892, 1899

Who Goes with Fergus?[1]

Who will go drive with Fergus now,
And pierce the deep wood's woven shade,
And dance upon the level shore?
Young man, lift up your russet brow,
5   And lift your tender eyelids, maid,
And brood on hopes and fear no more.

And no more turn aside and brood
Upon love's bitter mystery;
For Fergus rules the brazen cars,°   *bronze chariots*
10   And rules the shadows of the wood,
And the white breast of the dim sea
And all dishevelled wandering stars.

                                                          1893

The Man Who Dreamed of Faeryland

He stood among a crowd at Drumahair;[1]
His heart hung all upon a silken dress,

---

1. A poem suggested by a sonnet by the French poet Pierre de Ronsard (1524–1585); it begins: "Quand vous serez bien vieille, au soir, à la chandelle" (When you are quite old, in the evening by candlelight).
2. I.e., of the grate.
1. In a late version of this Irish heroic legend, Fergus, "king of the proud Red Branch Kings," gave up his throne voluntarily to King Conchubar of Ulster to learn by dreaming and meditating the bitter wisdom of the poet and philosopher.
1. This and other place-names in the poem refer to places in County Sligo.

And he had known at last some tenderness,
Before earth took him to her stony care;
5   But when a man poured fish into a pile,
It seemed they raised their little silver heads,
And sang what gold morning or evening sheds
Upon a woven world-forgotten isle
Where people love beside the ravelled[2] seas;
10   That Time can never mar a lover's vows
Under that woven changeless roof of boughs:
The singing shook him out of his new ease.

He wandered by the sands of Lissadell;
His mind ran all on money cares and fears,
15   And he had known at last some prudent years
Before they heaped his grave under the hill;
But while he passed before a plashy place,
A lug-worm with its grey and muddy mouth
Sang that somewhere to north or west or south
20   There dwelt a gay, exulting, gentle race
Under the golden or the silver skies;
That if a dancer stayed his hungry foot
It seemed the sun and moon were in the fruit:
And at that singing he was no more wise.
25   He mused beside the well of Scanavin,
He mused upon his mockers: without fail
His sudden vengeance were a country tale,
When earthy night had drunk his body in;
But one small knot-grass growing by the pool
30   Sang where—unnecessary cruel voice—
Old silence bids its chosen race rejoice,
Whatever ravelled waters rise and fall
Or stormy silver fret the gold of day,
And midnight there enfold them like a fleece
35   And lover there by lover be at peace.
The tale drove his fine angry mood away.

He slept under the hill of Lugnagall;
And might have known at last unhaunted sleep
Under that cold and vapour-turbaned steep,
40   Now that the earth had taken man and all:
Did not the worms that spired about his bones
Proclaim with that unwearied, reedy cry
That God has laid His fingers on the sky,
That from those fingers glittering summer runs
45   Upon the dancer by the dreamless wave.
Why should those lovers that no lovers miss
Dream, until God burn Nature with a kiss?
The man has found no comfort in the grave.

1891, 1930

___

2. Tangled; here turbulent.

Adam's Curse[1]

We sat together at one summer's end,
That beautiful mild woman, your close friend,
And you and I,[2] and talked of poetry.
I said, "A line will take us hours maybe;
5 Yet if it does not seem a moment's thought,
Our stitching and unstitching has been naught.
Better go down upon your marrow-bones
And scrub a kitchen pavement, or break stones
Like an old pauper, in all kinds of weather;
10 For to articulate sweet sounds together
Is to work harder than all these, and yet
Be thought an idler by the noisy set
Of bankers, schoolmasters, and clergymen
The martyrs call the world."

       And thereupon
15 That beautiful mild woman for whose sake
There's many a one shall find out all heartache
On finding that her voice is sweet and low
Replied, "To be born woman is to know—
Although they do not talk of it at school—
20 That we must labour to be beautiful."

I said, "It's certain there is no fine thing
Since Adam's fall but needs much labouring.
There have been lovers who thought love should be
So much compounded of high courtesy
25 That they would sigh and quote with learned looks
Precedents out of beautiful old books;
Yet now it seems an idle trade enough."

We sat grown quiet at the name of love;
We saw the last embers of daylight die,
30 And in the trembling blue-green of the sky
A moon, worn as if it had been a shell
Washed by time's waters as they rose and fell
About the stars and broke in days and years.

I had a thought for no one's but your ears:
35 That you were beautiful, and that I strove
To love you in the old high way of love;
That it had all seemed happy, and yet we'd grown
As weary-hearted as that hollow moon.

Nov. 1902   1902, 1922

1. When Adam was evicted from the Garden of
Eden, God cursed him with a life of toil and labor
(Genesis 3.17–19).

2. The two women in the poem are modeled on
Maud Gonne and her sister, Kathleen Pilcher
(1868–1919).

No Second Troy

Why should I blame her[1] that she filled my days
With misery, or that she would of late
Have taught to ignorant men most violent ways,
Or hurled the little streets upon the great,
5   Had they but courage equal to desire?
What could have made her peaceful with a mind
That nobleness made simple as a fire,
With beauty like a tightened bow, a kind
That is not natural in an age like this,
10   Being high and solitary and most stern?
Why, what could she have done, being what she is?
Was there another Troy for her to burn?[2]

Dec. 1908   1910

The Fascination of What's Difficult[1]

The fascination of what's difficult
Has dried the sap out of my veins, and rent
Spontaneous joy and natural content
Out of my heart. There's something ails our colt[2]
5   That must, as if it had not holy blood
Nor on Olympus[3] leaped from cloud to cloud,
Shiver under the lash, strain, sweat and jolt
As though it dragged road metal. My curse on plays
That have to be set up in fifty ways,
10   On the day's war with every knave and dolt,
Theatre business, management of men.
I swear before the dawn comes round again
I'll find the stable and pull out the bolt.

Sept. 1909–Mar. 1910   1910

A Coat

I made my song a coat
Covered with embroideries
Out of old mythologies
From heel to throat;

1. Maud Gonne, whose revolutionary activities are at issue in the poem.
2. Helen of Troy was the legendary cause of the Trojan War and thus of Troy's destruction.
1. Written when Yeats was director-manager of the Abbey Theatre. "Subject. To complain of the fascination of what's difficult. It spoils spontaneity and pleasure, and wastes time. Repeat the line ending difficult three times and rhyme on bolt, exalt, colt, jolt" [Yeats's diary for September 1909].
2. Pegasus, in Greek mythology a winged horse associated with poetry.
3. A mountain in Greece; the home of the gods.

5   But the fools caught it,
Wore it in the world's eyes
As though they'd wrought it.
Song, let them take it,
For there's more enterprise
10   In walking naked.

1912   1914

September 1913

What need you,[1] being come to sense,
But fumble in a greasy till°   *cash register*
And add the halfpence to the pence
And prayer to shivering prayer, until
5   You have dried the marrow from the bone;
For men were born to pray and save:
Romantic Ireland's dead and gone,
It's with O'Leary[2] in the grave.

Yet they were of a different kind,
10   The names that stilled your childish play,
They have gone about the world like wind,
But little time had they to pray
For whom the hangman's rope was spun,
And what, God help us, could they save?
15   Romantic Ireland's dead and gone,
It's with O'Leary in the grave.

Was it for this the wild geese[3] spread
The grey wing upon every tide;
For this that all that blood was shed,
20   For this Edward Fitzgerald died,
And Robert Emmet and Wolfe Tone,[4]
All that delirium of the brave?
Romantic Ireland's dead and gone,
It's with O'Leary in the grave.

25   Yet could we turn the years again,
And call those exiles as they were

1. Members of the new, largely Roman Catholic middle class. When the art dealer Hugh Lane (d. 1915) offered to give his collection of French impressionist paintings to the city of Dublin, provided they were permanently housed in a suitable gallery, Yeats became angry over fierce public opposition to funding the project.
2. John O'Leary (1830–1907), Irish nationalist, who, after five years' imprisonment and fifteen years' exile, returned to Dublin in 1885; he rallied the young Yeats to the cause of literary nationalism.
3. Popular name for the Irish who, because of the penal laws against Catholics (1695–1727), were forced to flee to the Continent.
4. Theobald Wolfe Tone (1763–1798), one of the chief founders of the United Irishmen (an Irish nationalist organization) and leader of the 1798 Irish Rising, committed suicide in prison. Lord Edward Fitzgerald (1763–1798), British officer who, after being dismissed from the army for disloyal activities, joined the United Irishmen, helped lead the 1798 Irish Rising, and died in prison. Robert Emmet (1778–1803), a leader of the abortive 1803 Irish Nationalist Revolt, was hanged for treason.

In all their loneliness and pain,
You'd cry, "Some woman's yellow hair
Has maddened every mother's son":
30   They weighed so lightly what they gave.
But let them be, they're dead and gone,
They're with O'Leary in the grave.

Sept. 1913   1913

Easter, 1916[1]

I have met them at close of day
Coming with vivid faces
From counter or desk among grey
Eighteenth-century houses.
5   I have passed with a nod of the head
Or polite meaningless words,
Or have lingered awhile and said
Polite meaningless words,
And thought before I had done
10 Of a mocking tale or a gibe
To please a companion
Around the fire at the club,
Being certain that they and I
But lived where motley[2] is worn:
15 All changed, changed utterly:
A terrible beauty is born.

That woman's days were spent
In ignorant good-will,
Her nights in argument
20 Until her voice grew shrill.
What voice more sweet than hers
When, young and beautiful,
She rode to harriers?[3]
This man had kept a school
25 And rode our wingèd horse;[4]
This other his helper and friend[5]
Was coming into his force;
He might have won fame in the end,
So sensitive his nature seemed,
30 So daring and sweet his thought.

1. During the Easter Rising of 1916, Irish nationalists revolted against the British government and proclaimed an Irish Republic. Nearly sixteen hundred Irish Volunteers and two hundred members of the Citizen Army seized buildings and a park in Dublin. The rebellion began on Easter Monday, April 24, 1916, and was crushed in six days. Over the next two weeks fifteen of the leaders were executed by firing squad. Yeats knew the chief nationalist leaders personally. For more on the Easter Rising, see "Imagining Ireland" at Norton Literature Online.

2. The multicolored clothes of a jester.
3. Constance Gore-Booth (1868–1927), afterward Countess Markievicz, took a prominent role in the uprising. Her death sentence was reduced to imprisonment. The other rebel leaders to whom Yeats refers were executed.
4. Padraic Pearse (1879–1916), founder of a boys' school in Dublin and poet—hence the "winged horse," or Pegasus, the horse of the Muses.
5. Thomas MacDonagh (1878–1916), poet and dramatist.

This other man I had dreamed
A drunken, vainglorious lout.[6]
He had done most bitter wrong
To some who are near my heart,
35 Yet I number him in the song;
He, too, has resigned his part
In the casual comedy;
He, too, has been changed in his turn,
Transformed utterly:
40 A terrible beauty is born.

Hearts with one purpose alone
Through summer and winter seem
Enchanted to a stone
To trouble the living stream.
45 The horse that comes from the road,
The rider, the birds that range
From cloud to tumbling cloud,
Minute by minute they change;
A shadow of cloud on the stream
50 Changes minute by minute;
A horse-hoof slides on the brim,
And a horse plashes within it;
The long-legged moor-hens dive,
And hens to moor-cocks call;
55 Minute by minute they live:
The stone's in the midst of all.

Too long a sacrifice
Can make a stone of the heart.
O when may it suffice?
60 That is Heaven's part, our part
To murmur name upon name,
As a mother names her child
When sleep at last has come
On limbs that had run wild.
65 What is it but nightfall?
No, no, not night but death;
Was it needless death after all?
For England may keep faith
For all that is done and said.[7]
70 We know their dream; enough
To know they dreamed and are dead;
And what if excess of love
Bewildered them till they died?
I write it out in a verse—
75 MacDonagh and MacBride
And Connolly[8] and Pearse

---

6. Major John MacBride (1865–1916), Irish revolutionary and estranged husband of Maud Gonne.
7. In 1914 the English government had passed Home Rule for Ireland into law, but because of World War I had suspended it, promising to implement it later.
8. James Connolly (1870–1916), a trade-union organizer and military commander of the rebellion.

Now and in time to be,
Wherever green is worn,
Are changed, changed utterly:
80 A terrible beauty is born.

May–Sept. 1916   1916, 1920

The Wild Swans at Coole[1]

The trees are in their autumn beauty,
The woodland paths are dry,
Under the October twilight the water
Mirrors a still sky;
5 Upon the brimming water among the stones
Are nine-and-fifty swans.

The nineteenth autumn has come upon me
Since I first made my count;[2]
I saw, before I had well finished,
10 All suddenly mount
And scatter wheeling in great broken rings
Upon their clamorous wings.

I have looked upon those brilliant creatures,
And now my heart is sore.
15 All's changed since I, hearing at twilight,
The first time on this shore,
The bell-beat of their wings above my head,
Trod with a lighter tread.

Unwearied still, lover by lover,
20 They paddle in the cold
Companionable streams or climb the air;
Their hearts have not grown old;
Passion or conquest, wander where they will,
Attend upon them still.

25 But now they drift on the still water,
Mysterious, beautiful;
Among what rushes will they build,
By what lake's edge or pool
Delight men's eyes when I awake some day
30 To find they have flown away?

Oct. 1916   1917

---

1. Coole Park, in County Galway, was the estate
of the Irish playwright Lady Augusta Gregory
(1852–1932).

2. Yeats made his first long visit to Coole in 1897;
from then on he spent summers there, often staying into the fall.

In Memory of Major Robert Gregory[1]

1

Now that we're almost settled in our house
I'll name the friends that cannot sup with us
Beside a fire of turf° in th' ancient tower,[2]   *peat*
And having talked to some late hour
5   Climb up the narrow winding stair to bed:
Discoverers of forgotten truth
Or mere companions of my youth,
All, all are in my thoughts to-night being dead.

2

Always we'd have the new friend meet the old
10   And we are hurt if either friend seem cold,
And there is salt to lengthen out the smart
In the affections of our heart,
And quarrels are blown up upon that head;
But not a friend that I would bring
15   This night can set us quarrelling,
For all that come into my mind are dead.

3

Lionel Johnson[3] comes the first to mind,
That loved his learning better than mankind,
Though courteous to the worst; much falling he
20   Brooded upon sanctity
Till all his Greek and Latin learning seemed
A long blast upon the horn that brought
A little nearer to his thought
A measureless consummation that he dreamed.

4

25   And that enquiring man John Synge[4] comes next,
That dying chose the living world for text
And never could have rested in the tomb
But that, long travelling, he had come
Towards nightfall upon certain set apart
30   In a most desolate stony place,
Towards nightfall upon a race
Passionate and simple like his heart.

---

1. Robert Gregory (1881–1918) was the only child of Lady Augusta Gregory. The first printing of this elegy included the following note: "(Major Robert Gregory, R.F.C. [Royal Flying Corps], M.C. [Military Cross], Legion of Honour, was killed in action on the Italian Front, January 23, 1918)." For another of Yeats's poems on Gregory's death, see "Representing the Great War" at Norton Literature Online.
2. In 1917 Yeats purchased the Norman tower Thor Ballylee, near Lady Gregory's home in Coole

Park. While that residence was being renovated, Yeats and his wife were living in a house that Lady Gregory had lent them.
3. English poet and scholar (1867–1902); he was "much falling" (line 19) because of his drinking.
4. Irish playwright (1871–1909), associated with the Irish literary renaissance and the Abbey Theatre. When Yeats first met Synge, in 1896, he encouraged him to travel to the Aran Islands ("a most desolate and stony place") and write about its rural residents.

5

And then I think of old George Pollexfen,[5]
In muscular youth well known to Mayo[6] men
35 For horsemanship at meets or at racecourses,
That could have shown how pure-bred horses
And solid men, for all their passion, live
But as the outrageous stars incline
By opposition, square and trine;[7]
40 Having grown sluggish and contemplative.

6

They were my close companions many a year,
A portion of my mind and life, as it were,
And now their breathless faces seem to look
Out of some old picture-book;
45 I am accustomed to their lack of breath,
But not that my dear friend's dear son,
Our Sidney[8] and our perfect man,
Could share in that discourtesy of death.

7

For all things the delighted eye now sees
50 Were loved by him;[9] the old storm-broken trees
That cast their shadows upon road and bridge;
The tower set on the stream's edge;
The ford where drinking cattle make a stir
Nightly, and startled by that sound
55 The water-hen must change her ground;
He might have been your heartiest welcomer.

8

When with the Galway foxhounds he would ride
From Castle Taylor to the Roxborough side[1]
Or Esserkelly plain, few kept his pace;
60 At Mooneen he had leaped a place
So perilous that half the astonished meet
Had shut their eyes; and where was it
He rode a race without a bit?
And yet his mind outran the horses' feet.

9

65 We dreamed that a great painter had been born[2]
To cold Clare[3] rock and Galway rock and thorn,
To that stern colour and that delicate line
That are our secret discipline

---

5. Yeats's maternal uncle (1839–1910), with whom he had spent holidays in Sligo as a young man.
6. County in western Ireland.
7. Terms from astrology, in which both Yeats and his uncle were interested.
8. Sir Philip Sidney (1554–1586), English poet and exemplar of the "Renaissance man"; like Gregory, he was killed in battle.

9. Robert Gregory encouraged Yeats to buy the tower.
1. Big country houses in County Galway. Roxborough was Lady Gregory's childhood home.
2. "Robert Gregory painted the Burren Hills and thereby found what promised to grow into a great style, but he had hardly found it before he was killed" (Yeats, "Ireland and the Arts").
3. County south of Galway.

Wherein the gazing heart doubles her might.
70 Soldier, scholar, horseman, he,
And yet he had the intensity
To have published all to be a world's delight.

10

What other could so well have counselled us
In all lovely intricacies of a house
75 As he that practised or that understood
All work in metal or in wood,
In moulded plaster or in carven stone?
Soldier, scholar, horseman, he,
And all he did done perfectly
80 As though he had but that one trade alone.

11

Some burn damp faggots,[4] others may consume
The entire combustible world in one small room
As though dried straw, and if we turn about
The bare chimney is gone black out
85 Because the work had finished in that flare.
Soldier, scholar, horseman, he,
As 'twere all life's epitome,
What made us dream that he could comb grey hair?

12

I had thought, seeing how bitter is that wind
90 That shakes the shutter, to have brought to mind
All those that manhood tried, or childhood loved
Or boyish intellect approved,
With some appropriate commentary on each;
Until imagination brought
95 A fitter welcome; but a thought
Of that late death took all my heart for speech.

June 1918   1918

The Second Coming

Turning and turning in the widening gyre[1]
The falcon cannot hear the falconer;
Things fall apart; the centre cannot hold;
Mere anarchy is loosed upon the world,
5 The blood-dimmed tide is loosed, and everywhere
The ceremony of innocence is drowned;
The best lack all conviction, while the worst
Are full of passionate intensity.[2]

4. Bundles of sticks.
1. Yeats's term (pronounced with a hard g) for a spiraling motion in the shape of a cone. He envisions the two-thousand-year cycle of the Christian age as spiraling toward its end and the next historical cycle as beginning after a violent reversal: "the end of an age, which always receives the revelation of the character of the next age, is represented by the coming of one gyre to its place of greatest expansion and of the other to that of its greatest contraction" [Yeats's note].
2. The poem was written in January 1919, in the aftermath of World War I and the Russian Revolution and on the eve of the Anglo-Irish War.

Surely some revelation is at hand;

10 Surely the Second Coming is at hand.
The Second Coming![3] Hardly are those words out
When a vast image out of *Spiritus Mundi*[4]
Troubles my sight: somewhere in sands of the desert
A shape with lion body and the head of a man,
15 A gaze blank and pitiless as the sun,
Is moving its slow thighs, while all about it
Reel shadows of the indignant desert birds.
The darkness drops again; but now I know
That twenty centuries of stony sleep
20 Were vexed to nightmare by a rocking cradle,
And what rough beast, its hour come round at last,
Slouches towards Bethlehem[5] to be born?

Jan. 1919   1920, 1921

A Prayer for My Daughter

Once more the storm is howling, and half hid
Under this cradle-hood and coverlid
My child sleeps on.[1] There is no obstacle
But Gregory's wood[2] and one bare hill
5 Whereby the haystack- and roof-levelling wind,
Bred on the Atlantic, can be stayed;
And for an hour I have walked and prayed
Because of the great gloom that is in my mind.

I have walked and prayed for this young child an hour
10 And heard the sea-wind scream upon the tower,
And under the arches of the bridge, and scream
In the elms above the flooded stream;
Imagining in excited reverie
That the future years had come,
15 Dancing to a frenzied drum,
Out of the murderous innocence of the sea.

May she be granted beauty and yet not
Beauty to make a stranger's eye distraught,
Or hers before a looking-glass, for such,
20 Being made beautiful overmuch,
Consider beauty a sufficient end,
Lose natural kindness and maybe
The heart-revealing intimacy
That chooses right, and never find a friend.

3. Christ's second coming is heralded by the coming of the Beast of the Apocalypse, or Antichrist (1 John 2.18).
4. The spirit of the universe (Latin); i.e., Yeats said, "a general storehouse of images," a collective unconscious or memory, in which the human race preserves its past memories.

5. Jesus' birthplace.
1. Yeats's daughter and first child, Anne Butler Yeats, was born on February 26, 1919, in Dublin and brought home to Yeats's refitted Norman tower of Thoor Ballylee in Galway.
2. Lady Gregory's wood at Coole, only a few miles from Thoor Ballylee.

25   Helen being chosen found life flat and dull
  And later had much trouble from a fool,[3]
  While that great Queen, that rose out of the spray,[4]
  Being fatherless could have her way
  Yet chose a bandy-leggèd smith for man.
30   It's certain that fine women eat
  A crazy salad with their meat
  Whereby the Horn of Plenty[5] is undone.

  In courtesy I'd have her chiefly learned;
  Hearts are not had as a gift but hearts are earned
35   By those that are not entirely beautiful;
  Yet many, that have played the fool
  For beauty's very self, has charm made wise,
  And many a poor man that has roved,
  Loved and thought himself beloved,
40   From a glad kindness cannot take his eyes.

  May she become a flourishing hidden tree
  That all her thoughts may like the linnet° be,   *small songbird*
  And have no business but dispensing round
  Their magnanimities of sound,
45   Not but in merriment begin a chase,
  Nor but in merriment a quarrel.
  O may she live like some green laurel
  Rooted in one dear perpetual place.

  My mind, because the minds that I have loved,
50   The sort of beauty that I have approved,
  Prosper but little, has dried up of late,
  Yet knows that to be choked with hate
  May well be of all evil chances chief.
  If there's no hatred in a mind
55   Assault and battery of the wind
  Can never tear the linnet from the leaf.

  An intellectual hatred is the worst,
  So let her think opinions are accursed.
  Have I not seen the loveliest woman[6] born
60   Out of the mouth of Plenty's horn,
  Because of her opinionated mind
  Barter that horn and every good
  By quiet natures understood
  For an old bellows full of angry wind?

65   Considering that, all hatred driven hence,
  The soul recovers radical innocence
  And learns at last that it is self-delighting,

---

3. Menelaus, Helen's husband. Her abduction by
Paris precipitated the Trojan War.
4. Venus, born from the sea, was the Roman goddess of love; her husband, Vulcan, was the lame
god of fire and metalwork (line 29).

5. In Greek mythology the goat's horn that suck-
led the god Zeus flowed with nectar and ambrosia;
the cornucopia thus became a symbol of plenty.
6. Maud Gonne.

Self-appeasing, self-affrighting,
And that its own sweet will is Heaven's will;
70   She can, though every face should scowl
And every windy quarter howl
Or every bellows burst, be happy still.

And may her bridegroom bring her to a house
Where all's accustomed, ceremonious;
75   For arrogance and hatred are the wares
Peddled in the thoroughfares.
How but in custom and in ceremony
Are innocence and beauty born?
Ceremony's a name for the rich horn,
80   And custom for the spreading laurel tree.

Feb.–June 1919   1919, 1921

Leda and the Swan[1]

A sudden blow: the great wings beating still
Above the staggering girl, her thighs caressed
By the dark webs, her nape caught in his bill,
He holds her helpless breast upon his breast.

5   How can those terrified vague fingers push
The feathered glory from her loosening thighs?
And how can body, laid in that white rush,
But feel the strange heart beating where it lies?

A shudder in the loins engenders there
10   The broken wall, the burning roof and tower[2]
And Agamemnon dead.
                    Being so caught up,
So mastered by the brute blood of the air,
Did she put on his knowledge with his power
Before the indifferent beak could let her drop?

Sept. 1923   1924, 1928

1. In Greek mythology the god Zeus, in the form of a swan, raped Leda, a mortal. Helen, Clytemnestra, Castor, and Pollux were the children of this union. Yeats saw Leda's rape as the beginning of a new age, analogous with the dove's annunciation to Mary of Jesus' conception: "I imagine the annunciation that founded Greece as made to Leda, remembering that they showed in a Spartan temple, strung up to the roof as a holy relic, an unhatched egg of hers, and that from one of her eggs came love and from the other war" (*A Vision*). For the author's revisions while composing the poem, see "Poems in Process," in the appendices to this volume.
2. I.e., the destruction of Troy, caused by Helen's abduction by Paris. Agamemnon, the leader of the Greek army that besieged Troy, was murdered by his wife, Clytemnestra, the other daughter of Leda and the swan.

Sailing to Byzantium[1]

1

That is no country for old men. The young
In one another's arms, birds in the trees,
—Those dying generations—at their song,
The salmon-falls, the mackerel-crowded seas,
5   Fish, flesh, or fowl, commend all summer long
Whatever is begotten, born, and dies.
Caught in that sensual music all neglect
Monuments of unageing intellect.

2

An aged man is but a paltry thing,
10 A tattered coat upon a stick, unless
Soul clap its hands and sing,[2] and louder sing
For every tatter in its mortal dress,
Nor is there singing school but studying
Monuments of its own magnificence;
15 And therefore I have sailed the seas and come
To the holy city of Byzantium.

3

O sages standing in God's holy fire
As in the gold mosaic of a wall,[3]
Come from the holy fire, perne in a gyre,[4]
20 And be the singing-masters of my soul.
Consume my heart away; sick with desire
And fastened to a dying animal
It knows not what it is; and gather me
Into the artifice of eternity.

4

25 Once out of nature I shall never take
My bodily form from any natural thing,
But such a form as Grecian goldsmiths make
Of hammered gold and gold enamelling
To keep a drowsy Emperor awake;[5]
30 Or set upon a golden bough to sing
To lords and ladies of Byzantium
Of what is past, or passing, or to come.

Sept. 1926   1927

1. Yeats wrote in *A Vision:* "I think that if I could be given a month of Antiquity and leave to spend it where I chose, I would spend it in Byzantium [now Istanbul] a little before Justinian opened St. Sophia and closed the Academy of Plato [in the 6th century C.E.]. . . . I think that in early Byzantium, maybe never before or since in recorded history, religious, aesthetic and practical life were one, that architect and artificers . . . spoke to the multitude and the few alike. The painter, the mosaic worker, the worker in gold and silver, the illuminator of sacred books, were almost impersonal, almost perhaps without the consciousness of individual design, absorbed in their subject-matter and that the vision of a whole people."

2. The poet William Blake (1757–1827) saw the soul of his dead brother rising to heaven, "clapping his hands for joy."

3. The mosaics in San Apollinaire Nuovo, in Ravenna, Italy, depict rows of Christian saints on a gold background; Yeats saw them in 1907.

4. I.e., whirl in a spiral.

5. I have read somewhere that in the Emperor's palace at Byzantium was a tree made of gold and silver, and artificial birds that sang [Yeats's note].

Among School Children

1

I walk through the long schoolroom questioning;
A kind old nun in a white hood replies;
The children learn to cipher° and to sing,   *do arithmetic*
To study reading-books and history,
5   To cut and sew, be neat in everything
In the best modern way—the children's eyes
In momentary wonder stare upon
A sixty-year-old smiling public man.[1]

2

I dream of a Ledaean[2] body, bent
10   Above a sinking fire, a tale that she
Told of a harsh reproof, or trivial event
That changed some childish day to tragedy—
Told, and it seemed that our two natures blent
Into a sphere from youthful sympathy,
15   Or else, to alter Plato's parable,
Into the yolk and white of the one shell.[3]

3

And thinking of that fit of grief or rage
I look upon one child or t'other there
And wonder if she stood so at that age—
20   For even daughters of the swan can share
Something of every paddler's heritage—
And had that colour upon cheek or hair,
And thereupon my heart is driven wild:
She stands before me as a living child.

4

25   Her present image floats into the mind—
Did Quattrocento[4] finger fashion it
Hollow of cheek as though it drank the wind
And took a mess of shadows for its meat?
And I though never of Ledaean kind
30   Had pretty plumage once—enough of that,
Better to smile on all that smile, and show
There is a comfortable kind of old scarecrow.

5

What youthful mother, a shape upon her lap
Honey of generation had betrayed,
35   And that must sleep, shriek, struggle to escape
As recollection or the drug decide,[5]

1. Yeats, as part of his work in the Irish Senate, visited a Montessori school in Waterford in 1926.
2. A body like Leda's. Yeats associated her daughter, Helen of Troy, with Maud Gonne.
3. In the *Symposium*, by the Greek philosopher Plato (ca. 428–ca. 348 B.C.E.), Aristophanes argues that "the primeval man" was both male and female but was divided (like an egg separated into yoke and white); the resulting two beings come together in love to become one again.
4. I.e., the skill of a 15th-century Italian painter.
5. I have taken the "honey of generation" from Porphyry's essay on "The Cave of Nymphs" [Yeats's note]. Porphyry (ca. 234–ca. 305 C.E.) was a Neoplatonic philosopher.

Would think her son, did she but see that shape
With sixty or more winters on its head,
A compensation for the pang of his birth,
40 Or the uncertainty of his setting forth?

6

Plato thought nature but a spume that plays
Upon a ghostly paradigm of things;[6]
Solider Aristotle played the taws
Upon the bottom of a king of kings;[7]
45 World-famous golden-thighed Pythagoras[8]
Fingered upon a fiddle-stick or strings
What a star sang and careless Muses heard:
Old clothes upon old sticks to scare a bird.

7

Both nuns and mothers worship images,
50 But those the candles light are not as those
That animate a mother's reveries,
But keep a marble or a bronze repose.
And yet they too break hearts—O Presences
That passion, piety or affection knows,
55 And that all heavenly glory symbolise—
O self-born mockers of man's enterprise;

8

Labour is blossoming or dancing where
The body is not bruised to pleasure soul,
Nor beauty born out of its own despair,
60 Nor blear-eyed wisdom out of midnight oil.
O chestnut tree, great-rooted blossomer,
Are you the leaf, the blossom or the bole?°   trunk
O body swayed to music, O brightening glance,
How can we know the dancer from the dance?

June 1926   1927

A Dialogue of Self and Soul[1]

I

My Soul. I summon to the winding ancient stair;
Set all your mind upon the steep ascent,
Upon the broken, crumbling battlement,
Upon the breathless starlit air,
5 Upon the star that marks the hidden pole;

---

6. Plato thought nature merely an image of an ideal world that exists elsewhere.
7. Plato's student Aristotle (384–322 B.C.E.) was "solider" because he regarded this world as the authentic one. He tutored Alexander the Great (356–323 B.C.E.), the "king of kings," and disciplined him with the "taws," or leather strap.
8. Greek philosopher (ca. 580–500 B.C.E.), known for his doctrine of the harmony of the spheres and

his discovery of the mathematical basis of musical intervals. His disciples, the Pythagoreans, venerated their master as a god with a golden thigh.
1. In a letter of October 2, 1923, Yeats wrote: "I am writing a new tower poem 'Sword and Tower,' which is a choice of rebirth rather than deliverance from birth. I make my Japanese sword and its silk covering my symbol of life." Junzo Sato, a friend, had given him the ceremonial sword in 1920.

Fix every wandering thought upon
That quarter where all thought is done:
Who can distinguish darkness from the soul?

My Self. The consecrated blade upon my knees
10   Is Sato's ancient blade, still as it was,
Still razor-keen, still like a looking-glass
Unspotted by the centuries;
That flowering, silken, old embroidery, torn
From some court-lady's dress and round
15   The wooden scabbard bound and wound,
Can, tattered, still protect, faded adorn.

My Soul. Why should the imagination of a man
Long past his prime remember things that are
Emblematical of love and war?
20   Think of ancestral night that can,
If but imagination scorn the earth
And intellect its wandering
To this and that and t'other thing,
Deliver from the crime of death and birth.

25   *My Self.* Montashigi, third of his family, fashioned it
Five hundred years ago, about it lie
Flowers from I know not what embroidery—
Heart's purple—and all these I set
For emblems of the day against the tower
30   Emblematical of the night,
And claim as by a soldier's right
A charter to commit the crime once more.

My Soul. Such fullness in that quarter overflows
And falls into the basin of the mind
35   That man is stricken deaf and dumb and blind,
For intellect no longer knows
Is from the *Ought,* or *Knower* from the *Known*—
That is to say, ascends to Heaven;
Only the dead can be forgiven;
40   But when I think of that my tongue's a stone.

2

My Self. A living man is blind and drinks his drop.
What matter if the ditches are impure?
What matter if I live it all once more?
Endure that toil of growing up;
45   The ignominy of boyhood; the distress
Of boyhood changing into man;
The unfinished man and his pain
Brought face to face with his own clumsiness;

The finished man among his enemies?—
50   How in the name of Heaven can he escape
That defiling and disfigured shape

The mirror of malicious eyes
Casts upon his eyes until at last
He thinks that shape must be his shape?
55 And what's the good of an escape
If honour find him in the wintry blast?

I am content to live it all again
And yet again, if it be life to pitch
Into the frog-spawn of a blind man's ditch,
60 A blind man battering blind men;
Or into that most fecund ditch of all,
The folly that man does
Or must suffer, if he woos
A proud woman not kindred of his soul.

65 I am content to follow to its source
Every event in action or in thought;
Measure the lot; forgive myself the lot!
When such as I cast out remorse
So great a sweetness flows into the breast
70 We must laugh and we must sing,
We are blest by everything,
Everything we look upon is blest.

July–Dec. 1927   1929

Byzantium[1]

The unpurged images of day recede;
The Emperor's drunken soldiery are abed;
Night resonance recedes, night-walkers' song
After great cathedral gong;
5 A starlit or a moonlit dome[2] disdains
All that man is,
All mere complexities,
The fury and the mire° of human veins.   *deep mud*

Before me floats an image, man or shade,
10 Shade more than man, more image than a shade;
For Hades' bobbin[3] bound in mummy-cloth
May unwind the winding path;[4]
A mouth that has no moisture and no breath

1. On October 4, 1930, Yeats sent his friend Sturge Moore a copy of this poem, saying: "The poem originates from a criticism of yours. You objected to the last verse of 'Sailing to Byzantium' because a bird made by a goldsmith was just as natural as anything else. That showed me that the idea needed exposition." The previous April, Yeats had noted in his diary: "Subject for a poem": "Describe Byzantium as it is in the system towards the end of the first Christian millennium. A walking mummy. Flames at the street corners where the soul is purified, birds of hammered gold singing in the golden trees, in the harbour [dolphins] offering their backs to the wailing dead that they may carry them to Paradise."
2. Of the great church of St. Sophia.
3. Spool. Hades was the Greek god of the underworld, the realm of the dead.
4. I.e., the spool of people's fate, which spins their destiny and which is wound like a mummy, may be unwound and lead to the timeless world of pure spirit.

Breathless mouths may summon;
15 I hail the superhuman;
I call it death-in-life and life-in-death.⁵

Miracle, bird or golden handiwork,
More miracle than bird or handiwork,
Planted on the starlit golden bough,
20 Can like the cocks of Hades crow,
Or, by the moon embittered, scorn aloud
In glory of changeless metal
Common bird or petal
And all complexities of mire or blood.

25 At midnight on the Emperor's pavement flit
Flames that no faggot° feeds, nor steel has lit,   *bundle of sticks*
Nor storm disturbs, flames begotten of flame,
Where blood-begotten spirits come
And all complexities of fury leave,
30 Dying into a dance,
An agony of trance,
An agony of flame that cannot singe a sleeve.

Astraddle on the dolphin's mire and blood,⁶
Spirit after spirit! The smithies break the flood,
35 The golden smithies of the Emperor!
Marbles of the dancing floor
Break bitter furies of complexity,
Those images that yet
Fresh images beget,
40 That dolphin-torn, that gong-tormented sea.

Sept. 1930   1932

Crazy Jane Talks with the Bishop¹

I met the Bishop on the road
And much said he and I.
"Those breasts are flat and fallen now
Those veins must soon be dry;
5 Live in a heavenly mansion,
Not in some foul sty."

"Fair and foul are near of kin,
And fair needs foul," I cried.
"My friends are gone, but that's a truth
10 Nor grave nor bed denied,

---

5. On Roman tombstones the cock is a herald of rebirth, thus of the continuing cycle of human life.
6. In ancient mythology dolphins were thought to carry the souls of the dead to the Isles of the Blessed.
1. One of a series of poems about an old woman partly modeled on Cracked Mary, an old woman who lived near Lady Gregory.

Learned in bodily lowliness
And in the heart's pride.

"A woman can be proud and stiff
When on love intent;
15   But Love has pitched his mansion in
The place of excrement;
For nothing can be sole or whole
That has not been rent."

Nov. 1931   1932

Lapis Lazuli

(For Harry Clifton)[1]

I have heard that hysterical women say
They are sick of the palette and fiddle-bow,
Of poets that are always gay,
For everybody knows or else should know
5   That if nothing drastic is done[2]
Aeroplane and Zeppelin[3] will come out,
Pitch like King Billy[4] bomb-balls in
Until the town lie beaten flat.

All perform their tragic play,
10   There struts Hamlet, there is Lear,
That's Ophelia, that Cordelia;
Yet they, should the last scene be there,
The great stage curtain about to drop,
If worthy their prominent part in the play,
15   Do not break up their lines to weep.
They know that Hamlet and Lear are gay;
Gaiety transfiguring all that dread.
All men have aimed at, found and lost;
Black out; Heaven blazing into the head:
20   Tragedy wrought to its uttermost.
Though Hamlet rambles and Lear rages,
And all the drop scenes drop at once
Upon a hundred thousand stages,
It cannot grow by an inch or an ounce.

25   On their own feet they came, or on shipboard,
Camel-back, horse-back, ass-back, mule-back,

1. The English writer Harry Clifton (1908–1978) gave Yeats for his seventieth birthday a piece of lapis lazuli, a deep blue stone, "carved by some Chinese sculptor into the semblance of a mountain with temple, trees, paths, and an ascetic and pupil about to climb the mountain. Ascetic, pupil, hard stone, eternal theme of the sensual east. The heroic cry in the midst of despair. But no, I am wrong, the east has its solutions always and therefore knows nothing of tragedy. It is we, not the east, that must raise the heroic cry" [Yeats to Dorothy Wellesley, July 6, 1935].
2. Because Europe was (in 1936) close to war.
3. German zeppelins, or airships, bombed London during World War I.
4. King William III (William of Orange), who defeated the army of King James II at the Battle of the Boyne, in Ireland, in 1690. In a popular ballad, "King William he threw his bomb-balls in, / And set them on fire."

Old civilisations put to the sword.
Then they and their wisdom went to rack:
No handiwork of Callimachus[5]
30 Who handled marble as if it were bronze,
Made draperies that seemed to rise
When sea-wind swept the corner, stands;
His long lamp chimney shaped like the stem
Of a slender palm, stood but a day;
35 All things fall and are built again
And those that build them again are gay.

Two Chinamen, behind them a third,
Are carved in Lapis Lazuli,
Over them flies a long-legged bird
40 A symbol of longevity;
The third, doubtless a serving-man,
Carries a musical instrument.

Every discolouration of the stone,
Every accidental crack or dent
45 Seems a water-course or an avalanche,
Or lofty slope where it still snows
Though doubtless plum or cherry-branch
Sweetens the little half-way house
Those Chinamen climb towards, and I
50 Delight to imagine them seated there;
There, on the mountain and the sky,
On all the tragic scene they stare.
One asks for mournful melodies;
Accomplished fingers begin to play.
55 Their eyes mid many wrinkles, their eyes,
Their ancient, glittering eyes, are gay.

July 1936   1938

Under Ben Bulben[1]

1

Swear by what the Sages spoke
Round the Mareotic Lake[2]
That the Witch of Atlas knew,
Spoke and set the cocks a-crow.

5. Athenian sculptor (5th century B.C.E.), supposedly the originator of the Corinthian column and
of the use of the running drill to imitate folds in
drapery in statues. Yeats wrote of him: "With Callimachus pure Ionic revives again . . . and upon
the only example of his work known to us, a marble
chair, a Persian is represented, and may one not
discover a Persian symbol in that bronze lamp,
shaped like a palm . . . ? But he was an archaistic
workman, and those who set him to work brought
back public life to an older form" (A Vision).
1. A mountain near Sligo; Yeats's grave is in sight
of it, in Drumcliff churchyard.
2. Lake Mareotis, near Alexandria, Egypt, was an
ancient center of Christian Neoplatonism and of
neo-Pythagorean philosophy. The lake is mentioned in Percy Bysshe Shelley's poem "The Witch
of Atlas." In an essay on Shelley, Yeats interprets
the witch as a symbol of timeless, absolute beauty;
passing in a boat by this and another lake, she "sees
all human life shadowed upon its waters . . . and
because she can see the reality of things she is
described as journeying 'in the calm depths' of 'the
wide lake' we journey over unpiloted."

5   Swear by those horsemen, by those women,
Complexion and form prove superhuman,[3]
That pale, long visaged company
That airs an immortality
Completeness of their passions won;
10   Now they ride the wintry dawn
Where Ben Bulben sets the scene.

Here's the gist of what they mean.

2

Many times man lives and dies
Between his two eternities,
15   That of race and that of soul,
And ancient Ireland knew it all.
Whether man dies in his bed
Or the rifle knocks him dead,
A brief parting from those dear
20   Is the worst man has to fear.
Though grave-diggers' toil is long,
Sharp their spades, their muscle strong,
They but thrust their buried men
Back in the human mind again.

3

25   You that Mitchel's prayer have heard
"Send war in our time, O Lord!"[4]
Know that when all words are said
And a man is fighting mad,
Something drops from eyes long blind
30   He completes his partial mind,
For an instant stands at ease,
Laughs aloud, his heart at peace,
Even the wisest man grows tense
With some sort of violence
35   Before he can accomplish fate
Know his work or choose his mate.

4

Poet and sculptor do the work
Nor let the modish painter shirk
What his great forefathers did,
40   Bring the soul of man to God,
Make him fill the cradles right.

---

3. Superhuman beings or fairies, like the Sidhe, believed to ride through the countryside near Ben Bulben.

4. From *Jail Journal,* by the Irish nationalist John Mitchel (1815–1875).

Measurement began our might:
Forms a stark Egyptian thought,
Forms that gentler Phidias[5] wrought.

45 Michael Angelo left a proof
On the Sistine Chapel roof,
Where but half-awakened Adam
Can disturb globe-trotting Madam
Till her bowels are in heat,
50 Proof that there's a purpose set
Before the secret working mind:
Profane perfection of mankind.

Quattrocento[6] put in paint,
On backgrounds for a God or Saint,
55 Gardens where a soul's at ease;
Where everything that meets the eye
Flowers and grass and cloudless sky
Resemble forms that are, or seem
When sleepers wake and yet still dream,
60 And when it's vanished still declare,
With only bed and bedstead there,
That Heavens had opened.

                    Gyres[7] run on;
When that greater dream had gone
Calvert and Wilson, Blake and Claude[8]
65 Prepared a rest for the people of God,
Palmer's[9] phrase, but after that
Confusion fell upon our thought.

5

Irish poets learn your trade
Sing whatever is well made,
70 Scorn the sort now growing up
All out of shape from toe to top,
Their unremembering hearts and heads
Base-born products of base beds.
Sing the peasantry, and then
75 Hard-riding country gentlemen,
The holiness of monks, and after
Porter-drinkers'[1] randy laughter;
Sing the lords and ladies gay
That were beaten into the clay

---

5. Greek sculptor (fl. ca. 490–430 B.C.E.).
6. 15th-century Italian art.
7. Yeats's term for conelike spirals or cycles of history.
8. Edward Calvert (1799–1883), English visionary artist and follower of William Blake (1757–1827), English mystical poet and artist. Richard

Wilson (1714–1782), English landscape painter and disciple of Claude Lorraine (1600–1682), French artist.
9. Samuel Palmer (1805–1881), English landscape painter who admired Blake.
1. Drinkers of dark brown bitter beer.

80 Through seven heroic centuries;[2]
Cast your mind on other days
That we in coming days may be
Still the indomitable Irishry.

6

Under bare Ben Bulben's head
85 In Drumcliff churchyard Yeats is laid,
An ancestor was rector there[3]
Long years ago; a church stands near,
By the road an ancient Cross.
No marble, no conventional phrase,
90 On limestone quarried near the spot
By his command these words are cut:

　　Cast a cold eye
　　On life, on death.
　　Horseman, pass by!

Sept. 1938   1939

Man and the Echo

Man. In a cleft that's christened Alt
　　Under broken stone I halt
　　At the bottom of a pit
　　That broad noon has never lit,
5 　　And shout a secret to the stone.
　　All that I have said and done,
　　Now that I am old and ill,
　　Turns into a question till
　　I lie awake night after night
10 　　And never get the answers right.
　　Did that play of mine[1] send out
　　Certain men the English shot?
　　Did words of mine put too great strain
　　On that woman's reeling brain?[2]
15 　　Could my spoken words have checked
　　That whereby a house[3] lay wrecked?
　　And all seems evil until I
　　Sleepless would lie down and die.

Echo. Lie down and die.

---

2. Since the Norman conquest of Ireland, in the
12th century.
3. Yeats's great-grandfather, the Reverend John
Yeats (1774–1846), was rector of Drumcliff
Church, Sligo.
1. *Cathleen ni Houlihan*, a nationalist play Yeats
wrote with Lady Gregory and in which Maud
Gonne played the title role in 1902. It helped

inspire the Easter Rising of 1916.
2. Margot Ruddock (1907–1951), a young poet
with whom Yeats had a brief affair in the 1930s
and to whom he offered financial support when
she suffered a nervous breakdown.
3. Coole Park, Lady Gregory's home, in disrepair
since her death in 1932.

Man.   That were to shirk
20   The spiritual intellect's great work
And shirk it in vain. There is no release
In a bodkin[4] or disease,
Nor can there be a work so great
As that which cleans man's dirty slate.
25   While man can still his body keep
Wine or love drug him to sleep,
Waking he thanks the Lord that he
Has body and its stupidity,
But body gone he sleeps no more
30   And till his intellect grows sure
That all's arranged in one clear view
Pursues the thoughts that I pursue,
Then stands in judgment on his soul,
And, all work done, dismisses all
35   Out of intellect and sight
And sinks at last into the night.

    Echo. Into the night.

    Man.   O rocky voice
Shall we in that great night rejoice?
What do we know but that we face
40   One another in this place?
But hush, for I have lost the theme
Its joy or night seem but a dream;
Up there some hawk or owl has struck
Dropping out of sky or rock,
45   A stricken rabbit is crying out
And its cry distracts my thought.

1938   1939

The Circus Animals' Desertion

1

I sought a theme and sought for it in vain,
I sought it daily for six weeks or so.
Maybe at last being but a broken man,
I must be satisfied with my heart, although
5 Winter and summer till old age began
My circus animals were all on show,
Those stilted boys, that burnished chariot,
Lion and woman and the Lord knows what.[1]

---

4. Dagger. Cf. *Hamlet* 3.1.77–78: "When he himself might his quietus make / With a bare bodkin."
1. Yeats refers to the ancient Irish heroes of his early work ("Those stilted boys"), the gilded carriage of his play *The Unicorn from the Stars* (1908), and the lion in several of his poems, including "The Second Coming."

2

What can I but enumerate old themes,
10 First that sea-rider Oisin[2] led by the nose
Through three enchanted islands, allegorical dreams,
Vain gaiety, vain battle, vain repose,
Themes of the embittered heart, or so it seems,
That might adorn old songs or courtly shows;
15 But what cared I that set him on to ride,
I, starved for the bosom of his fairy bride.

And then a counter-truth filled out its play,
"The Countess Cathleen"[3] was the name I gave it,
She, pity-crazed, had given her soul away,
20 But masterful Heaven had intervened to save it.
I thought my dear must her own soul destroy
So did fanaticism and hate enslave it,
And this brought forth a dream and soon enough
This dream itself had all my thought and love.

25 And when the Fool and Blind Man stole the bread
Cuchulain fought the ungovernable sea;[4]
Heart mysteries there, and yet when all is said
It was the dream itself enchanted me:
Character isolated by a deed
30 To engross the present and dominate memory.
Players and painted stage took all my love
And not those things that they were emblems of.

3

Those masterful images because complete
Grew in pure mind but out of what began?
35 A mound of refuse or the sweepings of a street,
Old kettles, old bottles, and a broken can,
Old iron, old bones, old rags, that raving slut
Who keeps the till. Now that my ladder's gone
I must lie down where all the ladders start
40 In the foul rag and bone shop of the heart.

1939

---

2. In the long title-poem of Yeats's first successful
book, *The Wanderings of Oisin and Other Poems*
(1889), the legendary poet warrior Oisin (pronounced *Usheen*) is enchanted by the beautiful
fairy woman Niamh (pronounced *Neeve*), who
leads him to the Islands of Delight, of Many Fears,
and of Forgetfulness.
3. A play (published in 1892) about an Irish
countess (an idealized version of Maud Gonne)
who sells her soul to the devil to buy food for the
starving Irish poor but is taken up to heaven (for
God "Looks always on the motive, not the deed").
4. In Yeats's play *On Baile's Strand* (1904), the
legendary warrior Cuchulain (pronounced *Cu-
HOOlin* by Yeats, *KooHULLin* in Irish), crazed by
his discovery that he has killed his son, fights with
the sea.

From Introduction
[A General Introduction for My Work][1]

I. The First Principle

A poet writes always of his personal life, in his finest work out of its tragedies, whatever it be, remorse, lost love or mere loneliness; he never speaks directly as to someone at the breakfast table, there is always a phantasmagoria. Dante and Milton had mythologies, Shakespeare the characters of English history, of traditional romance; even when the poet seems most himself, when Raleigh and gives potentates the lie,[2] or Shelley 'a nerve o'er which do creep the else unfelt oppressions of mankind',[3] or Byron when 'the heart wears out the breast as the sword wears out the sheath',[4] he is never the bundle of accident and incoherence that sits down to breakfast; he has been re-born as an idea, something intended, complete. A novelist might describe his accidence, his incoherence, he must not, he is more type than man, more passion than type. He is Lear, Romeo, Oedipus, Tiresias; he has stepped out of a play and even the woman he loves is Rosalind, Cleopatra, never The Dark Lady.[5] He is part of his own phantasmagoria and we adore him because nature has grown intelligible, and by so doing a part of our creative power. 'When mind is lost in the light of the Self', says the Prashna Upanishad,[6] 'it dreams no more; still in the body it is lost in happiness.' 'A wise man seeks in Self', says the Chāndôgya Upanishad, 'those that are alive and those that are dead and gets what the world cannot give.' The world knows nothing because it has made nothing, we know everything because we have made everything.

II. Subject-Matter

* * *

* * *I am convinced that in two or three generations it will become generally known that the mechanical theory[7] has no reality, that the natural and supernatural are knit together, that to escape a dangerous fanaticism we must study a new science; at that moment Europeans may find something attractive in a Christ posed against a background not of Judaism but of Druidism, not shut off in dead history, but flowing, concrete, phenomenal.

I was born into this faith, have lived in it, and shall die in it; my Christ, a legitimate deduction from the Creed of St Patrick[8] as I think, is that Unity of Being Dante compared to a perfectly proportioned human body, Blake's 'Imag-

---

1. Written in 1937 and originally printed as "A General Introduction for My Work" in Essays and Introductions (1961), the text is excerpted from Later Essays, ed. William H. O'Donnell (1994), vol. 5 of The Collected Works of W. B. Yeats.
2. From "The Lie," by the English writer and explorer Sir Walter Ralegh (1552–1618): "Tell potentates, they live / Acting by others' action; / Not loved unless they give, / Not strong but by a faction: / If potentates reply, / Give potentates the lie."
3. From "Julian and Maddalo," by the English poet Percy Bysshe Shelley (1792–1822).
4. Cf. "So, we'll go no more a roving," by the English poet George Gordon, Lord Byron (p. 616,

lines 5–6).
5. The woman to whom many of Shakespeare's de-idealizing sonnets are addressed. The rest of the names refer to characters in Shakespeare's plays and in Sophocles' ancient Greek drama Oedipus the King.
6. One of a series of ancient philosophical dialogues in Sanskrit. From Ten Principal Upanishads (1937), translated by Yeats and the Indian monk Shri Purohit Swami (1882–1941).
7. Theory explaining the universe in strictly naturalistic, Newtonian terms.
8. From the second paragraph of "The Confession of St. Patrick, or His Epistle to the Irish," by the fifth-century saint, the apostle of Ireland.

ination',[9] what the Upanishads have named 'Self': nor is this unity distant and therefore intellectually understandable, but imminent,[1] differing from man to man and age to age, taking upon itself pain and ugliness, 'eye of newt, and leg of frog'.[2]

Subconscious preoccupation with this theme brought me A Vision,[3] its harsh geometry an incomplete interpretation. The 'Irishry' have preserved their ancient 'deposit' through wars which, during the sixteenth and seventeenth centuries, became wars of extermination; no people, Lecky said at the opening of his Ireland in the Eighteenth Century,[4] have undergone greater persecution, nor did that persecution altogether cease up to our own day. No people hate as we do in whom that past is always alive; there are moments when hatred poisons my life and I accuse myself of effeminacy because I have not given it adequate expression. It is not enough to have put it into the mouth of a rambling peasant poet. Then I remind myself that, though mine is the first English marriage I know of in the direct line, all my family names are English and that I owe my soul to Shakespeare, to Spenser and to Blake, perhaps to William Morris,[5] and to the English language in which I think, speak and write, that everything I love has come to me through English; my hatred tortures me with love, my love with hate. I am like the Tibetan monk who dreams at his initiation that he is eaten by a wild beast and learns on waking that he himself is eater and eaten. This is Irish hatred and solitude, the hatred of human life that made Swift write Gulliver[6] and the epitaph upon his tomb, that can still make us wag between extremes and doubt our sanity.

Again and again I am asked why I do not write in Gaelic; some four or five years ago I was invited to dinner by a London society and found myself among London journalists, Indian students and foreign political refugees. An Indian paper says it was a dinner in my honour, I hope not; I have forgotten though I have a clear memory of my own angry mind. I should have spoken as men are expected to speak at public dinners; I should have paid and been paid conventional compliments; then they would speak of the refugees, from that on all would be lively and topical, foreign tyranny would be arraigned, England seem even to those confused Indians the protector of liberty; I grew angrier and angrier; Wordsworth, that typical Englishman, had published his famous sonnet to François Dominique Toussaint, a Santo Domingo negro:

> There's not a breathing of the common wind
> That will forget thee[7]

in the year when Emmet conspired and died, and he remembered that rebellion as little as the half hanging and the pitch cap that preceded it by half a

---

9. In Jerusalem the English poet William Blake (1757–1827) describes imagination as the "Divine body of the lord Jesus." Yeats's ideas about the Unity of Being are drawn from his reading of Dante's Il Convito.
1. In manuscript Yeats wrote "imanent" (a misspelling of "immanent"), but he allowed "imminent" to stand in the typescript.
2. Ingredients of the witches' cauldron in Shakespeare's Macbeth 4.1.
3. Yeats's mystical writings (1925, 1937), in which he sketches out and schematizes many of his theories.
4. A History of Ireland in the Eighteenth Century, by the Irish historian William Edward Hartpole Lecky (1838–1903).

5. English poet and designer (1834–1896). Edmund Spenser (1552–1599), English poet who, in addition to poetic works such as The Faerie Queene, wrote a treatise proposing the extermination of the Irish.
6. Gulliver's Travels, by the Irish satirist Jonathan Swift (1667–1745). Yeats's poem "Swift's Epitaph," a loose translation of the Latin on Swift's tomb, claims that "Swift has sailed into his rest; / Savage indignation there / Cannot lacerate his breast."
7. From "To Toussaint L'Ouverture," by the English poet William Wordsworth (1770–1850). L'Ouverture (1743–1803) died in prison after rebelling against France's rule in Haiti.

dozen years.[8] That there might be no topical speeches I denounced the oppression of the people of India; being a man of letters, not a politician, I told how they had been forced to learn everything, even their own Sanscrit, through the vehicle of English till the first discoverers of wisdom had become bywords for vague abstract facility. I begged the Indian writers present to remember that no man can think or write with music and vigour except in his mother tongue. I turned a friendly audience hostile, yet when I think of that scene I am unrepentant and angry.

I could no more have written in Gaelic than can those Indians write in English; Gaelic is my national language, but it is not my mother tongue.

III. Style and Attitude

Style is almost unconscious. I know what I have tried to do, little what I have done. Contemporary lyric poems, even those that moved me—'The Stream's Secret', 'Dolores'[9]—seemed too long, but an Irish preference for a swift current might be mere indolence, yet Burns may have felt the same when he read Thomson and Cowper.[1] The English mind is meditative, rich, deliberate; it may remember the Thames[2] valley. I planned to write short lyrics or poetic drama where every speech [would] be short and concentrated, knit by dramatic tension, and I did so with more confidence because young English poets were at that time writing out of emotion at the moment of crisis, though their old slow-moving meditation returned almost at once. Then, and in this English poetry has followed my lead, I tried to make the language of poetry coincide with that of passionate, normal speech. I wanted to write in whatever language comes most naturally when we soliloquise, as I do all day long, upon the events of our own lives or of any life where we can see ourselves for the moment. I sometimes compare myself with the mad old slum women I hear denouncing and remembering; 'how dare you,' I heard one say of some imaginary suitor, 'and you without health or a home'. If I spoke my thoughts aloud they might be as angry and as wild. It was a long time before I had made a language to my liking; I began to make it when I discovered some twenty years ago that I must seek, not as Wordsworth thought words in common use,[3] but a powerful and passionate syntax, and a complete coincidence between period and stanza. Because I need a passionate syntax for passionate subject-matter I compel myself to accept those traditional metres that have developed with the language. Ezra Pound, Turner, Lawrence, wrote admirable free verse, I could not.[4] I would lose myself, become joyless like those mad old women. The translators of the Bible, Sir Thomas Browne,[5] certain translators from the Greek when translators still bothered about rhythm, created a form midway between prose and verse that seems natural to impersonal meditation; but all

8. Paper caps filled with burning pitch were used for torture during the martial law preceding and following the Irish Rising of 1798. Robert Emmet (1778–1803), Irish nationalist executed after the Irish rebellion of 1803.
9. Long poems by Dante Gabriel Rossetti (1828–1882) and Algernon Charles Swinburne (1837–1909), respectively.
1. James Thomson (1700–1748) and William Cowper (1731–1800), poets most famous for their long poems. Robert Burns (1759–1796), Scottish poet of short lyrics.

2. English river that runs through London.
3. In the preface to Lyrical Ballads (1800), Wordsworth says that poetry should be written in "language really used by men."
4. In his Oxford Book of Modern Verse (1936), Yeats included free verse by the American poet Ezra Pound (1885–1972), the English poet Walter Turner (1889–1946), and the English poet and novelist D. H. Lawrence (1885–1930).
5. English physician and author (1605–1682) with an elaborate prose style.

that is personal soon rots; it must be packed in ice or salt. Once when I was in delirium from pneumonia I dictated a letter to George Moore[6] telling him to eat salt because it was a symbol of eternity; the delirium passed, I had no memory of that letter, but I must have meant what I now mean. If I wrote of personal love or sorrow in free verse, or in any rhythm that left it unchanged, amid all its accident, I would be full of self-contempt because of my egotism and indiscretion, and I foresee the boredom of my reader. I must choose a traditional stanza, even what I alter must seem traditional. I commit my emotion to shepherds, herdsmen, camel-drivers, learned men, Milton's or Shelley's Platonist, that tower Palmer drew.[7] Talk to me of originality and I will turn on you with rage. I am a crowd, I am a lonely man, I am nothing. Ancient salt is best packing. The heroes of Shakespeare convey to us through their looks, or through the metaphorical patterns of their speech, the sudden enlargement of their vision, their ecstasy at the approach of death, 'She should have died hereafter', 'Of many million kisses, the poor last', 'Absent thee from felicity awhile'; they have become God or Mother Goddess, the pelican, 'My baby at my breast',[8] but all must be cold; no actress has ever sobbed when she played Cleopatra, even the shallow brain of a producer has never thought of such a thing. The supernatural is present, cold winds blow across our hands, upon our faces, the thermometer falls, and because of that cold we are hated by journalists and groundlings. There may be in this or that detail painful tragedy, but in the whole work none. I have heard Lady Gregory say, rejecting some play in the modern manner sent to the Abbey Theatre, 'Tragedy must be a joy to the man who dies.' Nor is it any different with lyrics, songs, narrative poems; neither scholars nor the populace have sung or read anything generation after generation because of its pain. The maid of honour whose tragedy they sing must be lifted out of history with timeless pattern, she is one of the four Maries,[9] the rhythm is old and familiar, imagination must dance, must be carried beyond feeling into the aboriginal ice. Is ice the correct word? I once boasted, copying the phrase from a letter of my father's, that I would write a poem 'cold and passionate as the dawn'.[1]

When I wrote in blank verse I was dissatisfied; my vaguely mediaeval *Countess Cathleen* fitted the measure, but our Heroic Age went better, or so I fancied, in the ballad metre of *The Green Helmet*.[2] There was something in what I felt about Deirdre, about Cuchulain,[3] that rejected the Renaissance and its characteristic metres, and this was a principal reason why I created in dance plays the form that varies blank verse with lyric metres. When I speak blank verse and analyse my feelings I stand at a moment of history when instinct, its traditional songs and dances, its general agreement, is of the past. I have

6. Irish novelist (1852–1933).
7. The English artist Samuel Palmer (1805–1881) drew "The Lonely Tower" (1879) as an illustration of Milton's poem about the pensive man, "Il Penseroso" (1645), in which a scholar in a "high lonely tower" is dedicated to uncovering Plato's insights; in Shelley's "Prince Athanase," the idealistic hero searches for love.
8. From *Macbeth* 5.4, *Anthony and Cleopatra* 4.15, *Hamlet* 5.2, respectively. "Pelican": thought to feed its babies with its blood and thus often a symbol of self-sacrifice.
9. Mary, Queen of Scots (1542–1587) was served by four women named Mary.

1. From "The Fisherman" (1916): "Before I am old / I shall have written him one / Poem maybe as cold / And passionate as the dawn."
2. *The Countess Cathleen* (1892, later revised) is written in blank verse; *The Green Helmet* (1910), in iambic heptameter, which resembles the meter of a ballad (alternating between four- and three-stress lines).
3. The warrior hero of the Irish mythological Ulster Cycle; he also appears in Yeats's "dance" plays, derived from Japanese Noh drama. "Deirdre": in the Ulster Cycle, woman chosen to be queen of Ulster before she elopes with Naoise (pronounced *Neesha*).

been cast up out of the whale's belly though I still remember the sound and sway that came from beyond its ribs,[4] and, like the Queen in Paul Fort's ballad,[5] I smell of the fish of the sea. The contrapuntal structure of the verse, to employ a term adopted by Robert Bridges,[6] combines the past and present. If I repeat the first line of *Paradise Lost* so as to emphasise its five feet I am among the folk singers, 'Of mán's first disóbédience ánd the frúit', but speak it as I should I cross it with another emphasis, that of passionate prose, 'Of mán's first disobédience and the frúit', or 'Of mán's fírst dísobedience and the frúit', the folk song is still there, but a ghostly voice, an unvariable possibility, an unconscious norm. What moves me and my hearer is a vivid speech that has no laws except that it must not exorcise the ghostly voice. I am awake and asleep, at my moment of revelation, self-possessed in self-surrender; there is no rhyme, no echo of the beaten drum, the dancing foot, that would overset my balance. When I was a boy I wrote a poem upon dancing that had one good line: 'They snatch with their hands at the sleep of the skies.' If I sat down and thought for a year I would discover that but for certain syllabic limitations, a rejection or acceptance of certain elisions, I must wake or sleep.

The Countess Cathleen could speak a blank verse which I had loosened, almost put out of joint, for her need, because I thought of her as mediaeval and thereby connected her with the general European movement. For Deirdre and Cuchulain and all the other figures of Irish legend are still in the whale's belly.

IV. Whither?

The young English poets reject dream and personal emotion; they have thought out opinions that join them to this or that political party; they employ an intricate psychology, action in character, not as in the ballads character in action, and all consider that they have a right to the same close attention that men pay to the mathematician and the metaphysician. One of the more distinguished has just explained that man has hitherto slept but must now awake.[7] They are determined to express the factory, the metropolis, that they may be modern. Young men teaching school in some picturesque cathedral town, or settled for life in Capri or in Sicily, defend their type of metaphor by saying that it comes naturally to a man who travels to his work by Tube.[8] I am indebted to a man of this school who went through my work at my request, crossing out all conventional metaphors,[9] but they seem to me to have rejected also those dream associations which were the whole art of Mallarmé.[1] He had topped a previous wave. As they express not what the Upanishads call 'that ancient Self' but individual intellect, they have the right to choose the man in the Tube because of his objective importance. They attempt to kill the whale, push the Renaissance higher yet, out-think Leonardo;[2] their verse kills the folk

---

4. Cf. Jonah 2.10: "And the Lord spake unto the fish, and it vomited out Jonah upon the dry land."
5. "La Reine à la Mer" ("The Queen of the Sea," 1894–96), by the French poet Paul Fort (1872–1960).
6. English poet (1844–1930), who stressed the poetic tension of the counterpoint between regular meters and the rhythm of poetry as actually spoken.
7. Perhaps W. H. Auden (1907–1973) or C. Day

Lewis (1904–1972).
8. London's underground railway. Lewis taught in the spa town of Cheltenham in the early 1930s. D. H. Lawrence lived in Capri and Sicily in the early 1920s.
9. Ezra Pound did this circa 1910.
1. Stéphane Mallarmé (1842–1898), French poet.
2. Leonardo da Vinci (1452–1519), Italian artist and inventor.

ghost and yet would remain verse. I am joined to the 'Irishry' and I expect a counter-Renaissance. No doubt it is part of the game to push that Renaissance; I make no complaint; I am accustomed to the geometrical arrangement of history in *A Vision*, but I go deeper than 'custom' for my convictions. When I stand upon O'Connell Bridge[3] in the half-light and notice that discordant architecture, all those electric signs, where modern heterogeneity has taken physical form, a vague hatred comes up out of my own dark and I am certain that wherever in Europe there are minds strong enough to lead others the same vague hatred rises; in four or five or in less generations this hatred will have issued in violence and imposed some kind of rule of kindred. I cannot know the nature of that rule, for its opposite fills the light; all I can do to bring it nearer is to intensify my hatred. I am no Nationalist, except in Ireland for passing reasons; State and Nation are the work of intellect, and when you consider what comes before and after them they are, as Victor Hugo said of something or other, not worth the blade of grass God gives for the nest of the linnet.[4]

1937   1961

3. Over Dublin's river Liffey.
4. Small finch. Victor Hugo (1802–1885), French writer.

E. M. FORSTER
1879–1970

Born in London, Edward Morgan Forster was an infant when his father, an architect of Welsh extraction, died of consumption. An only child, Forster was raised by his paternal great-aunt and his mother, a member of a family distinguished over several generations for its evangelical religion and its philanthropic reformist activities. He was educated at Tonbridge School (the "Sawston" of his novel *The Longest Journey*), where he suffered from the cruelty of his classmates and other tribulations of being a day boy at a boarding school. As a student at King's College, Cambridge, he found an intellectual companionship that influenced his entire life. The friends he made were to become, with Forster, members of the "Bloomsbury Group"—so called because some of its prominent figures lived in the Bloomsbury district of London—which included the writers Lytton Strachey and Virginia Woolf, the art historians Clive Bell and Roger Fry, and the economist John Maynard Keynes. Forster's main interest was always in personal relations, the "little society" we make for ourselves with our friends. He cast a wary eye on society at large, his point of view being always that of the independent liberal, suspicious of political slogans and catchwords, critical of Victorian attitudes and British imperialism.

After graduation from Cambridge, Forster visited Greece and spent some time in Italy in 1901, and this experience influenced him permanently; throughout his life he tended to set Greek and Italian peasant life in symbolic contrast to the stuffy and repressed life of middle-class England. Both Greek mythology and Italian Renaissance art opened up to him a world of vital exuberance, and most of his work is concerned with ways of discovering such a quality in personal relationships amid the complexities and distortions of modern life. He began writing as a contributor to the newly founded liberal *Independent Review* in 1903, and in 1905 published his first novel, *Where*

Angels Fear to Tread, a tragicomic projection of conflicts between refined English gentility and coarse Italian vitality.

Forster's second novel, *The Longest Journey* (1907), examines the differences between living and dead relationships with much incidental satire of English public-school education and English notions of respectability. *A Room with a View* (1908) explores the nature of love with a great deal of subtlety, using (as with his first novel) Italy as a liberating agent for the British tourists whom he also satirizes. *Howards End* (1910) involves a conflict between two families, one interested in art and literature and the other only in money and business, and probes the relation between inward feeling and outward action, between the kinds of reality in which people live. "Only connect!" exclaims one of the characters. "Only connect the prose and the passion, and both will be exalted, and human love will soon be at its height." But no one knew better than Forster that this is more easily said than done and that false or premature connections, connections made by rule and not achieved through total realization of the personality, can destroy and corrupt.

A pacifist, Forster refused to fight in World War I and instead served in the International Red Cross in Egypt. In Alexandria he had his first significant sexual relationship, with Mohammed el Adl, an Egyptian tram conductor; he feared social disapproval less there than in England, where, not long after Oscar Wilde's infamous prosecution for homosexual offenses, he hid his personal life from public scrutiny.

He traveled to India in 1912 and 1922, and in his last (for Forster published no more fiction during his life) and best-known novel, *A Passage to India* (1924), he takes the fraught relations between British and colonized Indians in the subcontinent as a background for the most searching and complex of all his explorations of the possibilities and limitations, the promises and pitfalls, of human relationships. Published posthumously was another novel, *Maurice,* written more than fifty years before and circulated privately during his life, in which he tried to define and do justice to homosexual love, which had played an important part in his life. In addition to fiction Forster also wrote critical, autobiographical, and descriptive prose, notably *Aspects of the Novel* (1927), which, as a discussion of the techniques of fiction by a practicing novelist, has become a minor classic of criticism.

"The Other Boat," which concerns cross-ethnic homosexual attraction that collides with the sexual taboos and racial hierarchies of empire, is an unusually long and rich short story that Forster originally intended to turn into a novel, beginning it around 1913 but not completing it until 1957–58, and it was not published until after his death, first appearing in *The Life to Come and Other Stories* (1972). The first part of the story tells of a British family's journey by ship from India to England, and the rest of the story, set some years later, reverses direction, the journey into the Mediterranean and on toward India becoming the backdrop for the loosening—and then drastic reassertion—of British imperial norms of order, discipline, racial superiority, and heterosexuality. As in other of Forster's works, the passage into another cultural geography calls into question British middle-class values, which exact a high price in repression, tragically conflict with the protagonist's sensual and emotional desires, and ultimately explode into violence.

The Other Boat

I

'Cocoanut, come and play at soldiers.'
'I cannot, I am beesy.'
'But you must, Lion wants you.'

'Yes, come along, man,' said Lionel, running up with some paper cocked hats[1] and a sash. It was long long ago, and little boys still went to their deaths stiffly, and dressed in as many clothes as they could find.

'I cannot, I am beesy,' repeated Cocoanut.

'But man, what are you busy about?'

'I have soh many things to arrange, man.'

'Let's leave him and play by ourselves,' said Olive. 'We've Joan and Noel and Baby and Lieutenant Bodkin. Who wants Cocoanut?'

'Oh, shut up! I want him. We must have him. He's the only one who falls down when he's killed. All you others go on fighting long too long. The battle this morning was a perfect fast. Mother said so.'

'Well, I'll die.'

'So you say beforehand, but when it comes to the point you won't. Noel won't. Joan won't. Baby doesn't do anything properly—of course he's too little—and you can't expect Lieutenant Bodkin to fall down. Cocoanut, man, do.'

'I—weel—not.'

'Cocoanut cocoanut cocoanut cocoanut cocoanut cocoanut,' said Baby.

The little boy rolled on the deck screaming happily. He liked to be pressed by these handsome good-natured children. 'I must go and see the m'm m'm m'm,' he said.

'The what?'

'The m'm m'm m'm. They live—oh, so many of them—in the thin part of the ship.'

'He means the bow,'[2] said Olive. 'Oh, come along, Lion. He's hopeless.'

'What are m'm m'm m'm?'

'M'm.' He whirled his arms about, and chalked some marks on the planks.

'What are those?'

'M'm.'

'What's their name?'

'They have no name.'

'What do they do?'

'They just go so and oh! and so—ever—always——'

'Flying fish? . . . Fairies? . . . Noughts and crosses?'[3]

'They have no name.'

'Mother!' said Olive to a lady who was promenading with a gentleman, 'hasn't everything a name?'

'I suppose so.'

'Who's this?' asked the lady's companion.

'He's always hanging on to my children. I don't know.'

'Touch of the tar-brush,[4] eh?'

'Yes, but it doesn't matter on a voyage home. I would never allow it going to India.' They passed on, Mrs March calling back, 'Shout as much as you like, boys, but don't scream, don't scream.'

'They must have a name,' said Lionel, recollecting, 'because Adam named all the animals when the Bible was beginning.'

'They weren't in the Bible, m'm m'm m'm; they were all the time up in the

1. Triangular hats worn in navy and army.
2. Forward part of the ship.
3. Tic-tac-toe.
4. Appearance of having non-European ancestry, i.e., of having brown skin.

thin part of the sheep, and when you pop out they pop in, so how could Adam have?'

'Noah's ark is what he's got to now.'

Baby said 'Noah's ark, Noah's ark, Noah's ark,' and they all bounced up and down and roared. Then, without any compact, they drifted from the saloon[5] deck on to the lower, and from the lower down the staircase that led to the forecastle,[6] much as the weeds and jellies were drifting about outside in the tropical sea. Soldiering was forgotten, though Lionel said, 'We may as well wear our cocked hats.' They played with a fox-terrier, who was in the charge of a sailor, and asked the sailor himself if a roving life was a happy one. Then drifting forward again, they climbed into the bows, where the m'm m'm m'm were said to be.

Here opened a glorious country, much the best in the boat. None of the March children had explored there before, but Cocoanut, having few domesticities, knew it well. That bell that hung in the very peak—it was the ship's bell and if you rang it the ship would stop. Those big ropes were tied into knots—twelve knots an hour. This paint was wet, but only as far as there. Up that hole was coming a Lascar.[7] But of the m'm m'm he said nothing until asked. Then he explained in offhand tones that if you popped out they popped in, so that you couldn't expect to see them.

What treachery! How disappointing! Yet so ill-balanced were the children's minds that they never complained. Olive, in whom the instincts of a lady were already awaking, might have said a few well-chosen words, but when she saw her brothers happy she forgot too, and lifted Baby up on to a bollard[8] because he asked her to. They all screamed. Into their midst came the Lascar and laid down a mat for his three-o'clock prayer. He prayed as if he was still in India, facing westward, not knowing that the ship had rounded Arabia so that his holy places now lay behind him.[9] They continued to scream.

Mrs March and her escort remained on the saloon deck, inspecting the approach to Suez.[1] Two continents were converging with great magnificence of mountains and plain. At their junction, nobly placed, could be seen the smoke and the trees of the town. In addition to her more personal problems, she had become anxious about Pharaoh. 'Where exactly was Pharaoh drowned?'[2] she asked Captain Armstrong. 'I shall have to show my boys.' Captain Armstrong did not know, but he offered to ask Mr Hotblack, the Moravian[3] missionary. Mr Hotblack knew—in fact he knew too much. Somewhat snubbed by the military element in the earlier part of the voyage, he now bounced to the surface, became authoritative and officious, and undertook to wake Mrs March's little ones when they were passing the exact spot. He spoke of the origins of Christianity in a way that made her look down her nose, saying that the Canal was one long genuine Bible picture gallery, that donkeys could still be seen going down into Egypt carrying Holy Families,[4] and naked Arabs

---

5. Deck with large cabin(s) for passenger use.
6. Raised deck at the forward part of the ship.
7. An Indian sailor.
8. A thick post for securing ropes to.
9. Muslims pray facing Mecca.
1. Egyptian city at the south end of the Suez Canal (the shortest maritime route between Europe and India; it separates Asia from Africa).
2. In Exodus 14.21–23 Moses parts the Red Sea,

but after the Israelites have passed, the sea closes, drowning Pharoah and his army.
3. Member of a Protestant denomination, originally from a 15th-century reform religious movement in Moravia and Bohemia.
4. In Matthew 2.13–15 the family of the baby Jesus, fleeing from King Herod, travels from Bethlehem into Egypt; the journey is often depicted as taking place by donkey.

wading into the water to fish; 'Peter and Andrew by Galilee's shore, why, it hits the truth plumb.'[5] A clergyman's daughter and a soldier's wife, she could not admit that Christianity had ever been oriental. What good thing can come out of the Levant,[6] and is it likely that the apostles[7] ever had a touch of the tar-brush? Still, she thanked Mr Hotblack (for, having asked a favour of him, she had contracted an obligation towards him), and she resigned herself to greeting him daily until Southampton,[8] when their paths would part.

Then she observed, against the advancing land, her children playing in the bows without their topis[9] on. The sun in those far-off days was a mighty power and hostile to the Ruling Race.[1] Officers staggered at a touch of it, Tommies[2] collapsed. When the regiment was under canvas, it wore helmets at tiffin,[3] lest the rays penetrated the tent. She shouted at her doomed offspring, she gesticulated, Captain Armstrong and Mr Hotblack shouted, but the wind blew their cries backwards. Refusing company, she hurried forward alone; the children were far too excited and covered with paint.

'Lionel! Olive! Olive! What are you doing?'

'M'm m'm m'm, mummy—it's a new game.'

'Go back and play properly under the awning at once—it's far too hot. You'll have sunstroke every one of you. Come, Baby!'

'M'm m'm m'm.'

'Now, you won't want me to carry a great boy like you, surely.'

Baby flung himself round the bollard and burst into tears.

'It always ends like this,' said Mrs March as she detached him. 'You all behave foolishly and selfishly and then Baby cries. No, Olive—don't help me. Mother would rather do everything herself.'

'Sorry,' said Lionel gruffly. Baby's shrieks rent the air. Thoroughly naughty, he remained clasping an invisible bollard.[4] As she bent him into a portable shape, another mishap occurred. A sailor—an Englishman—leapt out of the hatchway with a piece of chalk and drew a little circle round her where she stood. Cocoanut screamed, 'He's caught you. He's come.'

'You're on dangerous ground, lady,' said the sailor respectfully. 'Men's quarters. Of course we leave it to your generosity.'

Tired with the voyage and the noise of the children, worried by what she had left in India and might find in England, Mrs March fell into a sort of trance. She stared at the circle stupidly, unable to move out of it, while Cocoanut danced round her and gibbered.

'Men's quarters—just to keep up the old custom.'

'I don't understand.'

'Passengers are often kind enough to pay their footing,' he said, feeling awkward; though rapacious he was independent. 'But of course there's no compulsion, lady. Ladies and gentlemen do as they feel.'

'I will certainly do what is customary—Baby, be quiet.'

'Thank you, lady. We divide whatever you give among the crew. Of course not those chaps.' He indicated the Lascar.

'The money shall be sent to you. I have no purse.'

---

5. Peter and Andrew, Jesus' disciples, were fishermen on the Sea of Galilee.
6. Historical term for region of the eastern Mediterranean.
7. Jesus' disciples.
8. Major port on the English Channel.

9. Pith helmets worn for protection from sun and heat.
1. I.e., the British.
2. Nickname for British soldiers.
3. Lunch (Anglo-Indian).
4. Post on a ship for securing ropes to.

He touched his forelock[5] cynically. He did not believe her. She stepped out of the circle and as she did so Cocoanut sprang into it and squatted grinning.

'You're a silly little boy and I shall complain to the stewardess about you,' she told him with unusual heat. 'You never will play any game properly and you stop the others. You're a silly idle useless unmanly little boy.'

II

S. S. Normannia
Red Sea
October, 191–

Hullo the Mater!

You may be thinking it is about time I wrote you a line, so here goes, however you should have got my wire sent before leaving Tilbury[6] with the glad news that I got a last minute passage on this boat when it seemed quite impossible I should do so. The Arbuthnots are on it too all right, so is a Lady Manning who claims acquaintance with Olive, not to mention several remarkably cheery subalterns,[7] poor devils, don't know what they are in for in the tropics. We make up two Bridge tables every night besides hanging together at other times, and get called the Big Eight, which I suppose must be regarded as a compliment. How I got my passage is curious. I was coming away from the S.S.[8] office after my final try in absolute despair when I ran into an individual whom you may or may not remember—he was a kid on that other boat when we cleared all out of India on that unlikely occasion over ten years ago—got called Cocoanut because of his peculiar shaped head. He has now turned into an equally weird youth, who has however managed to become influential in shipping circles, I can't think how some people manage to do things. He duly recognized me—dagoes[9] sometimes have marvellous memories—and on learning my sad plight fixed me up with a (single berth) cabin, so all is well. He is on board too, but our paths seldom cross. He has more than a touch of the tar-brush, so consorts with his own dusky fraternity, no doubt to their mutual satisfaction.

The heat is awful and I fear this is but a dull letter in consequence. Bridge I have already mentioned, and there are the usual deck games, betting on the ship's log, etc., still I think everyone will be glad to reach Bombay and get into harness.[1] Colonel and Mrs Arbuthnot are very friendly, and speaking confidentially I don't think it will do my prospects any harm having got to know them better. Well I will now conclude this screed[2] and I will write again when I have rejoined the regiment and contacted Isabel. Best love to all which naturally includes yourself from

Your affectionate first born,
Lionel March

PS. Lady Manning asks to be remembered to Olive, nearly forgot.

---

5. Lock of hair growing from the front of the head.
6. Port on the river Thames estuary.
7. Junior officers.
8. Steamship.

9. Disparaging term for foreigners.
1. Get to work, especially with military undertakings.
2. Gossipy letter.

When Captain March had posted this epistle he rejoined the Big Eight. Although he had spent the entire day with them they were happy to see him, for he exactly suited them. He was what any rising young officer ought to be—clean-cut, athletic, good-looking without being conspicuous. He had had wonderful professional luck, which no one grudged him: he had got into one of the little desert wars that were becoming too rare, had displayed dash and decision, had been wounded, and had been mentioned in despatches and got his captaincy early. Success had not spoiled him, nor was he vain of his personal appearance, although he must have known that thick fairish hair, blue eyes, glowing cheeks and strong white teeth constitute, when broad shoulders support them, a combination irresistible to the fair sex. His hands were clumsier than the rest of him, but bespoke hard honest work, and the springy gleaming hairs on them suggested virility. His voice was quiet, his demeanour assured, his temper equable. Like his brother officers he wore a mess[3] uniform slightly too small for him, which accentuated his physique—the ladies accentuating theirs by wearing their second best frocks and reserving their best ones for India.

Bridge proceeded without a hitch, as his mother had been given to understand it might. She had not been told that on either side of the players, violet darkening into black, rushed the sea, nor would she have been interested. Her son gazed at it occasionally, his forehead furrowed. For despite his outstanding advantages he was a miserable card-player, and he was having wretched luck. As soon as the Normannia entered the Mediterranean he had begun to lose, and the 'better luck after Port Said,'[4] always the case' that had been humorously promised him had never arrived. Here in the Red Sea he had lost the maximum the Big Eight's moderate stakes allowed. He couldn't afford it, he had no private means and he ought to be saving up for the future, also it was humiliating to let down his partner: Lady Manning herself. So he was thankful when play terminated and the usual drinks circulated. They sipped and gulped while the lighthouses on the Arabian coast winked at them and slid northwards. 'Bedfordshire!'[5] fell pregnantly from the lips of Mrs Arbuthnot. And they dispersed, with the certainty that the day which was approaching would exactly resemble the one that had died.

In this they were wrong.

Captain March waited until all was quiet, still frowning at the sea. Then with something alert and predatory about him, something disturbing and disturbed, he went down to his cabin.

'Come een,' said a sing-song voice.

For it was not a single cabin, as he had given his mother to understand. There were two berths, and the lower one contained Cocoanut. Who was naked. A brightly coloured scarf lay across him and contrasted with his blackish-grayish skin, and an aromatic smell came off him, not at all unpleasant. In ten years he had developed into a personable adolescent, but still had the same funny-shaped head. He had been doing his accounts and now he laid them down and gazed at the British officer adoringly.

'Man, I thought you was never coming,' he said, and his eyes filled with tears.

3. Mealtime.
4. Egyptian city at the northern entrance to the Suez Canal.

5. County in the southeastern Midlands of England.

'It's only those bloody Arbuthnots and their blasted bridge,' replied Lionel and closed the cabin door.

'I thought you was dead.'

'Well, I'm not.'

'I thought I should die.'

'So you will.' He sat down on the berth, heavily and with deliberate heaviness. The end of the chase was in sight. It had not been a long one. He had always liked the kid, even on that other boat, and now he liked him more than ever. Champagne in an ice-bucket too. An excellent kid. They couldn't associate on deck with that touch of the tar-brush, but it was a very different business down here, or soon would be. Lowering his voice, he said: 'The trouble is we're not supposed to do this sort of thing under any circumstances whatsoever, which you never seem to understand. If we got caught there'd be absolute bloody hell to pay, yourself as well as me, so for God's sake don't make a noise.'

'Lionel, O Lion of the Night, love me.'

'All right. Stay where you are.' Then he confronted the magic that had been worrying him on and off the whole evening and had made him inattentive at cards. A tang of sweat spread as he stripped and a muscle thickened up out of gold. When he was ready he shook off old Cocoanut, who was now climbing about like a monkey, and put him where he had to be, and manhandled him, gently, for he feared his own strength and was always gentle, and closed on him, and they did what they both wanted to do.

Wonderful, wonnerful . . .

They lay entwined, Nordic warrior and subtle supple boy, who belonged to no race and always got what he wanted. All his life he had wanted a toy that would not break, and now he was planning how he would play with Lionel for ever. He had longed for him ever since their first meeting, embraced him in dreams when only that was possible, met him again as the omens foretold, and marked him down, spent money to catch him and lime[6] him, and here he lay, caught, and did not know it.

There they lay caught, both of them, and did not know it, while the ship carried them inexorably towards Bombay.

III

It had not always been so wonderful, wonnerful. Indeed the start of the affair had been grotesque and nearly catastrophic. Lionel had stepped on board at Tilbury entirely the simple soldier man, without an inkling of his fate. He had thought it decent of a youth whom he had only known as a child to fix him up with a cabin, but had not expected to find the fellow on board too—still less to have to share the cabin with him. This gave him a nasty shock. British officers are never stabled with dagoes, never, it was too damn awkward for words. However, he could not very well protest under the circumstances, nor did he in his heart want to, for his colour-prejudices were tribal rather than personal, and only worked when an observer was present. The first half-hour together went most pleasantly, they were unpacking and sorting things out before the ship started, he found his childhood's acquaintance friendly

---

6. Ensnare.

2066 / E. M. Forster

and quaint, exchanged reminiscences, and even started teasing and bossing him as in the old days, and got him giggling delightedly. He sprang up to his berth and sat on its edge, swinging his legs. A hand touched them, and he thought no harm until it approached their junction. Then he became puzzled, scared and disgusted in quick succession, leapt down with a coarse barrack-room oath and a brow of thunder and went straight to the Master at Arms[7] to report an offence against decency. Here he showed the dash and decision that had so advantaged him in desert warfare: in other words he did not know what he was doing.

The Master at Arms could not be found, and during the delay Lionel's rage abated somewhat, and he reflected that if he lodged a formal complaint he would have to prove it, which he could not do, and might have to answer questions, at which he was never good. So he went to the Purser[8] instead, and he demanded to be given alternative accommodation, without stating any reason for the change. The Purser stared: the boat was chockablock full already, as Captain March must have known. 'Don't speak to me like that,' Lionel stormed, and shouldered his way to the gunwale[9] to see England recede. Here was the worst thing in the world, the thing for which Tommies got given the maximum, and here was he bottled up with it for a fortnight. What the hell was he to do? Go forward with the charge or blow his own brains out or what?

On to him thus desperately situated the Arbuthnots descended. They were slight acquaintances, their presence calmed him, and before long his light military guffaw rang out as if nothing had happened. They were pleased to see him, for they were hurriedly forming a group of sahibs[1] who would hang together during the voyage and exclude outsiders. With his help the Big Eight came into being, soon to be the envy of less happy passengers; introductions; drinks; jokes; difficulties of securing a berth. At this point Lionel made a shrewd move: everything gets known on a boat and he had better anticipate discovery. 'I got a passage all right,' he brayed, 'but at the cost of sharing my cabin with a wog.'[2] All condoled, and Colonel Arbuthnot in the merriest of moods exclaimed, 'Let's hope the blacks don't come off on the sheets,' and Mrs Arbuthnot, wittier still, cried, 'Of course they won't, dear, if it's a wog it'll be the coffees.' Everyone shouted with laughter, the good lady basked in the applause, and Lionel could not understand why he suddenly wanted to throw himself into the sea. It was so unfair, he was the aggrieved party, yet he felt himself in the wrong and almost a cad. If only he had found out the fellow's tastes in England he would never have touched him, no, not with tongs. But could he have found out? You couldn't tell by just looking. Or could you? Dimly, after ten years' forgetfulness, something stirred in that faraway boat of his childhood and he saw his mother . . . Well, she was always objecting to something or other, the poor Mater. No, he couldn't possibly have known.

The Big Eight promptly reserved tables for lunch and all future meals, and Cocoanut and his set were relegated to a second sitting—for it became evident that he too was in a set: the tagrag and coloured bobtail[3] stuff that accumulates in corners and titters and whispers, and may well be influential, but who cares?

---

7. Officer in charge of enforcing discipline on a ship.
8. Ship's officer who keeps accounts and manages provisions.
9. Upper edge of a ship's side.

1. Respectful term for Europeans in colonial India.
2. Offensive term for a foreign person of color.
3. "Tagrag and bobtail" is another version of "rag, tag, and bobtail," meaning the riffraff, or rabble.

Lionel regarded it with distaste and looked for a touch of the hangdog[4] in his unspeakable cabin-mate, but he was skipping and gibbering on the promenade deck as if nothing had occurred. He himself was safe for the moment, eating curry by the side of Lady Manning, and amusing her by his joke about the various names which the cook would give the same curry on successive days. Again something stabbed him and he thought: 'But what shall I do, *do,* when night comes? There will have to be some sort of showdown.' After lunch the weather deteriorated. England said farewell to her children with her choppiest seas, her gustiest winds, and the banging of invisible pots and pans in the empyrean.[5] Lady Manning thought she might do better in a deckchair. He squired her to it and then collapsed and re-entered his cabin as rapidly as he had left it a couple of hours earlier.

It now seemed full of darkies, who rose to their feet as he retched,[6] assisted him up to his berth and loosened his collar, after which the gong summoned them to their lunch. Presently Cocoanut and his elderly Parsee[7] secretary looked in to inquire and were civil and helpful and he could not but thank them. The showdown must be postponed. Later in the day he felt better and less inclined for it, and the night did not bring its dreaded perils or indeed anything at all. It was almost as if nothing had happened—almost but not quite. Master Cocoanut had learned his lesson, for he pestered no more, yet he skilfully implied that the lesson was an unimportant one. He was like someone who has been refused a loan and indicates that he will not apply again. He seemed positively not to mind his disgrace—incomprehensibly to Lionel, who expected either repentance or terror. Could it be that he himself had made too much fuss?

In this uneventful atmosphere the voyage across the Bay of Biscay[8] proceeded. It was clear that his favours would not again be asked, and he could not help wondering what would have happened if he had granted them. Propriety was re-established, almost monotonously; if he and Cocoanut ever overlapped in the cabin and had to settle (for instance) who should wash first, they solved the problem with mutual tact.

And then the ship entered the Mediterranean.

Resistance weakened under the balmier sky, curiosity increased. It was an exquisite afternoon—their first decent weather. Cocoanut was leaning out of the porthole to see the sunlit rock of Gibraltar.[9] Lionel leant against him to look too and permitted a slight, a very slight familiarity with his person. The ship did not sink nor did the heavens fall. The contact started something whirling about inside his head and all over him, he could not concentrate on after-dinner bridge, he felt excited, frightened and powerful all at once and kept looking at the stars. Cocoa, who said weird things sometimes, declared that the stars were moving into a good place and could be kept there.

That night champagne appeared in the cabin, and he was seduced. He never could resist champagne. Curse, oh curse! How on earth had it happened? Never again. More happened off the coast of Sicily, more, much more at Port Said, and here in the Red Sea they slept together as a matter of course.

4. Sneaky or despicable person.
5. Sky.
6. Stretched.
7. Indian follower of Zoroastrianism, an ancient religion originating in Iran.

8. Arm of the Atlantic bordered by the west coast of France and the north coast of Spain.
9. Limestone promontory at the southern tip of Spain.

IV

And this particular night they lay motionless for longer than usual, as though something in the fall of their bodies had enchanted them. They had never been so content with each other before, and only one of them realized that nothing lasts, that they might be more happy or less happy in the future, but would never again be exactly thus. He tried not to stir, not to breathe, not to live even, but life was too strong for him and he sighed.

'All right?' whispered Lionel.

'Yes.'

'Did I hurt?'

'Yes.'

'Sorry.'

'Why?'

'Can I have a drink?'

'You can have the whole world.'

'Lie still and I'll get you one too, not that you deserve it after making such a noise.'

'Was I again a noise?'

'You were indeed. Never mind, you shall have a nice drink.' Half Ganymede, half Goth,[1] he jerked a bottle out of the ice-bucket. Pop went a cork and hit the partition wall. Sounds of feminine protest became audible, and they both laughed. 'Here, hurry up, scuttle up and drink.' He offered the goblet, received it back, drained it, refilled. His eyes shone, any depths through which he might have passed were forgotten. 'Let's make a night of it,' he suggested. For he was of the conventional type who once the conventions are broken breaks them into little pieces, and for an hour or two there was nothing he wouldn't say or do.

Meanwhile the other one, the deep one, watched. To him the moment of ecstasy was sometimes the moment of vision, and his cry of delight when they closed had wavered into fear. The fear passed before he could understand what it meant or against what it warned him, against nothing perhaps. Still, it seemed wiser to watch. As in business, so in love, precautions are desirable, insurances must be effected. 'Man, shall we now perhaps have our cigarette?' he asked.

This was an established ritual, an assertion deeper than speech that they belonged to each other and in their own way. Lionel assented and lit the thing, pushed it between dusky lips, pulled it out, pulled at it, replaced it, and they smoked it alternately with their faces touching. When it was finished Cocoa refused to extinguish the butt in an ashtray but consigned it through the port-hole into the flying waters with incomprehensible words. He thought the words might protect them, though he could not explain how, or what they were.

'That reminds me . . .' said Lionel, and stopped. He had been reminded, and for no reason, of his mother. He did not want to mention her in his present state, the poor old Mater, especially after all the lies she had been told.

'Yes, of what did it remind you, our cigarette? Yes and please? I should know.'

---

1. An uncouth or uncivilized person. "Ganymede": in Greek mythology a Trojan boy whom Zeus, attracted by his great beauty, carried away to be the gods' cupbearer.

'Nothing.' And he stretched himself, flawless except for a scar down in the groin.

'Who gave you that?'

'One of your fuzzy-wuzzy cousins.'

'Does it hurt?'

'No.' It was a trophy from the little desert war. An assegai[2] had nearly unmanned him, nearly but not quite, which Cocoa said was a good thing. A dervish,[3] a very holy man, had once told him that what nearly destroys may bring strength and can be summoned in the hour of revenge. 'I've no use for revenge,' Lionel said.

'Oh Lion, why not when it can be so sweet?'

He shook his head and reached up for his pyjamas, a sultan's gift. It was presents all the time in these days. His gambling debts were settled through the secretary, and if he needed anything, or was thought to need it, something or other appeared. He had ceased to protest and now accepted indiscriminately. He could trade away the worst of the junk later on—some impossible jewelry for instance which one couldn't be seen dead in. He did wish, though, that he could have given presents in return, for he was anything but a sponger. He had made an attempt two nights previously, with dubious results. 'I seem always taking and never giving,' he had said. 'Is there nothing of mine you'd fancy? I'd be so glad if there was.' To receive the reply: 'Yes. Your hairbrush'— 'My *hairbrush*?'—and he was not keen on parting with this particular object, for it had been a coming-of-age gift from Isabel. His hesitation brought tears to the eyes, so he had to give in. 'You're welcome to my humble brush if you want it, of course. I'll just comb it out for you first'—'No, no, as it is uncombed,' and it was snatched away fanatically. Almost like a vulture snatching. Odd little things like this did happen occasionally, m'm m'm m'ms he called them, for they reminded him of oddities on the other boat. They did no one any harm, so why worry? Enjoy yourself while you can. He lolled at his ease and let the gifts rain on him as they would—a Viking at a Byzantine court, spoiled, adored and not yet bored.

This was certainly the life, and sitting on one chair with his feet on another he prepared for their usual talk, which might be long or short but was certainly the life. When Cocoanut got going it was fascinating. For all the day he had slipped around the ship, discovering people's weaknesses. More than that, he and his cronies were cognizant of financial possibilities that do not appear in the City columns,[4] and could teach one how to get rich if one thought it worth while. More than that, he had a vein of fantasy. In the midst of something ribald and scandalous—the discovery of Lady Manning, for instance: Lady Manning of all people in the cabin of the Second Engineer—he imagined the discovery being made by a flying fish who had popped through the Engineer's porthole, and he indicated the expression on the fish's face.

Yes, this was the life, and one that he had never experienced in his austere apprenticeship: luxury, gaiety, kindness, unusualness, and delicacy that did not exclude brutal pleasure. Hitherto he had been ashamed of being built like a brute: his preceptors had condemned carnality or had dismissed it as a waste

<hr>

2. Slender spear.
3. Member of any of various Muslim ascetic orders.

4. Newspapers of the City of London, the financial district.

of time, and his mother had ignored its existence in him and all her children; being hers, they had to be pure.

What to talk about this pleasurable evening? How about the passport scandal? For Cocoanut possessed two passports, not one like most people, and they confirmed a growing suspicion that he might not be altogether straight. In England Lionel would have sheered off at once from such a subject, but since Gibraltar they had become so intimate and morally so relaxed that he experienced nothing but friendly curiosity. The information on the passports was conflicting, so that it was impossible to tell the twister's[5] age, or where he had been born or indeed what his name was. 'You could get into serious trouble over this,' Lionel had warned him, to be answered by irresponsible giggles. 'You could, you know. However, you're no better than a monkey, and I suppose a monkey can't be expected to know it's own name.' To which the reply had been 'Lion, he don't know nothing at all. Monkey's got to come along to tell a Lion he's alive.' It was never easy to score. He had picked up his education, if that was the word for it, in London, and his financial beginnings in Amsterdam, one of the passports was Portuguese, the other Danish, and half the blood must be Asiatic, unless a drop was Negro.

'Now come along, tell me the truth and nothing but the truth for a change,' he began. 'Ah, that reminds me I've at last got off that letter to the Mater. She adores news. It was a bit difficult to think of anything to interest her, however I filled it up with tripe about the Arbuthnots, and threw you in at the end as a sort of makeweight.'

'To make what sort of weight?'

'Well, naturally I didn't say what we do. I'm not stark staring raving mad. I merely mentioned I'd run into you in the London office, and got a cabin through you, that is to say single-berth one. I threw dust in her eyes all right.'

'Dear Lionel, you don't know how to throw dust or even where it is. Of mud you know a little, good, but not dust. Why bring me into the matter at all?'

'Oh, for the sake of something to say.'

'Did you say I too was on board?'

'I did in passing,' he said irritably, for he now realized he had better not have. 'I was writing that damned epistle, not you, and I had to fill it up. Don't worry—she's forgotten your very existence by this time.'

The other was certain she hadn't. If he had foreseen this meeting and had worked towards it through dreams, why should not an anxious parent have foreseen it too? She had valid reasons for anxiety, for things had actually started on that other boat. A trivial collision between children had alerted them towards each other as men. Thence had their present happiness sprung, thither might it wither, for the children had been disturbed. That vengeful onswishing of skirts . . . ! 'What trick can I think of this time that will keep him from her? I love him, I am clever, I have money. I will try.' The first step was to contrive his exit from the Army. The second step was to dispose of that English girl in India, called Isabel, about whom too little was known. Marriage or virginity or concubinage for Isabel? He had no scruples at perverting Lionel's instincts in order to gratify his own, or at endangering his prospects of paternity. All that mattered was their happiness, and he thought he knew what that was. Much depended on the next few days: he had to work hard and to work with the stars. His mind played round approaching problems,

5. One who speaks or acts to evade the truth.

combining them, retreating from them, and aware all the time of a further problem, of something in the beloved which he did not understand. He half-closed his eyes and watched, and listened through half-closed ears. By not being too much on the spot and sacrificing shrewdness to vision he sometimes opened a door. And sure enough Lionel said, 'As a matter of fact the Mater never liked you,' and a door opened, slowly.

'Man, how should she? Oh, when the chalk went from the hand of the sailor round the feet of the lady and she could not move and we all knew it, and oh man how we mocked her.'

'I don't remember—well, I do a little. It begins to come back to me and does sound like the sort of thing that would put her off. She certainly went on about you after we landed, and complained that you made things interesting when they weren't, funny thing to say, still the Mater is pretty funny. So we put our heads together as children sometimes do——'

'Do they? Oh yes.'

'—and Olive who's pretty bossy herself decreed we shouldn't mention you again as it seemed to worry her extra and she had just had a lot of worry. He actually—I hadn't meant to tell you this, it's a dead secret.'

'It shall be. I swear. By all that is without me and within me I swear.' He became incomprehensible in his excitement and uttered words in that unknown tongue. Nearly all tongues were unknown to Lionel, and he was impressed.

'Well, he actually——'

'Man, of whom do you now speak?'

'Oh yes, the Mater's husband, my Dad. He was in the Army too, in fact he attained the rank of major, but a quite unspeakable thing happened—he went native somewhere out East and got cashiered[6]—deserted his wife and left her with five young children to bring up, and no money. She was taking us all away from him when you met us and still had a faint hope that he might pull himself together and follow her. Not he. He never even wrote—remember, this is absolutely secret.'

'Yes, yes,' but he thought the secret a very tame one: how else should a middle-aged husband behave? 'But, Lionel, one question to you the more. For whom did the Major desert the Mater?'

'He went native.'

'With a girl or with a boy?'

'A boy? Good God! Well, I mean to say, with a girl, naturally—I mean, it was somewhere right away in the depths of Burma.'

'Even in Burma there are boys. At least I once heard so. But the Dad went native with a girl. Ver' well. Might not therefore there be offspring?'

'If there were, they'd be half-castes.[7] Pretty depressing prospect. Well, you know what I mean. My family—Dad's, that's to say—can trace itself back nearly two hundred years, and the Mater's goes back to the War of the Roses. It's really pretty awful, Cocoa.'

The half-caste smiled as the warrior floundered. Indeed he valued him most when he fell full length. And the whole conversation—so unimportant in itself—gave him a sense of approaching victory which he had not so far entertained. He had a feeling that Lionel knew that he was in the net or almost in

6. Dishonorably discharged.
7. Offensive term for people of mixed racial descent.

it, and did not mind. Cross-question him further! Quick! Rattle him! 'Is Dad dead?' he snapped.

'I couldn't very well come East if he wasn't. He has made our name stink in these parts. As it is I've had to change my name, or rather drop half of it. He called himself Major Corrie March. We were all proud of the "Corrie" and had reason to be. Try saying "Corrie March" to the Big Eight here, and watch the effect.'

'You must get two passports, must you not, one with and one without a "Corrie" on it. I will fix it, yes? At Bombay?'

'So as I can cheat like you? No, thank you. My name is Lionel March and that's my name.' He poured out some more champagne.

'Are you like him?'

'I should hope not. I hope I'm not cruel and remorseless and selfish and self-indulgent and a liar as he was.'

'I don't mean unimportant things like that. I mean are you like him to look at?'

'You have the strangest ideas of what is important.'

'Was his body like yours?'

'How should I know?'—and he was suddenly shy. 'I was only a kid and the Mater's torn up every photograph of him she could lay her hands on. He was a hundred per cent Aryan all right and there was plenty of him as there certainly is of me—indeed there'll be too much of me if I continue swilling at this rate. Suppose we talk about your passports for a change.'

'Was he one in whom those who sought rest found fire, and fire rest?'

'I've not the least idea what you're talking about. Do you mean I'm such a one myself?'

'I do.'

'I've not the least idea——' Then he hesitated. 'Unless . . . no, you're daft[8] as usual, and in any case we've spent more than enough time in dissecting my unfortunate parent. I brought him up to show you how much the Mater has to put up with, one has to make endless allowances for her and you mustn't take it amiss if she's unreasonable about you. She'd probably like you if she got the chance. There was something else that upset her at the time . . . I seem to be bringing out all the family skeletons in a bunch, still they won't go any further, and I feel like chattering to someone about everything, once in a way. I've never had anyone to talk to like you. Never, and don't suppose I ever shall. Do you happen to remember the youngest of us all, the one we called Baby?'

'Ah, that pretty Baby!'

'Well, a fortnight after we landed and while we were up at my grandfather's looking for a house, that poor kid died.'

'Die what of?' he exclaimed, suddenly agitated. He raised his knees and rested his chin on them. With his nudity and his polished duskiness and his strange-shaped head, he suggested an image crouched outside a tomb.

'Influenza, quite straightforward. It was going through the parish and he caught it. But the worst of it was the Mater wouldn't be reasonable. She would insist that it was sunstroke, and that he got it running about with no topi on when she wasn't looking after him properly in this very same Red Sea.'

'Her poor pretty Baby. So I killed him for her.'

'Cocoa! How ever did you guess that? It's exactly what she twisted it round

8. Foolish.

to. We had quite a time with her. Olive argued, grandfather prayed . . . and I could only hang around and do the wrong thing, as I generally do.'

'But she—she saw me only, running in the sun with my devil's head, and m'm m'm m'm all you follow me till the last one the tiny one dies, and she, she talking to an officer, a handsome one, oh to sleep in his arms as I shall in yours, so she forgets the sun and it strikes the tiny one. I see.'

'Yes, you see in a wrong sort of way'; every now and then came these outbursts which ought to be rubbish yet weren't. Wrong of course about his mother, who was the very soul of purity, and over Captain Armstrong, who had become their valued family adviser. But right over Baby's death: she actually had declared that the idle unmanly imp had killed him, and designedly. Of recent years she had not referred to the disaster, and might have forgotten it. He was more than ever vexed with himself for mentioning Cocoanut in the letter he had recently posted to her.

'Did I kill him for you also?'

'For me? Of course not. I know the difference between influenza and sunstroke, and you don't develop the last-named after a three weeks' interval.'

'Did I kill him for anyone—or for anything?'

Lionel gazed into eyes that gazed through him and through cabin walls into the sea. A few days ago he would have ridiculed the question, but tonight he was respectful. This was because his affection, having struck earthward, was just trying to flower. 'Something's worrying you? Why not tell me about it?' he said.

'Did you love pretty Baby?'

'No, I was accustomed to see him around but he was too small to get interested in and I haven't given him a thought for years. So all's well.'

'There is nothing between us then?'

'Why should there be?'

'Lionel—dare I ask you one more question?'

'Yes, of course.'

'It is about blood. It is the last of all the questions. Have you ever shed blood?'

'No—oh, sorry, I should have said yes. I forgot that little war of mine. It goes clean out of my head between times. A battle's such a mess-up, you wouldn't believe, and this one had a miniature sandstorm raging to make confusion more confounded. Yes, I shed blood all right, or so the official report says. I didn't know at the time.' He was suddenly silent. Vividly and unexpectedly the desert surged up, and he saw it as a cameo,[9] from outside. The central figure—a grotesque one—was himself going berserk, and close to him was a dying savage who had managed to wound him and was trying to speak.

'I hope I never shed blood,' the other said. 'I do not blame others, but for me never.'

'I don't expect you ever will. You're not exactly cut out for a man of war. All the same, I've fallen for you.'

He had not expected to say this, and it was the unexpectedness that so delighted the boy. He turned away his face. It was distorted with joy and suffused with the odd purplish tint that denoted violent emotion. Everything had gone fairly right for a long time. Each step in the stumbling confession had brought him nearer to knowing what the beloved was like. But an open

9. Vividly carved stone.

avowal—he had not hoped for so much. 'Before morning I shall have enslaved him,' he thought, 'and he will begin doing whatever I put into his mind.' Even now he did not exult, for he knew by experience that though he always got what he wanted he seldom kept it, also that too much adoration can develop a flaw in the jewel. He remained impassive, crouched like a statue, chin on knees, hands round ankles, waiting for words to which he could safely reply.

'It seemed just a bit of foolery at first,' he went on. 'I woke up properly ashamed of myself after Gib, I don't mind telling you. Since then it's been getting so different, and now it's nothing but us. I tell you one thing though, one silly mistake I've made. I ought never to have mentioned you in that letter to the Mater. There's no advantage in putting her on the scent of something she can't understand; it's all right what we do, I don't mean that.'

'So you want the letter back?'

'But it's posted! Not much use wanting it.'

'Posted?' He was back to his normal and laughed gaily, his sharp teeth gleaming. 'What is posting? Nothing at all, even in a red English pillar-box. Even thence you can get most things out, and here is a boat. No! My secretary comes to you tomorrow morning: 'Excuse me, Captain March, sir, did you perhaps drop this unposted letter upon the deck?' You thank secretary, you take letter, you write Mater a better letter. Does anything trouble you now?'

'Not really. Except——'

'Except what?'

'Except I'm—I don't know. I'm fonder of you than I know how to say.'

'Should that trouble you?'

O calm mutual night, to one of them triumphant and promising both of them peace! O silence except for the boat throbbing gently! Lionel sighed, with a happiness he couldn't understand. 'You ought to have someone to look after you,' he said tenderly. Had he said this before to a woman and had she responded? No such recollection disturbed him, he did not even know that he was falling in love. 'I wish I could stay with you myself, but of course that's out of the question. If only things were a little different I——Come along, let's get our sleep.'

'You shall sleep and you shall awake.' For the moment was upon them at last, the flower opened to receive them, the appointed star mounted the sky, the beloved leaned against him to switch off the light over by the door. He closed his eyes to anticipate divine darkness. He was going to win. All was happening as he had planned, and when morning came and practical life had to be re-entered he would have won.

'Damn!'

The ugly stupid little word rattled out. 'Damn and blast,' Lionel muttered. As he stretched towards the switch, he had noticed the bolt close to it, and he discovered that he had left the door unbolted. The consequences could have been awkward. 'Pretty careless of me,' he reflected, suddenly wide awake. He looked round the cabin as a general might at a battlefield nearly lost by his own folly. The crouched figure was only a unit in it, and no longer the centre of desire. 'Cocoa, I'm awfully sorry,' he went on. 'As a rule it's you who take the risks, this time it's me. I apologize.'

The other roused himself from the twilight where he had hoped to be joined, and tried to follow the meaningless words. Something must have miscarried, but what? The sound of an apology was odious. He had always loathed the English trick of saying 'It's all my fault'; and if he encountered it in business it provided an extra incentive to cheat, and it was contemptible on the lips of a hero. When he grasped what the little trouble was and what the empty 'damns' signified, he closed his eyes again and said, 'Bolt the door therefore.'

'I have.'

'Turn out the light therefore.'

'I will. But a mistake like this makes one feel all insecure. It could have meant a courtmartial.'

'Could it, man?' he said sadly—sad because the moment towards which they were moving might be passing, because the chances of their convergence might be lost. What could he safely say? 'You was not to blame over the door, dear Lion,' he said. 'I mean we was both to blame. I knew it was unlocked all the time.' He said this hoping to console the beloved and to recall him to the entrance of night. He could not have made a more disastrous remark.

'You knew. But why didn't you say?'

'I had not the time.'

'Not the time to say "Bolt the door"?'

'No, I had not the time. I did not speak because there was no moment for such a speech.'

'No moment when I've been here for ages?'

'And when in that hour? When you come in first? Then? When you embrace me and summon my heart's blood. Is that the moment to speak? When I rest in your arms and you in mine, when your cigarette burns us, when we drink from one glass? When you are smiling? Do I interrupt then? Do I then say, "Captain March, sir, you have however forgotten to bolt the cabin door?" And when we talk of our faraway boat and of poor pretty Baby whom I never killed and I did not want to kill, and I never dreamt to kill—of what should we talk but of things far away? Lionel, no, no. Lion of the Night, come back to me before our hearts cool. Here is our place and we have so far no other and only we can guard each other. The door shut, the door unshut, is nothing, and is the same.'

'It wouldn't be nothing if the steward had come in,' said Lionel grimly.

'What harm if he did come in?'

'Give him the shock of his life, to say the least of it.'

'No shock at all. Such men are accustomed to far worse. He would be sure of a larger tip and therefore pleased. "Excuse me, gentlemen . . ." Then he goes and tomorrow my secretary tips him.'

'Cocoa, for God's sake, the things you sometimes say . . .' The cynicism repelled him. He noticed that it sometimes came after a bout of high faluting. It was a sort of backwash.[1] 'You never seem to realize the risks we run, either. Suppose I got fired from the Army through this.'

'Yes, suppose?'

'Well, what else could I do?'

'You could be my assistant manager at Basra.'[2]

'Not a very attractive alternative.' He was not sure whether he was being laughed at or not, which always rattled him, and the incident of the unbolted door increased in importance. He apologized again 'for my share in it' and added, 'You've not told that scruffy Parsee of yours about us, I do trust.'

'No. Oh no no no no and oh no. Satisfied?'

---

1. Motion of a receding wave.   2. City in what is now southeast Iraq.

'Nor the Goanese[3] steward?'

'Not told. Only tipped. Tip all. Of what other use is money?'

'I shall think you've tipped me next.'

'So I have.'

'That's not a pretty thing to say.'

'I am not pretty. I am not like you.' And he burst into tears. Lionel knew that nerves were on edge, but the suggestion that he was a hireling hurt him badly. He whose pride and duty it was to be independent and command! Had he been regarded as a male prostitute? 'What's upset you?' he said as kindly as possible. 'Don't take on so, Cocoa, there's no occasion for it.'

The sobs continued. He was weeping because he had planned wrongly. Rage rather than grief convulsed him. The bolt unbolted, the little snake not driven back into its hole—he had foreseen everything else and ignored the enemy at the gate. Bolt and double-bolt now—they would never complete the movement of love. As sometimes happened to him when he was unhinged, he could foretell the immediate future, and he knew before Lionel spoke exactly what he was going to say.

'I think I'll go on deck for a smoke.'

'Go.'

'I've a bit of a headache with this stupid misunderstanding, plus too much booze. I want a breath of fresh air. Then I'll come back.'

'When you come back you will not be you. And I may not be I.'

Further tears. Snivellings. 'We're both to blame,' said Lionel patiently, taking up the cigarette-case. 'I'm not letting myself off. I was careless. But why you didn't tell me at once I shall never understand, not if you talk till you're blue. I've explained to you repeatedly that this game we've been playing's a risky one, and honestly I think we'd better never have started it. However, we'll talk about that when you're not so upset.' Here he remembered that the cigarette-case was one of his patron's presents to him, so he substituted for it a favourite old pipe. The change was observed and it caused a fresh paroxysm. Like many men of the warm-blooded type, he was sympathetic to a few tears but exasperated when they persisted. Fellow crying and not trying to stop. Fellow crying as if he had the right to cry. Repeating 'I'll come back' as cordially as he could, he went up on deck to think the whole situation over. For there were several things about it he didn't like at all.

Cocoanut stopped weeping as soon as he was alone. Tears were a method of appeal which had failed, and he must seek comfort for his misery and desolation elsewhere. What he longed to do was to climb up into Lionel's berth above him and snuggle down there and dream that he might be joined. He dared not. Whatever else he ventured, it must not be that. It was forbidden to him, although nothing had ever been said. It was the secret place, the sacred place whence strength issued, as he had learned during the first half-hour of the voyage. It was the lair of a beast who might retaliate. So he remained down in his own berth, the safe one, where his lover would certainly never return. It was wiser to work and make money, and he did so for a time. It was still wiser to sleep, and presently he put his ledger aside and lay motionless. His eyes closed. His nostrils occasionally twitched as if responding to something which the rest of his body ignored. The scarf covered him. For it was one of

3. From Goa, India.

his many superstitions that it is dangerous to lie unclad when alone. Jealous of what she sees, the hag comes with her scimitar,[4] and she . . . Or she lifts up a man when he feels lighter than air.

V

Up on deck, alone with his pipe, Lionel began to recover his poise and his sense of leadership. Not that he and his pipe were really alone, for the deck was covered with passengers who had had their bedding carried up and now slept under the stars. They lay prone in every direction, and he had to step carefully between them on his way to the railing. He had forgotten that this migration happened nightly as soon as a boat entered the Red Sea; his nights had passed otherwise and elsewhere. Here lay a guileless subaltern, cherry-cheeked; there lay Colonel Arbuthnot, his bottom turned. Mrs Arbuthnot lay parted from her lord in the ladies' section. In the morning, very early, the Goanese stewards would awake the sahibs and carry their bedding back to their cabins. It was an old ritual—not practised in the English Channel or the Bay of Biscay or even in the Mediterranean—and on previous voyages he had taken part in it.

How decent and reliable they looked, the folk to whom he belonged! He had been born one of them, he had his work with them, he meant to marry into their caste. If he forfeited their companionship he would become nobody and nothing. The widened expanse of the sea, the winking lighthouse, helped to compose him, but what really recalled him to sanity was this quiet sleeping company of his peers. He liked his profession, and was rising in it thanks to that little war; it would be mad to jeopardize it, which he had been doing ever since he drank too much champagne at Gibraltar.

Not that he had ever been a saint. No—he had occasionally joined a brothel expedition, so as not to seem better than his fellow officers. But he had not been so much bothered by sex as were some of them. He hadn't had the time, what with his soldiering duties and his obligations at home as eldest son, and the doc said an occasional wet dream was nothing to worry about. Don't sleep on your back, though. On this simple routine he had proceeded since puberty. And during the past few months he had proceeded even further. Learning that he was to be posted to India, where he would contact Isabel, he had disciplined himself more severely and practised chastity even in thought. It was the least he could do for the girl he hoped to marry. Sex had entirely receded—only to come charging back like a bull. That infernal Cocoa—the mischief he had done. He had woken up so much that might have slept.

For Isabel's sake, as for his profession's, their foolish relationship must stop at once. He could not think how he had yielded to it, or why it had involved him so deeply. It would have ended at Bombay, it would have to end now, and Cocoanut must cry his eyes out if he thought it worth while. So far all was clear. But behind Isabel, behind the Army, was another power, whom he could not consider calmly; his mother, blind-eyed in the midst of the enormous web she had spun—filaments drifting everywhere, strands catching. There was no reasoning with her or about her, she understood nothing and controlled every-thing. She had suffered too much and was too high-minded to be judged like

4. Curved Asian sword.

other people, she was outside carnality and incapable of pardoning it. Earlier in the evening, when Cocoa mentioned her, he had tried to imagine her with his father, enjoying the sensations he was beginning to find so pleasant, but the attempt was sacrilegious and he was shocked at himself. From the great blank country she inhabited came a voice condemning him and all her children for sin, but condemning him most. There was no parleying[5] with her—she was a voice. God had not granted her ears—nor could she see, mercifully: the sight of him stripping[6] would have killed her. He, her first-born, set apart for the redemption of the family name. His surviving brother was too much a bookworm to be of any use, and the other two were girls.

He spat into the sea. He promised her 'Never again'. The words went out into the night like other enchantments. He said them aloud, and Colonel Arbuthnot, who was a light sleeper, woke up and switched on his torch.

'Hullo, who's that, what's there?'

'March, sir, Lionel March. I'm afraid I've disturbed you.'

'No, no, Lionel, that's all right, I wasn't asleep. Ye gods, what gorgeous pyjamas the fellow's wearing. What's he going about like a lone wolf for? Eh?'

'Too hot in my cabin, sir. Nothing sinister.'

'How goes the resident wog?'

'The resident wog he sleeps.'

'By the way, what's his name?'

'Moraes, I believe.'

'Exactly. Mr Moraes is in for trouble.'

'Oh. What for, sir?'

'For being on board. Lady Manning has just heard the story. It turns out that he gave someone in the London office a fat bribe to get him a passage though the boat was full, and as an easy way out they put him into your cabin. I don't care who gives or takes bribes. Doesn't interest me. But if the Company thinks it can treat a British officer like that it's very much mistaken. I'm going to raise hell at Bombay.'

'He's not been any particular nuisance,' said Lionel after a pause.

'I daresay not. It's the question of our prestige in the East, and it is also very hard luck on you, very hard. Why don't you come and sleep on deck like the rest of the gang?'

'Sound idea, I will.'

'We've managed to cordon off this section of the deck, and woe betide anything black that walks this way, if it's only a beetle. Good night.'

'Good night, sir.' Then something snapped and he heard himself shouting, 'Bloody rubbish, leave the kid alone.'

'Wh—what's that, didn't catch,' said the puzzled Colonel.

'Nothing sir, sorry sir.' And he was back in the cabin.

Why on earth had he nearly betrayed himself just as everything was going right? There seemed a sort of devil around. At the beginning of the voyage he had tempted him to throw himself overboard for no reason, but this was something more serious. 'When you come back to the cabin you will not be you,' Cocoa had said; and was it so?

However, the lower berth was empty, that was something, the boy must have gone to the lav, and he slipped out of his effeminate pyjamas and prepared

---

5. Mutual conversation.
6. Forster's substitution for his original phrase, "topping a dago." "Topping": copulating with.

to finish the night where he belonged—a good sleep there would steady him. His forearm was already along the rail, his foot poised for the upspring, when he saw what had happened.

'Hullo, Cocoanut, up in my berth for a change?' he said in clipped officer-tones, for it was dangerous to get angry. 'Stay there if you want to, I've just decided to sleep on deck.' There was no reply, but his own remarks pleased him and he decided to go further. 'As a matter of fact I shan't be using our cabin again except when it is absolutely necessary,' he continued. 'It's scarcely three days to Bombay, so I can easily manage, and I shan't, we shan't be meeting again after disembarkation. As I said earlier on, the whole thing has been a bit of a mistake. I wish we . . . ' He stopped. If only it wasn't so difficult to be kind! But his talk with the Colonel and his communion with the Mater prevented it. He must keep with his own people, or he would perish. He added, 'Sorry to have to say all this.'

'Kiss me.'

The words fell quietly after his brassiness and vulgarity and he could not answer them. The face was close to his now, the body curved away seductively into darkness.

'Kiss me.'

'No.'

'Noah? No? Then I kiss you.' And he lowered his mouth on to the muscular forearm and bit it.

Lionel yelped with the pain.

'Bloody bitch, wait till I . . . ' Blood oozed between the gold-bright hairs. 'You wait . . . ' And the scar in his groin reopened. The cabin vanished. He was back in a desert fighting savages. One of them asked for mercy, stumbled, and found none.

The sweet act of vengeance followed, sweeter than ever for both of them, and as ecstasy hardened into agony his hands twisted the throat. Neither of them knew when the end came, and he when he realized it felt no sadness, no remorse. It was part of a curve that had long been declining, and had nothing to do with death. He covered again with his warmth and kissed the closed eyelids tenderly and spread the bright-coloured scarf. Then he burst out of the stupid cabin on to the deck, and naked and with the seeds of love on him he dived into the sea.

The scandal was appalling. The Big Eight did their best, but it was soon all over the boat that a British officer had committed suicide after murdering a half-caste. Some of the passengers recoiled from such news. Others snuffled for more. The secretary of Moraes was induced to gossip and hint at proclivities, the cabin steward proved to have been overtipped, the Master at Arms had had complaints which he had managed to stifle, the Purser had been suspicious throughout, and the doctor who examined the injuries divulged that strangulation was only one of them, and that March had been a monster in human form, of whom the earth was well rid. The cabin was sealed up for further examination later, and the place where the two boys had made love and the tokens they had exchanged in their love went on without them to Bombay. For Lionel had been only a boy.

His body was never recovered—the blood on it quickly attracted the sharks. The body of his victim was consigned to the deep with all possible speed. There was a slight disturbance at the funeral. The native crew had become interested in it, no one understood why, and when the corpse was lowered were heard betting which way it would float. It moved northwards—contrary to the prevailing current—and there were clappings of hands and some smiles.

Finally Mrs March had to be informed. Colonel Arbuthnot and Lady Manning were deputed for the thankless task. Colonel Arbuthnot assured her that her son's death had been accidental, whatever she heard to the contrary; that he had stumbled overboard in the darkness during a friendly talk they had had together on deck. Lady Manning spoke with warmth and affection of his good looks and good manners and his patience 'with us old fogies at our Bridge.' Mrs March thanked them for writing but made no comment. She also received a letter from Lionel himself—the one that should have been intercepted in the post—and she never mentioned his name again.

1913–58   1972

VIRGINIA WOOLF
1882–1941

Virginia Woolf was born in London, daughter of Julia Jackson Duckworth, a member of the Duckworth publishing family, and Leslie (later Sir Leslie) Stephen, the Victorian critic, philosopher, biographer, and scholar. She grew up within a large and talented family, educating herself in her father's magnificent library, meeting in childhood many eminent Victorians, and learning Greek from the essayist and critic Walter Pater's sister. Writing and the intellectual life thus came naturally to her. But her youth was shadowed by suffering: her older half-brother sexually abused her; her mother died in 1895, precipitating the first of her mental breakdowns; a beloved half-sister died in childbirth two years later; her father died of cancer in 1904; and a brother died of typhoid in 1906.

After her father's death she settled with her sister and two brothers in Bloomsbury, the district of London that later became associated with the group among whom she moved. The "Bloomsbury Group" was an intellectual coterie frequented at various times by the biographer Lytton Strachey, the economist John Maynard Keynes, the art critic Roger Fry, and the novelist E. M. Forster. When her sister, Vanessa, a notable painter, married Clive Bell, an art critic, in 1907, Woolf and her brother Adrian took another house in Bloomsbury, and there they entertained their literary and artistic friends at evening gatherings, where the conversation sparkled. The Bloomsbury Group thrived at the center of the middle-class and upper-middle-class London intelligentsia. Their intelligence was equaled by their frankness, notably on sexual topics, and the sexual life of Bloomsbury provided ample material for discussion and contributed to Woolf's freedom of thinking about gender relations. The painter Duncan Grant, for example, was at different times the lover of Keynes, Woolf's brother Adrian, and her sister, whose daughter, Angelica, he fathered. Woolf too was bisexual; and thirteen years after her marriage to the journalist and essayist Leonard Woolf, she fell passionately in love with the poet Vita [Victoria] Sackville-West, wife of the bisexual diplomat and author Harold Nicolson. Woolf's relationship with this aristocratic lesbian inspired the most lighthearted and scintillating of her books, Orlando (1928), a novel about a transhistorical androgynous protagonist, whose identity shifts from masculine to feminine over centuries.

Underneath Woolf's liveliness and wit—qualities so well known among the Bloomsbury Group—lay psychological tensions created partly by her childhood wounds and partly by her perfectionism, she being her own most exacting critic. The public was unaware until her death that she had been subject to periods of severe depression, particularly after finishing a book. In March 1941 she drowned herself in a river, an act influenced by her dread of World War II (she and Leonard would have been arrested by the Gestapo had the Nazis invaded England) and her fear that she was about to lose her mind and become a burden on her husband, who had supported her emotionally and intellectually. (In 1917 the Woolfs had founded the Hogarth Press, which published some of the most interesting literature of their time, including T. S. Eliot's *Poems* [1919], fiction by Maxim Gorky, Katherine Mansfield, and E. M. Forster, the English translations of Freud, and Virginia's novels.)

As a fiction writer Woolf rebelled against what she called the "materialism" of novelists such as her contemporaries Arnold Bennett and John Galsworthy, who depicted suffering and social injustice through gritty realism, and she sought to render more delicately those aspects of consciousness in which she felt the truth of human experience lay. In her essay "Modern Fiction" she defines the task of the novelist as looking within, as conveying the mind receiving "a myriad impressions," as representing the "luminous halo" or "semi-transparent envelope surrounding us from the beginning of consciousness to the end." In her novels she abandoned linear narratives in favor of interior monologues and stream of consciousness narration, exploring with great subtlety problems of personal identity and personal relationships as well as the significance of time, change, loss, and memory for human personality. After two conventionally realistic novels, *The Voyage Out* (1915) and *Night and Day* (1919), she developed her own style, a carefully modulated flow that brought into prose fiction something of the rhythms and imagery of lyric poetry. While intensely psychological and interior, her novels also found inspiration and material in the physical realities of the body and in the heavily trafficked and populated streets of London. In *Monday or Tuesday* (1921), a series of sketches, she explored the possibilities of moving between action and contemplation, between retrospection and anticipation, between specific external events and delicate tracings of the flow of consciousness. These technical experiments made possible those later novels in which her characteristic method is fully developed—the elegiac *Jacob's Room* (1922); *Mrs. Dalloway* (1925), the first completely successful realization of her style; *To the Lighthouse* (1927), which in part memorializes her parents; *The Waves* (1931), the most experimental and difficult of her novels; and *Between the Acts* (1941), which includes a discontinuous pageant of English history and was published after her death.

Woolf was also a prodigious reviewer and essayist. She began to write criticism in 1905 for the *Times Literary Supplement* and published some five hundred reviews and essays for it and other periodicals, collected in *The Common Reader* (1925) and *The Second Common Reader* (1932); her prose presents itself as suggestive rather than authoritative and has an engaging air of spontaneity. In marked contrast to the formal language of the lecture hall or philosophical treatise, arenas and forms of learning from which women were historically barred, she writes in an informal, personal, playfully polemical tone, which is implicitly linked to her identity as a female writer. In her essays she is equally concerned with her own craft as a writer and with what it was like to be a quite different person living in a different age. At once more informal and more revealing are the six volumes of her *Letters* (1975–80) and five volumes of her *Diary* (1977–84), which she began to write in 1917. These, with their running commentary on her life and work, resemble a painter's sketchbooks and serve as a reminder that her writings, for all their variety, have the coherence found only in the work of the greatest literary artists.

Over the course of her career, Woolf grew increasingly concerned with the position of women, especially professional women, and the constrictions under which they suffered. She wrote several cogent essays on the subject, and women's social subjection also arises in her fiction. Her novel *The Years* (1937) was originally to have reflections on the position of women interspersed amid the action, but she later decided to publish them as a separate book, *Three Guineas* (1938). In *A Room of*

One's Own (1929), an essay based on two lectures on "Women and Fiction" delivered to female students at Cambridge, Woolf discusses various male institutions that historically either were denied to or oppressed women. Refused access to education, wealth, and property ownership, women lacked the conditions necessary to write and were unable to develop a literature of their own. Woolf advocated the creation of a literature that would include women's experience and ways of thinking, but instead of encouraging an exclusively female perspective, she proposed literature that would be "androgynous in mind" and resonate equally with men and women.

The Mark on the Wall

Perhaps it was the middle of January in the present year that I first looked up and saw the mark on the wall. In order to fix a date it is necessary to remember what one saw. So now I think of the fire; the steady film of yellow light upon the page of my book; the three chrysanthemums in the round glass bowl on the mantelpiece. Yes, it must have been the winter time, and we had just finished our tea, for I remember that I was smoking a cigarette when I looked up and saw the mark on the wall for the first time. I looked up through the smoke of my cigarette and my eye lodged for a moment upon the burning coals, and that old fancy of the crimson flag flapping from the castle tower came into my mind, and I thought of the cavalcade of red knights riding up the side of the black rock. Rather to my relief the sight of the mark interrupted the fancy, for it is an old fancy, an automatic fancy, made as a child perhaps. The mark was a small round mark, black upon the white wall, about six or seven inches above the mantelpiece.

How readily our thoughts swarm upon a new object, lifting it a little way, as ants carry a blade of straw so feverishly, and then leave it. . . . If that mark was made by a nail, it can't have been for a picture, it must have been for a miniature—the miniature of a lady with white powdered curls, powder-dusted cheeks, and lips like red carnations. A fraud of course, for the people who had this house before us would have chosen pictures in that way—an old picture for an old room. That is the sort of people they were—very interesting people, and I think of them so often, in such queer places, because one will never see them again, never know what happened next. They wanted to leave this house because they wanted to change their style of furniture, so he said, and he was in process of saying that in his opinion art should have ideas behind it when we were torn asunder, as one is torn from the old lady about to pour out tea and the young man about to hit the tennis ball in the back garden of the suburban villa as one rushes past in the train.

But for that mark, I'm not sure about it; I don't believe it was made by a nail after all; it's too big, too round, for that. I might get up, but if I got up and looked at it, ten to one I shouldn't be able to say for certain; because once a thing's done, no one ever knows how it happened. Oh! dear me, the mystery of life; the inaccuracy of thought! The ignorance of humanity! To show how very little control of our possessions we have—what an accidental affair this living is after all our civilisation—let me just count over a few of the things lost in one lifetime, beginning, for that seems always the most mysterious of losses—what cat would gnaw, what rat would nibble—three pale blue canisters of book-binding tools? Then there were the bird cages, the iron hoops, the steel skates, the Queen Anne coal-scuttle, the bagatelle[1] board, the hand organ—all gone, and jewels, too. Opals and emeralds, they lie about the roots of turnips. What a scraping paring affair it is to be sure! The wonder is that I've any clothes on my back, that I sit surrounded by solid furniture at this moment. Why, if one wants to compare life to anything, one must liken it to being blown through the Tube[2] at fifty miles an hour—landing at the other end without a single hairpin in one's hair! Shot out at the feet of God entirely naked! Tumbling head over heels in the asphodel meadows[3] like brown paper parcels pitched down a shoot in the post office! With one's hair flying back like the tail of a race-horse. Yes, that seems to express the rapidity of life, the perpetual waste and repair; all so casual, all so haphazard. . . .

But after life. The slow pulling down of thick green stalks so that the cup of the flower, as it turns over, deluges one with purple and red light. Why, after all, should one not be born there as one is born here, helpless, speechless, unable to focus one's eyesight, groping at the roots of the grass, at the toes of the Giants? As for saying which are trees, and which are men and women, or whether there are such things, that one won't be in a condition to do for fifty years or so. There will be nothing but spaces of light and dark, intersected by thick stalks, and rather higher up perhaps, rose-shaped blots of an indistinct colour—dim pinks and blues—which will, as time goes on, become more definite, become—I don't know what. . . .

And yet that mark on the wall is not a hole at all. It may even be caused by some round black substance, such as a small rose leaf, left over from the summer, and I, not being a very vigilant housekeeper—look at the dust on the mantelpiece, for example, the dust which, so they say, buried Troy[4] three times over, only fragments of pots utterly refusing annihilation, as one can believe.

The tree outside the window taps very gently on the pane. . . . . I want to think quietly, calmly, spaciously, never to be interrupted, never to have to rise from my chair, to slip easily from one thing to another, without any sense of hostility, or obstacle. I want to sink deeper and deeper, away from the surface, with its hard separate facts. To steady myself, let me catch hold of the first idea that passes . . . Shakespeare. . . . Well, he will do as well as another. A man who sat himself solidly in an arm-chair, and looked into the fire, so— A shower of ideas fell perpetually from some very high Heaven down through his mind. He leant his forehead on his hand, and people, looking in through the open door—for this scene is supposed to take place on a summer's evening— But how dull this is, this historical fiction! It doesn't interest me at all. I wish I could hit upon a pleasant track of thought, a track indirectly reflecting credit upon myself, for those are the pleasantest thoughts, and very frequent even in the minds of modest mouse-coloured people, who believe genuinely that they dislike to hear their own praises. They are not thoughts directly praising oneself; that is the beauty of them; they are thoughts like this:

"And then I came into the room. They were discussing botany. I said how I'd seen a flower growing on a dust heap on the site of an old house in Kingsway.[5] The seed, I said, must have been sown in the reign of Charles the First. What flowers grew in the reign of Charles the First?" I asked—(but I don't

---

1. Game played on oblong table with cue and balls. "Coal-scuttle": metal pail for carrying coal.
2. The London underground railway, or subway.
3. I.e., heaven, the next world (in Greek mythol-

ogy asphodel flowers grow in the Elysian fields).
4. Legendary site of ancient war chronicled in Homer's Greek epic *The Iliad*.
5. Street in London.

remember the answer). Tall flowers with purple tassels to them perhaps. And so it goes on. All the time I'm dressing up the figure of myself in my own mind, lovingly, stealthily, not openly adoring it, for if I did that, I should catch myself out, and stretch my hand at once for a book in self-protection. Indeed, it is curious how instinctively one protects the image of oneself from idolatry or any other handling that could make it ridiculous, or too unlike the original to be believed in any longer. Or is it not so very curious after all? It is a matter of great importance. Suppose the looking-glass smashes, the image disappears, and the romantic figure with the green of forest depths all about it is there no longer, but only that shell of a person which is seen by other people—what an airless, shallow, bald, prominent world it becomes! A world not to be lived in. As we face each other in omnibuses and underground railways we are looking into the mirror; that accounts for the vagueness, the gleam of glassiness, in our eyes. And the novelists in future will realise more and more the importance of these reflections, for of course there is not one reflection but an almost infinite number; those are the depths they will explore, those the phantoms they will pursue, leaving the description of reality more and more out of their stories, taking a knowledge of it for granted, as the Greeks did and Shakespeare perhaps—but these generalisations are very worthless. The military sound of the word is enough. It recalls leading articles, cabinet ministers—a whole class of things indeed which, as a child, one thought the thing itself, the standard thing, the real thing, from which one could not depart save at the risk of nameless damnation. Generalisations bring back somehow Sunday in London, Sunday afternoon walks, Sunday luncheons, and also ways of speaking of the dead, clothes, and habits—like the habit of sitting all together in one room until a certain hour, although nobody liked it. There was a rule for everything. The rule for tablecloths at that particular period was that they should be made of tapestry with little yellow compartments marked upon them, such as you may see in photographs of the carpets in the corridors of the royal palaces. Tablecloths of a different kind were not real tablecloths. How shocking, and yet how wonderful it was to discover that these real things, Sunday luncheons, Sunday walks, country houses, and tablecloths were not entirely real, were indeed half phantoms, and the damnation which visited the disbeliever in them was only a sense of illegitimate freedom. What now takes the place of those things I wonder, those real standard things? Men perhaps, should you be a woman; the masculine point of view which governs our lives, which sets the standard, which establishes Whitaker's Table of Precedency,[6] which has become, I suppose, since the war, half a phantom to many men and women, which soon, one may hope, will be laughed into the dustbin where the phantoms go, the mahogany sideboards and the Landseer[7] prints, Gods and Devils, Hell and so forth, leaving us all with an intoxicating sense of illegitimate freedom—if freedom exists. . . .

In certain lights that mark on the wall seems actually to project from the wall. Nor is it entirely circular. I cannot be sure, but it seems to cast a perceptible shadow, suggesting that if I ran my finger down that strip of the wall it would, at a certain point, mount and descend a small tumulus, a smooth

6. *Whitaker's Almanack*, an annual compendium of information, prints a "Table of Precedency," which shows the order in which the various ranks in public life and society proceed on formal occasions.

7. Sir Edwin Henry Landseer (1802–1873), English painter, reproductions of whose *Stag at Bay, Monarch of the Glen*, and similar animal paintings were often found in Victorian homes.

tumulus like those barrows on the South Downs[8] which are, they say, either tombs or camps. Of the two I should prefer them to be tombs, desiring melancholy like most English people, and finding it natural at the end of a walk to think of the bones stretched beneath the turf. . . . There must be some book about it. Some antiquary must have dug up those bones and given them a name. . . . What sort of a man is an antiquary, I wonder? Retired Colonels for the most part, I daresay, leading parties of aged labourers to the top here, examining clods of earth and stone, and getting into correspondence with the neighbouring clergy, which, being opened at breakfast time, gives them a feeling of importance, and the comparison of arrow-heads necessitates crosscountry journeys to the country towns, an agreeable necessity both to them and to their elderly wives, who wish to make plum jam or to clean out the study, and have every reason for keeping that great question of the camp or the tomb in perpetual suspension, while the Colonel himself feels agreeably philosophic in accumulating evidence on both sides of the question. It is true that he does finally incline to believe in the camp; and, being opposed, indites a pamphlet which he is about to read at the quarterly meeting of the local society when a stroke lays him low, and his last conscious thoughts are not of wife or child, but of the camp and that arrowhead there, which is now in the case at the local museum, together with the foot of a Chinese murderess, a handful of Elizabethan nails, a great many Tudor clay pipes, a piece of Roman pottery, and the wineglass that Nelson[9] drank out of—proving I really don't know what.

No, no, nothing is proved, nothing is known. And if I were to get up at this very moment and ascertain that the mark on the wall is really—what shall we say?—the head of a gigantic old nail, driven in two hundred years ago, which has now, owing to the patient attrition of many generations of housemaids, revealed its head above the coat of paint, and is taking its first view of modern life in the sight of a white-walled fire-lit room, what should I gain?— Knowledge? Matter for further speculation? I can think sitting still as well as standing up. And what is knowledge? What are our learned men save the descendants of witches and hermits who crouched in caves and in woods brewing herbs, interrogating shrew-mice and writing down the language of the stars? And the less we honour them as our superstitions dwindle and our respect for beauty and health of mind increases. . . . Yes, one could imagine a very pleasant world. A quiet, spacious world, with the flowers so red and blue in the open fields. A world without professors or specialists or house-keepers with the profiles of policemen, a world which one could slice with one's thought as a fish slices the water with his fin, grazing the stems of the water-lilies, hanging suspended over nests of white sea eggs. . . . How peaceful it is down here, rooted in the centre of the world and gazing up through the grey waters, with their sudden gleams of light, and their reflections—if it were not for Whitaker's Almanack—if it were not for the Table of Precedency!

I must jump up and see for myself what that mark on the wall really is—a nail, a rose-leaf, a crack in the wood?

Here is Nature once more at her old game of self-preservation. This train of thought, she perceives, is threatening mere waste of energy, even some

8. A range of low hills in southeastern England. "Barrows": mounds of earth or stones erected by prehistoric peoples, usually as burial places.

9. Horatio Nelson (1758–1805), British admiral. "Tudor": 15th-century English.

collision with reality, for who will ever be able to lift a finger against Whitaker's Table of Precedency? The Archbishop of Canterbury is followed by the Lord High Chancellor; the Lord High Chancellor is followed by the Archbishop of York. Everybody follows somebody, such is the philosophy of Whitaker; and the great thing is to know who follows whom. Whitaker knows, and let that, so Nature counsels, comfort you, instead of enraging you; and if you can't be comforted, if you must shatter this hour of peace, think of the mark on the wall.

I understand Nature's game—her prompting to take action as a way of ending any thought that threatens to excite or to pain. Hence, I suppose, comes our slight contempt for men of action—men, we assume, who don't think. Still, there's no harm in putting a full stop to one's disagreeable thoughts by looking at a mark on the wall.

Indeed, now that I have fixed my eyes upon it, I feel that I have grasped a plank in the sea; I feel a satisfying sense of reality which at once turns the two Archbishops and the Lord High Chancellor to the shadows of shades. Here is something definite, something real. Thus, waking from a midnight dream of horror, one hastily turns on the light and lies quiescent, worshipping the chest of drawers, worshipping solidity, worshipping reality, worshipping the impersonal world which is a proof of some existence other than ours. That is what one wants to be sure of. . . . Wood is a pleasant thing to think about. It comes from a tree; and trees grow, and we don't know how they grow. For years and years they grow, without paying any attention to us, in meadows, in forests, and by the side of rivers—all things one likes to think about. The cows swish their tails beneath them on hot afternoons; they paint rivers so green that when a moorhen dives one expects to see its feathers all green when it comes up again. I like to think of the fish balanced against the stream like flags blown out; and of water-beetles slowly raising domes of mud upon the bed of the river. I like to think of the tree itself: first of the close dry sensation of being wood; then the grinding of the storm; then the slow, delicious ooze of sap; I like to think of it, too, on winter's nights standing in the empty field with all leaves close-furled, nothing tender exposed to the iron bullets of the moon, a naked mast upon an earth that goes tumbling, tumbling, all night long. The song of birds must sound very loud and strange in June; and how cold the feet of insects must feel upon it, as they make laborious progresses up the creases of the bark, or sun themselves upon the thin green awning of the leaves, and look straight in front of them with diamond-cut red eyes. . . . One by one the fibres snap beneath the immense cold pressure of the earth, then the last storm comes and, falling, the highest branches drive deep into the ground again. Even so, life isn't done with; there are a million patient, watchful lives still for a tree, all over the world, in bedrooms, in ships, on the pavement, living rooms, where men and women sit after tea, smoking cigarettes. It is full of peaceful thoughts, happy thoughts, this tree. I should like to take each one separately—but something is getting in the way. . . . Where was I? What has it all been about? A tree? A river? The Downs?[1] Whitaker's Almanack? The fields of asphodel? I can't remember a thing. Everything's moving, falling, slipping, vanishing. . . . There is a vast upheaval of matter. Someone is standing over me and saying:

"I'm going out to buy a newspaper."

1. Part of the sea off the east coast of Kent.

"Yes?"

"Though it's no good buying newspapers. . . . Nothing ever happens. Curse this war; God damn this war! . . . All the same, I don't see why we should have a snail on our wall."

Ah, the mark on the wall! It was a snail.

1921

Modern Fiction

In making any survey, even the freest and loosest, of modern fiction, it is difficult not to take it for granted that the modern practice of the art is somehow an improvement upon the old. With their simple tools and primitive materials, it might be said, Fielding[1] did well and Jane Austen even better, but compare their opportunities with ours! Their masterpieces certainly have a strange air of simplicity. And yet the analogy between literature and the process, to choose an example, of making motor cars scarcely holds good beyond the first glance. It is doubtful whether in the course of the centuries, though we have learnt much about making machines, we have learnt anything about making literature. We do not come to write better; all that we can be said to do is to keep moving, now a little in this direction, now in that, but with a circular tendency should the whole course of the track be viewed from a sufficiently lofty pinnacle. It need scarcely be said that we make no claim to stand, even momentarily, upon that vantage-ground. On the flat, in the crowd, half blind with dust, we look back with envy to those happier warriors, whose battle is won and whose achievements wear so serene an air of accomplishment that we can scarcely refrain from whispering that the fight was not so fierce for them as for us. It is for the historian of literature to decide; for him to say if we are now beginning or ending or standing in the middle of a great period of prose fiction, for down in the plain little is visible. We only know that certain gratitudes and hostilities inspire us; that certain paths seem to lead to fertile land, others to the dust and the desert; and of this perhaps it may be worth while to attempt some account.

Our quarrel, then, is not with the classics, and if we speak of quarrelling with Mr Wells, Mr Bennett, and Mr Galsworthy;[2] it is partly that by the mere fact of their existence in the flesh their work has a living, breathing, everyday imperfection which bids us take what liberties with it we choose. But it is also true, that, while we thank them for a thousand gifts, we reserve our unconditional gratitude for Mr Hardy, for Mr Conrad, and in much lesser degree for the Mr Hudson of *The Purple Land, Green Mansions,* and *Far Away and Long Ago.*[3] Mr Wells, Mr Bennett, and Mr Galsworthy have excited so many hopes and disappointed them so persistently that our gratitude largely takes the form of thanking them for having shown us what they might have done but have not done; what we certainly could not do, but as certainly, perhaps, do not wish to do. No single phrase will sum up the charge or grievance which

---

1. Henry Fielding (1707–1754), English novelist.
2. H. G. Wells (1866–1946), Arnold Bennett (1867–1931), John Galsworthy (1867–1933), English novelists.
3. W. H. Hudson (1841–1922), naturalist and

writer, was born in Argentina, although he later lived in London. *The Purple Land* (1885) is about South America; *Green Mansions* (1904), a novel set in South America, was his first real success.

we have to bring against a mass of work so large in its volume and embodying so many qualities, both admirable and the reverse. If we tried to formulate our meaning in one word we should say that these three writers are materialists. It is because they are concerned not with the spirit but with the body that they have disappointed us, and left us with the feeling that the sooner English fiction turns its back upon them, as politely as may be, and marches, if only into the desert, the better for its soul. Naturally, no single word reaches the centre of three separate targets. In the case of Mr Wells it falls notably wide of the mark. And yet even with him it indicates to our thinking the fatal alloy in his genius, the great clod of clay that has got itself mixed up with the purity of his inspiration. But Mr Bennett is perhaps the worst culprit of the three, inasmuch as he is by far the best workman. He can make a book so well constructed and solid in its craftsmanship that it is difficult for the most exacting of critics to see through what chink or crevice decay can creep in. There is not so much as a draught between the frames of the windows, or a crack in the boards. And yet—if life should refuse to live there? That is a risk which the creator of *The Old Wives' Tale,* George Cannon, Edwin Clayhanger,[4] and hosts of other figures, may well claim to have surmounted. His characters live abundantly, even unexpectedly, but it remains to ask how do they live, and what do they live for? More and more they seem to us, deserting even the well-built villa in the Five Towns,[5] to spend their time in some softly padded first-class railway carriage, pressing bells and buttons innumerable; and the destiny to which they travel so luxuriously becomes more and more unquestionably an eternity of bliss spent in the very best hotel in Brighton.[6] It can scarcely be said of Mr Wells that he is a materialist in the sense that he takes too much delight in the solidity of his fabric. His mind is too generous in its sympathies to allow him to spend much time in making things shipshape and substantial. He is a materialist from sheer goodness of heart, taking upon his shoulders the work that ought to have been discharged by Government officials, and in the plethora of his ideas and facts scarcely having leisure to realize, or forgetting to think important, the crudity and coarseness of his human beings. Yet what more damaging criticism can there be both of his earth and of his Heaven than that they are to be inhabited here and hereafter by his Joans and his Peters?[7] Does not the inferiority of their natures tarnish whatever institutions and ideals may be provided for them by the generosity of their creator? Nor, profoundly though we respect the integrity and humanity of Mr Galsworthy, shall we find what we seek in his pages.

If we fasten, then, one label on all these books, on which is one word, materialists, we mean by it that they write of unimportant things; that they spend immense skill and immense industry making the trivial and the transitory appear the true and the enduring.

We have to admit that we are exacting, and, further, that we find it difficult to justify our discontent by explaining what it is that we exact. We frame our question differently at different times. But it reappears most persistently as we drop the finished novel on the crest of a sigh—Is it worth while? What is the point of it all? Can it be that, owing to one of those little deviations which

---

4. Characters in Arnold Bennett's novels; *The Old Wives' Tale* (1908) is the best-known.
5. The pottery towns of Staffordshire in which much of Bennett's fiction was set.
6. Once-fashionable seaside resort on the south-

west coast of England.
7. In his novel *Joan and Peter: The Story of an Education* (1918), Wells advocates education to address social problems.

the human spirit seems to make from time to time, Mr Bennett has come down with his magnificent apparatus for catching life just an inch or two on the wrong side? Life escapes; and perhaps without life nothing else is worth while. It is a confession of vagueness to have to make use of such a figure as this, but we scarcely better the matter by speaking, as critics are prone to do, of reality. Admitting the vagueness which afflicts all criticism of novels, let us hazard the opinion that for us at this moment the form of fiction most in vogue more often misses than secures the thing we seek. Whether we call it life or spirit, truth or reality, this, the essential thing, has moved off, or on, and refuses to be contained any longer in such ill-fitting vestments as we provide. Nevertheless, we go on perseveringly, conscientiously, constructing our two and thirty chapters after a design which more and more ceases to resemble the vision in our minds. So much of the enormous labour of proving the solidity, the likeness to life, of the story is not merely labour thrown away but labour misplaced to the extent of obscuring and blotting out the light of the conception. The writer seems constrained, not by his own free will but by some powerful and unscrupulous tyrant who has him in thrall, to provide a plot, to provide comedy, tragedy, love interest, and an air of probability embalming the whole so impeccable that if all his figures were to come to life they would find themselves dressed down to the last button of their coats in the fashion of the hour. The tyrant is obeyed; the novel is done to a turn. But sometimes, more and more often as time goes by, we suspect a momentary doubt, a spasm of rebellion, as the pages fill themselves in the customary way. Is life like this? Must novels be like this?

Look within and life, it seems, is very far from being "like this." Examine for a moment an ordinary mind on an ordinary day. The mind receives a myriad impressions—trivial, fantastic, evanescent, or engraved with the sharpness of steel. From all sides they come, an incessant shower of innumerable atoms; and as they fall, as they shape themselves into the life of Monday or Tuesday,[8] the accent falls differently from of old; the moment of importance came not here but there; so that, if a writer were a free man and not a slave, if he could write what he chose, not what he must, if he could base his work upon his own feeling and not upon convention, there would be no plot, no comedy, no tragedy, no love interest or catastrophe in the accepted style, and perhaps not a single button sewn on as the Bond Street[9] tailors would have it. Life is not a series of gig-lamps[1] symmetrically arranged; life is a luminous halo, a semi-transparent envelope surrounding us from the beginning of consciousness to the end. Is it not the task of the novelist to convey this varying, this unknown and uncircumscribed spirit, whatever aberration or complexity it may display, with as little mixture of the alien and external as possible? We are not pleading merely for courage and sincerity; we are suggesting that the proper stuff of fiction is a little other than custom would have us believe it.

It is, at any rate, in some such fashion as this that we seek to define the quality which distinguishes the work of several young writers, among whom Mr James Joyce is the most notable, from that of their predecessors. They attempt to come closer to life, and to preserve more sincerely and exactly what interests and moves them, even if to do so they must discard most of the conventions which are commonly observed by the novelist. Let us record the

---

8. *Monday or Tuesday* was Woolf's 1921 collection of experimental stories and sketches.

9. Fashionable shopping street in London.
1. Carriage lamps.

atoms as they fall upon the mind in the order in which they fall, let us trace the pattern, however disconnected and incoherent in appearance, which each sight or incident scores upon the consciousness. Let us not take it for granted that life exists more fully in what is commonly thought big than in what is commonly thought small. Anyone who has read *The Portrait of the Artist as a Young Man* or, what promises to be a far more interesting work, *Ulysses*,[2] now appearing in the *Little Review*, will have hazarded some theory of this nature as to Mr Joyce's intention. On our part, with such a fragment before us, it is hazarded rather than affirmed; but whatever the intention of the whole, there can be no question but that it is of the utmost sincerity and that the result, difficult or unpleasant as we may judge it, is undeniably important. In contrast with those whom we have called materialists, Mr Joyce is spiritual; he is concerned at all costs to reveal the flickerings of that innermost flame which flashes its messages through the brain, and in order to preserve it he disregards with complete courage whatever seems to him adventitious, whether it be probability, or coherence, or any other of these signposts which for generations have served to support the imagination of a reader when called upon to imagine what he can neither touch nor see. The scene in the cemetery,[3] for instance, with its brilliancy, its sordidity, its incoherence, its sudden lightning flashes of significance, does undoubtedly come so close to the quick of the mind that, on a first reading at any rate, it is difficult not to acclaim a masterpiece. If we want life itself, here surely we have it. Indeed, we find ourselves fumbling rather awkwardly if we try to say what else we wish, and for what reason a work of such originality yet fails to compare, for we must take high examples, with *Youth* or *The Mayor of Casterbridge*.[4] It fails because of the comparative poverty of the writer's mind, we might say simply and have done with it. But it is possible to press a little further and wonder whether we may not refer our sense of being in a bright yet narrow room, confined and shut in, rather than enlarged and set free, to some limitation imposed by the method as well as by the mind. Is it the method that inhibits the creative power? Is it due to the method that we feel neither jovial nor magnanimous, but centred in a self which, in spite of its tremor of susceptibility, never embraces or creates what is outside itself and beyond? Does the emphasis laid, perhaps didactically, upon indecency contribute to the effect of something angular and isolated? Or is it merely that in any effort of such originality it is much easier, for contemporaries especially, to feel what it lacks than to name what it gives? In any case it is a mistake to stand outside examining "methods". Any method is right, every method is right, that expresses what we wish to express, if we are writers; that brings us closer to the novelist's intention if we are readers. This method has the merit of bringing us closer to what we were prepared to call life itself; did not the reading of *Ulysses* suggest how much of life is excluded or ignored, and did it not come with a shock to open *Tristram Shandy* or even *Pendennis*[5] and be by them convinced that there are not only other aspects of life, but more important ones into the bargain.

However this may be, the problem before the novelist at present, as we suppose it to have been in the past, is to contrive means of being free to set down what he chooses. He has to have the courage to say that what interests

---

2. Written April, 1919 [Woolf's note].
3. The sixth episode ("Hades") of *Ulysses*, where Bloom goes to Paddy Dignam's funeral.
4. A story and a novel by, respectively, Joseph

Conrad and Thomas Hardy.
5. Novels by, respectively, the English writers Laurence Sterne (1713–1768) and William Makepeace Thackeray (1811–1863).

him is no longer "this" but "that": out of "that" alone must he construct his work. For the moderns "that", the point of interest, lies very likely in the dark places of psychology. At once, therefore, the accent falls a little differently; the emphasis is upon something hitherto ignored; at once a different outline of form becomes necessary, difficult for us to grasp, incomprehensible to our predecessors. No one but a modern, no one perhaps but a Russian, would have felt the interest of the situation which Tchekov has made into the short story which he calls "Gusev."[6] Some Russian soldiers lie ill on board a ship which is taking them back to Russia. We are given a few scraps of their talk and some of their thoughts; then one of them dies and is carried away; the talk goes on among the others for a time, until Gusev himself dies, and looking "like a carrot or a radish" is thrown overboard. The emphasis is laid upon such unexpected places that at first it seems as if there were no emphasis at all; and then, as the eyes accustom themselves to twilight and discern the shapes of things in a room we see how complete the story is, how profound, and how truly in obedience to his vision Tchekov has chosen this, that, and the other, and placed them together to compose something new. But it is impossible to say "this is comic," or "that is tragic," nor are we certain, since short stories, we have been taught, should be brief and conclusive, whether this, which is vague and inconclusive, should be called a short story at all.

The most elementary remarks upon modern English fiction can hardly avoid some mention of the Russian influence, and if the Russians are mentioned one runs the risk of feeling that to write of any fiction save theirs is waste of time. If we want understanding of the soul and heart where else shall we find it of comparable profundity? If we are sick of our own materialism the least considerable of their novelists has by right of birth a natural reverence for the human spirit. "Learn to make yourself akin to people. . . . But let this sympathy be not with the mind—for it is easy with the mind—but with the heart, with love towards them." In every great Russian writer we seem to discern the features of a saint, if sympathy for the sufferings of others, love towards them, endeavour to reach some goal worthy of the most exacting demands of the spirit constitute saintliness. It is the saint in them which confounds us with a feeling of our own irreligious triviality, and turns so many of our famous novels to tinsel and trickery. The conclusions of the Russian mind, thus comprehensive and compassionate, are inevitably, perhaps, of the utmost sadness. More accurately indeed we might speak of the inconclusiveness of the Russian mind. It is the sense that there is no answer, that if honestly examined life presents question after question which must be left to sound on and on after the story is over in hopeless interrogation that fills us with a deep, and finally it may be with a resentful, despair. They are right perhaps; unquestionably they see further than we do and without our gross impediments of vision. But perhaps we see something that escapes them, or why should this voice of protest mix itself with our gloom? The voice of protest is the voice of another and an ancient civilisation which seems to have bred in us the instinct to enjoy and fight rather than to suffer and understand. English fiction from Sterne to Meredith[7] bears witness to our natural delight in humour and comedy, in the beauty of earth, in the activities of the intellect, and in the splendour of the body. But any deductions that we may draw from the comparison of two fic-

---

6. 1890 story by the Russian writer Anton Pavlovich Chekhov (1860–1904).

7. George Meredith (1828–1909), English novelist.

tions so immeasurably far apart are futile save indeed as they flood us with a view of the infinite possibilities of the art and remind us that there is no limit to the horizon, and that nothing—no "method," no experiment, even of the wildest—is forbidden, but only falsity and pretence. "The proper stuff of fiction" does not exist; everything is the proper stuff of fiction, every feeling, every thought; every quality of brain and spirit is drawn upon; no perception comes amiss. And if we can imagine the art of fiction come alive and standing in our midst, she would undoubtedly bid us break her and bully her, as well as honour and love her, for so her youth is renewed and her sovereignty assured.

1925

A Room of One's Own[1]

Chapter One

But, you may say, we asked you to speak about women and fiction—what has that got to do with a room of one's own? I will try to explain. When you asked me to speak about women and fiction I sat down on the banks of a river and began to wonder what the words meant. They might mean simply a few remarks about Fanny Burney; a few more about Jane Austen; a tribute to the Brontës and a sketch of Haworth Parsonage under snow; some witticisms if possible about Miss Mitford; a respectful allusion to George Eliot; a reference to Mrs. Gaskell[2] and one would have done. But at second sight the words seemed not so simple. The title women and fiction might mean, and you may have meant it to mean, women and what they are like; or it might mean women and the fiction that they write; or it might mean women and the fiction that is written about them; or it might mean that somehow all three are inextricably mixed together and you want me to consider them in that light. But when I began to consider the subject in this last way, which seemed the most interesting, I soon saw that it had one fatal drawback. I should never be able to come to a conclusion. I should never be able to fulfil what is, I understand, the first duty of a lecturer—to hand you after an hour's discourse a nugget of pure truth to wrap up between the pages of your notebooks and keep on the mantelpiece for ever. All I could do was to offer you an opinion upon one minor point—a woman must have money and a room of her own if she is to write fiction; and that, as you will see, leaves the great problem of the true nature of woman and the true nature of fiction unsolved. I have shirked the duty of coming to a conclusion upon these two questions—women and fiction remain, so far as I am concerned, unsolved problems. But in order to make some amends I am going to do what I can to show you how I arrived at this opinion about the room and the money. I am going to develop in your presence as fully and freely as I can the train of thought which led me to think this. Perhaps if I lay bare the ideas, the prejudices, that lie behind this statement

---

1. This essay is based upon two papers read to the Arts Society at Newnham and the Odtaa at Girton in October 1928. The papers were too long to be read in full, and have since been altered and expanded [Woolf's note]. Newnham and Girton are women's colleges at Cambridge. Odtaa, or "One Damn Thing After Another," was an elite literary society.

2. All English writers: Frances Burney (1752–1840); Jane Austen (1775–1817); Charlotte (1816–1855), Emily (1818–1848), and Anne (1820–1849) Brontë, who grew up in the parsonage in Haworth (Yorkshire), where their father was curate; Mary Russell Mitford (1787–1855); George Eliot (pseudonym of Marian Evans, 1819–1880); and Elizabeth Gaskell (1810–1865).

you will find that they have some bearing upon women and some upon fiction. At any rate, when a subject is highly controversial—and any question about sex is that—one cannot hope to tell the truth. One can only show how one came to hold whatever opinion one does hold. One can only give one's audience the chance of drawing their own conclusions as they observe the limitations, the prejudices, the idiosyncrasies of the speaker. Fiction here is likely to contain more truth than fact. Therefore I propose, making use of all the liberties and licences of a novelist, to tell you the story of the two days that preceded my coming here—how, bowed down by the weight of the subject which you have laid upon my shoulders, I pondered it, and made it work in and out of my daily life. I need not say that what I am about to describe has no existence; Oxbridge[3] is an invention; so is Fernham; "I" is only a convenient term for somebody who has no real being. Lies will flow from my lips, but there may perhaps be some truth mixed up with them; it is for you to seek out this truth and to decide whether any part of it is worth keeping. If not, you will of course throw the whole of it into the wastepaper basket and forget all about it.

Here then was I (call me Mary Beton, Mary Seton, Mary Carmichael[4] or by any name you please—it is not a matter of any importance) sitting on the banks of a river a week or two ago in fine October weather, lost in thought. That collar I have spoken of, women and fiction, the need of coming to some conclusion on a subject that raises all sorts of prejudices and passions, bowed my head to the ground. To the right and left bushes of some sort, golden and crimson, glowed with the colour, even it seemed burnt with the heat, of fire. On the further bank the willows wept in perpetual lamentation, their hair about their shoulders. The river reflected whatever it chose of sky and bridge and burning tree, and when the undergraduate had oared his boat through the reflections they closed again, completely, as if he had never been. There one might have sat the clock round lost in thought. Thought—to call it by a prouder name than it deserved—had let its line down into the stream. It swayed, minute after minute, hither and thither among the reflections and the weeds, letting the water lift it and sink it, until—you know the little tug—the sudden conglomeration of an idea at the end of one's line: and then the cautious hauling of it in, and the careful laying of it out? Alas, laid on the grass how small, how insignificant this thought of mine looked; the sort of fish that a good fisherman puts back into the water so that it may grow fatter and be one day worth cooking and eating. I will not trouble you with that thought now, though if you look carefully you may find it for yourselves in the course of what I am going to say.

But however small it was, it had, nevertheless, the mysterious property of its kind—put back into the mind, it became at once very exciting, and important; and as it darted and sank, and flashed hither and thither, set up such a wash and tumult of ideas that it was impossible to sit still. It was thus that I found myself walking with extreme rapidity across a grass plot. Instantly a man's figure rose to intercept me. Nor did I at first understand that the gesticulations of a curious-looking object, in a cut-away coat and evening shirt, were aimed at me. His face expressed horror and indignation. Instinct rather than reason came to my help; he was a Beadle;[5] I was a woman. This was the

---

3. A common term blending Oxford and Cambridge.
4. Reference to the "Scottish Ballad of the Queen's Marys," also called "The Four Marys" (ca.

1563), a ballad about ladies-in-waiting to Mary, Queen of Scots.
5. Officer in a university who precedes public processions.

turf; there was the path. Only the Fellows and Scholars are allowed here; the gravel is the place for me. Such thoughts were the work of a moment. As I regained the path the arms of the Beadle sank, his face assumed its usual repose, and though turf is better walking than gravel, no very great harm was done. The only charge I could bring against the Fellows and Scholars of whatever the college might happen to be was that in protection of their turf, which has been rolled for 300 years in succession, they had sent my little fish into hiding.

What idea it had been that had sent me so audaciously trespassing I could not now remember. The spirit of peace descended like a cloud from heaven, for if the spirit of peace dwells anywhere, it is in the courts and quadrangles of Oxbridge on a fine October morning. Strolling through those colleges past those ancient halls the roughness of the present seemed smoothed away; the body seemed contained in a miraculous glass cabinet through which no sound could penetrate, and the mind, freed from any contact with facts (unless one trespassed on the turf again), was at liberty to settle down upon whatever meditation was in harmony with the moment. As chance would have it, some stray memory of some old essay about revisiting Oxbridge in the long vacation brought Charles Lamb to mind—Saint Charles, said Thackeray,[6] putting a letter of Lamb's to his forehead. Indeed, among all the dead (I give you my thoughts as they came to me), Lamb is one of the most congenial; one to whom one would have liked to say, Tell me then how you wrote your essays? For his essays are superior even to Max Beerbohm's,[7] I thought, with all their perfection, because of that wild flash of imagination, that lightning crack of genius in the middle of them which leaves them flawed and imperfect, but starred with poetry. Lamb then came to Oxbridge perhaps a hundred years ago. Certainly he wrote an essay—the name escapes me[8]—about the manuscript of one of Milton's poems which he saw here. It was *Lycidas* perhaps, and Lamb wrote how it shocked him to think it possible that any word in *Lycidas* could have been different from what it is. To think of Milton changing the words in that poem seemed to him a sort of sacrilege. This led me to remember what I could of *Lycidas* and to amuse myself with guessing which word it could have been that Milton had altered, and why. It then occurred to me that the very manuscript itself which Lamb had looked at was only a few hundred yards away, so that one could follow Lamb's footsteps across the quadrangle to that famous library[9] where the treasure is kept. Moreover, I recollected, as I put this plan into execution, it is in this famous library that the manuscript of Thackeray's *Esmond* is also preserved. The critics often say that *Esmond* is Thackeray's most perfect novel. But the affectation of the style, with its imitation of the eighteenth century, hampers one, so far as I remember; unless indeed the eighteenth-century style was natural to Thackeray—a fact that one might prove by looking at the manuscript and seeing whether the alterations were for the benefit of the style or of the sense. But then one would have to decide what is style and what is meaning, a question which— but here I was actually at the door which leads into the library itself. I must have opened it, for instantly there issued, like a guardian angel barring the way with a flutter of black gown instead of white wings, a deprecating, silvery,

---

6. William Makepeace Thackeray (1811–1863), English novelist, wrote *The History of Henry Esmond, Esquire* (1852), mentioned later. Charles Lamb (1775–1834), English critic and essayist.

7. English essayist and parodist (1872–1956).
8. "Oxford in the Vacation" (1823).
9. The library at Trinity College, Cambridge.

kindly gentleman, who regretted in a low voice as he waved me back that ladies are only admitted to the library if accompanied by a Fellow of the College or furnished with a letter of introduction.

That a famous library has been cursed by a woman is a matter of complete indifference to a famous library. Venerable and calm, with all its treasures safe locked within its breast, it sleeps complacently and will, so far as I am concerned, so sleep for ever. Never will I wake those echoes, never will I ask for that hospitality again, I vowed as I descended the steps in anger. Still an hour remained before luncheon, and what was one to do? Stroll on the meadows? sit by the river? Certainly it was a lovely autumn morning; the leaves were fluttering red to the ground; there was no great hardship in doing either. But the sound of music reached my ear. Some service or celebration was going forward. The organ complained magnificently as I passed the chapel door. Even the sorrow of Christianity sounded in that serene air more like the recollection of sorrow than sorrow itself; even the groanings of the ancient organ seemed lapped in peace. I had no wish to enter had I the right, and this time the verger might have stopped me, demanding perhaps my baptismal certificate, or a letter of introduction from the Dean. But the outside of these magnificent buildings is often as beautiful as the inside. Moreover, it was amusing enough to watch the congregation assembling, coming in and going out again, busying themselves at the door of the chapel like bees at the mouth of a hive. Many were in cap and gown; some had tufts of fur on their shoulders; others were wheeled in bath-chairs; others, though not past middle age, seemed creased and crushed into shapes so singular that one was reminded of those giant crabs and crayfish who heave with difficulty across the sand of an aquarium. As I leant against the wall the University indeed seemed a sanctuary in which are preserved rare types which would soon be obsolete if left to fight for existence on the pavement of the Strand.[1] Old stories of old deans and old dons came back to mind, but before I had summoned up courage to whistle—it used to be said that at the sound of a whistle old Professor —— instantly broke into a gallop—the venerable congregation had gone inside. The outside of the chapel remained. As you know, its high domes and pinnacles can be seen, like a sailing-ship always voyaging never arriving, lit up at night and visible for miles, far away across the hills. Once, presumably, this quadrangle with its smooth lawns, its massive buildings, and the chapel itself was marsh too, where the grasses waved and the swine rootled. Teams of horses and oxen, I thought, must have hauled the stone in wagons from far countries, and then with infinite labour the grey blocks in whose shade I was now standing were poised in order one on top of another, and then the painters brought their glass for the windows, and the masons were busy for centuries up on that roof with putty and cement, spade and trowel.[2] Every Saturday somebody must have poured gold and silver out of a leathern purse into their ancient fists, for they had their beer and skittles presumably of an evening. An unending stream of gold and silver, I thought, must have flowed into this court perpetually to keep the stones coming and the masons working; to level, to ditch, to dig and to drain. But it was then the age of faith, and money was poured liberally to set these stones on a deep foundation, and when the stones were raised, still more money was poured in from the coffers of kings and queens and great

1. A busy thoroughfare in London.
2. King's College Chapel, Cambridge, was built from 1446 to 1547.

nobles to ensure that hymns should be sung here and scholars taught. Lands were granted; tithes were paid. And when the age of faith was over and the age of reason had come, still the same flow of gold and silver went on; fellowships were founded; lectureships endowed; only the gold and silver flowed now, not from the coffers of the king, but from the chests of merchants and manufacturers, from the purses of men who had made, say, a fortune from industry, and returned, in their wills, a bounteous share of it to endow more chairs, more lectureships, more fellowships in the university where they had learnt their craft. Hence the libraries and laboratories; the observatories; the splendid equipment of costly and delicate instruments which now stands on glass shelves, where centuries ago the grasses waved and the swine rootled. Certainly, as I strolled round the court, the foundation of gold and silver seemed deep enough; the pavement laid solidly over the wild grasses. Men with trays on their heads went busily from staircase to staircase. Gaudy blossoms flowered in window-boxes. The strains of the gramophone blared out from the rooms within. It was impossible not to reflect—the reflection whatever it may have been was cut short. The clock struck. It was time to find one's way to luncheon.

It is a curious fact that novelists have a way of making us believe that luncheon parties are invariably memorable for something very witty that was said, or for something very wise that was done. But they seldom spare a word for what was eaten. It is part of the novelist's convention not to mention soup and salmon and ducklings, as if soup and salmon and ducklings were of no importance whatsoever, as if nobody ever smoked a cigar or drank a glass of wine. Here, however, I shall take the liberty to defy that convention and to tell you that the lunch on this occasion began with soles, sunk in a deep dish, over which the college cook had spread a counterpane of the whitest cream, save that it was branded here and there with brown spots like the spots on the flanks of a doe. After that came the partridges, but if this suggests a couple of bald, brown birds on a plate you are mistaken. The partridges, many and various, came with all their retinue of sauces and salads, the sharp and the sweet, each in its order; their potatoes, thin as coins but not so hard; their sprouts, foliated as rosebuds but more succulent. And no sooner had the roast and its retinue been done with than the silent serving-man, the Beadle himself perhaps in a milder manifestation, set before us, wreathed in napkins, a confection which rose all sugar from the waves. To call it pudding and so relate it to rice and tapioca would be an insult. Meanwhile the wineglasses had flushed yellow and flushed crimson; had been emptied; had been filled. And thus by degrees was lit, halfway down the spine, which is the seat of the soul, not that hard little electric light which we call brilliance, as it pops in and out upon our lips, but the more profound, subtle and subterranean glow, which is the rich yellow flame of rational intercourse. No need to hurry. No need to sparkle. No need to be anybody but oneself. We are all going to heaven and Vandyck[3] is of the company—in other words, how good life seemed, how sweet its rewards, how trivial this grudge or that grievance, how admirable friendship and the society of one's kind, as, lighting a good cigarette, one sunk among the cushions in the window-seat.

If by good luck there had been an ash-tray handy, if one had not knocked

---

3. Sir Anthony Van Dyck (1599–1641), born in Antwerp but lived for some years in England. He painted many grand portraits of the English royal family and court.

the ash out of the window in default, if things had been a little different from what they were, one would not have seen, presumably, a cat without a tail. The sight of that abrupt and truncated animal padding softly across the quadrangle changed by some fluke of the subconscious intelligence the emotional light for me. It was as if some one had let fall a shade. Perhaps the excellent hock[4] was relinquishing its hold. Certainly, as I watched the Manx cat pause in the middle of the lawn as if it too questioned the universe, something seemed lacking, something seemed different. But what was lacking, what was different, I asked myself, listening to the talk. And to answer that question I had to think myself out of the room, back into the past, before the war indeed, and to set before my eyes the model of another luncheon party held in rooms not very far distant from these; but different. Everything was different. Meanwhile the talk went on among the guests, who were many and young, some of this sex, some of that; it went on swimmingly, it went on agreeably, freely, amusingly. And as it went on I set it against the background of that other talk, and as I matched the two together I had no doubt that one was the descendant, the legitimate heir of the other. Nothing was changed; nothing was different save only—here I listened with all my ears not entirely to what was being said, but to the murmur or current behind it. Yes, that was it—the change was there. Before the war at a luncheon party like this people would have said precisely the same things but they would have sounded different, because in those days they were accompanied by a sort of humming noise, not articulate, but musical, exciting, which changed the value of the words themselves. Could one set that humming noise to words? Perhaps with the help of the poets one could. A book lay beside me and, opening it, I turned casually enough to Tennyson. And here I found Tennyson was singing:

> There has fallen a splendid tear
>   From the passion-flower at the gate.
> She is coming, my dove, my dear;
>   She is coming, my life, my fate;
> The red rose cries, "She is near, she is near";
>   And the white rose weeps, "She is late";
> The larkspur listens, "I hear, I hear";
>   And the lily whispers, "I wait."[5]

Was that what men hummed at luncheon parties before the war? And the women?

> My heart is like a singing bird
>   Whose nest is in a water'd shoot;
> My heart is like an apple tree
>   Whose boughs are bent with thick-set fruit;
> My heart is like a rainbow shell
>   That paddles in a halcyon sea;
> My heart is gladder than all these
>   Because my love is come to me.[6]

Was that what women hummed at luncheon parties before the war?

There was something so ludicrous in thinking of people humming such things even under their breath at luncheon parties before the war that I burst

---

4. Rhine wine.
5. *Maud* 1.22.10.

6. Christina Rossetti's *A Birthday*, first stanza.

out laughing, and had to explain my laughter by pointing at the Manx cat, who did look a little absurd, poor beast, without a tail, in the middle of the lawn. Was he really born so, or had he lost his tail in an accident? The tailless cat, though some are said to exist in the Isle of Man,[7] is rarer than one thinks. It is a queer animal, quaint rather than beautiful. It is strange what a difference a tail makes—you know the sort of things one says as a lunch party breaks up and people are finding their coats and hats.

This one, thanks to the hospitality of the host, had lasted far into the afternoon. The beautiful October day was fading and the leaves were falling from the trees in the avenue as I walked through it. Gate after gate seemed to close with gentle finality behind me. Innumerable beadles were fitting innumerable keys into well-oiled locks; the treasure-house was being made secure for another night. After the avenue one comes out upon a road—I forget its name—which leads you, if you take the right turning, along to Fernham. But there was plenty of time. Dinner was not till half-past seven. One could almost do without dinner after such a luncheon. It is strange how a scrap of poetry works in the mind and makes the legs move in time to it along the road. Those words—

> There has fallen a splendid tear
> From the passion-flower at the gate.
> She is coming, my dove, my dear—

sang in my blood as I stepped quickly along towards Headingley. And then, switching off into the other measure, I sang, where the waters are churned up by the weir:

> My heart is like a singing bird
> Whose nest is in a water'd shoot;
> My heart is like an apple tree . . .

What poets, I cried aloud, as one does in the dusk, what poets they were!

In a sort of jealousy, I suppose, for our own age, silly and absurd though these comparisons are, I went on to wonder if honestly one could name two living poets now as great as Tennyson and Christina Rossetti were then. Obviously it is impossible, I thought, looking into those foaming waters, to compare them. The very reason why the poetry excites one to such abandonment, such rapture, is that it celebrates some feeling that one used to have (at luncheon parties before the war perhaps), so that one responds easily, familiarly, without troubling to check the feeling, or to compare it with any that one has now. But the living poets express a feeling that is actually being made and torn out of us at the moment. One does not recognize it in the first place; often for some reason one fears it; one watches it with keenness and compares it jealously and suspiciously with the old feeling that one knew. Hence the difficulty of modern poetry; and it is because of this difficulty that one cannot remember more than two consecutive lines of any good modern poet. For this reason—that my memory failed me—the argument flagged for want of material. But why, I continued, moving on towards Headingley, have we stopped humming under our breath at luncheon parties? Why has Alfred ceased to sing

> She is coming, my dove, my dear?

---

7. One of the British Isles in the Irish Sea.

Why has Christina ceased to respond

> *My heart is gladder than all these*
> *Because my love is come to me?*

Shall we lay the blame on the war? When the guns fired in August 1914, did the faces of men and women show so plain in each other's eyes that romance was killed? Certainly it was a shock (to women in particular with their illusions about education, and so on) to see the faces of our rulers in the light of the shell-fire. So ugly they looked—German, English, French—so stupid. But lay the blame where one will, on whom one will, the illusion which inspired Tennyson and Christina Rossetti to sing so passionately about the coming of their loves is far rarer now than then. One has only to read, to look, to listen, to remember. But why say "blame"? Why, if it was an illusion, not praise the catastrophe, whatever it was, that destroyed illusion and put truth in its place? For truth . . . those dots mark the spot where, in search of truth, I missed the turning up to Fernham. Yes indeed, which was truth and which was illusion, I asked myself. What was the truth about these houses, for example, dim and festive now with their red windows in the dusk, but raw and red and squalid, with their sweets and their boot-laces, at nine o'clock in the morning? And the willows and the river and the gardens that run down to the river, vague now with the mist stealing over them, but gold and red in the sunlight—which was the truth, which was the illusion about them? I spare you the twists and turns of my cogitations, for no conclusion was found on the road to Headingley, and I ask you to suppose that I soon found out my mistake about the turning and retraced my steps to Fernham.

As I have said already that it was an October day, I dare not forfeit your respect and imperil the fair name of fiction by changing the season and describing lilacs hanging over garden walls, crocuses, tulips and other flowers of spring. Fiction must stick to facts, and the truer the facts the better the fiction—so we are told. Therefore it was still autumn and the leaves were still yellow and falling, if anything, a little faster than before, because it was now evening (seven twenty-three to be precise) and a breeze (from the southwest to be exact) had risen. But for all that there was something odd at work:

> *My heart is like a singing bird*
> *Whose nest is in a water'd shoot;*
> *My heart is like an apple tree*
> *Whose boughs are bent with thick-set fruit—*

perhaps the words of Christina Rossetti were partly responsible for the folly of the fancy—it was nothing of course but a fancy—that the lilac was shaking its flowers over the garden walls, and the brimstone butterflies were scudding hither and thither, and the dust of the pollen was in the air. A wind blew, from what quarter I know not, but it lifted the half-grown leaves so that there was a flash of silver grey in the air. It was the time between the lights when colours undergo their intensification and purples and golds burn in window-panes like the beat of an excitable heart; when for some reason the beauty of the world revealed and yet soon to perish (here I pushed into the garden, for, unwisely, the door was left open and no beadles seemed about), the beauty of the world which is so soon to perish, has two edges, one of laughter, one of anguish, cutting the heart asunder. The gardens of Fernham lay before me in the spring twilight, wild and open, and in the long grass, sprinkled and carelessly flung, were daffodils and bluebells, not orderly perhaps at the best of times, and now wind-blown and waving as they tugged at their roots. The windows of the building, curved like ships' windows among generous waves of red brick, changed from lemon to silver under the flight of the quick spring clouds. Somebody was in a hammock, somebody, but in this light they were phantoms only, half guessed, half seen, raced across the grass—would no one stop her?—and then on the terrace, as if popping out to breathe the air, to glance at the garden, came a bent figure, formidable yet humble, with her great forehead and her shabby dress—could it be the famous scholar, could it be J—— H—— herself?[8] All was dim, yet intense too, as if the scarf which the dusk had flung over the garden were torn asunder by star or sword—the flash of some terrible reality leaping, as its way is, out of the heart of the spring. For youth——

Here was my soup. Dinner was being served in the great dining-hall. Far from being spring it was in fact an evening in October. Everybody was assembled in the big dining-room. Dinner was ready. Here was the soup. It was a plain gravy soup. There was nothing to stir the fancy in that. One could have seen through the transparent liquid any pattern that there might have been on the plate itself. But there was no pattern. The plate was plain. Next came beef with its attendant greens and potatoes—a homely trinity, suggesting the rumps of cattle in a muddy market, and sprouts curled and yellowed at the edge, and bargaining and cheapening, and women with string bags on Monday morning. There was no reason to complain of human nature's daily food, seeing that the supply was sufficient and coal-miners doubtless were sitting down to less. Prunes and custard followed. And if any one complains that prunes, even when mitigated by custard, are an uncharitable vegetable (fruit they are not), stringy as a miser's heart and exuding a fluid such as might run in misers' veins who have denied themselves wine and warmth for eighty years and yet not given to the poor, he should reflect that there are people whose charity embraces even the prune. Biscuits and cheese came next, and here the water-jug was liberally passed round, for it is the nature of biscuits to be dry, and these were biscuits to the core. That was all. The meal was over. Everybody scraped their chairs back; the swing-doors swung violently to and fro; soon the hall was emptied of every sign of food and made ready no doubt for breakfast next morning. Down corridors and up staircases the youth of England went banging and singing. And was it for a guest, a stranger (for I had no more right here in Fernham than in Trinity or Somerville or Girton or Newnham or Christchurch),[9] to say, "The dinner was not good," or to say (we were now, Mary Seton and I, in her sitting-room), "Could we not have dined up here alone?" for if I had said anything of the kind I should have been prying and searching into the secret economies of a house which to the stranger wears so fine a front of gaiety and courage. No, one could say nothing of the sort. Indeed, conversation for a moment flagged. The human frame being what it is, heart, body and brain all mixed together, and not contained in separate compartments as they will be no doubt in another million years, a good dinner is of great importance to good talk. One cannot think well, love well, sleep well, if one has not dined well. The lamp in the spine does not light on beef and prunes. We are all *probably* going to heaven, and Vandyck is, we *hope*, to

---

8. Jane Harrison (1850–1928), fellow and lecturer in classical archaeology at Newnham College, Cambridge; author of *Ancient Art and Ritual* (1913) and other influential books.
9. Oxford college. Somerville is a women's college at Oxford.

meet us round the next corner—that is the dubious and qualifying state of mind that beef and prunes at the end of the day's work breed between them. Happily my friend, who taught science, had a cupboard where there was a squat bottle and little glasses—(but there should have been sole and partridge to begin with)—so that we were able to draw up to the fire and repair some of the damages of the day's living. In a minute or so we were slipping freely in and out among all those objects of curiosity and interest which form in the mind in the absence of a particular person, and are naturally to be discussed on coming together again—how somebody has married, another has not; one thinks this, another that; one has improved out of all knowledge, the other most amazingly gone to the bad—with all those speculations upon human nature and the character of the amazing world we live in which spring naturally from such beginnings. While these things were being said, however, I became shamefacedly aware of a current setting in of its own accord and carrying everything forward to an end of its own. One might be talking of Spain or Portugal, of book or racehorse, but the real interest of whatever was said was none of those things, but a scene of masons on a high roof some five centuries ago. Kings and nobles brought treasure in huge sacks and poured it under the earth. This scene was for ever coming alive in my mind and placing itself by another of lean cows and a muddy market and withered greens and the stringy hearts of old men—these two pictures, disjointed and disconnected and non-sensical as they were, were for ever coming together and combating each other and had me entirely at their mercy. The best course, unless the whole talk was to be distorted, was to expose what was in my mind to the air, when with good luck it would fade and crumble like the head of the dead king when they opened the coffin at Windsor.[1] Briefly, then, I told Miss Seton about the masons who had been all those years on the roof of the chapel, and about the kings and queens and nobles bearing sacks of gold and silver on their shoulders, which they shovelled into the earth; and then how the great financial magnates of our own time came and laid cheques and bonds, I suppose, where the others had laid ingots and rough lumps of gold. All that lies beneath the colleges down there, I said; but this college, where we are now sitting, what lies beneath its gallant red brick and the wild unkempt grasses of the garden? What force is behind the plain china off which we dined, and (here it popped out of my mouth before I could stop it) the beef, the custard and the prunes?

Well, said Mary Seton, about the year 1860—Oh, but you know the story, she said, bored, I suppose, by the recital. And she told me—rooms were hired. Committees met. Envelopes were addressed. Circulars were drawn up. Meetings were held; letters were read out; so-and-so has promised so much; on the contrary, Mr ——— won't give a penny. The *Saturday Review* has been very rude. How can we raise a fund to pay for offices? Shall we hold a bazaar? Can't we find a pretty girl to sit in the front row? Let us look up what John Stuart Mill[2] said on the subject. Can any one persuade the editor of the ——— to print a letter? Can we get Lady ——— to sign it? Lady ——— is out of town. That was the way it was done, presumably, sixty years ago, and it was a pro-digious effort, and a great deal of time was spent on it. And it was only after a long struggle and with the utmost difficulty that they got thirty thousand

---

1. Windsor Castle.
2. English philosopher and economist (1806–1873).

pounds together.[3] So obviously we cannot have wine and partridges and servants carrying tin dishes on their heads, she said. We cannot have sofas and separate rooms. "The amenities," she said, quoting from some book or other, "will have to wait."[4]

At the thought of all those women working year after year and finding it hard to get two thousand pounds together, and as much as they could do to get thirty thousand pounds, we burst out in scorn at the reprehensible poverty of our sex. What had our mothers been doing then that they had no wealth to leave us? Powdering their noses? Looking in at shop windows? Flaunting in the sun at Monte Carlo?[5] There were some photographs on the mantel-piece. Mary's mother—if that was her picture—may have been a wastrel in her spare time (she had thirteen children by a minister of the church), but if so her gay and dissipated life had left too few traces of its pleasures on her face. She was a homely body; an old lady in a plaid shawl which was fastened by a large cameo;[6] and she sat in a basket-chair, encouraging a spaniel to look at the camera, with the amused, yet strained expression of one who is sure that the dog will move directly the bulb is pressed. Now if she had gone into business; had become a manufacturer of artificial silk or a magnate on the Stock Exchange; if she had left two or three hundred thousand pounds to Fernham, we could have been sitting at our ease tonight and the subject of our talk might have been archaeology, botany, anthropology, physics, the nature of the atom, mathematics, astronomy, relativity, geography. If only Mrs Seton and her mother and her mother before her had learnt the great art of making money and had left their money, like their fathers and their grandfathers before them, to found fellowships and lectureships and prizes and scholarships appropriated to the use of their own sex, we might have dined very tolerably up here alone off a bird and a bottle of wine; we might have looked forward without undue confidence to a pleasant and honourable lifetime spent in the shelter of one of the liberally endowed professions. We might have been exploring or writing; mooning about the venerable places of the earth; sitting contemplative on the steps of the Parthenon, or going at ten to an office and coming home comfortably at half-past four to write a little poetry. Only, if Mrs Seton and her like had gone into business at the age of fifteen, there would have been—that was the snag in the argument—no Mary. What, I asked, did Mary think of that? There between the curtains was the October night, calm and lovely, with a star or two caught in the yellowing trees. Was she ready to resign her share of it and her memories (for they had been a happy family, though a large one) of games and quarrels up in Scotland, which she is never tired of praising for the fineness of its air and the quality of its cakes, in order that Fernham might have been endowed with fifty thousand pounds or so by a stroke of the pen? For, to endow a college would necessitate the suppression of families altogether. Making a fortune and bearing thirteen children—no human being could stand it. Consider the facts, we said. First there are nine months before

---

3. "We are told that we ought to ask for £30,000 at least. . . . It is not a large sum, considering that there is to be but one college of this sort for Great Britain, Ireland and the Colonies, and considering how easy it is to raise immense sums for boys' schools. But considering how few people really wish women to be educated, it is a good deal."— Lady Stephen, *Life of Miss Emily Davies* [Woolf's note]. Emily Davies (1830–1921), English educa-

tor, who established what was to become Girton College.
4. "Every penny which could be scraped together was set aside for building, and the amenities had to be postponed."—R. Strachey, *The Cause* [Woolf's note].
5. Resort town in Monaco, on the French Riviera.
6. Vividly carved stone.

the baby is born. Then the baby is born. Then there are three or four months spent in feeding the baby. After the baby is fed there are certainly five years spent in playing with the baby. You cannot, it seems, let children run about the streets. People who have seen them running wild in Russia say that the sight is not a pleasant one. People say, too, that human nature takes its shape in the years between one and five. If Mrs Seton, I said, had been making money, what sort of memories would you have had of games and quarrels? What would you have known of Scotland, and its fine air and cakes and all the rest of it? But it is useless to ask these questions, because you would never have come into existence at all. Moreover, it is equally useless to ask what might have happened if Mrs Seton and her mother and her mother before her had amassed great wealth and laid it under the foundations of college and library, because, in the first place, to earn money was impossible for them, and in the second, had it been possible, the law denied them the right to possess what money they earned. It is only for the last forty-eight years that Mrs Seton has had a penny of her own. For all the centuries before that it would have been her husband's property—a thought which, perhaps, may have had its share in keeping Mrs Seton and her mothers off the Stock Exchange. Every penny I earn, they may have said, will be taken from me and disposed of according to my husband's wisdom—perhaps to found a scholarship or to endow a fellowship in Balliol or Kings,[7] so that to earn money, even if I could earn money, is not a matter that interests me very greatly. I had better leave it to my husband.

At any rate, whether or not the blame rested on the old lady who was looking at the spaniel, there could be no doubt that for some reason or other our mothers had mismanaged their affairs very gravely. Not a penny could be spared for "amenities"; for partridges and wine, beadles and turf, books and cigars, libraries and leisure. To raise bare walls out of the bare earth was the utmost they could do.

So we talked standing at the window and looking, as so many thousands look every night, down on the domes and towers of the famous city beneath us. It was very beautiful, very mysterious in the autumn moonlight. The old stone looked very white and venerable. One thought of all the books that were assembled down there; of the pictures of old prelates and worthies hanging in the panelled rooms; of the painted windows that would be throwing strange globes and crescents on the pavement; of the tablets and memorials and inscriptions; of the fountains and the grass; of the quiet rooms looking across the quiet quadrangles. And (pardon me the thought) I thought, too, of the admirable smoke and drink and the deep armchairs and the pleasant carpets: of the urbanity, the geniality, the dignity which are the offspring of luxury and privacy and space. Certainly our mothers had not provided us with anything comparable to all this—our mothers who found it difficult to scrape together thirty thousand pounds, our mothers who bore thirteen children to ministers of religion at St Andrews.[8]

So I went back to my inn, and as I walked through the dark streets I pondered this and that, as one does at the end of the day's work. I pondered why it was that Mrs Seton had no money to leave us; and what effect poverty has

---

7. Colleges at Oxford and Cambridge, respectively.
8. Perhaps St. Andrew Holborn, a church in Lon-

don designed by Sir Christopher Wren (1632–1723).

on the mind; and what effect wealth has on the mind; and I thought of the queer old gentlemen I had seen that morning with tufts of fur upon their shoulders; and I remembered how if one whistled one of them ran; and I thought of the organ booming in the chapel and of the shut doors of the library; and I thought how unpleasant it is to be locked out; and I thought how it is worse perhaps to be locked in; and, thinking of the safety and prosperity of the one sex and of the poverty and insecurity of the other and of the effect of tradition and of the lack of tradition upon the mind of a writer, I thought at last that it was time to roll up the crumpled skin of the day, with its arguments and its impressions and its anger and its laughter, and cast it into the hedge. A thousand stars were flashing across the blue wastes of the sky. One seemed alone with an inscrutable society. All human beings were laid asleep—prone, horizontal, dumb. Nobody seemed stirring in the streets of Oxbridge. Even the door of the hotel sprang open at the touch of an invisible hand—not a boots was sitting up to light me to bed, it was so late.

Chapter Two

The scene, if I may ask you to follow me, was now changed. The leaves were still falling, but in London now, not Oxbridge; and I must ask you to imagine a room, like many thousands, with a window looking across people's hats and vans and motor-cars to other windows, and on the table inside the room a blank sheet of paper on which was written in large letters WOMEN AND FICTION, but no more. The inevitable sequel to lunching and dining at Oxbridge seemed, unfortunately, to be a visit to the British Museum. One must strain off what was personal and accidental in all these impressions and so reach the pure fluid, the essential oil of truth. For that visit to Oxbridge and the luncheon and the dinner had started a swarm of questions. Why did men drink wine and women water? Why was one sex so prosperous and the other so poor? What effect has poverty on fiction? What conditions are necessary for the creation of works of art?—a thousand questions at once suggested themselves. But one needed answers, not questions; and an answer was only to be had by consulting the learned and the unprejudiced, who have removed themselves above the strife of tongue and the confusion of body and issued the result of their reasoning and research in books which are to be found in the British Museum. If truth is not to be found on the shelves of the British Museum, where, I asked myself, picking up a notebook and a pencil, is truth?

Thus provided, thus confident and enquiring, I set out in the pursuit of truth. The day, though not actually wet, was dismal, and the streets in the neighbourhood of the Museum were full of open coal-holes, down which sacks were showering; four-wheeled cabs were drawing up and depositing on the pavement corded boxes containing, presumably, the entire wardrobe of some Swiss or Italian family seeking fortune or refuge or some other desirable commodity which is to be found in the boarding-houses of Bloomsbury in the winter. The usual hoarse-voiced men paraded the streets with plants on barrows. Some shouted; others sang. London was like a workshop. London was like a machine. We were all being shot backwards and forwards on this plain foundation to make some pattern. The British Museum was another department of the factory. The swing-doors swung open; and there one stood under the vast dome, as if one were a thought in the huge bald forehead which is so splendidly encircled by a band of famous names. One went to the counter;

one took a slip of paper; one opened a volume of the catalogue, and . . . . . the five dots here indicate five separate minutes of stupefaction, wonder and bewilderment. Have you any notion how many books are written about women in the course of one year? Have you any notion how many are written by men? Are you aware that you are, perhaps, the most discussed animal in the universe? Here had I come with a notebook and a pencil proposing to spend a morning reading, supposing that at the end of the morning I should have transferred the truth to my notebook. But I should need to be a herd of elephants, I thought, and a wilderness of spiders, desperately referring to the animals that are reputed longest lived and most multitudinously eyed, to cope with all this. I should need claws of steel and beak of brass even to penetrate the husk. How shall I ever find the grains of truth embedded in all this mass of paper, I asked myself, and in despair began running my eye up and down the long list of titles. Even the names of the books gave me food for thought. Sex and its nature might well attract doctors and biologists; but what was surprising and difficult of explanation was the fact that sex—woman, that is to say—also attracts agreeable essayists, light-fingered novelists, young men who have taken the M.A. degree; men who have taken no degree; men who have no apparent qualification save that they are not women. Some of these books were, on the face of it, frivolous and facetious; but many, on the other hand, were serious and prophetic, moral and hortatory. Merely to read the titles suggested innumerable schoolmasters, innumerable clergymen mounting their platforms and pulpits and holding forth with a loquacity which far exceeded the hour usually allotted to such discourse on this one subject. It was a most strange phenomenon; and apparently—here I consulted the letter M—one confined to male sex. Women do not write books about men—a fact that I could not help welcoming with relief, for if I had first to read all that men have written about women, then all that women have written about men, the aloe that flowers once in a hundred years would flower twice before I could set pen to paper. So, making a perfectly arbitrary choice of a dozen volumes or so, I sent my slips of paper to lie in the wire tray, and waited in my stall, among the other seekers for the essential oil of truth.

What could be the reason, then, of this curious disparity, I wondered, drawing cart-wheels on the slips of paper provided by the British taxpayer for other purposes. Why are women, judging from this catalogue, so much more interesting to men than men are to women? A very curious fact it seemed, and my mind wandered to picture the lives of men who spend their time in writing books about women; whether they were old or young, married or unmarried, red-nosed or hump-backed—anyhow, it was flattering, vaguely, to feel oneself the object of such attention, provided that it was not entirely bestowed by the crippled and the infirm—so I pondered until all such frivolous thoughts were ended by an avalanche of books sliding down on to the desk in front of me. Now the trouble began. The student who has been trained in research at Oxbridge has no doubt some method of shepherding his question past all distractions till it runs into its answer as a sheep runs into its pen. The student by my side, for instance, who was copying assiduously from a scientific manual was, I felt sure, extracting pure nuggets of the essential ore every ten minutes or so. His little grunts of satisfaction indicated so much. But if, unfortunately, one has had no training in a university, the question far from being shepherded to its pen flies like a frightened flock hither and thither, helter-skelter, pursued by a whole pack of hounds. Professors, schoolmasters, sociologists, clergymen, novelists, essayists, journalists, men who had no qualification save that they were not women, chased my simple and single question—Why are women poor?—until it became fifty questions; until the fifty questions leapt frantically into mid-stream and were carried away. Every page in my notebook was scribbled over with notes. To show the state of mind I was in, I will read you a few of them, explaining that the page was headed quite simply, WOMEN AND POVERTY, in block letters; but what followed was something like this:

> Condition in Middle Ages of,
> Habits in the Fiji Islands of,
> Worshipped as goddesses by,
> Weaker in moral sense than,
> Idealism of,
> Greater conscientiousness of,
> South Sea Islanders, age of puberty among,
> Attractiveness of,
> Offered as sacrifice to,
> Small size of brain of,
> Profounder sub-consciousness of,
> Less hair on the body of,
> Mental, moral and physical inferiority of,
> Love of children of,
> Greater length of life of,
> Weaker muscles of,
> Strength of affections of,
> Vanity of,
> Higher education of,
> Shakespeare's opinion of,
> Lord Birkenhead's opinion of,
> Dean Inge's opinion of,
> La Bruyère's opinion of,
> Dr Johnson's opinion of,
> Mr Oscar Browning's[9] opinion of, . . .

Here I drew breath and added, indeed, in the margin, Why does Samuel Butler[1] say, "Wise men never say what they think of women"? Wise men never say anything else apparently. But, I continued, leaning back in my chair and looking at the vast dome in which I was a single but by now somewhat harassed thought, what is so unfortunate is that wise men never think the same thing about women. Here is Pope:

> Most women have no character at all.[2]

And here is La Bruyère:

> Les femmes sont extrêmes; elles sont meilleures ou pires que les hommes—[3]

9. Famous history lecturer (1837–1923) at King's College, Cambridge. F. E. Smith, earl of Birkenhead (1872–1930), was lord chancellor (1919–22) and an opponent of women's suffrage. William Ralph Inge (1860–1954) was dean of St. Paul's Cathedral in London (1911–34). Woolf quotes the opinions of the French moralist Jean de La Bruyère

(1645–1696) and of the English writer Samuel Johnson (1609–1784) below.
1. English writer (1835–1902).
2. From "Epistle to a Lady," by the English poet Alexander Pope (1688–1744).
3. Women are extreme: they are better or worse than men (French).

a direct contradiction by keen observers who were contemporary. Are they capable of education or incapable? Napoleon thought them incapable. Dr Johnson thought the opposite.[4] Have they souls or have they not souls? Some savages say they have none. Others, on the contrary, maintain that women are half divine and worship them on that account.[5] Some sages hold that they are shallower in the brain; others that they are deeper in the consciousness. Goethe honoured them; Mussolini[6] despises them. Wherever one looked men thought about women and thought differently. It was impossible to make head or tail of it all, I decided, glancing with envy at the reader next door who was making the neatest abstracts, headed often with an A or a B or a C, while my own notebook rioted with the wildest scribble of contradictory jottings. It was distressing, it was bewildering, it was humiliating. Truth had run through my fingers. Every drop had escaped.

I could not possibly go home, I reflected, and add as a serious contribution to the study of women and fiction that women have less hair on their bodies than men, or that the age of puberty among the South Sea Islanders is nine— or is it ninety?—even the handwriting had become in its distraction indecipherable. It was disgraceful to have nothing more weighty or respectable to show after a whole morning's work. And if I could not grasp the truth about W. (as for brevity's sake I had come to call her) in the past, why bother about W. in the future? It seemed pure waste of time to consult all those gentlemen who specialise in woman and her effect on whatever it may be—politics, children, wages, morality—numerous and learned as they are. One might as well leave their books unopened.

But while I pondered I had unconsciously, in my listlessness, in my desperation, been drawing a picture where I should, like my neighbour, have been writing a conclusion. I had been drawing a face, a figure. It was the face and the figure of Professor von X. engaged in writing his monumental work entitled *The Mental, Moral, and Physical Inferiority of the Female Sex.* He was not in my picture a man attractive to women. He was heavily built; he had a great jowl; to balance that he had very small eyes; he was very red in the face. His expression suggested that he was labouring under some emotion that made him jab his pen on the paper as if he were killing some noxious insect as he wrote, but even when he had killed it that did not satisfy him; he must go on killing it; and even so, some cause for anger and irritation remained. Could it be his wife, I asked, looking at my picture. Was she in love with a cavalry officer? Was the cavalry officer slim and elegant and dressed in astrachan? Had he been laughed at, to adopt the Freudian theory, in his cradle by a pretty girl? For even in his cradle the professor, I thought, could not have been an attractive child. Whatever the reason, the professor was made to look very angry and very ugly in my sketch, as he wrote his great book upon the mental, moral and physical inferiority of women. Drawing pictures was an idle way of

4. " 'Men know that women are an overmatch for them, and therefore they choose the weakest or the most ignorant. If they did not think so, they never could be afraid of women knowing as much as themselves.' . . . In justice to the sex, I think it but candid to acknowledge that, in a subsequent conversation, he told me that he was serious in what he said."—Boswell, *The Journal of a Tour to the Hebrides* [Woolf's note]. James Boswell (1740–1795), Scottish lawyer, diarist, and writer, renowned for his biography of Samuel Johnson.

5. "The ancient Germans believed that there was something holy in women, and accordingly consulted them as oracles."—Frazer, *Golden Bough* [Woolf's note]. Sir James Frazer (1854–1941), Scottish anthropologist.

6. Italian Fascist dictator (1883–1945). Johann Wolfgang von Goethe (1749–1832), German poet, novelist, and playwright.

finishing an unprofitable morning's work. Yet it is in our idleness, in our dreams, that the submerged truth sometimes comes to the top. A very elementary exercise in psychology, not to be dignified by the name of psychoanalysis, showed me, on looking at my notebook, that the sketch of the angry professor had been made in anger. Anger had snatched my pencil while I dreamt. But what was anger doing there? Interest, confusion, amusement, boredom—all these emotions I could trace and name as they succeeded each other throughout the morning. Had anger, the black snake, been lurking among them? Yes, said the sketch, anger had. It referred me unmistakably to the one book, to the one phrase, which had roused the demon; it was the professor's statement about the mental, moral and physical inferiority of women. My heart had leapt. My cheeks had burnt. I had flushed with anger. There was nothing specially remarkable, however foolish, in that. One does not like to be told that one is naturally the inferior of a little man—I looked at the student next me—who breathes hard, wears a ready-made tie, and has not shaved this fortnight. One has certain foolish vanities. It is only human nature, I reflected, and began drawing cartwheels and circles over the angry professor's face till he looked like a burning bush or a flaming comet—anyhow, an apparition without human semblance or significance. The professor was nothing now but a faggot burning on the top of Hampstead Heath.[7] Soon my own anger was explained and done with; but curiosity remained. How explain the anger of the professors? Why were they angry? For when it came to analysing the impression left by these books there was always an element of heat. This heat took many forms; it showed itself in satire, in sentiment, in curiosity, in reprobation. But there was another element which was often present and could not immediately be identified. Anger, I called it. But it was anger that had gone underground and mixed itself with all kinds of other emotions. To judge from its odd effects, it was anger disguised and complex, not anger simple and open.

Whatever the reason, all these books, I thought, surveying the pile on the desk, are worthless for my purposes. They were worthless scientifically, that is to say, though humanly they were full of instruction, interest, boredom, and very queer facts about the habits of the Fiji Islanders. They had been written in the red light of emotion and not in the white light of truth. Therefore they must be returned to the central desk and restored each to his own cell in the enormous honeycomb. All that I had retrieved from that morning's work had been the one fact of anger. The professors—I lumped them together thus— were angry. But why, I asked myself, having returned the books, why, I repeated, standing under the colonnade among the pigeons and the prehistoric canoes, why are they angry? And, asking myself this question, I strolled off to find a place for luncheon. What is the real nature of what I call for the moment their anger? I asked. Here was a puzzle that would last all the time that it takes to be served with food in a small restaurant somewhere near the British Museum. Some previous luncher had left the lunch edition of the evening paper on a chair, and, waiting to be served, I began idly reading the headlines. A ribbon of very large letters ran across the page. Somebody had made a big score in South Africa. Lesser ribbons announced that Sir Austen Chamberlain was at Geneva.[8] A meat axe with human hair on it had been found in a cellar.

---

7. An extensive area of open land on a hill overlooking London. "Faggot": a bundle of sticks.

8. Headquarters of the League of Nations. Chamberlain (1863–1937) was a British statesman and

Mr Justice ———— commented in the Divorce Courts upon the Shamelessness of Women. Sprinkled about the paper were other pieces of news. A film actress had been lowered from a peak in California and hung suspended in mid-air. The weather was going to be foggy. The most transient visitor to this planet, I thought, who picked up this paper could not fail to be aware, even from this scattered testimony, that England is under the rule of a patriarchy. Nobody in their senses could fail to detect the dominance of the professor. His was the power and the money and the influence. He was the proprietor of the paper and its editor and sub-editor. He was the Foreign Secretary and the Judge. He was the cricketer; he owned the racehorses and the yachts. He was the director of the company that pays two hundred per cent to its shareholders. He left millions to charities and colleges that were ruled by himself. He suspended the film actress in mid-air. He will decide if the hair on the meat axe is human; he it is who will acquit or convict the murderer, and hang him, or let him go free. With the exception of the fog he seemed to control everything. Yet he was angry. I knew that he was angry by this token. When I read what he wrote about women I thought, not of what he was saying, but of himself. When an arguer argues dispassionately he thinks only of the argument; and the reader cannot help thinking of the argument too. If he had written dispassionately about women, had used indisputable proofs to establish his argument and had shown no trace of wishing that the result should be one thing rather than another, one would not have been angry either. One would have accepted the fact, as one accepts the fact that a pea is green or a canary yellow. So be it, I should have said. But I had been angry because he was angry. Yet it seemed absurd, I thought, turning over the evening paper, that a man with all this power should be angry. Or is anger, I wondered, somehow, the familiar, the attendant sprite[9] on power? Rich people, for example, are often angry because they suspect that the poor want to seize their wealth. The professors, or patriarchs, as it might be more accurate to call them, might be angry for that reason partly, but partly for one that lies a little less obviously on the surface. Possibly they were not "angry" at all; often, indeed, they were admiring, devoted, exemplary in the relations of private life. Possibly when the professor insisted a little too emphatically upon the inferiority of women, he was concerned not with their inferiority, but with his own superiority. That was what he was protecting rather hot-headedly and with too much emphasis, because it was a jewel to him of the rarest price. Life for both sexes—and I looked at them, shouldering their way along the pavement—is arduous, difficult, a perpetual struggle. It calls for gigantic courage and strength. More than anything, perhaps, creatures of illusion as we are, it calls for confidence in oneself. Without self-confidence we are as babes in the cradle. And how can we generate this imponderable quality, which is yet so invaluable, most quickly? By thinking that other people are inferior to oneself. By feeling that one has some innate superiority—it may be wealth, or rank, a straight nose, or the portrait of a grandfather by Romney[1]—for there is no end to the pathetic devices of the human imagination—over other people. Hence the enormous importance to a patriarch who has to conquer, who has to rule, of feeling that great numbers of people, half the human race indeed, are by nature inferior to himself. It

---

brother of Neville Chamberlain, British prime minister (1937–40).
9. Spirit.

1. George Romney (1734–1802), fashionable English portrait painter.

must indeed be one of the chief sources of his power. But let me turn the light of this observation on to real life, I thought. Does it help to explain some of those psychological puzzles that one notes in the margin of daily life? Does it explain my astonishment the other day when Z, most humane, most modest of men, taking up some book by Rebecca West[2] and reading a passage in it, exclaimed, "The arrant feminist! She says that men are snobs!" The exclamation, to me so surprising—for why was Miss West an arrant feminist for making a possibly true if uncomplimentary statement about the other sex?—was not merely the cry of wounded vanity; it was a protest against some infringement of his power to believe in himself. Women have served all these centuries as looking-glasses possessing the magic and delicious power of reflecting the figure of man at twice its natural size. Without that power probably the earth would still be swamp and jungle. The glories of all our wars would be unknown. We should still be scratching the outlines of deer on the remains of mutton bones and bartering flints for sheepskins or whatever simple ornament took our unsophisticated taste. Supermen and Fingers of Destiny would never have existed. The Czar and the Kaiser[3] would never have worn their crowns or lost them. Whatever may be their use in civilised societies, mirrors are essential to all violent and heroic action. That is why Napoleon and Mussolini[4] both insist so emphatically upon the inferiority of women, for if they were not inferior, they would cease to enlarge. That serves to explain in part the necessity that women so often are to men. And it serves to explain how restless they are under her criticism; how impossible it is for her to say to them this book is bad, this picture is feeble, or whatever it may be, without giving far more pain and rousing far more anger than a man would do who gave the same criticism. For if she begins to tell the truth, the figure in the looking-glass shrinks; his fitness for life is diminished. How is he to go on giving judgement, civilising natives, making laws, writing books, dressing up and speechifying at banquets, unless he can see himself at breakfast and at dinner at least twice the size he really is? So I reflected, crumbling my bread and stirring my coffee and now and again looking at the people in the street. The looking-glass vision is of supreme importance because it charges the vitality; it stimulates the nervous system. Take it away and man may die, like the drug fiend deprived of his cocaine. Under the spell of that illusion, I thought, looking out of the window, half the people on the pavement are striding to work. They put on their hats and coats in the morning under its agreeable rays. They start the day confident, braced, believing themselves desired at Miss Smith's tea party; they say to themselves as they go into the room, I am the superior of half the people here, and it is thus that they speak with that self-confidence, that self-assurance, which have had such profound consequences in public life and lead to such curious notes in the margin of the private mind.

But these contributions to the dangerous and fascinating subject of the psychology of the other sex—it is one, I hope, that you will investigate when you have five hundred a year of your own—were interrupted by the necessity of paying the bill. It came to five shillings and ninepence. I gave the waiter a ten-shilling note and he went to bring me change. There was another ten-shilling note in my purse; I noticed it, because it is a fact that still takes my breath away—the power of my purse to breed ten-shillings notes automati-

2. Adopted name of Cicily Isabel Fairfield (1892–1983), English feminist, journalist, and novelist.

3. Rulers of Russia and Germany, respectively.

4. I.e., dictators.

cally. I open it and there they are. Society gives me chicken and coffee, bed and lodging, in return for a certain number of pieces of paper which were left me by an aunt, for no other reason than that I share her name.

My aunt, Mary Beton, I must tell you, died by a fall from her horse when she was riding out to take the air in Bombay. The news of my legacy reached me one night about the same time that the act was passed that gave votes to women. A solicitor's letter fell into the post-box and when I opened it I found that she had left me five hundred pounds a year for ever. Of the two—the vote and the money—the money, I own, seemed infinitely the more important. Before that I had made my living by cadging odd jobs from newspapers, by reporting a donkey show here or a wedding there; I had earned a few pounds by addressing envelopes, reading to old ladies, making artificial flowers, teaching the alphabet to small children in a kindergarten. Such were the chief occupations that were open to women before 1918. I need not, I am afraid, describe in any detail the hardness of the work, for you know perhaps women who have done it; nor the difficulty of living on the money when it was earned, for you may have tried. But what still remains with me as a worse infliction than either was the poison of fear and bitterness which those days bred in me. To begin with, always to be doing work that one did not wish to do, and to do it like a slave, flattering and fawning, not always necessarily perhaps, but it seemed necessary and the stakes were too great to run risks; and then the thought of that one gift which it was death to hide—a small one but dear to the possessor—perishing and with it myself, my soul—all this became like a rust eating away the bloom of the spring, destroying the tree at its heart. However, as I say, my aunt died; and whenever I change a ten-shilling note a little of that rust and corrosion is rubbed off; fear and bitterness go. Indeed, I thought, slipping the silver into my purse, it is remarkable, remembering the bitterness of those days, what a change of temper a fixed income will bring about. No force in the world can take from me my five hundred pounds. Food, house and clothing are mine for ever. Therefore not merely do effort and labour cease, but also hatred and bitterness. I need not hate any man; he cannot hurt me. I need not flatter any man; he has nothing to give me. So imperceptibly I found myself adopting a new attitude towards the other half of the human race. It was absurd to blame any class or any sex, as a whole. Great bodies of people are never responsible for what they do. They are driven by instincts which are not within their control. They too, the patriarchs, the professors, had endless difficulties, terrible drawbacks to contend with. Their education had been in some ways as faulty as my own. It had bred in them defects as great. True, they had money and power, but only at the cost of harbouring in their breasts an eagle, a vulture, for ever tearing the liver out and plucking at the lungs—the instinct for possession, the rage for acquisition which drives them to desire other people's fields and goods perpetually; to make frontiers and flags; battleships and poison gas; to offer up their own lives and their children's lives. Walk through the Admiralty Arch[5] (I had reached that monument), or any other avenue given up to trophies and cannon, and reflect upon the kind of glory celebrated there. Or watch in the spring sunshine the stockbroker and the great barrister going indoors to make money and more money and more money when it is a fact that five hundred pounds a year will

5. Between the Mall and Trafalgar Square in London, constructed 1906–11 to commemorate Britain's imperial successes.

keep one alive in the sunshine. These are unpleasant instincts to harbour, I reflected. They are bred of the conditions of life; of the lack of civilisation, I thought, looking at the statue of the Duke of Cambridge,[6] and in particular at the feathers in his cocked hat, with a fixity that they have scarcely ever received before. And, as I realised these drawbacks, by degrees fear and bitterness modified themselves into pity and toleration; and then in a year or two, pity and toleration went, and the greatest release of all came, which is freedom to think of things in themselves. That building, for example, do I like it or not? Is that picture beautiful or not? Is that in my opinion a good book or a bad? Indeed my aunt's legacy unveiled the sky to me, and substituted for the large and imposing figure of a gentleman, which Milton recommended for my perpetual adoration, a view of the open sky.

So thinking, so speculating, I found my way back to my house by the river. Lamps were being lit and an indescribable change had come over London since the morning hour. It was as if the great machine after labouring all day had made with our help a few yards of something very exciting and beautiful— a fiery fabric flashing with red eyes, a tawny monster roaring with hot breath. Even the wind seemed flung like a flag as it lashed the houses and rattled the hoardings.

In my little street, however, domesticity prevailed. The house painter was descending his ladder; the nursemaid was wheeling the perambulator carefully in and out back to nursery tea; the coal-heaver was folding his empty sacks on top of each other; the woman who keeps the green-grocer's shop was adding up the day's takings with her hands in red mittens. But so engrossed was I with the problem you have laid upon my shoulders that I could not see even these usual sights without referring them to one centre. I thought how much harder it is now than it must have been even a century ago to say which of these employments is the higher, the more necessary. Is it better to be a coal-heaver or a nursemaid; is the charwoman[7] who has brought up eight children of less value to the world than the barrister who has made a hundred thousand pounds? It is useless to ask such questions; for nobody can answer them. Not only do the comparative values of charwomen and lawyers rise and fall from decade to decade, but we have no rods with which to measure them even as they are at the moment. I had been foolish to ask my professor to furnish me with "indisputable proofs" of this or that in his argument about women. Even if one could state the value of any one gift at the moment, those values will change; in a century's time very possibly they will have changed completely. Moreover, in a hundred years, I thought, reaching my own doorstep, women will have ceased to be the protected sex. Logically they will take part in all the activities and exertions that were once denied them. The nursemaid will heave coal. The shop-woman will drive an engine. All assumptions founded on the facts observed when women were the protected sex will have disappeared— as, for example (here a squad of soldiers marched down the street), that women and clergymen and gardeners live longer than other people. Remove that protection, expose them to the same exertions and activities, make them soldiers and sailors and engine-drivers and dock labourers, and will not women die off so much younger, so much quicker, than men that one will say, "I saw a woman today," as one used to say, "I saw an aeroplane." Anything may happen when

6. On Whitehall Lane, directly off Trafalgar Square. 7. Household worker.

womanhood has ceased to be a protected occupation, I thought, opening the door. But what bearing has all this upon the subject of my paper, Women and Fiction? I asked, going indoors.

Chapter Three

It was disappointing not to have brought back in the evening some important statement, some authentic fact. Women are poorer than men because—this or that. Perhaps now it would be better to give up seeking for the truth, and receiving on one's head an avalanche of opinion hot as lava, discoloured as dish-water. It would be better to draw the curtains; to shut out distractions; to light the lamp; to narrow the enquiry and to ask the historian, who records not opinions but facts, to describe under what conditions women lived, not throughout the ages, but in England, say in the time of Elizabeth.[8]

For it is a perennial puzzle why no woman wrote a word of that extraordinary literature when every other man, it seemed, was capable of song or sonnet. What were the conditions in which women lived, I asked myself; for fiction, imaginative work that is, is not dropped like a pebble upon the ground, as science may be; fiction is like a spider's web, attached ever so lightly perhaps, but still attached to life at all four corners. Often the attachment is scarcely perceptible; Shakespeare's plays, for instance, seem to hang there complete by themselves. But when the web is pulled askew, hooked up at the edge, torn in the middle, one remembers that these webs are not spun in midair by incorporeal creatures, but are the work of suffering human beings, and are attached to grossly material things, like health and money and the houses we live in.

I went, therefore, to the shelf where the histories stand and took down one of the latest, Professor Trevelyan's *History of England*.[9] Once more I looked up Women, found "position of," and turned to the pages indicated. "Wife-beating," I read, "was a recognised right of man, and was practised without shame by high as well as low. . . . Similarly," the historian goes on, "the daughter who refused to marry the gentleman of her parents' choice was liable to be locked up, beaten and flung about the room, without any shock being inflicted on public opinion. Marriage was not an affair of personal affection, but of family avarice, particularly in the 'chivalrous' upper classes. . . . Betrothal often took place while one or both of the parties was in the cradle, and marriage when they were scarcely out of the nurses' charge." That was about 1470, soon after Chaucer's time. The next reference to the position of women is some two hundred years later, in the time of the Stuarts.[1] "It was still the exception for women of the upper and middle class to choose their own husbands, and when the husband had been assigned, he was lord and master, so far at least as law and custom could make him. Yet even so," Professor Trevelyan concludes, "neither Shakespeare's women nor those of authentic seventeenth-century memoirs, like the Verneys and the Hutchinsons,[2] seem wanting in personality and character." Certainly, if we consider

8. She reigned from 1558 to 1603.
9. G. M. Trevelyan's *History of England* (1926) long held its place as the standard one-volume history of the country.
1. I.e., during the reign of the British house of Stuart (1603–49, 1660–1714).
2. "The ideal family life of the period [1640–50]

that ended in such tragic political division has been recorded once for all in the *Memoirs of the Verney Family*" (Trevelyan, *History of England*). Lucy Hutchinson (1620–after 1675) wrote the biography of her husband, Col. John Hutchinson (1615–1664); it was first published in 1806.

it, Cleopatra must have had a way with her; Lady Macbeth, one would suppose, had a will of her own; Rosalind,[3] one might conclude, was an attractive girl. Professor Trevelyan is speaking no more than the truth when he remarks that Shakespeare's women do not seem wanting in personality and character. Not being a historian, one might go even further and say that women have burnt like beacons in all the works of all the poets from the beginning of time—Clytemnestra, Antigone, Cleopatra, Lady Macbeth, Phèdre, Cressida, Rosalind, Desdemona, the Duchess of Malfi, among the dramatists; then among the prose writers: Millamant, Clarissa, Becky Sharp, Anna Karenina, Emma Bovary, Madame de Guermantes[4]—the names flock to mind, nor do they recall women "lacking in personality and character." Indeed, if woman had no existence save in the fiction written by men, one would imagine her a person of the utmost importance, very various; heroic and mean; splendid and sordid; infinitely beautiful and hideous in the extreme; as great as a man, some think even greater.[5] But this is woman in fiction. In fact, as Professor Trevelyan points out, she was locked up, beaten and flung about the room.

A very queer, composite being thus emerges. Imaginatively she is of the highest importance; practically she is completely insignificant. She pervades poetry from cover to cover; she is all but absent from history. She dominates the lives of kings and conquerors in fiction; in fact she was the slave of any boy whose parents forced a ring upon her finger. Some of the most inspired words, some of the most profound thoughts in literature fall from her lips; in real life she could hardly read, could scarcely spell, and was the property of her husband.

It was certainly an odd monster that one made up by reading the historians first and the poets afterwards—a worm winged like an eagle; the spirit of life and beauty in a kitchen chopping up suet. But these monsters, however amusing to the imagination, have no existence in fact. What one must do to bring her to life was to think poetically and prosaically at one and the same moment, thus keeping in touch with fact—that she is Mrs Martin, aged thirty-six, dressed in blue, wearing a black hat and brown shoes; but not losing sight of fiction either—that she is a vessel in which all sorts of spirits and forces are coursing and flashing perpetually. The moment, however, that one tries this method with the Elizabethan woman, one branch of illumination fails; one is held up by the scarcity of facts. One knows nothing detailed, nothing perfectly true and substantial about her. History scarcely mentions her. And I turned

3. These three Shakespearean heroines are, respectively, in *Antony and Cleopatra, Macbeth,* and *As You Like It.*
4. Characters in, respectively, Aeschylus's *Agamemnon;* Sophocles' *Antigone;* Shakespeare's *Antony and Cleopatra* and *Macbeth;* Racine's *Phèdre;* Shakespeare's *Troilus and Cressida, As You Like It,* and *Othello;* Webster's *The Duchess of Malfi;* Congreve's *Way of the World;* Richardson's *Clarissa;* Thackeray's *Vanity Fair;* Tolstoy's *Anna Karenina;* Flaubert's *Madame Bovary;* and Proust's *A la Recherche du Temps Perdu (In Search of Lost Time).*
5. "It remains a strange and almost inexplicable fact that in Athena's city, where women were kept in almost Oriental suppression as odalisques or drudges, the stage should yet have produced figures like Clytemnestra and Cassandra, Atossa and Antigone, Phèdre and Medea, and all the other heroines who dominate play after play of the 'misogynist' Euripides. But the paradox of this world where in real life a respectable woman could hardly show her face alone in the street, and yet on the stage woman equals or surpasses man, has never been satisfactorily explained. In modern tragedy the same predominance exists. At all events, a very cursory survey of Shakespeare's work (similarly with Webster, though not with Marlowe or Jonson) suffices to reveal how this dominance, this initiative of women, persists from Rosalind to Lady Macbeth. So too in Racine; six of his tragedies bear their heroines' names; and what male characters of his shall we set against Hermione and Andromaque, Bérénice and Roxane, Phèdre and Athalie? So again with Ibsen; what men shall we match with Solveig and Nora, Hedda and Hilda Wangel and Rebecca West?"—F. L. Lucas, *Tragedy,* pp. 114–15 [Woolf's note].

to Professor Trevelyan again to see what history meant to him. I found by looking at his chapter headings that it meant—

"The Manor Court and the Methods of Open-field Agriculture . . . The Cistercians and Sheep-farming . . . The Crusades . . . The University . . . The House of Commons . . . The Hundred Years' War . . . The Wars of the Roses . . . The Renaissance Scholars . . . The Dissolution of the Monasteries . . . Agrarian and Religious Strife . . . The Origin of English Sea-power . . . The Armada . . ." and so on. Occasionally an individual woman is mentioned, an Elizabeth, or a Mary; a queen or a great lady. But by no possible means could middle-class women with nothing but brains and character at their command have taken part in any one of the great movements which, brought together, constitute the historian's view of the past. Nor shall we find her in any collection of anecdotes. Aubrey[6] hardly mentions her. She never writes her own life and scarcely keeps a diary; there are only a handful of her letters in existence. She left no plays or poems by which we can judge her. What one wants, I thought—and why does not some brilliant student at Newnham or Girton supply it?—is a mass of information; at what age did she marry; how many children had she as a rule; what was her house like; had she a room to herself; did she do the cooking; would she be likely to have a servant? All these facts lie somewhere, presumably, in parish registers and account books; the life of the average Elizabethan woman must be scattered about somewhere, could one collect it and make a book of it. It would be ambitious beyond my daring, I thought, looking about the shelves for books that were not there, to suggest to the students of those famous colleges that they should re-write history, though I own that it often seems a little queer as it is, unreal, lop-sided; but why should they not add a supplement to history? calling it, of course, by some inconspicuous name so that women might figure there without impropriety? For one often catches a glimpse of them in the lives of the great, whisking away into the background, concealing, I sometimes think, a wink, a laugh, perhaps a tear. And, after all, we have lives enough of Jane Austen; it scarcely seems necessary to consider again the influence of the tragedies of Joanna Baillie[7] upon the poetry of Edgar Allan Poe; as for myself, I should not mind if the homes and haunts of Mary Russell Mitford[8] were closed to the public for a century at least. But what I find deplorable, I continued, looking about the bookshelves again, is that nothing is known about women before the eighteenth century. I have no model in my mind to turn about this way and that. Here am I asking why women did not write poetry in the Elizabethan age, and I am not sure how they were educated; whether they were taught to write; whether they had sitting-rooms to themselves; how many women had children before they were twenty-one; what, in short, they did from eight in the morning till eight at night. They had no money evidently; according to Professor Trevelyan they were married whether they liked it or not before they were out of the nursery, at fifteen or sixteen very likely. It would have been extremely odd, even upon this showing, had one of them suddenly written the plays of Shakespeare, I concluded, and I thought of that old gentleman, who is dead now, but was a bishop, I think, who declared that it was impossible for any woman, past, present, or to come, to have the genius of Shakespeare. He wrote to the

---

6. John Aubrey (1626–1697), English writer, especially of short biographies.
7. English poet and dramatist (1762–1851).

8. Poet and novelist (1787–1855), best-known for sketches of country life.

papers about it. He also told a lady who applied to him for information that cats do not as a matter of fact go to heaven, though they have, he added, souls of a sort. How much thinking those old gentlemen used to save one! How the borders of ignorance shrank back at their approach! Cats do not go to heaven. Women cannot write the plays of Shakespeare.

Be that as it may, I could not help thinking, as I looked at the works of Shakespeare on the shelf, that the bishop was right at least in this; it would have been impossible, completely and entirely, for any woman to have written the plays of Shakespeare in the age of Shakespeare. Let me imagine, since facts are so hard to come by, what would have happened had Shakespeare had a wonderfully gifted sister, called Judith,[9] let us say. Shakespeare himself went, very probably—his mother was an heiress—to the grammar school, where he may have learnt Latin—Ovid, Virgil and Horace—and the elements of grammar and logic. He was, it is well known, a wild boy who poached rabbits, perhaps shot a deer, and had, rather sooner than he should have done, to marry a woman in the neighbourhood, who bore him a child rather quicker than was right. That escapade sent him to seek his fortune in London. He had, it seemed, a taste for the theatre; he began by holding horses at the stage door. Very soon he got work in the theatre, became a successful actor, and lived at the hub of the universe, meeting everybody, knowing everybody, practising his art on the boards, exercising his wits in the streets, and even getting access to the palace of the queen. Meanwhile his extraordinarily gifted sister, let us suppose, remained at home. She was as adventurous, as imaginative, as agog to see the world as he was. But she was not sent to school. She had no chance of learning grammar and logic, let alone of reading Horace and Virgil. She picked up a book now and then, one of her brother's perhaps, and read a few pages. But then her parents came in and told her to mend the stockings or mind the stew and not moon about with books and papers. They would have spoken sharply but kindly, for they were substantial people who knew the conditions of life for a woman and loved their daughter—indeed, more likely than not she was the apple of her father's eye. Perhaps she scribbled some pages up in an apple loft on the sly, but was careful to hide them or set fire to them. Soon, however, before she was out of her teens, she was to be betrothed to the son of a neighbouring wool-stapler.[1] She cried out that marriage was hateful to her, and for that she was severely beaten by her father. Then he ceased to scold her. He begged her instead not to hurt him, not to shame him in this matter of her marriage. He would give her a chain of beads or a fine petticoat, he said; and there were tears in his eyes. How could she disobey him? How could she break his heart? The force of her own gift alone drove her to it. She made up a small parcel of her belongings, let herself down by a rope one summer's night and took the road to London. She was not seventeen. The birds that sang in the hedge were not more musical than she was. She had the quickest fancy, a gift like her brother's, for the tune of words. Like him, she had a taste for the theatre. She stood at the stage door; she wanted to act, she said. Men laughed in her face. The manager—a fat, loose-lipped man—guffawed. He bellowed something about poodles dancing and women acting—no woman, he said, could possibly be an actress. He hinted—

---

9. Shakespeare had a daughter named Judith.
1. A stapler is a dealer in staple goods (i.e., established goods in trade and marketing); hence a

wool-stapler is a dealer in wool (one of the "staple" products of 16th-century England).

you can imagine what. She could get no training in her craft. Could she even seek her dinner in a tavern or roam the streets at midnight? Yet her genius was for fiction and lusted to feed abundantly upon the lives of men and women and the study of their ways. At last—for she was very young, oddly like Shakespeare the poet in her face, with the same grey eyes and rounded brows—at last Nick Greene the actor-manager took pity on her; she found herself with child by that gentleman and so—who shall measure the heat and violence of the poet's heart when caught and tangled in a woman's body?—killed herself one winter's night and lies buried at some cross-roads where the omnibuses now stop outside the Elephant and Castle.[2]

That, more or less, is how the story would run, I think, if a woman in Shakespeare's day had had Shakespeare's genius. But for my part, I agree with the deceased bishop, if such he was—it is unthinkable that any woman in Shakespeare's day should have had Shakespeare's genius. For genius like Shakespeare's is not born among labouring, uneducated, servile people. It was not born in England among the Saxons and the Britons. It is not born today among the working classes. How, then, could it have been born among women whose work began, according to Professor Trevelyan, almost before they were out of the nursery, who were forced to it by their parents and held to it by all the power of law and custom? Yet genius of a sort must have existed among women as it must have existed among the working classes. Now and again an Emily Brontë or a Robert Burns[3] blazes out and proves its presence. But certainly it never got itself on to paper. When, however, one reads of a witch being ducked, of a woman possessed by devils, of a wise woman selling herbs, or even of a very remarkable man who had a mother, then I think we are on the track of a lost novelist, a suppressed poet, of some mute and inglorious[4] Jane Austen, some Emily Brontë who dashed her brains out on the moor or mopped and mowed about the highways crazed with the torture that her gift had put her to. Indeed, I would venture to guess that Anon, who wrote so many poems without signing them, was often a woman. It was a woman Edward Fitzgerald,[5] I think, suggested who made the ballads and the folk-songs, crooning them to her children, beguiling her spinning with them, or the length of the winter's night.

This may be true or it may be false—who can say?—but what is true in it, so it seemed to me, reviewing the story of Shakespeare's sister as I had made it, is that any woman born with a great gift in the sixteenth century would certainly have gone crazed, shot herself, or ended her days in some lonely cottage outside the village, half witch, half wizard, feared and mocked at. For it needs little skill in psychology to be sure that a highly gifted girl who had tried to use her gift for poetry would have been so thwarted and hindered by other people, so tortured and pulled asunder by her own contrary instincts, that she must have lost her health and sanity to a certainty. No girl could have walked to London and stood at a stage door and forced her way into the presence of actor-managers without doing herself a violence and suffering an anguish which may have been irrational—for chastity may be a fetish invented by certain societies for unknown reasons—but were none the less inevitable.

---

2. Suicides were buried at crossroads. The Elephant and Castle was a tavern south of the river Thames, where roads went off to different parts of southern England.
3. Scottish poet (1759–1796).

4. An echo of Thomas Gray's "Elegy Written in a Country Churchyard" (1751), line 59: "Some mute inglorious Milton here may rest."
5. Poet and translator (1809–1883).

Chastity had then, it has even now, a religious importance in a woman's life, and has so wrapped itself round with nerves and instincts that to cut it free and bring it to the light of day demands courage of the rarest. To have lived a free life in London in the sixteenth century would have meant for a woman who was poet and playwright a nervous stress and dilemma which might well have killed her. Had she survived, whatever she had written would have been twisted and deformed, issuing from a strained and morbid imagination. And undoubtedly, I thought, looking at the shelf where there are no plays by women, her work would have gone unsigned. That refuge she would have sought certainly. It was the relic of the sense of chastity that dictated anonymity to women even so late as the nineteenth century. Currer Bell, George Eliot, George Sand,[6] all the victims of inner strife as their writings prove, sought ineffectively to veil themselves by using the name of a man. Thus they did homage to the convention, which if not implanted by the other sex was liberally encouraged by them (the chief glory of a woman is not to be talked of, said Pericles,[7] himself a much-talked-of man), that publicity in women is detestable. Anonymity runs in their blood. The desire to be veiled still possesses them. They are not even now as concerned about the health of their fame as men are, and, speaking generally, will pass a tombstone or a signpost without feeling an irresistible desire to cut their names on it, as Alf, Bert or Chas. must do in obedience to their instinct, which murmurs if it sees a fine woman go by, or even a dog, Ce chien est à moi.[8] And, of course, it may not be a dog, I thought, remembering Parliament Square, the Sieges Allee[9] and other avenues; it may be a piece of land or a man with curly black hair. It is one of the great advantages of being a woman that one can pass even a very fine negress without wishing to make an Englishwoman of her.

That woman, then, who was born with a gift of poetry in the sixteenth century, was an unhappy woman, a woman at strife against herself. All the conditions of her life, all her own instincts, were hostile to the state of mind which is needed to set free whatever is in the brain. But what is the state of mind that is most propitious to the act of creation, I asked. Can one come by any notion of the state that furthers and makes possible that strange activity? Here I opened the volume containing the Tragedies of Shakespeare. What was Shakespeare's state of mind, for instance, when he wrote *Lear* and *Antony and Cleopatra*? It was certainly the state of mind most favourable to poetry that there has ever existed. But Shakespeare himself said nothing about it. We only know casually and by chance that he "never blotted a line."[1] Nothing indeed was ever said by the artist himself about his state of mind until the eighteenth century perhaps. Rousseau[2] perhaps began it. At any rate, by the nineteenth century self-consciousness had developed so far that it was the habit for men of letters to describe their minds in confessions and autobiographies. Their lives also were written, and their letters were printed after their deaths. Thus, though we do not know what Shakespeare went through when he wrote *Lear*, we do know what Carlyle went through when he wrote the *French Revolution*; what Flaubert went through when he wrote *Madame Bovary*; what Keats was

6. Male pseudonyms, respectively, of Charlotte Brontë, Marian Evans, and Amandine-Aurore-Lucie Dupin (1804–1876).
7. Athenian statesman (ca. 495–429 B.C.E.).
8. This dog is mine (French).
9. Avenue of Victory, a busy thoroughfare in Berlin. "Parliament Square": London intersection.

1. Ben Jonson, *Timber* (1640): "I remember, the players have often mentioned it as an honour to Shakespeare that in his writing (whatsoever he penned) he never blotted out a line."
2. Jean-Jacques Rousseau (1712–1778), early-Romantic French philosopher and memoirist.

going through when he tried to write poetry against the coming of death and the indifference of the world.

And one gathers from this enormous modern literature of confession and self-analysis that to write a work of genius is almost always a feat of prodigious difficulty. Everything is against the likelihood that it will come from the writer's mind whole and entire. Generally material circumstances are against it. Dogs will bark; people will interrupt; money must be made; health will break down. Further, accentuating all these difficulties and making them harder to bear is the world's notorious indifference. It does not ask people to write poems and novels and histories; it does not need them. It does not care whether Flaubert finds the right word or whether Carlyle scrupulously verifies this or that fact. Naturally, it will not pay for what it does not want. And so the writer, Keats, Flaubert, Carlyle, suffers, especially in the creative years of youth, every form of distraction and discouragement. A curse, a cry of agony, rises from those books of analysis and confession. "Mighty poets in their misery dead"[3]—that is the burden of their song. If anything comes through in spite of all this, it is a miracle, and probably no book is born entire and uncrippled as it was conceived.

But for women, I thought, looking at the empty shelves, these difficulties were infinitely more formidable. In the first place, to have a room of her own, let alone a quiet room or a sound-proof room, was out of the question, unless her parents were exceptionally rich or very noble, even up to the beginning of the nineteenth century. Since her pin money, which depended on the good will of her father, was only enough to keep her clothed, she was debarred from such alleviations as came even to Keats or Tennyson or Carlyle, all poor men, from a walking tour, a little journey to France, from the separate lodging which, even if it were miserable enough, sheltered them from the claims and tyrannies of their families. Such material difficulties were formidable; but much worse were the immaterial. The indifference of the world which Keats and Flaubert and other men of genius have found so hard to bear was in her case not indifference but hostility. The world did not say to her as it said to them, Write if you choose; it makes no difference to me. The world said with a guffaw, Write? What's the good of your writing? Here the psychologists of Newnham and Girton might come to our help, I thought, looking again at the blank spaces on the shelves. For surely it is time that the effect of discouragement upon the mind of the artist should be measured, as I have seen a dairy company measure the effect of ordinary milk and Grade A milk upon the body of the rat. They set two rats in cages side by side, and of the two one was furtive, timid and small, and the other was glossy, bold and big. Now what food do we feed women as artists upon? I asked, remembering, I suppose, that dinner of prunes and custard. To answer that question I had only to open the evening paper and to read that Lord Birkenhead is of opinion—but really I am not going to trouble to copy out Lord Birkenhead's opinion upon the writing of women. What Dean Inge says I will leave in peace. The Harley Street specialist[4] may be allowed to rouse the echoes of Harley Street with his vociferations without raising a hair on my head. I will quote, however, Mr Oscar Browning, because Mr Oscar Browning was a great figure in Cambridge at one time, and used to examine the students at Girton and Newnham. Mr Oscar

---

3. From Wordsworth's "Resolution and Independence" (1807), line 116.

4. On Harley Street in London many medical specialists have their consulting rooms.

Browning was wont to declare "that the impression left on his mind, after looking over any set of examination papers, was that, irrespective of the marks he might give, the best woman was intellectually the inferior of the worst man." After saying that Mr Browning went back to his rooms—and it is this sequel that endears him and makes him a human figure of some bulk and majesty—he went back to his rooms and found a stable-boy lying on the sofa—"a mere skeleton, his cheeks were cavernous and sallow, his teeth were black, and he did not appear to have the full use of his limbs. . . . 'That's Arthur' [said Mr Browning]. 'He's a dear boy really and most high-minded.' " The two pictures always seem to me to complete each other. And happily in this age of biography the two pictures often do complete each other, so that we are able to interpret the opinions of great men not only by what they say, but by what they do.

But though this is possible now, such opinions coming from the lips of important people must have been formidable enough even fifty years ago. Let us suppose that a father from the highest motives did not wish his daughter to leave home and become writer, painter or scholar. "See what Mr Oscar Browning says," he would say; and there was not only Mr Oscar Browning; there was the *Saturday Review*; there was Mr Greg[5]—the "essentials of a woman's being," said Mr Greg emphatically, "are that *they are supported by, and they minister to, men*"—there was an enormous body of masculine opinion to the effect that nothing could be expected of women intellectually. Even if her father did not read out loud these opinions, any girl could read them for herself; and the reading, even in the nineteenth century, must have lowered her vitality, and told profoundly upon her work. There would always have been that assertion—you cannot do this, you are incapable of doing that—to protest against, to overcome. Probably for a novelist this germ is no longer of much effect; for there have been women novelists of merit. But for painters it must still have some sting in it; and for musicians, I imagine, is even now active and poisonous in the extreme. The woman composer stands where the actress stood in the time of Shakespeare. Nick Greene, I thought, remembering the story I had made about Shakespeare's sister, said that a woman acting put him in mind of a dog dancing. Johnson repeated the phrase two hundred years later of women preaching. And here, I said, opening a book about music, we have the very words used again in this year of grace, 1928, of women who try to write music. "Of Mlle Germaine Tailleferre one can only repeat Dr Johnson's dictum concerning a woman preacher, transposed into terms of music. 'Sir, a woman's composing is like a dog's walking on his hind legs. It is not done well, but you are surprised to find it done at all.' "[6] So accurately does history repeat itself.

Thus, I concluded, shutting Mr Oscar Browning's life and pushing away the rest, it is fairly evident that even in the nineteenth century a woman was not encouraged to be an artist. On the contrary, she was snubbed, slapped, lectured and exhorted. Her mind must have been strained and her vitality lowered by the need of opposing this, of disproving that. For here again we come within range of that very interesting and obscure masculine complex which has had so much influence upon the woman's movement; that deepseated desire, not so much that *she* shall be inferior as that *he* shall be superior, which plants him wherever one looks, not only in front of the arts, but barring the way to

5. Sir W. W. Greg (1875–1959), bibliographer and literary scholar.

6. *A Survey of Contemporary Music*, Cecil Gray, p. 246 [Woolf's note].

politics too, even when the risk to himself seems infinitesimal and the suppliant humble and devoted. Even Lady Bessborough, I remembered, with all her passion for politics, must humbly bow herself and write to Lord Granville Leveson-Gower:[7] ". . . notwithstanding all my violence in politics and talking so much on that subject, I perfectly agree with you that no woman has any business to meddle with that or any other serious business, farther than giving her opinion (if she is ask'd)." And so she goes on to spend her enthusiasm where it meets with no obstacle whatsoever upon that immensely important subject, Lord Granville's maiden speech in the House of Commons. The spectacle is certainly a strange one, I thought. The history of men's opposition to women's emancipation is more interesting perhaps than the story of that emancipation itself. An amusing book might be made of it if some young student at Girton or Newnham would collect examples and deduce a theory—but she would need thick gloves on her hands, and bars to protect her of solid gold.

But what is amusing now, I recollected, shutting Lady Bessborough, had to be taken in desperate earnest once. Opinions that one now pastes in a book labelled cock-a-doodle-dum and keeps for reading to select audiences on summer nights once drew tears, I can assure you. Among your grandmothers and great-grandmothers there were many that wept their eyes out. Florence Nightingale shrieked loud in her agony.[8] Moreover, it is all very well for you, who have got yourselves to college and enjoy sitting-rooms—or is it only bed-sitting-rooms?—of your own to say that genius should disregard such opinions; that genius should be above caring what is said of it. Unfortunately, it is precisely the men or women of genius who mind most what is said of them. Remember Keats. Remember the words he had cut on his tombstone.[9] Think of Tennyson; think—but I need hardly multiply instances of the undeniable, if very unfortunate, fact that it is the nature of the artist to mind excessively what is said about him. Literature is strewn with the wreckage of men who have minded beyond reason the opinions of others.

And this susceptibility of theirs is doubly unfortunate, I thought, returning again to my original enquiry into what state of mind is most propitious for creative work, because the mind of an artist, in order to achieve the prodigious effort of freeing whole and entire the work that is in him, must be incandescent, like Shakespeare's mind, I conjectured, looking at the book which lay open at *Antony and Cleopatra*. There must be no obstacle in it, no foreign matter unconsumed.

For though we say that we know nothing about Shakespeare's state of mind, even as we say that, we are saying something about Shakespeare's state of mind. The reason perhaps why we know so little of Shakespeare—compared with Donne or Ben Jonson or Milton—is that his grudges and spites and antipathies are hidden from us. We are not held up by some "revelation" which reminds us of the writer. All desire to protest, to preach, to proclaim an injury, to pay off a score, to make the world the witness of some hardship or grievance was fired out of him and consumed. Therefore his poetry flows from him free and unimpeded. If ever a human being got his work expressed completely, it

---

7. English statesman (1773–1846). Lady Bessborough is Henrietta, countess of Bessborough (1761–1821).
8. See *Cassandra*, by Florence Nightingale, printed in *The Cause*, by R. Strachey [Woolf's note]. Florence Nightingale (1820–1910), English nurse, who originated and directed a group of field nurses during the Crimean War and is considered the founder of modern nursing.
9. "Here lies one whose name was writ in water."

was Shakespeare. If ever a mind was incandescent, unimpeded, I thought, turning again to the bookcase, it was Shakespeare's mind.

Chapter Four

That one would find any woman in that state of mind in the sixteenth century was obviously impossible. One has only to think of the Elizabethan tombstones with all those children kneeling with clasped hands; and their early deaths; and to see their houses with their dark, cramped rooms, to realise that no woman could have written poetry then. What one would expect to find would be that rather later perhaps some great lady would take advantage of her comparative freedom and comfort to publish something with her name to it and risk being thought a monster. Men, of course, are not snobs, I continued, carefully eschewing "the arrant feminism" of Miss Rebecca West; but they appreciate with sympathy for the most part the efforts of a countess to write verse. One would expect to find a lady of title meeting with far greater encouragement than an unknown Miss Austen or a Miss Brontë at that time would have met with. But one would also expect to find that her mind was disturbed by alien emotions like fear and hatred and that her poems showed traces of that disturbance. Here is Lady Winchilsea,[1] for example, I thought, taking down her poems. She was born in the year 1661; she was noble both by birth and by marriage; she was childless; she wrote poetry, and one has only to open her poetry to find her bursting out in indignation against the position of women:

> How are we fallen! fallen by mistaken rules,
> And Education's more than Nature's fools;
> Debarred from all improvements of the mind,
> And to be dull, expected and designed;
> And if some one would soar above the rest,
> With warmer fancy, and ambition pressed,
> So strong the opposing faction still appears,
> The hopes to thrive can ne'er outweigh the fears.

Clearly her mind has by no means "consumed all impediments and become incandescent." On the contrary, it is harrassed and distracted with hates and grievances. The human race is split up for her into two parties. Men are the "opposing faction"; men are hated and feared, because they have the power to bar her way to what she wants to do—which is to write.

> Alas! a woman that attempts the pen,
> Such a presumptuous creature is esteemed,
> The fault can by no virtue be redeemed.
> They tell us we mistake our sex and way;
> Good breeding, fashion, dancing, dressing, play,
> Are the accomplishments we should desire;
> To write, or read, or think, or to enquire,
> Would cloud our beauty, and exhaust our time,
> And interrupt the conquests of our prime,
> Whilst the dull manage of a servile house
> Is held by some our utmost art and use.

1. Anne Finch, countess of Winchilsea (1661–1720); the quotations are from her poem "The Introduction."

Indeed she has to encourage herself to write by supposing that what she writes will never be published; to soothe herself with the sad chant:

> To some few friends, and to thy sorrows sing,
> For groves of laurel thou wert never meant;
> Be dark enough thy shades, and be thou there content.

Yet it is clear that could she have freed her mind from hate and fear and not heaped it with bitterness and resentment, the fire was hot within her. Now and again words issue of pure poetry:

> Nor will in fading silks compose,
> Faintly the inimitable rose.

—they are rightly praised by Mr Murry,[2] and Pope, it is thought, remembered and appropriated those others:

> Now the jonquille o'ercomes the feeble brain;
> We faint beneath the aromatic pain.

It was a thousand pities that the woman who could write like that, whose mind was turned to nature and reflection, should have been forced to anger and bitterness. But how could she have helped herself? I asked, imagining the sneers and the laughter, the adulation of the toadies,[3] the scepticism of the professional poet. She must have shut herself up in a room in the country to write, and been torn asunder by bitterness and scruples perhaps, though her husband was of the kindest, and their married life perfection. She "must have," I say, because when one comes to seek out the facts about Lady Winchilsea, one finds, as usual, that almost nothing is known about her. She suffered terribly from melancholy, which we can explain at least to some extent when we find her telling us how in the grip of it she would imagine:

> My lines decried, and my employment thought,
> An useless folly or presumptuous fault:

The employment, which was thus censured, was, as far as one can see, the harmless one of rambling about the fields and dreaming:

> My hand delights to trace unusual things,
> And deviates from the known and common way,
> Nor will in fading silks compose,
> Faintly the inimitable rose.

Naturally, if that was her habit and that was her delight, she could only expect to be laughed at; and, accordingly, Pope or Gay[4] is said to have satirised her "as a blue-stocking with an itch for scribbling." Also it is thought that she offended Gay by laughing at him. She said that his *Trivia* showed that "he was more proper to walk before a chair than to ride in one." But this is all "dubious gossip" and, says Mr Murry, "uninteresting." But there I do not agree with him, for I should have liked to have had more even of dubious gossip so that I might have found out or made up some image of this melancholy lady, who loved wandering in the fields and thinking about unusual things and scorned, so rashly, so unwisely, "the dull manage of a servile house." But she became

2. John Middleton Murry (1889–1957), English literary critic.
3. Sycophants.
4. John Gay (1685–1732), English poet and play-wright, author of the poem "Trivia, or The Art of Walking the Streets of London" (1716), mentioned below.

diffuse, Mr Murry says. Her gift is all grown about with weeds and bound with briars. It had no chance of showing itself for the fine distinguished gift it was. And so, putting her back on the shelf, I turned to the other great lady, the Duchess whom Lamb loved, hare-brained, fantastical Margaret of Newcastle,[5] her elder, but her contemporary. They were very different, but alike in this that both were noble and both childless, and both were married to the best of husbands. In both burnt the same passion for poetry and both are disfigured and deformed by the same causes. Open the Duchess and one finds the same outburst of rage, "Women live like Bats or Owls, labour like Beasts, and die like Worms. . . ." Margaret too might have been a poet; in our day all that activity would have turned a wheel of some sort. As it was, what could bind, tame or civilise for human use that wild, generous, untutored intelligence? It poured itself out, higgledy-piggledy, in torrents of rhyme and prose, poetry and philosophy which stand congealed in quartos and folios that nobody ever reads. She should have had a microscope put in her hand. She should have been taught to look at the stars and reason scientifically. Her wits were turned with solitude and freedom. No one checked her. No one taught her. The professors fawned on her. At Court they jeered at her. Sir Egerton Brydges[6] complained of her coarseness—"as flowing from a female of high rank brought up in the Courts." She shut herself up at Welbeck[7] alone.

What a vision of loneliness and riot the thought of Margaret Cavendish brings to mind! as if some giant cucumber had spread itself over all the roses and carnations in the garden and choked them to death. What a waste that the woman who wrote "the best bred women are those whose minds are civilest" should have frittered her time away scribbling nonsense and plunging ever deeper into obscurity and folly till the people crowded round her coach when she issued out. Evidently the crazy Duchess became a bogey to frighten clever girls with. Here, I remembered, putting away the Duchess and opening Dorothy Osborne's[8] letters, is Dorothy writing to Temple about the Duchess's new book. "Sure the poore woman is a little distracted, shee could never bee soe rediculous else as to venture at writeing book's and in verse too, if I should not sleep this fortnight I should not come to that."

And so, since no woman of sense and modesty could write books, Dorothy, who was sensitive and melancholy, the very opposite of the Duchess in temper, wrote nothing. Letters did not count. A woman might write letters while she was sitting by her father's sick-bed. She could write them by the fire whilst the men talked without disturbing them. The strange thing is, I thought, turning over the pages of Dorothy's letters, what a gift that untaught and solitary girl had for the framing of a sentence, for the fashioning of a scene. Listen to her running on:

"After dinner wee sitt and talk till Mr B. com's in question and then I am gon. the heat of the day is spent in reading or working and about sixe or seven a Clock, I walke out into a Common that lyes hard by the house where a great many young wenches keep Sheep and Cow's and sitt in the shades singing of Ballads; I goe to them and compare their voyces and Beauty's to some Ancient Shepherdesses that I have read of and finde a vaste difference there, but trust mee I think these are as innocent as those could bee. I talke to them, and

---

5. Margaret Lucas Cavendish, duchess of Newcastle (1623–1673), author of "Female Orations," quoted below.
6. English writer (1762–1837).

7. Estate of Margaret's husband, in Nottinghamshire.
8. Later, Lady Temple (1627–1695), famous for her letters to her future husband.

finde they want nothing to make them the happiest People in the world, but the knoledge that they are soe. most commonly when we are in the middest of our discourse one looks aboute her and spyes her Cow's goeing into the Corne and then away they all run, as if they had wing's at theire heels. I that am not soe nimble stay behinde, and when I see them driveing home theire Cattle I think tis time for mee to retyre too. when I have supped I goe into the Garden and soe to the syde of a small River that runs by it where I sitt downe and wish you with mee. . . ."

One could have sworn that she had the makings of a writer in her. But "if I should not sleep this fortnight I should not come to that"—one can measure the opposition that was in the air to a woman writing when one finds that even a woman with a great turn for writing has brought herself to believe that to write a book was to be ridiculous, even to show oneself distracted. And so we come, I continued, replacing the single short volume of Dorothy Osborne's letters upon the shelf, to Mrs Behn.[9]

And with Mrs Behn we turn a very important corner on the road. We leave behind, shut up in their parks among their folios, those solitary great ladies who wrote without audience or criticism, for their own delight alone. We come to town and rub shoulders with ordinary people in the streets. Mrs Behn was a middle-class woman with all the plebeian virtues of humour, vitality and courage; a woman forced by the death of her husband and some unfortunate adventures of her own to make her living by her wits. She had to work on equal terms with men. She made, by working very hard, enough to live on. The importance of that fact outweighs anything that she actually wrote, even the splendid "A Thousand Martyrs I have made," or "Love in Fantastic Triumph sat," for here begins the freedom of the mind, or rather the possibility that in the course of time the mind will be free to write what it likes. For now that Aphra Behn had done it, girls could go to their parents and say, You need not give me an allowance; I can make money by my pen. Of course the answer for many years to come was, Yes, by living the life of Aphra Behn! Death would be better! and the door was slammed faster than ever. That profoundly interesting subject, the value that men set upon women's chastity and its effect upon their education, here suggests itself for discussion, and might provide an interesting book if any student at Girton or Newnham cared to go into the matter. Lady Dudley, sitting in diamonds among the midges of a Scottish moor, might serve for frontispiece. Lord Dudley, *The Times* said when Lady Dudley died the other day, "a man of cultivated taste and many accomplishments, was benevolent and bountiful, but whimsically despotic. He insisted upon his wife's wearing full dress, even at the remotest shooting-lodge in the Highlands; he loaded her with gorgeous jewels," and so on, "he gave her everything—always excepting any measure of responsibility." Then Lord Dudley had a stroke and she nursed him and ruled his estates with supreme competence for ever after. That whimsical despotism was in the nineteenth century too.

But to return. Aphra Behn proved that money could be made by writing at the sacrifice, perhaps, of certain agreeable qualities; and so by degrees writing became not merely a sign of folly and a distracted mind, but was of practical importance. A husband might die, or some disaster overtake the family. Hundreds of women began as the eighteenth century drew on to add to their pin

---

9. Aphra Behn (ca. 1640–1689), English poet and playwright, and author of *Oroonoko*.

money, or to come to the rescue of their families by making translations or writing the innumerable bad novels which have ceased to be recorded even in text-books, but are to be picked up in the fourpenny boxes in the Charing Cross Road.[1] The extreme activity of mind which showed itself in the later eighteenth century among women—the talking, and the meeting, the writing of essays on Shakespeare, the translating of the classics—was founded on the solid fact that women could make money by writing. Money dignifies what is frivolous if unpaid for. It might still be well to sneer at "blue stockings with an itch for scribbling," but it could not be denied that they could put money in their purses. Thus, towards the end of the eighteenth century a change came about which, if I were rewriting history, I should describe more fully and think of greater importance than the Crusades or the Wars of the Roses. The middle-class woman began to write. For if *Pride and Prejudice* matters, and *Middlemarch* and *Villette* and *Wuthering Heights*[2] matter, then it matters far more than I can prove in an hour's discourse that women generally, and not merely the lonely aristocrat shut up in her country house among her folios and her flatterers, took to writing. Without those forerunners, Jane Austen and the Brontës and George Eliot could no more have written than Shakespeare could have written without Marlowe, or Marlowe without Chaucer, or Chaucer without those forgotten poets who paved the ways and tamed the natural savagery of the tongue. For masterpieces are not single and solitary births; they are the outcome of many years of thinking in common, of thinking by the body of the people, so that the experience of the mass is behind the single voice. Jane Austen should have laid a wreath upon the grave of Fanny Burney, and George Eliot done homage to the robust shade of Eliza Carter[3]— the valiant old woman who tied a bell to her bedstead in order that she might wake early and learn Greek. All women together ought to let flowers fall upon the tomb of Alphra Behn which is, most scandalously but rather appropriately, in Westminster Abbey,[4] for it was she who earned them the right to speak their minds. It is she—shady and amorous as she was—who makes it not quite fantastic for me to say to you tonight: Earn five hundred a year by your wits.

Here, then, one had reached the early nineteenth century. And here, for the first time, I found several shelves given up entirely to the works of women. But why, I could not help asking, as I ran my eyes over them, were they, with very few exceptions, all novels? The original impulse was to poetry. The "supreme head of song" was a poetess. Both in France and in England the women poets precede the women novelists. Moreover, I thought, looking at the four famous names, what had George Eliot in common with Emily Brontë? Did not Charlotte Brontë fail entirely to understand Jane Austen? Save for the possibly relevant fact that not one of them had a child, four more incongruous characters could not have met together in a room—so much so that it is tempting to invent a meeting and a dialogue between them. Yet by some strange force they were all compelled, when they wrote, to write novels. Had it something to do with being born of the middle class, I asked; and with the fact, which Miss Emily Davies[5] a little later was so strikingly to demonstrate, that the middle-class family in the early nineteenth century was possessed only of a single sitting-room between them? If a woman wrote, she would have to

---

1. A street in London famed for its bookshops.
2. Novels by, respectively, Jane Austen, George Eliot, Charlotte Brontë, and Emily Brontë. *Emma,* mentioned below, is by Austen.

3. English poet and translator (1717–1806).
4. Site of Poet's Corner, which contains the tombs of many notable authors.
5. See n. 3, p. 2102.

write in the common sitting-room. And, as Miss Nightingale was so vehemently to complain,—"women never have an half hour . . . that they can call their own"—she was always interrupted. Still it would be easier to write prose and fiction there than to write poetry or a play. Less concentration is required. Jane Austen wrote like that to the end of her days. "How she was able to effect all this," her nephew writes in his Memoir, "is surprising, for she had no separate study to repair to, and most of the work must have been done in the general sitting-room, subject to all kinds of casual interruptions. She was careful that her occupation should not be suspected by servants or visitors or any persons beyond her own family party."[6] Jane Austen hid her manuscripts or covered them with a piece of blotting-paper. Then, again, all the literary training that a woman had in the early nineteenth century was training in the observation of character, in the analysis of emotion. Her sensibility had been educated for centuries by the influences of the common sitting-room. People's feelings were impressed on her; personal relations were always before her eyes. Therefore, when the middle-class woman took to writing, she naturally wrote novels, even though, as seems evident enough, two of the four famous women here named were not by nature novelists. Emily Brontë should have written poetic plays; the overflow of George Eliot's capacious mind should have spread itself when the creative impulse was spent upon history or biography. They wrote novels, however; one may even go further, I said, taking *Pride and Prejudice* from the shelf, and say that they wrote good novels. Without boasting or giving pain to the opposite sex, one may say that *Pride and Prejudice* is a good book. At any rate, one would not have been ashamed to have been caught in the act of writing *Pride and Prejudice*. Yet Jane Austen was glad that a hinge creaked, so that she might hide her manuscript before any one came in. To Jane Austen there was something discreditable in writing *Pride and Prejudice*. And, I wondered, would *Pride and Prejudice* have been a better novel if Jane Austen had not thought it necessary to hide her manuscript from visitors? I read a page or two to see; but I could not find any signs that her circumstances had harmed her work in the slightest. That, perhaps, was the chief miracle about it. Here was a woman about the year 1800 writing without hate, without bitterness, without fear, without protest, without preaching. That was how Shakespeare wrote, I thought, looking at *Antony and Cleopatra*; and when people compare Shakespeare and Jane Austen, they may mean that the minds of both had consumed all impediments; and for that reason we do not know Jane Austen and we do not know Shakespeare, and for that reason Jane Austen pervades every word that she wrote, and so does Shakespeare. If Jane Austen suffered in any way from her circumstances it was in the narrowness of life that was imposed upon her. It was impossible for a woman to go about alone. She never travelled; she never drove through London in an omnibus or had luncheon in a shop by herself. But perhaps it was the nature of Jane Austen not to want what she had not. Her gift and her circumstances matched each other completely. But I doubt whether that was true of Charlotte Brontë, I said, opening *Jane Eyre* and laying it beside *Pride and Prejudice*.

I opened it at chapter twelve and my eye was caught by the phrase, "Anybody may blame me who likes." What were they blaming Charlotte Brontë for, I wondered? And I read how Jane Eyre used to go up on to the roof when Mrs. Fairfax was making jellies and looked over the fields at the distant view. And

---

6. *Memoir of Jane Austen*, by her nephew, James Edward Austen-Leigh [Woolf's note].

then she longed—and it was for this that they blamed her—that "then I longed for a power of vision which might overpass that limit; which might reach the busy world, towns, regions full of life I had heard of but never seen: that then I desired more of practical experience than I possessed; more of intercourse with my kind, of acquaintance with variety of character than was here within my reach. I valued what was good in Mrs. Fairfax, and what was good in Adèle; but I believed in the existence of other and more vivid kinds of goodness, and what I believed in I wished to behold.

"Who blames me? Many, no doubt, and I shall be called discontented. I could not help it: the restlessness was in my nature; it agitated me to pain sometimes. . . .

"It is vain to say human beings ought to be satisfied with tranquillity: they must have action; and they will make it if they cannot find it. Millions are condemned to a stiller doom than mine, and millions are in silent revolt against their lot. Nobody knows how many rebellions ferment in the masses of life which people earth. Women are supposed to be very calm generally: but women feel just as men feel; they need exercise for their faculties and a field for their efforts as much as their brothers do; they suffer from too rigid a restraint, too absolute a stagnation, precisely as men would suffer; and it is narrow-minded in their more privileged fellow-creatures to say that they ought to confine themselves to making puddings and knitting stockings, to playing on the piano and embroidering bags. It is thoughtless to condemn them, or laugh at them, if they seek to do more or learn more than custom has pronounced necessary for their sex.

"When thus alone I not unfrequently heard Grace Poole's laugh. . . ."

That is an awkward break, I thought. It is upsetting to come upon Grace Poole all of a sudden. The continuity is disturbed. One might say, I continued, laying the book down beside *Pride and Prejudice*, that the woman who wrote those pages had more genius in her than Jane Austen; but if one reads them over and marks that jerk in them, that indignation, one sees that she will never get her genius expressed whole and entire. Her books will be deformed and twisted. She will write in a rage where she should write calmly. She will write foolishly where she should write wisely. She will write of herself where she should write of her characters. She is at war with her lot. How could she help but die young, cramped and thwarted?

One could not but play for a moment with the thought of what might have happened if Charlotte Brontë had possessed say three hundred a year—but the foolish woman sold the copyright of her novels outright for fifteen hundred pounds; had somehow possessed more knowledge of the busy world, and towns and regions full of life; more practical experience, and intercourse with her kind and acquaintance with a variety of character. In those words she puts her finger exactly not only upon her own defects as a novelist but upon those of her sex at that time. She knew, no one better, how enormously her genius would have profited if it had not spent itself in solitary visions over distant fields; if experience and intercourse and travel had been granted her. But they were not granted; they were withheld; and we must accept the fact that all those good novels, *Villette, Emma, Wuthering Heights, Middlemarch*, were written by women without more experience of life than could enter the house of a respectable clergyman; written too in the common sitting-room of that respectable house and by women so poor that they could not afford to buy more than a few quires of paper at a time upon which to write *Wuthering*

Heights or *Jane Eyre*. One of them, it is true, George Eliot, escaped after much tribulation, but only to a secluded villa in St John's Wood.[7] And there she settled down in the shadow of the world's disapproval. "I wish it to be understood," she wrote, "that I should never invite any one to come and see me who did not ask for the invitation"; for was she not living in sin with a married man and might not the sight of her damage the chastity of Mrs Smith or whoever it might be that chanced to call? One must submit to the social convention, and be "cut off from what is called the world." At the same time, on the other side of Europe, there was a young man living freely with this gipsy or with that great lady; going to the wars; picking up unhindered and uncensored all that varied experience of human life which served him so splendidly later when he came to write his books. Had Tolstoi[8] lived at the Priory in seclusion with a married lady "cut off from what is called the world," however edifying the moral lesson, he could scarcely, I thought, have written *War and Peace*.

But one could perhaps go a little deeper into the question of novel-writing and the effect of sex upon the novelist. If one shuts one's eyes and thinks of the novel as a whole, it would seem to be a creation owning a certain looking-glass likeness to life, though of course with simplifications and distortions innumerable. At any rate, it is a structure leaving a shape on the mind's eye, built now in squares, now pagoda shaped, now throwing out wings and arcades, now solidly compact and domed like the Cathedral of Saint Sofia at Constantinople. This shape, I thought, thinking back over certain famous novels, starts in one the kind of emotion that is appropriate to it. But that emotion at once blends itself with others, for the "shape" is not made by the relation of stone to stone, but by the relation of human being to human being. Thus a novel starts in us all sorts of antagonistic and opposed emotions. Life conflicts with something that is not life. Hence the difficulty of coming to any agreement about novels, and the immense sway that our private prejudices have upon us. On the one hand, we feel You—John the hero—must live, or I shall be in the depths of despair. On the other, we feel, Alas, John, you must die, because the shape of the book requires it. Life conflicts with something that is not life. Then since life it is in part, we judge it as life. James is the sort of man I most detest, one says. Or, This is a farrago of absurdity. I could never feel anything of the sort myself. The whole structure, it is obvious, thinking back on any famous novel, is one of infinite complexity, because it is thus made up of so many different judgments, of so many different kinds of emotion. The wonder is that any book so composed holds together for more than a year or two, or can possibly mean to the English reader what it means for the Russian or the Chinese. But they do hold together occasionally very remarkably. And what holds them together in these rare instances of survival (I was thinking of *War and Peace*) is something that one calls integrity, though it has nothing to do with paying one's bills or behaving honourably in an emergency. What one means by integrity, in the case of the novelist, is the conviction that he gives one that this is the truth. Yes, one feels, I should never have thought that this could be so; I have never known people behaving like that. But you have convinced me that so it is, so it happens. One holds every phrase, every scene to the light as one reads—for Nature seems, very oddly, to have provided us with an inner light by which to judge of the novelist's

---

7. A suburb in northwest London that developed in the 1840s.

8. Leo Tolstoy (1828–1910), Russian novelist.

integrity or disintegrity. Or perhaps it is rather that Nature, in her most irrational mood, has traced in invisible ink on the walls of the mind a premonition which these great artists confirm; a sketch which only needs to be held to the fire of genius to become visible. When one so exposes it and sees it come to life one exclaims in rapture, But this is what I have always felt and known and desired! And one boils over with excitement, and, shutting the book even with a kind of reverence as if it were something very precious, a stand-by to return to as long as one lives, one puts it back on the shelf, I said, taking *War and Peace* and putting it back in its place. If, on the other hand, these poor sentences that one takes and tests rouse first a quick and eager response with their bright colouring and their dashing gestures but there they stop: something seems to check them in their development: or if they bring to light only a faint scribble in that corner and a blot over there, and nothing appears whole and entire, then one heaves a sigh of disappointment and says, Another failure. This novel has come to grief somewhere.

And for the most part, of course, novels do come to grief somewhere. The imagination falters under the enormous strain. The insight is confused; it can no longer distinguish between the true and the false; it has no longer the strength to go on with the vast labour that calls at every moment for the use of so many different faculties. But how would all this be affected by the sex of the novelist, I wondered, looking at *Jane Eyre* and the others. Would the fact of her sex in any way interfere with the integrity of a woman novelist— that integrity which I take to be the backbone of the writer? Now, in the passages I have quoted from *Jane Eyre,* it is clear that anger was tampering with the integrity of Charlotte Brontë the novelist. She left her story, to which her entire devotion was due, to attend to some personal grievance. She remembered that she had been starved of her proper due of experience—she had been made to stagnate in a parsonage mending stockings when she wanted to wander free over the world. Her imagination swerved from indignation and we feel it swerve. But there were many more influences than anger tugging at her imagination and deflecting it from its path. Ignorance, for instance. The portrait of Rochester is drawn in the dark. We feel the influence of fear in it; just as we constantly feel an acidity which is the result of oppression, a buried suffering smouldering beneath her passion, a rancour which contracts those books, splendid as they are, with a spasm of pain.

And since a novel has this correspondence to real life, its values are to some extent those of real life. But it is obvious that the values of women differ very often from the values which have been made by the other sex; naturally, this is so. Yet it is the masculine values that prevail. Speaking crudely, football and sport are "important"; the worship of fashion, the buying of clothes "trivial." And these values are inevitably transferred from life to fiction. This is an important book, the critic assumes, because it deals with war. This is an insignificant book because it deals with the feelings of women in a drawing-room. A scene in a battlefield is more important than a scene in a shop—everywhere and much more subtly the difference of value persists. The whole structure, therefore, of the early nineteenth-century novel was raised, if one was a woman, by a mind which was slightly pulled from the straight, and made to alter its clear vision in deference to external authority. One has only to skim those old forgotten novels and listen to the tone of voice in which they are written to divine that the writer was meeting criticism; she was saying this by way of aggression, or that by way of conciliation. She was admitting that she was "only a woman," or protesting that she was "as good as a man." She met that criticism as her temperament dictated, with docility and diffidence, or with anger and emphasis. It does not matter which it was; she was thinking of something other than the thing itself. Down comes her book upon our heads. There was a flaw in the centre of it. And I thought of all the women's novels that lie scattered, like small pock-marked apples in an orchard, about the secondhand book shops of London. It was the flaw in the centre that had rotted them. She had altered her values in deference to the opinion of others.

But how impossible it must have been for them not to budge either to the right or to the left. What genius, what integrity it must have required in face of all that criticism, in the midst of that purely patriarchal society, to hold fast to the thing as they saw it without shrinking. Only Jane Austen did it and Emily Brontë. It is another feather, perhaps the finest, in their caps. They wrote as women write, not as men write. Of all the thousand women who wrote novels then, they alone entirely ignored the perpetual admonitions of the eternal pedagogue—write this, think that. They alone were deaf to that persistent voice, now grumbling, now patronising, now domineering, now grieved, now shocked, now angry, now avuncular, that voice which cannot let women alone, but must be at them, like some too conscientious governess, adjuring them, like Sir Egerton Brydges, to be refined; dragging even into the criticism of poetry criticism of sex;[9] admonishing them, if they would be good and win, as I suppose, some shiny prize, to keep within certain limits which the gentleman in question thinks suitable: ". . . female novelists should only aspire to excellence by courageously acknowledging the limitations of their sex."[1] That puts the matter in a nutshell, and when I tell you, rather to your surprise, that this sentence was written not in August 1828 but in August 1928, you will agree, I think, that however delightful it is to us now, it represents a vast body of opinion—I am not going to stir those old pools, I take only what chance has floated to my feet—that was far more vigorous and far more vocal a century ago. It would have needed a very stalwart young woman in 1828 to disregard all those snubs and chidings and promises of prizes. One must have been something of a firebrand to say to oneself, Oh, but they can't buy literature too. Literature is open to everybody. I refuse to allow you, Beadle though you are, to turn me off the grass. Lock up your libraries if you like; but there is no gate, no lock, no bolt that you can set upon the freedom of my mind.

But whatever effect discouragement and criticism had upon their writing—and I believe that they had a very great effect—that was unimportant compared with the other difficulty which faced them (I was still considering those early nineteenth-century novelists) when they came to set their thoughts on paper—that is that they had no tradition behind them, or one so short and partial that it was of little help. For we think back through our mothers if we are women. It is useless to go to the great men writers for help, however much one may go to them for pleasure. Lamb, Browne, Thackeray, Newman, Sterne, Dickens, De Quincey—whoever it may be—never helped a woman yet, though

---

9. "[She] has a metaphysical purpose, and that is a dangerous obsession, especially with a woman, for women rarely possess men's healthy love of rhetoric. It is a strange lack in the sex which is in other things more primitive and more materialistic."—*New Criterion*, June 1928 [Woolf's note].

1. "If, like the reporter, you believe that female novelists should only aspire to excellence by courageously acknowledging the limitations of their sex (Jane Austen [has] demonstrated how gracefully this gesture can be accomplished). . . ."—*Life and Letters*, August 1928 [Woolf's note].

she may have learnt a few tricks of them and adapted them to her use. The weight, the pace, the stride of a man's mind are too unlike her own for her to lift anything substantial from him successfully. The ape is too distant to be sedulous. Perhaps the first thing she would find, setting pen to paper, was that there was no common sentence ready for her use. All the great novelists like Thackeray and Dickens and Balzac have written a natural prose, swift but not slovenly, expressive but not precious, taking their own tint without ceasing to be common property. They have based it on the sentence that was current at the time. The sentence that was current at the beginning of the nineteenth century ran something like this perhaps: "The grandeur of their works was an argument with them, not to stop short, but to proceed. They could have no higher excitement or satisfaction than in the exercise of their art and endless generations of truth and beauty. Success prompts to exertion; and habit facilitates success." That is a man's sentence; behind it one can see Johnson, Gibbon[2] and the rest. It was a sentence that was unsuited for a woman's use. Charlotte Brontë, with all her splendid gift for prose, stumbled and fell with that clumsy weapon in her hands. George Eliot committed atrocities with it that beggar description. Jane Austen looked at it and laughed at it and devised a perfectly natural, shapely sentence proper for her own use and never departed from it. Thus, with less genius for writing than Charlotte Brontë, she got infinitely more said. Indeed, since freedom and fullness of expression are of the essence of the art, such a lack of tradition, such a scarcity and inadequacy of tools, must have told enormously upon the writing of women. Moreover, a book is not made of sentences laid end to end, but of sentences built, if an image helps, into arcades or domes. And this shape too has been made by men out of their own needs for their own uses. There is no reason to think that the form of the epic or of the poetic play suits a woman any more than the sentence suits her. But all the older forms of literature were hardened and set by the time she became a writer. The novel alone was young enough to be soft in her hands—another reason, perhaps, why she wrote novels. Yet who shall say that even now "the novel" (I give it inverted commas to mark my sense of the words' inadequacy), who shall say that even this most pliable of all forms is rightly shaped for her use? No doubt we shall find her knocking that into shape for herself when she has the free use of her limbs; and providing some new vehicle, not necessarily in verse, for the poetry in her. For it is the poetry that is still denied outlet. And I went on to ponder how a woman nowadays would write a poetic tragedy in five acts—would she use verse— would she not use prose rather?

But these are difficult questions which lie in the twilight of the future. I must leave them, if only because they stimulate me to wander from my subject into trackless forests where I shall be lost and, very likely, devoured by wild beasts. I do not want, and I am sure that you do not want me, to broach that very dismal subject, the future of fiction, so that I will only pause here one moment to draw your attention to the great part which must be played in that future so far as women are concerned by physical conditions. The book has somehow to be adapted to the body, and at a venture one would say that women's books should be shorter, more concentrated, than those of men, and framed so that they do not need long hours of steady and uninterrupted work.

---

2. Edward Gibbon (1737–1794), English historian, author of *The History of the Decline and Fall of the Roman Empire*.

For interruptions there will always be. Again, the nerves that feed the brain would seem to differ in men and women, and if you are going to make them work their best and hardest, you must find out what treatment suits them—whether these hours of lectures, for instance, which the monks devised, presumably, hundreds of years ago, suit them—what alternations of work and rest they need, interpreting rest not as doing nothing but as doing something but something that is different; and what should that difference be? All this should be discussed and discovered; all this is part of the question of women and fiction. And yet, I continued, approaching the bookcase again, where shall I find that elaborate study of the psychology of women by a woman? If through their incapacity to play football women are not going to be allowed to practise medicine——

Happily my thoughts were now given another turn.

Chapter Five

I had come at last, in the course of this rambling, to the shelves which hold books by the living; by women and by men; for there are almost as many books written by women now as by men. Or if that is not yet quite true, if the male is still the voluble sex, it is certainly true that women no longer write novels solely. There are Jane Harrison's books on Greek archaeology; Vernon Lee's books on aesthetics; Gertrude Bell's[3] books on Persia. There are books on all sorts of subjects which a generation ago no woman could have touched. There are poems and plays and criticism; there are histories and biographies, books of travel and books of scholarship and research; there are even a few philosophies and books about science and economics. And though novels predominate, novels themselves may very well have changed from association with books of a different feather. The natural simplicity, the epic age of women's writing, may have gone. Reading and criticism may have given her a wider range, a greater subtlety. The impulse towards autobiography may be spent. She may be beginning to use writing as an art, not as a method of self-expression. Among these new novels one might find an answer to several such questions.

I took down one of them at random. It stood at the very end of the shelf, was called *Life's Adventure*, or some such title, by Mary Carmichael,[4] and was published in this very month of October. It seems to be her first book, I said to myself, but one must read it as if it were the last volume in a fairly long series, continuing all those other books that I have been glancing at—Lady Winchilsea's poems and Aphra Behn's plays and the novels of the four great novelists. For books continue each other, in spite of our habit of judging them separately. And I must also consider her—this unknown woman—as the descendant of all those other women whose circumstances I have been glancing at and see what she inherits of their characteristics and restrictions. So, with a sigh, because novels so often provide an anodyne and not an antidote, glide one into torpid slumbers instead of rousing one with a burning brand, I settled down with a notebook and a pencil to make what I could of Mary Carmichael's first novel, *Life's Adventure*.

3. English archaeologist and writer (1868–1926). Harrison (1850–1928), scholar and lecturer at Cambridge. Lee (1856–1935), essayist and art critic.
4. The novel *Love's Creation* was published in London in 1928 under the name Marie Carmichael, the pseudonym for Marie Stopes, a crusader for birth control. The plot and characters resemble those mentioned by Woolf.

To begin with, I ran my eye up and down the page. I am going to get the hang of her sentences first, I said, before I load my memory with blue eyes and brown and the relationship that there may be between Chloe and Roger. There will be time for that when I have decided whether she has a pen in her hand or a pickaxe. So I tried a sentence or two on my tongue. Soon it was obvious that something was not quite in order. The smooth gliding of sentence after sentence was interrupted. Something tore, something scratched; a single word here and there flashed its torch in my eyes. She was "unhanding" herself as they say in the old plays. She is like a person striking a match that will not light, I thought. But why, I asked her as if she were present, are Jane Austen's sentences not of the right shape for you? Must they all be scrapped because Emma and Mr Woodhouse are dead? Alas, I sighed, that it should be so. For while Jane Austen breaks from melody to melody as Mozart from song to song, to read this writing was like being out at sea in an open boat. Up one went, down one sank. This terseness, this shortwindedness, might mean that she was afraid of something; afraid of being called "sentimental" perhaps; or she remembers that women's writing has been called flowery and so provides a superfluity of thorns; but until I have read a scene with some care, I cannot be sure whether she is being herself or some one else. At any rate, she does not lower one's vitality, I thought, reading more carefully. But she is heaping up too many facts. She will not be able to use half of them in a book of this size. (It was about half the length of *Jane Eyre.*) However, by some means or other she succeeded in getting us all—Roger, Chloe, Olivia, Tony and Mr Bigham—in a canoe up the river. Wait a moment, I said, leaning back in my chair, I must consider the whole thing more carefully before I go any further.

I am almost sure, I said to myself, that Mary Carmichael is playing a trick on us. For I feel as one feels on a switchback railway when the car, instead of sinking, as one has been led to expect, swerves up again. Mary is tampering with the expected sequence. First she broke the sentence; now she has broken the sequence. Very well, she has every right to do both these things if she does them not for the sake of breaking, but for the sake of creating. Which of the two it is I cannot be sure until she has faced herself with a situation. I will give her every liberty, I said, to choose what that situation shall be; she shall make it of tin cans and old kettles if she likes; but she must convince me that she believes it to be a situation; and then when she has made it she must face it. She must jump. And, determined to do my duty by her as reader if she would do her duty by me as writer, I turned the page and read . . . I am sorry to break off so abruptly. Are there no men present? Do you promise me that behind that red curtain over there the figure of Sir Chartres Biron[5] is not concealed? We are all women, you assure me? Then I may tell you that the very next words I read were these—"Chloe liked Olivia . . ." Do not start. Do not blush. Let us admit in the privacy of our own society that these things sometimes happen. Sometimes women do like women.

"Chloe liked Olivia," I read. And then it struck me how immense a change was there. Chloe liked Olivia perhaps for the first time in literature. Cleopatra did not like Octavia. And how completely *Antony and Cleopatra* would have been altered had she done so! As it is, I thought, letting my mind, I am afraid, wander a little from *Life's Adventure,* the whole thing is simplified, conven-

5. Chief magistrate of London who in 1928 judged that the novel *The Well of Loneliness,* by the lesbian writer Radclyffe Hall, was an "obscene libel" and ordered all copies destroyed.

tionalised, if one dared say it, absurdly. Cleopatra's only feeling about Octavia is one of jealousy. Is she taller than I am? How does she do her hair? The play, perhaps, required no more. But how interesting it would have been if the relationship between the two women had been more complicated. All these relationships between women, I thought, rapidly recalling the splendid gallery of fictitious women, are too simple. So much has been left out, unattempted. And I tried to remember any case in the course of my reading where two women are represented as friends. There is an attempt at it in *Diana of the Crossways*. They are confidantes, of course, in Racine[6] and the Greek tragedies. They are now and then mothers and daughters. But almost without exception they are shown in their relation to men. It was strange to think that all the great women of fiction were, until Jane Austen's day, not only seen by the other sex, but seen only in relation to the other sex. And how small a part of a woman's life is that; and how little can a man know even of that when he observes it through the black or rosy spectacles which sex puts upon his nose. Hence, perhaps, the peculiar nature of woman in fiction; the astonishing extremes of her beauty and horror; her alternations between heavenly good-ness and hellish depravity—for so a lover would see her as his love rose or sank, was prosperous or unhappy. This is not so true of the nineteenth-century novelists, of course. Woman becomes much more various and complicated there. Indeed it was the desire to write about women perhaps that led men by degrees to abandon the poetic drama which, with its violence, could make so little use of them, and to devise the novel as a more fitting receptacle. Even so it remains obvious, even in the writing of Proust,[7] that a man is terribly hampered and partial in his knowledge of women, as a woman in her knowl-edge of men.

Also, I continued, looking down at the page again, it is becoming evident that women, like men, have other interests besides the perennial interests of domesticity. "Chloe liked Olivia. They shared a laboratory together. . . ." I read on and discovered that these two young women were engaged in mincing liver, which is, it seems, a cure for pernicious anaemia: although one of them was married and had—I think I am right in stating—two small children. Now all that, of course, has had to be left out, and thus the splendid portrait of the fictitious woman is much too simple and much too monotonous. Suppose, for instance, that men were only represented in literature as the lovers of women, and were never the friends of men, soldiers, thinkers, dreamers; how few parts in the plays of Shakespeare could be allotted to them; how literature would suffer! We might perhaps have most of Othello; and a good deal of Antony; but no Caesar, no Brutus, no Hamlet, no Lear, no Jaques—literature would be incredibly impoverished, as indeed literature is impoverished beyond our counting by the doors that have been shut upon women. Married against their will, kept in one room, and to one occupation, how could a dramatist give a full or interesting or truthful account of them? Love was the only possible interpreter. The poet was forced to be passionate or bitter, unless indeed he chose to "hate women," which meant more often than not that he was unat-tractive to them.

Now if Chloe likes Olivia and they share a laboratory, which of itself will

6. Jean Racine (1639–1699), French dramatist. *"Diana of the Crossways"*: 1885 novel by the English author George Meredith (1828–1909).

7. Marcel Proust (1871–1922), French novelist and author of the seven-volume *A la Recherche du Temps Perdu* (1913–27).

make their friendship more varied and lasting because it will be less personal; if Mary Carmichael knows how to write, and I was beginning to enjoy some quality in her style; if she has a room to herself, of which I am not quite sure; if she has five hundred a year of her own—but that remains to be proved— then I think that something of great importance has happened.

For if Chloe likes Olivia and Mary Carmichael knows how to express it she will light a torch in that vast chamber where nobody has yet been. It is all half lights and profound shadows like those serpentine caves where one goes with a candle peering up and down, not knowing where one is stepping. And I began to read the book again, and read how Chloe watched Olivia put a jar on a shelf and say how it was time to go home to her children. That is a sight that has never been seen since the world began, I exclaimed. And I watched too, very curiously. For I wanted to see how Mary Carmichael set to work to catch those unrecorded gestures, those unsaid or half-said words, which form themselves, no more palpably than the shadows of moths on the ceiling, when women are alone, unlit by the capricious and coloured light of the other sex. She will need to hold her breath, I said, reading on, if she is to do it; for women are so suspicious of any interest that has not some obvious motive behind it, so terribly accustomed to concealment and suppression, that they are off at the flicker of an eye turned observingly in their direction. The only way for you to do it, I thought, addressing Mary Carmichael as if she were there, would be to talk of something else, looking steadily out of the window, and thus note, not with a pencil in a notebook, but in the shortest of shorthand, in words that are hardly syllabled yet, what happens when Olivia—this organism that has been under the shadow of the rock these million years—feels the light fall on it, and sees coming her way a piece of strange food—knowledge, adventure, art. And she reaches out for it, I thought, again raising my eyes from the page, and has to devise some entirely new combination of her resources, so highly developed for their purposes, so as to absorb the new into the old without disturbing the infinitely intricate and elaborate balance of the whole.

But, alas, I had done what I had determined not to do; I had slipped unthinkingly into praise of my own sex. "Highly developed"—"infinitely intricate"— such are undeniably terms of praise, and to praise one's own sex is always suspect, often silly; moreover, in this case, how could one justify it? One could not go to the map and say Columbus discovered America and Columbus was a woman; or take an apple and remark, Newton discovered the laws of gravitation and Newton was a woman; or look into the sky and say aeroplanes are flying overhead and aeroplanes were invented by women. There is no mark on the wall to measure the precise height of women. There are no yard measures, neatly divided into the fractions of an inch, that one can lay against the qualities of a good mother or the devotion of a daughter, or the fidelity of a sister, or the capacity of a housekeeper. Few women even now have been graded at the universities; the great trials of the professions, army and navy, trade, politics and diplomacy have hardly tested them. They remain even at this moment almost unclassified. But if I want to know all that a human being can tell me about Sir Hawley Butts, for instance, I have only to open Burke or Debrett[8] and I shall find that he took such and such a degree; owns a hall; has an heir; was Secretary to a Board; represented Great Britain in Canada; and has

---

8. Annual reference works of genealogy and the peerage. Sir Hawley Butts, however, seems to be Woolf's invention.

received a certain number of degrees, offices, medals and other distinctions by which his merits are stamped upon him indelibly. Only Providence can know more about Sir Hawley Butts than that.

When, therefore, I say "highly developed," "infinitely intricate," of women, I am unable to verify my words either in Whitaker, Debrett or the University Calendar. In this predicament what can I do? And I looked at the bookcase again. There were the biographies: Johnson and Goethe and Carlyle and Sterne and Cowper and Shelley and Voltaire and Browning and many others. And I began thinking of all those great men who have for one reason or another admired, sought out, lived with, confided in, made love to, written of, trusted in, and shown what can only be described as some need of and dependence upon certain persons of the opposite sex. That all these relationships were absolutely Platonic I would not affirm, and Sir William Joynson Hicks[9] would probably deny. But we should wrong these illustrious men very greatly if we insisted that they got nothing from these alliances but comfort, flattery and the pleasures of the body. What they got, it is obvious, was something that their own sex was unable to supply; and it would not be rash, perhaps, to define it further, without quoting the doubtless rhapsodical words of the poets, as some stimulus, some renewal of creative power which is in the gift only of the opposite sex to bestow. He would open the door of drawing-room or nursery, I thought, and find her among her children perhaps, or with a piece of embroidery on her knee—at any rate, the centre of some different order and system of life, and the contrast between this world and his own, which might be the law courts or the House of Commons, would at once refresh and invigorate; and there would follow, even in the simplest talk, such a natural difference of opinion that the dried ideas in him would be fertilised anew; and the sight of her creating in a different medium from his own would so quicken his creative power that insensibly his sterile mind would begin to plot again, and he would find the phrase or the scene which was lacking when he put on his hat to visit her. Every Johnson has his Thrale,[1] and holds fast to her for some such reasons as these, and when the Thrale marries her Italian music master Johnson goes half mad with rage and disgust, not merely that he will miss his pleasant evenings at Streatham, but that the light of his life will be "as if gone out."

And without being Dr Johnson or Goethe or Carlyle or Voltaire, one may feel, though very differently from these great men, the nature of this intricacy and the power of this highly developed creative faculty among women. One goes into the room—but the resources of the English language would be much put to the stretch, and whole flights of words would need to wing their way illegitimately into existence before a woman could say what happens when she goes into a room. The rooms differ so completely; they are calm or thunderous; open on to the sea, or, on the contrary, give on to a prison yard; are hung with washing; or alive with opals and silks; are hard as horsehair or soft as feathers—one has only to go into any room in any street for the whole of that extremely complex force of femininity to fly in one's face. How should it be otherwise? For women have sat indoors all these millions of years, so that by this time the very walls are permeated by their creative force, which has,

---

9. English Conservative politician and evangelical religious figure (1865–1932).
1. Hester Lynch Thrale (1741–1821), who with her husband, Henry, was for many years friend and hostess to Samuel Johnson at their home in Streatham Place. After Henry's death she married an Italian musician, much to Johnson's distress; his reaction helped end their friendship.

indeed, so overcharged the capacity of bricks and mortar that it must needs harness itself to pens and brushes and business and politics. But this creative power differs greatly from the creative power of men. And one must conclude that it would be a thousand pities if it were hindered or wasted, for it was won by centuries of the most drastic discipline, and there is nothing to take its place. It would be a thousand pities if women wrote like men, or lived like men, or looked like men, for if two sexes are quite inadequate, considering the vastness and variety of the world, how should we manage with one only? Ought not education to bring out and fortify the differences rather than the similarities? For we have too much likeness as it is, and if an explorer should come back and bring word of other sexes looking through the branches of other trees at other skies, nothing would be of greater service to humanity; and we should have the immense pleasure into the bargain of watching Professor X rush for his measuring-rods to prove himself "superior."

Mary Carmichael, I thought, still hovering at a little distance above the page, will have her work cut out for her merely as an observer. I am afraid indeed that she will be tempted to become, what I think the less interesting branch of the species—the naturalist-novelist, and not the contemplative. There are so many new facts for her to observe. She will not need to limit herself any longer to the respectable houses of the upper middle classes. She will go without kindness or condescension, but in the spirit of fellowship into those small, scented rooms where sit the courtesan, the harlot and the lady with the pug dog. There they still sit in the rough and ready-made clothes that the male writer has had perforce to clap upon their shoulders. But Mary Carmichael will have out her scissors and fit them close to every hollow and angle. It will be a curious sight, when it comes, to see these women as they are, but we must wait a little, for Mary Carmichael will still be encumbered with that self-consciousness in the presence of "sin" which is the legacy of our sexual barbarity. She will still wear the shoddy old fetters of class on her feet.

However, the majority of women are neither harlots nor courtesans; nor do they sit clasping pug dogs to dusty velvet all through the summer afternoon. But what do they do then? and there came to my mind's eye one of those long streets somewhere south of the river whose infinite rows are innumerably populated. With the eye of the imagination I saw a very ancient lady crossing the street on the arm of a middle-aged woman, her daughter, perhaps, both so respectably booted and furred that their dressing in the afternoon must be a ritual, and the clothes themselves put away in cupboards with camphor, year after year, throughout the summer months. They cross the road when the lamps are being lit (for the dusk is their favourite hour), as they must have done year after year. The elder is close on eighty; but if one asked her what her life has meant to her, she would say that she remembered the streets lit for the battle of Balaclava, or had heard the guns fire in Hyde Park for the birth of King Edward the Seventh.[2] And if one asked her, longing to pin down the moment with date and season, but what were you doing on the fifth of April 1868, or the second of November 1875, she would look vague and say that she could remember nothing. For all the dinners are cooked; the plates and cups washed; the children set to school and gone out into the world.

2. In 1841 (since Woolf is writing in 1928, Edward's birth would actually have been before the birth of a woman "close on eighty"). The "battle of Balaclava," famous for the Charge of the Light Brigade, occurred in 1854.

Nothing remains of it all. All has vanished. No biography or history has a word to say about it. And the novels, without meaning to, inevitably lie.

All these infinitely obscure lives remain to be recorded, I said, addressing Mary Carmichael as if she were present; and went on in thought through the streets of London feeling in imagination the pressure of dumbness, the accumulation of unrecorded life, whether from the women at the street corners with their arms akimbo, and the rings embedded in their fat swollen fingers, talking with a gesticulation like the swing of Shakespeare's words; or from the violet-sellers and match-sellers and old crones stationed under doorways; or from drifting girls whose faces, like waves in sun and cloud, signal the coming of men and women and the flickering lights of shop windows. All that you will have to explore, I said to Mary Carmichael, holding your torch firm in your hand. Above all, you must illumine your own soul with its profundities and its shallows, and its vanities and its generosities, and say what your beauty means to you or your plainness, and what is your relation to the everchanging and turning world of gloves and shoes and stuffs swaying up and down among the faint scents that come through chemists' bottles down arcades of dress material over a floor of pseudo-marble. For in imagination I had gone into a shop; it was laid with black and white paving; it was hung, astonishingly beautifully, with coloured ribbons. Mary Carmichael might well have a look at that in passing, I thought, for it is a sight that would lend itself to the pen as fittingly as any snowy peak or rocky gorge in the Andes. And there is the girl behind the counter too—I would as soon have her true history as the hundred and fiftieth life of Napoleon or seventieth study of Keats and his use of Miltonic inversion which old Professor Z and his like are now inditing. And then I went on very warily, on the very tips of my toes (so cowardly am I, so afraid of the lash that was once almost laid on my own shoulders), to murmur that she should also learn to laugh, without bitterness, at the vanities—say rather at the peculiarities, for it is a less offensive word—of the other sex. For there is a spot the size of a shilling at the back of the head which one can never see for oneself. It is one of the good offices that sex can discharge for sex—to describe that spot the size of a shilling at the back of the head. Think how much women have profited by the comments of Juvenal; by the criticism of Strindberg.[3] Think with what humanity and brilliancy men, from the earliest ages, have pointed out to women that dark place at the back of the head! And if Mary were very brave and very honest, she would go behind the other sex and tell us what she found there. A true picture of man as a whole can never be painted until a woman has described that spot the size of a shilling. Mr Woodhouse and Mr Casaubon[4] are spots of that size and nature. Not of course that any one in their senses would counsel her to hold up to scorn and ridicule of set purpose—literature shows the futility of what is written in that spirit. Be truthful, one would say, and the result is bound to be amazingly interesting. Comedy is bound to be enriched. New facts are bound to be discovered.

However, it was high time to lower my eyes to the page again. It would be better, instead of speculating what Mary Carmichael might write and should write, to see what in fact Mary Carmichael did write. So I began to read again. I remembered that I had certain grievances against her. She had broken up

3. August Strindberg (1849–1912), Swedish play-wright. Juvenal (55 to 60–ca. 127), Roman satirist.
4. The husband of the heroine in George Eliot's

Middlemarch. Woodhouse is the father of the heroine in Jane Austen's *Emma*.

Jane Austen's sentence, and thus given me no chance of pluming myself upon my impeccable taste, my fastidious ear. For it was useless to say, "Yes, yes, this is very nice; but Jane Austen wrote much better than you do," when I had to admit that there was no point of likeness between them. Then she had gone further and broken the sequence—the expected order. Perhaps she had done this unconsciously, merely giving things their natural order, as a woman would, if she wrote like a woman. But the effect was somehow baffling; one could not see a wave heaping itself, a crisis coming round the next corner. Therefore I could not plume myself either upon the depths of my feelings and my profound knowledge of the human heart. For whenever I was about to feel the usual things in the usual places, about love, about death, the annoying creature twitched me away, as if the important point were just a little further on. And thus she made it impossible for me to roll out my sonorous phrases about "elemental feelings," the "common stuff of humanity," "depths of the human heart," and all those other phrases which support us in our belief that, however clever we may be on top, we are very serious, very profound and very humane underneath. She made me feel, on the contrary, that instead of being serious and profound and humane, one might be—and the thought was far less seductive—merely lazy minded and conventional into the bargain.

But I read on, and noted certain other facts. She was no "genius"—that was evident. She had nothing like the love of Nature, the fiery imagination, the wild poetry, the brilliant wit, the brooding wisdom of her great predecessors, Lady Winchilsea, Charlotte Brontë, Jane Austen and George Eliot; she could not write with the melody and the dignity of Dorothy Osborne—indeed she was no more than a clever girl whose books will no doubt be pulped by the publishers in ten years' time. But, nevertheless, she had certain advantages which women of far greater gift lacked even half a century ago. Men were no longer to her "the opposing faction"; she need not waste her time railing against them; she need not climb on to the roof and ruin her peace of mind longing for travel, experience and a knowledge of the world and character that were denied her. Fear and hatred were almost gone, or traces of them showed only in a slight exaggeration of the joy of freedom, a tendency to the caustic and satirical, rather than to the romantic, in her treatment of the other sex. Then there could be no doubt that as a novelist she enjoyed some natural advantages of a high order. She had a sensibility that was very wide, eager and free. It responded to an almost imperceptible touch on it. It feasted like a plant newly stood in the air on every sight and sound that came its way. It ranged, too, very subtly and curiously, among almost unknown or unrecorded things; it lighted on small things and showed that perhaps they were not small after all. It brought buried things to light and made one wonder what need there had been to bury them. Awkward though she was and without the unconscious bearing of long descent which makes the least turn of the pen of a Thackeray or a Lamb delightful to the ear, she had—I began to think—mastered the first great lesson; she wrote as a woman, but as a woman who has forgotten that she is a woman, so that her pages were full of that curious sexual quality which comes only when sex is unconscious of itself.

All this was to the good. But no abundance of sensation or fineness of perception would avail unless she could build up out of the fleeting and the personal the lasting edifice which remains unthrown. I had said that I would wait until she faced herself with "a situation." And I meant by that until she proved by summoning, beckoning and getting together that she was not a skimmer of surfaces merely, but had looked beneath into the depths. Now is the time, she would say to herself at a certain moment, when without doing anything violent I can show the meaning of all this. And she would begin— how unmistakable that quickening is!—beckoning and summoning, and there would rise up in memory, half forgotten, perhaps quite trivial things in other chapters dropped by the way. And she would make their presence felt while some one sewed or smoked a pipe as naturally as possible, and one would feel, as she went on writing, as if one had gone to the top of the world and seen it laid out, very majestically, beneath.

At any rate, she was making the attempt. And as I watched her lengthening out for the test, I saw, but hoped that she did not see, the bishops and the deans, the doctors and the professors, the patriarchs and the pedagogues all at her shouting warning and advice. You can't do this and you shan't do that! Fellows and scholars only allowed on the grass! Ladies not admitted without a letter of introduction! Aspiring and graceful female novelists this way! So they kept at her like the crowd at a fence on the race-course, and it was her trial to take her fence without looking to right or left. If you stop to curse you are lost, I said to her; equally, if you stop to laugh. Hesitate or fumble and you are done for. Think only of the jump, I implored her, as if I had put the whole of my money on her back; and she went over it like a bird. But there was a fence beyond that and a fence beyond that. Whether she had the staying power I was doubtful, for the clapping and the crying were fraying to the nerves. But she did her best. Considering that Mary Carmichael was no genius, but an unknown girl writing her first novel in a bed-sitting-room, without enough of those desirable things, time, money and idleness, she did not do so badly, I thought.

Give her another hundred years, I concluded, reading the last chapter— people's noses and bare shoulders showed naked against a starry sky, for some one had twitched the curtain in the drawing-room—give her a room of her own and five hundred a year, let her speak her mind and leave out half that she now puts in, and she will write a better book one of these days. She will be a poet, I said, putting *Life's Adventure,* by Mary Carmichael, at the end of the shelf, in another hundred years' time.

Chapter Six

Next day the light of the October morning was falling in dusty shafts through the uncurtained windows, and the hum of traffic rose from the street. London then was winding itself up again; the factory was astir; the machines were beginning. It was tempting, after all this reading, to look out of the window and see what London was doing on the morning of the twenty-sixth of October 1928. And what was London doing? Nobody, it seemed, was reading *Antony and Cleopatra.* London was wholly indifferent, it appeared, to Shakespeare's plays. Nobody cared a straw—and I do not blame them—for the future of fiction, the death of poetry or the development by the average woman of a prose style completely expressive of her mind. If opinions upon any of these matters had been chalked on the pavement, nobody would have stooped to read them. The nonchalance of the hurrying feet would have rubbed them out in half an hour. Here came an errand-boy; here a woman with a dog on a lead. The fascination of the London street is that no two people are ever alike; each seems bound on some private affair of his own. There were the business-like, with their little bags; there were the drifters rattling sticks upon area railings; there were affable characters to whom the streets serve for clubroom, hailing men in carts and giving information without being asked for it. Also there were funerals to which men, thus suddenly reminded of the passing of their own bodies, lifted their hats. And then a very distinguished gentleman came slowly down a doorstep and paused to avoid collision with a bustling lady who had, by some means or other, acquired a splendid fur coat and a bunch of Parma violets. They all seemed separate, self-absorbed, on business of their own.

At this moment, as so often happens in London, there was a complete lull and suspension of traffic. Nothing came down the street; nobody passed. A single leaf detached itself from the plane tree at the end of the street, and in that pause and suspension fell. Somehow it was like a signal falling, a signal pointing to a force in things which one had overlooked. It seemed to point to a river, which flowed past, invisibly, round the corner, down the street, and took people and eddied them along, as the stream at Oxbridge had taken the undergraduate in his boat and the dead leaves. Now it was bringing from one side of the street to the other diagonally a girl in patent leather boots, and then a young man in a maroon overcoat; it was also bringing a taxi-cab; and it brought all three together at a point directly beneath my window; where the taxi stopped; and the girl and the young man stopped; and they got into the taxi; and then the cab glided off as if it were swept on by the current elsewhere.

The sight was ordinary enough; what was strange was the rhythmical order with which my imagination had invested it; and the fact that the ordinary sight of two people getting into a cab had the power to communicate something of their own seeming satisfaction. The sight of two people coming down the street and meeting at the corner seems to ease the mind of some strain, I thought, watching the taxi turn and make off. Perhaps to think, as I had been thinking these two days, of one sex as distinct from the other is an effort. It interferes with the unity of the mind. Now that effort had ceased and that unity had been restored by seeing two people come together and get into a taxi-cab. The mind is certainly a very mysterious organ, I reflected, drawing my head in from the window, about which nothing whatever is known, though we depend upon it so completely. Why do I feel that there are severances and oppositions in the mind, as there are strains from obvious causes on the body? What does one mean by "the unity of the mind," I pondered, for clearly the mind has so great a power of concentrating at any point at any moment that it seems to have no single state of being. It can separate itself from the people in the street, for example, and think of itself as apart from them, at an upper window looking down on them. Or it can think with other people spontaneously, as, for instance, in a crowd waiting to hear some piece of news read out. It can think back through its fathers or through its mothers, as I have said that a woman writing thinks back through her mothers. Again if one is a woman one is often surprised by a sudden splitting off of consciousness, say in walking down Whitehall,[5] when from being the natural inheritor of that civilisation, she becomes, on the contrary, outside of it, alien and critical. Clearly the mind is always altering its focus, and bringing the world into different perspectives. But some of these states of mind seem, even if adopted spontaneously, to be less comfortable than others. In order to keep oneself continuing in them one is unconsciously holding something back, and gradually the repression

5. London thoroughfare along which are located the chief offices of the British government.

becomes an effort. But there may be some state of mind in which one could continue without effort because nothing is required to be held back. And this perhaps, I thought, coming in from the window, is one of them. For certainly when I saw the couple get into the taxi-cab the mind felt as if, after being divided, it had come together again in a natural fusion. The obvious reason would be that it is natural for the sexes to co-operate. One has a profound, if irrational, instinct in favour of the theory that the union of man and woman makes for the greatest satisfaction, the most complete happiness. But the sight of the two people getting into the taxi and the satisfaction it gave me made me also ask whether there are two sexes in the mind corresponding to the two sexes in the body, and whether they also require to be united in order to get complete satisfaction and happiness. And I went on amateurishly to sketch a plan of the soul so that in each of us two powers preside, one male, one female; and in the man's brain, the man predominates over the woman, and in the woman's brain, the woman predominates over the man. The normal and comfortable state of being is that when the two live in harmony together, spiritually cooperating. If one is a man, still the woman part of the brain must have effect; and a woman also must have intercourse with the man in her. Coleridge perhaps meant this when he said that a great mind is androgynous. It is when this fusion takes place that the mind is fully fertilised and uses all its faculties. Perhaps a mind that is purely masculine cannot create, any more than a mind that is purely feminine, I thought. But it would be well to test what one meant by man-womanly, and conversely by woman-manly, by pausing and looking at a book or two.

Coleridge certainly did not mean, when he said that a great mind is androgynous, that it is a mind that has any special sympathy with women; a mind that takes up their cause or devotes itself to their interpretation. Perhaps the androgynous mind is less apt to make these distinctions than the single-sexed mind. He meant, perhaps, that the androgynous mind is resonant and porous; that it transmits emotion without impediment; that it is naturally creative, incandescent and undivided. In fact one goes back to Shakespeare's mind as the type of the androgynous, of the man-womanly mind, though it would be impossible to say what Shakespeare thought of women. And if it be true that it is one of the tokens of the fully developed mind that it does not think specially or separately of sex, how much harder it is to attain that condition now than ever before. Here I came to the books by living writers, and there paused and wondered if this fact were not at the root of something that had long puzzled me. No age can ever have been as stridently sex-conscious as our own; those innumerable books by men about women in the British Museum are a proof of it. The Suffrage campaign[6] was no doubt to blame. It must have roused in men an extraordinary desire for self-assertion; it must have made them lay an emphasis upon their own sex and its characteristics which they would not have troubled to think about had they not been challenged. And when one is challenged, even by a few women in black bonnets, one retaliates, if one has never been challenged before, rather excessively. That perhaps accounts for some of the characteristics that I remember to have found here, I thought, taking down a new novel by Mr A, who is in the prime of life and very well thought of, apparently, by the reviewers. I opened it. Indeed, it was delightful to read a man's writing again. It was so direct, so straightforward

---

6. Movement of the 19th and early-20th centuries seeking the right for women to vote.

after the writing of women. It indicated such freedom of mind, such liberty of person, such confidence in himself. One had a sense of physical well-being in the presence of this well-nourished, well-educated, free mind, which had never been thwarted or opposed, but had had full liberty from birth to stretch itself in whatever way it liked. All this was admirable. But after reading a chapter or two a shadow seemed to lie across the page. It was a straight dark bar, a shadow shaped something like the letter "I." One began dodging this way and that to catch a glimpse of the landscape behind it. Whether that was indeed a tree or a woman walking I was not quite sure. Back one was always hailed to the letter "I." One began to be tired of "I." Not but what this "I" was a most respectable "I"; honest and logical; as hard as a nut, and polished for centuries by good teaching and good feeding. I respect and admire that "I" from the bottom of my heart. But—here I turned a page or two, looking for something or other—the worst of it is that in the shadow of the letter "I" all is shapeless as mist. Is that a tree? No, it is a woman. But . . . she has not a bone in her body, I thought, watching Phoebe, for that was her name, coming across the beach. Then Alan got up and the shadow of Alan at once obliterated Phoebe. For Alan had views and Phoebe was quenched in the flood of his views. And then Alan, I thought, had passions; and here I turned page after page very fast, feeling that the crisis was approaching, and so it was. It took place on the beach under the sun. It was done very openly. It was done very vigorously. Nothing could have been more indecent. But . . . I had said "but" too often. One cannot go on saying "but." One must finish the sentence some- how, I rebuked myself. Shall I finish it, "But—I am bored!" But why was I bored? Partly because of the dominance of the letter "I" and the aridity, which, like the giant beech tree, it casts within its shade. Nothing will grow there. And partly for some more obscure reason. There seemed to be some obstacle, some impediment of Mr A's mind which blocked the fountain of creative energy and shored it within narrow limits. And remembering the lunch party at Oxbridge, and the cigarette ash and the Manx cat and Tennyson and Chris- tina Rossetti all in a bunch, it seemed possible that the impediment lay there. As he no longer hums under his breath, "There has fallen a splendid tear from the passion-flower at the gate," when Phoebe crosses the beach, and she no longer replies, "My heart is like a singing bird whose nest is in a water'd shoot," when Alan approaches what can he do? Being honest as the day and logical as the sun, there is only one thing he can do. And that he does, to do him justice, over and over (I said, turning the pages) and over again. And that, I added, aware of the awful nature of the confession, seems somehow dull. Shakespeare's indecency uproots a thousand other things in one's mind, and is far from being dull. But Shakespeare does it for pleasure; Mr A, as the nurses say, does it on purpose. He does it in protest. He is protesting against the equality of the other sex by asserting his own superiority. He is therefore impeded and inhibited and self-conscious as Shakespeare might have been if he too had known Miss Clough[7] and Miss Davies. Doubtless Elizabethan lit- erature would have been very different from what it is if the woman's move- ment had begun in the sixteenth century and not in the nineteenth.

What, then, it amounts to, if this theory of the two sides of the mind holds good, is that virility has now become self-conscious—men, that is to say, are

7. Anne Jemima Clough (1820–1892), first principal of Newnham College, Cambridge, and advocate for women's suffrage and higher education.

now writing only with the male side of their brains. It is a mistake for a woman to read them, for she will inevitably look for something that she will not find. It is the power of suggestion that one most misses, I thought, taking Mr B the critic in my hand and reading, very carefully and very dutifully, his remarks upon the art of poetry. Very able they were, acute and full of learning; but the trouble was, that his feelings no longer communicated; his mind seemed separated into different chambers; not a sound carried from one to the other. Thus, when one takes a sentence of Mr B into the mind it falls plump to the ground—dead; but when one takes a sentence of Coleridge into the mind, it explodes and gives birth to all kinds of other ideas, and that is the only sort of writing of which one can say that it has the secret of perpetual life.

But whatever the reason may be, it is a fact that one must deplore. For it means—here I had come to rows of books by Mr Galsworthy and Mr Kipling[8] —that some of the finest works of our greatest living writers fall upon deaf ears. Do what she will a woman cannot find in them that fountain of perpetual life which the critics assure her is there. It is not only that they celebrate male virtues, enforce male values and describe the world of men; it is that the emotion with which these books are permeated is to a woman incomprehensible. It is coming, it is gathering, it is about to burst on one's head, one begins saying long before the end. That picture will fall on old Jolyon's head;[9] he will die of the shock; the old clerk will speak over him two or three obituary words; and all the swans on the Thames will simultaneously burst out singing. But one will rush away before that happens and hide in the gooseberry bushes, for the emotion which is so deep, so subtle, so symbolical to a man moves a woman to wonder. So with Mr Kipling's officers who turn their backs; and his Sowers who sow the Seed; and his Men who are alone with their Work; and the Flag— one blushes at all these capital letters as if one had been caught eavesdropping at some purely masculine orgy. The fact is that neither Mr Galsworthy nor Mr Kipling has a spark of the woman in him. Thus all their qualities seem to a woman, if one may generalise, crude and immature. They lack suggestive power. And when a book lacks suggestive power, however hard it hits the surface of the mind it cannot penetrate within.

And in that restless mood in which one takes books out and puts them back again without looking at them I began to envisage an age to come of pure, of self-assertive virility, such as the letters of professors (take Sir Walter Raleigh's letters, for instance) seem to forebode, and the rulers of Italy have already brought into being. For one can hardly fail to be impressed in Rome by the sense of unmitigated masculinity; and whatever the value of unmitigated masculinity upon the state, one may question the effect of it upon the art of poetry. At any rate, according to the newspapers, there is a certain anxiety about fiction in Italy. There has been a meeting of academicians whose object it is "to develop the Italian novel." "Men famous by birth, or in finance, industry or the Fascist corporations" came together the other day and discussed the matter, and a telegram was sent to the Duce[1] expressing the hope "that the Fascist era would soon give birth to a poet worthy of it." We may all join in that pious hope, but it is doubtful whether poetry can come out of an incubator. Poetry ought to have a mother as well as a father. The Fascist poem,

---

8. John Galsworthy (1867–1933) and Rudyard Kipling (1865–1936), English novelists.
9. A reference to an event in John Galsworthy's

popular fictional series *The Forsyte Saga* (1922).
1. "The leader," i.e., Mussolini.

one may fear, will be a horrid little abortion such as one sees in a glass jar in the museum of some county town. Such monsters never live long, it is said; one has never seen a prodigy of that sort cropping grass in a field. Two heads on one body do not make for length of life.

However, the blame for all this, if one is anxious to lay blame, rests no more upon one sex than upon the other. All seducers and reformers are responsible, Lady Bessborough when she lied to Lord Granville; Miss Davies when she told the truth to Mr Greg. All who have brought about a state of sex-consciousness are to blame, and it is they who drive me, when I want to stretch my faculties on a book, to seek it in that happy age, before Miss Davies and Miss Clough were born, when the writer used both sides of his mind equally. One must turn back to Shakespeare then, for Shakespeare was androgynous; and so was Keats and Sterne and Cowper and Lamb and Coleridge. Shelley perhaps was sexless. Milton and Ben Jonson had a dash too much of the male in them. So had Wordsworth and Tolstoi. In our time Proust was wholly androgynous, if not perhaps a little too much of a woman. But that failing is too rare for one to complain of it, since without some mixture of the kind the intellect seems to predominate and the other faculties of the mind harden and become barren. However, I consoled myself with the reflection that this is perhaps a passing phase; much of what I have said in obedience to my promise to give you the course of my thoughts will seem out of date; much of what flames in my eyes will seem dubious to you who have not yet come of age.

Even so, the very first sentence that I would write here, I said, crossing over to the writing-table and taking up the page headed Women and Fiction, is that it is fatal for any one who writes to think of their sex. It is fatal to be a man or woman pure and simple; one must be woman-manly or man-womanly. It is fatal for a woman to lay the least stress on any grievance; to plead even with justice any cause; in any way to speak consciously as a woman. And fatal is no figure of speech; for anything written with that conscious bias is doomed to death. It ceases to be fertilised. Brilliant and effective, powerful and masterly, as it may appear for a day or two, it must wither at nightfall; it cannot grow in the minds of others. Some collaboration has to take place in the mind between the woman and the man before the act of creation can be accomplished. Some marriage of opposites has to be consummated. The whole of the mind must lie wide open if we are to get the sense that the writer is communicating his experience with perfect fullness. There must be freedom and there must be peace. Not a wheel must grate, not a light glimmer. The curtains must be close drawn. The writer, I thought, once his experience is over, must lie back and let his mind celebrate its nuptials in darkness. He must not look or question what is being done. Rather, he must pluck the petals from a rose or watch the swans float calmly down the river. And I saw again the current which took the boat and the undergraduate and the dead leaves; and the taxi took the man and the woman, I thought, seeing them come together across the street, and the current swept them away, I thought, hearing far off the roar of London's traffic, into that tremendous stream.

Here, then, Mary Beton ceases to speak. She has told you how she reached the conclusion—the prosaic conclusion—that it is necessary to have five hundred a year and a room with a lock on the door if you are to write fiction or poetry. She has tried to lay bare the thoughts and impressions that led her to think this. She has asked you to follow her flying into the arms of a Beadle, lunching here, dining there, drawing pictures in the British Museum, taking books from the shelf, looking out of the window. While she has been doing all these things, you no doubt have been observing her failings and foibles and deciding what effect they have had on her opinions. You have been contradicting her and making whatever additions and deductions seem good to you. That is all as it should be, for in a question like this truth is only to be had by laying together many varieties of error. And I will end now in my own person by anticipating two criticisms, so obvious that you can hardly fail to make them.

No opinion has been expressed, you may say, upon the comparative merits of the sexes even as writers. That was done purposely, because, even if the time had come for such a valuation—and it is far more important at the moment to know how much money women had and how many rooms than to theorise about their capacities—even if the time had come I do not believe that gifts, whether of mind or character, can be weighed like sugar and butter, not even in Cambridge, where they are so adept at putting people into classes and fixing caps on their heads and letters after their names. I do not believe that even the Table of Precedency which you will find in Whitaker's *Almanac* represents a final order of values, or that there is any sound reason to suppose that a Commander of the Bath will ultimately walk in to dinner behind a Master in Lunacy. All this pitting of sex against sex, of quality against quality; all this claiming of superiority and imputing of inferiority, belong to the private-school stage of human existence where there are "sides," and it is necessary for one side to beat another side, and of the utmost importance to walk up to a platform and receive from the hands of the Headmaster himself a highly ornamental pot. As people mature they cease to believe in sides or in Headmasters or in highly ornamental pots. At any rate, where books are concerned, it is notoriously difficult to fix labels of merit in such a way that they do not come off. Are not reviews of current literature a perpetual illustration of the difficulty of judgement? "This great book," "this worthless book," the same book is called by both names. Praise and blame alike mean nothing. No, delightful as the pastime of measuring may be, it is the most futile of all occupations, and to submit to the decrees of the measurers the most servile of attitudes. So long as you write what you wish to write, that is all that matters; and whether it matters for ages or only for hours, nobody can say. But to sacrifice a hair of the head of your vision, a shade of its colour, in deference to some Headmaster with a silver pot in his hand or to some professor with a measuring-rod up his sleeve, is the most abject treachery, and the sacrifice of wealth and chastity which used to be said to be the greatest of human disasters, a mere flea-bite in comparison.

Next I think that you may object that in all this I have made too much of the importance of material things. Even allowing a generous margin for symbolism, that five hundred a year stands for the power to contemplate, that a lock on the door means the power to think for oneself, still you may say that the mind should rise above such things; and that great poets have often been poor men. Let me then quote to you the words of your own Professor of Literature, who knows better than I do what goes to the making of a poet. Sir Arthur Quiller-Couch writes:[2]

"What are the great poetical names of the last hundred years or so? Cole-

2. *The Art of Writing*, by Sir Arthur Quiller-Couch [Woolf's note].

ridge, Wordsworth, Byron, Shelley, Landor, Keats, Tennyson, Browning, Arnold, Morris, Rossetti, Swinburne—we may stop there. Of these, all but Keats, Browning, Rossetti were University men; and of these three, Keats, who died young, cut off in his prime, was the only one not fairly well to do. It may seem a brutal thing to say, and it is a sad thing to say: but, as a matter of hard fact, the theory that poetical genius bloweth where it listeth, and equally in poor and rich, holds little truth. As a matter of hard fact, nine out of those twelve were University men: which means that somehow or other they procured the means to get the best education England can give. As a matter of hard fact, of the remaining three you know that Browning was well to do, and I challenge you that, if he had not been well to do, he would no more have attained to write *Saul* or *The Ring and the Book* than Ruskin would have attained to writing *Modern Painters* if his father had not dealt prosperously in business. Rossetti had a small private income; and, moreover, he painted. There remains but Keats; whom Atropos slew young, as she slew John Clare in a mad-house, and James Thomson[3] by the laudanum he took to drug disappointment. These are dreadful facts, but let us face them. It is—however dishonouring to us as a nation—certain that, by some fault in our commonwealth, the poor poet has not in these days, nor has had for two hundred years, a dog's chance. Believe me—and I have spent a great part of ten years in watching some three hundred and twenty elementary schools—we may prate of democracy, but actually, a poor child in England has little more hope than had the son of an Athenian slave to be emancipated into that intellectual freedom of which great writings are born."

Nobody could put the point more plainly. "The poor poet has not in these days, nor has had for two hundred years, a dog's chance . . . a poor child in England has little more hope than had the son of an Athenian slave to be emancipated into that intellectual freedom of which great writings are born." That is it. Intellectual freedom depends upon material things. Poetry depends upon intellectual freedom. And women have always been poor, not for two hundred years merely, but from the beginning of time. Women have had less intellectual freedom than the sons of Athenian slaves. Women, then, have not had a dog's chance of writing poetry. That is why I have laid so much stress on money and a room of one's own. However, thanks to the toils of those obscure women in the past, of whom I wish we knew more, thanks, curiously enough, to two wars, the Crimean which let Florence Nightingale out of her drawing-room, and the European War which opened the doors to the average woman some sixty years later, these evils are in the way to be bettered. Otherwise you would not be here tonight, and your chance of earning five hundred pounds a year, precarious as I am afraid that it still is, would be minute in the extreme.

Still, you may object, why do you attach so much importance to this writing of books by women when, according to you, it requires so much effort, leads perhaps to the murder of one's aunts, will make one almost certainly late for luncheon, and may bring one into very grave disputes with certain very good fellows? My motives, let me admit, are partly selfish. Like most uneducated Englishwomen, I like reading—I like reading books in the bulk. Lately my diet has become a trifle monotonous; history is too much about wars; biography

---

3. Scottish pre-Romantic poet (1700–1748). Atropos: in Greek mythology the Fate who cut the thread of life. Clare (1793–1864), English Romantic poet.

too much about great men; poetry has shown, I think, a tendency to sterility, and fiction—but I have sufficiently exposed my disabilities as a critic of modern fiction and will say no more about it. Therefore I would ask you to write all kinds of books, hesitating at no subject however trivial or however vast. By hook or by crook, I hope that you will possess yourselves of money enough to travel and to idle, to contemplate the future or the past of the world, to dream over books and loiter at street corners and let the line of thought dip deep into the stream. For I am by no means confining you to fiction. If you would please me—and there are thousands like me—you would write books of travel and adventure, and research and scholarship, and history and biography, and criticism and philosophy and science. By so doing you will certainly profit the art of fiction. For books have a way of influencing each other. Fiction will be much the better for standing cheek by jowl with poetry and philosophy. Moreover, if you consider any great figure of the past, like Sappho, like the Lady Murasaki,[4] like Emily Brontë, you will find that she is an inheritor as well as an originator, and has come into existence because women have come to have the habit of writing naturally; so that even as a prelude to poetry such activity on your part would be invaluable.

But when I look back through these notes and criticise my own train of thought as I made them, I find that my motives were not altogether selfish. There runs through these comments and discursions the conviction—or is it the instinct?—that good books are desirable and that good writers, even if they show every variety of human depravity, are still good human beings. Thus when I ask you to write more books I am urging you to do what will be for your good and for the good of the world at large. How to justify this instinct or belief I do not know, for philosophic words, if one has not been educated at a university, are apt to play one false. What is meant by "reality"? It would seem to be something very erratic, very undependable—now to be found in a dusty road, now in a scrap of newspaper in the street, now in a daffodil in the sun. It lights up a group in a room and stamps some casual saying. It overwhelms one walking home beneath the stars and makes the silent world more real than the world of speech—and then there it is again in an omnibus in the uproar of Piccadilly.[5] Sometimes, too, it seems to dwell in shapes too far away for us to discern what their nature is. But whatever it touches, it fixes and makes permanent. That is what remains over when the skin of the day has been cast into the hedge; that is what is left of past time and of our loves and hates. Now the writer, as I think, has the chance to live more than other people in the presence of this reality. It is his business to find it and collect it and communicate it to the rest of us. So at least I infer from reading *Lear* or *Emma* or *La Recherche du Temps Perdu*. For the reading of these books seems to perform a curious couching operation on the senses; one sees more intensely afterwards; the world seems bared of its covering and given an intenser life. Those are the enviable people who live at enmity with unreality; and those are the pitiable who are knocked on the head by the thing done without knowing or caring. So that when I ask you to earn money and have a room of your own, I am asking you to live in the presence of reality, an invigorating life, it would appear, whether one can impart it or not.

4. Shikibu Murasaki (978?–?1026), Japanese court lady, author of *The Tale of Genji*. Sappho (fl. ca. 610–ca. 580 B.C.E.), Greek lyric poet, who lived on the island of Lesbos.

5. London street that ends in the bustling intersection of Piccadilly Circus.

Here I would stop, but the pressure of convention decrees that every speech must end with a peroration. And a peroration addressed to women should have something, you will agree, particularly exalting and ennobling about it. I should implore you to remember your responsibilities, to be higher, more spiritual; I should remind you how much depends upon you, and what an influence you can exert upon the future. But those exhortations can safely, I think, be left to the other sex, who will put them, and indeed have put them, with far greater eloquence than I can compass. When I rummage in my own mind I find no noble sentiments about being companions and equals and influencing the world to higher ends. I find myself saying briefly and prosaically that it is much more important to be oneself than anything else. Do not dream of influencing other people, I would say, if I knew how to make it sound exalted. Think of things in themselves.

And again I am reminded by dipping into newspapers and novels and biographies that when a woman speaks to women she should have something very unpleasant up her sleeve. Women are hard on women. Women dislike women. Women—but are you not sick to death of the word? I can assure you that I am. Let us agree, then, that a paper read by a woman to women should end with something particularly disagreeable.

But how does it go? What can I think of? The truth is, I often like women. I like their unconventionality. I like their subtlety. I like their anonymity. I like—but I must not run on in this way. That cupboard there,—you say it holds clean table-napkins only; but what if Sir Archibald Bodkin[6] were concealed among them? Let me then adopt a sterner tone. Have I, in the preceding words, conveyed to you sufficiently the warnings and reprobation of mankind? I have told you the very low opinion in which you were held by Mr Oscar Browning. I have indicated what Napoleon once thought of you and what Mussolini thinks now. Then, in case any of you aspire to fiction, I have copied out for your benefit the advice of the critic about courageously acknowledging the limitations of your sex. I have referred to Professor X and given prominence to his statement that women are intellectually, morally and physically inferior to men. I have handed on all that has come my way without going in search of it, and here is a final warning—from Mr John Langdon Davies.[7] Mr John Langdon Davies warns women "that when children cease to be altogether desirable, women cease to be altogether necessary." I hope you will make a note of it.

How can I further encourage you to go about the business of life? Young women, I would say, and please attend, for the peroration is beginning, you are, in my opinion, disgracefully ignorant. You have never made a discovery of any sort of importance. You have never shaken an empire or led an army into battle. The plays of Shakespeare are not by you, and you have never introduced a barbarous race to the blessings of civilisation. What is your excuse? It is all very well for you to say, pointing to the streets and squares and forests of the globe swarming with black and white and coffee-coloured inhabitants, all busily engaged in traffic and enterprise and love-making, we have had other work on our hands. Without our doing, those seas would be unsailed and those fertile lands a desert. We have borne and bred and washed

6. British director of public prosecutions who decided to ban James Joyces's *Ulysses* for obscenity in 1922.

7. *A Short History of Women*, by John Langdon Davies [Woolf's note].

and taught, perhaps to the age of six or seven years, the one thousand six hundred and twenty-three million human beings who are, according to statistics, at present in existence, and that, allowing that some had help, takes time.

There is truth in what you say—I will not deny it. But at the same time may I remind you that there have been at least two colleges for women in existence in England since the year 1866; that after the year 1880 a married woman was allowed by law to possess her own property; and that in 1919—which is a whole nine years ago—she was given a vote? May I also remind you that the most of the professions have been open to you for close on ten years now? When you reflect upon these immense privileges and the length of time during which they have been enjoyed, and the fact that there must be at this moment some two thousand women capable of earning over five hundred a year in one way or another, you will agree that the excuse of lack of opportunity, training, encouragement, leisure and money no longer holds good. Moreover, the economists are telling us that Mrs Seton has had too many children. You must, of course, go on bearing children, but, so they say, in twos and threes, not in tens and twelves.

Thus, with some time on your hands and with some book learning in your brains—you have had enough of the other kind, and are sent to college partly, I suspect, to be uneducated—surely you should embark upon another stage of your very long, very laborious and highly obscure career. A thousand pens are ready to suggest what you should do and what effect you will have. My own suggestion is a little fantastic, I admit; I prefer, therefore, to put it in the form of fiction.

I told you in the course of this paper that Shakespeare had a sister; but do not look for her in Sir Sidney Lee's[8] life of the poet. She died young—alas, she never wrote a word. She lies buried where the omnibuses now stop, opposite the Elephant and Castle. Now my belief is that this poet who never wrote a word and was buried at the crossroads still lives. She lives in you and in me, and in many other women who are not here tonight, for they are washing up the dishes and putting the children to bed. But she lives; for great poets do not die; they are continuing presences; they need only the opportunity to walk among us in the flesh. This opportunity, as I think, it is now coming within your power to give her. For my belief is that if we live another century or so—I am talking of the common life which is the real life and not of the little separate lives which we live as individuals—and have five hundred a year each of us and rooms of our own; if we have the habit of freedom and the courage to write exactly what we think; if we escape a little from the common sitting-room and see human beings not always in their relation to each other but in relation to reality; and the sky, too, and the trees or whatever it may be in themselves; if we look past Milton's bogey,[9] for no human being should shut out the view; if we face the fact, for it is a fact, that there is no arm to cling to, but that we go alone and that our relation is to the world of reality and not only to the world of men and women, then the opportunity will come and the dead poet who was Shakespeare's sister will put on the body which she has so often laid down. Drawing her life from the lives of the unknown who were her

8. Biographer and Shakespeare scholar (1859–1926), author of *Life of William Shakespeare* (1898).
9. Milton, with his unhappy first marriage, his campaign for freedom of divorce, and his deliberate subordination of Eve to Adam in *Paradise Lost*, was and often still is held to be (not altogether accurately) what the present age calls a male chauvinist.

forerunners, as her brother did before her, she will be born. As for her coming without that preparation, without that effort on our part, without that determination that when she is born again she shall find it possible to live and write her poetry, that we cannot expect, for that would be impossible. But I maintain that she would come if we worked for her, and that so to work, even in poverty and obscurity, is worth while.

1929

Professions for Women[1]

When your secretary invited me to come here, she told me that your Society is concerned with the employment of women and she suggested that I might tell you something about my own professional experiences. It is true I am a woman; it is true I am employed; but what professional experiences have I had? It is difficult to say. My profession is literature; and in that profession there are fewer experiences for women than in any other, with the exception of the stage—fewer, I mean, that are peculiar to women. For the road was cut many years ago—by Fanny Burney, by Aphra Behn, by Harriet Martineau,[2] by Jane Austen, by George Eliot—many famous women, and many more unknown and forgotten, have been before me, making the path smooth, and regulating my steps. Thus, when I came to write, there were very few material obstacles in my way. Writing was a reputable and harmless occupation. The family peace was not broken by the scratching of a pen. No demand was made upon the family purse. For ten and sixpence one can buy paper enough to write all the plays of Shakespeare—if one has a mind that way. Pianos and models, Paris, Vienna, and Berlin, masters and mistresses, are not needed by a writer. The cheapness of writing paper is, of course, the reason why women have succeeded as writers before they have succeeded in the other professions.

But to tell you my story—it is a simple one. You have only got to figure to yourselves a girl in a bedroom with a pen in her hand. She had only to move that pen from left to right—from ten o'clock to one. Then it occurred to her to do what is simple and cheap enough after all—to slip a few of those pages into an envelope, fix a penny stamp in the corner, and drop the envelope into the red box at the corner. It was thus that I became a journalist; and my effort was rewarded on the first day of the following month—a very glorious day it was for me—by a letter from an editor containing a cheque for one pound ten shillings and sixpence. But to show you how little I deserve to be called a professional woman, how little I know of the struggles and difficulties of such lives, I have to admit that instead of spending that sum upon bread and butter, rent, shoes and stockings, or butcher's bills, I went out and bought a cat—a beautiful cat, a Persian cat, which very soon involved me in bitter disputes with my neighbours.

What could be easier than to write articles and to buy Persian cats with the profits? But wait a moment. Articles have to be about something. Mine, I seem to remember, was about a novel by a famous man. And while I was writ-

---

1. A paper read to the Women's Service League [Woolf's note]. Woolf here echoes her points in *A Room of One's Own* about a woman's needing money (specifically, five hundred British pounds) and a room in which to write.

2. Economist, moralist, journalist, and novelist (1802–1876). Burney (1752–1840), author of *Evelina* and other novels. Behn (1640–1689), writer of romances and plays.

ing this review, I discovered that if I were going to review books I should need to do battle with a certain phantom. And the phantom was a woman, and when I came to know her better I called her after the heroine of a famous poem, The Angel in the House.[3] It was she who used to come between me and my paper when I was writing reviews. It was she who bothered and wasted my time and so tormented me that at last I killed her. You who come of a younger and happier generation may not have heard of her—you may not know what I mean by The Angel in the House. I will describe her as shortly as I can. She was intensely sympathetic. She was immensely charming. She was utterly unselfish. She excelled in the difficult arts of family life. She sacrificed herself daily. If there was chicken, she took the leg; if there was a draught she sat in it—in short she was so constituted that she never had a mind or a wish of her own, but preferred to sympathise always with the minds and wishes of others. Above all—I need not say it—she was pure. Her purity was supposed to be her chief beauty—her blushes, her great grace. In those days—the last of Queen Victoria—every house had its Angel. And when I came to write I encountered her with the very first words. The shadow of her wings fell on my page; I heard the rustling of her skirts in the room. Directly, that is to say, I took my pen in my hand to review that novel by a famous man, she slipped behind me and whispered: 'My dear, you are a young woman. You are writing about a book that has been written by a man. Be sympathetic; be tender; flatter; deceive; use all the arts and wiles of our sex. Never let anybody guess that you have a mind of your own. Above all, be pure.' And she made as if to guide my pen. I now record the one act for which I take some credit to myself, though the credit rightly belongs to some excellent ancestors of mine who left me a certain sum of money—shall we say five hundred pounds a year?—so that it was not necessary for me to depend solely on charm for my living. I turned upon her and caught her by the throat. I did my best to kill her. My excuse, if I were to be had up in a court of law, would be that I acted in self-defence. Had I not killed her she would have killed me. She would have plucked the heart out of my writing. For, as I found, directly I put pen to paper, you cannot review even a novel without having a mind of your own, without expressing what you think to be the truth about human relations, morality, sex. And all these questions, according to the Angel of the House, cannot be dealt with freely and openly by women; they must charm, they must conciliate, they must—to put it bluntly—tell lies if they are to succeed. Thus, whenever I felt the shadow of her wing or the radiance of her halo upon my page, I took up the inkpot and flung it at her. She died hard. Her fictitious nature was of great assistance to her. It is far harder to kill a phantom than a reality. She was always creeping back when I thought I had despatched her. Though I flatter myself that I killed her in the end, the struggle was severe; it took much time that had better have been spent upon learning Greek grammar; or in roaming the world in search of adventures. But it was a real experience; it was an experience that was bound to befall all women writers at that time. Killing the Angel in the House was part of the occupation of a woman writer.

But to continue my story. The Angel was dead; what then remained? You may say that what remained was a simple and common object—a young woman in a bedroom with an inkpot. In other words, now that she had rid herself of falsehood, that young woman had only to be herself. Ah, but what

3. By Coventry Patmore (1823–1896), published 1854–62.

is 'herself'? I mean, what is a woman? I assure you, I do not know. I do not believe that you know. I do not believe that anybody can know until she has expressed herself in all the arts and professions open to human skill. That indeed is one of the reasons why I have come here—out of respect for you, who are in process of showing us by your experiments what a woman is, who are in process of providing us, by your failures and successes, with that extremely important piece of information.

But to continue the story of my professional experiences. I made one pound ten and six by my first review; and I bought a Persian cat with the proceeds. Then I grew ambitious. A Persian cat is all very well, I said; but a Persian cat is not enough. I must have a motor-car. And it was thus that I became a novelist—for it is a very strange thing that people will give you a motor-car if you will tell them a story. It is a still stranger thing that there is nothing so delightful in the world as telling stories. It is far pleasanter than writing reviews of famous novels. And yet, if I am to obey your secretary and tell you my professional experiences as a novelist, I must tell you about a very strange experience that befell me as a novelist. And to understand it you must try first to imagine a novelist's state of mind. I hope I am not giving away professional secrets if I say that a novelist's chief desire is to be as unconscious as possible. He has to induce in himself a state of perpetual lethargy. He wants life to proceed with the utmost quiet and regularity. He wants to see the same faces, to read the same books, to do the same things day after day, month after month, while he is writing, so that nothing may break the illusion in which he is living—so that nothing may disturb or disquiet the mysterious nosings about, feelings round, darts, dashes, and sudden discoveries of that very shy and illusive spirit, the imagination. I suspect that this state is the same both for men and women. Be that as it may, I want you to imagine me writing a novel in a state of trance. I want you to figure to yourselves a girl sitting with a pen in her hand, which for minutes, and indeed for hours, she never dips into the inkpot. The image that comes to my mind when I think of this girl is the image of a fisherman lying sunk in dreams on the verge of a deep lake with a rod held out over the water. She was letting her imagination sweep unchecked round every rock and cranny of the world that lies submerged in the depths of our unconscious being. Now came the experience that I believe to be far commoner with women writers than with men. The line raced through the girl's fingers. Her imagination had rushed away. It had sought the pools, the depths, the dark places where the largest fish slumber. And then there was a smash. There was an explosion. There was foam and confusion. The imagination had dashed itself against something hard. The girl was roused from her dream. She was indeed in a state of the most acute and difficult distress. To speak without figure, she had thought of something, something about the body, about the passions which it was unfitting for her as a woman to say. Men, her reason told her, would be shocked. The consciousness of what men will say of a woman who speaks the truth about her passions had roused her from her artist's state of unconsciousness. She could write no more. The trance was over. Her imagination could work no longer. This I believe to be a very common experience with women writers—they are impeded by the extreme conventionality of the other sex. For though men sensibly allow themselves great freedom in these respects, I doubt that they realize or can control the extreme severity with which they condemn such freedom in women.

These then were two very genuine experiences of my own. These were two of the adventures of my professional life. The first—killing the Angel in the House—I think I solved. She died. But the second, telling the truth about my own experiences as a body, I do not think I solved. I doubt that any woman has solved it yet. The obstacles against her are still immensely powerful—and yet they are very difficult to define. Outwardly, what is simpler than to write books? Outwardly, what obstacles are there for a woman rather than for a man? Inwardly, I think, the case is very different; she has still many ghosts to fight, many prejudices to overcome. Indeed it will be a long time still, I think, before a woman can sit down to write a book without finding a phantom to be slain, a rock to be dashed against. And if this is so in literature, the freest of all professions for women, how is it in the new professions which you are now for the first time entering?

Those are the questions that I should like, had I time, to ask you. And indeed, if I have laid stress upon these professional experiences of mine, it is because I believe that they are, though in different forms, yours also. Even when the path is nominally open—when there is nothing to prevent a woman from being a doctor, a lawyer, a civil servant—there are many phantoms and obstacles, as I believe, looming in her way. To discuss and define them is I think of great value and importance; for thus only can the labour be shared, the difficulties be solved. But besides this, it is necessary also to discuss the ends and the aims for which we are fighting, for which we are doing battle with these formidable obstacles. Those aims cannot be taken for granted; they must be perpetually questioned and examined. The whole position, as I see it—here in this hall surrounded by women practising for the first time in history I know not how many different professions—is one of extraordinary interest and importance. You have won rooms of your own in the house hitherto exclusively owned by men. You are able, though not without great labour and effort, to pay the rent. You are earning your five hundred pounds a year. But this freedom is only a beginning; the room is your own, but it is still bare. It has to be furnished; it has to be decorated; it has to be shared. How are you going to furnish it, how are you going to decorate it? With whom are you going to share it, and upon what terms? These, I think are questions of the utmost importance and interest. For the first time in history you are able to ask them; for the first time you are able to decide for yourselves what the answers should be. Willingly would I stay and discuss those questions and answers—but not tonight. My time is up; and I must cease.

1942

From A Sketch of the Past[1]

[MOMENTS OF BEING AND NON-BEING]

—I begin: the first memory.

This was of red and purple flowers on a black ground—my mother's dress; and she was sitting either in a train or in an omnibus, and I was on her lap. I

1. The autobiographical essay from which this extract is taken was published in *Moments of Being*, ed. Jeanne Schulkind (1976). Woolf began it on April 18, 1939, as a relief from the labor of writing *Roger Fry: A Biography* (1940). The last date entered in the manuscript is November 17, 1940, some four months before her death. Under the shadow of approaching war, she gropes back for the bright memories of childhood, especially those associated with the Stephens' summer home, Talland House, at St. Ives in Cornwall, the setting for her novel *To the Lighthouse* (1927).

therefore saw the flowers she was wearing very close; and can still see purple and red and blue, I think, against the black; they must have been anemones, I suppose. Perhaps we were going to St Ives; more probably, for from the light it must have been evening, we were coming back to London. But it is more convenient artistically to suppose that we were going to St Ives, for that will lead to my other memory, which also seems to be my first memory, and in fact it is the most important of all my memories. If life has a base that it stands upon, if it is a bowl that one fills and fills and fills—then my bowl without a doubt stands upon this memory. It is of lying half asleep, half awake, in bed in the nursery at St Ives. It is of hearing the waves breaking, one, two, one, two, and sending a splash of water over the beach; and then breaking, one, two, one, two, behind a yellow blind. It is of hearing the blind draw its little acorn[2] across the floor as the wind blew the blind out. It is of lying and hearing this splash and seeing this light, and feeling, it is almost impossible that I should be here; of feeling the purest ecstasy I can conceive.

I could spend hours trying to write that as it should be written, in order to give the feeling which is even at this moment very strong in me. But I should fail (unless I had some wonderful luck); I dare say I should only succeed in having the luck if I had begun by describing Virginia herself.

Here I come to one of the memoir writer's difficulties—one of the reasons why, though I read so many, so many are failures. They leave out the person to whom things happened. The reason is that it is so difficult to describe any human being. So they say: "This is what happened"; but they do not say what the person was like to whom it happened. And the events mean very little unless we know first to whom they happened. Who was I then? Adeline Virginia Stephen, the second daughter of Leslie and Julia Prinsep Stephen, born on 25th January 1882, descended from a great many people, some famous, others obscure; born into a large connection, born not of rich parents, but of well-to-do parents, born into a very communicative, literate, letter writing, visiting, articulate, late nineteenth century world; so that I could if I liked to take the trouble, write a great deal here not only about my mother and father but about uncles and aunts, cousins and friends. But I do not know how much of this, or what part of this, made me feel what I felt in the nursery at St Ives. I do not know how far I differ from other people. That is another memoir writer's difficulty. Yet to describe oneself truly one must have some standard of comparison; was I clever, stupid, good looking, ugly, passionate, cold—? Owing partly to the fact that I was never at school, never competed in any way with children of my own age, I have never been able to compare my gifts and defects with other people's. But of course there was one external reason for the intensity of this first impression: the impression of the waves and the acorn on the blind; the feeling, as I describe it sometimes to myself, of lying in a grape and seeing through a film of semi-transparent yellow—it was due partly to the many months we spent in London. The change of nursery was a great change. And there was the long train journey; and the excitement. I remember the dark; the lights; the stir of the going up to bed.

But to fix my mind upon the nursery—it had a balcony; there was a partition, but it joined the balcony of my father's and mother's bedroom. My mother would come out onto her balcony in a white dressing gown. There were passion

---

2. I.e., the acorn-shaped button on the end of the blind cord.

flowers growing on the wall; they were great starry blossoms, with purple streaks, and large green buds, part empty, part full.

If I were a painter I should paint these first impressions in pale yellow, silver, and green. There was the pale yellow blind; the green sea; and the silver of the passion flowers. I should make a picture that was globular; semi-transparent. I should make a picture of curved petals; of shells; of things that were semi-transparent; I should make curved shapes, showing the light through, but not giving a clear outline. Everything would be large and dim; and what was seen would at the same time be heard; sounds would come through this petal or leaf—sounds indistinguishable from sights. Sound and sight seem to make equal parts of these first impressions. When I think of the early morning in bed I also hear the caw of rooks[3] falling from a great height. The sound seems to fall through an elastic, gummy air; which holds it up; which prevents it from being sharp and distinct. The quality of the air above Talland House seemed to suspend sound, to let it sink down slowly, as if it were caught in a blue gummy veil. The rooks cawing is part of the waves breaking—one, two, one, two—and the splash as the wave drew back and then it gathered again, and I lay there half awake, half asleep, drawing in such ecstasy as I cannot describe.

The next memory—all these colour-and-sound memories hang together at St Ives—was much more robust; it was highly sensual. It was later. It still makes me feel warm; as if everything were ripe; humming; sunny; smelling so many smells at once; and all making a whole that even now makes me stop—as I stopped then going down to the beach; I stopped at the top to look down at the gardens. They were sunk beneath the road. The apples were on a level with one's head. The gardens gave off a murmur of bees; the apples were red and gold; there were also pink flowers; and grey and silver leaves. The buzz, the croon, the smell, all seemed to press voluptuously against some membrane; not to burst it; but to hum round one such a complete rapture of pleasure that I stopped, smelt; looked. But again I cannot describe that rapture. It was rapture rather than ecstasy.

The strength of these pictures—but sight was always then so much mixed with sound that picture is not the right word—the strength anyhow of these impressions makes me again digress. Those moments—in the nursery, on the road to the beach—can still be more real than the present moment. This I have just tested. For I got up and crossed the garden. Percy was digging the asparagus bed; Louie[4] was shaking a mat in front of the bedroom door. But I was seeing them through the sight I saw here—the nursery and the road to the beach. At times I can go back to St Ives more completely than I can this morning. I can reach a state where I seem to be watching things happen as if I were there. That is, I suppose, that my memory supplies what I had forgotten, so that it seems as if it were happening independently, though I am really making it happen. In certain favourable moods, memories—what one has forgotten—come to the top. Now if this is so, is it not possible—I often wonder—that things we have felt with great intensity have an existence independent of our minds; are in fact still in existence? And if so, will it not be possible, in time, that some device will be invented by which we can tap them? I see it—the past—as an avenue lying behind; a long ribbon of scenes, emotions. There at

3. Black crows.
4. The gardener and "daily help," respectively, at Monks House, the Woolfs' country home in Rodmell, Sussex.

the end of the avenue still, are the garden and the nursery. Instead of remembering here a scene and there a sound, I shall fit a plug into the wall;[5] and listen in to the past. I shall turn up August 1890. I feel that strong emotion must leave its trace; and it is only a question of discovering how we can get ourselves again attached to it, so that we shall be able to live our lives through from the start.

But the peculiarity of these two strong memories is that each was very simple. I am hardly aware of myself, but only of the sensation. I am only the container of the feeling of ecstasy, of the feeling of rapture. Perhaps this is characteristic of all childhood memories; perhaps it accounts for their strength. Later we add to feelings much that makes them more complex; and therefore less strong; or if not less strong, less isolated, less complete. But instead of analysing this, here is an instance of what I mean—my feeling about the looking-glass in the hall.

There was a small looking-glass in the hall at Talland House. It had, I remember, a ledge with a brush on it. By standing on tiptoe I could see my face in the glass. When I was six or seven perhaps, I got into the habit of looking at my face in the glass. But I only did this if I was sure that I was alone. I was ashamed of it. A strong feeling of guilt seemed naturally attached to it. But why was this so? One obvious reason occurs to me—Vanessa and I were both what was called tomboys; that is, we played cricket, scrambled over rocks, climbed trees, were said not to care for clothes and so on. Perhaps therefore to have been found looking in the glass would have been against our tomboy code. But I think that my feeling of shame went a great deal deeper. I am almost inclined to drag in my grandfather—Sir James, who once smoked a cigar, liked it, and so threw away his cigar and never smoked another. I am almost inclined to think that I inherited a streak of the puritan, of the Clapham Sect.[6] At any rate, the looking-glass shame has lasted all my life, long after the tomboy phase was over. I cannot now powder my nose in public. Everything to do with dress—to be fitted, to come into a room wearing a new dress—still frightens me; at least makes me shy, self-conscious, uncomfortable. "Oh to be able to run, like Julian Morrell,[7] all over the garden in a new dress", I thought not many years ago at Garsington; when Julian undid a parcel and put on a new dress and scampered round and round like a hare. Yet femininity was very strong in our family. We were famous for our beauty—my mother's beauty, Stella's beauty, gave me as early as I can remember, pride and pleasure. What then gave me this feeling of shame, unless it were that I inherited some opposite instinct? My father was spartan, ascetic, puritanical. He had I think no feeling for pictures; no ear for music; no sense of the sound of words. This leads me to think that my—I would say 'our' if I knew enough about Vanessa, Thoby and Adrian[8]—but how little we know even about brothers and sisters— this leads me to think that my natural love for beauty was checked by some ancestral dread. Yet this did not prevent me from feeling ecstasies and raptures spontaneously and intensely and without any shame or the least sense of guilt, so long as they were disconnected with my own body. I thus detect another

---

5. I.e., as if plugging in a radio.
6. In marrying Jane Catherine Venn, Woolf's grandfather, James Stephen, had allied himself with the heart of the so-called Clapham sect. John and Henry Venn, respectively rector and curate of Clapham in south London, were prominent members of this evangelical society, which, in the early

19th century, was instrumental in bringing about the abolition of the slave trade.
7. Daughter of Philip Morrell, member of Parliament, and his wife, Ottoline, the celebrated literary hostess. Garsington Manor was their house in Oxfordshire.
8. Woolf's brothers and sister.

element in the shame which I had in being caught looking at myself in the glass in the hall. I must have been ashamed or afraid of my own body. Another memory, also of the hall, may help to explain this. There was a slab outside the dining room door for standing dishes upon. Once when I was very small George Duckworth[9] lifted me onto this, and as I sat there he began to explore my body. I can remember the feel of his hand going under my clothes; going firmly and steadily lower and lower. I remember how I hoped that he would stop; how I stiffened and wriggled as his hand approached my private parts. But it did not stop. His hand explored my private parts too. I remember resenting, disliking it—what is the word for so dumb and mixed a feeling? It must have been strong, since I still recall it. This seems to show that a feeling about certain parts of the body; how they must not be touched; how it is wrong to allow them to be touched; must be instinctive. It proves that Virginia Stephen was not born on the 25th January 1882, but was born many thousands of years ago; and had from the very first to encounter instincts already acquired by thousands of ancestresses in the past.

And this throws light not merely on my own case, but upon the problem that I touched on the first page; why it is so difficult to give any account of the person to whom things happen. The person is evidently immensely complicated. Witness the incident of the looking-glass. Though I have done my best to explain why I was ashamed of looking at my own face I have only been able to discover some possible reasons; there may be others; I do not suppose that I have got at the truth; yet this is a simple incident; and it happened to me personally; and I have no motive for lying about it. In spite of all this, people write what they call "lives" of other people; that is, they collect a number of events, and leave the person to whom it happened unknown. Let me add a dream; for it may refer to the incident of the looking-glass. I dreamt that I was looking in a glass when a horrible face—the face of an animal—suddenly showed over my shoulder. I cannot be sure if this was a dream, or if it happened. Was I looking in the glass one day when something in the background moved, and seemed to me alive? I cannot be sure. But I have always remembered the other face in the glass, whether it was a dream or a fact, and that it frightened me.

These then are some of my first memories. But of course as an account of my life they are misleading, because the things one does not remember are as important; perhaps they are more important. If I could remember one whole day I should be able to describe, superficially at least, what life was like as a child. Unfortunately, one only remembers what is exceptional. And there seems to be no reason why one thing is exceptional and another not. Why have I forgotten so many things that must have been, one would have thought, more memorable than what I do remember? Why remember the hum of bees in the garden going down to the beach, and forget completely being thrown naked by father into the sea? (Mrs Swanwick says she saw that happen.)[1]

This leads to a digression, which perhaps may explain a little of my own psychology; even of other people's. Often when I have been writing one of my so-called novels I have been baffled by this same problem; that is, how to

9. Woolf's half-brother and the subject of her autobiographical essay "22 Hyde Park Gate," written in 1920 and published in *Moments of Being* (1978).
1. In Mrs. Swanwick's autobiography, *I Have Been Young* (1935), she recalls having known Leslie Stephen at St. Ives: "We watched with delight his naked babies running about the beach or being towed into the sea between his legs, and their beautiful mother."

describe what I call in my private shorthand—"non-being." Every day includes much more non-being than being. Yesterday for example, Tuesday the 18th of April, was [as] it happened a good day; above the average in "being." It was fine; I enjoyed writing these first pages; my head was relieved of the pressure of writing about Roger; I walked over Mount Misery[2] and along the river; and save that the tide was out, the country, which I notice very closely always, was coloured and shaded as I like—there were the willows, I remember, all plumy and soft green and purple against the blue. I also read Chaucer with pleasure; and began a book—the memoirs of Madame de la Fayette[3]—which interested me. These separate moments of being were however embedded in many more moments of non-being. I have already forgotten what Leonard[4] and I talked about at lunch; and at tea; although it was a good day the goodness was embedded in a kind of nondescript cotton wool. This is always so. A great part of every day is not lived consciously. One walks, eats, sees things, deals with what has to be done; the broken vacuum cleaner; ordering dinner; writing orders to Mabel;[5] washing; cooking dinner; bookbinding. When it is a bad day the proportion of non-being is much larger. I had a slight temperature last week; almost the whole day was non-being. The real novelist can somehow convey both sorts of being. I think Jane Austen can; and Trollope; perhaps Thackeray and Dickens and Tolstoy. I have never been able to do both. I tried—in *Night and Day*; and in *The Years*.[6] But I will leave the literary side alone for the moment.

As a child then, my days, just as they do now, contained a large proportion of this cotton wool, this non-being. Week after week passed at St Ives and nothing made any dint upon me. Then, for no reason that I know about, there was a sudden violent shock; something happened so violently that I have remembered it all my life. I will give a few instances. The first: I was fighting with Thoby on the lawn. We were pommelling each other with our fists. Just as I raised my fist to hit him, I felt: why hurt another person? I dropped my hand instantly, and stood there, and let him beat me. I remember the feeling. It was a feeling of hopeless sadness. It was as if I became aware of something terrible; and of my own powerlessness. I slunk off alone, feeling horribly depressed. The second instance was also in the garden at St Ives. I was looking at the flower bed by the front door; "That is the whole," I said. I was looking at a plant with a spread of leaves; and it seemed suddenly plain that the flower itself was a part of the earth; that a ring enclosed what was the flower; and that was the real flower; part earth; part flower. It was a thought I put away as being likely to be very useful to me later. The third case was also at St Ives. Some people called Valpy had been staying at St Ives, and had left. We were waiting at dinner one night, when somehow I overheard my father or my mother say that Mr Valpy had killed himself. The next thing I remember is being in the garden at night and walking on the path by the apple tree. It seemed to me that the apple tree was connected with the horror of Mr Valpy's suicide. I could not pass it. I stood there looking at the grey-green creases of the bark—it was a moonlit night—in a trance of horror. I seemed to be dragged

2. Two cottages on the hillside between Southease and Piddinghoe known locally as Mount Misery.
3. French novelist (1634–1693).
4. Her husband, the English writer Leonard Woolf (1880–1969). In 1917 the Woolfs founded the Hogarth Press, a literary publisher.

5. Instructions to the Woolfs' maid.
6. Novels published in 1919 and 1938, respectively. Anthony Trollope (1815–1882), English novelist. William Makepeace Thackeray (1811–1863), English novelist. Leo Tolstoy (1828–1910), Russian novelist.

down, hopelessly, into some pit of absolute despair from which I could not escape. My body seemed paralysed.

These are three instances of exceptional moments. I often tell them over, or rather they come to the surface unexpectedly. But now that for the first time I have written them down, I realise something that I have never realised before. Two of these moments ended in a state of despair. The other ended, on the contrary, in a state of satisfaction. When I said about the flower "That is the whole," I felt that I had made a discovery. I felt that I had put away in my mind something that I should go back [to], to turn over and explore. It strikes me now that this was a profound difference. It was the difference in the first place between despair and satisfaction. This difference I think arose from the fact that I was quite unable to deal with the pain of discovering that people hurt each other; that a man I had seen had killed himself. The sense of horror held me powerless. But in the case of the flower I found a reason; and was thus able to deal with the sensation. I was not powerless. I was conscious—if only at a distance—that I should in time explain it. I do not know if I was older when I saw the flower than I was when I had the other two experiences. I only know that many of these exceptional moments brought with them a peculiar horror and a physical collapse; they seemed dominant; myself passive. This suggests that as one gets older one has a greater power through reason to provide an explanation; and that this explanation blunts the sledge-hammer force of the blow. I think this is true, because though I still have the peculiarity that I receive these sudden shocks, they are now always welcome; after the first surprise, I always feel instantly that they are particularly valuable. And so I go on to suppose that the shock-receiving capacity is what makes me a writer. I hazard the explanation that a shock is at once in my case followed by the desire to explain it. I feel that I have had a blow; but it is not, as I thought as a child, simply a blow from an enemy hidden behind the cotton wool of daily life; it is or will become a revelation of some order; it is a token of some real thing behind appearances; and I make it real by putting it into words. It is only by putting it into words that I make it whole; this wholeness means that it has lost its power to hurt me; it gives me, perhaps because by doing so I take away the pain, a great delight to put the severed parts together. Perhaps this is the strongest pleasure known to me. It is the rapture I get when in writing I seem to be discovering what belongs to what; making a scene come right; making a character come together. From this I reach what I might call a philosophy; at any rate it is a constant idea of mine; that behind the cotton wool is hidden a pattern; that we—I mean all human beings—are connected with this; that the whole world is a work of art; that we are parts of the work of art. *Hamlet* or a Beethoven quartet is the truth about this vast mass that we call the world. But there is no Shakespeare, there is no Beethoven; certainly and emphatically there is no God; we are the words; we are the music; we are the thing itself. And I see this when I have a shock.

This intuition of mine—it is so instinctive that it seems given to me, not made by me—has certainly given its scale to my life ever since I saw the flower in the bed by the front door at St Ives. If I were painting myself I should have to find some—rod, shall I say—something that would stand for the conception. It proves that one's life is not confined to one's body and what one says and does; one is living all the time in relation to certain background rods or conceptions. Mine is that there is a pattern hid behind the cotton wool. And this conception affects me every day. I prove this, now, by spending the morning writing, when I might be walking, running a shop, or learning to do something that will be useful if war comes. I feel that by writing I am doing what is far more necessary than anything else.

All artists I suppose feel something like this. It is one of the obscure elements in life that has never been much discussed. It is left out in almost all biographies and autobiographies, even of artists. Why did Dickens spend his entire life writing stories? What was his conception? I bring in Dickens partly because I am reading *Nicholas Nickleby* at the moment; also partly because it struck me, on my walk yesterday, that these moments of being of mine were scaffolding in the background; were the invisible and silent part of my life as a child. But in the foreground there were of course people; and these people were very like characters in Dickens. They were caricatures; they were very simple; they were immensely alive. They could be made with three strokes of the pen, if I could do it. Dickens owes his astonishing power to make characters alive to the fact that he saw them as a child sees them; as I saw Mr Wolstenholme; C. B. Clarke, and Mr Gibbs.

I name these three people because they all died when I was a child. Therefore they have never been altered. I see them exactly as I saw them then. Mr Wolstenholme was a very old gentleman who came every summer to stay with us. He was brown; he had a beard and very small eyes in fat cheeks; and he fitted into a brown wicker beehive chair as if it had been his nest. He used to sit in this beehive chair smoking and reading. He had only one characteristic—that when he ate plum tart he spurted the juice through his nose so that it made a purple stain on his grey moustache. This seemed enough to cause us perpetual delight. We called him "The Woolly One." By way of shading him a little I remember that we had to be kind to him because he was not happy at home; that he was very poor, yet once gave Thoby half a crown; that he had a son who was drowned in Australia; and I know too that he was a great mathematician. He never said a word all the time I knew him. But he still seems to me a complete character; and whenever I think of him I begin to laugh.

Mr Gibbs was perhaps less simple. He wore a tie ring; had a bald, benevolent head; was dry; neat; precise; and had folds of skin under his chin. He made father groan—"why can't you go—why can't you go?" And he gave Vanessa and myself two ermine skins, with slits down the middle out of which poured endless wealth—streams of silver. I also remember him lying in bed, dying; husky; in a night shirt; and showing us drawings by Retzsch.[7] The character of Mr Gibbs also seems to me complete and amuses me very much.

As for C. B. Clarke, he was an old botanist; and he said to my father "All you young botanists like Osmunda."[8] He had an aunt aged eighty who went for a walking tour in the New Forest. That is all—that is all I have to say about these three old gentlemen. But how real they were! How we laughed at them! What an immense part they played in our lives!

One more caricature comes into my mind; though pity entered into this one. I am thinking of Justine Nonon. She was immensely old. Little hairs sprouted on her long bony chin. She was a hunchback; and walked like a spider, feeling her way with her long dry fingers from one chair to another. Most of the time she sat in the arm-chair beside the fire. I used to sit on her knee; and her knee

---

7. Friedrich Retzsch (1779–1857), German engraver.

8. Flowering ferns.

jogged up and down; and she sang in a hoarse cracked voice "Ron ron ron—et plon plon plon—" and then her knee gave and I was tumbled onto the floor. She was French; she had been with the Thackerays. She only came to us on visits. She lived by herself at Shepherd's Bush; and used to bring Adrian a glass jar of honey. I got the notion that she was extremely poor; and it made me uncomfortable that she brought this honey, because I felt she did it by way of making her visit acceptable. She said too: "I have come in my carriage and pair"—which meant the red omnibus. For this too I pitied her; also because she began to wheeze; and the nurses said she would not live much longer; and soon she died. That is all I know about her; but I remember her as if she were a completely real person, with nothing left out, like the three old men.

Apr. 1939–Nov. 1940   1978

JAMES JOYCE
1882–1941

James Joyce was born in Dublin, son of a talented but feckless father, who is accurately described in Joyce's novel *A Portrait of the Artist as a Young Man* (1916) as having been "a medical student, an oarsman, a tenor, an amateur actor, a shouting politician, a small landlord, a small investor, a drinker, a good fellow, a storyteller, somebody's secretary, something in a distillery, a tax-gatherer, a bankrupt, and at present a praiser of his own past." The elder Joyce drifted steadily down the financial and social scale, his family moving from house to house, each one less genteel and more shabby than the previous. James Joyce's primary education was Catholic, from the age of six to the age of nine at Clongowes Wood College and from eleven to sixteen at Belvedere College. Both were Jesuit institutions and were normal roads to the priesthood. He then studied modern languages at University College, Dublin.

From a comparatively young age Joyce regarded himself as a rebel against the shabbiness and philistinism of Dublin. In his last year of school at Belvedere he began to reject his Catholic faith in favor of a literary mission that he saw as involving rebellion and exile. He refused to play any part in the nationalist or other popular activities of his fellow students, and he created some stir by his outspoken articles, one of which, on the Norwegian playwright Henrik Ibsen, appeared in London's *Fortnightly Review* when Joyce was eighteen. He taught himself Dano-Norwegian in order to read Ibsen and to write to him. When an article by Joyce, significantly titled "The Day of the Rabblement," was refused, on instructions of the faculty adviser, by the student magazine that had commissioned it, he had it printed privately. By 1902, when he received his A.B. degree, he was already committed to a career as exile and writer. For Joyce, as for his character Stephen Dedalus, the latter implied the former. To preserve his integrity, to avoid involvement in popular causes, to devote himself to the life of the artist, he felt that he had to go abroad.

Joyce went to Paris after graduation, was recalled to Dublin by his mother's fatal illness, had a short spell there as a schoolteacher, then returned to the Continent in 1904 to teach English at Trieste and then at Zurich. He took with him Nora Barnacle, a woman from Galway with no interest in literature; her vivacity and wit charmed Joyce, and the two lived in devoted companionship until his death, although they were not married until 1931. In 1920 Joyce and Barnacle settled in Paris, where they lived until December 1940, when the war forced them to take refuge in Switzerland; he died in Zurich a few weeks later.

Proud, obstinate, absolutely convinced of his genius, given to fits of sudden gaiety and of sudden silence, Joyce was not always an easy person to get along with, yet he never lacked friends, and throughout his thirty-six years on the Continent he was always the center of a literary circle. Life was hard at first. In Trieste he had very little money, and he did not improve matters by drinking heavily, a habit checked somewhat by his brother Stanislaus, who came out from Dublin to act (as Stanislaus put it much later) as his "brother's keeper." Joyce also suffered from eye diseases and, blind for brief periods, underwent twenty-five operations. In 1917 Edith Rockefeller McCormick and then the lawyer John Quinn, steered in Joyce's direction by Ezra Pound, helped out financially, but a more permanent benefactor was the English feminist and editor Harriet Shaw Weaver, who not only subsidized Joyce generously from 1917 to the end of his life but also occupied herself indefatigably with arrangements for publishing his work.

In spite of doing most of his writing in Trieste, Zurich, and Paris, Joyce paradoxically wrote only and always about Dublin. No writer has ever been more soaked in Dublin, its atmosphere, its history, its topography. He devised ways of expanding his accounts of Dublin, however, so that they became microcosms of human history, geography, and experience.

Joyce began his career by writing a series of stories etching with extraordinary clarity aspects of Dublin life. These stories—published as *Dubliners* in 1914—are sharp realistic sketches of what Joyce called the "paralysis" that beset the lives of people in then-provincial Ireland. The language is crisp, lucid, and detached, and the details are chosen and organized so that carefully interacting symbolic meanings are set up. Some of the stories, such as "Araby," are built around what Joyce called an "epiphany," a dramatic but fleeting moment of revelation about the self or the world. Many end abruptly, without conventional narrative closure, or they lack overt connectives and transitions, leaving multiple possibilities in suspension. The last story in *Dubliners*, "The Dead," was not part of the original draft of the book but was added later, when Joyce was preoccupied with the nature of artistic objectivity. At a festive event, attended by guests whose portraits Joyce draws with precision and economy, a series of jolting events frees the protagonist, Gabriel, from his possessiveness and egotism. The view he attains at the end is the mood of supreme neutrality that Joyce saw as the beginning of artistic awareness. It is the view of art developed by Stephen Dedalus in *A Portrait of the Artist as a Young Man*.

Dubliners represents Joyce's first phase: he had to come to terms with the life he had rejected. Next he had to come to terms with the meaning of his own growth as a man dedicated to imaginative writing, and he did so by writing a novel about the youth and development of an artist, a kind of novel known by the German term *Künstlerroman* (a variation on the *Bildungsroman*). The book's narrative style changes to evoke developments in Stephen's consciousness, from the bare record of a child's tactile experiences to the ironically lush descriptions of artistic illumination to the self-sufficiency of the final diary entries. Joyce wove his autobiography into a novel so finely chiseled and carefully organized, so stripped of everything superfluous, that each word contributes to the presentation of the theme: the parallel movement toward art and toward exile. A part of his first draft was published posthumously under the original title, *Stephen Hero* (1944), and a comparison between it and the final version, *Portrait of the Artist*, shows how carefully Joyce reworked and compressed his material for maximum effect.

In *Portrait* Stephen works out a theory in which art moves from the lyrical form (the simplest, the personal expression of an instant of emotion) through the narrative form (no longer purely personal) to the dramatic (the highest and most nearly perfect form, where "the artist, like the God of creation, remains within or behind or beyond or above his handiwork, invisible, refined out of existence, indifferent, paring his fingernails"). This view of art, which involves the objectivity, even the exile, of the artist—even though the artist uses only the materials provided for him or her by his or her own life—overlaps with the emphasis on masks, impersonality, and ironic detachment in the work of other modernist writers, such as Pound, W. B. Yeats, and T. S. Eliot. Joyce's next novel, *Ulysses* (1922), and his last, *Finnegans Wake* (1939), represent the most consummate craftsmanship, put at the service of a humanely comic vision. His innovations in organization, style, and narrative technique have influenced countless other writers, but these books are unique.

From the beginning Joyce had trouble getting into print. Publication of *Dubliners* was held up for many years while he fought with both English and Irish publishers about words and phrases that they wished to eliminate. *Ulysses* was banned in Britain and America on publication; its earlier serialization in an American magazine, *The Little Review* (March 1918–December 1920), had been stopped abruptly when the U.S. Post Office brought a charge of obscenity against the work. Fortunately Judge John Woolsey's history-making decision in a U.S. district court on December 6, 1933, resulted in the lifting of the ban and the free circulation of *Ulysses* first in America and soon afterward in Britain.

ULYSSES

Ulysses is an account of one day in the lives of Dubliners; it thus describes a limited number of events involving a limited number of people in a limited environment. Yet Joyce's ambition—which took him seven years to realize—is to present the events in such a manner that depth and implication are given to them and they become symbolic. The episodes in *Ulysses* correspond to episodes in Homer's ancient Greek epic *Odyssey*. Joyce regarded Homer's Odysseus, or Ulysses, as the most "complete" man in literature, shown in all his aspects—coward and hero, cautious and reckless, weak and strong, husband and philanderer, father and son, dignified and ridiculous; so he makes his hero, Leopold Bloom, an Irish Jew, into a modern Ulysses. The parallels between the Homeric archetypes and the modern-day characters and events create a host of interpretive complexities. They can seem tight or loose, deflating or ennobling, ironic or heroic, epic or mock-epic, depending on their specific use in different episodes and, to some extent, on the propensities of the reader.

Ulysses opens at eight o'clock on the morning of June 16, 1904. Stephen Dedalus (the same character as in *Portrait*, but two years after the last glimpse of him there) had been summoned back to Dublin by his mother's fatal illness and now lives in an old military tower on the shore with Buck Mulligan, a rollicking medical student, and an Englishman called Haines. In the first three episodes of *Ulysses*, which concentrate on Stephen, he is built up as an aloof, uncompromising artist, rejecting all advances by representatives of the normal world, the incomplete man, to be contrasted later with the complete Leopold Bloom, who is much more "normal" and conciliatory. After tracing Stephen through his early-morning activities and learning the main currents of his mind, we go, in the fourth episode, to the home of Bloom. We follow closely his every activity: attending a funeral, transacting business, eating lunch, walking through the Dublin streets, worrying about his wife's infidelity with Blazes Boylan— and at each point the contents of his mind, including retrospect and anticipation, are presented to us, until his past history is revealed. Finally Bloom and Stephen, who have been just missing each other all day, get together. By this time it is late, and Stephen, who has been drinking with some medical students, is the worse for liquor. Bloom, moved by a paternal feeling toward Stephen (his own son had died in infancy and in a symbolic way Stephen takes his place), follows him during subsequent adventures in the role of protector. The climax of the book comes when Stephen, far gone in drink, and Bloom, worn out with fatigue, succumb to a series of hallucinations, where their unconscious minds surface in dramatic form and their personalities are revealed with a completeness and a frankness unique in literature. Then Bloom takes the unresponsive Stephen home and gives him a meal. After Stephen's departure Bloom retires to bed—it is now two in the morning, June 17—while his wife, Molly, lying in bed, closes the book with a long monologue in which she recalls her romantic and other experiences. Her monologue unfolds in eight flowing, unpunctuated paragraphs, which culminate in the book's final, resonant affirmation, a memory of her response to Bloom's marriage proposal: "and yes I said yes I will Yes."

On the level of realistic description, Ulysses pulses with life and can be enjoyed for its evocation of early-twentieth-century Dublin. On the level of psychological exploration, it gives a profound and moving presentation of the personalities and consciousnesses of Leopold Bloom, Stephen Dedalus, and Molly Bloom. On the level of style, it exhibits the most fascinating linguistic virtuosity, many an episode written in a distinctive way that reflects its subject—e.g., newspaper headlines intruding in a chapter set in a newspaper office (the "Aeolus" episode), the sentimental language of women's magazines dominating a chapter set on a beach where girls are playing ("Nausicaa"), and the pastiche of styles of English literature from its Anglo-Saxon birth to the twentieth century taking over in a chapter set in a maternity hospital ("Oxen of the Sun"). On a deeper symbolic level, the novel explores the paradoxes of human loneliness and sociability (for Bloom is both Jew and Dubliner, both exile and citizen), and it explores the problems posed by the relations between parent and child, between the generations, and between the sexes. At the same time, through its use of themes from Homer, Dante, and Shakespeare and from literature, philosophy, and history, the book weaves a subtle pattern of allusion and suggestion. The more one reads Ulysses the more one finds in it, but at the same time one does not need to probe into the symbolic meaning to relish both its literary artistry and its emotional richness. At the forefront stands Bloom, from one point of view a frustrated and confused outsider in the society in which he moves, from another a champion of kindness and justice whose humane curiosity about his fellows redeems him from mere vulgarity and gives the book its positive human foundation.

Readers who come to Ulysses with expectations about the way the story is to be presented derived from their reading of Victorian novels or even of twentieth-century novelists such as Conrad and Lawrence will find much that is at first puzzling. Joyce presents the consciousness of his characters directly, without any explanatory comment that tells the reader whose consciousness is being rendered (this is the stream of consciousness method, also known as interior monologue). He may move, in the same paragraph and without any sign that he is making such a transition, from a description of a character's action—e.g., Stephen walking along the shore or Bloom entering a restaurant—to an evocation of the character's mental response to this action. That response is always multiple: it derives partly from the character's immediate situation and partly from the whole complex of attitudes created by a personal past history. To suggest this multiplicity, Joyce may vary his style, from the flippant to the serious or from a realistic description to a suggestive set of images that indicate what might be called the general tone of the character's consciousness. Past and present mingle in the texture of the prose because they mingle in the texture of consciousness, and this mingling can be indicated by puns, by sudden breaks into a new kind of style or a new kind of subject matter, or by some other device for keeping the reader constantly in sight of the shifting, kaleidoscopic nature of human awareness. With a little experience the reader learns to follow the implications of Joyce's shifts in manner and content—even to follow that initially bewildering passage in the "Proteus" episode in which Stephen does not go to visit his uncle and aunt but, passing the road that leads to their house, imagines the kind of conversation that would take place in his home if he had gone to visit his uncle and had then returned home and reported that he had done so. Ulysses must not be approached as though it were a traditional novel; we must set aside our preconceptions, follow wherever the author leads us, and let the language tell us what it has to say.

FINNEGANS WAKE

Joyce's final work, *Finnegans Wake* took more than fourteen years to write, and Joyce considered it his masterpiece. In *Ulysses* he had made the symbolic aspect of the novel at least as important as the realistic aspect, but in *Finnegans Wake* he gave up realism altogether. This vast story of a symbolic Irishman's cosmic dream develops by enormous reverberating puns a continuous expansion of meaning, the elements in the puns deriving from every conceivable source in history, literature, mythology, and Joyce's personal experience. The whole book being (on one level at least) a dream, Joyce invents his own dream language, in which words are combined, distorted, created by fitting together bits of other words, used with several different meanings at once, often drawn from several different languages at once, and fused in all sorts of ways to achieve whole clusters of meaning simultaneously. In fact, so many echoing suggestions can be found in every word or phrase that a full annotation of even a few pages would require a large book. Over time, readers and critics of *Finnegans Wake* have sorted out the complex interactions of the multiple puns and pun clusters through which the ideas are projected, and every rereading reveals new meanings. Many readers find the efforts of explication too arduous, but the book has great beauty and fascination even for the casual reader. Newcomers are advised to read aloud— or to listen to the recording of Joyce reading aloud—the extract printed here to appreciate the degree to which the rhythms of the prose assist in conveying the meaning.

To an even greater extent than *Ulysses*, *Finnegans Wake* aims to embrace all of human history. The title comes from an Irish American ballad about Tom Finnegan, a hod carrier who falls off a ladder when drunk and is apparently killed, but who revives when during the wake (the watch by his dead body) someone spills whiskey on him. The theme of death and resurrection, of cycles of change coming round in the course of history, is central to *Finnegans Wake,* which derives one of its main principles of organization from the cyclical theory of history put forward in 1725 by the Italian philosopher Giambattista Vico. Vico held that history passes through four phases: the divine, or theocratic, when people are governed by their awe of the supernatural; the aristocratic (the "heroic age" reflected in Homer and in *Beowulf*); the democratic and individualistic; and the final stage of chaos, a fall into confusion that startles humanity back into supernatural reverence and starts the process once again. Joyce, like Yeats, saw his own generation as in the final stage awaiting the shock that will bring humans back to the first.

A mere account of the narrative line of *Finnegans Wake* cannot give any idea of the content of the work. If one explains that it opens with Finnegan's fall, then introduces his successor, Humphrey Chimpden Earwicker, who keeps a pub in Chapelizod, a Dublin suburb on the river Liffey, near Phoenix Park; that HCE is feeling guilty about an indecency he committed (or may have committed) in Phoenix Park; that his dream constitutes the novel; that his wife, Anna Livia Plurabelle, or ALP (who is also Eve, Iseult, Ireland, the Liffey), changes her role just as he does; that HCE and ALP have two sons, Shem and Shaun (or Jerry and Kevin), who represent introvert and extrovert, artist and practical man, creator and popularizer, and who symbolize this dichotomy in human nature by all kinds of metamorphoses; and if one adds that, in the four books into which *Finnegans Wake* is divided (after Vico's pattern), actions comic or grotesque or sad or tender or desperate or passionate or terribly ordinary (and very often several of these things at the same time) take place with all the shifting meanings of a dream, so that characters change into others or into inanimate objects and the setting keeps shifting—still one has said very little about what makes *Finnegans Wake* what it is. The dreamer is at once a particular person and a universal figure, his initials also standing for "Here Comes Everybody." His mysterious misdemeanor in Phoenix Park is in a sense Original Sin: Earwicker is Adam as well as a primeval giant, the Hill of Howth, the Great Parent ("Haveth Childers Everywhere" is another expansion of HCE), and Man in History. Other characters who flit and change through the book, such as the Twelve Customers (who are also twelve jurymen and public opinion) and the Four Old Men (who are also judges, the authors of the four Gospels, and the four elements), help weave the texture of multiple significance so characteristic of the work. But always it is the punning language, extending significance downward—rather than the plot, developing it lengthwise—that bears the main load of meaning.

Araby[1]

North Richmond Street, being blind, was a quiet street except at the hour when the Christian Brothers' School[2] set the boys free. An uninhabited house of two storeys stood at the blind end, detached from its neighbours in a square ground. The other houses of the street, conscious of decent lives within them, gazed at one another with brown imperturbable faces.

The former tenant of our house, a priest, had died in the back drawing-room. Air, musty from having been long enclosed, hung in all the rooms, and the waste room behind the kitchen was littered with old useless papers. Among these I found a few paper-covered books, the pages of which were curled and damp: *The Abbot*, by Walter Scott, *The Devout Communicant* and *The Memoirs of Vidocq*.[3] I liked the last best because its leaves were yellow. The wild garden behind the house contained a central apple-tree and a few straggling bushes under one of which I found the late tenant's rusty bicycle-pump. He had been a very charitable priest; in his will he had left all his money to institutions and the furniture of his house to his sister.

When the short days of winter came dusk fell before we had well eaten our dinners. When we met in the street the houses had grown sombre. The space of sky above us was the colour of ever-changing violet and towards it the lamps of the street lifted their feeble lanterns. The cold air stung us and we played till our bodies glowed. Our shouts echoed in the silent street. The career of our play brought us through the dark muddy lanes behind the houses where we ran the gantlet of the rough tribes from the cottages, to the back doors of the dark dripping gardens where odours arose from the ashpits, to the dark odorous stables where a coachman smoothed and combed the horse or shook music from the buckled harness. When we returned to the street light from the kitchen windows had filled the areas. If my uncle was seen turning the corner we hid in the shadow until we had seen him safely housed. Or if Mangan's sister came out on the doorstep to call her brother in to his tea we watched her from our shadow peer up and down the street. We waited to see

---

1. The third of the fifteen stories in *Dubliners*. This tale of the frustrated quest for beauty in the midst of drabness is both meticulously realistic in its handling of details of Dublin life and the Dublin scene and highly symbolic in that almost every image and incident suggests some particular aspect of the theme (e.g., the suggestion of the Holy Grail in the image of the chalice, mentioned in the fifth paragraph). Joyce was drawing on his own childhood recollections, and the uncle in the story is a reminiscence of Joyce's father. But in all the stories in *Dubliners* dealing with childhood, the child lives not with his parents but with an uncle and aunt—a symbol of that isolation and lack of proper relation between "consubstantial" (in the flesh) parents

and children that is a major theme in Joyce's work.
2. The Joyce family moved to 17 North Richmond Street, Dublin, in 1894; and Joyce had earlier briefly attended the Christian Brothers' school a few doors away (the Christian Brothers are a Catholic religious community). The details of the house described here correspond exactly to those of number 17.
3. François Eugéne Vidocq (1775–1857) had an extraordinary career as soldier, thief, chief of the French detective force, and private detective. *The Abbot* is a historical novel dealing with Mary, Queen of Scots. *The Devout Communicant* is a Catholic religious manual.

whether she would remain or go in and, if she remained, we left our shadow and walked up to Mangan's steps resignedly. She was waiting for us, her figure defined by the light from the half-opened door. Her brother always teased her before he obeyed and I stood by the railings looking at her. Her dress swung as she moved her body and the soft rope of her hair tossed from side to side.

Every morning I lay on the floor in the front parlour watching her door. The blind was pulled down to within an inch of the sash so that I could not be seen. When she came out on the doorstep my heart leaped. I ran to the hall, seized my books and followed her. I kept her brown figure always in my eye and, when we came near the point at which our ways diverged, I quickened my pace and passed her. This happened morning after morning. I had never spoken to her, except for a few casual words, and yet her name was like a summons to all my foolish blood.

Her image accompanied me even in places the most hostile to romance. On Saturday evenings when my aunt went marketing I had to go to carry some of the parcels. We walked through the flaring streets, jostled by drunken men and bargaining women, amid the curses of labourers, the shrill litanies of shop-boys who stood on guard by the barrels of pigs' cheeks, the nasal chanting of street-singers, who sang a *come-all-you*[4] about O'Donovan Rossa, or a ballad about the troubles in our native land. These noises converged in a single sensation of life for me: I imagined that I bore my chalice safely through a throng of foes. Her name sprang to my lips at moments in strange prayers and praises which I myself did not understand. My eyes were often full of tears (I could not tell why) and at times a flood from my heart seemed to pour itself out into my bosom. I thought little of the future. I did not know whether I would ever speak to her or not or, if I spoke to her, how I could tell her of my confused adoration. But my body was like a harp and her words and gestures were like fingers running upon the wires.

One evening I went into the back drawing-room in which the priest had died. It was a dark rainy evening and there was no sound in the house. Through one of the broken panes I heard the rain impinge upon the earth, the fine incessant needles of water playing in the sodden beds. Some distant lamp or lighted window gleamed below me. I was thankful that I could see so little. All my senses seemed to desire to veil themselves and, feeling that I was about to slip from them, I pressed the palms of my hands together until they trembled, murmuring: *O love! O love!* many times.

At last she spoke to me. When she addressed the first words to me I was so confused that I did not know what to answer. She asked me was I going to *Araby*.[5] I forgot whether I answered yes or no. It would be a splendid bazaar, she said; she would love to go.

—And why can't you? I asked.

While she spoke she turned a silver bracelet round and round her wrist. She could not go, she said, because there would be a retreat that week in her convent.[6] Her brother and two other boys were fighting for their caps and I was alone at the railings. She held one of the spikes, bowing her head towards me. The light from the lamp opposite our door caught the white curve of her

4. Street ballad, so called from its opening words. This one was about the 19th-century Irish nationalist Jeremiah Donovan, popularly known as O'Donovan Rossa.
5. The bazaar, described by its "official catalogue"

as a "Grand Oriental Fête," was actually held in Dublin on May 14–19, 1894.
6. I.e., her convent school. "Retreat": period of seclusion from ordinary activities devoted to religious exercises.

neck, lit up her hair that rested there and, falling, lit up the hand upon the railing. It fell over one side of her dress and caught the white border of a petticoat, just visible as she stood at ease.

—It's well for you, she said.

—If I go, I said, I will bring you something.

What innumerable follies laid waste my waking and sleeping thoughts after that evening! I wished to annihilate the tedious intervening days. I chafed against the work of school. At night in my bedroom and by day in the classroom her image came between me and the page I strove to read. The syllables of the word *Araby* were called to me through the silence in which my soul luxuriated and cast an Eastern enchantment over me. I asked for leave to go to the bazaar on Saturday night. My aunt was surprised and hoped it was not some Freemason affair.[7] I answered few questions in class. I watched my master's face pass from amiability to sternness; he hoped I was not beginning to idle. I could not call my wandering thoughts together. I had hardly any patience with the serious work of life which, now that it stood between me and my desire, seemed to me child's play, ugly monotonous child's play.

On Saturday morning I reminded my uncle that I wished to go to the bazaar in the evening. He was fussing at the hallstand, looking for the hat-brush, and answered me curtly:

—Yes, boy, I know.

As he was in the hall I could not go into the front parlour and lie at the window. I left the house in bad humour and walked slowly towards the school. The air was pitilessly raw and already my heart misgave me.

When I came home to dinner my uncle had not yet been home. Still it was early. I sat staring at the clock for some time and, when its ticking began to irritate me, I left the room. I mounted the staircase and gained the upper part of the house. The high cold empty gloomy rooms liberated me and I went from room to room singing. From the front window I saw my companions playing below in the street. Their cries reached me weakened and indistinct and, leaning my forehead against the cool glass, I looked over at the dark house where she lived. I may have stood there for an hour, seeing nothing but the brown-clad figure cast by my imagination, touched discreetly by the lamplight at the curved neck, at the hand upon the railings and at the border below the dress.

When I came downstairs again I found Mrs Mercer sitting at the fire. She was an old garrulous woman, a pawn-broker's widow, who collected used stamps for some pious purpose. I had to endure the gossip of the tea-table. The meal was prolonged beyond an hour and still my uncle did not come. Mrs Mercer stood up to go: she was sorry she couldn't wait any longer, but it was after eight o'clock and she did not like to be out late, as the night air was bad for her. When she had gone I began to walk up and down the room, clenching my fists. My aunt said:

—I'm afraid you may put off your bazaar for this night of Our Lord.

At nine o'clock I heard my uncle's latchkey in the halldoor. I heard him talking to himself and heard the hallstand rocking when it had received the weight of his overcoat. I could interpret these signs. When he was midway through his dinner I asked him to give me the money to go to the bazaar. He had forgotten.

---

7. His aunt shares her Church's distrust of the Freemasons, an old European secret society, reputedly anti-Catholic.

—The people are in bed and after their first sleep now, he said.

I did not smile. My aunt said to him energetically:

—Can't you give him the money and let him go? You've kept him late enough as it is.

My uncle said he was very sorry he had forgotten. He said he believed in the old saying: *All work and no play makes Jack a dull boy*. He asked me where I was going and, when I had told him a second time he asked me did I know *The Arab's Farewell to his Steed*.[8] When I left the kitchen he was about to recite the opening lines of the piece to my aunt.

I held a florin[9] tightly in my hand as I strode down Buckingham Street towards the station. The sight of the streets thronged with buyers and glaring with gas recalled to me the purpose of my journey. I took my seat in a third-class carriage of a deserted train. After an intolerable delay the train moved out of the station slowly. It crept onward among ruinous houses and over the twinkling river. At Westland Row Station a crowd of people pressed to the carriage doors; but the porters moved them back, saying that it was a special train for the bazaar. I remained alone in the bare carriage. In a few minutes the train drew up beside an improvised wooden platform. I passed out on to the road and saw by the lighted dial of a clock that it was ten minutes to ten. In front of me was a large building which displayed the magical name.

I could not find any sixpenny entrance and, fearing that the bazaar would be closed, I passed in quickly through a turnstile, handing a shilling to a weary-looking man. I found myself in a big hall girdled at half its height by a gallery. Nearly all the stalls were closed and the greater part of the hall was in darkness. I recognized a silence like that which pervades a church after a service. I walked into the centre of the bazaar timidly. A few people were gathered about the stalls which were still open. Before a curtain, over which the words *Café Chantant*[1] were written in coloured lamps, two men were counting money on a salver. I listened to the fall of the coins.

Remembering with difficulty why I had come I went over to one of the stalls and examined porcelain vases and flowered tea-sets. At the door of the stall a young lady was talking and laughing with two young gentlemen. I remarked their English accents and listened vaguely to their conversation.

—O, I never said such a thing!

—O, but you did!

—O, but I didn't!

—Didn't she say that?

—Yes. I heard her.

—O, there's a . . . fib!

Observing me the young lady came over and asked me did I wish to buy anything. The tone of her voice was not encouraging; she seemed to have spoken to me out of a sense of duty. I looked humbly at the great jars that stood like eastern guards at either side of the dark entrance to the stall and murmured:

—No, thank you.

The young lady changed the position of one of the vases and went back to the two young men. They began to talk of the same subject. Once or twice the young lady glanced at me over her shoulder.

8. Once-popular sentimental poem by Caroline Norton.
9. A silver coin, now obsolete, worth two shillings.

1. Singing café (French; literal trans.); a café that provided musical entertainment, popular early in the 20th century.

I lingered before her stall, though I knew my stay was useless, to make my interest in her wares seem the more real. Then I turned away slowly and walked down the middle of the bazaar. I allowed the two pennies to fall against the sixpence in my pocket. I heard a voice call from one end of the gallery that the light was out. The upper part of the hall was now completely dark.

Gazing up into the darkness I saw myself as a creature driven and derided by vanity; and my eyes burned with anguish and anger.

1905   1914

The Dead

Lily, the caretaker's daughter, was literally run off her feet. Hardly had she brought one gentleman into the little pantry behind the office on the ground floor and helped him off with his overcoat than the wheezy hall-door bell clanged again and she had to scamper along the bare hallway to let in another guest. It was well for her she had not to attend to the ladies also. But Miss Kate and Miss Julia had thought of that and had converted the bathroom upstairs into a ladies' dressing-room. Miss Kate and Miss Julia were there, gossiping and laughing and fussing, walking after each other to the head of the stairs, peering down over the banisters and calling down to Lily to ask her who had come.

It was always a great affair, the Misses Morkan's annual dance. Everybody who knew them came to it, members of the family, old friends of the family, the members of Julia's choir, any of Kate's pupils that were grown up enough and even some of Mary Jane's pupils too. Never once had it fallen flat. For years and years it had gone off in splendid style as long as anyone could remember; ever since Kate and Julia, after the death of their brother Pat, had left the house in Stoney Batter and taken Mary Jane, their only niece, to live with them in the dark gaunt house on Usher's Island, the upper part of which they had rented from Mr Fulham, the cornfactor[1] on the ground floor. That was a good thirty years ago if it was a day. Mary Jane, who was then a little girl in short clothes, was now the main prop of the household for she had the organ in Haddington Road.[2] She had been through the Academy and gave a pupils' concert every year in the upper room of the Antient Concert Rooms.[3] Many of her pupils belonged to better-class families on the Kingstown and Dalkey line. Old as they were, her aunts also did their share. Julia, though she was quite grey, was still the leading soprano in Adam and Eve's, and Kate, being too feeble to go about much, gave music lessons to beginners on the old square piano in the back room. Lily, the caretaker's daughter, did housemaid's work for them. Though their life was modest they believed in eating well; the best of everything: diamond-bone sirloins, three-shilling tea and the best bottled stout.[4] But Lily seldom made a mistake in the orders so that she got on well with her three mistresses. They were fussy, that was all. But the only thing they would not stand was back answers.

Of course they had good reason to be fussy on such a night. And then it

---

1. Grain merchant.
2. Haddington Road, like Adam and Eve's below, is a church.

3. Concert hall in Dublin. The academy was the Royal Irish Academy of Music.
4. A dark brown malt liquor, akin to beer.

was long after ten o'clock and yet there was no sign of Gabriel and his wife. Besides they were dreadfully afraid that Freddy Malins might turn up screwed.[5] They would not wish for worlds that any of Mary Jane's pupils should see him under the influence; and when he was like that it was sometimes very hard to manage him. Freddy Malins always came late but they wondered what could be keeping Gabriel: and that was what brought them every two minutes to the banisters to ask Lily had Gabriel or Freddy come.

—O, Mr Conroy, said Lily to Gabriel when she opened the door for him, Miss Kate and Miss Julia thought you were never coming. Good-night, Mrs Conroy.

—I'll engage[6] they did, said Gabriel, but they forget that my wife here takes three mortal hours to dress herself.

He stood on the mat, scraping the snow from his goloshes, while Lily led his wife to the foot of the stairs and called out:

—Miss Kate, here's Mrs Conroy.

Kate and Julia came toddling down the dark stairs at once. Both of them kissed Gabriel's wife, said she must be perished alive and asked was Gabriel with her.

—Here I am as right as the mail, Aunt Kate! Go on up. I'll follow, called out Gabriel from the dark.

He continued scraping his feet vigorously while the three women went upstairs, laughing, to the ladies' dressing-room. A light fringe of snow lay like a cape on the shoulders of his overcoat and like toecaps on the toes of his goloshes; and, as the buttons of his overcoat slipped with a squeaking noise through the snow-stiffened frieze,[7] a cold fragrant air from out-of-doors escaped from crevices and folds.

—Is it snowing again, Mr Conroy? asked Lily.

She had preceded him into the pantry to help him off with his overcoat. Gabriel smiled at the three syllables she had given his surname and glanced at her. She was a slim, growing girl, pale in complexion and with hay-coloured hair. The gas in the pantry made her look still paler. Gabriel had known her when she was a child and used to sit on the lowest step nursing a rag doll.

—Yes, Lily, he answered, and I think we're in for a night of it.

He looked up at the pantry ceiling, which was shaking with the stamping and shuffling of feet on the floor above, listened for a moment to the piano and then glanced at the girl, who was folding his overcoat carefully at the end of a shelf.

—Tell me, Lily, he said in a friendly tone, do you still go to school?

—O no, sir, she answered. I'm done schooling this year and more.

—O, then, said Gabriel gaily, I suppose we'll be going to your wedding one of these fine days with your young man, eh?

The girl glanced back at him over her shoulder and said with great bitterness:

—The men that is now is only all palaver[8] and what they can get out of you.

Gabriel coloured as if he felt he had made a mistake and, without looking at her, kicked off his goloshes and flicked actively with his muffler at his patent-leather shoes.

He was a stout tallish young man. The high colour of his cheeks pushed

5. Drunk.
6. Bet.
7. A kind of coarse woolen cloth.
8. Empty and deceptive talk.

upwards even to his forehead where it scattered itself in a few formless patches of pale red; and on his hairless face there scintillated restlessly the polished lenses and the bright gilt rims of the glasses which screened his delicate and restless eyes. His glossy black hair was parted in the middle and brushed in a long curve behind his ears where it curled slightly beneath the groove left by his hat.

When he had flicked lustre into his shoes he stood up and pulled his waistcoat down more tightly on his plump body. Then he took a coin rapidly from his pocket.

—O Lily, he said, thrusting it into her hands, it's Christmas-time, isn't it? Just . . . here's a little. . . .

He walked rapidly towards the door.

—O no, sir! cried the girl, following him. Really, sir, I wouldn't take it.

—Christmas-time! Christmas-time! said Gabriel, almost trotting to the stairs and waving his hand to her in deprecation.

The girl, seeing that he had gained the stairs, called out after him:

—Well, thank you, sir.

He waited outside the drawing-room door until the waltz should finish, listening to the skirts that swept against it and to the shuffling of feet. He was still discomposed by the girl's bitter and sudden retort. It had cast a gloom over him which he tried to dispel by arranging his cuffs and the bows of his tie. Then he took from his waistcoat pocket a little paper and glanced at the headings he had made for his speech. He was undecided about the lines from Robert Browning for he feared they would be above the heads of his hearers. Some quotation that they could recognise from Shakespeare or from the Melodies[9] would be better. The indelicate clacking of the men's heels and the shuffling of their soles reminded him that their grade of culture differed from his. He would only make himself ridiculous by quoting poetry to them which they could not understand. They would think that he was airing his superior education. He would fail with them just as he had failed with the girl in the pantry. He had taken up a wrong tone. His whole speech was a mistake from first to last, an utter failure.

Just then his aunts and his wife came out of the ladies' dressing-room. His aunts were two small plainly dressed old women. Aunt Julia was an inch or so the taller. Her hair, drawn low over the tops of her ears, was grey; and grey also, with darker shadows, was her large flaccid face. Though she was stout in build and stood erect her slow eyes and parted lips gave her the appearance of a woman who did not know where she was or where she was going. Aunt Kate was more vivacious. Her face, healthier than her sister's, was all puckers and creases, like a shrivelled red apple, and her hair, braided in the same old-fashioned way, had not lost its ripe nut colour.

They both kissed Gabriel frankly. He was their favourite nephew, the son of their dead elder sister, Ellen, who had married T. J. Conroy of the Port and Docks.[1]

—Gretta tells me you're not going to take a cab back to Monkstown tonight, Gabriel, said Aunt Kate.

—No, said Gabriel, turning to his wife, we had quite enough of that last year, hadn't we? Don't you remember, Aunt Kate, what a cold Gretta got out

9. *Irish Melodies* by Dublin-born Thomas Moore (1779–1852), a collection of songs—including one called "O Ye Dead"—that was extremely popular

in late-19th- and early-20th-century Ireland.
1. Board managing the Port of Dublin.

of it? Cab windows rattling all the way, and the east wind blowing in after we passed Merrion. Very jolly it was. Gretta caught a dreadful cold.

Aunt Kate frowned severely and nodded her head at every word.

—Quite right, Gabriel, quite right, she said. You can't be too careful.

—But as for Gretta there, said Gabriel, she'd walk home in the snow if she were let.

Mrs Conroy laughed.

—Don't mind him, Aunt Kate, she said. He's really an awful bother, what with green shades for Tom's eyes at night and making him do the dumb-bells, and forcing Eva to eat the stirabout.[2] The poor child! And she simply hates the sight of it! . . . O, but you'll never guess what he makes me wear now!

She broke out into a peal of laughter and glanced at her husband, whose admiring and happy eyes had been wandering from her dress to her face and hair. The two aunts laughed heartily too, for Gabriel's solicitude was a standing joke with them.

—Goloshes! said Mrs Conroy. That's the latest. Whenever it's wet underfoot I must put on my goloshes. To-night even he wanted me to put them on, but I wouldn't. The next thing he'll buy me will be a diving suit.

Gabriel laughed nervously and patted his tie reassuringly while Aunt Kate nearly doubled herself, so heartily did she enjoy the joke. The smile soon faded from Aunt Julia's face and her mirthless eyes were directed towards her nephew's face. After a pause she asked:

—And what are goloshes, Gabriel?

—Goloshes, Julia! exclaimed her sister. Goodness me, don't you know what goloshes are? You wear them over your . . . over your boots, Gretta, isn't it?

—Yes, said Mrs Conroy. Guttapercha things. We both have a pair now. Gabriel says everyone wears them on the continent.

—O, on the continent, murmured Aunt Julia, nodding her head slowly.

Gabriel knitted his brows and said, as if he were slightly angered:

—It's nothing very wonderful but Gretta thinks it very funny because she says the word reminds her of Christy Minstrels.[3]

—But tell me, Gabriel, said Aunt Kate, with brisk tact. Of course, you've seen about the room. Gretta was saying . . .

—O, the room is all right, replied Gabriel. I've taken one in the Gresham.[4]

—To be sure, said Aunt Kate, by far the best thing to do. And the children, Gretta, you're not anxious about them?

—O, for one night, said Mrs Conroy. Besides, Bessie will look after them.

—To be sure, said Aunt Kate again. What a comfort it is to have a girl like that, one you can depend on! There's that Lily, I'm sure I don't know what has come over her lately. She's not the girl she was at all.

Gabriel was about to ask his aunt some questions on this point but she broke off suddenly to gaze after her sister who had wandered down the stairs and was craning her neck over the banisters.

—Now, I ask you, she said, almost testily, where is Julia going? Julia! Julia! Where are you going?

2. Porridge made by stirring oatmeal in boiling milk or water.
3. Originally the name of a troupe of entertainers imitating African Americans, founded by George Christy of New York. By Joyce's time the meaning had become extended to any group with blackened faces who sang what were known as Negro melodies to banjo accompaniment, interspersed with jokes.
4. The Gresham Hotel, still one of the best hotels in Dublin.

Julia, who had gone halfway down one flight, came back and announced blandly:

—Here's Freddy.

At the same moment a clapping of hands and a final flourish of the pianist told that the waltz had ended. The drawing-room door was opened from within and some couples came out. Aunt Kate drew Gabriel aside hurriedly and whispered into his ear:

—Slip down, Gabriel, like a good fellow and see if he's all right, and don't let him up if he's screwed. I'm sure he's screwed. I'm sure he is.

Gabriel went to the stairs and listened over the banisters. He could hear two persons talking in the pantry. Then he recognised Freddy Malins' laugh. He went down the stairs noisily.

—It's such a relief, said Aunt Kate to Mrs Conroy, that Gabriel is here. I always feel easier in my mind when he's here. . . . Julia, there's Miss Daly and Miss Power will take some refreshment. Thanks for your beautiful waltz, Miss Daly. It made lovely time.

A tall wizen-faced man, with a stiff grizzled moustache and swarthy skin, who was passing out with his partner said:

—And may we have some refreshment, too, Miss Morkan?

—Julia, said Aunt Kate summarily, and here's Mr Browne and Miss Furlong. Take them in, Julia, with Miss Daly and Miss Power.

—I'm the man for the ladies, said Mr Browne, pursing his lips until his moustache bristled and smiling in all his wrinkles. You know, Miss Morkan, the reason they are so fond of me is—

He did not finish his sentence, but, seeing that Aunt Kate was out of earshot, at once led the three young ladies into the back room. The middle of the room was occupied by two square tables placed end to end, and on these Aunt Julia and the caretaker were straightening and smoothing a large cloth. On the sideboard were arrayed dishes and plates, and glasses and bundles of knives and forks and spoons. The top of the closed square piano served also as a sideboard for viands and sweets. At a smaller sideboard in one corner two young men were standing, drinking hop-bitters.

Mr Browne led his charges thither and invited them all, in jest, to some ladies' punch, hot, strong and sweet. As they said they never took anything strong he opened three bottles of lemonade for them. Then he asked one of the young men to move aside, and, taking hold of the decanter, filled out for himself a goodly measure of whisky. The young men eyed him respectfully while he took a trial sip.

—God help me, he said, smiling, it's the doctor's orders.

His wizened face broke into a broader smile, and the three young ladies laughed in musical echo to his pleasantry, swaying their bodies to and fro, with nervous jerks of their shoulders. The boldest said:

—O, now, Mr Browne, I'm sure the doctor never ordered anything of the kind.

Mr Browne took another sip of his whisky and said, with sidling mimicry:

—Well, you see, I'm like the famous Mrs Cassidy, who is reported to have said: *Now, Mary Grimes, if I don't take it, make me take it, for I feel I want it.*

His hot face had leaned forward a little too confidentially and he had assumed a very low Dublin accent so that the young ladies, with one instinct, received his speech in silence. Miss Furlong, who was one of Mary Jane's pupils, asked Miss Daly what was the name of the pretty waltz she had played;

and Mr Browne, seeing that he was ignored, turned promptly to the two young men who were more appreciative.

A red-faced young woman, dressed in pansy, came into the room, excitedly clapping her hands and crying:

—Quadrilles![5] Quadrilles!

Close on her heels came Aunt Kate, crying:

—Two gentlemen and three ladies, Mary Jane!

—O, here's Mr Bergin and Mr Kerrigan, said Mary Jane. Mr Kerrigan, will you take Miss Power? Miss Furlong, may I get you a partner, Mr Bergin. O, that'll just do now.

—Three ladies, Mary Jane, said Aunt Kate.

The two young gentlemen asked the ladies if they might have the pleasure, and Mary Jane turned to Miss Daly.

—O, Miss Daly, you're really awfully good, after playing for the last two dances, but really we're so short of ladies to-night.

—I don't mind in the least, Miss Morkan.

—But I've a nice partner for you, Mr Bartell D'Arcy, the tenor. I'll get him to sing later on. All Dublin is raving about him.

—Lovely voice, lovely voice! said Aunt Kate.

As the piano had twice begun the prelude to the first figure Mary Jane led her recruits quickly from the room. They had hardly gone when Aunt Julia wandered slowly into the room, looking behind her at something.

—What is the matter, Julia? asked Aunt Kate anxiously. Who is it?

Julia, who was carrying in a column of table-napkins, turned to her sister and said, simply, as if the question had surprised her:

—It's only Freddy, Kate, and Gabriel with him.

In fact right behind her Gabriel could be seen piloting Freddy Malins across the landing. The latter, a young man of about forty, was of Gabriel's size and build, with very round shoulders. His face was fleshy and pallid, touched with colour only at the thick hanging lobes of his ears and at the wide wings of his nose. He had coarse features, a blunt nose, a convex and receding brow, tumid and protruded lips. His heavy-lidded eyes and the disorder of his scanty hair made him look sleepy. He was laughing heartily in a high key at a story which he had been telling Gabriel on the stairs and at the same time rubbing the knuckles of his left fist backwards and forwards into his left eye.

—Good-evening, Freddy, said Aunt Julia.

Freddy Malins bade the Misses Morkan good-evening in what seemed an offhand fashion by reason of the habitual catch in his voice and then, seeing that Mr Browne was grinning at him from the sideboard, crossed the room on rather shaky legs and began to repeat in an undertone the story he had just told to Gabriel.

—He's not so bad, is he? said Aunt Kate to Gabriel.

Gabriel's brows were dark but he raised them quickly and answered:

—O no, hardly noticeable.

—Now, isn't he a terrible fellow! she said. And his poor mother made him take the pledge[6] on New Year's Eve. But come on, Gabriel, into the drawing-room.

Before leaving the room with Gabriel she signalled to Mr Browne by frown-

---

5. A square dance usually performed by four couples.

6. Sign a solemn promise not to drink alcohol.

ing and shaking her forefinger in warning to and fro. Mr Browne nodded in answer and, when she had gone, said to Freddy Malins:

—Now, then, Teddy, I'm going to fill you out a good glass of lemonade just to buck you up.

Freddy Malins, who was nearing the climax of his story, waved the offer aside impatiently but Mr Browne, having first called Freddy Malins' attention to a disarray in his dress, filled out and handed him a full glass of lemonade. Freddy Malins' left hand accepted the glass mechanically, his right hand being engaged in the mechanical readjustment of his dress. Mr Browne, whose face was once more wrinkling with mirth, poured out for himself a glass of whisky while Freddy Malins exploded, before he had well reached the climax of his story, in a kink of high-pitched bronchitic laughter and, setting down his untasted and overflowing glass, began to rub the knuckles of his left fist backwards and forwards into his left eye, repeating words of his last phrase as well as his fit of laughter would allow him.

Gabriel could not listen while Mary Jane was playing her Academy piece, full of runs and difficult passages, to the hushed drawing-room. He liked music but the piece she was playing had no melody for him and he doubted whether it had any melody for the other listeners, though they had begged Mary Jane to play something. Four young men, who had come from the refreshment-room to stand in the door-way at the sound of the piano, had gone away quietly in couples after a few minutes. The only persons who seemed to follow the music were Mary Jane herself, her hands racing along the key-board or lifted from it at the pauses like those of a priestess in momentary imprecation, and Aunt Kate standing at her elbow to turn the page.

Gabriel's eyes, irritated by the floor, which glittered with beeswax under the heavy chandelier, wandered to the wall above the piano. A picture of the balcony scene in *Romeo and Juliet* hung there and beside it was a picture of the two murdered princes in the Tower[7] which Aunt Julia had worked in red, blue and brown wools when she was a girl. Probably in the school they had gone to as girls that kind of work had been taught, for one year his mother had worked for him as a birthday present a waistcoat of purple tabinet,[8] with little foxes' heads upon it, lined with brown satin and having round mulberry buttons. It was strange that his mother had had no musical talent though Aunt Kate used to call her the brains carrier of the Morkan family. Both she and Julia had always seemed a little proud of their serious and matronly sister. Her photograph stood before the pierglass.[9] She held an open book on her knees and was pointing out something in it to Constantine who, dressed in a man-o'-war suit,[1] lay at her feet. It was she who had chosen the names for her sons for she was very sensible of the dignity of family life. Thanks to her, Constantine was now senior curate[2] in Balbriggan and, thanks to her, Gabriel himself had taken his degree in the Royal University. A shadow passed over his face as he remembered her sullen opposition to his marriage. Some slighting phrases she had used still rankled in his memory; she had once spoken of Gretta as being country cute and that was not true of Gretta at all. It was

7. Probably Edward V and his brother Richard, duke of York, reputedly murdered in 1483 by their uncle and successor, Richard III.
8. Silk and wool fabric made chiefly in Ireland.
9. Large tall mirror.
1. Sailor suit, favorite wear for children of both sexes early in the 20th century.
2. Clergyman appointed to assist a parish priest.

Gretta who had nursed her during all her last long illness in their house at Monkstown.

He knew that Mary Jane must be near the end of her piece for she was playing again the opening melody with runs of scales after every bar and while he waited for the end the resentment died down in his heart. The piece ended with a trill of octaves in the treble and a final deep octave in the bass. Great applause greeted Mary Jane as, blushing and rolling up her music nervously, she escaped from the room. The most vigorous clapping came from the four young men in the doorway who had gone away to the refreshment-room at the beginning of the piece but had come back when the piano had stopped.

Lancers[3] were arranged. Gabriel found himself partnered with Miss Ivors. She was a frank-mannered talkative young lady, with a freckled face and prominent brown eyes. She did not wear a low-cut bodice and the large brooch which was fixed in the front of her collar bore on it an Irish device.

When they had taken their places she said abruptly:

—I have a crow to pluck with you.

—With me? said Gabriel.

She nodded her head gravely.

—What is it? asked Gabriel, smiling at her solemn manner.

—Who is G. C.? answered Miss Ivors, turning her eyes upon him.

Gabriel coloured and was about to knit his brows, as if he did not understand, when she said bluntly:

—O, innocent Amy! I have found out that you write for *The Daily Express*. Now, aren't you ashamed of yourself?

—Why should I be ashamed of myself? asked Gabriel, blinking his eyes and trying to smile.

—Well, I'm ashamed of you, said Miss Ivors frankly. To say you'd write for a rag like that. I didn't think you were a West Briton.[4]

A look of perplexity appeared on Gabriel's face. It was true that he wrote a literary column every Wednesday in *The Daily Express*, for which he was paid fifteen shillings. But that did not make him a West Briton surely. The books he received for review were almost more welcome than the paltry cheque. He loved to feel the covers and turn over the pages of newly printed books. Nearly every day when his teaching in the college was ended he used to wander down the quays to the second-hand booksellers, to Hickey's on Bachelor's Walk, to Webb's, or Massey's on Aston's Quay, or to O'Clohissey's in the by-street. He did not know how to meet her charge. He wanted to say that literature was above politics. But they were friends of many years' standing and their careers had been parallel, first at the University and then as teachers: he could not risk a grandiose phrase with her. He continued blinking his eyes and trying to smile and murmured lamely that he saw nothing political in writing reviews of books.

When their turn to cross had come he was still perplexed and inattentive. Miss Ivors promptly took his hand in a warm grasp and said in a soft friendly tone:

—Of course, I was only joking. Come, we cross now.

When they were together again she spoke of the University question[5] and

3. A square dance for four or more couples.
4. A pejorative term for one who denies a separate Irish nationality and sees Ireland as simply a west-ern extension of Great Britain.
5. Namely, whether Ireland's elite Protestant universities should be open to Catholics.

Gabriel felt more at ease. A friend of hers had shown her his review of Browning's poems. That was how she had found out the secret: but she liked the review immensely. Then she said suddenly:

—O, Mr Conroy, will you come for an excursion to the Aran Isles[6] this summer? We're going to stay there a whole month. It will be splendid out in the Atlantic. You ought to come. Mr Clancy is coming, and Mr Kilkelly and Kathleen Kearney. It would be splendid for Gretta too if she'd come. She's from Connacht,[7] isn't she?

—Her people are, said Gabriel shortly.

—But you will come, won't you? said Miss Ivors, laying her warm hand eagerly on his arm.

—The fact is, said Gabriel, I have already arranged to go—

—Go where? asked Miss Ivors.

—Well, you know, every year I go for a cycling tour with some fellows and so—

—But where? asked Miss Ivors.

—Well, we usually go to France or Belgium or perhaps Germany, said Gabriel awkwardly.

—And why do you go to France and Belgium, said Miss Ivors, instead of visiting your own land?

—Well, said Gabriel, it's partly to keep in touch with the languages and partly for a change.

—And haven't you your own language to keep in touch with—Irish? asked Miss Ivors.

—Well, said Gabriel, if it comes to that, you know, Irish is not my language.

Their neighbours had turned to listen to the cross-examination. Gabriel glanced right and left nervously and tried to keep his good humour under the ordeal which was making a blush invade his forehead.

—And haven't you your own land to visit, continued Miss Ivors, that you know nothing of, your own people, and your own country?

—O, to tell you the truth, retorted Gabriel suddenly, I'm sick of my own country, sick of it!

—Why? asked Miss Ivors.

Gabriel did not answer for his retort had heated him.

—Why? repeated Miss Ivors.

They had to go visiting together and, as he had not answered her, Miss Ivors said warmly:

—Of course, you've no answer.

Gabriel tried to cover his agitation by taking part in the dance with great energy. He avoided her eyes for he had seen a sour expression on her face. But when they met in the long chain he was surprised to feel his hand firmly pressed. She looked at him from under her brows for a moment quizzically[8] until he smiled. Then, just as the chain was about to start again, she stood on tiptoe and whispered into his ear:

—West Briton!

When the lancers were over Gabriel went away to a remote corner of the room where Freddy Malins' mother was sitting. She was a stout feeble old woman with white hair. Her voice had a catch in it like her son's and she

---

6. Three small islands lying across the entrance to Galway Bay, on the west coast of Ireland.
7. Or Connaught, a rural region on the west coast of Ireland.
8. Teasingly.

stuttered slightly. She had been told that Freddy had come and that he was nearly all right. Gabriel asked her whether she had had a good crossing. She lived with her married daughter in Glasgow and came to Dublin on a visit once a year. She answered placidly that she had had a beautiful crossing and that the captain had been most attentive to her. She spoke also of the beautiful house her daughter kept in Glasgow, and of all the nice friends they had there. While her tongue rambled on Gabriel tried to banish from his mind all memory of the unpleasant incident with Miss Ivors. Of course the girl or woman, or whatever she was, was an enthusiast but there was a time for all things. Perhaps he ought not to have answered her like that. But she had no right to call him a West Briton before people, even in joke. She had tried to make him ridiculous before people, heckling him and staring at him with her rabbit's eyes.

He saw his wife making her way towards him through the waltzing couples. When she reached him she said into his ear:

—Gabriel, Aunt Kate wants to know won't you carve the goose as usual. Miss Daly will carve the ham and I'll do the pudding.

—All right, said Gabriel.

—She's sending in the younger ones first as soon as this waltz is over so that we'll have the table to ourselves.

—Were you dancing? asked Gabriel.

—Of course I was. Didn't you see me? What words had you with Molly Ivors?

—No words. Why? Did she say so?

—Something like that. I'm trying to get that Mr D'Arcy to sing. He's full of conceit, I think.

—There were no words, said Gabriel moodily, only she wanted me to go for a trip to the west of Ireland and I said I wouldn't.

His wife clasped her hands excitedly and gave a little jump.

—O, do go, Gabriel, she cried. I'd love to see Galway again.

—You can go if you like, said Gabriel coldly.

She looked at him for a moment, then turned to Mrs Malins and said:

—There's a nice husband for you, Mrs Malins.

While she was threading her way back across the room Mrs Malins, without adverting to the interruption, went on to tell Gabriel what beautiful places there were in Scotland and beautiful scenery. Her son-in-law brought them every year to the lakes and they used to go fishing. Her son-in-law was a splendid fisher. One day he caught a fish, a beautiful big big fish, and the man in the hotel boiled it for their dinner.

Gabriel hardly heard what she said. Now that supper was coming near he began to think again about his speech and about the quotation. When he saw Freddy Malins coming across the room to visit his mother Gabriel left the chair free for him and retired into the embrasure[9] of the window. The room had already cleared and from the back room came the clatter of plates and knives. Those who still remained in the drawing-room seemed tired of dancing and were conversing quietly in little groups. Gabriel's warm trembling fingers tapped the cold pane of the window. How cool it must be outside! How pleasant it would be to walk out alone, first along by the river and then through the park! The snow would be lying on the branches of the trees and forming a

9. Opening for a window in a thick wall.

bright cap on the top of the Wellington Monument.[1] How much more pleasant it would be there than at the supper-table!

He ran over the headings of his speech: Irish hospitality, sad memories, the Three Graces, Paris,[2] the quotation from Browning. He repeated to himself a phrase he had written in his review: *One feels that one is listening to a thought-tormented music.* Miss Ivors had praised the review. Was she sincere? Had she really any life of her own behind all her propagandism? There had never been any ill-feeling between them until that night. It unnerved him to think that she would be at the supper-table, looking up at him while he spoke with her critical quizzing eyes. Perhaps she would not be sorry to see him fail in his speech. An idea came into his mind and gave him courage. He would say, alluding to Aunt Kate and Aunt Julia: *Ladies and Gentlemen, the generation which is now on the wane among us may have had its faults but for my part I think it had certain qualities of hospitality, of humour, of humanity, which the new and very serious and hypereducated generation that is growing up around us seems to me to lack.* Very good: that was one for Miss Ivors. What did he care that his aunts were only two ignorant old women?

A murmur in the room attracted his attention. Mr Browne was advancing from the door, gallantly escorting Aunt Julia, who leaned upon his arm, smiling and hanging her head. An irregular musketry of applause escorted her also as far as the piano and then, as Mary Jane seated herself on the stool, and Aunt Julia, no longer smiling, half turned so as to pitch her voice fairly into the room, gradually ceased. Gabriel recognised the prelude. It was that of an old song of Aunt Julia's—*Arrayed for the Bridal.*[3] Her voice, strong and clear in tone, attacked with great spirit the runs which embellish the air and though she sang very rapidly she did not miss even the smallest of the grace notes. To follow the voice, without looking at the singer's face, was to feel and share the excitement of swift and secure flight. Gabriel applauded loudly with all the others at the close of the song and loud applause was borne in from the invisible supper-table. It sounded so genuine that a little colour struggled into Aunt Julia's face as she bent to replace in the music-stand the old leather-bound song-book that had her initials on the cover. Freddy Malins, who had listened with his head perched sideways to hear her better, was still applauding when everyone else had ceased and talking animatedly to his mother who nodded her head gravely and slowly in acquiescence. At last, when he could clap no more, he stood up suddenly and hurried across the room to Aunt Julia whose hand he seized and held in both his hands, shaking it when words failed him or the catch in his voice proved too much for him.

—I was just telling my mother, he said, I never heard you sing so well, never. No, I never heard your voice so good as it is to-night. Now! Would you believe that now? That's the truth. Upon my word and honour that's the truth. I never heard your voice sound so fresh and so . . . so clear and fresh, never.

Aunt Julia smiled broadly and murmured something about compliments as

1. Tribute to Arthur Wellesley (1769–1852), 1st duke of Wellington, Dublin-born hero of the British army. The obelisk stands in Dublin's Phoenix Park.

2. In Greek mythology Paris was selected by Zeus to choose which of three goddesses was the most beautiful. The Graces were three sister-goddesses—Aglaia, splendor; Euphrosyne, festivity; and Thalia, rejoicing—who together represented loveliness

and joy. Gabriel is making a mental note to refer to his two aunts and Mary Jane in a complimentary way.

3. This old song (beginning "Arrayed for the bridal, in beauty behold her") "is replete with long and complicated runs, requiring a sophisticated and gifted singer" (Bowen, *Musical Allusions in the Works of James Joyce*, 1974); the suggestion is that Aunt Julia was a really accomplished singer.

she released her hand from his grasp. Mr Browne extended his open hand
towards her and said to those who were near him in the manner of a showman
introducing a prodigy to an audience:

—Miss Julia Morkan, my latest discovery!

He was laughing very heartily at this himself when Freddy Malins turned
to him and said:

—Well, Browne, if you're serious you might make a worse discovery. All I
can say is I never heard her sing half so well as long as I am coming here. And
that's the honest truth.

—Neither did I, said Mr Browne. I think her voice has greatly improved.

Aunt Julia shrugged her shoulders and said with meek pride:

—Thirty years ago I hadn't a bad voice as voices go.

—I often told Julia, said Aunt Kate emphatically, that she was simply thrown
away in that choir. But she never would be said by me.

She turned as if to appeal to the good sense of the others against a refractory
child while Aunt Julia gazed in front of her, a vague smile of reminiscence
playing on her face.

—No, continued Aunt Kate, she wouldn't be said or led by anyone, slaving
there in that choir night and day, night and day. Six o'clock on Christmas
morning! And all for what?

—Well, isn't it for the honour of God, Aunt Kate? asked Mary Jane, twisting
round on the piano-stool and smiling.

Aunt Kate turned fiercely on her niece and said:

—I know all about the honour of God, Mary Jane, but I think it's not at all
honourable for the pope to turn out the women out of the choirs that have
slaved there all their lives and put little whipper-snappers of boys over their
heads. I suppose it is for the good of the Church if the pope does it. But it's
not just, Mary Jane, and it's not right.

She had worked herself into a passion and would have continued in defence
of her sister for it was a sore subject with her but Mary Jane, seeing that all
the dancers had come back, intervened pacifically:

—Now, Aunt Kate, you're giving scandal to Mr Browne who is of the other
persuasion.[4]

Aunt Kate turned to Mr Browne, who was grinning at this allusion to his
religion, and said hastily:

—O, I don't question the pope's being right. I'm only a stupid old woman
and I wouldn't presume to do such a thing. But there's such a thing as common
everyday politeness and gratitude. And if I were in Julia's place I'd tell that
Father Healy straight up to his face . . .

—And besides, Aunt Kate, said Mary Jane, we really are all hungry and
when we are hungry we are all very quarrelsome.

—And when we are thirsty we are also quarrelsome, added Mr Browne.

—So that we had better go to supper, said Mary Jane, and finish the discussion afterwards.

On the landing outside the drawing-room Gabriel found his wife and Mary
Jane trying to persuade Miss Ivors to stay for supper. But Miss Ivors, who had
put on her hat and was buttoning her cloak, would not stay. She did not feel
in the least hungry and she had already overstayed her time.

—But only for ten minutes, Molly, said Mrs Conroy. That won't delay you.

---

4. I.e., Protestant.

—To take a pick itself, said Mary Jane, after all your dancing.

—I really couldn't, said Miss Ivors.

—I am afraid you didn't enjoy yourself at all, said Mary Jane hopelessly.

—Ever so much, I assure you, said Miss Ivors, but you really must let me run off now.

—But how can you get home? asked Mrs Conroy.

—O, it's only two steps up the quay.

Gabriel hesitated a moment and said:

—If you will allow me, Miss Ivors, I'll see you home if you really are obliged to go.

But Miss Ivors broke away from them.

—I won't hear of it, she cried. For goodness sake go in to your suppers and don't mind me. I'm quite well able to take care of myself.

—Well, you're the comical girl, Molly, said Mrs Conroy frankly.

—*Beannacht libh*,[5] cried Miss Ivors, with a laugh, as she ran down the staircase.

Mary Jane gazed after her, a moody puzzled expression on her face, while Mrs Conroy leaned over the banisters to listen for the hall-door. Gabriel asked himself was he the cause of her abrupt departure. But she did not seem to be in ill humour: she had gone away laughing. He stared blankly down the staircase.

At that moment Aunt Kate came toddling out of the supper-room, almost wringing her hands in despair.

—Where is Gabriel? she cried. Where on earth is Gabriel? There's everyone waiting in there, stage to let, and nobody to carve the goose!

—Here I am, Aunt Kate! cried Gabriel, with sudden animation, ready to carve a flock of geese, if necessary.

A fat brown goose lay at one end of the table and at the other end, on a bed of creased paper strewn with sprigs of parsley, lay a great ham, stripped of its outer skin and peppered over with crust crumbs, a neat paper frill round its shin and beside this was a round of spiced beef. Between these rival ends ran parallel lines of side-dishes: two little minsters of jelly, red and yellow; a shallow dish full of blocks of blancmange[6] and red jam, a large green leaf-shaped dish with a stalk-shaped handle, on which lay bunches of purple raisins and peeled almonds, a companion dish on which lay a solid rectangle of Smyrna figs, a dish of custard topped with grated nutmeg, a small bowl full of chocolates and sweets wrapped in gold and silver papers and a glass vase in which stood some tall celery stalks. In the centre of the table there stood, as sentries to a fruit-stand which upheld a pyramid of oranges and American apples, two squat old-fashioned decanters of cut glass, one containing port and the other dark sherry. On the closed square piano a pudding in a huge yellow dish lay in waiting and behind it were three squads of bottles of stout and ale and minerals, drawn up according to the colours of their uniforms, the first two black, with brown and red labels, the third and smallest squad white, with transverse green sashes.

Gabriel took his seat boldly at the head of the table and, having looked to the edge of the carver, plunged his fork firmly into the goose. He felt quite at ease now for he was an expert carver and liked nothing better than to find himself at the head of a well-laden table.

5. Blessing on you (Gaelic; literal trans.); good-bye. 6. Sweet almond-flavored pudding.

—Miss Furlong, what shall I send you? he asked. A wing or a slice of the breast?

—Just a small slice of the breast.

—Miss Higgins, what for you?

—O, anything at all, Mr Conroy.

While Gabriel and Miss Daly exchanged plates of goose and plates of ham and spiced beef Lily went from guest to guest with a dish of hot floury potatoes wrapped in a white napkin. This was Mary Jane's idea and she had also suggested apple sauce for the goose but Aunt Kate had said that plain roast goose without apple sauce had always been good enough for her and she hoped she might never eat worse. Mary Jane waited on her pupils and saw that they got the best slices and Aunt Kate and Aunt Julia opened and carried across from the piano bottles of stout and ale for the gentlemen and bottles of minerals for the ladies. There was a great deal of confusion and laughter and noise, the noise of orders and counter-orders, of knives and forks, of corks and glass-stoppers. Gabriel began to carve second helpings as soon as he had finished the first round without serving himself. Everyone protested loudly so that he compromised by taking a long draught of stout for he had found the carving hot work. Mary Jane settled down quietly to her supper but Aunt Kate and Aunt Julia were still toddling round the table, walking on each other's heels, getting in each other's way and giving each other unheeded orders. Mr Browne begged of them to sit down and eat their suppers and so did Gabriel but they said there was time enough so that, at last, Freddy Malins stood up and, capturing Aunt Kate, plumped her down on her chair amid general laughter.

When everyone had been well served Gabriel said, smiling:

—Now, if anyone wants a little more of what vulgar people call stuffing let him or her speak.

A chorus of voices invited him to begin his own supper and Lily came forward with three potatoes which she had reserved for him.

—Very well, said Gabriel amiably, as he took another preparatory draught, kindly forget my existence, ladies and gentlemen, for a few minutes.

He set to his supper and took no part in the conversation with which the table covered Lily's removal of the plates. The subject of talk was the opera company which was then at the Theatre Royal. Mr Bartell D'Arcy, the tenor, a dark-complexioned young man with a smart moustache, praised very highly the leading contralto of the company but Miss Furlong thought she had a rather vulgar style of production. Freddy Malins said there was a negro chieftain singing in the second part of the Gaiety pantomime who had one of the finest tenor voices he had every heard.

—Have you heard him? he asked Mr Bartell D'Arcy across the table.

—No, answered Mr Bartell D'Arcy carelessly.

—Because, Freddy Malins explained, now I'd be curious to hear your opinion of him. I think he has a grand voice.

—It takes Teddy to find out the really good things, said Mr Browne familiarly to the table.

—And why couldn't he have a voice too? asked Freddy Malins sharply. Is it because he's only a black?

Nobody answered this question and Mary Jane led the table back to the legitimate opera. One of her pupils had given her a pass for *Mignon*.[7] Of course it was very fine, she said, but it made her think of poor Georgina Burns. Mr

7. Opera by Ambroise Thomas first produced in Paris in 1866 and in London in 1870.

Browne could go back farther still, to the old Italian companies that used to come to Dublin—Tietjens, Ilma de Murzka, Campanini, the great Trebelli, Giuglini, Ravelli, Aramburo. Those were the days, he said, when there was something like singing to be heard in Dublin. He told too of how the top gallery of the old Royal used to be packed night after night, of how one night an Italian tenor had sung five encores to *Let Me Like a Soldier Fall,*[8] introducing a high C every time, and of how the gallery boys would sometimes in their enthusiasm unyoke the horses from the carriage of some great *prima donna* and pull her themselves through the streets to her hotel. Why did they never play the grand old operas now, he asked, *Dinorah, Lucrezia Borgia?*[9] Because they could not get the voices to sing them: that was why.

—O, well, said Mr Bartell D'Arcy, I presume there are as good singers to-day as there were then.

—Where are they? asked Mr Browne defiantly.

—In London, Paris, Milan, said Mr Bartell d'Arcy warmly. I suppose Caruso,[1] for example, is quite as good, if not better than any of the men you have mentioned.

—Maybe so, said Mr Browne. But I may tell you I doubt it strongly.

—O, I'd give anything to hear Caruso sing, said Mary Jane.

—For me, said Aunt Kate, who had been picking a bone, there was only one tenor. To please me, I mean. But I suppose none of you ever heard of him.

—Who was he, Miss Morkan? asked Mr Bartell D'Arcy politely.

—His name, said Aunt Kate, was Parkinson. I heard him when he was in his prime and I think he had then the purest tenor voice that was ever put into a man's throat.

—Strange, said Mr Bartell d'Arcy. I never even heard of him.

—Yes, yes, Miss Morkan is right, said Mr Browne. I remember hearing of old Parkinson but he's too far back for me.

—A beautiful pure sweet mellow English tenor, said Aunt Kate with enthusiasm.

Gabriel having finished, the huge pudding was transferred to the table. The clatter of forks and spoons began again. Gabriel's wife served out spoonfuls of the pudding and passed the plates down the table. Midway down they were held up by Mary Jane, who replenished them with raspberry or orange jelly or with blancmange and jam. The pudding was of Aunt Julia's making and she received praises for it from all quarters. She herself said that it was not quite brown enough.

—Well, I hope, Miss Morkan, said Mr Browne, that I'm brown enough for you because, you know, I'm all brown.

All the gentlemen, except Gabriel, ate some of the pudding out of compliment to Aunt Julia. As Gabriel never ate sweets the celery had been left for him. Freddy Malins also took a stalk of celery and ate it with his pudding. He had been told that celery was a capital thing for the blood and he was just then under doctor's care. Mrs Malins, who had been silent all through the

8. This song, from the opera *Maritana* by W. Wallace (it actually begins "Yes! let me like a soldier fall"), ends on middle C; it would be a piece of exhibitionism to end on a high C, as Joyce's father, who had a good voice, used to do. Joyce's brother Stanislaus remembered the song as insufferable rubbish. Mr. Browne is not to be taken seriously as a music critic.
9. An opera by Donizetti, first produced at La Scala, Milan, in 1833. *Dinorah* is an opera by Meyerbeer, first produced in Paris in 1859.
1. Enrico Caruso (1873–1921), the great Italian dramatic tenor.

supper, said that her son was going down to Mount Melleray in a week or so. The table then spoke of Mount Melleray, how bracing the air was down there, how hospitable the monks were and how they never asked for a penny-piece from their guests.

—And do you mean to say, asked Mr Browne incredulously, that a chap can go down there and put up there as if it were a hotel and live on the fat of the land and then come away without paying a farthing?

—O, most people give some donation to the monastery when they leave, said Mary Jane.

—I wish we had an institution like that in our Church, said Mr Browne candidly.

He was astonished to hear that the monks never spoke, got up at two in the morning and slept in their coffins. He asked what they did it for.

—That's the rule of the order, said Aunt Kate firmly.

—Yes, but why? asked Mr Browne.

Aunt Kate repeated that it was the rule, that was all. Mr Browne still seemed not to understand. Freddy Malins explained to him, as best he could, that the monks were trying to make up for the sins committed by all the sinners in the outside world. The explanation was not very clear for Mr Browne grinned and said:

—I like that idea very much but wouldn't a comfortable spring bed do them as well as a coffin?

—The coffin, said Mary Jane, is to remind them of their last end.

As the subject had grown lugubrious it was buried in a silence of the table during which Mrs Malins could be heard saying to her neighbour in an indistinct undertone:

—They are very good men, the monks, very pious men.

The raisins and almonds and figs and apples and oranges and chocolates and sweets were now passed about the table and Aunt Julia invited all the guests to have either port or sherry. At first Mr Bartell D'Arcy refused to take either but one of his neighbours nudged him and whispered something to him upon which he allowed his glass to be filled. Gradually as the last glasses were being filled the conversation ceased. A pause followed, broken only by the noise of the wine and by unsettlings of chairs. The Misses Morkan, all three, looked down at the tablecloth. Someone coughed once or twice and then a few gentlemen patted the table gently as a signal for silence. The silence came and Gabriel pushed back his chair and stood up.

The patting at once grew louder in encouragement and then ceased altogether. Gabriel leaned his ten trembling fingers on the tablecloth and smiled nervously at the company. Meeting a row of upturned faces he raised his eyes to the chandelier. The piano was playing a waltz tune and he could hear the skirts sweeping against the drawing-room door. People, perhaps, were standing in the snow on the quay outside, gazing up at the lighted windows and listening to the waltz music. The air was pure there. In the distance lay the park where the trees were weighted with snow. The Wellington Monument wore a gleaming cap of snow that flashed westward over the white field of Fifteen Acres.

He began:

—Ladies and Gentlemen.

—It has fallen to my lot this evening, as in years past, to perform a very pleasing task but a task for which I am afraid my poor powers as a speaker are all too inadequate.

—No, no! said Mr Browne.

—But, however that may be, I can only ask you to-night to take the will for the deed and to lend me your attention for a few moments while I endeavour to express to you in words what my feelings are on this occasion.

—Ladies and Gentlemen. It is not the first time that we have gathered together under this hospitable roof, around this hospitable board. It is not the first time that we have been the recipients—or perhaps, I had better say, the victims—of the hospitality of certain good ladies.

He made a circle in the air with his arm and paused. Everyone laughed or smiled at Aunt Kate and Aunt Julia and Mary Jane who all turned crimson with pleasure. Gabriel went on more boldly:

—I feel more strongly with every recurring year that our country has no tradition which does it so much honour and which it should guard so jealously as that of its hospitality. It is a tradition that is unique as far as my experience goes (and I have visited not a few places abroad) among the modern nations. Some would say, perhaps, that with us it is rather a failing than anything to be boasted of. But granted even that, it is, to my mind, a princely failing, and one that I trust will long be cultivated among us. Of one thing, at least, I am sure. As long as this one roof shelters the good ladies aforesaid—and I wish from my heart it may do so for many and many a long year to come—the tradition of genuine warm-hearted courteous Irish hospitality, which our fore-fathers have handed down to us and which we in turn must hand down to our descendants, is still alive among us.

A hearty murmur of assent ran round the table. It shot through Gabriel's mind that Miss Ivors was not there and that she had gone away discourteously: and he said with confidence in himself:

—Ladies and Gentlemen.

—A new generation is growing up in our midst, a generation actuated by new ideas and new principles. It is serious and enthusiastic for these new ideas and its enthusiasm, even when it is misdirected, is, I believe, in the main sincere. But we are living in a sceptical and, if I may use the phrase, a thought-tormented age: and sometimes I fear that this new generation, educated or hypereducated as it is, will lack those qualities of humanity, of hospitality, of kindly humour which belonged to an older day. Listening to-night to the names of all those great singers of the past it seemed to me, I must confess, that we were living in a less spacious age. Those days might, without exaggeration, be called spacious days: and if they are gone beyond recall let us hope, at least, that in gatherings such as this we shall still speak of them with pride and affection, still cherish in our hearts the memory of those dead and gone great ones whose fame the world will not willingly let die.

—Hear, hear! said Mr Browne loudly.

—But yet, continued Gabriel, his voice falling into a softer inflection, there are always in gatherings such as this sadder thoughts that will recur to our minds: thoughts of the past, of youth, of changes, of absent faces that we miss here to-night. Our path through life is strewn with many such sad memories: and were we to brood upon them always we could not find the heart to go on bravely with our work among the living. We have all of us living duties and living affections which claim, and rightly claim, our strenuous endeavours.

—Therefore, I will not linger on the past. I will not let any gloomy moralising intrude upon us here to-night. Here we are gathered together for a brief moment from the bustle and rush of our everyday routine. We are met here as friends, in the spirit of good-fellowship, as colleagues, also to a certain extent, in the true spirit of *camaraderie*, and as the guests of—what shall I call them?—the Three Graces of the Dublin musical world.

The table burst into applause and laughter at this sally. Aunt Julia vainly asked each of her neighbours in turn to tell her what Gabriel had said.

—He says we are the Three Graces,[2] Aunt Julia, said Mary Jane.

Aunt Julia did not understand but she looked up, smiling, at Gabriel, who continued in the same vein:

—Ladies and Gentlemen.

—I will not attempt to play to-night the part that Paris played on another occasion. I will not attempt to choose between them. The task would be an invidious one and one beyond my poor powers. For when I view them in turn, whether it be our chief hostess herself, whose good heart, whose too good heart, has become a byword with all who know her, or her sister, who seems to be gifted with perennial youth and whose singing must have been a surprise and a revelation to us all to-night, or, last but not least, when I consider our youngest hostess, talented, cheerful, hard-working and the best of nieces, I confess, Ladies and Gentlemen, that I do not know to which of them I should award the prize.

Gabriel glanced down at his aunts and, seeing the large smile on Aunt Julia's face and the tears which had risen to Aunt Kate's eyes, hastened to his close. He raised his glass of port gallantly, while every member of the company fingered a glass expectantly, and said loudly:

—Let us toast them all three together. Let us drink to their health, wealth, long life, happiness and prosperity and may they long continue to hold the proud and self-won position which they hold in their profession and the position of honour and affection which they hold in our hearts.

All the guests stood up, glass in hand, and, turning towards the three seated ladies, sang in unison, with Mr Browne as leader:

> *For they are jolly gay fellows,*
> *For they are jolly gay fellows,*
> *For they are jolly gay fellows,*
> *Which nobody can deny.*

Aunt Kate was making frank use of her handkerchief and even Aunt Julia seemed moved. Freddy Malins beat time with his pudding-fork and the singers turned towards one another, as if in melodious conference, while they sang, with emphasis:

> *Unless he tells a lie,*
> *Unless he tells a lie.*

Then, turning once more towards their hostesses, they sang:

> *For they are jolly gay fellows,*
> *For they are jolly gay fellows,*
> *For they are jolly gay fellows,*
> *Which nobody can deny.*

The acclamation which followed was taken up beyond the door of the supper-room by many of the other guests and renewed time after time, Freddy Malins acting as officer with his fork on high.

2. See n. 2, p. 2182.

The piercing morning air came into the hall where they were standing so that Aunt Kate said:

—Close the door, somebody. Mrs Malins will get her death of cold.

—Browne is out there, Aunt Kate, said Mary Jane.

—Browne is everywhere, said Aunt Kate, lowering her voice.

Mary Jane laughed at her tone.

—Really, she said archly, he is very attentive.

—He has been laid on here like the gas, said Aunt Kate in the same tone, all during the Christmas.

She laughed herself this time good-humouredly and then added quickly:

—But tell him to come in, Mary Jane, and close the door. I hope to goodness he didn't hear me.

At that moment the hall-door was opened and Mr Browne came in from the doorstep, laughing as if his heart would break. He was dressed in a long green overcoat with mock astrakhan cuffs and collar and wore on his head an oval fur cap. He pointed down the snow-covered quay from where the sound of shrill prolonged whistling was borne in.

—Teddy will have all the cabs in Dublin out, he said.

Gabriel advanced from the little pantry behind the office, struggling into his overcoat and, looking round the hall, said:

—Gretta not down yet?

—She's getting on her things, Gabriel, said Aunt Kate.

—Who's playing up there? asked Gabriel.

—Nobody. They're all gone.

—O no, Aunt Kate, said Mary Jane. Bartell D'Arcy and Miss O'Callaghan aren't gone yet.

—Someone is strumming at the piano, anyhow, said Gabriel.

Mary Jane glanced at Gabriel and Mr Browne and said with a shiver:

—It makes me feel cold to look at you two gentlemen muffled up like that. I wouldn't like to face your journey home at this hour.

—I'd like nothing better this minute, said Mr Browne stoutly, than a rattling fine walk in the country or a fast drive with a good spanking goer between the shafts.

—We used to have a very good horse and trap[3] at home, said Aunt Julia sadly.

—The never-to-be-forgotten Johnny, said Mary Jane, laughing.

Aunt Kate and Gabriel laughed too.

—Why, what was wonderful about Johnny? asked Mr Browne.

—The late lamented Patrick Morkan, our grandfather, that is, explained Gabriel, commonly known in his later years as the old gentleman, was a glue-boiler.[4]

—O, now, Gabriel, said Aunt Kate, laughing, he had a starch mill.

—Well, glue or starch, said Gabriel, the old gentleman had a horse by the name of Johnny. And Johnny used to work in the old gentleman's mill, walking round and round in order to drive the mill. That was all very well; but now comes the tragic part about Johnny. One fine day the old gentleman thought he'd like to drive out with the quality[5] to a military review in the park.

—The Lord have mercy on his soul, said Aunt Kate compassionately.

3. A two-wheeled horse-drawn carriage on springs.
4. Glue was made by boiling animal hides and hoofs.
5. People of rank or high social position.

—Amen, said Gabriel. So the old gentleman, as I said, harnessed Johnny and put on his very best tall hat and his very best stock collar and drove out in grand style from his ancestral mansion somewhere near Back Lane, I think.

Everyone laughed, even Mrs Malins, at Gabriel's manner and Aunt Kate said:

—O now, Gabriel, he didn't live in Back Lane, really. Only the mill was there.

—Out from the mansion of his forefathers, continued Gabriel, he drove with Johnny. And everything went on beautifully until Johnny came in sight of King Billy's statue:[6] and whether he fell in love with the horse King Billy sits on or whether he thought he was back again in the mill, anyhow he began to walk round the statue.

Gabriel paced in a circle round the hall in his goloshes amid the laughter of the others.

—Round and round he went, said Gabriel, and the old gentleman, who was a very pompous old gentleman, was highly indignant. *Go on, sir! What do you mean, sir! Johnny! Johnny! Most extraordinary conduct! Can't understand the horse!*

The peals of laughter which followed Gabriel's imitation of the incident were interrupted by a resounding knock at the hall-door. Mary Jane ran to open it and let in Freddy Malins. Freddy Malins, with his hat well back on his head and his shoulders humped with cold, was puffing and steaming after his exertions.

—I could only get one cab, he said.

—O, we'll find another along the quay, said Gabriel.

—Yes, said Aunt Kate. Better not keep Mrs Malins standing in the draught.

Mrs Malins was helped down the front steps by her son and Mr Browne and, after many manœuvres, hoisted into the cab. Freddy Malins clambered in after her and spent a long time settling her on the seat, Mr Browne helping him with advice. At last she was settled comfortably and Freddy Malins invited Mr Browne into the cab. There was a good deal of confused talk, and then Mr Browne got into the cab. The cabman settled his rug over his knees, and bent down for the address. The confusion grew greater and the cabman was directed differently by Freddy Malins and Mr Browne, each of whom had his head out through a window of the cab. The difficulty was to know where to drop Mr Browne along the route and Aunt Kate, Aunt Julia and Mary Jane helped the discussion from the doorstep with cross-directions and contradictions and abundance of laughter. As for Freddy Malins he was speechless with laughter. He popped his head in and out of the window every moment, to the great danger of his hat, and told his mother how the discussion was progressing till at last Mr Browne shouted to the bewildered cabman above the din of everybody's laughter:

—Do you know Trinity College?

—Yes, sir, said the cabman.

—Well, drive bang up against Trinity College gates, said Mr Browne, and then we'll tell you where to go. You understand now?

—Yes, sir, said the cabman.

—Make like a bird for Trinity College.

—Right, sir, cried the cabman.

6. Statue of King William III of England in front of Trinity College, Dublin. He defeated predominantly Irish Catholic forces in the 1690 Battle of the Boyne.

The horse was whipped up and the cab rattled off along the quay amid a chorus of laughter and adieus.

Gabriel had not gone to the door with the others. He was in a dark part of the hall gazing up the staircase. A woman was standing near the top of the first flight, in the shadow also. He could not see her face but he could see the terracotta and salmonpink panels of her skirt which the shadow made appear black and white. It was his wife. She was leaning on the banisters, listening to something. Gabriel was surprised at her stillness and strained his ear to listen also. But he could hear little save the noise of laughter and dispute on the front steps, a few chords struck on the piano and a few notes of a man's voice singing.

He stood still in the gloom of the hall, trying to catch the air that the voice was singing and gazing up at his wife. There was grace and mystery in her attitude as if she were a symbol of something. He asked himself what is a woman standing on the stairs in the shadow, listening to distant music, a symbol of. If he were a painter he would paint her in that attitude. Her blue felt hat would show off the bronze of her hair against the darkness and the dark panels of her skirt would show off the light ones. *Distant Music* he would call the picture if he were a painter.

The hall-door was closed; and Aunt Kate, Aunt Julia and Mary Jane came down the hall, still laughing.

—Well, isn't Freddy terrible? said Mary Jane. He's really terrible.

Gabriel said nothing but pointed up the stairs towards where his wife was standing. Now that the hall-door was closed the voice and the piano could be heard more clearly. Gabriel held up his hand for them to be silent. The song seemed to be in the old Irish tonality and the singer seemed uncertain both of his words and of his voice. The voice, made plaintive by distance and by the singer's hoarseness, faintly illuminated the cadence of the air with words expressing grief:

> *O, the rain falls on my heavy locks*
> *And the dew wets my skin,*
> *My babe lies cold . . .*

—O, exclaimed Mary Jane. It's Bartell D'Arcy singing and he wouldn't sing all the night. O, I'll get him to sing a song before he goes.

—O do, Mary Jane, said Aunt Kate.

Mary Jane brushed past the others and ran to the staircase but before she reached it the singing stopped and the piano was closed abruptly.

—O, what a pity! she cried. Is he coming down, Gretta?

Gabriel heard his wife answer yes and saw her come down towards them. A few steps behind her were Mr Bartell D'Arcy and Miss O'Callaghan.

—O, Mr D'Arcy, cried Mary Jane, it's downright mean of you to break off like that when we were all in raptures listening to you.

—I have been at him all the evening, said Miss O'Callaghan, and Mrs Conroy too and he told us he had a dreadful cold and couldn't sing.

—O, Mr D'Arcy, said Aunt Kate, now that was a great fib to tell.

—Can't you see that I'm as hoarse as a crow? said Mr D'Arcy roughly.

He went into the pantry hastily and put on his overcoat. The others, taken aback by his rude speech, could find nothing to say. Aunt Kate wrinkled her brows and made signs to the others to drop the subject. Mr D'Arcy stood swathing his neck carefully and frowning.

—It's the weather, said Aunt Julia, after a pause.

—Yes, everybody has colds, said Aunt Kate readily, everybody.

—They say, said Mary Jane, we haven't had snow like it for thirty years; and I read this morning in the newspapers that the snow is general all over Ireland.

—I love the look of snow, said Aunt Julia sadly.

—So do I, said Miss O'Callaghan. I think Christmas is never really Christmas unless we have the snow on the ground.

—But poor Mr D'Arcy doesn't like the snow, said Aunt Kate, smiling.

Mr D'Arcy came from the pantry, full swathed and buttoned, and in a repentant tone told them the history of his cold. Everyone gave him advice and said it was a great pity and urged him to be very careful of his throat in the night air. Gabriel watched his wife who did not join in the conversation. She was standing right under the dusty fanlight and the flame of the gas lit up the rich bronze of her hair which he had seen her drying at the fire a few days before. She was in the same attitude and seemed unaware of the talk about her. At last she turned towards them and Gabriel saw that there was colour on her cheeks and that her eyes were shining. A sudden tide of joy went leaping out of his heart.

—Mr D'Arcy, she said, what is the name of that song you were singing?

—It's called The Lass of Aughrim,[7] said Mr D'Arcy, but I couldn't remember it properly. Why? Do you know it?

—The Lass of Aughrim, she repeated. I couldn't think of the name.

—It's a very nice air, said Mary Jane. I'm sorry you were not in voice tonight.

—Now, Mary Jane, said Aunt Kate, don't annoy Mr D'Arcy. I won't have him annoyed.

Seeing that all were ready to start she shepherded them to the door where good-night was said:

—Well, good-night, Aunt Kate, and thanks for the pleasant evening.

—Good-night, Gabriel. Good-night, Gretta!

—Good-night, Aunt Kate, and thanks ever so much. Good-night, Aunt Julia.

—O, good-night, Gretta, I didn't see you.

—Good-night, Mr D'Arcy. Good-night, Miss O'Callaghan.

—Good-night, Miss Morkan.

—Good-night, again.

—Good-night, all. Safe home.

—Good-night. Good-night.

The morning was still dark. A dull yellow light brooded over the houses and the river; and the sky seemed to be descending. It was slushy underfoot; and only streaks and patches of snow lay on the roofs, on the parapets of the quay and on the area railings. The lamps were still burning redly in the murky air and, across the river, the palace of the Four Courts stood out menacingly against the heavy sky.

She was walking on before him with Mr Bartell D'Arcy, her shoes in a brown parcel tucked under one arm and her hands holding her skirt up from the slush. She had no longer any grace of attitude but Gabriel's eyes were still bright with happiness. The blood went bounding along his veins; and the thoughts went rioting through his brain, proud, joyful, tender, valorous.

7. An Irish version of a ballad about a girl deserted by her lover, whom she later tries to find, bringing the baby she had by him. Other versions are called "Love Gregory" and "Lord Gregory" (the name of the deserting lover), "The Lass of Lochryan," and "The Lass of Ocram."

She was walking on before him so lightly and so erect that he longed to run after her noiselessly, catch her by the shoulders and say something foolish and affectionate into her ear. She seemed to him so frail that he longed to defend her against something and then to be alone with her. Moments of their secret life together burst like stars upon his memory. A heliotrope[8] envelope was lying beside his breakfast-cup and he was caressing it with his hand. Birds were twittering in the ivy and the sunny web of the curtain was shimmering along the floor: he could not eat for happiness. They were standing on the crowded platform and he was placing a ticket inside the warm palm of her glove. He was standing with her in the cold, looking in through a grated window at a man making bottles in a roaring furnace. It was very cold. Her face, fragrant in the cold air, was quite close to his; and suddenly she called out to the man at the furnace:

—Is the fire hot, sir?

But the man could not hear her with the noise of the furnace. It was just as well. He might have answered rudely.

A wave of yet more tender joy escaped from his heart and went coursing in warm flood along his arteries. Like the tender fires of stars moments of their life together, that no one knew of or would ever know of, broke upon and illumined his memory. He longed to recall to her those moments, to make her forget the years of their dull existence together and remember only their moments of ecstasy. For the years, he felt, had not quenched his soul or hers. Their children, his writing, her household cares had not quenched all their souls' tender fire. In one letter that he had written to her then he had said: *Why is it that words like these seem to me so dull and cold? Is it because there is no word tender enough to be your name?*

Like distant music these words that he had written years before were borne towards him from the past. He longed to be alone with her. When the others had gone away, when he and she were in their room in the hotel, then they would be alone together. He would call her softly:

—Gretta!

Perhaps she would not hear at once: she would be undressing. Then something in his voice would strike her. She would turn and look at him. . . .

At the corner of Winetavern Street they met a cab. He was glad of its rattling noise as it saved him from conversation. She was looking out of the window and seemed tired. The others spoke only a few words, pointing out some building or street. The horse galloped along wearily under the murky morning sky, dragging his old rattling box after his heels, and Gabriel was again in a cab with her, galloping to catch the boat, galloping to their honeymoon.

As the cab drove across O'Connell[9] Bridge Miss O'Callaghan said:

—They say you never cross O'Connell Bridge without seeing a white horse.

—I see a white man this time, said Gabriel.

—Where? asked Mr Bartell D'Arcy.

Gabriel pointed to the statue, on which lay patches of snow. Then he nodded familiarly to it and waved his hand.

—Good-night, Dan, he said gaily.

When the cab drew up before the hotel Gabriel jumped out and, in spite of Mr Bartell D'Arcy's protest, paid the driver. He gave the man a shilling over his fare. The man saluted and said:

---

8. Grayish purple.
9. Daniel O'Connell (1775–1847), Irish nationalist, statesman, and orator. His statue stands by
O'Connell Bridge in Dublin.

—A prosperous New Year to you, sir.

—The same to you, said Gabriel cordially.

She leaned for a moment on his arm in getting out of the cab and while standing at the curbstone, bidding the others good-night. She leaned lightly on his arm, as lightly as when she had danced with him a few hours before. He had felt proud and happy then, happy that she was his, proud of her grace and wifely carriage. But now, after the kindling again of so many memories, the first touch of her body, musical and strange and perfumed, sent through him a keen pang of lust. Under cover of her silence he pressed her arm closely to his side; and, as they stood at the hotel door, he felt that they had escaped from their lives and duties, escaped from home and friends and run away together with wild and radiant hearts to a new adventure.

An old man was dozing in a great hooded chair in the hall. He lit a candle in the office and went before them to the stairs. They followed him in silence, their feet falling in soft thuds on the thickly carpeted stairs. She mounted the stairs behind the porter, her head bowed in the ascent, her frail shoulders curved as with a burden, her skirt girt tightly about her. He could have flung his arms about her hips and held her still for his arms were trembling with desire to seize her and only the stress of his nails against the palms of his hands held the wild impulse of his body in check. The porter halted on the stairs to settle his guttering candle. They halted too on the steps below him. In the silence Gabriel could hear the falling of the molten wax into the tray and the thumping of his own heart against his ribs.

The porter led them along a corridor and opened a door. Then he set his unstable candle down on a toilet-table and asked at what hour they were to be called in the morning.

—Eight, said Gabriel.

The porter pointed to the tap of the electric-light and began a muttered apology but Gabriel cut him short.

—We don't want any light. We have light enough from the street. And I say, he added, pointing to the candle, you might remove that handsome article, like a good man.

The porter took up his candle again, but slowly for he was surprised by such a novel idea. Then he mumbled good-night and went out. Gabriel shot the lock to.

A ghostly light from the street lamp lay in a long shaft from one window to the door. Gabriel threw his overcoat and hat on a couch and crossed the room towards the window. He looked down into the street in order that his emotion might calm a little. Then he turned and leaned against a chest of drawers with his back to the light. She had taken off her hat and cloak and was standing before a large swinging mirror, unhooking her waist.[1] Gabriel paused for a few moments, watching her, and then said:

—Gretta!

She turned away from the mirror slowly and walked along the shaft of light towards him. Her face looked so serious and weary that the words would not pass Gabriel's lips. No, it was not the moment yet.

—You looked tired, he said.

—I am a little, she answered.

—You don't feel ill or weak?

—No, tired: that's all.

---

1. Shirtwaist; a tailored blouse.

She went on to the window and stood there, looking out. Gabriel waited again and then, fearing that diffidence was about to conquer him, he said abruptly:

—By the way, Gretta!

—What is it?

—You know that poor fellow Malins? he said quickly.

—Yes. What about him?

—Well, poor fellow, he's a decent sort of chap after all, continued Gabriel in a false voice. He gave me back that sovereign I lent him and I didn't expect it really. It's a pity he wouldn't keep away from that Browne, because he's not a bad fellow at heart.

He was trembling now with annoyance. Why did she seem so abstracted? He did not know how he could begin. Was she annoyed, too, about something? If she would only turn to him or come to him of her own accord! To take her as she was would be brutal. No, he must see some ardour in her eyes first. He longed to be master of her strange mood.

—When did you lend him the pound? she asked, after a pause.

Gabriel strove to restrain himself from breaking out into brutal language about the sottish Malins and his pound. He longed to cry to her from his soul, to crush her body against his, to overmaster her. But he said:

—O, at Christmas, when he opened that little Christmas-card shop in Henry Street.

He was in such a fever of rage and desire that he did not hear her come from the window. She stood before him for an instant, looking at him strangely. Then, suddenly raising herself on tiptoe and resting her hands lightly on his shoulders, she kissed him.

—You are a very generous person, Gabriel, she said.

Gabriel, trembling with delight at her sudden kiss and at the quaintness of her phrase, put his hands on her hair and began smoothing it back, scarcely touching it with his fingers. The washing had made it fine and brilliant. His heart was brimming over with happiness. Just when he was wishing for it she had come to him of her own accord. Perhaps her thoughts had been running with his. Perhaps she had felt the impetuous desire that was in him and then the yielding mood had come upon her. Now that she had fallen to him so easily he wondered why he had been so diffident.

He stood, holding her head between his hands. Then, slipping one arm swiftly about her body and drawing her towards him, he said softly:

—Gretta dear, what are you thinking about?

She did not answer nor yield wholly to his arm. He said again, softly:

—Tell me what it is, Gretta. I think I know what is the matter. Do I know?

She did not answer at once. Then she said in an outburst of tears:

—O, I am thinking about that song, *The Lass of Aughrim*.

She broke loose from him and ran to the bed and, throwing her arms across the bed-rail, hid her face. Gabriel stood stock-still for a moment in astonishment and then followed her. As he passed in the way of the cheval-glass[2] he caught sight of himself in full length, his broad, well-filled shirt-front, the face whose expression always puzzled him when he saw it in a mirror and his glimmering gilt-rimmed eyeglasses. He halted a few paces from her and said:

—What about the song? Why does that make you cry?

___

2. Full-length mirror that can be tilted.

She raised her head from her arms and dried her eyes with the back of her hand like a child. A kinder note than he had intended went into his voice.

—Why, Gretta? he asked.

—I am thinking about a person long ago who used to sing that song.

—And who was the person long ago? asked Gabriel, smiling.

—It was a person I used to know in Galway when I was living with my grandmother, she said.

The smile passed away from Gabriel's face. A dull anger began to gather again at the back of his mind and the dull fires of his lust began to glow angrily in his veins.

—Someone you were in love with? he asked ironically.

—It was a young boy I used to know, she answered, named Michael Furey. He used to sing that song, *The Lass of Aughrim*. He was very delicate.

Gabriel was silent. He did not wish her to think that he was interested in this delicate boy.

—I can see him so plainly, she said after a moment. Such eyes as he had: big dark eyes! And such an expression in them—an expression!

—O then, you were in love with him? said Gabriel.

—I used to go out walking with him, she said, when I was in Galway.

A thought flew across Gabriel's mind.

—Perhaps that was why you wanted to go to Galway with that Ivors girl? he said coldly.

She looked at him and asked in surprise:

—What for?

Her eyes made Gabriel feel awkward. He shrugged his shoulders and said:

—How do I know! To see him perhaps.

She looked away from him along the shaft of light towards the window in silence.

—He is dead, she said at length. He died when he was only seventeen. Isn't it a terrible thing to die so young as that?

—What was he? asked Gabriel, still ironically.

—He was in the gasworks,[3] she said.

Gabriel felt humiliated by the failure of his irony and by the evocation of this figure from the dead, a boy in the gasworks. While he had been full of memories of their secret life together, full of tenderness and joy and desire, she had been comparing him in her mind with another. A shameful consciousness of his own person assailed him. He saw himself as a ludicrous figure, acting as a pennyboy for his aunts, a nervous well-meaning sentimentalist, orating to vulgarians and idealising his own clownish lusts, the pitiable fatuous fellow he had caught a glimpse of in the mirror. Instinctively he turned his back more to the light lest she might see the shame that burned upon his forehead.

He tried to keep up his tone of cold interrogation but his voice when he spoke was humble and indifferent.

—I suppose you were in love with this Michael Furey, Gretta, he said.

—I was great with him at that time, she said.

Her voice was veiled and sad. Gabriel, feeling now how vain it would be to try to lead her whither he had purposed, caressed one of her hands and said, also sadly:

3. Factory where coal gas for heating and lighting is produced.

—And what did he die of so young, Gretta? Consumption, was it?

—I think he died for me, she answered.

A vague terror seized Gabriel at this answer as if, at that hour when he had hoped to triumph, some impalpable and vindictive being was coming against him, gathering forces against him in its vague world. But he shook himself free of it with an effort of reason and continued to caress her hand. He did not question her again for he felt that she would tell him of herself. Her hand was warm and moist: it did not respond to his touch but he continued to caress it just as he had caressed her first letter to him that spring morning.

—It was in the winter, she said, about the beginning of the winter when I was going to leave my grandmother's and come up here to the convent. And he was ill at the time in his lodgings in Galway and wouldn't be let out and his people in Oughterard were written to. He was in decline, they said, or something like that. I never knew rightly.

She paused for a moment and sighed.

—Poor fellow, she said. He was very fond of me and he was such a gentle boy. We used to go out together, walking, you know, Gabriel, like the way they do in the country. He was going to study singing only for his health. He had a very good voice, poor Michael Furey.

—Well; and then? asked Gabriel.

—And then when it came to the time for me to leave Galway and come up to the convent he was much worse and I wouldn't be let see him so I wrote a letter saying I was going up to Dublin and would be back in the summer and hoping he would be better then.

She paused for a moment to get her voice under control and then went on:

—Then the night before I left I was in my grandmother's house in Nuns' Island, packing up, and I heard gravel thrown up against the window. The window was so wet I couldn't see so I ran downstairs as I was and slipped out the back into the garden and there was the poor fellow at the end of the garden, shivering.

—And did you not tell him to go back? asked Gabriel.

—I implored him to go home at once and told him he would get his death in the rain. But he said he did not want to live. I can see his eyes as well as well! He was standing at the end of the wall where there was a tree.

—And did he go home? asked Gabriel.

—Yes, he went home. And when I was only a week in the convent he died and he was buried in Oughterard where his people came from. O, the day I heard that, that he was dead!

She stopped, choking with sobs, and overcome by emotion, flung herself face downward on the bed, sobbing in the quilt. Gabriel held her hand for a moment longer, irresolutely, and then, shy of intruding on her grief, let it fall gently and walked quietly to the window.

She was fast asleep.

Gabriel, leaning on his elbow, looked for a few moments unresentfully on her tangled hair and half-open mouth, listening to her deep-drawn breath. So she had had that romance in her life: a man had died for her sake. It hardly pained him now to think how poor a part he, her husband, had played in her life. He watched her while she slept as though he and she had never lived together as man and wife. His curious eyes rested long upon her face and on her hair: and, as he thought of what she must have been then, in that time of her first girlish beauty, a strange friendly pity for her entered his soul. He did not like to say even to himself that her face was no longer beautiful but he knew that it was no longer the face for which Michael Furey had braved death.

Perhaps she had not told him all the story. His eyes moved to the chair over which she had thrown some of her clothes. A petticoat string dangled to the floor. One boot stood upright, its limp upper fallen down: the fellow of it lay upon its side. He wondered at his riot of emotions of an hour before. From what had it proceeded? From his aunt's supper, from his own foolish speech, from the wine and dancing, the merry-making when saying good-night in the hall, the pleasure of the walk along the river in the snow. Poor Aunt Julia! She, too, would soon be a shade with the shade of Patrick Morkan and his horse. He had caught that haggard look upon her face for a moment when she was singing *Arrayed for the Bridal*. Soon, perhaps, he would be sitting in that same drawing-room, dressed in black, his silk hat on his knees. The blinds would be drawn down and Aunt Kate would be sitting beside him, crying and blowing her nose and telling him how Julia had died. He would cast about in his mind for some words that might console her, and would find only lame and useless ones. Yes, yes: that would happen very soon.

The air of the room chilled his shoulders. He stretched himself cautiously along under the sheets and lay down beside his wife. One by one they were all becoming shades. Better pass boldly into that other world, in the full glory of some passion, than fade and wither dismally with age. He thought of how she who lay beside him had locked in her heart for so many years that image of her lover's eyes when he had told her that he did not wish to live.

Generous tears filled Gabriel's eyes. He had never felt like that himself towards any woman but he knew that such a feeling must be love. The tears gathered more thickly in his eyes and in the partial darkness he imagined he saw the form of a young man standing under a dripping tree. Other forms were near. His soul had approached that region where dwell the vast hosts of the dead. He was conscious of, but could not apprehend, their wayward and flickering existence. His own identity was fading out into a grey impalpable world: the solid world itself which these dead had one time reared and lived in was dissolving and dwindling.

A few light taps upon the pane made him turn to the window. It had begun to snow again. He watched sleepily the flakes, silver and dark, falling obliquely against the lamplight. The time had come for him to set out on his journey westward. Yes, the newspapers were right: snow was general all over Ireland. It was falling on every part of the dark central plain, on the treeless hills, falling softly upon the Bog of Allen[4] and, farther westward, softly falling into the dark mutinous Shannon waves. It was falling, too, upon every part of the lonely churchyard on the hill where Michael Furey lay buried. It lay thickly drifted on the crooked crosses and headstones, on the spears of the little gate, on the barren thorns. His soul swooned slowly as he heard the snow falling faintly through the universe and faintly falling, like the descent of their last end, upon all the living and the dead.

1914

4. The name given to many separate peat bogs between the rivers Liffey (which runs through Dublin) and Shannon (which runs through the central plain of Ireland).

From Ulysses[1]

[PROTEUS][2]

Ineluctable modality of the visible: at least that if no more, thought through my eyes.[3] Signatures of all things[4] I am here to read, seaspawn and seawrack, the nearing tide, that rusty boot. Snotgreen, bluesilver, rust: coloured signs. Limits of the diaphane.[5] But he adds: in bodies. Then he was aware of them bodies before of them coloured. How? By knocking his sconce against them, sure. Go easy. Bald he was and a millionaire, *maestro di color che sanno.*[6] Limit of the diaphane in. Why in? Diaphane, adiaphane.[7] If you can put your five fingers through it, it is a gate, if not a door. Shut your eyes and see.

Stephen closed his eyes to hear his boots crush crackling wrack and shells. You are walking through it howsomever. I am, a stride at a time. A very short space of time through very short times of space. Five, six: the *Nacheinander.*[8] Exactly: and that is the ineluctable modality of the audible. Open your eyes. No. Jesus! If I fell over a cliff that beetles o'er his base,[9] fell through the *Nebeneinander*[1] ineluctably. I am getting on nicely in the dark. My ash sword hangs at my side. Tap with it: they do.[2] My two feet in his boots[3] are at the

---

1. *Ulysses* was first published in book form on Feb. 2, 1922, Joyce's fortieth birthday. The text given here has been collated with the 1932 Odyssey Press edition.

2. "Proteus," the third of the novel's eigtheen episodes, is so titled because of the deliberate analogies that exist between it and the description of Proteus in Homer's *Odyssey* 4. (Joyce did not title any of the episodes in *Ulysses,* but the names are his; he used them in correspondence and in talk with friends.)

In the *Odyssey* Proteus is the sea god, who continually alters his shape: when Telemachus, Ulysses' son, asks Menelaus for help in finding his father, Menelaus tells him that he encountered Proteus by the seashore on the island of Pharos "in front of Egypt," and that, by holding on to him while he changed from one shape to another, he was able to force him to tell what had happened to Ulysses and the other Greek heroes of the Trojan War. In Joyce's narrative Stephen Dedalus (who, like Homer's Telemachus, is looking for a father, but not in the literal "consubstantial" sense) is walking alone by the Dublin shore, "along Sandymount strand," speculating on the shifting shapes of things and the possibility of knowing truth by appearances.

Stephen meditates first on the "modality of the visible" and on the mystical notion that the Demiurge, God's subordinate, writes his signature on all things; then on the "modality of the audible," closing his eyes and trying to know reality through the sense of hearing. As he continues his walk, the people and objects he sees mingle in his thoughts with memories of his past relations with his family, of his schooldays, of his residence in Paris (from where he was recalled by his mother's fatal illness), of his feeling guilty about his mother's death (he had refused to kneel down and pray at her bedside, because he considered it a betrayal of his integrity as an unbeliever), and also with a variety of speculations about life and reality often derived from mystical works he had read "in the stagnant bay of

Marsh's library" (in Dublin). Stephen's highly theoretical, inquiring, musing mind contrasts sharply with the practical, humane, sensual, concrete imagination of the book's real hero, Leopold Bloom, but significant parallels exist between the streams of consciousness of the two. Some of the more important themes that emerge in Stephen's reverie are pointed out in the footnotes.

3. I.e., the sense of sight provides an unavoidable way ("ineluctable modality") of knowing reality, the knowledge thus provided being a kind of "thought through [the] eyes."

4. From Jakob Böhme (1575–1624), German mystic.

5. Transparency. Stephen is speculating on Aristotle's view of perception as developed in his *De Anima.*

6. One tradition held that Aristotle was bald, with thin legs, small eyes, and a lisp. Aristotle is also traditionally supposed to have inherited considerable wealth and to have been presented with a fortune by his former pupil Alexander the Great. The Italian phrase, Dante's description of Aristotle in the *Inferno,* means "the master of them that know."

7. What is not transparent (opposite of "diaphane").

8. After one another (German). Stephen, with eyes shut, is now sensing reality through the sense of sound only: unlike sight, sound falls on the sense of hearing in chronological sequence, one sound after another.

9. "What if it tempt you toward the flood, my lord, / Or to the dreadful summit of the cliff / That beetles o'er his base into the sea" (*Hamlet* 1.4.50–52). Allusions to *Hamlet* occur often in *Ulysses.*

1. Beside one another (German).

2. Stephen is still walking with his eyes shut, tapping with his "ash sword" (the ash-wood walking stick he carries), as "they" (i.e., blind people) do.

3. I.e., his friend Buck Mulligan's. Stephen, lacking boots of his own, had borrowed a cast-off pair of Mulligan's.

ends of my legs, *nebeneinander*. Sounds solid: made by the mallet of *Los demiurgos*.[4] Am I walking into eternity along Sandymount strand? Crush, crack, crik, crick. Wild sea money. Dominie Deasy kens them a'.[5]

> *Won't you come to Sandymount,*
> *Madeline the mare?*

Rhythm begins, you see. I hear. A catalectic tetrameter[6] of iambs marching. No, agallop: *deline the mare*.

Open your eyes now. I will. One moment. Has all vanished since? If I open and am for ever in the black adiaphane. *Basta!*[7] I will see if I can see.

See now. There all the time without you: and ever shall be, world without end.

They came down the steps from Leahy's terrace prudently, *Frauenzimmer*:[8] and down the shelving shore flabbily, their splayed feet sinking in the silted sand. Like me, like Algy,[9] coming down to our mighty mother. Number one swung lourdily[1] her midwife's bag, the other's gamp[2] poked in the beach. From the liberties, out for the day. Mrs Florence MacCabe, relict of the late Patk MacCabe,[3] deeply lamented, of Bride Street. One of her sisterhood lugged me squealing into life. Creation from nothing. What has she in the bag? A misbirth with a trailing navelcord, hushed in ruddy wool. The cords of all link back, strandentwining cable of all flesh. That is why mystic monks. Will you be as gods? Gaze in your *omphalos*. Hello. Kinch here. Put me on to Edenville. Aleph, alpha: nought, nought, one.[4]

Spouse and helpmate of Adam Kadmon: Heva,[5] naked Eve. She had no navel. Gaze. Belly without blemish, bulging big, a buckler of taut vellum, no, whiteheaped corn, orient and immortal, standing from everlasting to everlasting. Womb of sin.[6]

---

4. The Demiurge, or demiurgos, supernatural being who, according to Gnostic philosophy, made the world in subordination to God. The mystical notion of the Demiurge, whose mallet fashioned all things and who writes his signature on them, haunts Stephen's mind. The world, sensed by the ear only, "sounds solid," as though made by the Demiurge's hammer. The ending *-os* gives the word the appearance of a Spanish plural, so Joyce whimsically writes "*Los demiurgos*," which in Spanish would be "the demiurges."

5. "Dominie": schoolmaster. Mr. Deasy was the headmaster of the school where Stephen taught (the previous episode has shown Stephen teaching). "Kens them a' ": knows them all; Stephen is putting Deasy into a mock-Scottish folk song.

6. The first of the two lines of popular verse that have come into Stephen's head consists metrically of four iambic feet ("tetrameter") with the last foot unlike the first, not defective ("catalectic").

7. Enough! (Italian).

8. Dames, wenches (German). Here, midwives. Stephen sees them coming from Leahy's Terrace, which runs by the beach.

9. Algernon Charles Swinburne, who wrote: "I will go back to the great sweet mother, / Mother and lover of men, the sea. / I will go down to her, I and none other" ("The Triumph of Time," lines 1–3).

1. Heavily (coined by Stephen from the French *lourd*). Stephen, like Joyce, had studied modern languages at University College, Dublin, and his preoccupation with words and languages is part of his character as potential literary artist.

2. Umbrella; and perhaps reference to Mrs. Gamp, the nurse in Dickens's *Martin Chuzzlewit*.

3. Stephen imagines the first midwife is called Mrs. MacCabe. "Relict": widow.

4. Stephen is speculating on the mystical significance of the navel cord, seeing it as linking the generations, the combined navel cords stretching back to Adam and Eve. A mystic gazed in his *omphalos* (navel) to make contact with the first man. Stephen thinks of himself ("Kinch," his nickname) calling up Adam in "Edenville" through his navel, using the line of linked navel cords as a telephone line. Adam's telephone number, "Aleph, alpha: nought, nought, one," begins with the first letters of the Hebrew and of the Greek alphabet to suggest the great primeval number.

5. Hebrew for Eve. Because she was not born in the regular way, but created from Adam's rib, she had no navel. "Adam Kadmon": Adam the Beginner, so called in Hebrew cabalistic literature of the Middle Ages.

6. Stephen is led, through reflection on Eve's navel-less "belly without blemish," to a recollection of the description of the original Eden (Paradise) by Thomas Traherne (ca. 1637–1674), from whose prose *Centuries of Meditation* he quotes: "The corn was orient and immortal wheat, which should never be reaped, nor was ever sown. I thought it had stood from everlasting to everlasting." But immediately afterward Stephen reflects that such language is inappropriate to Eve's body, as hers was the "womb of sin"—i.e., she first ate the fatal apple and brought forth sin.

Wombed in sin darkness I was too, made not begotten. By them, the man with my voice and my eyes and a ghostwoman with ashes on her breath.[7] They clasped and sundered, did the coupler's will. From before the ages He willed me and now may not will me away or ever. A *lex eterna*[8] stays about Him. Is that then the divine substance wherein Father and Son are consubstantial? Where is poor dear Arius[9] to try conclusions? Warring his life long on the contransmagnificandjewbangtantiality.[1] Illstarred heresiarch.[2] In a Greek watercloset he breathed his last: *euthanasia*. With beaded mitre and with crozier, stalled upon his throne, widower of a widowed see, with upstiffed omophorion, with clotted hinderparts.

Airs romped round him, nipping and eager airs. They are coming, waves. The whitemaned seahorses, champing, brightwindbridled, the steeds of Mananaan.[3]

I mustn't forget his letter for the press. And after? The Ship, half twelve. By the way go easy with that money like a good young imbecile. Yes, I must.[4]

His pace slackened. Here. Am I going to aunt Sara's or not? My consubstantial father's voice. Did you see anything of your artist brother Stephen lately? No? Sure he's not down in Strasburg terrace with his aunt Sally? Couldn't he fly a bit higher than that, eh? And and and and tell us Stephen, how is uncle Si? O weeping God, the things I married into. De boys up in de hayloft. The drunken little costdrawer and his brother, the cornet player. Highly respectable gondoliers. And skeweyed Walter sirring his father, no less. Sir. Yes, sir. No, sir. Jesus wept: and no wonder, by Christ.[5]

I pull the wheezy bell of their shuttered cottage: and wait. They take me for a dun, peer out from a coign of vantage.[6]

—It's Stephen, sir.

—Let him in. Let Stephen in.

A bolt drawn back and Walter welcomes me.

—We thought you were someone else.

In his broad bed nuncle Richie, pillowed and blanketed, extends over the

---

7. Stephen is haunted by thoughts of his mother in this guise.

8. Eternal law (Latin). God's eternal law, Stephen reflects, willed his birth from the beginning. He then goes on to speculate on the nature of the divine substance and whether God the Father and God the Son are of the same substance ("consubstantial").

9. Third-century theologian who "tried conclusions" on this matter, maintaining that Christ was less divine than God (Arius's views were condemned as heretical by the Council of Nicaea in 325).

1. Ironic "portmanteau word" made up of terms connected with the Arian controversy—"consubstantial," "transubstantial" (of a substance that changes into another)—and with the facts of Christ's nature (e.g., "Jew"; Jesus was a Jew, as Leopold Bloom in a later episode reminds an anti-Semitic Irishman).

2. Arch-heretic. Arius died suddenly in Constantinople in 336. He was never a bishop, and Stephen's image of him at the moment of death in full episcopal attire seems to combine recollections of other early "heresiarchs." In an earlier reverie Stephen had conjured up in his mind "a horde of heresies fleeing with mitres awry." These heretics

are connected in Stephen's mind with argument about the relation between God the Father and God the Son and so with the problem of the true nature of paternity, which haunts him constantly.

3. Mananaan MacLir, Celtic sea god; his steeds are the "whitemaned seahorses." ("White horses" is still the name in Britain for the white foam atop waves.)

4. Mr. Deasy had given Stephen a letter to the press to be taken to the newspaper office. After that he has an appointment with Mulligan at The Ship, a tavern. "That money" is Mr. Deasy's last payment to him.

5. Stephen has been wondering whether to call on his uncle and aunt, Richie and Sara Goulding. He imagines his father interrogating him about the visit as if he had gone; he then pictures his cousins asking after his father, Simon Dedalus (his cousins' "uncle Si"). Simon is contemptuous of his wife's relations (Sara Goulding is his wife's sister). Stephen knows that any mention of them will bring on the familiar abuse of "the things I married into"—at best "highly respectable gondoliers" (from Gilbert and Sullivan's opera *The Gondoliers*). The scene that follows is also Stephen's purely imaginary picture of what the visit would be like.

6. Favorable corner.

hillock of his knees a sturdy forearm. Cleanchested. He has washed the upper moiety.

—Morrow, nephew.

He lays aside the lapboard whereon he drafts his bills of costs for the eyes of master Goff and master Shapland Tandy, filing consents and common searches and a writ of *Duces Tecum.*[7] A bogoak frame over his bald head: Wilde's *Requiescat.*[8] The drone of his misleading whistle brings Walter back.

—Yes, sir?

—Malt[9] for Richie and Stephen, tell mother. Where is she?

—Bathing Crissie, sir.

Papa's little bedpal. Lump of love.

—No, uncle Richie . . .

—Call me Richie. Damn your lithia water.[1] It lowers. Whusky!

—Uncle Richie, really. . . .

—Sit down or by the law Harry I'll knock you down.

Walter squints vainly for a chair.

—He has nothing to sit down on, sir.

—He has nowhere to put it, you mug. Bring in our chippendale chair. Would you like a bite of something? None of your damned lawdeedaw air here: the rich of a rasher fried with a herring? Sure? So much the better. We have nothing in the house but backache pills.

All'erta![2] He drones bars of Ferrando's *aria di sortita.* The grandest number, Stephen, in the whole opera. Listen.

His tuneful whistle sounds again, finely shaded, with rushes of the air, his fists bigdrumming on his padded knees.

This wind is sweeter.

Houses of decay, mine, his and all. You told the Clongowes gentry you had an uncle a judge and an uncle a general in the army.[3] Come out of them, Stephen. Beauty is not there. Nor in the stagnant bay of Marsh's library where you read the fading prophecies of Joachim Abbas.[4] For whom? The hundred-headed rabble of the cathedral close.[5] A hater of his kind ran from them to the wood of madness, his mane foaming in the moon, his eyeballs stars. Houyhnhnm, horsenostrilled.[6] The oval equine faces, Temple, Buck Mulligan, Foxy Campbell. Lantern jaws. Abbas[7] father, furious dean, what offence laid fire to their brains? Paff! *Descende, calve, ut nimium decalveris.*[8] A garland of

7. You shall take with you (Latin); opening words of a search warrant. Goulding was a law clerk with Messrs. Goff and Tandy.
8. Poem by Oscar Wilde.
9. Whiskey.
1. Mineral water containing lithium salts, often used therapeutically.
2. Look out! (Italian); the first words of the *aria di sortita* (aria sung by a character about to leave the stage) sung by Ferrando, captain of the guard, in Verdi's opera *Il Trovatore.*
3. Stephen, reflecting on the steady social decline of his family, is remembering that, while at school at Clongowes Wood College, he had pretended to have important relations.
4. Abbot Joachim of Floris (the monastery of San Giovanni in Fiore, Italy), 12th-century mystic and theologian, whose prophetic work *Expositio in Apocalypsin* Stephen (like Joyce) had read in Marsh's Library.

5. I.e., the precinct of a cathedral (Marsh's Library is in the close of St. Patrick's Cathedral).
6. St. Patrick's Close has recalled Jonathan Swift, who was dean of St. Patrick's. Stephen remembers Swift's misanthropy (he was "a hater of his kind") and his creation of the Houyhnhnms (noble horses) in book 4 of *Gulliver's Travels.* Then he thinks of people he knew who have horse faces.
7. Literally: father.
8. Go down, bald-head, lest you become even balder (Latin). This sentence, from Joachim's *Concordia* of the Old and New Testaments, is based on the mocking cry of the children to the prophet Elisha (2 Kings 2.23: "Go up, thou bald head"); Joachim saw Elisha as a forerunner of St. Benedict—both had shaven or baldish heads. Stephen goes on to imagine the "comminated" (threatened) head of Joachim descending, clutching a "monstrance" (receptacle in which the Host [consecrated bread or wafer] is exposed for adoration), in

grey hair on his comminated head see him me clambering down to the footpace (*descende*), clutching a monstrance, basiliskeyed. Get down, bald poll! A choir gives back menace and echo, assisting about the altar's horns, the snorted Latin of jackpriests moving burly in their albs, tonsured and oiled and gelded, fat with the fat of kidneys of wheat.

And at the same instant perhaps a priest round the corner is elevating it. Dringdring! And two streets off another locking it into a pyx.[9] Dringadring! And in a ladychapel another taking housel all to his own cheek. Dringdring! Down, up, forward, back. Dan Occam[1] thought of that, invincible doctor. A misty English morning the imp hypostasis tickled his brain. Bringing his host down and kneeling he heard twine with his second bell the first bell in the transept (he is lifting his) and, rising, heard (now I am lifting) their two bells (he is kneeling) twang in diphthong.

Cousin Stephen, you will never be a saint.[2] Isle of saints.[3] You were awfully holy, weren't you? You prayed to the Blessed Virgin that you might not have a red nose. You prayed to the devil in Serpentine avenue that the fubsy widow in front might lift her clothes still more from the wet street. O si, certo![4] Sell your soul for that, do, dyed rags pinned round a squaw. More tell me, more still! On the top of the Howth tram alone crying to the rain: Naked women! What about that, eh?

What about what? What else were they invented for?

Reading two pages apiece of seven books every night, eh? I was young. You bowed to yourself in the mirror, stepping forward to applause earnestly, striking face. Hurray for the Goddamned idiot! Hray! No-one saw: tell no-one. Books you were going to write with letters for titles. Have you read his F? O yes, but I prefer Q. Yes, but W is wonderful. O yes, W. Remember your epiphanies[5] on green oval leaves, deeply deep, copies to be sent if you died to all the great libraries of the world, including Alexandria? Someone was to read them there after a few thousand years, a mahamanvantara.[6] Pico della Mirandola[7] like. Ay, very like a whale.[8] When one reads these strange pages of one long gone one feels that one is at one with one who once . . .

The grainy sand had gone from under his feet. His boots trod again a damp crackling mast, razorshells, squeaking pebbles, that on the unnumbered pebbles beats, wood sieved by the shipworm, lost Armada. Unwholesome sandflats waited to suck his treading soles, breathing upward sewage breath. He coasted

---

the midst of a nightmare church service.

9. Vessel in which the Host is kept. Stephen is imagining such a service, with himself officiating (he almost became a priest).

1. William of Occam or Ockham ("Dan" means "master"), 14th-century English theologian, who held that the individual thing is the reality and its name, the universal, an abstraction; he was concerned with hypostasis—the essential part of a thing as distinct from its attributes.

2. A parody of the words of Dryden to his distant relative Swift: "Cousin, you will never make a poet."

3. Ireland was called "*insula sanctorum*" (isle of saints) in the Middle Ages.

4. Oh yes, certainly! (Italian).

5. Joyce's term for the prose poems he wrote as a young man. An epiphany, he said, was the sudden "revelation of the whatness of a thing"—of a gesture, a phrase, or a thought he had experienced;

he attempted to express, in the writing, the moment at which "the soul of the commonest object . . . seems to us radiant." Stephen's recollection of early and exotic literary ambitions is drawn directly from Joyce's ambitions at the same age.

6. Cycle of change and recurrence, in Indian mystical thought. It is connected in Stephen's mind with the constant ebb and flow of the sea by which he is walking.

7. 15th-century mystical philosopher; his *Heptaplus* is a mystical account of the Creation, much influenced by Jewish cabalistic thought.

8. Polonius to Hamlet (*Hamlet* 3.2.351) with reference to the changing shape of a cloud. The Protean theme of constant change, of ebb and flow, and of metempsychosis (i.e., transmigration of souls: a major theme in *Ulysses*), is working in Stephen's mind. The following sentence is a parody of an elegant, condescending modern essay on Pico or some other early mystic.

them, walking warily. A porterbottle stood up, stogged to its waist, in the cakey sand dough. A sentinel: isle of dreadful thirst.[9] Broken hoops on the shore; at the land a maze of dark cunning nets; farther away chalkscrawled backdoors and on the higher beach a dryingline with two crucified shirts. Ringsend: wigwams of brown steersmen and master mariners. Human shells.

He halted. I have passed the way to aunt Sara's. Am I not going there? Seems not. No-one about. He turned northeast and crossed the firmer sand towards the Pigeonhouse.[1]

—*Qui vous a mis dans cette fichue position?*

—*C'est le pigeon, Joseph.*

Patrice, home on furlough, lapped warm milk with me in the bar Mac-Mahon. Son of the wild goose, Kevin Egan of Paris. My father's a bird, he lapped the sweet *lait chaud* with pink young tongue, plump bunny's face. Lap, *lapin*. He hopes to win in the *gros lots*. About the nature of women he read in Michelet. But he must send me *La Vie de Jésus* by M. Léo Taxil. Lent it to his friend.[2]

—*C'est tordant, vous savez. Moi, je suis socialiste. Je ne crois pas en l'existence de Dieu. Faut pas le dire à mon père.*

—*Il croit?*

—*Mon père, oui.*

Schluss.[3] He laps.

My Latin quarter hat. God, we simply must dress the character. I want puce gloves. You were a student, weren't you? Of what in the other devil's name? Paysayenn. P. C. N., you know: *physiques, chimiques et naturelles.*[4] Aha. Eating your groatsworth of *mou en civet,*[5] fleshpots of Egypt, elbowed by belching cabmen. Just say in the most natural tone: when I was in Paris, *boul'Mich',*[6] I used to. Yes, used to carry punched tickets to prove an alibi if they arrested you for murder somewhere. Justice. On the night of the seventeenth of February 1904 the prisoner was seen by two witnesses. Other fellow did it: other me. Hat, tie, overcoat, nose. *Lui, c'est moi.*[7] You seem to have enjoyed yourself.

Proudly walking. Whom were you trying to walk like? Forget: a dispossessed. With mother's money order, eight shillings, the banging door of the post office slammed in your face by the usher. Hunger toothache. *Encore deux minutes.*

---

9. The atmosphere of the sandflats reminds Stephen of a desert island where people die of thirst. (The island of Pharos, where Menelaus found Proteus, was an "island of dreadful hunger.")

1. The Pigeon House in Ringsend, an old structure built on a breakwater in Dublin Bay and which in the course of time has served a great variety of purposes, suggests to Stephen the Dove, which is the symbol of the Holy Spirit, and this in turn suggests an irreverent dialogue (supposedly between Joseph and Mary when Mary is found to be pregnant: "Who has got you into this wretched condition?" "It was the pigeon [i.e., the Holy Dove], Joseph"). This he had picked up in Paris from the blasphemous M. Léo Taxil, whose book *La Vie de Jésus* ("The Life of Jesus") is mentioned in the next paragraph.

2. Stephen had first met Léo Taxil through Patrice, the son of "Kevin Egan of Paris," who in real life was the exiled nationalist Joseph Casey. The phrase "my father's a bird" comes from *The Song of the Cheerful Jesus*, a blasphemous poem by Buck Mulligan (based on Joyce's friend Oliver

Gogarty, who really wrote the poem); Stephen recalls Patrice reciting it as he drank warm milk ("*lait chaud*"), lapping it like a "*lapin*" (rabbit), and expressing the hope that he would win something substantial in the French national lottery (*gros lot*: "first prize"). Jules Michelet (1798–1874), French historian.

3. End (German). Conversation in French between Stephen and Patrice: "It's screamingly funny, you know. I'm a socialist myself. I don't believe in the existence of God. Mustn't tell my father." "He is a believer?" "My father, yes."

4. I.e., the faculty of physics, chemistry, and biology at the École de Médecine in Paris, where Stephen, like Joyce, took a premedical course for a short time. The faculty was popularly known as "P.C.N." (pronounced "Paysayenn").

5. Stew.

6. Popular Parisian abbreviation for the Boulevard Saint Michel.

7. "He is me"—a parody of Louis XIV's remark "*L'état c'est moi*" (I am the state).

Look clock. Must get. *Fermé*. Hired dog! Shoot him to bloody bits with a bang shotgun, bits man spattered walls all brass buttons. Bits all khrrrrklak in place clack back. Not hurt? O, that's all right. Shake hands. See what I meant, see? O, that's all right. Shake a shake. O, that's all only all right.[8]

You were going to do wonders, what? Missionary to Europe after fiery Columbanus. Fiacre and Scotus on their creepystools[9] in heaven spilt from their pintpots, loudlatinlaughing: *Euge!*[1] *Euge!* Pretending to speak broken English as you dragged your valise, porter threepence, across the slimy pier at Newhaven. *Comment?* Rich booty you brought back; *Le Tutu*, five tattered numbers of *Pantalon Blanc et Culotte Rouge*,[2] a blue French telegram, curiosity to show:

—Mother dying come home father.[3]

The aunt thinks you killed your mother. That's why she won't.[4]

> Then here's a health to Mulligan's aunt
> And I'll tell you the reason why.
> She always kept things decent in
> The Hannigan famileye.

His feet marched in sudden proud rhythm over the sand furrows, along by the boulders of the south wall. He stared at them proudly, piled stone mammoth skulls. Gold light on sea, on sand, on boulders. The sun is there, the slender trees, the lemon houses.

Paris rawly waking, crude sunlight on her lemon streets. Moist pith of farls[5] of bread, the froggreen wormwood, her matin incense, court the air. Belluomo rises from the bed of his wife's lover's wife, the kerchiefed housewife is astir, a saucer of acetic acid in her hand. In Rodot's Yvonne and Madeleine newmake their tumbled beauties, shattering with gold teeth *chaussons* of pastry, their mouths yellowed with the *pus* of *flan breton*.[6] Faces of Paris men go by, their wellpleased pleasers, curled *conquistadores*.[7]

Noon slumbers. Kevin Egan rolls gunpowder cigarettes through fingers smeared with printer's ink,[8] sipping his green fairy as Patrice his white. About us gobblers fork spiced beans down their gullets. *Un demi setier!*[9] A jet of coffee steam from the burnished caldron. She serves me at his beck. *Il est irlandais. Hollandais? Non fromage. Deux irlandais, nous, Irlande, vous savez? Ah, oui!*[1] She thought you wanted a cheese *hollandais*. Your postprandial, do you know

---

8. A recollection of the occasion when, desperate for money, Stephen had received a money order for eight shillings from his mother. Afflicted with both hunger and toothache, he had gone to cash it at the post office—which was closed, even though, as he expostulated with the man at the door, there were still two minutes (*"encore deux minutes"*) until the official closing time. In his retrospective rage he imagines himself shooting the "hired dog" to bits, and then in a revulsion of feeling has a mental reconciliation with him.
9. Low stools. "Columbanus": 6th-century Irish missionary on the Continent. Fiacre was a 6th-century Irish saint. John Duns Scotus (1266–1308), Scottish scholastic theologian and philosopher.
1. Well done!
2. Like *Le Tutu*, the name of a French popular periodical.
3. This telegram was actually received by Joyce in Paris.

4. Stephen recalls Buck Mulligan's telling him that his (Mulligan's) aunt disapproved of Stephen because, by refusing to pray at his dying mother's bedside, he had hastened her death. Stephen then tries to laugh away his guilty feeling by quoting mentally a (slightly parodied) verse of a popular song.
5. Thin circular cakes.
6. Memories of a restaurant in Paris. "*Chaussons*": pastry turnovers. "*Flan breton*": pastry filled with custard.
7. Conquerors (Spanish).
8. Egan (i.e., Joseph Casey) became a typesetter for the Parisian edition of the *New York Herald*.
9. Abusive Parisian slang for a liquid measure (about one-fourth of a liter)—here, presumably, of wine or beer. "Green Fairy": absinthe, a strong green liqueur.
1. He is Irish. Dutch? Not cheese. We are two Irishmen, Ireland, you understand? Oh, yes!

that word? Postprandial. There was a fellow I knew once in Barcelona, queer fellow, used to call it his postprandial. Well: *slainte!*[2] Around the slabbed tables the tangle of wined breaths and grumbling gorges. His breath hangs over our saucestained plates, the green fairy's fang thrusting between his lips. Of Ireland, the Dalcassians, of hopes, conspiracies, of Arthur Griffith now.[3] To yoke me as his yokefellow, our crimes our common cause. You're your father's son. I know the voice. His fustian shirt, sanguineflowered, trembles its Spanish tassels at his secrets. M. Drumont,[4] famous journalist, Drumont, know what he called queen Victoria? Old hag with the yellow teeth. *Vieille ogresse* with the *dents jaunes.* Maud Gonne, beautiful woman, *la Patrie*, M. Millevoye, Félix Faure,[5] know how he died? Licentious men. The *froeken, bonne à tout faire,*[6] who rubs male nakedness in the bath at Upsala. *Moi faire*, she said, *tous les messieurs.*[7] Not this *monsieur*, I said. Most licentious custom. Bath a most private thing. I wouldn't let my brother, not even my own brother, most lascivious thing. Green eyes, I see you. Fang, I feel. Lascivious people.

The blue fuse burns deadly between hands and burns clear. Loose tobacco shreds catch fire: a flame and acrid smoke light our corner. Raw facebones under his peep of day boy's hat. How the head centre got away, authentic version. Got up as a young bride, man, veil, orangeblossoms, drove out the road to Malahide. Did, faith. Of lost leaders, the betrayed, wild escapes. Disguises, clutched at, gone not here.[8]

Spurned lover. I was a strapping young gossoon[9] at that time, I tell you. I'll show you my likeness one day. I was, faith. Lover, for her love he prowled with colonel Richard Burke, tanist of his sept,[1] under the walls of Clerkenwell[2] and, crouching, saw a flame of vengeance hurl them upward in the fog. Shattered glass and toppling masonry. In gay Paree he hides, Egan of Paris, unsought by any save by me. Making his day's stations, the dingy printing-case, his three taverns, the Montmartre lair he sleeps short night in, *rue de la Goutte-d'Or,* damascened with flyblown faces of the gone. Loveless, landless, wifeless. She is quite nicey comfy without her outcast man,[3] madame in *rue Gît-le-Cœur,* canary and two buck lodgers. Peachy cheeks, a zebra skirt, frisky as a young thing's. Spurned and undespairing. Tell Pat[4] you saw me, won't you? I wanted to get poor Pat a job one time. *Mon fils*, soldier of France. I taught him to sing *The boys of Kilkenny are stout roaring blades.* Know that old lay? I taught Patrice that. Old Kilkenny: saint Canice, Strongbow's castle on the Nore.[5] Goes like this. O, O. He takes me, Napper Tandy,[6] by the hand.

---

2. Your health! (Gaelic).
3. Two extremes of Irish history. From the Dalcassian line came the early kings of Munster (from 300 c.e. on). Arthur Griffith (1872–1922) was an Irish revolutionary leader, founder of the Sinn Fein ("Ourselves Alone") movement.
4. Edouard Drumont (1844–1917), French politician and bitter anti-Semite.
5. 19th-century French statesman. "Maud Gonne," the beautiful actress and violent Irish nationalist whom W. B. Yeats loved. "La Patrie": journal edited by Lucien Millevoye, French nationalist deputy and Maud Gonne's lover.
6. Maid-of-all-work (French). "Froeken": fröken, unmarried woman or Miss (Swedish).
7. I do all the gentlemen (in broken French).
8. Another Protean theme of change. Egan had told Stephen of his cousin James Stephens's escape from prison disguised as a bride.

9. Boy.
1. Clan. "Tanist": successor-apparent to a Celtic chief.
2. District in east-central London. Stephen is recalling Egan's conversation about the Fenian violence in London that necessitated his fleeing to France.
3. I.e., Egan's wife, who is "quite nicey comfy" in the metaphorical "*rue Gît-le-Cœur*" (i.e., the street where the heart lies dead) back home in Ireland.
4. Patrice, Egan's son.
5. Kilkenny is called after the Irish Saint Canice (its Irish name is Cill Chainnigh), on the river Nore, where Strongbow (the second earl of Pembroke, who invaded Ireland in the 12th century), had his stronghold.
6. James Napper Tandy (1740–1803), Irish revolutionary hero of the song "The Wearing of the Green."

> *O, O the boys of*
> *Kilkenny . . .*

Weak wasting hand on mine. They have forgotten Kevin Egan, not he them.
Remembering thee, O Sion.[7]

He had come nearer the edge of the sea and wet sand slapped his boots.
The new air greeted him, harping in wild nerves, wind of wild air of seeds of
brightness. Here, I am not walking out to the Kish lightship, am I? He stood
suddenly, his feet beginning to sink slowly in the quaking soil. Turn back.

Turning, he scanned the shore south, his feet sinking again slowly in new
sockets. The cold domed room of the tower[8] waits. Through the barbicans[9]
the shafts of light are moving ever, slowly ever as my feet are sinking, creeping
duskward over the dial floor. Blue dusk, nightfall, deep blue night. In the
darkness of the dome they wait, their pushedback chairs, my obelisk valise,
around a board of abandoned platters. Who to clear it? He has the key.[1] I will
not sleep there when this night comes. A shut door of a silent tower, entombing
their blind bodies, the panthersahib and his pointer.[2] Call: no answer. He lifted
his feet up from the suck and turned back by the mole of boulders. Take all,
keep all. My soul walks with me, form of forms. So in the moon's midwatches
I pace the path above the rocks, in sable silvered, hearing Elsinore's tempting
flood.[3]

The flood is following me. I can watch it flow past from here. Get back then
by the Poolbeg road to the strand there. He climbed over the sedge and eely
oarweeds and sat on a stool of rock, resting his ashplant in a grike.[4]

A bloated carcass of a dog lay lolled on bladderwrack. Before him the gunwale of a boat, sunk in sand. *Un coche ensablé*[5] Louis Veuillot called Gautier's[6]
prose. These heavy sands are language tide and wind have silted here. And
there, the stoneheaps of dead builders, a warren of weasel rats. Hide gold
there. Try it. You have some. Sands and stones. Heavy of the past. Sir Lout's
toys. Mind you don't get one bang on the ear. I'm the bloody well gigant rolls
all them bloody well boulders, bones for my steppingstones. Feefawfum. I
zmellz de bloodz oldz an Iridzman.[7]

A point, live dog, grew into sight running across the sweep of sand. Lord,
is he going to attack me? Respect his liberty. You will not be master of others
or their slave. I have my stick. Sit tight. From farther away, walking shoreward
across from the crested tide, figures, two. The two maries. They have tucked
it safe mong the bulrushes. Peekaboo. I see you. No, the dog. He is running
back to them. Who?

Galleys of the Lochlanns[8] ran here to beach, in quest of prey, their blood-
beaked prows riding low on a molten pewter surf. Dane vikings, torcs of toma-

---

7. Cf. Psalm 137.1 (in the King James Bible): "we
wept, when we remembered Zion." But "Zion" in
the Douay (Roman Catholic) Bible, is spelled
"Sion," and the Book of Common Prayer has
"When we remembered thee, O Sion."
8. Where Stephen lived with Buck Mulligan.
9. Outworks of a castle.
1. In the preceding episode Mulligan asked for
and got the key of the tower from Stephen.
2. I.e., Mulligan and the Englishman Haines, who
lived with Stephen in the tower. Stephen thinks of
them as calling for him in vain, because he has
decided not to return.
3. Cf. *Hamlet* 1.2.241, where the ghost of Hamlet's murdered father is described as having a beard
of "sable silver'd."

4. Chink, crevice.
5. A coach embedded in the sand (French).
6. Théophile Gautier, 19th-century French poet,
novelist, and critic. Veuillot, 19th-century French
journalist.
7. Stephen is thinking of the boulders on the
shore as the work of a large but clumsy giant ("Sir
Lout"). "They [Sir Lout and his family] were giants
right enough. . . . My Sir Lout has rocks in his
mouth instead of teeth. He articulates badly"
(Joyce to Frank Budgen, reported in Budgen's
James Joyce and the Making of Ulysses, 1934).
8. Scandinavians (Gaelic). Stephen is meditating
on the Vikings who settled Dublin; it was here that
they came ashore, he thinks. Malachi (below), king
of Meath, had their first leader drowned.

hawks aglitter on their breasts when Malachi wore the collar of gold. A school of turlehide whales stranded in hot noon, spouting, hobbling in the shallows. Then from the starving cagework city a horde of jerkined dwarfs, my people, with flayers' knives, running, scaling, hacking in green blubbery whalemeat. Famine, plague and slaughters. Their blood is in me, their lusts my waves. I moved among them on the frozen Liffey, that I, a changeling, among the spluttering resin fires. I spoke to no-one: none to me.

The dog's bark ran towards him, stopped, ran back. Dog of my enemy. I just simply stood pale, silent, bayed about. *Terribilia meditans.*[9] A primrose doublet, fortune's knave, smiled on my fear. For that are you pining, the bark of their applause? Pretenders: live their lives. The Bruce's brother, Thomas Fitzgerald, silken knight, Perkin Warbeck, York's false scion, in breeches of silk of whiterose ivory, wonder of a day, and Lambert Simnel, with a tail of nans and sutlers, a scullion crowned.[1] All kings' sons. Paradise of pretenders then and now. He saved men from drowning[2] and you shake at a cur's yelping. But the courtiers who mocked Guido in Or san Michele were in their own house. House of . . . We don't want any of your medieval abstrusiosities. Would you do what he did? A boat would be near, a lifebuoy. *Natürlich,*[3] put there for you. Would you or would you not? The man that was drowned nine days ago off Maiden's rock. They are waiting for him now. The truth, spit it out. I would want to. I would try. I am not a strong swimmer. Water cold soft. When I put my face into it in the basin at Clongowes. Can't see! Who's behind me? Out quickly, quickly! Do you see the tide flowing quickly in on all sides, sheeting the lows of sands quickly, shellcocoacoloured? If I had land under my feet. I want his life still to be his, mine to be mine. A drowning man. His human eyes scream to me out of horror of his death. I . . . With him together down . . . I could not save her.[4] Waters: bitter death: lost.

A woman and a man. I see her skirties. Pinned up, I bet.

Their dog ambled about a bank of dwindling sand, trotting, sniffing on all sides. Looking for something lost in a past life. Suddenly he made off like a bounding hare, ears flung back, chasing the shadow of a lowskimming gull. The man's shrieked whistle struck his limp ears. He turned, bounded back, came nearer, trotted on twinkling shanks. On a field tenney a buck, trippant, proper, unattired.[5] At the lacefringe of the tide he halted with stiff forehoofs, seawardpointed ears. His snout lifted barked at the wavenoise, herds of seamorse.[6] They serpented towards his feet, curling, unfurling many crests, every ninth, breaking, plashing, from far, from farther out, waves and waves.

Cocklepickers.[7] They waded a little way in the water and, stooping, soused their bags, and, lifting them again, waded out. The dog yelped running to them, reared up and pawed them, dropping on all fours, again reared up at them with mute bearish fawning. Unheeded he kept by them as they came towards the drier sand, a rag of wolf's tongue redpanting from his jaws. His speckled body ambled ahead of them and then loped off at a calf's gallop. The carcass

9. Meditating terrible things (Latin).
1. Stephen is meditating on pretenders (i.e., false claimants): the names here are those of pretenders who have figured in English history.
2. Mulligan had saved a man from drowning.
3. Of course (German).
4. A man had been drowned off the coast, and his body had not yet been recovered. As Stephen thinks of the horror of drowning, he recalls once

again his mother's death.
5. The dog is described in the language of heraldry. "On an orange-brown (tawny) background, a buck, tripping, in natural colors, without horns."
6. Seahorses, with a pun on Morse code.
7. Stephen recognizes the man and woman on the beach as gypsy cockle pickers (cockles are edible shellfish, like mussels).

lay on his path. He stopped, sniffed, stalked round it, brother, nosing closer, went round it, sniffing rapidly like a dog all over the dead dog's bedraggled fell. Dogskull, dogsniff, eyes on the ground, moves to one great goal. Ah, poor dogsbody. Here lies poor dogsbody's body.

—Tatters! Outofthat, you mongrel.

The cry brought him skulking back to his master and a blunt bootless kick sent him unscathed across a spit of sand, crouched in flight. He slunk back in a curve. Doesn't see me. Along by the edge of the mole he lolloped, dawdled, smelt a rock and from under a cocked hindleg pissed against it. He trotted forward and, lifting his hindleg, pissed quick short at an unsmelt rock. The simple pleasures of the poor. His hindpaws then scattered sand: then his fore-paws dabbled and delved. Something he buried there, his grandmother.[8] He rooted in the sand, dabbling, delving and stopped to listen to the air, scraped up the sand again with a fury of his claws, soon ceasing, a pard,[9] a panther, got in spousebreach,[1] vulturing the dead.

After he woke me last night same dream or was it? Wait. Open hallway. Street of harlots. Remember. Haroun al Raschid.[2] I am almosting it. That man led me, spoke. I was not afraid. The melon he had he held against my face. Smiled: creamfruit smell. That was the rule, said. In. Come. Red carpet spread. You will see who.

Shouldering their bags they trudged, the red Egyptians.[3] His blued feet out of turnedup trousers slapped the clammy sand, a dull brick muffler strangling his unshaven neck. With woman steps she followed: the ruffian and his strolling mort. Spoils[4] slung at her back. Loose sand and shellgrit crusted her bare feet. About her windraw face her hair trailed. Behind her lord his helpmate, bing awast, to Romeville.[5] When night hides her body's flaws calling under her brown shawl from an archway where dogs have mired. Her fancyman is treating two Royal Dublins in O'Loughlin's of Blackpitts. Buss her, wap in rogues' rum lingo, for, O, my dimber wapping dell.[6] A shefiend's whiteness under her rancid rags. Fumbally's lane that night: the tanyard smells.

> White thy fambles, red thy gan
> And thy quarrons dainty is.
> Couch a hogshead with me then.
> In the darkmans clip and kiss.[7]

Morose delectation Aquinas tunbelly calls this, *frate porcospino*.[8] Unfallen Adam rode and not rutted. Call away let him:[9] *thy quarrons dainty is.* Language no whit worse than his. Monkwords, marybeads jabber on their girdles: rogue-words, tough nuggets patter in their pockets.

8. Reference to a joke Stephen had made to his pupils in school that morning about "the fox burying his grandmother under a hollybush."
9. Leopard or panther.
1. I.e., begotten in adultery.
2. Stephen's dream of the famous Caliph of Baghdad, of the "street of harlots," and of his meeting a man with a melon foreshadows his meeting later in the day with Leopold Bloom and his visit to the brothel area of Dublin.
3. I.e., gypsies. As Stephen watches the gypsy cockle pickers with their dog he imagines their vagabond life and recalls fragments of gypsy speech and of thieves' slang.
4. The association of gypsy ("mort": free gypsy woman; harlot) with Egyptian reminds Stephen of the Israelites "spoiling the Egyptians" (Exodus

12.36).
5. Go away to London.
6. 17th-century thieves' slang. "Buss": kiss. "Wap": copulate with. "Rum": good. "Dimber": pretty. "Wapping dell": whore.
7. More thieves' slang. "Fambles": hands. "Gan": mouth. "Quarrons": body. "Couch a hogshead": come to bed. "Darkmans": night. "Clip": kiss. These four lines and some of the phrases in the preceding paragraph are quoted from a song of the period, "The Rogue's Delight in Praise of His Strolling Mort" (cf. n. 3 and n. 4, this page).
8. Brother porcupine (Italian), a reference to the fat ("tunbelly") but prickly 13-century philosopher, St. Thomas Aquinas.
9. The gypsy is calling his dog.

Passing now.

A side-eye at my Hamlet hat. If I were suddenly naked here as I sit? I am not. Across the sands of all the world, followed by the sun's flaming sword, to the west, trekking to evening lands. She trudges, schlepps, trains, drags, trascines her load.[1] A tide westering, moondrawn, in her wake. Tides, myriadislanded, within her, blood not mine, *oinopa ponton*,[2] a winedark sea. Behold the handmaid of the moon. In sleep the wet sign calls her hour, bids her rise. Bridebed, childbed, bed of death, ghostcandled.[3] *Omnis caro ad te veniet.* He comes, pale vampire, through storm his eyes, his bat sails bloodying the sea, mouth to her mouth's kiss.[4]

Here. Put a pin in that chap, will you? My tablets.[5] Mouth to her kiss. No. Must be two of em. Glue em well. Mouth to her mouth's kiss.

His lips lipped and mouthed fleshless lips of air: mouth to her womb. Oomb, allwombing tomb.[6] His mouth moulded issuing breath, unspeeched: ooeeehah: roar of cataractic planets, globed, blazing, roaring wayawayawayawayawayaway. Paper. The banknotes, blast them. Old Deasy's letter. Here. Thanking you for the hospitality tear the blank end off. Turning his back to the sun he bent over far to a table of rock and scribbled words.[7] That's twice I forgot to take slips from the library counter.

His shadow lay over the rocks as he bent, ending. Why not endless till the farthest star? Darkly they are there behind this light, darkness shining in the brightness, delta of Cassiopeia, worlds. Me sits there with his augur's rod of ash, in borrowed sandals, by day beside a livid sea, unbeheld, in violet night walking beneath a reign of uncouth stars.[8] I throw this ended shadow from me, manshape ineluctable, call it back. Endless, would it be mine, form of my form? Who watches me here? Who ever anywhere will read these written words? Signs on a white field. Somewhere to someone in your flutiest voice. The good bishop of Cloyne[9] took the veil of the temple out of his shovel hat: veil of space with coloured emblems hatched on its field. Hold hard. Coloured on a flat: yes, that's right. Flat I see, then think distance, near, far, flat I see, east, back. Ah, see now. Falls back suddenly, frozen in stereoscope. Click does the trick. You find my words dark. Darkness is in our souls, do you not think? Flutier. Our souls, shamewounded by our sins, cling to us yet more, a woman to her lover clinging, the more the more.

She trusts me, her hand gentle, the longlashed eyes. Now where the blue hell am I bringing her beyond the veil?[1] Into the ineluctable modality of the ineluctable visuality. She, she, she. What she? The virgin at Hodges Figgis' window on Monday looking in for one of the alphabet books you were going

---

1. All words suggesting moving or dragging. " 'I like that crescendo of verbs,' he [Joyce] said. 'The irresistible tug of the tides' " (Budgen).
2. Winedark sea (Homer).
3. He is thinking of his mother again. The following Latin (from the burial service) means: All flesh will come to thee.
4. Death comes like the Flying Dutchman in a phantom ship to give the fatal kiss.
5. Cf. *Hamlet* 1.5.107: "My tablets."
6. Cf. Blake's poem "The Gates of Paradise," esp. the lines "The door of death I open found / And the worm weaving in the ground: / Thou'rt my mother from the womb, / Wife, sister, daughter, to the tomb." Cf. also *Romeo and Juliet* 2.2.9–10: "the earth, that's nature's mother, is her tomb. / What is her burying grave, that is her womb."
7. Stephen tears off the blank end of Mr. Deasy's

letter to the press and writes a poem, which is quoted later in the novel.
8. He imagines himself as the constellation Cassiopeia, supposed to represent the wife of Cepheus (an Ethiopian king) seated in a chair and holding up her arms. His ash walking stick he thinks of as an "augur's [Roman soothsayer's] rod of ash."
9. George Berkeley (1685–1753), bishop of Cloyne (in Ireland), who argued that the external world has no objective reality but exists only in the mind of the perceiver. Stephen (as at the opening of this episode) is experimenting again with ways of sensing reality.
1. "She" is Psyche, the soul, whom he is bringing from "beyond the veil." But from metaphysical speculations on reality and the soul Stephen is led (by the Psyche association) to think of "the virgin at Hodges Figgis' [a bookseller's] window."

to write. Keen glance you gave her. Wrist through the braided jess of her sunshade. She lives in Leeson park with a grief and kickshaws, a lady of letters. Talk that to some else, Stevie: a pickmeup. Bet she wears those curse of God stays suspenders and yellow stockings, darned with lumpy wool. Talk about apple dumplings, *piuttosto*.[2] Where are your wits?

Touch me. Soft eyes. Soft soft soft hand. I am lonely here. O, touch me soon, now. What is that word known to all men? I am quiet here alone. Sad too. Touch, touch me.

He lay back at full stretch over the sharp rocks, cramming the scribbled note and pencil into a pocket, his hat tilted down on his eyes. That is Kevin Egan's movement I made, nodding for his nap, sabbath sleep. *Et vidit Deus. Et erant valde bona.*[3] Alo! *Bonjour.* Welcome as the flowers in May. Under its leaf he watched through peacocktwittering lashes the southing sun. I am caught in this burning scene. Pan's hour, the faunal noon. Among gumheavy serpentplants, milkoozing fruits, where on the tawny waters leaves lie wide. Pain is far.

And no more turn aside and brood.[4]

His gaze brooded on his broadtoed boots, a buck's castoffs, *nebeneinander*. He counted the creases of rucked leather wherein another's foot had nested warm. The foot that beat the ground in tripudium, foot I dislove. But you were delighted when Esther Osvalt's shoe went on you: girl I knew in Paris. *Tiens, quel petit pied!*[5] Staunch friend, a brother soul: Wilde's love that dare not speak its name.[6] He now will leave me. And the blame? As I am. As I am. All or not at all.

In long lassoes from the Cock lake the water flowed full, covering green-goldenly lagoons of sand, rising, flowing. My ashplant will float away. I shall wait. No, they will pass on, passing chafing against the low rocks, swirling, passing. Better get this job over quick. Listen: a fourworded wavespeech: seesoo, hrss, rsseeiss ooos. Vehement breath of waters amid seasnakes, rearing horses, rocks. In cups of rocks it slops: flop, slop, slap: bounded in barrels. And, spent, its speech ceases. It flows purling, widely flowing, floating foam-pool, flower unfurling.

Under the upswelling tide he saw the writhing weeds lift languidly and sway reluctant arms, hising up their petticoats,[7] in whispering water swaying and upturning coy silver fronds. Day by day: night by night: lifted, flooded and let fall. Lord, they are weary: and, whispered to, they sigh. Saint Ambrose heard it, sigh of leaves and waves, waiting, awaiting the fullness of their times, *diebus ac noctibus iniurias patiens ingemiscit*.[8] To no end gathered; vainly then released, forthflowing, wending back: loom of the moon. Weary too in sight of lovers, lascivious men, a naked woman shining in her courts, she draws a toil of waters.

Five fathoms out there. Full fathom five thy father lies.[9] At one he said.

---

2. Rather, sooner (Italian).

3. Connecting two phrases from the Vulgate (Latin Bible): "And God saw" (Genesis 1.4) and "And they were very good" (Genesis 1.31).

4. The first line of the second (and last) stanza of Yeats's poem "Who Goes with Fergus?" which is often in Stephen's mind. The line expresses for him the mood, of noontide stillness and of lotos eating in a lush Asian scene, that overcomes him momentarily when he realizes that it is twelve o'clock, the hour of the Greek nature god Pan, "faunal noon." This Asian lotos-eating theme, which is associated

also with Bloom, is important in the *Odyssey*.

5. Look, what a little foot! (French).

6. Asked at his 1895 trial for homosexuality what this line meant, Oscar Wilde defined it as the great spiritual affection of an elder man for a younger man.

7. A phrase from a vulgar song sung by Mulligan earlier that morning.

8. Night and day he patiently groaned forth his wrongs (St. Ambrose).

9. From Ariel's song (*The Tempest* 1.2.400).

Found drowned. High water at Dublin bar. Driving before it a loose drift of rubble, fanshoals of fishes, silly shells. A corpse rising salt-white from the undertow, bobbing landward a pace a pace a porpoise. There he is. Hook it quick. Sunk though he be beneath the watery floor. We have him. Easy now.

Bag of corpsegas sopping in foul brine. A quiver of minnows, fat of a spongy titbit, flash through the slits of his buttoned trouserfly. God becomes man becomes fish becomes barnacle goose becomes featherbed mountain. Dead breaths I living breathe, tread dead dust, devour a urinous offal from all dead. Hauled stark over the gunwhale he breathes upward the stench of his green grave, his leprous nosehole snoring to the sun.

A seachange[1] this, brown eyes saltblue. Seadeath, mildest of all deaths known to man. Old Father Ocean. *Prix de Paris:*[2] beware of imitations. Just you give it a fair trial. We enjoyed ourselves immensely.

Come. I thirst. Clouding over. No black clouds anywhere, are there? Thunderstorm. Allbright he falls, proud lightning of the intellect, *Lucifer, dico, qui nescit occasum.*[3] No. My cockle hat and staff and hismy sandal shoon.[4] Where? To evening lands. Evening will find itself.

He took the hilt of his ashplant, lunging with it softly, dallying still. Yes, evening will find itself in me, without me. All days make their end. By the way next when is it? Tuesday will be the longest day. Of all the glad new year, mother,[5] the rum tum tiddledy tum. Lawn Tennyson,[6] gentleman poet. *Già.*[7] For the old hag with the yellow teeth. And Monsieur Drumont, gentleman journalist. *Già.* My teeth are very bad. Why, I wonder? Feel. That one is going too. Shells. Ought I go to a dentist, I wonder, with what money? That one. Toothless Kinch, the superman. Why is that, I wonder, or does it mean something perhaps?

My handkerchief. He threw it. I remember. Did I not take it up?

His hand groped vainly in his pockets. No, I didn't. Better buy one.

He laid the dry snot picked from his nostril on a ledge of rock, carefully. For the rest let look who will.

Behind. Perhaps there is someone.

He turned his face over a shoulder, rere regardant.[8] Moving through the air high spars of a threemaster, her sails brailed up on the crosstrees, homing, upstream, silently moving, a silent ship.

[LESTRYGONIANS][9]

Pineapple rock, lemon platt, butter scotch. A sugarsticky girl shovelling scoopfuls of creams for a christian brother. Some school treat. Bad for their

---

1. Another quotation from Ariel's song (1.2.404).
2. Prize of Paris. The reference is probably to the Paris Exposition of 1889, where prizes were awarded in various categories of food and other commodities; the winners bore the seal of the prize on the label (hence, "beware of imitations"). Stephen mentally awards the prize to death by drowning.
3. Lucifer, I say, who knows not his fall (Latin). Thunder and lightning recall the fall of Lucifer.
4. From Ophelia's mad song (*Hamlet* 4.5.23–26): "How should I your true love know / From another one?— / By his cockle hat and staff, / And his sandal shoon." Ophelia, too, was drowned.
5. Cf. Alfred, Lord Tennyson, "The May Queen": "You must wake and call me early, call me early, mother dear; / Tomorrow 'ill be the happiest time of all the glad New Year."
6. A parody of the poet's name, punning on "lawn

tennis," attributed to W. B. Yeats.
7. Let's go (Italian).
8. Looking behind him (heraldic terminology). Stephen, as we leave him sitting by the shore, is described in a highly stylized, heraldic language.
9. The eighth of the novel's eighteen episodes. It is lunchtime in Dublin, and Leopold Bloom, as he walks through the city in no great hurry (for he likes to linger and watch what goes on around him), thinks of food. The Lestrygonians in book 10 of the *Odyssey* are cannibals, and throughout this episode there are suggestions of the slaughter of living creatures for food or of food as something disgusting, which make somewhat tenuous contact with Homer's description of the cannibals spearing Ulysses' men for food. This episode shows us Bloom's consciousness responding to the sights and sounds of Dublin. His humane curiosity, his desire to learn and to improve the human lot, his

tummies. Lozenge and comfit manufacturer to His Majesty the King. God. Save. Our. Sitting on his throne sucking red jujubes white.

A sombre Y. M. C. A. young man, watchful among the warm sweet fumes of Graham Lemon's, placed a throwaway in a hand of Mr Bloom.

Heart to heart talks.

Bloo . . . Me? No.

Blood of the Lamb.[1]

His slow feet walked him riverward, reading. Are you saved? All are washed in the blood of the lamb. God wants blood victim. Birth, hymen, martyr, war, foundation of a building, sacrifice, kidney burntoffering, druids' altars. Elijah is coming. Dr John Alexander Dowie,[2] restorer of the church in Zion, is coming.

> *Is coming! Is coming!! Is coming!!!*
> *All heartily welcome.*

Paying game. Torry and Alexander last year. Polygamy. His wife will put the stopper on that. Where was that ad some Birmingham firm the luminous crucifix. Our Saviour. Wake up in the dead of night and see him on the wall, hanging. Pepper's ghost idea.[3] Iron Nails Ran In.

Phosphorus it must be done with. If you leave a bit of codfish for instance. I could see the bluey silver over it. Night I went down to the pantry in the kitchen. Don't like all the smells in it waiting to rush out. What was it she[4] wanted? The Malaga raisins. Thinking of Spain. Before Rudy[5] was born. The phosphorescence, that bluey greeny. Very good for the brain.

From Butler's monument house corner he glanced along Bachelor's walk. Dedalus' daughter there still outside Dillon's auctionrooms. Must be selling off some old furniture. Knew her eyes at once from the father. Lobbing about waiting for him. Home always breaks up when the mother goes. Fifteen children he had. Birth every year almost. That's in their theology or the priest won't give the poor woman the confession, the absolution. Increase and multiply. Did you ever hear such an idea? Eat you out of house and home. No families themselves to feed. Living on the fat of the land. Their butteries and larders. I'd like to see them do the black fast Yom Kippur.[6] Crossbuns. One meal and a collation for fear he'd collapse on the altar. A housekeeper of one of those fellows if you could pick it out of her. Never pick it out of her. Like getting L s. d.[7] out of him. Does himself well. No guests. All for number one. Watching his water. Bring your own bread and butter. His reverence. Mum's the word.

---

sympathetic concern for Mrs. Breen and Mrs. Purefoy, his feeding the gulls, his recollections of a happier time when his daughter was a baby and his relations with his wife were thoroughly satisfactory, his interest in opera, his continuous shying away from thoughts of his wife's rendezvous with the dashing Blazes Boylan—all this helps to build up his character in depth and to differentiate him sharply from Stephen. Unlike Stephen, Bloom's interest in language is confined to simple puns and translations; his interest in poetry is obvious and sentimental; his interest in the nature of reality takes the form of half-forgotten fragments of science remaining in his mind from school days. Everything about him is concrete, practical, sensual, and middlebrow or lowbrow, as distinct from the abstract, theoretical, esoteric speculations of Stephen in the "Proteus" episode.

1. Bloom has been handed a religious leaflet ("throwaway") containing the phrase "Blood of the Lamb." He at first mistakes "Blood" for "Bloom."

2. Scottish American evangelist (1847–1907), who established the "Christian Catholic Apostolic Church in Zion" in 1896 and founded Zion City, IL, in 1901.

3. A dramatic troupe advertising as "The original Pepper's Ghost! and Spectral Opera Company" was popular in the late-19th century; it seems to have specialized in ghostly special effects, possibly achieved through the use of phosphorescent material on its costumes.

4. I.e., Bloom's wife, Molly, born in Gibraltar.

5. Their son, who had died in infancy eleven years before.

6. Jewish Day of Atonement.

7. I.e., cash: L, s., d. are the abbreviations, respectively, for pounds, shillings, and pence.

Good Lord, that poor child's dress is in flitters. Underfed she looks too. Potatoes and marge, marge and potatoes. It's after they feel it. Proof of the pudding. Undermines the constitution.

As he set foot on O'Connell bridge a puffball of smoke plumed up from the parapet. Brewery barge with export stout. England. Sea air sours it, I heard. Be interesting some day get a pass through Hancock to see the brewery. Regular world in itself. Vats of porter, wonderful. Rats get in too. Drink themselves bloated as big as a collie floating. Dead drunk on the porter. Drink till they puke again like christians. Imagine drinking that! Rats: vats. Well of course if we knew all the things.

Looking down he saw flapping strongly, wheeling between the gaunt quaywalls, gulls. Rough weather outside. If I threw myself down? Reuben J's son must have swallowed a good bellyful of that sewage.[8] One and eightpence too much. Hhhhm. It's the droll way he comes out with the things. Knows how to tell a story too.

They wheeled lower. Looking for grub. Wait.

He threw down among them a crumpled paper ball. Elijah thirtytwo feet per sec is com.[9] Not a bit. The ball bobbed unheeded on the wake of swells, floated under by the bridgepiers. Not such damn fools. Also the day I threw that stale cake out of the Erin's King picked it up in the wake fifty yards astern. Live by their wits. They wheeled, flapping.

> The hungry famished gull
> Flaps o'er the waters dull.

That is how poets write, the similar sounds. But then Shakespeare has no rhymes: blank verse. The flow of the language it is. The thoughts. Solemn.

> Hamlet, I am thy father's spirit
> Doomed for a certain time to walk the earth.[1]

—Two apples a penny! Two for a penny!

His gaze passed over the glazed apples serried on her stand. Australians they must be this time of year. Shiny peels: polishes them up with a rag or a handkerchief.

Wait. Those poor birds.

He halted again and bought from the old applewoman two Banbury cakes for a penny and broke the brittle paste and threw its fragments down into the Liffey. See that? The gulls swooped silently two, then all from their heights, pouncing on prey. Gone. Every morsel.

Aware of their greed and cunning he shook the powdery crumb from his hands. They never expected that. Manna.[2] Live on fishy flesh they have to, all seabirds, gulls, seagoose. Swans from Anna Liffey[3] swim down here sometimes to preen themselves. No accounting for tastes. Wonder what kind is swanmeat. Robinson Crusoe had to live on them.

They wheeled, flapping weakly. I'm not going to throw any more. Penny quite enough. Lot of thanks I get. Not even a caw. They spread foot and mouth

8. The son of Reuben J. Dodd, Dublin solicitor (lawyer), had been rescued from the river Liffey by a man to whom Reuben J. had given two shillings as a reward—"one and eightpence too much," as Simon Dedalus had remarked to Bloom earlier that morning when they were discussing the incident. In the following sentences Bloom is thinking of Dedalus's comment.
9. I.e., Elijah is coming, accelerating at the rate of

thirty-two feet per second per second, the acceleration rate of falling bodies. ("Elijah is coming" is the legend on the handbill Bloom is tossing away).
1. *Hamlet* 1.5.9–10 (slightly misquoted).
2. The divine food (small, round, and white) that the children of Israel ate in the wilderness (Exodus 16.14–15).
3. The Liffey flows from the Wicklow Mountains northeast and east to Dublin Bay.

disease too. If you cram a turkey, say, on chestnutmeal it tastes like that. Eat pig like pig. But then why is it that saltwater fish are not salty? How is that?

His eyes sought answer from the river and saw a rowboat rock at anchor on the treacly swells lazily its plastered board.

Kino's

11 / -

Trousers[4]

Good idea that. Wonder if he pays rent to the corporation. How can you own water really? It's always flowing in a stream, never the same, which in the stream of life we trace. Because life is a stream. All kinds of places are good for ads. That quack doctor for the clap used to be stuck up in all the greenhouses. Never see it now. Strictly confidential. Dr Hy Franks. Didn't cost him a red like Maginni the dancing master self advertisement. Got fellows to stick them up or stick them up himself for that matter on the q.t. running in to loosen a button. Flybynight. Just the place too. POST NO BILLS. POST NO PILLS.[5] Some chap with a dose burning him.

If he . . .

O!

Eh?

No . . . No.

No, no. I don't believe it. He wouldn't surely?

No, no.[6]

Mr Bloom moved forward, raising his troubled eyes. Think no more about that. After one. Timeball on the ballastoffice is down. Dunsink time. Fascinating little book that is of Sir Robert Ball's. Parallax. I never exactly understood.[7] There's a priest. Could ask him. Par it's Greek: parallel, parallax. Met him pike hoses[8] she called it till I told her about the transmigration. O rocks!

Mr Bloom smiled O rocks at two windows of the ballastoffice. She's right after all. Only big words for ordinary things on account of the sound. She's not exactly witty. Can be rude too. Blurt out what I was thinking. Still I don't know. She used to say Ben Dollard had a base barreltone voice. He has legs like barrels and you'd think he was singing into a barrel. Now isn't that wit? They used to call him big Ben. Not half as witty as calling him base barreltone. Appetite like an albatross. Get outside of a baron of beef. Powerful man he was at stowing away number one Bass.[9] Barrel of Bass. See? It all works out.

A procession of whitesmocked men marched slowly towards him along the gutter, scarlet sashes across their boards. Bargains. Like that priest they are this morning: we have sinned: we have suffered. He read the scarlet letters on

---

4. I.e., eleven shillings ("11 / -") for Kino's Trousers. Bloom is a canvasser for advertisements: he receives commissions from newspapers for getting tradesmen to place advertisements with them.
5. The revised text edited by John Kidd (1993) reads, POST NO BILLS. POST 110 PILLS. "Post no bills" can mean either "do not affix any posters" or "mail no accounts." Bloom is punning to himself on the quack doctor's advertising (by posting bills), collecting his money (by mailing accounts), and sending pills to patients by mail.
6. Blazes Boylan, flashy philanderer, is due to call on Molly Bloom that afternoon, to discuss the program of a concert that he is managing for her (Molly is a singer). Bloom knows that Boylan and his wife will commit adultery together. Here it suddenly occurs to him that Boylan might give Molly

a "dose" of veneral disease, but he puts the thought from him as incredible.
7. The "timeball on the ballastoffice" registers the official time of the observatory at Dunsink (Dublin). Noticing that the timeball is down, which means that it is after one o'clock, Bloom is reminded of the observatory, then of the Irish astronomer Sir Robert Ball's popular book on astronomy, The Story of the Heavens (1886), and of the astronomical term parallax, which he found in the book but "never exactly understood."
8. Molly's way of pronouncing metempsychosis. When Bloom had explained metempsychosis to her that morning, she had exclaimed "O rocks!" at the pretentious term. He now mentally repeats "O rocks!" at the thought of the word parallax.
9. A popular British ale.

their five tall white hats: H. E. L. Y. S. Wisdom Hely's. Y lagging behind drew
a chunk of bread from under his foreboard, crammed it into his mouth and
munched as he walked. Our staple food. Three bob a day, walking along the
gutters, street after street. Just keep skin and bone together, bread and skilly.
They are not Boyl: no: M'Glade's men. Doesn't bring in any business either. I
suggested to him about a transparent showcart with two smart girls sitting
inside writing letters, copybooks, envelopes, blottingpaper. I bet that would
have caught on. Smart girls writing something catch the eye at once. Everyone
dying to know what she's writing. Get twenty of them round you if you stare
at nothing. Have a finger in the pie. Women too. Curiosity. Pillar of salt.[1]
Wouldn't have it of course because he didn't think of it himself first. Or the
inkbottle I suggested with a false stain of black celluloid. His ideas for ads like
Plumtree's potted under the obituaries, cold meat department. You can't lick
'em. What? Our envelopes. Hello! Jones, where are you going? Can't stop,
Robinson, I am hastening to purchase the only reliable inkeraser *Kansell*, sold
by Hely's Ltd, 85 Dame street. Well out of that ruck I am. Devil of a job it
was collecting accounts of those convents. Tranquilla convent. That was a
nice nun there, really sweet face. Wimple suited her small head. Sister? Sister?
I am sure she was crossed in love by her eyes. Very hard to bargain with that
sort of a woman. I disturbed her at her devotions that morning. But glad to
communicate with the outside world. Our great day, she said. Feast of Our
Lady of Mount Carmel. Sweet name too: caramel. She knew, I think she knew
by the way she. If she had married she would have changed. I suppose they
really were short of money. Fried everything in the best butter all the same.
No lard for them. My heart's broke eating dripping. They like buttering themselves in and out. Molly tasting it, her veil up. Sister? Pat Claffey, the pawn-
broker's daughter. It was a nun they say invented barbed wire.

He crossed Westmoreland street when apostrophe S had plodded by. Rover
cycleshop. Those races are on today. How long ago is that? Year Phil Gilligan
died. We were in Lombard street west. Wait, was in Thom's. Got the job in
Wisdom Hely's year we married. Six years. Ten years ago: ninetyfour he died,
yes that's right the big fire at Arnott's. Val Dillon was lord mayor. The Glencree
dinner. Alderman Robert O'Reilly emptying the port into his soup before the
flag fell, Bobbob lapping it for the inner alderman. Couldn't hear what the
band played. For what we have already received may the Lord make us. Milly[2]
was a kiddy then. Molly had that elephantgrey dress with the braided frogs.
Mantailored with selfcovered buttons. She didn't like it because I sprained my
ankle first day she wore choir picnic at the Sugarloaf. As if that. Old Goodwin's
tall hat done up with some sticky stuff. Flies' picnic too. Never put a dress on
her back like it. Fitted her like a glove, shoulder and hips. Just beginning to
plump it out well. Rabbitpie we had that day. People looking after her.

Happy. Happier then. Snug little room that was with the red wallpaper,
Dockrell's, one and ninepence a dozen. Milly's tubbing night. American soap
I bought: elderflower. Cosy smell of her bathwater. Funny she looked soaped
all over. Shapely too. Now photography.[3] Poor papa's daguerreotype atelier he
told me of. Hereditary taste.

He walked along the curbstone.

---

1. Cf. Genesis 19.1–26, where Lot's wife defies
God's order to "look not behind thee" and is turned
into "a pillar of salt."

2. Bloom's fifteen-year-old daughter. "For . . . us":
cf. the Lord's Prayer, often said before meals.

3. Milly is working at a photographer's.

Stream of life. What was the name of that priestlylooking chap was always squinting in when he passed? Weak eyes, woman. Stopped in Citron's saint Kevin's parade. Pen something. Pendennis? My memory is getting. Pen . . . ? Of course it's years ago. Noise of the trams probably. Well, if he couldn't remember the dayfather's name that he sees every day.

Bartell d'Arcy was the tenor, just coming out then. Seeing her home after practice. Conceited fellow with his waxedup moustache. Gave her that song *Winds that blow from the south.*

Windy night that was I went to fetch her there was that lodge meeting on about those lottery tickets after Goodwin's concert in the supperroom or oakroom of the Mansion house. He and I behind. Sheet of her music blew out of my hand against the High school railings. Lucky it didn't. Thing like that spoils the effect of a night for her. Professor Goodwin linking her in front. Shaky on his pins, poor old sot. His farewell concerts. Positively last appearance on any stage. May be for months and may be for never. Remember her laughing at the wind, her blizzard collar up. Corner of Harcourt road remember that gust. Brrfoo! Blew up all her skirts and her boa nearly smothered old Goodwin. She did get flushed in the wind. Remember when we got home raking up the fire and frying up those pieces of lap of mutton for her supper with the Chutney sauce she liked. And the mulled rum. Could see her in the bedroom from the hearth unclamping the busk of her stays: white.

Swish and soft flop her stays made on the bed. Always warm from her. Always liked to let her self out. Sitting there after till near two taking out her hairpins. Milly tucked up in beddyhouse. Happy. Happy. That was the night . . .

—O, Mr Bloom, how do you do?

—O, how do you do, Mrs Breen?[4]

—No use complaining. How is Molly those times? Haven't seen her for ages.

—In the pink, Mr Bloom said gaily, Milly has a position down in Mullingar, you know.

—Go away! Isn't that grand for her?

—Yes, in a photographer's there. Getting on like a house on fire. How are all your charges?

—All on the baker's list, Mrs Breen said.

How many has she? No other in sight.

—You're in black I see. You have no . . .

—No, Mr. Bloom said. I have just come from a funeral.

Going to crop up all day, I foresee. Who's dead, when and what did he die of? Turn up like a bad penny.

—O dear me, Mrs Breen said, I hope it wasn't any near relation.

May as well get her sympathy.

—Dignam, Mr Bloom said. An old friend of mine. He died quite suddenly, poor fellow. Heart trouble, I believe. Funeral was this morning.

> *Your funeral's tomorrow*
> *While you're coming through the rye.*
> *Diddlediddle dumdum*
> *Diddlediddle . . .*

—Sad to lose the old friends, Mrs Breen's womaneyes said melancholily. Now that's quite enough about that. Just quietly: husband.

---

4. Mrs. Breen had been an old sweetheart of Bloom's.

—And your lord and master?

Mrs Breen turned up her two large eyes. Hasn't lost them anyhow.

—O, don't be talking, she said. He's a caution to rattlesnakes. He's in there now with his lawbooks finding out the law of libel. He has me heartscalded. Wait till I show you.

Hot mockturtle vapour and steam of newbaked jampuffs rolypoly poured out from Harrison's. The heavy noonreek tickled the top of Mr Bloom's gullet. Want to make good pastry, butter, best flour, Demerara sugar, or they'd taste it with the hot tea. Or is it from her? A barefoot arab stood over the grating, breathing in the fumes. Deaden the gnaw of hunger that way. Pleasure or pain is it? Penny dinner. Knife and fork chained to the table.

Opening her handbag, chipped leather, hatpin: ought to have a guard on those things. Stick it in a chap's eye in the tram. Rummaging. Open. Money. Please take one. Devils if they lose sixpence. Raise Cain. Husband barging. Where's the ten shillings I gave you on Monday? Are you feeding your little brother's family? Soiled handkerchief: medicinebottle. Pastille that was fell. What is she? . . .

—There must be a new moon out, she said. He's always bad then.[5] Do you know what he did last night?

Her hand ceased to rummage. Her eyes fixed themselves on him, wide in alarm, yet smiling.

—What? Mr. Bloom asked.

Let her speak. Look straight in her eyes. I believe you. Trust me.

—Woke me up in the night, she said. Dream he had, a nightmare.

Indiges.[6]

—Said the ace of spades[7] was walking up the stairs.

—The ace of spades! Mr Bloom said.

She took a folded postcard from her handbag.

—Read that, she said. He got it this morning.

—What is it? Mr Bloom asked, taking the card. U. P.?[8]

—U.p.: up, she said. Someone taking a rise out of him. It's a great shame for them whoever he is.

—Indeed it is, Mr Bloom said.

She took back the card, sighing.

—And now he's going round to Mr Menton's office. He's going to take an action for ten thousand pounds, he says.

She folded the card into her untidy bag and snapped the catch.

Same blue serge dress she had two years ago, the nap bleaching. Seen its best days. Wispish hair over her ears. And that dowdy toque: three old grapes to take the harm out of it. Shabby genteel. She used to be a tasty dresser. Lines round her mouth. Only a year or so older than Molly.

See the eye that woman gave her, passing. Cruel. The unfair sex.

He looked still at her, holding back behind his look his discontent. Pungent mockturtle oxtail mulligatawny. I'm hungry too. Flakes of pastry on the gusset of her dress: daub of sugary flour stuck to her cheek. Rhubarb tart with liberal fillings, rich fruit interior. Josie Powell that was. In Luke Doyle's long ago, Dolphin's Barn, the charades. U.p.: up.

Change the subject.

---

5. Mr. Breen is mentally disturbed.
6. I.e., indigestion, which Bloom thinks caused Mr. Breen's nightmare.
7. A symbol of death.

8. Expression used in Charles Dickens's *Oliver Twist* (1838) to announce the approaching death of an old woman. It also suggests "you're crazy" or "you've been screwed."

—Do you ever see anything of Mrs Beaufoy, Mr Bloom asked.

—Mina Purefoy? she said.

Philip Beaufoy I was thinking. Playgoers' Club[9] Matcham often thinks of the masterstroke. Did I pull the chain? Yes. The last act.

—Yes.

—I just called to ask on the way in is she over it. She's in the lying-in hospital in Holles street. Dr Horne got her in. She's three days bad now.

—O, Mr Bloom said. I'm sorry to hear that.

—Yes, Mrs Breen said. And a houseful of kids at home. It's a very stiff birth, the nurse told me.

—O, Mr Bloom said.

His heavy pitying gaze absorbed her news. His tongue clacked in compassion. Dth! Dth!

—I'm sorry to hear that, he said. Poor thing! Three days! That's terrible for her.

Mrs Breen nodded

—She was taken bad on the Tuesday . . .

Mr Bloom touched her funnybone gently, warning her.

—Mind! Let this man pass.

A bony form strode along the curbstone from the river, staring with a rapt gaze into the sunlight through a heavystringed glass. Tight as a skullpiece a tiny hat gripped his head. From his arm a folded dustcoat, a stick and an umbrella dangled to his stride.

—Watch him, Mr Bloom said. He always walks outside the lampposts. Watch!

—Who is he if it's a fair question? Mrs Breen asked. Is he dotty?

—His name is Cashel Boyle O'Connor Fitzmaurice Tisdall Farrell, Mr Bloom said smiling. Watch!

—He has enough of them, she said. Denis will be like that one of these days.

She broke off suddenly.

—There he is, she said. I must go after him. Goodbye. Remember me to Molly, won't you?

—I will, Mr Bloom said.

He watched her dodge through passers towards the shopfronts. Denis Breen in skimpy frockcoat and blue canvas shoes shuffled out of Harrison's hugging two heavy tomes to his ribs. Blown in from the bay. Like old times. He suffered her to overtake him without surprise and thrust his dull grey beard towards her, his loose jaw wagging as he spoke earnestly.

Meshuggah.[1] Off his chump.

Mr Bloom walked on again easily, seeing ahead of him in sunlight the tight skullpiece, the dangling stick, umbrella, dustcoat. Going the two days. Watch him! Out he goes again. One way of getting on in the world. And that other old mosey lunatic in those duds. Hard time she must have with him.

U.p.: up. I'll take my oath that's Alf Bergan or Richie Goulding. Wrote it for a lark in the Scotch house, I bet anything. Round to Menton's office. His oyster eyes staring at the postcard. Be a feast for the gods.

9. Bloom is thinking of the story "Matcham's Masterstroke," by "Mr. Philip Beaufoy, Playgoers' Club, London," which he had read on the toilet that morning. He then mentally quotes the opening sentence.

1. Mad (Yiddish).

He passed the *Irish Times*. There might be other answers lying there. Like to answer them all. Good system for criminals. Code. At their lunch now. Clerk with the glasses there doesn't know me. O, leave them there to simmer. Enough bother wading through fortyfour of them. Wanted smart lady typist to aid gentleman in literary work. I called you naughty darling because I do not like that other world. Please tell me what is the meaning. Please tell me what perfume does your wife. Tell me who made the world.[2] The way they spring those questions on you. And the other one Lizzie Twigg.[3] My literary efforts have had the good fortune to meet with the approval of the eminent poet A. E. (Mr Geo. Russell).[4] No time to do her hair drinking sloppy tea with a book of poetry.

Best paper by long chalks for a small ad. Got the provinces now. Cook and general, exc cuisine, housemaid kept. Wanted live man for spirit counter. Resp. girl (R. C.) wishes to hear of post in fruit or pork shop. James Carlisle made that. Six and a half per cent dividend. Made a big deal on Coates's shares. Ca' canny. Cunning old Scotch hunks. All the toady news. Our gracious and popular vicereine.[5] Bought the *Irish Field* now. Lady Mountcashel has quite recovered after her confinement and rode out with the Ward Union staghounds at the enlargement yesterday at Rathoath. Uneatable fox. Pothunters too. Fear injects juices make it tender enough for them. Riding astride. Sit her horse like a man. Weightcarrying huntress. No sidesaddle or pillion for her, not for Joe. First to the meet and in at the death. Strong as a broodmare some of those horsey women. Swagger around livery stables. Toss off a glass of brandy neat while you'd say knife. That one at the Grosvenor this morning. Up with her on the car: wishswish. Stonewall or fivebarred gate put her mount to it. Think that pugnosed driver did it out of spite. Who is this she was like? O yes! Mrs Miriam Dandrade that sold me her old wraps and black underclothes in the Shelbourne hotel. Divorced Spanish American. Didn't take a feather out of her my handling them. As if I was her clotheshorse. Saw her in the viceregal party when Stubbs the park ranger got me in with Whelan of the *Express*. Scavenging what the quality left. High tea. Mayonnaise I poured on the plums thinking it was custard. Her ears ought to have tingled for a few weeks after. Want to be a bull for her. Born courtesan. No nursery work for her, thanks.

Poor Mrs Purefoy! Methodist husband. Method in his madness. Saffron bun and milk and soda lunch in the educational dairy. Eating with a stopwatch, thirtytwo chews to the minute. Still his muttonchop whiskers grew. Supposed to be well connected. Theodore's cousin in Dublin Castle. One tony relative in every family. Hardy annuals he presents her with. Saw him out at the Three Jolly Topers marching along bareheaded and his eldest boy carrying one in a marketnet. The squallers. Poor thing! Then having to give the breast year after

---

2. Cf. Marlowe's *The Tragical History of Doctor Faustus* 5, lines 237–44:

FAUSTUS   . . . Tell me who made the world?
MEPHASTOPHILIS   I will not.
     . . . Think on hell Faustus, for thou art damned.
FAUSTUS   Think, Faustus, upon God, that made the world.

3. Bloom is mentally quoting a letter written to him by the typist Martha Clifford, with whom he is carrying on a purely epistolary love affair (she had misspelled *word* as *world*: "I do not like that other world"). Lizzie Twigg was one of the other typists who had answered his advertisement for a secretary "to aid gentleman in literary work" (Bloom's pretext for beginning such an affair).

4. Æ (George Russell, 1867–1935), the Irish poet mentioned as a reference by Lizzie Twigg when she answered Bloom's advertisement, is later encountered by Bloom with a woman who Bloom speculates might be Lizzie.

5. Wife of the viceroy, who represented the British Crown in Ireland; Bloom is thinking of the society column in the *Irish Times*.

year all hours of the night. Selfish those t.t's[6] are. Dog in the manger. Only one lump of sugar in my tea, if you please.

He stood at Fleet street crossing. Luncheon interval a sixpenny at Rowe's? Must look up that ad in the national library.[7] An eightpenny in the Burton. Better. On my way.

He walked on past Bolton's Westmoreland house. Tea. Tea. Tea. I forgot to tap Tom Kernan.[8]

Sss. Dth, dth, dth! Three days imagine groaning on a bed with a vinegared handkerchief round her forehead, her belly swollen out. Phew! Dreadful simply! Child's head too big: forceps. Doubled up inside her trying to butt its way out blindly, groping for the way out. Kill me that would. Lucky Molly got over hers lightly. They ought to invent something to stop that. Life with hard labour. Twilightsleep idea: queen Victoria was given that. Nine she had. A good layer. Old woman that lived in a shoe she had so many children. Suppose he was consumptive. Time someone thought about it instead of gassing about the what was it the pensive bosom of the silver effulgence.[9] Flapdoddle to feed fools on. They could easily have big establishments. Whole thing quite painless out of all the taxes give every child born five quid at compound interest up to twentyone, five per cent is a hundred shillings and five tiresome pounds, multiply by twenty decimal system, encourage people to put by money save hundred and ten and a bit twentyone years want to work it out on paper come to a tidy sum, more than you think.

Not stillborn of course. They are not even registered. Trouble for nothing.

Funny sight two of them together, their bellies out. Molly and Mrs Moisel. Mothers' meeting. Phthisis retires for the time being, then returns. How flat they look after all of a sudden! Peaceful eyes. Weight off their mind. Old Mrs Thornton was a jolly old soul. All my babies, she said. The spoon of pap in her mouth before she fed them. O, that's nyumyum. Got her hand crushed by old Tom Wall's son. His first bow to the public. Head like a prize pumpkin. Snuffy Dr Murren. People knocking them up at all hours. For God's sake doctor. Wife in her throes. Then keep them waiting months for their fee. To attendance on your wife. No gratitude in people. Humane doctors, most of them.

Before the huge high door of the Irish house of parliament a flock of pigeons flew. Their little frolic after meals. Who will we do it on? I pick the fellow in black. Here goes. Here's good luck. Must be thrilling from the air. Apjohn, myself and Owen Goldberg up in the trees near Goose green playing the monkeys. Mackerel they called me.

A squad of constables debouched from College street, marching in Indian file. Goosestep. Foodheated faces, sweating helmets, patting their truncheons. After their feed with a good load of fat soup under their belts. Policeman's lot is oft a happy one.[1] They split up into groups and scattered, saluting towards their beats. Let out to graze. Best moment to attack one in pudding time. A punch in his dinner. A squad of others, marching irregularly, rounded Trinity[2] railings, making for the station. Bound for their troughs. Prepare to receive cavalry. Prepare to receive soup.

---

6. Abbreviation of *teetotalers*, total abstainers from alcohol.
7. Bloom's goal, on his walk through Dublin, is the National Library, where he wants to look up an advertisement in a back number of the *Kilkenny People*.
8. A Dublin tea merchant and friend of Bloom's, whom Bloom had earlier intended to ask ("tap") for some tea.
9. "Pensive bosom" and "silver effulgence": Bloom recalls two phrases from a public speech that is quoted (via a newspaper account) in "Aeolus," the novel's seventh episode.
1. Cf. W. S. Gilbert, *Pirates of Penzance*: "The policeman's lot is not a happy one."
2. Trinity College, Dublin.

He crossed under Tommy Moore's roguish finger. They did right to put him up over a urinal: meeting of the waters.[3] Ought to be places for women. Running into cakeshops. Settle my hat straight. *There is not in this wide world a vallee.* Great song of Julia Morkan's. Kept her voice up to the very last. Pupil of Michael Balfe's wasn't she?

He gazed after the last broad tunic. Nasty customers to tackle. Jack Power could a tale unfold: father a G man. If a fellow gave them trouble being lagged they let him have it hot and heavy in the bridewell.[4] Can't blame them after all with the job they have especially the young hornies. That horsepoliceman the day Joe Chamberlain was given his degree in Trinity he got a run for his money.[5] My word he did! His horse's hoofs clattering after us down Abbey street. Luck I had the presence of mind to dive into Manning's or I was souped. He did come a wallop, by George. Must have cracked his skull on the cobblestones. I oughtn't to have got myself swept along with those medicals. And the Trinity jibs[6] in their mortarboards. Looking for trouble. Still I got to know that young Dixon who dressed that sting for me in the Mater and now he's in Holles street where Mrs Purefoy. Wheels within wheels. Police whistle in my ears still. All skedaddled. Why he fixed on me. Give me in charge. Right here it began.

—Up the Boers!

—Three cheers for De Wet![7]

—We'll hang Joe Chamberlain on a sourapple tree.

Silly billies: mob of young cubs yelling their guts out. Vinegar hill. The Butter exchange band. Few years' time half of them magistrates and civil servants. War comes on: into the army helterskelter: same fellows used to. Whether on the scaffold high.

Never know who you're talking to. Corny Kelleher he has Harvey Duff in his eye. Like that Peter or Denis or James Carey that blew the gaff on the invincibles. Member of the corporation too. Egging raw youths on to get in the know. All the time drawing secret service pay from the castle.[8] Drop him like a hot potato. Why those plainclothes men are always courting slaveys. Easily twig a man used to uniform. Squarepushing up against a backdoor. Maul her a bit. Then the next thing on the menu. And who is the gentleman does be visiting there? Was the young master saying anything? Peeping Tom through the keyhole. Decoy duck. Hotblooded young student fooling round her fat arms ironing.

—Are those yours, Mary?

—I don't wear such things . . . Stop or I'll tell the missus on you. Out half the night.

—There are great times coming, Mary. Wait till you see.

—Ah, get along with your great times coming.

Barmaids too. Tobaccoshopgirls.

James Stephens'[9] idea was the best. He knew them. Circles of ten so that a fellow couldn't round on more than his own ring. Sinn Fein.[1] Back out you

3. "The Meeting of the Waters" was a famous poem by the much-loved Irish poet Thomas Moore (1779–1852), whose statue Bloom now passes.
4. Prison.
5. When Joseph Chamberlain, the British colonial secretary, came to Dublin to receive an honorary degree from Trinity College, a group of medical students rioted against him and against the Anglo-Boer War (1899–1902), in which the Boers, or Afrikaners, fought and lost to the British Empire.
6. Trinity College students.
7. Boer general. "Up" here as in "up with."
8. I.e., from the British government, whose representative lived at Dublin Castle.
9. Irish nationalist revolutionary.
1. Ourselves Alone (Gaelic); Irish revolutionary movement.

get the knife. Hidden hand. Stay in. The firing squad. Turnkey's daughter got him out of Richmond, off from Lusk. Putting up in the Buckingham Palace hotel under their very noses. Garibaldi.[2]

You must have a certain fascination: Parnell. Arthur Griffith[3] is a square-headed fellow but he has no go in him for the mob. Want to gas about our lovely land. Gammon[4] and spinach. Dublin Bakery Company's tearoom. Debating societies. That republicanism is the best form of government. That the language question should take precedence of the economic question. Have your daughters inveigling them to your house. Stuff them up with meat and drink. Michaelmas goose. Here's a good lump of thyme seasoning under the apron for you. Have another quart of goosegrease before it gets too cold. Half-fed enthusiasts. Penny roll and a walk with the band. No grace for the carver. The thought that the other chap pays best sauce in the world. Make themselves thoroughly at home. Show us over those apricots, meaning peaches. The not far distant day. Home Rule sun rising up in the northwest.[5]

His smile faded as he walked, a heavy cloud hiding the sun slowly, shadowing Trinity's surly front. Trams passed one another, ingoing, outgoing, clanging. Useless words. Things go on same; day after day: squads of police marching out, back: trams in, out. Those two loonies mooching about. Dignam carted off. Mina Purefoy swollen belly on a bed groaning to have a child tugged out of her. One born every second somewhere. Other dying every second. Since I fed the birds five minutes. Three hundred kicked the bucket. Other three hundred born, washing the blood off, all are washed in the blood of the lamb, bawling maaaaaa.

Cityful passing away, other cityful coming, passing away too: other coming on, passing on. Houses, lines of houses, streets, miles of pavements, piledup bricks, stones. Changing hands. This owner, that. Landlord never dies they say. Other steps into his shoes when he gets his notice to quit. They buy the place up with gold and still they have all the gold. Swindle in it somewhere. Piled up in cities, worn away age after age. Pyramids in sand. Built on bread and onions. Slaves Chinese wall. Babylon. Big stones left. Round towers. Rest rubble, sprawling suburbs, jerrybuilt, Kerwan's mushroom houses built of breeze. Shelter for the night.

No-one is anything.

This is the very worst hour of the day. Vitality. Dull, gloomy: hate this hour. Feel as if I had been eaten and spewed.

Provost's house. The reverend Dr Salmon: tinned salmon. Well tinned in there. Wouldn't live in it if they paid me. Hope they have liver and bacon today. Nature abhors a vacuum.

The sun freed itself slowly and lit glints of light among the silverware in Walter Sexton's window opposite by which John Howard Parnell[6] passed, unseeing.

There he is: the brother. Image of him. Haunting face. Now that's a coincidence. Course hundreds of times you think of a person and don't meet him. Like a man walking in his sleep. No-one knows him. Must be a corporation

2. Bloom is thinking of a variety of nationalist conspirators who escaped from danger, among them the 19th-century Italian patriot and general Giuseppe Garibaldi.
3. Founder of Sinn Fein (1872–1922). Charles Stewart Parnell (1846–1891), Irish nationalist political leader.

4. Ham, bacon.
5. Reference to Griffith's comment on the *Freeman's Journal* masthead, which showed the sun rising in the northwest from behind the Bank of Ireland. Bloom has a *Freeman* in his pocket.
6. Charles Parnell's brother.

meeting today. They say he never put on the city marshal's uniform since he got the job. Charley Beulger used to come out on his high horse, cocked hat, puffed, powdered and shaved. Look at the woebegone walk of him. Eaten a bad egg. Poached eyes on ghost. I have a pain. Great man's brother: his brother's brother. He'd look nice on the city charger. Drop into the D. B. C. probably for his coffee, play chess there. His brother used men as pawns. Let them all go to pot. Afraid to pass a remark on him. Freeze them up with that eye of his. That's the fascination: the name. All a bit touched. Mad Fanny and his other sister Mrs Dickinson driving about with scarlet harness. Bolt upright like surgeon M'Ardle. Still David Sheehy beat him for south Meath. Apply for the Chiltern Hundreds[7] and retire into public life. The patriot's banquet. Eating orangepeels in the park. Simon Dedalus said when they put him in parliament that Parnell would come back from the grave and lead him out of the House of Commons by the arm.

—Of the twoheaded octopus, one of whose heads is the head upon which the ends of the world have forgotten to come while the other speaks with a Scotch accent. The tentacles . . .

They passed from behind Mr Bloom along the curbstone. Beard and bicycle. Young woman.

And there he is too. Now that's really a coincidence: second time. Coming events cast their shadows before. With the approval of the eminent poet, Mr Geo Russell. That might be Lizzie Twigg with him.[8] A. E.: what does that mean? Initials perhaps. Albert Edward, Arthur Edmund, Alphonsus Eb Ed El Esquire. What was he saying? The ends of the world with a Scotch accent. Tentacles: octopus. Something occult: symbolism. Holding forth. She's taking it all in. Not saying a word. To aid gentleman in literary work.

His eyes followed the high figure in homespun, beard and bicycle, a listening woman at his side. Coming from the vegetarian. Only weggebobbles and fruit. Don't eat a beefsteak. If you do the eyes of that cow will pursue you through all eternity. They say it's healthier. Wind and watery though. Tried it. Keep you on the run all day. Bad as a bloater. Dreams all night. Why do they call that thing they gave me nutsteak? Nutarians. Fruitarians. To give you the idea you are eating rumpsteak. Absurd. Salty too. They cook in soda. Keep you sitting by the tap all night.

Her stockings are loose over her ankles. I detest that: so tasteless. Those literary etherial people they are all. Dreamy, cloudy, symbolistic. Esthetes they are. I wouldn't be surprised if it was that kind of food you see produces the like waves of the brain the poetical. For example one of those policemen sweating Irish stew into their shirts; you couldn't squeeze a line of poetry out of him. Don't know what poetry is even. Must be in a certain mood.

> *The dreamy cloudy gull*
> *Waves o'er the waters dull.*

He crossed at Nassau street corner and stood before the window of Yeates and Son, pricing the fieldglasses. Or will I drop into old Harris's and have a chat with young Sinclair? Wellmannered fellow. Probably at his lunch. Must

---

7. The stewardship of the Chiltern Hundreds (a tract of land in central England owned by the British Crown) is by a legal figment held to be an office of profit under the Crown and is conferred on members of Parliament wishing to resign, which by law they cannot do. Members of Parliament who accept an office of profit under the Crown must vacate their seats.

8. Bloom wonders whether the woman with A. E. might be Lizzie Twigg and then goes on to speculate on the meaning of "A. E." and on Russell's mystical ideas.

get those old glasses of mine set right. Gœrz lenses six guineas. Germans making their way everywhere. Sell on easy terms to capture trade. Undercutting. Might chance on a pair in the railway lost property office. Astonishing the things people leave behind them in trains and cloakrooms. What do they be thinking about? Women too. Incredible. Last year travelling to Ennis had to pick up that farmer's daughter's bag and hand it to her at Limerick junction. Unclaimed money too. There's a little watch up there on the roof of the bank to test those glasses by.

His lids came down on the lower rims of his irides. Can't see it. If you imagine it's there you can almost see it. Can't see it.

He faced about and, standing between the awnings, held out his right hand at arm's length towards the sun. Wanted to try that often. Yes: completely. The tip of his little finger blotted out the sun's disk. Must be the focus where the rays cross. If I had black glasses. Interesting. There was a lot of talk about those sunspots when we were in Lombard street west. Terrific explosions they are. There will be a total eclipse this year: autumn some time.

Now that I come to think of it, that ball falls at Greenwich time. It's the clock is worked by an electric wire from Dunsink. Must go out there some first Saturday of the month. If I could get an introduction to professor Joly or learn up something about his family. That would do to: man always feels complimented. Flattery where least expected. Nobleman proud to be descended from some king's mistress. His foremother. Lay it on with a trowel. Cap in hand goes through the land. Not go in and blurt out what you know you're not to: what's parallax? Show this gentleman the door.

Ah.

His hand fell again to his side.

Never know anything about it. Waste of time. Gasballs spinning about, crossing each other, passing. Same old dingdong always. Gas, then solid, then world, then cold, then dead shell drifting around, frozen rock like that pineapple rock. The moon. Must be a new moon out, she said. I believe there is.

He went on by la maison Claire.

Wait. The full moon was the night we were Sunday fortnight exactly there is a new moon. Walking down by the Tolka. Not bad for a Fairview moon. She was humming. The young May moon she's beaming, love. He other side of her. Elbow, arm. He. Glowworm's la-amp is gleaming, love. Touch. Fingers. Asking. Answer. Yes.

Stop. Stop. If it was it was.[9] Must.

Mr Bloom, quickbreathing, slowlier walking passed Adam court.

With deep quiet relief, his eyes took note: this is street here middle of the day Bob Doran's bottle shoulders. On his annual bend, M'Coy said. They drink in order to say or do something or *cherchez la femme*.[1] Up in the Coombe with chummies and streetwalkers and then the rest of the year as sober as a judge.

Yes. Thought so. Sloping into the Empire. Gone. Plain soda would do him good. Where Pat Kinsella had his Harp theatre before Whitbread ran the Queen's.[2] Broth of a boy. Dion Boucicault[3] business with his harvestmoon face in a poky bonnet. Three Purty Maids from School. How time flies eh? Showing long red pantaloons under his skirts. Drinkers, drinking, laughed spluttering, their drink against their breath. More power, Pat. Coarse red: fun

---

9. Bloom is thinking again of his wife's infidelity.
1. Look for the woman, i.e., in the case (French).
2. The Queen's Theatre.

3. Irish-born American dramatist, manager, and actor.

for drunkards: guffaw and smoke. Take off that white hat. His parboiled eyes. Where is he now? Beggar somewhere. The harp that once did starve us all.[4]

I was happier then. Or was that I? Or am I now I? Twentyeight I was. She twentythree when we left Lombard street west something changed. Could never like it again after Rudy. Can't bring back time. Like holding water in your hand. Would you go back to then? Just beginning then. Would you? Are you not happy in your home, you poor little naughty boy? Wants to sew on buttons for me. I must answer. Write it in the library.

Grafton street gay with housed awnings lured his senses. Muslin prints silk, dames and dowagers, jingle of harnesses, hoofthuds lowringing in the baking causeway. Thick feet that woman has in the white stockings. Hope the rain mucks them up on her. Countrybred chawbacon. All the beef to the heels were in. Always gives a woman clumsy feet. Molly looks out of plumb.

He passed, dallying, the windows of Brown Thomas, silk mercers. Cascades of ribbons. Flimsy China silks. A tilted urn poured from its mouth a flood of bloodhued poplin: lustrous blood. The huguenots brought that here. *La causa è santa!*[5] *Tara tara.* Great chorus that. *Tara.* Must be washed in rainwater. Meyerbeer. *Tara: bom bom bom.*

Pincushions. I'm a long time threatening to buy one. Stick them all over the place. Needles in window curtains.

He bared slightly his left forearm. Scrape: nearly gone. Not today anyhow. Must go back for that lotion. For her birthday perhaps. Junejuly augseptember eighth. Nearly three months off. Then she mightn't like it. Women won't pick up pins. Say it cuts lo.

Gleaming silks, petticoats on slim brass rails, rays of flat silk stockings.

Useless to go back. Had to be. Tell me all.

High voices. Sunwarm silk. Jingling harnesses. All for a woman, home and houses, silkwebs, silver, rich fruits, spicy from Jaffa. Agendath Netaim.[6] Wealth of the world.

A warm human plumpness settled down on his brain. His brain yielded. Perfume of embraces all him assailed. With hungered flesh obscurely, he mutely craved to adore.

Duke street. Here we are. Must eat. The Burton. Feel better then.

He turned Combridge's corner, still pursued. Jingling hoofthuds. Perfumed bodies, warm, full. All kissed, yielded: in deep summer fields, tangled pressed grass, in trickling hallways of tenements, along sofas, creaking beds.

—Jack, love!

—Darling!

—Kiss me, Reggy!

—My boy!

—Love![7]

4. A reference to the lack of financial success of the Harp Theatre through a punning reworking of Moore's famous "Harp That Once Through Tara's Halls."

5. "The cause is sacred," chorus from Meyerbeer's opera *Les Huguenots*, which Bloom is recalling. The Huguenots were 16th- and 17th-century French Protestants, many of whom fled to Britain to escape persecution.

6. Planters' Company (Hebrew). Bloom recalls a leaflet, which he had seen that morning and is still carrying in his pocket, advertising an early Zionist settlement

7. Sensual images are leading Bloom to imagine love scenes from a sentimental novel as he enters Burton's restaurant. In the *Odyssey*, the Lestrygonians had used "the handsome daughter of Lestrygonian Antiphates" as a decoy to lure Ulysses' men to her father.

His heart astir he pushed in the door of the Burton restaurant. Stink gripped his trembling breath: pungent meatjuice, slop of greens. See the animals feed.

Men, men, men.

Perched on high stools by the bar, hats shoved back, at the tables calling for more bread no charge, swilling, wolfing gobfuls of sloppy food, their eyes bulging, wiping wetted moustaches. A pallid suetfaced young man polished his tumbler knife fork and spoon with his napkin. New set of microbes. A man with an infant's saucestained napkin tucked round him shovelled gurgling soup down his gullet. A man spitting back on his plate: halfmasticated gristle: no teeth to chewchewchew it. Chump chop from the grill. Bolting to get it over. Sad booser's eyes. Bitten off more than he can chew. Am I like that? See ourselves as others see us. Hungry man is an angry man. Working tooth and jaw. Don't! O! A bone! That last pagan king of Ireland Cormac in the school-poem choked himself at Sletty southward of the Boyne.[8] Wonder what he was eating. Something galoptious.[9] Saint Patrick converted him to Christianity. Couldn't swallow it all however.

—Roast beef and cabbage.

—One stew.

Smells of men. His gorge rose. Spaton sawdust, sweetish warmish cigarette-smoke, reek of plug, spilt beer, men's beery piss, the stale of ferment.

Couldn't eat a morsel here. Fellow sharpening knife and fork, to eat all before him, old chap picking his tootles. Slight spasm, full, chewing the cud. Before and after. Grace after meals. Look on this picture then on that. Scoffing up stewgravy with sopping sippets of bread. Lick it off the plate, man! Get out of this.

He gazed round the stooled and tabled eaters, tightening the wings of his nose.

—Two stouts here.

—One corned and cabbage.

That fellow ramming a knifeful of cabbage down as if his life depended on it. Good stroke. Give me the fidgets to look. Safer to eat from his three hands. Tear it limb from limb. Second nature to him. Born with a silver knife in his mouth. That's witty, I think. Or no. Silver means born rich. Born with a knife. But then the allusion is lost.

An illgirt server gathered sticky clattering plates. Rock, the bailiff, standing at the bar blew the foamy crown from his tankard. Well up: it splashed yellow near his boot. A diner, knife and fork upright, elbows on table, ready for a second helping stared towards the food-lift across his stained square of news-paper. Other chap telling him something with his mouth full. Sympathetic listener. Table talk. I munched hum un thu Unchster Bunk un Munchday. Ha? Did you, faith?

Mr Bloom raised two fingers doubtfully to his lips. His eyes said:

—Not here. Don't see him.[1]

Out. I hate dirty eaters.

He backed towards the door. Get a light snack in Davy Byrne's. Stopgap. Keep me going. Had a good breakfast.

—Roast and mashed here.

---

8. Bloom is recalling a "schoolpoem" about a leg-endary incident in Irish history.
9. I.e., "goluptious," slang for delicious.

1. He pretends he is looking for someone he can-not see, so that he has an excuse to leave without eating.

—Pint of stout.

Every fellow for his own, tooth and nail. Gulp. Grub. Gulp. Gobstuff.

He came out into clearer air and turned back towards Grafton street. Eat or be eaten. Kill! Kill!

Suppose that communal kitchen years to come perhaps. All trotting down with porringers and tommycans to be filled. Devour contents in the street. John Howard Parnell example the provost of Trinity every mother's son don't talk of your provosts and provost of Trinity women and children, cabmen, priests, parsons, fieldmarshals, archbishops. From Ailesbury road, Clyde road, artisans' dwellings north Dublin union, lord mayor in his gingerbread coach, old queen in a bathchair. My plate's empty. After you with our incorporated drinking cup. Like sir Philip Crampton's fountain. Rub off the microbes with your handkerchief. Next chap rubs on a new batch with his. Father O'Flynn would make hares of them all. Have rows all the same. All for number one. Children fighting for the scrapings of the pot. Want a souppot as big as the Phoenix park. Harpooning flitches and hindquarters out of it. Hate people all round you. City Arms hotel *table d'hôte* she called it. Soup, joint and sweet. Never know whose thoughts you're chewing. Then who'd wash up all the plates and forks? Might be all feeding on tabloids that time. Teeth getting worse and worse.

After all there's a lot in that vegetarian fine flavour of things from the earth garlic, of course, it stinks Italian organgrinders crisp of onions mushrooms truffles. Pain to animal too. Pluck and draw fowl. Wretched brutes there at the cattlemarket waiting for the poleaxe to split their skulls open. Moo. Poor trembling calves. Meh. Staggering bob. Bubble and squeak. Butchers' buckets wobble lights. Give us that brisket off the hook. Plup. Rawhead and bloody bones. Flayed glasseyed sheep hung from their haunches, sheepsnouts bloody-papered snivelling nosejam on sawdust. Top and lashers going out. Don't maul them pieces, young one.

Hot fresh blood they prescribe for decline. Blood always needed. Insidious. Lick it up smokinghot, thick sugary. Famished ghosts.

Ah, I'm hungry.

He entered Davy Byrne's. Moral pub. He doesn't chat. Stands a drink now and then. But in leapyear once in four. Cashed a cheque for me once.

What will I take now? He drew his watch. Let me see now. Shandygaff?

—Hello, Bloom, Nosey Flynn said from his nook.

—Hello, Flynn.

—How's things?

—Tiptop . . . Let me see. I'll take a glass of burgundy and . . . let me see.

Sardines on the shelves. Almost taste them by looking. Sandwich? Ham and his descendants mustered and bred there. Potted meats. What is home without Plumtree's potted meat? Incomplete. What a stupid ad! Under the obituary notices they stuck it. All up a plumtree. Dignam's potted mat. Cannibals would with lemon and rice. White missionary too salty. Like pickled pork. Expect the chief consumes the parts of honour. Ought to be tough from exercise. His wives in a row to watch the effect. *There was a right royal old nigger. Who ate or something the somethings of the reverend Mr MacTrigger.* With it an abode of bliss. Lord knows what concoction. Cauls mouldy tripes windpipes faked and minced up. Puzzle find the meat. Kosher. No meat and milk together. Hygiene that was what they call now, Yom Kippur fast spring cleaning of inside. Peace and war depend on some fellow's digestion. Religions. Christmas turkeys and geese. Slaughter of innocents.[2] Eat, drink and be merry. Then casual wards full after. Heads bandaged. Cheese digests all but itself. Mighty cheese.

—Have you a cheese sandwich?

—Yes, sir.

Like a few olives too if they had them. Italian I prefer. Good glass of burgundy; take away that. Lubricate. A nice salad, cool as a cucumber. Tom Kernan can dress. Puts gusto into it. Pure olive oil. Milly served me that cutlet with a sprig of parsley. Take one Spanish onion. God made food, the devil the cooks. Devilled crab.

—Wife well?

—Quite well, thanks . . . A cheese sandwich, then. Gorgonzola, have you?

—Yes, sir.

Nosey Flynn sipped his grog.

—Doing any singing those times?

Look at his mouth. Could whistle in his own ear. Flap ears to match. Music. Knows as much about it as my coachman. Still better tell him. Does no harm. Free ad.

—She's engaged for a big tour end of this month. You may have heard perhaps.

—No. O, that's the style. Who's getting it up?

The curate[3] served.

—How much is that?

—Seven d., sir . . . Thank you, sir.

Mr Bloom cut his sandwich into slender strips. *Mr MacTrigger*. Easier than the dreamy creamy stuff. *His five hundred wives. Had the time of their lives.*

—Mustard, sir?

—Thank you.

He studded under each lifted strip yellow blobs. *Their lives*. I have it. *It grew bigger and bigger and bigger.*

—Getting it up? he said. Well, it's like a company idea, you see. Part shares and part profits.

—Ay, now I remember, Nosey Flynn said, putting his hand in his pocket to scratch his groin. Who is this was telling me? Isn't Blazes Boylan mixed up in it?

A warm shock of air heat of mustard hanched on Mr Bloom's heart. He raised his eyes and met the stare of a bilious clock. Two. Pub clock five minutes fast. Time going on. Hands moving. Two. Not yet.[4]

His midriff yearned then upward, sank within him, yearned more longly, longingly.

Wine.

He smellsipped the cordial juice and, bidding his throat strongly to speed it, set his wineglass delicately down.

—Yes, he said. He's the organiser in point of fact.

No fear: no brains.

Nosey Flynn snuffled and scratched. Flea having a good square meal.

—He had a good slice of luck, Jack Mooney was telling me, over that boxing match Myler Keogh won again that soldier in the Portobello barracks. By God, he had the little kipper down in the country Carlow he was telling me. . . .

---

2. Cf. Herod's massacre of innocent children after hearing prophecies of Jesus' birth (Matthew 2.16).

3. Bartender.

4. I.e., not yet time for Boylan to visit Molly.

Hope that dewdrop doesn't come down into his glass. No, snuffled it up.

—For near a month, man, before it came off. Sucking duck eggs by God till further orders. Keep him off the boose, see? O, by God, Blazes is a hairy chap.

Davy Byrne came forward from the hindbar in tuckstitched shirtsleeves, cleaning his lips with two wipes of his napkin. Herring's blush. Whose smile upon each feature plays with such and such replete. Too much fat on the parsnips.

—And here's himself and pepper on him, Nosey Flynn said. Can you give us a good one for the Gold cup?

—I'm off that, Mr Flynn, Davy Byrne answered. I never put anything on a horse.

—You're right there, Nosey Flynn said.

Mr Bloom ate his strips of sandwich, fresh clean bread, with relish of disgust, pungent mustard, the feety savour of green cheese. Sips of his wine soothed his palate. Not logwood that. Tastes fuller this weather with the chill off.

Nice quiet bar. Nice piece of wood in that counter. Nicely planed. Like the way it curves there.

—I wouldn't do anything at all in that line, Davy Byrne said. It ruined many a man, the same horses.

Vintners' sweepstake. Licensed for the sale of beer, wine and spirits for consumption on the premises. Heads I win tails you lose.

—True for you, Nosey Flynn said. Unless you're in the know. There's no straight sport going now. Lenehan gets some good ones. He's giving Sceptre today. Zinfandel's the favourite, lord Howard de Walden's, won at Epsom. Morny Cannon is riding him. I could have got seven to one against Saint Amant a fortnight before.

—That so? Davy Byrne said. . . .

He went towards the window and, taking up the petty cash book, scanned its pages.

—I could, faith, Nosey Flynn said, snuffling. That was a rare bit of horseflesh. Saint Frusquin was her sire. She won in a thunderstorm, Rothschild's filly, with wadding in her ears. Blue jacket and yellow cap. Bad luck to big Ben Dollard and his John O'Gaunt. He put me off it. Ay.

He drank resignedly from his tumbler, running his fingers down the flutes.

—Ay, he said, sighing.

Mr Bloom, champing standing, looked upon his sigh. Nosey numbskull. Will I tell him that horse Lenehan?[5] He knows already. Better let him forget. Go and lose more. Fool and his money. Dewdrop coming down again. Cold nose he'd have kissing a woman. Still they might like. Prickly beards they like. Dogs' cold noses. Old Mrs Riordan with the rumbling stomach's Skye terrier in the City Arms hotel. Molly fondling him in her lap. O, the big doggybowwowsywowsy!

Wine soaked and softened rolled pith of bread mustard a moment mawkish cheese. Nice wine it is. Taste it better because I'm not thirsty. Bath of course does that. Just a bite or two. Then about six o'clock I can. Six. Six. Time will be gone then. She . . .

Mild fire of wine kindled his veins. I wanted that badly. Felt so off colour. His eyes unhungrily saw shelves of tins, sardines, gaudy lobsters' claws. All

5. Bloom is wondering whether to pass on a tip from Lenehan, who wrote for the racing paper *Sport*.

the odd things people pick up for food. Out of shells, periwinkles with a pin, off trees, snails out of the ground the French eat, out of the sea with bait on a hook. Silly fish learn nothing in a thousand years. If you didn't know risky putting anything into your mouth. Poisonous berries. Johnny Magories. Roundness you think good. Gaudy colour warns you off. One fellow told another and so on. Try it on the dog first. Led on by the smell or the look. Tempting fruit. Ice cones. Cream. Instinct. Orangegroves for instance. Need artificial irrigation. Bleibtreustrasse.[6] Yes but what about oysters. Unsightly like a clot of phlegm. Filthy shells. Devil to open them too. Who found them out? Garbage, sewage they feed on. Fizz and Red bank oysters. Effect on the sexual. Aphrodis. He was in the Red bank this morning. Was he oyster old fish at table. Perhaps he young flesh in bed. No. June has no ar no oysters. But there are people like tainted game. Jugged hare. First catch your hare. Chinese eating eggs fifty years old, blue and green again. Dinner of thirty courses. Each dish harmless might mix inside. Idea for a poison mystery. That archduke Leopold was it. No. Yes, or was it Otto one of those Habsburgs? Or who was it used to eat the scruff off his own head? Cheapest lunch in town. Of course, aristocrats, then the others copy to be in the fashion. Milly too rock oil and flour. Raw pastry I like myself. Half the catch of oysters they throw back in the sea to keep up the price. Cheap. No-one would buy. Caviare. Do the grand. Hock in green glasses. Swell blowout. Lady this. Powdered bosom pearls. The *élite. Crème de la crème.*[7] They want special dishes to pretend they're. Hermit with a platter of pulse keep down the stings of the flesh. Know me come eat with me. Royal sturgeon. High sheriff, Coffey, the butcher, right to venisons of the forest from his ex.[8] Send him back the half of a cow. Spread I saw down in the Master of the Rolls' kitchen area. Whitehatted *Chef* like a rabbi. Combustible duck. Curly cabbage *à la duchesse de Parme.* Just as well to write it on the bill of fare so you can know what you've eaten too many drugs spoil the broth. I know it myself. Dosing it with Edwards' desicated soup. Geese stuffed silly for them. Lobsters boiled alive. Do ptake some ptarmigan. Wouldn't mind being a waiter in a swell hotel. Tips, evening dress, halfnaked ladies. May I tempt you to a little more filleted lemon sole, miss Dubedat? Yes, do bedad. And she did bedad. Huguenot name I expect that. A miss Dubedat lived in Killiney, I remember. *Du, de la,* French. Still it's the same fish, perhaps old Micky Hanlon of Moore street ripped the guts out of making money, hand over fist, finger in fishes' gills, can't write his name on a cheque, think he was painting the landscape with his mouth twisted. Moooikill A Aitcha Ha. Ignorant as a kish of brogues,[9] worth fifty thousand pounds.

Stuck on the pane two flies buzzed, stuck.

Glowing wine on his palate lingered swallowed. Crushing in the winepress grapes of Burgundy. Sun's heat it is. Seems to a secret touch telling me memory. Touched his sense moistened remembered. Hidden under wild ferns on Howth. Below us bay sleeping sky. No sound. The sky. The bay purple by the Lion's head. Green by Drumleck. Yellowgreen towards Sutton. Fields of undersea, the lines faint brown in grass, buried cities. Pillowed on my coat

---

6. The Berlin street that contained the offices of the "Planters' Company" (see n. 6, p. 2227).
7. Cream of the cream (i.e., the very best, socially).
8. All sturgeon caught in or off Britain were the property of the king, according to the ancient tra-

ditional rights to certain kinds of fish or game. Bloom goes on to imagine a Dublin butcher having a "right to venisons of the forest from his ex[cellency]"—i.e., the viceroy.
9. A basket of shoes.

she had her hair, earwigs in the heather scrub my hand under her nape, you'll toss me all. O wonder! Coolsoft with ointments her hand touched me, caressed: her eyes upon me did not turn away. Ravished over her I lay, full lips full open, kissed her mouth. Yum. Softly she gave me in my mouth the seedcake warm and chewed. Mawkish pulp her mouth had mumbled sweet and sour with spittle. Joy: I ate it: joy. Young life, her lips that gave me pouting. Soft, warm, sticky gumjelly lips. Flowers her eyes were, take me, willing eyes. Pebbles fell. She lay still. A goat. No-one. High on Ben Howth rhododendrons a nannygoat walking surefooted, dropping currants. Screened under ferns she laughed warmfolded. Wildly I lay on her, kissed her, eyes, her lips, her stretched neck, beating, woman's breasts full in her blouse of nun's veiling, fat nipples upright. Hot I tongued her. She kissed me. I was kissed. All yielding she tossed my hair. Kissed, she kissed me.[1]

Me. And me now.

Stuck, the flies buzzed.

His downcast eyes followed the silent veining of the oaken slab. Beauty: it curves: curves are beauty. Shapely goddesses, Venus, Juno: curves the world admires. Can see them library museum standing in the round hall, naked goddesses. Aids to digestion. They don't care what man looks. All to see. Never speaking, I mean to say to fellows like Flynn. Suppose she did Pygmalion and Galatea[2] what would she say first? Mortal! Put you in your proper place. Quaffing nectar at mess with gods, golden dishes, all ambrosial. Not like a tanner lunch we have, boiled mutton, carrots and turnips, bottle of Allsop. Nectar, imagine it drinking electricity: god's food. Lovely forms of women sculped Junonian. Immortal lovely. And we stuffing food in one hole and out behind: food, chyle, blood, dung, earth, food: have to feed it like stoking an engine. They have no. Never looked. I'll look today. Keeper won't see. Bend down let something see if she.

Dribbling a quiet message from his bladder came to go to do not to do there to do. A man and ready he drained his glass to the lees and walked, to men too they gave themselves, manly conscious, lay with men lovers, a youth enjoyed her, to the yard.

When the sound of his boots had ceased Davy Byrne said from his book:

—What is this he is? Isn't he in the insurance line?

—He's out of that long ago, Nosey Flynn said. He does canvassing for the *Freeman*.

—I know him well to see, Davy Byrne said. Is he in trouble?

—Trouble? Nosey Flynn said. Not that I heard of. Why?

—I noticed he was in mourning.

—Was he? Nosey Flynn said. So he was, faith. I asked him how was all at home. You're right, by God. So he was.

—I never broach the subject, Davy Byrne said humanely, if I see a gentleman is in trouble that way. It only brings it up fresh in their minds.

—It's not the wife anyhow, Nosey Flynn said. I met him the day before yesterday and he coming out of that Irish farm dairy John Wyse Nolan's wife

---

1. Bloom is remembering when he first proposed to Molly, on the Hill of Howth, near Dublin. Molly also recalls this in the final episode ("Penelope"), which is her soliloquy: "we were lying among the rhododendrons on Howth head in the gray tweed suit and his straw hat the day I got him to propose to me yes . . . my God after that long kiss I near lost my breath . . . I saw he understood or felt what a woman is and I knew I could always get round him and I gave him all the pleasure I could leading him on."

2. In Greek mythology Pygmalion, king of Cyprus, sculpted a statue of the goddess Aphrodite that became a mortal woman, Galatea.

has in Henry street with a jar of cream in his hand taking it home to his better half. She's well nourished, I tell you. Plovers on toast.

—And is he doing for the *Freeman*? Davy Byrne said.

Nosey Flynn pursed his lips.

—He doesn't buy cream on the ads he picks up. You can make bacon of that.

—How so? Davy Byrne asked, coming from his book.

Nosey Flynn made swift passes in the air with juggling fingers. He winked.

—He's in the craft,[3] he said.

—Do you tell me so? Davy Byrne said.

—Very much so, Nosey Flynn said. Ancient free and accepted order. Light, life and love, by God. They give him a leg up. I was told that by a, well, I won't say who.

—Is that a fact?

—O, it's a fine order, Nosey Flynn said. They stick to you when you're down. I know a fellow was trying to get into it, but they're as close as damn it. By God they did right to keep the women out of it.

Davy Byrne smiledyawnednodded all in one:

—Iiiiiichaaaaaaach!

—There was one woman, Nosey Flynn said, hid herself in a clock to find out what they do be doing. But be damned but they smelt her out and swore her in on the spot a master mason. That was one of the Saint Legers of Doneraile.

Davy Byrne, sated after his yawn, said with tearwashed eyes:

—And is that a fact? Decent quiet man he is. I often saw him in here and I never once saw him, you know, over the line.

—God Almighty couldn't make him drunk, Nosey Flynn said firmly. Slips off when the fun gets too hot. Didn't you see him look at his watch? Ah, you weren't there. If you ask him to have a drink first thing he does he outs with the watch to see what he ought to imbibe. Declare to God he does.

—There are some like that, Davy Byrne said. He's a safe man, I'd say.

—He's not too bad, Nosey Flynn said, snuffling it up. He has been known to put his hand down too to help a fellow. Give the devil his due. O, Bloom has his good points. But there's one thing he'll never do.

His hand scrawled a dry pen signature beside his grog.

—I know, Davy Byrne said.

—Nothing in black and white, Nosey Flynn said.

Paddy Leonard and Bantam Lyons came in. Tom Rochford followed frowning, a plaining hand on his claret waistcoat.

—Day, Mr Byrne.

—Day, gentlemen.

They paused at the counter.

—Who's standing? Paddy Leonard asked.

—I'm sitting anyhow, Nosey Flynn answered.

—Well, what'll it be? Paddy Leonard asked.

—I'll take a stone ginger, Bantam Lyons said.

—How much? Paddy Leonard cried. Since when, for God's sake? What's yours, Tom?

—How is the main drainage? Nosey Flynn asked, sipping.

---

3. I.e., in the "free and accepted order" of Freemasons, one of the oldest European secret societies; it was not in good repute in predominantly Roman Catholic countries like Ireland.

For answer Tom Rochford pressed his hand to his breastbone and hiccupped.

—Would I trouble you for a glass of fresh water, Mr Byrne? he said.

—Certainly, sir.

Paddy Leonard eyed his alemates.

—Lord love a duck, he said, look at what I'm standing drinks to! Cold water and gingerpop! Two fellows that would suck whisky off a sore leg. He has some bloody horse up his sleeve for the Gold cup. A dead snip.

—Zinfandel is it? Nosey Flynn asked.

Tom Rochford spilt powder from a twisted paper into the water set before him.

—That cursed dyspepsia, he said before drinking.

—Breadsoda is very good, Davy Byrne said.

Tom Rochford nodded and drank.

—Is it Zinfandel?

—Say nothing, Bantam Lyons winked. I'm going to plunge five bob on my own.

—Tell us if you're worth your salt and be damned to you, Paddy Leonard said. Who gave it to you?

Mr Bloom on his way out raised three fingers in greeting.

—So long, Nosey Flynn said.

The others turned.

—That's the man now that gave it to me, Bantam Lyons whispered.

—Prrwht! Paddy Leonard said with scorn. Mr Byrne, sir, we'll take two of your small Jamesons[4] after that and a . . . .

—Stone ginger, Davy Byrne added civilly.

—Ay, Paddy Leonard said. A suckingbottle for the baby.

Mr Bloom walked towards Dawson street, his tongue brushing his teeth smooth. Something green it would have to be: spinach say. Then with those Röntgen rays[5] searchlight you could.

At Duke lane a ravenous terrier choked up a sick knuckly cud on the cobblestones and lapped it with new zest. Surfeit. Returned with thanks having fully digested the contents. First sweet then savoury. Mr Bloom coasted warily. Ruminants. His second course. Their upper jaw they move. Wonder if Tom Rochford will do anything with that invention of his. Wasting time explaining it to Flynn's mouth. Lean people long mouths. Ought to be a hall or a place where inventors could go in and invent free. Course then you'd have all the cranks pestering.

He hummed, prolonging in solemn echo, the closes of the bars:

> Don Giovanni, a cenar teco
> M'invitasti.[6]

Feel better. Burgundy. Good pick me up. Who distilled first? Some chap in the blues. Dutch courage. That *Kilkenny People* in the national library now I must.

Bare clean closestools, waiting, in the window of William Miller, plumber,

4. Brand of Irish whiskey.
5. X-rays.
6. Because Molly is a singer, Bloom is familiar with opera. Here he recalls the song sung by the Commendatore's statue in Mozart's *Don Giovanni* and below he translates accurately the Italian words he quotes, except for *"teco"* (with thee). This opera supplies some of the key themes in *Ulysses,* and the famous duet between Don Giovanni and Zerlina, *"Là ci darèm la mano"* (There we will join hands), haunts Bloom's mind throughout the day. It is on the program of Molly's concert that she is discussing with Boylan that afternoon, and Bloom associates it with her adultery with Boylan.

turned back his thoughts. They could: and watch it all the way down, swallow a pin sometimes come out of the ribs years after, tour round the body, changing biliary duct, spleen squirting liver, gastric juice coils of intestines like pipes. But the poor buffer would have to stand all the time with his insides entrails on show. Science.

—*A cenar teco.*

What does that *teco* mean? Tonight perhaps.

> *Don Giovanni, thou hast me invited*
> *To come to supper tonight,*
> *The rum the rumdum.*

Doesn't go properly.

Keyes: two months if I get Nannetti[7] to. That'll be two pounds ten, about two pounds eight. Three Hynes owes me. Two eleven. Prescott's ad. Two fifteen. Five guineas about. On the pig's back.

Could buy one of those silk petticoats for Molly, colour of her new garters. Today. Today. Not think.[8]

Tour the south then. What about English wateringplaces? Brighton, Margate. Piers by moonlight. Her voice floating out. Those lovely seaside girls. Against John Long's a drowsing loafer lounged in heavy thought, gnawing a crusted knuckle. Handy man wants job. Small wages. Will eat anything.

Mr Bloom turned at Gray's confectioner's window of unbought tarts and passed the reverend Thomas Connellan's bookstore. *Why I left the church of Rome? Birds' Nest.* Women run him. They say they used to give pauper children soup to change to protestants in the time of the potato blight. Society over the way papa went to for the conversion of poor jews. Same bait. *Why we left the church of Rome?*

A blind stripling stood tapping the curbstone with his slender cane. No tram in sight. Wants to cross.

—Do you want to cross? Mr Bloom asked.

The blind stripling did not answer. His wallface frowned weakly. He moved his head uncertainly.

—You're in Dawson street, Mr Bloom said. Molesworth street is opposite. Do you want to cross? There's nothing in the way.

The cane moved out trembling to the left. Mr Bloom's eye followed its line and saw again the dyeworks' van drawn up before Drago's. Where I saw his brillantined hair just when I was. Horse drooping. Driver in John Long's. Slaking his drouth.

—There's a van there, Mr Bloom said, but it's not moving. I'll see you across. Do you want to go to Molesworth street?

—Yes, the stripling answered. South Frederick street.

—Come, Mr Bloom said.

He touched the thin elbow gently: then took the limp seeing hand to guide it forward.

Say something to him. Better not do the condescending. They mistrust what you tell them. Pass a common remark.

—The rain kept off.

---

7. Proofreader and business manager of the *Freeman's Journal* and in charge of the advertising Bloom is trying to get for the paper. If he will add a complimentary reference to Keyes, a grocer, in a gossip column, Keyes promises to renew his advertisement, which means a commission for Bloom.
8. I.e., of Molly and Boylan.

No answer.

Stains on his coat. Slobbers his food, I suppose. Tastes all different for him. Have to be spoonfed first. Like a child's hand, his hand. Like Milly's was. Sensitive. Sizing me up I daresay from my hand. Wonder if he has a name. Van. Keep his cane clear of the horse's legs tired drudge get his doze. That's right. Clear. Behind a bull: in front of a horse.

—Thanks, sir.

Knows I'm a man. Voice.

—Right now? First turn to the left.

The blind stripling tapped the curbstone and went on his way, drawing his cane back, feeling again.

Mr Bloom walked behind the eyeless feet, a flatcut suit of herringbone tweed. Poor young fellow! How on earth did he know that van was there? Must have felt it. See things in their foreheads perhaps. Kind of sense of volume. Weight would he feel it if something was removed. Feel a gap. Queer idea of Dublin he must have, tapping his way round by the stones. Could he walk in a beeline if he hadn't that cane? Bloodless pious face like a fellow going in to be a priest.

Penrose! That was that chap's name.

Look at all the things they can learn to do. Read with their fingers. Tune pianos. Or we are surprised they have any brains. Why we think a deformed person or a hunchback clever if he says something we might say. Of course the other senses are more. Embroider. Plait baskets. People ought to help. Workbasket I could buy Molly's birthday. Hates sewing. Might take an objection. Dark men they call them.

Sense of smell must be stronger too. Smells on all sides bunched together. Each person too. Then the spring, the summer: smells. Tastes. They say you can't taste wines with your eyes shut or a cold in the head. Also smoke in the dark they say get no pleasure.

And with a woman, for instance. More shameless not seeing. That girl passing the Stewart institution, head in the air. Look at me. I have them all on. Must be strange not to see her. Kind of a form in his mind's eye. The voice temperature when he touches her with fingers must almost see the lines, the curves. His hands on her hair, for instance. Say it was black for instance. Good. We call it black. Then passing over her white skin. Different feel perhaps. Feeling of white.

Postoffice. Must answer.[9] Fag[1] today. Send her a postal order two shillings half a crown. Accept my little present. Stationer's just here too. Wait. Think over it.

With a gentle finger he felt ever so slowly the hair combed back above his ears. Again. Fibres of fine fine straw. Then gently his finger felt the skin of his right cheek. Downy hair there too. Not smooth enough. The belly is the smoothest. No-one about. There he goes into Frederick street. Perhaps to Levenston's dancing academy piano. Might be settling my braces.

Walking by Doran's public house he slid his hand between waistcoat and trousers and, pulling aside his shirt gently, felt a slack fold of his belly. But I know it's whitey yellow. Want to try in the dark to see.

He withdrew his hand and pulled his dress to.

Poor fellow! Quite a boy. Terrible. Really terrible. What dreams would he

9. Martha Clifford's letter.   1. Nuisance.

have, not seeing. Life a dream for him. Where is the justice being born that way. All those women and children excursion beanfeast burned and drowned in New York.[2] Holocaust. Karma they call that transmigration for sins you did in a past life the reincarnation met him pike hoses.[3] Dear, dear, dear. Pity of course: but somehow you can't cotton on to them someway.

Sir Frederick Falkiner going into the freemasons' hall. Solemn as Troy. After his good lunch in Earlsfort terrace. Old legal cronies cracking a magnum. Tales of the bench and assizes and annals of the bluecoat school.[4] I sentenced him to ten years. I suppose he'd turn up his nose at that stuff I drank. Vintage wine for them, the year marked on a dusty bottle. Has his own ideas of justice in the recorder's court. Wellmeaning old man. Police charge sheets crammed with cases get their percentage manufacturing crime. Sends them to the rightabout. The devil on moneylenders. Gave Reuben J. a great strawcalling. Now he's really what they call a dirty jew. Power those judges have. Crusty old topers in wigs. Bear with a sore paw. And may the Lord have mercy on your soul.

Hello, placard. Mirus bazaar. His excellency the lord lieutenant. Sixteenth today it is. In aid of funds for Mercer's hospital. The *Messiah* was first given for that. Yes. Handel. What about going out there. Ballsbridge. Drop in on Keyes. No use sticking to him like a leech. Wear out my welcome. Sure to know someone on the gate.

Mr Bloom came to Kildare street. First I must. Library.

Straw hat in sunlight. Tan shoes. Turnedup trousers. It is. It is.[5]

His heart quopped[6] softly. To the right. Museum. Goddesses. He swerved to the right.

Is it? Almost certain. Won't look. Wine in my face. Why did I? Too heady. Yes, it is. The walk. Not see. Not see. Get on.

Making for the museum gate with long windy strides he lifted his eyes. Handsome building. Sir Thomas Deane designed. Not following me?

Didn't see me perhaps. Light in his eyes.

The flutter of his breath came forth in short sighs. Quick. Cold statues: quiet there. Safe in a minute.

No, didn't see me. After two. Just at the gate.

My heart!

His eyes beating looked steadfastly at cream curves of stone. Sir Thomas Deane was the Greek architecture.

Look for something I.

His hasty hand went quick into a pocket, took out, read unfolded Agendath Netaim. Where did I?

Busy looking for.

He thrust back quickly Agendath.

Afternoon she said.

I am looking for that. Yes, that. Try all pockets. Handker. *Freeman.* Where did I? Ah, yes. Trousers. Purse. Potato. Where did I?

Hurry. Walk quietly. Moment more. My heart.

---

2. This terrible disaster on an excursion steamer on a New York City river took place on June 15, 1904, and was reported in the Dublin papers on June 16.

3. I.e., metempsychosis. Bloom is remembering again their morning conversation on this subject, when Molly exclaimed, "O rocks!"

4. Sir Frederick Falkiner wrote the history of the "bluecoat school," in Oxmantown, Dublin, founded by Charles II for poor children.

5. Bloom catches a glimpse of Boylan and tries to avoid an encounter.

6. Throbbed, quivered (dialect, now obsolete).

His hand looking for the where did I put found in his hip pocket soap lotion have to call tepid paper stuck. Ah, soap there! Yes. Gate.[7] Safe!

1914–21   1922

Finnegans Wake   Because the meanings in *Finnegans Wake* are developed not by action but by language—a great network of multiple puns that echo themes back and forth throughout the book—the careful reading of a single passage, even out of context, will convey more than any summary of the "plot" (some discussion of the general plan of the work is given in the Joyce headnote). The passage printed here was one of Joyce's favorites, and there exists an audio recording of it made by him. It consists of the closing pages of chapter 8 of book 1; the chapter was published separately as "Anna Livia Plurabelle" in 1928 and 1930, although the finished book omits this title.

The entire chapter is a dialogue, and the scene is the river Liffey: two washerwomen are washing in public the dirty linen of HCE and ALP (the "hero" and "heroine") and gossiping as they work. As this excerpt opens, it is growing dark; things become gradually less and less distinct, so that the washerwomen cannot be sure what the objects seen in the dusk really are. As it grows darker, the river becomes wider (we get nearer its mouth) and the wind rises, so that the women have more and more difficulty hearing each other. At last, as night falls, they become part of the landscape, an elm tree and a stone on the river bank. Toward the end of the dialogue they ask to hear a tale of Shem and Shaun (the two sons of HCE and ALP), and this question points the way to book 2, which opens with the boys (metamorphosed for the moment into Glugg and Chuff) playing in front of the tavern in the evening.

A complete annotation of even this brief passage is, of course, a physical impossibility in this anthology. The notes that are provided are intended to indicate the nature of what Joyce does with language and to enable the reader to see some of what is going on. But all sorts of suggestions built up in the language are not referred to in the notes; all readers will find some for themselves.

From Finnegans Wake

From *Anna Livia Plurabelle*

* * * Well, you know or don't you kennet[1] or haven't I told you every telling has a taling and that's the he and the she of it. Look, look, the dusk is growing! My branches lofty are taking root. And my cold cher's gone ashley.[2] Fieluhr?

---

7. Anxious to avoid Boylan, Bloom pretends to admire the architecture of the Museum and National Library building and then pretends to be looking for something in his pockets, where he finds the "Agendath Netaim" leaflet. He continues to search desperately in his pockets to avoid looking up and seeing Boylan, discovers the potato he carries as a remedy against rheumatism and a cake of soap he had bought that morning (the soap reminds him that he must call at the chemist's to collect a face lotion he had ordered for Molly). At last he goes through the National Library gate and feels safe.

1. Ken it ("know it") + Kennet (river in England). Rivers in *Finnegans Wake* symbolize the flow of life, and thousands of river names are suggested throughout the book in allusive pun combinations, as here.

2. "Cold cher": cold cheer (i.e., cold comfort) + cold chair + (perhaps) culture. "Gone ashley": gone to ashes. Going to ashes suggests the fiery death and rebirth of the mythical bird called the phoenix: from the ashes of the dead phoenix rises a new one. Modern culture, which can provide only cold cheer, is in the state of decay, the "going to ashes," which precedes the stage of rebirth into a new cultural cycle (according to Giambattista Vico's cyclical theory of history, which is important to *Finnegans Wake*). "Gone ashley" also means "turned into an ash tree" (i.e., it is so cold that the speaker feels herself turning into a tree).

Filou![3] What age is at? It saon[4] is late. 'Tis endless now senne[5] eye or erewone[6] last saw Waterhouse's clogh.[7] They took it asunder, I hurd thum sigh. When will they reassemble it? O, my back, my back, my bach![8] I'd want to go to Aches-les-Pains.[9] Pingpong! There's the Belle for Sexaloitez![10] And Concepta de Send-us-pray! Pang! Wring out the Clothes! Wring in the dew![11] Godavari,[12] vert the showers![13] And grant thaya grace! Aman. Will we spread them here now? Ay, we will. Flip! Spread on your bank and I'll spread mine on mine. Flep! It's what I'm doing. Spread! It's churning chill. Der went[14] is rising. I'll lay a few stones on the hostel sheets. A man and his bride embraced between them. Else I'd have sprinkled and folded them only. And I'll tie my butcher's apron here. It's suety yet. The strollers will pass it by. Six shifts, ten kerchiefs, nine to hold to the fire and this for the code,[15] the convent napkins, twelve, one baby's shawl. Good mother Jossiph[16] knows, she said. Whose head? Mutter snores? Deataceas![17] Wharnow are alle her childer, say? In kingdome gone or power to come or gloria be to them farther? Allalivial, allalluvial![18] Some here, more no more, more again lost alla stranger.[19] I've heard tell that same brooch of the Shannons[20] was married into a family in Spain. And all the Dunders de Dunnes[21] in Markland's[22] Vineland beyond the Brendan's herring pool[23] takes number nine in yangsee's[24] hats. And one of Biddy's[25] beads went bobbing till she rounded up lost histereve[26] with a marigold and a cobbler's candle in a side strain of a main drain of a manzinahurries[27] off Bachelor's Walk. But all that's left to the last of the Meaghers[28] in the loup[29] of the years prefixed and between is one kneebuckle and two hooks in the front. Do you tell me that now? I do in troth. Orara por Orbe and poor Las Animals![30] Ussa, Ulla, we're

3. Pickpocket; thief (French). "Fieluhr": *Viel Uhr?* (What's the time?; German). From an old anecdote of a German soldier and a French soldier shouting at each other across the Rhine. They mishear each other as the washerwomen will later.

4. Soon + Saône (river in France).

5. Since + Senne (river in Belgium).

6. E'er a one + *Erewhon* (novel by Samuel Butler—an anagram for *Nowhere*).

7. Waterhouse's clock, a well-known clock on Dame Street, Dublin.

8. "Brook" (German) + "dear" (Welsh).

9. Cf. Aix-les-Bains, France.

10. "Sachselüte," a Zurich fertility rite (literally, the ringing of six o'clock), which celebrates the burial of winter.

11. Tennyson, *In Memoriam*: "Ring out the old, ring in the new."

12. God of Eire + the name of a river in India.

13. "Vert": avert + *vert* (green; French), for "the showers" make grass green.

14. *Der Wind* (the wind; German) + Derwent (river in England).

15. Cold + code (i.e., the code in which the book is written). The numbers in this sentence have special meanings indicated in other episodes.

16. Joseph + *joss* (God; pidgin English) + gossip (which derives from "god-sib," Middle English, "godparent").

17. A play on *Deo gratias* ("thanks be to God") and on *Dea Tacita* ("silent-goddess"), a name from Roman mythology.

18. Multiple punning—Anna Livia + all alive + *la lluvia* (rain; Spanish) + alluvial—suggesting the mother-river-fertility associations of ALP. At least two other meanings are also present: All alive O! (street cry of shellfish vendors) + Alleluia (Vulgate Latin form of *Hallelujah*).

19. Cf. *à l'étranger* (abroad; French).

20. Same ornament and branch of the Shannons (family and river).

21. The form of the name suggests an aristocratic Anglo-Norman family. "Dunder" suggests thunder. *Dun* is an Irish word meaning "hill," "fort on a hill."

22. Borderland + land of the mark (i.e., land of money, or America; Markland's Vineland was one of Leif Eriksson's names for America). Both King Mark of Cornwall (a character in the Tristan and Iseult story) and Mark of the Gospels are primary symbolic characters in *Finnegans Wake*.

23. The Atlantic Ocean. St. Brendan was an Irish monk who sailed out into the Atlantic to find the terrestrial paradise.

24. Yankees' + Yangtze (river in China). The de Dunnes have swollen heads now that they have emigrated to America.

25. Diminutive form of the name Bridget. St. Brigid (or Bridget) is a patron saint of Ireland. "Biddy" is also a term for an Irish maidservant.

26. Yester eve (last night) + eve of history. The sentence may be paraphrased: "Irish history got lost when she went off in a side branch of the main Roman Catholic Church, and Biddy (i.e., Ireland) landed herself in the dirt." Also, hysteria + eve.

27. A urinal + Manzanares (river in Spain). Also, man's in a hurry.

28. Thomas Francis Meagher, Irish patriot and revolutionary, who was transported to Van Diemen's Land in 1849 and escaped to America in 1852.

29. Loop + *loup* ("wolf" and also "solitary man"; French). Cf. Wolfe Tone, the ill-fated Irish revolutionist.

30. Souls (Spanish) + the name of a river in Colorado. *Ora pro nobis* (pray for us; Latin) + Orara (river in New South Wales) + *pro orbe* (for the world; Latin) + Orbe (river in France). The entire sentence may be read: "Pray for us and for all souls."

umbas[31] all! Mezha, didn't you hear it a deluge of times, ufer[32] and ufer, respund to spond?[33] You deed, you deed! I need, I need! It's that irrawaddyng[34] I've stoke in my aars. It all but husheth the lethest zswound. Oronoko![35] What's your trouble? Is that the great Finnleader[36] himself in his joakimono[37] on his statue riding the high horse there forehengist?[38] Father of Otters,[39] it is himself! Yonne there! Isset that? On Fallareen Common? You're thinking of Astley's Amphitheayter where the bobby restrained you making sugarstuck pouts to the ghostwhite horse of the Peppers.[40] Throw the cobwebs from your eyes, woman, and spread your washing proper! It's well I know your sort of slop. Flap! Ireland sober is Ireland stiff.[41] Lord help you, Maria, full of grease, the load is with me! Your prayers. I sonht zo![42] Madammangut! Were you lifting your elbow, tell us, glazy cheeks, in Conway's Carrigacurra canteen? Was I what, hobbledyhips?[43] Flop! Your rere gait's creakorheuman bitts your butts disagrees.[44] Amn't I up since the damp dawn, marthared mary allacook, with Corrigan's pulse and varicoarse veins, my pramaxle smashed, Alice Jane in decline and my oneeyed mongrel twice run over, soaking and bleaching boiler rags, and sweating cold, a widow like me, for to deck my tennis champion son, the laundryman with the lavandier flannels? You won your limpopo[45] limp from the husky[46] hussars when Collars and Cuffs was heir to the town and your slur gave the stink to Carlow.[47] Holy Scamander,[48] I sar[49] it again! Near the golden falls. Icis on us! Seints of light! Zezere![50] Subdue your noise, you hamble creature! What is it but a blackburry growth or the dwyergray ass them four old codgers[51] owns. Are you meanam[52] Tarpey and Lyons and Gregory?[53] I meyne now, thank all, the four of them, and the roar of them, that draves[54] that stray in the mist and old Johnny MacDougal along with them. Is that the Poolbeg flasher beyant,[55] pharphar, or a fireboat coasting nyar[56] the Kishtna[57] or a glow I behold within a hedge or my Garry come back from the Indes? Wait till the honeying of the lune,[58] love! Die eve, little eve, die![59] We see that

31. *Umbra* (shade; Latin) + Umba (river in Africa). "Ussa," "Ulla," and "Mezha" are also river names; each contains a number of other meanings.
32. Bank (of river).
33. *Spund* (bung; German).
34. A multiple pun: Irrawady (river in Burma) + irritating + wadding. This and the following sentence may be paraphrased: "It's that wadding I've stuck in my ears. It hushes the least sound."
35. *Oroonoko* (novel by Aphra Behn about a "noble savage," published ca. 1678) + Orinoco (river in Venezuela).
36. Fionn mac Cumhail (Finn MacCool), legendary hero of ancient Ireland.
37. Comic kimono. *Joki* is the Finnish word for river; the name Joachim is perhaps also implied.
38. According to tradition, Hengist was the Jute invader of England (with Horsa), ca. 449; he founded the kingdom of Kent.
39. Father of Waters (i.e., the Mississippi) + Father of Orders (i.e., Saint Patrick).
40. Philip Astley's Royal Amphitheatre was a famous late-18th-century English circus, specializing in trained horses. "Pepper's Ghost" was a popular circus act. One of the washerwomen has been reproving the other, who thought she saw the great Finn himself riding his high horse, by telling her that once before she had to be restrained by a policeman for making "sugarstuck pouts" at a circus horse.
41. The temperance reformer Father Matthew had as his slogan "Ireland sober is Ireland free."
42. I thought so + Izonzo (river in Italy).

43. Hobbledehoy + wobbly hips.
44. The sentence is a punning discussion of her hard work and ailments.
45. A river in south Africa.
46. Cf. *uisge* (whiskey, but literally "water [of life]"; Gaelic).
47. I.e., "You got a slur on your reputation carrying on with soldiers in the Age of Elegance, and the scandal was all over Ireland" (ALP is being addressed and some of her many lovers are mentioned). "Carlow": a county in Ireland.
48. River near Troy, famous in classical legend.
49. I saw + Isar (river in Germany).
50. See there + Zezere (river in Portugal).
51. The Four Old Men, who represent, among other things, the authors of the Gospels, and the four elements.
52. Meaning + Menam (river in Thailand).
53. Tarpey, Lyons, Gregory, and MacDougal (next sentence) are the "four old codgers."
54. Drives + Drave (river in Hungary).
55. I.e., the Poolbeg Lighthouse beyond (this lighthouse is in Dublin Bay). "Pharphar": far far + Pharphar (river in Damascus) + *pharos* (lighthouse; Greek).
56. Near + Nyar (river in India).
57. City in ancient Mesopotamia, traditionally the ruling city after the Flood + Krishna (Hindu god of joy) + Kistna (river in India) + the Kish lightship (in Dublin Bay).
58. Loon (boy; Scottish) + *luna* (moon; Latin). "Honeying of the lune": honeymoon, etc.
59. From a children's game in which a swing is

wonder in your eye. We'll meet again, we'll part once more. The spot I'll seek if the hour you'll find. My chart shines high where the blue milk's upset. Forgivemequick. I'm going! Bubye! And you, pluck your watch, forgetmenot. Your evenlode.[60] So save to jurna's[61] end! My sights are swimming thicker on me by the shadows to this place. I sow[62] home slowly now by own way, moy-valley way. Towy I too, rathmine.[63]

Ah, but she was the queer old skeowsha[64] anyhow, Anna Livia, trinkettoes! And sure he was the quare old buntz too, Dear Dirty Dumpling,[65] foosther-father of fingalls[66] and dotthergills. Gammer and gaffer we're all their gang-sters. Hadn't he seven dams to wive him? And every dam had her seven crutches. And every crutch had its seven hues.[67] And each hue had a differing cry. Sudds[68] for me and supper for you and the doctor's bill for Joe John. Befor! Bifur![69] He married his markets, cheap by foul, I know, like any Etrurian Catholic Heathen, in their pinky limony creamy birnies[70] and their turkiss indienne mauves. But at milkidmass[71] who was the spouse? Then all that was was fair. Tys Elvenland![72] Teems of times and happy returns. The seim anew.[73] Ordovico or viricordo. Anna was, Livia is, Plurabelle's to be.[74] Northmen's thing made southfolk's place but howmulty plurators made each one in per-son?[75] Latin me that, my trinity scholard, out of eure sanscreed into oure eryan![76] *Hircus Civis Eblanensis!*[77] He had buckgoat paps on him, soft ones for orphans. Ho,[78] Lord! Twins of his bosom. Lord save us! And ho! Hey? What all men. Hot? His tittering daughters of. Whawk?

Can't hear with the waters of. The chittering waters of. Flittering bats, fieldmice bawk talk. Ho! Are you not gone ahome? What Thom Malone? Can't hear with bawk of bats, all thim liffeying waters of. Ho, talk save us! My foos won't moos.[79] I feel as old as yonder elm. A tale told of Shaun or Shem? All

---

allowed to slow down to the refrain "She's dead, little Eva, little Eva, she's dead."

60. Evening load + Evenlode (river in England).

61. Journey + Jurna (river in Brazil).

62. Sow (river in England).

63. Moy is the name of an Irish river; Towy, a Welsh river. Moyvalley and Rathmine are names of Dublin suburbs.

64. Old timer, in Dublin.

65. "Dumpling" suggests Humpty Dumpty, whose fall is one of the many involved in the vastly sym-bolic fall of Finnegan. The phrase "Dear Dirty Dublin" occurs in *Ulysses.*

66. Blond and dark Scandinavian invaders of Ire-land.

67. Colors of the rainbow (suggested a few lines later by "pinky limony creamy" and "turkiss indienne mauves"). In these sentences Joyce is par-odying the nursery rhyme "As I was going to St. Ives / I met a man with seven wives."

68. Suds (slang for beer) + soap suds + sudd (the floating vegetable matter that often obstructs nav-igation on the White Nile).

69. Bifurcated creature! This image of human as a forked being suggests HCE (cf. "Etrurian Cath-olic Heathen," next sentence). HCE's marital his-tory, in his role as the Great Parent or generator, is one theme in this passage.

70. Coats of mail.

71. Milking time + Michaelmas (September 29).

72. 'Tis the land of Elves + Tys Elv (Norway).

73. The same again + Seim (river in Ireland).

74. The Ordovices were an ancient British tribe in northern Wales, and *Ordovician* is a term for a geo-

logical period. "Ordovico" is also a pun on Vico and his order of historical phases. Joyce is suggesting the cyclical nature of things: the marital history of HCE is the history of ever-renewing life ("the seim anew"), and HCE's bride is Everywoman, past, present, and future ("Anna was, Livia is, Plura-belle's to be"). "Viricordo" is another verbal twist to Vico and his cycles, suggesting his *ricorso* ("recurrence," i.e., the fourth stage of the cycle that brings back the first), as well as overtones from the Latin *vir* (man) and *cor* (heart): the heart of the individual beats on, through all phases of civ-ilization.

75. This sentence may be paraphrased: "The Northmen's assembly (thing) is now in Suffolk Place, but how many ancestors went into the mak-ing of each one of us?"

76. I.e., out of your Sanskrit into your Aryan. "Sanscreed" has further punning meanings: *sans* screed (without script) + *sans* creed (without faith). Thus the phrase can read: "out of your illit-eracy or faithlessness into Irish" (Eire-an). I.e., the greatest skeptic must pause in reverence before the endless flow of life, represented by Irish history. "Trinity": Trinity College, Dublin.

77. The Goat-Citizen of Dublin! (Latin). The goat is the symbol of lust and so of fecundity; "*Ebla-nensis*" is the adjective form of Eblana, the name given by the 3rd-century Alexandrian geographer Ptolemy to what may have been the site of the modern Dublin.

78. River (Chinese).

79. Move + *Moos* (moss; German). Her foot ("foos") won't move; it is also turning to moss.

Livia's daughter-sons. Dark hawks hear us. Night! Night! My ho head halls. I feel as heavy as yonder stone. Tell me of John or Shaun? Who were Shem and Shaun the living sons or daughters of? Night now! Tell me, tell me, tell me, elm! Night night! Telmetale of stem or stone.[80] Beside the rivering waters of, hitherandthithering waters of. Night!

1923–38   1939

---

80. Stone and elm tree are important symbols in *Finnegans Wake*. Signifying permanence and change, time and space, mercy and justice, they undergo many changes of symbolic meaning throughout the book.

D. H. LAWRENCE
1885–1930

David Herbert Lawrence was born in the midland mining village of Eastwood, Nottinghamshire. His father was a miner; his mother, better educated than her husband and self-consciously genteel, fought all her married life to lift her children out of the working class. Lawrence was aware from a young age of the struggle between his parents, and allied himself with his mother's delicacy and refinement, resenting his father's coarse and sometimes drunken behavior. In his early novel *Sons and Lovers* (1913), against a background of paternal coarseness conflicting with maternal refinement, Lawrence sets the theme of the demanding mother who has given up the prospect of achieving a true emotional life with her husband and turns to her sons with a stultifying and possessive love. Many years later Lawrence came to feel that he had failed to appreciate his father's vitality and wholeness, even if they were distorted by the culture in which he lived.

Spurred on by his mother, Lawrence escaped from the mining world through education. He won a scholarship to Nottingham high school and later, after working first as a clerk and then as an elementary-school teacher, studied for two years at University College, Nottingham, where he obtained his teacher's certificate. Meanwhile he was reading on his own a great deal of literature and some philosophy and was working on his first novel. Publishing a group of poems in 1909, his first short story and his first novel, *The White Peacock*, in 1910, he was regarded in London literary circles as a promising young writer. He taught school from 1908 to 1912 in Croydon, a southern suburb of London, but he gave this up after falling in love with Frieda von Richthofen Weekley, the German wife of a professor at Nottingham. They went to Germany together and married in 1914, after Frieda's divorce.

Abroad with Frieda, Lawrence finished *Sons and Lovers*, at which he had been working off and on for years. The war brought them back to England, where Frieda's German origins and Lawrence's pacifist objection to the war gave him trouble with the authorities. More and more—especially after the almost immediate banning for indecency of his next novel, *The Rainbow*, in 1915—Lawrence came to feel that the forces of modern civilization were arrayed against him. As soon as he could leave England after the war, he sought refuge in Italy, Australia, Mexico, then again in Italy, and finally in the south of France, often desperately ill, restlessly searching for an ideal, or at least a tolerable, community in which to live. He died of tuberculosis in the south of France at the age of forty-four.

In his poetry and his fiction, Lawrence seeks to express the deep-rooted, the elemental, the instinctual in people and nature. He is at constant war with the mechanical and artificial, with the constraints and hypocrisies that civilization imposes. Because he had new things to say and a new way of saying them, he was not easily or quickly appreciated. Although his early novels are more conventional in style and treatment, from the publication of *The Rainbow* the critics turned away in bewilderment and condemnation. The rest of his life, during which he produced about a dozen more novels and many poems, short stories, sketches, and miscellaneous articles, was, in his own words, "a savage enough pilgrimage," marked by incessant struggle and by periods of frustration and despair. Phrases such as "supreme impulse" and "quickening spontaneous emotion" were characteristic of Lawrence's belief in intuition, in the dark forces of the inner self, that must not be allowed to be swamped by the rational faculties but must be brought into a harmonious relation with them.

The genteel culture of Lawrence's mother came more and more to represent death for Lawrence. In much of his later work, and especially in some of his short stories, he sets the deadening restrictiveness of middle-class conventional living against the forces of liberation that are often represented by an outsider—a peasant, a gypsy, a worker, a primitive of some kind, someone free by circumstance or personal effort. The recurring theme of his short stories—which contain some of his best work—is the distortion of love by possessiveness or gentility or a false romanticism or a false conception of the life of the artist and the achievement of a living relation between a man and a woman against the pressure of class-feeling or tradition or habit or prejudice.

In his two masterpieces, *The Rainbow* and *Women in Love* (both of which developed out of what was originally conceived as a single novel to be called *The Sisters*), Lawrence probes with both subtlety and power into various aspects of relationship— the relationship between humans and their environment, the relationship between the generations, the relationship between man and woman, the relationship between instinct and intellect, and above all the proper basis for the marriage relationship as he conceived it. Lawrence's view of marriage as a struggle, bound up with the deepest rhythms and most profound instincts, derived from his own relationship with his strong-minded wife. He explores this and other kinds of human relationships with a combination of uncanny psychological precision and intense poetic feeling. His novels have an acute surface realism, a sharp sense of time and place, and brilliant topographical detail; at the same time their high symbolism, both of the total pattern of action and of incidents and objects within it, establishes a formal and emotional rhythm.

In poetry as in fiction Lawrence sought out new modes of expression. He began writing in traditional verse forms but, especially after 1912, came to feel that poetry had to be unshackled from habit and fixed form, if it is to make contact with what he called the "insurgent naked throb of the instant moment." Harkening back to the experiments of the American poet Walt Whitman and anticipating the more "open" and "organic" forms of the later twentieth century, Lawrence claimed poetry must be spontaneous, flexible, alive, "direct utterance from the instant, whole man," and should express the "pulsating, carnal self" ("The Poetry of the Present," 1919). To convey the dynamism of animals and people, the emotional intensity of human relationships, his poems repeat and develop symbols or layer clauses in ritualistic cadences or unfold parallels with ancient myths. Vehemently autobiographical, the vital and even ecstatic encounters with nature, sex, and raw feeling in his poems assert the primacy of the unconscious and instinctual self, from which he felt the cerebral-intellectual self had alienated the English middle classes.

In the late 1950s the critic A. Alvarez judged: "The only native English poet of any importance to survive the First World War was D. H. Lawrence." Although there are complex reasons for the posthumous critical triumph of this writer who was so much reviled in his lifetime, there is also a simple and striking reason that must not be forgotten. Lawrence had vision; he responded intensely to life; he had a keen ear and a piercing eye for vitality and color and sound, for landscape—be it of England or Italy or New Mexico—for the individuality and concreteness of things in nature, and for the individuality and concreteness of people. His travel sketches are as impressive in their way as his novels and poems; he seizes both on the symbolic incident and on the concrete reality, and each is interpreted in terms of the other. He looked at the world freshly, with his own eyes, avoiding formulas and clichés; and he forged for himself a kind of utterance that, at his best, was able to convey powerfully and vividly what his original vision showed him. A restless pilgrim, he had uncanny perceptions into the depths of physical things and an uncompromising honesty in his view of human beings and the world.

Odour of Chrysanthemums

I

The small locomotive engine, Number 4, came clanking, stumbling down from Selston with seven full wagons. It appeared round the corner with loud threats of speed, but the colt that it startled from among the gorse,[1] which still flickered indistinctly in the raw afternoon, out-distanced it at a canter. A woman, walking up the railway line to Underwood, drew back into the hedge, held her basket aside, and watched the footplate of the engine advancing. The trucks[2] thumped heavily past, one by one, with slow inevitable movement, as she stood insignificantly trapped between the jolting black wagons and the hedge; then they curved away towards the coppice[3] where the withered oak leaves dropped noiselessly, while the birds, pulling at the scarlet hips beside the track, made off into the dusk that had already crept into the spinney.[4] In the open, the smoke from the engine sank and cleaved to the rough grass. The fields were dreary and forsaken, and in the marshy strip that led to the whimsey,[5] a reedy pit-pond, the fowls had already abandoned their run among the alders, to roost in the tarred fowl-house. The pit-bank loomed up beyond the pond, flames like red sores licking its ashy sides, in the afternoon's stagnant light. Just beyond rose the tapering chimneys and the clumsy black headstocks of Brinsley Colliery.[6] The two wheels were spinning fast up against the sky, and the winding engine rapped out its little spasms. The miners were being turned up.

The engine whistled as it came into the wide bay of railway lines beside the colliery, where rows of trucks stood in harbour.

Miners, single, trailing and in groups, passed like shadows diverging home. At the edge of the ribbed level of sidings squat a low cottage, three steps down from the cinder track. A large bony vine clutched at the house, as if to claw down the tiled roof. Round the bricked yard grew a few wintry primroses. Beyond, the long garden sloped down to a bush-covered brook course. There were some twiggy apple trees, winter-crack trees, and ragged cabbages. Beside the path hung disheveled pink chrysanthemums, like pink cloths hung on bushes. A woman came stooping out of the felt-covered fowl-house, half-way down the garden. She closed and padlocked the door, then drew herself erect, having brushed some bits from her white apron.

She was a tall woman of imperious mien, handsome, with definite black eyebrows. Her smooth black hair was parted exactly. For a few moments she stood steadily watching the miners as they passed along the railway: then she

---

1. Common prickly bush with yellow flowers.
2. Open freight cars.
3. A wood of small trees or shrubs.
4. Thicket.

5. Machine for raising ore or water from a mine.
6. Coal mine. "Headstocks" support revolving parts of a machine.

turned towards the brook course. Her face was calm and set, her mouth was closed with disillusionment. After a moment she called:

"John!" There was no answer. She waited, and then said distinctly:

"Where are you?"

"Here!" replied a child's sulky voice from among the bushes. The woman looked piercingly through the dusk.

"Are you at that brook?" she asked sternly.

For answer the child showed himself before the raspberry-canes that rose like whips. He was a small, sturdy boy of five. He stood quite still, defiantly.

"Oh!" said the mother, conciliated. "I thought you were down at that wet brook—and you remember what I told you——"

The boy did not move or answer.

"Come, come on in," she said more gently, "it's getting dark. There's your grandfather's engine coming down the line!"

The lad advanced slowly, with resentful, taciturn movement. He was dressed in trousers and waistcoat of cloth that was too thick and hard for the size of the garments. They were evidently cut down from a man's clothes.

As they went slowly towards the house he tore at the ragged wisps of chrysanthemums and dropped the petals in handfuls along the path.

"Don't do that—it does look nasty," said his mother. He refrained, and she, suddenly pitiful, broke off a twig with three or four wan flowers and held them against her face. When mother and son reached the yard her hand hesitated, and instead of laying the flower aside, she pushed it in her apron-band. The mother and son stood at the foot of the three steps looking across the bay of lines at the passing home of the miners. The trundle of the small train was imminent. Suddenly the engine loomed past the house and came to a stop opposite the gate.

The engine-driver, a short man with round grey beard, leaned out of the cab high above the woman.

"Have you got a cup of tea?" he said in a cheery, hearty fashion.

It was her father. She went in, saying she would mash.[7] Directly, she returned.

"I didn't come to see you on Sunday," began the little grey-bearded man.

"I didn't expect you," said his daughter.

The engine-driver winced; then, reassuming his cheery, airy manner, he said:

"Oh, have you heard then? Well, and what do you think——?"

"I think it is soon enough," she replied.

At her brief censure the little man made an impatient gesture, and said coaxingly, yet with dangerous coldness:

"Well, what's a man to do? It's no sort of life for a man of my years, to sit at my own hearth like a stranger. And if I'm going to marry again it may as well be soon as late—what does it matter to anybody?"

The woman did not reply, but turned and went into the house. The man in the engine-cab stood assertive, till she returned with a cup of tea and a piece of bread and butter on a plate. She went up the steps and stood near the footplate of the hissing engine.

"You needn't 'a' brought me bread an' butter," said her father. "But a cup of tea"—he sipped appreciatively—"it's very nice." He sipped for a moment or

---

7. Steep the tea.

two, then: "I hear as Walter's got another bout[8] on," he said.

"When hasn't he?" said the woman bitterly.

"I heerd tell of him in the 'Lord Nelson' braggin' as he was going to spend that b—— afore he went: half a sovereign[9] that was."

"When?" asked the woman.

"A' Sat'day night—I know that's true."

"Very likely," she laughed bitterly. "He gives me twenty-three shillings."

"Aye, it's a nice thing, when a man can do nothing with his money but make a beast of himself!" said the grey-whiskered man. The woman turned her head away. Her father swallowed the last of his tea and handed her the cup.

"Aye," he sighed, wiping his mouth. "It's a settler,[1] it is——"

He put his hand on the lever. The little engine strained and groaned, and the train rumbled towards the crossing. The woman again looked across the metals. Darkness was settling over the spaces of the railway and trucks: the miners, in grey somber groups, were still passing home. The winding engine pulsed hurriedly, with brief pauses. Elizabeth Bates looked at the dreary flow of men, then she went indoors. Her husband did not come.

The kitchen was small and full of firelight; red coals piled glowing up the chimney mouth. All the life of the room seemed in the white, warm hearth and the steel fender reflecting the red fire. The cloth was laid for tea; cups glinted in the shadows. At the back, where the lowest stairs protruded into the room, the boy sat struggling with a knife and a piece of white wood. He was almost hidden in the shadow. It was half-past four. They had but to await the father's coming to begin tea. As the mother watched her son's sullen little struggle with the wood, she saw herself in his silence and pertinacity; she saw the father in her child's indifference to all but himself. She seemed to be occupied by her husband. He had probably gone past his home, slunk past his own door, to drink before he came in, while his dinner spoiled and wasted in waiting. She glanced at the clock, then took the potatoes to strain them in the yard. The garden and fields beyond the brook were closed in uncertain darkness. When she rose with the saucepan, leaving the drain steaming into the night behind her, she saw the yellow lamps were lit along the high road that went up the hill away beyond the space of the railway lines and the field. Then again she watched the men trooping home, fewer now and fewer.

Indoors the fire was sinking and the room was dark red. The woman put her saucepan on the hob,[2] and set a batter-pudding near the mouth of the oven. Then she stood unmoving. Directly, gratefully, came quick young steps to the door. Someone hung on the latch a moment, then a little girl entered and began pulling off her outdoor things, dragging a mass of curls, just ripening from gold to brown, over her eyes with her hat.

Her mother chid her for coming late from school, and said she would have to keep her at home the dark winter days.

"Why, mother, it's hardly a bit dark yet. The lamp's not lighted, and my father's not home."

"No, he isn't. But it's a quarter to five! Did you see anything of him?"

The child became serious. She looked at her mother with large, wistful blue eyes.

---

8. Session; i.e., bout of drinking.
9. Gold coin worth twenty shillings. Half a sovereign is worth ten. Lord Nelson is the name of a

public house (pub).
1. Crushing (or final) blow.
2. Part of the fireplace.

"No, mother, I've never seen him. Why? Has he come up an' gone past, to Old Brinsley? He hasn't, mother, 'cos I never saw him."

"He'd watch that," said the mother bitterly, "he'd take care as you didn't see him. But you may depend upon it, he's seated in the 'Prince o' Wales.'[3] He wouldn't be this late."

The girl looked at her mother piteously.

"Let's have our teas, mother, should we?" said she.

The mother called John to table. She opened the door once more and looked out across the darkness of the lines. All was deserted: she could not hear the winding-engines.

"Perhaps," she said to herself, "he's stopped to get some ripping[4] done."

They sat down to tea. John, at the end of the table near the door, was almost lost in the darkness. Their faces were hidden from each other. The girl crouched against the fender[5] slowly moving a thick piece of bread before the fire. The lad, his face a dusky mark on the shadow, sat watching her who was transfigured in the red glow.

"I do think it's beautiful to look in the fire," said the child.

"Do you?" said her mother. "Why?"

"It's so red, and full of little caves—and it feels so nice, and you can fair smell it."

"It'll want mending directly," replied her mother, "and then if your father comes he'll carry on and say there never is a fire when a man comes home sweating from the pit. A public-house is always warm enough."

There was silence till the boy said complainingly: "Make haste, our Annie."

"Well, I am doing! I can't make the fire do it no faster, can I?"

"She keeps wafflin' it about so's to make 'er slow," grumbled the boy.

"Don't have such an evil imagination, child," replied the mother.

Soon the room was busy in the darkness with the crisp sound of crunching. The mother ate very little. She drank her tea determinedly, and sat thinking. When she rose her anger was evident in the stern unbending of her head. She looked at the pudding in the fender, and broke out:

"It is a scandalous thing as a man can't even come home to his dinner! If it's crozzled[6] up to a cinder I don't see why I should care. Past his very door he goes to get to a public-house, and here I sit with his dinner waiting for him——"

She went out. As she dropped piece after piece of coal on the red fire, the shadows fell on the walls, till the room was almost in total darkness.

"I canna see," grumbled the invisible John. In spite of herself, the mother laughed.

"You know the way to your mouth," she said. She set the dust pan outside the door. When she came again like a shadow on the hearth, the lad repeated, complaining sulkily:

"I canna see."

"Good gracious!" cried the mother irritably, "you're as bad as your father if it's a bit dusk!"

Nevertheless, she took a paper spill from a sheaf on the mantelpiece and proceeded to light the lamp that hung from the ceiling in the middle of the

---

3. Name of a pub.
4. Taking out or cutting away coal or stone (a mining and quarrying term).
5. Frame that keeps coals in the fireplace.
6. Curled.

room. As she reached up, her figure displayed itself just rounding with maternity.

"Oh, mother——!" exclaimed the girl.

"What?" said the woman, suspended in the act of putting the lamp-glass over the flame. The copper reflector shone handsomely on her, as she stood with uplifted arm, turning to face her daughter.

"You've got a flower in your apron!" said the child, in a little rapture at this unusual event.

"Goodness me!" exclaimed the woman, relieved. "One would think the house was afire." She replaced the glass and waited a moment before turning up the wick. A pale shadow was seen floating vaguely on the floor.

"Let me smell!" said the child, still rapturously, coming forward and putting her face to her mother's waist.

"Go along, silly!" said the mother, turning up the lamp. The light revealed their suspense so that the woman felt it almost unbearable. Annie was still bending at her waist. Irritably, the mother took the flowers out from her apron-band.

"Oh, mother—don't take them out!" Annie cried, catching her hand and trying to replace the sprig.

"Such nonsense!" said the mother, turning away. The child put the pale chrysanthemums to her lips, murmuring:

"Don't they smell beautiful!"

Her mother gave a short laugh.

"No," she said, "not to me. It was chrysanthemums when I married him, and chrysanthemums when you were born, and the first time they ever brought him home drunk, he'd got brown chrysanthemums in his buttonhole."

She looked at the children. Their eyes and their parted lips were wondering. The mother sat rocking in silence for some time. Then she looked at the clock.

"Twenty minutes to six!" In a tone of fine bitter carelessness she continued: "Eh, he'll not come now till they bring him. There he'll stick! But he needn't come rolling in here in his pit-dirt, for *I* won't wash him. He can lie on the floor——Eh, what a fool I've been, what a fool! And this is what I came here for, to this dirty hole, rats and all, for him to slink past his very door. Twice last week—he's begun now——"

She silenced herself and rose to clear the table.

While for an hour or more the children played, subduedly intent, fertile of imagination, united in fear of the mother's wrath, and in dread of their father's home-coming, Mrs Bates sat in her rocking chair making a "singlet" of thick cream-coloured flannel, which gave a dull wounded sound as she tore off the grey edge. She worked at her sewing with energy, listening to the children, and her anger wearied itself, lay down to rest, opening its eyes from time to time and steadily watching, its ears raised to listen. Sometimes even her anger quailed and shrank, and the mother suspended her sewing, tracing the footsteps that thudded along the sleepers[7] outside; she would lift her head sharply to bid the children "hush," but she recovered herself in time, and the footsteps went past the gate, and the children were not flung out of their play-world.

But at last Annie sighed, and gave in. She glanced at her wagon of slippers, and loathed the game. She turned plaintively to her mother.

"Mother!"—but she was inarticulate.

7. Railroad ties.

John crept out like a frog from under the sofa. His mother glanced up.

"Yes," she said, "just look at those shirt-sleeves!"

The boy held them out to survey them, saying nothing. Then somebody called in a hoarse voice away down the line, and suspense bristled in the room, till two people had gone by outside, talking.

"It is time for bed," said the mother.

"My father hasn't come," wailed Annie plaintively. But her mother was primed with courage.

"Never mind. They'll bring him when he does come—like a log." She meant there would be no scene. "And he may sleep on the floor till he wakes himself. I know he'll not go to work to-morrow after this!"

The children had their hands and faces wiped with a flannel. They were very quiet. When they had put on their night-dresses, they said their prayers, the boy mumbling. The mother looked down at them, at the brown silken bush of intertwining curls in the nape of the girl's neck, at the little black head of the lad, and her heart burst with anger at their father, who caused all three such distress. The children hid their faces in her skirts for comfort.

When Mrs Bates came down, the room was strangely empty, with a tension of expectancy. She took up her sewing and stitched for some time without raising her head. Meantime her anger was tinged with fear.

II

The clock struck eight and she rose suddenly, dropping her sewing on her chair. She went to the stair-foot door, opened it, listening. Then she went out, locking the door behind her.

Something scuffled in the yard, and she started, though she knew it was only the rats with which the place was over-run. The night was very dark. In the great bay of railway lines, bulked with trucks, there was no trace of light, only away back she could see a few yellow lamps at the pit-top, and the red smear of the burning pit-bank on the night. She hurried along the edge of the track, then, crossing the converging lines, came to the stile by the white gates, whence she emerged on the road. Then the fear which had led her shrank. People were walking up to New Brinsley; she saw the lights in the houses; twenty yards farther on were the broad windows of the "Prince of Wales," very warm and bright, and the loud voices of men could be heard distinctly. What a fool she had been to imagine that anything had happened to him! He was merely drinking over there at the "Prince of Wales." She faltered. She had never yet been to fetch him, and she never would go. So she continued her walk towards the long straggling line of houses, standing back on the highway. She entered a passage between the dwellings.

"Mr Rigley?—Yes! Did you want him? No, he's not in at this minute."

The raw-boned woman leaned forward from her dark scullery[8] and peered at the other, upon whom fell a dim light through the blind of the kitchen window.

"Is it Mrs Bates?" she asked in a tone tinged with respect.

"Yes. I wondered if your Master was at home. Mine hasn't come yet."

" 'Asn't 'e! Oh, Jack's been 'ome an' 'ad 'is dinner an' gone out. 'E's just gone for 'alf an hour afore bed-time. Did you call at the 'Prince of Wales'?"

8. Back kitchen.

"No——"

"No, you didn't like——! It's not very nice." The other woman was indulgent. There was an awkward pause. "Jack never said nothink about—about your Master," she said.

"No!—I expect he's stuck in there!"

Elizabeth Bates said this bitterly, and with recklessness. She knew that the woman across the yard was standing at her door listening, but she did not care. As she turned:

"Stop a minute! I'll just go an' ask Jack if 'e knows anythink," said Mrs Rigley.

"Oh no—I wouldn't like to put——!"

"Yes, I will, if you'll just step inside an' see as th' childer doesn't come downstairs and set theirselves afire."

Elizabeth Bates, murmuring a remonstrance, stepped inside. The other woman apologised for the state of the room.

The kitchen needed apology. There were little frocks and trousers and childish undergarments on the squab[9] and on the floor, and a litter of playthings everywhere. On the black American cloth[1] of the table were pieces of bread and cake, crusts, slops, and a teapot with cold tea.

"Eh, ours is just as bad," said Elizabeth Bates, looking at the woman, not at the house. Mrs Rigley put a shawl over her head and hurried out, saying:

"I shanna be a minute."

The other sat, noting with faint disapproval the general untidiness of the room. Then she fell to counting the shoes of various sizes scattered over the floor. There were twelve. She sighed and said to herself: "No wonder!"—glancing at the litter. There came the scratching of two pairs of feet on the yard, and the Rigleys entered. Elizabeth Bates rose. Rigley was a big man, with very large bones. His head looked particularly bony. Across his temple was a blue scar, caused by a wound got in the pit, a wound in which the coal dust remained blue like tattooing.

" 'Asna 'e come whoam yit?" asked the man, without any form of greeting, but with deference and sympathy. "I couldna say wheer he is—'e's non ower theer!"—he jerked his head to signify the "Prince of Wales."

" 'E's 'appen gone up to th' Yew,"[2] said Mrs Rigley.

There was another pause. Rigley had evidently something to get off his mind: "Ah left 'im finishin' a stint," he began. "Loose-all[3] 'ad bin gone about ten minutes when we com'n away, an' I shouted: 'Are ter comin', Walt?' an' 'e said: 'Go on, Ah shanna be but a'ef a minnit,' so we com'n ter th' bottom, me an' Bowers, thinkin' as 'e wor just behint, an' 'ud come up i' th' next bantle[4]——"

He stood perplexed, as if answering a charge of deserting his mate. Elizabeth Bates, now again certain of disaster, hastened to reassure him:

"I expect 'e's gone up to th' 'Yew Tree,' as you say. It's not the first time. I've fretted myself into a fever before now. He'll come home when they carry him."

"Ay, isn't it too bad!" deplored the other woman.

"I'll just step up to Dick's an' see if 'e is theer," offered the man, afraid of appearing alarmed, afraid of taking liberties.

---

9. Couch.
1. Oilcloth.
2. I.e., the Yew Tree (a pub).

3. Signal for end of work.
4. Group.

"Oh, I wouldn't think of bothering you that far," said Elizabeth Bates, with emphasis, but he knew she was glad of his offer.

As they stumbled up the entry, Elizabeth Bates heard Rigley's wife run across the yard and open her neighbour's door. At this, suddenly all the blood in her body seemed to switch away from her heart.

"Mind!" warned Rigley. "Ah've said many a time as Ah'd fill up them ruts in this entry, sumb'dy 'll be breakin' their legs yit."

She recovered herself and walked quickly along with the miner.

"I don't like leaving the children in bed, and nobody in the house," she said.

"No, you dunna!" he replied courteously. They were soon at the gate of the cottage.

"Well, I shanna be many minnits. Dunna you be frettin' now, 'e'll be all right," said the butty.[5]

"Thank you very much, Mr Rigley," she replied.

"You're welcome!" he stammered, moving away. "I shanna be many minnits."

The house was quiet. Elizabeth Bates took off her hat and shawl, and rolled back the rug. When she had finished, she sat down. It was a few minutes past nine. She was startled by the rapid chuff of the winding-engine at the pit, and the sharp whirr of the brakes on the rope as it descended. Again she felt the painful sweep of her blood, and she put her hand to her side, saying aloud: "Good gracious!—it's only the nine o'clock deputy[6] going down," rebuking herself.

She sat still, listening. Half an hour of this, and she was wearied out.

"What am I working myself up like this for?" she said pitiably to herself, "I s'll only be doing myself some damage."

She took out her sewing again.

At a quarter to ten there were footsteps. One person! She watched for the door to open. It was an elderly woman, in a black bonnet and a black woollen shawl—his mother. She was about sixty years old, pale, with blue eyes, and her face all wrinkled and lamentable. She shut the door and turned to her daughter-in-law peevishly.

"Eh, Lizzie, whatever shall we do, whatever shall we do!" she cried.

Elizabeth drew back a little, sharply.

"What is it, mother?" she said.

The elder woman seated herself on the sofa.

"I don't know, child, I can't tell you!"—she shook her head slowly. Elizabeth sat watching her, anxious and vexed.

"I don't know," replied the grandmother, sighing very deeply. "There's no end to my troubles, there isn't. The things I've gone through, I'm sure it's enough——!" She wept without wiping her eyes, the tears running.

"But, mother," interrupted Elizabeth, "what do you mean? What is it?"

The grandmother slowly wiped her eyes. The fountains of her tears were stopped by Elizabeth's directness. She wiped her eyes slowly.

"Poor child! Eh, you poor thing!" she moaned. "I don't know what we're going to do, I don't—and you as you are—it's a thing, it is indeed!"

Elizabeth waited.

"Is he dead?" she asked, and at the words her heart swung violently, though

---

5. Workmate (cf. "buddy"). Among English coal miners it means a supervisor intermediary between the employers and the men.
6. Minor coal-mine official.

she felt a slight flush of shame at the ultimate extravagance of the question. Her words sufficiently frightened the old lady, almost brought her to herself.

"Don't say so, Elizabeth! We'll hope it's not as bad as that; no, may the Lord spare us that, Elizabeth. Jack Rigley came just as I was sittin' down to a glass afore going to bed, an' 'e said: ' 'Appen you'll go down th' line, Mrs. Bates. Walt's had an accident. 'Appen you'll go an' sit wi' 'er till we can get him home.' I hadn't time to ask him a word afore he was gone. An' I put my bonnet on an' come straight down, Lizzie. I thought to myself: 'Eh, that poor blessed child, if anybody should come an' tell her of a sudden, there's no knowin' what'll 'appen to 'er.' You mustn't let it upset you, Lizzie—or you know what to expect. How long is it, six months—or is it five, Lizzie? Ay!"—the old woman shook her head—"time slips on, it slips on! Ay!"

Elizabeth's thoughts were busy elsewhere. If he was killed—would she be able to manage on the little pension and what she could earn?—she counted up rapidly. If he was hurt—they wouldn't take him to the hospital—how tiresome he would be to nurse!—but perhaps she'd be able to get him away from the drink and his hateful ways. She would—while he was ill. The tears offered to come to her eyes at the picture. But what sentimental luxury was this she was beginning? She turned to consider the children. At any rate she was absolutely necessary for them. They were her business.

"Ay!" repeated the old woman, "it seems but a week or two since he brought me his first wages. Ay—he was a good lad, Elizabeth, he was, in his way. I don't know why he got to be such a trouble, I don't. He was a happy lad at home, only full of spirits. But there's no mistake he's been a handful of trouble, he has! I hope the Lord'll spare him to mend his ways. I hope so, I hope so. You've had a sight o' trouble with him, Elizabeth, you have indeed. But he was a jolly enough lad wi' me, he was, I can assure you. I don't know how it is. . . ."

The old woman continued to muse aloud, a monotonous irritating sound, while Elizabeth thought concentratedly, startled once, when she heard the winding-engine chuff quickly, and the brakes skirr with a shriek. Then she heard the engine more slowly, and the brakes made no sound. The old woman did not notice. Elizabeth waited in suspense. The mother-in-law talked, with lapses into silence.

"But he wasn't your son, Lizzie, an' it makes a difference. Whatever he was, I remember him when he was little, an' I learned to understand him and to make allowances. You've got to make allowances for them——"

It was half-past ten, and the old woman was saying: "But it's trouble from beginning to end; you're never too old for trouble, never too old for that——" when the gate banged back, and there were heavy feet on the steps.

"I'll go, Lizzie, let me go," cried the old woman, rising. But Elizabeth was at the door. It was a man in pit-clothes.

"They're bringin' 'im, Missis," he said. Elizabeth's heart halted a moment. Then it surged on again, almost suffocating her.

"Is he—is it bad?" she asked.

The man turned away, looking at the darkness:

"The doctor says 'e'd been dead hours. 'E saw 'im i' th' lamp-cabin."

The old woman, who stood just behind Elizabeth, dropped into a chair, and folded her hands, crying: "Oh, my boy, my boy!"

"Hush!" said Elizabeth, with a sharp twitch of a frown. "Be still, mother, don't waken th' children: I wouldn't have them down for anything!"

The old woman moaned softly, rocking herself. The man was drawing away. Elizabeth took a step forward.

"How was it?" she asked.

"Well, I couldn't say for sure," the man replied, very ill at ease. " 'E wor finishin' a stint an' th' butties 'ad gone, an' a lot o' stuff come down atop 'n 'im."

"And crushed him?" cried the widow, with a shudder.

"No," said the man, "it fell at th' back of 'im. 'E wor under th' face an' it niver touched 'im. It shut 'im in. It seems 'e wor smothered."

Elizabeth shrank back. She heard the old woman behind her cry:

"What?—what did 'e say it was?"

The man replied, more loudly: " 'E wor smothered!"

Then the old woman wailed aloud, and this relieved Elizabeth.

"Oh, mother," she said, putting her hand on the old woman, "don't waken th' children, don't waken th' children."

She wept a little, unknowing, while the old mother rocked herself and moaned. Elizabeth remembered that they were bringing him home, and she must be ready. "They'll lay him in the parlour," she said to herself, standing a moment pale and perplexed.

Then she lighted a candle and went into the tiny room. The air was cold and damp, but she could not make a fire, there was no fireplace. She set down the candle and looked round. The candlelight glittered on the lustre-glasses, on the two vases that held some of the pink chrysanthemums, and on the dark mahogany. There was a cold, deathly smell of chrysanthemums in the room. Elizabeth stood looking at the flowers. She turned away, and calculated whether there would be room to lay him on the floor, between the couch and the chiffonier. She pushed the chairs aside. There would be room to lay him down and to step round him. Then she fetched the old red tablecloth, and another old cloth, spreading them down to save her bit of carpet. She shivered on leaving the parlour; so, from the dresser drawer she took a clean shirt and put it at the fire to air. All the time her mother-in-law was rocking herself in the chair and moaning.

"You'll have to move from there, mother," said Elizabeth. "They'll be bringing him in. Come in the rocker."

The old mother rose mechanically, and seated herself by the fire, continuing to lament. Elizabeth went into the pantry for another candle, and there, in the little pent-house under the naked tiles, she heard them coming. She stood still in the pantry doorway, listening. She heard them pass the end of the house, and come awkwardly down the three steps, a jumble of shuffling footsteps and muttering voices. The old woman was silent. The men were in the yard.

Then Elizabeth heard Matthews, the manager of the pit, say: "You go in first, Jim. Mind!"

The door came open, and the two women saw a collier backing into the room, holding one end of a stretcher, on which they could see the nailed pit-boots of the dead man. The two carriers halted, the man at the head stooping to the lintel of the door.

"Wheer will you have him?" asked the manager, a short, white-bearded man.

Elizabeth roused herself and came from the pantry carrying the unlighted candle.

"In the parlour," she said.

"In there, Jim!" pointed the manager, and the carriers backed round into the tiny room. The coat with which they had covered the body fell off as they awkwardly turned through the two doorways, and the women saw their man, naked to the waist, lying stripped for work. The old woman began to moan in a low voice of horror.

"Lay th' stretcher at th' side," snapped the manager, "an' put 'im on th' cloths. Mind now, mind! Look you now——!"

One of the men had knocked off a vase of chrysanthemums. He stared awkwardly, then they set down the stretcher. Elizabeth did not look at her husband. As soon as she could get in the room, she went and picked up the broken vase and the flowers.

"Wait a minute!" she said.

The three men waited in silence while she mopped up the water with a duster.

"Eh, what a job, what a job, to be sure!" the manager was saying, rubbing his brow with trouble and perplexity. "Never knew such a thing in my life, never! He'd no business to ha' been left. I never knew such a thing in my life! Fell over him clean as a whistle, an' shut him in. Not four foot of space, there wasn't—yet it scarce bruised him."

He looked down at the dead man, lying prone, half naked, all grimed with coal-dust.

" ' 'Sphyxiated,' the doctor said. It is the most terrible job I've ever known. Seems as if it was done o' purpose. Clean over him, an' shut 'im in, like a mouse-trap"—he made a sharp, descending gesture with his hand.

The colliers standing by jerked aside their heads in hopeless comment.

The horror of the thing bristled upon them all.

Then they heard the girl's voice upstairs calling shrilly: "Mother, mother—who is it? Mother, who is it?"

Elizabeth hurried to the foot of the stairs and opened the door:

"Go to sleep!" she commanded sharply. "What are you shouting about? Go to sleep at once—there's nothing——"

Then she began to mount the stairs. They could hear her on the boards, and on the plaster floor of the little bedroom. They could hear her distinctly:

"What's the matter now?—what's the matter with you, silly thing?"—her voice was much agitated, with an unreal gentleness.

"I thought it was some men come," said the plaintive voice of the child. "Has he come?"

"Yes, they've brought him. There's nothing to make a fuss about. Go to sleep now, like a good child."

They could hear her voice in the bedroom, they waited whilst she covered the children under the bedclothes.

"Is he drunk?" asked the girl, timidly, faintly.

"No! No—he's not! He—he's asleep."

"Is he asleep downstairs?"

"Yes—and don't make a noise."

There was silence for a moment, then the men heard the frightened child again:

"What's that noise?"

"It's nothing, I tell you, what are you bothering for?"

The noise was the grandmother moaning. She was oblivious of everything, sitting on her chair rocking and moaning. The manager put his hand on her arm and bade her "Sh—sh! !"

The old woman opened her eyes and looked at him. She was shocked by this interruption, and seemed to wonder.

"What time is it?" the plaintive thin voice of the child, sinking back unhappily into sleep, asked this last question.

"Ten o'clock," answered the mother more softly. Then she must have bent down and kissed the children.

Matthews beckoned to the men to come away. They put on their caps and took up the stretcher. Stepping over the body, they tiptoed out of the house. None of them spoke till they were far from the wakeful children.

When Elizabeth came down she found her mother alone on the parlour floor, leaning over the dead man, the tears dropping on him.

"We must lay him out," the wife said. She put on the kettle, then returning knelt at the feet, and began to unfasten the knotted leather laces. The room was clammy and dim with only one candle, so that she had to bend her face almost to the floor. At last she got off the heavy boots and put them away.

"You must help me now," she whispered to the old woman. Together they stripped the man.

When they arose, saw him lying in the naïve dignity of death, the women stood arrested in fear and respect. For a few moments they remained still, looking down, the old mother whimpering. Elizabeth felt countermanded.[7] She saw him, how utterly inviolable he lay in himself. She had nothing to do with him. She could not accept it. Stooping, she laid her hand on him, in claim. He was still warm, for the mine was hot where he had died. His mother had his face between her hands, and was murmuring incoherently. The old tears fell in succession as drops from wet leaves; the mother was not weeping, merely her tears flowed. Elizabeth embraced the body of her husband, with cheek and lips. She seemed to be listening, inquiring, trying to get some connection. But she could not. She was driven away. He was impregnable.

She rose, went into the kitchen where she poured warm water into a bowl, brought soap and flannel and a soft towel. "I must wash him," she said.

Then the old mother rose stiffly, and watched Elizabeth as she carefully washed his face, carefully brushing his big blond moustache from his mouth with the flannel. She was afraid with a bottomless fear, so she ministered to him. The old woman, jealous, said:

"Let me wipe him!"—and she kneeled on the other side drying slowly as Elizabeth washed, her big black bonnet sometimes brushing the dark head of her daughter-in-law. They worked thus in silence for a long time. They never forgot it was death, and the touch of the man's dead body gave them strange emotions, different in each of the women; a great dread possessed them both, the mother felt the lie was given to her womb, she was denied; the wife felt the utter isolation of the human soul, the child within her was a weight apart from her.

At last it was finished. He was a man of handsome body, and his face showed no traces of drink. He was blond, full-fleshed, with fine limbs. But he was dead.

"Bless him," whispered his mother, looking always at his face, and speaking out of sheer terror. "Dear lad—bless him!" She spoke in a faint, sibilant ecstasy of fear and mother love.

Elizabeth sank down again to the floor, and put her face against his neck, and trembled and shuddered. But she had to draw away again. He was dead, and her living flesh had no place against his. A great dread and weariness held her: she was so unavailing. Her life was gone like this.

---

7. Contradicted.

"White as milk he is, clear as a twelve-month baby, bless him, the darling!" the old mother murmured to herself. "Not a mark on him, clear and clean and white, beautiful as ever a child was made," she murmured with pride. Elizabeth kept her face hidden.

"He went peaceful, Lizzie—peaceful as sleep. Isn't he beautiful, the lamb? Ay—he must ha' made his peace, Lizzie. 'Appen he made it all right, Lizzie, shut in there. He'd have time. He wouldn't look like this if he hadn't made his peace. The lamb, the dear lamb. Eh, but he had a hearty laugh. I loved to hear it. He had the heartiest laugh, Lizzie, as a lad——"

Elizabeth looked up. The man's mouth was fallen back, slightly open under the cover of the moustache. The eyes, half shut, did not show glazed in the obscurity. Life with its smoky burning gone from him, had left him apart and utterly alien to her. And she knew what a stranger he was to her. In her womb was ice of fear, because of this separate stranger with whom she had been living as one flesh. Was this what it all meant—utter, intact separateness, obscured by heat of living? In dread she turned her face away. The fact was too deadly. There had been nothing between them, and yet they had come together, exchanging their nakedness repeatedly. Each time he had taken her, they had been two isolated beings, far apart as now. He was no more responsible than she. The child was like ice in her womb. For as she looked at the dead man, her mind, cold and detached, said clearly: "Who am I? What have I been doing? I have been fighting a husband who did not exist. *He* existed all the time. What wrong have I done? What was that I have been living with? There lies the reality, this man." And her soul died in her for fear: she knew she had never seen him, he had never seen her, they had met in the dark and had fought in the dark, not knowing whom they met or whom they fought. And now she saw, and turned silent in seeing. For she had been wrong. She had said he was something he was not; she had felt familiar with him. Whereas he was apart all the while, living as she never lived, feeling as she never felt.

In fear and shame she looked at his naked body, that she had known falsely. And he was the father of her children. Her soul was torn from her body and stood apart. She looked at his naked body and was ashamed, as if she had denied it. After all, it was itself. It seemed awful to her. She looked at his face, and she turned her own face to the wall. For his look was other than hers, his way was not her way. She had denied him what he was—she saw it now. She had refused him as himself. And this had been her life, and his life. She was grateful to death, which restored the truth. And she knew she was not dead.

And all the while her heart was bursting with grief and pity for him. What had he suffered? What stretch of horror for this helpless man! She was rigid with agony. She had not been able to help him. He had been cruelly injured, this naked man, this other being, and she could make no reparation. There were the children—but the children belonged to life. This dead man had nothing to do with them. He and she were only channels through which life had flowed to issue in the children. She was a mother—but how awful she knew it now to have been a wife. And he, dead now, how awful he must have felt it to be a husband. She felt that in the next world he would be a stranger to her. If they met there, in the beyond, they would only be ashamed of what had been before. The children had come, for some mysterious reason, out of both of them. But the children did not unite them. Now he was dead, she knew how eternally he was apart from her, how eternally he had nothing more to do with her. She saw this episode of her life closed. They had denied each other in life. Now he had withdrawn. An anguish came over her. It was finished then: it had become hopeless between them long before he died. Yet he had been her husband. But how little!

"Have you got his shirt, 'Lizabeth?"

Elizabeth turned without answering, though she strove to weep and behave as her mother-in-law expected. But she could not, she was silenced. She went into the kitchen and returned with the garment.

"It is aired," she said, grasping the cotton shirt here and there to try. She was almost ashamed to handle him; what right had she or anyone to lay hands on him; but her touch was humble on his body. It was hard work to clothe him. He was so heavy and inert. A terrible dread gripped her all the while: that he could be so heavy and utterly inert, unresponsive, apart. The horror of the distance between them was almost too much for her—it was so infinite a gap she must look across.

At last it was finished. They covered him with a sheet and left him lying, with his face bound. And she fastened the door of the little parlour, lest the children should see what was lying there. Then, with peace sunk heavy on her heart, she went about making tidy the kitchen. She knew she submitted to life, which was her immediate master. But from death, her ultimate master, she winced with fear and shame.

1911, 1914

The Horse Dealer's Daughter

"Well, Mabel, and what are you going to do with yourself?" asked Joe, with foolish flippancy. He felt quite safe himself. Without listening for an answer, he turned aside, worked a grain of tobacco to the tip of his tongue, and spat it out. He did not care about anything, since he felt safe himself.

The three brothers and the sister sat round the desolate breakfast-table, attempting some sort of desultory consultation. The morning's post had given the final tap to the family fortunes, and all was over. The dreary dining-room itself, with its heavy mahogany furniture, looked as if it were waiting to be done away with.

But the consultation amounted to nothing. There was a strange air of ineffectuality about the three men, as they sprawled at table, smoking and reflecting vaguely on their own condition. The girl was alone, a rather short, sullen-looking young woman of twenty-seven. She did not share the same life as her brothers. She would have been good-looking, save for the impressive fixity of her face, "bull-dog," as her brothers called it.

There was a confused tramping of horses' feet outside. The three men all sprawled round in their chairs to watch. Beyond the dark holly bushes that separated the strip of lawn from the high-road, they could see a cavalcade of shire horses swinging out of their own yard, being taken for exercise. This was the last time. These were the last horses that would go through their hands. The young men watched with critical, callous look. They were all frightened at the collapse of their lives, and the sense of disaster in which they were involved left them no inner freedom.

Yet they were three fine, well-set fellows enough. Joe, the eldest, was a man of thirty-three, broad and handsome in a hot, flushed way. His face was red, he twisted his black moustache over a thick finger, his eyes were shallow and restless. He had a sensual way of uncovering his teeth when he laughed, and his bearing was stupid. Now he watched the horses with a glazed look of helplessness in his eyes, a certain stupor of downfall.

The great draught horses swung past. They were tied head to tail, four of them, and they heaved along to where a lane branched off from the high-road, planting their great hoofs floutingly in the fine black mud, swinging their great rounded haunches sumptuously, and trotting a few sudden steps as they were led into the lane, round the corner. Every movement showed a massive, slumbrous strength, and a stupidity which held them in subjection. The groom at the head looked back, jerking the leading rope. And the cavalcade moved out of sight up the lane, the tail of the last horse, bobbed up tight and stiff, held out taut from the swinging great haunches as they rocked behind the hedges in a motion-like sleep.

Joe watched with glazed hopeless eyes. The horses were almost like his own body to him. He felt he was done for now. Luckily he was engaged to a woman as old as himself, and therefore her father, who was steward of a neighbouring estate, would provide him with a job. He would marry and go into harness. His life was over, he would be a subject animal now.

He turned uneasily aside, the retreating steps of the horses echoing in his ears. Then, with foolish restlessness, he reached for the scraps of bacon-rind from the plates, and making a faint whistling sound, flung them to the terrier that lay against the fender. He watched the dog swallow them, and waited till the creature looked into his eyes. Then a faint grin came on his face, and in a high, foolish voice he said:

"You won't get much more bacon, shall you, you little b——?"

The dog faintly and dismally wagged its tail, then lowered its haunches, circled round, and lay down again.

There was another helpless silence at the table. Joe sprawled uneasily in his seat, not willing to go till the family conclave was dissolved. Fred Henry, the second brother, was erect, clean-limbed, alert. He had watched the passing of the horses with more *sang-froid*.[1] If he was an animal, like Joe, he was an animal which controls, not one which is controlled. He was master of any horse, and he carried himself with a well-tempered air of mastery. But he was not master of the situations of life. He pushed his coarse brown moustache upwards, off his lip, and glanced irritably at his sister, who sat impassive and inscrutable.

"You'll go and stop with Lucy for a bit, shan't you?" he asked. The girl did not answer.

"I don't see what else you can do," persisted Fred Henry.

"Go as a skivvy,"[2] Joe interpolated laconically.

The girl did not move a muscle.

"If I was her, I should go in for training for a nurse," said Malcolm, the youngest of them all. He was the baby of the family, a young man of twenty-two, with a fresh, jaunty *museau*.[3]

But Mabel did not take any notice of him. They had talked at her and round her for so many years, that she hardly heard them at all.

1. Cold blood (French, literal trans.); here calm detachment.
2. Servant girl.
3. Muzzle (French); here face.

The marble clock on the mantelpiece softly chimed the half-hour, the dog rose uneasily from the hearth-rug and looked at the party at the breakfast-table. But still they sat in an ineffectual conclave.

"Oh, all right," said Joe suddenly, apropos of nothing. "I'll get a move on."

He pushed back his chair, straddled his knees with a downward jerk, to get them free, in horsey fashion, and went to the fire. Still he did not go out of the room; he was curious to know what the others would do or say. He began to charge his pipe, looking down at the dog and saying in a high, affected voice:

"Going wi' me? Going wi' me are ter? Tha'rt goin' further than tha counts on just now, dost hear?"

The dog faintly wagged his tail, the man stuck out his jaw and covered his pipe with his hands, and puffed intently, losing himself in the tobacco, looking down all the while at the dog with an absent brown eye. The dog looked up at him in mournful distrust. Joe stood with his knees stuck out, in real horsey fashion.

"Have you had a letter from Lucy?" Fred Henry asked of his sister.

"Last week," came the neutral reply.

"And what does she say?"

There was no answer.

"Does she *ask* you to go and stop there?" persisted Fred Henry.

"She says I can if I like."

"Well, then, you'd better. Tell her you'll come on Monday."

This was received in silence.

"That's what you'll do then, is it?" said Fred Henry, in some exasperation.

But she made no answer. There was a silence of futility and irritation in the room. Malcolm grinned fatuously.

"You'll have to make up your mind between now and next Wednesday," said Joe loudly, "or else find yourself lodgings on the kerbstone."

The face of the young woman darkened, but she sat on immutable.

"Here's Jack Ferguson!" exclaimed Malcolm, who was looking aimlessly out of the window.

"Where?" exclaimed Joe loudly.

"Just gone past."

"Coming in?"

Malcolm craned his neck to see the gate.

"Yes," he said.

There was a silence. Mabel sat on like one condemned, at the head of the table. Then a whistle was heard from the kitchen. The dog got up and barked sharply. Joe opened the door and shouted:

"Come on."

After a moment a young man entered. He was muffled up in overcoat and a purple woollen scarf, and his tweed cap, which he did not remove, was pulled down on his head. He was of medium height, his face was rather long and pale, his eyes looked tired.

"Hello, Jack! Well, Jack!" exclaimed Malcolm and Joe. Fred Henry merely said: "Jack."

"What's doing?" asked the newcomer, evidently addressing Fred Henry.

"Same. We've got to be out by Wednesday. Got a cold?"

"I have—got it bad, too."

"Why don't you stop in?"

"*Me* stop in? When I can't stand on my legs, perhaps I shall have a chance." The young man spoke huskily. He had a slight Scotch accent.

"It's a knock-out, isn't it," said Joe, boisterously, "if a doctor goes round croaking with a cold. Looks bad for the patients, doesn't it?"

The young doctor looked at him slowly.

"Anything the matter with *you*, then?" he asked sarcastically.

"Not as I know of. Damn your eyes, I hope not. Why?"

"I thought you were very concerned about the patients, wondered if you might be one yourself."

"Damn it, no, I've never been patient to no flaming doctor, and hope I never shall be," returned Joe.

At this point Mabel rose from the table, and they all seemed to become aware of her existence. She began putting the dishes together. The young doctor looked at her, but did not address her. He had not greeted her. She went out of the room with the tray, her face impassive and unchanged.

"When are you off then, all of you?" asked the doctor.

"I'm catching the eleven-forty," replied Malcolm. "Are you goin' down wi' th' trap, Joe?"

"Yes, I've told you I'm going down wi' th' trap, haven't I?"

"We'd better be getting her in then. So long Jack, if I don't see you before I go," said Malcolm, shaking hands.

He went out, followed by Joe, who seemed to have his tail between his legs.

"Well, this is the devil's own," exclaimed the doctor, when he was left alone with Fred Henry. "Going before Wednesday, are you?"

"That's the orders," replied the other.

"Where, to Northampton?"

"That's it."

"The devil!" exclaimed Ferguson, with quiet chagrin.

And there was silence between the two.

"All settled up, are you?" asked Ferguson.

"About."

There was another pause.

"Well, I shall miss yer, Freddy, boy," said the young doctor.

"And I shall miss thee, Jack," returned the other.

"Miss you like hell," mused the doctor.

Fred Henry turned aside. There was nothing to say. Mabel came in again, to finish clearing the table.

"What are *you* going to do, then, Miss Pervin?" asked Ferguson. "Going to your sister's, are you?"

Mabel looked at him with her steady, dangerous eyes, that always made him uncomfortable, unsettling his superficial ease.

"No," she said.

"Well, what in the name of fortune *are* you going to do? Say what you mean to do," cried Fred Henry, with futile intensity.

But she only averted her head, and continued her work. She folded the white table-cloth, and put on the chenille cloth.

"The sulkiest bitch that ever trod!" muttered her brother.

But she finished her task with perfectly impassive face, the young doctor watching her interestedly all the while. Then she went out.

Fred Henry stared after her, clenching his lips, his blue eyes fixing in sharp antagonism, as he made a grimace of sour exasperation.

"You could bray⁴ her into bits, and that's all you'd get out of her," he said, in a small, narrowed tone.

The doctor smiled faintly.

"What's she *going* to do, then?" he asked.

"Strike me if *I* know!" returned the other.

There was a pause. Then the doctor stirred.

"I'll be seeing you tonight, shall I?" he said to his friend.

"Ay—where's it to be? Are we going over to Jessdale?"

"I don't know. I've got such a cold on me. I'll come round to the 'Moon and Stars,'⁵ anyway."

"Let Lizzie and May miss their night for once, eh?"

"That's it—if I feel as I do now."

"All's one——"

The two young men went through the passage and down to the back door together. The house was large, but it was servantless now, and desolate. At the back was a small bricked house-yard and beyond that a big square, gravelled fine and red, and having stables on two sides. Sloping, dank, winter-dark fields stretched away on the open sides.

But the stables were empty. Joseph Pervin, the father of the family, had been a man of no education, who had become a fairly large horse dealer. The stables had been full of horses, there was a great turmoil and come-and-go of horses and of dealers and grooms. Then the kitchen was full of servants. But of late things had declined. The old man had married a second time, to retrieve his fortunes. Now he was dead and everything was gone to the dogs,⁶ there was nothing but debt and threatening.

For months, Mabel had been servantless in the big house, keeping the home together in penury for her ineffectual brothers. She had kept house for ten years. But previously it was with unstinted means. Then, however brutal and coarse everything was, the sense of money had kept her proud, confident. The men might be foul-mouthed, the women in the kitchen might have had reputations, her brothers might have illegitimate children. But so long as there was money, the girl felt herself established, and brutally proud, reserved.

No company came to the house, save dealers and coarse men. Mabel had no associates of her own sex, after her sister went away. But she did not mind. She went regularly to church, she attended to her father. And she lived in the memory of her mother, who had died when she was fourteen, and whom she had loved. She had loved her father, too, in a different way, depending upon him, and feeling secure in him, until at the age of fifty-four, he married again. And then she had set hard against him. Now he had died and left them all hopelessly in debt.

She had suffered badly during the period of poverty. Nothing, however, could shake the curious, sullen, animal pride that dominated each member of the family. Now, for Mabel, the end had come. Still she would not cast about her. She would follow her own way just the same. She would always hold the keys of her own situation. Mindless and persistent, she endured from day to day. Why should she think? Why should she answer anybody? It was enough that this was the end, and there was no way out. She need not pass any more darkly along the main street of the small town, avoiding every eye. She need

4. Grind.
5. Name of a public house (pub).
6. Gone wrong (slang).

not demean herself any more, going into the shops and buying the cheapest food. This was at an end. She thought of nobody, not even of herself. Mindless and persistent, she seemed in a sort of ecstasy to be coming nearer to her fulfilment, her own glorification, approaching her dead mother, who was glorified.

In the afternoon, she took a little bag, with shears and sponge and a small scrubbing-brush, and went out. It was a grey, wintry day, with saddened, dark green fields and an atmosphere blackened by the smoke of foundries not far off. She went quickly, darkly along the causeway, heeding nobody, through the town to the churchyard.

There she always felt secure, as if no one could see her, although as a matter of fact she was exposed to the stare of everyone who passed along under the churchyard wall. Nevertheless, once under the shadow of the great looming church, among the graves, she felt immune from the world, reserved within the thick churchyard wall as in another country.

Carefully she clipped the grass from the grave, and arranged the pinky-white, small chrysanthemums in the tin cross. When this was done, she took an empty jar from a neighbouring grave, brought water, and carefully, most scrupulously sponged the marble headstone and the coping-stone.

It gave her sincere satisfaction to do this. She felt in immediate contact with the world of her mother. She took minute pains, went through the park in a state bordering on pure happiness, as if in performing this task she came into a subtle, intimate connection with her mother. For the life she followed here in the world was far less real than the world of death she inherited from her mother.

The doctor's house was just by the church. Ferguson, being a mere hired assistant, was slave to the country-side. As he hurried now to attend to the out-patients in the surgery, glancing across the graveyard with his quick eye, he saw the girl at her task at the grave. She seemed so intent and remote, it was like looking into another world. Some mystical element was touched in him. He slowed down as he walked, watching her as if spellbound.

She lifted her eyes, feeling him looking. Their eyes met. And each looked away again at once, each feeling, in some way, found out by the other. He lifted his cap and passed on down the road. There remained distinct in his consciousness, like a vision, the memory of her face, lifted from the tombstone in the churchyard, and looking at him with slow, large, portentous eyes. It *was* portentous, her face. It seemed to mesmerise him. There was a heavy power in her eyes which laid hold of his whole being, as if he had drunk some powerful drug. He had been feeling weak and done before. Now the life came back into him, he felt delivered from his own fretted, daily self.

He finished his duties at the surgery as quickly as might be, hastily filling up the bottles of the waiting people with cheap drugs. Then, in perpetual haste, he set off again to visit several cases in another part of his round, before tea-time. At all times he preferred to walk if he could, but particularly when he was not well. He fancied the motion restored him.

The afternoon was falling. It was grey, deadened, and wintry, with a slow, moist, heavy coldness sinking in and deadening all the faculties. But why should he think or notice? He hastily climbed the hill and turned across the dark green fields, following the black cinder-track. In the distance, across a shallow dip in the country, the small town was clustered like smouldering ash, a tower, a spire, a heap of low, raw, extinct houses. And on the nearest fringe of the town, sloping into the dip, was Oldmeadow, the Pervins' house. He could see the stables and the outbuildings distinctly, as they lay towards him on the slope. Well, he would not go there many more times! Another resource would be lost to him, another place gone: the only company he cared for in the alien, ugly little town he was losing. Nothing but work, drudgery, constant hastening from dwelling to dwelling among the colliers and the iron-workers. It wore him out, but at the same time he had a craving for it. It was a stimulant to him to be in the homes of the working people, moving, as it were, through the innermost body of their life. His nerves were excited and gratified. He could come so near, into the very lives of the rough, inarticulate, powerfully emotional men and women. He grumbled, he said he hated the hellish hole. But as a matter of fact it excited him, the contact with the rough, strongly-feeling people was a stimulant applied direct to his nerves.

Below Oldmeadow, in the green, shallow, soddened hollow of fields, lay a square, deep pond. Roving across the landscape, the doctor's quick eye detected a figure in black passing through the gate of the field, down towards the pond. He looked again. It would be Mabel Pervin. His mind suddenly became alive and attentive.

Why was she going down there? He pulled up on the path on the slope above, and stood staring. He could just make sure of the small black figure moving in the hollow of the failing day. He seemed to see her in the midst of such obscurity, that he was like a clairvoyant, seeing rather with the mind's eye than with ordinary sight. Yet he could see her positively enough, whilst he kept his eye attentive. He felt, if he looked away from her, in the thick, ugly falling dusk, he would lose her altogether.

He followed her minutely as she moved, direct and intent, like something transmitted rather than stirring in voluntary activity, straight down the field towards the pond. There she stood on the bank for a moment. She never raised her head. Then she waded slowly into the water.

He stood motionless as the small black figure walked slowly and deliberately towards the centre of the pond, very slowly, gradually moving deeper into the motionless water, and still moving forward as the water got up to her breast. Then he could see her no more in the dusk of the dead afternoon.

"There!" he exclaimed. "Would you believe it?"

And he hastened straight down, running over the wet, soddened fields, pushing through the hedges, down into the depression of callous wintry obscurity. It took him several minutes to come to the pond. He stood on the bank, breathing heavily. He could see nothing. His eyes seemed to penetrate the dead water. Yes, perhaps that was the dark shadow of her black clothing beneath the surface of the water.

He slowly ventured into the pond. The bottom was deep, soft clay, he sank in, and the water clasped dead cold round his legs. As he stirred he could smell the cold, rotten clay that fouled up into the water. It was objectionable in his lungs. Still, repelled and yet not heeding, he moved deeper into the pond. The cold water rose over his thighs, over his loins, upon his abdomen. The lower part of his body was all sunk in the hideous cold element. And the bottom was so deeply soft and uncertain, he was afraid of pitching with his mouth underneath. He could not swim, and was afraid.

He crouched a little, spreading his hands under the water and moving them round, trying to feel for her. The dead cold pond swayed upon his chest. He moved again, a little deeper, and again, with his hands underneath, he felt all around under the water. And he touched her clothing. But it evaded his fingers. He made a desperate effort to grasp it.

And so doing he lost his balance and went under, horribly, suffocating in the foul earthy water, struggling madly for a few moments. At last, after what seemed an eternity, he got his footing, rose again into the air and looked around. He gasped, and knew he was in the world. Then he looked at the water. She had risen near him. He grasped her clothing, and drawing her nearer, turned to take his way to land again.

He went very slowly, carefully, absorbed in the slow progress. He rose higher, climbing out of the pond. The water was now only about his legs; he was thankful, full of relief to be out of the clutches of the pond. He lifted her and staggered on to the bank, out of the horror of wet, grey clay.

He laid her down on the bank. She was quite unconscious and running with water. He made the water come from her mouth, he worked to restore her. He did not have to work very long before he could feel the breathing begin again in her; she was breathing naturally. He worked a little longer. He could feel her live beneath his hands; she was coming back. He wiped her face, wrapped her in his overcoat, looked round into the dim, dark grey world, then lifted her and staggered down the bank and across the fields.

It seemed an unthinkably long way, and his burden so heavy he felt he would never get to the house. But at last he was in the stable-yard, and then in the house-yard. He opened the door and went into the house. In the kitchen he laid her down on the hearth-rug and called. The house was empty. But the fire was burning in the grate.

Then again he kneeled to attend to her. She was breathing regularly, her eyes were wide open and as if conscious, but there seemed something missing in her look. She was conscious in herself, but unconscious of her surroundings.

He ran upstairs, took blankets from a bed, and put them before the fire to warm. Then he removed her saturated, earthy-smelling clothing, rubbed her dry with a towel, and wrapped her naked in the blankets. Then he went into the dining room, to look for spirits. There was a little whisky. He drank a gulp himself, and put some into her mouth.

The effect was instantaneous. She looked full into his face, as if she had been seeing him for some time, and yet had only just become conscious of him.

"Dr. Ferguson?" she said.

"What?" he answered.

He was divesting himself of his coat, intending to find some dry clothing upstairs. He could not bear the smell of the dead, clayey water, and he was mortally afraid for his own health.

"What did I do?" she asked.

"Walked into the pond," he replied. He had begun to shudder like one sick, and could hardly attend to her. Her eyes remained full on him, he seemed to be going dark in his mind, looking back at her helplessly. The shuddering became quieter in him, his life came back to him, dark and unknowing, but strong again.

"Was I out of my mind?" she asked, while her eyes were fixed on him all the time.

"Maybe, for the moment," he replied. He felt quiet, because his strength had come back. The strange fretful strain had left him.

"Am I out of my mind now?" she asked.

"Are you?" he reflected a moment. "No," he answered truthfully. "I don't see that you are." He turned his face aside. He was afraid now, because he felt dazed, and felt dimly that her power was stronger than his, in this issue. And she continued to look at him fixedly all the time. "Can you tell me where I shall find some dry things to put on?" he asked.

"Did you dive into the pond for me?" she asked.

"No," he answered. "I walked in. But I went in overhead as well."

There was silence for a moment. He hesitated. He very much wanted to go upstairs to get into dry clothing. But there was another desire in him. And she seemed to hold him. His will seemed to have gone to sleep, and left him, standing there slack before her. But he felt warm inside himself. He did not shudder at all, though his clothes were sodden on him.

"Why did you?" she asked.

"Because I didn't want you to do such a foolish thing," he said.

"It wasn't foolish," she said, still gazing at him as she lay on the floor, with a sofa cushion under her head. "It was the right thing to do. *I* knew best, then."

"I'll go and shift these wet things," he said. But still he had not the power to move out of her presence, until she sent him. It was as if she had the life of his body in her hands, and he could not extricate himself. Or perhaps he did not want to.

Suddenly she sat up. Then she became aware of her own immediate condition. She felt the blankets about her, she knew her own limbs. For a moment it seemed as if her reason were going. She looked round, with wild eye, as if seeking something. He stood still with fear. She saw her clothing lying scattered.

"Who undressed me?" she asked, her eyes resting full and inevitable on his face.

"I did," he replied, "to bring you round."

For some moments she sat and gazed at him awfully, her lips parted.

"Do you love me, then?" she asked.

He only stood and stared at her, fascinated. His soul seemed to melt.

She shuffled forward on her knees, and put her arms round him, round his legs, as he stood there, pressing her breasts against his knees and thighs, clutching him with strange, convulsive certainty, pressing his thighs against her, drawing him to her face, her throat, as she looked up at him with flaring, humble eyes of transfiguration, triumphant in first possession.

"You love me," she murmured, in strange transport, yearning and triumphant and confident. "You love me. I know you love me, I know."

And she was passionately kissing his knees, through the wet clothing, passionately and indiscriminately kissing his knees, his legs, as if unaware of everything.

He looked down at the tangled wet hair, the wild, bare, animal shoulders. He was amazed, bewildered, and afraid. He had never thought of loving her. He had never wanted to love her. When he rescued her and restored her, he was a doctor, and she was a patient. He had had no single personal thought of her. Nay, this introduction of the personal element was very distasteful to him, a violation of his professional honour. It was horrible to have her there embracing his knees. It was horrible. He revolted from it, violently. And yet—and yet—he had not the power to break away.

She looked at him again, with the same supplication of powerful love, and that same transcendent, frightening light of triumph. In view of the delicate flame which seemed to come from her face like a light, he was powerless. And yet he had never intended to love her. He had never intended. And something stubborn in him could not give way.

"You love me," she repeated, in a murmur of deep, rhapsodic assurance. "You love me."

Her hands were drawing him, drawing him down to her. He was afraid, even a little horrified. For he had, really, no intention of loving her. Yet her hands were drawing him towards her. He put out his hand quickly to steady himself, and grasped her bare shoulder. A flame seemed to burn the hand that grasped her soft shoulder. He had no intention of loving her: his whole will was against his yielding. It was horrible. And yet wonderful was the touch of her shoulders, beautiful the shining of her face. Was she perhaps mad? He had a horror of yielding to her. Yet something in him ached also.

He had been staring away at the door, away from her. But his hand remained on her shoulder. She had gone suddenly very still. He looked down at her. Her eyes were now wide with fear, with doubt, the light was dying from her face, a shadow of terrible greyness was returning. He could not bear the touch of her eyes' question upon him, and the look of death behind the question.

With an inward groan he gave way, and let his heart yield towards her. A sudden gentle smile came on his face. And her eyes, which never left his face, slowly, slowly filled with tears. He watched the strange water rise in her eyes, like some slow fountain coming up. And his heart seemed to burn and melt away in his breast.

He could not bear to look at her any more. He dropped on his knees and caught her head with his arms and pressed her face against his throat. She was very still. His heart, which seemed to have broken, was burning with a kind of agony in his breast. And he felt her slow, hot tears wetting his throat. But he could not move.

He felt the hot tears wet his neck and the hollows of his neck, and he remained motionless, suspended through one of man's eternities. Only now it had become indispensable to him to have her face pressed close to him; he could never let her go again. He could never let her head go away from the close clutch of his arm. He wanted to remain like that for ever, with his heart hurting him in a pain that was also life to him. Without knowing, he was looking down on her damp, soft brown hair.

Then, as it were suddenly, he smelt the horrid stagnant smell of that water. And at the same moment she drew away from him and looked at him. Her eyes were wistful and unfathomable. He was afraid of them, and he fell to kissing her, not knowing what he was doing. He wanted her eyes not to have that terrible, wistful, unfathomable look.

When she turned her face to him again, a faint delicate flush was glowing, and there was again dawning that terrible shining of joy in her eyes, which really terrified him, and yet which he now wanted to see, because he feared the look of doubt still more.

"You love me?" she said, rather faltering.

"Yes." The word cost him a painful effort. Not because it wasn't true. But because it was too newly true, the *saying* seemed to tear open again his newly-torn heart. And he hardly wanted it to be true, even now.

She lifted her face to him, and he bent forward and kissed her on the mouth, gently, with the one kiss that is an eternal pledge. And as he kissed her his heart strained again in his breast. He never intended to love her. But now it was over. He had crossed over the gulf to her, and all that he had left behind had shrivelled and become void.

After the kiss, her eyes again slowly filled with tears. She sat still, away from him, with her face drooped aside, and her hands folded in her lap. The tears fell very slowly. There was complete silence. He too sat there motionless and silent on the hearth-rug. The strange pain of his heart that was broken seemed to consume him. That he should love her? That this was love! That he should be ripped open in this way! Him, a doctor! How they would all jeer if they knew! It was agony to him to think they might know.

In the curious naked pain of the thought he looked again to her. She was sitting there drooped into a muse. He saw a tear fall, and his heart flared hot. He saw for the first time that one of her shoulders was quite uncovered, one arm bare, he could see one of her small breasts; dimly, because it had become almost dark in the room.

"Why are you crying?" he asked, in an altered voice.

She looked up at him, and behind her tears the consciousness of her situation for the first time brought a dark look of shame to her eyes.

"I'm not crying, really," she said, watching him, half frightened.

He reached his hand, and softly closed it on her bare arm.

"I love you! I love you!" he said in a soft, low vibrating voice, unlike himself.

She shrank, and dropped her head. The soft, penetrating grip of his hand on her arm distressed her. She looked up at him.

"I want to go," she said. "I want to go and get you some dry things."

"Why?" he said. "I'm all right."

"But I want to go," she said. "And I want you to change your things."

He released her arm, and she wrapped herself in the blanket, looking at him, rather frightened. And still she did not rise.

"Kiss me," she said wistfully.

He kissed her, but briefly, half in anger.

Then, after a second, she rose nervously, all mixed up in the blanket. He watched her in her confusion as she tried to extricate herself and wrap herself up so that she could walk. He watched her relentlessly, as she knew. And as she went, the blanket trailing, and as he saw a glimpse of her feet and her white leg, he tried to remember her as she was when he had wrapped her in the blanket. But then he didn't want to remember, because she had been nothing to him then, and his nature revolted from remembering her as she was when she was nothing to him.

A tumbling muffled noise from within the dark house startled him. Then he heard her voice: "There are clothes." He rose and went to the foot of the stairs, and gathered up the garments she had thrown down. Then he came back to the fire, to rub himself down and dress. He grinned at his own appearance when he had finished.

The fire was sinking, so he put on coal. The house was now quite dark, save for the light of a street-lamp that shone in faintly from beyond the holly trees. He lit the gas with matches he found on the mantelpiece. Then he emptied the pockets of his own clothes, and threw all his wet things in a heap into the scullery. After which he gathered up her sodden clothes, gently, and put them in a separate heap on the copper-top in the scullery.

It was six o'clock on the clock. His own watch had stopped. He ought to go back to the surgery. He waited, and still she did not come down. So he went to the foot of the stairs and called:

"I shall have to go."

Almost immediately he heard her coming down. She had on her best dress of black voile, and her hair was tidy, but still damp. She looked at him—and in spite of herself, smiled.

"I don't like you in those clothes," she said.

"Do I look a sight?" he answered.

They were shy of one another.

"I'll make you some tea," she said.

"No, I must go."

"Must you?" And she looked at him again with the wide, strained, doubtful eyes. And again, from the pain of his breast, he knew how he loved her. He went and bent to kiss her, gently, passionately, with his heart's painful kiss.

"And my hair smells so horrible," she murmured in distraction. "And I'm so awful, I'm so awful! Oh no, I'm too awful." And she broke into bitter, heart-broken sobbing. "You can't want to love me, I'm horrible."

"Don't be silly, don't be silly," he said, trying to comfort her, kissing her, holding her in his arms. "I want you, I want to marry you, we're going to be married, quickly, quickly—to-morrow if I can."

But she only sobbed terribly, and cried:

"I feel awful. I feel awful. I feel I'm horrible to you."

"No, I want you, I want you," was all he answered, blindly, with that terrible intonation which frightened her almost more than her horror lest he should *not* want her.

1922

Why the Novel Matters

We have curious ideas of ourselves. We think of ourselves as a body with a spirit in it, or a body with a soul in it, or a body with a mind in it. *Mens sana in corpore sano.*[1] The years drink up the wine, and at last throw the bottle away, the body, of course, being the bottle.

It is a funny sort of superstition. Why should I look at my hand, as it so cleverly writes these words, and decide that it is a mere nothing compared to the mind that directs it? Is there really any huge difference between my hand and my brain? Or my mind? My hand is alive, it flickers with a life of its own. It meets all the strange universe in touch, and learns a vast number of things, and knows a vast number of things. My hand, as it writes these words, slips gaily along, jumps like a grasshopper to dot an *i*, feels the table rather cold, gets a little bored if I write too long, has its own rudiments of thought, and is just as much *me* as is my brain, my mind, or my soul. Why should I imagine that there is a *me* which is more *me* than my hand is? Since my hand is absolutely alive, me alive.

Whereas, of course, as far as I am concerned, my pen isn't alive at all. My pen *isn't me* alive. Me alive ends at my finger tips.

Whatever is me alive is me. Every tiny bit of my hands is alive, every little

1. A healthy mind in a healthy body (Latin).

freckle and hair and fold of skin. And whatever is me alive is me. Only my finger-nails, those ten little weapons between me and an inanimate universe, they cross the mysterious Rubicon[2] between me alive and things like my pen, which are not alive, in my own sense.

So, seeing my hand is all alive, and me alive, wherein is it just a bottle, or a jug, or a tin can, or a vessel of clay, or any of the rest of that nonsense? True, if I cut it it will bleed, like a can of cherries. But then the skin that is cut, and the veins that bleed, and the bones that should never be seen, they are all just as alive as the blood that flows. So the tin can business, or vessel of clay, is just bunk.

And that's what you learn, when you're a novelist. And that's what you are very liable *not* to know, if you're a parson, or a philosopher, or a scientist, or a stupid person. If you're a parson, you talk about souls in heaven. If you're a novelist, you know that paradise is in the palm of your hand, and on the end of your nose, because both are alive; and alive, and man alive, which is more than you can say, for certain, of paradise. Paradise is after life, and I for one am not keen on anything that is *after* life. If you are a philosopher, you talk about infinity, and the pure spirit which knows all things. But if you pick up a novel, you realise immediately that infinity is just a handle to this self-same jug of a body of mine; while as for knowing, if I find my finger in the fire, I know that fire burns, with a knowledge so emphatic and vital, it leaves Nirvana[3] merely a conjecture. Oh, yes, my body, me alive, *knows*, and knows intensely. And as for the sum of all knowledge, it can't be anything more than an accumulation of all the things I know in the body, and you, dear reader, know in the body.

These damned philosophers, they talk as if they suddenly went off in steam, and were then much more important than they are when they're in their shirts. It is nonsense. Every man, philosopher included, ends in his own finger-tips. That's the end of his man alive. As for the words and thoughts and sighs and aspirations that fly from him, they are so many tremulations in the ether, and not alive at all. But if the tremulations reach another man alive, he may receive them into his life, and his life may take on a new colour, like a chameleon creeping from a brown rock on to a green leaf. All very well and good. It still doesn't alter the fact that the so-called spirit, the message or teaching of the philosopher or the saint, isn't alive at all, but just a tremulation upon the ether, like a radio message. All this spirit stuff is just tremulations upon the ether. If you, as man alive, quiver from the tremulation of the ether into new life, that is because you are man alive, and you take sustenance and stimulation into your alive man in a myriad ways. But to say that the message, or the spirit which is communicated to you, is more important than your living body, is nonsense. You might as well say that the potato at dinner was more important.

Nothing is important but life. And for myself, I can absolutely see life nowhere but in the living. Life with a capital L is only man alive. Even a cabbage in the rain is cabbage alive. All things that are alive are amazing. And all things that are dead are subsidiary to the living. Better a live dog than a dead lion. But better a live lion than a live dog. *C'est la vie!*

---

2. When Julius Caesar crossed the river Rubicon (near Rimini, Italy) in 49 B.C.E., in defiance of the Senate, he indicated his intention of advancing against Pompey and thus involving the country in civil war. Hence to "cross the Rubicon" means to take an important and irrevocable decision.

3. In Buddhist theology the extinction of the self and its desires and the attainment of perfect beatitude.

It seems impossible to get a saint, or a philosopher, or a scientist, to stick to this simple truth. They are all, in a sense, renegades. The saint wishes to offer himself up as spiritual food for the multitude. Even Francis of Assisi[4] turns himself into a sort of angel-cake, of which anyone may take a slice. But an angel-cake is rather less than man alive. And poor St Francis might well apologise to his body, when he is dying: "Oh, pardon me, my body, the wrong I did you through the years!" It was no wafer,[5] for others to eat.

The philosopher, on the other hand, because he can think, decides that nothing but thoughts matter. It is as if a rabbit, because he can make little pills, should decide that nothing but little pills matter. As for the scientist, he has absolutely no use for me so long as I am man alive. To the scientist, I am dead. He puts under the microscope a bit of dead me, and calls it me. He takes me to pieces, and says first one piece, and then another piece, is me. My heart, my liver, my stomach have all been scientifically me, according to the scientist; and nowadays I am either a brain, or nerves, or glands, or something more up-to-date in the tissue line.

Now I absolutely flatly deny that I am a soul, or a body, or a mind, or an intelligence, or a brain, or a nervous system, or a bunch of glands, or any of the rest of these bits of me. The whole is greater than the part. And therefore, I, who am man alive, am greater than my soul, or spirit, or body, or mind, or consciousness, or anything else that is merely a part of me. I am a man, and alive. I am man alive, and as long as I can, I intend to go on being man alive.

For this reason I am a novelist. And being a novelist, I consider myself superior to the saint, the scientist, the philosopher, and the poet, who are all great masters of different bits of man alive, but never get the whole hog.

The novel is the one bright book of life. Books are not life. They are only tremulations on the ether. But the novel as a tremulation can make the whole man alive tremble. Which is more than poetry, philosophy, science, or any other book-tremulation can do.

The novel is the book of life. In this sense, the Bible is a great confused novel. You may say, it is about God. But it is really about man alive. Adam, Eve, Sarai, Abraham, Isaac, Jacob, Samuel, David, Bath-Sheba, Ruth, Esther, Solomon, Job, Isaiah, Jesus, Mark, Judas, Paul, Peter: what is it but man alive, from start to finish? Man alive, not mere bits. Even the Lord is another man alive, in a burning bush, throwing the tablets of stone at Moses's head.

I do hope you begin to get my idea, why the novel is supremely important, as a tremulation on the ether. Plato makes the perfect ideal being tremble in me. But that's only a bit of me. Perfection is only a bit, in the strange make-up of man alive. The Sermon on the Mount[6] makes the selfless spirit of me quiver. But that, too, is only a bit of me. The Ten Commandments set the old Adam shivering in me, warning me that I am a thief and a murderer, unless I watch it. But even the old Adam is only a bit of me.

I very much like all these bits of me to be set trembling with life and the wisdom of life. But I do ask that the whole of me shall tremble in its wholeness, some time or other.

And this, of course, must happen in me, living.

But as far as it can happen from a communication, it can only happen when

---

4. Roman Catholic saint (1181 or 1182–1226).   Communion.
5. Consumed as Christ's body in Roman Catholic   6. See Matthew 5.7.

a whole novel communicates itself to me. The Bible—but *all* the Bible—and Homer, and Shakespeare: these are the supreme old novels. These are all things to all men. Which means that in their wholeness they affect the whole man alive, which is the man himself, beyond any part of him. They set the whole tree trembling with a new access of life, they do not just stimulate growth in one direction.

I don't want to grow in any one direction any more. And, if I can help it, I don't want to stimulate anybody else into some particular direction. A particular direction ends in a *cul-de-sac*. We're in a *cul-de-sac* at present.

I don't believe in any dazzling revelation, or in any supreme Word. "The grass withereth, the flower fadeth, but the Word of the Lord shall stand for ever."[7] That's the kind of stuff we've drugged ourselves with. As a matter of fact, the grass withereth, but comes up all the greener for that reason, after the rains. The flower fadeth, and therefore the bud opens. But the Word of the Lord, being man-uttered and a mere vibration on the ether, becomes staler and staler, more and more boring, till at last we turn a deaf ear and it ceases to exist, far more finally than any withered grass. It is grass that renews its youth like the eagle, not any Word.

We should ask for no absolutes, or absolute. Once and for all and for ever, let us have done with the ugly imperialism of any absolute. There is no absolute good, there is nothing absolutely right. All things flow and change, and even change is not absolute. The whole is a strange assembly of apparently incongruous parts, slipping past one another.

Me, man alive, I am a very curious assembly of incongruous parts. My yea! of today is oddly different from my yea! of yesterday. My tears of to-morrow will have nothing to do with my tears of a year ago. If the one I love remains unchanged and unchanging, I shall cease to love her. It is only because she changes and startles me into change and defies my inertia, and is herself staggered in her inertia by my changing, that I can continue to love her. If she stayed put, I might as well love the pepper pot.

In all this change, I maintain a certain integrity. But woe betide me if I try to put my finger on it. If I say of myself, I am this, I am that!—then, if I stick to it, I turn into a stupid fixed thing like a lamp-post. I shall never know wherein lies my integrity, my individuality, my me. I *can* never know it. It is useless to talk about my ego. That only means that I have made up an *idea* of myself, and that I am trying to cut myself out to pattern. Which is no good. You can cut your cloth to fit your coat, but you can't clip bits off your living body, to trim it down to your idea. True, you can put yourself into ideal corsets. But even in ideal corsets, fashions change.

Let us learn from the novel. In the novel, the characters can do nothing but *live*. If they keep on being good, according to pattern, or bad, according to pattern, or even volatile, according to pattern, they cease to live, and the novel falls dead. A character in a novel has got to live, or it is nothing.

We, likewise, in life have got to live, or we are nothing.

What we mean by living is, of course, just as indescribable as what we mean by *being*. Men get ideas into their heads, of what they mean by Life, and they proceed to cut life out to pattern. Sometimes they go into the desert to seek God, sometimes they go into the desert to seek cash, sometimes it is wine, woman, and song, and again it is water, political reform, and votes. You never

7. Isaiah 40.8.

know what it will be next: from killing your neighbour with hideous bombs and gas that tears the lungs, to supporting a Foundlings' Home[8] and preaching infinite Love, and being co-respondent in a divorce.

In all this wild welter, we need some sort of guide. It's no good inventing Thou Shalt Nots!

What then? Turn truly, honourably to the novel, and see wherein you are man alive, and wherein you are dead man in life. You may love a woman as man alive, and you may be making love to a woman as sheer dead man in life. You may eat your dinner as man alive, or as a mere masticating corpse. As man alive you may have shot at your enemy. But as a ghastly simulacrum of life you may be firing bombs into men who are neither your enemies nor your friends, but just things you are dead to. Which is criminal, when the things happen to be alive.

To be alive, to be man alive, to be whole man alive: that is the point. And at its best, the novel, and the novel supremely, can help you. It can help you not to be dead man in life. So much of a man walks about dead and a carcass in the street and house, to-day: so much of women is merely dead. Like a pianoforte with half the notes mute.

But the novel you can see, plainly, when the man goes dead, the woman goes inert. You can develop an instinct for life, if you will, instead of a theory of right and wrong, good and bad.

In life, there is right and wrong, good and bad, all the time. But what is right in one case is wrong in another. And in the novel you see one man becoming a corpse, because of his so-called goodness, another going dead because of his so-called wickedness. Right and wrong is an instinct: but an instinct of the whole consciousness in a man, bodily, mental, spiritual at once. And only in the novel are *all* things given full play, or at least, they may be given full play, when we realize that life itself, and not inert safety, is the reason for living. For out of the full play of all things emerges the only thing that is anything, the wholeness of a man, the wholeness of a woman, man live, and live woman.

1936

Love on the Farm[1]

What large, dark hands are those at the window
Grasping in the golden light
Which weaves its way through the evening wind
    At my heart's delight?

5   Ah, only the leaves! But in the west
I see a redness suddenly come
Into the evening's anxious breast—
    'Tis the wound of love goes home!

8. Orphanage.
1. Called "Cruelty and Love" when first published in 1913 and "Love on the Farm" when it appeared in *Collected Poems* (1928).

The woodbine° creeps abroad   *honeysuckle*
10 Calling low to her lover:
    The sunlit flirt who all the day
    Has poised above her lips in play
    And stolen kisses, shallow and gay
    Of pollen, now has gone away—
15   She woos the moth with her sweet, low word;
And when above her his moth-wings hover
Then her bright breast she will uncover
And yield her honey-drop to her lover.

Into the yellow, evening glow
20 Saunters a man from the farm below;
Leans, and looks in at the low-built shed
Where the swallow has hung her marriage bed.
    The bird lies warm against the wall.
    She glances quick her startled eyes
25   Towards him, then she turns away
    Her small head, making warm display
    Of red upon the throat. Her terrors sway
Her out of the nest's warm, busy ball,
Whose plaintive cry is heard as she flies
30 In one blue stoop from out the sties°   *pens for animals*
Into the twilight's empty hall.
Oh, water-hen, beside the rushes
Hide your quaintly scarlet blushes,
Still your quick tail, lie still as dead,
35 Till the distance folds over his ominous tread!

The rabbit presses back her ears,
Turns back her liquid, anguished eyes
And crouches low; then with wild spring
Spurts from the terror of *his* oncoming;
40 To be choked back, the wire ring
Her frantic effort throttling:
    Piteous brown ball of quivering fears!
Ah, soon in his large, hard hands she dies,
And swings all loose from the swing of his walk!
45 Yet calm and kindly are his eyes
And ready to open in brown surprise
Should I not answer to his talk
Or should he my tears surmise.

I hear his hand on the latch, and rise from my chair
50 Watching the door open; he flashes bare
His strong teeth in a smile, and flashes his eyes
In a smile like triumph upon me; then careless-wise
He flings the rabbit soft on the table board
And comes towards me: ah! the uplifted sword
55 Of his hand against my bosom! and oh, the broad
Blade of his glance that asks me to applaud
His coming! With his hand he turns my face to him
And caresses me with his fingers that still smell grim

Of the rabbit's fur! God, I am caught in a snare!
60 I know not what fine wire is round my throat;
I only know I let him finger there
My pulse of life, and let him nose like a stoat°   weasel
Who sniffs with joy before he drinks the blood.

And down his mouth comes to my mouth! and down
65 His bright dark eyes come over me, like a hood
Upon my mind! his lips meet mine, and a flood
Of sweet fire sweeps across me, so I drown
Against him, die, and find death good.

1913, 1928

Piano[1]

Softly, in the dusk, a woman is singing to me;
Taking me back down the vista of years, till I see
A child sitting under the piano, in the boom of the tingling strings
And pressing the small, poised feet of a mother who smiles as she sings.

5 In spite of myself, the insidious mastery of song
Betrays me back, till the heart of me weeps to belong
To the old Sunday evenings at home, with winter outside
And hymns in the cozy parlour, the tinkling piano our guide.

So now it is vain for the singer to burst into clamour
10 With the great black piano appassionato.° The glamour   played with passion
Of childish days is upon me, my manhood is cast
Down in the flood of remembrance, I weep like a child for the past.

1918

Tortoise Shout

I thought he was dumb,
I said he was dumb,
Yet I've heard him cry.

First faint scream,
5 Out of life's unfathomable dawn,
Far off, so far, like a madness, under the horizon's dawning rim,
Far, far off, far scream.

Tortoise *in extremis.*[1]

1. For an earlier version of this poem, see "Poems in Process," in the appendices to this volume.

1. At the point of death (Latin).

Why were we crucified into sex?
10 Why were we not left rounded off, and finished in ourselves.
As we began,
As he certainly began, so perfectly alone?

A far, was-it-audible scream,
Or did it sound on the plasm direct?

15 Worse than the cry of the new-born,
A scream,
A yell,
A shout,
A pæan,
20 A death-agony,
A birth-cry,
A submission,
All, tiny, far away, reptile under the first dawn.

War-cry, triumph, acute-delight, death-scream reptilian,
25 Why was the veil torn?[2]
The silken shriek of the soul's torn membrane?
The male soul's membrane
Torn with a shriek half music, half horror.

Crucifixion.
30 Male tortoise, cleaving behind the hovel-wall of that dense female,
Mounted and tense, spread-eagle, outreaching out of the shell
In tortoise-nakedness,
Long neck, and long vulnerable limbs extruded, spread-eagle over her
    house-roof,
And the deep, secret, all-penetrating tail curved beneath her walls,
35 Reaching and gripping tense, more reaching anguish in uttermost tension
Till suddenly, in the spasm of coition, tupping[3] like a jerking leap, and oh!
Opening its clenched face from his outstretched neck
And giving that fragile yell, that scream,
Super-audible,
40 From his pink, cleft, old-man's mouth,
Giving up the ghost,
Or screaming in Pentecost,[4] receiving the ghost.

His scream, and his moment's subsidence,
The moment of eternal silence,
45 Yet unreleased, and after the moment, the sudden, startling jerk of coition,
    and at once
The inexpressible faint yell—
And so on, till the last plasm of my body was melted back
To the primeval rudiments of life, and the secret.

---

2. Cf. Matthew 27.50–51, describing Jesus' death: "Jesus, when he had cried again with a loud voice, yielded up the ghost. And, behold, the veil [curtain] of the temple was rent in twain, from the top to the bottom; and the earth did quake, and the rocks rent."
3. Copulating.
4. The religious holiday celebrating the descent of the Holy Ghost on Jesus' apostles.

So he tups, and screams
50   Time after time that frail, torn scream
After each jerk, the longish interval,
The tortoise eternity,
Age-long, reptilian persistence,
Heart-throb, slow heart-throb, persistent for the next spasm.

55   I remember, when I was a boy,
I heard the scream of a frog, which was caught with his foot in the mouth
    of an up-starting snake;
I remember when I first heard bull-frogs break into sound in the spring;
I remember hearing a wild goose out of the throat of night
Cry loudly, beyond the lake of waters;
60   I remember the first time, out of a bush in the darkness, a nightingale's
    piercing cries and gurgles startled the depths of my soul;
I remember the scream of a rabbit as I went through a wood at midnight;
I remember the heifer in her heat, blorting and blorting through the hours,
    persistent and irrepressible;
I remember my first terror hearing the howl of weird, amorous cats;
I remember the scream of a terrified, injured horse, the sheet lightning,
65   And running away from the sound of a woman in labour, something like an
    owl whooing,
And listening inwardly to the first bleat of a lamb,
The first wail of an infant,
And my mother singing to herself,
And the first tenor singing of the passionate throat of a young
    collier,° who has long since drunk himself to death,   *coal miner*
70   The first elements of foreign speech
On wild dark lips.

And more than all these,
And less than all these,
This last,
75   Strange, faint coition yell
Of the male tortoise at extremity,
Tiny from under the very edge of the farthest far-off horizon of life.

The cross,
The wheel on which our silence first is broken,
80   Sex, which breaks up our integrity, our single inviolability, our deep silence,
Tearing a cry from us.

Sex, which breaks us into voice, sets us calling across the deeps, calling,
    calling for the complement,
Singing, and calling, and singing again, being answered, having found.
Torn, to become whole again, after long seeking for what is lost,
85   The cry from the tortoise as from Christ, the Osiris⁵-cry of abandonment,
That which is whole, torn asunder,
That which is in part, finding its whole again throughout the universe.

                                  1921

5. The Egyptian vegetation god, murdered by his brother Set, who cut the corpse into fourteen pieces and scattered them throughout Egypt. Osi- ris, like Christ, was resurrected, and became an important ruler in the other world.

Bavarian Gentians

Not every man has gentians in his house
in soft September, at slow, sad Michaelmas.[1]

Bavarian gentians, big and dark, only dark
darkening the daytime torchlike with the smoking blueness of Pluto's[2]
    gloom,
5 ribbed and torchlike, with their blaze of darkness spread blue
down flattening into points, flattened under the sweep of white day
torch-flower of the blue-smoking darkness, Pluto's dark-blue daze,
black lamps from the halls of Dis, burning dark blue,
giving off darkness, blue darkness, as Demeter's pale lamps give off light,
10 lead me then, lead me the way.

Reach me a gentian, give me a torch
let me guide myself with the blue, forked torch of this flower
down the darker and darker stairs, where blue is darkened on blueness
even where Persephone goes, just now, from the frosted September
15 to the sightless realm where darkness was awake upon the dark
and Persephone herself is but a voice
or a darkness invisible enfolded in the deeper dark
of the arms Plutonic, and pierced with the passion of dense gloom,
among the splendour of torches of darkness, shedding darkness on the lost
      bride and her groom.

1923

Snake

A snake came to my water-trough
On a hot, hot day, and I in pyjamas for the heat,
To drink there.

In the deep, strange-scented shade of the great dark
    carob-tree°   *Mediterranean evergreen*
5 I came down the steps with my pitcher
And must wait, must stand and wait, for there he was at the trough before
    me.

He reached down from a fissure in the earth-wall in the gloom
And trailed his yellow-brown slackness soft-bellied down, over the edge of
    the stone trough
And rested his throat upon the stone bottom,
10 And where the water had dripped from the tap, in a small clearness,

---

1. September 29, the feast celebrating the Archangel Michael.
2. God of the underworld in classical mythology.
Also called Dis, he abducted Persephone, daughter
of the goddess of agriculture, Demeter. Persephone was allowed to return to the earth every spring,
but had to descend again to Hades in the autumn,
"the frosted September" (line 14). Demeter and
Persephone were central figures in ancient fertility
myths, where Persephone's annual descent and
return were linked with the death and rebirth of
vegetation.

He sipped with his straight mouth,
Softly drank through his straight gums, into his slack long body,
Silently.

Someone was before me at my water-trough,
15 And I, like a second comer, waiting.

He lifted his head from his drinking, as cattle do,
And looked at me vaguely, as drinking cattle do,
And flickered his two-forked tongue from his lips, and mused a moment,
And stooped and drank a little more,
20 Being earth-brown, earth-golden from the burning bowels of
        the earth
On the day of Sicilian July, with Etna° smoking.   *the volcano*

The voice of my education said to me
He must be killed,
For in Sicily the black, black snakes are innocent, the gold are venomous.

25 And voices in me said, If you were a man
You would take a stick and break him now, and finish him off.

But must I confess how I liked him,
How glad I was he had come like a guest in quiet, to drink at my water-
        trough
And depart peaceful, pacified, and thankless
30 Into the burning bowels of this earth?

Was it cowardice, that I dared not kill him?
Was it perversity, that I longed to talk to him?
Was it humility, to feel so honoured?
I felt so honoured.

35 And yet those voices:
If you were not afraid, you would kill him!

And truly I was afraid, I was most afraid,
But even so, honoured still more
That he should seek my hospitality
40 From out the dark door of the secret earth.

He drank enough
And lifted his head, dreamily, as one who has drunken,
And flickered his tongue like a forked night on the air, so black;
Seeming to lick his lips,
45 And looked around like a god, unseeing, into the air,
And slowly turned his head,
And slowly, very slowly, as if thrice adream
Proceeded to draw his slow length curving round
And climb the broken bank of my wall-face.

50 And as he put his head into that dreadful hole,
And as he slowly drew up, snake-easing his shoulders, and entered farther,

A sort of horror, a sort of protest against his withdrawing into that horrid
    black hole,
Deliberately going into the blackness, and slowly drawing himself after,
Overcame me now his back was turned.

55   I looked round, I put down my pitcher,
I picked up a clumsy log
And threw it at the water-trough with a clatter.

I think it did not hit him;
But suddenly that part of him that was left behind convulsed in undignified
    haste,
60   Writhed like lightning, and was gone
Into the black hole, the earth-lipped fissure in the wall-front
At which, in the intense still noon, I stared with fascination.

And immediately I regretted it.
I thought how paltry, how vulgar, what a mean act!
65   I despised myself and the voices of my accursed human education.

And I thought of the albatross,[1]
And I wished he would come back, my snake.

For he seemed to me again like a king,
Like a king in exile, uncrowned in the underworld,
70   Now due to be crowned again.

And so, I missed my chance with one of the lords
Of life.
And I have something to expiate;
A pettiness.

1923

Cypresses[1]

Tuscan cypresses,
What is it?

Folded in like a dark thought,
For which the language is lost,
5   Tuscan cypresses,
Is there a great secret?
Are our words no good?

The undeliverable secret,
Dead with a dead race and a dead speech, and yet
10   Darkly monumental in you,
Etruscan cypresses.

---

1. In Coleridge's *Rime of the Ancient Mariner.*   1. Tall dark coniferous evergreen trees, associated

Ah, how I admire your fidelity,
Dark cypresses!

Is it the secret of the long-nosed Etruscans?[2]
15 The long-nosed, sensitive-footed, subtly-smiling Etruscans,
Who made so little noise outside the cypress groves?

Among the sinuous, flame-tall cypresses
That swayed their length of darkness all around
Etruscan-dusky, wavering men of old Etruria:
20 Naked except for fanciful long shoes,
Going with insidious, half-smiling quietness
And some of Africa's imperturbable sang-froid[3]
About a forgotten business.

What business, then?
25 Nay, tongues are dead, and words are hollow as hollow seed-pods,
Having shed their sound and finished all their echoing
Etruscan syllables,
That had the telling.

Yet more I see you darkly concentrate,
30 Tuscan cypresses,
On one old thought:
On one old slim imperishable thought, while you remain
Etruscan cypresses;
Dusky, slim marrow-thought of slender, flickering men of Etruria,
35 Whom Rome called vicious.

Vicious, dark cypresses:
Vicious, you supple, brooding, softly-swaying pillars of dark flame.
Monumental to a dead, dead race
Embowered in you!

40 Were they then vicious, the slender, tender-footed
Long-nosed men of Etruria?
Or was their way only evasive and different, dark, like cypress-trees in a
    wind?

They are dead, with all their vices,
And all that is left
45 Is the shadowy monomania of some cypresses
And tombs.

The smile, the subtle Etruscan smile still lurking
Within the tombs,
Etruscan cypresses.

50 He laughs longest who laughs last;°   (*proverbial*)
Nay, Leonardo[4] only bungled the pure Etruscan smile.

---

2. The most important of the pre-Roman inhabitants of Italy.
3. Cold blood (French, literal trans.); here calm detachment.

4. Leonardo da Vinci (1452–1519), Italian painter whose portrait known as the *Mona Lisa* or *La Gioconda* has a famous mysterious smile.

What would I not give
To bring back the rare and orchid-like
Evil-yclept° Etruscan?   °called (archaic)
55 For as to the evil
We have only Roman word for it,
Which I, being a little weary of Roman virtue,
Don't hang much weight on.

For oh, I know, in the dust where we have buried
60 The silenced races and all their abominations,
We have buried so much of the delicate magic of life.

There in the deeps
That churn the frankincense and ooze the myrrh,
Cypress shadowy,
65 Such an aroma of lost human life!

They say the fit survive,
But I invoke the spirits of the lost.
Those that have not survived, the darkly lost,
To bring their meaning back into life again,
70 Which they have taken away
And wrap inviolable in soft cypress-trees,
Etruscan cypresses.

Evil, what is evil?
There is only one evil, to deny life
75 As Rome denied Etruria
And mechanical America Montezuma⁵ still.

Fiesole.   1923

How Beastly the Bourgeois Is

How beastly the bourgeois is
especially the male of the species—

Presentable, eminently presentable—
shall I make you a present of him?

5 Isn't he handsome? Isn't he healthy? Isn't he a fine specimen?
Doesn't he look the fresh clean englishman, outside?
Isn't it god's own image? tramping his thirty miles a day
after partridges, or a little rubber ball?
wouldn't you like to be like that, well off, and quite the thing?

10 Oh, but wait!
Let him meet a new emotion, let him be faced with another man's need,
let him come home to a bit of moral difficulty, let life face him with a new
        demand on his understanding

---

5. Aztec war chief or emperor of ancient Mexico at the time of the Spanish conquest early 16th century.

and then watch him go soggy, like a wet meringue.
Watch him turn into a mess, either a fool or a bully.
15 Just watch the display of him, confronted with a new demand on his
      intelligence,
a new life-demand.

How beastly the bourgeois is
especially the male of the species—
Nicely groomed, like a mushroom
20 standing there so sleek and erect and eyeable—
and like a fungus, living on the remains of bygone life
sucking his life out of the dead leaves of greater life than his own.

And even so, he's stale, he's been there too long.
Touch him, and you'll find he's all gone inside
25 just like an old mushroom, all wormy inside, and hollow ·
under a smooth skin and an upright appearance.

Full of seething, wormy, hollow feelings
rather nasty—
How beastly the bourgeois is!

30 Standing in their thousands, these appearances, in damp England
what a pity they can't all be kicked over
like sickening toadstools, and left to melt back, swiftly
into the soil of England.

                                                1929

The Ship of Death[1]

I

Now it is autumn and the falling fruit
and the long journey towards oblivion.

The apples falling like great drops of dew
to bruise themselves an exit from themselves.

5 And it is time to go, to bid farewell
to one's own self, and find an exit
from the fallen self.

II

Have you built your ship of death, O have you?
O build your ship of death, for you will need it.

10 The grim frost is at hand, when the apples will fall
thick, almost thundrous, on the hardened earth.

---

1. Lawrence is remembering "the sacred treasures of the dead, the little bronze ship of death that should bear him over to the other world," found in Etruscan tombs and described in his book *Etruscan Places* (1932).

2284 / D. H. LAWRENCE

And death is on the air like a smell of ashes!
Ah! can't you smell it?

And in the bruised body, the frightened soul
15 finds itself shrinking, wincing from the cold
that blows upon it through the orifices.

III

And can a man his own quietus make
with a bare bodkin?[2]

With daggers, bodkins, bullets, man can make
20 a bruise or break of exit for his life;
but is that a quietus, O tell me, is it quietus?

Surely not so! for how could murder, even self-murder
ever a quietus make?

IV

O let us talk of quiet that we know,
25 that we can know, the deep and lovely quiet
of a strong heart at peace!

How can we this, our own quietus, make?

V

Build then the ship of death, for you must take
the longest journey, to oblivion.

30 And die the death, the long and painful death
that lies between the old self and the new.

Already our bodies are fallen, bruised, badly bruised,
already our souls are oozing through the exit
of the cruel bruise.

35 Already the dark and endless ocean of the end
is washing in through the breaches of our wounds,
already the flood is upon us.

Oh build your ship of death, your little ark
and furnish it with food, with little cakes, and wine
40 for the dark flight down oblivion.

VI

Piecemeal the body dies, and the timid soul
has her footing washed away, as the dark flood rises.

---

2. Cf. Shakespeare's *Hamlet* 3.1.70–76: "For who would bear the whips and scorns of time, / . . . When
he himself might his quietus make / With a bare bodkin?" "Bodkin": dagger.

We are dying, we are dying, we are all of us dying
and nothing will stay the death-flood rising within us
45   and soon it will rise on the world, on the outside world.

We are dying, we are dying, piecemeal our bodies are dying
and our strength leaves us,
and our soul cowers naked in the dark rain over the flood,
cowering in the last branches of the tree of our life.

VII

50   We are dying, we are dying, so all we can do
is now to be willing to die, and to build the ship
of death to carry the soul on the longest journey.

A little ship, with oars and food
and little dishes, and all accoutrements
55   fitting and ready for the departing soul.

Now launch the small ship, now as the body dies
and life departs, launch out, the fragile soul
in the fragile ship of courage, the ark of faith
with its store of food and little cooking pans
60   and change of clothes,
upon the flood's black waste
upon the waters of the end
upon the sea of death, where still we sail
darkly, for we cannot steer, and have no port.

65   There is no port, there is nowhere to go
only the deepening blackness darkening still
blacker upon the soundless, ungurgling flood
darkness at one with darkness, up and down
and sideways utterly dark, so there is no direction any more
70   and the little ship is there; yet she is gone.
She is not seen, for there is nothing to see her by.
She is gone! gone! and yet
somewhere she is there.
Nowhere!

VIII

75   And everything is gone, the body is gone
completely under, gone, entirely gone.
The upper darkness is heavy as the lower,
between them the little ship
is gone
80   she is gone.

It is the end, it is oblivion.

IX

And yet out of eternity a thread
separates itself on the blackness,

a horizontal thread
85 that fumes a little with pallor upon the dark.

Is it illusion? or does the pallor fume
A little higher?
Ah wait, wait, for there's the dawn,
the cruel dawn of coming back to life
90 out of oblivion.

Wait, wait, the little ship
drifting, beneath the deathly ashy grey
of a flood-dawn.

Wait, wait! even só, a flush of yellow
95 and strangely, O chilled wan soul, a flush of rose.

A flush of rose, and the whole thing starts again.

X

The flood subsides, and the body, like a worn sea-shell
emerges strange and lovely.
And the little ship wings home, faltering and lapsing
100 on the pink flood,
and the frail soul steps out, into her house again
filling the heart with peace.

Swings the heart renewed with peace
even of oblivion.

105 Oh build your ship of death, oh build it!
for you will need it.
For the voyage of oblivion awaits you.

1929–30   1933

T. S. ELIOT
1888–1965

Thomas Stearns Eliot was born in St. Louis, Missouri, of New England stock. He entered Harvard in 1906 and was influenced there by the anti-Romanticism of Irving Babbitt and the philosophical and critical interests of George Santayana, as well as by the enthusiastic study of Renaissance literature and of South Asian religions. He wrote his Harvard dissertation on the English idealist philosopher F. H. Bradley, whose emphasis on the private nature of individual experience, "a circle enclosed on the outside," influenced Eliot's poetry considerably. He also studied literature and philosophy in France and Germany, before going to England shortly after the outbreak of World War I in 1914. He studied Greek philosophy at Oxford, taught school in London, and then obtained a position with Lloyd's Bank. In 1915 he married an English writer, Vivienne Haigh-Wood, but the marriage was not a success. She suffered from poor emotional and physical health. The strain told on Eliot, too. By November 1921 distress and worry had brought him to the verge of a nervous breakdown, and on medical advice he went to recuperate in a Swiss sanitorium. Two months later he returned, pausing in Paris long enough to give his early supporter and adviser Ezra Pound the manuscript of *The Waste Land.* Eliot left his wife in 1933, and she was eventually committed to a mental home, where she died in 1947. Ten years later he was happily remarried to his secretary, Valerie Fletcher.

Eliot started writing literary and philosophical reviews soon after settling in London and was assistant editor of *The Egoist* magazine from 1917 to 1919. In 1922 he founded the influential quarterly *The Criterion,* which he edited until it ceased publication in 1939. His poetry first appeared in 1915, when, at Pound's urging, "The Love Song of J. Alfred Prufrock" was printed in *Poetry* magazine (Chicago) and a few other short poems were published in the short-lived periodical *Blast.* His first published collection of poems was *Prufrock and Other Observations,* 1917; two other small collections followed in 1919 and 1920; in 1922 *The Waste Land* appeared, first in *The Criterion* in October, then in *The Dial* (in America) in November, and finally in book form. Meanwhile he was also publishing collections of his critical essays. In 1925 he joined the London publishing firm Faber & Gwyer, and he was made a director when the firm was renamed Faber & Faber. He became a British subject and joined the Church of England in 1927.

"Our civilization comprehends great variety and complexity, and this variety and complexity, playing upon a refined sensibility, must produce various and complex results. The poet must become more and more comprehensive, more allusive, more indirect, in order to force, to dislocate if necessary, language into his meaning." This remark, from Eliot's essay "The Metaphysical Poets" (1921), gives one clue to his poetic method from "Prufrock" through *The Waste Land.* When he settled in London he saw poetry in English as exhausted, with no verbal excitement or original craftsmanship. He sought to make poetry more subtle, more suggestive, and at the same time more precise. Like the imagists, he emphasized the necessity of clear and precise images. From the philosopher poet T. E. Hulme and from Pound, he learned to fear what was seen as Romantic self-indulgence and vagueness, and to regard the poetic medium rather than the poet's personality as the important factor. At the same time the "hard, dry" images advocated by Hulme were not enough for him; he wanted wit, allusiveness, irony. He saw in the Metaphysical poets how wit and passion could be combined, and he saw in the French symbolists, such as Charles Baudelaire, Stéphane Mallarmé, Paul Verlaine, and Arthur Rimbaud, how an image could be both absolutely precise in what it referred to physically and endlessly suggestive in its meanings because of its relationship to other images. The combination of precision, symbolic suggestion, and ironic mockery in the poetry of the late-nineteenth-century French poet Jules Laforgue attracted and influenced him, as did Laforgue's verse technique that Eliot described in an interview as "rhyming lines of irregular length, with the rhymes coming in irregular places." He also found in the Jacobean dramatists, such as Thomas Middleton, Cyril Tourneur, and John Webster, a flexible blank verse with overtones of colloquial movement, a way of counterpointing the accent of conversation and the note of terror. Eliot's fluency in French and German, his study of Western and non-Western literary and religious texts in their original languages, his rigorous knowledge of philosophy, his exacting critical intellect, his keen sensitivity to colloquial rhythm and idiom, his ability to fuse anguished emotional states with sharply etched intellectual satire—all of these contributed to his crafting one of the twentieth century's most distinctive and influential bodies of poetry.

Hulme's protests against the Romantic concept of poetry reinforced what Eliot had learned from Babbitt at Harvard; yet for all his severity with poets such as Percy Shelley and Walt Whitman, for all his cultivation of a classical viewpoint and his insistence on order and discipline rather than on mere self-expression in art, one side of Eliot's poetic genius is Romantic. The symbolist influence on his imagery, his elegiac lamentation over loss and fragmentation, his interest in the evocative and the suggestive, lines such as "And fiddled whisper music on those strings / And bats with baby faces in the violet light / Whistled, and beat their wings," and recurring images such as the hyacinth girl and the rose garden show what could be called a Romantic element in his poetry. But it is combined with a dry ironic allusiveness, a play of wit and satire, and a colloquial element, which are not normally found in poets of the Romantic tradition.

Eliot's real novelty—and the cause of much bewilderment when his poems first appeared—was his deliberate elimination of all merely connective and transitional passages, his building up of the total pattern of meaning through the immediate juxtaposition of images without overt explanation of what they are doing, together with his use of oblique references to other works of literature (some of them quite obscure to most readers of his time). "Prufrock" presents a symbolic landscape where the meaning emerges from the mutual interaction of the images, and that meaning is enlarged by echoes, often ironic, of Hesiod and Dante and Shakespeare. The Waste Land is a series of scenes and images with no author's voice intervening to tell us where we are but with the implications developed through multiple contrasts and through analogies with older literary works often referred to in a distorted quotation or half-concealed allusion. Furthermore, the works referred to are not necessarily central in the Western literary tradition: besides Dante and Shakespeare there are pre-Socratic philosophers; major and minor seventeenth-century poets and drama-tists; works of anthropology, history, and philosophy; texts of Buddhism and Hinduism; even popular songs and vaudeville. Ancient and modern voices, high and low art, Western and non-Western languages clash, coincide, jostle alongside one another. In a culture where the poet's public might lack a common cultural heritage, a shared knowledge of works of the past, Eliot felt it necessary to accumulate his own body of references. In this his use of earlier literature differs from, say, John Milton's. Both poets are difficult for the modern reader, who needs editorial assistance in recognizing and understanding many of the allusions—but Milton was drawing on a body of knowledge common to educated people in his day. Nevertheless, this aspect of Eliot can be exaggerated; his imagery and the movement of his verse set the tone he requires, establish the area of meaning to be developed, so that even a reader ignorant of most of the literary allusions can often get the feel of the poem and achieve some understanding of what it says.

Eliot's early poetry, until at least the middle 1920s, is mostly concerned in one way or another with the Waste Land, with aspects of cultural decay in the modern Western world. After his formal acceptance of Anglican Christianity, a penitential note appears in much of his verse, a note of quiet searching for spiritual peace, with considerable allusion to biblical, liturgical, and mystical religious literature and to Dante. Ash Wednesday (1930), a poem in six parts, much less fiercely concentrated in style than the earlier poetry, explores with gentle insistence a mood both penitential and ques-tioning. The Ariel poems (so called because published in Faber's Ariel pamphlet series) present or explore aspects of religious doubt or discovery or revelation, some-times, as in "Journey of the Magi," drawing on biblical incident. In Four Quartets (of which the first, "Burnt Norton," appeared in the Collected Poems of 1936, though all four were not completed until 1943, when they were published together), Eliot fur-ther explored essentially religious moods, dealing with the relation between time and eternity and the cultivation of that selfless passivity that can yield the moment of timeless revelation in the midst of time. The mocking irony, the savage humor, the collage of quotations, the deliberately startling juxtaposition of the sordid and the romantic give way in these later poems to a quieter poetic idiom that is less jagged and more abstract, less fragmentary and more formally patterned.

As a critic Eliot worked out in his reading of older literature what he needed as a poet to hold and to admire. He lent the growing weight of his authority to a shift in literary taste that replaced Milton by John Donne as the great seventeenth-century English poet and replaced Alfred, Lord Tennyson in the nineteenth century by Gerard Manley Hopkins. Rewriting English literary history, he saw the late-seventeenth-century "dissociation of sensibility"—the segregation of intellect and emotion—as determining the course of English poetry throughout the eighteenth and nineteenth centuries. This theory also explained what he was aiming at in his own poetry: the reestablishment of that *unified* sensibility he found in Donne and other early-seventeenth-century poets and dramatists, who were able, he suggests in "The Metaphysical Poets," to "feel their thought as immediately as the odour of a rose." His view of tradition, his dislike of the poetic exploitation of the author's personality, his advocacy of what he called "orthodoxy," made him suspicious of what he considered eccentric geniuses such as William Blake and D. H. Lawrence. On the other side, his dislike of the grandiloquent and his insistence on complexity and on the mingling of the formal with the conversational made him distrust Milton's influence on English poetry. He considered himself a "classicist in literature, royalist in politics, and Anglo-Catholic in religion" (*For Lancelot Andrewes*, 1928), in favor of order against chaos, tradition against eccentricity, authority against rampant individualism; yet his own poetry is in many respects untraditional and certainly highly individual in tone. His conservative and even authoritarian habit of mind, his anti-Semitic remarks and missionary zeal, alienated some who admire—and some whose own poetry has been much influenced by—his poetry.

Eliot's plays address, directly or indirectly, religious themes. *Murder in the Cathedral* (1935) deals in an appropriately ritual manner with the killing of Archbishop Thomas à Becket, using a chorus and presenting its central speech as a sermon by the archbishop. *The Family Reunion* (1939) deals with the problem of guilt and redemption in a modern upper-class English family; combining choric devices from Greek tragedy with a poetic idiom subdued to the accents of drawing-room conversation. In his three later plays, all written in the 1950s, *The Cocktail Party*, *The Confidential Clerk*, and *The Elder Statesman*, he achieved popular success by casting a serious religious theme in the form of a sophisticated modern social comedy, using a verse that is so conversational in movement that when spoken in the theater it does not sound like verse at all.

Critics differ on the degree to which Eliot succeeded in his last plays in combining box-office success with dramatic effectiveness. But there is no disagreement on his importance as one of the great renovators of poetry in English, whose influence on a whole generation of poets, critics, and intellectuals was enormous. His range as a poet is limited, and his interest in the great middle ground of human experience (as distinct from the extremes of saint and sinner) deficient; but when in 1948 he was awarded the rare honor of the Order of Merit by King George VI and also gained the Nobel Prize in literature, his positive qualities were widely and fully recognized—his poetic cunning, his fine craftsmanship, his original accent, his historical importance as *the* poet of the modern symbolist-Metaphysical tradition.

The Love Song of J. Alfred Prufrock[1]

S'io credesse che mia risposta fosse
a persona che mai tornasse al mondo,
questa fiamma staria senza più scosse.
Ma per cio cche giammai di questo fondo
non torno vivo alcun, s'i'odo il vero,
senza tema d'infamia ti rispondo.[2]

---

1. The title implies an ironic contrast between the romantic suggestions of "love song" and the dully prosaic name "J. Alfred Prufrock."

2. "If I thought that my reply would be to one who would ever return to the world, this flame would stay without further movement; but since none has

Let us go then, you and I,
When the evening is spread out against the sky
Like a patient etherised upon a table;
Let us go, through certain half-deserted streets,
5   The muttering retreats
Of restless nights in one-night cheap hotels
And sawdust restaurants with oyster shells:
Streets that follow like a tedious argument
Of insidious intent
10   To lead you to an overwhelming question . . .
Oh, do not ask, 'What is it?'
Let us go and make our visit.

In the room the women come and go
Talking of Michelangelo.

15   The yellow fog that rubs its back upon the window-panes,
The yellow smoke that rubs its muzzle on the window-panes
Licked its tongue into the corners of the evening,
Lingered upon the pools that stand in drains,
Let fall upon its back the soot that falls from chimneys,
20   Slipped by the terrace, made a sudden leap,
And seeing that it was a soft October night,
Curled once about the house, and fell asleep.

And indeed there will be time[3]
For the yellow smoke that slides along the street,
25   Rubbing its back upon the window-panes;
There will be time, there will be time
To prepare a face to meet the faces that you meet;
There will be time to murder and create,
And time for all the works and days of hands[4]
30   That lift and drop a question on your plate;
Time for you and time for me,
And time yet for a hundred indecisions,
And for a hundred visions and revisions,
Before the taking of a toast and tea.

35   In the room the women come and go
Talking of Michelangelo.

And indeed there will be time
To wonder, 'Do I dare?' and, 'Do I dare?'
Time to turn back and descend the stair,
40   With a bald spot in the middle of my hair—
(They will say: 'How his hair is growing thin!')
My morning coat, my collar mounting firmly to the chin,

---

ever returned alive from this depth, if what I hear
is true, I answer you without fear of infamy"
(Dante, *Inferno* 27.61–66). Guido da Montefeltro,
shut up in his flame (the punishment given to false
counselors), tells the shame of his evil life to Dante
because he believes Dante will never return to
earth to report it.

3. Cf. Andrew Marvell, "To His Coy Mistress,"
line 1: "Had we but world enough, and time."
4. *Works and Days* is a poem about the farming
year by the Greek poet Hesiod (8th century B.C.E.).
Eliot contrasts useful agricultural labor with the
futile "works and days of hands" engaged in meaningless social gesturing.

My necktie rich and modest, but asserted by a simple pin—
(They will say: 'But how his arms and legs are thin!')
45 Do I dare
Disturb the universe?
In a minute there is time
For decisions and revisions which a minute will reverse.

For I have known them all already, known them all—
50 Have known the evenings, mornings, afternoons,
I have measured out my life with coffee spoons;
I know the voices dying with a dying fall[5]
Beneath the music from a farther room.
        So how should I presume?

55 And I have known the eyes already, known them all—
The eyes that fix you in a formulated phrase,
And when I am formulated, sprawling on a pin,
When I am pinned and wriggling on the wall,
Then how should I begin
60 To spit out all the butt-ends of my days and ways?
        And how should I presume?

And I have known the arms already, known them all—
Arms that are braceleted and white and bare
(But in the lamplight, downed with light brown hair!)
65 Is it perfume from a dress
That makes me so digress?
Arms that lie along a table, or wrap about a shawl.
        And should I then presume?
        And how should I begin?

                    · · · · ·

70 Shall I say, I have gone at dusk through narrow streets
And watched the smoke that rises from the pipes
Of lonely men in shirt-sleeves, leaning out of windows? . . .
I should have been a pair of ragged claws
Scuttling across the floors of silent seas.[6]

                    · · · · ·

75 And the afternoon, the evening, sleeps so peacefully!
Smoothed by long fingers,
Asleep . . . tired . . . or it malingers,
Stretched on the floor, here beside you and me.
Should I, after tea and cakes and ices,
80 Have the strength to force the moment to its crisis?
But though I have wept and fasted, wept and prayed,
Though I have seen my head (grown slightly bald) brought in upon a
        platter,[7]

5. Cf. Shakespeare's *Twelfth Night* 1.1.4: "That strain again, it had a dying fall."
6. I.e., he would have been better as a crab on the ocean bed. Perhaps, too, the motion of a crab suggests futility and growing old. Cf. Shakespeare's *Hamlet* 2.2.201–02: "for you yourself, sir, should be old as I am—if, like a crab, you could go backward."
7. Like that of John the Baptist. See Mark 6.17–28 and Matthew 14.3–11.

I am no prophet—and here's no great matter;
I have seen the moment of my greatness flicker,
85   And I have seen the eternal Footman hold my coat, and snicker,
And in short, I was afraid.

And would it have been worth it, after all,
After the cups, the marmalade, the tea,
Among the porcelain, among some talk of you and me,
90   Would it have been worth while,
To have bitten off the matter with a smile,
To have squeezed the universe into a ball[8]
To roll it toward some overwhelming question,
To say: 'I am Lazarus,[9] come from the dead,
95   Come back to tell you all, I shall tell you all'—
If one, settling a pillow by her head,
      Should say: 'That is not what I meant at all.
      That is not it, at all.'

And would it have been worth it, after all,
100 Would it have been worth while,
After the sunsets and the dooryards and the sprinkled streets,
After the novels, after the teacups, after the skirts that trail along the floor—
And this, and so much more?—
It is impossible to say just what I mean!
105 But as if a magic lantern threw the nerves in patterns on a screen:
Would it have been worth while
If one, settling a pillow or throwing off a shawl,
And turning toward the window, should say:
      'That is not it at all,
110   That is not what I meant, at all.'

                              . . . . .

No! I am not Prince Hamlet, nor was meant to be;
Am an attendant lord, one that will do
To swell a progress,[1] start a scene or two,
Advise the prince; no doubt, an easy tool,
115 Deferential, glad to be of use,
Politic, cautious, and meticulous;
Full of high sentence,[2] but a bit obtuse;
At times, indeed, almost ridiculous—
Almost, at times, the Fool.

120 I grow old . . . I grow old . . .
I shall wear the bottoms of my trousers rolled.

Shall I part my hair behind? Do I dare to eat a peach?
I shall wear white flannel trousers, and walk upon the beach.
I have heard the mermaids singing, each to each.

---

8. Cf. "To His Coy Mistress," lines 41–44: "Let us
roll all our strength and all / Our sweetness up into
one ball, / And tear our pleasures with rough strife
/ Thorough the iron gates of life."
9. Raised by Jesus from the dead (Luke 16.19–31
and John 11.1–44).
1. In the Elizabethan sense of a state journey

made by a royal or noble person. Elizabethan plays
sometimes showed such "progresses" crossing the
stage. Cf. Chaucer's General Prologue to The Canterbury Tales, line 308.
2. In its older meanings: "opinions," "sententious-
ness."

125   I do not think that they will sing to me.

I have seen them riding seaward on the waves
Combing the white hair of the waves blown back
When the wind blows the water white and black.

We have lingered in the chambers of the sea
130   By sea-girls wreathed with seaweed red and brown
Till human voices wake us, and we drown.

1910–11   1915, 1917

Sweeney among the Nightingales

ὤμοι, πέπληγμαι καιρίαν πληγὴν ἔσω.[1]

Apeneck Sweeney spreads his knees
Letting his arms hang down to laugh,
The zebra stripes along his jaw
Swelling to maculate° giraffe.   *spotted, stained*

5   The circles of the stormy moon
Slide westward toward the River Plate,[2]
Death and the Raven[3] drift above
And Sweeney guards the hornèd gate.[4]

Gloomy Orion and the Dog
10   Are veiled;[5] and hushed the shrunken seas;
The person in the Spanish cape
Tries to sit on Sweeney's knees

Slips and pulls the table cloth
Overturns a coffee-cup,
15   Reorganized upon the floor
She yawns and draws a stocking up;

The silent man in mocha brown
Sprawls at the window-sill and gapes;
The waiter brings in oranges
20   Bananas figs and hothouse grapes;

The silent vertebrate in brown
Contracts and concentrates, withdraws;
Rachel *née* Rabinovitch
Tears at the grapes with murderous paws;

1. "Alas, I am struck with a mortal blow within"
(Aeschylus, *Agamemnon*, line 1343); the voice of
Agamemnon heard crying out from the palace as
he is murdered by his wife, Clytemnestra.
2. Or Rio de la Plata, an estuary on the South
American coast between Argentina and Uruguay,
formed by the Uruguay and Paraná rivers.

3. The constellation Corvus.
4. The gates of horn, in Hades, through which
true dreams come to the upper world.
5. For Sweeney and his female friend, the gate of
vision is blocked and the great myth-making constellations—"Orion and the Dog"—are "veiled."

25 She and the lady in the cape
 Are suspect, thought to be in league;
 Therefore the man with heavy eyes
 Declines the gambit, shows fatigue,

 Leaves the room and reappears
30 Outside the window, leaning in,
 Branches of wistaria
 Circumscribe a golden grin;

 The host with someone indistinct
 Converses at the door apart,
35 The nightingales are singing near
 The Convent of the Sacred Heart,

 And sang within the bloody wood
 When Agamemnon cried aloud[6]
 And let their liquid siftings fall
40 To stain the stiff dishonoured shroud.

1918, 1919

The Waste Land

In the essay "*Ulysses,* Order, and Myth" (1923), Eliot hinted at the ambitions of *The Waste Land* when he declared that others would follow James Joyce "in manipulating a continuous parallel between contemporaneity and antiquity. . . . It is simply a way of controlling, of ordering, of giving a shape and a significance to the immense panorama of futility and anarchy which is contemporary history. . . . It is, I seriously believe, a step toward making the modern world possible in art." Eliot labeled this new technique "the mythical method."

He gave another clue to the theme and structure of *The Waste Land* in a general note, in which he stated that "not only the title, but the plan and a good deal of the symbolism of the poem were suggested by Miss Jessie L. Weston's book on the Grail legend: *From Ritual to Romance* [1920]." He further acknowledged a general indebtedness to Sir James Frazer's *Golden Bough* (thirteen volumes, 1890–1915), "especially the . . . volumes *Adonis, Attis, Osiris,*" in which Frazer deals with ancient vegetation myths and fertility ceremonies. Drawing on material from Frazer and other anthropologists, Weston traces the relationship of these myths and rituals to Christianity and especially to the legend of the Holy Grail. She finds an archetypal fertility myth in the story of the Fisher King, whose death, infirmity, or impotence (there are many forms of the myth) brought drought and desolation to the land and failure of the power to reproduce themselves among both humans and beasts. This symbolic Waste Land can be revived only if a "questing knight" goes to the Chapel Perilous, situated in the heart of it, and there asks certain ritual questions about the Grail (or Cup) and the Lance—originally fertility symbols, female and male, respectively. The proper asking of these questions revives the king and restores fertility to the land. The relation of this original Grail myth to fertility cults and rituals found in many different civilizations, and represented by stories of a god who dies and is later resurrected (e.g., Tammuz, Adonis, Attis), shows their common origin in a response to

6. Agamemnon is murdered not in a "bloody wood" but in his bath. Eliot here telescopes Agamemnon's murder with the wood where, in Greek myth, Philomela was raped by her sister's husband, Tereus (she was subsequently turned into a nightingale), and also with the ancient "bloody wood" of Nemi, where the old priest was slain by his successor (as described in the first chapter of Sir James Frazer's *Golden Bough*).

the cyclical movement of the seasons, with vegetation dying in winter to be resurrected again in the spring. Christianity, according to Weston, gave its own spiritual meaning to the myth; it "did not hesitate to utilize the already existing medium of instruction, but boldly identified the Deity of Vegetation, regarded as Life Principle, with the God of the Christian Faith." The Fisher King is related to the use of the fish symbol in early Christianity. Weston states "with certainty that the Fish is a Life symbol of immemorial antiquity, and that the title of Fisher has, from the earliest ages, been associated with the Deities who were held to be specially connected with the origin and preservation of Life." Eliot, following Weston, thus uses a great variety of mythological and religious material, both Western and Eastern, to paint a symbolic picture of the modern Waste Land and the need for regeneration. He vividly presents the terror of that desiccated life—its loneliness, emptiness, and irrational apprehensions—as well as its misuse of sexuality, but he paradoxically ends the poem with a benediction. The mass death and social collapse of World War I inform the poem's vision of a Waste Land strewn with corpses, wreckage, and ruin. Another significant general source for the poem is the German composer Richard Wagner's operas *Götterdämmerung* (*Twilight of the Gods*), *Parsifal*, *Das Rheingold*, and *Tristan und Isolde*.

The poem as published owes a great deal to the severe pruning of Ezra Pound; the original manuscript, with Pound's excisions and comments, provides fascinating information about the genesis and development of the poem, and was reproduced in facsimile in 1971, edited by Eliot's widow, Valerie Eliot. Reprinted below is the text as first published in book form in December 1922, including Eliot's notes, which are supplemented by the present editors' notes.

The Waste Land

"NAM Sibyllam quidem Cumis ego ipse oculis meis vidi in ampulla pendere, et cum illi pueri dicerent: Σίβυλλα τί θέλεις; respondebat illa: ἀποθανειν θέλω."[1]

FOR EZRA POUND
il miglior fabbro[2]

I. The Burial of the Dead[3]

April is the cruellest month, breeding
Lilacs out of the dead land, mixing
Memory and desire, stirring
Dull roots with spring rain.
5   Winter kept us warm, covering
Earth in forgetful snow, feeding
A little life with dried tubers.
Summer surprised us, coming over the Starnbergersee[4]

1. From the *Satyricon* of Petronius (1st century C.E.): "For once I myself saw with my own eyes the Sibyl at Cumae hanging in a cage, and when the boys said to her 'Sibyl, what do you want?' she replied, 'I want to die.' " (The Greek may be transliterated, "Síbylla tí théleis?" and "apothanéin thélo.") The Cumaean Sibyl was the most famous of the Sibyls, the prophetic old women of Greek mythology; she guided Aeneas through Hades in Virgil's *Aeneid*. She had been granted immortality by Apollo, but because she forgot to ask for perpetual youth, she shrank into withered old age and her authority declined.
2. The better craftsman (Italian); a tribute origi-

nally paid to the Provençal poet Arnaut Daniel in Dante's *Purgatorio* 26.117. Ezra Pound (1885–1972), American expatriate poet who was a key figure in the modern movement in poetry, helped Eliot massively revise the manuscript.
3. The title comes from the Anglican burial service.
4. Lake a few miles south of Munich, where the "mad" King Ludwig II of Bavaria drowned in 1886 in mysterious circumstances. This romantic, melancholy king passionately admired Richard Wagner and especially Wagner's opera *Tristan und Isolde*, which plays a significant part in *The Waste Land*. Ludwig's suffering of "death by water" in the

With a shower of rain; we stopped in the colonnade,
10   And went on in sunlight, into the Hofgarten,[5]
And drank coffee, and talked for an hour.
Bin gar keine Russin, stamm' aus Litauen, echt deutsch.[6]
And when we were children, staying at the archduke's,
My cousin's, he took me out on a sled,
15   And I was frightened. He said, Marie,
Marie, hold on tight. And down we went.
In the mountains, there you feel free.
I read, much of the night, and go south in the winter.

What are the roots that clutch, what branches grow
20   Out of this stony rubbish? Son of man,[7]
You cannot say, or guess, for you know only
A heap of broken images, where the sun beats,
And the dead tree gives no shelter, the cricket no relief,[8]
And the dry stone no sound of water. Only
25   There is shadow under this red rock,[9]
(Come in under the shadow of this red rock),
And I will show you something different from either
Your shadow at morning striding behind you
Or your shadow at evening rising to meet you;
30   I will show you fear in a handful of dust.

> *Frisch weht der Wind*
> *Der Heimat zu,*
> *Mein Irisch Kind,*
> *Wo weilest du?*[1]

35   "You gave me hyacinths first a year ago;
"They called me the hyacinth girl."
—Yet when we came back, late, from the Hyacinth[2] garden,
Yours arms full, and your hair wet, I could not
Speak, and my eyes failed, I was neither
40   Living nor dead, and I knew nothing,
Looking into the heart of light, the silence.
Oed' und leer das Meer.[3]

Starnbergersee thus evokes a cluster of themes central to the poem. Eliot had met King Ludwig's second cousin Countess Marie Larisch and talked with her. Although he had probably not read the countess's book *My Past*, which discusses King Ludwig at length, he got information about her life and times from her in person, and the remarks made in lines 8–18 are hers.
5. A small public park in Munich.
6. I am not Russian at all; I come from Lithuania, a true German (German).
7. Cf. Ezekiel II, i [Eliot's note]. God, addressing Ezekiel, continues: "stand upon thy feet, and I will speak unto thee."
8. Cf. Ecclesiastes XII, v [Eliot's note]. The verse Eliot cites is part of the preacher's picture of the desolation of old age, "when they shall be afraid of that which is high, and fears shall be in the way and the almond tree shall flourish, and the grass-

hopper shall be a burden, and desire shall fail."
9. Cf. Isaiah 32.2: the "righteous king" "shall be . . . as rivers of water in a dry place, as the shadow of a great rock in a weary land."
1. V. [see] *Tristan und Isolde*, I, verses 5–8 [Eliot's note]. In Wagner's opera a sailor recalls the girl he has left behind: "Fresh blows the wind to the homeland; my Irish child, where are you waiting?"
2. Name of a young man loved and accidentally killed by Apollo in Greek mythology; from his blood sprang the flower named for him, inscribed with "AI," a cry of grief.
3. Id. [Ibid] III, verse 24 [Eliot's note]. In act 3 of *Tristan und Isolde*, Tristan lies dying. He is waiting for Isolde to come to him from Cornwall, but a shepherd, appointed to watch for her sail, can report only, "Waste and empty is the sea." *Oed'* (or *Öd'*) was originally misspelled *Od'*.

Madame Sosostris,⁴ famous clairvoyante,
Had a bad cold, nevertheless
45 Is known to be the wisest woman in Europe,
With a wicked pack of cards.⁵ Here, said she,
Is your card, the drowned Phoenician Sailor,⁶
(Those are pearls that were his eyes. Look!)
Here is Belladonna,⁷ the Lady of the Rocks,
50 The lady of situations.
Here is the man with three staves, and here the Wheel,⁸
And here is the one-eyed merchant,⁹ and this card,
Which is blank, is something he carries on his back,
Which I am forbidden to see. I do not find
55 The Hanged Man.¹ Fear death by water.
I see crowds of people, walking round in a ring.
Thank you. If you see dear Mrs. Equitone,
Tell her I bring the horoscope myself:
One must be so careful these days.

60 Unreal City,²
Under the brown fog of a winter dawn,
A crowd flowed over London Bridge, so many,³
I had not thought death had undone so many.
Sighs, short and infrequent, were exhaled,⁴

4. A mock Egyptian name (suggested to Eliot by "Sesostris, the Sorceress of Ecbatana," the name assumed by a character in Aldous Huxley's novel *Crome Yellow* [1921] who dresses up as a gypsy to tell fortunes at a fair).
5. I.e., the deck of Tarot cards. The four suits of the Tarot pack, discussed by Jessie Weston in *From Ritual to Romance*, are the cup, lance, sword, and dish—the life symbols found in the Grail story. Weston noted that "today the Tarot has fallen somewhat into disrepute, being principally used for purposes of divination." Some of the cards mentioned in lines 46–56 are discussed by Eliot in his note to this passage: "I am not familiar with the exact constitution of the Tarot pack of cards, from which I have obviously departed to suit my own convenience. The Hanged Man, a member of the traditional pack, fits my purpose in two ways: because he is associated in my mind with the Hanged God of Frazer, and because I associate him with the hooded figure in the passage of the disciples to Emmaus in part V. The Phoenician Sailor and the Merchant appear later; also the 'crowds of people,' and Death by Water is executed in part IV. The Man with Three Staves (an authentic member of the Tarot pack) I associate, quite arbitrarily, with the Fisher King himself."
6. See part 4. Phlebas the Phoenician and Mr. Eugenides, the Smyrna merchant—both of whom appear later in the poem—are different phases of the same symbolic character, here identified as the "Phoenician Sailor." Mr. Eugenides exports "currants" (line 210); the drowned Phlebas floats in the "current" (line 315). Line 48 draws from Ariel's song in Shakespeare's *The Tempest* (1.2.400–08) to the shipwrecked Ferdinand, who was "sitting on a bank / Weeping again the King my father's wrack," when "this music crept by me on the waters." The song is about the supposed drowning of Ferdinand's father, Alonso. *The Waste Land* contains many references to *The Tempest*. Ferdi-

nand is associated with Phlebas and Mr. Eugenides and, therefore, with the "drowned Phoenician Sailor."
7. Beautiful lady (Italian). The word also suggests Madonna (the Virgin Mary) and, therefore, the Madonna of the Rocks (as in Leonardo da Vinci's painting); the rocks symbolize the Church. Belladonna is also an eye cosmetic and a poison—the deadly nightshade.
8. I.e., the wheel of fortune, whose turning represents the reversals of human life.
9. I.e., Mr. Eugenides, "one-eyed" because the figure is in profile on the card. Unlike the man with three staves and the wheel, which are Tarot cards, he is Eliot's creation.
1. On his card in the Tarot pack he is shown hanging by one foot from a T-shaped cross. He symbolizes the self-sacrifice of the fertility god who is killed so that his resurrection may restore fertility to land and people.
2. Cf. Baudelaire: "Fourmillante cité, cité pleine de rêves, / Où le spectre en plein jour raccroche le passant" [Eliot's note]. The lines are quoted from "Les Sept Vieillards" ("The Seven Old Men") of *Les Fleurs du Mal* (*The Flowers of Evil*), by the French poet Charles Baudelaire (1821–1867): "Swarming city, city full of dreams, / Where the specter in broad daylight accosts the passerby." The word *rêve* was originally misspelled *rève*.
3. Cf. Inferno III, 55–57 [Eliot's note]. The note goes on to quote Dante's lines, which may be translated: "So long a train of people, / that I should never have believed / That death had undone so many." Dante, just outside the gate of hell, has seen "the wretched souls of those who lived without disgrace and without praise."
4. Cf. Inferno IV, 25–27 [Eliot's note]. In Limbo, the first circle of hell, Dante has found the virtuous heathens, who lived before Christianity and are, therefore, eternally unable to achieve their desire

65　And each man fixed his eyes before his feet.
　　Flowed up the hill and down King William Street,
　　To where Saint Mary Woolnoth kept the hours
　　With a dead sound on the final stroke of nine.[5]
　　There I saw one I knew, and stopped him, crying: "Stetson![6]
70　"You who were with me in the ships at Mylae![7]
　　"That corpse you planted last year in your garden,
　　"Has it begun to sprout?[8] Will it bloom this year?
　　"Or has the sudden frost disturbed its bed?
　　"Oh keep the Dog far hence, that's friend to men,
75　"Or with his nails he'll dig it up again![9]
　　"You! hypocrite lecteur!—mon semblable—mon frère!"[1]

II. A Game of Chess[2]

　　The Chair she sat in, like a burnished throne,[3]
　　Glowed on the marble, where the glass
　　Held up by standards wrought with fruited vines
80　From which a golden Cupidon peeped out
　　(Another hid his eyes behind his wing)
　　Doubled the flames of sevenbranched candelabra
　　Reflecting light upon the table as
　　The glitter of her jewels rose to meet it,
85　From satin cases poured in rich profusion;
　　In vials of ivory and coloured glass
　　Unstoppered, lurked her strange synthetic perfumes,
　　Unguent, powdered, or liquid—troubled, confused
　　And drowned the sense in odours; stirred by the air
90　That freshened from the window, these ascended
　　In fattening the prolonged candle-flames,
　　Flung their smoke into the laquearia,[4]
　　Stirring the pattern on the coffered ceiling.

---

of seeing God. Dante's lines, cited by Eliot, mean "Here, so far as I could tell by listening, / there was no lamentation except sighs, / which caused the eternal air to tremble."
5. A phenomenon which I have often noticed [Eliot's note]. St. Mary Woolnoth is a church in the City of London (the financial district); the crowd is flowing across London Bridge to work in the City. According to the Bible, Jesus died at the ninth hour.
6. Presumably representing the "average business-man."
7. The battle of Mylae (260 B.C.E.) in the First Punic War, which, in some measure like World War I, was fought for economic reasons.
8. A distortion of the fertility god's ritual death, which heralded rebirth.
9. Cf. the Dirge in Webster's *White Devil* [Eliot's note]. In the play by John Webster (d. 1625), the dirge, sung by Cornelia, has the lines "But keep the wolf far thence, that's foe to men, / For with his nails he'll dig them up again." Eliot makes the "wolf" into a "dog," which is not a foe but a friend to humans.
1. V. Baudelaire, Preface to *Fleurs du Mal* [Eliot's note]. The passage is the last line of the introductory poem "Au Lecteur" ("To the Reader"), in Baudelaire's *Fleurs du Mal*; it may be translated:

"Hypocrite reader!—my likeness—my brother!" "Au Lecteur" describes humans as sunk in stupidity, sin, and evil, but the worst in "each man's foul menagerie of sin" is boredom, the *"monstre déli-cat"*—"You know him, reader."
2. The title suggests two plays by Thomas Middleton (1580–1627): *A Game at Chess* and, more significant, *Women Beware Women*, which has a scene in which a mother-in-law is distracted by a game of chess while her daughter-in-law is seduced: every move in the chess game represents a move in the seduction.
3. Cf. *Antony and Cleopatra*, II, ii, l. 190 [Eliot's note]. In Shakespeare's play, Enobarbus's famous description of the first meeting of Antony and Cleopatra begins, "The barge she sat in, like a burnish'd throne, / Burn'd on the water." Eliot's language in the opening lines of part 2 echoes ironically Enobarbus's speech.
4. Laquearia. V. *Aeneid*, I, 726 [Eliot's note]. *Laquearia* means "a paneled ceiling," and Eliot's note quotes the passage in the *Aeneid* that was his source for the word. The passage may be translated: "Blazing torches hang from the gold-paneled ceiling [*laquearibus aureis*], and torches conquer the night with flames." Virgil is describing the banquet given by Dido, queen of Carthage, for Aeneas, with whom she fell in love.

Huge sea-wood fed with copper
95 Burned green and orange, framed by the coloured stone,
In which sad light a carvèd dolphin swam.
Above the antique mantel was displayed
As though a window gave upon the sylvan scene[5]
The change of Philomel,[6] by the barbarous king
100 So rudely forced; yet there the nightingale
Filled all the desert with inviolable voice
And still she cried, and still the world pursues,
"Jug Jug"[7] to dirty ears.
And other withered stumps of time
105 Were told upon the walls; staring forms
Leaned out, leaning, hushing the room enclosed.
Footsteps shuffled on the stair.
Under the firelight, under the brush, her hair
Spread out in fiery points
110 Glowed into words, then would be savagely still.

"My nerves are bad tonight. Yes, bad. Stay with me.
"Speak to me. Why do you never speak. Speak.
"What are you thinking of? What thinking? What?
"I never know what you are thinking. Think."

115 I think we are in rats' alley[8]
Where the dead men lost their bones.

"What is that noise?"
                    The wind under the door.[9]
"What is that noise now? What is the wind doing?"
120   Nothing again nothing.
                                        "Do
"You know nothing? Do you see nothing? Do you remember
"Nothing?"

        I remember
125 Those are pearls that were his eyes.[1]
"Are you alive, or not? Is there nothing in your head?"
                                        But
O O O O that Shakespeherian Rag[2]—
It's so elegant
130 So intelligent

"What shall I do now? What shall I do?"
"I shall rush out as I am, and walk the street

5. Sylvan scene. V. Milton, *Paradise Lost*, IV, 140 [Eliot's note]. The phrase is part of the first description of Eden, seen through Satan's eyes.
6. V. Ovid, *Metamorphoses*, VI, Philomela [Eliot's note]. Philomela was raped by "the barbarous king" Tereus, husband of her sister, Procne. Philomela was then transformed into a nightingale. Eliot's note for line 100 refers ahead to his elaboration of the nightingale's song.
7. Conventional representation of nightingale's song in Elizabethan poetry.

8. Cf. Part III, l. 195 [Eliot's note].
9. Cf. Webster: "Is the wind in that door still?" [Eliot's note]. In John Webster's *The Devil's Law Case* (3.2.162), a physician asks this question on finding that the victim of a murderous attack is still breathing, meaning "Is he still alive?"
1. Cf. Part I, l. 37, 48 [Eliot's note].
2. American ragtime song, which was a hit of Ziegfeld's Follies in 1912. The chorus is "That Shakespherean Rag, most intelligent, very elegant."

"With my hair down, so. What shall we do tomorrow?
"What shall we ever do?"
135   The hot water at ten.
And if it rains, a closed car at four.
And we shall play a game of chess,[3]
Pressing lidless eyes and waiting for a knock upon the door.

When Lil's husband got demobbed,[4] I said—
140 I didn't mince my words, I said to her myself,
HURRY UP PLEASE ITS TIME[5]
Now Albert's coming back, make yourself a bit smart.
He'll want to know what you done with that money he gave you
To get yourself some teeth. He did, I was there.
145 You have them all out, Lil, and get a nice set,
He said, I swear, I can't bear to look at you.
And no more can't I, I said, and think of poor Albert,
He's been in the army four years, he wants a good time,
And if you dont give it him, there's others will, I said.
150 Oh is there, she said. Something o' that, I said.
Then I'll know who to thank, she said, and give me a straight look.
HURRY UP PLEASE ITS TIME
If you dont like it you can get on with it, I said,
Others can pick and choose if you can't.
155 But if Albert makes off, it wont be for lack of telling.
You ought to be ashamed, I said, to look so antique.
(And her only thirty-one.)
I can't help it, she said, pulling a long face,
It's them pills I took, to bring it off, she said.
160 (She's had five already, and nearly died of young George.)
The chemist[6] said it would be alright, but I've never been the same.
You *are* a proper fool, I said.
Well, if Albert wont leave you alone, there it is, I said,
What you get married for if you dont want children?
165 HURRY UP PLEASE ITS TIME
Well, that Sunday Albert was home, they had a hot gammon,°   *ham, bacon*
And they asked me in to dinner, to get the beauty of it hot—
HURRY UP PLEASE ITS TIME
HURRY UP PLEASE ITS TIME
170 Goonight Bill. Goonight Lou. Goonight May. Goonight.
Ta ta. Goonight. Goonight.
Good night, ladies, good night, sweet ladies, good night, good night.[7]

III. The Fire Sermon[8]

The river's tent is broken: the last fingers of leaf
Clutch and sink into the wet bank. The wind

3. Cf. the game of chess in Middleton's *Women Beware Women* [Eliot's note]. The significance of this chess game is discussed in the first note to part 2.
4. British slang for "demobilized" (discharged from the army after World War I).
5. The traditional call of the British bartender at closing time.
6. Pharmacist. "To bring it off": to cause an abortion.
7. Cf. the mad Ophelia's departing words (Shakespeare, *Hamlet* 4.5.69–70). Ophelia, too, met "death by water." Cf. also the popular song lyric "Good night ladies, we're going to leave you now."
8. The Buddha preached the Fire Sermon, against the fires of lust and other passions that destroy people and prevent their regeneration.

175 Crosses the brown land, unheard. The nymphs are departed.
Sweet Thames, run softly, till I end my song.[9]
The river bears no empty bottles, sandwich papers,
Silk handkerchiefs, cardboard boxes, cigarette ends
Or other testimony of summer nights. The nymphs are departed.
180 And their friends, the loitering heirs of city directors;
Departed, have left no addresses.
By the waters of Leman I sat down and wept[1] . . .
Sweet Thames, run softly till I end my song,
Sweet Thames, run softly, for I speak not loud or long.
185 But at my back in a cold blast I hear[2]
The rattle of the bones, and chuckle spread from ear to ear.

A rat crept softly through the vegetation
Dragging its slimy belly on the bank
While I was fishing in the dull canal
190 On a winter evening round behind the gashouse
Musing upon the king my brother's wreck
And on the king my father's death before him.[3]
White bodies naked on the low damp ground
And bones cast in a little low dry garret,
195 Rattled by the rat's foot only, year to year.
But at my back from time to time I hear
The sound of horns and motors,[4] which shall bring
Sweeney to Mrs. Porter in the spring.[5]
O the moon shone bright on Mrs. Porter
200 And on her daughter
They wash their feet in soda water[6]
Et O ces voix d'enfants, chantant dans la coupole![7]

Twit twit twit
Jug jug jug jug jug jug
205 So rudely forc'd.
Tereu[8]

9. V. Spenser, *Prothalamion* [Eliot's note]. Eliot's line is the refrain from Edmund Spenser's marriage song, which is also set by the river Thames in London.
1. Cf. Psalms 137.1, in which the exiled Hebrews mourn for their homeland: "By the rivers of Babylon, there we sat down, yea, we wept, when we remembered Zion." Lake Leman is another name for Lake Geneva, in Switzerland; Eliot wrote *The Waste Land* in Lausanne, by that lake. The noun *leman* is an archaic word meaning lover.
2. An ironic distortion of Andrew Marvell's "To His Coy Mistress," lines 21–22: "But at my back I always hear / Time's wingèd chariot hurrying near." Cf. lines 196–97.
3. Cf. *The Tempest*, I, ii [Eliot's note]. See line 48.
4. Cf. Marvell, *To His Coy Mistress* [Eliot's note].
5. Cf. Day, *Parliament of Bees*: "When of the sudden, listening, you shall hear, / A noise of horns and hunting, which shall bring / Actaeon to Diana in the spring, / Where all shall see her naked skin" [Eliot's note]. Actaeon was changed to a stag and hunted to death after he saw Diana, the goddess of chastity, bathing with her nymphs. John Day

(1574–ca. 1640), English poet.
6. I do not know the origin of the ballad from which these lines are taken; it was reported to me from Sydney, Australia [Eliot's note]. One of the less bawdy versions of the song, which was popular among Australian troops in World War I, went as follows: "O the moon shines bright on Mrs. Porter / And on the daughter / Of Mrs. Porter. / They wash their feet in soda water / And so they oughter / To keep them clean."
7. V. Verlaine, *Parsifal* [Eliot's note]: "And O those children's voices singing in the dome!" The sonnet by the French poet Paul Verlaine (1844–1896) describes Parsifal, the questing knight, resisting all sensual temptations to keep himself pure for the Grail and heal the Fisher King; Wagner's Parsifal had his feet washed before entering the castle of the Grail.
8. A reference to Tereus, who "rudely forc'd" Philomela; it was also one of the conventional words for a nightingale's song in Elizabethan poetry. Cf. the song from John Lyly's *Alexander and Campaspe* (1564): "Oh, 'tis the ravished nightingale. / Jug, jug, jug, jug, tereu! she cries." Cf. also lines 100ff.

Unreal City
Under the brown fog of a winter noon
Mr. Eugenides, the Smyrna[9] merchant
210 Unshaven, with a pocket full of currants
C.i.f.[1] London: documents at sight,
Asked me in demotic° French   *colloquial*
To luncheon at the Cannon Street Hotel
Followed by a weekend at the Metropole.[2]

215 At the violet hour, when the eyes and back
Turn upward from the desk, when the human engine waits
Like a taxi throbbing waiting,
I Tiresias,[3] though blind, throbbing between two lives,
Old man with wrinkled female breasts, can see
220 At the violet hour, the evening hour that strives
Homeward, and brings the sailor home from sea,[4]
The typist home at teatime, clears her breakfast, lights
Her stove, and lays out food in tins.
Out of the window perilously spread
225 Her drying combinations° touched by the sun's last rays,   *undergarments*
On the divan are piled (at night her bed)
Stockings, slippers, camisoles, and stays.°   *corset*
I Tiresias, old man with wrinkled dugs
Perceived the scene, and foretold the rest—
230 I too awaited the expected guest.
He, the young man carbuncular,° arrives,   *pimply*
A small house agent's clerk, with one bold stare,
One of the low on whom assurance sits
As a silk hat on a Bradford[5] millionaire.

9. Now Izmir, a seaport in western Turkey; here associated with Carthage and the ancient Phoenician and Syrian merchants, who spread the old mystery cults.

1. The currants were quoted at a price "carriage and insurance free to London"; and the Bill of Lading etc. were to be handed to the buyer upon payment of the sight draft [Eliot's note]. Another gloss of C.i.f. is "cost, insurance and freight."

2. Luxury hotel in the seaside resort of Brighton. Cannon Street Hotel, near the station that was then chief terminus for travelers to the Continent, was a favorite meeting place for businesspeople going or coming from abroad; it was also a locale for homosexual liaisons.

3. Tiresias, although a mere spectator and not indeed a "character," is yet the most important personage in the poem, uniting all the rest. Just as the one-eyed merchant, seller of currants, melts into the Phoenician Sailor, and the latter is not wholly distinct from Ferdinand Prince of Naples, so all the women are one woman, and the two sexes meet in Tiresias. What Tiresias sees, in fact, is the substance of the poem. The whole passage from Ovid is of great anthropological interest [Eliot's note]. The note then quotes, from the Latin text of Ovid's *Metamorphoses*, the story of Tiresias's change of sex: "[The story goes that once Jove, having drunk a great deal,] jested with Juno. He said, 'Your pleasure in love is really greater than that enjoyed by men.' She denied it; so they decided to seek the opinion of the wise Tiresias, for he knew both

aspects of love. For once, with a blow of his staff, he had committed violence on two huge snakes as they copulated in the green forest; and—wonderful to tell—was turned from a man into a woman and thus spent seven years. In the eighth year he saw the same snakes again and said: 'If a blow struck at you is so powerful that it changes the sex of the giver, I will now strike at you again.' With these words she struck the snakes, and again became a man. So he was appointed arbitrator in the playful quarrel, and supported Jove's statement. It is said that Saturnia [i.e., Juno] was quite disproportionately upset, and condemned the arbitrator to perpetual blindness. But the almighty father (for no god may undo what has been done by another god), in return for the sight that was taken away, gave him the power to know the future and so lightened the penalty paid by the honor."

4. This may not appear as exact as Sappho's lines, but I had in mind the "longshore" or "dory" fisherman, who returns at nightfall [Eliot's note]. Sappho's poem addressed Hesperus, the evening star, as the star that brings everyone home from work to evening rest; her poem is here distorted by Eliot. There is also an echo of the 19th-century Scottish writer Robert Louis Stevenson's "Requiem," line 221: "Home is the sailor, home from sea."

5. Either the Yorkshire woolen manufacturing town, where many fortunes were made in World War I, or the pioneer oil town of Bradford, Pennsylvania, the home of one of Eliot's wealthy Harvard contemporaries, T. E. Hanley.

235 The time is now propitious, as he guesses,
The meal is ended, she is bored and tired,
Endeavours to engage her in caresses
Which still are unreproved, if undesired.
Flushed and decided, he assaults at once;
240 Exploring hands encounter no defence;
His vanity requires no response,
And makes a welcome of indifference.
(And I Tiresias have foresuffered all
Enacted on this same divan or bed;
245 I who have sat by Thebes[6] below the wall
And walked among the lowest of the dead.)
Bestows one final patronising kiss,
And gropes his way, finding the stairs unlit . . .

She turns and looks a moment in the glass,
250 Hardly aware of her departed lover;
Her brain allows one half-formed thought to pass:
"Well now that's done: and I'm glad it's over."
When lovely woman stoops to folly and
Paces about her room again, alone,
255 She smoothes her hair with automatic hand,
And puts a record on the gramophone.[7]

"This music crept by me upon the waters"[8]
And along the Strand, up Queen Victoria Street.
O City, City, I can sometimes hear
260 Beside a public bar in Lower Thames Street,
The pleasant whining of a mandoline
And a clatter and a chatter from within
Where fishmen lounge at noon: where the walls
Of Magnus Martyr hold
265 Inexplicable splendour of Ionian white and gold.[9]

The river sweats[1]
Oil and tar
The barges drift
With the turning tide

6. For many generations, Tiresias lived in Thebes, where he witnessed the tragic fates of Oedipus and Creon; he prophesied in the marketplace by the wall of Thebes.
7. V. Goldsmith, the song in *The Vicar of Wakefield* [Eliot's note]. Olivia, a character in Oliver Goldsmith's 1766 novel, sings the following song when she returns to the place where she was seduced: "When lovely woman stoops to folly / And finds too late that men betray / What charm can soothe her melancholy, / What art can wash her guilt away? / The only art her guilt to cover, / To hide her shame from every eye, / To give repentance to her lover / And wring his bosom—is to die."
8. V. *The Tempest*, as above [Eliot's note]. Cf. line 48. The line is from Ferdinand's speech, continuing after "weeping again the King my father's wrack."

9. The interior of St. Magnus Martyr is to my mind one of the finest among [Sir Christopher] Wren's interiors. See *The Proposed Demolition of Nineteen City Churches*: (P. S. King & Son, Ltd.) [Eliot's note]. In these lines the "pleasant" music, the "fishmen" resting after labor, and the splendor of the church interior suggest a world of true values, where work and relaxation are both real and take place in a context of religious meaning.
1. The Song of the (three) Thames-daughters begins here. From line 292 to 306 inclusive they speak in turn. V. *Götterdämmerung*, III, i: the Rhinedaughters [Eliot's note]. Eliot parallels the Thames-daughters with the Rhinemaidens in Wagner's opera *Götterdämmerung* (*The Twilight of the Gods*), who lament that, with the gold of the Rhine stolen, the beauty of the river is gone. The refrain in lines 277–78 is borrowed from Wagner.

Red sails
Wide
To leeward, swing on the heavy spar.
The barges wash
Drifting logs
Down Greenwich reach
Past the Isle of Dogs.[2]
            Weialala leia
            Wallala leialala

Elizabeth and Leicester[3]
Beating oars
The stern was formed
A gilded shell
Red and gold
The brisk swell
Rippled both shores
Southwest wind
Carried down stream
The peal of bells
White towers
            Weialala leia
            Wallala leialala

"Trams and dusty trees.
Highbury bore me. Richmond and Kew
Undid me.[4] By Richmond I raised my knees
Supine on the floor of a narrow canoe."

"My feet are at Moorgate,[5] and my heart
Under my feet. After the event
He wept. He promised 'a new start.'
I made no comment. What should I resent?"

"On Margate[6] Sands.
I can connect
Nothing with nothing.
The broken fingernails of dirty hands.
My people humble people who expect
Nothing."
            la la

To Carthage then I came[7]

2. Greenwich is a borough in London on the south side of the Thames; opposite is the Isle of Dogs (a peninsula).

3. The fruitless love of Queen Elizabeth and the earl of Leicester (Robert Dudley) is recalled in Eliot's note: "V. [J. A.] Froude, *Elizabeth*, Vol. I, ch. iv, letter of De Quadra to Philip of Spain: 'In the afternoon we were in a barge, watching the games on the river. (The queen) was alone with Lord Robert and myself on the poop, when they began to talk nonsense, and went so far that Lord Robert at last said, as I was on the spot there was no reason why they should not be married if the queen pleased.'" Queen Elizabeth I was born in the old Greenwich House, by the river, where

Greenwich Hospital now stands.

4. Cf. *Purgatorio*, V, 133 [Eliot's note]. The *Purgatorio* lines, which Eliot here parodies, may be translated: "Remember me, who am La Pia. / Siena made me, Maremma undid me." "Highbury": a residential London suburb. "Richmond": a pleasant part of London westward up the Thames, with boating and riverside hotels. "Kew": adjoining Richmond, has the famous Kew Gardens.

5. Underground (i.e., subway) station Eliot used daily while working at Lloyds Bank.

6. Popular seaside resort on the Thames estuary.

7. V. St. Augustine's *Confessions*: "to Carthage then I came, where a caldron of unholy loves sang all about mine ears" [Eliot's note]. The passage

Burning burning burning burning[8]
O Lord Thou pluckest me out[9]
310 O Lord Thou pluckest

burning

IV. Death by Water[1]

Phlebas the Phoenician, a fortnight dead,
Forgot the cry of gulls, and the deep sea swell
And the profit and loss.
315   A current under sea
Picked his bones in whispers. As he rose and fell
He passed the stages of his age and youth
Entering the whirlpool.
                    Gentile or Jew
320 O you who turn the wheel and look to windward,
Consider Phlebas, who was once handsome and tall as you.

V. What the Thunder Said[2]

After the torchlight red on sweaty faces
After the frosty silence in the gardens
After the agony in stony places
325 The shouting and the crying
Prison and palace and reverberation
Of thunder of spring over distant mountains
He who was living is now dead[3]
We who were living are now dying
330 With a little patience

Here is no water but only rock
Rock and no water and the sandy road
The road winding above among the mountains
Which are mountains of rock without water
335 If there were water we should stop and drink
Amongst the rock one cannot stop or think
Sweat is dry and feet are in the sand
If there were only water amongst the rock

---

from the *Confessions* quoted here occurs in St. Augustine's account of his youthful life of lust. Cf. line 92 and its note.

8. The complete text of the Buddha's Fire Sermon (which corresponds in importance to the Sermon on the Mount) from which these words are taken, will be found translated in the late Henry Clarke Warren's *Buddhism in Translation* (Harvard Oriental Series). Mr. Warren was one of the great pioneers of Buddhist studies in the occident [Eliot's note]. In the sermon, the Buddha instructs his priests that all things "are on fire. . . . The eye . . . is on fire; forms are on fire; eye-consciousness is on fire; impressions received by the eye are on fire; and whatever sensation, pleasant, unpleasant, or indifferent, originates in dependence on impressions received by the eye, that also is on fire. And with what are these on fire? With the fire of passion, say I, with the fire of hatred, with the fire of

infatuation." For Jesus' Sermon on the Mount, see Matthew 5–7.

9. From St. Augustine's *Confessions* again. The collocation of these two representatives of eastern and western asceticism, as the culmination of this part of the poem, is not an accident [Eliot's note].

1. This section has been interpreted as signifying death by water without resurrection or as symbolizing the sacrificial death that precedes rebirth.

2. In the first part of Part V three themes are employed: the journey to Emmaus, the approach to the Chapel Perilous (see Miss Weston's book), and the present decay of eastern Europe [Eliot's note]. On the journey to Emmaus, the resurrected Jesus walks alongside and converses with two disciples, who think he is a stranger until he reveals his identity (Luke 24.13–14).

3. These lines allude to Jesus' agony in the Garden of Gethsemane, his trial, and his crucifixion.

Dead mountain mouth of carious° teeth that cannot spit   °decayed
340 Here one can neither stand nor lie nor sit
There is not even silence in the mountains
But dry sterile thunder without rain
There is not even solitude in the mountains
But red sullen faces sneer and snarl
345 From doors of mudcracked houses
                If there were water

      And no rock
      If there were rock
      And also water
350   And water
      A spring
      A pool among the rock
      If there were the sound of water only
      Not the cicada[4]
355   And dry grass singing
      But sound of water over a rock
      Where the hermit-thrush[5] sings in the pine trees
      Drip drop drip drop drop drop drop
      But there is no water

360 Who is the third who walks always beside you?[6]
When I count, there are only you and I together
But when I look ahead up the white road
There is always another one walking beside you
Gliding wrapt in a brown mantle, hooded
365 I do not know whether a man or a woman
—But who is that on the other side of you?

What is that sound high in the air[7]
Murmur of maternal lamentation
Who are those hooded hordes swarming
370 Over endless plains, stumbling in cracked earth
Ringed by the flat horizon only
What is the city over the mountains
Cracks and reforms and bursts in the violet air
Falling towers
375 Jerusalem Athens Alexandria
Vienna London
Unreal

---

4. Cf. Ecclesiastes' prophecy "the grasshopper shall be a burden, and desire shall fail." Cf. also line 23 and its note.
5. This is *Turdus aonalaschkae pallasii*, the hermit-thrush which I have heard in Quebec County. Chapman says (*Handbook of Birds of Eastern North America*) "it is most at home in secluded woodland and thickety retreats. . . . Its notes are not remarkable for variety or volume, but in purity and sweetness of tone and exquisite modulation they are unequaled." Its "water-dripping song" is justly celebrated [Eliot's note].
6. The following lines were stimulated by the account of one of the Antarctic expeditions (I forget which, but I think one of Shackleton's): it was related that the party of explorers, at the extremity

of their strength, had the constant delusion that there was *one more member* than could actually be counted [Eliot's note]. This reminiscence is associated with Jesus' unrecognized presence on the way to Emmaus.
7. Eliot's note for lines 367–77 is: "Cf. Herman Hesse, *Blick ins Chaos* ["A Glimpse into Chaos"]." The note then quotes a passage from the German text, which is translated: "Already half of Europe, already at least half of Eastern Europe, on the way to Chaos, drives drunk in sacred infatuation along the edge of the precipice, sings drunkenly, as though hymn singing, as Dmitri Karamazov [in Dostoyevsky's *Brothers Karamazov*] sang. The offended bourgeois laughs at the songs; the saint and the seer hear them with tears."

A woman drew her long black hair out tight
And fiddled whisper music on those strings
380   And bats with baby faces in the violet light
Whistled, and beat their wings
And crawled head downward down a blackened wall
And upside down in air were towers
Tolling reminiscent bells, that kept the hours
385   And voices singing out of empty cisterns and exhausted wells.

In this decayed hole among the mountains
In the faint moonlight, the grass is singing
Over the tumbled graves, about the chapel
There is the empty chapel, only the wind's home.[8]
390   It has no windows, and the door swings,
Dry bones can harm no one.
Only a cock stood on the rooftree
Co co   rico   co co   rico[9]
In a flash of lightning. Then a damp gust
395   Bringing rain

Ganga[1] was sunken, and the limp leaves
Waited for rain, while the black clouds
Gathered far distant, over Himavant.[2]
The jungle crouched, humped in silence.
400   Then spoke the thunder
Da[3]
Datta: what have we given?
My friend, blood shaking my heart
The awful daring of a moment's surrender
405   Which an age of prudence can never retract
By this, and this only, we have existed
Which is not to be found in our obituaries
Or in memories draped by the beneficent spider[4]
Or under seals broken by the lean solicitor[o]   lawyer
410   In our empty rooms
Da
Dayadhvam: I have heard the key[5]

8. Suggesting the moment of near despair before
the Chapel Perilous, when the questing knight
sees nothing there but decay. This illusion of noth-
ingness is the knight's final test.
9. The crowing of the cock signals the departure
of ghosts and evil spirits. Cf. *Hamlet* 1.1.157ff. In
Matthew 26.34 and 74 the cock crows after Peter
betrays Jesus three times.
1. Sanskrit name for the major sacred river in
India.
2. I.e., snowy mountain (Sanskrit); usually applied
to the Himalayas.
3. Datta, dayadhvam, damyata (Give, sympathize,
control). The fable of the meaning of the Thunder
is found in the *Brihadaranyaka—Upanishad*, 5, 1.
A translation is found in Deussen's *Sechzig Upanishads des Veda*, p. 489 [Eliot's note]. In the Old
Indian fable The Three Great Disciplines, the Creator God Prajapati utters the enigmatic syllable *DA*
to three groups. Lesser gods, naturally unruly,
interpret it as "Control yourselves" (*Damyata*);
humans, naturally greedy, as "Give" (*Datta*);

demons, naturally cruel, as "Be compassionate"
(*Dayadhvam*); "That very thing is repeated even
today by the heavenly voice, in the form of thunder
as '*DA*' '*DA*' '*DA*,' which means 'Control yourselves,' 'Give,' and 'Have compassion.' Therefore
one should practice these three things: self-
control, giving, and mercy." The Upanishads are
ancient philosophical dialogues in Sanskrit. They
are primary texts for an early form of Hinduism
sometimes called Brahminism.
4. Cf. Webster, *The White Devil*, V, vi: ". . . they'll
remarry / Ere the worm pierce your winding-sheet,
ere the spider / Make a thin curtain for your epi-
taphs" [Eliot's note].
5. Cf. *Inferno*, XXXIII, 46 [Eliot's note]. In this
passage from the *Inferno* Ugolino recalls his
imprisonment in the tower with his children,
where they starved to death: "And I heard below
the door of the horrible tower being nailed shut."
Eliot's note for this line goes on to quote F. H.
Bradley, *Appearance and Reality*, p. 346: " 'My
external sensations are no less private to myself

Turn in the door once and turn once only
We think of the key, each in his prison
415 Thinking of the key, each confirms a prison
Only at nightfall, æthereal rumours
Revive for a moment a broken Coriolanus[6]
DA
Damyata: The boat responded
420 Gaily, to the hand expert with sail and oar
The sea was calm, your heart would have responded
Gaily, when invited, beating obedient
To controlling hands

                    I sat upon the shore
425 Fishing,[7] with the arid plain behind me
Shall I at least set my lands in order?[8]

London Bridge is falling down falling down falling down[9]
Poi s'ascose nel foco che gli affina[1]
Quando fiam uti chelidon[2]—O swallow swallow[3]
430 *Le Prince d'Aquitaine à la tour abolie*[4]
These fragments I have shored against my ruins
Why then Ile fit you. Hieronymo's mad againe.[5]
Datta. Dayadhvam. Damyata.

      Shantih   shantih   shantih[6]

1921   1922

---

than are my thoughts or my feelings. In either case my experience falls within my own circle, a circle closed on the outside; and, with all its elements alike, every sphere is opaque to the others which surround it. . . . In brief, regarded as an existence which appears in a soul, the whole world for each is peculiar and private to that soul.'" Eliot wrote his doctoral thesis on Bradley's philosophy.

6. Coriolanus, who acted out of pride rather than duty, exemplifies a man locked in the prison of himself. He led the enemy against his native city out of injured pride (cf. Shakespeare's *Coriolanus*).

7. V. Weston: *From Ritual to Romance*; chapter on the Fisher King [Eliot's note].

8. Cf. Isaiah 38.1: "Thus saith the Lord, Set thine house in order, for thou shalt die, and not live."

9. One of the later lines of this nursery rhyme is "Take the key and lock her up, my fair lady."

1. V. *Purgatorio*, XXVI, 148 [Eliot's note]. The note goes on to quote lines 145–148 of the *Purgatorio*, in which the Provençal poet Arnaut Daniel addresses Dante: "'Now I pray you, by that virtue which guides you to the summit of the stairway, be mindful in due time of my pain.'" Then (in the line Eliot quotes here) "he hid himself in the fire which refines them."

2. V. *Pervigilium Veneris*. Cf. Philomela in parts II and III [Eliot's note]. The Latin phrase in the text, originally misquoting *uti* as *ceu*, means, "When shall I be as the swallow?" It comes from

the late Latin poem "*Pervigilium Veneris*" ("Vigil of Venus"), "When will my spring come? When shall I be as the swallow that I may cease to be silent? I have lost the Muse in silence, and Apollo regards me not."

3. Cf. A. C. Swinburne's "Itylus," which begins, "Swallow, my sister, O sister swallow, / How can thine heart be full of spring?" and Tennyson's lyric in *The Princess*: "O Swallow, Swallow, flying, flying south."

4. V. Gerard de Nerval, Sonnet *El Desdichado* [Eliot's note]. The French line may be translated: "The Prince of Aquitaine in the ruined tower." One of the cards in the Tarot pack is "the tower struck by lightning."

5. V. Kyd's *Spanish Tragedy* [Eliot's note]. Subtitled *Hieronymo's Mad Againe*, Kyd's play (1594) is an early example of the Elizabethan tragedy of revenge. Hieronymo, driven mad by the murder of his son, has his revenge when he is asked to write a court entertainment. He replies, "Why then Ile fit you!" (i.e., accommodate you), and assigns the parts in the entertainment so that, in the course of the action, his son's murderers are killed.

6. Shantih. Repeated as here, a formal ending to an Upanishad. "The Peace which passeth understanding" is a feeble translation of the content of this word [Eliot's note]. On the Upanishads see the note to line 401 above.

The Hollow Men

Mistah Kurtz—he dead.[1]
A penny for the Old Guy[2]

I

We are the hollow men
We are the stuffed men
Leaning together
Headpiece filled with straw. Alas!
5   Our dried voices, when
We whisper together
Are quiet and meaningless
As wind in dry glass
Or rats' feet over broken glass
10   In our dry cellar[3]

Shape without form, shade without colour,
Paralysed force, gesture without motion;

Those who have crossed
With direct eyes, to death's other Kingdom
15   Remember us—if at all—not as lost
Violent souls, but only
As the hollow men
The stuffed men.

II

Eyes I dare not meet in dreams
20   In death's dream kingdom[4]
These do not appear:
There, the eyes are
Sunlight on a broken column
There, is a tree swinging
25   And voices are
In the wind's singing
More distant and more solemn
Than a fading star.

Let me be no nearer
30   In death's dream kingdom
Let me also wear
Such deliberate disguises
Rat's coat, crowskin, crossed staves

---

1. From Joseph Conrad's *Heart of Darkness* (see p. 1941).
2. Every year on Nov. 5, British children build bonfires, on which they burn a scarecrow effigy of the traitor Guido [Guy] Fawkes, who in 1605 attempted to blow up the Parliament buildings.
For some days before this, they ask people in the streets for pennies with which to buy fireworks.
3. Cf. *The Waste Land*, lines 115 and 195.
4. At the end of Dante's *Purgatorio* and in *Paradiso* 4, he cannot meet the gaze of Beatrice (see Eliot's 1929 essay "Dante").

In a field[5]
35 Behaving as the wind behaves
No nearer—

Not that final meeting
In the twilight kingdom[6]

III

This is the dead land
40 This is cactus land
Here the stone images[7]
Are raised, here they receive
The supplication of a dead man's hand
Under the twinkle of a fading star.

45 Is it like this
In death's other kingdom
Waking alone
At the hour when we are
Trembling with tenderness
50 Lips that would kiss
Form prayers to broken stone.

IV

The eyes are not here
There are no eyes here
In this valley of dying stars
55 In this hollow valley
This broken jaw of our lost kingdoms

In this last of meeting places
We grope together
And avoid speech
60 Gathered on this beach of the tumid river[8]

Sightless, unless
The eyes reappear
As the perpetual star
Multifoliate rose[9]
65 Of death's twilight kingdom
The hope only
Of empty men.

---

5. The traditional British scarecrow is made from two sticks tied in the form of a cross (the vertical one stuck in the ground), dressed in cast-off clothes, and sometimes draped with dead vermin.
6. Perhaps a reference to Dante's meeting with Beatrice after he has crossed the river Lethe. There reminded of his sins, he is allowed to proceed to Paradise (Purgatorio 30).
7. Cf. The Waste Land, line 22.
8. Dante's Acheron, which encircles hell, and the Congo of Conrad's Heart of Darkness.
9. The image of heaven in Dante's Paradiso 32.

V

Here we go round the prickly pear
Prickly pear prickly pear
70 Here we go round the prickly pear
At five o'clock in the morning.[1]

Between the idea
And the reality
Between the motion
75 And the act[2]
Falls the Shadow[3]
                    For Thine is the Kingdom[4]

Between the conception
And the creation
80 Between the emotion
And the response
Falls the Shadow
                    Life is very long

Between the desire
85 And the spasm
Between the potency
And the existence
Between the essence
And the descent
90 Falls the Shadow
                    For Thine is the Kingdom

For Thine is
Life is
For Thine is the

95 This is the way the world ends
This is the way the world ends
This is the way the world ends
Not with a bang but a whimper.

1924–25   1925

1. Parodic version of the children's rhyme ending "Here we go round the mulberry bush / On a cold and frosty morning."
2. Cf. Shakespeare's Julius Caesar 2.1.63–5: "Between the acting of a dreadful thing / And the first motion, all the interim is / Like a phantasma or a hideous dream."
3. Cf. Ernest Dowson's "Non sum qualis eram bonae sub regno Cynarae," lines 1–2: "Last night, ah, yesternight, betwixt her lips and mine / There fell thy shadow, Cynara!"
4. Cf. The Lord's Prayer.

Journey of the Magi[1]

'A cold coming we had of it,
Just the worst time of the year
For a journey, and such a long journey:
The ways deep and the weather sharp,
5   The very dead of winter.'[2]
And the camels galled, sore-footed, refractory,
Lying down in the melting snow.
There were times we regretted
The summer palaces on slopes, the terraces,
10   And the silken girls bringing sherbet.
Then the camel men cursing and grumbling
And running away, and wanting their liquor and women,
And the night-fires going out, and the lack of shelters,
And the cities hostile and the towns unfriendly
15   And the villages dirty and charging high prices:
A hard time we had of it.
At the end we preferred to travel all night,
Sleeping in snatches,
With the voices singing in our ears, saying
20   That this was all folly.

    Then at dawn we came down to a temperate valley,
Wet, below the snow line, smelling of vegetation;
With a running stream and a water mill beating the darkness,
And three trees on the low sky.[3]
25   And an old white horse galloped away in the meadow.
Then we came to a tavern with vine-leaves over the lintel,
Six hands at an open door dicing for pieces of silver,
And feet kicking the empty wine-skins.
But there was no information, and so we continued
30   And arrived at evening, not a moment too soon
Finding the place; it was (you may say) satisfactory.

    All this was a long time ago, I remember,
And I would do it again, but set down
This set down
35   This: were we led all that way for
Birth or Death? There was a Birth, certainly,
We had evidence and no doubt. I had seen birth and death,
But had thought they were different; this Birth was
Hard and bitter agony for us, like Death, our death.
40   We returned to our places, these Kingdoms,
But no longer at ease here, in the old dispensation,

1. One of the wise men who came from the east to Jerusalem to do homage to the infant Jesus (Matthew 2.1–12) is recalling in old age the meaning of the experience.
2. Adapted from a passage in a 1622 Christmas sermon by Bishop Lancelot Andrewes: "A cold coming they had of it at this time of the year, just the worst time of the year to take a journey, and specially a long journey in. The ways deep, the weather sharp, the days short, the sun farthest off, *in solstitio brumali,* 'the very dead of winter.' "
3. The "three trees" suggest the three crosses, with Jesus crucified on the center one; the men "dicing for pieces of silver" (line 27) suggest the soldiers dicing for Jesus' garments and Judas's betrayal of him for thirty pieces of silver; the empty wineskins recall one of Jesus' parables of old and new (Mark 2.22).

With an alien people clutching their gods.
I should be glad of another death.

1927

Little Gidding[1]

I

Midwinter spring is its own season
Sempiternal° though sodden towards sundown,   *eternal, everlasting*
Suspended in time, between pole and tropic,
When the short day is brightest, with frost and fire,
5   The brief sun flames the ice, on pond and ditches,
In windless cold that is the heart's heat,
Reflecting in a watery mirror
A glare that is blindness in the early afternoon.
And glow more intense than blaze of branch, or brazier,
10   Stirs the dumb spirit: no wind, but pentecostal fire[2]
In the dark time of the year. Between melting and freezing
The soul's sap quivers. There is no earth smell
Or smell of living thing. This is the springtime
But not in time's covenant. Now the hedgerow
15   Is blanched for an hour with transitory blossom
Of snow, a bloom more sudden
Than that of summer, neither budding nor fading,
Not in the scheme of generation.
Where is the summer, the unimaginable
Zero summer?

20   If you came this way,
Taking the route you would be likely to take
From the place you would be likely to come from,
If you came this way in may time, you would find the hedges
White again, in May, with voluptuary sweetness.
25   It would be the same at the end of the journey,
If you came at night like a broken king,[3]

---

1. This is the last of Eliot's *Four Quartets*, four related poems each divided into five "movements" in a manner reminiscent of the structure of a quartet or a sonata and each dealing with some aspect of the relation of time and eternity, the meaning of history, the achievement of the moment of timeless insight. Although the *Four Quartets* constitute a unified sequence, they were each written separately and can be read as individual poems. "*Little Gidding* can be understood by itself, without reference to the preceding poems, which it yet so beautifully completes" (Helen Gardner, *The Composition of Four Quartets*). Each of the four is named after a place. Little Gidding is a village in Huntingdonshire where in 1625 Nicholas Ferrar established an Anglican religious community; the community was broken up in 1647, toward the end of the English Civil War, by the victorious Puritans; the chapel, however, was rebuilt in the 19th century and still exists. Eliot wrote the poem in 1942, when he was taking his turn as a nighttime fire-watcher during the incendiary bombings of London in World War II.

2. On the Pentecost day after the death and resurrection of Jesus, there appeared to his apostles "cloven tongues like as of fire . . . And they were all filled with the Holy Ghost" (Acts 2).

3. King Charles I visited Ferrar's community more than once and is said to have paid his last visit in secret after his final defeat at the battle of Naseby in the civil war.

If you came by day not knowing what you came for,
It would be the same, when you leave the rough road
And turn behind the pig-sty to the dull façade
30 And the tombstone. And what you thought you came for
Is only a shell, a husk of meaning
From which the purpose breaks only when it is fulfilled
If at all. Either you had no purpose
Or the purpose is beyond the end you figured
35 And is altered in fulfilment. There are other places
Which also are the world's end, some at the sea jaws,
Or over a dark lake, in a desert or a city[4]—
But this is the nearest, in place and time,
Now and in England.

                    If you came this way,
40 Taking any route, starting from anywhere,
At any time or at any season,
It would always be the same: you would have to put off
Sense and notion. You are not here to verify,
Instruct yourself, or inform curiosity
45 Or carry report. You are here to kneel
Where prayer has been valid. And prayer is more
Than an order of words, the conscious occupation
Of the praying mind, or the sound of the voice praying.
And what the dead had no speech for, when living,
50 They can tell you, being dead: the communication
Of the dead is tongued with fire beyond the language of the living.
Here, the intersection of the timeless moment
Is England and nowhere. Never and always.

II

Ash on an old man's sleeve
55 Is all the ash the burnt roses leave.
Dust in the air suspended
Marks the place where a story ended.[5]
Dust inbreathed was a house—
The wall, the wainscot, and the mouse.
60 The death of hope and despair,
    This is the death of air.[6]

There are flood and drouth
Over the eyes and in the mouth,
Dead water and dead sand

---

4. "The 'sea jaws' [Eliot] associated with Iona and St. Columba and with Lindisfarne and St. Cuthbert: the 'dark lake' with the lake of Glendalough and St. Kevin's hermitage in County Wicklow: the desert with the hermits of the Thebaid and St. Antony: the city with Padua and the other St. Antony" (Gardner).
5. Eliot wrote to a friend: "During the Blitz [bombing] the accumulated debris was suspended in the London air for hours after a bombing. Then it would slowly descend and cover one's sleeves and coat with a fine white ash."
6. "The death of air," like that of "earth" and of "water and fire" in the succeeding stanzas, recalls the theory of the creative strife of the four elements propounded by Heraclitus (Greek philosopher of 4th and 5th centuries B.C.E.): "Fire lives in the death of air; water lives in the death of earth; and earth lives in the death of water."

65   Contending for the upper hand.
     The parched eviscerate soil
     Gapes at the vanity of toil,
     Laughs without mirth.
         This is the death of earth.

70   Water and fire succeed
     The town, the pasture, and the weed.
     Water and fire deride
     The sacrifice that we denied.
     Water and fire shall rot
75   The marred foundations we forgot,
     Of sanctuary and choir.
         This is the death of water and fire.

     In the uncertain hour before the morning[7]
       Near the ending of interminable night
80   At the recurrent end of the unending
    After the dark dove with the flickering tongue[8]
       Had passed below the horizon of his homing
       While the dead leaves still rattled on like tin
    Over the asphalt where no other sound was
85   Between three districts whence the smoke arose
       I met one walking, loitering and hurried
    As if blown towards me like the metal leaves
       Before the urban dawn wind unresisting.
       And as I fixed upon the down-turned face
90   That pointed scrutiny with which we challenge
       The first-met stranger in the waning dusk
       I caught the sudden look of some dead master
    Whom I had known, forgotten, half recalled
       Both one and many; in the brown baked features
95   The eyes of a familiar compound ghost[9]
    Both intimate and unidentifiable.
       So I assumed a double part, and cried
       And heard another's voice cry: 'What! are *you* here?'
    Although we were not. I was still the same,
100   Knowing myself yet being someone other—
       And he a face still forming; yet the words sufficed
    To compel the recognition they preceded.
       And so, compliant to the common wind,
       Too strange to each other for misunderstanding,
105   In concord at this intersection time
       Of meeting nowhere, no before and after,
       We trod the pavement in a dead patrol.
     I said: 'The wonder that I feel is easy,
       Yet ease is cause of wonder. Therefore speak:

---

7. The pattern of indentation in the left margin of lines 78–149, their movement and elevated diction, are meant to suggest the terza rima of Dante's *Divine Comedy*.
8. The German dive bomber.
9. This encounter with a ghost "compounded" of W. B. Yeats and his fellow Irishman Jonathan Swift is modeled on Dante's meeting with Brunetto Latini (*Inferno* 15), including a direct translation (line 98) of Dante's cry of horrified recognition: *"Siete voi qui, ser Brunetto?"* Cf. also Shakespeare's sonnet 86, line 9: "that affable familiar ghost."

110   I may not comprehend, may not remember.'
      And he: 'I am not eager to rehearse
         My thought and theory which you have forgotten.
         These things have served their purpose: let them be.
      So with your own, and pray they be forgiven

115   By others, as I pray you to forgive
      Both bad and good. Last season's fruit is eaten
      And the fullfed beast shall kick the empty pail.
         For last year's words belong to last year's language
         And next year's words await another voice.

120   But, as the passage now presents no hindrance
         To the spirit unappeased and peregrine°   *foreign, wandering*
         Between two worlds become much like each other,
      So I find words I never thought to speak
         In streets I never thought I should revisit

125   When I left my body on a distant shore.[1]
      Since our concern was speech, and speech impelled us
         To purify the dialect of the tribe[2]
         And urge the mind to aftersight and foresight,
      Let me disclose the gifts reserved for age

130   To set a crown upon your lifetime's effort.
         First, the cold friction of expiring sense
      Without enchantment, offering no promise
         But bitter tastelessness of shadow fruit
         As body and soul begin to fall asunder.

135   Second, the conscious impotence of rage[3]
         At human folly, and the laceration
         Of laughter at what ceases to amuse.[4]
      And last, the rending pain of re-enactment
         Of all that you have done, and been;[5] the shame

140   Of motives late revealed, and the awareness
      Of things ill done and done to others' harm
         Which once you took for exercise of virtue.
         Then fools' approval stings, and honour stains.
      From wrong to wrong the exasperated spirit

145   Proceeds, unless restored by that refining fire[6]
         Where you must move in measure, like a dancer.'[7]
      The day was breaking. In the disfigured street
         He left me, with a kind of valediction,
         And faded on the blowing of the horn.[8]

---

1. Yeats died on Jan. 28, 1939, at Roquebrune in the south of France.
2. A rendering of the line *"Donner un sens plus pur aux mots de la tribu"* in Stéphane Mallarmé's 1877 sonnet "Le Tombeau d'Edgar Poe" ("The Tomb of Edgar Poe").
3. Cf. Yeats's "The Spur": "You think it horrible that lust and rage / Should dance attention upon my old age."
4. Cf. Yeats's "Swift's Epitaph" (translated from Swift's own Latin): "Savage indignation there / Cannot lacerate his breast."
5. Cf. Yeats's "Man and the Echo": "All that I have said and done, / Now that I am old and ill, / Turns into a question till / I lie awake night after night / And never get the answer right. / Did that play of mine send out / Certain men the English shot?"

6. Cf. *The Waste Land*, line 428 and its note; also the refining fire in Yeats's "Byzantium," lines 25–32.
7. Cf. Yeats's "Among School Children," line 64: "How can we know the dancer from the dance?"
8. Cf. *Hamlet* 1.2.157: "It faded on the crowing of the cock." The horn is the all-clear signal after an air raid (the dialogue has taken place between the dropping of the last bomb and the sounding of the all clear). Eliot called the section that ends with this line "the nearest equivalent to a canto of the *Inferno* or *Purgatorio*" that he could achieve and spoke of his intention to present "a parallel, by means of contrast, between the *Inferno* and the *Purgatorio* . . . and a hallucinated scene after an air raid."

III

150 There are three conditions which often look alike
Yet differ completely, flourish in the same hedgerow:
Attachment to self and to things and to persons, detachment
From self and from things and from persons; and, growing between
them, indifference
Which resembles the others as death resembles life,
155 Being between two lives—unflowering, between
The live and the dead nettle.[9] This is the use of memory:
For liberation—not less of love but expanding
Of love beyond desire, and so liberation
From the future as well as the past. Thus, love of a country
160 Begins as attachment to our own field of action
And comes to find that action of little importance
Though never indifferent. History may be servitude,
History may be freedom. See, now they vanish,
The faces and places, with the self which, as it could, loved them,
165 To become renewed, transfigured, in another pattern.

Sin is Behovely, but
All shall be well, and
All manner of thing shall be well.[1]
If I think, again, of this place,
170 And of people, not wholly commendable,
Of no immediate kin or kindness,
But some of peculiar genius,
All touched by a common genius,
United in the strife which divided them;
175 If I think of a king at nightfall,[2]
Of three men, and more, on the scaffold
And a few who died forgotten
In other places, here and abroad,
And of one who died blind and quiet[3]
180 Why should we celebrate
These dead men more than the dying?
It is not to ring the bell backward
Nor is it an incantation
To summon the spectre of a Rose.
185 We cannot revive old factions
We cannot restore old policies
Or follow an antique drum.
These men, and those who opposed them
And those whom they opposed
190 Accept the constitution of silence
And are folded in a single party.

9. Eliot wrote to a friend: "The dead nettle is the family of flowering plants of which the White Archangel is one of the commonest and closely resembles the stinging nettle and is found in its company."
1. A quotation from the 14th-century English mystic Dame Julian of Norwich: "Sin is behovabil [inevitable and fitting], but all shall be well and all

shall be well and all manner of thing shall be well."
2. I.e., Charles I. He died "on the scaffold" in 1649, while his principal advisers, Archbishop Laud and Thomas Wentworth, earl of Strafford, were both executed earlier by the victorious parliamentary forces.
3. I.e., Milton, who sided with Cromwell against the king.

Whatever we inherit from the fortunate
We have taken from the defeated
What they had to leave us—a symbol:
195   A symbol perfected in death.
And all shall be well and
All manner of thing shall be well
By the purification of the motive
In the ground of our beseeching.[4]

IV

200   The dove[5] descending breaks the air
With flame of incandescent terror
Of which the tongues declare
The one discharge from sin and error.
The only hope, or else despair
205   Lies in the choice of pyre or pyre—
    To be redeemed from fire by fire.

Who then devised the torment? Love.
Love is the unfamiliar Name
Behind the hands that wove
210   The intolerable shirt of flame[6]
Which human power cannot remove.
    We only live, only suspire°   *breathe, sigh*
    Consumed by either fire or fire.

V

  What we call the beginning is often the end
215   And to make an end is to make a beginning.
The end is where we start from. And every phrase
And sentence that is right (where every word is at home,
Taking its place to support the others,
The word neither diffident nor ostentatious,
220   And easy commerce of the old and the new,
The common word exact without vulgarity,
The formal word precise but not pedantic,
The complete consort[7] dancing together)
Every phrase and every sentence is an end and a beginning,
225   Every poem an epitaph. And any action
Is a step to the block, to the fire, down the sea's throat
Or to an illegible stone: and that is where we start.
We die with the dying:
See, they depart, and we go with them.
230   We are born with the dead:
See, they return, and bring us with them.
The moment of the rose and the moment of the yew-tree[8]

---

4. Dame Julian of Norwich was instructed in a vision that "the ground of our beseeching" is love.
5. Both a dive bomber and the Holy Spirit with its Pentecostal tongues of fire.
6. Out of love for her husband, Hercules, Deianira gave him the poisoned shirt of Nessus. She had been told that it would increase his love for her, but instead it so corroded his flesh that in his agony he mounted a funeral pyre and burned himself to death.
7. Company; also harmony of sounds.
8. Traditional symbol of death and grief.

Are of equal duration. A people without history
Is not redeemed from time, for history is a pattern
235 Of timeless moments. So, while the light fails
On a winter's afternoon, in a secluded chapel
History is now and England.

With the drawing of this Love and the voice of this Calling[9]

We shall not cease from exploration
240 And the end of all our exploring
Will be to arrive where we started
And know the place for the first time.
Through the unknown, remembered gate
When the last of earth left to discover
245 Is that which was the beginning;
At the source of the longest river
The voice of the hidden waterfall
And the children in the apple tree
Not known, because not looked for
250 But heard, half-heard, in the stillness
Between two waves of the sea.[1]
Quick now, here, now, always—
A condition of complete simplicity
(Costing not less than everything)
255 And all shall be well and
All manner of thing shall be well
When the tongues of flame are in-folded
Into the crowned knot of fire
And the fire and the rose are one.

1942   1942, 1943

Tradition and the Individual Talent[1]

I

In English writing we seldom speak of tradition, though we occasionally apply its name in deploring its absence. We cannot refer to 'the tradition' or to 'a tradition'; at most, we employ the adjective in saying that the poetry of So-and-so is 'traditional' or even 'too traditional.' Seldom, perhaps, does the word appear except in a phrase of censure. If otherwise, it is vaguely approbative, with the implication, as to the work approved, of some pleasing archæological reconstruction. You can hardly make the word agreeable to English ears without this comfortable reference to the reassuring science of archæology.

Certainly the word is not likely to appear in our appreciations of living or dead writers. Every nation, every race, has not only its own creative, but its

9. This line is from the *Cloud of Unknowing,* an anonymous 14th-century mystical work.
1. The voices of the children in the apple tree symbolize the sudden moment of insight. Cf. the conclusion to "Burnt Norton" (the first of the *Four Quartets*), where the laughter of the children in the garden has a like meaning: "Sudden in a shaft of sunlight / Even while the dust moves / There rises the hidden laughter / Of children in the foliage / Quick now, here, now, always."
1. First published in *The Egoist* magazine (1919) and later collected in *The Sacred Wood* (1920).

own critical turn of mind; and is even more oblivious of the shortcomings and limitations of its critical habits than of those of its creative genius. We know, or think we know, from the enormous mass of critical writing that has appeared in the French language the critical method or habit of the French; we only conclude (we are such unconscious people) that the French are 'more critical' than we, and sometimes even plume ourselves a little with the fact, as if the French were the less spontaneous. Perhaps they are; but we might remind ourselves that criticism is as inevitable as breathing, and that we should be none the worse for articulating what passes in our minds when we read a book and feel an emotion about it, for criticizing our own minds in their work of criticism. One of the facts that might come to light in this process is our tendency to insist, when we praise a poet, upon those aspects of his work in which he least resembles anyone else. In these aspects or parts of his work we pretend to find what is individual, what is the peculiar essence of the man. We dwell with satisfaction upon the poet's difference from his predecessors, especially his immediate predecessors; we endeavour to find something that can be isolated in order to be enjoyed. Whereas if we approach a poet without this prejudice we shall often find that not only the best, but the most individual parts of his work may be those in which the dead poets, his ancestors, assert their immortality most vigorously. And I do not mean the impressionable period of adolescence, but the period of full maturity.

Yet if the only form of tradition, of handing down, consisted in following the ways of the immediate generation before us in a blind or timid adherence to its successes, 'tradition' should positively be discouraged. We have seen many such simple currents soon lost in the sand; and novelty is better than repetition. Tradition is a matter of much wider significance. It cannot be inherited, and if you want it you must obtain it by great labour. It involves, in the first place, the historical sense, which we may call nearly indispensable to any one who would continue to be a poet beyond his twenty-fifth year; and the historical sense involves a perception, not only of the pastness of the past, but of its presence; the historical sense compels a man to write not merely with his own generation in his bones, but with a feeling that the whole of the literature of Europe from Homer and within it the whole of the literature of his own country has a simultaneous existence and composes a simultaneous order. This historical sense, which is a sense of the timeless as well as of the temporal and of the timeless and of the temporal together, is what makes a writer traditional. And it is at the same time what makes a writer most acutely conscious of his place in time, of his own contemporaneity.

No poet, no artist of any art, has his complete meaning alone. His significance, his appreciation is the appreciation of his relation to the dead poets and artists. You cannot value him alone; you must set him, for contrast and comparison, among the dead. I mean this as a principle of æsthetic, not merely historical, criticism. The necessity that he shall conform, that he shall cohere, is not one-sided; what happens when a new work of art is created is something that happens simultaneously to all the works of art which preceded it. The existing monuments form an ideal order among themselves, which is modified by the introduction of the new (the really new) work of art among them. The existing order is complete before the new work arrives; for order to persist after the supervention of novelty, the *whole* existing order must be, if ever so slightly, altered; and so the relations, proportions, values of each work of art toward the whole are readjusted; and this is conformity between the old and the new.

Whoever has approved this idea of order, of the form of European, of English literature will not find it preposterous that the past should be altered by the present as much as the present is directed by the past. And the poet who is aware of this will be aware of great difficulties and responsibilities.

In a peculiar sense he will be aware also that he must inevitably be judged by the standards of the past. I say judged, not amputated, by them; not judged to be as good as, or worse or better than, the dead; and certainly not judged by the canons of dead critics. It is a judgment, a comparison, in which two things are measured by each other. To conform merely would be for the new work not really to conform at all; it would not be new, and would therefore not be a work of art. And we do not quite say that the new is more valuable because it fits in; but its fitting in is a test of its value—a test, it is true, which can only be slowly and cautiously applied, for we are none of us infallible judges of conformity. We say: it appears to conform, and is perhaps individual, or it appears individual, and may conform; but we are hardly likely to find that it is one and not the other.

To proceed to a more intelligible exposition of the relation of the poet to the past: he can neither take the past as a lump, an indiscriminate bolus,[2] nor can he form himself wholly on one or two private admirations, nor can he form himself wholly upon one preferred period. The first course is inadmissible, the second is an important experience of youth, and the third is a pleasant and highly desirable supplement. The poet must be very conscious of the main current, which does not at all flow invariably through the most distinguished reputations. He must be quite aware of the obvious fact that art never improves, but that the material of art is never quite the same. He must be aware that the mind of Europe—the mind of his own country—a mind which he learns in time to be much more important than his own private mind—is a mind which changes, and that this change is a development which abandons nothing en route, which does not superannuate either Shakespeare, or Homer, or the rock drawing of the Magdalenian[3] draftsmen. That this development, refinement perhaps, complication certainly, is not, from the point of view of the artist, any improvement. Perhaps not even an improvement from the point of view of the psychologist or not to the extent which we imagine; perhaps only in the end based upon a complication in economics and machinery. But the difference between the present and the past is that the conscious present is an awareness of the past in a way and to an extent which the past's awareness of itself cannot show.

Someone said: 'The dead writers are remote from us because we know so much more than they did.' Precisely, and they are that which we know.

I am alive to a usual objection to what is clearly part of my programme for the métier[4] of poetry. The objection is that the doctrine requires a ridiculous amount of erudition (pedantry), a claim which can be rejected by appeal to the lives of poets in any pantheon. It will even be affirmed that much learning deadens or perverts poetic sensibility. While, however, we persist in believing that a poet ought to know as much as will not encroach upon his necessary receptivity and necessary laziness, it is not desirable to confine knowledge to whatever can be put into a useful shape for examinations, drawing-rooms, or the still more pretentious modes of publicity. Some can absorb knowledge,

---

2. A round mass of anything: a large pill.
3. The most advanced culture of the European Paleolithic period (from discoveries at La Madeleine, France).
4. Vocation (French).

the more tardy must sweat for it. Shakespeare acquired more essential history from Plutarch[5] than most men could from the whole British Museum. What is to be insisted upon is that the poet must develop or procure the consciousness of the past and that he should continue to develop this consciousness throughout his career.

What happens is a continual surrender of himself as he is at the moment to something which is more valuable. The progress of an artist is a continual self-sacrifice, a continual extinction of personality.

There remains to define this process of depersonalisation and its relation to the sense of tradition. It is in this depersonalization that art may be said to approach the condition of science. I, therefore, invite you to consider, as a suggestive analogy, the action which takes place when a bit of finely filiated[6] platinum is introduced into a chamber containing oxygen and sulphur dioxide.

II

Honest criticism and sensitive appreciation are directed not upon the poet but upon the poetry. If we attend to the confused cries of the newspaper critics and the susurrus[7] of popular repetition that follows, we shall hear the names of poets in great numbers; if we seek not Blue-book[8] knowledge but the enjoyment of poetry, and ask for a poem, we shall seldom find it. I have tried to point out the importance of the relation of the poem to other poems by other authors, and suggested the conception of poetry as a living whole of all the poetry that has ever been written. The other aspect of this Impersonal theory of poetry is the relation of the poem to its author. And I hinted, by an analogy, that the mind of the mature poet differs from that of the immature one not precisely in any valuation of 'personality,' not being necessarily more interesting, or having 'more to say,' but rather by being a more finely perfected medium in which special, or very varied, feelings are at liberty to enter into new combinations.

The analogy was that of the catalyst.[9] When the two gases previously mentioned are mixed in the presence of a filament of platinum, they form sulphurous acid. This combination takes place only if the platinum is present; nevertheless the newly formed acid contains no trace of platinum, and the platinum itself is apparently unaffected; has remained inert, neutral, and unchanged. The mind of the poet is the shred of platinum. It may partly or exclusively operate upon the experience of the man himself; but, the more perfect the artist, the more completely separate in him will be the man who suffers and the mind which creates; the more perfectly will the mind digest and transmute the passions which are its material.

The experience, you will notice, the elements which enter the presence of the transforming catalyst, are of two kinds: emotions and feelings. The effect of a work of art upon the person who enjoys it is an experience different in kind from any experience not of art. It may be formed out of one emotion, or may be a combination of several; and various feelings, inhering for the writer

---

5. Greek biographer (1st century C.E.) of famous Greeks and Romans; from his work Shakespeare drew the plots of his Roman plays.
6. Drawn out like a thread.

7. Murmuring, buzzing (Latin).
8. British government publication.
9. Substance that triggers a chemical change without being affected by the reaction.

in particular words or phrases or images, may be added to compose the final result. Or great poetry may be made without the direct use of any emotion whatever: composed out of feelings solely. Canto XV of the *Inferno* (Brunetto Latini)[1] is a working up of the emotion evident in the situation; but the effect, though single as that of any work of art, is obtained by considerable complexity of detail. The last quatrain gives an image, a feeling attaching to an image, which 'came,' which did not develop simply out of what precedes, but which was probably in suspension in the poet's mind until the proper combination arrived for it to add itself to.[2] The poet's mind is in fact a receptacle for seizing and storing up numberless feelings, phrases, images, which remain there until all the particles which can unite to form a new compound are present together.

If you compare several representative passages of the greatest poetry you see how great is the variety of types of combination, and also how completely any semi-ethical criterion of 'sublimity' misses the mark. For it is not the 'greatness,' the intensity, of the emotions, the components, but the intensity of the artistic process, the pressure, so to speak, under which the fusion takes place, that counts. The episode of Paolo and Francesca[3] employs a definite emotion, but the intensity of the poetry is something quite different from whatever intensity in the supposed experience it may give the impression of. It is no more intense, furthermore, than Canto XXVI,[4] the voyage of Ulysses, which has not the direct dependence upon an emotion. Great variety is possible in the process of transmutation of emotion: the murder of Agamemnon, or the agony of Othello,[5] gives an artistic effect apparently closer to a possible original than the scenes from Dante. In the *Agamemnon*, the artistic emotion approximates to the emotion of an actual spectator; in *Othello* to the emotion of the protagonist himself. But the difference between art and the event is always absolute; the combination which is the murder of Agamemnon is probably as complex as that which is the voyage of Ulysses. In either case there has been a fusion of elements. The ode of Keats contains a number of feelings which have nothing particular to do with the nightingale, but which the nightingale, partly, perhaps, because of its attractive name, and partly because of its reputation, served to bring together.

The point of view which I am struggling to attack is perhaps related to the metaphysical theory of the substantial unity of the soul: for my meaning is, that the poet has, not a 'personality' to express, but a particular medium, which is only a medium and not a personality, in which impressions and experiences combine in peculiar and unexpected ways. Impressions and experiences which are important for the man may take no place in the poetry, and those which become important in the poetry may play quite a negligible part in the man, the personality.

I will quote a passage which is unfamiliar enough to be regarded with fresh attention in the light—or darkness—of these observations:

1. Dante meets in hell his old master, Brunetto Latini, suffering eternal punishment for unnatural lust yet still loved and admired by Dante, who addresses him with affectionate courtesy.
2. Dante's strange interview with Brunetto is over, and Brunetto moves off to continue his punishment: "Then he turned round, and seemed like one of those / Who run for the green cloth [in the footrace] at Verona / In the field; and he seemed among them / Not the loser but the winner."

3. Illicit lovers whom Dante meets in the second circle of hell (*Inferno* 5) and at whose punishment and sorrows he swoons with pity.
4. Of the *Inferno*. Ulysses, suffering in hell for "false counseling," tells Dante of his final voyage.
5. Shakespeare's character kills himself after being duped into jealously murdering his wife. In Aeschylus's play *Agamemnon* the title character is murdered by his wife, Clytemnestra.

> And now methinks I could e'en chide myself
> For doating on her beauty, though her death
> Shall be revenged after no common action.
> Does the silkworm expend her yellow labours
> For thee? For thee does she undo herself?
> Are lordships sold to maintain ladyships
> For the poor benefit of a bewildering minute?
> Why does yon fellow falsify highways,
> And put his life between the judge's lips,
> To refine such a thing—keeps horse and men
> To beat their valours for her? . . . [6]

In this passage (as is evident if it is taken in its context) there is a combination of positive and negative emotions: an intensely strong attraction toward beauty and an equally intense fascination by the ugliness which is contrasted with it and which destroys it. This balance of contrasted emotion is in the dramatic situation to which the speech is pertinent, but that situation alone is inadequate to it. This is, so to speak, the structural emotion, provided by the drama. But the whole effect, the dominant tone, is due to the fact that a number of floating feelings, having an affinity to this emotion by no means superficially evident, have combined with it to give us a new art emotion.

It is not in his personal emotions, the emotions provoked by particular events in his life, that the poet is in any way remarkable or interesting. His particular emotions may be simple, or crude, or flat. The emotion in his poetry will be a very complex thing, but not with the complexity of the emotions of people who have very complex or unusual emotions in life. One error, in fact, of eccentricity in poetry is to seek for new human emotions to express; and in this search for novelty in the wrong place it discovers the perverse. The business of the poet is not to find new emotions, but to use the ordinary ones and, in working them up into poetry, to express feelings which are not in actual emotions at all. And emotions which he has never experienced will serve his turn as well as those familiar to him. Consequently, we must believe that 'emotion recollected in tranquillity'[7] is an inexact formula. For it is neither emotion, nor recollection, nor, without distortion of meaning, tranquility. It is a concentration, and a new thing resulting from the concentration, of a very great number of experiences which to the practical and active person would not seem to be experiences at all; it is a concentration which does not happen consciously or of deliberation. These experiences are not 'recollected,' and they finally unite in an atmosphere which is 'tranquil' only in that it is a passive attending upon the event. Of course this is not quite the whole story. There is a great deal, in the writing of poetry, which must be conscious and deliberate. In fact, the bad poet is usually unconscious where he ought to be conscious, and conscious where he ought to be unconscious. Both errors tend to make him 'personal.' Poetry is not a turning loose of emotion, but an escape from emotion; it is not the expression of personality, but an escape from personality. But, of course, only those who have personality and emotions know what it means to want to escape from these things.

---

6. From Cyril Tourneur's *Revenger's Tragedy* 3.4 (1607).
7. In his preface to *Lyrical Ballads* (2nd ed., 1800), Wordsworth writes that poetry "takes its origin from emotion recollected in tranquility."

III

ὁ δὲ νοῦζ ἴσωζ θειό τερόν τι καὶ ἀπαθέζ ἐστιν.[8]

This essay proposes to halt at the frontier of metaphysics or mysticism, and confine itself to such practical conclusions as can be applied by the responsible person interested in poetry. To divert interest from the poet to the poetry is a laudable aim: for it would conduce to a juster estimation of actual poetry, good and bad. There are many people who appreciate the expression of sincere emotion in verse, and there is a smaller number of people who can appreciate technical excellence. But very few know when there is an expression of *significant* emotion, emotion which has its life in the poem and not in the history of the poet. The emotion of art is impersonal. And the poet cannot reach this impersonality without surrendering himself wholly to the work to be done. And he is not likely to know what is to be done unless he lives in what is not merely the present, but the present moment of the past, unless he is conscious, not of what is dead, but of what is already living.

1919, 1920

The Metaphysical Poets

By collecting these poems[1] from the work of a generation more often named than read, and more often read than profitably studied, Professor Grierson has rendered a service of some importance. Certainly the reader will meet with many poems already preserved in other anthologies, at the same time that he discovers poems such as those of Aurelian Townshend or Lord Herbert of Cherbury here included. But the function of such an anthology as this is neither that of Professor Saintsbury's admirable edition of Caroline poets nor that of the *Oxford Book of English Verse*. Mr. Grierson's book is in itself a piece of criticism and a provocation of criticism; and we think that he was right in including so many poems of Donne, elsewhere (though not in many editions) accessible, as documents in the case of 'metaphysical poetry.' The phrase has long done duty as a term of abuse or as the label of a quaint and pleasant taste. The question is to what extent the so-called metaphysicals formed a school (in our own time we should say a 'movement'), and how far this so-called school or movement is a digression from the main current.

Not only is it extremely difficult to define metaphysical poetry, but difficult to decide what poets practise it and in which of their verses. The poetry of Donne (to whom Marvell and Bishop King are sometimes nearer than any of the other authors) is late Elizabethan, its feeling often very close to that of Chapman. The 'courtly' poetry is derivative from Jonson, who borrowed liberally from the Latin; it expires in the next century with the sentiment and witticism of Prior. There is finally the devotional verse of Herbert, Vaughan, and Crashaw (echoed long after by Christina Rossetti and Francis Thompson); Crashaw, sometimes more profound and less sectarian than the others, has a

---

8. Aristotle's "De Anima" ("On the Soul") 1.4: "The mind is doubtless something more divine and unimpressionable."
1. *Metaphysical Lyrics and Poems of the Seven-*

teenth Century: Donne to Butler (1921), selected and edited, with an essay, by Herbert J. C. Grierson. Eliot's essay was originally a review of this book in the London *Times Literary Supplement*.

quality which returns through the Elizabethan period to the early Italians. It is difficult to find any precise use of metaphor, simile, or other conceit, which is common to all the poets and at the same time important enough as an element of style to isolate these poets as a group. Donne, and often Cowley, employ a device which is sometimes considered characteristically 'metaphysical'; the elaboration (contrasted with the condensation) of a figure of speech to the furthest stage to which ingenuity can carry it. Thus Cowley develops the commonplace comparison of the world to a chess-board through long stanzas (*To Destiny*), and Donne, with more grace, in *A Valediction,*[2] the comparison of two lovers to a pair of compasses. But elsewhere we find, instead of the mere explication of the content of a comparison, a development by rapid association of thought which requires considerable agility on the part of the reader.

> On a round ball
> A workeman that hath copies by, can lay
> An Europe, Afrique, and an Asia,
> And quickly make that, which was nothing, All,
> > So doth each teare,
> > Which thee doth weare,
> A globe, yea world by that impression grow,
> Till thy tears mixt with mine doe overflow
> This world, by waters sent from thee, my heaven dissolved so.[3]

Here we find at least two connexions which are not implicit in the first figure, but are forced upon it by the poet: from the geographer's globe to the tear, and the tear to the deluge. On the other hand, some of Donne's most successful and characteristic effects are secured by brief words and sudden contrasts:

> A bracelet of bright hair about the bone,[4]

where the most powerful effect is produced by the sudden contrast of associations of 'bright hair' and of 'bone'. This telescoping of images and multiplied associations is characteristic of the phrase of some of the dramatists of the period which Donne knew: not to mention Shakespeare, it is frequent in Middleton, Webster, and Tourneur, and is one of the sources of the vitality of their language.

Johnson, who employed the term 'metaphysical poets', apparently having Donne, Cleveland, and Cowley chiefly in mind, remarks of them that 'the most heterogeneous ideas are yoked by violence together'.[5] The force of this impeachment lies in the failure of the conjunction, the fact that often the ideas are yoked but not united; and if we are to judge of styles of poetry by their abuse, enough examples may be found in Cleveland to justify Johnson's condemnation. But a degree of heterogeneity of material compelled into unity by the operation of the poet's mind is omnipresent in poetry. We need not select for illustration such a line as:

> Notre âme est un trois-mâts cherchant son Icarie;[6]

2. I.e., "A Valediction: Forbidding Mourning."
3. Donne's "A Valediction: Of Weeping," lines 10–18.
4. "The Relic," line 6.
5. See Samuel Johnson's *Cowley.*

6. From Charles Baudelaire's "Le Voyage": "Our soul is a three-masted ship searching for her Icarie"; Icarie is an imaginary utopia in *Voyage en Icarie* (1840), a novel by the French socialist Etienne Cabet.

we may find it in some of the best lines of Johnson himself (*The Vanity of Human Wishes*):

> His fate was destined to a barren strand,
> A petty fortress, and a dubious hand;
> He left a name at which the world grew pale,
> To point a moral, or adorn a tale.

where the effect is due to a contrast of ideas, different in degree but the same in principle, as that which Johnson mildly reprehended. And in one of the finest poems of the age (a poem which could not have been written in any other age), the *Exequy* of Bishop King, the extended comparison is used with perfect success: the idea and the simile become one, in the passage in which the Bishop illustrates his impatience to see his dead wife, under the figure of a journey:

> Stay for me there; I will not faile
> To meet thee in that hollow Vale.
> And think not much of my delay;
> I am already on the way,
> And follow thee with all the speed
> Desire can make, or sorrows breed.
> Each minute is a short degree,
> And ev'ry hour a step towards thee,
> At night when I betake to rest,
> Next morn I rise nearer my West
> Of life, almost by eight houres sail,
> Than when sleep breath'd his drowsy gale. . . .
> But heark! My Pulse, like a soft Drum
> Beats my approach, tells Thee I come;
> And slow howere my marches be,
> I shall at last sit down by Thee.

(In the last few lines there is that effect of terror which is several times attained by one of Bishop King's admirers, Edgar Poe.) Again, we may justly take these quatrains from Lord Herbert's Ode,[7] stanzas which would, we think, be immediately pronounced to be of the metaphysical school:

> So when from hence we shall be gone,
>   And be no more, nor you, nor I,
>   As one another's mystery,
> Each shall be both, yet both but one.
>
> This said, in her up-lifted face,
>   Her eyes, which did that beauty crown,
>   Were like two stars, that having faln down,
> Look up again to find their place:
>
> While such a moveless silent peace
>   Did seize on their becalmed sense,
>   One would have thought some influence
> Their ravished spirits did possess.

7. Edward, Lord Herbert of Cherbury (1583–1648), brother of George Herbert. The "Ode" is his "Ode upon a Question moved, whether Love should continue forever?"

There is nothing in these lines (with the possible exception of the stars, a simile not at once grasped, but lovely and justified) which fits Johnson's general observations on the metaphysical poets in his essay on Cowley. A good deal resides in the richness of association which is at the same time borrowed from and given to the word 'becalmed'; but the meaning is clear, the language simple and elegant. It is to be observed that the language of these poets is as a rule simple and pure; in the verse of George Herbert this simplicity is carried as far as it can go—a simplicity emulated without success by numerous modern poets. The *structure* of the sentences, on the other hand, is sometimes far from simple, but this is not a vice; it is a fidelity to thought and feeling. The effect, at its best, is far less artificial than that of an ode by Gray. And as this fidelity induces variety of thought and feeling, so it induces variety of music. We doubt whether, in the eighteenth century, could be found two poems in nominally the same metre, so dissimilar as Marvell's *Coy Mistress* and Crashaw's *Saint Teresa;* the one producing an effect of great speed by the use of short syllables, and the other an ecclesiastical solemnity by the use of long ones:

> *Love, thou art absolute sole lord*
> *Of life and death.*

If so shrewd and sensitive (though so limited) a critic as Johnson failed to define metaphysical poetry by its faults, it is worth while to inquire whether we may not have more success by adopting the opposite method: by assuming that the poets of the seventeenth century (up to the Revolution)[8] were the direct and normal development of the precedent age; and, without prejudicing their case by the adjective 'metaphysical', consider whether their virtue was not something permanently valuable, which subsequently disappeared, but ought not to have disappeared. Johnson has hit, perhaps by accident, on one of their peculiarities, when he observes that 'their attempts were always analytic'; he would not agree that, after the dissociation, they put the material together again in a new unity.

It is certain that the dramatic verse of the later Elizabethan and early Jacobean poets expresses a degree of development of sensibility which is not found in any of the prose, good as it often is. If we except Marlowe, a man of prodigious intelligence, these dramatists were directly or indirectly (it is at least a tenable theory) affected by Montaigne.[9] Even if we except also Jonson and Chapman, these two were probably erudite, and were notably men who incorporated their erudition into their sensibility: their mode of feeling was directly and freshly altered by their reading and thought. In Chapman especially there is a direct sensuous apprehension of thought, or a recreation of thought into feeling, which is exactly what we find in Donne:

> *in this one thing, all the discipline*
> *Of manners and of manhood is contained;*
> *A man to join himself with th' Universe*
> *In his main sway, and make in all things fit*
> *One with that All, and go on, round as it;*
> *Not plucking from the whole his wretched part,*
> *And into straits, or into nought revert,*

---

8. Of 1688; when James II was replaced by William and Mary.

9. Michel de Montaigne (1533–1592), French essayist.

> Wishing the complete Universe might be
> Subject to such a rag of it as he;
> But to consider great Necessity.[1]

We compare this with some modern passage:

> No, when the fight begins within himself,
> A man's worth something. God stoops o'er his head,
> Satan looks up between his feet—both tug—
> He's left, himself, i' the middle; the soul wakes
> And grows. Prolong that battle through his life![2]

It is perhaps somewhat less fair, though very tempting (as both poets are concerned with the perpetuation of love by offspring), to compare with the stanzas already quoted from Lord Herbert's Ode the following from Tennyson:

> One walked between his wife and child,
> With measured footfall firm and mild,
> And now and then he gravely smiled.
>   The prudent partner of his blood
>   Leaned on him, faithful, gentle, good,
>   Wearing the rose of womanhood.
> And in their double love secure,
> The little maiden walked demure,
> Pacing with downward eyelids pure.
>   These three made unity so sweet,
>   My frozen heart began to beat,
>   Remembering its ancient heat.[3]

The difference is not a simple difference of degree between poets. It is something which had happened to the mind of England between the time of Donne or Lord Herbert of Cherbury and the time of Tennyson and Browning; it is the difference between the intellectual poet and the reflective poet. Tennyson and Browning are poets, and they think; but they do not feel their thought as immediately as the odour of a rose. A thought to Donne was an experience; it modified his sensibility. When a poet's mind is perfectly equipped for its work, it is constantly amalgamating disparate experience; the ordinary man's experience is chaotic, irregular, fragmentary. The latter falls in love, or reads Spinoza,[4] and these two experiences have nothing to do with each other, or with the noise of the typewriter or the smell of cooking; in the mind of the poet these experiences are always forming new wholes.

We may express the difference by the following theory: The poets of the seventeenth century, the successors of the dramatists of the sixteenth, possessed a mechanism of sensibility which could devour any kind of experience. They are simple, artificial, difficult, or fantastic, as their predecessors were; no less nor more than Dante, Guido Cavalcanti, Guinicelli, or Cino.[5] In the seventeenth century a dissociation of sensibility set in, from which we have never recovered; and this dissociation, as is natural, was aggravated by the influence of the two most powerful poets of the century, Milton and Dryden.

---

1. From *The Revenge of Bussy d'Ambois* (4.1.137–46).
2. Robert Browning, "Bishop Blougram's Apology," lines 693–97.
3. "The Two Voices," lines 412–23.
4. 17th-century Dutch philosopher.

5. These last three poets, all of whom lived in the 13th century, were members of the Tuscan school of lyric love poets. Guido Guinicelli was hailed by Dante in the *Purgatorio* as "father of Italian poets." Cino da Pistoia was a friend of Dante and Petrarch.

Each of these men performed certain poetic functions so magnificently well that the magnitude of the effect concealed the absence of others. The language went on and in some respects improved; the best verse of Collins, Gray, Johnson, and even Goldsmith satisfies some of our fastidious demands better than that of Donne or Marvell or King. But while the language became more refined, the feeling became more crude. The feeling, the sensibility, expressed in the *Country Churchyard*[6] (to say nothing of Tennyson and Browning) is cruder than that in the *Coy Mistress*.

The second effect of the influence of Milton and Dryden followed from the first, and was therefore slow in manifestation. The sentimental age began early in the eighteenth century, and continued. The poets revolted against the ratiocinative, the descriptive; they thought and felt by fits, unbalanced; they reflected. In one or two passages of Shelley's *Triumph of Life,* in the second *Hyperion,* there are traces of a struggle toward unification of sensibility. But Keats and Shelley died, and Tennyson and Browning ruminated.

After this brief exposition of a theory—too brief, perhaps, to carry conviction—we may ask, what would have been the fate of the 'metaphysical' had the current of poetry descended in a direct line from them, as it descended in a direct line to them? They would not, certainly, be classified as metaphysical. The possible interests of a poet are unlimited; the more intelligent he is the better; the more intelligent he is the more likely that he will have interests: our only condition is that he turn them into poetry, and not merely meditate on them poetically. A philosophical theory which has entered into poetry is established, for its truth or falsity in one sense ceases to matter, and its truth in another sense is proved. The poets in question have, like other poets, various faults. But they were, at best, engaged in the task of trying to find the verbal equivalent for states of mind and feeling. And this means both that they are more mature, and that they wear better, than later poets of certainly not less literary ability.

It is not a permanent necessity that poets should be interested in philosophy, or in any other subject. We can only say that it appears likely that poets in our civilization, as it exists at present, must be *difficult.* Our civilization comprehends great variety and complexity, and this variety and complexity, playing upon a refined sensibility, must produce various and complex results. The poet must become more and more comprehensive, more allusive, more indirect, in order to force, to dislocate if necessary, language into his meaning. (A brilliant and extreme statement of this view, with which it is not requisite to associate oneself, is that of M Jean Epstein, *La Poésie d'aujourd'hui.*[7]) Hence we get something which looks very much like the conceit—we get, in fact, a method curiously similar to that of the 'metaphysical poets', similar also in its use of obscure words and of simple phrasing.

> O géraniums diaphanes, guerroyeurs sortilèges,
> Sacrilèges monomanes!
> Emballages, dévergondages, douches! O pressoirs
> Des vendanges des grands soirs!
> Layettes aux abois,
> Thyrses au fond des bois!
> Transfusions, représailles,

---

6. I.e., "An Elegy Written in a Country Church-yard," by Thomas Gray (1716–1771).

7. Poetry of today (French).

> *Relevailles, compresses et l'éternal potion,*
> *Angélus! n'en pouvoir plus*
> *De débâcles nuptiales! de débâcles nuptiales!*[8]

The same poet could write also simply:

> *Elle est bien loin, elle pleure,*
> *Le grand vent se lamente aussi . . .*[9]

Jules Laforgue, and Tristan Corbière[1] in many of his poems, are nearer to the 'school of Donne' than any modern English poet. But poets more classical than they have the same essential quality of transmuting ideas into sensations, of transforming an observation into a state of mind.

> *Pour l'enfant, amoureux de cartes et d'estampes,*
> *L'univers est égal à son vaste appétit.*
> *Ah, que le monde est grand à la clarté des lampes!*
> *Aux yeux du souvenir que le monde est petit!*[2]

In French literature the great master of the seventeenth century—Racine— and the great master of the nineteenth—Baudelaire—are in some ways more like each other than they are like anyone else. The greatest two masters of diction are also the greatest two psychologists, the most curious explorers of the soul. It is interesting to speculate whether it is not a misfortune that two of the greatest masters of diction in our language, Milton and Dryden, triumph with a dazzling disregard of the soul. If we continued to produce Miltons and Drydens it might not so much matter, but as things are it is a pity that English poetry has remained so incomplete. Those who object to the 'artificiality' of Milton or Dryden sometimes tell us to 'look into our hearts and write.'[3] But that is not looking deep enough; Racine or Donne looked into a good deal more than the heart. One must look into the cerebral cortex, the nervous system, and the digestive tracts.

May we not conclude, then, that Donne, Crashaw, Vaughan, Herbert and Lord Herbert, Marvell, King, Cowley at his best, are in the direct current of English poetry, and that their faults should be reprimanded by this standard rather than coddled by antiquarian affection? They have been enough praised in terms which are implicit limitations because they are 'metaphysical' or 'witty,' 'quaint' or 'obscure,' though at their best they have not these attributes more than other serious poets. On the other hand, we must not reject the criticism of Johnson (a dangerous person to disagree with) without having mastered it, without having assimilated the Johnsonian canons of taste. In reading the celebrated passage in his essay on Cowley we must remember that by wit he clearly means something more serious than we usually mean to-day; in his criticism of their versification we must remember in what a narrow discipline he was trained, but also how well trained; we must remember that

---

8. From *Derniers Vers* (*Last Poems*, 1890) 10, by Jules Laforgue (1860–1887): "O transparent geraniums, warrior incantations, / Monomaniac sacrileges! / Packing materials, shamelessnesses, shower baths! O wine presses / Of great evening vintages! / Hard-pressed baby linen, / Thyrsis in the depths of the woods! / Transfusions, reprisals, / Churchings, compresses, and the eternal potion, / Angelus! no longer to be borne [are] / Catastrophic marriages! catastrophic marriages!"
9. From *Derniers Vers* 11, "Sur une Défunte" ("On a Dead Woman"): "She is far away, she weeps / The great wind mourns also."
1. French symbolist poet (1845–1875).
2. From Charles Baudelaire's "Le Voyage": "For the child, in love with maps and prints, / The universe matches his vast appetite. / Ah, how big the world is by lamplight! How small the world is to the eyes of memory!"
3. An adaptation of the last line of the first sonnet of *Astrophil and Stella*, by Sir Philip Sidney (1554– 1586).

Johnson tortures chiefly the chief offenders, Cowley and Cleveland. It would be a fruitful work, and one requiring a substantial book, to break up the classification of Johnson (for there has been none since) and exhibit these poets in all their difference of kind and of degree, from the massive music of Donne to the faint, pleasing tinkle of Aurelian Townshend—whose *Dialogue between a Pilgrim and Time* is one of the few regrettable omissions from the excellent anthology of Professor Grierson.

1921

KATHERINE MANSFIELD
1888–1923

Kathleen Mansfield Beauchamp was born in Wellington, New Zealand, daughter of a respected businessman who was later knighted. In 1903 the family moved to London, where Kathleen and her sisters entered Queen's College, the first institution in England founded expressly for the higher education of women. The family returned to New Zealand, leaving the girls in London, but the Beauchamps brought their daughters home in 1906. By this time Kathleen had written a number of poems, sketches, and stories; and after experimenting with different pen names, she adopted that of Katherine Mansfield. She was restless and ambitious and chafed against the narrowness of middle-class life in New Zealand, at that time still very much a new country in the shadow of the British Empire.

In July 1908 Mansfield left again for London; she never returned to New Zealand. In 1909 she suddenly married G. C. Bowden, a teacher of singing and elocution, but left him the same evening. Shortly afterward she became pregnant by another man and went to Germany to await the birth, but she had a miscarriage there. Her experiences in Germany are told in carefully observed sketches full of ironic detail in her first published book, *In a German Pension* (1911).

In 1910 she briefly resumed life with Bowden, who put her in touch with A. R. Orage, editor of the avant-garde periodical *The New Age*. There she published a number of her stories and sketches. At the end of 1911 she met the critic John Middleton Murry, editor of the modernist magazine *Rhythm,* and eventually married him. She developed intense but conflicted friendships with D. H. Lawrence, Virginia Woolf, and other writers of the day. During all this time Mansfield experimented in technique and refined her art, attempting within the short story to illuminate the ambivalences and complexities of friendship and family, gender and class. The death in World War I in October 1915 of her much-loved younger brother sent her imagination back to their childhood days in New Zealand and in doing so gave a fresh charge and significance to her writing. Using her newly developed style with an ever greater subtlety and sensitivity, she now produced her best stories, including "Prelude," "Daughters of the Late Colonel," "At the Bay," and "The Garden Party." With the publication of *The Garden Party and Other Stories* in February 1922, Mansfield's place as a master of the modern short story was ensured. But she was gravely ill with tuberculosis and died suddenly at the age of thirty-four in Fontainebleau, France, where she had gone to try to find a cure by adopting the methods of the controversial mystic George Ivanovich Gurdjieff.

Mansfield produced her best and most characteristic work in her last years, when she combined incident, image, symbol, and structure in a way comparable with, yet interestingly different from, James Joyce's method in *Dubliners,* both writers sharing an influence in the precise and understated art of the Russian writer Anton Chekhov. "Daughters of the Late Colonel," a story of two middle-aged sisters and their devotion to a tyrannical father, shows her working characteristically through suggestion rather than explicit development to illuminate a late-Victorian world, with the subdued elegiac sense of female lives wasted in the service of an outmoded patriarchal order, although the story's ironic surface is restrained comedy. The meaning is achieved most of all through the atmosphere, built up by the accumulation of small strokes, none of which seems more than a shrewdly observed realistic detail. Mansfield also manipulates time masterfully: she makes particularly effective use of the unobtrusive flashback, where we find ourselves in an earlier phase of the action without quite knowing how we got there but fully aware of its relevance to the total action and atmosphere.

The Daughters of the Late Colonel

I

The week after was one of the busiest weeks of their lives. Even when they went to bed it was only their bodies that lay down and rested; their minds went on, thinking things out, talking things over, wondering, deciding, trying to remember where . . .

Constantia lay like a statue, her hands by her sides, her feet just overlapping each other, the sheet up to her chin. She stared at the ceiling.

'Do you think father would mind if we gave his top-hat to the porter?'

'The porter?' snapped Josephine. 'Why ever the porter? What a very extraordinary idea!'

'Because,' said Constantia slowly, 'he must often have to go to funerals. And I noticed at—at the cemetery that he only had a bowler.' She paused. 'I thought then how very much he'd appreciate a top-hat. We ought to give him a present, too. He was always very nice to father.'

'But,' cried Josephine, flouncing on her pillow and staring across the dark at Constantia, 'father's head!' And suddenly, for one awful moment, she nearly giggled. Not, of course, that she felt in the least like giggling. It must have been habit. Years ago, when they had stayed awake at night talking, their beds had simply heaved. And now the porter's head, disappearing, popped out, like a candle, under father's hat. . . . The giggle mounted, mounted; she clenched her hands; she fought it down; she frowned fiercely at the dark and said 'Remember' terribly sternly.

'We can decide tomorrow,' she sighed.

Constantia had noticed nothing; she sighed.

'Do you think we ought to have our dressing-gowns dyed as well?'

'Black?' almost shrieked Josephine.

'Well, what else?' said Constantia. 'I was thinking—it doesn't seem quite sincere, in a way, to wear black out of doors and when we're fully dressed, and then when we're at home—'

'But nobody sees us,' said Josephine. She gave the bedclothes such a twitch that both her feet became uncovered and she had to creep up the pillows to get them well under again.

'Kate does,' said Constantia. 'And the postman very well might.'

Josephine thought of her dark-red slippers, which matched her dressing-gown, and of Constantia's favourite indefinite green ones which went with hers. Black! Two black dressing-gowns and two pairs of black woolly slippers, creeping off to the bathroom like black cats.

'I don't think it's absolutely necessary,' said she.

Silence. Then Constantia said, 'We shall have to post the papers with the notice in them tomorrow to catch the Ceylon mail. . . . How many letters have we had up till now?'

'Twenty-three.'

Josephine had replied to them all, and twenty-three times when she came to 'We miss our dear father so much' she had broken down and had to use her handkerchief, and on some of them even to soak up a very light-blue tear with an edge of blotting-paper. Strange! She couldn't have put it on—but twenty-three times. Even now, though, when she said over to herself sadly 'We miss our dear father *so* much,' she could have cried if she'd wanted to.

'Have you got enough stamps?' came from Constantia.

'Oh, how can I tell?' said Josephine crossly. 'What's the good of asking me that now?'

'I was just wondering,' said Constantia mildly.

Silence again. There came a little rustle, a scurry, a hop.

'A mouse,' said Constantia.

'It can't be a mouse because there aren't any crumbs,' said Josephine.

'But it doesn't know there aren't,' said Constantia.

A spasm of pity squeezed her heart. Poor little thing! She wished she'd left a tiny piece of biscuit on the dressing-table. It was awful to think of it not finding anything. What would it do?

'I can't think how they manage to live at all,' she said slowly.

'Who?' demanded Josephine.

And Constantia said more loudly than she meant to, 'Mice.'

Josephine was furious. 'Oh, what nonsense, Con!' she said. 'What have mice got to do with it? You're asleep.'

'I don't think I am,' said Constantia. She shut her eyes to make sure. She was.

Josephine arched her spine, pulled up her knees, folded her arms so that her fists came under her ears, and pressed her cheek hard against the pillow.

II

Another thing which complicated matters was they had Nurse Andrews staying on with them that week. It was their own fault; they had asked her. It was Josephine's idea. On the morning—well, on the last morning, when the doctor had gone, Josephine had said to Constantia, 'Don't you think it would be rather nice if we asked Nurse Andrews to stay on for a week as our guest?'

'Very nice,' said Constantia.

'I thought,' went on Josephine quickly, 'I should just say this afternoon, after I've paid her, "My sister and I would be very pleased, after all you've done for us, Nurse Andrews, if you would stay on for a week as our guest." I'd have to put that in about being our guest in case—'

'Oh, but she could hardly expect to be paid!' cried Constantia.

'One never knows,' said Josephine sagely.

Nurse Andrews had, of course, jumped at the idea. But it was a bother. It meant they had to have regular sit-down meals at the proper times, whereas if they'd been alone they could just have asked Kate if she wouldn't have minded bringing them a tray wherever they were. And meal-times now that the strain was over were rather a trial.

Nurse Andrews was simply fearful about butter. Really they couldn't help feeling that about butter, at least, she took advantage of their kindness. And she had that maddening habit of asking for just an inch more bread to finish what she had on her plate, and then, at the last mouthful, absent-mindedly—of course it wasn't absent-mindedly—taking another helping. Josephine got very red when this happened, and she fastened her small, bead-like eyes on the tablecloth as if she saw a minute strange insect creeping through the web of it. But Constantia's long, pale face lengthened and set, and she gazed away—away—far over the desert, to where that line of camels unwound like a thread of wool. . . .

'When I was with Lady Tukes,' said Nurse Andrews, 'she had such a dainty little contrayvance for the buttah. It was a silvah cupid balanced on the—on the bordah of a glass dish, holding a tayny fork. And when you wanted some buttah you simply pressed his foot and he bent down and speared you a piece. It was quite a gayme.'

Josephine could hardly bear that. But 'I think those things are very extravagant' was all she said.

'But whey?' asked Nurse Andrews, beaming through her eyeglasses. 'No one, surely, would take more buttah than one wanted—would one?'

'Ring, Con,' cried Josephine. She couldn't trust herself to reply.

And proud young Kate, the enchanted princess, came in to see what the old tabbies wanted now. She snatched away their plates of mock something or other and slapped down a white terrified blancmange.[1]

'Jam, please, Kate,' said Josephine kindly.

Kate knelt and burst open the sideboard, lifted the lid of the jam-pot, saw it was empty, put it on the table, and stalked off.

'I'm afraid,' said Nurse Andrews a moment later, 'there isn't any.'

'Oh, what a bother!' said Josephine. She bit her lip. 'What had we better do?'

Constantia looked dubious. 'We can't disturb Kate again,' she said softly.

Nurse Andrews waited, smiling at them both. Her eyes wandered, spying at everything behind her eyeglasses. Constantia in despair went back to her camels. Josephine frowned heavily—concentrated. If it hadn't been for this idiotic woman she and Con would, of course, have eaten their blancmange without. Suddenly the idea came.

'I know,' she said. 'Marmalade. There's some marmalade in the sideboard. Get it, Con.'

'I hope,' laughed Nurse Andrews—and her laugh was like a spoon tinkling against a medicine glass—'I hope it's not very bittah marmalayde.'

III

But, after all, it was not long now, and then she'd be gone for good. And there was no getting over the fact that she had been very kind to father. She had nursed him day and night at the end. Indeed, both Constantia and Josephine felt privately she had rather overdone the not leaving him at the very last. For when they had gone in to say goodbye Nurse Andrews had sat beside

1. A gelatinous dessert.

his bed the whole time, holding his wrist and pretending to look at her watch. It couldn't have been necessary. It was so tactless, too. Supposing father had wanted to say something—something private to them. Not that he had. Oh, far from it! He lay there, purple, a dark, angry purple in the face, and never even looked at them when they came in. Then, as they were standing there, wondering what to do, he had suddenly opened one eye. Oh, what a difference it would have made, what a difference to their memory of him, how much easier to tell people about it, if he had only opened both! But no—one eye only. It glared at them a moment and then . . . went out.

IV

It had made it very awkward for them when Mr Farolles, of St John's, called the same afternoon.

'The end was quite peaceful, I trust?' were the first words he said as he glided towards them through the dark drawing-room.

'Quite,' said Josephine faintly. They both hung their heads. Both of them felt certain that eye wasn't at all a peaceful eye.

'Won't you sit down?' said Josephine.

'Thank you, Miss Pinner,' said Mr Farolles gratefully. He folded his coattails and began to lower himself into father's armchair, but just as he touched it he almost sprang up and slid into the next chair instead.

He coughed. Josephine clasped her hands; Constantia looked vague.

'I want you to feel, Miss Pinner,' said Mr Farolles, 'and you, Miss Constantia, that I'm trying to be helpful. I want to be helpful to you both, if you will let me. These are the times,' said Mr Farolles, very simply and earnestly, 'when God means us to be helpful to one another.'

'Thank you very much, Mr Farolles,' said Josephine and Constantia.

'Not at all,' said Mr Farolles gently. He drew his kid gloves through his fingers and leaned forward. 'And if either of you would like a little Communion, either or both of you, here and now, you have only to tell me. A little Communion is often very help—a great comfort,' he added tenderly.

But the idea of a little Communion terrified them. What! In the drawing room by themselves—with no—no altar or anything! The piano would be much too high, thought Constantia, and Mr Farolles could not possibly lean over it with the chalice. And Kate would be sure to come bursting in and interrupt them, thought Josephine. And supposing the bell rang in the middle? It might be somebody important—about their mourning. Would they get up reverently and go out, or would they have to wait . . . in torture?

'Perhaps you will send round a note by your good Kate if you would care for it later,' said Mr Farolles.

'Oh yes, thank you very much!' they both said.

Mr Farolles got up and took his black straw hat from the round table.

'And about the funeral,' he said softly. 'I may arrange that—as your dear father's old friend and yours, Miss Pinner—and Miss Constantia?'

Josephine and Constantia got up too.

'I should like it to be quite simple,' said Josephine firmly, 'and not too expensive. At the same time, I should like—'

'A good one that will last,' thought dreamy Constantia, as if Josephine were buying a nightgown. But of course Josephine didn't say that. 'One suitable to our father's position.' She was very nervous.

'I'll run round to our good friend Mr Knight,' said Mr Farolles soothingly. 'I will ask him to come and see you. I am sure you will find him very helpful indeed.'

V

Well, at any rate, all that part of it was over, though neither of them could possibly believe that father was never coming back. Josephine had had a moment of absolute terror at the cemetery, while the coffin was lowered, to think that she and Constantia had done this thing without asking his permission. What would father say when he found out? For he was bound to find out sooner or later. He always did. 'Buried. You two girls had me buried?' She heard his stick thumping. Oh, what would they say? What possible excuse could they make? It sounded such an appallingly heartless thing to do. Such a wicked advantage to take of a person because he happened to be helpless at the moment. The other people seemed to treat it all as a matter of course. They were strangers; they couldn't be expected to understand that father was the very last person for such a thing to happen to. No, the entire blame for it all would fall on her and Constantia. And the expense, she thought, stepping into the tight-buttoned cab. When she had to show him the bills. What would he say then?

She heard him absolutely roaring, 'And do you expect me to pay for this gimcrack excursion of yours?'

'Oh,' groaned poor Josephine aloud, 'we shouldn't have done it, Con!'

And Constantia, pale as a lemon in all that blackness, said in a frightened whisper, 'Done what, Jug?'

'Let them bu-bury father like that,' said Josephine, breaking down and crying into her new, queer-smelling mourning handkerchief.

'But what else could we have done?' asked Constantia wonderingly. 'We couldn't have kept him unburied. At any rate, not in a flat that size.'

Josephine blew her nose; the cab was dreadfully stuffy.

'I don't know,' she said forlornly. 'It is all so dreadful. I feel we ought to have tried to, just for a time at least. To make perfectly sure. One thing's certain'—and her tears sprang out again—'father will never forgive us for this—never!'

VI

Father would never forgive them. That was what they felt more than ever when, two mornings later, they went into his room to go through his things. They had discussed it quite calmly. It was even down on Josephine's list of things to be done. Go through father's things and settle about them. But that was a very different matter from saying after breakfast:

'Well, are you ready, Con?'

'Yes, Jug—when you are.'

'Then I think we'd better get it over.'

It was dark in the hall. It had been a rule for years never to disturb father in the morning, whatever happened. And now they were going to open the door without knocking even . . . . Constantia's eyes were enormous at the idea; Josephine felt weak in the knees.

'You—you go first,' she gasped, pushing Constantia.

But Constantia said, as she always had said on those occasions, 'No, Jug, that's not fair. You're the eldest.'

Josephine was just going to say—what at other times she wouldn't have owned to for the world—what she kept for her very last weapon, 'But you're the tallest,' when they noticed that the kitchen door was open, and there stood Kate. . . .

'Very stiff,' said Josephine, grasping the door-handle and doing her best to turn it. As if anything ever deceived Kate!

It couldn't be helped. That girl was . . . Then the door was shut behind them, but—but they weren't in father's room at all. They might have suddenly walked through the wall by mistake into a different flat altogether. Was the door just behind them? They were too frightened to look. Josephine knew that if it was it was holding itself tight shut; Constantia felt that, like the doors in dreams, it hadn't any handle at all. It was the coldness which made it so awful. Or the whiteness—which? Everything was covered. The blinds were down, a cloth hung over the mirror, a sheet hid the bed, a huge fan of white paper filled the fireplace. Constantia timidly put out her hand; she almost expected a snowflake to fall. Josephine felt a queer tingling in her nose, as if her nose was freezing. Then a cab klop-klopped over the cobbles below, and the quiet seemed to shake into little pieces.

'I had better pull up a blind,' said Josephine bravely.

'Yes, it might be a good idea,' whispered Constantia.

They only gave the blind a touch, but it flew up and the cord flew after, rolling round the blind-stick, and the little tassel tapped as if trying to get free. That was too much for Constantia.

'Don't you think—don't you think we might put it off for another day?' she whispered.

'Why?' snapped Josephine, feeling, as usual, much better now that she knew for certain that Constantia was terrified. 'It's got to be done. But I do wish you wouldn't whisper, Con.'

'I didn't know I was whispering,' whispered Constantia.

'And why do you keep on staring at the bed?' said Josephine, raising her voice almost defiantly. 'There's nothing on the bed.'

'Oh, Jug, don't say so!' said poor Connie. 'At any rate, not so loudly.'

Josephine felt herself that she had gone too far. She took a wide swerve over to the chest of drawers, put out her hand, but quickly drew it back again.

'Connie!' she gasped, and she wheeled round and leaned with her back against the chest of drawers.

'Oh, Jug—what?'

Josephine could only glare. She had the most extraordinary feeling that she had just escaped something simply awful. But how could she explain to Constantia that father was in the chest of drawers? He was in the top drawer with his handkerchiefs and neckties, or in the next with his shirts and pyjamas, or in the lowest of all with his suits. He was watching there, hidden away—just behind the door-handle—ready to spring.

She pulled a funny old-fashioned face at Constantia, just as she used to in the old days when she was going to cry.

'I can't open,' she nearly wailed.

'No, don't, Jug,' whispered Constantia earnestly. 'It's much better not to. Don't let's open anything. At any rate, not for a long time.'

'But—but it seems so weak,' said Josephine, breaking down.

'But why not be weak for once, Jug?' argued Constantia, whispering quite fiercely. 'If it is weak.' And her pale stare flew from the locked writing-table—so safe—to the huge glittering wardrobe, and she began to breathe in a queer, panting way. 'Why shouldn't we be weak for once in our lives, Jug? It's quite excusable. Let's be weak—be weak, Jug. It's much nicer to be weak than to be strong.'

And then she did one of those amazingly bold things that she'd done about twice before in their lives: she marched over to the wardrobe, turned the key, and took it out of the lock. Took it out of the lock and held it up to Josephine, showing Josephine by her extraordinary smile that she knew what she'd done—she'd risked deliberately father being in there among his overcoats.

If the huge wardrobe had lurched forward, had crashed down on Constantia, Josephine wouldn't have been surprised. On the contrary, she would have thought it the only suitable thing to happen. But nothing happened. Only the room seemed quieter than ever, and bigger flakes of cold air fell on Josephine's shoulders and knees. She began to shiver.

'Come, Jug,' said Constantia, still with that awful callous smile; and Josephine followed just as she had that last time, when Constantia had pushed Benny into the round pond.

VII

But the strain told on them when they were back in the dining-room. They sat down, very shaky, and looked at each other.

'I don't feel I can settle to anything,' said Josephine, 'until I've had something. Do you think we could ask Kate for two cups of hot water?'

'I really don't see why we shouldn't,' said Constantia carefully. She was quite normal again. 'I won't ring. I'll go to the kitchen door and ask her.'

'Yes, do,' said Josephine, sinking down into a chair. 'Tell her, just two cups, Con, nothing else—on a tray.'

'She needn't even put the jug on, need she?' said Constantia, as though Kate might very well complain if the jug had been there.

'Oh, no, certainly not! The jug's not at all necessary. She can pour it direct out of the kettle,' cried Josephine, feeling that would be a labour-saving indeed.

Their cold lips quivered at the greenish brims. Josephine curved her small red hands round the cup; Constantia sat up and blew on the wavy stream, making it flutter from one side to the other.

'Speaking of Benny,' said Josephine.

And though Benny hadn't been mentioned Constantia immediately looked as though he had.

'He'll expect us to send him something of father's, of course. But it's so difficult to know what to send to Ceylon.'

'You mean things get unstuck so on the voyage,' murmured Constantia.

'No, lost,' said Josephine sharply. 'You know there's no post. Only runners.'

Both paused to watch a black man in white linen drawers running through the pale fields for dear life, with a large brown-paper parcel in his hands. Josephine's black man was tiny; he scurried along glistening like an ant. But there was something blind and tireless about Constantia's tall, thin fellow, which made him, she decided, a very unpleasant person indeed . . . . On the veranda, dressed all in white and wearing a cork helmet, stood Benny. His right hand shook up and down, as father's did when he was impatient. And behind him, not in the least interested, sat Hilda, the unknown sister-in-law. She swung in a cane rocker and flicked over the leaves of the *Tatler*.

'I think his watch would be the most suitable present,' said Josephine.

Constantia looked up; she seemed surprised.

'Oh, would you trust a gold watch to a native?'

'But of course I'd disguise it,' said Josephine. 'No one would know it was a watch.' She liked the idea of having to make a parcel such a curious shape that no one could possibly guess what it was. She even thought for a moment of hiding the watch in a narrow cardboard corset-box that she'd kept by her for a long time, waiting for it to come in for something. It was such beautiful firm cardboard. But, no, it wouldn't be appropriate for this occasion. It had lettering on it: *Medium Women's 28. Extra Firm Busks.* It would be almost too much of a surprise for Benny to open that and find father's watch inside.

'And of course it isn't as though it would be going—ticking, I mean,' said Constantia, who was still thinking of the native love of jewelery. 'At least,' she added, 'it would be very strange if after all that time it was.'

VIII

Josephine made no reply. She had flown off on one of her tangents. She had suddenly thought of Cyril. Wasn't it more usual for the only grandson to have the watch? And then dear Cyril was so appreciative and a gold watch meant so much to a young man. Benny, in all probability, had quite got out of the habit of watches; men so seldom wore waistcoats in those hot climates. Whereas Cyril in London wore them from year's end to year's end. And it would be so nice for her and Constantia, when he came to tea, to know it was there. 'I see you've got on grandfather's watch, Cyril.' It would be somehow so satisfactory.

Dear boy! What a blow his sweet, sympathetic little note had been! Of course they quite understood; but it was most unfortunate.

'It would have been such a point, having him,' said Josephine.

'And he would have enjoyed it so,' said Constantia, not thinking what she was saying.

However, as soon as he got back he was coming to tea with his aunties. Cyril to tea was one of their rare treats.

'Now, Cyril, you mustn't be frightened of our cakes. Your Auntie Con and I bought them at Buszard's this morning. We know what a man's appetite is. So don't be ashamed of making a good tea.'

Josephine cut recklessly into the rich dark cake that stood for her winter gloves or the soling and heeling of Constantia's only respectable shoes. But Cyril was most unmanlike in appetite.

'I say, Aunt Josephine, I simply can't. I've only just had lunch, you know.'

'Oh, Cyril, that can't be true! It's after four,' cried Josephine. Constantia sat with her knife poised over the chocolate-roll.

'It is, all the same,' said Cyril. 'I had to meet a man at Victoria,[2] and he kept me hanging about till . . . there was only time to get lunch and to come on here. And he gave me—phew'—Cyril put his hand to his forehead—'a terrific blow-out,'[3] he said.

2. London railroad station, connecting with the Channel ports.　　3. Feast.

It was disappointing—today of all days. But still he couldn't be expected to know.

'But you'll have a meringue, won't you, Cyril?' said Aunt Josephine. 'These meringues were bought specially for you. Your dear father was so fond of them. We were sure you are, too.'

'I *am*, Aunt Josephine,' cried Cyril ardently. 'Do you mind if I take half to begin with?'

'Not at all, dear boy; but we mustn't let you off with that.'

'Is your dear father still so fond of meringues?' asked Auntie Con gently. She winced faintly as she broke through the shell of hers.

'Well, I don't quite know, Auntie Con,' said Cyril breezily.

At that they both looked up.

'Don't know?' almost snapped Josephine. 'Don't know a thing like that about your own father, Cyril?'

'Surely,' said Auntie Con softly.

Cyril tried to laugh it off. 'Oh, well,' he said, 'it's such a long time since—' He faltered. He stopped. Their faces were too much for him.

'Even *so*,' said Josephine.

And Auntie Con looked.

Cyril put down his teacup. 'Wait a bit,' he cried. 'Wait a bit, Aunt Josephine. What am I thinking of?'

He looked up. They were beginning to brighten. Cyril slapped his knee.

'Of course,' he said, 'it was meringues. How could I have forgotten? Yes, Aunt Josephine, you're perfectly right. Father's most frightfully keen on meringues.'

They didn't only beam. Aunt Josephine went scarlet with pleasure; Auntie Con gave a deep, deep sigh.

'And now, Cyril, you must come and see father,' said Josephine. 'He knows you were coming today.'

'Right,' said Cyril, very firmly and heartily. He got up from his chair; suddenly he glanced at the clock.

'I say, Auntie Con, isn't your clock a bit slow? I've got to meet a man at—at Paddington[4] just after five. I'm afraid I shan't be able to stay very long with grandfather.'

'Oh, he won't expect you to stay *very* long!' said Aunt Josephine.

Constantia was still gazing at the clock. She couldn't make up her mind if it was fast or slow. It was one or the other, she felt almost certain of that. At any rate, it had been.

Cyril still lingered. 'Aren't you coming along, Auntie Con?'

'Of course,' said Josephine, 'we shall all go. Come on, Con.'

IX

They knocked at the door, and Cyril followed his aunts into grandfather's hot, sweetish room.

'Come on,' said Grandfather Pinner. 'Don't hang about. What is it? What've you been up to?'

He was sitting in front of a roaring fire, clasping his stick. He had a thick

---

4. London railroad station, serving the west of England and Wales.

rug over his knees. On his lap there lay a beautiful pale yellow silk handkerchief.

'It's Cyril, father,' said Josephine shyly. And she took Cyril's hand and led him forward.

'Good afternoon, grandfather,' said Cyril, trying to take his hand out of Aunt Josephine's. Grandfather Pinner shot his eyes at Cyril in the way he was famous for. Where was Auntie Con? She stood on the other side of Aunt Josephine; her long arms hung down in front of her; her hands were clasped. She never took her eyes off grandfather.

'Well,' said Grandfather Pinner, beginning to thump, 'what have you got to tell me?'

What had he, what had he got to tell him? Cyril felt himself smiling like a perfect imbecile. The room was stifling, too.

But Aunt Josephine came to his rescue. She cried brightly, 'Cyril says his father is still very fond of meringues, father dear.'

'Eh?' said Grandfather Pinner, curving his hand like a purple meringue-shell over one ear.

Josephine repeated, 'Cyril says his father is still very fond of meringues.'

'Can't hear,' said old Colonel Pinner. And he waved Josephine away with his stick, then pointed with his stick to Cyril. 'Tell me what she's trying to say,' he said.

(My God!) 'Must I?' said Cyril, blushing and staring at Aunt Josephine.

'Do, dear,' she smiled. 'It will please him so much.'

'Come on, out with it!' cried Colonel Pinner testily, beginning to thump again.

And Cyril leaned forward and yelled, 'Father's still very fond of meringues.'

At that Grandfather Pinner jumped as though he had been shot.

'Don't shout!' he cried. 'What's the matter with the boy? Meringues! What about 'em?'

'Oh, Aunt Josephine, must we go on?' groaned Cyril desperately.

'It's quite all right, dear boy,' said Aunt Josephine, as though he and she were at the dentist's together. 'He'll understand in a minute.' And she whispered to Cyril, 'He's getting a bit deaf, you know.' Then she leaned forward and really bawled at Grandfather Pinner, 'Cyril only wanted to tell you, father dear, that his father is still very fond of meringues.'

Colonel Pinner heard that time, heard and brooded, looking Cyril up and down.

'What an esstrordinary thing!' said old Grandfather Pinner. 'What an esstrordinary thing to come all this way here to tell me!'

And Cyril felt it *was*.

'Yes, I shall send Cyril the watch,' said Josephine.

'That would be very nice,' said Constantia. 'I seem to remember last time he came there was some little trouble about the time.'

X

They were interrupted by Kate bursting through the door in her usual fashion, as though she had discovered some secret panel in the wall.

'Fried or boiled?' asked the bold voice.

Fried or boiled? Josephine and Constantia were quite bewildered for the moment. They could hardly take it in.

'Fried or boiled what, Kate?' asked Josephine, trying to begin to concentrate. Kate gave a loud sniff. 'Fish.'

'Well, why didn't you say so immediately?' Josephine reproached her gently. 'How could you expect us to understand, Kate? There are a great many things in this world, you know, which are fried or boiled.' And after such a display of courage she said quite brightly to Constantia, 'Which do you prefer, Con?'

'I think it might be nice to have it fried,' said Constantia. 'On the other hand, of course boiled fish is very nice. I think I prefer both equally well . . . Unless you . . . In that case—'

'I shall fry it,' said Kate, and she bounced back, leaving their door open and slamming the door of her kitchen.

Josephine gazed at Constantia; she raised her pale eyebrows until they rippled away into her pale hair. She got up. She said in a very lofty, imposing way, 'Do you mind following me into the drawing-room, Constantia? I've something of great importance to discuss with you.'

For it was always to the drawing-room they retired when they wanted to talk over Kate.

Josephine closed the door meaningly. 'Sit down, Constantia,' she said, still very grand. She might have been receiving Constantia for the first time. And Con looked round vaguely for a chair, as though she felt indeed quite a stranger.

'Now the question is,' said Josephine, bending forward, 'whether we shall keep her or not.'

'That is the question,' agreed Constantia.

'And this time,' said Josephine firmly, 'we must come to a definite decision.'

Constantia looked for a moment as though she might begin going over all the other times, but she pulled herself together and said, 'Yes, Jug.'

'You see, Con,' explained Josephine, 'everything is so changed now.' Constantia looked up quickly. 'I mean,' went on Josephine, 'we're not dependent on Kate as we were.' And she blushed faintly. 'There's not father to cook for.'

'That is perfectly true,' agreed Constantia. 'Father certainly doesn't want any cooking now, whatever else—'

Josephine broke in sharply, 'You're not sleepy, are you, Con?'

'Sleepy, Jug?' Constantia was wide-eyed.

'Well, concentrate more,' said Josephine sharply, and she returned to the subject. 'What it comes to is, if we did'—and this she barely breathed, glancing at the door—'give Kate notice'—she raised her voice again—'we could manage our own food.'

'Why not?' cried Constantia. She couldn't help smiling. The idea was so exciting. She clasped her hands. 'What should we live on, Jug?'

'Oh, eggs in various forms!' said Jug, lofty again. 'And, besides, there are all the cooked foods.'

'But I've always heard,' said Constantia, 'they are considered so very expensive.'

'Not if one buys them in moderation,' said Josephine. But she tore herself away from this fascinating bypath and dragged Constantia after her.

'What we've got to decide now, however, is whether we really do trust Kate or not.'

Constantia leaned back. Her flat little laugh flew from her lips.

'Isn't it curious, Jug,' said she, 'that just on this one subject I've never been able to quite make up my mind?'

XI

She never had. The whole difficulty was to prove anything. How did one prove things, how could one? Suppose Kate had stood in front of her and deliberately made a face. Mightn't she very well have been in pain? Wasn't it impossible, at any rate, to ask Kate if she was making a face at her? If Kate answered 'No'—and of course she would say 'No'—what a position! How undignified! Then again Constantia suspected, she was almost certain that Kate went to her chest of drawers when she and Josephine were out, not to take things but to spy. Many times she had come back to find her amethyst cross in the most unlikely places, under her lace ties or on top of her evening Bertha.[5] More than once she had laid a trap for Kate. She had arranged things in a special order and then called Josephine to witness.

'You see, Jug?'

'Quite, Con.'

'Now we shall be able to tell.'

But, oh dear, when she did go to look, she was as far off from a proof as ever! If anything was displaced, it might so very well have happened as she closed the drawer; a jolt might have done it so easily.

'You come, Jug, and decide. I really can't. It's too difficult.'

But after a pause and a long glare Josephine would sigh. 'Now you've put the doubt into my mind, Con, I'm sure I can't tell myself.'

'Well, we can't postpone it again,' said Josephine. 'If we postpone it this time—'

XII

But at that moment in the street below a barrel-organ struck up. Josephine and Constantia sprang to their feet together.

'Run, Con,' said Josephine. 'Run quickly. There's sixpence on the—'

Then they remembered. It didn't matter. They would never have to stop the organ-grinder again. Never again would she and Constantia be told to make that monkey take his noise somewhere else. Never would sound that loud, strange bellow when father thought they were not hurrying enough. The organ-grinder might play there all day and the stick would not thump.

It never will thump again,
It never will thump again,

played the barrel-organ.

What was Constantia thinking? She had such a strange smile; she looked different. She couldn't be going to cry.

'Jug, Jug,' said Constantia softly, pressing her hands together. 'Do you know what day it is? It's Saturday. It's a week today, a whole week.'

A week since father died,
A week since father died,

---

5. Detachable lace collar for low-necked dresses.

cried the barrel-organ. And Josephine, too, forgot to be practical and sensible; she smiled faintly, strangely. On the Indian carpet there fell a square of sunlight, pale red; it came and went and came—and stayed, deepened—until it shone almost golden.

'The sun's out,' said Josephine, as though it really mattered.

A perfect fountain of bubbling notes shook from the barrel-organ, round, bright notes, carelessly scattered.

Constantia lifted her big, cold hands as if to catch them, and then her hands fell again. She walked over to the mantelpiece to her favourite Buddha. And the stone and gilt image, whose smile always gave her such a queer feeling, almost a pain and yet a pleasant pain, seemed today to be more than smiling. He knew something; he had a secret. 'I know something that you don't know,' said her Buddha. Oh, what was it, what could it be? And yet she had always felt there was . . . something.

The sunlight pressed through the windows, thieved its way in, flashed its light over the furniture and the photographs. Josephine watched it. When it came to mother's photograph, the enlargement over the piano, it lingered as though puzzled to find so little remained of mother, except the ear-rings shaped like tiny pagodas and a black feather boa. Why did the photographs of dead people always fade so? wondered Josephine. As soon as a person was dead their photograph died too. But, of course, this one of mother was very old. It was thirty-five years old. Josephine remembered standing on a chair and pointing out that feather boa to Constantia and telling her that it was a snake that had killed their mother in Ceylon . . . . Would everything have been different if mother hadn't died? She didn't see why. Aunt Florence had lived with them until they had left school, and they had moved three times and had their yearly holiday and . . . and there'd been changes of servants, of course.

Some little sparrows, young sparrows they sounded, chirped on the window-ledge. *Yeep—eyeep—yeep.* But Josephine felt they were not sparrows, not on the window-ledge. It was inside her, that queer little crying noise. *Yeep—eyeep—yeep.* Ah, what was it crying, so weak and forlorn?

If mother had lived, might they have married? But there had been nobody for them to marry. There had been father's Anglo-Indian friends before he quarreled with them. But after that she and Constantia never met a single man except clergymen. How did one meet men? Or even if they'd met them, how could they have got to know men well enough to be more than strangers? One read of people having adventures, being followed, and so on. But nobody had ever followed Constantia and her. Oh yes, there had been one year at Eastbourne[6] a mysterious man at their boarding-house who had put a note on the jug of hot water outside their bedroom door! But by the time Connie had found it the steam had made the writing too faint to read; they couldn't even make out to which of them it was addressed. And he had left next day. And that was all. The rest had been looking after father and at the same time keeping out of father's way. But now? But now? The thieving sun touched Josephine gently. She lifted her face. She was drawn over to the window by gentle beams . . . .

Until the barrel-organ stopped playing Constantia stayed before the Buddha, wondering, but not as usual, not vaguely. This time her wonder was like longing. She remembered the times she had come in here, crept out of bed in

---

6. Seaside resort on Sussex coast.

her nightgown when the moon was full, and lain on the floor with her arms outstretched, as though she was crucified. Why? The big, pale moon had made her do it. The horrible dancing figures on the carved screen had leered at her and she hadn't minded. She remembered too how, whenever they were at the seaside, she had gone off by herself and got as close to the sea as she could, and sung something, something she had made up, while she gazed all over that restless water. There had been this other life, running out, bringing things home in bags, getting things on approval, discussing them with Jug, and taking them back to get more things on approval, and arranging father's trays and trying not to annoy father. But it all seemed to have happened in a kind of tunnel. It wasn't real. It was only when she came out of the tunnel into the moonlight or by the sea or into a thunderstorm that she really felt herself. What did it mean? What was it she was always wanting? What did it all lead to? Now? Now?

She turned away from the Buddha with one of her vague gestures. She went over to where Josephine was standing. She wanted to say something to Josephine, something frightfully important, about—about the future and what . . . 'Don't you think perhaps—' she began.

But Josephine interrupted her. 'I was wondering if now—' she murmured. They stopped; they waited for each either.

'Go on, Con,' said Josephine.

'No, no, Jug; after you,' said Constantia.

'No, say what you were going to say. You began,' said Josephine.

'I . . . I'd rather hear what you were going to say first,' said Constantia.

'Don't be absurd, Con.'

'Really, Jug.'

'Connie!'

'Oh, Jug!'

A pause. Then Constantia said faintly, 'I can't say what I was going to say, Jug, because I've forgotten what it was . . . that I was going to say.'

Josephine was silent for a moment. She stared at a big cloud where the sun had been. Then she replied shortly, 'I've forgotten too.'

1920   1922

The Garden Party[1]

And after all the weather was ideal. They could not have had a more perfect day for a garden party if they had ordered it. Windless, warm, the sky without a cloud. Only the blue was veiled with a haze of light gold, as it is sometimes in early summer. The gardener had been up since dawn, mowing the lawns and sweeping them, until the grass and the dark flat rosettes where the daisy plants had been seemed to shine. As for the roses, you could not help feeling they understood that roses are the only flowers that impress people at garden parties; the only flowers that everybody is certain of knowing. Hundreds, yes, literally hundreds, had come out in a single night; the green bushes bowed down as though they had been visited by archangels.

1. This story draws on an incident from Mansfield's life. In March 1907 her mother gave a garden party in their Wellington house, but a street accident befell a neighbor living in a poor quarter nearby.

Breakfast was not yet over before the men came to put up the marquee.

'Where do you want the marquee put, mother?'

'My dear child, it's no use asking me. I'm determined to leave everything to you children this year. Forget I am your mother. Treat me as an honoured guest.'

But Meg could not possibly go and supervise the men. She had washed her hair before breakfast, and she sat drinking her coffee in a green turban, with a dark wet curl stamped on each cheek. Jose, the butterfly, always came down in a silk petticoat and a kimono jacket.

'You'll have to go, Laura; you're the artistic one.'

Away Laura flew, still holding her piece of bread-and-butter. It's so delicious to have an excuse for eating out of doors, and besides, she loved having to arrange things; she always felt she could do it so much better than anybody else.

Four men in their shirt-sleeves stood grouped together on the garden path. They carried staves covered with rolls of canvas, and they had big tool-bags slung on their backs. They looked impressive. Laura wished now that she had not got the bread-and-butter, but there was nowhere to put it, and she couldn't possibly throw it away. She blushed and tried to look severe and even a little bit short-sighted as she came up to them.

'Good morning,' she said, copying her mother's voice. But that sounded so fearfully affected that she was ashamed, and stammered like a little girl, 'Oh—er—have you come—is it about the marquee?'

'That's right, miss,' said the tallest of the men, a lanky, freckled fellow, and he shifted his tool-bag, knocked back his straw hat and smiled down at her. 'That's about it.'

His smile was so easy, so friendly that Laura recovered. What nice eyes he had, small, but such a dark blue! And now she looked at the others, they were smiling too. 'Cheer up, we won't bite,' their smile seemed to say. How very nice workmen were! And what a beautiful morning! She mustn't mention the morning; she must be business-like. The marquee.

'Well, what about the lily-lawn? Would that do?'

And she pointed to the lily-lawn with the hand that didn't hold the bread-and-butter. They turned, they stared in the direction. A little fat chap thrust out his under-lip, and the tall fellow frowned.

'I don't fancy it,' said he. 'Not conspicuous enough. You see, with a thing like a marquee,' and he turned to Laura in his easy way, 'you want to put it somewhere where it'll give you a bang slap in the eye, if you follow me.'

Laura's upbringing made her wonder for a moment whether it was quite respectful of a workman to talk to her of bangs slap in the eye. But she did quite follow him.

'A corner of the tennis-court,' she suggested. 'But the band's going to be in one corner.'

'H'm, going to have a band, are you?' said another of the workmen. He was pale. He had a haggard look as his dark eyes scanned the tennis-court. What was he thinking?

'Only a very small band,' said Laura gently. Perhaps he wouldn't mind so much if the band was quite small. But the tall fellow interrupted.

'Look here, miss, that's the place. Against those trees. Over there. That'll do fine.'

Against the karakas. Then the karaka-trees would be hidden. And they were so lovely, with their broad, gleaming leaves, and their clusters of yellow fruit. They were like trees you imagined growing on a desert island, proud, solitary, lifting their leaves and fruits to the sun in a kind of silent splendour. Must they be hidden by a marquee?

They must. Already the men had shouldered their staves and were making for the place. Only the tall fellow was left. He bent down, pinched a sprig of lavender, put his thumb and forefinger to his nose and snuffed up the smell. When Laura saw that gesture she forgot all about the karakas in her wonder at him caring for things like that—caring for the smell of lavender. How many men that she knew would have done such a thing? Oh, how extraordinarily nice workmen were, she thought. Why couldn't she have workmen for friends rather than the silly boys she danced with and who came to Sunday night supper? She would get on much better with men like these.

It's all the fault, she decided, as the tall fellow drew something on the back of an envelope, something that was to be looped up or left to hang, of these absurd class distinctions. Well, for her part, she didn't feel them. Not a bit, not an atom . . . And now there came the chock-chock of wooden hammers. Some one whistled, some one sang out, 'Are you right there, matey?' 'Matey!' The friendliness of it, the—the—Just to prove how happy she was, just to show the tall fellow how at home she felt, and how she despised stupid conventions, Laura took a big bite of her bread-and-butter as she stared at the little drawing. She felt just like a work-girl.

'Laura, Laura, where are you? Telephone, Laura!' a voice cried from the house.

'Coming!' Away she skimmed, over the lawn, up the path, up the steps, across the veranda, and into the porch. In the hall her father and Laurie were brushing their hats ready to go to the office.

'I say, Laura,' said Laurie very fast, 'you might just give a squiz[2] at my coat before this afternoon. See if it wants pressing.'

'I will,' said she. Suddenly she couldn't stop herself. She ran at Laurie and gave him a small, quick squeeze. 'Oh, I do love parties, don't you?' gasped Laura.

'Ra-ther,' said Laurie's warm, boyish voice, and he squeezed his sister too, and gave her a gentle push. 'Dash off to the telephone, old girl.'

The telephone. 'Yes, yes; oh yes. Kitty? Good morning, dear. Come to lunch? Do, dear. Delighted of course. It will only be a very scratch meal—just the sandwich crusts and broken meringue-shells and what's left over. Yes, isn't it a perfect morning? Your white? Oh, I certainly should. One moment—hold the line. Mother's calling.' And Laura sat back. 'What, mother? Can't hear.'

Mrs Sheridan's voice floated down the stairs. 'Tell her to wear that sweet hat she had on last Sunday.'

'Mother says you're to wear that sweet hat you had on last Sunday. Good. One o'clock. Bye-bye.'

Laura put back the receiver, flung her arms over her head, took a deep breath, stretched and let them fall. 'Huh,' she sighed, and the moment after the sigh she sat up quickly. She was still, listening. All the doors in the house seemed to be open. The house was alive with soft, quick steps and running voices. The green baize[3] door that led to the kitchen regions swung open and

---

2. Glance.
3. Coarse woolen.

shut with a muffled thud. And now there came a long, chuckling absurd sound. It was the heavy piano being moved on its stiff castors. But the air! If you stopped to notice, was the air always like this? Little faint winds were playing chase in at the tops of the windows, out at the doors. And there were two tiny spots of sun, one on the inkpot, one on a silver photograph frame, playing too. Darling little spots. Especially the one on the inkpot lid. It was quite warm. A warm little silver star. She could have kissed it.

The front door bell pealed, and there sounded the rustle of Sadie's print skirt on the stairs. A man's voice murmured; Sadie answered, careless, 'I'm sure I don't know. Wait. I'll ask Mrs Sheridan.'

'What is it, Sadie?' Laura came into the hall.

'It's the florist, Miss Laura.'

It was, indeed. There, just inside the door, stood a wide, shallow tray full of pots of pink lilies. No other kind. Nothing but lilies—canna lilies, big pink flowers, wide open, radiant, almost frighteningly alive on bright crimson stems.

'O-oh, Sadie!' said Laura, and the sound was like a little moan. She crouched down as if to warm herself at that blaze of lilies; she felt they were in her fingers, on her lips, growing in her breast.

'It's some mistake,' she said faintly. 'Nobody ever ordered so many. Sadie, go and find mother.'

But at that moment Mrs Sheridan joined them.

'It's quite right,' she said calmly. 'Yes, I ordered them. Aren't they lovely?' She pressed Laura's arm. 'I was passing the shop yesterday, and I saw them in the window. And I suddenly thought for once in my life I shall have enough canna lilies. The garden party will be a good excuse.'

'But I thought you said you didn't mean to interfere,' said Laura. Sadie had gone. The florist's man was still outside at his van. She put her arm round her mother's neck and gently, very gently, she bit her mother's ear.

'My darling child, you wouldn't like a logical mother, would you? Don't do that. Here's the man.'

He carried more lilies still, another whole tray.

'Bank them up, just inside the door, on both sides of the porch, please,' said Mrs Sheridan. 'Don't you agree, Laura?'

'Oh, I *do* mother.'

In the drawing-room Meg, Jose and good little Hans had at last succeeded in moving the piano.

'Now, if we put this chesterfield against the wall and move everything out of the room except the chairs, don't you think?'

'Quite.'

'Hans, move these tables into the smoking-room, and bring a sweeper to take these marks off the carpet and—one moment, Hans—' Jose loved giving orders to the servants, and they loved obeying her. She always made them feel they were taking part in some drama. 'Tell mother and Miss Laura to come here at once.'

'Very good, Miss Jose.'

She turned to Meg. 'I want to hear what the piano sounds like, just in case I'm asked to sing this afternoon. Let's try over "This life is Weary."'

Pom! Ta-ta-ta *Tee*-ta! The piano burst out so passionately that Jose's face changed. She clasped her hands. She looked mournfully and enigmatically at her mother and Laura as they came in.

> This Life is *Wee*-ary,
> A Tear—a Sigh.
> A Love that *Chan*-ges,
> This Life is *Wee*-ary,
> A Tear—a Sigh.
> A Love that *Chan*-ges,
> And then . . . Good-bye!

But at the word 'Good-bye,' and although the piano sounded more desperate than ever, her face broke into a brilliant, dreadfully unsympathetic smile.

'Aren't I in good voice, mummy?' she beamed.

> This Life is *Wee*-ary,
> Hope comes to Die.
> A Dream—a *Wa*-kening.

But now Sadie interrupted them. 'What is it, Sadie?'

'If you please, m'm, cook says have you got the flags[4] for the sandwiches?'

'The flags for the sandwiches, Sadie?' echoed Mrs Sheridan dreamily. And the children knew by her face that she hadn't got them. 'Let me see.' And she said to Sadie firmly, 'Tell cook I'll let her have them in ten minutes.'

Sadie went.

'Now, Laura,' said her mother quickly. 'Come with me into the smoking-room. I've got the names[5] somewhere on the back of an envelope. You'll have to write them out for me. Meg, go upstairs this minute and take that wet thing off your head. Jose, run and finish dressing this instant. Do you hear me, children, or shall I have to tell your father when he comes home to-night? And—and, Jose, pacify cook if you do go into the kitchen, will you? I'm terrified of her this morning.'

The envelope was found at last behind the dining-room clock, though how it had got there Mrs Sheridan could not imagine.

'One of you children must have stolen it out of my bag, because I remember vividly—cream cheese and lemon-curd. Have you done that?'

'Yes.'

'Egg and—' Mrs Sheridan held the envelope away from her. 'It looks like mice. It can't be mice, can it?'

'Olive, pet,' said Laura, looking over her shoulder.

'Yes, of course, olive. What a horrible combination it sounds. Egg and olive.'

They were finished at last, and Laura took them off to the kitchen. She found Jose there pacifying the cook, who did not look at all terrifying.

'I have never seen such exquisite sandwiches,' said Jose's rapturous voice. 'How many kinds did you say there were, cook? Fifteen?'

'Fifteen, Miss Jose.'

'Well, cook, I congratulate you.'

Cook swept up crusts with the long sandwich knife and smiled broadly.

'Godber's has come,' announced Sadie, issuing out of the pantry. She had seen the man pass the window.

That meant the cream puffs had come. Godber's were famous for their cream puffs. Nobody ever thought of making them at home.

---

4. Little paper flags stuck in a plate of small tri-angular sandwiches indicating what is inside the sandwiches on each plate—an English custom adopted by the New Zealand middle class as a sign of gentility.

5. I.e., the names of the sandwich fillings to be written on each flag.

'Bring them in and put them on the table, my girl,' ordered cook.

Sadie brought them in and went back to the door. Of course Laura and Jose were far too grown-up to really care about such things. All the same, they couldn't help agreeing that the puffs looked very attractive. Very. Cook began arranging them, shaking off the extra icing sugar.

'Don't they carry one back to all one's parties?' said Laura.

'I suppose they do,' said practical Jose, who never liked to be carried back. 'They look beautifully light and feathery, I must say.'

'Have one each, my dears,' said cook in her comfortable voice. 'Yer ma won't know.'

Oh, impossible. Fancy cream puffs so soon after breakfast. The very idea made one shudder. All the same, two minutes later Jose and Laura were licking their fingers with that absorbed inward look that only comes from whipped cream.

'Let's go into the garden, out by the back way,' suggested Laura. 'I want to see how the men are getting on with the marquee. They're such awfully nice men.'

But the back door was blocked by cook, Sadie, Godber's man and Hans.

Something had happened.

'Tuk-tuk-tuk,' clucked cook like an agitated hen. Sadie had her hand clapped to her cheek as though she had toothache. Hans's face was screwed up in the effort to understand. Only Godber's man seemed to be enjoying himself; it was his story.

'What's the matter? What's happened?'

'There's been a horrible accident,' said cook. 'A man killed.'

'A man killed! Where? How? When?'

But Godber's man wasn't going to have his story snatched from under his very nose.

'Know those little cottages just below here, miss?' Know them? Of course, she knew them. 'Well, there's a young chap living there, name of Scott, a carter. His horse shied at a traction-engine, corner of Hawke Street this morning, and he was thrown out on the back of his head. Killed.'

'Dead!' Laura stared at Godber's man.

'Dead when they picked him up,' said Godber's man with relish. 'They were taking the body home as I come up here.' And he said to the cook, 'He's left a wife and five little ones.'

'Jose, come here.' Laura caught hold of her sister's sleeve and dragged her through the kitchen to the other side of the green baize door. There she paused and leaned against it. 'Jose!' she said, horrified, 'however are we going to stop everything?'

'Stop everything, Laura!' cried Jose in astonishment. 'What do you mean?'

'Stop the garden party, of course.' Why did Jose pretend?

But Jose was still more amazed. 'Stop the garden party? My dear Laura, don't be so absurd. Of course we can't do anything of the kind. Nobody expects us to. Don't be so extravagant.'

'But we can't possibly have a garden party with a man dead just outside the front gate.'

That really was extravagant, for the little cottages were in a lane to themselves at the very bottom of a steep rise that led up to the house. A broad road ran between. True, they were far too near. They were the greatest possible eyesore, and they had no right to be in that neighbourhood at all. They were little mean dwellings painted a chocolate brown. In the garden patches there was nothing but cabbage stalks, sick hens and tomato cans. The very smoke coming out of their chimneys was poverty-stricken. Little rags and shreds of smoke, so unlike the great silvery plumes that uncurled from the Sheridans' chimneys. Washerwomen lived in the lane and sweeps and a cobbler, and a man whose house-front was studded all over with minute bird-cages. Children swarmed. When the Sheridans were little they were forbidden to set foot there because of the revolting language and of what they might catch. But since they were grown up, Laura and Laurie on their prowls sometimes walked through. It was disgusting and sordid. They came out with a shudder. But still one must go everywhere; one must see everything. So through they went.

'And just think of what the band would sound like to that poor woman,' said Laura.

'Oh, Laura!' Jose began to be seriously annoyed. 'If you're going to stop a band playing every time some one has an accident, you'll lead a very strenuous life. I'm every bit as sorry about it as you. I feel just as sympathetic.' Her eyes hardened. She looked at her sister just as she used to when they were little and fighting together. 'You won't bring a drunken workman back to life by being sentimental,' she said softly.

'Drunk! Who said he was drunk?' Laura turned furiously on Jose. She said, just as they had used to say on those occasions, 'I'm going straight up to tell mother.'

'Do, dear,' cooed Jose.

'Mother, can I come into your room?' Laura turned the big glass door-knob.

'Of course, child. Why, what's the matter? What's given you such a colour?' And Mrs Sheridan turned round from her dressing-table. She was trying on a new hat.

'Mother, a man's been killed,' began Laura.

'Not in the garden?' interrupted her mother.

'No, no!'

'Oh, what a fright you gave me!' Mrs Sheridan sighed with relief, and took off the big hat and held it on her knees.

'But listen, mother,' said Laura. Breathless, half-choking, she told the dreadful story. 'Of course, we can't have our party, can we?' she pleaded. 'The band and everybody arriving. They'd hear us, mother; they're nearly neighbours!'

To Laura's astonishment her mother behaved just like Jose; it was harder to bear because she seemed amused. She refused to take Laura seriously.

'But, my dear child, use your common sense. It's only by accident we've heard of it. If some one had died there normally—and I can't understand how they keep alive in those poky little holes—we should still be having our party, shouldn't we?'

Laura had to say 'yes' to that, but she felt it was all wrong. She sat down on her mother's sofa and pinched the cushion frill.

'Mother, isn't it really terribly heartless of us?' she asked.

'Darling!' Mrs Sheridan got up and came over to her, carrying the hat. Before Laura could stop her she had popped it on. 'My child!' said her mother, 'the hat is yours. It's made for you. It's much too young for me. I have never seen you look such a picture. Look at yourself!' And she held up her hand-mirror.

'But, mother,' Laura began again. She couldn't look at herself; she turned aside.

This time Mrs Sheridan lost patience just as Jose had done.

'You are being very absurd, Laura,' she said coldly. 'People like that don't expect sacrifices from us. And it's not very sympathetic to spoil everybody's enjoyment as you're doing now.'

'I don't understand,' said Laura, and she walked quickly out of the room into her own bedroom. There, quite by chance, the first thing she saw was this charming girl in the mirror, in her black hat trimmed with gold daisies, and a long black velvet ribbon. Never had she imagined she could look like that. Is mother right? she thought. And now she hoped her mother was right. Am I being extravagant? Perhaps it was extravagant. Just for a moment she had another glimpse of that poor woman and those little children, and the body being carried into the house. But it all seemed blurred, unreal, like a picture in the newspaper. I'll remember it again after the party's over, she decided. And somehow that seemed quite the best plan . . .

Lunch was over by half past one. By half past two they were all ready for the fray. The green-coated band had arrived and was established in a corner of the tennis-court.

'My dear!' trilled Kitty Maitland, 'aren't they too like frogs for words? You ought to have arranged them round the pond with the conductor in the middle on a leaf.'

Laurie arrived and hailed them on his way to dress. At the sight of him Laura remembered the accident again. She wanted to tell him. If Laurie agreed with the others, then it was bound to be all right. And she followed him into the hall.

'Laurie!'

'Hallo!' He was half-way upstairs, but when he turned round and saw Laura he suddenly puffed out his cheeks and goggled his eyes at her. 'My word, Laura! You do look stunning,' said Laurie. 'What an absolutely topping hat!'

Laura said faintly 'Is it?' and smiled up at Laurie, and didn't tell him after all.

Soon after that people began coming in streams. The band struck up; the hired waiters ran from the house to the marquee. Wherever you looked there were couples strolling, bending to the flowers, greeting, moving on over the lawn. They were like bright birds that had alighted in the Sheridans' garden for this one afternoon, on their way to—where? Ah, what happiness it is to be with people who all are happy, to press hands, press cheeks, smile into eyes.

'Darling Laura, how well you look!'

'What a becoming hat, child!'

'Laura, you look quite Spanish. I've never seen you look so striking.'

And Laura, glowing, answered softly, 'Have you had tea? Won't you have an ice? The passion-fruit ices really are rather special.' She ran to her father and begged him. 'Daddy darling, can't the band have something to drink?'

And the perfect afternoon slowly ripened, slowly faded, slowly its petals closed.

'Never a more delightful garden party . . . ' 'The greatest success . . . ' 'Quite the most . . . '

Laura helped her mother with the goodbyes. They stood side by side in the porch till it was all over.

'All over, all over, thank heaven,' said Mrs Sheridan. 'Round up the others, Laura. Let's go and have some fresh coffee. I'm exhausted. Yes, it's been very successful. But oh, these parties, these parties! Why will you children insist on giving parties!' And they all of them sat down in the deserted marquee.

'Have a sandwich, daddy dear. I wrote the flag.'

'Thanks.' Mr Sheridan took a bite and the sandwich was gone. He took another. 'I suppose you didn't hear of a beastly accident that happened to-day?' he said.

'My dear,' said Mrs Sheridan, holding up her hand, 'we did. It nearly ruined the party. Laura insisted we should put it off.'

'Oh, mother!' Laura didn't want to be teased about it.

'It was a horrible affair all the same,' said Mr Sheridan. 'The chap was married too. Lived just below in the lane, and leaves a wife and half a dozen kiddies, so they say.'

An awkward little silence fell. Mrs Sheridan fidgeted with her cup. Really, it was very tactless of father . . .

Suddenly she looked up. There on the table were all those sandwiches, cakes, puffs, all un-eaten, all going to be wasted. She had one of her brilliant ideas.

'I know,' she said. 'Let's make up a basket. Let's send that poor creature some of this perfectly good food. At any rate, it will be the greatest treat for the children. Don't you agree? And she's sure to have neighbours calling in and so on. What a point to have it all ready prepared. Laura!' She jumped up. 'Get me the big basket out of the stairs cupboard.'

'But, mother, do you really think it's a good idea?' said Laura.

Again, how curious, she seemed to be different from them all. To take scraps from their party. Would the poor woman really like that?

'Of course! What's the matter with you today? An hour or two ago you were insisting on us being sympathetic, and now—'

Oh well! Laura ran for the basket. It was filled, it was heaped by her mother.

'Take it yourself, darling,' said she. 'Run down just as you are. No, wait, take the arum lilies too. People of that class are so impressed by arum lilies.'

'The stems will ruin her lace frock,' said practical Jose.

So they would. Just in time. 'Only the basket, then. And, Laura!'—her mother followed her out of the marquee—'don't on any account—'

'What mother?'

No, better not put such ideas into the child's head! 'Nothing! Run along.'

It was just growing dusky as Laura shut their garden gates. A big dog ran by like a shadow. The road gleamed white, and down below in the hollow the little cottages were in deep shade. How quiet it seemed after the afternoon. Here she was going down the hill to somewhere where a man lay dead, and she couldn't realize it. Why couldn't she? She stopped a minute. And it seemed to her that kisses, voices, tinkling spoons, laughter, the smell of crushed grass were somehow inside her. She had no room for anything else. How strange! She looked up at the pale sky, and all she thought was, 'Yes, it was the most successful.'

Now the broad road was crossed. The lane began, smoky and dark. Women in shawls and men's tweed caps hurried by. Men hung over the palings; the children played in the doorways. A low hum came from the mean little cottages. In some of them there was a flicker of light, and a shadow, crab-like, moved across the window. Laura bent her head and hurried on. She wished now she had put on a coat. How her frock shone! And the big hat with the velvet streamer—if only it was another hat! Were the people looking at her? They must be. It was a mistake to have come; she knew all along it was a mistake. Should she go back even now?

No, too late. This was the house. It must be. A dark knot of people stood outside. Beside the gate an old, old woman with a crutch sat in a chair, watching. She had her feet on a newspaper. The voices stopped as Laura drew near. The group parted. It was as though she was expected, as though they had known she was coming here.

Laura was terribly nervous. Tossing the velvet ribbon over her shoulder, she said to a woman standing by, 'Is this Mrs Scott's house?' and the woman, smiling queerly, said, 'It is, my lass.'

Oh, to be away from this! She actually said, 'Help me, God,' as she walked up the tiny path and knocked. To be away from those staring eyes, or to be covered up in anything, one of those women's shawls even. I'll just leave the basket and go, she decided. I shan't even wait for it to be emptied.

Then the door opened. A little woman in black showed in the gloom.

Laura said, 'Are you Mrs Scott?' But to her horror the woman answered, 'Walk in please, miss,' and she was shut in the passage.

'No,' said Laura, 'I don't want to come in. I only want to leave this basket. Mother sent—'

The little woman in the gloomy passage seemed not to have heard her. 'Step this way, please, miss,' she said in an oily voice, and Laura followed her.

She found herself in a wretched little low kitchen, lighted by a smoky lamp. There was a woman sitting before the fire.

'Em,' said the little creature who had let her in. 'Em! It's a young lady.' She turned to Laura. She said meaningly, 'I'm her sister, Miss. You'll excuse 'er, won't you?'

'Oh, but of course!' said Laura. 'Please, please don't disturb her. I—I only want to leave—'

But at that moment the woman at the fire turned round. Her face, puffed up, red, with swollen eyes and swollen lips, looked terrible. She seemed as though she couldn't understand why Laura was there. What did it mean? Why was this stranger standing in the kitchen with a basket? What was it all about? And the poor face puckered up again.

'All right, my dear,' said the other. 'I'll thenk the young lady.'

And again she began, 'You'll excuse her, miss, I'm sure,' and her face, swollen too, tried an oily smile.

Laura only wanted to get out, to get away. She was back in the passage. The door opened. She walked straight through into the bedroom where the dead man was lying.

'You'd like a look at 'im, wouldn't you?' said Em's sister, and she brushed past Laura over to the bed. 'Don't be afraid, my lass,'—and now her voice sounded fond and sly, and fondly she drew down the sheet—' 'e looks a picture. There's nothing to show. Come along, my dear.'

Laura came.

There lay a young man, fast asleep—sleeping so soundly, so deeply, that he was far, far away from them both. Oh, so remote, so peaceful. He was dreaming. Never wake him up again. His head was sunk in the pillow, his eyes were closed; they were blind under the closed eyelids. He was given up to his dream. What did garden parties and baskets and lace frocks matter to him? He was far from all those things. He was wonderful, beautiful. While they were laughing and while the band was playing, this marvel had come to the lane. Happy . . . happy . . . All is well, said that sleeping face. This is just as it should be. I am content.

But all the same you had to cry, and she couldn't go out of the room without saying something to him. Laura gave a loud childish sob.

'Forgive my hat,' she said.

And this time she didn't wait for Em's sister. She found her way out of the door, down the path, past all those dark people. At the corner of the lane she met Laurie.

He stepped out of the shadow. 'Is that you, Laura?'

'Yes.'

'Mother was getting anxious. Was it all right?'

'Yes, quite. Oh, Laurie!' She took his arm, she pressed up against him.

'I say, you're not crying, are you?' asked her brother.

Laura shook her head. She was.

Laurie put his arm round her shoulder. 'Don't cry,' he said in his warm, loving voice. 'Was it awful?'

'No,' sobbed Laura. 'It was simply marvellous. But, Laurie—' She stopped, she looked at her brother. 'Isn't life,' she stammered, 'isn't life—' But what life was she couldn't explain. No matter. He quite understood.

'Isn't it, darling?' said Laurie.

1921   1922

JEAN RHYS
1890–1979

Jean Rhys was born Ella Gwendolen Rees Williams on the small island of Dominica in the West Indies. Her father was a Welsh doctor; her mother, a Creole (that is, a white West Indian) descended from wealthy, slave-holding plantation owners. Rhys was educated at a convent school in Roseau, Dominica, before, at the age of seventeen, leaving Dominica to attend the Perse School in Cambridge, England; she returned to her birthplace only once, in 1936. Her feelings toward her Caribbean background and childhood were mixed: she deeply appreciated the rich sensations and cross-racial engagements of her tropical experience, yet she was haunted by the knowledge of her violent heritage and carried a heavy burden of historical guilt. As a West Indian she felt estranged from mainstream European culture and identified with the suffering of Afro-Caribbeans, yet as a white Creole she grew up feeling out of place amid the predominantly black population of Dominica.

After studying briefly at the Academy of Dramatic Art in London, Rhys worked as a traveling chorus girl, mannequin, film extra, and—during World War I—volunteer cook. In 1919 she left England to marry the first of three husbands, and for many years she lived abroad, mainly in Paris, where she began to write the stories of her first book, *The Left Bank: Sketches and Studies of Present-Day Bohemian Paris* (1927). It was published with an introduction by the established novelist and poet Ford Madox Ford, who was for a time her lover. Ford grasped the link between her vulnerability as a person and her strength as a writer; he perceived her "terrifying insight . . . and passion for stating the case of the underdog." Rhys declared, "I have only ever written about myself," and indeed much of her writing is semiautobiographical. Her fiction frequently depicts single, economically challenged women, rootless outsiders living in bohemian London or Paris. Her early "sketches" were followed by her first novel, *Postures* (1928, reprinted as *Quartet* in 1969), in part an account of her affair with Ford; *After Leaving Mr. Mackenzie* (1930), about sexual betrayal; *Voyage in the Dark*

(1934), an account of a nineteen-year-old chorus girl in London who has come from Dominica; and *Good Morning, Midnight* (1939), another first-person narrative of a lonely drifter, this time in Paris.

She published nothing more for many years, dropping out of sight and often living in poverty, until, following the enthusiastic reception of a radio adaptation of *Good Morning, Midnight* in 1957, she began to work in earnest on her masterpiece, *Wide Sargasso Sea* (1966). In this novel, set in Jamaica and Dominica in the 1830s and 1840s, Rhys returns to her Caribbean childhood and, in a brilliant act of imaginative sympathy, creates a West Indian prehistory for the first Mrs. Rochester, the madwoman in the attic of Charlotte Brontë's *Jane Eyre*. Altogether Rhys worked on the novel for twenty-one years, amid bouts of depression, loneliness, and alcoholism, but its immediate acclaim gave her the recognition she had so long been denied. She continued to publish works of fiction and autobiography and in the year before her death received the Commander of the Order of the British Empire.

During the long period when she was writing *Wide Sargasso Sea,* Rhys produced only two published stories, both of which draw like the novel on her Caribbean youth. In "The Day They Burned the Books," set in the West Indies, a white girl who only partly understands the painful entanglements of class, race, and cultural prejudice tells how a lower-class Englishman has accumulated a trove of books he values for their cultural prestige, while his mulatto wife, embittered by her husband's racism, comes to despise them as emblems of British imperial oppression. "Let Them Call It Jazz" also has a first-person female narrator, but this time she is a West Indian mulatto, who speaks in West Indian English of her struggle against racial and class barriers after immigrating to London, an outsider in the metropolitan heart of the empire, ultimately jailed—as was Rhys for a few days after assaulting a neighbor—in Royal Holloway Prison. The shattering of a stained-glass window in this story—like the book burning in the first story and the house burning in *Wide Sargasso Sea*—represents an eruption of Afro-Caribbean rage in response to the circumscriptions and deceptions of white racism.

Whether working in Standard or West Indian English, Rhys is one of the great prose stylists of the twentieth century, her language spare yet lyrical, her sentences exactingly written and rewritten to suggest the most in the fewest possible words. Her writing is almost painfully alert to sensory detail, sensitive to the terrible fears and frustrated longings of marginalized people, and fierce in its unmasking of the social and psychic consequences of racial and gender oppression.

The Day They Burned the Books

My friend Eddie was a small, thin boy. You could see the blue veins in his wrists and temples. People said that he had consumption[1] and wasn't long for this world. I loved, but sometimes despised him.

His father, Mr Sawyer, was a strange man. Nobody could make out what he was doing in our part of the world at all. He was not a planter or a doctor or a lawyer or a banker. He didn't keep a store. He wasn't a schoolmaster or a government official. He wasn't—that was the point—a gentleman. We had several resident romantics who had fallen in love with the moon on the Caribees[2]—they were all gentlemen and quite unlike Mr Sawyer who hadn't an 'h' in his composition.[3] Besides, he detested the moon and everything else about the Caribbean and he didn't mind telling you so.

---

1. Wasting of the body associated with tuberculosis.
2. Or Caribbees: old term for the group of islands in the southeastern West Indies, now called the Lesser Antilles.
3. His pronunciation marks him as lower-class.

He was agent for a small steamship line which in those days linked up Venezuela and Trinidad[4] with the smaller islands, but he couldn't make much out of that. He must have a private income, people decided, but they never decided why he had chosen to settle in a place he didn't like and to marry a coloured woman. Though a decent, respectable, nicely educated coloured woman, mind you.

Mrs Sawyer must have been very pretty once but, what with one thing and another, that was in days gone by.

When Mr Sawyer was drunk—this often happened—he used to be very rude to her. She never answered him.

'Look at the nigger showing off,' he would say; and she would smile as if she knew she ought to see the joke but couldn't. 'You damned, long-eyed, gloomy half-caste,[5] you don't smell right,' he would say; and she never answered, not even to whisper, 'You don't smell right to me, either.'

The story went that once they had ventured to give a dinner party and that when the servant, Mildred, was bringing in coffee, he had pulled Mrs Sawyer's hair. 'Not a wig, you see,' he bawled. Even then, if you can believe it, Mrs Sawyer had laughed and tried to pretend that it was all part of the joke, this mysterious, obscure, sacred English joke.

But Mildred told the other servants in the town that her eyes had gone wicked, like a soucriant's[6] eyes, and that afterwards she had picked up some of the hair he pulled out and put it in an envelope, and that Mr Sawyer ought to look out (hair is obeah[7] as well as hands).

Of course, Mrs Sawyer had her compensations. They lived in a very pleasant house in Hill Street. The garden was large and they had a fine mango tree, which bore prolifically. The fruit was small, round, very sweet and juicy—a lovely, red-and-yellow colour when it was ripe. Perhaps it was one of the compensations, I used to think.

Mr Sawyer built a room on to the back of this house. It was unpainted inside and the wood smelt very sweet. Bookshelves lined the walls. Every time the Royal Mail steamer[8] came in it brought a package for him, and gradually the empty shelves filled.

Once I went there with Eddie to borrow *The Arabian Nights*.[9] That was on a Saturday afternoon, one of those hot, still afternoons when you felt that everything had gone to sleep, even the water in the gutters. But Mrs Sawyer was not asleep. She put her head in at the door and looked at us, and I knew that she hated the room and hated the books.

It was Eddie with the pale blue eyes and straw-coloured hair—the living image of his father, though often as silent as his mother—who first infected me with doubts about 'home', meaning England. He would be so quiet when others who had never seen it—none of us had ever seen it—were talking about its delights, gesticulating freely as we talked—London, the beautiful, rosy-cheeked ladies, the theatres, the shops, the fog, the blazing coal fires in winter, the exotic food (whitebait[1] eaten to the sound of violins), strawberries and

---

4. Formerly British, Caribbean island off north-east Venezuela.
5. Offensive term for a person of mixed racial descent.
6. Female vampire, in Caribbean legend.
7. A charm or fetish used in Afro-Caribbean witchcraft or sorcery.
8. Ship, owned by the Royal Mail Steam Packet

Company, that ferried mail from London to the West Indies beginning in 1841.
9. Also called *The Thousand and One Nights*, a collection of old stories, largely Persian, Arabian, and Indian in origin.
1. Young of a small fish, such as herring, considered a delicacy when cooked whole.

cream—the word 'strawberries' always spoken with a guttural and throaty sound which we imagined to be the proper English pronunciation.

'I don't like strawberries,' Eddie said on one occasion.

'You *don't like* strawberries?'

'No, and I don't like daffodils either. Dad's always going on about them. He says they lick the flowers here into a cocked hat[2] and I bet that's a lie.'

We were all too shocked to say, 'You don't know a thing about it.' We were so shocked that nobody spoke to him for the rest of the day. But I for one admired him. I also was tired of learning and reciting poems in praise of daffodils, and my relations with the few 'real' English boys and girls I had met were awkward. I had discovered that if I called myself English they would snub me haughtily: 'You're not English; you're a horrid colonial.' 'Well, I don't much want to be English,' I would say. 'It's much more fun to be French or Spanish or something like that—and, as a matter of fact, I am a bit.' Then I was too killingly funny, quite ridiculous. Not only a horrid colonial, but also ridiculous. Heads I win, tails you lose—that was the English. I had thought about all this, and thought hard, but I had never dared to tell anybody what I thought and I realized that Eddie had been very bold.

But he was bold, and stronger than you would think. For one thing, he never felt the heat; some coldness in his fair skin resisted it. He didn't burn red or brown, he didn't freckle much.

Hot days seemed to make him feel especially energetic. 'Now we'll run twice round the lawn and then you can pretend you're dying of thirst in the desert and that I'm an Arab chieftain bringing you water.'

'You must drink slowly,' he would say, 'for if you're very thirsty and you drink quickly you die.'

So I learnt the voluptuousness of drinking slowly when you are very thirsty— small mouthful by small mouthful, until the glass of pink, iced Coca-Cola was empty.

Just after my twelfth birthday Mr Sawyer died suddenly, and as Eddie's special friend I went to the funeral, wearing a new white dress. My straight hair was damped with sugar and water the night before and plaited into tight little plaits, so that it should be fluffy for the occasion.

When it was all over everybody said how nice Mrs Sawyer had looked, walking like a queen behind the coffin and crying her eyeballs out at the right moment, and wasn't Eddie a funny boy? He hadn't cried at all.

After this Eddie and I took possession of the room with the books. No one else ever entered it, except Mildred to sweep and dust in the mornings, and gradually the ghost of Mr Sawyer pulling Mrs Sawyer's hair faded, though this took a little time. The blinds were always halfway down and going in out of the sun was like stepping into a pool of brown-green water. It was empty except for the bookshelves, a desk with a green baize[3] top and a wicker rocking-chair.

'My room,' Eddie called it. 'My books,' he would say, 'my books.'

I don't know how long this lasted. I don't know whether it was weeks after Mr Sawyer's death or months after, that I see myself and Eddie in the room. But there we are and there, unexpectedly, are Mrs Sawyer and Mildred. Mrs Sawyer's mouth tight, her eyes pleased. She is pulling all the books out of the

---

2. From *knocked into a cocked hat*: make them look terrible by comparison. Daffodils are common in English poetry, but do not grow in the West Indies.

3. Feltlike fabric.

shelves and piling them into two heaps. The big, fat glossy ones—the good-looking ones, Mildred explains in a whisper—lie in one heap. The *Encyclopaedia Britannica, British Flowers, Birds and Beasts,* various histories, books with maps, Froude's *English in the West Indies*[4] and so on—they are going to be sold. The unimportant books, with paper covers or damaged covers or torn pages, lie in another heap. They are going to be burnt—yes, burnt.

Mildred's expression was extraordinary as she said that—half hugely delighted, half shocked, even frightened. And as for Mrs Sawyer—well, I knew bad temper (I had often seen it), I knew rage, but this was hate. I recognized the difference at once and stared at her curiously. I edged closer to her so that I could see the titles of the books she was handling.

It was the poetry shelf. *Poems,* Lord Byron, *Poetical Works,* Milton, and so on. Vlung, vlung, vlung—all thrown into the heap that were to be sold. But a book by Christina Rossetti, though also bound in leather, went into the heap that was to be burnt, and by a flicker in Mrs Sawyer's eyes I knew that worse than men who wrote books were women who wrote books—infinitely worse. Men could be mercifully shot; women must be tortured.

Mrs Sawyer did not seem to notice that we were there, but she was breathing free and easy and her hands had got the rhythm of tearing and pitching. She looked beautiful, too—beautiful as the sky outside which was a very dark blue, or the mango tree, long sprays of brown and gold.

When Eddie said 'no', she did not even glance at him.

'No,' he said again in a high voice. 'Not that one. I was reading that one.'

She laughed and he rushed at her, his eyes starting out of his head, shrieking, 'Now I've got to hate you too. Now I hate you too.'

He snatched the book out of her hand and gave her a violent push. She fell into the rocking-chair.

Well, I wasn't going to be left out of all this, so I grabbed a book from the condemned pile and dived under Mildred's outstretched arm.

Then we were both in the garden. We ran along the path, bordered with crotons.[5] We pelted down the path though they did not follow us and we could hear Mildred laughing—kyah, kyah, kyah, kyah. As I ran I put the book I had taken into the loose front of my brown holland dress. It felt warm and alive.

When we got into the street we walked sedately, for we feared the black children's ridicule. I felt very happy, because I had saved this book and it was my book and I would read it from the beginning to the triumphant words 'The End'. But I was uneasy when I thought of Mrs Sawyer.

'What will she do?' I said.

'Nothing,' Eddie said. 'Not to me.'

He was white as a ghost in his sailor suit, a blue-white even in the setting sun, and his father's sneer was clamped on his face.

'But she'll tell your mother all sorts of lies about you,' he said. 'She's an awful liar. She can't make up a story to save her life, but she makes up lies about people all right.'

'My mother won't take any notice of her,' I said. Though I was not at all sure.

'Why not? Because she's . . . because she isn't white?'

Well, I knew the answer to that one. Whenever the subject was brought

4. Published in 1888 by the English historian 5. Tropical plants.
James Anthony Froude (1818–1894).

up—people's relations and whether they had a drop of coloured blood or whether they hadn't—my father would grow impatient and interrupt. 'Who's white?' he would say. 'Damned few.'

So I said, 'Who's white? Damned few.'

'You can go to the devil,' Eddie said. 'She's prettier than your mother. When she's asleep her mouth smiles and she has your curling eyelashes and quantities and quantities and *quantities* of hair.'

'Yes,' I said truthfully. 'She's prettier than my mother.'

It was a red sunset that evening, a huge, sad, frightening sunset.

'Look, let's go back,' I said. 'If you're sure she won't be vexed with you, let's go back. It'll be dark soon.'

At his gate he asked me not to go. 'Don't go yet, don't go yet.'

We sat under the mango tree and I was holding his hand when he began to cry. Drops fell on my hand like the water from the dripstone in the filter[6] in our yard. Then I began to cry too and when I felt my own tears on my hand I thought, 'Now perhaps we're married.'

'Yes, certainly, now we're married,' I thought. But I didn't say anything. I didn't say a thing until I was sure he had stopped. Then I asked, 'What's your book?'

'It's *Kim*,'[7] he said. 'But it got torn. It starts at page twenty now. What's the one you took?'

'I don't know, it's too dark to see,' I said.

When I got home I rushed into my bedroom and locked the door because I knew that this book was the most important thing that had ever happened to me and I did not want anybody to be there when I looked at it.

But I was very disappointed, because it was in French and seemed dull. *Fort Comme La Mort*,[8] it was called. . . .

1960

Let Them Call It Jazz

One bright Sunday morning in July I have trouble with my Notting Hill[1] landlord because he ask for a month's rent in advance. He tell me this after I live there since winter, settling up every week without fail. I have no job at the time, and if I give the money he want there's not much left. So I refuse. The man drunk already at that early hour, and he abuse me—all talk, he can't frighten me. But his wife is a bad one—now she walk in my room and say she must have cash. When I tell her no, she give my suitcase one kick and it burst open. My best dress fall out, then she laugh and give another kick. She say month in advance is usual, and if I can't pay find somewhere else.

Don't talk to me about London. Plenty people there have heart like stone. Any complaint—the answer is 'prove it'. But if nobody see and bear witness for me, how to prove anything? So I pack up and leave. I think better not have dealings with that woman. She too cunning, and Satan don't lie worse.

---

6. Dripstone is a sandstone used as a filter to clean water for household use.
7. Novel (1901) by the English writer Rudyard Kipling (1865–1936), about an Irish orphan boy growing up in India.

8. *Strong as Death*, 1889 novel by the French writer Guy de Maupassant (1850–1893).
1. Area of London, then slums with Afro-Caribbean immigrants.

I walk about till a place nearby is open where I can have coffee and a sandwich. There I start talking to a man at my table. He talk to me already, I know him, but I don't know his name. After a while he ask, 'What's the matter? Anything wrong?' and when I tell him my trouble he say I can use an empty flat he own till I have time to look around.

This man is not at all like most English people. He see very quick, and he decide very quick. English people take long time to decide—you three-quarter dead before they make up their mind about you. Too besides, he speak very matter of fact, as if it's nothing. He speak as if he realize well what it is to live like I do—that's why I accept and go.

He tell me somebody occupy the flat till last week, so I find everything all right, and he tell me how to get there—three-quarters of an hour from Victoria Station,[2] up a steep hill, turn left, and I can't mistake the house. He give me the keys and an envelope with a telephone number on the back. Underneath is written 'After 6 P.M. ask for Mr Sims'.

In the train that evening I think myself lucky, for to walk about London on a Sunday with nowhere to go—that take the heart out of you.

I find the place and the bedroom of the downstairs flat is nicely furnished—two looking glass, wardrobe, chest of drawers, sheets, everything. It smell of jasmine scent, but it smell strong of damp too.

I open the door opposite and there's a table, a couple chairs, a gas stove and a cupboard, but this room so big it look empty. When I pull the blind up I notice the paper peeling off and mushrooms growing on the walls—you never see such a thing.

The bathroom the same, all the taps rusty. I leave the two other rooms and make up the bed. Then I listen, but I can't hear one sound. Nobody come in, nobody go out of that house. I lie awake for a long time, then I decide not to stay and in the morning I start to get ready quickly before I change my mind. I want to wear my best dress, but it's a funny thing—when I take up that dress and remember how my landlady kick it I cry. I cry and I can't stop. When I stop I feel tired to my bones, tired like old woman. I don't want to move again—I have to force myself. But in the end I get out in the passage and there's a postcard for me. 'Stay as long as you like. I'll be seeing you soon—Friday probably. Not to worry.' It isn't signed, but I don't feel so sad and I think, 'All right, I wait here till he come. Perhaps he know of a job for me.'

Nobody else live in the house but a couple on the top floor—quiet people and they don't trouble me. I have no word to say against them.

First time I meet the lady she's opening the front door and she give me a very inquisitive look. But next time she smile a bit and I smile back—once she talk to me. She tell me the house very old, hundred and fifty year old, and she had her husband live there since long time. 'Valuable property,' she says, 'it could have been saved, but nothing done of course.' Then she tells me that as to the present owner—if he is the owner—well he have to deal with local authorities and she believe they make difficulties. 'These people are determined to pull down all the lovely old houses—it's shameful.'

So I agree that many things shameful. But what to do? What to do? I say it have an elegant shape, it make the other houses in the street look cheap trash, and she seem pleased. That's true too. The house sad and out of place, especially at night. But it have style. The second floor shut up, and as for my flat, I go in the two empty rooms once, but never again.

2. Train station in London.

Underneath was the cellar, full of old boards and broken-up furniture—I see a big rat there one day. It was no place to be alone in I tell you, and I get the habit of buying a bottle of wine most evenings, for I don't like whisky and the rum here no good. It don't even *taste* like rum. You wonder what they do to it.

After I drink a glass or two I can sing and when I sing all the misery goes from my heart. Sometimes I make up songs but next morning I forget them, so other times I sing the old ones like 'Tantalizin' ' or 'Don't Trouble Me Now.'

I think I go but I don't go. Instead I wait for the evening and the wine and that's all. Everywhere else I live—well, it doesn't matter to me, but this house is different—empty and no noise and full of shadows, so that sometimes you ask yourself what make all those shadows in an empty room.

I eat in the kitchen, then I clean up everything and have a bath for coolness. Afterwards I lean my elbows on the windowsill and look at the garden. Red and blue flowers mix up with the weeds and there are five-six apple trees. But the fruit drop and lie in the grass, so sour nobody want it. At the back, near the wall, is a bigger tree—this garden certainly take up a lot of room, perhaps that's why they want to pull the place down.

Not much rain all the summer, but not much sunshine either. More of a glare. The grass get brown and dry, the weeds grow tall, the leaves on the trees hang down. Only the red flowers—the poppies—stand up to that light, everything else look weary.

I don't trouble about money, but what with wine and shillings for the slot-meters,[3] it go quickly; so I don't waste much on food. In the evening I walk outside—not by the apple trees but near the street—it's not so lonely.

There's no wall here and I can see the woman next door looking at me over the hedge. At first I say good evening, but she turn away her head, so afterwards I don't speak. A man is often with her, he wear a straw hat with a black ribbon and goldrim spectacles. His suit hang on him like it's too big. He's the husband it seems and he stare at me worse than his wife—he stare as if I'm wild animal let loose. Once I laugh in his face because why these people have to be like that? I don't bother them. In the end I get that I don't even give them one single glance. I have plenty other things to worry about.

To show you how I felt. I don't remember exactly. But I believe it's the second Saturday after I come that when I'm at the window just before, I go for my wine I feel somebody's hand on my shoulder and it's Mr Sims. He must walk very quiet because I don't know a thing till he touch me.

He says hullo, then he tells me I've got terrible thin, do I ever eat. I say of course I eat but he goes on that it doesn't suit me at all to be so thin and he'll buy some food in the village. (That's the way he talk. There's no village here. You don't get away from London so quick.)

It don't seem to me he look very well himself, but I just say bring a drink instead, as I am not hungry.

He come back with three bottles—vermouth, gin and red wine. Then he ask if the little devil who was here last smash all the glasses and I tell him she smash some, I find the pieces. But not all. 'You fight with her, eh?'

He laugh, and he don't answer. He pour out the drinks then he says, 'Now, you eat up those sandwiches.'

Some men when they are there you don't worry so much. These sort of men you do all they tell you blindfold because they can take the trouble from your

---

3. Coin-fed meters for gas and electricity.

heart and make you think you're safe. It's nothing they say or do. It's a feeling they can give you. So I don't talk with him seriously—I don't want to spoil that evening. But I ask about the house and why it's so empty and he says:

'Has the old trout upstairs been gossiping?'

I tell him, 'She suppose they make difficulties for you.'

'It was a damn bad buy,' he says and talks about selling the lease or something. I don't listen much.

We were standing by the window then and the sun low. No more glare. He puts his hand over my eyes. 'Too big—much too big for your face,' he says and kisses me like you kiss a baby. When he takes his hand away I see he's looking out at the garden and he says this—'It gets you. My God it does.'

I know very well it's not me he means, so I ask him, 'Why sell it then? If you like it, keep it.'

'Sell what?' he says. 'I'm not talking about this damned house.'

I ask what he's talking about. 'Money,' he says. 'Money. That's what I'm talking about. Ways of making it.'

'I don't think so much of money. It don't like me and what do I care?' I was joking, but he turns around, his face quite pale and he tells me I'm a fool. He tells me I'll get pushed around all my life and die like a dog, only worse because they'd finish off a dog, but they'll let me live till I'm a caricature of myself. That's what he say, 'Caricature of yourself.' He say I'll curse the day I was born and everything and everybody in this bloody world before I'm done.

I tell him, 'No I'll never feel like that,' and he smiles, if you can call it a smile, and says he's glad I'm content with my lot. 'I'm disappointed in you, Selina. I thought you had more spirit.'

'If I contented that's all right,' I answer him. 'I don't see very many looking contented over here.' We're standing staring at each other when the doorbell rings. 'That's a friend of mine,' he says. 'I'll let him in.'

As to the friend, he's all dressed up in stripe pants and a black jacket and he's carrying a brief-case. Very ordinary looking but with a soft kind of voice.

'Maurice, this is Selina Davis,' says Mr Sims, and Maurice smiles very kind but it don't mean much, then he looks at his watch and says they ought to be getting along.

At the door Mr Sims tells me he'll see me next week and I answer straight out, 'I won't be here next week because I want a job and I won't get one in this place.'

'Just what I'm going to talk about. Give it a week longer, Selina.'

I say, 'Perhaps I stay a few more days. Then I go. Perhaps I go before.'

'Oh no you won't go,' he says.

They walk to the gates quickly and drive off in a yellow car. Then I feel eyes on me and it's the woman and her husband in the next door garden watching. The man make some remark and she look at me so hateful, so hating I shut the front door quick.

I don't want more wine. I want to go to bed early because I must think. I must think about money. It's true I don't care for it. Even when somebody steal my savings—this happen soon after I get to the Notting Hill house—I forget it soon. About thirty pounds they steal. I keep it roll up in a pair of stockings, but I go to the drawer one day, and no money. In the end I have to tell the police. They ask me exact sum and I say I don't count it lately, about thirty pounds. 'You don't know how much?' they say. 'When did you count it last? Do you remember? Was it before you move or after?'

I get confuse, and I keep saying, 'I don't remember,' though I remember well I see it two days before. They don't believe me and when a policeman come to the house I hear the landlady tell him, 'She certainly had no money when she came here. She wasn't able to pay a month's rent in advance for her room though it's a rule in this house.' 'These people terrible liars,' she say and I think 'it's you a terrible liar, because when I come you tell me weekly or monthly as you like.' It's from that time she don't speak to me and perhaps it's she take it. All I know is I never see one penny of my savings again, all I know is they pretend I never have any, but as it's gone, no use to cry about it. Then my mind goes to my father, for my father is a white man and I think a lot about him. If I could see him only once, for I too small to remember when he was there. My mother is fair coloured woman, fairer than I am they say, and she don't stay long with me either. She have a chance to go to Venezuela when I three-four year old and she never come back. She send money instead. It's my grandmother take care of me. She's quite dark and what we call 'country-cookie' but she's the best I know.

She save up all the money my mother send, she don't keep one penny for herself—that's how I get to England. I was a bit late in going to school regular, getting on for twelve years, but I can sew very beautiful, excellent—so I think I get a good job—in London perhaps.

However, here they tell me all this fine handsewing take too long. Waste of time—too slow. They want somebody to work quick and to hell with the small stitches. Altogether it don't look so good for me, I must say, and I wish I could see my father. I have his name—Davis. But my grandmother tell me, 'Every word that comes out of that man's mouth a damn lie. He is certainly first class liar, though no class otherwise.' So perhaps I have not even his real name.

Last thing I see before I put the light out is the postcard on the dressing table. 'Not to worry.'

Not to worry! Next day is Sunday, and it's on the Monday the people next door complain about me to the police. That evening the woman is by the hedge, and when I pass her she says in very sweet quiet voice, '*Must* you stay? *Can't* you go?' I don't answer. I walk out in the street to get rid of her. But she run inside her house to the window, she can still see me. Then I start to sing, so she can understand I'm not afraid of her. The husband call out: 'If you don't stop that noise I'll send for the police.' I answer them quite short. I say, 'You go to hell and take your wife with you.' And I sing louder.

The police come pretty quick—two of them. Maybe they just round the corner. All I can say about police, and how they behave is I think it all depends who they dealing with. Of my own free will I don't want to mix up with police. No.

One man says, you can't cause this disturbance here. But the other asks a lot of questions. What is my name? Am I tenant of a flat in No. 17? How long have I lived there? Last address and so on. I get vexed the way he speak and I tell him, 'I come here because somebody steal my savings. Why you don't look for my money instead of bawling at me? I work hard for my money. All-you don't do one single thing to find it.'

'What's she talking about?' the first one says, and the other one tells me, 'You can't make that noise here. Get along home. You've been drinking.'

I see that woman looking at me and smiling, and other people at their windows, and I'm so angry I bawl at them too. I say, 'I have absolute and perfect right to be in the street same as anybody else, and I have absolute and perfect right to ask the police why they don't even look for my money when it disappear. It's because a dam' English thief take it you don't look,' I say. The end of all this is that I have to go before a magistrate, and he fine me five pounds for drunk and disorderly, and he give me two weeks to pay.

When I get back from the court I walk up and down the kitchen, up and down, waiting for six o'clock because I have no five pounds left, and I don't know what to do. I telephone at six and a woman answers me very short and sharp, then Mr Sims comes along and he don't sound too pleased either when I tell him what happen. 'Oh Lord!' he says, and I say I'm sorry. 'Well don't panic,' he says, 'I'll pay the fine. But look, I don't think. . . .' Then he breaks off and talk to some other person in the room. He goes on, 'Perhaps better not stay at No. 17. I think I can arrange something else. I'll call for you Wednesday—Saturday latest. Now behave till then.' And he hang up before I can answer that I don't want to wait till Wednesday, much less Saturday. I want to get out of that house double quick and with no delay. First I think I ring back, then I think better now as he sound so vex.

I get ready, but Wednesday he don't come, and Saturday he don't come. All the week I stay in the flat. Only once I go out and arrange for bread, milk and eggs to be left at the door, and seems to me I meet up with a lot of policemen. They don't look at me, but they see me all right. I don't want to drink—I'm all the time listening, listening and thinking, how can I leave before I know if my fine is paid? I tell myself the police let me know, that's certain. But I don't trust them. What they care? The answer is Nothing. Nobody care. One afternoon I knock at the old lady's flat upstairs, because I get the idea she give me good advice. I can hear her moving about and talking, but she don't answer and I never try again.

Nearly two weeks pass like that, then I telephone. It's the woman speaking and she say, 'Mr Sims is not in London at present.' I ask, 'When will he be back—it's urgent,' and she hang up. I'm not surprised. Not at all. I knew that would happen. All the same I feel heavy like lead. Near the phone box is a chemist's shop, so I ask him for something to make me sleep, the day is bad enough, but to lie awake all night—Ah no! He gives me a little bottle marked 'One or two tablets only' and I take three when I go to bed because more and more I think that sleeping is better than no matter what else. However, I lie there, eyes wide open as usual, so I take three more. Next thing I know the room is full of sunlight, so it must be late afternoon, but the lamp is still on. My head turn around and I can't think well at all. At first I ask myself how I get to the place. Then it comes to me, but in pictures—like the landlady kicking my dress, and when I take my ticket at Victoria Station, and Mr Sims telling me to eat the sandwiches, but I can't remember everything clear, and I feel very giddy and sick. I take in the milk and eggs at the door, go in the kitchen, and try to eat but the food hard to swallow.

It's when I'm putting the things away that I see the bottles—pushed back on the lowest shelf in the cupboard.

There's a lot of drink left, and I'm glad I tell you. Because I can't bear the way I feel. Not any more. I mix a gin and vermouth and I drink it quick, then I mix another and drink it slow by the window. The garden looks different, like I never see it before. I know quite well what I must do, but it's late now—tomorrow I have one more drink, of wine this time, and then a song comes in my head, I sing it and I dance it, and more I sing, more I am sure this is the best tune that has ever come to me in all my life.

The sunset light from the window is gold colour. My shoes sound loud on the boards. So I take them off, my stockings too and go on dancing but the room feel shut in, I can't breathe, and I go outside still singing. Maybe I dance a bit too. I forget all about that woman till I hear her saying, 'Henry, look at this.' I turn around and I see her at the window. 'Oh yes, I wanted to speak with you,' I say, 'Why bring the police and get me in bad trouble? Tell me that.'

'And you tell me what you're doing here at all,' she says. 'This is a respectable neighbourhood.'

Then the man come along. 'Now young woman, take yourself off. You ought to be ashamed of this behaviour.'

'It's disgraceful,' he says, talking to his wife, but loud so I can hear, and she speaks loud too—for once. 'At least the other tarts that crook installed here were *white* girls,' she says.

'You a dam' fouti[4] liar,' I say. 'Plenty of those girls in your country already. Numberless as the sands on the shore. You don't need me for that.'

'You're not a howling success at it certainly.' Her voice sweet sugar again. 'And you won't be seeing much more of your friend Mr Sims. He's in trouble too. Try somewhere else. Find somebody else. If you can, of course.' When she say that my arm moves of itself. I pick up a stone and bam! through the window. Not the one they are standing at but the next, which is of coloured glass, green and purple and yellow.

I never see a woman look so surprise. Her mouth fall open she so full of surprise. I start to laugh, louder and louder—I laugh like my grandmother, with my hands on my hips and my head back. (When she laugh like that you can hear her to the end of our street.) At last I say, 'Well, I'm sorry. An accident. I get it fixed tomorrow early.' 'That glass is irreplaceable,' the man says. 'Irreplaceable.' 'Good thing,' I say, 'those colours look like they sea-sick to me. I buy you a better windowglass.'

He shake his fist at me. 'You won't be let off with a fine this time,' he says. Then they draw the curtains, I call out at them. 'You run away. Always you run away. Ever since I come here you hunt me down because I don't answer back. It's you shameless.' I try to sing 'Don't Trouble Me Now'.

> *Don't trouble me now*
> *You without honour*
> *Don't walk in my footstep*
> *You without shame.*

But my voice don't sound right, so I get back indoors and drink one more glass of wine—still wanting to laugh, and still thinking of my grandmother for that is one of her songs.

It's about a man whose doudou give him the go-by[5] when she find somebody rich and he sail away to Panama. Plenty people die there of fever when they make that Panama canal so long ago. But he don't die. He come back with dollars and the girl meet him on the jetty, all dressed up and smiling. Then he sing to her, 'You without honour, you without shame'. It sound good in Martinique patois too: *'Sans honte'.*[6]

Afterwards I ask myself, 'Why I do that? It's not like me. But if they treat

---

4. West Indian expletive.
5. Intentionally snub by leaving behind. "Dou-

dou": darling (French Creole).
6. Without shame (French Creole).

you wrong over and over again the hour strike when you burst out that's what.'

Too besides, Mr Sims can't tell me now I have no spirit I don't care, I sleep quickly and I'm glad I break the woman's ugly window. But as to my own song it go *right* away and it never come back. A pity.

Next morning the doorbell ringing wake me up. The people upstairs don't come down, and the bell keeps on like fury self. So I go to look, and there is a policeman and a policewoman outside. As soon as I open the door the woman put her foot in it. She wear sandals and thick stockings and I never see a foot so big or so bad. It look like it want to mash up the whole world. Then she come in after the foot, and her face not so pretty either. The policeman tell me my fine is not paid and people make serious complaints about me, so they're taking me back to the magistrate. He show me a paper and I look at it, but I don't read it. The woman push me in the bedroom, and tell me to get dress quickly, but I just stare at her, because I think perhaps I wake up soon. Then I ask her what I must wear. She say she suppose I had some clothes on yesterday. Or not? 'What's it matter, wear anything,' she says. But I find clean underclothes and stockings and my shoes with high heels and I comb my hair. I start to file my nails, because I think they too long for magistrate's court but she get angry. 'Are you coming quietly or aren't you?' she says. So I go with them and we get in a car outside.

I wait for a long time in a room full of policemen. They come in, they go out, they telephone, they talk in low voices. Then it's my turn, and first thing I notice in the court room is a man with frowning black eyebrows. He sit below the magistrate, he dressed in black and he so handsome I can't take my eyes off him. When he see that he frowns worse than before.

First comes a policeman to testify I cause disturbance, and then comes the old gentleman from next door. He repeat that bit about nothing but the truth so help me God. Then he says I make dreadful noise at night and use abominable language, and dance in obscene fashion. He says when they try to shut the curtains because his wife so terrify of me, I throw stones and break a valuable stain-glass window. He say his wife get serious injury if she'd been hit, and as it is she in terrible nervous condition and the doctor is with her. I think, 'Believe me, if I aim at your wife I hit your wife—that's certain.' 'There was no provocation,' he says. 'None at all.' Then another lady from across the street says this is true. She heard no provocation whatsoever, and she swear that they shut the curtains but I go on insulting them and using filthy language and she saw all this and heard it.

The magistrate is a little gentleman with a quiet voice, but I'm very suspicious of these quiet voices now. He ask me why I don't pay any fine, and I say because I haven't the money. I get the idea they want to find out all about Mr Sims—they listen so very attentive. But they'll find out nothing from me. He ask how long I have the flat and I say I don't remember. I know they want to trip me up like they trip me up about my savings so I won't answer. At last he ask if I have anything to say as I can't be allowed to go on being a nuisance. I think, 'I'm nuisance to you because I have no money that's all.' I want to speak up and tell him how they steal all my savings, so when my landlord asks for month's rent I haven't got it to give. I want to tell him the woman next door provoke me since long time and call me bad names but she have a soft sugar voice and nobody hear—that's why I broke her window, but I'm ready to buy another after all. I want to say all I do is sing in that old garden, and I want to say this in decent quiet voice. But I hear myself talking loud and I see my hands wave in the air. Too besides it's no use, they won't believe me, so I don't finish. I stop, and I feel the tears on my face. 'Prove it.' That's all they will say. They whisper, they whisper. They nod, they nod.

Next thing I'm in a car again with a different policewoman, dressed very smart. Not in uniform. I ask her where she's taking me and she says 'Holloway' just that 'Holloway'.[7]

I catch hold of her hand because I'm afraid. But she takes it away. Cold and smooth her hand slide away and her face is china face—smooth like a doll and I think, 'This is the last time I ask anything from anybody. So help me God.'

The car come up to a black castle and little mean streets are all round it. A lorry was blocking up the castle gates. When it get by we pass through and I am in jail. First I stand in a line with others who are waiting to give up handbags and all belongings to a woman behind bars like in a post office. The girl in front bring out a nice compact, look like gold to me, lipstick to match and a wallet full of notes. The woman keep the money, but she give back the powder and lipstick and she half-smile. I have two pounds seven shillings and sixpence in pennies. She take my purse, then she throw me my compact (which is cheap) my comb and my handkerchief like everything in my bag is dirty. So I think, 'Here too, here too.' But I tell myself, 'Girl, what you expect, eh? They all like that. All.'

Some of what happen afterwards I forget, or perhaps better not remember. Seems to me they start by trying to frighten you. But they don't succeed with me for I don't care for nothing now, it's as if my heart hard like a rock and I can't feel.

Then I'm standing at the top of a staircase with a lot of women and girls. As we are going down I notice the railing very low on one side, very easy to jump, and a long way below there's the grey stone passage like it's waiting for you.

As I'm thinking this a uniform woman step up alongside quick and grab my arm. She say, 'Oh no you don't.'

I was just noticing the railing very low that's all—but what's the use of saying so.

Another long line waits for the doctor. It move forward slowly and my legs terrible tired. The girl in front is very young and she cry and cry. 'I'm scared,' she keeps saying. She's lucky in a way—as for me I never will cry again. It all dry up and hard in me now. That, and a lot besides. In the end I tell her to stop, because she doing just what these people want her to do.

She stop crying and start a long story, but while she is speaking her voice get very far away, and I find I can't see her face clear at all.

Then I'm in a chair, and one of those uniform women is pushing my head down between my knees, but let her push—everything go away from me just the same.

They put me in the hospital because the doctor say I'm sick. I have cell by myself and it's all right except I don't sleep. The things they say you mind I don't mind.

When they clang the door on me I think, 'You shut me in, but you shut all those other dam' devils *out*. They can't reach me now.'

At first it bothers me when they keep on looking at me all through the night.

---

7. Prison in London.

They open a little window in the doorway to do this. But I get used to it and get used to the night chemise[8] they give me. It very thick, and to my mind it not very clean either—but what's that matter to me? Only the food I can't swallow—especially the porridge. The woman ask me sarcastic, 'Hunger striking?' But afterwards I can leave most of it, and she don't say nothing.

One day a nice girl comes around with books and she give me two, but I don't want to read so much. Beside one is about a murder, and the other is about a ghost and I don't think it's at all like those books tell you.

There is nothing I want now. It's no use. If they leave me in peace and quiet that's all I ask. The window is barred but not small, so I can see a little thin tree through the bars, and I like watching it.

After a week they tell me I'm better and I can go out with the others for exercise. We walk round and round one of the yards in that castle—it is fine weather and the sky is a kind of pale blue, but the yard is a terrible sad place. The sunlight fall down and die there. I get tired walking in high heels and I'm glad when that's over.

We can talk, and one day an old woman come up and ask me for dog-ends. I don't understand, and she start muttering at me like she very vexed. Another woman tell me she mean cigarette ends, so I say I don't smoke. But the old woman still look angry, and when we're going in she give me one push and I nearly fall down. I'm glad to get away from these people, and hear the door clang and take my shoes off.

Sometimes I think, 'I'm here because I wanted to sing' and I have to laugh. But there's a small looking glass in my cell and I see myself and I'm like somebody else. Like some strange new person. Mr Sims tells me I too thin, but what he say now to this person in the looking glass? So I don't laugh again.

Usually I don't think at all. Everything and everybody seem small and far away, that is the only trouble.

Twice the doctor come to see me. He don't say much and I don't say anything, because a uniform woman is always there. She looks like she thinking, 'Now the lies start.' So I prefer not to speak. Then I'm sure they can't trip me up. Perhaps I there still, or in a worse place. But one day this happen.

We were walking round and round in the yard and I hear a woman singing— the voice come from high up, from one of the small barred windows. At first I don't believe it. Why should anybody sing here? Nobody want to sing in jail, nobody want to do anything. There's no reason, and you have no hope. I think I must be asleep, dreaming, but I'm awake all right and I see all the others are listening too. A nurse is with us that afternoon, not a policewoman. She stop and look up at the window.

It's a smoky kind of voice, and a bit rough sometimes, as if those old dark walls theyselves are complaining, because they see too much misery—too much. But it don't fall down and die in the courtyard; seems to me it could jump the gates of the jail easy and travel far, and nobody could stop it. I don't hear the words—only the music. She sing one verse and she begin another, then she break off sudden. Everybody starts walking again, and nobody says one word. But as we go in I ask the woman in front who was singing. 'That's the Holloway song,' she says. 'Don't you know it yet? She was singing from the punishment cells, and she tell the girls cheerio and never say die.' Then I have to go one way to the hospital block and she goes another so we don't speak again.

8. Loosely fitting nightgown.

When I'm back in my cell I can't just wait for bed. I walk up and down and I think. 'One day I hear that song on trumpets and these walls will fall and rest.'[9] I want to get out so bad I could hammer on the door, for I know now that anything can happen, and I don't want to stay lock up here and miss it.

Then I'm hungry. I eat everything they bring and in the morning I'm still so hungry I eat the porridge. Next time the doctor come he tells me I seem much better. Then I say a little of what really happen in that house. Not much. Very careful.

He look at me hard and kind of surprised. At the door he shake his finger and says, 'Now don't let me see you here again.'

That evening the woman tells me I'm going, but she's so upset about it I don't ask questions. Very early, before it's light she bangs the door open and shouts at me to hurry up. As we're going along the passages I see the girl who gave me the books. She's in a row with others doing exercises. Up Down, Up Down, Up. We pass quite close and I notice she's looking very pale and tired. It's crazy, it's all crazy. This up down business and everything else too. When they give me my money I remember I leave my compact in the cell, so I ask if I can go back for it. You should see that policewoman's face as she shoo me on.

There's no car, there's a van and you can't see through the windows. The third time it stop I get out with one other, a young girl, and it's the same magistrates' court as before.

The two of us wait in a small room, nobody else there, and after a while the girl say, 'What the hell are they doing? I don't want to spend all day here.' She go to the bell and she keep her finger press on it. When I look at her she say, 'Well, what are they *for*?' That girl's face is hard like a board—she could change faces with many and you wouldn't know the difference. But she get results certainly. A policeman comes in, all smiling, and we go in the court. The same magistrate, the same frowning man sits below, and when I hear my fine is paid I want to ask who paid it, but he yells at me, 'Silence.'

I think I will never understand the half of what happen, but they tell me I can go, and I understand that. The magistrate ask if I'm leaving the neighbourhood and I say yes, then I'm out in the streets again, and it's the same fine weather, same feeling I'm dreaming.

When I get to the house I see two men talking in the garden. The front door and the door of the flat are both open. I go in, and the bedroom is empty, nothing but the glare streaming inside because they take the Venetian blinds away. As I'm wondering where my suitcase is, and the clothes I leave in the wardrobe, there's a knock and it's the old lady from upstairs carrying my case packed, and my coat is over her arm. She says she sees me come in. 'I kept your things for you.' I start to thank her but she turn her back and walk away. They like that here, and better not expect too much. Too besides, I bet they tell her I'm terrible person.

I go in the kitchen, but when I see they are cutting down the big tree at the back I don't stay to watch.

At the station I'm waiting for the train and a woman asks if I feel well. 'You look so tired,' she says. 'Have you come a long way?' I want to answer, 'I come so far I lose myself on that journey.' But I tell her, 'Yes, I am quite well. But I can't stand the heat.' She says she can't stand it either, and we talk about the weather till the train come in.

9. The walls of Jericho fall when trumpets sound (Joshua 6).

I'm not frightened of them any more—after all what else can they do? I know what to say and everything go like a clock works.

I get a room near Victoria where the landlady accept one pound in advance, and next day I find a job in the kitchen of a private hotel close by. But I don't stay there long. I hear of another job going in a big store—altering ladies' dresses and I get that. I lie and tell them I work in very expensive New York shop. I speak bold and smooth faced, and they never check up on me. I make a friend there—Clarice—very light coloured, very smart, she have a lot to do with the customers and she laugh at some of them behind their backs. But I say it's not their fault if the dress don't fit. Special dress for one person only— that's very expensive in London. So it's take in, or let out all the time. Clarice have two rooms not far from the store. She furnish herself gradual and she gives parties sometimes Saturday nights. It's there I start whistling the Holloway Song. A man comes up to me and says, 'Let's hear that again.' So I whistle it again (I never sing now) and he tells me 'Not bad'. Clarice have an old piano somebody give her to store and he plays the tune, jazzing it up. I say, 'No, not like that,' but everybody else say the way he do it is first class. Well I think no more of this till I get a letter from him telling me he has sold the song and as I was quite a help he encloses five pounds with thanks.

I read the letter and I could cry. For after all, that song was all I had. I don't belong nowhere really, and I haven't money to buy my way to belonging. I don't want to either.

But when that girl sing, she sing to me and she sing for me. I was there because I was *meant* to be there. It was *meant* I should hear it—this I *know*.

Now I've let them play it wrong, and it will go from me like all the other songs—like everything. Nothing left for me at all.

But then I tell myself all this is foolishness. Even if they played it on trumpets, even if they played it just right, like I wanted—no walls would fall so soon. 'So let them call it jazz,' I think, and let them play it wrong. That won't make no difference to the song I heard.

I buy myself a dusty pink dress with the money.

1961   1962

STEVIE SMITH
1902–1971

Stevie Smith's real name was Florence Margaret Smith, but she was nicknamed "Stevie" after a famous jockey because of her small stature. She was born in Hull, Yorkshire, but at the age of three went with her mother and sister to live with an aunt in Palmer's Green, a suburb north of London. She worked as a secretary at the magazine-publishing firm of Newnes, Pearson, while continuing to live with her aunt, to whom she was devoted. When her aunt grew old and infirm, Smith gave up her job to look after her, although she herself was often in ill health. At the same time she managed to lead a lively social life in London and was known for the vividness and range of her conversation.

Smith brought out her first novel, *Novel on Yellow Paper* (1936), at the suggestion of a publisher who rejected a collection of poems. This was followed by her first volume of poetry, *A Good Time Was Had by All* (1937), and in due course by eight further poetry collections and two further novels.

Smith's work is utterly original, fitting into no category and showing none of the characteristic influences of the age. Her poetry sometimes seems to be light verse, and it draws on nursery rhyme and often employs simple language, but its humor can shade into dread, its whimsy into metaphysical pondering. She illustrated many of her poems with line drawings (she called them "doodles") that reinforce the effect of mock-naïveté. This stance is akin to the cunning innocence of the fool or the trickster, and can be seen, in part, as a gendered deflection and subversion of masculine cultural norms. Her diction ranges from the matter-of-fact to the archaic, from colloquialism ("Poor chap"), slang ("you ass"), and nonsense ("Our Bog Is Dood") to didacticism ("My point which upon this has been obscured") and foreign phrases ("Sunt Leones"). Her verse moves from free conversational rhythms to traditional verse patterns, on occasion becoming—to ironic effect—almost doggerel. Her tone can be satiric, solemn, or both at once. A poem such as "Not Waving but Drowning" belies the apparent guilelessness of Smith's art. Like the dying man's ambiguous gesture here, her poetry waves to us, with its songlike lyricism and comedy, and yet also reveals much about "drowning"—about death, suicide, and other painful human issues. A religious skeptic, Smith said she was always in danger of falling into belief, and her poetry shows her to be fascinated by theological speculation, the language of the Bible, and religious experience.

Sunt Leones[1]

    The lions who ate the Christians on the sands of the arena
    By indulging native appetites played what has now been seen a
    Not entirely negligible part
    In consolidating at the very start
5   The position of the Early Christian Church.
    Initiatory rites are always bloody
    And the lions, it appears
    From contemporary art, made a study
    Of dyeing Coliseum sands a ruddy
10   Liturgically sacrificial hue
    And if the Christians felt a little blue—
    Well people being eaten often do.
    Theirs was the death, and theirs the crown undying,[2]
    A state of things which must be satisfying.
15   My point which up to this has been obscured
    Is that it was the lions who procured
    By chewing up blood gristle flesh and bone
    The martyrdoms on which the Church has grown.
    I only write this poem because I thought it rather looked
20   As if the part the lions played was being overlooked.
    By lions' jaws great benefits and blessings were begotten
    And so our debt to Lionhood must never be forgotten.

1937

1. There be lions (Latin). Christians were attacked and eaten by lions in the public games held in the Colosseum during the Roman Empire.

2. I.e., of martyrdom, in heaven. The Christian liturgy, or system of worship, prescribes certain colors for certain festivals (line 10).

Our Bog Is Dood

Our Bog is dood, our Bog is dood,
They lisped in accents mild,
But when I asked them to explain
They grew a little wild.
How do you know your Bog is dood   5
My darling little child?

We know because we wish it so
That is enough, they cried,
And straight within each infant eye
Stood up the flame of pride,   10
And if you do not think it so
You shall be crucified.

Then tell me, darling little ones,
What's dood, suppose Bog is?
Just what we think, the answer came,   15
Just what we think it is.
They bowed their heads. Our Bog is ours
And we are wholly his.

But when they raised them up again
They had forgotten me   20
Each one upon each other glared
In pride and misery
For what was dood, and what their Bog
They never could agree.

Oh sweet it was to leave them then,   25
And sweeter not to see,
And sweetest of all to walk alone
Beside the encroaching sea,
The sea that soon should drown them all,
That never yet drowned me.   30

1950

Not Waving but Drowning

Nobody heard him, the dead man,
But still he lay moaning:
I was much further out than you thought
And not waving but drowning.

Poor chap, he always loved larking   5
And now he's dead
It must have been too cold for him his heart gave way,
They said.

Oh, no no no, it was too cold always
10 (Still the dead one lay moaning)
I was much too far out all my life
And not waving but drowning.

1957

Thoughts About the Person from Porlock[1]

Coleridge received the Person from Porlock
And ever after called him a curse,
Then why did he hurry to let him in?
He could have hid in the house.

5 It was not right of Coleridge in fact it was wrong
(But often we all do wrong)
As the truth is I think he was already stuck
With Kubla Khan.

He was weeping and wailing: I am finished, finished,
10 I shall never write another word of it,

1. See Coleridge, "Kubla Khan," (p. 446).

When along comes the Person from Porlock
And takes the blame for it.

It was not right, it was wrong,
But often we all do wrong.

       • • •

15   May we inquire the name of the Person from Porlock?
Why, Porson, didn't you know?
He lived at the bottom of Porlock Hill
So had a long way to go,

He wasn't much in the social sense
20   Though his grandmother was a Warlock,
One of the Ruthlandshire ones I fancy
And nothing to do with Porlock.

And he lived at the bottom of the hill as I said
And had a cat named Flo,
25   And had a cat named Flo.

I long for the Person from Porlock
To bring my thoughts to an end,
I am becoming impatient to see him
I think of him as a friend,

30   Often I look out of the window
Often I run to the gate
I think, He will come this evening,
I think it is rather late.

I am hungry to be interrupted
35   Forever and ever amen
O Person from Porlock come quickly
And bring my thoughts to an end.

       • • •

I felicitate the people who have a Person from Porlock
To break up everything and throw it away
40   Because then there will be nothing to keep them
And they need not stay.

       • • •

Why do they grumble so much?
He comes like a benison
They should be glad he has not forgotten them
45   They might have had to go on.

       • • •

These thoughts are depressing I know. They are depressing,
I wish I was more cheerful, it is more pleasant,
Also it is a duty, we should smile as well as submitting
To the purpose of One Above who is experimenting

50 With various mixtures of human character which goes best,
All is interesting for him it is exciting, but not for us.
There I go again, Smile, smile, and get some work to do
Then you will be practically unconscious without positively having to go.

1962

Pretty

Why is the word pretty so underrated?
In November the leaf is pretty when it falls
The stream grows deep in the woods after rain
And in the pretty pool the pike stalks

5   He stalks his prey, and this is pretty too,
The prey escapes with an underwater flash
But not for long, the great fish has him now
The pike is a fish who always has his prey

And this is pretty. The water rat is pretty
10 His paws are not webbed, he cannot shut his nostrils
As the otter can and the beaver, he is torn between
The land and water, Not "torn," he does not mind.

The owl hunts in the evening and it is pretty
The lake water below him rustles with ice
15 There is frost coming from the ground, in the air mist
All this is pretty, it could not be prettier.

Yes, it could always be prettier, the eye abashes
It is becoming an eye that cannot see enough,
Out of the wood the eye climbs. This is prettier
20 A field in the evening, tilting up.

The field tilts to the sky. Though it is late
The sky is lighter than the hill field
All this looks easy but really it is extraordinary
Well, it is extraordinary to be so pretty.

25 And it is careless, and that is always pretty
This field, this owl, this pike, this pool are careless,
As Nature is always careless and indifferent
Who sees, who steps, means nothing, and this is pretty.

So a person can come along like a thief—pretty!—
30 Stealing a look, pinching the sound and feel,
Lick the icicle broken from the bank
And still say nothing at all, only cry pretty.

Cry pretty, pretty, pretty and you'll be able
Very soon not even to cry pretty

35 And so be delivered entirely from humanity
This is prettiest of all, it is very pretty.

1966

GEORGE ORWELL
1903–1950

"George Orwell" was the pseudonym of Eric Blair, who was born in the village of
Motihari in Bengal, India, where his father was a British civil servant. He was sent
to private school in England and won a scholarship to Eton, the foremost "public
school" (i.e., private boarding school) in the country. At these schools he became
conscious of the difference between his own background and the wealthy backgrounds of many of his schoolmates. On leaving school he joined the Imperial Police
in Burma (both Burma—now called Myanmar—and India were then still part of the
British Empire). His service in Burma from 1922 to 1927 produced a sense of guilt
about British colonialism and a feeling that he had to make some personal expiation
for it. This he would later do with an anticolonial novel, *Burmese Days* (1934), and
essays such as "Shooting an Elephant" (1936), which subordinates lingering colonial
attitudes to fiercely anti-imperial insights. He returned to England determined to be
a writer and adopted his pseudonym as one way of escaping from the class position
in which his elite education placed him. He went to Paris to try to earn a living by
teaching while he made his first attempts at writing. His extremely difficult time in
Paris was followed by a spell as a tramp in England, and he vividly recorded both
experiences in his first book, *Down and Out in Paris and London* (1933). Orwell did
not have to suffer the dire poverty that he seems to have courted (he had influential
friends who would have been glad to help him); he wanted, however, to learn firsthand
about the life of the poor, both out of humane curiosity and because, as he wrote, if
he did so "part of my guilt would drop from me."

The Road to Wigan Pier (1937) discusses the experiences Orwell shared with unemployed miners in the north of England. The book pleased neither the left nor the
right, for by now Orwell was showing what was to become his characteristic independence of mind on political and social questions: he wrote of what he knew first-
hand to be true and was contemptuous of ideologies. He never joined a political party
but regarded himself as a man of the uncommitted and independent left.

When the Spanish Civil War broke out in 1936 after General Franco raised his
military rebellion against the elected government, Orwell went there as a reporter
and stayed to fight on the Republican side, rising to the rank of second lieutenant
and suffering a throat wound. His *Homage to Catalonia* (1938) strongly criticized the
Communist part in the civil war and showed from his own experience how the Communist Party in Spain was out to destroy anarchists, Trotskyists, and any others on
the Republican side who were suspected of not toeing the Stalinist line; it aroused
great indignation on the left in Britain and elsewhere, for many leftists believed that
they should solidly support the Soviet Union and the Communist Party as the natural
leaders in the struggle against international fascism. Orwell never wavered in his
belief that while profound social change was necessary and desirable in capitalist
countries of the West, the so-called socialism established in Soviet Russia was a
perversion of socialism and a wicked tyranny. In *Animal Farm* (1945) he wrote a fable
showing how such a perversion of socialism could develop, while in *Nineteen-Eighty-
Four* (1949), when he was an embittered man dying of tuberculosis, he wrote a savagely powerful novel depicting a totalitarian future, where the government uses the

language of socialism to cover a tyranny that systematically destroys the human spirit. In that vision of hell on Earth, language has become one of the principal instruments of oppression. The Ministry of Truth is there concerned with the transmission of untruth, and the white face of its pyramidal structure proclaims in "Newspeak" the three slogans of the party: "WAR IS PEACE / FREEDOM IS SLAVERY / IGNORANCE IS STRENGTH." Three years before Orwell formulated "Newspeak," "doublespeak," and "Big Brother is watching you," he had explored in one of his most influential essays, "Politics and the English Language," the decay of language and the ways in which that decay might be resisted. The fifty years that have passed since he wrote the piece have only confirmed the accuracy of its diagnosis and the value of its prescription.

Orwell was an outstanding journalist, and the essays he wrote regularly for the left-wing British journal *Tribune* and other periodicals include some of his best work. His independent eye made him both a permanent misfit politically and a brilliantly original writer.

Shooting an Elephant

In Moulmein, in Lower Burma, I was hated by large numbers of people—the only time in my life that I have been important enough for this to happen to me. I was sub-divisional police officer of the town, and in an aimless, petty kind of way anti-European feeling was very bitter. No one had the guts to raise a riot, but if a European woman went through the bazaars alone somebody would probably spit betel[1] juice over her dress. As a police officer I was an obvious target and was baited whenever it seemed safe to do so. When a nimble Burman tripped me up on the football field and the referee (another Burman) looked the other way, the crowd yelled with hideous laughter. This happened more than once. In the end the sneering yellow faces of young men that met me everywhere, the insults hooted after me when I was at a safe distance, got badly on my nerves. The young Buddhist priests were the worst of all. There were several thousands of them in the town and none of them seemed to have anything to do except stand on street corners and jeer at Europeans.

All this was perplexing and upsetting. For at that time I had already made up my mind that imperialism was an evil thing and the sooner I chucked up my job and got out of it the better. Theoretically—and secretly, of course—I was all for the Burmese and all against their oppressors, the British. As for the job I was doing, I hated it more bitterly than I can perhaps make clear. In a job like that you see the dirty work of Empire at close quarters. The wretched prisoners huddling in the stinking cages of the lock-ups, the grey, cowed faces of the long-term convicts, the scarred buttocks of the men who had been flogged with bamboos—all these oppressed me with an intolerable sense of guilt. But I could get nothing into perspective. I was young and ill-educated and I had had to think out my problems in the utter silence that is imposed on every Englishman in the East. I did not even know that the British Empire is dying, still less did I know that it is a great deal better than the younger empires that are going to supplant it. All I knew was that I was stuck between my hatred of the empire I served and my rage against the evil-spirited little beasts who tried to make my job impossible. With one part of my mind I

---

1. Leaf of a plant chewed as a delicacy in Burma and other Eastern countries.

thought of the British Raj as an unbreakable tyranny, as something clamped down, *in saecula saeculorum*,[2] upon the will of prostrate peoples; with another part I thought that the greatest joy in the world would be to drive a bayonet into a Buddhist priest's guts. Feelings like these are the normal by-products of imperialism; ask any Anglo-Indian official, if you can catch him off duty.

One day something happened which in a roundabout way was enlightening. It was a tiny incident in itself, but it gave me a better glimpse than I had had before of the real nature of imperialism—the real motives for which despotic governments act. Early one morning the sub-inspector at a police station the other end of the town rang me up on the phone and said that an elephant was ravaging the bazaar. Would I please come and do something about it? I did not know what I could do, but I wanted to see what was happening and I got on to a pony and started out. I took my rifle, an old .44 Winchester and much too small to kill an elephant, but I thought the noise might be useful *in terrorem*.[3] Various Burmans stopped me on the way and told me about the elephant's doings. It was not, of course, a wild elephant, but a tame one which had gone "must."[4] It had been chained up as tame elephants always are when their attack of "must" is due, but on the previous night it had broken its chain and escaped. Its mahout,[5] the only person who could manage it when it was in that state, had set out in pursuit, but he had taken the wrong direction and was now twelve hours' journey away, and in the morning the elephant had suddenly reappeared in the town. The Burmese population had no weapons and were quite helpless against it. It had already destroyed somebody's bamboo hut, killed a cow and raided some fruit-stalls and devoured the stock; also it had met the municipal rubbish van, and, when the driver jumped out and took to his heels, had turned the van over and inflicted violence upon it.

The Burmese sub-inspector and some Indian constables were waiting for me in the quarter where the elephant had been seen. It was a very poor quarter, a labyrinth of squalid bamboo huts, thatched with palm-leaf, winding all over a steep hillside. I remember that it was a cloudy stuffy morning at the beginning of the rains. We began questioning the people as to where the elephant had gone, and, as usual, failed to get any definite information. That is invariably the case in the East; a story always sounds clear enough at a distance, but the nearer you get to the scene of events the vaguer it becomes. Some of the people said that the elephant had gone in one direction, some said that he had gone in another, some professed not even to have heard of any elephant. I had almost made up my mind that the whole story was a pack of lies, when we heard yells a little distance away. There was a loud, scandalised cry of "Go away, child! Go away this instant!" and an old woman with a switch in her hand came round the corner of a hut, violently shooing away a crowd of naked children. Some more women followed, clicking their tongues and exclaiming; evidently there was something there that the children ought not to have seen. I rounded the hut and saw a man's dead body sprawling in the mud. He was an Indian, a black Dravidian coolie,[6] almost naked, and he could not have been dead many minutes. The people said that the elephant had come suddenly upon him round the corner of the hut, caught him with its trunk, put its foot on his back and ground him into the earth. This was the

2. For ever and ever (Latin). "Raj": rule (Hindi).
3. To frighten it (Latin).
4. A state of sexual frenzy to which certain animals are subject at irregular intervals.

5. Elephant driver (Hindi).
6. Hired laborer (disputed origin). "Dravidian": a South Asian people.

rainy season and the ground was soft, and his face had scored a trench a foot deep and a couple of yards long. He was lying on his belly with arms crucified and head sharply twisted to one side. His face was coated with mud, the eyes wide open, the teeth bared and grinning with an expression of unendurable agony. (Never tell me, by the way, that the dead look peaceful. Most of the corpses I have seen looked devilish.) The friction of the great beast's foot had stripped the skin from his back as neatly as one skins a rabbit. As soon as I saw the dead man I sent an orderly to a friend's house nearby to borrow an elephant rifle. I had already sent back the pony, not wanting it to go mad with fright and throw me if it smelled the elephant.

The orderly came back in a few minutes with a rifle and five cartridges, and meanwhile some Burmans had arrived and told us that the elephant was in the paddy fields below, only a few hundred yards away. As I started forward practically the whole population of the quarter flocked out of their houses and followed me. They had seen the rifle and were all shouting excitedly that I was going to shoot the elephant. They had not shown much interest in the elephant when he was merely ravaging their homes, but it was different now that he was going to be shot. It was a bit of fun to them, as it would be to an English crowd; besides, they wanted the meat. It made me vaguely uneasy. I had no intention of shooting the elephant—I had merely sent for the rifle to defend myself if necessary—and it is always unnerving to have a crowd following you. I marched down the hill, looking and feeling a fool, with the rifle over my shoulder and an ever-growing army of people jostling at my heels. At the bottom, when you got away from the huts, there was a metalled road and beyond that a miry waste of paddy fields a thousand yards across, not yet ploughed but soggy from the first rains and dotted with coarse grass. The elephant was standing eighty yards from the road, his left side towards us. He took not the slightest notice of the crowd's approach. He was tearing up bunches of grass, beating them against his knees to clean them and stuffing them into his mouth.

I had halted on the road. As soon as I saw the elephant I knew with perfect certainty that I ought not to shoot him. It is a serious matter to shoot a working elephant—it is comparable to destroying a huge and costly piece of machinery—and obviously one ought not to do it if it can possibly be avoided. And at that distance, peacefully eating, the elephant looked no more dangerous than a cow. I thought then and I think now that his attack of "must" was already passing off; in which case he would merely wander harmlessly about until the mahout came back and caught him. Moreover, I did not in the least want to shoot him. I decided that I would watch him for a little while to make sure that he did not turn savage again, and then go home.

But at that moment I glanced round at the crowd that had followed me. It was an immense crowd, two thousand at the least and growing every minute. It blocked the road for a long distance on either side. I looked at the sea of yellow faces above the garish clothes—faces all happy and excited over this bit of fun, all certain that the elephant was going to be shot. They were watching me as they would watch a conjuror about to perform a trick. They did not like me, but with the magical rifle in my hands I was momentarily worth watching. And suddenly I realised that I should have to shoot the elephant after all. The people expected it of me and I had got to do it; I could feel their two thousand wills pressing me forward, irresistibly. And it was at this moment, as I stood there with the rifle in my hands, that I first grasped the hollowness, the futility of the white man's dominion in the East. Here was I,

the white man with his gun, standing in front of the unarmed native crowd—
seemingly the leading actor of the piece; but in reality I was only an absurd
puppet pushed to and fro by the will of those yellow faces behind. I perceived
in this moment that when the white man turns tyrant it is his own freedom
that he destroys. He becomes a sort of hollow, posing dummy, the conven-
tionalised figure of a sahib.[7] For it is the condition of his rule that he shall
spend his life in trying to impress the "natives" and so in every crisis he has
got to do what the "natives" expect of him. He wears a mask, and his face
grows to fit it. I had got to shoot the elephant. I had committed myself to doing
it when I sent for the rifle. A sahib has got to act like a sahib; he has got to
appear resolute, to know his own mind and do definite things. To come all
that way, rifle in hand, with two thousand people marching at my heels, and
then to trail feebly away, having done nothing—no, that was impossible. The
crowd would laugh at me. And my whole life, every white man's life in the
East, was one long struggle not to be laughed at.

But I did not want to shoot the elephant. I watched him beating his bunch
of grass against his knees, with that preoccupied grandmotherly air that elephants have. It seemed to me that it would be murder to shoot him. At that
age I was not squeamish about killing animals, but I had never shot an elephant and never wanted to. (Somehow it always seems worse to kill a *large*
animal.) Besides, there was the beast's owner to be considered. Alive, the
elephant was worth at least a hundred pounds; dead, he would only be worth
the value of his tusks—five pounds, possibly. But I had got to act quickly. I
turned to some experienced-looking Burmans who had been there when we
arrived, and asked them how the elephant had been behaving. They all said
the same thing: he took no notice of you if you left him alone, but he might
charge if you went too close to him.

It was perfectly clear to me what I ought to do. I ought to walk up to within,
say, twenty-five yards of the elephant and test his behaviour. If he charged I
could shoot, if he took no notice of me it would be safe to leave him until the
mahout came back. But also I knew that I was going to do no such thing. I
was a poor shot with a rifle and the ground was soft mud into which one would
sink at every step. If the elephant charged and I missed him, I should have
about as much chance as a toad under a steam-roller. But even then I was not
thinking particularly of my own skin, only the watchful yellow faces behind.
For at that moment, with the crowd watching me, I was not afraid in the
ordinary sense, as I would have been if I had been alone. A white man mustn't
be frightened in front of "natives"; and so, in general, he isn't frightened. The
sole thought in my mind was that if anything went wrong those two thousand
Burmans would see me pursued, caught, trampled on and reduced to a grinning corpse like that Indian up the hill. And if that happened it was quite
probable that some of them would laugh. That would never do. There was
only one alternative. I shoved the cartridges into the magazine and lay down
on the road to get a better aim.

The crowd grew very still, and a deep, low, happy sigh, as of people who see
the theatre curtain go up at last, breathed from innumerable throats. They
were going to have their bit of fun after all. The rifle was a beautiful German
thing with cross-hair sights. I did not then know that in shooting an elephant
one should shoot to cut an imaginary bar running from ear-hole to ear-hole.
I ought therefore, as the elephant was sideways on, to have aimed straight at

---

7. White gentleman (Urdu).

his ear-hole; actually I aimed several inches in front of this, thinking the brain would be further forward.

When I pulled the trigger I did not hear the bang or feel the kick—one never does when a shot goes home—but I heard the devilish roar of glee that went up from the crowd. In that instant, in too short a time, one would have thought, even for the bullet to get there, a mysterious, terrible change had come over the elephant. He neither stirred nor fell, but every line of his body had altered. He looked suddenly stricken, shrunken, immensely old, as though the frightful impact of the bullet had paralysed him without knocking him down. At last, after what seemed a long time—it might have been five seconds, I dare say—he sagged flabbily to his knees. His mouth slobbered. An enormous senility seemed to have settled upon him. One could have imagined him thousands of years old. I fired again into the same spot. At the second shot he did not collapse but climbed with desperate slowness to his feet and stood weakly upright, with legs sagging and head drooping. I fired a third time. That was the shot that did for him. You could see the agony of it jolt his whole body and knock the last remnant of strength from his legs. But in falling he seemed for a moment to rise, for as his hind legs collapsed beneath him he seemed to tower upwards like a huge rock toppling, his trunk reaching skyward like a tree. He trumpeted, for the first and only time. And then down he came, his belly towards me, with a crash that seemed to shake the ground even where I lay.

I got up. The Burmans were already racing past me across the mud. It was obvious that the elephant would never rise again, but he was not dead. He was breathing very rhythmically with long rattling gasps, his great mound of a side painfully rising and falling. His mouth was wide open—I could see far down into caverns of pale pink throat. I waited a long time for him to die, but his breathing did not weaken. Finally I fired my two remaining shots into the spot where I thought his heart must be. The thick blood welled out of him like red velvet, but still he did not die. His body did not even jerk when the shots hit him, the tortured breathing continued without a pause. He was dying, very slowly and in great agony, but in some world remote from me where not even a bullet could damage him further. I felt that I had got to put an end to that dreadful noise. It seemed dreadful to see the great beast lying there, powerless to move and yet powerless to die, and not even to be able to finish him. I sent back for my small rifle and poured shot after shot into his heart and down his throat. They seemed to make no impression. The tortured gasps continued as steadily as the ticking of a clock.

In the end I could not stand it any longer and went away. I heard later that it took him half an hour to die. Burmans were arriving with dahs[8] and baskets even before I left, and I was told they had stripped his body almost to the bones by the afternoon.

Afterwards, of course, there were endless discussions about the shooting of the elephant. The owner was furious, but he was only an Indian and could do nothing. Besides, legally I had done the right thing, for a mad elephant has to be killed, like a mad dog, if its owner fails to control it. Among the Europeans opinion was divided. The older men said I was right, the younger men said it was a damn shame to shoot an elephant for killing a coolie, because an elephant was worth more than any damn Coringhee[9] coolie. And afterwards I

---

8. Short heavy swords (Burmese).
9. From the seaport Coringa, on the east coast of Madras in British India.

was very glad that the coolie had been killed; it put me legally in the right and it gave me a sufficient pretext for shooting the elephant. I often wondered whether any of the others grasped that I had done it solely to avoid looking a fool.

1936

Politics and the English Language

Most people who bother with the matter at all would admit that the English language is in a bad way, but it is generally assumed that we cannot by conscious action do anything about it. Our civilisation is decadent, and our language—so the argument runs—must inevitably share in the general collapse. It follows that any struggle against the abuse of language is a sentimental archaism, like preferring candles to electric light or hansom cabs to aeroplanes. Underneath this lies the half-conscious belief that language is a natural growth and not an instrument which we shape for our own purposes.

Now, it is clear that the decline of a language must ultimately have political and economic causes: it is not due simply to the bad influence of this or that individual writer. But an effect can become a cause, reinforcing the original cause and producing the same effect in an intensified form, and so on indefinitely. A man may take to drink because he feels himself to be a failure, and then fail all the more completely because he drinks. It is rather the same thing that is happening to the English language. It becomes ugly and inaccurate because our thoughts are foolish, but the slovenliness of our language makes it easier for us to have foolish thoughts. The point is that the process is reversible. Modern English, especially written English, is full of bad habits which spread by imitation and which can be avoided if one is willing to take the necessary trouble. If one gets rid of these habits one can think more clearly, and to think clearly is a necessary first step towards political regeneration: so that the fight against bad English is not frivolous and is not the exclusive concern of professional writers. I will come back to this presently, and I hope that by that time the meaning of what I have said here will have become clearer. Meanwhile, here are five specimens of the English language as it is now habitually written.

These five passages have not been picked out because they are especially bad—I could have quoted far worse if I had chosen—but because they illustrate various of the mental vices from which we now suffer. They are a little below the average, but are fairly representative samples. I number them so that I can refer back to them when necessary:

> 1. I am not, indeed, sure whether it is not true to say that the Milton who once seemed not unlike a seventeenth-century Shelley had not become, out of an experience ever more bitter in each year, more alien (sic)[1] to the founder of that Jesuit sect which nothing could induce him to tolerate.
>
> Professor Harold Laski (Essay in *Freedom of Expression*).

---

1. Thus, i.e., that's the way it was written.

2. Above all, we cannot play ducks and drakes with a native battery of idioms which prescribes such egregious collocations of vocables as the Basic *put up with* for *tolerate* or *put at a loss* for *bewilder*.

Professor Lancelot Hogben (Interglossa).

3. On the one side we have the free personality: by definition it is not neurotic, for it has neither conflict nor dream. Its desires, such as they are, are transparent, for they are just what institutional approval keeps in the forefront of consciousness; another institutional pattern would alter their number and intensity; there is little in them that is natural, irreducible, or culturally dangerous. But *on the other side,* the social bond itself is nothing but the mutual reflection of these self-secure integrities. Recall the definition of love. Is not this the very picture of a small academic? Where is there a place in this hall of mirrors for either personality or fraternity?

Essay on psychology in Politics (New York).

4. All the "best people" from the gentlemen's clubs, and all the frantic Fascist captains, united in common hatred of Socialism and bestial horror of the rising tide of the mass revolutionary movement, have turned to acts of provocation, to foul incendiarism, to medieval legends of poisoned wells, to legalise their own destruction to proletarian organisations, and rouse the agitated petty-bourgeoisie to chauvinistic fervour on behalf of the fight against the revolutionary way out of the crisis.

Communist pamphlet.

5. If a new spirit *is* to be infused into this old country, there is one thorny and contentious reform which must be tackled, and that is the humanisation and galvanisation of the BBC.[2] Timidity here will bespeak canker and atrophy of the soul. The heart of Britain may be sound and of strong beat, for instance, but the British lion's roar at present is like that of Bottom in Shakespeare's *Midsummer Night's Dream*—as gentle as any sucking dove. A virile new Britain cannot continue indefinitely to be traduced in the eyes, or rather ears, of the world by the effete languors of Langham Place, brazenly masquerading as "standard English." When the Voice of Britain is heard at nine o'clock, better far and infinitely less ludicrous to hear aitches[3] honestly dropped than the present priggish, inflated, inhibited, school-ma'amish arch braying of blameless bashful mewing maidens!

Letter in Tribune.

Each of these passages has faults of its own, but, quite apart from avoidable ugliness, two qualities are common to all of them. The first is staleness of imagery: the other is lack of precision. The writer either has a meaning and cannot express it, or he inadvertently says something else, or he is almost indifferent as to whether his words mean anything or not. This mixture of vagueness and sheer incompetence is the most marked characteristic of mod-

---

2. British Broadcasting Corporation.
3. I.e., *h* sounds, which are not aspirated in colloquial speech. During—and for some time after— World War II, few programs had a larger audience than the evening nine o'clock news. Langham Place is the location of the BBC's main offices in London.

ern English prose, and especially of any kind of political writing. As soon as certain topics are raised, the concrete melts into the abstract and no one seems able to think of turns of speech that are not hackneyed: prose consists less and less of *words* chosen for the sake of their meaning, and more of *phrases* tacked together like the sections of a prefabricated hen-house. I list below, with notes and examples, various of the tricks by means of which the work of prose construction is habitually dodged:

Dying metaphors. A newly invented metaphor assists thought by evoking a visual image, while on the other hand a metaphor which is technically "dead" (e.g., *iron resolution*) has in effect reverted to being an ordinary word and can generally be used without loss of vividness. But in between these two classes there is a huge dump of worn-out metaphors which have lost all evocative power and are merely used because they save people the trouble of inventing phrases for themselves. Examples are: *Ring the changes on, take up the cudgels for, toe the line, ride roughshod over, stand shoulder to shoulder with, play into the hands of, no axe to grind, grist to the mill, fishing in troubled waters, rift within the lute, on the order of the day, Achilles' heel, swan song, hotbed.* Many of these are used without knowledge of their meaning (What is a "rift," for instance?), and incompatible metaphors are frequently mixed, a sure sign that the writer is not interested in what he is saying. Some metaphors now current have been twisted out of their original meaning without those who use them even being aware of the fact. For example, *toe the line* is sometimes written *tow the line.* Another example is *the hammer and the anvil,* now always used with the implication that the anvil gets the worst of it. In real life it is always the anvil that breaks the hammer, never the other way about: a writer who stopped to think what he was saying would be aware of this, and would avoid perverting the original phrase.

Operators, or *verbal false limbs.* These save the trouble of picking out appropriate verbs and nouns, and at the same time pad each sentence with extra syllables which give it an appearance of symmetry. Characteristic phrases are: *render inoperative, militate against, prove unacceptable, make contact with, be subjected to, give rise to, give grounds for, have the effect of, play a leading part (rôle) in, make itself felt, take effect, exhibit a tendency to, serve the purpose of,* etc etc. The keynote is the elimination of simple verbs. Instead of being a single word, such as *break, stop, spoil, mend, kill,* a verb becomes a *phrase,* made up of a noun or adjective tacked on to some general-purposes verb such as *prove, serve, form, play, render.* In addition, the passive voice is wherever possible used in preference to the active, and noun constructions are used instead of gerunds (*by examination of* instead of *by examining*). The range of verbs is further cut down by means of the *-ise* and *de-* formations, and banal statements are given an appearance of profundity by means of the *not un-* formation. Simple conjunctions and prepositions are replaced by such phrases as *with respect to, having regard to, the fact that, by dint of, in view of, in the interests of, on the hypothesis that;* and the ends of sentences are saved from anticlimax by such resounding commonplaces as *greatly to be desired, cannot be left out of account, a development to be expected in the near future, deserving of serious consideration, brought to a satisfactory conclusion,* and so on and so forth.

Pretentious diction. Words like *phenomenon, element, individual* (as noun), *objective, categorical, effective, virtual, basic, primary, promote, constitute, exhibit, exploit, utilise, eliminate, liquidate,* are used to dress up simple statements and give an air of scientific impartiality to biassed judgements. Adjectives like *epoch-making, epic, historic, unforgettable, triumphant, age-old, inevitable, inexorable, veritable,* are used to dignify the sordid processes of international politics, while writing that aims at glorifying war usually takes on an archaic colour, its characteristic words being: *realm, throne, chariot, mailed fist, trident, sword, shield, buckler, banner, jackboot, clarion.* Foreign words and expressions such as *cul de sac, ancien régime, deus ex machina, mutatis mutandis, status quo, Gleichschaltung, Weltanschauung,*[4] are used to give an air of culture and elegance. Except for the useful abbreviations *i.e., e.g.,* and *etc.,* there is no real need for any of the hundreds of foreign phrases now current in English. Bad writers, and especially scientific, political and sociological writers, are nearly always haunted by the notion that Latin or Greek words are grander than Saxon ones, and unnecessary words like *expedite, ameliorate, predict, extraneous, deracinated, clandestine, sub-aqueous* and hundreds of others constantly gain ground from their Anglo-Saxon opposite numbers.[5] The jargon peculiar to Marxist writing (*hyena, hangman, cannibal, petty bourgeois, these gentry, lacquey, flunkey, mad dog, White Guard,* etc.) consists largely of words and phrases translated from Russian, German or French; but the normal way of coining a new word is to use a Latin or Greek root with the appropriate affix and, where necessary, the *-ise* formation. It is often easier to make up words of this kind (*deregionalise, impermissible, extramarital, non-fragmentatory* and so forth) than to think up the English words that will cover one's meaning. The result, in general, is an increase in slovenliness and vagueness.

Meaningless words. In certain kinds of writing, particularly in art criticism and literary criticism, it is normal to come across long passages which are almost completely lacking in meaning.[6] Words like *romantic, plastic, values, human, dead, sentimental, natural, vitality,* as used in art criticism, are strictly meaningless, in the sense that they not only do not point to any discoverable object, but are hardly even expected to do so by the reader. When one critic writes, "The outstanding features of Mr X's work is its living quality," while another writes, "The immediately striking thing about Mr X's work is its peculiar deadness," the reader accepts this as a simple difference of opinion. If words like *black* and *white* were involved, instead of the jargon words *dead* and *living,* he would see at once that language was being used in an improper way. Many political words are similarly abused. The word *Fascism* has now no meaning

4. Respectively: dead end (French), former system of government (French), the god from the machine (Latin), with the necessary changes (Latin), the existing state of things (Latin), standardization of political institutions among authoritarian states (German), and philosophy of life (German).
5. An interesting illustration of this is the way in which the English flower names which were in use till very recently are being ousted by Greek ones, *snapdragon* becoming *antirrhinum, forget-me-not* becoming *myosotis,* etc. It is hard to see any practical reason for this change of fashion: it is probably due to an instinctive turning-away from the more homely word and a vague feeling that the Greek word is scientific [Orwell's note].
6. Example: "Comfort's catholicity of perception and image, strangely Whitmanesque in range, almost the exact opposite in aesthetic compulsion, continues to evoke that trembling atmospheric accumulative hinting at a cruel, an inexorably serene timelessness . . . Wrey Gardiner scores by aiming at simple bullseyes with precision. Only they are not so simple, and through this contented sadness runs more than the surface bitter-sweet of resignation." (*Poetry Quarterly.*) [Orwell's note].

except in so far as it signifies "something not desirable." The words *democracy, socialism, freedom, patriotic, realistic, justice,* have each of them several different meanings which cannot be reconciled with one another. In the case of a word like *democracy,* not only is there no agreed definition, but the attempt to make one is resisted from all sides. It is almost universally felt that when we call a country democratic we are praising it: consequently the defenders of every kind of régime claim that it is a democracy, and fear that they might have to stop using the word if it were tied down to any one meaning. Words of this kind are often used in a consciously dishonest way. That is, the person who uses them has his own private definition, but allows his hearer to think he means something quite different. Statements like *Marshal Pétain*[7] *was a true patriot, The Soviet press is the freest in the world, The Catholic Church is opposed to persecution,* are almost always made with intent to deceive. Other words used in variable meanings, in most cases more or less dishonestly, are: *class, totalitarian, science, progressive, reactionary, bourgeois, equality.*

Now that I have made this catalogue of swindles and perversions, let me give another example of the kind of writing that they lead to. This time it must of its nature be an imaginary one. I am going to translate a passage of good English into modern English of the worst sort. Here is a well-known verse from *Ecclesiastes:*

> I returned, and saw under the sun, that the race is not to the swift, nor the battle to the strong, neither yet bread to the wise, nor yet riches to men of understanding, nor yet favour to men of skill; but time and chance happeneth to them all.

Here it is in modern English:

> Objective consideration of contemporary phenomena compels the conclusion that success or failure in competitive activities exhibits no tendency to be commensurate with innate capacity, but that a considerable element of the unpredictable must invariably be taken into account.

This is a parody, but not a very gross one. Exhibit 3, above, for instance, contains several patches of the same kind of English. It will be seen that I have not made a full translation. The beginning and ending of the sentence follow the original meaning fairly closely, but in the middle the concrete illustrations—race, battle, bread—dissolve into the vague phrase "success or failure in competitive activities". This had to be so, because no modern writer of the kind I am discussing—no one capable of using phrases like "objective consideration of contemporary phenomena"—would ever tabulate his thoughts in that precise and detailed way. The whole tendency of modern prose is away from concreteness. Now analyse these two sentences a little more closely. The first contains 49 words but only 60 syllables, and all its words are those of everyday life. The second contains 38 words of 90 syllables: 18 of its words are from Latin roots, and one from Greek. The first sentence contains six vivid images, and only one phrase ("time and chance") that could be called vague. The second contains not a single fresh, arresting phrase, and in spite of its 90 syllables it gives only a shortened version of the meaning contained in the first. Yet without a doubt it is the second kind of sentence

7. French army officer (1856–1951), head of the Vichy government that collaborated with Germany in World War II.

that is gaining ground in modern English. I do not want to exaggerate. This kind of writing is not yet universal, and outcrops of simplicity will occur here and there in the worst-written page. Still, if you or I were told to write a few lines on the uncertainty of human fortunes, we should probably come much nearer to my imaginary sentence than to the one from *Ecclesiastes*.

As I have tried to show, modern writing at its worst does not consist in picking out words for the sake of their meaning and inventing images in order to make the meaning clearer. It consists in gumming together long strips of words which have already been set in order by someone else, and making the results presentable by sheer humbug. The attraction of this way of writing is that it is easy. It is easier—even quicker, once you have the habit—to say *In my opinion it is a not unjustifiable assumption that* than to say *I think*. If you use ready-made phrases, you not only don't have to hunt about for words; you also don't have to bother with the rhythms of your sentences, since these phrases are generally so arranged as to be more or less euphonious. When you are composing in a hurry—when you are dictating to a stenographer, for instance, or making a public speech—it is natural to fall into a pretentious, latinised style. Tags like *a consideration which we should do well to bear in mind* or *a conclusion to which all of us would readily assent* will save many a sentence from coming down with a bump. By using stale metaphors, similes and idioms, you save much mental effort, at the cost of leaving your meaning vague, not only for your reader but for yourself. This is the significance of mixed metaphors. The sole aim of a metaphor is to call up a visual image. When these images clash—as in *The Fascist octopus has sung its swan song, the jackboot is thrown into the melting-pot*—it can be taken as certain that the writer is not seeing a mental image of the objects he is naming; in other words he is not really thinking. Look again at the examples I gave at the beginning of this essay. Professor Laski (1) uses five negatives in 53 words. One of these is superfluous, making nonsense of the whole passage, and in addition there is the slip *alien* for akin, making further nonsense, and several avoidable pieces of clumsiness which increase the general vagueness. Professor Hogben (2) plays ducks and drakes with a battery which is able to write prescriptions, and, while disapproving of the everyday phrase *put up with*, is unwilling to look *egregious* up in the dictionary and see what it means. (3), if one takes an uncharitable attitude towards it, is simply meaningless: probably one could work out its intended meaning by reading the whole of the article in which it occurs. In (4) the writer knows more or less what he wants to say, but an accumulation of stale phrases chokes him like tea-leaves blocking a sink. In (5) words and meaning have almost parted company. People who write in this manner usually have a general emotional meaning—they dislike one thing and want to express solidarity with another—but they are not interested in the detail of what they are saying. A scrupulous writer, in every sentence that he writes, will ask himself at least four questions, thus: What am I trying to say? What words will express it? What image or idiom will make it clearer? Is this image fresh enough to have an effect? And he will probably ask himself two more: Could I put it more shortly? Have I said anything that is avoidably ugly? But you are not obliged to go to all this trouble. You can shirk it by simply throwing your mind open and letting the ready-made phrases come crowding in. They will construct your sentences for you—even think your thoughts for you, to a certain extent—and at need they will perform the important service of partially concealing your meaning even from yourself. It is at this point that the special connection between politics and the debasement of language becomes clear.

In our time it is broadly true that political writing is bad writing. Where it is not true, it will generally be found that the writer is some kind of rebel, expressing his private opinions, and not a "party line." Orthodoxy, of whatever colour, seems to demand a lifeless, imitative style. The political dialects to be found in pamphlets, leading articles, manifestos, White Papers and the speeches of Under-Secretaries[8] do, of course, vary from party to party, but they are all alike in that one almost never finds in them a fresh, vivid, home-made turn of speech. When one watches some tired hack on the platform mechanically repeating the familiar phrases—*bestial atrocities, iron heel, blood-stained tyranny, free peoples of the world, stand shoulder to shoulder*— one often has a curious feeling that one is not watching a live human being but some kind of dummy: a feeling which suddenly becomes stronger at moments when the light catches the speaker's spectacles and turns them into blank discs which seem to have no eyes behind them. And this is not altogether fanciful. A speaker who uses that kind of phraseology has gone some distance towards turning himself into a machine. The appropriate noises are coming out of his larynx, but his brain is not involved as it would be if he were choosing his words for himself. If the speech he is making is one that he is accustomed to make over and over again, he may be almost unconscious of what he is saying, as one is when one utters the responses in church. And this reduced state of consciousness, if not indispensable, is at any rate favourable to political conformity.

In our time, political speech and writing are largely the defence of the indefensible. Things like the continuance of British rule in India,[9] the Russian purges and deportations, the dropping of the atom bombs on Japan, can indeed be defended, but only by arguments which are too brutal for most people to face, and which do not square with the professed aims of political parties. Thus political language has to consist largely of euphemism, question-begging and sheer cloudy vagueness. Defenceless villages are bombarded from the air, the inhabitants driven out into the countryside, the cattle machine-gunned, the huts set on fire with incendiary bullets: this is called *pacification*. Millions of peasants are robbed of their farms and sent trudging along the roads with no more than they can carry: this is called *transfer of population* or *rectification of frontiers*. People are imprisoned for years without trial, or shot in the back of the neck or sent to die of scurvy in Arctic lumber camps: this is called *elimination of unreliable elements*. Such phraseology is needed if one wants to name things without calling up mental pictures of them. Consider for instance some comfortable English professor defending Russian totalitarianism. He cannot say outright, "I believe in killing off your opponents when you can get good results by doing so." Probably, therefore, he will say something like this:

> While freely conceding that the Soviet régime exhibits certain features which the humanitarian may be inclined to deplore, we must, I think, agree that a certain curtailment of the right to political opposition is an unavoidable concomitant of transitional periods, and that the rigours which the Russian people have been called upon to undergo have been amply justified in the sphere of concrete achievement.

8. Senior British civil servants. "White Papers": official documents, each on a particular topic, issued by the British government.
9. This ended in 1947.

The inflated style is itself a kind of euphemism. A mass of Latin words falls upon the facts like soft snow, blurring the outlines and covering up all the details. The great enemy of clear language is insincerity. When there is a gap between one's real and one's declared aims, one turns as it were instinctively to long words and exhausted idioms, like a cuttlefish squirting out ink. In our age there is no such thing as "keeping out of politics." All issues are political issues, and politics itself is a mass of lies, evasions, folly, hatred and schizophrenia. When the general atmosphere is bad, language must suffer. I should expect to find—this is a guess which I have not sufficient knowledge to verify—that the German, Russian and Italian languages have all deteriorated in the last ten or fifteen years, as a result of dictatorship.

But if thought corrupts language, language can also corrupt thought. A bad usage can spread by tradition and imitation, even among people who should and do know better. The debased language that I have been discussing is in some ways very convenient. Phrases like a *not unjustifiable assumption, leaves much to be desired, would serve no good purpose, a consideration which we should do well to bear in mind,* are a continuous temptation, a packet of aspirins always at one's elbow. Look back through this essay, and for certain you will find that I have again and again committed the very faults I am protesting against. By this morning's post I have received a pamphlet dealing with conditions in Germany. The author tells me that he "felt impelled" to write it. I open it at random, and here is almost the first sentence that I see: "(The Allies) have an opportunity not only of achieving a radical transformation of Germany's social and political structure in such a way as to avoid a nationalistic reaction in Germany itself, but at the same time of laying the foundations of a co-operative and unified Europe." You see, he "feels impelled" to write—feels, presumably, that he has something new to say—and yet his words, like cavalry horses answering the bugle, group themselves automatically into the familiar dreary pattern. This invasion of one's mind by ready-made phrases (*lay the foundations, achieve a radical transformation*) can only be prevented if one is constantly on guard against them, and every such phrase anaesthetises a portion of one's brain.

I said earlier that the decadence of our language is probably curable. Those who deny this would argue, if they produced an argument at all, that language merely reflects existing social conditions, and that we cannot influence its development by any direct tinkering with words and constructions. So far as the general tone or spirit of a language goes, this may be true, but it is not true in detail. Silly words and expressions have often disappeared, not through any evolutionary process but owing to the conscious action of a minority. Two recent examples were *explore every avenue* and *leave no stone unturned,* which were killed by the jeers of a few journalists. There is a long list of fly-blown metaphors which could similarly be got rid of if enough people would interest themselves in the job; and it should also be possible to laugh the *not un-* formation out of existence,[1] to reduce the amount of Latin and Greek in the average sentence, to drive out foreign phrases and strayed scientific words, and, in general, to make pretentiousness unfashionable. But all these are minor points. The defence of the English language implies more than this, and perhaps it is best to start by saying what it does *not* imply.

To begin with, it has nothing to do with archaism, with the salvaging of

---

1. One can cure oneself of the *not un-* formation by memorising this sentence: *A not unblack dog was chasing a not unsmall rabbit across a not ungreen field* [Orwell's note].

obsolete words and turns of speech, or with the setting-up of a "standard English" which must never be departed from. On the contrary, it is especially concerned with the scrapping of every word or idiom which has outworn its usefulness. It has nothing to do with correct grammar and syntax, which are of no importance so long as one makes one's meaning clear, or with the avoidance of Americanisms, or with having what is called a "good prose style." On the other hand it is not concerned with fake simplicity and the attempt to make written English colloquial. Nor does it even imply in every case preferring the Saxon word to the Latin one, though it does imply using the fewest and shortest words that will cover one's meaning. What is above all needed is to let the meaning choose the word, and not the other way about. In prose, the worst thing one can do with words is to surrender to them. When you think of a concrete object, you think wordlessly, and then, if you want to describe the thing you have been visualising, you probably hunt about till you find the exact words that seem to fit it. When you think of something abstract you are more inclined to use words from the start, and unless you make a conscious effort to prevent it, the existing dialect will come rushing in and do the job for you, at the expense of blurring or even changing your meaning. Probably it is better to put off using words as long as possible and get one's meaning as clear as one can through pictures or sensations. Afterwards one can choose—not simply *accept*—the phrases that will best cover the meaning, and then switch round and decide what impression one's words are likely to make on another person. This last effort of the mind cuts out all stale or mixed images, all prefabricated phrases, needless repetitions, and humbug and vagueness generally. But one can often be in doubt about the effect of a word or a phrase, and one needs rules that one can rely on when instinct fails. I think the following rules will cover most cases:

    i. Never use a metaphor, simile or other figure of speech which you are used to seeing in print.

    ii. Never use a long word where a short one will do.

    iii. If it is possible to cut a word out, always cut it out.

    iv. Never use the passive where you can use the active.

    v. Never use a foreign phrase, a scientific word or a jargon word if you can think of an everyday English equivalent.

    vi. Break any of these rules sooner than say anything outright barbarous.

These rules sound elementary, and so they are, but they demand a deep change of attitude in anyone who has grown used to writing in the style now fashionable. One could keep all of them and still write bad English, but one could not write the kind of stuff that I quoted in those five specimens at the beginning of this article.

I have not here been considering the literary use of language, but merely language as an instrument for expressing and not for concealing or preventing thought. Stuart Chase and others have come near to claiming that all abstract words are meaningless, and have used this as a pretext for advocating a kind of political quietism. Since you don't know what Fascism is, how can you struggle against Fascism? One need not swallow such absurdities as this, but one ought to recognise that the present political chaos is connected with the decay of language, and that one can probably bring about some improvement by starting at the verbal end. If you simplify your English, you are freed from the worst follies of orthodoxy. You cannot speak any of the necessary dialects, and when you make a stupid remark its stupidity will be obvious, even to yourself. Political language—and with variations this is true of all political parties, from Conservatives to Anarchists—is designed to make lies sound truthful and murder respectable, and to give an appearance of solidity to pure wind. One cannot change this all in a moment, but one can at least change one's own habits, and from time to time one can even, if one jeers loudly enough, send some worn-out and useless phrase—some *jackboot, Achilles' heel, hotbed, melting pot, acid test, veritable inferno* or other lump of verbal refuse—into the dustbin where it belongs.

1946, 1947

SAMUEL BECKETT
1906–1989

Samuel Beckett was born near Dublin. Like W. B. Yeats, Bernard Shaw, and Oscar Wilde, he came from an Anglo-Irish Protestant family. He received a B.A. from Trinity College, Dublin, and after teaching English at the École Normale Supérieure in Paris for two years, returned to Trinity College to take his M.A. in 1931. He gave up teaching in 1932 to write, and having produced an insightful essay on the early stages of James Joyce's *Finnegans Wake* in 1929, he also worked as Joyce's amanuensis (secretary) and translator. In 1937 he settled permanently in Paris, where during World War II he joined an underground group in the anti-Nazi resistance and, after his group was betrayed, barely escaped into unoccupied France. From the mid-1940s he generally wrote in French and subsequently translated some of his work into an eloquent Irish-inflected English. His early novels—*Murphy* (1938; Eng. trans., 1957), *Watt* (1953), and the trilogy, *Molloy* (1951; 1955), *Malone Dies* (1951; 1956), and *The Unnameable* (1953; 1958)—have been hailed as masterpieces and precursors of postmodern fiction; but he is best-known for his plays, especially *Waiting for Godot* (1952; 1954) and *Endgame* (1957; 1958). He received the Nobel Prize in Literature in 1969.

Not much happens in a Beckett play; there is little plot, little incident, and little characterization. Characters engage in dialogue or dialectical monologues that go nowhere. There is no progression, no development, no resolution. Rambling exchanges and repetitive actions enact the lack of a fixed center, of meaning, of purpose, in the lives depicted. Yet the characters persist in their habitual, almost ritualistic, activities; they go on talking, even if only to themselves. In spite of a reiterated theme of nonexistence, the characters go on existing—if minimally: a stream of discourse, of thought and will, a consciousness questioning its own meaning and purpose. In *Waiting for Godot* the main characters wait for an arrival that is constantly deferred. They inhabit a bleak landscape seemingly confined to one road, one tree; they talk of moving on, yet never leave. Subsequent plays restrict the acting space to a room, to urns, to a mound in which the actor is buried; characters are physically confined or disabled, until *Not I* (1973) presents the most minimal embodiment of human consciousness available to theatrical representation: a disembodied mouth.

Beckett focuses his work on fundamental questions of existence and nonexistence, the mind and the body, the self as known from within and as seen from the outside or in retrospect. Joyce's artistic integrity and stream-of-consciousness technique influenced him, but the minimalism of Beckett's plays and fiction contrast with the maximalism of Joyce's *Ulysses* and *Finnegans Wake*. "I realised that Joyce had gone as far as one could in the direction of knowing more, in control of one's material," he told the biographer James Knowlson. "I realised my own way was in impoverishment, in lack of knowledge and in taking away, in subtracting rather than adding."

At the heart of *Endgame* is the vexed relationship between Hamm, the master, and Clov, his servant and nurse. These irritable, resentful, spiteful characters talk of leaving, dying, or otherwise ending, but they continue repetitively in their peevish ways. They live inside a room with two high windows that afford ambiguous views of an exterior world, where everything may or may not be dead. The play's only other characters are Hamm's parents, Nell and Nagg, but they live in two garbage cans and appear from the shoulders up; their relationship is hardly robust. Like other Beckett plays, this one juxtaposes vaudeville, slapstick, and other comic traditions with the intellectual and the grotesque. While denying the audience the comfortable security of a recognizable world, *Endgame* provides laughs, sometimes at the audience's expense. It shares its tragicomic quality with absurdist drama, which disrupts the conventions of realist drama, draws attention to its own fictionality, and refuses to provide hierarchies of significance. Reduced to bare essentials, the maimed, struggling, incomplete characters of *Endgame*—though often behaving as if they were the bumbling protagonists of a farce—raise unsettling questions about meaning and absurdity, power and dependency, time and repetition, language and the void.

Endgame[1]

For Roger Blin[2]

THE CHARACTERS

NAGG
NELL
HAMM
CLOV

Bare interior.
Grey light.
Left and right back, high up, two small windows, curtains drawn.
Front right, a door. Hanging near door, its face to wall, a picture.
Front left, touching each other, covered with an old sheet, two ashbins.
Centre, in an armchair on castors, covered with an old sheet, HAMM.
Motionless by the door, his eyes fixed on HAMM, CLOV. *Very red face.*
Brief tableau.

[CLOV *goes and stands under window left. Stiff, staggering walk. He looks up at window left. He turns and looks at window right. He goes and stands under window right. He looks up at window right. He turns and looks at window left. He goes out, comes back immediately with a small step-ladder, carries it over and sets it down under window left, gets up on it, draws back curtain. He gets down, takes six steps (for example) towards window right, goes back for ladder, carries it over and sets it down under window right, gets up on it, draws back curtain. He gets down, takes three steps towards window left, goes back for ladder,*

---

1. Translated by the author.
2. Frenchman (1907–1984), who directed the premieres of *Waiting for Godot*, *Endgame*, and other Beckett plays.

carries it over and sets it down under window left, gets up on it, looks out of window. Brief laugh. He gets down, takes one step towards window right, goes back for ladder, carries it over and sets it down under window right, gets up on it, looks out of window. Brief laugh. He gets down, goes with ladder towards ashbins, halts, turns, carries back ladder and sets it down under window right, goes to ashbins, removes sheet covering them, folds it over his arm. He raises one lid, stoops and looks into bin. Brief laugh. He closes lid. Same with other bin. He goes to HAMM, *removes sheet covering him, folds it over his arm. In a dressing-gown, a stiff toque[3] on his head, a large blood-stained handkerchief over his face, a whistle hanging from his neck, a rug over his knees, thick socks on his feet,* HAMM *seems to be asleep.* CLOV *looks him over. Brief laugh. He goes to door, halts, turns towards auditorium.*]

CLOV   [*Fixed gaze, tonelessly.*] Finished, it's finished, nearly finished, it must be nearly finished. [*Pause.*] Grain upon grain, one by one, and one day, suddenly, there's a heap, a little heap, the impossible heap. [*Pause.*] I can't be punished any more. [*Pause.*] I'll go now to my kitchen, ten feet by ten feet by ten feet, and wait for him to whistle me. [*Pause.*] Nice dimensions, nice proportions, I'll lean on the table, and look at the wall, and wait for him to whistle me. [*He remains a moment motionless, then goes out. He comes back immediately, goes to window right, takes up the ladder and carries it out. Pause.* HAMM *stirs. He yawns under the handkerchief. He removes the handkerchief from his face. Very red face. Black glasses.*]

HAMM   Me—[*He yawns.*]—to play.[4] [*He holds the handkerchief spread out before him.*] Old Stancher![5] [*He takes off his glasses, wipes his eyes, his face, the glasses, puts them on again, folds the handkerchief and puts it back neatly in the breast-pocket of his dressing-gown. He clears his throat, joins the tips of his fingers.*] Can there be misery—[*He yawns.*]—loftier than mine? No doubt. Formerly. But now? [*Pause.*] My father? [*Pause.*] My mother? [*Pause.*] My . . . dog? [*Pause.*] Oh I am willing to believe they suffer as much as such creatures can suffer. But does that mean their sufferings equal mine? No doubt. [*Pause.*] No, all is a—[*He yawns.*]—bsolute, [*Proudly.*] the bigger a man is the fuller he is. [*Pause. Gloomily.*] And the emptier. [*He sniffs.*] Clov! [*Pause.*] No, alone. [*Pause.*] What dreams! Those forests! [*Pause.*] Enough, it's time it ended, in the shelter too. [*Pause.*] And yet I hesitate, I hesitate to . . . to end. Yes, there it is, it's time it ended and yet I hesitate to—[*He yawns.*]—to end. [*Yawns.*] God, I'm tired, I'd be better off in bed. [*He whistles. Enter* CLOV *immediately. He halts beside the chair.*] You pollute the air! [*Pause.*] Get me ready, I'm going to bed.

CLOV   I've just got you up.

HAMM   And what of it?

CLOV   I can't be getting you up and putting you to bed every five minutes, I have things to do. [*Pause.*]

HAMM   Did you ever see my eyes?

CLOV   No.

HAMM   Did you never have the curiosity, while I was sleeping, to take off my glasses and look at my eyes?

3. Small cap with no brim.
4. Hamm announces that it is his move, as it were in a game of chess, of which the final stage is called the "endgame."
5. Handkerchief that stanches (checks the flow of) blood.

CLOV   Pulling back the lids? [*Pause.*] No.

HAMM   One of these days I'll show them to you. [*Pause.*] It seems they've gone all white. [*Pause.*] What time is it?

CLOV   The same as usual.

HAMM   [*Gesture towards window right.*] Have you looked?

CLOV   Yes.

HAMM   Well?

CLOV   Zero.

HAMM   It'd need to rain.

CLOV   It won't rain. [*Pause.*]

HAMM   Apart from that, how do you feel?

CLOV   I don't complain.

HAMM   You feel normal?

CLOV   [*Irritably.*] I tell you I don't complain.

HAMM   I feel a little queer. [*Pause.*] Clov!

CLOV   Yes.

HAMM   Have you not had enough?

CLOV   Yes! [*Pause.*] Of what?

HAMM   Of this . . . this . . . thing.

CLOV   I always had. [*Pause.*] Not you?

HAMM   [*Gloomily.*] Then there's no reason for it to change.

CLOV   It may end. [*Pause.*] All life long the same questions, the same answers.

HAMM   Get me ready. [CLOV *does not move.*] Go and get the sheet. [CLOV *does not move.*] Clov!

CLOV   Yes.

HAMM   I'll give you nothing more to eat.

CLOV   Then we'll die.

HAMM   I'll give you just enough to keep you from dying. You'll be hungry all the time.

CLOV   Then we won't die. [*Pause.*] I'll go and get the sheet. [*He goes towards the door.*]

HAMM   No! [CLOV *halts.*] I'll give you one biscuit per day. [*Pause.*] One and a half. [*Pause.*] Why do you stay with me?

CLOV   Why do you keep me?

HAMM   There's no one else.

CLOV   There's nowhere else. [*Pause.*]

HAMM   You're leaving me all the same.

CLOV   I'm trying.

HAMM   You don't love me.

CLOV   No.

HAMM   You loved me once.

CLOV   Once!

HAMM   I've made you suffer too much. [*Pause.*] Haven't I?

CLOV   It's not that.

HAMM   [*Shocked.*] I haven't made you suffer too much?

CLOV   Yes!

HAMM   [*Relieved.*] Ah you gave me a fright! [*Pause. Coldly.*] Forgive me. [*Pause. Louder.*] I said, Forgive me.

CLOV   I heard you. [*Pause.*] Have you bled?

HAMM   Less. [*Pause.*] Is it not time for my pain-killer?

CLOV   No. [*Pause.*]

HAMM   How are your eyes?

CLOV Bad.

HAMM How are your legs?

CLOV Bad.

HAMM But you can move.

CLOV Yes.

HAMM [*Violently.*] Then move! [CLOV *goes to back wall, leans against it with his forehead and hands.*] Where are you?

CLOV Here.

HAMM Come back! [CLOV *returns to his place beside the chair.*] Where are you?

CLOV Here.

HAMM Why don't you kill me?

CLOV I don't know the combination of the cupboard. [*Pause.*]

HAMM Go and get two bicycle-wheels.

CLOV There are no more bicycle-wheels.

HAMM What have you done with your bicycle?

CLOV I never had a bicycle.

HAMM The thing is impossible.

CLOV When there were still bicycles I wept to have one. I crawled at your feet. You told me to go to hell. Now there are none.

HAMM And your rounds? When you inspected my paupers. Always on foot?

CLOV Sometimes on horse. [*The lid of one of the bins lifts and the hands of* NAGG *appear, gripping the rim. Then his head emerges. Nightcap. Very white face.* NAGG *yawns, then listens.*] I'll leave you, I have things to do.

HAMM In your kitchen?

CLOV Yes.

HAMM Outside of here it's death. [*Pause.*] All right, be off. [*Exit* CLOV. *Pause.*] We're getting on.

NAGG Me Pap![6]

HAMM Accursed progenitor![7]

NAGG Me pap!

HAMM The old folks at home! No decency left! Guzzle, guzzle, that's all they think of. [*He whistles. Enter* CLOV. *He halts beside the chair.*] Well! I thought you were leaving me.

CLOV Oh not just yet, not just yet.

NAGG Me pap!

HAMM Give him his pap.

CLOV There's no more pap.

HAMM [*To* NAGG.] Do you hear that? There's no more pap. You'll never get any more pap.

NAGG I want me pap!

HAMM Give him a biscuit. [*Exit* CLOV.] Accursed fornicator! How are your stumps?

NAGG Never mind me stumps. [*Enter* CLOV *with biscuit.*]

CLOV I'm back again, with the biscuit. [*He gives biscuit to* NAGG *who fingers it, sniffs it.*]

NAGG [*Plaintively.*] What is it?

CLOV Spratt's medium.[8]

NAGG [*As before.*] It's hard! I can't!

---

6. Mushy food.   8. Brand name of a biscuit (cookie).
7. Parent.

HAMM Bottle him! [CLOV *pushes* NAGG *back into the bin, closes the lid.*]

CLOV [*Returning to his place beside the chair.*] If age but knew!

HAMM Sit on him!

CLOV I can't sit.

HAMM True. And I can't stand.

CLOV So it is.

HAMM Every man his speciality. [*Pause.*] No phone calls? [*Pause.*] Don't we laugh?

CLOV [*After reflection.*] I don't feel like it.

HAMM [*After reflection.*] Not I. [*Pause.*] Clov!

CLOV Yes.

HAMM Nature has forgotten us.

CLOV There's no more nature.

HAMM No more nature! You exaggerate.

CLOV In the vicinity.

HAMM But we breathe, we change! We lose our hair, our teeth! Our bloom! Our ideals!

CLOV Then she hasn't forgotten us.

HAMM But you say there is none.

CLOV [*Sadly.*] No one that ever lived ever thought so crooked as we.

HAMM We do what we can.

CLOV We shouldn't. [*Pause.*]

HAMM You're a bit of all right,[9] aren't you?

CLOV A smithereen. [*Pause.*]

HAMM This is slow work. [*Pause.*] Is it not time for my pain-killer?

CLOV No. [*Pause.*] I'll leave you, I have things to do.

HAMM In your kitchen?

CLOV Yes.

HAMM What, I'd like to know.

CLOV I look at the wall.

HAMM The wall! And what do you see on your wall? Mene, mene?[1] Naked bodies?

CLOV I see my light dying.

HAMM Your light dying! Listen to that! Well, it can die just as well here, *your* light. Take a look at me and then come back and tell me what you think of *your* light. [*Pause.*]

CLOV You shouldn't speak to me like that. [*Pause.*]

HAMM [*Coldly.*] Forgive me. [*Pause. Louder.*] I said, Forgive me.

CLOV I heard you. [*The lid of* NAGG'S *bin lifts. His hands appear, gripping the rim. Then his head emerges. In his mouth the biscuit. He listens.*]

HAMM Did your seeds come up?

CLOV No.

HAMM Did you scratch round them to see if they had sprouted?

CLOV They haven't sprouted.

HAMM Perhaps it's still too early.

CLOV If they were going to sprout they would have sprouted. [*Violently.*] They'll never sprout! [*Pause.* NAGG *takes biscuit in his hand.*]

---

9. You're pretty good (British slang).
1. "Mene mene, tekel, upharsin": words written by a heavenly hand on the wall during the feast of Balshazzar, king of Babylon. Translated as "Thou art weighed in the balance and found wanting," it foretells his ruin (Daniel 5.25–28).

HAMM   This is not much fun. [*Pause.*] But that's always the way at the end of the day, isn't it, Clov?

CLOV   Always.

HAMM   It's the end of the day like any other day, isn't it, Clov?

CLOV   Looks like it. [*Pause.*]

HAMM   [*Anguished.*] What's happening, what's happening?

CLOV   Something is taking its course. [*Pause.*]

HAMM   All right, be off. [*He leans back in his chair, remains motionless.* CLOV *does not move, heaves a great groaning sigh.* HAMM *sits up.*] I thought I told you to be off.

CLOV   I'm trying. [*He goes to door, halts.*] Ever since I was whelped.[2] [*Exit* CLOV.]

HAMM   We're getting on. [*He leans back in his chair, remains motionless.* NAGG *knocks on the lid of the other bin. Pause. He knocks harder. The lid lifts and the hands of* NELL *appear, gripping the rim. Then her head emerges. Lace cap. Very white face.*]

NELL   What is it, my pet? [*Pause.*] Time for love?

NAGG   Were you asleep?

NELL   Oh no!

NAGG   Kiss me.

NELL   We can't.

NAGG   Try. [*Their heads strain towards each other, fail to meet, fall apart again.*]

NELL   Why this farce, day after day? [*Pause.*]

NAGG   I've lost me tooth.

NELL   When?

NAGG   I had it yesterday.

NELL   [*Elegiac.*[3]] Ah yesterday! [*They turn painfully towards each other.*]

NAGG   Can you see me?

NELL   Hardly. And you?

NAGG   What?

NELL   Can you see me?

NAGG   Hardly.

NELL   So much the better, so much the better.

NAGG   Don't say that. [*Pause.*] Our sight has failed.

NELL   Yes. [*Pause. They turn away from each other.*]

NAGG   Can you hear me?

NELL   Yes. And you?

NAGG   Yes. [*Pause.*] Our hearing hasn't failed.

NELL   Our what?

NAGG   Our hearing.

NELL   No. [*Pause.*] Have you anything else to say to me?

NAGG   Do you remember—

NELL   No.

NAGG   When we crashed on our tandem[4] and lost our shanks. [*They laugh heartily.*]

NELL   It was in the Ardennes. [*They laugh less heartily.*]

NAGG   On the road to Sedan.[5] [*They laugh still less heartily.*] Are you cold?

2. Born (usually applied to puppies: whelps).
3. As though lamenting something lost.
4. A bicycle made for two.
5. Town in northern France where the French Army was defeated in 1870 during the Franco-Prussian War. Ardennes is a forest in northern France, which was the scene of fierce fighting in both World Wars.

NELL   Yes, perished. And you?

NAGG   [*Pause.*] I'm freezing. [*Pause.*] Do you want to go in?

NELL   Yes.

NAGG   Then go in. [NELL *does not move.*] Why don't you go in?

NELL   I don't know. [*Pause.*]

NAGG   Has he changed your sawdust?

NELL   It isn't sawdust. [*Pause. Wearily.*] Can you not be a little accurate, Nagg?

NAGG   Your sand then. It's not important.

NELL   It is important. [*Pause.*]

NAGG   It was sawdust once.

NELL   Once!

NAGG   And now it's sand. [*Pause.*] From the shore. [*Pause. Impatiently.*] Now it's sand he fetches from the shore.

NELL   Now it's sand.

NAGG   Has he changed yours?

NELL   No.

NAGG   Nor mine. [*Pause.*] I won't have it! [*Pause. Holding up the biscuit.*] Do you want a bit?

NELL   No. [*Pause.*] Of what?

NAGG   Biscuit. I've kept you half. [*He looks at the biscuit. Proudly.*] Three quarters. For you. Here. [*He proffers the biscuit.*] No? [*Pause.*] Do you not feel well?

HAMM   [*Wearily.*] Quiet, quiet, you're keeping me awake. [*Pause.*] Talk softer. [*Pause.*] If I could sleep I might make love. I'd go into the woods. My eyes would see . . . the sky, the earth. I'd run, run, they wouldn't catch me. [*Pause.*] Nature! [*Pause.*] There's something dripping in my head. [*Pause.*] A heart, a heart in my head. [*Pause.*]

NAGG   [*Soft.*] Do you hear him? A heart in his head! [*He chuckles cautiously.*]

NELL   One mustn't laugh at those things, Nagg. Why must you always laugh at them?

NAGG   Not so loud!

NELL   [*Without lowering her voice.*] Nothing is funnier than unhappiness, I grant you that. But—

NAGG   [*Shocked.*] Oh!

NELL   Yes, yes, it's the most comical thing in the world. And we laugh, we laugh, with a will, in the beginning. But it's always the same thing. Yes, it's like the funny story we have heard too often, we still find it funny, but we don't laugh any more. [*Pause.*] Have you anything else to say to me?

NAGG   No.

NELL   Are you quite sure? [*Pause.*] Then I'll leave you.

NAGG   Do you not want your biscuit? [*Pause.*] I'll keep it for you. [*Pause.*] I thought you were going to leave me.

NELL   I am going to leave you.

NAGG   Could you give me a scratch before you go?

NELL   No. [*Pause.*] Where?

NAGG   In the back.

NELL   No. [*Pause.*] Rub yourself against the rim.

NAGG   It's lower down. In the hollow.

NELL   What hollow?

NAGG   The hollow! [*Pause.*] Could you not? [*Pause.*] Yesterday you scratched me there.

NELL   [*Elegiac.*] Ah yesterday!

NAGG   Could you not? [*Pause.*] Would you like me to scratch you? [*Pause.*]
Are you crying again?

NELL   I was trying. [*Pause.*]

HAMM   Perhaps it's a little vein. [*Pause.*]

NAGG   What was that he said?

NELL   Perhaps it's a little vein.

NAGG   What does that mean? [*Pause.*] That means nothing. [*Pause.*] Will I
tell you the story of the tailor?

NELL   No. [*Pause.*] What for?

NAGG   To cheer you up.

NELL   It's not funny.

NAGG   It always made you laugh. [*Pause.*] The first time I thought you'd die.

NELL   It was on Lake Como.[6] [*Pause.*] One April afternoon. [*Pause.*] Can you
believe it?

NAGG   What?

NELL   That we once went out rowing on Lake Como. [*Pause.*] One April
afternoon.

NAGG   We had got engaged the day before.

NELL   Engaged!

NAGG   You were in such fits that we capsized. By rights we should have been
drowned.

NELL   It was because I felt happy.

NAGG   [*Indignant.*] It was not, it was not, it was my story and nothing else.
Happy! Don't you laugh at it still? Every time I tell it. Happy!

NELL   It was deep, deep. And you could see down to the bottom. So white.
So clean.

NAGG   Let me tell it again. [*Raconteur's voice.*] An Englishman, needing a pair
of striped trousers in a hurry for the New Year festivities, goes to his tailor
who takes his measurements. [*Tailor's voice.*] "That's the lot, come back in
four days, I'll have it ready." Good. Four days later. [*Tailor's voice.*] "So sorry,
come back in a week, I've made a mess of the seat." Good, that's all right,
a neat seat can be very ticklish. A week later. [*Tailor's voice.*] "Frightfully
sorry, come back in ten days. I've made a hash of the crotch." Good, can't
be helped, a snug crotch is always a teaser. Ten days later. [*Tailor's voice.*]
"Dreadfully sorry, come back in a fortnight, I've made a balls of the fly."
Good, at a pinch, a smart fly is a stiff proposition. [*Pause. Normal voice.*] I
never told it worse. [*Pause. Gloomy.*] I tell this story worse and worse. [*Pause.
Raconteur's voice.*] Well, to make it short, the bluebells are blowing and he
ballockses[7] the buttonholes. [*Customer's voice.*] "God damn you to hell, Sir,
no, it's indecent, there are limits! In six days, do you hear me, six days, God
made the world. Yes Sir, no less Sir, the WORLD! And you are not bloody
well capable of making me a pair of trousers in three months!" [*Tailor's voice,
scandalised.*] "But my dear Sir, my dear Sir, look—[*Disdainful gesture, dis-
gustedly.*]—at the world—[*Pause.*] and look—[*Loving gesture, proudly.*]—at
my TROUSERS!" [*Pause. He looks at NELL who has remained impassive, her
eyes unseeing, breaks into a high forced laugh, cuts it short, pokes his head
towards NELL, launches his laugh again.*]

HAMM   Silence!

   [NAGG *starts, cuts short his laugh.*]

---

6. Large lake in northern Italy.   7. Botches.

NELL   You could see down to the bottom.

HAMM   [*Exasperated.*] Have you not finished? Will you never finish? [*With sudden fury.*] Will this never finish? [NAGG *disappears into his bin, closes the lid behind him.* NELL *does not move. Frenziedly.*] My kingdom for a night-man![8] [*He whistles. Enter* CLOV.] Clear away this muck! Chuck it in the sea! [CLOV *goes to bins, halts.*]

NELL   So white.

HAMM   What? What's she blathering about? [CLOV *stoops, takes* NELL's *hand, feels her pulse.*]

NELL   [*To* CLOV.] Desert! [CLOV *lets go her hand, pushes her back in the bin, closes the lid.*]

CLOV   [*Returning to his place beside the chair.*] She has no pulse.

HAMM   What was she drivelling about?

CLOV   She told me to go away, into the desert.

HAMM   Damn busybody! Is that all?

CLOV   No.

HAMM   What else?

CLOV   I didn't understand.

HAMM   Have you bottled her?

CLOV   Yes.

HAMM   Are they both bottled?

CLOV   Yes.

HAMM   Screw down the lids. [CLOV *goes towards door.*] Time enough. [CLOV *halts.*] My anger subsides, I'd like to pee.

CLOV   [*With alacrity.*] I'll go and get the catheter. [*He goes towards door.*]

HAMM   Time enough. [CLOV *halts.*] Give me my pain-killer.

CLOV   It's too soon. [*Pause.*] It's too soon on top of your tonic, it wouldn't act.

HAMM   In the morning they brace you up and in the evening they calm you down. Unless it's the other way round. [*Pause.*] That old doctor, he's dead naturally?

CLOV   He wasn't old.

HAMM   But he's dead?

CLOV   Naturally. [*Pause.*] You ask me that? [*Pause.*]

HAMM   Take me for a little turn. [CLOV *goes behind the chair and pushes it forward.*] Not too fast! [CLOV *pushes chair.*] Right round the world! [CLOV *pushes chair.*] Hug the walls, then back to the centre again. [CLOV *pushes chair.*] I was right in the centre, wasn't I?

CLOV   [*Pushing.*] Yes.

HAMM   We'd need a proper wheel-chair. With big wheels. Bicycle wheels! [*Pause.*] Are you hugging?

CLOV   [*Pushing.*] Yes.

HAMM   [*Groping for wall.*] It's a lie! Why do you lie to me?

CLOV   [*Bearing closer to wall.*] There! There!

HAMM   Stop! [CLOV *stops chair close to back wall.* HAMM *lays his hand against wall.*] Old wall! [*Pause.*] Beyond is the . . . other hell. [*Pause. Violently.*] Closer! Closer! Up against!

CLOV   Take away your hand. [HAMM *withdraws his hand.* CLOV *rams chair against wall.*] There! [HAMM *leans towards wall, applies his ear to it.*]

8. A collector of nightsoil (excrement). Cf. Shakespeare's *Richard III* 5.7.7: "A horse! A horse! My kingdom for a horse!"

HAMM   Do you hear? [*He strikes the wall with his knuckles.*] Do you hear?
Hollow bricks! [*He strikes again.*] All that's hollow! [*Pause. He straightens
up. Violently.*] That's enough. Back!

CLOV   We haven't done the round.

HAMM   Back to my place! [CLOV *pushes chair back to centre.*] Is that my place?

CLOV   Yes, that's your place.

HAMM   Am I right in the centre?

CLOV   I'll measure it.

HAMM   More or less! More or less!

CLOV   [*Moving chair slightly.*] There!

HAMM   I'm more or less in the centre?

CLOV   I'd say so.

HAMM   You'd say so! Put me right in the centre!

CLOV   I'll go and get the tape.

HAMM   Roughly! Roughly! [CLOV *moves chair slightly.*] Bang in the centre!

CLOV   There! [*Pause.*]

HAMM   I feel a little too far to the left. [CLOV *moves chair slightly.*] Now I feel
a little too far to the right. [CLOV *moves chair slightly.*] I feel a little too far
forward. [CLOV *moves chair slightly.*] Now I feel a little too far back. [CLOV
moves chair slightly.] Don't stay there, [*I.e., behind the chair.*] you give me
the shivers. [CLOV *returns to his place beside the chair.*]

CLOV   If I could kill him I'd die happy. [*Pause.*]

HAMM   What's the weather like?

CLOV   As usual.

HAMM   Look at the earth.

CLOV   I've looked.

HAMM   With the glass?

CLOV   No need of the glass.

HAMM   Look at it with the glass.

CLOV   I'll go and get the glass. [*Exit CLOV.*]

HAMM   No need of the glass! [*Enter CLOV with telescope.*]

CLOV   I'm back again, with the glass. [*He goes to window right, looks up at it.*]
I need the steps.

HAMM   Why? Have you shrunk? [*Exit CLOV with telescope.*] I don't like that,
I don't like that. [*Enter CLOV with ladder, but without telescope.*]

CLOV   I'm back again, with the steps. [*He sets down ladder under window right,
gets up on it, realises he has not the telescope, gets down.*] I need the glass.
[*He goes towards door.*]

HAMM   [*Violently.*] But you have the glass!

CLOV   [*Halting, violently.*] No, I haven't the glass! [*Exit CLOV.*]

HAMM   This is deadly. [*Enter CLOV with telescope. He goes towards ladder.*]

CLOV   Things are livening up. [*He gets up on ladder, raises the telescope, lets
it fall.*] I did it on purpose. [*He gets down, picks up the telescope, turns it on
auditorium.*] I see . . . a multitude . . . in transports . . . of joy.[9] [*Pause.*]
That's what I call a magnifier. [*He lowers the telescope, turns towards HAMM.*]
Well? Don't we laugh?

HAMM   [*After reflection.*] I don't.

CLOV   [*After reflection.*] Nor I. [*He gets up on ladder, turns the telescope on

---

9. Cf. Revelation 7.9–10: "After this I beheld, and lo, a great multitude, which . . . cried with a loud voice
. . . Salvation."

the without.] Let's see. [*He looks, moving the telescope.*] Zero . . . [*He looks.*]
. . . zero . . . [*He looks.*] . . . and zero.

HAMM   Nothing stirs. All is—

CLOV   Zer—

HAMM   [*Violently.*] Wait till you're spoke to! [*Normal voice.*] All is . . . all is
. . . all is what? [*Violently.*] All is what?

CLOV   What all is? In a word? Is that what you want to know? Just a moment.
[*He turns the telescope on the without, looks, lowers the telescope, turns
towards* HAMM.] Corpsed. [*Pause.*] Well? Content?

HAMM   Look at the sea.

CLOV   It's the same.

HAMM   Look at the ocean! [CLOV *gets down, takes a few steps towards window
left, goes back for ladder, carries it over and sets it down under window left,
gets up on it, turns the telescope on the without, looks at length. He starts,
lowers the telescope, examines it, turns it again on the without.*]

CLOV   Never seen anything like that!

HAMM   [*Anxious.*] What? A sail? A fin? Smoke?

CLOV   [*Looking.*] The light is sunk.

HAMM   [*Relieved.*] Pah! We all knew that.

CLOV   [*Looking.*] There was a bit left.

HAMM   The base.

CLOV   [*Looking.*] Yes.

HAMM   And now?

CLOV   [*Looking.*] All gone.

HAMM   No gulls?

CLOV   [*Looking.*] Gulls!

HAMM   And the horizon? Nothing on the horizon?

CLOV   [*Lowering the telescope, turning towards* HAMM, *exasperated.*] What in
God's name could there be on the horizon? [*Pause.*]

HAMM   The waves, how are the waves?

CLOV   The waves? [*He turns the telescope on the waves.*] Lead.

HAMM   And the sun?

CLOV   [*Looking.*] Zero.

HAMM   But it should be sinking. Look again.

CLOV   [*Looking.*] Damn the sun.

HAMM   Is it night already then?

CLOV   [*Looking.*] No.

HAMM   Then what is it?

CLOV   [*Looking.*] Grey. [*Lowering the telescope, turning towards* HAMM,
louder.] Grey! [*Pause. Still louder.*] GRREY! [*Pause. He gets down,
approaches* HAMM *from behind, whispers in his ear.*]

HAMM   [*Starting.*] Grey! Did I hear you say grey?

CLOV   Light black. From pole to pole.

HAMM   You exaggerate. [*Pause.*] Don't stay there, you give me the shivers.
[CLOV *returns to his place beside the chair.*]

CLOV   Why this farce, day after day?

HAMM   Routine. One never knows. [*Pause.*] Last night I saw inside my breast.
There was a big sore.

CLOV   Pah! You saw your heart.

HAMM   No, it was living. [*Pause. Anguished.*] Clov!

CLOV   Yes.

HAMM What's happening?

CLOV Something is taking its course. [*Pause.*]

HAMM Clov!

CLOV [*Impatiently.*] What is it?

HAMM We're not beginning to . . . to . . . mean something?

CLOV Mean something! You and I, mean something! [*Brief laugh.*] Ah that's a good one!

HAMM I wonder. [*Pause.*] Imagine if a rational being came back to earth, wouldn't he be liable to get ideas into his head if he observed us long enough. [*Voice of rational being.*] Ah, good, now I see what it is, yes, now I understand what they're at! [CLOV *starts, drops the telescope and begins to scratch his belly with both hands. Normal voice.*] And without going so far as that, we ourselves . . . [*With emotion.*] . . . we ourselves . . . at certain moments . . . [*Vehemently.*] To think perhaps it won't all have been for nothing!

CLOV [*Anguished, scratching himself.*] I have a flea!

HAMM A flea! Are there still fleas?

CLOV On me there's one. [*Scratching.*] Unless it's a crablouse.

HAMM [*Very perturbed.*] But humanity might start from there all over again! Catch him, for the love of God!

CLOV I'll go and get the powder. [*Exit CLOV.*]

HAMM A flea! This is awful! What a day! [*Enter CLOV with a sprinkling-tin.*]

CLOV I'm back again, with the insecticide.

HAMM Let him have it! [CLOV *loosens the top of his trousers, pulls it forward and shakes powder into the aperture. He stoops, looks, waits, starts, frenziedly shakes more powder, stoops, looks, waits.*]

CLOV The bastard!

HAMM Did you get him?

CLOV Looks like it. [*He drops the tin and adjusts his trousers.*] Unless he's laying doggo.

HAMM Laying! Lying you mean. Unless he's *lying* doggo.

CLOV Ah? One says lying? One doesn't say laying?

HAMM Use your head, can't you. If he was laying we'd be bitched.

CLOV Ah. [*Pause.*] What about that pee?

HAMM I'm having it.

CLOV Ah that's the spirit, that's the spirit! [*Pause.*]

HAMM [*With ardour.*] Let's go from here, the two of us! South! You can make a raft and the currents will carry us away, far away, to other . . . mammals!

CLOV God forbid!

HAMM Alone, I'll embark alone! Get working on that raft immediately. Tomorrow I'll be gone for ever.

CLOV [*Hastening towards door.*] I'll start straight away.

HAMM Wait! [CLOV *halts.*] Will there be sharks, do you think?

CLOV Sharks? I don't know. If there are there will be. [*He goes towards door.*]

HAMM Wait! [CLOV *halts.*] Is it not yet time for my pain-killer?

CLOV [*Violently.*] No! [*He goes towards door.*]

HAMM Wait! [CLOV *halts.*] How are your eyes?

CLOV Bad.

HAMM But you can see.

CLOV All I want.

HAMM How are your legs?

CLOV Bad.

HAMM   But you can walk.

CLOV   I come . . . and go.

HAMM   In my house. [*Pause. With prophetic relish.*] One day you'll be blind, like me. You'll be sitting there, a speck in the void, in the dark, for ever, like me. [*Pause.*] One day you'll say to yourself, I'm tired, I'll sit down, and you'll go and sit down. Then you'll say, I'm hungry, I'll get up and get something to eat. But you won't get up. You'll say, I shouldn't have sat down, but since I have I'll sit on a little longer, then I'll get up and get something to eat. But you won't go up and you won't get anything to eat. [*Pause.*] You'll look at the wall a while, then you'll say, I'll close my eyes, perhaps have a little sleep, after that I'll feel better, and you'll close them. And when you open them again there'll be no wall any more. [*Pause.*] Infinite emptiness will be all around you, all the resurrected dead of all the ages wouldn't fill it, and there you'll be like a little bit of grit in the middle of the steppe.[1] [*Pause.*] Yes, one day you'll know what it is, you'll be like me, except that you won't have anyone with you, because you won't have had pity on anyone and because there won't be anyone left to have pity on. [*Pause.*]

CLOV   It's not certain. [*Pause.*] And there's one thing you forget.

HAMM   Ah?

CLOV   I can't sit down.

HAMM   [*Impatiently.*] Well you'll lie down then, what the hell! Or you'll come to a standstill, simply stop and stand still, the way you are now. One day you'll say, I'm tired, I'll stop. What does the attitude matter? [*Pause.*]

CLOV   So you all want me to leave you.

HAMM   Naturally.

CLOV   Then I'll leave you.

HAMM   You can't leave us.

CLOV   Then I won't leave you. [*Pause.*]

HAMM   Why don't you finish us? [*Pause.*] I'll tell you the combination of the cupboard if you promise to finish me.

CLOV   I couldn't finish you.

HAMM   Then you won't finish me. [*Pause.*]

CLOV   I'll leave you, I have things to do.

HAMM   Do you remember when you came here?

CLOV   No. Too small, you told me.

HAMM   Do you remember your father?

CLOV   [*Wearily.*] Same answer. [*Pause.*] You've asked me these questions millions of times.

HAMM   I love the old questions. [*With fervour.*] Ah the old questions, the old answers, there's nothing like them! [*Pause.*] It was I was a father to you.

CLOV   Yes. [*He looks at* HAMM *fixedly.*] You were that to me.

HAMM   My house a home for you.

CLOV   Yes. [*He looks about him.*] This was that for me.

HAMM   [*Proudly.*] But for me, [*Gesture towards himself.*] no father. But for Hamm, [*Gesture towards surroundings.*] no home. [*Pause.*]

CLOV   I'll leave you.

HAMM   Did you ever think of one thing?

CLOV   Never.

HAMM   That here we're down in a hole. [*Pause.*] But beyond the hills? Eh?

---

1. Level grassy plain devoid of forest, especially in southeast Europe and Siberia.

Perhaps it's still green. Eh? [*Pause.*] Flora! Pomona! [*Ecstatically.*] Ceres![2]
[*Pause.*] Perhaps you won't need to go very far.

CLOV   I can't go very far. [*Pause.*] I'll leave you.

HAMM   Is my dog ready?

CLOV   He lacks a leg.

HAMM   Is he silky?

CLOV   He's a kind of Pomeranian.

HAMM   Go and get him.

CLOV   He lacks a leg.

HAMM   Go and get him! [*Exit* CLOV.] We're getting on. [*Enter* CLOV *holding by one of its three legs a black toy dog.*]

CLOV   Your dogs are here. [*He hands the dog to* HAMM *who feels it, fondles it.*]

HAMM   He's white, isn't he?

CLOV   Nearly.

HAMM   What do you mean, nearly? Is he white or isn't he?

CLOV   He isn't. [*Pause.*]

HAMM   You've forgotten the sex.

CLOV   [*Vexed.*] But he isn't finished. The sex goes on at the end. [*Pause.*]

HAMM   You haven't put on his ribbon.

CLOV   [*Angrily.*] But he isn't finished, I tell you! First you finish your dog and then you put on his ribbon! [*Pause.*]

HAMM   Can he stand?

CLOV   I don't know.

HAMM   Try. [*He hands the dog to* CLOV *who places it on the ground.*] Well?

CLOV   Wait! [*He squats down and tries to get the dog to stand on its three legs, fails, lets it go. The dog falls on its side.*]

HAMM   [*Impatiently.*] Well?

CLOV   He's standing.

HAMM   [*Groping for the dog.*] Where? Where is he? [CLOV *holds up the dog in a standing position.*]

CLOV   There. [*He takes* HAMM's *hand and guides it towards the dog's head.*]

HAMM   [*His hand on the dog's head.*] Is he gazing at me?

CLOV   Yes.

HAMM   [*Proudly.*] As if he were asking me to take him for a walk?

CLOV   If you like.

HAMM   [*As before.*] Or as if he were begging me for a bone. [*He withdraws his hand.*] Leave him like that, standing there imploring me. [CLOV *straightens up. The dog falls on its side.*]

CLOV   I'll leave you.

HAMM   Have you had your visions?

CLOV   Less.

HAMM   Is Mother Pegg's light on?

CLOV   Light! How could anyone's light be on?

HAMM   Extinguished!

CLOV   Naturally it's extinguished. If it's not on it's extinguished.

HAMM   No, I mean Mother Pegg.

CLOV   But naturally she's extinguished! [*Pause.*] What's the matter with you today?

HAMM   I'm taking my course. [*Pause.*] Is she buried?

---

2. In Roman mythology, respectively, the goddesses of flowers, fruit, and crops.

CLOV Buried! Who would have buried her?

HAMM You.

CLOV Me! Haven't I enough to do without burying people?

HAMM But you'll bury me.

CLOV No I won't bury you. [*Pause.*]

HAMM She was bonny once, like a flower of the field. [*With reminiscent leer.*] And a great one for the men!

CLOV We too were bonny—once. It's a rare thing not to have been bonny—once. [*Pause.*]

HAMM Go and get the gaff.[3] [CLOV *goes to door, halts.*]

CLOV Do this, do that, and I do it. I never refuse. Why?

HAMM You're not able to.

CLOV Soon I won't do it any more.

HAMM You won't be able to any more. [*Exit* CLOV.] Ah the creatures, the creatures, everything has to be explained to them. [*Enter* CLOV *with gaff.*]

CLOV Here's your gaff. Stick it up. [*He gives the gaff to* HAMM *who, wielding it like a puntpole,[4] tries to move his chair.*]

HAMM Did I move?

CLOV No. [HAMM *throws down the gaff.*]

HAMM Go and get the oilcan.

CLOV What for?

HAMM To oil the castors.

CLOV I oiled them yesterday.

HAMM Yesterday! What does that mean? Yesterday!

CLOV [*Violently.*] That means that bloody awful day, long ago, before this bloody awful day. I use the words you taught me. If they don't mean anything any more, teach me others. Or let me be silent. [*Pause.*]

HAMM I once knew a madman who thought the end of the world had come. He was a painter—and engraver. I had a great fondness for him. I used to go and see him, in the asylum. I'd take him by the hand and drag him to the window. Look! There! All that rising corn! And there! Look! The sails of the herring fleet! All that loveliness! [*Pause.*] He'd snatch away his hand and go back into his corner. Appalled. All he had seen was ashes. [*Pause.*] He alone had been spared. [*Pause.*] Forgotten. [*Pause.*] It appears the case is . . . was not so . . . so unusual.

CLOV A madman! When was that?

HAMM Oh way back, way back, you weren't in the land of the living.

CLOV God be with the days! [*Pause.* HAMM *raises his toque.*]

HAMM I had a great fondness for him. [*Pause. He puts on his toque again.*] He was a painter—and engraver.

CLOV There are so many terrible things.

HAMM No, no, there are not so many now. [*Pause.*] Clov!

CLOV Yes.

HAMM Do you not think this has gone on long enough?

CLOV Yes! [*Pause.*] What?

HAMM This . . . this . . . thing.

CLOV I've always thought so. [*Pause.*] You not?

HAMM [*Gloomily.*] Then it's a day like any other day.

---

3. Barbed fishing spear.
4. Long pole, pushed against the bottom of a river to propel a punt (a shallow flat-bottomed boat).

CLOV As long as it lasts. [*Pause.*] All life long the same inanities.

HAMM I can't leave you.

CLOV I know. And you can't follow me. [*Pause.*]

HAMM If you leave me how shall I know?

CLOV [*Briskly.*] Well you simply whistle me and if I don't come running it means I've left you. [*Pause.*]

HAMM You won't come and kiss me goodbye?

CLOV Oh I shouldn't think so. [*Pause.*]

HAMM But you might be merely dead in your kitchen.

CLOV The result would be the same.

HAMM Yes, but how would I know, if you were merely dead in your kitchen?

CLOV Well . . . sooner or later I'd start to stink.

HAMM You stink already. The whole place stinks of corpses.

CLOV The whole universe.

HAMM [*Angrily.*] To hell with the universe. [*Pause.*] Think of something.

CLOV What?

HAMM An idea, have an idea. [*Angrily.*] A bright idea!

CLOV Ah good. [*He starts pacing to and fro, his eyes fixed on the ground, his hands behind his back. He halts.*] The pains in my legs! It's unbelievable! Soon I won't be able to think any more.

HAMM You won't be able to leave me. [CLOV *resumes his pacing.*] What are you doing?

CLOV Having an idea. [*He paces.*] Ah! [*He halts.*]

HAMM What a brain! [*Pause.*] Well?

CLOV Wait! [*He meditates. Not very convinced.*] Yes . . . [*Pause. More convinced.*] Yes! [*He raises his head.*] I have it! I set the alarm. [*Pause.*]

HAMM This is perhaps not one of my bright days, but frankly—

CLOV You whistle me. I don't come. The alarm rings. I'm gone. It doesn't ring. I'm dead. [*Pause.*]

HAMM Is it working? [*Pause. Impatiently.*] The alarm, is it working?

CLOV Why wouldn't it be working?

HAMM Because it's worked too much.

CLOV But it's hardly worked at all.

HAMM [*Angrily.*] Then because it's worked too little!

CLOV I'll go and see. [*Exit* CLOV. *Brief ring of alarm off. Enter* CLOV *with alarm-clock. He holds it against* HAMM'*s ear and releases alarm. They listen to it ringing to the end. Pause.*] Fit to wake the dead! Did you hear it?

HAMM Vaguely.

CLOV The end is terrific!

HAMM I prefer the middle. [*Pause.*] Is it not time for my pain-killer?

CLOV No! [*He goes to door, turns.*] I'll leave you.

HAMM It's time for my story. Do you want to listen to my story.

CLOV No.

HAMM Ask my father if he wants to listen to my story. [CLOV *goes to bins, raises the lid of* NAGG'*s, stoops, looks into it. Pause. He straightens up.*]

CLOV He's asleep.

HAMM Wake him. [CLOV *stoops, wakes* NAGG *with the alarm. Unintelligible words.* CLOV *straightens up.*]

CLOV He doesn't want to listen to your story.

HAMM I'll give him a bon-bon. [CLOV *stoops. As before.*]

CLOV He wants a sugar-plum.

HAMM   He'll get a sugar-plum. [CLOV *stoops. As before.*]

CLOV   It's a deal. [*He goes towards door.* NAGG*'s hands appear, gripping the rim. Then the head emerges.* CLOV *reaches door, turns.*] Do you believe in the life to come?

HAMM   Mine was always that. [*Exit* CLOV.] Got him that time!

NAGG   I'm listening.

HAMM   Scoundrel! Why did you engender me?

NAGG   I didn't know.

HAMM   What? What didn't you know?

NAGG   That it'd be you. [*Pause.*] You'll give me a sugar-plum?

HAMM   After the audition.

NAGG   You swear?

HAMM   Yes.

NAGG   On what?

HAMM   My honour. [*Pause. They laugh heartily.*]

NAGG   Two.

HAMM   One.

NAGG   One for me and one for—

HAMM   One! Silence! [*Pause.*] Where was I? [*Pause. Gloomily.*] It's finished, we're finished. [*Pause.*] Nearly finished. [*Pause.*] There'll be no more speech. [*Pause.*] Something dripping in my head, ever since the fontanelles.[5] [*Stifled hilarity of* NAGG.] Splash, splash, always on the same spot. [*Pause.*] Perhaps it's a little vein. [*Pause.*] A little artery. [*Pause. More animated.*] Enough of that, it's story time, where was I? [*Pause. Narrative tone.*] The man came crawling towards me, on his belly. Pale, wonderfully pale and thin, he seemed on the point of—[*Pause. Normal tone.*] No, I've done that bit. [*Pause. Narrative tone.*] I calmly filled my pipe—the meerschaum, lit it with . . . let us say a vesta,[6] drew a few puffs. Aah! [*Pause.*] Well, what is it you want? [*Pause.*] It was an extra-ordinarily bitter day, I remember, zero by the thermometer. But considering it was Christmas Eve there was nothing . . . extra-ordinary about that. Seasonable weather, for once in a way. [*Pause.*] Well, what ill wind blows you my way? He raised his face to me, black with mingled dirt and tears. [*Pause. Normal tone.*] That should do it. [*Narrative tone.*] No, no, don't look at me, don't look at me. He dropped his eyes and mumbled something, apologies I presume. [*Pause.*] I'm a busy man, you know, the final touches, before the festivities, you know what it is. [*Pause. Forcibly.*] Come on now, what is the object of this invasion? [*Pause.*] It was a glorious bright day, I remember, fifty by the heliometer,[7] but already the sun was sinking down into the . . . down among the dead. [*Normal tone.*] Nicely put, that. [*Narrative tone.*] Come on now, come on, present your petition and let me resume my labours. [*Pause. Normal tone.*] There's English for you. Ah well . . . [*Narrative tone.*] It was then he took the plunge. It's my little one, he said. Tsstss, a little one, that's bad. My little boy, he said, as if the sex mattered. Where did he come from? He named the hole. A good half-day, on horse. What are you insinuating? That the place is still inhabited? No no, not a soul, except himself and the child—assuming he existed. Good. I enquired about the situation at Kov,[8] beyond the gulf. Not

---

5. Membranous space in infant's skull at the angles of the parietal bones.
6. Vesta is the brand name of a type of match (from Vesta, Roman goddess of the hearth).

7. Literally, a sun meter.
8. Conceivably the town of Kova in southern Siberia (except that it has no gulf); more probably Hamm's invention.

a sinner. Good. And you expect me to believe you have left your little one back there, all alone, and alive into the bargain? Come now! [*Pause.*] It was a howling wild day, I remember, a hundred by the anemometer.[9] The wind was tearing up the dead pines and sweeping them . . . away. [*Pause. Normal tone.*] A bit feeble, that. [*Narrative tone.*] Come on, man, speak up, what is it you want from me, I have to put up my holly. [*Pause.*] Well to make it short it finally transpired that what he wanted from me was . . . bread for his brat? Bread? But I have no bread, it doesn't agree with me. Good. Then perhaps a little corn? [*Pause. Normal tone.*] That should do it. [*Narrative tone.*] Corn, yes, I have corn, it's true, in my granaries. But use your head. I give you some corn, a pound, a pound and a half, you bring it back to your child and you make him—if he's still alive—a nice pot of porridge, [NAGG *reacts.*] a nice pot and a half of porridge, full of nourishment. Good. The colours come back into his little cheeks—perhaps. And then? [*Pause.*] I lost patience. [*Violently.*] Use your head, can't you, use your head, you're on earth, there's no cure for that! [*Pause.*] It was an exceedingly dry day, I remember, zero by the hygrometer. Ideal weather, for my lumbago.[1] [*Pause. Violently.*] But what in God's name do you imagine? That the earth will awake in spring? That the rivers and seas will run with fish again? That there's manna in heaven still for imbeciles like you? [*Pause.*] Gradually I cooled down, sufficiently at least to ask him how long he had taken on the way. Three whole days. Good. In what condition he had left the child. Deep in sleep. [*Forcibly.*] But deep in what sleep, deep in what sleep already? [*Pause.*] Well to make it short I finally offered to take him into my service. He had touched a chord. And then I imagined already that I wasn't much longer for this world. [*He laughs. Pause.*] Well? [*Pause.*] Well? Here if you were careful you might die a nice natural death, in peace and comfort. [*Pause.*] Well? [*Pause.*] In the end he asked me would I consent to take in the child as well—if he were still alive. [*Pause.*] It was the moment I was waiting for. [*Pause.*] Would I consent to take in the child . . . [*Pause.*] I can see him still, down on his knees, his hands flat on the ground, glaring at me with his mad eyes, in defiance of my wishes. [*Pause. Normal tone.*] I'll soon have finished with this story. [*Pause.*] Unless I bring in other characters. [*Pause.*] But where would I find them? [*Pause.*] Where would I look for them? [*Pause. He whistles. Enter* CLOV.] Let us pray to God.

NAGG Me sugar-plum!

CLOV There's a rat in the kitchen!

HAMM A rat! Are there still rats?

CLOV In the kitchen there's one.

HAMM And you haven't exterminated him?

CLOV Half. You disturbed us.

HAMM He can't get away?

CLOV No.

HAMM You'll finish him later. Let us pray to God.

CLOV Again!

NAGG Me sugar-plum!

HAMM God first! [*Pause.*] Are you right?

CLOV [*Resigned.*] Off we go.

---

9. A wind meter.
1. Rheumatic pain in the lumbar region of the lower back. "Hygrometer": a moisture meter.

HAMM [*To* NAGG.] And you?

NAGG [*Clasping his hands, closing his eyes, in a gabble.*] Our Father which art—

HAMM Silence! In silence! Where are your manners? [*Pause.*] Off we go. [*Attitudes of prayer. Silence. Abandoning his attitude, discouraged.*] Well?

CLOV [*Abandoning his attitude.*] What a hope! And you?

HAMM Sweet damn all! [*To* NAGG.] And you?

NAGG Wait! [*Pause. Abandoning his attitude.*] Nothing doing!

HAMM The bastard! He doesn't exist!

CLOV Not yet.

NAGG Me sugar-plum!

HAMM There are no more sugar-plums! [*Pause.*]

NAGG It's natural. After all I'm your father. It's true if it hadn't been me it would have been someone else. But that's no excuse. [*Pause.*] Turkish Delight,[2] for example, which no longer exists, we all know that, there is nothing in the world I love more. And one day I'll ask you for some, in return for a kindness, and you'll promise it to me. One must live with the times. [*Pause.*] Whom did you call when you were a tiny boy, and were frightened, in the dark? Your mother? No. Me. We let you cry. Then we moved you out of earshot, so that we might sleep in peace. [*Pause.*] I was asleep, as happy as a king, and you woke me up to have me listen to you. It wasn't indispensable, you didn't really need to have me listen to you. [*Pause.*] I hope the day will come when you'll really need to have me listen to you, and need to hear my voice, any voice. [*Pause.*] Yes, I hope I'll live till then, to hear you calling me like when you were a tiny boy, and were frightened, in the dark, and I was your only hope. [*Pause.* NAGG *knocks on lid of* NELL's *bin. Pause.*] Nell! [*Pause. He knocks louder. Pause. Louder.*] Nell! [*Pause.* NAGG *sinks back into his bin, closes the lid behind him. Pause.*]

HAMM Our revels now are ended.[3] [*He gropes for the dog*] The dog's gone.

CLOV He's not a real dog, he can't go.

HAMM [*Groping.*] He's not there.

CLOV He's lain down.

HAMM Give him up to me. [CLOV *picks up the dog and gives it to* HAMM. HAMM *holds it in his arms. Pause.* HAMM *throws away the dog.*] Dirty brute! [CLOV *begins to pick up the objects lying on the ground.*] What are you doing?

CLOV Putting things in order. [*He straightens up. Fervently.*] I'm going to clear everything away! [*He starts picking up again.*]

HAMM Order!

CLOV [*Straightening up.*] I love order. It's my dream. A world where all would be silent and still and each thing in its last place, under the last dust. [*He starts picking up again.*]

HAMM [*Exasperated.*] What in God's name do you think you are doing?

CLOV [*Straightening up.*] I'm doing my best to create a little order.

HAMM Drop it! [CLOV *drops the objects he has picked up.*]

CLOV After all, there or elsewhere. [*He goes towards door.*]

HAMM [*Irritably.*] What's wrong with your feet?

CLOV My feet?

HAMM Tramp! Tramp!

---

2. A sticky sweet candy (originally from Turkey).
3. Words spoken by Prospero in Shakespeare's *The Tempest* 4.1.148.

CLOV   I must have put on my boots.

HAMM   Your slippers were hurting you? [*Pause.*]

CLOV   I'll leave you.

HAMM   No!

CLOV   What is there to keep me here?

HAMM   The dialogue. [*Pause.*] I've got on with my story. [*Pause.*] I've got on with it well. [*Pause. Irritably.*] Ask me where I've got to.

CLOV   Oh, by the way, your story?

HAMM   [*Surprised.*] What story?

CLOV   The one you've been telling yourself all your days.

HAMM   Ah you mean my chronicle?

CLOV   That's the one. [*Pause.*]

HAMM   [*Angrily.*] Keep going, can't you, keep going!

CLOV   You've got on with it, I hope.

HAMM   [*Modestly.*] Oh not very far, not very far. [*He sighs.*] There are days like that, one isn't inspired. [*Pause.*] Nothing you can do about it, just wait for it to come. [*Pause.*] No forcing, no forcing, it's fatal. [*Pause.*] I've got on with it a little all the same. [*Pause.*] Technique, you know. [*Pause. Irritably.*] I say I've got on with it a little all the same.

CLOV   [*Admiringly.*] Well I never! In spite of everything you were able to get on with it!

HAMM   [*Modestly.*] Oh not very far, you know, not very far, but nevertheless, better than nothing.

CLOV   Better than nothing! Is it possible?

HAMM   I'll tell you how it goes. He comes crawling on his belly—

CLOV   Who?

HAMM   What?

CLOV   Who do you mean, he?

HAMM   Who do I mean! Yet another.

CLOV   Ah him! I wasn't sure.

HAMM   Crawling on his belly, whining for bread for his brat. He's offered a job as gardener. Before— [CLOV *bursts out laughing.*] What is there so funny about that?

CLOV   A job as gardener!

HAMM   Is that what tickles you?

CLOV   It must be that.

HAMM   It wouldn't be the bread?

CLOV   Or the brat. [*Pause.*]

HAMM   The whole thing is comical, I grant you that. What about having a good guffaw the two of us together?

CLOV   [*After reflection.*] I couldn't guffaw again today.

HAMM   [*After reflection.*] Nor I. [*Pause.*] I continue then. Before accepting with gratitude he asks if he may have his little boy with him.

CLOV   What age?

HAMM   Oh tiny.

CLOV   He would have climbed the trees.

HAMM   All the little odd jobs.

CLOV   And then he would have grown up.

HAMM   Very likely. [*Pause.*]

CLOV   Keep going, can't you, keep going!

HAMM   That's all. I stopped there. [*Pause.*]

CLOV Do you see how it goes on.

HAMM More or less.

CLOV Will it not soon be the end?

HAMM I'm afraid it will.

CLOV Pah! You'll make up another.

HAMM I don't know. [*Pause.*] I feel rather drained. [*Pause.*] The prolonged creative effort. [*Pause.*] If I could drag myself down to the sea! I'd make a pillow of sand for my head and the tide would come.

CLOV There's no more tide. [*Pause.*]

HAMM Go and see is she dead. [CLOV *goes to bins, raises the lid of* NELL'*s, stoops, looks into it. Pause.*]

CLOV Looks like it. [*He closes the lid, straightens up.* HAMM *raises his toque. Pause. He puts it on again.*]

HAMM [*With his hand to his toque.*] And Nagg? [CLOV *raises lid of* NAGG'*s bin, stoops, looks into it. Pause.*]

CLOV Doesn't look like it. [*He closes the lid, straightens up.*]

HAMM [*Letting go his toque.*] What's he doing? [CLOV *raises lid of* NAGG'*s bin, stoops, looks into it. Pause.*]

CLOV He's crying. [*He closes lid, straightens up.*]

HAMM Then he's living. [*Pause.*] Did you ever have an instant of happiness?

CLOV Not to my knowledge. [*Pause.*]

HAMM Bring me under the window. [CLOV *goes towards chair.*] I want to feel the light on my face. [CLOV *pushes chair.*] Do you remember, in the beginning, when you took me for a turn? You used to hold the chair too high. At every step you nearly tipped me out. [*With senile quaver.*] Ah great fun, we had, the two of us, great fun. [*Gloomily.*] And then we got into the way of it. [CLOV *stops the chair under window right.*] There already? [*Pause. He tilts back his head.*] Is it light?

CLOV It isn't dark.

HAMM [*Angrily*] I'm asking you is it light.

CLOV Yes. [*Pause.*]

HAMM The curtain isn't closed?

CLOV No.

HAMM What window is it?

CLOV The earth.

HAMM I knew it! [*Angrily.*] But there's no light there! The other! [CLOV *stops the chair under window left.* HAMM *tilts back his head.*] That's what I call light! [*Pause.*] Feels like a ray of sunshine. [*Pause.*] No?

CLOV No.

HAMM It isn't a ray of sunshine I feel on my face?

CLOV No. [*Pause.*]

HAMM Am I very white? [*Pause. Angrily.*] I'm asking you am I very white!

CLOV Not more so than usual. [*Pause.*]

HAMM Open the window.

CLOV What for?

HAMM I want to hear the sea.

CLOV You wouldn't hear it.

HAMM Even if you opened the window?

CLOV No.

HAMM Then it's not worth while opening it?

CLOV No.

HAMM [*Violently*] Then open it! [CLOV *gets up on the ladder, opens the window. Pause.*] Have you opened it?

CLOV Yes. [*Pause.*]

HAMM You swear you've opened it?

CLOV Yes. [*Pause.*]

HAMM Well . . . ! [*Pause.*] It must be very calm. [*Pause. Violently.*] I'm asking you is it very calm!

CLOV Yes.

HAMM It's because there are no more navigators. [*Pause.*] You haven't much conversation all of a sudden. Do you not feel well?

CLOV I'm cold.

HAMM What month are we? [*Pause.*] Close the window, we're going back. [CLOV *closes the window, gets down, pushes the chair back to its place, remains standing behind it, head bowed.*] Don't stay there, you give me the shivers! [CLOV *returns to his place beside the chair.*] Father! [*Pause. Louder.*] Father! [*Pause.*] Go and see did he hear me. [CLOV *goes to* NAGG's *bin, raises the lid, stoops. Unintelligible words.* CLOV *straightens up.*]

CLOV Yes.

HAMM Both times? [CLOV *stoops. As before.*]

CLOV Once only.

HAMM The first time or the second? [CLOV *stoops. As before.*]

CLOV He doesn't know.

HAMM It must have been the second.

CLOV We'll never know. [*He closes lid.*]

HAMM Is he still crying?

CLOV No.

HAMM The dead go fast. [*Pause.*] What's he doing?

CLOV Sucking his biscuit.

HAMM Life goes on. [CLOV *returns to his place beside the chair.*] Give me a rug. I'm freezing.

CLOV There are no more rugs. [*Pause.*]

HAMM Kiss me. [*Pause.*] Will you not kiss me?

CLOV No.

HAMM On the forehead.

CLOV I won't kiss you anywhere. [*Pause.*]

HAMM [*Holding out his hand.*] Give me your hand at least. [*Pause.*] Will you not give me your hand?

CLOV I won't touch you. [*Pause.*]

HAMM Give me the dog. [CLOV *looks round for the dog.*] No!

CLOV Do you not want your dog?

HAMM No.

CLOV Then I'll leave you.

HAMM [*Head bowed, absently.*] That's right. [CLOV *goes to door, turns.*]

CLOV If I don't kill that rat he'll die.

HAMM [*As before.*] That's right. [*Exit* CLOV. *Pause.*] Me to play. [*He takes out his handkerchief, unfolds it, holds it spread out before him.*] We're getting on. [*Pause.*] You weep, and weep, for nothing, so as not to laugh, and little by little . . . you begin to grieve. [*He folds the handkerchief, puts it back in his pocket, raises his head.*] All those I might have helped. [*Pause.*] Helped! [*Pause.*] Saved. [*Pause.*] Saved! [*Pause.*] The place was crawling with them! [*Pause. Violently.*] Use your head, can't you, use your head, you're on earth, there's no cure for that! [*Pause.*] Get out of here and love one another! Lick your neighbour as yourself![4] [*Pause. Calmer.*] When it wasn't bread they wanted it was crumpets. [*Pause. Violently.*] Out of my sight and back to your petting parties! [*Pause.*] All that, all that! [*Pause.*] Not even a real dog! [*Calmer.*] The end is in the beginning and yet you go on. [*Pause.*] Perhaps I could go on with my story, end it and begin another. [*Pause.*] Perhaps I could throw myself out on the floor. [*He pushes himself painfully off his seat, falls back again.*] Dig my nails into the cracks and drag myself forward with my fingers. [*Pause.*] It will be the end and there I'll be, wondering what can have brought it on and wondering what can have . . . [*He hesitates.*] . . . why it was so long coming. [*Pause.*] There I'll be, in the old shelter, alone against the silence and . . . [*He hesitates.*] . . . the stillness. If I can hold my peace, and sit quiet, it will be all over with sound, and motion, all over and done with. [*Pause.*] I'll have called my father and I'll have called my . . . [*He hesitates.*] . . . my son. And even twice, or three times, in case they shouldn't have heard me, the first time, or the second. [*Pause.*] I'll say to myself, He'll come back. [*Pause.*] And then? [*Pause.*] And then? [*Pause.*] He couldn't, he has gone too far. [*Pause.*] And then? [*Pause. Very agitated.*] All kinds of fantasies! That I'm being watched! A rat! Steps! Breath held and then . . . [*He breathes out.*] Then babble, babble, words, like the solitary child who turns himself into children, two, three, so as to be together, and whisper together, in the dark. [*Pause.*] Moment upon moment, pattering down, like the millet grains of . . . [*He hesitates.*] . . . that old Greek,[5] and all life long you wait for that to mount up to a life. [*Pause. He opens his mouth to continue, renounces.*] Ah let's get it over! [*He whistles. Enter* CLOV *with alarm-clock. He halts beside the chair.*] What? Neither gone nor dead?

CLOV   In spirit only.

HAMM   Which?

CLOV   Both.

HAMM   Gone from me you'd be dead.

CLOV   And vice versa.

HAMM   Outside of here it's death! [*Pause.*] And the rat?

CLOV   He's got away.

HAMM   He can't go far. [*Pause. Anxious.*] Eh?

CLOV   He doesn't need to go far. [*Pause.*]

HAMM   Is it not time for my pain-killer?

CLOV   Yes.

HAMM   Ah! At last! Give it to me! Quick! [*Pause.*]

CLOV   There's no more pain-killer. [*Pause.*]

HAMM   [*Appalled.*] Good . . . ! [*Pause.*] No more pain-killer!

CLOV   No more pain-killer. You'll never get any more pain-killer. [*Pause.*]

HAMM   But the little round box. It was full!

CLOV   Yes. But now it's empty. [*Pause.* CLOV *starts to move about the room. He is looking for a place to put down the alarm-clock.*]

HAMM   [*Soft.*] What'll I do? [*Pause. In a scream.*] What'll I do? [CLOV *sees the picture, takes it down, stands it on the floor with its face to the wall, hangs up the alarm-clock in its place.*] What are you doing?

4. Parody of Jesus' instruction: "Thou shalt love thy neighbor as thyself" (Matthew 19.19).
5. Zeno of Elea (ca. 450 B.C.E.), a Greek philosopher famous for his paradoxes; e.g., "If a grain of millet falling makes no sound, how can a bushel of grains make any sound?" (reported by Aristotle in his *Physics* 5:250 a.19).

CLOV Winding up.

HAMM   Look at the earth.

CLOV Again!

HAMM   Since it's calling to you.

CLOV Is your throat sore? [*Pause.*] Would you like a lozenge? [*Pause.*] No. [*Pause.*] Pity. [CLOV *goes, humming, towards window right, halts before it, looks up at it.*]

HAMM   Don't sing.

CLOV [*Turning towards* HAMM.] One hasn't the right to sing any more?

HAMM   No.

CLOV Then how can it end?

HAMM   You want it to end?

CLOV I want to sing.

HAMM   I can't prevent you. [*Pause.* CLOV *turns towards window right.*]

CLOV What did I do with that steps? [*He looks around for ladder.*] You didn't see that steps? [*He sees it.*] Ah, about time. [*He goes towards window left.*] Sometimes I wonder if I'm in my right mind. Then it passes over and I'm as lucid as before. [*He gets up on ladder, looks out of window.*] Christ, she's under water! [*He looks.*] How can that be? [*He pokes forward his head, his hand above his eyes.*] It hasn't rained. [*He wipes the pane, looks. Pause.*] Ah what a fool I am! I'm on the wrong side! [*He gets down, takes a few steps towards window right.*] Under water! [*He goes back for ladder.*] What a fool I am! [*He carries ladder towards window right.*] Sometimes I wonder if I'm in my right senses. Then it passes off and I'm as intelligent as ever. [*He sets down ladder under window right, gets up on it, looks out of window. He turns towards* HAMM.] Any particular sector you fancy? Or merely the whole thing?

HAMM   Whole thing.

CLOV The general effect? Just a moment. [*He looks out of window. Pause.*]

HAMM   Clov.

CLOV [*Absorbed.*] Mmm.

HAMM   Do you know what it is?

CLOV [*As before.*] Mmm.

HAMM   I was never there. [*Pause.*] Clov!

CLOV [*Turning towards* HAMM, *exasperated.*] What is it?

HAMM   I was never there.

CLOV Lucky for you. [*He looks out of window.*]

HAMM   Absent, always. It all happened without me. I don't know what's happened. [*Pause.*] Do you know what's happened? [*Pause.*] Clov!

CLOV [*Turning towards* HAMM, *exasperated.*] Do you want me to look at this muckheap, yes or no?

HAMM   Answer me first.

CLOV What?

HAMM   Do you know what's happened?

CLOV When? Where?

HAMM   [*Violently.*] When! What's happened? Use your head, can't you! What has happened?

CLOV What for Christ's sake does it matter? [*He looks out of window.*]

HAMM   I don't know. [*Pause.* CLOV *turns towards* HAMM.]

CLOV [*Harshly.*] When old Mother Pegg asked you for oil for her lamp and you told her to get out to hell, you knew what was happening then, no? [*Pause.*] You know what she died of, Mother Pegg? Of darkness.

HAMM   [*Feebly.*] I hadn't any.

CLOV   [*As before.*] Yes, you had. [*Pause.*]

HAMM   Have you the glass?

CLOV   No, it's clear enough as it is.

HAMM   Go and get it. [*Pause.* CLOV *casts up his eyes, brandishes his fists. He loses balance, clutches on to the ladder. He starts to get down, halts.*]

CLOV   There's one thing I'll never understand. [*He gets down.*] Why I always obey you. Can you explain that to me?

HAMM   No. . . . Perhaps it's compassion. [*Pause.*] A kind of great compassion. [*Pause.*] Oh you won't find it easy, you won't find it easy. [*Pause.* CLOV *begins to move about the room in search of the telescope.*]

CLOV   I'm tired of our goings on, very tired. [*He searches.*] You're not sitting on it? [*He moves the chair, looks at the place where it stood, resumes his search.*]

HAMM   [*Anguished.*] Don't leave me there! [*Angrily* CLOV *restores the chair to its place.*] Am I right in the centre?

CLOV   You'd need a microscope to find this— [*He sees the telescope.*] Ah, about time. [*He picks up the telescope, gets up on the ladder, turns the telescope on the without.*]

HAMM   Give me the dog.

CLOV   [*Looking.*] Quiet!

HAMM   [*Angrily.*] Give me the dog! [CLOV *drops the telescope, clasps his hands to his head. Pause. He gets down precipitately, looks for the dog, sees it, picks it up, hastens towards* HAMM *and strikes him violently on the head with the dog.*]

CLOV   There's your dog for you! [*The dog falls to the ground. Pause.*]

HAMM   He hit me!

CLOV   You drive me mad, I'm mad!

HAMM   If you must hit me, hit me with the axe. [*Pause.*] Or with the gaff, hit me with the gaff. Not with the dog. With the gaff. Or with the axe. [CLOV *picks up the dog and gives it to* HAMM *who takes it in his arms.*]

CLOV   [*Imploringly.*] Let's stop playing!

HAMM   Never! [*Pause.*] Put me in my coffin.

CLOV   There are no more coffins.

HAMM   Then let it end! [CLOV *goes towards ladder.*] With a bang! [CLOV *gets up on ladder, gets down again, looks for telescope, sees it, picks it up, gets up ladder, raises telescope.*] Of darkness! And me? Did anyone ever have pity on me?

CLOV   [*Lowering the telescope, turning towards* HAMM.] What? [*Pause.*] Is it me you're referring to?

HAMM   [*Angrily.*] An aside, ape! Did you never hear an aside before? [*Pause.*] I'm warming up for my last soliloquy.

CLOV   I warn you. I'm going to look at this filth since it's an order. But it's the last time. [*He turns the telescope on the without.*] Let's see. [*He moves the telescope.*] Nothing . . . nothing . . . good . . . good . . . nothing . . . goo— [*He starts, lowers the telescope, examines it, turns it again on the without. Pause.*] Bad luck to it!

HAMM   More complications! [CLOV *gets down.*] Not an underplot, I trust. [CLOV *moves ladder nearer window, gets up on it, turns telescope on the without.*]

CLOV   [*Dismayed.*] Looks like a small boy!

HAMM   [*Sarcastic.*] A small . . . boy!

CLOV   I'll go and see. [*He gets down, drops the telescope, goes towards door, turns.*] I'll take the gaff. [*He looks for the gaff, sees it, picks it up, hastens towards door.*]

HAMM   No! [CLOV *halts.*]

CLOV   No? A potential procreator?

HAMM   If he exists he'll die there or he'll come here. And if he doesn't . . . [*Pause.*]

CLOV   You don't believe me? You think I'm inventing? [*Pause.*]

HAMM   It's the end, Clov, we've come to the end. I don't need you any more. [*Pause.*]

CLOV   Lucky for you. [*He goes towards door.*]

HAMM   Leave me the gaff. [CLOV *gives him the gaff, goes towards door, halts, looks at alarm-clock, takes it down, looks round for a better place to put it, goes to bins, puts it on lid of* NAGG's *bin. Pause.*]

CLOV   I'll leave you. [*He goes towards door.*]

HAMM   Before you go . . . [CLOV *halts near door.*] . . . say something.

CLOV   There is nothing to say.

HAMM   A few words . . . to ponder . . . in my heart.

CLOV   Your heart!

HAMM   Yes. [*Pause. Forcibly.*] Yes! [*Pause.*] With the rest, in the end, the shadows, the murmurs, all the trouble, to end up with. [*Pause.*] Clov. . . . He never spoke to me. Then, in the end, before he went, without my having asked him, he spoke to me. He said . . .

CLOV   [*Despairingly.*] Ah . . . !

HAMM   Something . . . from your heart.

CLOV   My heart!

HAMM   A few words . . . from your heart. [*Pause.*]

CLOV   [*Fixed gaze, tonelessly, towards auditorium.*] They said to me, That's love, yes, yes, not a doubt, now you see how—

HAMM   Articulate!

CLOV   [*As before.*] How easy it is. They said to me, That's friendship, yes, yes, no question, you've found it. They said to me, Here's the place, stop, raise your head and look at all that beauty. That order! They said to me. Come now, you're not a brute beast, think upon these things and you'll see how all becomes clear. And simple! They said to me, What skilled attention they get, all these dying of their wounds.

HAMM   Enough!

CLOV   [*As before.*] I say to myself—sometimes, Clov, you must learn to suffer better than that if you want them to weary of punishing you—one day. I say to myself—sometimes, Clov, you must be there better than that if you want them to let you go—one day. But I feel too old, and too far, to form new habits. Good, it'll never end, I'll never go. [*Pause.*] Then one day, suddenly, it ends, it changes, I don't understand, it dies, or it's me, I don't understand, that either. I ask the words that remain—sleeping, waking, morning, evening. They have nothing to say. [*Pause.*] I open the door of the cell and go. I am so bowed I only see my feet, if I open my eyes, and between my legs a little trail of black dust. I say to myself that the earth is extinguished, though I never saw it lit. [*Pause.*] It's easy going. [*Pause.*] When I fall I'll weep for happiness. [*Pause. He goes towards door.*]

HAMM   Clov! [CLOV *halts, without turning.*] Nothing. [CLOV *moves on.*] Clov! [CLOV *halts, without turning.*]

CLOV   This is what we call making an exit.

HAMM   I'm obliged to you, Clov. For your services.

CLOV   [*Turning, sharply.*] Ah pardon, it's I am obliged to you.

HAMM   It's we are obliged to each other. [*Pause.* CLOV *goes towards door.*] One thing more. [CLOV *halts.*] A last favour. [*Exit* CLOV.] Cover me with the sheet. [*Long pause.*] No? Good. [*Pause.*] Me to play. [*Pause. Wearily.*] Old endgame lost of old, play and lose and have done with losing. [*Pause. More animated.*] Let me see. [*Pause.*] Ah yes! [*He tries to move the chair, using the gaff as before. Enter* CLOV, *dressed for the road. Panama hat, tweed coat, raincoat over his arm, umbrella, bag. He halts by the door and stands there, impassive and motionless, his eyes fixed on* HAMM, *till the end.* HAMM *gives up.*] Good. [*Pause.*] Discard. [*He throws away the gaff, makes to throw away the dog, thinks better of it.*] Take it easy. [*Pause.*] And now? [*Pause.*] Raise hat. [*He raises his toque.*] Peace to our . . . arses. [*Pause.*] And put on again. [*He puts on his toque.*] Deuce. [*Pause. He takes off his glasses.*] Wipe. [*He takes out his handkerchief and, without unfolding it, wipes his glasses.*] And put on again. [*He puts on his glasses, puts back the handkerchief in his pocket.*] We're coming. A few more squirms like that and I'll call. [*Pause.*] A little poetry. [*Pause.*] You prayed— [*Pause. He corrects himself.*] You CRIED for night; it comes— [*Pause. He corrects himself.*] It FALLS: now cry in darkness. [*He repeats, chanting.*] You cried for night; it falls: now cry in darkness.[6] [*Pause.*] Nicely put, that. [*Pause.*] And now? [*Pause.*] Moments for nothing, now as always, time was never and time is over, reckoning closed and story ended. [*Pause. Narrative tone.*] If he could have his child with him. . . . [*Pause.*] It was the moment I was waiting for. [*Pause.*] You don't want to abandon him? You want him to bloom while you are withering? Be there to solace your last million last moments? [*Pause.*] He doesn't realize, all he knows is hunger, and cold, and death to crown it all. But you! You ought to know what the earth is like, nowadays. Oh I put him before his responsibilities! [*Pause. Normal tone.*] Well, there we are, there I am, that's enough. [*He raises the whistle to his lips, hesitates, drops it. Pause.*] Yes, truly! [*He whistles. Pause. Louder. Pause.*] Good. [*Pause.*] Father! [*Pause. Louder.*] Father! [*Pause.*] Good. [*Pause.*] We're coming. [*Pause.*] And to end up with? [*Pause.*] Discard. [*He throws away the dog. He tears the whistle from his neck.*] With my compliments. [*He throws whistle towards auditorium. Pause. He sniffs. Soft.*] Clov! [*Long pause.*] No? Good. [*He takes out the handkerchief.*] Since that's the way we're playing it . . . [*He unfolds handkerchief.*] . . . let's play it that way . . . [*He unfolds.*] . . . and speak no more about it . . . [*He finishes unfolding.*] . . . speak no more. [*He holds handkerchief spread out before him.*] Old stancher! [*Pause.*] You . . . remain. [*Pause. He covers his face with handkerchief, lowers his arms to armrests, remains motionless.*] [*Brief tableau.*]

CURTAIN

1958

---

6. Parody of a line from Charles Baudelaire's poem "Meditation" that can be translated as: "You were calling for evening; it falls; it is here."

W. H. AUDEN
1907–1973

Wystan Hugh Auden was born in York, England, the son of a doctor and of a former nurse. He was educated at private schools and Christ Church, Oxford. After graduation from Oxford he traveled abroad, taught school in England from 1930 to 1935, and later worked for a government film unit. His sympathies in the 1930s were with the left, like those of most intellectuals of his age, and he went to Spain during its Civil War, intending to serve as an ambulance driver on the left-wing Republican side. To his surprise he felt so disturbed by the sight of the many Roman Catholic churches gutted and looted by the Republicans that he returned to England without fulfilling his ambition. He traveled in Iceland and China before moving to the United States in 1939; in 1946 he became an American citizen. He taught at a number of American colleges and was professor of poetry at Oxford from 1956 to 1960. Most of his later life was shared between residences in New York City and in Europe—first in southern Italy, then in Austria.

Auden was the most prominent of the young English poets who, in the late 1920s and early 1930s, saw themselves bringing new techniques and attitudes to English poetry. Stephen Spender, C. Day Lewis, and Louis MacNeice were other liberal and leftist poets in this loosely affiliated group. Auden learned metrical and verbal techniques from Gerard Manley Hopkins and Wilfred Owen, and from T. S. Eliot he took a conversational and ironic tone, an acute inspection of cultural decay. Thomas Hardy's metrical variety, formal irregularity, and fusion of panoramic and intimate perspectives also proved a useful example, and Auden admired W. B. Yeats's "serious reflective" poems of "personal and public interest," though he later came to disavow Yeats's grand aspirations and rhetoric. Auden's English studies at Oxford familiarized him with the rhythms and long alliterative line of Anglo-Saxon poetry. He learned, too, from popular and folk culture, particularly the songs of the English music hall and, later, American blues singers.

The Depression that hit America in 1929 hit England soon afterward, and Auden and his contemporaries looked out at an England of industrial stagnation and mass unemployment, seeing not Eliot's metaphorical Waste Land but a more literal Waste Land of poverty and "depressed areas." Auden's early poetry diagnoses the ills of his country. This diagnosis, conducted in a verse that combines irreverence with craftsmanship, draws on both Freud and Marx to show England now as a nation of neurotic invalids, now as the victim of an antiquated economic system. The intellectual liveliness and nervous force of this work made a great impression, even though the compressed, elliptical, impersonal style created difficulties of interpretation.

Gradually Auden sought to clarify his imagery and syntax, and in the late 1930s he produced "Lullaby," "Musée des Beaux Arts," "In Memory of W. B. Yeats," and other poems of finely disciplined movement, pellucid clarity, and deep yet unsentimental feeling. Some of the poems he wrote at this time, such as "Spain" and "September 1, 1939," aspire to a visionary perspective on political and social change; but as Auden became increasingly skeptical of poetry in the grand manner, of poetry as revelation or as a tool for political change, he removed these poems from his canon. (He came to see as false his claim in "September 1, 1939" that "We must love one another or die.") "Poetry is not magic," he said in the essay "Writing," but a form of truth telling that should "disenchant and disintoxicate." As he continued to remake his style during World War II, he created a voice that, in contrast not only to Romanticism but also to the authoritarianism devastating Europe, was increasingly flat, ironic, and conversational. He never lost his ear for popular speech or his ability to combine elements from popular art with technical formality. He daringly mixed the grave and the flippant, vivid detail and allegorical abstraction. He always experimented, particularly in ways of bringing together high artifice and a colloquial tone.

The poems of Auden's last phase are increasingly personal in tone and combine an air of offhand informality with remarkable technical skill in versification. He turned out, as if effortlessly, poems in numerous verse forms, including sestinas, sonnets, ballads, canzones, syllabics, haiku, the blues, even limericks. As he became ever more mistrustful of a prophetic role for the poet, he embraced the ordinary—the hours of the day, the rooms of a house, a changeable landscape. He took refuge in love and friendship, particularly the love and friendship he shared with the American writer Chester Kallmann. Like Eliot, Auden became a member of the Church of England, and the emotions of his late poetry—sometimes comic, sometimes solemn—were grounded in an ever deepening but rarely obtrusive religious feeling. In the last year of his life he returned to England to live in Oxford, feeling the need to be part of a university community as a protection against loneliness. Auden is now generally recognized as one of the masters of twentieth-century English poetry, a thoughtful, seriously playful poet, combining extraordinary intelligence and immense craftsmanship.

A note on the texts: Auden heavily revised his poems, sometimes omitting stanzas (as in "Spain" and "In Memory of W. B. Yeats") or even entire poems ("Spain" and "September 1, 1939"). The texts below are reprinted as they first appeared in book form and again in his *Selected Poems: A New Edition*, ed. Edward Mendelson (1989).

Petition[1]

> Sir, no man's enemy, forgiving all
> But will his negative inversion, be prodigal:
> Send to us power and light, a sovereign touch[2]
> Curing the intolerable neural itch,
> 5 The exhaustion of weaning, the liar's quinsy,°   *tonsillitis*
> And the distortions of ingrown virginity.
> Prohibit sharply the rehearsed response
> And gradually correct the coward's stance;
> Cover in time with beams those in retreat
> 10 That, spotted, they turn though the reverse were great;
> Publish each healer that in city lives
> Or country houses at the end of drives;
> Harrow the house of the dead; look shining at
> New styles of architecture, a change of heart.

Oct. 1929   1930

On This Island[1]

> Look, stranger, at this island now
> The leaping light for your delight discovers,
> Stand stable here
> And silent be,

---

1. This title, by which the poem is widely known, is from Auden's later collections. Many of his early poems first appeared without titles.
2. The king's touch was often regarded as miraculous cure for disease (cf. "sovereign" as an adjective, meaning "supreme, all-dominating").
1. The title is from Auden's later collections.

5   That through the channels of the ear
    May wander like a river
    The swaying sound of the sea.

    Here at the small field's ending pause
    Where the chalk wall falls to the foam, and its tall ledges
10   Oppose the pluck
    And knock of the tide,
    And the shingle scrambles after the suck-
    ing surf, and the gull lodges
    A moment on its sheer side.

15   Far off like floating seeds the ships
    Diverge on urgent voluntary errands;
    And the full view
    Indeed may enter
    And move in memory as now these clouds do,
20   That pass the harbour mirror
    And all the summer through the water saunter.

Nov. 1935   1936

Lullaby[1]

    Lay your sleeping head, my love,
    Human on my faithless arm;
    Time and fevers burn away
    Individual beauty from
5   Thoughtful children, and the grave
    Proves the child ephemeral:
    But in my arms till break of day
    Let the living creature lie,
    Mortal, guilty, but to me
10   The entirely beautiful.

    Soul and body have no bounds:
    To lovers as they lie upon
    Her tolerant enchanted slope
    In their ordinary swoon,
15   Grave the vision Venus° sends   *Roman goddess of love*
    Of supernatural sympathy,
    Universal love and hope;
    While an abstract insight wakes
    Among the glaciers and the rocks
20   The hermit's sensual ecstasy.

    Certainty, fidelity
    On the stroke of midnight pass

1. Title from Auden's later collections.

Like vibrations of a bell,
And fashionable madmen raise
25   Their pedantic boring cry:
Every farthing[2] of the cost,
All the dreaded cards foretell,
Shall be paid, but from this night
Not a whisper, not a thought,
30   Not a kiss nor look be lost.

Beauty, midnight, vision dies:
Let the winds of dawn that blow
Softly round your dreaming head
Such a day of sweetness show
35   Eye and knocking heart may bless,
Find the mortal world enough;
Noons of dryness see you fed
By the involuntary powers,
Nights of insult let you pass
40   Watched by every human love.

Jan. 1937   1937, 1940

Spain[1]

Yesterday all the past. The language of size
Spreading to China along the trade-routes; the diffusion
           Of the counting-frame and the cromlech;[2]
Yesterday the shadow-reckoning in the sunny climates.

5   Yesterday the assessment of insurance by cards,
The divination of water; yesterday the invention
           Of cartwheels and clocks, the taming of
Horses. Yesterday the bustling world of the navigators.

Yesterday the abolition of fairies and giants,
10   The fortress like a motionless eagle eyeing the valley,
           The chapel built in the forest;
Yesterday the carving of angels and alarming gargoyles;

The trial of heretics among the columns of stone;
Yesterday the theological feuds in the taverns
15   And the miraculous cure at the fountain;
Yesterday the Sabbath of witches; but to-day the struggle.

2. At one time the smallest and least valuable British coin.
1. The Spanish Civil War, which began in 1936 as a rebellion by General Franco's right-wing army against the left-wing, elected Spanish government, was viewed by British liberal intellectuals as a testing struggle between fascism and democracy. Written while the war was raging this poem appeared separately in 1937, the proceeds of its sale going to Medical Aid for Spain. In 1940 Auden retitled the poem "Spain 1937," deleted lines 69–76, and made other changes; later he removed the poem from his canon.
2. Ancient stone circle.

Yesterday the installation of dynamos and turbines,
The construction of railways in the colonial desert;
      Yesterday the classic lecture
20 On the origin of Mankind. But to-day the struggle.

Yesterday the belief in the absolute value of Greek,
The fall of the curtain upon the death of a hero;
      Yesterday the prayer to the sunset
And the adoration of madmen. But to-day the struggle.

25 As the poet whispers, startled among the pines,
Or where the loose waterfall sings compact, or upright
      On the crag by the leaning tower:
"O my vision. O send me the luck of the sailor."

And the investigator peers through his instruments
30 At the inhuman provinces, the virile bacillus
      Or enormous Jupiter finished:
"But the lives of my friends. I inquire. I inquire."

And the poor in their fireless lodgings, dropping the sheets
Of the evening paper: "Our day is our loss, O show us
35   History the operator, the
Organiser, Time the refreshing river."

And the nations combine each cry, invoking the life
That shapes the individual belly and orders
      The private nocturnal terror:
40 "Did you not found the city state of the sponge,

"Raise the vast military empires of the shark
And the tiger, establish the robin's plucky canton?°   *district*
      Intervene. O descend as a dove or
A furious papa or a mild engineer,[3] but descend."

45 And the life, if it answers at all, replies from the heart
And the eyes and the lungs, from the shops and squares of the city
      "O no, I am not the mover;
Not to-day; not to you. To you, I'm the

"Yes-man, the bar-companion, the easily-duped;
50 I am whatever you do. I am your vow to be
      Good, your humorous story.
I am your business voice. I am your marriage.

"What's your proposal? To build the just city? I will.
I agree. Or is it the suicide pact, the romantic
55   Death? Very well, I accept, for
I am your choice, your decision. Yes, I am Spain."

---

3. Auden plays on the idea of a *deus ex machina*, literally a god from a machine, who appears suddenly in a play to resolve an impasse. "Dove": in the Bible the form taken by the Holy Spirit when descending to Earth.

Many have heard it on remote peninsulas,
On sleepy plains, in the aberrant fishermen's islands
    Or the corrupt heart of the city,
60   Have heard and migrated like gulls or the seeds of a flower.

They clung like burrs to the long expresses that lurch
Through the unjust lands, through the night, through the alpine tunnel;
    They floated over the oceans;
They walked the passes. All presented their lives.

65   On that arid square, that fragment nipped off from hot
Africa, soldered so crudely to inventive Europe;
    On that tableland scored by rivers,
Our thoughts have bodies; the menacing shapes of our fever

Are precise and alive. For the fears which made us respond
70   To the medicine ad. and the brochure of winter cruises
    Have become invading battalions;
And our faces, the institute-face, the chain-store, the ruin

Are projecting their greed as the firing squad and the bomb.
Madrid is the heart. Our moments of tenderness blossom
75   As the ambulance and the sandbag;
Our hours of friendship into a people's army.

To-morrow, perhaps the future. The research on fatigue
And the movements of packers; the gradual exploring of all the
    Octaves of radiation;
80   To-morrow the enlarging of consciousness by diet and breathing.

To-morrow the rediscovery of romantic love,
The photographing of ravens; all the fun under
    Liberty's masterful shadow;
To-morrow the hour of the pageant-master and the musician,

85   The beautiful roar of the chorus under the dome;
To-morrow the exchanging of tips on the breeding of terriers,
    The eager election of chairmen
By the sudden forest of hands. But to-day the struggle.

To-morrow for the young the poets exploding like bombs,
90   The walks by the lake, the weeks of perfect communion;
    To-morrow the bicycle races
Through the suburbs on summer evenings. But to-day the struggle.

To-day the deliberate increase in the chances of death,
The conscious acceptance of guilt in the necessary murder;[4]
95   To-day the expending of powers
On the flat ephemeral pamphlet and the boring meeting.

---

4. After these two lines were criticized by George Orwell, Auden revised them to read "the inevitable increase" and "the fact of murder."

To-day the makeshift consolations: the shared cigarette,
The cards in the candlelit barn, and the scraping concert,
    The masculine jokes; to-day the
100 Fumbled and unsatisfactory embrace before hurting.

The stars are dead. The animals will not look.
We are left alone with our day, and the time is short, and
    History to the defeated
May say Alas but cannot help nor pardon.

Mar. 1937   1937

As I Walked Out One Evening[1]

As I walked out one evening,
    Walking down Bristol Street,
The crowds upon the pavement
    Were fields of harvest wheat.

5 And down by the brimming river
    I heard a lover sing
Under an arch of the railway:
    "Love has no ending.

"I'll love you, dear, I'll love you
10   Till China and Africa meet
And the river jumps over the mountain
    And the salmon sing in the street.

"I'll love you till the ocean
    Is folded and hung up to dry
15 And the seven stars[2] go squawking
    Like geese about the sky.

"The years shall run like rabbits
    For in my arms I hold
The Flower of the Ages
20   And the first love of the world."

But all the clocks in the city
    Began to whirr and chime:
"O let not Time deceive you,
    You cannot conquer Time.

25 "In the burrows of the Nightmare
    Where Justice naked is,
Time watches from the shadow
    And coughs when you would kiss.

1. Title from Auden's later collections.
2. The constellation of the Pleiades, supposed by the ancients to be seven sisters.

"In headaches and in worry
30   Vaguely life leaks away,
And Time will have his fancy
        To-morrow or to-day.

"Into many a green valley
        Drifts the appalling[3] snow;
35 Time breaks the threaded dances
        And the diver's brilliant bow.

"O plunge your hands in water,
        Plunge them in up to the wrist;
Stare, stare in the basin
40   And wonder what you've missed.

"The glacier knocks in the cupboard,
        The desert sighs in the bed,
And the crack in the tea-cup opens
        A lane to the land of the dead.

45 "Where the beggars raffle the banknotes
        And the Giant is enchanting to Jack,
And the Lily-white Boy is a Roarer
        And Jill goes down on her back.[4]

"O look, look in the mirror,
50   O look in your distress;
Life remains a blessing
        Although you cannot bless.

"O stand, stand at the window
        As the tears scald and start;
55 You shall love your crooked neighbour
        With your crooked heart."

It was late, late in the evening,
        The lovers they were gone;
The clocks had ceased their chiming
60   And the deep river ran on.

Nov. 1937   1938, 1940

Musée des Beaux Arts[1]

About suffering they were never wrong,
The Old Masters: how well they understood
Its human position; how it takes place

---

3. Literally, making white.
4. The giant of "Jack and the Bean Stalk" is trying
to seduce Jack; the "lily-white Boy" (presumably

pure) becomes a boisterous reveler; Jill, of "Jack
and Jill," is seduced.
1. Museum of Fine Arts (French).

While someone else is eating or opening a window or just walking dully
    along;
5 How, when the aged are reverently, passionately waiting
For the miraculous birth, there always must be
Children who did not specially want it to happen, skating
On a pond at the edge of the wood:
They never forgot
10 That even the dreadful martyrdom must run its course
Anyhow in a corner, some untidy spot
Where the dogs go on with their doggy life and the torturer's horse
Scratches its innocent behind on a tree.

In Brueghel's *Icarus*,[2] for instance: how everything turns away
15 Quite leisurely from the disaster; the ploughman may
Have heard the splash, the forsaken cry,
But for him it was not an important failure; the sun shone
As it had to on the white legs disappearing into the green
Water; and the expensive delicate ship that must have seen
20 Something amazing, a boy falling out of the sky,
Had somewhere to get to and sailed calmly on.

Dec. 1938   1940

In Memory of W. B. Yeats[1]

(d. January 1939)

I

He disappeared in the dead of winter:
The brooks were frozen, the air-ports almost deserted,
And snow disfigured the public statues;
The mercury sank in the mouth of the dying day.
5 O all the instruments agree
The day of his death was a dark cold day.

Far from his illness
The wolves ran on through the evergreen forests,
The peasant river was untempted by the fashionable quays;
10 By mourning tongues
The death of the poet was kept from his poems.

But for him it was his last afternoon as himself,
An afternoon of nurses and rumours;

---

2. *The Fall of Icarus*, by the Flemish painter Pieter Brueghel (ca. 1525–1569), in the Musées Royaux des Beaux Arts in Brussels. In one corner of Brueghel's painting, Icarus's legs are seen disappearing into the sea, his wings having melted when he flew too close to the sun. Auden also alludes to other paintings by Brueghel: the nativity scene in *The* *Numbering at Bethlehem*, skaters in *Winter Landscape with Skaters and a Bird Trap*, a horse scratching its behind in *The Massacre of the Innocents*.
1. The Irish poet William Butler Yeats, born in 1865, died on January 29, 1939, in Roquebrune (southern France).

The provinces of his body revolted,
15 The squares of his mind were empty,
Silence invaded the suburbs,
The current of his feeling failed: he became his admirers.

Now he is scattered among a hundred cities
And wholly given over to unfamiliar affections;
20 To find his happiness in another kind of wood[2]
And be punished under a foreign code of conscience.
The words of a dead man
Are modified in the guts of the living.

But in the importance and noise of to-morrow
25 When the brokers are roaring like beasts on the floor of the Bourse,[3]
And the poor have the sufferings to which they are fairly accustomed,
And each in the cell of himself is almost convinced of his freedom;
A few thousand will think of this day
As one thinks of a day when one did something slightly unusual.

30 O all the instruments agree
The day of his death was a dark cold day.

II

You were silly like us: your gift survived it all;
The parish of rich women,[4] physical decay,
Yourself; mad Ireland hurt you into poetry.
35 Now Ireland has her madness and her weather still,
For poetry makes nothing happen: it survives
In the valley of its saying where executives
Would never want to tamper; it flows south
From ranches of isolation and the busy griefs,
40 Raw towns that we believe and die in; it survives,
A way of happening, a mouth.

III[5]

Earth, receive an honoured guest;
William Yeats is laid to rest:
Let the Irish vessel lie
45 Emptied of its poetry.

Time that is intolerant
Of the brave and innocent,
And indifferent in a week
To a beautiful physique,

---

2. Cf. the beginning of Dante's *Inferno:* "In the middle of the journey of our life I came to myself in a dark wood where the straight way was lost" (1.1–3).
3. The French stock exchange.
4. Several wealthy women, including Lady

Augusta Gregory (1852–1932), provided financial help to Yeats.
5. The stanza pattern of this section echoes that of Yeats's late poem "Under Ben Bulben." Auden later omitted the section's second, third, and fourth stanzas.

50 Worships language and forgives
Everyone by whom it lives;
Pardons cowardice, conceit,
Lays its honours at their feet.

Time that with this strange excuse
55 Pardoned Kipling[6] and his views,
And will pardon Paul Claudel,[7]
Pardons him for writing well.

In the nightmare of the dark
All the dogs of Europe bark,[8]
60 And the living nations wait,
Each sequestered in its hate;

Intellectual disgrace
Stares from every human face,
And the seas of pity lie
65 Locked and frozen in each eye.

Follow, poet, follow right
To the bottom of the night,
With your unconstraining voice
Still persuade us to rejoice;

70 With the farming of a verse
Make a vineyard of the curse,
Sing of human unsuccess
In a rapture of distress;

In the deserts of the heart
75 Let the healing fountain start,
In the prison of his days
Teach the free man how to praise.

Feb. 1939   1939, 1940

The Unknown Citizen

To JS/07/M/378
This Marble Monument is Erected by the State

He was found by the Bureau of Statistics to be
One against whom there was no official complaint,
And all the reports on his conduct agree
That, in the modern sense of an old-fashioned word, he was a saint,
5 For in everything he did he served the Greater Community.

---

6. The British writer Rudyard Kipling (1865–1936) championed imperialism.
7. French author (1868–1955) with extremely conservative politics. Yeats was at times anti-democratic and appeared to favor dictatorship.
8. World War II began in September 1939.

Except for the War till the day he retired
He worked in a factory and never got fired,
But satisfied his employers, Fudge Motors Inc.
Yet he wasn't a scab or odd in his views,
10 For his Union reports that he paid his dues,
(Our report on his Union shows it was sound)
And our Social Psychology workers found
That he was popular with his mates and liked a drink.
The Press are convinced that he bought a paper every day
15 And that his reactions to advertisements were normal in every way.
Policies taken out in his name prove that he was fully insured,
And his Health-card shows he was once in hospital but left it cured.
Both Producers Research and High-Grade Living declare
He was fully sensible to the advantages of the Installment Plan
20 And had everything necessary to the Modern Man,
A gramophone, a radio, a car and a frigidaire.
Our researchers into Public Opinion are content
That he held the proper opinions for the time of year;
When there was peace, he was for peace; when there was war, he
            went.
25 He was married and added five children to the population,
Which our Eugenist[1] says was the right number for a parent of his
            generation,
And our teachers report that he never interfered with their education.
Was he free? Was he happy? The question is absurd:
Had anything been wrong, we should certainly have heard.

Mar. 1939   1939, 1940

September 1, 1939[1]

I sit in one of the dives
On Fifty-Second Street[2]
Uncertain and afraid
As the clever hopes expire
5   Of a low dishonest decade:
Waves of anger and fear
Circulate over the bright
And darkened lands of the earth,
Obsessing our private lives;
10   The unmentionable odour of death
Offends the September night.

Accurate scholarship can
Unearth the whole offence
From Luther[3] until now
15   That has driven a culture mad,
Find what occurred at Linz,[4]

1. An expert in eugenics, a pseudoscience for the genetic "improvement" of humans.
1. The date of Germany's invasion of Poland and the outbreak of World War II.

2. In New York City, where Auden was living.
3. Martin Luther (1483–1546), founder of the Protestant Reformation.
4. Austrian city where Hitler spent his childhood.

What huge imago[5] made
A psychopathic god:
I and the public know
20   What all schoolchildren learn,
Those to whom evil is done
Do evil in return.

Exiled Thucydides[6] knew
All that a speech can say
25   About Democracy,
And what dictators do,
The elderly rubbish they talk
To an apathetic grave;
Analysed all in his book,
30   The enlightenment driven away,
The habit-forming pain,
Mismanagement and grief:
We must suffer them all again.

Into this neutral air
35   Where blind skyscrapers use
Their full height to proclaim
The strength of Collective Man,
Each language pours its vain
Competitive excuse:
40   But who can live for long
In an euphoric dream;
Out of the mirror they stare,
Imperialism's face
And the international wrong.

45   Faces along the bar
Cling to their average day:
The lights must never go out,
The music must always play,
All the conventions conspire
50   To make this fort assume
The furniture of home;
Lest we should see where we are,
Lost in a haunted wood,
Children afraid of the night
55   Who have never been happy or good.

The windiest militant trash
Important Persons shout
Is not so crude as our wish:
What mad Nijinsky wrote
60   About Diaghilev[7]
Is true of the normal heart;

5. Psychoanalytic term for the unconscious representation of a parental figure.
6. Greek general (d. ca. 401 B.C.E.) and historian of the Peloponnesian War, exiled from Athens

because he failed to prevent the Spartans from seizing a colony.
7. The Russian dancer and choreographer Vaslav Nijinsky (1890–1950) wrote that his former lover

For the error bred in the bone
Of each woman and each man
Craves what it cannot have,
65 Not universal love
But to be loved alone.

From the conservative dark
Into the ethical life
The dense commuters come,
70 Repeating their morning vow,
"I *will* be true to the wife,
I'll concentrate more on my work,"
And helpless governors wake
To resume their compulsory game:
75 Who can release them now,
Who can reach the deaf,
Who can speak for the dumb?[8]

All I have is a voice
To undo the folded lie,
80 The romantic lie in the brain
Of the sensual man-in-the-street
And the lie of Authority
Whose buildings grope the sky:
There is no such thing as the State
85 And no one exists alone;
Hunger allows no choice
To the citizen or the police;
We must love one another or die.[9]

Defenceless under the night
90 Our world in stupor lies;
Yet, dotted everywhere,
Ironic points of light
Flash out wherever the Just
Exchange their messages:
95 May I, composed like them
Of Eros° and of dust,   *Greek god of desire*
Beleaguered by the same
Negation and despair,
Show an affirming flame.

Sept. 1939   1939, 1940

---

the ballet impresario Sergey Diaghilev (1872–
1929) "does not want universal love, but to be
loved alone."
8. Proverbs 31.8.

9. Auden later revised this line, which struck him
as "dishonest." In one version of the poem the line
reads "We must love one another and die." Another
version leaves out the entire stanza.

The Twentieth Century and After

Les Demoiselles d'Avignon, Pablo Picasso, 1907

This masterpiece by Spanish expatriate painter Pablo Picasso helped unleash the experimental energies of modern art. The painting breaks with formal traditions of one-point perspective and human modeling, violently fracturing space in jagged planes. At the same time it defies conventions of sexual decorum in the visual arts, confronting the viewer with five naked prostitutes in a brothel. The masklike faces, particularly of the women to the right, echo African art; they suggest the crucial role non-Western art will play in the development of modernism. The abstract faces, angular forms, and formally fragmented bodies intimate the revolutionary techniques of analytic cubism that Picasso and his French collaborator Georges Braque would develop in Paris from 1907 to 1914. THE MUSEUM OF MODERN ART/LICENSED BY SCALA/ART RESOURCE, NY.

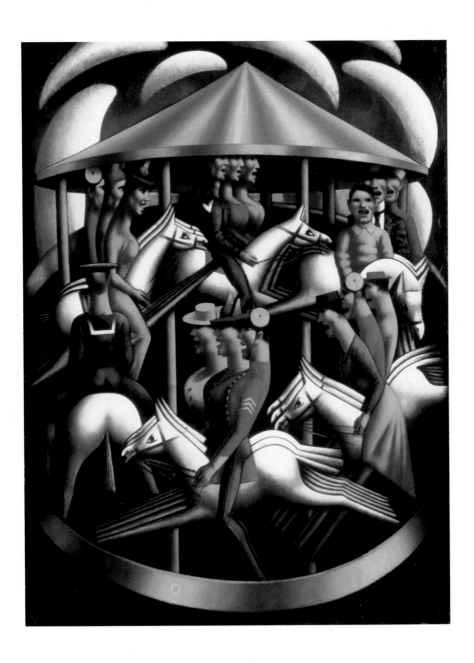

The Merry-Go-Round, Mark Gertler, 1916

Painted in the midst of World War I, *The Merry-Go-Round* explores the insufferable condition of life on the home front and on the battlefields. Its circularity describes the frustration of the deadlock on the Western Front, while its mingling of automatized soldiers and women conveys the sense of psychological menace pervading civilian society. The grinning puppet-like figures and the fun-fair setting convey an atmosphere of ghastly levity, in which war becomes a game. Glaring artificial colors contribute to the impression of a violent and confined world, where even nature is mechanical. Tate Gallery, London/Art Resource, NY.

Over the Top, 1st Artists' Rifles at Marcoing, 30th December 1917,
John Northcote Nash, 1918

John Nash enlisted in the Artists' Rifles in 1916 and survived several attempts at going "over the top" before his appointment as a War Artist two years later. In this painting he powerfully recollects the futile danger of an attack near Cambrai in 1917. A line of soldiers clambers out of a crude, wound-red trench to trudge through snow toward an unseen enemy. Several men are killed immediately, then fall prostrate or fall back into the ready-made grave of their recent refuge. Years later Nash recalled that the advance had from the outset been doomed, "was in fact pure murder," designed to divert attention from a bombing raid elsewhere. Of the eighty men who set out, only twelve, including Nash, returned. IMPERIAL WAR MUSEUM, LONDON, UK/BRIDGEMAN ART LIBRARY.

Tube Shelter Perspective (1941) and *Family Group* (1947), Henry Moore

In their disparate treatments of space and community, these works powerfully demonstrate the antithetic atmospheres of war and peace. Moore took up sketching during World War I because of a scarcity of sculpting material. His impression of crowds sheltering in the London Underground during an air raid, ranged in parallel lines down a seemingly endless tunnel, evokes the involuntary intimacy of strangers—forced into proximity, yet still isolated and anonymous. *Family Group,* by contrast, expresses a postwar moment of relative security, when the birth of Moore's only daughter coincided with the government's promotion of traditional family values, and Moore's return to sculpture found a ready market for large-scale public art. Two parents, infants on their knees, sit in a cozy circle, their bodies merging in a physical expression of unity. The holes within the sculpture recall the wartime tunnel, transforming it from a void that swallows masses of people to a harmonious space controlled by the bodies. *FAMILY GROUP*: CHRISTIE'S IMAGES/CORBIS; *TUBE SHELTER PERSPECTIVE*: HENRY MOORE FOUNDATION; TATE GALLERY, LONDON/ART RESOURCE, NY.

Painting, Francis Bacon, 1946

Bacon's nightmarish association of the slaughterhouse with the emblems of political and religious power conjures both the suffering and the hypocrisy of the twentieth century. The bust of a man, his face overshadowed by an open umbrella, surrounded by microphones, the whole superimposed upon a butcher's display, evokes the discrepancy between rhetoric and means of power. While the umbrella offers a ludicrous symbol of respectability, the visual parallels between man and meat draw attention to the brutal foundations of political influence. The man's broad shoulders resemble the squared outline of the carcass behind him. The red and white of his face, and his exposed teeth, suggest the flesh and bone of the beef. Incongruous religious references, in the cruciform spread of the carcass and the churchlike decorations on the walls, augment the painting's insinuations of corruption. THE ESTATE OF FRANCIS BACON/ARS, NY/DACS, LONDON; DIGITAL IMAGE; THE MUSEUM OF MODERN ART/LICENSED BY SCALA/ART RESOURCE, NY.

Model with Unfinished Self-Portrait, David Hockney, 1977

In *Model with Unfinished Self-Portrait* layers of illusion, realism undermined by artifice, and pictures within pictures draw our attention to the deceptive nature of painting. At first we seem to see in mirror image a model (Gregory Evans, Hockney's lover) sleeping while the artist paints; but as the title implies, the figure in fact lies in front of *Self-Portrait with Blue Guitar,* a painting developed concurrently with *Model,* depicting Hockney as Picasso, drawing a guitar. Hockney used the relationship between the canvases to reinforce his persona: *Model* invokes Picasso's technique of combining naturalistic with stylized or unfinished elements; while *Self-Portrait,* which eventually incorporated a bust of Dora Maar, Picasso's mistress, encourages an analogy between Picasso, Hockney, and their respective muses. Private Collection/Bridgeman Art Library.

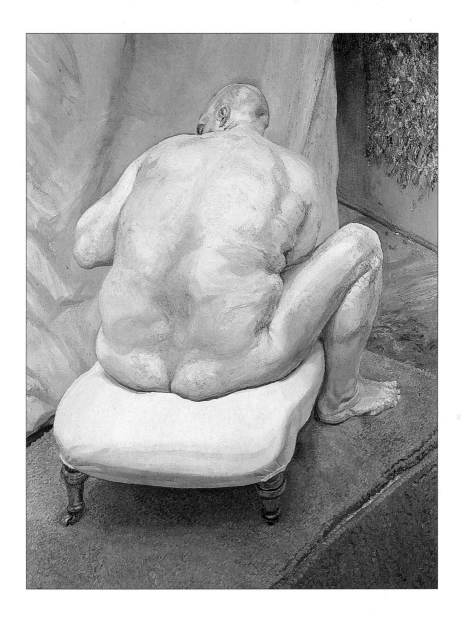

Naked Man, Back View, Lucian Freud, 1993

Freud's nudes study the details of the human body with an unflinching fascination that is modern in its refusal to censor or sentimentalize. Bowery, Freud's model, was a two-hundred-pound nightclub performer, famous for the gorgeous and outrageous costumes he used to reinvent himself in public. Yet Freud, recalling their first encounter, remembered the shape of his lower limbs rather than his outfit, observing that "his calves went right down to his feet, almost avoiding the whole business of ankles altogether." His depiction of Bowery in the nude strongly evokes the magnificence and the vulnerability of a body better known for its sartorial transformations. COURTESY OF ACQUAVELLA GALLERIES, INC. © 1993 THE METROPOL-ITAN MUSEUM OF ART, PURCHASE LILA ACHESON WALLACE GIFT (1993.71).

Marsyas, Anish Kapoor, October 9, 2002–April 6, 2003

Designed as a temporary installation to fill the vast central Turbine Hall at London's Tate Modern, *Marsyas* consists of a dark-red plastic membrane joining together three steel rings, two positioned vertically at either end and the third hung horizontally between. Its title refers to Marsyas, the satyr whom, in Greek mythology, Apollo flayed alive, and the membrane's color and contortions evoke flesh, even mutilated flesh. Yet the whole structure also has an ethereal quality, opening around each ring like the throat of an enormous flower. Suspended in the air, its intense, monochromatic surface resisting spatial recession, it seeks, as Kapoor has commented, "to make body into sky." Copyright 2002 Anish Kapoor; Tate Gallery, London/Art Resource, NY.

In Praise of Limestone[1]

If it form the one landscape that we the inconstant ones
  Are consistently homesick for, this is chiefly
Because it dissolves in water. Mark these rounded slopes
  With their surface fragrance of thyme and beneath
5 A secret system of caves and conduits; hear these springs
  That spurt out everywhere with a chuckle
Each filling a private pool for its fish and carving
  Its own little ravine whose cliffs entertain
The butterfly and the lizard; examine this region
10   Of short distances and definite places:
What could be more like Mother or a fitter background
  For her son, for the nude young male who lounges
Against a rock displaying his dildo,° never doubting   *penis*
  That for all his faults he is loved, whose works are but
15 Extensions of his power to charm? From weathered outcrop
  To hill-top temple, from appearing waters to
Conspicuous fountains, from a wild to a formal vineyard,
  Are ingenious but short steps that a child's wish
To receive more attention than his brothers, whether
20   By pleasing or teasing, can easily take.

Watch, then, the band of rivals as they climb up and down
  Their steep stone gennels[2] in twos and threes, sometimes
Arm in arm, but never, thank God, in step; or engaged
  On the shady side of a square at midday in
25 Voluble discourse, knowing each other too well to think
  There are any important secrets, unable
To conceive a god whose temper-tantrums are moral
  And not to be pacified by a clever line
Or a good lay: for, accustomed to a stone that responds,
30   They have never had to veil their faces in awe
Of a crater whose blazing fury could not be fixed;
  Adjusted to the local needs of valleys
Where everything can be touched or reached by walking,
  Their eyes have never looked into infinite space
35 Through the lattice-work of a nomad's comb; born lucky,
  Their legs have never encountered the fungi
And insects of the jungle, the monstrous forms and lives
  With which we have nothing, we like to hope, in common.
So, when one of them goes to the bad, the way his mind works
40   Remains comprehensible: to become a pimp
Or deal in fake jewelry or ruin a fine tenor voice
  For effects that bring down the house could happen to all
But the best and the worst of us . . .
                    That is why, I suppose,
  The best and worst never stayed here long but sought

1. Inspired by the limestone landscape outside
Florence, Italy, where Auden and his longtime
companion Chester Kallman (1921–1975) were
staying; the poem also recalls the poet's native
Yorkshire. In a letter to Elizabeth Mayer, Auden
wrote: "I hadn't realised till I came how like Italy
is to my 'Mutterland', the Pennines [hills in the
north of England]. Am in fact starting on a poem,
'In Praise of Limestone', the theme of which is that
rock creates the only truly human landscape."
2. Narrow passages between houses (Yorkshire
dialect) or, as here, rocks.

45   Immoderate soils where the beauty was not so external,
     The light less public and the meaning of life
  Something more than a mad camp. "Come!" cried the granite wastes,
     "How evasive is your humor, how accidental
  Your kindest kiss, how permanent is death." (Saints-to-be
50   Slipped away sighing.) "Come!" purred the clays and gravels
  "On our plains there is room for armies to drill; rivers
     Wait to be tamed and slaves to construct you a tomb
  In the grand manner: soft as the earth is mankind and both
     Need to be altered." (Intendant Caesars rose and
55   Left, slamming the door.) But the really reckless were fetched
     By an older colder voice, the oceanic whisper:
  "I am the solitude that asks and promises nothing;
     That is how I shall set you free. There is no love;
  There are only the various envies, all of them sad."

60   They were right, my dear, all those voices were right
  And still are; this land is not the sweet home that it looks,
     Nor its peace the historical calm of a site
  Where something was settled once and for all: A backward
     And dilapidated province, connected
65   To the big busy world by a tunnel, with a certain
     Seedy appeal, is that all it is now? Not quite:
  It has a worldly duty which in spite of itself
     It does not neglect, but calls into question
  All the Great Powers assume; it disturbs our rights. The poet,
70   Admired for his earnest habit of calling
  The sun the sun, his mind Puzzle, is made uneasy
     By these solid statues which so obviously doubt
  His antimythological myth; and these gamins,°   *urchins*
     Pursuing the scientist down the tiled colonnade
75   With such lively offers, rebuke his concern for Nature's
     Remotest aspects: I, too, am reproached, for what
  And how much you know. Not to lose time, not to get caught,
     Not to be left behind, not, please! to resemble
  The beasts who repeat themselves, or a thing like water
80   Or stone whose conduct can be predicted, these
  Are our Common Prayer,[3] whose greatest comfort is music
     Which can be made anywhere, is invisible,
  And does not smell. In so far as we have to look forward
     To death as a fact, no doubt we are right: But if
85   Sins can be forgiven, if bodies rise from the dead,
     These modifications of matter into
  Innocent athletes and gesticulating fountains,
     Made solely for pleasure, make a further point:
  The blessed will not care what angle they are regarded from,
90   Having nothing to hide. Dear, I know nothing of
  Either, but when I try to imagine a faultless love
     Or the life to come, what I hear is the murmur
  Of underground streams, what I see is a limestone landscape.

May 1948   1948, 1951

3. The Book of Common Prayer is the liturgical book of the Anglican Church.

The Shield of Achilles[1]

She looked over his shoulder
    For vines and olive trees,
Marble well-governed cities,
    And ships upon untamed seas,
5   But there on the shining metal
      His hands had put instead
An artificial wilderness
    And a sky like lead.

A plain without a feature, bare and brown,
10   No blade of grass, no sign of neighborhood,
Nothing to eat and nowhere to sit down,
    Yet, congregated on its blankness, stood
    An unintelligible multitude,
A million eyes, a million boots in line,
15   Without expression, waiting for a sign.

Out of the air a voice without a face
    Proved by statistics that some cause was just
In tones as dry and level as the place:
    No one was cheered and nothing was discussed;
20   Column by column in a cloud of dust
They marched away enduring a belief
Whose logic brought them, somewhere else, to grief.

She looked over his shoulder
    For ritual pieties,
25   White flower-garlanded heifers,
    Libation and sacrifice,[2]
But there on the shining metal
    Where the altar should have been,
She saw by his flickering forge-light
30   Quite another scene.

Barbed wire enclosed an arbitrary spot
    Where bored officials lounged (one cracked a joke)
And sentries sweated, for the day was hot:
    A crowd of ordinary decent folk
35   Watched from without and neither moved nor spoke
As three pale figures were led forth and bound
To three posts driven upright in the ground.

---

1. In Homer's *Iliad* Achilles, the chief Greek hero in the war with Troy, lends his armor to his great friend Patroclus and loses it when Patroclus is killed by Hector. While Achilles is mourning the death of his friend, his mother, the goddess Thetis, goes to Mt. Olympus to beg Hephaestos, the god of fire, to forge new armor for Achilles. The splendid shield of Achilles that Hephaestos then makes is described in book 18 (lines 478–608). On it he depicts the earth, the heavens, the sea, and the planets; a city in peace (with a wedding and a trial) and a city at war; scenes from country life, animal life, and the joyful life of young men and women. The ocean, as the outer border, flows around all these scenes.

2. Cf. John Keats's "Ode on a Grecian Urn" (1820): "Who are these coming to the sacrifice? / To what green altar, O mysterious priest, / Lead'st thou that heifer lowing at the skies, / And all her silken flanks with garlands dressed?" "Libation": sacrifice of wine or other liquid.

The mass and majesty of this world, all
    That carries weight and always weighs the same,
40 Lay in the hands of others; they were small
    And could not hope for help and no help came:
What their foes liked to do was done, their shame
Was all the worst could wish; they lost their pride
And died as men before their bodies died.

45   She looked over his shoulder
        For athletes at their games,
      Men and women in a dance
        Moving their sweet limbs
        Quick, quick, to music,
50   But there on the shining shield
      His hands had set no dancing-floor
        But a weed-choked field.

A ragged urchin, aimless and alone,
    Loitered about that vacancy; a bird
55 Flew up to safety from his well-aimed stone:
    That girls are raped, that two boys knife a third,
Were axioms to him, who'd never heard
Of any world where promises were kept
Or one could weep because another wept.

60   The thin-lipped armorer,
        Hephaestos, hobbled away;
      Thetis of the shining breasts
        Cried out in dismay
      At what the god had wrought
65   To please her son, the strong
      Iron-hearted man-slaying Achilles
        Who would not live long.

1952   1952, 1955

[Poetry as Memorable Speech][1]

    Of the many definitions of poetry, the simplest is still the best: 'memorable speech.' That is to say, it must move our emotions, or excite our intellect, for only that which is moving or exciting is memorable, and the stimulus is the audible spoken word and cadence, to which in all its power of suggestion and incantation we must surrender, as we do when talking to an intimate friend. We must, in fact, make exactly the opposite kind of mental effort to that we make in grasping other verbal uses, for in the case of the latter the aura of suggestion round every word through which, like the atom radiating lines of force through the whole of space and time, it becomes ultimately a sign for the sum of all possible meanings, must be rigorously suppressed and its meaning confined to a single dictionary one. For this reason the exposition of a

1. Excerpted from Auden and John Garrett's introduction to their anthology of verse, *The Poet's Tongue*.

scientific theory is easier to read than to hear. No poetry, on the other hand, which when mastered is not better heard than read is good poetry.

All speech has rhythm, which is the result of the combination of the alternating periods of effort and rest necessary to all living things, and the laying of emphasis on what we consider important; and in all poetry there is a tension between the rhythm due to the poet's personal values, and those due to the experiences of generations crystallised into habits of language such as the English tendency to alternate weak and accented syllables, and conventional verse forms like the hexameter, the heroic pentameter, or the French Alexandrine. Similes, metaphors of image or idea, and auditory metaphors such as rhyme, assonance, and alliteration help further to clarify and strengthen the pattern and internal relations of the experience described.

Poetry, in fact, bears the same kind of relation to Prose, using prose simply in the sense of all those uses of words that are not poetry, that algebra bears to arithmetic. The poet writes of personal or fictitious experiences, but these are not important in themselves until the reader has realised them in his own consciousness.

> Soldier from the war returning,
> Spoiler of the taken town.[2]

It is quite unimportant, though it is the kind of question not infrequently asked, who the soldier is, what regiment he belongs to, what war he had been fighting in, etc. The soldier is you or me, or the man next door. Only when it throws light on our own experience, when these lines occur to us as we see, say, the unhappy face of a stockbroker in the suburban train, does poetry convince us of its significance. The test of a poet is the frequency and diversity of the occasions on which we remember his poetry.

Memorable speech then. About what? Birth, death, the Beatific Vision,[3] the abysses of hatred and fear, the awards and miseries of desire, the unjust walking the earth and the just scratching miserably for food like hens, triumphs, earthquakes, deserts of boredom and featureless anxiety, the Golden Age promised or irrevocably past, the gratifications and terrors of childhood, the impact of nature on the adolescent, the despairs and wisdoms of the mature, the sacrificial victim, the descent into Hell, the devouring and the benign mother? Yes, all of these, but not these only. Everything that we remember no matter how trivial: the mark on the wall, the joke at luncheon, word games, these, like the dance of a stoat[4] or the raven's gamble, are equally the subject of poetry.

We shall do poetry a great disservice if we confine it only to the major experiences of life:

> The soldier's pole is fallen,
> Boys and girls are level now with men,
> And there is nothing left remarkable
> Beneath the visiting moon.

> They had a royal wedding.
> All his courtiers wished him well.

---

2. Beginning lines of a poem (in which "war" is plural) by the English poet A. E. Housman (1859–1936).

3. A sight of the glories of heaven.

4. Weasel.

> The horses pranced and the dancers danced.
> O Mister it was swell.

> And masculine is found to be
> Hadria the Adriatic Sea,[5]

have all their rightful place, and full appreciation of one depends on full appreciation of the others.

A great many people dislike the idea of poetry as they dislike over-earnest people, because they imagine it is always worrying about the eternal verities.

Those, in Mr Spender's[6] words, who try to put poetry on a pedestal only succeed in putting it on the shelf. Poetry is no better and no worse than human nature; it is profound and shallow, sophisticated and naïve, dull and witty, bawdy and chaste in turn.

In spite of the spread of education and the accessibility of printed matter, there is a gap between what is commonly called 'highbrow' and 'lowbrow' taste, wider perhaps than it has ever been.

The industrial revolution broke up the agricultural communities, with their local conservative cultures, and divided the growing population into two classes: those whether employers or employees who worked and had little leisure, and a small class of shareholders who did no work, had leisure but no responsibilities or roots, and were therefore preoccupied with themselves. Literature has tended therefore to divide into two streams, one providing the first with a compensation and escape, the other the second with a religion and a drug. The Art for Art's sake[7] of the London drawing-rooms of the '90's, and towns like Burnley and Rochdale,[8] are complementary.

Nor has the situation been much improved by the increased leisure and educational opportunities which the population to-day as a whole possess. Were leisure all, the unemployed would have created a second Athens.

Artistic creations may be produced by individuals, and because their work is only appreciated by a few it does not necessarily follow that it is not good; but a universal art can only be the product of a community united in sympathy, sense of worth, and aspiration; and it is improbable that the artist can do his best except in such a society.

* * *

The 'average' man says: 'When I get home I want to spend my time with my wife or in the nursery; I want to get out on to the links[9] or go for a spin in the car, not to read poetry. Why should I? I'm quite happy without it.' We must be able to point out to him that whenever, for example, he makes a good joke he is creating poetry, that one of the motives behind poetry is curiosity, the wish to know what we feel and think, and how, as E. M. Forster[1] says, can I know what I think till I see what I say, and that curiosity is the only human passion that can be indulged in for twenty-four hours a day without satiety.

The psychologist maintains that poetry is a neurotic symptom, an attempt

---

5. A mnemonic to help remember that Hadria, Latin for the Adriatic Sea, is masculine, despite its typically feminine ending. The first quotation is a remembered version of Cleopatra's speech after Antony dies in Shakespeare's *Antony and Cleopatra* (4.16.67–70). The source of the middle quotation has not been identified.

6. Stephen Spender (1909–1995), English poet.
7. Phrase associated with aestheticism.
8. Once industrial mill towns in Lancashire, England.
9. Ground on which golf is played.
1. English novelist (1879–1970).

to compensate by phantasy for a failure to meet reality. We must tell him that phantasy is only the beginning of writing; that, on the contrary, like psychology, poetry is a struggle to reconcile the unwilling subject and object; in fact, that since psychological truth depends so largely on context, poetry, the parabolic[2] approach, is the only adequate medium for psychology.

The propagandist, whether moral or political, complains that the writer should use his powers over words to persuade people to a particular course of action, instead of fiddling while Rome burns.[3] But Poetry is not concerned with telling people what to do, but with extending our knowledge of good and evil, perhaps making the necessity for action more urgent and its nature more clear, but only leading us to the point where it is possible for us to make a rational and moral choice.

*   *   *

1935

2. I.e., akin to parable.
3. The Roman emperor Nero (37–68) reputedly fiddled while Rome burned.

LOUIS MacNEICE
1907–1963

Born in Belfast, the son of a strong-willed Anglican rector (later to become a courageously independent bishop), Louis MacNeice illustrates the English critic Cyril Connolly's dictum that "the one golden recipe for Art is the ferment of an unhappy childhood working through a noble imagination." MacNeice's mother fell ill and died. "When I was five the black dreams came; / Nothing after was quite the same." Sent to English schools, where he lost his Irish accent, he was educated at Marlborough College and Merton College, Oxford. He became a lecturer in classics at Birmingham University and, later, at Bedford College, London. Following the breakup of his first marriage, he traveled to Iceland with his friend the poet W. H. Auden, then to Spain on the eve of—and again during—the Spanish Civil War, and to the United States at the beginning of World War II. After returning to England in 1940, he joined the British Broadcasting Corporation as a feature writer and producer and, except for a year and a half spent in Athens as director of the British Institute, worked for the BBC for the rest of his life.

He was a pioneer of radio drama, a playwright, a translator (of Aeschylus' *Agamemnon* and Goethe's *Faust*), and a literary critic. Best-known as a poet, however, he was early identified with the other liberal and leftist Oxford poets, Auden, Stephen Spender, and C. Day Lewis. Openness, honesty, and a consistently high level of craft characterize his poems. In a responsive, flexible voice, they ruminate tentatively and ponder without resolution. MacNeice delights in the surface of the world his senses apprehend and celebrates "the drunkenness of things being various," often (as in "Bagpipe Music") with wit and a wild gaiety. In love with life's irreducible multiplicity, he strives to embrace life's flux, despite an underlying sense of sadness and, sometimes, tragedy: "All our games are funeral games."

Sunday Morning

Down the road someone is practising scales,
The notes like little fishes vanish with a wink of tails,
Man's heart expands to tinker with his car
For this is Sunday morning, Fate's great bazaar,
5 Regard these means as ends, concentrate on this Now,
And you may grow to music or drive beyond Hindhead[1] anyhow,
Take corners on two wheels until you go so fast
That you can clutch a fringe or two of the windy past,
That you can abstract this day and make it to the week of time
10 A small eternity, a sonnet self-contained in rhyme.

But listen, up the road, something gulps, the church spire
Opens its eight bells out, skulls' mouths which will not tire
To tell how there is no music or movement which secures
Escape from the weekday time. Which deadens and endures.

1933   1935

The Sunlight on the Garden

The sunlight on the garden
Hardens and grows cold,
We cannot cage the minute
Within its nets of gold,
5 When all is told
We cannot beg for pardon.

Our freedom as free lances
Advances towards its end;
The earth compels, upon it
10 Sonnets and birds descend;
And soon, my friend,
We shall have no time for dances.

The sky was good for flying
Defying the church bells
15 And every evil iron
Siren and what it tells:
The earth compels,
We are dying, Egypt, dying[1]

And not expecting pardon,
20 Hardened in heart anew,
But glad to have sat under
Thunder and rain with you,

---

1. An upland district in Surrey popular for outings.

1. Cf. Antony's speech in Shakespeare's *Antony
and Cleopatra* 4.16.19: "I am dying, Egypt, dying."

And grateful too
For sunlight on the garden.

1937, 1938

Bagpipe Music

It's no go the merrygoround, it's no go the rickshaw,
All we want is a limousine and a ticket for the peepshow.
Their knickers° are made of crêpe-de-chine,° their   *panties / silky material*
    shoes are made of python,
Their halls are lined with tiger rugs and their walls with heads of bison.

5 John MacDonald found a corpse, put it under the sofa,
Waited till it came to life and hit it with a poker,
Sold its eyes for souvenirs, sold its blood for whisky,
Kept its bones for dumb-bells to use when he was fifty.

It's no go the Yogi-Man, it's no go Blavatsky,[1]
10 All we want is a bank balance and a bit of skirt in a taxi.
Annie MacDougall went to milk, caught her foot in the heather,
Woke to hear a dance record playing of Old Vienna.
It's no go your maidenheads, it's no go your culture,
All we want is a Dunlop tyre and the devil mend the puncture.

15 The Laird o' Phelps spent Hogmanay[2] declaring he was sober,
Counted his feet to prove the fact and found he had one foot over.
Mrs Carmichael had her fifth, looked at the job with repulsion,
Said to the midwife "Take it away; I'm through with overproduction."

It's no go the gossip column, it's no go the Ceilidh,[3]
20 All we want is a mother's help and a sugar-stick for the baby.

Willie Murray cut his thumb, couldn't count the damage,
Took the hide of an Ayrshire cow and used it for a bandage.
His brother caught three hundred cran[4] when the seas were lavish,
Threw the bleeders back in the sea and went upon the parish.[5]

25 It's no go the Herring Board, it's no go the Bible,
All we want is a packet of fags° when our hands are idle.   *cigarettes*

It's no go the picture palace, it's no go the stadium,
It's no go the country cot° with a pot of pink geraniums.   *cottage*
It's no go the Government grants, it's no go the elections,
30 Sit on your arse for fifty years and hang your hat on a pension.

1. Madame Blavatsky (1831–1891), famous theosophist whose ideas were popular in some quarters in 1930s Britain. The poem is set in Depression-era Scotland, before World War II.
2. New Year's Eve (Scots).
3. A Scottish Gaelic word pronounced *kaley* for a social evening spent singing and storytelling.
4. A measure of fresh herrings, about 750 fish. The Scottish herring industry failed in the 1930s; the Herring Board (line 25) was a government attempt to provide direction.
5. I.e., "went on the county" (on relief).

It's no go my honey love, it's no go my poppet;
Work your hands from day to day, the winds will blow the profit.
The glass is falling hour by hour, the glass will fall forever,
But if you break the bloody glass you won't hold up the weather.

1937

Star-Gazer

Forty-two years ago (to me if to no one else
The number is of some interest) it was a brilliant starry night
And the westward train was empty and had no corridors
So darting from side to side I could catch the unwonted sight
5   Of those almost intolerably bright
Holes, punched in the sky, which excited me partly because
Of their Latin names and partly because I had read in the textbooks
How very far off they were, it seemed their light
Had left them (some at least) long years before I was.

10   And this remembering now I mark that what
Light was leaving some of them at least then,
Forty-two years ago, will never arrive
In time for me to catch it, which light when
It does get here may find that there is not
15   Anyone left alive
To run from side to side in a late night train
Admiring it and adding noughts in vain.

Jan. 1963   1963

DYLAN THOMAS
1914–1953

Dylan Thomas was born in Swansea, Wales, and educated at Swansea Grammar
School. After working for a time as a newspaper reporter, he was "discovered" as a
poet in 1933 through a poetry contest in a popular newspaper. The following year his
Eighteen Poems caused considerable excitement because of their powerfully suggestive obscurity and the strange violence of their imagery. It looked as though a new
kind of visionary Romanticism had been restored to English poetry after the deliberately muted ironic tones of T. S. Eliot and his followers. Over time it became clear
that Thomas was also a master of poetic craft, not merely a shouting rhapsodist. His
verbal panache played against strict verse forms, such as the villanelle ("Do Not Go
Gentle into That Good Night"). "I am a painstaking, conscientious, involved and
devious craftsman in words," he wrote in his "Poetic Manifesto." His images were
carefully ordered in a patterned sequence, and his major theme was the unity of all
life, the continuing *process* of life and death and new life that linked the generations.
Thomas saw the workings of biology as a magical transformation producing unity out
of diversity, and again and again in his poetry he sought a poetic ritual to celebrate

this unity ("The force that through the green fuse drives the flower / Drives my green age"). He saw men and women locked in cycles of growth, love, procreation, new growth, death, and new life again. Hence each image engenders its opposite in what he called "my dialectical method": "Each image holds within it the seed of its own destruction." Thomas derives his closely woven, sometimes self-contradictory images from the Bible, Welsh folklore and preaching, and Freud. In his poems of reminiscence and autobiographical emotion, such as "Poem in October," he communicates more immediately through compelling use of lyrical feeling and simple natural images. His autobiographical work *Portrait of the Artist as a Young Dog* (1940) and his radio play *Under Milk Wood* (1954) reveal a vividness of observation and a combination of violence and tenderness in expression that show he could handle prose as excitingly as verse.

Thomas was a brilliant talker, an alcoholic, a reckless and impulsive man whose short life was packed with emotional ups and downs. His poetry readings in the United States between 1950 and 1953 were enormous successes, in spite of his sometimes reckless antics. He died suddenly in New York of what was diagnosed as "an insult to the brain," precipitated by alcohol. He played the part of the wild bohemian poet, and while some thought this behavior wonderful, others deplored it. He was a stirring reader of his own and others' poems, and many people who do not normally read poetry were drawn to Thomas's by the magic of his own reading. After his premature death a reaction set in: some critics declared that he had been overrated as a poet because of his sensational life. The "Movement" poets, such as Philip Larkin, repudiated his rhetorical extravagance. Even so, Thomas is still considered an original poet of great power and beauty.

The Force That Through the Green Fuse Drives the Flower

The force that through the green fuse drives the flower
Drives my green age; that blasts the roots of trees
Is my destroyer.
And I am dumb to tell the crooked rose
5   My youth is bent by the same wintry fever.

The force that drives the water through the rocks
Drives my red blood; that dries the mouthing streams
Turns mine to wax.
And I am dumb to mouth unto my veins
10   How at the mountain spring the same mouth sucks.

The hand that whirls the water in the pool[1]
Stirs the quicksand; that ropes the blowing wind
Hauls my shroud sail.
And I am dumb to tell the hanging man
15   How of my clay is made the hangman's lime.[2]

The lips of time leech to the fountain head;
Love drips and gathers, but the fallen blood
Shall calm her sores.

---

1. The hand of the angel who troubles the water of the pool Bethesda, thus rendering it curative, in John 5.1–4.

2. Quicklime was sometimes poured into the graves of public hangmen's victims to accelerate decomposition.

And I am dumb to tell a weather's wind
20 How time has ticked a heaven round the stars.

And I am dumb to tell the lover's tomb
How at my sheet goes the same crooked worm.

1933

The Hunchback in the Park

The hunchback in the park
A solitary mister
Propped between trees and water
From the opening of the garden lock
5   That lets the trees and water enter
Until the Sunday sombre bell at dark[1]

Eating bread from a newspaper
Drinking water from the chained cup
That the children filled with gravel
10 In the fountain basin where I sailed my ship
Slept at night in a dog kennel
But nobody chained him up.

Like the park birds he came early
Like the water he sat down
15 And Mister they called Hey mister
The truant boys from the town
Running when he had heard them clearly
On out of sound

Past lake and rockery°   rock garden
20 Laughing when he shook his paper
Hunchbacked in mockery
Through the loud zoo of the willow groves
Dodging the park keeper
With his stick that picked up leaves.

25 And the old dog sleeper
Alone between nurses and swans
While the boys among willows
Made the tigers jump out of their eyes
To roar on the rockery stones
30 And the groves were blue with sailors

Made all day until bell time
A woman figure without fault
Straight as a young elm
Straight and tall from his crooked bones

1. The bell indicates the park's closing for the night.

35 That she might stand in the night
    After the locks and chains

    All night in the unmade park
    After the railings and shrubberies
    The birds the grass the trees the lake
40 And the wild boys innocent as strawberries
    Had followed the hunchback
    To his kennel in the dark.

1941   1946

Poem in October

    It was my thirtieth year to heaven
Woke to my hearing from harbour and neighbour wood
    And the mussel pooled and the heron
        Priested shore
5   The morning beckon
With water praying and call of seagull and rook°   *crow*
And the knock of sailing boats on the net webbed wall
        Myself to set foot
        That second
10 In the still sleeping town and set forth.

    My birthday began with the water-
Birds and the birds of the winged trees flying my name
    Above the farms and the white horses
        And I rose
15   In rainy autumn
And walked abroad in a shower of all my days.
High tide and the heron dived when I took the road
        Over the border
        And the gates
20 Of the town closed as the town awoke.

    A springful of larks in a rolling
Cloud and the roadside bushes brimming with whistling
    Blackbirds and the sun of October
        Summery
25   On the hill's shoulder,
Here were fond climates and sweet singers suddenly
Come in the morning where I wandered and listened
        To the rain wringing
        Wind blow cold
30 In the wood faraway under me.

    Pale rain over the dwindling harbour
And over the sea wet church the size of a snail
    With its horns through mist and the castle
        Brown as owls

35   But all the gardens
Of spring and summer were blooming in the tall tales
Beyond the border and under the lark full cloud.
                   There could I marvel
                       My birthday
40   Away but the weather turned around.

It turned away from the blithe country
And down the other air and the blue altered sky
             Streamed again a wonder of summer
                   With apples
45   Pears and red currants
And I saw in the turning so clearly a child's
Forgotten mornings when he walked with his mother
             Through the parables
                Of sun light
50   And the legends of the green chapels

And the twice told fields of infancy
That his tears burned my cheeks and his heart moved in mine.
         These were the woods the river and sea
             Where a boy
55   In the listening
Summertime of the dead whispered the truth of his joy
To the trees and the stones and the fish in the tide.
          And the mystery
           Sang alive
60   Still in the water and singingbirds.

And there could I marvel my birthday
Away but the weather turned around. And the true
         Joy of the long dead child sang burning
           In the sun.
65   It was my thirtieth
Year to heaven stood there then in the summer noon
Though the town below lay leaved with October blood.
         O may my heart's truth
         Still be sung
70   On this high hill in a year's turning.

1944   1946

Fern Hill[1]

Now as I was young and easy under the apple boughs
About the lilting house and happy as the grass was green,
         The night above the dingle[2] starry,
           Time let me hail and climb

---

1. Name of the Welsh farmhouse, home of his aunt Ann Jones, where Thomas spent summer holidays as a boy.
2. Deep dell or hollow, usually wooded.

5   Golden in the heydays of his eyes,
And honoured among wagons I was prince of the apple towns
And once below a time I lordly had the trees and leaves
      Trail with daisies and barley
      Down the rivers of the windfall light.

10   And as I was green and carefree, famous among the barns
About the happy yard and singing as the farm was home,
      In the sun that is young once only,
        Time let me play and be
      Golden in the mercy of his means,
15 And green and golden I was huntsman and herdsman, the calves
Sang to my horn, the foxes on the hills barked clear and cold,
       And the sabbath rang slowly
      In the pebbles of the holy streams.

All the sun long it was running, it was lovely, the hay
20 Fields high as the house, the tunes from the chimneys, it was air
      And playing, lovely and watery
        And fire green as grass.
      And nightly under the simple stars
As I rode to sleep the owls were bearing the farm away,
25 All the moon long I heard, blessed among stables, the night-jars[3]
      Flying with the ricks,° and the horses   *haystacks*
       Flashing into the dark.

And then to awake, and the farm, like a wanderer white
With the dew, come back, the cock on his shoulder: it was all
30   Shining, it was Adam and maiden,[4]
       The sky gathered again
      And the sun grew round that very day.
So it must have been after the birth of the simple light
In the first, spinning place, the spellbound horses walking warm
35   Out of the whinnying green stable
       On to the fields of praise.

And honoured among foxes and pheasants by the gay house
Under the new made clouds and happy as the heart was long,
      In the sun born over and over,
40   I ran my heedless ways,
      My wishes raced through the house high hay
And nothing I cared, at my sky blue trades, that time allows
In all his tuneful turning so few and such morning songs
      Before the children green and golden
45   Follow him out of grace,

Nothing I cared, in the lamb white days, that time would take me
Up to the swallow thronged loft by the shadow of my hand,
      In the moon that is always rising,
       Nor that riding to sleep

3. Species of bird.   4. Cf. Genesis 1.

50   I should hear him fly with the high fields
    And wake to the farm forever fled from the childless land.
   Oh as I was young and easy in the mercy of his means,
        Time held me green and dying
   Though I sang in my chains like the sea.

1945   1946

Do Not Go Gentle into That Good Night

Do not go gentle into that good night,
Old age should burn and rave at close of day;
Rage, rage against the dying of the light.

Though wise men at their end know dark is right,
5   Because their words had forked no lightning they
Do not go gentle into that good night.

Good men, the last wave by, crying how bright
Their frail deeds might have danced in a green bay,
Rage, rage against the dying of the light.

10   Wild men who caught and sang the sun in flight,
And learn, too late, they grieved it on its way,
Do not go gentle into that good night.

Grave men, near death, who see with blinding sight
Blind eyes could blaze like meteors and be gay,
15   Rage, rage against the dying of the light.

And you, my father, there on the sad height,
Curse, bless, me now with your fierce tears, I pray.
Do not go gentle into that good night.
Rage, rage against the dying of the light.

1951   1952

Voices from World War II

In December 1939, a few months after the start of World War II, a leading article in *The Times Literary Supplement* urged poets to do their duty: "it is for the poets to sound the trumpet call. . . . The monstrous threat to belief and freedom which we are fighting should urge new psalmists to fresh songs of deliverance." The biblical diction reveals the underlying expectation that the poets of 1940 would come forward, like those of 1914, to sanctify the cause with images of sacrifice derived from Jesus Christ's precedent and precept: "greater love hath no man than this, that a man lay down his life for his friends." Far from taking up trumpets, the poets responded bitterly—C. Day Lewis with the poem "Where Are the War Poets?":

> They who in folly or mere greed
> Enslaved religion, markets, laws,
> Borrow our language now and bid
> Us to speak up in freedom's cause.
>
> It is the logic of our times,
> No subject for immortal verse—
> That we who lived by honest dreams
> Defend the bad against the worse.

Stephen Spender responded with an essay, in which he wrote: "At the beginning of the last war Rupert Brooke and others were 'trumpets singing to battle.' Why did not Rupert Brooke step forward 'young and goldenhaired' this time? No doubt, in part, precisely because one had done so last time. There is another reason: the poetry of the war of democracy versus fascism had already been written by English, French, Spanish, German and Italian émigré poets during the Spanish war."

With few exceptions the British poets of the 1930s had been born shortly before the outbreak of World War I, and those who were to be the poets of World War II were born during that earlier conflict. They grew up not, as Rupert Brooke, in the sunlit peace of Georgian England but amid wars and rumors of wars. They lived through the Great Depression and the rise of fascism. Introduced to the horrors of the last war—increased to mythic proportions by their fathers, uncles, and elder brothers—they were continually reminded of it by a flood of best-selling battle memoirs: Edmund Blunden's *Undertones of War* (1928), Robert Graves's *Goodbye to All That* (1929), Siegfried Sassoon's *Memoirs of an Infantry Officer* (1930) and *Sherston's Progress* (1936), and David Jones's *In Parenthesis* (1937). By then another myth, that of the Next War, was taking even more terrifying shape. Western intellectuals' last hope for the 1930s rested with the ragged troops of the left-wing Spanish Republic in their civil war against the right-wing Spanish Army that had mutinied in 1936 against the country's elected government. Democracy and fascism were at last in the open, fighting a war that many thought would determine not simply the future of Spain but the future of Europe. The conscience of the West was aroused as never since the Greek War of Independence against the Turks in 1821–29, in which Byron had lost his life. With the final defeat of the Spanish Republicans in 1938, the Next War ceased to be a myth so much as an all-but-inescapable certainty. At the start of W. B. Yeats's poem "Lapis Lazuli" (1938), "hysterical women say":

> everybody knows or else should know
> That if nothing drastic is done

> Aeroplane and Zeppelin will come out,
> Pitch like King Billy bomb-balls in
> Until the town lie beaten flat.

World War I had been fought, for the most part, on the land, and its emblem in popular mythology was the trench. After the indiscriminate killing of civilians in a bombing raid—by German aircraft—on the Spanish town of Guernica in 1937, everyone knew or else should have known that the emblem of the Next War would be the bomb, the fire from heaven.

So it proved. On September 1, 1939, Germany, in pursuit of imperial ambitions and without warning, launched a savage attack on Poland by land and air. Two days later Britain and France declared war on Germany. By the end of the month, Germany and its ally Russia had between them defeated and partitioned Poland. Russia then attacked Finland, and in April 1940 Germany invaded Denmark and Norway. For Britain and France the period of inactivity that came to be known as "The Phoney War" ended in May, when the German Army overran Luxembourg and invaded The Netherlands and Belgium; their armored columns raced for the English Channel. Cut off, the British forces were evacuated by sea, with heavy losses, from Dunkirk, and in June France signed an armistice with Germany. In August, as prelude to an invasion, the German *Luftwaffe* (Air Force) attacked England. Over the months that followed, the fighter pilots of the Royal Air Force (RAF) challenged the enemy bombers' nightly blitz of London and other major cities. The Battle of Britain, as it came to be called, cost the *Luftwaffe* twenty-three hundred planes and the RAF, nine hundred and caused the Germans to abandon their plans for invasion.

In 1941, Virginia Woolf imagined the coming fury, which would be a factor in her suicide. At the end of Woolf's novel *Between the Acts,* the village pageant of English history is over, and Mr. Streatfield's speech of thanks is interrupted: "A zoom severed it. Twelve aeroplanes in perfect formation like a flight of wild duck came overhead." The following year Edith Sitwell depicted the blitz in "Still Falls the Rain," as did T. S. Eliot in part 2 of "Little Gidding." The Battle of Britain, however, was not the only battle, and British poets were already responding to war on land and at sea as well as in the air. Some of their work shows the influence of their predecessors: Alun Lewis acknowledges a debt to Edward Thomas, whereas the diction and pararhyming of Keith Douglas's poems clearly owe something to Wilfred Owen's. Their voices, however, are their own, and the dominant mood of their poetry is strikingly unlike that from and about the trenches of the Western Front. Just as the heroics of 1914 were impossible in 1940 (although there was no lack of heroism), so too was the antipropagandist indignation of a Siegfried Sassoon. Now that everybody knew about the Battle of the Somme, the bombing of Guernica, London, Dresden, who could be surprised by evidence of "Man's inhumanity to man"? In the draft preface to his poems, one of the more influential poetic manifestos of the twentieth century, Owen had written: "All a poet can do today is warn. That is why the true poets must be truthful." His warnings and those of his contemporaries had been uttered in vain, but the poets of World War II knew they must be truthful, true to their wartime experience of boredom and brutality, true to their humanity, and above all resistant to the murderous inhumanity of the machines.

EDITH SITWELL
1887–1964

Edith Sitwell's father was an extremely eccentric English baronet; her mother, the daughter of an earl. Sitwell, an eccentrically gifted poet, objected to the subdued rural descriptions and reflections of the Georgian poets (of whom Rupert Brooke was the most popular) and reacted in favor of a highly abstract verbal experimentation that exploited the sounds and rhythms and suggestions of words and phrases, often with remarkable pyrotechnic display. She edited and was a substantial contributor to the six "cycles" of *Wheels* (1916–21), an annual anthology of modern poems, in which she displayed her verbal and rhythmic virtuosity and encouraged others to follow her example. Her poem sequence *Façade* (1922), with its cunning exploration of rhymes and rhythms, was set to music by the composer Sir William Walton, whose intensely sympathetic treatment of the words enhanced their impact. The 1923 performance in London's Aeolian Hall was a sensation: Sitwell intoned the poems from behind a screen, and Walton conducted the orchestra.

But Sitwell was more than a flashy manipulator of surfaces. Throughout her poetry she hints at profounder meanings, sometimes with mocking laughter, sometimes with anguish, and in her later work she attacks the pettiness and philistinism of the high society of her time. In still later poems, influenced by William Blake, W. B. Yeats, and her friend Dylan Thomas, Sitwell wished to achieve, she said in her autobiography, "a greater expressiveness, a greater formality, and a return to rhetoric," rejecting "the outcry for understatement, for quietness, for neutral tints in poetry." These poems, such as "Still Falls the Rain," are much concerned with the horrors of war, the varieties of human suffering produced by modern civilization, and the healing powers of a faith in God, combined with a sense of the richness and variety of nature.

Still Falls the Rain

The Raids, 1940.[1] *Night and Dawn*

Still falls the Rain—
Dark as the world of man, black as our loss—
Blind as the nineteen hundred and forty nails
Upon the Cross.

5   Still falls the Rain
With a sound like the pulse of the heart that is changed to the hammer-
    beat
In the Potter's Field,[2] and the sound of the impious feet
On the Tomb:
          Still falls the Rain
In the Field of Blood where the small hopes breed and the human brain
10 Nurtures its greed, that worm with the brow of Cain.[3]

Still falls the Rain
At the feet of the Starved Man hung upon the Cross.
Christ that each day, each night, nails there, have mercy on us—
On Dives and on Lazarus:[4]
15 Under the Rain the sore and the gold are as one.

1. During the Battle of Britain the German air force carried out many raids on London, often with incendiary bombs (see lines 27 and 30).
2. Cf. Matthew 27.3–8: "Then Judas, which betrayed [Jesus], when he saw that he was condemned, repented himself, and brought back the 30 pieces of silver to the chief priests and elders, saying, I have sinned in that I betrayed innocent blood. But they said, What is that to us? see thou to it. And he cast down the pieces of silver into the sanctuary, and departed; and he went away and hanged himself. And the chief priests took the pieces of silver . . . and bought with them the potter's field, to bury strangers in. Wherefore that field was called, The field of blood, unto this day."
3. The first murderer (Genesis 4).
4. In Jesus' parable the rich man Dives was sent to hell, while the leprous beggar Lazarus went to heaven (Luke 16.19–31). This is not the same Lazarus who was raised from the dead.

Still falls the Rain—
Still falls the Blood from the Starved Man's wounded Side:
He bears in His Heart all wounds,—those of the light that died,
The last faint spark
20   In the self-murdered heart, the wounds of the sad uncomprehending dark,
The wounds of the baited bear,[5]—
The blind and weeping bear whom the keepers beat
On his helpless flesh . . . the tears of the hunted hare.

Still falls the Rain—
25   Then—O Ile leape up to my God: who pulles me doune—
See, see where Christ's blood streames in the firmament:[6]
It flows from the Brow we nailed upon the tree
Deep to the dying, to the thirsting heart
That holds the fires of the world,—dark-smirched with pain
30   As Caesar's laurel crown.[7]

Then sounds the voice of One who like the heart of man
Was once a child who among beasts has lain—
"Still do I love, still shed my innocent light, my Blood, for thee."

                                                                          1942

---

5. A medieval and Elizabethan sport in which dogs fought a bear chained to a post.
6. Faustus's despairing cry at the end of Christopher Marlowe's play *Doctor Faustus* (1604), when he realizes that he has been damned for his pact with Mephistopheles.
7. Traditionally worn by victorious generals, and perhaps here associated with Jesus' crown of thorns (Matthew 27.29).

HENRY REED
1914–1986

Henry Reed was born and educated in Birmingham, at the King Edward VI School and at Birmingham University, where he gained a first-class degree in classics (having taught himself Greek) and began an M.A. thesis on Thomas Hardy. After leaving the university in 1934, he tried teaching, like many other British writers of the 1930s, but, again like most of them, hated it and left to make his way as a freelance writer and critic. During World War II he served—"or rather *studied*," as he put it—in the Royal Army Ordnance Corps for a year. A notable mimic, he would entertain his friends with a comic imitation of a sergeant instructing new recruits. After a few performances he noticed that the words of the weapon-training instructor, couched in the style of the military manual, fell into certain rhythmic patterns. His fascination with these patterns eventually informed his *Lessons of the War,* the first of which, "Naming of Parts," is probably the most anthologized poem prompted by World War II.

From 1942 to 1945 Reed worked as a cryptographer and translator at the Government Code and Cypher School at Bletchley. In the evenings he wrote much of his first radio play—an adaptation of Melville's *Moby-Dick*—and many of the poems to be published in *A Map of Verona* (1946). After the war, he produced a number of other successful—and often funny—radio plays, verse translations of the Italian poet Giacomo Leopardi (1798–1837), and more fine poems. Many of the best of these were found in manuscript at his death, and with the posthumous publication of his *Collected Poems* (1991), he emerged as a poet whose lifelong quest for lasting homosexual love—which he never found—led him through Edenic landscapes of desire, like the setting of "Naming of Parts."

From Lessons of the War

To Alan Michell

Vixi duellis nuper idoneus
Et militavi non sine gloria[1]

1. Naming of Parts

Today we have naming of parts. Yesterday,
We had daily cleaning. And tomorrow morning,
We shall have what to do after firing. But today,
Today we have naming of parts. Japonica[2]
5 Glistens like coral in all of the neighbouring gardens,
     And today we have naming of parts.

This is the lower sling swivel. And this
Is the upper sling swivel, whose use you will see,
When you are given your slings. And this is the piling swivel,
10 Which in your case you have not got. The branches
Hold in the gardens their silent, eloquent gestures,
     Which in our case we have not got.

This is the safety-catch, which is always released
With an easy flick of the thumb. And please do not let me
15 See anyone using his finger. You can do it quite easy
If you have any strength in your thumb. The blossoms
Are fragile and motionless, never letting anyone see
     Any of them using their finger.

And this you can see is the bolt. The purpose of this
20 Is to open the breech, as you see. We can slide it
Rapidly backwards and forwards: we call this
Easing the spring.[3] And rapidly backwards and forwards
The early bees are assaulting and fumbling the flowers:
     They call it easing the Spring.

25 They call it easing the Spring: it is perfectly easy
If you have any strength in your thumb; like the bolt,
And the breech, and the cocking-piece, and the point of balance,
Which in our case we have not got; and the almond-blossom

---

1. "Lately I have lived in the midst of battles, creditably enough, / and have soldiered, not without glory" (Horace's *Odes* 3.26.1–2, with the letter *p* of *puellis*—girls—turned upside down to produce *duellis*—battles; an emendation, an exchange, that encapsulates the theme of the *Lessons*).
2. A shrub with brilliant scarlet flowers.
3. An operation that, by ejecting the bullets from the magazine of a rifle, takes the pressure off the magazine spring.

Silent in all of the gardens and the bees going backwards and forwards,
30   For today we have naming of parts.

1945

KEITH DOUGLAS
1920–1944

Keith Douglas was born in Tunbridge Wells, the son of a regular army officer, who had won the Military Cross in World War I and who, in 1927, deserted his wife and son. Like Byron, whose army officer father died in the poet's youth, Douglas developed an almost obsessive interest in warfare. At the age of ten he wrote a poem about the Battle of Waterloo, and later, at Christ's Hospital School in London, he divided his leisure time between developing his precocious talents as poet and artist, riding, playing rugby football, and participating enthusiastically in the Officer Cadet Corps. At Merton College, Oxford, he was tutored by Edmund Blunden, a distinguished soldier poet of World War I. In 1940 Douglas enlisted in a cavalry regiment that was soon obliged to exchange its horses for tanks and in August 1942 he went into battle against German field marshal Rommel's Africa Corps in the Egyptian desert. Forced to remain in reserve behind the lines, Douglas commandeered a truck and, directly disobeying orders, drove off to join his regiment.

His subsequent achievement as a poet and as the author of a brilliant memoir of the desert campaign, *Alamein to Zem Zem* (1966), was to celebrate the last stand of the chivalric hero. His poem "Aristocrats" ends perhaps with a distant echo of Roland's horn, sounded in the Pass of Roncevalles at the end of the twelfth-century French chivalric epic *La Chanson de Roland* (*The Song of Roland*). Douglas's poem succeeds where most of the would-be heroic poems of 1914 and 1915 fail. Sharply focused, it acknowledges both the stupidity and the chivalry, the folly and the glamour of cavalrymen on mechanical mounts, dueling in the desert. Douglas's language, spare and understated, finely responsive to his theme, fuses ancient and modern: his heroes are "gentle"—like Chaucer's "verray parfit gentil knight" in *The Canterbury Tales*— and at the same time "obsolescent."

Douglas survived the desert campaign, but was killed in the assault on the Normandy beaches, on June 6, 1944.

Gallantry

The Colonel[1] in a casual voice
spoke into the microphone a joke
Which through a hundred earphones broke
into the ears of a doomed race.[2]

---

1. Lt. Col. J. D. Player, killed in Tunisia, Enfidaville, February 1943, left £3,000 to the Beaufort Hunt, and directed that the incumbent of the living in his gift [i.e., the church whose vicar he was entitled to appoint] should be a 'man who approves of hunting, shooting, and all manly sports, which are the backbone of the nation.' [Douglas's note on one of the manuscripts of "Aristocrats." Player was in fact killed in April.]

2. Cf. Wilfred Owen's "Anthem for Doomed Youth" (p. 1971).

5   Into the ears of the doomed boy, the fool
    whose perfectly mannered flesh fell
    in opening the door for a shell
    as he had learnt to do at school.

    Conrad luckily survived the winter:
10   he wrote a letter to welcome
    the auspicious spring: only his silken
    intentions severed with a single splinter.

    Was George fond of little boys?
    We always suspected it,
15   but who will say: since George was hit
    we never mention our surmise.

    It was a brave thing the Colonel said,
    but the whole sky turned too hot
    and the three heroes never heard what
20   it was, gone deaf with steel and lead.

    But the bullets cried with laughter,
    the shells were overcome with mirth,
    plunging their heads in steel and earth—
    (the air commented in a whisper).

El Ballah, General Hospital, Apr. 1943   1949

Vergissmeinnicht[1]

    Three weeks gone and the combatants gone
    returning over the nightmare ground
    we found the place again, and found
    the soldier sprawling in the sun.

5   The frowning barrel of his gun
    overshadowing. As we came on
    that day, he hit my tank with one
    like the entry of a demon.

    Look. Here in the gunpit spoil
10   the dishonoured picture of his girl
    who has put: *Steffi. Vergissmeinnicht*
    in a copybook gothic script.

    We see him almost with content,
    abased, and seeming to have paid
15   and mocked at by his own equipment
    that's hard and good when he's decayed.

---

1. Forget me not (German).

But she would weep to see today
how on his skin the swart° flies move;   *black*
the dust upon the paper eye
20   and the burst stomach like a cave.

For here the lover and killer are mingled
who had one body and one heart.
And death who had the soldier singled
has done the lover mortal hurt.

Tunisia, 1943   1944

Aristocrats[1]

"I think I am becoming a God"[2]

The noble horse with courage in his eye
clean in the bone, looks up at a shellburst:
away fly the images of the shires[3]
but he puts the pipe back in his mouth.

5   Peter was unfortunately killed by an 88:[4]
it took his leg away, he died in the ambulance.
I saw him crawling on the sand; he said
It's most unfair, they've shot my foot off.

How can I live among this gentle
10   obsolescent breed of heroes, and not weep?
Unicorns, almost,
for they are falling into two legends
in which their stupidity and chivalry
are celebrated. Each, fool and hero, will be an immortal.

15   The plains were their cricket pitch[5]
and in the mountains the tremendous drop fences[6]
brought down some of the runners. Here then
under the stones and earth they dispose themselves,
I think with their famous unconcern.
20   It is not gunfire I hear but a hunting horn.[7]

Enfidaville, Tunisia, 1943   1946

---

1. Another version of this poem is entitled "Sportsmen."
2. The dying words of Roman Emperor Vespasian were supposedly "Alas! I suppose I am turning into a god."
3. Counties. Cf. Owen's "Anthem for Doomed Youth," line 8 (p. 1971).
4. A German tank fitted with an eighty-eight-millimeter gun.
5. Field on which the game of cricket is played.
6. Fences in the course of a steeplechase horse race.
7. See n. 1, p. 2456.

CHARLES CAUSLEY
1917–2003

Born and educated in Launceston, Cornwall, Charles Causley followed the tradition of his seafaring people and served in the Royal Navy from 1940 to 1946. His experiences on a destroyer and an aircraft carrier had a catalytic effect on him as a poet. "It was Hitler who pushed a subject under my nose," he wrote. "I think the event that affected me more than anything else in those years was the fact that the companion who had left my home-town with me for the navy in 1940 was later lost in a convoy to Russia. From the moment I heard this news, I found myself haunted by the words in the twenty-fourth chapter of St Matthew: 'Then shall two be in the field; the one shall be taken, and the other left.' If my poetry is 'about' anything, it is this."

Causley's Cornishness shows in his skillful use of verse forms and narrative strategies drawn from an oral folk tradition. A formally conservative poet, he was a master of the ballad told in a voice that is at once impersonal—the voice of the anonymous early balladeers—and unmistakably his own. Causley's seeming simplicity, like that of the early balladeers, can be misleading; his jaunty cadences, his spry interweaving of ancient and modern diction, heighten the poignancy of elegies such as the ones printed here.

From 1947 to 1976 he taught at a school in Cornwall. He wrote many volumes of poems and several plays—some of each, with great success, for children.

At the British War Cemetery, Bayeux[1]

I walked where in their talking graves
And shirts of earth five thousand lay,
When history with ten feasts of fire
Had eaten the red air away.

5 I am Christ's boy, I cried, I bear
In iron hands the bread, the fishes.[2]
I hang with honey and with rose
This tidy wreck of all your wishes.

On your geometry of sleep
10 The chestnut and the fir-tree fly,
And lavender and marguerite
Forge with their flowers an English sky.

Turn now towards the belling town
Your jigsaws of impossible bone,
15 And rising read your rank of snow
Accurate as death upon the stone.

About your easy heads my prayers
I said with syllables of clay.
What gift, I asked, shall I bring now
20 Before I weep and walk away?

1. Near the coast of northwest France, the scene of heavy fighting following the Normandy landings in June 1944.
2. Cf. Matthew 14.19–20.

Take, they replied, the oak and laurel.[3]
Take our fortune of tears and live
Like a spendthrift lover. All we ask
Is the one gift you cannot give.

1957

Armistice Day

I stood with three comrades in Parliament Square[1]
November her freights of grey fire unloading,
No sound from the city upon the pale air
Above us the sea-bell eleven exploding.

5   Down by the bands and the burning memorial
Beats all the brass in a royal array,
But at our end we are not so sartorial:
Out of (as usual) the rig of the day.

Starry is wearing a split pusser's flannel[2]
10   Rubbed, as he is, by the regular tide;
Oxo the ducks[3] that he ditched in the Channel
In June, 1940 (when he was inside).

Kitty recalls his abandon-ship station,
Running below at the Old Man's salute[4]
15   And (with a deck-watch) going down for duration[5]
Wearing his oppo's pneumonia-suit.[6]

Comrades, for you the black captain of carracks[7]
Writes in Whitehall[8] his appalling decisions,
But as was often the case in the Barracks
20   Several ratings are not at Divisions.[9]

Into my eyes the stiff sea-horses stare,
Over my head sweeps the sun like a swan.
As I stand alone in Parliament Square
A cold bugle calls, and the city moves on.

1957

---

3. Trees whose leaves are traditionally taken as emblems of courage and victory, respectively.
1. An annual "Remembrance Sunday" service is held at the Cenotaph, a stone memorial to the dead of the two World Wars, in London's Parliament Square. It includes a two-minute silence after the last stroke of eleven o'clock.
2. A torn navy-issue shirt.
3. Sailor's white tunic and trousers.
4. A British naval tradition calls for the Captain (Old Man) of a sinking ship to go down saluting.
5. I.e., for the duration of the war; a phrase common during World War II.
6. Canvas suit—belonging to his friend ("opposite number")—worn while painting the ship.
7. Large merchant ships equipped for warfare.
8. London street in which stands the Admiralty (navy headquarters).
9. I.e., noncommissioned sailors are absent from church parade, the religious service on board ship.

Nation and Language

Armies and navies, cannons and guns helped spread and consolidate British rule across vast areas of the earth's surface, but so too did the English language. Over many years, in many different parts of the world, the language of the British Empire displaced or commingled with indigenous languages. Then the twentieth century witnessed the decolonization and devolution of the British Empire, from early-century Ireland to midcentury India and Africa and the Caribbean to late-century Hong Kong. Imaginative writers from these and other regions have thus had to wrestle with questions of nation and language. Should they write stories, plays, and poems in the language and traditions of the colonizer, or should they repudiate English and employ their indigenous languages? Is English an enabling tool by which peoples of different nationalities can express their identities, or is it contaminated by a colonial history and mentality that it insidiously perpetuates? If English is chosen for imaginative writing, should it be a standardized English of the imperial center or an English inflected by contact with indigenous languages—a creole, patois, pidgin, even a synthetic composite of a local vernacular and Standard English? Since American power has sustained the global reach of English long after the withdrawal of British colonial administrators and armies, debates over such questions have persisted in many parts of the world where English still thrives in the aftermath of a dead empire.

Having tried to subdue the Irish people for centuries, the British outlawed the use of the Irish language (or Gaelic) in Ireland, and Brian Friel explores the painful effects of the forcible displacement of Irish in his important historical play, *Translations*. Because of Ireland's long and bloody colonial history and the flowering there of cultural nationalism, early-twentieth-century Irish writers were already expressing a powerful ambivalence toward English as both a vital literary inheritance and the language of colonial subjugation. Recalling the sixteenth- and seventeenth-century English "wars of extermination" against the Irish, W. B. Yeats acknowledges a historical hatred of the English but then reminds himself that, as an English-language writer, "I owe my soul to Shakespeare, to Spenser and to Blake, perhaps to William Morris, and to the English language in which I think, speak and write, that everything I love has come to me through English; my hatred tortures me with love, my love with hate" (see his "Introduction," excerpted in this volume). In the novel *A Portrait of the Artist as a Young Man*, James Joyce's autobiographical persona, Stephen Dedalus, reflects on his conversation with an academic dean, an Englishman: "The language in which we are speaking is his before it is mine. . . . I cannot speak or write these [English] words without unrest of spirit. His language, so familiar and so foreign, will always be for me an acquired speech. I have not made or accepted its words. My voice holds them at bay. My soul frets in the shadow of his language." Yet Yeats and Joyce, despite this vexed relation to the language, wrote some of the most innovative English-language poetry and fiction of the twentieth century. Indeed, their conflicted relation to the English language and its literary inheritance—that "unrest of spirit" in its shadow—may paradoxically have impelled their massive literary achievements.

Transplanted in different parts of the world, English has sometimes seemed strange and estranging. When African and Caribbean schoolchildren with British colonial educations tried to write poems, as Kamau Brathwaite and other writers have attested, they would follow the conventions of English poetry, composing iambic pentameter verse about snowfall or daffodils, which they had never seen. English language and

2461

English literature thus risked alienating colonized peoples from their local environments and distinctive cultural histories.

The feeling that the English language is alienating, inextricably bound to colonialism, has led some nativist writers, such as the Kenyan novelist Ngũgĩ wa Thiong'o, to reject it outright. If language is a "collective memory bank," then a people cannot recover its colonially suppressed identity and history without returning to an indigenous language. But the novelist Salman Rushdie, who often writes in an Indianized, or "chutnified," English, takes the opposite stance: "The English language ceased to be the sole possession of the English some time ago," he asserts. English has become a local language even in parts of the world, such as India, where it was once imposed. Rushdie and other cosmopolitan writers reject the assumption that the English language has an inherent relationship to only one kind of national or ethnic experience. "The English language is nobody's special property," asserts the Caribbean poet Derek Walcott.

For the colonial or postcolonial writer who embraces English, the question remains, Which English? The imported standard or a local vernacular? Or if both, should they be intermingled or kept apart? At one end of the spectrum are writers, such as V. S. Naipaul and Wole Soyinka, who think Standard English, perhaps slightly altered, can bespeak a postcolonial experience of race, identity, and history. At the other end are vernacular writers who feel the language of the center cannot do justice to their experience at the margins of empire. The poet Louise Bennett, for example, gives voice to everyday Jamaican experience in her witty and wily use of Jamaican Creole or Patois; she mocks its denigration as a "corruption of the English language," pointing out that Standard English is but an amalgam of dialects and foreign languages. "It was in language that the slave was perhaps most successfully imprisoned by his master," Brathwaite has written, "and it was in his (mis-)use of it that he perhaps most effectively rebelled."

Between the Standard English writer and the vernacular writer range a host of other possibilities. Some poets and novelists, such as the Jamaican-born Claude McKay and the Scottish nationalist Hugh MacDiarmid, spend a substantial part of their careers writing in one version of English and then shift dramatically to another. Others employ either Standard English or a local vernacular depending on the perspective they are presenting. Two of Caribbean-born writer Jean Rhys's stories written during the same period offer two distinct points of view, one in the normative English of a white West Indian child, the other in the creolized (or hybridized) English of a mulatto immigrant in London. Finally, many writers, such as Walcott, Brathwaite, and the Yorkshire poet Tony Harrison, switch between standard and "dialect" within or across individual works, creating juxtapositions, tensions, and new relationships between languages that have traditionally been kept hierarchically discrete. They linguistically embody their interstitial experience of living in between metropolis and margin, canon and creole, schoolbooks and the street.

Whether using slightly or heavily creolized English, or a medley of both, writers from across the world—Barbadians and Bombayites and "Black Britons"—have employed a diverse array of distinctive idioms, dialects, creoles to defy imperial norms, express emerging cultural identities, and inaugurate rich new possibilities for literature in English.

CLAUDE McKAY
1890–1948

Claude McKay was born into a poor farmworking family in Sunny Ville, Clarendon Parish, Jamaica, and spent the first half of his life on the British Caribbean island. He was apprenticed to a cabinetmaker and then a wheelwright and served for less than a year as a police constable in Kingston. An English linguist and folklorist, Walter Jekyll, encouraged him to write in Jamaican dialect, or Creole. Drawing on the example of the Scottish-dialect poet Robert Burns, McKay harnessed Jamaican idiom in poems collected in two books published in 1912, *Constab Ballads* and *Songs of Jamaica*, including "Old England," a seemingly reverent imaginative journey, in a new literary language, to the imperial "homeland." The first major poet to make effective literary use of Jamaican English, he influenced many later Afro-Caribbean poets who went further, such as Louise Bennett.

For his poetry McKay won a prize that enabled him to travel to the United States and study at Alabama's Tuskegee Institute and at Kansas State College, before moving to Harlem in 1914. Switching in his poetry from Jamaican to Standard English, he helped precipitate the Harlem Renaissance with his *Harlem Shadows* (1922), which included sonnets addressing the vexed racial experience of an Afro-Caribbean immigrant. For most of the 1920s into the mid-1930s, McKay, identifying with the radical left, lived and wrote novels and short stories mainly in England, France, and Morocco. He died in poverty in Chicago, where he taught in his last years for a Catholic youth organization. His sonnet "If We Must Die," written in response to the American antiblack riots of the summer of 1919, became a World War II rallying cry after Winston Churchill read it, without attribution, to the British people.

Old England

I've a longin' in me dept's of heart dat I can conquer not,
'Tis a wish dat I've been havin' from since I could form a t'o't,°   *thought*
'Tis to sail athwart the ocean an' to hear de billows roar,
When dem ride aroun' de steamer,° when dem beat on England's   *steamship*
    shore.

5   Just to view de homeland England, in de streets of London walk,
An' to see de famous sights dem 'bouten which dere's so much talk,
An' to watch de fact'ry chimneys pourin' smoke up to de sky,
An' to see de matches-children, dat I hear 'bout, passin' by.[1]

    I would see Saint Paul's Cathedral,[2] an' would hear some of de great
10   Learnin' comin' from de bishops, preachin' relics of old fait';
I would ope me mout' wid wonder at de massive organ soun',
An' would 'train me eyes to see de beauty lyin' all aroun'.

    I'd go to de City Temple,[3] where de old fait' is a wreck,
An' de parson is a-preachin' views dat most folks will not tek;
15   I'd go where de men of science meet togeder in deir hall,
To give light unto de real truths, to obey king Reason's call.

---

1. Cf. the short story "The Little-Match Seller," by the Danish writer Hans Christian Andersen (1805–1875), and the poem "The Little Match Girl," by the Scottish writer William McGonagall (1830?–1902), both about a poor match-selling girl who freezes to death on New Year's Eve.
2. In London, cathedral of the Anglican bishop.
3. Victorian church in central London.

I would view Westminster Abbey,[4] where de great of England sleep,
An' de solemn marble statues o'er deir ashes vigil keep;
I would see immortal Milton an' de wul'-famous Shakespeare,
20 Past'ral Wordswort', gentle Gray,[5] an' all de great souls buried dere.

I would see de ancient chair where England's kings deir crowns put on,
Soon to lay dem by again when all de vanity is done;
An' I'd go to view de lone spot where in peaceful solitude
Rests de body of our Missis Queen,[6] Victoria de Good.

25 An' dese places dat I sing of now shall afterwards impart
All deir solemn sacred beauty to a weary searchin' heart;
So I'll rest glad an' contented in me min[10] for evermore,   *mind*
When I sail across de ocean back to my own native shore.

                                                                    1912

If We Must Die

If we must die, let it not be like hogs
Hunted and penned in an inglorious spot,
While round us bark the mad and hungry dogs,
Making their mock at our accursed lot.
5   If we must die, O let us nobly die,
So that our precious blood may not be shed
In vain; then even the monsters we defy
Shall be constrained to honor us though dead!
O kinsmen! we must meet the common foe!
10 Though far outnumbered let us show us brave,
And for their thousand blows deal one deathblow!
What though before us lies the open grave?
Like men we'll face the murderous, cowardly pack,
Pressed to the wall, dying, but fighting back!

                                                              1919, 1922

4. London church, where monarchs are crowned
and the famous, including poets, are buried.
5. Thomas Gray (1716–1771), English poet and
author of "Elegy Written in a Country Churchyard."
6. So-called in Jamaica, Victoria reigned during
the emancipation of slaves in 1837.

HUGH MacDIARMID
1892–1978

Hugh MacDiarmid, often said to be the greatest Scottish poet since Robert Burns,
was born Christopher Murray Grieve in the Scottish border town of Langholm. After
a short period of training as a teacher, he turned to journalism. His political convictions made for a turbulent life. He was a founding member of the National Party of
Scotland, but it expelled him in 1933 because of his communism. He then joined the

Communist Party of Great Britain, but it expelled him as well, because of his Scottish nationalism.

From the 1920s MacDiarmid was the central figure of the Scottish Renaissance movement. He published short lyrics in a revived Scots, or "Lallans" (i.e., Lowland Scots), a language that fused the rich vocabulary of medieval Scottish poets, modern dialect Scots, and Standard English. In *A Drunk Man Looks at the Thistle* (1926), he built up an epic statement about Scotland out of a series of related lyrics and passages of descriptive and reflective poetry. In such early poems MacDiarmid proved the vigor and robust physicality of Scots as a medium for modern poetry, after the Burns tradition had declined into sentimentality and imitation. In essays such as "English Ascendancy in British Literature" (excerpted below), he argued vehemently against confining "British literature" to the Standard English literature of England, championing instead the varieties of Scottish, Irish, and Welsh literatures written in locally distinctive forms of English and other languages of the British Isles.

MacDiarmid wrote little poetry in Scots after the mid-1930s, when he turned to an ambitious "poetry of fact and first-hand experience and scientific knowledge," including the long poem *In Memoriam James Joyce* (1955), written in colloquial English but formally patterned by carefully controlled shifts in tempo. In it he affirms the essential kinship of everything in the world that is fully realized and properly possessed of its identity—a theme that clearly bears on his lifelong preoccupation with Scottish nationality, language, and culture.

[The Splendid Variety of Languages and Dialects][1]

* * * Burns[2] knew what he was doing when he reverted from 18th century English to a species of synthetic Scots and was abundantly justified in the result. He was not contributing to English literature but to a clearly defined and quite independent tradition of Scottish poetry hailing from the days of Dunbar and the other great 15th century 'makars'[3]—the golden age of Scottish poetry when the English impulse seemed to have gone sterile and Scotland, not England, was apparently destined to produce the great poetry of the United Kingdom. To ask why this promise was not redeemed and why English, a far less concentrated and expressive language, became the medium of such an incomparably greater succession of poets, involves deep questions of the relationship of literature to economic, political and other considerations and both the causal and the casual in history: but at the moment it is more germane to my point to ask if the potentialities of the Scottish literary tradition can yet be realized? There are signs that they may be. The problem of the British Isles is the problem of English Ascendancy. Ireland after a protracted struggle has won a considerable measure of autonomy;[4] Scotland and Wales may succeed in doing the same; but what is of importance to my point in the meantime is that, in breaking free (or fairly free) politically, Ireland not only experienced the Literary Revival associated with the names of Yeats, 'A. E.', Synge[5] and the others, but has during the past half century recovered almost entirely her ancient Gaelic literature. * * *

1. Excerpted from "English Ascendancy in British Literature," first published in T. S. Eliot's journal *The Criterion.* "Ascendancy": dominance.
2. Robert Burns (1759–1796), Scottish poet.
3. Poets (Scots); term used for the courtly poets known as the Scottish Chaucerians. William Dunbar (1460?–1530?) was the dominant poet among them.
4. The Irish Free State was established in 1922, though Northern Ireland remained part of the U.K.
5. John Millington Synge (1871–1909), Irish playwright. William Butler Yeats (1865–1939), Irish poet. "A. E." was the pseudonym of the Irish poet and mystic George Russell (1867–1935).

* * * * * *

* * * Literature, so far from manifesting any trend towards uniformity or standardization, is evolving in the most disparate ways; and there are few literatures in which dialect elements, and even such extreme employments of—and plays upon—them as render them permanently untranslatable and unintelligible to all but a handful of readers in their own countries, are not peculiarly and significantly active. On this account (as isolating it from general contemporary tendency which must have some deep-seated relation to the needs of modern, and prospective, consciousness) it is a pity that English literature is maintaining a narrow ascendancy tradition instead of broad-basing itself on all the diverse cultural elements and the splendid variety of languages and dialects, in the British Isles. (I do not refer here to the Empire, and the United States of America, though the evolution of genuine independent literatures in all of these is a matter of no little consequence and, already clearly appreciated in America, is being increasingly so realized in most of the Dominions,[6] which is perhaps the cultural significance of the anti-English and other tendencies in most of them which are making for those changes in the Imperial organization which will deprive England of the hegemony it has maintained too long.) To recognize and utilize these, instead of excluding them, could only make for its enrichment. It is absurd that intelligent readers of English, who would be ashamed not to know something (if only the leading names, and roughly, what they stand for) of most Continental literatures, are content to ignore Scottish, Irish, and Welsh Gaelic literatures, and Scots Vernacular literature. Surely the latter are nearer to them than the former, and the language difficulty no greater. These Gaelic, and Scots dialect poets were products of substantially the same environment and concerned for the most part with the same political, psychological, and practical issues, the same traditions and tendencies, the same landscapes, as poets in English to whom, properly regarded, they are not only valuably complementary, but (in view of their linguistic, technical, and other divergencies) corrective. Confinement to the English central stream is like refusing to hear all but one side of a complicated case—and in view of the extent to which the English language is definitely adscripted[7] in certain important moral and psychological directions, and incapable of dealing with certain types of experience which form no inconsiderable part of certain other European literatures and may well be of far greater consequence to the future of humanity as a whole than the more 'normal matters' with which it is qualified to deal, becomes a sort of self-infliction of an extensive spiritual and psychological blindness. * * *

1931

From A Drunk Man Looks at the Thistle

1. Farewell to Dostoevski[1]

The wan leafs shak, atour° us like the snaw.   °around
Here is the cavaburd[2] in which Earth's tint.°   °lost

---

6. Self-governing nations in the British Commonwealth.

7. Attached (to the soil).

1. Fyodor Dostoyevsky (1821–1881), Russian novelist.

2. Dense snowstorm.

There's naebody but Oblivion and us,
Puir gangrel° buddies, waunderin' hameless in't.   *wanderer*

5   The stars are larochs° o' auld cottages,   *foundations*
And a' Time's glen is fu' o' blinnin'° stew.°   *blinding / storm*
Nae freen'ly lozen° skimmers:° and the wund°   *window / gleams / wind*
Rises and separates even me and you.

I ken nae Russian and you ken nae Scots.
10 We canna tell oor voices frae the wund.
The snaw is seekin' everywhere: oor herts
At last like roofless ingles° it has f'und.   *hearths*

And gethers there in drift on endless drift,
Oor broken herts that it can never fill;
15 And still—its leafs like snaw, its growth like wund—
The thistle[3] rises and forever will!

                                                        1926

2. *Yet Ha'e I Silence Left*

Yet ha'e I Silence left, the croon° o' a'.   *crown*

No' her, wha on the hills langsyne° I saw   *long ago*
Liftin' a foreheid o' perpetual snaw.

No' her, wha in the how-dumb-deid o' nicht[4]
5   Kyths,[5] like Eternity in Time's despite.

No' her, withooten° shape, wha's name is Daith,°   *without / death*
No' Him, unkennable° abies° to faith   *unknowable / except*

—God whom, gin° e'er He saw a Man,'ud be   *if*
E'en mair dumfooner'd[6] at the sicht° than he.   *sight*

10 —But Him, whom nocht° in man or Deity,   *nothing*
Or Daith or Dreid or Laneliness can touch,
Wha's deed owre often and has seen owre much.[7]

O I ha'e Silence left.

                                                        1926

From In Memoriam James Joyce

We Must Look at the Harebell[1]

We must look at the harebell as if
We had never seen it before.

---

3. The emblem of Scotland.
4. The still center of night.
5. Makes herself known, appears.
6. More dumbfounded.

7. Who has died too often and seen too much.
1. The Scottish bluebell, a blue flower with a bell-shaped blossom.

Remembrance gives an accumulation of satisfaction
Yet the desire for change is very strong in us
5   And change is in itself a recreation.
To those who take any pleasure
In flowers, plants, birds, and the rest
An ecological change is recreative.
(Come. Climb with me. Even the sheep are different
10   And of new importance.
The coarse-fleeced, hardy Herdwick,
The Hampshire Down, artificially fed almost from birth,
And butcher-fat from the day it is weaned,
The Lincoln-Longwool, the biggest breed in England,
15   With the longest fleece, and the Southdown
Almost the smallest—and between them thirty other breeds,
Some whitefaced, some black,
Some with horns and some without,
Some long-wooled, some short-wooled,
20   In England where the men, and women too,
Are almost as interesting as the sheep.)
Everything is different, everything changes,
Except for the white bedstraw which climbs all the way
Up from the valleys to the tops of the high passes
25   The flowers are all different and more precious
Demanding more search and particularity of vision.
Look! Here and there a pinguicula² eloquent of the Alps
Still keeps a purple-blue flower
On the top of its straight and slender stem.
30   Bog-asphodel, deep-gold, and comely in form,
The queer, almost diabolical, sundew,
And when you leave the bog for the stag moors and the rocks
The parsley fern—a lovelier plant
Than even the proud Osmunda Regalis³—
35   Flourishes in abundance
Showing off oddly contrasted fronds
From the cracks of the lichened stones.
It is pleasant to find the books
Describing it as "very local."
40   Here is a change indeed!
The universal *is* the particular.

                                                                    1955

Another Epitaph on an Army of Mercenaries¹

It is a God-damned lie to say that these
Saved, or knew, anything worth any man's pride.
They were professional murderers and they took
Their blood money and impious risks and died.

---

2. The butterwort, a genus of small herbs whose leaves secrete a sticky substance in which small insects are caught.
3. The flowering, or royal, fern; a plant with large fronds.

1. Cf. A. E. Housman's "Epitaph on an Army of Mercenaries" (p. 1953), to which this is a response.

5   In spite of all their kind some elements of worth
     With difficulty persist here and there on earth.

1935

LOUISE BENNETT
1919–2006

Louise Bennett, the preeminent West Indian poet of Creole verse, was born and grew up in Kingston, Jamaica, in the British West Indies, her mother a dressmaker, her father a baker. After she had published her first book of poetry, *Dialect Verses* (1942), she attended London's Royal Academy of Dramatic Art. As "Miss Lou" she won a mass following in the Caribbean through her vibrant stage performances of her poetry and of folk song; her weekly "dialect" poems published from 1943 in Jamaica's national newspaper, the *Gleaner;* her radio show, "Miss Lou's Views" (1966–82); and her children's-television program, "Ring Ding" (1970–82).

Bennett helped dismantle the view that Jamaican English is a corruption of Standard English, a prejudice she lambastes in radio monologues such as "Jamaica Language" and in poems such as "Dry-Foot Bwoy," which humorously juxtaposes a metaphor-rich Creole with a hollowly imitative British English. From a young age she felt the humor, wit, and vigor of Creole were largely untapped possibilities for writing and performing poetry, even though this commitment to Jamaican English prevented her from being recognized as a poet until after the black cultural revolution of the late 1960s and 1970s. In her poetry she often assumed the perspective of a West Indian trickster, such as the woman who cunningly subverts gender and geographic hierarchies in "Jamaica Oman [Woman]." Bennett made wily and ebullient use of received forms, employing the ironic possibilities of dramatic monologue, the contrasts and inversions afforded by the ballad stanza, and the time-tested wisdom and pith of Jamaican proverbs. Both on the page and in her recorded performances, Bennett's vital characters and robust imagination help win over readers unfamiliar with Jamaican English, who can join in the laughing seriousness of poems such as "Colonization in Reverse," which ironically inverts Britain's xenophobic apprehension at the postwar influx of Jamaican immigrants, while also casting a suspicious eye on some Jamaicans' reverse exploitation of their exploiters. No one is safe from the multiple ironies and carnivalesque irreverence of Bennett's verse.

Jamaica Language[1]

Listen, na!

My Aunty Roachy seh dat it bwile[2] her temper an really bex[3] her fi true anytime she hear anybody a style we Jamaican dialec as "corruption of the English language." For if dat be de case, den dem shoulda call English Language corruption of Norman French an Latin an all dem tarra[4] language what dem seh dat English is derived from.

Oonoo[5] hear de wud? "Derived." English is a derivation but Jamaica Dialec is corruption! What a unfairity!

---

1. Originally broadcast sometime between 1979 and 1981, this radio monologue has been reprinted from *Aunty Roachy Seh* (1993), ed. Mervyn Morris.
2. Boils.
3. Vexes.
4. Other.
5. You (plural).

Aunty Roachy seh dat if Jamaican Dialec is corruption of de English Language, den it is also a corruption of de African Twi Language to, a oh!

For Jamaican Dialec did start when we English forefahders did start musan-boun[6] we African ancestors fi stop talk fi-dem African Language altogedder an learn fi talk so-so[7] English, because we English forefahders couldn understan what we African ancestors-dem wasa seh to dem one anodder when dem wasa talk eena dem African Language to dem one annodder!

But we African ancestors-dem pop[8] we English forefahders-dem. Yes! Pop dem an disguise up de English Language fi projec fi-dem African Language in such a way dat we English forefahders-dem still couldn understan what we African ancestors-dem wasa talk bout when dem wasa talk to dem one annodder!

Yes, bwoy!

So till now, aldoah plenty a we Jamaica Dialec wuds-dem come from English wuds, yet, still an for all, de talkin is so-so Jamaican, an when we ready we can meck it soun like it no got no English at all eena it! An no so-so English-talkin smaddy cyaan[9] understan weh we a seh if we doan want dem to understan weh we a seh, a oh!

An we fix up we dialec wud fi soun like whatsoever we a talk bout, look like! For instance, when we seh sinting "kooroo-kooroo"[1] up, yuh know seh dat it mark-up mark-up. An if we seh one house "rookoo-rookoo"[2] up, it is plain to see dat it ole an shaky-shaky. An when we seh smaddy "boogoo-yagga", everybody know seh dat him outa-order; an if we seh dem "boonoonoonoos",[3] yuh know seh dat dem nice an we like dem. Mmmm.

Aunty Roachy seh dat Jamaica Dialec is more direc an to de point dan English. For all like how English smaddy would seh "Go away", Jamaican jus seh "Gweh!" An de only time we use more wuds dan English is when we want fi meck someting soun strong: like when dem seh sinting "batter-batter" up, it soun more expressive dan if yuh seh "it is battered." But most of all we fling weh all de bangarang an trimmins[4]-dem an only lef what wantin, an dat's why when English smaddy seh "I got stuck by a prickle" Jamaican jus seh "Macca[5] jook me"!

So fi-we Jamaica Language is not no English Language corruption at all, a oh! An we no haffi shame a it, like one gal who did go a Englan go represent we Jamaican folk-song "One shif me got" as "De sole underwear garment I possess", and go sing "Mumma, Mumma, dem ketch Puppa" as "Mother, Mother, they apprehended Father"!

Ay ya yie!

1979–81   1993

Dry-Foot Bwoy[1]

Wha wrong wid Mary dry-foot bwoy?
Dem gal got him fi mock,°   *The girls are mocking him*

---

6. Compel.
7. Only.
8. Outwitted.
9. Can't. "Smaddy": people.
1. Rough; rocky. "Sinting": something.
2. Unsteady.

3. Beautiful; wonderful (term of endearment). "Boogoo-yagga": ill-mannered.
4. Miscellaneous trash and trimmings.
5. A prickly plant.
1. Thin-legged (inexperienced) boy.

An when me meet him tarra night
De bwoy gi me a shock!

5   Me tell him seh him auntie an
Him cousin dem sen howdy[2]
An ask him how him getting awn.
Him seh, 'Oh, jolley, jolley!'

Me start fi feel so sorry fi
10   De po bad-lucky soul,
Me tink him come a foreign lan
Come ketch bad foreign cole!

Me tink him got a bad sore-troat,
But as him chat-chat gwan
15   Me fine out seh is foreign twang
De bwoy wasa put awn![3]

For me notice dat him answer
To nearly all me seh
Was 'Actually', 'What', 'Oh deah!'
20   An all dem sinting deh.°   *All of them things there*

Me gi a joke, de gal dem laugh;
But hear de bwoy, 'Haw-haw!
I'm sure you got that bally-dash°   *nonsense, balderdash*
Out of the cinema!'

25   Same time me laas me temper, an
Me holler, 'Bwoy, kirout!°   *clear out*
No chat to me wid no hot pittata
Eena yuh mout!'

Him tan° up like him stunted, den   *stand*
30   Hear him no, 'How silley!
I don't think that I really
Understand you, actually.'

Me seh, 'Yuh understan me, yaw!
No yuh name Cudjoe Scoop?
35   Always visit Nana kitchen an
Gi laugh fi gungoo soup![4]

'An now all yuh can seh is "actually"?
Bwoy, but tap!
Wha happen to dem sweet Jamaica
40   Joke yuh use fi pop?'

2. I told him that his auntie and his cousins sent
[or send] greetings.
3. But as he kept talking I realized his foreign
accent was put on.

4. Chastising the boy for his pretensions, the
speaker reminds him that he is Afro-Jamaican.
Cudjoe and Nana are African names used in
Jamaica. "Gungoo": congo pea.

Him get bex° and walk tru de door,   *vexed*
Him head eena de air;
De gal-dem bawl out affa him,[5]
'Not going? What! Oh deah!'

45   An from dat night till tedeh, mah,
Dem all got him fi mock.
Miss Mary dry-foot bwoy!
Cyaan get over de shock!

1957

Colonization in Reverse

What a joyful news, Miss Mattie;
Ah feel like me heart gwine burs—
Jamaica people colonizin
Englan in reverse.[1]

5   By de hundred, by de tousan,
From country an from town,
By de ship-load, by de plane-load,
Jamaica is Englan boun.

Dem a pour out a Jamaica;
10   Everybody future plan
Is fi get a big-time job
An settle in de motherlan.

What a islan! What a people!
Man an woman, ole an young
15   Jussa pack dem bag an baggage
An tun history upside dung!°   *down*

Some people doan like travel,
But fi show dem loyalty
Dem all a open up cheap-fare-
20   To-Englan agency;

An week by week dem shippin off
Dem countryman like fire
Fi immigrate an populate
De seat a de Empire.

25   Oonoo° se how life is funny,   *you (plural)*
Oonoo see de tunabout?
Jamaica live fi box bread
Out a English people mout.

5. The girls went crying after him.
1. Encouraged by the postwar labor shortage in England and the scarcity of work at home, three hundred thousand Jamaicans migrated to Britain from 1948 to 1962.

For when dem catch a Englan
30 An start play dem different role
Some will settle down to work
An some will settle fi de dole.°   *for unemployment benefits*

Jane seh de dole is not too bad
Because dey payin she
35 Two pounds a week fi seek a job
Dat suit her dignity.

Me seh Jane will never fine work
At de rate how she dah look
For all day she stay pon Aunt Fan couch
40 An read love-story book.

What a devilment a Englan!
Dem face war an brave de worse;
But ah wonderin how dem gwine stan
Colonizin in reverse.

                                        1957

Jamaica Oman[1]

Jamaica oman cunny, sah!°   *cunning, sir*
Is how dem jinnal so?°   *how are they so tricky?*
Look how long dem liberated
An de man dem never know!

5 Look how long Jamaica oman
—Modder, sister, wife, sweetheart—
Outa road an eena yard° deh pon   *home*
A dominate her part!

From Maroon Nanny[2] teck her body
10 Bounce bullet back pon man,
To when nowadays gal-pickney° tun   *girl-child*
Spellin-Bee champion.

From de grass root to de hill-top,
In profession, skill an trade,
15 Jamaica oman teck her time
Dah mount an meck de grade.

Some backa man a push, some side-a
Man a hole him han,
Some a lick sense eena man head,
20 Some a guide him pon him plan!

1. Woman.
2. Jamaican national hero who led the Maroons,
fugitive slaves, in battle during the eighteenth century. Bullets reputedly ricocheted off her and killed
her enemies.

Neck an neck an foot an foot wid man
She buckle hole° her own;   *she take hold*
While man a call her 'so-so rib'
Oman a tun backbone![3]

25   An long before Oman Lib[4] bruck out
Over foreign lan
Jamaica female wasa work
Her liberated plan!

Jamaica oman know she strong,
30   She know she tallawah,°   *sturdy*
But she no want her pickney° dem   *children*
Fi start call her 'Puppa'.°   *Papa*

So de cunny Jamma° oman   *Jamaican*
Gwan like pants-suit is a style,
35   An Jamaica man no know she wear
De trousiz all de while!

So Jamaica oman coaxin
Fambly budget from explode
A so Jamaica man a sing
40   'Oman a heaby load!'[5]

But de cunny Jamma oman
Ban her belly,[6] bite her tongue,
Ketch water, put pot pon fire
An jus dig her toe a grung.[7]

45   For 'Oman luck deh a dungle',[8]
Some rooted more dan some,
But as long as fowl a scratch dungle heap
Oman luck mus come!

Lickle by lickle man start praise her,
50   Day by day de praise a grow;
So him praise her, so it sweet her,
For she wonder if him know.

1975

3. Eve is said to have come from Adam's rib (Genesis 2.21–22).
4. Women's Liberation Movement.
5. A folk song often sung while working in the fields.

6. Binds her belly (a practice associated with grief; also a suggestion of belt tightening, as in hunger).
7. And just digs her toes into the ground.
8. I.e., woman's luck will be rediscovered (proverbial). "Dungle": garbage dump.

BRIAN FRIEL
b. 1929

For the renowned playwright Brian Friel, as for his Irish predecessors W. B. Yeats and James Joyce, the vexed issue of language and national identity has been a central preoccupation. His play *Translations* (1980), which reimagines the transitional moment when the language of the colonizer is supplanting the language of the colonized, is one of the richest late-twentieth century meditations on the role of the English language in British colonialism.

Set in 1833 in the rural village of Baile Beag, County Donegal, on the northwest corner of Ireland, the play dramatizes two key processes in the linguistic transformation of a colonized nation: remapping and education. Captain Lancey and Lieutenant Yolland, English officers in the Royal Engineers, have been sent to Ireland to help remap it with anglicized and standardized place-names. An intermediary figure, Owen, originally from Baile Beag but employed by the English as an interpreter, is helping the imperial military, as he puts it, "to translate the quaint, archaic tongue" of the Irish "into the King's good English." To produce Britain's first Ordnance Survey of Ireland, ordered by Parliament in 1824, each Gaelic name is replaced either by a translated English equivalent (Cnoc na Ri becomes Kings Head) or a similar English sound (Druim Dubh becomes Dromduff). Language is crucial in claiming the land for the British crown—ridding it of ambiguity and opacity, making it readable, knowable, taxable, militarily penetrable, evacuating its linguistically embodied history and memory. After Lieutenant Yolland and the Irishwoman Maire fall in love—a cross-linguistic and cross-ethnic romance with tragic consequences—the psychic violence of this colonial renaming becomes a matter of brutal physical force. The play widens the scope of its profound reflection on naming and identity through suggestive parallels with other acts of nomination—the nearly mute Sarah's vocalizing her name, the ritual naming of a baby, Owen's accidental renaming as Roland by the English officers, even an allusion to Adam's naming of the animals.

At the very time when the Ordnance Survey is remaking Irish topography, a new English-language system of National Education is being put into place, and it will supplant the local Irish-speaking schools, or hedge schools, greatly accelerating the anglicization of the still-Gaelic-speaking regions of Ireland. Hugh O'Donnell presides over the hedge school, and while his classroom is a barn where the English language and its literary canon (e.g., William Wordsworth) are unknown, the ancient Greek and Roman gods and goddesses, such as flashing-eyed Athena, are vital and immediate presences in classical languages. The conflicted schoolmaster, who initially dismisses English as useful "for the purposes of commerce" and then seeks employment in the new English schools, foresees the loss of an educational system and, to a significant degree, of a culture; he muses elegiacally but realistically that a community's language cannot remain frozen in the face of massive historical change: "We must learn where we live. We must learn to make [the new English names] our own. We must make them our new home." The English language, the play evocatively suggests, has both dispossessed and rehoused, unified and fragmented, advanced and oppressed the Irish, like the many other peoples remapped and reeducated by the empire.

Friel was born in Omagh, County Tyrone, Northern Ireland, and spent much of his youth in Derry (or Londonderry), Northern Ireland, with vacations across the border in County Donegal, in the Irish Republic, with his maternal relatives. He attended St. Patrick's College, Ireland's national seminary, in Maynooth, but instead of becoming a Roman Catholic priest, taught school in Derry for ten years, before turning full-time to writing in 1960. Having published short stories, essays, and radio plays, he increasingly devoted himself to writing stage dramas, such as *Philadelphia, Here I Come!* (first produced in 1964), *Faith Healer* (1979), and *Dancing at Lughnasa*

(1990), which have been performed and garnered prizes in Derry, Dublin, New York, London, and elsewhere. In 1969 Friel moved across the border from Northern Ireland into Derry's hinterland in County Donegal, and in 1980 he cofounded the Field Day Theatre Company, which has brought professional drama to many parts of Ireland and Northern Ireland, while seeking to break down calcified polarities of Northern Irish politics (Catholic vs. Protestant, Unionist vs. Republican, etc.). *Translations* was Field Day's first production, with the company's cofounder, the actor Stephen Rea, playing the role of Owen, and Liam Neeson playing Doalty.

PRONOUNCING GLOSSARY

As an aid for performance and reading, the following phonetic spellings provide a rough guide to the pronunciation of Irish names and words. Standard Irish diacritical marks are given in the glossary, though omitted by Friel in the playscript.

Anna na mBréag: ANN-na nuh MRAYG

Baile Beag: BOLL-ya bYUG (BOLL rhymes with *doll*)

Baile na gGall: BOLL-ya nuh NOWL (NOWL rhymes with *owl; nuh* has the *u* sound as in English *up*)

Beann na Gaoithe: bYOWN na GWEE-ha (YOWN rhymes with *town*)

Buncrana: bunn KRAAH-na (where *AA* is an elongated version of the *a* sound in *apple*)

Bun na hAbhann: BUNN nuh HOW-un

Caitlín Dubh Nic Reactainn: katt-LEEN DUV neek ROK-tin

Carraig na Rí: KORR-ig nuh REE (KORR: the *o* sound as in English *on* and *off*)

Carraig an Phoill: KORR-ig on f-WEEL

Catach: KOTT-ukh

Ceann Balor: kYOWN BA-lor (YOWN as above; "Balor" rhymes with *valor*)

Cnoc na Móna: k-NUKH nuh MOW-na (MOW as in English)

Cnoc na nGabhar: k-NUKH nuh NOW-er (NOW as in English)

Cnoc na Rí: k-NUCK nuh REE

Cúchulainn: KOO-kuhl-lin

Diarmuid: DEER-med

Donegal: dunny-GAWL

Druim Dubh: drimm DUV (the *u* sound of the English *un-*)

Druim Luachra: Drim LOO-krah

Éamon: AIM-en

Grania: GRAW-nya

Inis Meadhon: IN-ish MAAN (where *AA* is an elongated version of the *a* sound in *apple*)

Lag: log (exactly like the English word *log*)

Lis Maol: liss MAY-ull (*liss* rhymes with English *kiss*)

Lis na Muc: LISS nuh MUK

Lis na nGall: Liss nuh nALL

Lis na nGradh: LISS nuh nRAW (a gentle little *n* sound before the *RAW*)

Loch an Iubhair: LUKH un OO-er

Loch na nÉan: LUKH nuh NAY-un

Luachra: LOO-akh-ra

Machaire bán: MOKH-ur-uh BAWN

Machaire Buidhe: MOKH-i-reh bWEE (the middle *i* is short like the English *in*)

Machaire Mór: MOKH-i-reh MOOR

Máire Chatach: MAW-reh KHOTT-ukh

Manus: MAAH-nuss

Mullach Dearg: MULL-ukh JA-rug (hard *J* as in *John*)

Poll na gCaorach: POWL nuh GAY-rukh (POWL rhymes with *cowl*)

Port: purt (rhymes with *hurt*)

Poteen: puh-TCHEEN

Ruadh: ROO-uh

Séamus: SHAY-muss

Seán: shawn

Tobair Bhriain: TUB-er vr-EE-un

Tobair Vree: TUB-er vrEE (the letter V is
an anglicization)

Tor: tur (as in the first syllable of the
English word *turret*)

Trá Bhán: trAW VAWN

Tulach Álainn: TULL-ukh AW-linn

Translations

MANUS	BRIDGET
SARAH	HUGH
JIMMY JACK	OWEN
MAIRE	CAPTAIN LANCEY
DOALTY	LIEUTENANT YOLLAND

The action takes place in a hedge-school[1] *in the townland of Baile Beag/Ballybeg,
an Irish-speaking community in County Donegal.*[2]

ACT ONE   *An afternoon in late August 1833.*
ACT TWO   *A few days later.*
ACT THREE   *The evening of the following day.*

Act One

   *The hedge-school is held in a disused barn or hay-shed or byre. Along the back
wall are the remains of five or six stalls—wooden posts and chains—where cows
were once milked and bedded. A double door left, large enough to allow a cart
to enter. A window right. A wooden stairway without a banister leads to the
upstairs living-quarters (off) of the schoolmaster and his son. Around the room
are broken and forgotten implements: a cart-wheel, some lobster-pots, farming
tools, a battle*[3] *of hay, a churn, etc. There are also the stools and bench-seats
which the pupils use and a table and chair for the master. At the door a pail of
water and a soiled towel. The room is comfortless and dusty and functional—
there is no trace of a woman's hand.*
   When the play opens, MANUS *is teaching* SARAH *to speak. He kneels beside her.
She is sitting on a low stool, her head down, very tense, clutching a slate on her
knees. He is coaxing her gently and firmly and—as with everything he does—
with a kind of zeal.*
   MANUS *is in his late twenties/early thirties; the master's older son. He is pale-
faced, lightly built, intense, and works as an unpaid assistant—a monitor—to his
father. His clothes are shabby; and when he moves we see that he is lame.*
   SARAH's *speech defect is so bad that all her life she has been considered locally
to be dumb and she has accepted this: when she wishes to communicate, she
grunts and makes unintelligible nasal sounds. She has a waiflike*[4] *appearance
and could be any age from seventeen to thirty-five.*
   JIMMY JACK CASSIE—*known as the Infant Prodigy—sits by himself, contentedly
reading Homer in Greek and smiling to himself. He is a bachelor in his sixties,*

---

1. Peasant school in which the Irish language was
the primary medium of instruction; the hedge
school was so called because it was beside a hedge
(or in the open air or in a barn). Such schools were
formed because education of Roman Catholics in
Ireland had been officially proscribed by the Penal
Laws passed in the 17th and 18th centuries.

2. In the northwest corner of Ireland, now in the
Republic of Ireland. Baile Beag/Ballybeg is the
imaginary community in which many of Friel's
plays are set.
3. Compact bundle.
4. Like a homeless child.

lives alone, and comes to these evening classes partly for the company and partly for the intellectual stimulation. He is fluent in Latin and Greek but is in no way pedantic—to him it is perfectly normal to speak these tongues.[5] He never washes. His clothes—heavy top coat, hat, mittens, which he wears now—are filthy and he lives in them summer and winter, day and night. He now reads in a quiet voice and smiles in profound satisfaction. For JIMMY the world of the gods and the ancient myths is as real and as immediate as everyday life in the townland of Baile Beag.

    MANUS holds SARAH's hands in his and he articulates slowly and distinctly into her face.

MANUS We're doing very well. And we're going to try it once more—just once more. Now—relax and breathe in . . . deep . . . and out . . . in . . . and out . . .
> [SARAH *shakes her head vigorously and stubbornly.*]

MANUS Come on, Sarah. This is our secret.
> [*Again vigorous and stubborn shaking of* SARAH's *head.*]

MANUS Nobody's listening. Nobody hears you.

JIMMY *'Ton d'emeibet epeita thea glaukopis Athene . . .'*[6]

MANUS Get your tongue and your lips working. 'My name—' Come on. One more try. 'My name is—' Good girl.

SARAH My . . .

MANUS Great. 'My name—'

SARAH My . . . my . . .

MANUS Raise your head. Shout it out. Nobody's listening.

JIMMY *'. . . alla hekelos estai en Atreidao domois . . .'*[7]

MANUS Jimmy, please! Once more—just once more—'My name—' Good girl. Come on now. Head up. Mouth open.

SARAH My . . .

MANUS Good.

SARAH My . . .

MANUS Great.

SARAH My name . . .

MANUS Yes?
> [SARAH *pauses. Then in a rush.*]

SARAH My name is Sarah.

MANUS Marvellous! Bloody marvellous!
> [MANUS *hugs* SARAH. *She smiles in shy, embarrassed pleasure.*]

  Did you hear that, Jimmy?—'My name is Sarah'—clear as a bell. [*To* SARAH.] The Infant Prodigy doesn't know what we're at.
> [SARAH *laughs at this.* MANUS *hugs her again and stands up.*]

  Now we're really started! Nothing'll stop us now! Nothing in the wide world!
> [JIMMY, *chuckling at his text, comes over to them.*]

JIMMY Listen to this, Manus.

MANUS Soon you'll be telling me all the secrets that have been in that head of yours all these years.

---

5. Latin and Greek were taught and used in the hedge schools.
6. But the grey-eyed goddess Athene then replied to him (*Odyssey*, XIII, 420) [Friel's note]. Athena, ancient Greek goddess of war, wisdom, and the city, was a tutelary god to the hero Odysseus, also known by the Roman name Ulysses. In this scene of Homer's epic, she plots Odysseus' return home, after his ten-year absence. A disguise, as a dirty and shriveled old man, will enable him to trick and kill the suitors to his wife, Penelope.
7. But he sits at ease in the halls of the Sons of Athens (*Odyssey*, XIII, 423–4) [Friel's note].

Certainly, James—what is it?

[*To* SARAH.] Maybe you'd set out the stools?

[MANUS *runs up the stairs.*]

JIMMY   Wait till you hear this, Manus.

MANUS   Go ahead. I'll be straight down.

JIMMY   '*Hos ara min phamene rabdo epemassat Athene*—' 'After Athene had said this, she touched Ulysses with her wand. She withered the fair skin of his supple limbs and destroyed the flaxen[8] hair from off his head and about his limbs she put the skin of an old man . . . '! The divil! The divil!

[MANUS *has emerged again with a bowl of milk and a piece of bread.*]

JIMMY   And wait till you hear! She's not finished with him yet!

[*As* MANUS *descends the stairs he toasts* SARAH *with his bowl.*]

JIMMY   '*Knuzosen de oi osse*—' 'She dimmed his two eyes that were so beautiful and clothed him in a vile ragged cloak begrimed with filthy smoke . . .'! D'you see! Smoke! Smoke! D'you see! Sure look at what the same turf-smoke has done to myself! [*He rapidly removes his hat to display his bald head.*] Would you call that flaxen hair?

MANUS   Of course I would.

JIMMY   'And about him she cast the great skin of a filthy hind,[9] stripped of the hair, and into his hand she thrust a staff and a wallet'! Ha-ha-ha! Athene did that to Ulysses! Made him into a tramp! Isn't she the tight one?

MANUS   You couldn't watch her, Jimmy.

JIMMY   You know what they call her?

MANUS   '*Glaukopis Athene.*'

JIMMY   That's it! The flashing-eyed Athene! By God, Manus, sir, if you had a woman like that about the house, it's not stripping a turf[1]-bank you'd be thinking about—eh?

MANUS   She was a goddess, Jimmy.

JIMMY   Better still. Sure isn't our own Grania a class of a goddess and—

MANUS   Who?

JIMMY   Grania—Grania—Diarmuid's Grania.[2]

MANUS   Ah.

JIMMY   And sure she can't get her fill of men.

MANUS   Jimmy, you're impossible.

JIMMY   I was just thinking to myself last night: if you had the choosing between Athene and Artemis and Helen of Troy—all three of them Zeus's girls[3]—imagine three powerful-looking daughters like that all in the one parish of Athens!—now, if you had the picking between them, which would you take?

MANUS   [*To* SARAH.]   Which should I take, Sarah?

JIMMY   No harm to Helen; and no harm to Artemis; and indeed no harm to our own Grania, Manus. But I think I've no choice but to go bull-straight for Athene. By God, sir, them flashing eyes would fair keep a man jigged[4] up constant!

---

8. A pale strawlike color. Jimmy is continuing with the same scene of the *Odyssey*.
9. Female red deer.
1. Peat; dried and used for fuel.
2. Young and beautiful Irish princess betrothed to the aged but powerful Fionn mac Cumhaill; many medieval stories recount the flight of Grania and her lover, Dairmud, over the Irish countryside in

their attempt to escape capture by Fionn.
3. I.e., daughters of the most powerful Greek god. As goddess of wild animals, vegetation, and the hunt, Artemis was contrasted with Athena, goddess of the city. Helen's abduction was the legendary cause of the Trojan War.
4. Jerked, caught.

[*Suddenly and momentarily, as if in spasm,* JIMMY *stands to attention and salutes, his face raised in pained ecstasy.*

MANUS *laughs. So does* SARAH. JIMMY *goes back to his seat, and his reading.*]

MANUS   You're a dangerous bloody man, Jimmy Jack.

JIMMY   'Flashing-eyed'! Hah! Sure Homer knows it all, boy. Homer knows it all.

[MANUS *goes to the window and looks out.*]

MANUS   Where the hell has he got to?

[SARAH *goes to* MANUS *and touches his elbow. She mimes rocking a baby.*]

MANUS   Yes, I know he's at the christening; but it doesn't take them all day to put a name on a baby, does it?

[SARAH *mimes pouring drinks and tossing them back quickly.*]

MANUS   You may be sure. Which pub?

[SARAH *indicates.*]

MANUS   Gracie's?

[*No. Further away.*]

MANUS   Con Connie Tim's?

[*No. To the right of there.*]

MANUS   Anna na mBreag's?

[*Yes. That's it.*]

MANUS   Great. She'll fill him up. I suppose I may take the class then.

[MANUS *begins to distribute some books, slates and chalk, texts etc. beside the seats.*

SARAH *goes over to the straw and produces a bunch of flowers she has hidden there.*

During this.]

JIMMY   '*Autar o ek limenos prosebe—*' 'But Ulysses went forth from the harbour and through the woodland to the place where Athene had shown him he could find the good swineherd who—*o oi biotoio malista kedeto*'—what's that, Manus?

MANUS   'Who cared most for his substance'.

JIMMY   That's it! 'The good swineherd who cared most for his substance above all the slaves that Ulysses possessed . . .'[5]

[SARAH *presents the flowers to* MANUS.]

MANUS   Those are lovely, Sarah.

[*But* SARAH *has fled in embarrassment to her seat and has her head buried in a book.* MANUS *goes to her.*]

MANUS   Flow–ers.

[*Pause.* SARAH *does not look up.*]

MANUS   Say the word: flow–ers. Come on—flow–ers.

SARAH   Flowers.

MANUS   You see?—you're off!

[MANUS *leans down and kisses the top of* SARAH's *head.*]

MANUS   And they're beautiful flowers. Thank you.

[MAIRE *enters, a strong-minded, strong-bodied woman in her twenties with a head of curly hair. She is carrying a small can of milk.*]

---

5. At the beginning of book 14 of the *Odyssey*, Odysseus seeks, at Athena's instruction, the field hand who has been most attentive to the hero's estate in his absence.

MAIRE   Is this all's here? Is there no school this evening?

MANUS   If my father's not back, I'll take it.

    [MANUS *stands awkwardly, having been caught kissing* SARAH *and with the flowers almost formally at his chest.*]

MAIRE   Well now, isn't that a pretty sight. There's your milk. How's Sarah?

    [SARAH *grunts a reply.*]

MANUS   I saw you out at the hay.

    [MAIRE *ignores this and goes to* JIMMY.]

MAIRE   And how's Jimmy Jack Cassie?

JIMMY   Sit down beside me, Maire.

MAIRE   Would I be safe?

JIMMY   No safer man in Donegal.

    [MAIRE *flops on a stool beside* JIMMY.]

MAIRE   Ooooh. The best harvest in living memory, they say; but I don't want to see another like it. [*Showing* JIMMY *her hands.*] Look at the blisters.

JIMMY   *Esne fatigata?*

MAIRE   *Sum fatigatissima.*

JIMMY   *Bene! Optime!*[6]

MAIRE   That's the height of my Latin. Fit me better if I had even that much English.

JIMMY   English? I thought you had some English?

MAIRE   Three words. Wait—there was a spake[7] I used to have off by heart. What's this it was?

    [*Her accent is strange because she is speaking a foreign language and because she does not understand what she is saying.*]

    'In Norfolk[8] we besport ourselves around the maypoll.' What about that!

MANUS   Maypole.[9]

    [*Again* MAIRE *ignores* MANUS.]

MAIRE   God have mercy on my Aunt Mary—she taught me that when I was about four, whatever it means. Do you know what it means, Jimmy?

JIMMY   Sure you know I have only Irish like yourself.

MAIRE   And Latin. And Greek.

JIMMY   I'm telling you a lie: I know one English word.

MAIRE   What?

JIMMY   Bo–som.

MAIRE   What's a bo–som?

JIMMY   You know—[*He illustrates with his hands.*]—bo–som—bo–som—you know—Diana, the huntress,[1] she has two powerful bosom.

MAIRE   You may be sure that's the one English word you would know. [*Rises.*] Is there a drop of water about?

    [MANUS *gives* MAIRE *his bowl of milk.*]

MANUS   I'm sorry I couldn't get up last night.

MAIRE   Doesn't matter.

MANUS   Biddy Hanna sent for me to write a letter to her sister in Nova Scotia. All the gossip of the parish. 'I brought the cow to the bull three times last week but no good. There's nothing for it now but Big Ned Frank.'

MAIRE   [*Drinking.*]   That's better.

---

6. Are you tired? / I am very tired. / Good! Excellent! [Friel's note].
7. Speech.
8. County of eastern England.

9. Tall decorated pole around which traditional English dances were conducted in springtime.
1. Roman goddess, comparable to the Greek Artemis.

MANUS   And she got so engrossed in it that she forgot who she was dictating to: 'The aul drunken schoolmaster and that lame son of his are still footering about in the hedge-school, wasting people's good time and money.'

[MAIRE *has to laugh at this.*]

MAIRE   She did not!

MANUS   And me taking it all down. 'Thank God one of them new national schools² is being built above at Poll na gCaorach.' It was after midnight by the time I got back.

MAIRE   Great to be a busy man.

[MAIRE *moves away.* MANUS *follows.*]

MANUS   I could hear music on my way past but I thought it was too late to call.

MAIRE   [*To* SARAH.]   Wasn't your father in great voice last night?

[SARAH *nods and smiles.*]

MAIRE   It must have been near three o'clock by the time you got home?

[SARAH *holds up four fingers.*]

MAIRE   Was it four? No wonder we're in pieces.

MANUS   I can give you a hand at the hay tomorrow.

MAIRE   That's the name of a hornpipe,³ isn't it?—'The Scholar In The Hay-field'—or is it a reel?⁴

MANUS   If the day's good.

MAIRE   Suit yourself. The English soldiers below in the tents, them sapper⁵ fellas, they're coming up to give us a hand. I don't know a word they're saying, nor they me; but sure that doesn't matter, does it?

MANUS   What the hell are you so crabbed⁶ about?!

[DOALTY *and* BRIDGET *enter noisily. Both are in their twenties.*

DOALTY *is brandishing a surveyor's pole. He is an open-minded, open-hearted, generous and slightly thick young man.*

BRIDGET *is a plump, fresh young girl, ready to laugh, vain, and with a countrywoman's instinctive cunning.*

DOALTY *enters doing his imitation of the master.*]

DOALTY   Vesperal⁷ salutations to you all.

BRIDGET   He's coming down past Carraig na Ri and he's as full as a pig!

DOALTY   *Ignari, stulti, rustici*⁸—pot-boys and peasant whelps⁹—semi-literates and illegitimates.

BRIDGET   He's been on the batter¹ since this morning; he sent the wee ones home at eleven o'clock.

DOALTY   Three questions. Question A—Am I drunk? Question B—Am I sober? [*Into* MAIRE'*s face.*] *Responde—responde!*²

BRIDGET   Question C, Master—When were you last sober?

MAIRE   What's the weapon, Doalty?

BRIDGET   I warned him. He'll be arrested one of these days.

DOALTY   Up in the bog with Bridget and her aul fella, and the Red Coats were

---

2. In 1831, two years earlier, a new system of English-speaking schools had been introduced; these would eventually supplant the hedge schools.
3. Vigorous dance performed by a sole person to a wind instrument.
4. Lively dance performed by couples facing each other.
5. Soldier who works in saps, i.e., fortifications, or does field work.

6. Annoyed.
7. Evening.
8. Ignoramuses, fools, peasants [Latin; Friel's note].
9. Young wild animals. "Pot-boys": assistants who serve beer in a pub.
1. On the bottle.
2. Answer—answer! [Latin; Friel's note].

just across at the foot of Cnoc na Mona, dragging them aul chains and peeping through that big machine they lug about everywhere with them— you know the name of it, Manus?

MAIRE   Theodolite.[3]

BRIDGET   How do you know?

MAIRE   They leave it in our byre[4] at night sometimes if it's raining.

JIMMY   Theodolite—what's the etymology of that word, Manus?

MANUS   No idea.

BRIDGET   Get on with the story.

JIMMY   *Theo—theos*[5]—something to do with a god. Maybe *thea*—a goddess! What shape's the yoke?

DOALTY   'Shape!' Will you shut up, you aul eejit[6] you! Anyway, every time they'd stick one of these poles into the ground and move across the bog, I'd creep up and shift it twenty or thirty paces to the side.

BRIDGET   God!

DOALTY   Then they'd come back and stare at it and look at their calculations and stare at it again and scratch their heads. And Cripes[7], d'you know what they ended up doing?

BRIDGET   Wait till you hear!

DOALTY   They took the bloody machine apart! [*And immediately he speaks in gibberish—an imitation of two very agitated and confused sappers in rapid conversation.*]

BRIDGET   That's the image of them!

MAIRE   You must be proud of yourself, Doalty.

DOALTY   What d'you mean?

MAIRE   That was a very clever piece of work.

MANUS   It was a gesture.

MAIRE   What sort of a gesture?

MANUS   Just to indicate . . . a presence.

MAIRE   Hah!

BRIDGET   I'm telling you—you'll be arrested.

[*When* DOALTY *is embarrassed—or pleased—he reacts physically. He now grabs* BRIDGET *around the waist.*]

DOALTY   What d'you make of that for an implement, Bridget? Wouldn't that make a great aul shaft for your churn?

BRIDGET   Let go of me, you dirty brute! I've a headline to do before Big Hughie comes.

MANUS   I don't think we'll wait for him. Let's get started.

[*Slowly, reluctantly they begin to move to their seats and specific tasks.* DOALTY *goes to the bucket of water at the door and washes his hands.* BRIDGET *sets up a hand-mirror and combs her hair.*]

BRIDGET   Nellie Ruadh's baby was to be christened this morning. Did any of yous hear what she called it? Did you, Sarah?

[SARAH *grunts: No.*]

BRIDGET   Did you, Maire?

MAIRE   No.

BRIDGET   Our Seamus says she was threatening she was going to call it after its father.

---

3. A portable instrument for surveying.
4. Barn.
5. God (Greek).

6. Idiot.
7. Christ (mild oath).

DOALTY Who's the father?

BRIDGET That's the point, you donkey you!

DOALTY Ah.

BRIDGET So there's a lot of uneasy bucks about Baile Beag this day.

DOALTY She told me last Sunday she was going to call it Jimmy.

BRIDGET You're a liar, Doalty.

DOALTY Would I tell you a lie? Hi, Jimmy, Nellie Ruadh's aul fella's looking for you.

JIMMY For me?

MAIRE Come on, Doalty.

DOALTY Someone told him . . .

MAIRE Doalty!

DOALTY He heard you know the first book of the Satires of Horace[8] off by heart . . .

JIMMY That's true.

DOALTY . . . and he wants you to recite it for him.

JIMMY I'll do that for him certainly, certainly.

DOALTY He's busting to hear it.

[JIMMY *fumbles in his pockets.*]

JIMMY I came across this last night—this'll interest you—in Book Two of Virgil's *Georgics.*[9]

DOALTY Be God, that's my territory alright.

BRIDGET You clown you! [*To* SARAH.] Hold this for me, would you? [*Her mirror.*]

JIMMY Listen to this, Manus. '*Nigra fere et presso pinguis sub vomere terra . . .*'

DOALTY Steady on now—easy, boys, easy—don't rush me, boys—[*He mimes great concentration.*]

JIMMY Manus?

MANUS 'Land that is black and rich beneath the pressure of the plough . . .'

DOALTY Give *me* a chance!

JIMMY 'And with *cui putre*—with crumbly soil—is in the main best for corn.' There you are!

DOALTY There you are.

JIMMY 'From no other land will you see more wagons wending homeward behind slow bullocks.'[1] Virgil! There!

DOALTY 'Slow bullocks'!

JIMMY Isn't that what I'm always telling you? Black soil for corn. *That's* what you should have in that upper field of yours—corn, not spuds.

DOALTY Would you listen to that fella! Too lazy be Jasus to wash himself and he's lecturing me on agriculture! Would you go and take a running race at yourself, Jimmy Jack Cassie! [*Grabs* SARAH.] Come away out of this with me, Sarah, and we'll plant some corn together.

MANUS Alright—alright. Let's settle down and get some work done. I know Sean Beag isn't coming—he's at the[2] salmon. What about the Donnelly twins? [*To* DOALTY.] Are the Donnelly twins not coming any more?

---

8. Latin lyric poet (65–8 B.C.E.).
9. Four books of poems on farming and rural life by the Roman poet (70–19 B.C.E.).

1. Bulls or, loosely, cattle.
2. Fishing for.

[DOALTY *shrugs and turns away.*]
Did you ask them?

DOALTY Haven't seen them. Not about these days.

[DOALTY *begins whistling through his teeth.*
Suddenly the atmosphere is silent and alert.]

MANUS Aren't they at home?

DOALTY No.

MANUS Where are they then?

DOALTY How would I know?

BRIDGET Our Seamus says two of the soldiers' horses were found last night
at the foot of the cliffs at Machaire Buide and . . .

[*She stops suddenly and begins writing with chalk on her slate.*]
D'you hear the whistles of this aul slate? Sure nobody could write on an aul
slippery thing like that.

MANUS What headline did my father set you?

BRIDGET 'It's easier to stamp out learning than to recall it.'

JIMMY Book Three, the *Agricola* of Tacitus.[3]

BRIDGET God but you're a dose.[4]

MANUS Can you do it?

BRIDGET There. Is it bad? Will he ate me?

MANUS It's very good. Keep your elbow in closer to your side. Doalty?

DOALTY I'm at the seven-times table. I'm perfect, skipper.

[MANUS *moves to* SARAH.]

MANUS Do you understand those sums?

[SARAH *nods: Yes.* MANUS *leans down to her ear.*]

MANUS My name is Sarah.

[MANUS *goes to* MAIRE. *While he is talking to her the others swop books,*
talk quietly, etc.]

MANUS Can I help you? What are you at?

MAIRE Map of America. [*Pause.*] The passage money came last Friday.

MANUS You never told me that.

MAIRE Because I haven't seen you since, have I?

MANUS You don't want to go. You said that yourself.

MAIRE There's ten below me to be raised and no man in the house. What do
you suggest?

MANUS Do you want to go?

MAIRE Did you apply for that job in the new national school?

MANUS No.

MAIRE You said you would.

MANUS I said I might.

MAIRE When it opens, this is finished: nobody's going to pay to go to a hedge-
school.

MANUS I know that and I . . . [*He breaks off because he sees* SARAH, *obviously*
listening, at his shoulder. She moves away again.] I was thinking that maybe
I could . . .

MAIRE It's £56 a year you're throwing away.

MANUS I can't apply for it.

---

3. Roman historian (ca. 56–ca. 120 C.E.), author
of *De Vita Julii Agricolae* (*The Life of Julius Agric-*
ola), or the *Agricola*, a biography of his father-in-

law, including an account of his career in Britain.
4. I.e., a dose of medicine, or an unpleasant experience.

MAIRE   You *promised* me you would.

MANUS   My father has applied for it.

MAIRE   He has not!

MANUS   Day before yesterday.

MAIRE   For God's sake, sure you know he'd never—

MANUS   I couldn't—I can't go in against him.

[MAIRE *looks at him for a second. Then.*]

MAIRE   Suit yourself. [*To* BRIDGET.] I saw your Seamus heading off to the Port fair early this morning.

BRIDGET   And wait till you hear this—I forgot to tell you this. He said that as soon as he crossed over the gap at Cnoc na Mona—just beyond where the soldiers are making the maps—the sweet smell was everywhere.

DOALTY   You never told me that.

BRIDGET   It went out of my head.

DOALTY   He saw the crops in Port?

BRIDGET   Some.

MANUS   How did the tops look?

BRIDGET   Fine—I think.

DOALTY   In flower?

BRIDGET   I don't know. I think so. He didn't say.

MANUS   Just the sweet smell—that's all?

BRIDGET   They say that's the way it snakes in, don't they? First the smell; and then one morning the stalks are all black and limp.

DOALTY   Are you stupid? It's the rotting stalks makes the sweet smell for God's sake. That's what the smell is—rotting stalks.

MAIRE   Sweet smell! Sweet smell! Every year at this time somebody comes back with stories of the sweet smell. Sweet God, did the potatoes ever fail in Baile Beag? Well, did they ever—ever? Never! There was never blight here. Never. Never. But we're always sniffing about for it, aren't we?—looking for disaster. The rents are going to go up again—the harvest's going to be lost—the herring have gone away for ever—there's going to be evictions. Honest to God, some of you people aren't happy unless you're miserable and you'll not be right content until you're dead!

DOALTY   Bloody right, Maire. And sure St. Colmcille prophesied there'd never be blight here. He said:

> The spuds will bloom in Baile Beag
> Till rabbits grow an extra lug.[5]

And sure that'll never be. So we're alright.

Seven threes are twenty-one; seven fours are twenty-eight; seven fives are forty-nine— Hi, Jimmy, do you fancy my chances as boss of the new national school?

JIMMY   What's that?—what's that?

DOALTY   Agh, g'way back home to Greece, son.

MAIRE   You ought to apply, Doalty.

DOALTY   D'you think so? Cripes, maybe I will. Hah!

BRIDGET   Did you know that you start at the age of six and you have to stick

5. Ear. St. Comcille (521–597), also known as St. Columba, was born in Donegal and established monasteries and churches throughout Ireland and Scotland. Cf. Friel's play about his life, *The Enemy Within* (1962).

at it until you're twelve at least—no matter how smart you are or how much you know.

DOALTY   Who told you that yarn?

BRIDGET   And every child from every house has to go all day, every day, summer or winter. That's the law.

DOALTY   I'll tell you something—nobody's going to go near them—they're not going to take on—law or no law.

BRIDGET   And everything's free in them. You pay for nothing except the books you use; that's what our Seamus says.

DOALTY   'Our Seamus'. Sure your Seamus wouldn't pay anyway. She's making this all up.

BRIDGET   Isn't that right, Manus?

MANUS   I think so.

BRIDGET   And from the very first day you go, you'll not hear one word of Irish spoken. You'll be taught to speak English and every subject will be taught through English and everyone'll end up as cute as the Buncrana[6] people.

[SARAH *suddenly grunts and mimes a warning that the master is coming. The atmosphere changes. Sudden business. Heads down.*]

DOALTY   He's here, boys. Cripes, he'll make yella meal out of me for those bloody tables.

BRIDGET   Have you any extra chalk, Manus?

MAIRE   And the atlas for me.

[DOALTY *goes to* MAIRE *who is sitting on a stool at the back.*]

DOALTY   Swop you seats.

MAIRE   Why?

DOALTY   There's an empty one beside the Infant Prodigy.

MAIRE   I'm fine here.

DOALTY   Please, Maire. I want to jouk[7] in the back here.

[MAIRE *rises.*]

God love you. [*Aloud.*] Anyone got a bloody table-book? Cripes, I'm wrecked.

[SARAH *gives him one.*]

God, I'm dying about you.

[*In his haste to get to the back seat* DOALTY *bumps into* BRIDGET *who is kneeling on the floor and writing laboriously on a slate resting on top of a bench-seat.*]

BRIDGET   Watch where you're going, Doalty!

[DOALTY *gooses*[8] BRIDGET. *She squeals.*

Now the quiet hum of work: JIMMY *reading Homer in a low voice;* BRIDGET *copying her headline;* MAIRE *studying the atlas;* DOALTY, *his eyes shut tight, mouthing his tables;* SARAH *doing sums.*

After a few seconds.]—

BRIDGET   Is this 'g' right, Manus? How do you put a tail on it?

DOALTY   Will you shut up! I can't concentrate!

[*A few more seconds of work. Then* DOALTY *opens his eyes and looks around.*]

False alarm, boys. The bugger's[9] not coming at all. Sure the bugger's hardly fit to walk.

---

6. Small coastal town northwest of Derry.
7. Perch.
8. Pokes or tickles in an erogenous place.
9. Vulgar term of abuse.

[*And immediately* HUGH *enters. A large man, with residual dignity, shabbily dressed, carrying a stick. He has, as always, a large quantity of drink taken, but he is by no means drunk. He is in his early sixties.*]

HUGH *Adsum*, Doalty, *adsum*.[1] Perhaps not in *sobrietate perfecta*[2] but adequately *sobrius*[3] to overhear your quip. Vesperal salutations to you all.

[*Various responses.*]

JIMMY *Ave*,[4] Hugh.

HUGH James.

[*He removes his hat and coat and hands them and his stick to* MANUS, *as if to a footman.*]

Apologies for my late arrival: we were celebrating the baptism of Nellie Ruadh's baby.

BRIDGET [*Innocently.*] What name did she put on it, Master?

HUGH Was it Eamon? Yes, it was Eamon.

BRIDGET Eamon Donal from Tor! Cripes!

HUGH And after the *caerimonia nominationis*[5]—Maire?

MAIRE The ritual of naming.

HUGH Indeed—we then had a few libations to mark the occasion. Altogether very pleasant. The derivation of the word 'baptise'?—where are my Greek scholars? Doalty?

DOALTY Would it be—ah—ah—

HUGH Too slow. James?

JIMMY 'Baptizein'—to dip or immerse.

HUGH Indeed—our friend Pliny Minor[6] speaks of the 'baptisterium'—the cold bath.

DOALTY Master.

HUGH Doalty?

DOALTY I suppose you could talk then about baptising a sheep at sheep-dipping, could you?

[*Laughter. Comments.*]

HUGH Indeed—the precedent is there—the day you were appropriately named Doalty—seven nines?

DOALTY What's that, Master?

HUGH Seven times nine?

DOALTY Seven nines—seven nines—seven times nine—seven times nine are—Cripes, it's on the tip of my tongue, Master—I knew it for sure this morning—funny that's the only one that foxes[7] me—

BRIDGET [*Prompt.*] Sixty-three.

DOALTY What's wrong with me: sure seven nines are fifty-three, Master.

HUGH Sophocles from Colonus would agree with Doalty Dan Doalty from Tulach Alainn: 'To know nothing is the sweetest life.'[8] Where's Sean Beag?

MANUS He's at the salmon.

HUGH And Nora Dan?

MAIRE She says she's not coming back any more.

---

1. I am present [Latin; Friel's note].
2. With complete sobriety [Latin; Friel's note].
3. Sober [Latin; Friel's note].
4. Hail [Latin; Friel's note].
5. Ceremony of naming [Latin; Friel's note].
6. Or Pliny the Younger (61 or 62–ca. 113 C.E.),

Roman administrator who wrote an important collection of letters.
7. Befuddles.
8. From *Ajax*, by the ancient Greek playwright Sophocles (ca. 496–406 B.C.E.), born in the village of Colonus, near Athens.

HUGH Ah. Nora Dan can now write her name—Nora Dan's education is complete. And the Donnelly twins?

[*Brief pause. Then.*]

BRIDGET They're probably at the turf.⁹ [*She goes to* HUGH.] There's the one-and-eight I owe you for last quarter's arithmetic and there's my one-and-six¹ for this quarter's writing.

HUGH *Gratias tibi ago.*² [*He sits at his table.*] Before we commence our *studia*³ I have three items of information to impart to you—[*To* MANUS.] a bowl of tea, strong tea, black—

[MANUS *leaves.*]

Item A: on my perambulations today—Bridget? Too slow. Maire?

MAIRE *Perambulare*—to walk about.

HUGH Indeed—I encountered Captain Lancey of the Royal Engineers who is engaged in the ordnance survey of this area. He tells me that in the past few days two of his horses have strayed and some of his equipment seems to be mislaid. I expressed my regret and suggested he address you himself on these matters. He then explained that he does not speak Irish. Latin? I asked. None. Greek? Not a syllable. He speaks—on his own admission—only English; and to his credit he seemed suitably verecund—James?

JIMMY *Verecundus*—humble.

HUGH Indeed—he voiced some surprise that we did not speak his language. I explained that a few of us did, on occasion—outside the parish of course—and then usually for the purposes of commerce, a use to which his tongue seemed particularly suited—[*Shouts.*] and a slice of soda bread—and I went on to propose that our own culture and the classical tongues made a happier conjugation—Doalty?

DOALTY *Conjugo*—I join together.

[DOALTY *is so pleased with himself that he prods and winks at* BRIDGET.]

HUGH Indeed—English, I suggested, couldn't really express us. And again to his credit he acquiesced to my logic. Acquiesced—Maire?

[MAIRE *turns away impatiently.* HUGH *is unaware of the gesture.*]

Too slow. Bridget?

BRIDGET *Acquiesco.*⁴

HUGH *Procede.*

BRIDGET *Acquiesco, acquiescere, acquievi, acquietum.*

HUGH Indeed—and Item B . . .

MAIRE Master.

HUGH Yes?

[MAIRE *gets to her feet uneasily but determinedly. Pause.*]

Well, girl?

MAIRE We should all be learning to speak English. That's what my mother says. That's what I say. That's what Dan O'Connell⁵ said last month in Ennis. He said the sooner we all learn to speak English the better.

[*Suddenly several speak together.*]

---

9. I.e., cutting turf.
1. One and a half shillings—eighteen pennies—in the old British currency. "One-and-eight": one shilling and eight pence, or twenty pennies.
2. I thank you [Latin; Friel's note].
3. Studies [Latin; Friel's note].
4. Acquiescere: to rest, to find comfort in [Latin; Friel's note].

5. Irish lawyer and nationalist leader (1775–1847), born in Kerry and known as the Liberator, who argued for Ireland's adoption of the English language. The first Roman Catholic member of Parliament, he regained civil rights for Irish Catholics and urged the reestablishment of the Irish Parliament in Dublin.

JIMMY   What's she saying? What? What?

DOALTY   It's Irish he uses when he's travelling around scrounging votes.

BRIDGET   And sleeping with married women. Sure no woman's safe from that fella.

JIMMY   Who-who-who? Who's this? Who's this?

HUGH   *Silentium!* [*Pause.*] Who is she talking about?

MAIRE   I'm talking about Daniel O'Connell.

HUGH   Does she mean that little Kerry politician?

MAIRE   I'm talking about the Liberator, Master, as you well know. And what he said was this: 'The old language is a barrier to modern progress.' He said that last month. And he's right. I don't want Greek. I don't want Latin. I want English.

[MANUS *reappears on the platform above.*]

I want to be able to speak English because I'm going to America as soon as the harvest's all saved.

[MAIRE *remains standing.* HUGH *puts his hand into his pocket and produces a flask of whisky. He removes the cap, pours a drink into it, tosses it back, replaces the cap, puts the flask back into his pocket. Then.*]

HUGH   We have been diverted—*diverto*—*divertere*—Where were we?

DOALTY   Three items of information, Master. You're at Item B.

HUGH   Indeed—Item B—Item B—yes—On my way to the christening this morning I chanced to meet Mr George Alexander, Justice of the Peace. We discussed the new national school. Mr Alexander invited me to take charge of it when it opens. I thanked him and explained that I could do that only if I were free to run it as I have run this hedge-school for the past thirty-five years—filling what our friend Euripides[6] calls the '*aplestos pithos*'—James?

JIMMY   'The cask that cannot be filled'.

HUGH   Indeed—and Mr Alexander retorted courteously and emphatically that he hopes that is how it will be run.

[MAIRE *now sits.*]

Indeed. I have had a strenuous day and I am weary of you all. [*He rises.*] Manus will take care of you.

[HUGH *goes towards the steps.*

OWEN *enters.* OWEN *is the younger son, a handsome, attractive young man in his twenties. He is dressed smartly—a city man. His manner is easy and charming: everything he does is invested with consideration and enthusiasm. He now stands framed in the doorway, a travelling bag across his shoulder.*]

OWEN   Could anybody tell me is this where Hugh Mor O'Donnell holds his hedge-school?

DOALTY   It's Owen—Owen Hugh! Look, boys—it's Owen Hugh!

[OWEN *enters. As he crosses the room he touches and has a word for each person.*]

OWEN   Doalty! [*Playful punch.*] How are you, boy? *Jacobe, quid agis?*[7] Are you well?

JIMMY   Fine. Fine.

OWEN   And Bridget! Give us a kiss. Aaaaaah!

BRIDGET   You're welcome, Owen.

6. Greek playwright (ca. 484–406 B.C.E.).   7. James, how are you? [Latin; Friel's note].

OWEN   It's not—? Yes, it *is* Maire Chatach! God! A young woman!

MAIRE   How are you, Owen?

[OWEN *is now in front of* HUGH. *He puts his two hands on his father's shoulders.*]

OWEN   And how's the old man himself?

HUGH   Fair—fair.

OWEN   Fair? For God's sake you never looked better! Come here to me. [*He embraces* HUGH *warmly and genuinely.*] Great to see you, Father. Great to be back.

[HUGH's *eyes are moist—partly joy, partly the drink.*]

HUGH   I—I'm—I'm—pay no attention to—

OWEN   Come on—come on—come on—[*He gives* HUGH *his handkerchief.*] Do you know what you and I are going to do tonight? We are going to go up to Anna na mBreag's . . .

DOALTY   Not there, Owen.

OWEN   Why not?

DOALTY   Her poteen's[8] worse than ever.

BRIDGET   They say she puts frogs in it!

OWEN   All the better. [*To* HUGH.] And you and I are going to get footless drunk. That's arranged.

[OWEN *sees* MANUS *coming down the steps with tea and soda bread. They meet at the bottom.*]

And Manus!

MANUS   You're welcome, Owen.

OWEN   I know I am. And it's great to be here. [*He turns round, arms outstretched.*] I can't believe it. I come back after six years and everything's just as it was! Nothing's changed! Not a thing! [*Sniffs.*] Even that smell—that's the same smell this place always had. What is it anyway? Is it the straw?

DOALTY   Jimmy Jack's feet.

[*General laughter. It opens little pockets of conversation round the room.*]

OWEN   And Doalty Dan Doalty hasn't changed either!

DOALTY   Bloody right, Owen.

OWEN   Jimmy, are you well?

JIMMY   Dodging about.

OWEN   Any word of the big day?

[*This is greeted with 'ohs' and 'ahs'.*]

Time enough, Jimmy. Homer's easier to live with, isn't he?

MAIRE   We heard stories that you own ten big shops in Dublin[9]—is it true?

OWEN   Only nine.

BRIDGET   And you've twelve horses and six servants.

OWEN   Yes—that's true. God Almighty, would you listen to them—taking a hand at me!

MANUS   When did you arrive?

OWEN   We left Dublin yesterday morning, spent last night in Omagh and got here half an hour ago.

MANUS   You're hungry then.

HUGH   Indeed—get him food—get him a drink.

---

8. Local whiskey illegally distilled to evade British taxation.

9. Ireland's capital was the site of English military and political power.

OWEN   Not now, thanks; later. Listen—am I interrupting you all?

HUGH   By no means. We're finished for the day.

OWEN   Wonderful. I'll tell you why. Two friends of mine are waiting outside the door. They'd like to meet you and I'd like you to meet them. May I bring them in?

HUGH   Certainly. You'll all eat and have . . .

OWEN   Not just yet, Father. You've seen the sappers working in this area for the past fortnight, haven't you? Well, the older man is Captain Lancey . . .

HUGH   I've met Captain Lancey.

OWEN   Great. He's the cartographer in charge of this whole area. Cartographer—James?

> [OWEN *begins to play this game—his father's game—partly to involve his classroom audience, partly to show he has not forgotten it, and indeed partly because he enjoys it.*]

JIMMY   A maker of maps.

OWEN   Indeed—and the younger man that I travelled with from Dublin, his name is Lieutenant Yolland and he is attached to the toponymic department—Father?—*responde—responde!*

HUGH   He gives names to places.

OWEN   Indeed—although he is in fact an orthographer—Doalty?—too slow—Manus?

MANUS   The correct spelling of those names.

OWEN   Indeed—indeed!

> [OWEN *laughs and claps his hands. Some of the others join in.*]

Beautiful! Beautiful! Honest to God, it's such a delight to be back here with you all again—'*civilised*' people. Anyhow—may I bring them in?

HUGH   Your friends are our friends.

OWEN   I'll be straight back.

> [*There is general talk as* OWEN *goes towards the door. He stops beside* SARAH.]

OWEN   That's a new face. Who are you?

> [*A very brief hesitation. Then.*]

SARAH   My name is Sarah.

OWEN   Sarah who?

SARAH   Sarah Johnny Sally.

OWEN   Of course! From Bun na hAbhann! I'm Owen—Owen Hugh Mor. From Baile Beag. Good to see you.

> [*During this* OWEN–SARAH *exchange.*]

HUGH   Come on now. Let's tidy this place up. [*He rubs the top of his table with his sleeve.*] Move, Doalty—lift those books off the floor.

DOALTY   Right, Master; certainly, Master; I'm doing my best, Master.

> [OWEN *stops at the door.*]

OWEN   One small thing, Father.

HUGH   *Silentium!*

OWEN   I'm on their pay-roll.

> [SARAH, *very elated at her success, is beside* MANUS.]

SARAH   I said it, Manus!

> [MANUS *ignores* SARAH. *He is much more interested in* OWEN *now.*]

MANUS   You haven't enlisted, have you?!

> [SARAH *moves away.*]

OWEN   Me a soldier? I'm employed as a part-time, underpaid, civilian interpreter. My job is to translate the quaint, archaic tongue you people persist in speaking into the King's good English. [*He goes out.*]

HUGH Move—move—move! Put some order on things! Come on, Sarah— hide that bucket. Whose are these slates? Somebody take these dishes away. *Festinate! Festinate!*[1]

    [HUGH *pours another drink.*

      MANUS *goes to* MAIRE *who is busy tidying.*]

MANUS You didn't tell me you were definitely leaving.

MAIRE Not now.

HUGH Good girl, Bridget. That's the style.

MANUS You might at least have told me.

HUGH Are these your books, James?

JIMMY Thank you.

MANUS Fine! Fine! Go ahead! Go ahead!

MAIRE You talk to me about getting married—with neither a roof over your head nor a sod of ground under your foot. I suggest you go for the new school; but no—'My father's in for that.' Well now he's got it and now this is finished and now you've nothing.

MANUS I can always . . .

MAIRE What? Teach classics to the cows? Agh—

    [MAIRE *moves away from* MANUS.

      OWEN *enters with* LANCEY *and* YOLLAND. CAPTAIN LANCEY *is middle-aged; a small, crisp officer, expert in his field as cartographer but uneasy with people—especially civilians, especially these foreign civilians. His skill is with deeds, not words.*

      LIEUTENANT YOLLAND *is in his late twenties/early thirties. He is tall and thin and gangling, blond hair, a shy, awkward manner. A soldier by accident.*]

OWEN Here we are. Captain Lancey—my father.

LANCEY Good evening.

    [HUGH *becomes expansive, almost courtly with his visitors.*]

HUGH You and I have already met, sir.

LANCEY Yes.

OWEN And Lieutenant Yolland—both Royal Engineers—my father.

HUGH You're very welcome, gentlemen.

YOLLAND How do you do.

HUGH *Gaudeo vos hic adesse.*[2]

OWEN And I'll make no other introductions except that these are some of the people of Baile Beag and—what?—well you're among the best people in Ireland now. [*He pauses to allow* LANCEY *to speak.* LANCEY *does not.*] Would you like to say a few words, Captain?

HUGH What about a drop, sir?

LANCEY A what?

HUGH Perhaps a modest refreshment? A little sampling of our aqua vitae?[3]

LANCEY No, no.

HUGH Later perhaps when . . .

LANCEY I'll say what I have to say, if I may, and as briefly as possible. Do they speak *any* English, Roland?

---

1. Hurry! [Latin; Friel's note].
2. Welcome! [Latin; Friel's note].

3. "Aqua vitae": spirits; literally, in Latin, water of life.

OWEN   Don't worry. I'll translate.

LANCEY   I see. [*He clears his throat. He speaks as if he were addressing children—a shade too loudly and enunciating excessively.*] You may have seen
me—seen me—working in this section—section?—working. We are here—
here—in this place—you understand?—to make a map—a map—a map
and—

JIMMY   *Nonne Latine loquitur?*[4]

[*HUGH holds up a restraining hand.*]

HUGH   James.

LANCEY   [*To JIMMY.*]   I do not speak Gaelic, sir. [*He looks at OWEN.*]

OWEN   Carry on.

LANCEY   A map is a representation on paper—a picture—you understand picture?—a paper picture—showing, representing this country—yes?—showing your country in miniature—a scaled drawing on paper of—of—of—

[*Suddenly DOALTY sniggers. Then BRIDGET. Then SARAH. OWEN leaps in
quickly.*]

OWEN   It might be better if you *assume* they understand you—

LANCEY   Yes?

OWEN   And I'll translate as you go along.

LANCEY   I see. Yes. Very well. Perhaps you're right. Well. What we are doing
is this. [*He looks at OWEN. OWEN nods reassuringly.*] His Majesty's government has ordered the first ever comprehensive survey of this entire country—a general triangulation which will embrace detailed hydrographic and
topographic information and which will be executed to a scale of six inches
to the English mile.

HUGH   [*Pouring a drink.*]   Excellent—excellent.

[*LANCEY looks at OWEN.*]

OWEN   A new map is being made of the whole country.

[*LANCEY looks to OWEN: Is that all? OWEN smiles reassuringly and indicates to proceed.*]

LANCEY   This enormous task has been embarked on so that the military
authorities will be equipped with up-to-date and accurate information on
every corner of this part of the Empire.

OWEN   The job is being done by soldiers because they are skilled in this work.

LANCEY   And also so that the entire basis of land valuation can be reassessed
for purposes of more equitable taxation.

OWEN   This new map will take the place of the estate-agent's map so that
from now on you will know exactly what is yours in law.

LANCEY   In conclusion I wish to quote two brief extracts from the white paper
which is our governing charter: [*Reads.*] 'All former surveys of Ireland originated in forfeiture and violent transfer of property; the present survey has
for its object the relief which can be afforded to the proprietors and occu-
piers of land from unequal taxation.'

OWEN   The captain hopes that the public will cooperate with the sappers and
that the new map will mean that taxes are reduced.

HUGH   A worthy enterprise—*opus honestum!* And Extract B?

LANCEY   'Ireland is privileged. No such survey is being undertaken in England.
So this survey cannot but be received as proof of the disposition of this
government to advance the interests of Ireland.' My sentiments, too.

---

4. Does he not speak Latin? [Friel's note].

OWEN   This survey demonstrates the government's interest in Ireland and the captain thanks you for listening so attentively to him.

HUGH   Our pleasure, Captain.

LANCEY   Lieutenant Yolland?

YOLLAND   I—I—I've nothing to say—really—

OWEN   The captain is the man who actually makes the new map. George's task is to see that the place-names on this map are . . . correct. [To YOLLAND.] Just a few words—they'd like to hear you. [To class.] Don't you want to hear George, too?

MAIRE   Has he anything to say?

YOLLAND [To MAIRE.]   Sorry—sorry?

OWEN   She says she's dying to hear you.

YOLLAND [To MAIRE.]   Very kind of you—thank you . . . [To class.] I can only say that I feel—I feel very foolish to—to be working here and not to speak your language. But I intend to rectify that—with Roland's help—indeed I do.

OWEN   He wants me to teach him Irish!

HUGH   You are doubly welcome, sir.

YOLLAND   I think your countryside is—is—is—is very beautiful. I've fallen in love with it already. I hope we're not too—too crude an intrusion on your lives. And I know that I'm going to be happy, very happy, here.

OWEN   He is already a committed Hibernophile[5]—

JIMMY   He loves—

OWEN   Alright, Jimmy—we know—he loves Baile Beag; and he loves you all.

HUGH   Please . . . May I . . . ?

[HUGH is now drunk. He holds on to the edge of the table.]

OWEN   Go ahead, Father. [Hands up for quiet.] Please—please.

HUGH   And we, gentlemen, we in turn are happy to offer you our friendship, our hospitality, and every assistance that you may require. Gentlemen— welcome!

[A few desultory[6] claps. The formalities are over. General conversation. The soldiers meet the locals.

MANUS and OWEN meet down stage.]

OWEN   Lancey's a bloody ramrod but George's alright. How are you anyway?

MANUS   What sort of a translation was that, Owen?

OWEN   Did I make a mess of it?

MANUS   You weren't saying what Lancey was saying!

OWEN   'Uncertainty in meaning is incipient poetry'—who said that?

MANUS   There was nothing uncertain about what Lancey said: it's a bloody military operation, Owen! And what's Yolland's function? What's 'incorrect' about the place-names we have here?

OWEN   Nothing at all. They're just going to be standardised.

MANUS   You mean changed into English?

OWEN   Where there's ambiguity, they'll be Anglicised.

MANUS   And they call you Roland! They both call you Roland!

OWEN   Shhhhh. Isn't it ridiculous? They seemed to get it wrong from the very beginning—or else they can't pronounce Owen. I was afraid some of you bastards would laugh.

MANUS   Aren't you going to tell them?

---

5. Lover of Ireland (in Latin, Hibernia).   6. Scattered.

OWEN Yes—yes—soon—soon.

MANUS But they . . .

OWEN Easy, man, easy. Owen—Roland—what the hell. It's only a name. It's the same me, isn't it? Well, isn't it?

MANUS Indeed it is. It's the same Owen.

OWEN And the same Manus. And in a way we complement each other.

> [*He punches* MANUS *lightly, playfully and turns to join the others. As he goes.*]

Alright—who has met whom? Isn't this a job for the go-between?

> [MANUS *watches* OWEN *move confidently across the floor, taking* MAIRE *by the hand and introducing her to* YOLLAND.
>
> HUGH *is trying to negotiate the steps.*
>
> JIMMY *is lost in a text.*
>
> DOALTY *and* BRIDGET *are reliving their giggling.*
>
> SARAH *is staring at* MANUS.]

Act Two

SCENE ONE

The sappers have already mapped most of the area. YOLLAND'*s official task, which* OWEN *is now doing, is to take each of the Gaelic names—every hill, stream, rock, even every patch of ground which possessed its own distinctive Irish name— and Anglicise it, either by changing it into its approximate English sound or by translating it into English words. For example, a Gaelic name like Cnoc Ban could become Knockban or—directly translated—Fair Hill. These new standardised names were entered into the Name-Book, and when the new maps appeared they contained all these new Anglicised names.* OWEN'*s official function as translator is to pronounce each name in Irish and then provide the English translation.*

The hot weather continues. It is late afternoon some days later.

Stage right: an improvised clothes-line strung between the shafts of the cart and a nail in the wall; on it are some shirts and socks.

A large map—one of the new blank maps—is spread out on the floor. OWEN *is on his hands and knees, consulting it. He is totally engrossed in his task, which he pursues with great energy and efficiency.*

YOLLAND'*s hesitancy has vanished—he is at home here now. He is sitting on the floor, his long legs stretched out before him, his back resting against a creel,[7] his eyes closed. His mind is elsewhere. One of the reference books—a church registry—lies open on his lap.*

Around them are various reference books, the Name-Book, a bottle of poteen, some cups etc.

OWEN *completes an entry in the Name-Book and returns to the map on the floor.*

OWEN Now. Where have we got to? Yes—the point where that stream enters the sea—that tiny little beach there. George!

YOLLAND Yes. I'm listening. What do you call it? Say the Irish name again?

OWEN Bun na hAbhann.

YOLLAND Again.

OWEN Bun na hAbhann.

---

7. Large wicker basket.

YOLLAND Bun na hAbhann.

OWEN That's terrible, George.

YOLLAND I know. I'm sorry. Say it again.

OWEN Bun na hAbhann.

YOLLAND Bun na hAbhann.

OWEN That's better. Bun is the Irish word for bottom. And Abha means river. So it's literally the mouth of the river.

YOLLAND Let's leave it alone. There's no English equivalent for a sound like that.

OWEN What is it called in the church registry?

[*Only now does* YOLLAND *open his eyes.*]

YOLLAND Let's see . . . Banowen.

OWEN That's wrong. [*Consults text.*] The list of freeholders calls it Owen-more—that's completely wrong: Owenmore's the big river at the west end of the parish. [*Another text.*] And in the grand jury lists it's called—God!—Binhone!—wherever they got that. I suppose we could Anglicize it to Bun-owen; but somehow that's neither fish nor flesh.

[YOLLAND *closes his eyes again.*]

YOLLAND I give up.

OWEN [*At map.*] Back to first principles. What are we trying to do?

YOLLAND Good question.

OWEN We are trying to denominate and at the same time describe that tiny area of soggy, rocky, sandy ground where that little stream enters the sea, an area known locally as Bun na hAbhann . . . Burnfoot![8] What about Burnfoot?

YOLLAND [*Indifferently.*] Good, Roland. Burnfoot's good.

OWEN George, my name isn't . . .

YOLLAND B-u-r-n-f-o-o-t?

OWEN I suppose so. What do you think?

YOLLAND Yes.

OWEN Are you happy with that?

YOLLAND Yes.

OWEN Burnfoot it is then. [*He makes the entry into the Name-Book.*] Bun na nAbhann—B-u-r-n-

YOLLAND You're becoming very skilled at this.

OWEN We're not moving fast enough.

YOLLAND [*Opens eyes again.*] Lancey lectured me again last night.

OWEN When does he finish here?

YOLLAND The sappers are pulling out at the end of the week. The trouble is, the maps they've completed can't be printed without these names. So London screams at Lancey and Lancey screams at me. But I wasn't intimidated.

[MANUS *emerges from upstairs and descends.*]

'I'm sorry, sir,' I said, 'But certain tasks demand their own tempo. You cannot rename a whole country overnight.' Your Irish air has made me bold. [*To* MANUS.] Do you want us to leave?

MANUS Time enough. Class won't begin for another half-hour.

YOLLAND Sorry—sorry?

OWEN Can't you speak English?

[MANUS *gathers the things off the clothes-line.* OWEN *returns to the map.*]

---

8. "Burn" is an Ulster-Scots word for river.

OWEN We now come across that beach . . .

YOLLAND Tra—that's the Irish for beach. [*To* MANUS.] I'm picking up the odd word, Manus.

MANUS So.

OWEN . . . on past Burnfoot; and there's nothing around here that has any name that I know of until we come down here to the south end, just about here . . . and there should be a ridge of rocks there . . . Have the sappers marked it? They have. Look, George.

YOLLAND Where are we?

OWEN There.

YOLLAND I'm lost.

OWEN Here. And the name of that ridge is Druim Dubh. Put English on that, Lieutenant.

YOLLAND Say it again.

OWEN Druim Dubh.

YOLLAND Dubh means black.

OWEN Yes.

YOLLAND And Druim means . . . what? a fort?

OWEN We met it yesterday in Druim Luachra.

YOLLAND A ridge! The Black Ridge! [*To* MANUS.] You see, Manus?

OWEN We'll have you fluent at the Irish before the summer's over.

YOLLAND Oh I wish I were. [*To* MANUS *as he crosses to go back upstairs.*] We got a crate of orange from Dublin today. I'll send some up to you.

MANUS Thanks. [*To* OWEN.] Better hide that bottle. Father's just up and he'd be better without it.

OWEN Can't you speak English before your man?

MANUS Why?

OWEN Out of courtesy.

MANUS Doesn't he want to learn Irish? [*To* YOLLAND.] Don't you want to learn Irish?

YOLLAND Sorry—sorry? I—I—

MANUS I understand the Lanceys perfectly but people like you puzzle me.

OWEN Manus, for God's sake!

MANUS [*Still to* YOLLAND.] How's the work going?

YOLLAND The work?—the work? Oh, it's—it's staggering along—I think—[*To* OWEN.]—isn't it? But we'd be lost without Roland.

MANUS [*Leaving.*] I'm sure. But there are always the Rolands, aren't there? [*He goes upstairs and exits.*]

YOLLAND What was that he said?—something about Lancey, was it?

OWEN He said we should hide that bottle before Father gets his hands on it.

YOLLAND Ah.

OWEN He's always trying to protect him.

YOLLAND Was he lame from birth?

OWEN An accident when he was a baby: Father fell across his cradle. That's why Manus feels so responsible for him.

YOLLAND Why doesn't he marry?

OWEN Can't afford to, I suppose.

YOLLAND Hasn't he a salary?

OWEN What salary? All he gets is the odd shilling Father throws him—and that's seldom enough. I got out in time, didn't I?

[YOLLAND *is pouring a drink.*]

Easy with that stuff—it'll hit you suddenly.

YOLLAND   I like it.

OWEN   Let's get back to the job. Druim Dubh—what's it called in the jury lists? [*Consults texts.*]

YOLLAND   Some people here resent us.

OWEN   Dramduff—wrong as usual.

YOLLAND   I was passing a little girl yesterday and she spat at me.

OWEN   And it's Drimdoo here. What's it called in the registry?

YOLLAND   Do you know the Donnelly twins?

OWEN   Who?

YOLLAND   The Donnelly twins.

OWEN   Yes. Best fishermen about here. What about them?

YOLLAND   Lancey's looking for them.

OWEN   What for?

YOLLAND   He wants them for questioning.

OWEN   Probably stolen somebody's nets. Dramduffy! Nobody ever called it Dramduffy. Take your pick of those three.

YOLLAND   My head's addled. Let's take a rest. Do you want a drink?

OWEN   Thanks. Now, every Dubh we've come across we've changed to Duff. So if we're to be consistent, I suppose Druim Dubh has to become Dromduff.

[YOLLAND *is now looking out the window.*]

You can see the end of the ridge from where you're standing. But D-r-u-m or D-r-o-m? [*Name-Book.*] Do you remember—which did we agree on for Druim Luachra?

YOLLAND   That house immediately above where we're camped—

OWEN   Mm?

YOLLAND   The house where Maire lives.

OWEN   Maire? Oh, Maire Chatach.

YOLLAND   What does that mean?

OWEN   Curly-haired; the whole family are called the Catachs. What about it?

YOLLAND   I hear music coming from that house almost every night.

OWEN   Why don't you drop in?

YOLLAND   Could I?

OWEN   Why not? We used D-r-o-m then. So we've got to call it D-r-o-m-d-u-f-f—alright?

YOLLAND   Go back up to where the new school is being built and just say the names again for me, would you?

OWEN   That's a good idea. Poolkerry, Ballybeg—

YOLLAND   No, no; as they still are—in your own language.

OWEN   Poll na gCaorach,

[YOLLAND *repeats the names silently after him.*]

Baile Beag, Ceann Balor, Lis Maol, Machaire Buidhe, Baile na gGall, Carraig na Ri, Mullach Dearg—

YOLLAND   Do you think I could live here?

OWEN   What are you talking about?

YOLLAND   Settle down here—live here.

OWEN   Come on, George.

YOLLAND   I mean it.

OWEN   Live on what? Potatoes? Buttermilk?

YOLLAND   It's really heavenly.

OWEN For God's sake! The first hot summer in fifty years and you think it's Eden. Don't be such a bloody romantic. You wouldn't survive a mild winter here.

YOLLAND Do you think not? Maybe you're right.

> [DOALTY *enters in a rush.*]

DOALTY Hi, boys, is Manus about?

OWEN He's upstairs. Give him a shout.

DOALTY Manus!

The cattle's going mad in that heat—Cripes, running wild all over the place.

> [*To* YOLLAND.] How are you doing, skipper?

> [MANUS *appears.*]

YOLLAND Thank you for—I—I'm very grateful to you for—

DOALTY Wasting your time. I don't know a word you're saying. Hi, Manus, there's two bucks down the road there asking for you.

MANUS [*Descending.*] Who are they?

DOALTY Never clapped eyes on them. They want to talk to you.

MANUS What about?

DOALTY They wouldn't say. Come on. The bloody beasts'll end up in Loch an Iubhair if they're not capped.[9] Good luck, boys!

> [DOALTY *rushes off.* MANUS *follows him.*]

OWEN Good luck! What were you thanking Doalty for?

YOLLAND I was washing outside my tent this morning and he was passing with a scythe across his shoulder and he came up to me and pointed to the long grass and then cut a pathway round my tent and from the tent down to the road—so that my feet won't get wet with the dew. Wasn't that kind of him? And I have no words to thank him . . .

I suppose you're right: I suppose I couldn't live here . . .

Just before Doalty came up to me this morning, I was thinking that at that moment I might have been in Bombay instead of Ballybeg. You see, my father was at his wits end with me and finally he got me a job with the East India Company[1]—some kind of a clerkship. This was ten, eleven months ago. So I set off for London. Unfortunately I—I—I missed the boat. Literally. And since I couldn't face Father and hadn't enough money to hang about until the next sailing, I joined the Army. And they stuck me into the Engineers and posted me to Dublin. And Dublin sent me here. And while I was washing this morning and looking across the Tra Bhan, I was thinking how very, very lucky I am to be here and not in Bombay.

OWEN Do you believe in fate?

YOLLAND Lancey's so like my father. I was watching him last night. He met every group of sappers as they reported in. He checked the field kitchens. He examined the horses. He inspected every single report—even examining the texture of the paper and commenting on the neatness of the handwriting. The perfect colonial servant: not only must the job be done—it must be done with excellence. Father has that drive, too; that dedication; that indefatigable energy. He builds roads—hopping from one end of the Empire to the other. Can't sit still for five minutes. He says himself the longest time

---

9. Surpassed.
1. English trade company in India, South Asia, and Southeast Asia, chartered in 1600 and central to 18th- and 19th-century British imperialism in the region.

he ever sat still was the night before Waterloo when they were waiting for
Wellington to make up his mind to attack.[2]

OWEN What age is he?

YOLLAND Born in 1789—the very day the Bastille fell.[3] I've often thought
maybe that gave his whole life its character. Do you think it could? He
inherited a new world the day he was born—the Year One. Ancient time
was at an end. The world had cast off its old skin. There were no longer any
frontiers to man's potential. Possibilities were endless and exciting. He still
believes that. The Apocalypse is just about to happen . . . I'm afraid I'm a
great disappointment to him. I've neither his energy, nor his coherence, nor
his belief. Do I believe in fate? The day I arrived in Ballybeg,—no, Baile
Beag—the moment you brought me in here, I had a curious sensation. It's
difficult to describe. It was a momentary sense of discovery; no—not quite
a sense of discovery—a sense of recognition, of confirmation of something
I half knew instinctively as if I had stepped . . .

OWEN Back into ancient time?

YOLLAND No, no. It wasn't an awareness of *direction* being changed but of
experience being of a totally different order. I had moved into a consciousness that wasn't striving nor agitated, but at its ease and with its own conviction and assurance. And when I heard Jimmy Jack and your father
swopping stories about Apollo and Cuchulain and Paris and Ferdia[4]—as if
they lived down the road—it was then that I thought—I knew—perhaps I
could live here . . . [*Now embarrassed.*] Where's the pot-een?

OWEN Poteen.

YOLLAND Poteen—poteen—poteen. Even if I did speak Irish I'd always be an
outsider here, wouldn't I? I may learn the password but the language of the
tribe will always elude me, won't it? The private will always be . . . hermetic,[5]
won't it?

OWEN You can learn to decode us.

[HUGH *emerges from upstairs and descends. He is dressed for the road.
Today he is physically and mentally jaunty and alert—almost self-
consciously jaunty and alert. Indeed, as the scene progresses, one has
the sense that he is deliberately parodying himself.*

The moment HUGH *gets to the bottom of the steps* YOLLAND *leaps
respectfully to his feet.*]

HUGH [*As he descends.*]

  Quantumvis cursum longum fessumque moratur
  Sol, sacro tandem carmine vesper adest.

I dabble in verse, Lieutenant, after the style of Ovid.[6]

  [*To* OWEN.] A drop of that to fortify me.

YOLLAND You'll have to translate it for me.

HUGH Let's see—

  No matter how long the sun may linger on his long and weary journey
  At length evening comes with its sacred song.

---

2. Dublin-born Arthur Wellesley (1769–1852),
duke of Wellington, vanquished the French
emperor Napoleon's army on June 18, 1815, in
Waterloo, Belgium.
3. The French Revolution began on July 14, 1789,
with the storming of the Bastille (a jail in Paris).
The French monarchy was later overthrown and
replaced by the First Republic.
4. Mythical Irish warrior, slain by his foster

brother, Cuchulainn, the greatest hero of the
medieval Ulster Cycle, an extensive series of stories
focused on the warriors of King Conchobar's court
in Northern Ireland. "Apollo": Greek god of arts,
music, and prophecy, who helped the Trojan
prince Paris kill the greatest Greek hero, Achilles,
in the Trojan War.
5. Secret, hidden.
6. Roman poet (43 B.C.E.–17? C.E.).

YOLLAND   Very nice, sir.

HUGH   English succeeds in making it sound . . . plebeian.[7]

OWEN   Where are you off to, Father?

HUGH   An *expeditio*[8] with three purposes. Purpose A: to acquire a testimonial from our parish priest—[*To* YOLLAND.] a worthy man but barely literate; and since he'll ask me to write it myself, how in all modesty can I do myself justice?

   [*To* OWEN.] Where did this [*Drink.*] come from?

OWEN   Anna na mBreag's.

HUGH [*To* YOLLAND.]   In that case address yourself to it with circumspection.

   [*And* HUGH *instantly tosses the drink back in one gulp and grimaces.*]
   Aaaaaaagh!

   [*Holds out his glass for a refill.*]

   Anna na mBreag means Anna of the Lies. And Purpose B: to talk to the builders of the new school about the kind of living accommodation I will require there. I have lived too long like a journeyman[9] tailor.

YOLLAND   Some years ago we lived fairly close to a poet—well, about three miles away.

HUGH   His name?

YOLLAND   Wordsworth—William Wordsworth.[1]

HUGH   Did he speak of me to you?

YOLLAND   Actually I never talked to him. I just saw him out walking—in the distance.

HUGH   Wordsworth? . . . no. I'm afraid we're not familiar with your literature, Lieutenant. We feel closer to the warm Mediterranean.[2] We tend to overlook your island.

YOLLAND   I'm learning to speak Irish, sir.

HUGH   Good.

YOLLAND   Roland's teaching me.

HUGH   Splendid.

YOLLAND   I mean—I feel so cut off from the people here. And I was trying to explain a few minutes ago how remarkable a community this is. To meet people like yourself and Jimmy Jack who actually converse in Greek and Latin. And your place-names—what was the one we came across this morning?—Termon, from Terminus, the god of boundaries.[3] It—it—it's really astonishing.

HUGH   We like to think we endure around truths immemorially posited.

YOLLAND   And your Gaelic literature—you're a poet yourself—

HUGH   Only in Latin, I'm afraid.

YOLLAND   I understand it's enormously rich and ornate.

HUGH   Indeed, Lieutenant. A rich language. A rich literature. You'll find, sir, that certain cultures expend on their vocabularies and syntax acquisitive energies and ostentations entirely lacking in their material lives. I suppose you could call us a spiritual people.

OWEN [*Not unkindly; more out of embarrassment before* YOLLAND.]   Will you stop that nonsense, Father.

HUGH   Nonsense? What nonsense?

---

7. Of the common people.
8. Expedition [Latin; Friel's note].
9. Hireling, subservient.
1. Romantic poet (1770–1850), who composed

poetry while walking through England's Lake District.
2. I.e., Greek and Latin literature.
3. In Roman mythology.

OWEN Do you know where the priest lives?

HUGH At Lis na Muc, over near . . .

OWEN No, he doesn't. Lis na Muc, the Fort of the Pigs, has become Swine-fort. [*Now turning the pages of the Name-Book—a page per name.*] And to get to Swinefort you pass through Greencastle and Fair Head and Strandhill and Gort and Whiteplains. And the new school isn't at Poll na gCaorach—it's at Sheepsrock. Will you be able to find your way?

[HUGH *pours himself another drink. Then.*]

HUGH Yes, it is a rich language, Lieutenant, full of the mythologies of fantasy and hope and self-deception—a syntax opulent with tomorrows. It is our response to mud cabins and a diet of potatoes; our only method of replying to . . . inevitabilities.

[*To* OWEN.] Can you give me the loan of half-a-crown? I'll repay you out of the subscriptions I'm collecting for the publication of my new book. [*To* YOLLAND.] It is entitled: 'The Pentaglot Preceptor[4] or Elementary Institute of the English, Greek, Hebrew, Latin and Irish Languages; Particularly Calculated for the Instruction of Such Ladies and Gentlemen as may Wish to Learn without the Help of a Master'.

YOLLAND [*Laughs.*] That's a wonderful title!

HUGH Between ourselves—the best part of the enterprise. Nor do I, in fact, speak Hebrew. And that last phrase—'without the Help of a Master'—that was written before the new national school was thrust upon me—do you think I ought to drop it now? After all you don't dispose of the cow just because it has produced a magnificent calf, do you?

YOLLAND You certainly do not.

HUGH The phrase goes. And I'm interrupting work of moment. [*He goes to the door and stops there.*]

To return briefly to that other matter, Lieutenant. I understand your sense of exclusion, of being cut off from a life here; and I trust you will find access to us with my son's help. But remember that words are signals, counters. They are not immortal. And it can happen—to use an image you'll understand—it can happen that a civilisation can be imprisoned in a linguistic contour which no longer matches the landscape of . . . fact.

Gentlemen. [*He leaves.*]

OWEN 'An *expeditio* with three purposes': the children laugh at him: he always promises three points and he never gets beyond A and B.

YOLLAND He's an astute man.

OWEN He's bloody pompous.

YOLLAND But so astute.

OWEN And he drinks too much. Is it astute not to be able to adjust for survival? Enduring around truths immemorially posited—hah!

YOLLAND He knows what's happening.

OWEN What is happening?

YOLLAND I'm not sure. But I'm concerned about my part in it. It's an eviction of sorts.

OWEN We're making a six-inch map of the country. Is there something sinister in that?

YOLLAND Not in . . .

OWEN And we're taking place-names that are riddled with confusion and . . .

---

4. I.e., the five-tongued head teacher.

YOLLAND Who's confused? Are the people confused?

OWEN . . . and we're standardising those names as accurately and as sensitively as we can.

YOLLAND Something is being eroded.

OWEN Back to the romance again. Alright! Fine! Fine! Look where we've got to. [*He drops on his hands and knees and stabs a finger at the map.*] We've come to this crossroads. Come here and look at it, man! Look at it! And we call that crossroads Tobair Vree. And why do we call it Tobair Vree? I'll tell you why. Tobair means a well. But what does Vree mean? It's a corruption of Brian—[*Gaelic pronunciation.*] Brian—an erosion of Tobair Bhriain. Because a hundred-and-fifty years ago there used to be a well there, not at the crossroads, mind you—that would be too simple—but in a field close to the crossroads. And an old man called Brian, whose face was disfigured by an enormous growth, got it into his head that the water in that well was blessed; and every day for seven months he went there and bathed his face in it. But the growth didn't go away; and one morning Brian was found drowned in that well. And ever since that crossroads is known as Tobair Vree—even though that well has long since dried up. I know the story because my grandfather told it to me. But ask Doalty—or Maire—or Bridget—even my father—even Manus—why it's called Tobair Vree; and do you think they'll know? I know they don't know. So the question I put to you, Lieutenant, is this: What do we do with a name like that? Do we scrap Tobair Vree altogether and call it—what?—The Cross? Crossroads? Or do we keep piety with a man long dead, long forgotten, his name 'eroded' beyond recognition, whose trivial little story nobody in the parish remembers?

YOLLAND Except you.

OWEN I've left here.

YOLLAND You remember it.

OWEN I'm asking you: what do we write in the Name-Book?

YOLLAND Tobair Vree.

OWEN Even though the well is a hundred yards from the actual crossroads—and there's no well anyway—and what the hell does Vree mean?

YOLLAND Tobair Vree.

OWEN That's what you want?

YOLLAND Yes.

OWEN You're certain?

YOLLAND Yes.

OWEN Fine. Fine. That's what you'll get.

YOLLAND That's what you want, too, Roland.
  [*Pause.*]

OWEN [*Explodes.*] George! For God's sake! *My name is not Roland!*

YOLLAND What?

OWEN [*Softly.*] My name is Owen.
  [*Pause.*]

YOLLAND Not Roland?

OWEN Owen.

YOLLAND You mean to say—?

OWEN Owen.

YOLLAND But I've been—

OWEN O-w-e-n.

YOLLAND Where did Roland come from?

OWEN I don't know.

YOLLAND It was never Roland?

OWEN Never.

YOLLAND O my God!

[*Pause. They stare at one another. Then the absurdity of the situation strikes them suddenly. They explode with laughter.* OWEN *pours drinks. As they roll about their lines overlap.*]

YOLLAND Why didn't you tell me?

OWEN Do I look like a Roland?

YOLLAND Spell Owen again.

OWEN I was getting fond of Roland.

YOLLAND O my God!

OWEN O-w-e-n.

YOLLAND What'll we write—

OWEN —in the Name-Book?!

YOLLAND R-o-w-e-n!

OWEN Or what about Ol-

YOLLAND Ol- what?

OWEN Oland!

[*And again they explode.*
MANUS *enters. He is very elated.*]

MANUS What's the celebration?

OWEN A christening!

YOLLAND A baptism!

OWEN A hundred christenings!

YOLLAND A thousand baptisms! Welcome to Eden!

OWEN Eden's right! We name a thing and—bang!—it leaps into existence![5]

YOLLAND Each name a perfect equation with its roots.

OWEN A perfect congruence with its reality.
[*To* MANUS.] Take a drink.

YOLLAND Poteen—beautiful.

OWEN Lying Anna's poteen.

YOLLAND Anna na mBreag's poteen.

OWEN Excellent, George.

YOLLAND I'll decode you yet.

OWEN [*Offers drink.*] Manus?

MANUS Not if that's what it does to you.

OWEN You're right. Steady—steady—sober up—sober up.

YOLLAND Sober as a judge, Owen.
[MANUS *moves beside* OWEN.]

MANUS I've got good news! Where's Father?

OWEN He's gone out. What's the good news?

MANUS I've been offered a job.

OWEN Where? [*Now aware of* YOLLAND.] Come on, man—speak in English.

MANUS For the benefit of the colonist?

OWEN He's a decent man.

MANUS Aren't they all at some level?

OWEN Please.

---

5. Cf. Adam's naming of every creature (Genesis 2.19–20).

[MANUS *shrugs.*]

He's been offered a job.

YOLLAND   Where?

OWEN   Well—tell us!

MANUS   I've just had a meeting with two men from Inis Meadhon.[6] They want me to go there and start a hedge-school. They're giving me a free house, free turf, and free milk; a rood[7] of standing corn; twelve drills[8] of potatoes; and— [*He stops.*]

OWEN   And what?

MANUS   A salary of £42 a year!

OWEN   Manus, that's wonderful!

MANUS   You're talking to a man of substance.

OWEN   I'm delighted.

YOLLAND   Where's Inis Meadhon?

OWEN   An island south of here. And they came looking for you?

MANUS   Well, I mean to say . . .

[OWEN *punches* MANUS.]

OWEN   Aaaaagh! This calls for a real celebration.

YOLLAND   Congratulations.

MANUS   Thank you.

OWEN   Where are you, Anna?

YOLLAND   When do you start?

MANUS   Next Monday.

OWEN   We'll stay with you when we're there.

[*To* YOLLAND.] How long will it be before we reach Inis Meadhon?

YOLLAND   How far south is it?

MANUS   About fifty miles.

YOLLAND   Could we make it by December?

OWEN   We'll have Christmas together. [*Sings.*] 'Christmas Day on Inis Meadhon . . .'

YOLLAND   [*Toast.*]   I hope you're very content there, Manus.

MANUS   Thank you.

[YOLLAND *holds out his hand.* MANUS *takes it. They shake warmly.*]

OWEN   [*Toast.*]   Manus.

MANUS   [*Toast.*]   To Inis Meadhon. [*He drinks quickly and turns to leave.*]

OWEN   Hold on—hold on—refills coming up.

MANUS   I've got to go.

OWEN   Come on, man; this is an occasion. Where are you rushing to?

MANUS   I've got to tell Maire.

[MAIRE *enters with her can of milk.*]

MAIRE   You've got to tell Maire what?

OWEN   He's got a job!

MAIRE   Manus?

OWEN   He's been invited to start a hedge-school in Inis Meadhon.

MAIRE   Where?

MANUS   Inis Meadhon—the island! They're giving me £42 a year and . . .

OWEN   A house, fuel, milk, potatoes, corn, pupils, what-not!

---

6. Middle Island; one of the three Aran Islands, off the west coast of Ireland, south of Donegal.

7. A cubic measure.
8. Rows.

MANUS   I start on Monday.
OWEN   You'll take a drink. Isn't it great?
MANUS   I want to talk to you for . . .
MAIRE   There's your milk. I need the can back.
    [MANUS *takes the can and runs up the steps.*]
MANUS [*As he goes.*]   How will you like living on an island?
OWEN   You know George, don't you?
MAIRE   We wave to each other across the fields.
YOLLAND   Sorry-sorry?
OWEN   She says you wave to each other across the fields.
YOLLAND   Yes, we do; oh yes, indeed we do.
MAIRE   What's he saying?
OWEN   He says you wave to each other across the fields.
MAIRE   That's right. So we do.
YOLLAND   What's she saying?
OWEN   Nothing—nothing—nothing.
    [*To* MAIRE.] What's the news?
      [MAIRE *moves away, touching the text books with her toe.*]
MAIRE   Not a thing. You're busy, the two of you.
OWEN   We think we are.
MAIRE   I hear the Fiddler O'Shea's about. There's some talk of a dance tomor-
    row night.
OWEN   Where will it be?
MAIRE   Maybe over the road. Maybe at Tobair Vree.
YOLLAND   Tobair Vree!
MAIRE   Yes.
YOLLAND   Tobair Vree! Tobair Vree!
MAIRE   Does he know what I'm saying?
OWEN   Not a word.
MAIRE   Tell him then.
OWEN   Tell him what?
MAIRE   About the dance.
OWEN   Maire says there may be a dance tomorrow night.
YOLLAND [*To* OWEN.]   Yes? May I come?
    [*To* MAIRE.] Would anybody object if I came?
MAIRE [*To* OWEN.]   What's he saying?
OWEN [*To* YOLLAND.]   Who would object?
MAIRE [*To* OWEN.]   Did you tell him?
YOLLAND [*To* MAIRE.]   Sorry-sorry?
OWEN [*To* MAIRE.]   He says may he come?
MAIRE [*To* YOLLAND.]   That's up to you.
YOLLAND [*To* OWEN.]   What does she say?
OWEN [*To* YOLLAND.]   She says—
YOLLAND [*To* MAIRE.]   What-what?
MAIRE [*To* OWEN.]   Well?
YOLLAND [*To* OWEN.]   Sorry-sorry?
OWEN [*To* YOLLAND.]   Will you go?
YOLLAND [*To* MAIRE.]   Yes, yes, if I may.
MAIRE [*To* OWEN.]   What does he say?
YOLLAND [*To* OWEN.]   What is she saying?

OWEN   O for God's sake!

> [*To* MANUS *who is descending with the empty can.*] You take on this job, Manus.

MANUS   I'll walk you up to the house. Is your mother at home? I want to talk to her.

MAIRE   What's the rush? [*To* OWEN.] Didn't you offer me a drink?

OWEN   Will you risk Anna na mBreag?

MAIRE   Why not.

> [YOLLAND *is suddenly intoxicated. He leaps up on a stool, raises his glass and shouts.*]

YOLLAND   Anna na mBreag! Baile Beag! Inis Meadhon! Bombay! Tobair Vree! Eden! And poteen—correct, Owen?

OWEN   Perfect.

YOLLAND   And bloody marvellous stuff it is, too. I love it! Bloody, bloody, bloody marvellous!

> [*Simultaneously with his final 'bloody marvellous' bring up very loud the introductory music of the reel. Then immediately go to black.*
> *Retain the music throughout the very brief interval.*]

SCENE TWO

The following night.

This scene may be played in the schoolroom, but it would be preferable to lose—by lighting—as much of the schoolroom as possible, and to play the scene down front in a vaguely 'outside' area.

The music rises to a crescendo. Then in the distance we hear MAIRE *and* YOLLAND *approach—laughing and running. They run on, hand-in-hand. They have just left the dance.*

Fade the music to distant background. Then after a time it is lost and replaced by guitar music.

MAIRE *and* YOLLAND *are now down front, still holding hands and excited by their sudden and impetuous escape from the dance.*

MAIRE   O my God, that leap across the ditch nearly killed me.

YOLLAND   I could scarcely keep up with you.

MAIRE   Wait till I get my breath back.

YOLLAND   We must have looked as if we were being chased.

> [*They now realise they are alone and holding hands—the beginnings of embarrassment. The hands disengage. They begin to drift apart. Pause.*]

MAIRE   Manus'll wonder where I've got to.

YOLLAND   I wonder did anyone notice us leave.

> [*Pause. Slightly further apart.*]

MAIRE   The grass must be wet. My feet are soaking.

YOLLAND   Your feet must be wet. The grass is soaking.

> [*Another pause. Another few paces apart. They are now a long distance from one another.*]

YOLLAND [*Indicating himself.*]   George.

> [MAIRE *nods: Yes—yes. Then.*]

MAIRE   Lieutenant George.

YOLLAND   Don't call me that. I never think of myself as Lieutenant.

MAIRE   What-what?

YOLLAND   Sorry-sorry? [*He points to himself again.*] George.

[MAIRE *nods: Yes-yes. Then points to herself.*]

MAIRE   Maire.

YOLLAND   Yes, I know you're Maire. Of course I know you're Maire. I mean
I've been watching you night and day for the past . . .

MAIRE [*Eagerly.*]   What—what?

YOLLAND [*Points.*]   Maire. [*Points.*] George. [*Points both.*] Maire and George.
[MAIRE *nods: Yes-yes-yes.*]
I—I—I—

MAIRE   Say anything at all. I love the sound of your speech.

YOLLAND [*Eagerly.*]   Sorry-sorry?
[*In acute frustration he looks around, hoping for some inspiration that
will provide him with communicative means. Now he has a thought: he
tries raising his voice and articulating in a staccato style and with equal
and absurd emphasis on each word.*]
Every-morning-I-see-you-feeding-brown-hens-and-giving-meal-to-black-
calf—[*The futility of it.*]—O my God.
[MAIRE *smiles. She moves towards him. She will try to communicate in
Latin.*]

MAIRE   *Tu es centurio in—in—in exercitu Britannico—*[9]

YOLLAND   Yes-yes? Go on—go on—say anything at all—I love the sound of
your speech.

MAIRE   *—et es in castris quae—quae—quae sunt in agro*[1]—[*The futility of
it.*]—O my God.
[YOLLAND *smiles. He moves towards her.
Now for her English words.*] George—water.

YOLLAND   'Water'? Water! Oh yes—water—water—very good—water—good—
good.

MAIRE   Fire.

YOLLAND   Fire—indeed—wonderful—fire, fire, fire—splendid—splendid!

MAIRE   Ah . . . ah . . .

YOLLAND   Yes? Go on.

MAIRE   Earth.

YOLLAND   'Earth'?

MAIRE   Earth. Earth.
[YOLLAND *still does not understand.*
MAIRE *stoops down and picks up a handful of clay. Holding it out.*]
Earth.

YOLLAND   Earth! Of course—earth! Earth. Earth. Good Lord, Maire, your
English is perfect!

MAIRE [*Eagerly.*]   What—what?

YOLLAND   Perfect English. English perfect.

MAIRE   George—

YOLLAND   That's beautiful—oh that's really beautiful.

MAIRE   George—

YOLLAND   Say it again—say it again—

MAIRE   Shhh. [*She holds her hand up for silence—she is trying to remember
her one line of English. Now she remembers it and she delivers the line as if*

---

9. You are a centurion in the British Army [Latin;
Friel's note]. "Centurion": an officer in command
of a hundred soldiers.

1. And you are in the camp in the field [Latin;
Friel's note].

English were her language—easily, fluidly, conversationally.] George, in Norfolk we besport ourselves around the maypoll.

YOLLAND   Good God, do you? That's where my mother comes from—Norfolk.
Norwich actually. Not exactly Norwich town but a small village called Little
Walsingham close beside it. But in our own village of Winfarthing we have
a maypole too and every year on the first of May— [*He stops abruptly, only
now realising. He stares at her. She in turn misunderstands his excitement.*]

MAIRE   [*To herself.*]   Mother of God, my Aunt Mary wouldn't have taught me
something dirty, would she?

[*Pause.*

YOLLAND *extends his hand to* MAIRE. *She turns away from him and
moves slowly across the stage.*]

YOLLAND   Maire.

[*She still moves away.*]

YOLLAND   Maire Chatach.

[*She still moves away.*]

YOLLAND   Bun na hAbhann?[2] [*He says the name softly, almost privately, very
tentatively, as if he were searching for a sound she might respond to. He tries
again.*] Druim Dubh?[3]

[MAIRE *stops. She is listening.* YOLLAND *is encouraged.*]

Poll na gCaorach. Lis Maol.[4]

[MAIRE *turns towards him.*]

Lis na nGall.[5]

MAIRE   Lis na nGradh.[6]

[*They are now facing each other and begin moving—almost imperceptibly—towards one another.*]

MAIRE   Carraig an Phoill.[7]

YOLLAND   Carraig na Ri. Loch na nEan.[8]

MAIRE   Loch an Iubhair. Machaire Buidhe.[9]

YOLLAND   Machaire Mor. Cnoc na Mona.[1]

MAIRE   Cnoc na nGabhar.[2]

YOLLAND   Mullach.[3]

MAIRE   Port.[4]

YOLLAND   Tor.[5]

MAIRE   Lag.[6] [*She holds out her hands to* YOLLAND. *He takes them. Each now
speaks almost to himself/herself.*]

YOLLAND   I wish to God you could understand me.

MAIRE   Soft hands; a gentleman's hands.

YOLLAND   Because if you could understand me I could tell you how I spend
my days either thinking of you or gazing up at your house in the hope that
you'll appear even for a second.

MAIRE   Every evening you walk by yourself along the Tra Bhan and every
morning you wash yourself in front of your tent.

YOLLAND   I would tell you how beautiful you are, curly-headed Maire. I would
so like to tell you how beautiful you are.

---

2. Mouth of the River?
3. Black Ridge?
4. Pit of the Sheep. Bald Fairy Fort.
5. Fairy Fort of the Foreigner.
6. Fairy Fort of Love.
7. Rock of the Hole.
8. Rock of the King. Lake of the Bird.

9. Lake of the Yew Tree. The Great Plain.
1. The Big Plain. Hill of the Nobles.
2. Hill of the Goat.
3. Summit.
4. Port (i.e., same meaning in Gaelic and English).
5. Bush or heavy.
6. Weak.

MAIRE   Your arms are long and thin and the skin on your shoulders is very white.

YOLLAND   I would tell you . . .

MAIRE   Don't stop—I know what you're saying.

YOLLAND   I would tell you how I want to be here—to live here—always—with you—always, always.

MAIRE   'Always'? What is that word—'always'?

YOLLAND   Yes-yes; always.

MAIRE   You're trembling.

YOLLAND   Yes, I'm trembling because of you.

MAIRE   I'm trembling, too. [*She holds his face in her hand.*]

YOLLAND   I've made up my mind . . .

MAIRE   Shhhh.

YOLLAND   I'm not going to leave here . . .

MAIRE   Shhh—listen to me. I want you, too, soldier.

YOLLAND   Don't stop—I know what you're saying.

MAIRE   I want to live with you—anywhere—anywhere at all—always—always.

YOLLAND   'Always'? What is that word—'always'?

MAIRE   Take me away with you, George.
   [*Pause.*
      Suddenly they kiss.
      SARAH *enters. She sees them. She stands shocked, staring at them. Her mouth works. Then almost to herself.*]

SARAH   Manus . . . Manus!
   [SARAH *runs off.*
      Music to crescendo.]

Act Three

The following evening. It is raining.

SARAH *and* OWEN *alone in the schoolroom.* SARAH, *more waiflike than ever, is sitting very still on a stool, an open book across her knee. She is pretending to read but her eyes keep going up to the room upstairs.* OWEN *is working on the floor as before, surrounded by his reference books, map, Name-Book etc. But he has neither concentration nor interest; and like* SARAH *he glances up at the upstairs room.*

After a few seconds MANUS *emerges and descends, carrying a large paper bag which already contains his clothes. His movements are determined and urgent. He moves around the classroom, picking up books, examining each title carefully, and choosing about six of them which he puts into his bag. As he selects these books.*

OWEN   You know that old limekiln[7] beyond Con Connie Tim's pub, the place we call The Murren?—do you know why it's called The Murren?
   [MANUS *does not answer.*]
I've only just discovered: it's a corruption of Saint Muranus. It seems Saint Muranus had a monastery somewhere about there at the beginning of the seventh century. And over the years the name became shortened to The Murren. Very unattractive name, isn't it? I think we should go back to the

---

7. Furnace for making lime out of shells or limestone.

original—Saint Muranus. What do you think? The original's Saint Muranus.
Don't you think we should go back to that?

> [*No response.* OWEN *begins writing the name into the Name-Book.*
> MANUS *is now rooting about among the forgotten implements for a piece
> of rope. He finds a piece. He begins to tie the mouth of the flimsy,
> overloaded bag—and it bursts, the contents spilling out on the floor.*]

MANUS   Bloody, bloody, bloody hell!

> [*His voice breaks in exasperation: he is about to cry.*
> OWEN *leaps to his feet.*]

OWEN   Hold on. I've a bag upstairs.

> [*He runs upstairs.* SARAH *waits until* OWEN *is off. Then.*]

SARAH   Manus . . . Manus, I . . .

> [MANUS *hears* SARAH *but makes no acknowledgement. He gathers up his
> belongings.*
> OWEN *reappears with the bag he had on his arrival.*]

OWEN   Take this one—I'm finished with it anyway. And it's supposed to keep
out the rain.

> [MANUS *transfers his few belongings.* OWEN *drifts back to his task. The
> packing is now complete.*]

MANUS   You'll be here for a while? For a week or two anyhow?

OWEN   Yes.

MANUS   You're not leaving with the army?

OWEN   I haven't made up my mind. Why?

MANUS   Those Inis Meadhon men will be back to see why I haven't turned
up. Tell them—tell them I'll write to them as soon as I can. Tell them I still
want the job but that it might be three or four months before I'm free to go.

OWEN   You're being damned stupid, Manus.

MANUS   Will you do that for me?

OWEN   Clear out now and Lancey'll think you're involved somehow.

MANUS   Will you do that for me?

OWEN   Wait a couple of days even. You know George—he's a bloody romantic—maybe he's gone out to one of the islands and he'll suddenly reappear
tomorrow morning. Or maybe the search party'll find him this evening lying
drunk somewhere in the sandhills. You've seen him drinking that poteen—
doesn't know how to handle it. Had he drink on him last night at the dance?

MANUS   I had a stone in my hand when I went out looking for him—I was
going to fell him. The lame scholar turned violent.

OWEN   Did anybody see you?

MANUS   [*Again close to tears.*]   But when I saw him standing there at the side
of the road—smiling—and her face buried in his shoulder—I couldn't even
go close to them. I just shouted something stupid—something like, 'You're
a bastard, Yolland.' If I'd even said it in English . . . 'cos he kept saying
'Sorry-sorry?' The wrong gesture in the wrong language.

OWEN   And you didn't see him again?

MANUS   'Sorry?'

OWEN   Before you leave tell Lancey that—just to clear yourself.

MANUS   What have I to say to Lancey? You'll give that message to the island-
men?

OWEN   I'm warning you: run away now and you're bound to be . . .

MANUS   [*To* SARAH.]   Will you give that message to the Inis Meadhon men?

SARAH   I will.

[MANUS *picks up an old sack and throws it across his shoulders.*]

OWEN   Have you any idea where you're going?

MANUS   Mayo, maybe. I remember Mother saying she had cousins somewhere away out in the Erris Peninsula.[8] [*He picks up his bag.*] Tell father I took only the Virgil and the Caesar and the Aeschylus[9] because they're mine anyway—I bought them with the money I get for that pet lamb I reared— do you remember that pet lamb? And tell him that Nora Dan never returned the dictionary and that she still owes him two-and-six[1] for last quarter's reading—he always forgets those things.

OWEN   Yes.

MANUS   And his good shirt's ironed and hanging up in the press and his clean socks are in the butter-box under the bed.

OWEN   Alright.

MANUS   And tell him I'll write.

OWEN   If Maire asks where you've gone . . . ?

MANUS   He'll need only half the amount of milk now, won't he? Even less than half—he usually takes his tea black. [*Pause.*] And when he comes in at night—you'll hear him; he makes a lot of noise—I usually come down and give him a hand up. Those stairs are dangerous without a banister. Maybe before you leave you'd get Big Ned Frank to put up some sort of a handrail. [*Pause.*] And if you can bake, he's very fond of soda bread.

OWEN   I can give you money. I'm wealthy. Do you know what they pay me? Two shillings a day for this—this—this—

[MANUS *rejects the offer by holding out his hand.*]

Goodbye, Manus.

[MANUS *and* OWEN *shake hands.*

Then MANUS *picks up his bag briskly and goes towards the door. He stops a few paces beyond* SARAH, *turns, comes back to her. He addresses her as he did in Act One but now without warmth or concern for her.*]

MANUS   What is your name? [*Pause.*] Come on. What is your name?

SARAH   My name is Sarah.

MANUS   Just Sarah? Sarah what? [*Pause.*] Well?

SARAH   Sarah Johnny Sally.

MANUS   And where do you live? Come on.

SARAH   I live in Bun na hAbhann. [*She is now crying quietly.*]

MANUS   Very good, Sarah Johnny Sally. There's nothing to stop you now— nothing in the wide world. [*Pause. He looks down at her.*] It's alright—it's alright—you did no harm—you did no harm at all. [*He stoops over her and kisses the top of her head—as if in absolution. Then briskly to the door and off.*]

OWEN   Good luck, Manus!

SARAH   [*Quietly.*] I'm sorry . . . I'm sorry . . . I'm so sorry, Manus . . .

[OWEN *tries to work but cannot concentrate. He begins folding up the map. As he does.*]

OWEN   Is there class this evening?

[SARAH *nods: yes.*]

I suppose Father knows. Where is he anyhow?

---

8. Northwest corner of County Mayo, south of Donegal.
9. Ancient Greek playwright (525–456 B.C.E.). The surviving works of the Roman general and

statesman Julius Caesar (100–44 B.C.E) are his military commentaries.
1. Two shillings and sixpence—thirty pennies—in the old British currency.

[SARAH *points.*]

Where?

[SARAH *mimes rocking a baby.*]

I don't understand—where?

[SARAH *repeats the mime and wipes away tears.* OWEN *is still puzzled.*]

It doesn't matter. He'll probably turn up.

[BRIDGET *and* DOALTY *enter, sacks over their heads against the rain. They are self-consciously noisier, more ebullient, more garrulous than ever—brimming over with excitement and gossip and brio.*]

DOALTY You're missing the crack,[2] boys! Cripes, you're missing the crack! Fifty more soldiers arrived an hour ago!

BRIDGET And they're spread out in a big line from Sean Neal's over to Lag and they're moving straight across the fields towards Cnoc na nGabhar!

DOALTY Prodding every inch of the ground in front of them with their bayonets and scattering animals and hens in all directions!

BRIDGET And tumbling everything before them—fences, ditches, hay-stacks, turf-stacks!

DOALTY They came to Barney Petey's field of corn—straight through it be God as if it was heather![3]

BRIDGET Not a blade of it left standing!

DOALTY And Barney Petey just out of his bed and running after them in his drawers: 'You hoors[4] you! Get out of my corn, you hoors you!'

BRIDGET First time he ever ran in his life.

DOALTY Too lazy, the wee get,[5] to cut it when the weather was good.

[SARAH *begins putting out the seats.*]

BRIDGET Tell them about Big Hughie.

DOALTY Cripes, if you'd seen your aul fella, Owen.

BRIDGET They were all inside in Anna na mBreag's pub—all the crowd from the wake—

DOALTY And they hear the commotion and they all come out to the street—

BRIDGET Your father in front; the Infant Prodigy footless[6] behind him!

DOALTY And your aul fella, he sees the army stretched across the countryside—

BRIDGET O my God!

DOALTY And Cripes he starts roaring at them!

BRIDGET 'Visigoths! Huns! Vandals!'[7]

DOALTY '*Ignari! Stulti! Rustici!*'[8]

BRIDGET And wee Jimmy Jack jumping up and down and shouting, 'Thermopylae! Thermopylae!'[9]

DOALTY You never saw crack like it in your life, boys. Come away on out with me, Sarah, and you'll see it all.

BRIDGET Big Hughie's fit to take no class. Is Manus about?

OWEN Manus is gone.

BRIDGET Gone where?

OWEN He's left—gone away.

2. Excitement.
3. Plant with small leaves and flowers.
4. Whores.
5. Little bastard or little fool.
6. Barefoot.
7. Nomadic tribes that militarily challenged the (Western) Roman Empire in the 4th and 5th cen-

turies.
8. Ignoramuses! Fools! Peasants! [Latin; Friel's note].
9. A narrow valley on the Aegean Sea, where in 480 B.C.E. a small number of Greek soldiers attempted to stave off a much larger Persian force.

DOALTY Where to?

OWEN He doesn't know. Mayo, maybe.

DOALTY What's on in Mayo?

OWEN [*To* BRIDGET.] Did you see George and Maire Chatach leave the dance last night?

BRIDGET We did. Didn't we, Doalty?

OWEN Did you see Manus following them out?

BRIDGET I didn't see him going out but I saw him coming in by himself later.

OWEN Did George and Maire come back to the dance?

BRIDGET No.

OWEN Did you see them again?

BRIDGET He left her home. We passed them going up the back road—didn't we, Doalty?

OWEN And Manus stayed till the end of the dance?

DOALTY We know nothing. What are you asking us for?

OWEN Because Lancey'll question me when he hears Manus's gone. [*Back to* BRIDGET.] That's the way George went home? By the back road? That's where you saw him?

BRIDGET Leave me alone, Owen. I know nothing about Yolland. If you want to know about Yolland, ask the Donnelly twins.

[*Silence.* DOALTY *moves over to the window.*]

[*To* SARAH.] He's a powerful fiddler, O'Shea, isn't he? He told our Seamus he'll come back for a night at Hallowe'en.

[OWEN *goes to* DOALTY *who looks resolutely out the window.*]

OWEN What's this about the Donnellys? [*Pause.*] Were they about last night?

DOALTY Didn't see them if they were. [*Begins whistling through his teeth.*]

OWEN George is a friend of mine.

DOALTY So.

OWEN I want to know what's happened to him.

DOALTY Couldn't tell you.

OWEN What have the Donnelly twins to do with it? [*Pause.*] Doalty!

DOALTY I know nothing, Owen—nothing at all—I swear to God. All I know is this: on my way to the dance I saw their boat beached at Port. It wasn't there on my way home, after I left Bridget. And that's all I know. As God's my judge.

The half-dozen times I met him I didn't know a word he said to me; but he seemed a right enough sort . . . [*With sudden excessive interest in the scene outside.*] Cripes, they're crawling all over the place! Cripes, there's millions of them! Cripes, they're levelling the whole land!

[OWEN *moves away.*

MAIRE *enters. She is bareheaded and wet from the rain; her hair in disarray. She attempts to appear normal but she is in acute distress, on the verge of being distraught. She is carrying the milk-can.*]

MAIRE Honest to God, I must be going off my head. I'm half-way here and I think to myself, 'Isn't this can very light?' and I look into it and isn't it empty.

OWEN It doesn't matter.

MAIRE How will you manage for tonight?

OWEN We have enough.

MAIRE Are you sure?

OWEN Plenty, thanks.

MAIRE It'll take me no time at all to go back up for some.

OWEN   Honestly, Maire.

MAIRE   Sure it's better you have it than that black calf that's . . . that . . . [*She looks around.*] Have you heard anything?

OWEN   Nothing.

MAIRE   What does Lancey say?

OWEN   I haven't seen him since this morning.

MAIRE   What does he *think*?

OWEN   We really didn't talk. He was here for only a few seconds.

MAIRE   He left me home, Owen. And the last thing he said to me—he tried to speak in Irish—he said, 'I'll see you yesterday'—he meant to say 'I'll see you tomorrow.' And I laughed that much he pretended to get cross and he said 'Maypoll! Maypoll!' because I said that word wrong. And off he went, laughing—laughing, Owen! Do you think he's alright? What do *you* think?

OWEN   I'm sure he'll turn up, Maire.

MAIRE   He comes from a tiny wee place called Winfarthing. [*She suddenly drops on her hands and knees on the floor—where* OWEN *had his map a few minutes ago—and with her finger traces out an outline map.*]

Come here till you see. Look. There's Winfarthing. And there's two other wee villages right beside it; one of them's called Barton Bendish—it's there; and the other's called Saxingham Nethergate—it's about there. And there's Little Walsingham—that's his mother's townland. Aren't they odd names? Sure they make no sense to me at all. And Winfarthing's near a big town called Norwich. And Norwich is in a county called Norfolk. And Norfolk is in the east of England. He drew a map for me on the wet strand and wrote the names on it. I have it all in my head now: Winfarthing—Barton Bendish—Saxingham Nethergate—Little Walsingham—Norwich—Norfolk. Strange sounds, aren't they? But nice sounds; like Jimmy Jack reciting his Homer.

[*She gets to her feet and looks around; she is almost serene now. To* SARAH.] You were looking lovely last night, Sarah. Is that the dress you got from Boston? Green suits you.

[*To* OWEN.] Something very bad's happened to him, Owen. I know. He wouldn't go away without telling me. Where is he, Owen? You're his friend—where is he? [*Again she looks around the room; then sits on a stool.*]

I didn't get a chance to do my geography last night. The master'll be angry with me. [*She rises again.*]

I think I'll go home now. The wee ones have to be washed and put to bed and that black calf has to be fed . . .

My hands are that rough; they're still blistered from the hay. I'm ashamed of them. I hope to God there's no hay to be saved in Brooklyn.

[*She stops at the door.*] Did you hear? Nellie Ruadh's baby died in the middle of the night. I must go up to the wake. It didn't last long, did it?

[MAIRE *leaves. Silence. Then.*]

OWEN   I don't think there'll be any class. Maybe you should . . .

[OWEN *begins picking up his texts.* DOALTY *goes to him.*]

DOALTY   Is he long gone?—Manus.

OWEN   Half an hour.

DOALTY   Stupid bloody fool.

OWEN   I told him that.

DOALTY   Do they know he's gone?

OWEN   Who?

DOALTY   The army.

OWEN   Not yet.

DOALTY   They'll be after him like bloody beagles. Bloody, bloody fool, limping along the coast. They'll overtake him before night for Christ's sake.

[DOALTY *returns to the window.* LANCEY *enters—now the commanding officer.*]

OWEN   Any news? Any word?

[LANCEY *moves into the centre of the room, looking around as he does.*]

LANCEY   I understood there was a class. Where are the others?

OWEN   There was to be a class but my father . . .

LANCEY   This will suffice. I will address them and it will be their responsibility to pass on what I have to say to every family in this section.

[LANCEY *indicates to* OWEN *to translate.* OWEN *hesitates, trying to assess the change in* LANCEY's *manner and attitude.*]

I'm in a hurry, O'Donnell.

OWEN   The captain has an announcement to make.

LANCEY   Lieutenant Yolland is missing. We are searching for him. If we don't find him, or if we receive no information as to where he is to be found, I will pursue the following course of action. [*He indicates to* OWEN *to translate.*]

OWEN   They are searching for George. If they don't find him—

LANCEY   Commencing twenty-four hours from now we will shoot all livestock in Ballybeg.

[OWEN *stares at* LANCEY.]

At once.

OWEN   Beginning this time tomorrow they'll kill every animal in Baile Beag— unless they're told where George is.

LANCEY   If that doesn't bear results, commencing forty-eight hours from now we will embark on a series of evictions and levelling of every abode in the following selected areas—

OWEN   You're not—!

LANCEY   Do your job. Translate.

OWEN   If they still haven't found him in two days' time they'll begin evicting and levelling every house starting with these townlands.

[LANCEY *reads from his list.*]

LANCEY   Swinefort.

OWEN   Lis na Muc.

LANCEY   Burnfoot.

OWEN   Bun na hAbhann.

LANCEY   Dromduff.

OWEN   Druim Dubh.

LANCEY   Whiteplains.

OWEN   Machaire Ban.

LANCEY   Kings Head.

OWEN   Cnoc na Ri.

LANCEY   If by then the lieutenant hasn't been found, we will proceed until a complete clearance is made of this entire section.

OWEN   If Yolland hasn't been got by then, they will ravish the whole parish.

LANCEY   I trust they know exactly what they've got to do.

[*Pointing to* BRIDGET.] I know you. I know where you live.

[*Pointing to* SARAH.] Who are you? Name!

[SARAH's *mouth opens and shuts, opens and shuts. Her face becomes contorted.*]
What's your name?
[*Again* SARAH *tries frantically.*]

OWEN Go on, Sarah. You can tell him.
[*But* SARAH *cannot. And she knows she cannot. She closes her mouth. Her head goes down.*]

OWEN Her name is Sarah Johnny Sally.

LANCEY Where does she live?

OWEN Bun na hAbhann.

LANCEY Where?

OWEN Burnfoot.

LANCEY I want to talk to your brother—is he here?

OWEN Not at the moment.

LANCEY Where is he?

OWEN He's at a wake.

LANCEY What wake?
[DOALTY, *who has been looking out the window all through* LANCEY's *announcements, now speaks—calmly, almost casually.*]

DOALTY Tell him his whole camp's on fire.

LANCEY What's your name? [*To* OWEN.] Who's that lout?

OWEN Doalty Dan Doalty.

LANCEY Where does he live?

OWEN Tulach Alainn.

LANCEY What do we call it?

OWEN Fair Hill. He says your whole camp is on fire.
[LANCEY *rushes to the window and looks out. Then he wheels on* DOALTY.]

LANCEY I'll remember you, Mr Doalty. [*To* OWEN.] You carry a big responsibility in all this. [*He goes off.*]

BRIDGET Mother of God, does he mean it, Owen?

OWEN Yes, he does.

BRIDGET We'll have to hide the beasts somewhere—our Seamus'll know where. Maybe at the back of Lis na nGradh—or in the caves at the far end of the Tra Bhan. Come on, Doalty! Come on! Don't be standing about there!
[DOALTY *does not move.* BRIDGET *runs to the door and stops suddenly. She sniffs the air. Panic.*]
The sweet smell! Smell it! It's the sweet smell! Jesus, it's the potato blight!

DOALTY It's the army tents burning, Bridget.

BRIDGET Is it? Are you sure? Is that what it is? God, I thought we were destroyed altogether. Come on! Come on!
[*She runs off* OWEN *goes to* SARAH *who is preparing to leave.*]

OWEN How are you? Are you alright?
[SARAH *nods: Yes.*]

OWEN Don't worry. It will come back to you again.
[SARAH *shakes her head.*]

OWEN It will. You're upset now. He frightened you. That's all's wrong.
[*Again* SARAH *shakes her head, slowly, emphatically, and smiles at* OWEN. *Then she leaves.*
OWEN *busies himself gathering his belongings.* DOALTY *leaves the window and goes to him.*]

DOALTY   He'll do it, too.

OWEN   Unless Yolland's found.

DOALTY   Hah!

OWEN   Then he'll certainly do it.

DOALTY   When my grandfather was a boy they did the same thing. [*Simply, altogether without irony.*] And after all the trouble you went to, mapping the place and thinking up new names for it.

> [OWEN *busies himself. Pause.*
>
> DOALTY *almost dreamily.*]

I've damned little to defend but he'll not put me out without a fight. And there'll be others who think the same as me.

OWEN   That's a matter for you.

DOALTY   If we'd all stick together. If we knew how to defend ourselves.

OWEN   Against a trained army.

DOALTY   The Donnelly twins know how.

HUGH   If they could be found.

DOALTY   If they could be found. [*He goes to the door.*] Give me a shout after you've finished with Lancey. I might know something then. [*He leaves.*]

> [OWEN *picks up the Name-Book. He looks at it momentarily, then puts it on top of the pile he is carrying. It falls to the floor. He stoops to pick it up—hesitates—leaves it. He goes upstairs.*
>
> *As* OWEN *ascends,* HUGH *and* JIMMY JACK *enter. Both wet and drunk.* JIMMY *is very unsteady. He is trotting behind* HUGH, *trying to break in on* HUGH's *declamation.*
>
> HUGH *is equally drunk but more experienced in drunkenness: there is a portion of his mind which retains its clarity.*]

HUGH   There I was, appropriately dispositioned to proffer my condolences to the bereaved mother . . .

JIMMY   Hugh—

HUGH   . . . and about to enter the *domus lugubris*[1]—Maire Chatach?

JIMMY   The wake house.

HUGH   Indeed—when I experience a plucking at my elbow: Mister George Alexander, Justice of the Peace. 'My tidings are infelicitous,' said he— Bridget? Too slow. Doalty?

JIMMY   *Infelix*—unhappy.

HUGH   Unhappy indeed. 'Master Bartley Timlin has been appointed to the new national school.'

'Timlin? Who is Timlin?'

'A schoolmaster from Cork.[2] And he will be a major asset to the community: he is also a very skilled bacon-curer'!

JIMMY   Hugh—

HUGH   Ha-ha-ha-ha-ha! The Cork bacon-curer! *Barbarus hic ego sum quia non intelligor ulli*—James?

JIMMY   Ovid.

HUGH   *Procede.*

JIMMY   'I am a barbarian in this place because I am not understood by anyone.'[3]

---

1. House of mourning [Latin; Friel's note].
2. Influential city on Ireland's south coast.
3. From Ovid's *Tristia,* written after the Roman

poet was exiled to live by the Black Sea in what is Romania today.

HUGH   Indeed—[*Shouts.*] Manus! Tea!

    I will compose a satire on Master Bartley Timlin, schoolmaster and bacon-curer. But it will be too easy, won't it?

    [*Shouts.*] Strong tea! Black!

    [*The only way* JIMMY *can get* HUGH's *attention is by standing in front of him and holding his arms.*]

JIMMY   Will you listen to me, Hugh!

HUGH   James.

    [*Shouts.*] And a slice of soda bread.

JIMMY   I'm going to get married.

HUGH   Well!

JIMMY   At Christmas.

HUGH   Splendid.

JIMMY   To Athene.

HUGH   Who?

JIMMY   Pallas Athene.

HUGH   *Glaukopis Athene?*

JIMMY   Flashing-eyed, Hugh, flashing-eyed! [*He attempts the gesture he has made before: standing to attention, the momentary spasm, the salute, the face raised in pained ecstasy—but the body does not respond efficiently this time. The gesture is grotesque.*]

HUGH   The lady has assented?

JIMMY   She asked *me*—I assented.

HUGH   Ah. When was this?

JIMMY   Last night.

HUGH   What does her mother say?

JIMMY   Metis from Hellespont?[4] Decent people—good stock.

HUGH   And her father?

JIMMY   I'm meeting Zeus tomorrow. Hugh, will you be my best man?

HUGH   Honoured, James; profoundly honoured.

JIMMY   You know what I'm looking for, Hugh, don't you? I mean to say—you know—I—I—I joke like the rest of them—you know?—[*Again he attempts the pathetic routine but abandons it instantly.*] You know yourself, Hugh—don't you?—You know all that. But what I'm really looking for, Hugh—what I really want—companionship, Hugh—at my time of life, companionship, company, someone to talk to. Away up in Beann na Gaoithe—you've no idea how lonely it is. Companionship—correct, Hugh? Correct?

HUGH   Correct.

JIMMY   And I always liked her, Hugh. Correct?

HUGH   Correct, James.

JIMMY   Someone to talk to.

HUGH   Indeed.

JIMMY   That's all, Hugh. The whole story. You know it all now, Hugh. You know it all.

    [*As* JIMMY *says those last lines he is crying, shaking his head, trying to keep his balance, and holding a finger up to his lips in absurd gestures of secrecy and intimacy. Now he staggers away, tries to sit on a stool,*

---

4. Renowned for her wisdom, Metis was impregnated by and then swallowed by Zeus, whose head began to ache until Athena sprang from his head.

misses it, slides to the floor, his feet in front of him, his back against the broken cart. Almost at once he is asleep.

     HUGH *watches all of this. Then he produces his flask and is about to pour a drink when he sees the Name-Book on the floor. He picks it up and leafs through it, pronouncing the strange names as he does. Just as he begins,* OWEN *emerges and descends with two bowls of tea.*]

HUGH   Ballybeg. Burnfoot. Kings Head. Whiteplains. Fair Hill. Dunboy. Green Bank.

     [OWEN *snatches the book from* HUGH.]

OWEN   I'll take that. [*In apology.*] It's only a catalogue of names.

HUGH   I know what it is.

OWEN   A mistake—my mistake—nothing to do with us. I hope that's strong enough. [*Tea.*]

     [*He throws the book on the table and crosses over to* JIMMY.]

Jimmy. Wake up, Jimmy. Wake up, man.

JIMMY   What—what-what?

OWEN   Here. Drink this. Then go on away home. There may be trouble. Do you hear me, Jimmy? There may be trouble.

HUGH   [*Indicating Name-Book.*]   We must learn those new names.

OWEN [*Searching around.*]   Did you see a sack lying about?

HUGH   We must learn where we live. We must learn to make them our own. We must make them our new home.

     [OWEN *finds a sack and throws it across his shoulders.*]

OWEN   I know where I live.

HUGH   James thinks he knows, too. I look at James and three thoughts occur to me: A—that it is not the literal past, the 'facts' of history, that shape us, but images of the past embodied in language. James has ceased to make that discrimination.

OWEN   Don't lecture me, Father.

HUGH   B—we must never cease renewing those images; because once we do, we fossilise. Is there no soda bread?

OWEN   And C, Father—one single, unalterable 'fact': if Yolland is not found, we are all going to be evicted. Lancey has issued the order.

HUGH   Ah. *Edictum imperatoris.*[5]

OWEN   You should change out of those wet clothes. I've got to go. I've got to see Doalty Dan Doalty.

HUGH   What about?

OWEN   I'll be back soon.

     [*As* OWEN *exits.*]

HUGH   Take care, Owen. To remember everything is a form of madness. [*He looks around the room, carefully, as if he were about to leave it forever. Then he looks at* JIMMY, *asleep again.*]

    The road to Sligo.[6] A spring morning. 1798.[7] Going into battle. Do you remember, James? Two young gallants with pikes across their shoulders and the *Aeneid*[8] in their pockets. Everything seemed to find definition that

---

5. The decree of the commander [Latin; Friel's note].

6. Port town south of County Donegal.

7. That year a force of Catholics and Protestants known as the United Irishmen launched a rebellion throughout Ireland. After the British quashed the uprising, the Irish Parliament was abolished, and two years later the Act of Union incorporated Ireland into the United Kingdom.

8. Virgil's epic, about the Trojan hero Aeneas, who escapes the destruction of Troy and founds Rome.

spring—a congruence, a miraculous matching of hope and past and present and possibility. Striding across the fresh, green land. The rhythms of perception heightened. The whole enterprise of consciousness accelerated. We were gods that morning, James; and I had recently married *my* goddess, Caitlin Dubh Nic Reactainn, may she rest in peace. And to leave her and my infant son in his cradle—that was heroic, too. By God, sir, we were magnificent. We marched as far as—where was it?—Glenties![9] All of twenty-three miles in one day. And it was there, in Phelan's pub, that we got homesick for Athens, just like Ulysses. The *desiderium nostrorum*—the need for our own. Our *pietas*,[1] James, was for older, quieter things. And that was the longest twenty-three miles back I ever made. [*Toasts* JIMMY.] My friend, confusion is not an ignoble condition.

[MAIRE *enters.*]

MAIRE   I'm back again. I set out for somewhere but I couldn't remember where. So I came back here.

HUGH   Yes, I will teach you English, Maire Chatach.

MAIRE   Will you, Master? I must learn it. I need to learn it.

HUGH   Indeed you may well be my only pupil. [*He goes towards the steps and begins to ascend.*]

MAIRE   When can we start?

HUGH   Not today. Tomorrow, perhaps. After the funeral. We'll begin tomorrow. [*Ascending.*] But don't expect too much. I will provide you with the available words and the available grammar. But will that help you to interpret between privacies? I have no idea. But it's all we have. I have no idea at all. [*He is now at the top.*]

MAIRE   Master, what does the English word 'always' mean?

HUGH   *Semper—per omnia saecula.*[2] The Greeks called it *'aei'*. It's not a word I'd start with. It's a silly word, girl. [*He sits.*]

[JIMMY *is awake. He gets to his feet.*

MAIRE *sees the Name-Book, picks it up, and sits with it on her knee.*]

MAIRE   When he comes back, this is where he'll come to. He told me this is where he was happiest.

[JIMMY *sits beside* MAIRE.]

JIMMY   Do you know the Greek word *endogamein*? It means to marry within the tribe. And the word *exogamein* means to marry outside the tribe. And you don't cross those borders casually—both sides get very angry. Now, the problem is this: Is Athene sufficiently mortal or am I sufficiently godlike for the marriage to be acceptable to her people and to my people? You think about that.

HUGH   *Urbs antiqua fuit*—there was an ancient city which,'tis said, Juno[3] loved above all the lands. And it was the goddess's aim and cherished hope that here should be the capital of all nations—should the fates perchance allow that. Yet in truth she discovered that a race was springing from Trojan

---

9. A region of intersecting glens on the coast of central Donegal.
1. Piety [Friel's note]. The Latin term for the trait associated especially with Virgil's dutiful hero Aeneas. The story of Ulysses', or Odysseus', ten-year wandering on the way home is told in Homer's *Odyssey*.
2. Always—for all time. *Aei*, always [Friel's note].
3. In Roman mythology queen of the gods, who loved ancient Carthage (now in Tunisia) above all. Hugh's recitation is from the beginning of the nar-

rative of Virgil's *Aeneid*. Here Juno angrily foresees the destruction of Carthage by Aeneas's Roman descendants ("a race was springing from Trojan blood") and the extension of Roman rule over this North African colony (Rome and Carthage fought the Punic Wars in the 3rd and 2nd centuries B.C.E.). While vaunting Rome's imperial mission to civilize the world, Virgil's epic also includes a tragic love story: Aeneas and the Carthaginian queen Dido fall in love, but she commits suicide after he abandons her for his imperial duty.

blood to overthrow some day these Tyrian[4] towers—a people *late regem belloque superbum*—kings of broad realms and proud in war who would come forth for Lybia's[5] downfall—such was—such was the course—such was the course ordained—ordained by fate . . . What the hell's wrong with me? Sure I know it backwards. I'll begin again. *Urbs antiqua fuit*—there was an ancient city which,'tis said, Juno loved above all the lands.

[*Begin to bring down the lights.*]

And it was the goddess's aim and cherished hope that here should be the capital of all nations—should the fates perchance allow that. Yet in truth she discovered that a race was springing from Trojan blood to overthrow some day these Tyrian towers—a people kings of broad realms and proud in war who would come forth for Lybia's downfall . . .

[*Black.*]

4. I.e., Carthaginian. Carthage had been founded by Phoenicians from the city of Tyre (now in Leb- anon).
5. Carthage's.

KAMAU BRATHWAITE
b. 1930

As a poet and historian Kamau Brathwaite has been the most prominent West Indian spokesman for "the literature of reconnection": he has sought to recover and revalue the African inheritance in the Caribbean—a religious, linguistic, and cultural inheritance seen as embarrassing or taboo through most of the twentieth century. In *History of the Voice*, a lecture first delivered in 1979, Brathwaite argues that Afro-Caribbeans, their ancestors uprooted by slavery, were further cut off from their specific history and their local environment by Standard English models of language and literature. He proposes "nation language," a creolized English saturated with African words, rhythms, even grammar, as a crucial tool for writers to recuperate Afro-Caribbean history and experience. His own poetry draws on West Indian syncopations, orality, and musical traditions, but also adapts imported models, such as the modernist dislocations of persona, rhythm, and tone in T. S. Eliot's verse.

He was born Lawson Edward Brathwaite in Bridgetown, Barbados, at the eastern edge of the West Indies. His undergraduate studies in history were at Cambridge University; his graduate studies, at the University of Sussex. He worked as an education officer for the Ministry of Education in Ghana (1955–62) and taught history at the University of the West Indies, before taking a position in comparative literature at New York University in 1991. His many books of poetry include a work of epic scope and scale, *The Arrivants: A New World Trilogy* (1973), which gathers *Rights of Passage* (1967), *Masks* (1968), and *Islands* (1969).

[Nation Language][1]

What I am going to talk about this morning is language from the Caribbean, the process of using English in a different way from the "norm". English in a new sense as I prefer to call it. English in an ancient sense. English

1. First printed separately in 1984, Brathwaite's lecture *History of the Voice* was slightly modified and incorporated in his essay collection *Roots* (1986, 1993), from which this selection is excerpted.

in a very traditional sense. And sometimes not English at all, but *language*.

I start my thoughts, taking up from the discussion that developed after Dennis Brutus's[2] very excellent presentation. Without logic, and through instinct, the people who spoke with Dennis from the floor yesterday brought up the question of language.* * * In his case, it was English, and English as spoken by Africans, and the native languages as spoken by Africans.

We in the Caribbean have a similar kind of plurality: we have English, which is the imposed language on much of the archipelago. English is an imperial language, as are French, Dutch, and Spanish. We have what we call creole English, which is a mixture of English and an adaptation that English took in the new environment of the Caribbean when it became mixed with the other imported languages. We have also what is called *nation language*, which is the kind of English spoken by the people who were brought to the Caribbean, not the official English now, but the language of slaves and labourers, the servants who were brought in by the conquistadors. Finally, we have the remnants of ancestral languages still persisting in the Caribbean. There is Amerindian, which is active in certain parts of Central America but not in the Caribbean because the Amerindians are a destroyed people, and their languages were practically destroyed. We have Hindi, spoken by some of the more traditional East Indians who live in the Caribbean, and there are also varieties of Chinese. And, miraculously, there are survivals of African languages still persisting in the Caribbean. So we have that spectrum—that prism—of languages similar to the kind of structure that Dennis described for South Africa. Now, I have to give you some kind of background to the development of these languages, the historical development of this plurality, because I can't take it for granted that you know and understand the history of the Caribbean.

The Caribbean is a set of islands stretching out from Florida in a mighty curve. You must know of the Caribbean at least from television, at least now with hurricane David (—) coming right into it. The islands stretch out on an arc of some two thousand miles from Florida through the Atlantic to the South American coast, and they were originally inhabited by Amerindian people, Taino, Siboney, Carib, Arawak. In 1492, Columbus "discovered" (as it is said) the Caribbean, and with that discovery came the intrusion of European culture and peoples and a fragmentation of the original Amerindian culture. We had Europe "nationalizing" itself into Spanish, French, English and Dutch so that people had to start speaking (and *thinking*) in four metropolitan languages rather than possibly a single native language. Then, with the destruction of the Amerindians, which took place within 30 years of Columbus' discovery (one million dead a year), it was necessary for the Europeans to import new labour bodies into the Caribbean. And the most convenient form of labour was the labour on the very edge of the trade winds—the labour on the edge of the *slave* trade winds, the labour on the edge of the hurricane, the labour on the edge of West Africa—. And so the peoples of Ashanti,[3] Congo, Nigeria, from all that mighty coast of western Africa were imported into the Caribbean. And we had the arrival in that area of a new language structure. It consisted of many languages, but basically they had a common semantic and stylistic form. What these languages had to do, however, was to submerge themselves, because officially the conquering peoples—the Spaniards, the English, the French, and the Dutch—did not wish to hear people speaking Ashanti or any

2. South African poet (b. 1924).   3. Region in present-day central Ghana.

of the Congolese languages. So there was a submergence of this imported language. Its status became one of inferiority. Similarly, its speakers were slaves. They were conceived of as inferiors—nonhuman, in fact—. But this very submergence served an interesting intercultural purpose, because although people continued to speak English as it was spoken in Elizabethan times and on through the Romantic and Victorian ages, that English was, nonetheless, still being influenced by the underground language, the submerged language that the slaves had brought. And that underground language was itself constantly transforming itself into new forms. It was moving from a purely African form to a form that was African, but which was adapting to the new environment and to the cultural imperatives of the European languages. And it was influencing the way in which the French, Dutch, and Spanish spoke their own languages. So there was a very complex process taking place which is now beginning to surface in our literature.

In the Caribbean, as in South Africa (and in any area of cultural imperialism for that matter), the educational system did not recognize the presence of these various languages. What our educational system did was to recognize and maintain the language of the conquistador—the language of the planter, the language of the official, the language of the Anglican preacher—. It insisted that not only would English be spoken in the anglophone Caribbean, but that the educational system would carry the contours of an English heritage. Hence, as Dennis said, Shakespeare, George Eliot, Jane Austen—British literature and literary forms, the models that were intimate to Great Britain, that had very little to do, really, with the environment and the reality of the Caribbean—were dominant in the Caribbean educational system. People were forced to learn things that had no relevance to themselves. Paradoxically, in the Caribbean (as in many other "cultural disaster" areas), the people educated in this system came to know more, even today, about English kings and queens than they do about our own national heroes, our own slave rebels—the people who helped to build and to destroy our society—. We are more excited by English literary models, by the concept of, say, Sherwood Forest and Robin Hood, than we are by Nanny of the Maroons,[4] a name some of us didn't even know until a few years ago. And in terms of what we write, our perceptual models, we are more conscious (in terms of sensibility) of the falling of snow for instance—the models are all there for the falling of the snow—than of the force of the hurricanes that take place every year. In other words, we haven't got the syllables, the syllabic intelligence, to describe the hurricane, which is our own experience; whereas we can describe the imported alien experience of the snowfall. It is that kind of situation that we are in.

Now the creole adaptation to all this is the child who, instead of writing in an essay "The snow was falling on the fields of Shropshire"[5] (which is what our children literally were writing until a few years ago, below drawings they made of white snow fields and the corn-haired people who inhabited such a landscape), wrote "The snow was falling on the cane fields." The child had not yet reached the obvious statement that it wasn't snow at all, but rain that

4. The Maroons were Africans and escaped slaves who, after running away or participating in successful rebellions, set up autonomous societies throughout plantation America in marginal and certainly inaccessible areas outside European influence. . . . Nanny of the Maroons, an ex-

Ashanti (?) Queen Mother, is regarded as one of the greatest of the Jamaican freedom fighters [Brathwaite's note].
5. Region of western England on the Welsh border, written about by the English poet A. E. Housman (1859–1936).

was probably falling on the cane fields. She was trying to have both cultures at the same time. But that is creolization.

What is even more important, as we develop this business of emergent language in the Caribbean, is the actual rhythm and the syllables, the very body work, in a way, of the language. What English has given us as a model for poetry, and to a lesser extent, prose (but poetry is the basic tool here), is the pentameter: "The curfew tolls the knell of parting day."[6] There have, of course, been attempts to break it. And there were other dominant forms like, for example, *Beowulf* (c. 750), *The Seafarer*,[7] and what Langland (1322?–1400) had produced:

> For trewthe telleth that love. is triacle of hevene;
> May no synne be on him sene. that useth that spise,
> And alle his werkes he wrougte. with love as him liste.

Or, from *Piers the Plowman* (which does not make it into *Palgrave's Golden Treasury*,[8] but which we all had to "do" at school) the haunting prologue:

> In a somer seson. whan soft was the sonne
> I shope me into shroudes. as I a shepe were

Which has recently inspired our own Derek Walcott to his first major nation language effort:

> In idle August, while the sea soft,
> and leaves of brown islands stick to the rim
> of this Caribbean, I blow out the light
> by the dreamless face of Maria Concepcion
> to ship as a seaman on the schooner Flight.[9]

But by the time we reach Chaucer (1345–1400), the pentameter prevails. Over in the New World, the Americans—Walt Whitman—tried to bridge or to break the pentameter through a cosmic movement, a large movement of sound. Cummings tried to fragment it. And Marianne Moore attacked it with syllabics.[1] But basically the pentameter remained, and it carries with it a certain kind of experience, which is not the experience of a hurricane. The hurricane does not roar in pentameter. And that's the problem: how do you get a rhythm that approximates the natural experience, the environmental experience. We have been trying to break out of the entire pentametric model in the Caribbean and to move into a system that more closely and intimately approaches our own experience. So that is what we are talking about now.

It is nation language in the Caribbean that, in fact, largely ignores the pentameter. Nation language is the language that is influenced very strongly by the African model, the African aspect of our New World/Caribbean heritage. English it may be in terms of its lexicon, but it is not English in terms of its syntax. And English it certainly is not in terms of its rhythm and timbre, its own sound explosion. In its contours, it is not English, even though the words, as you hear them, would be English to a greater or lesser degree. And this brings us back to the question that some of you raised yesterday: can English be a rev-

---

6. The opening line of "Elegy Written in a Country Churchyard," by the English poet Thomas Gray (1716–1771).
7. Poem in Old English.
8. Collection of songs and lyric poems published in London. *Piers the Plowman*: Middle English poem believed to have been written by William

Langland (ca. 1330–1387).
9. Beginning of "The Schooner *Flight*," by the Saint Lucian poet Derek Walcott (b. 1930).
1. Verses based on the number of syllables, not accents, in a line. E. E. Cummings (1894–1962), American poet. Marianne Moore (1887–1972), American poet.

olutionary language? And the lovely answer that came back was: it is not English that is the agent. It is not language, but people, who make revolutions.

I think, however, that language does really have a role to play here, certainly in the Caribbean. But it is an English that is not the standard, imported, educated English, but that of the submerged, surrealist experience and sensibility, which has always been there and which is now increasingly coming to the surface and influencing the perception of contemporary Caribbean people. It is what I call, as I say, *nation language.* I use the term in contrast to *dialect.* The word dialect has been bandied about for a long time, and it carries very pejorative overtones. Dialect is thought of as "bad" English. Dialect is "inferior" English. Dialect is the language when you want to make fun of someone. Caricature speaks in dialect. Dialect has a long history coming from the plantation where people's dignity was distorted through their languages and the descriptions that the dialect gave to them. Nation language, on the other hand, is the submerged area of that dialect that is much more closely allied to the African aspect of experience in the Caribbean. It may be in English, but often it is in an English which is like a howl, or a shout, or a machine-gun, or the wind, or a wave. It is also like the blues. And sometimes it is English and African at the same time.* * *

           *   *   *

The mainstream poets who were moving from standard English to nation language were influenced basically, I think (again the models are important), by T. S. Eliot. What T. S. Eliot did for Caribbean poetry and Caribbean literature was to introduce the notion of the speaking voice, the conversational tone.[2] That is what really attracted us to Eliot. And you can see how the Caribbean poets introduced here have been influenced by him, although they eventually went on to create their own environmental expression.

           *   *   *

1979–81   1984, 1986

Calypso[1]

1

The stone had skidded arc'd and bloomed into islands:
Cuba and San Domingo
Jamaica and Puerto Rico
Grenada Guadeloupe Bonaire[2]

5   curved stone hissed into reef
       wave teeth fanged into clay

---

2. For those of us who really made the breakthrough, it was Eliot's actual voice—or rather his recorded voice, property of the British Council (Barbados)—reading "Preludes", "The Love Song of J. Alfred Prufrock", *The Waste Land,* and later the *Four Quartets*—not the texts—which turned us on. In that dry deadpan delivery, the "riddims" of St. Louis (though we did not know the source then) were stark and clear for those of us who at the same time were listening to the dislocations of Bird, Dizzy, and Klook. And it is interesting that, on the whole, the establishment could not stand Eliot's voice—and far less jazz [Brathwaite's note].

Bird: American jazz musician Charlie "Bird" Parker (1920–1955). Dizzy: American jazz trumpeter Dizzy Gillespie (1917–1993). Klook: American jazz drummer Kenny Clarke (1914–1985).
1. Type of folk song originating in Trinidad, often involving commentary on current events and improvised wordplay with syncopated rhythms. This poem is from *Rights of Passage,* the first of three books collected as *The Arrivants.*
2. Caribbean Islands. The first two stanzas suggest a creation myth in which the islands are formed in a rock-skipping game called ducks and drakes.

white splash flashed into spray
Bathsheba Montego Bay[3]

bloom of the arcing summers . . .

2

10 The islands roared into green plantations
ruled by silver sugar cane
sweat and profit
cutlass profit
islands ruled by sugar cane

15 And of course it was a wonderful time
a profitable hospitable well-worth-your-time
when captains carried receipts for rices
letters spices wigs
opera glasses swaggering asses
20 debtors vices pigs

O it was a wonderful time
an elegant benevolent redolent time—
and young Mrs. P.'s quick irrelevant crime
at four o'clock in the morning . . .

3

25 But what of black Sam
with the big splayed toes
and the shoe black shiny skin?

He carries bucketfulls of water
'cause his Ma's just had another daughter.

30 And what of John with the European name
who went to school and dreamt of fame
his boss one day called him a fool
and the boss hadn't even been to school . . .

4

Steel drum steel drum
35 hit the hot calypso dancing
hot rum hot rum
who goin' stop this bacchanalling?[4]

For we glance the banjo
dance the limbo
40 grow our crops by maljo[5]

---

3. Jamaican city and tourist resort. "Bathsheba":
seaside resort in Barbados.
4. From *Bacchanalia*: festival of Bacchus, the
Roman god of wine, celebrated with song, dancing,
and revelry.
5. Evil eye (Trinidadian dialect; from the French
mal yeux).

have loose morals
gather corals
father our neighbour's quarrels

perhaps when they come
45   with their cameras and straw
hats: sacred pink tourists from the frozen Nawth

we should get down to those
white beaches
where if we don't wear breeches

50   it becomes an island dance
Some people doin' well
while others are catchin' hell

o the boss gave our Johnny the sack
though we beg him please
55   please to take 'im back

so the boy now nigratin' overseas . . .

1967

WOLE SOYINKA
b. 1934

Wole Soyinka was born in Abeokuta, near Ibadan, in western Nigeria, and educated
at Government College and University College, in Ibadan. In 1954 he began his
studies at the University of Leeds. After six years in England he returned to Nigeria,
where he founded a national theater in 1960 and, at the cost of repeated imprisonment, intervened in tumultuous political struggles. He has taught at universities in
Ibadan, Lagos, and Ife, as well as at North American universities. In 1986 he became
the first black African writer to receive the Nobel Prize in Literature, recognized for
plays, such as *Death and the King's Horseman* (1975), that inventively hybridize
Yoruba oral traditions with European literary paradigms, fuse African rhetoric, myth,
and ritual with the verbal extravagance of Elizabethan and Jacobean theater. He has
also written poems, including "Telephone Conversation," a mini verse drama of sorts
in which two characters, a racist English landlady and an African trying to rent an
apartment, are wittily pitted against one another.

Telephone Conversation

The price seemed reasonable, location
Indifferent. The landlady swore she lived
Off premises. Nothing remained
But self-confession. 'Madam', I warned,
5   'I hate a wasted journey—I am African.'

Silence. Silenced transmission of
Pressurised good-breeding. Voice, when it came,
Lip-stick coated, long gold-rolled
Cigarette-holder pipped. Caught I was, foully.

10 'HOW DARK?' . . . I had not misheard . . . 'ARE YOU LIGHT
'OR VERY DARK?' Button B. Button A.[1] Stench
Of rancid breath of public hide-and-speak.
Red booth. Red pillar-box.° Red double-tiered   *mailbox*
Omnibus° squelching tar. It *was* real! Shamed   *double-decker bus*
15 By ill-mannered silence, surrender
Pushed dumbfoundment to beg simplification.
Considerate she was, varying the emphasis—

'ARE YOU DARK? OR VERY LIGHT?' Revelation came.
'You mean—like plain or milk chocolate?'
20 Her assent was clinical, crushing in its light
Impersonality. Rapidly, wave-length adjusted,
I chose. 'West African sepia'°—and as afterthought,   *reddish brown*
'Down in my passport.' Silence for spectroscopic[2]
Flight of fancy, till truthfulness clanged her accent
25 Hard on the mouthpiece. 'WHAT'S THAT?' conceding
'DON'T KNOW WHAT THAT IS.' 'Like brunette.'

'THAT'S DARK, ISN'T IT?' 'Not altogether.
'Facially, I am brunette, but madam, you should see
'The rest of me. Palm of my hand, soles of my feet
30 'Are a peroxide blonde. Friction, caused—
'Foolishly madam—by sitting down, has turned
'My bottom raven black—One moment madam'—sensing
Her receiver rearing on the thunderclap
About my ears—'Madam', I pleaded, 'Wouldn't you rather
35 'See for yourself?'

1960, 1962

---

1. Buttons on old British telephones.   2. Related to study of the spectrum.

TONY HARRISON
b. 1937

Tony Harrison was born in Leeds, where his father was a baker, and where he learned a regional Yorkshire dialect from his mother. At the age of eleven, a scholarship to the prestigious Leeds Grammar School dislocated him from his working-class background: he was told he would have to learn to speak "properly" and forbidden, because of his accent, to read his poetry aloud in the classroom. He later studied classics at Leeds University. While a lecturer in English at Ahmadu Bello University in northern Nigeria, he translated (with fellow poet James Simmons) Aristophanes' *Lysistrata* into the pidgin English of the Hausa people; at the same time he wrote poems in the voices of working-class British expatriates. He has been resident dramatist at the

National Theatre in London, has undertaken commissions for the Metropolitan Opera in New York, and has published verse translations of classical Greek and French plays.

As a poet Harrison has been faithful to his modest origins. His poems give speech to the speechless, to the exploited and oppressed—the two uncles of "Heredity," for example, or a bereaved father unable to articulate his grief, or a terrified convict— exposing their predicaments with passion and indignation. Attributing to working-class speech of the north of England a "richer engagement, a more sensual engagement, with language," he brings that sensual vigor, wit, and immediacy of working-class Yorkshire speech into an exciting amalgam with literary English. Like Caribbean poets, Irish poets, Scottish poets, and others, he combines Standard English with nonstandard oral sounds, with the diction, syntax, and grammar of regional speech, in an unstable, sometimes explosive compound. His sixteen-line near-sonnets from the long work called *The School of Eloquence,* like his important long poem *v.,* richly interweave the literary and the oral, learned allusion and raw directness, Standard English and working-class Yorkshire speech.

Heredity

How you became a poet's a mystery!
Wherever did you get your talent from?

I say: I had two uncles, Joe and Harry—
one was a stammerer, the other dumb.

1978

National Trust[1]

Bottomless pits. There's one in Castleton,[2]
and stout upholders of our law and order
one day thought its depth worth wagering on
and borrowed a convict hush-hush from his warder
5   and winched him down; and back, flayed, grey, mad, dumb.

Not even a good flogging made him holler!

O gentlemen, a better way to plumb
the depths of Britain's dangling a scholar,
say, here at the booming shaft at Towanroath,[3]
10 now National Trust, a place where they got tin,
those gentlemen who silenced the men's oath
and killed the language that they swore it in.

The dumb go down in history and disappear
and not one gentleman's been brought to book:

---

1. A British association to preserve places of natural beauty or buildings of architectural or historical importance.

2. In the Derby coalfields.
3. A tin mine in Cornwall.

15   *Mes den hep tavas a-gollas y dyr*

(Cornish)—

            "the tongueless man gets his land took."

1978

Book Ends

I

Baked the day she suddenly dropped dead
we chew it slowly that last apple pie.

Shocked into sleeplessness you're scared of bed.
We never could talk much, and now don't try.

5   *You're like book ends, the pair of you,* she'd say,
      Hog that grate, say nothing, sit, sleep, stare . . .

The "scholar" me, you, worn out on poor pay,
only our silence made us seem a pair.

Not as good for staring in, blue gas,
10   too regular each bud, each yellow spike.[1]

A night you need my company to pass
and she not here to tell us we're alike!

Your life's all shattered into smithereens.

Back in our silences and sullen looks,
15   for all the Scotch we drink, what's still between's
not the thirty or so years, but books, books, books.

1978

II

The stone's too full. The wording must be terse.
There's scarcely room to carve the FLORENCE on it—

Come on, it's not as if we're wanting verse.
It's not as if we're wanting a whole sonnet!

5   After tumblers of neat *Johnny Walker*
      (I think that both of us were on our third)

you said you'd always been a clumsy talker
and couldn't find another, shorter word
for "beloved" or for "wife" in the inscription,
10   but not too clumsy that you can't still cut:

---

1. Flames from the gas fire common in lower-class English homes.

You're supposed to be the bright boy at description
and you can't tell them what the fuck to put!

I've got to find the right words on my own.

I've got the envelope that he'd been scrawling,
15 mis-spelt, mawkish, stylistically appalling
but I can't squeeze more love into their stone.

1981

Long Distance

I

Your bed's got two wrong sides. Your life's all grouse.°   grumble
I let your phone-call take its dismal course:

Ah can't stand it no more, this empty house!

Carrots choke us wi'out your mam's white sauce!

5 *Them sweets you brought me, you can have 'em back.*
Ah'm diabetic now. Got all the facts.
(The diabetes comes hard on the track
of two coronaries and cataracts.)

Ah've allus liked things sweet! But now ah push
10 *food down mi throat! Ah'd sooner do wi'out.*
And t'only reason now for beer 's to flush
(*so t'dietician said*) *mi kidneys out.*

When I come round, they'll be laid out, the sweets,
Lifesavers, my father's New World treats,
15 still in the big brown bag, and only bought
rushing through JFK[1] as a last thought.

II

Though my mother was already two years dead
Dad kept her slippers warming by the gas,
put hot water bottles her side of the bed
and still went to renew her transport pass.

5 You couldn't just drop in. You had to phone.
He'd put you off an hour to give him time
to clear away her things and look alone
as though his still raw love were such a crime.

He couldn't risk my blight of disbelief
10 though sure that very soon he'd hear her key

1. A New York airport.

scrape in the rusted lock and end his grief.
He *knew* she'd just popped out to get the tea.

I believe life ends with death, and that is all.
You haven't both gone shopping; just the same,
in my new black leather phone book there's your name
and the disconnected number I still call.

15

1981

Turns

I thought it made me look more "working class"
(as if a bit of chequered cloth could bridge that gap!)
I did a turn in it before the glass.
My mother said: *It suits you, your dad's cap.*
(She preferred me to wear suits and part my hair:
You're every bit as good as that lot are!)

5

All the pension queue[1] came out to stare.
Dad was sprawled beside the postbox (still VR),[2]
his cap turned inside up beside his head,
smudged H A H in purple Indian ink
and Brylcreem slicks[3] displayed so folk might think
he wanted charity for dropping dead.

10

He never begged. For nowt![4] Death's reticence
crowns his life's, and *me*, I'm opening my trap
to busk[5] the class that broke him for the pence
that splash like brackish tears into our cap.

15

1981

Marked with D.[1]

When the chilled dough of his flesh went in an oven
not unlike those he fuelled all his life,
I thought of his cataracts ablaze with Heaven
and radiant with the sight of his dead wife,
light streaming from his mouth to shape her name,
"not Florence and not Flo but always Florrie."
I thought how his cold tongue burst into flame
but only literally, which makes me sorry,

5

1. Line of retired people waiting for their pension
(social security) payments.
2. Sidewalk mailbox dating from the reign of
Queen Victoria and carrying the initials of her
name and Latin title: Victoria Regina.
3. Play on Brylcreem Sticks, a hairstyling wax.
4. Nothing (northern dialect).

5. Take around the hat; i.e., solicit money for
street entertainment (from members of the middle
class, in this case).
1. Cf. the anonymous nursery rhyme "Pat-a-cake,
pat-a-cake, baker's man / Bake me a cake as fast as
you can / Pat it and prick it, and mark it with B, /
Put it in the oven for baby and me."

sorry for his sake there's no Heaven to reach.
10 I get it all from Earth my daily bread
but he hungered for release from mortal speech
that kept him down, the tongue that weighed like lead.

The baker's man that no-one will see rise
and England made to feel like some dull oaf
15 is smoke, enough to sting one person's eyes
and ash (not unlike flour) for one small loaf.

1981

NGŨGĨ WA THIONG'O
b. 1938

Ngũgĩ wa Thiong'o was born in Limuru, Kenya, where his father was a peasant farmer. He was educated at the Alliance High School in Kikuyu, Kenya; Makerere University in Kampala, Uganda; and Leeds University in England. In the late 1960s, while teaching at University College, Nairobi, Kenya, he was one of the prime movers behind the abolition of the college's English department, arguing for its replacement by a Department of African Literature and Languages (two departments were formed, one of literature, the other of language). His novels include *Weep Not, Child* (1964), about the 1950s Mau Mau rebellion against British rule in Kenya, *A Grain of Wheat* (1967), about the war's aftermath, and *Petals of Blood* (1977), about the failure of the East African state, and he has written plays and novels in his native Gĩkũyũ, also sharply critical of post-independence Kenya, such as the novel *Matigarima Njiruungi* (1986). In 1982, after his imprisonment in Kenya and the banning of his books there, Ngũgĩ left to teach abroad, most recently at New York University.

At the beginning of *Decolonising the Mind* (1986), Ngũgĩ declares the book "my farewell to English as a vehicle for any of my writings. From now on it is Gĩkũyũ and Kiswahili all the way." Although Ngũgĩ has subsequently modified this position, he lays out starkly the case against English language and literature as tools of colonialism, which continue to have insidious effects long after formal decolonization. As the student of a British colonial education, Ngũgĩ came to feel that, because of the close relation between language and cultural memory, the imposition of English language and literature severs colonized peoples from their cultural experience—an experience best recovered and explored in indigenous languages.

From Decolonising the Mind
From *The Language of African Literature*

III

I was born into a large peasant family: father, four wives and about twenty-eight children. I also belonged, as we all did in those days, to a wider extended family and to the community as a whole.

We spoke Gĩkũyũ[1] as we worked in the fields. We spoke Gĩkũyũ in and

---

1. Bantu language spoken in western Kenya by approximately five million people.

outside the home. I can vividly recall those evenings of story-telling around the fireside. It was mostly the grown-ups telling the children but everybody was interested and involved. We children would re-tell the stories the following day to other children who worked in the fields picking the pyrethrum flowers,[2] tea-leaves or coffee beans of our European and African landlords.

The stories, with mostly animals as the main characters, were all told in Gĩkũyũ. Hare, being small, weak but full of innovative wit and cunning, was our hero. We identified with him as he struggled against the brutes of prey like lion, leopard, hyena. His victories were our victories and we learnt that the apparently weak can outwit the strong. We followed the animals in their struggle against hostile nature—drought, rain, sun, wind—a confrontation often forcing them to search for forms of co-operation. But we were also interested in their struggles amongst themselves, and particularly between the beasts and the victims of prey. These twin struggles, against nature and other animals, reflected real-life struggles in the human world.

Not that we neglected stories with human beings as the main characters. There were two types of characters in such human-centred narratives: the species of truly human beings with qualities of courage, kindness, mercy, hatred of evil, concern for others; and a man-eat-man two-mouthed species with qualities of greed, selfishness, individualism and hatred of what was good for the larger co-operative community. Co-operation as the ultimate good in a community was a constant theme. It could unite human beings with animals against ogres and beasts of prey, as in the story of how dove, after being fed with castor-oil seeds, was sent to fetch a smith working far away from home and whose pregnant wife was being threatened by these man-eating two-mouthed ogres.

There were good and bad story-tellers. A good one could tell the same story over and over again, and it would always be fresh to us, the listeners. He or she could tell a story told by someone else and make it more alive and dramatic. The differences really were in the use of words and images and the inflexion of voices to effect different tones.

We therefore learnt to value words for their meaning and nuances. Language was not a mere string of words. It had a suggestive power well beyond the immediate and lexical meaning. Our appreciation of the suggestive magical power of language was reinforced by the games we played with words through riddles, proverbs, transpositions of syllables, or through nonsensical but musically arranged words. So we learnt the music of our language on top of the content. The language, through images and symbols, gave us a view of the world, but it had a beauty of its own. The home and the field were then our pre-primary school but what is important, for this discussion, is that the language of our evening teach-ins, and the language of our immediate and wider community, and the language of our work in the fields were one.

And then I went to school, a colonial school, and this harmony was broken. The language of my education was no longer the language of my culture. I first went to Kamaandura, missionary run, and then to another called Maan-guuũ run by nationalists grouped around the Gĩkũyũ Independent and Karinga Schools Association. Our language of education was still Gĩkũyũ. The very first time I was ever given an ovation for my writing was over a composition in Gĩkũyũ. So for my first four years there was still harmony between the language of my formal education and that of the Limuru peasant community.

2. Flower used to produce a natural insecticide.

It was after the declaration of a state of emergency over Kenya in 1952[3] that all the schools run by patriotic nationalists were taken over by the colonial regime and were placed under District Education Boards chaired by Englishmen. English became the language of my formal education. In Kenya, English became more than a language: it was *the* language, and all the others had to bow before it in deference.

Thus one of the most humiliating experiences was to be caught speaking Gĩkũyũ in the vicinity of the school. The culprit was given corporal punishment—three to five strokes of the cane on bare buttocks—or was made to carry a metal plate around the neck with inscriptions such as I AM STUPID or I AM A DONKEY. Sometimes the culprits were fined money they could hardly afford. And how did the teachers catch the culprits? A button was initially given to one pupil who was supposed to hand it over to whoever was caught speaking his mother tongue. Whoever had the button at the end of the day would sing who had given it to him and the ensuing process would bring out all the culprits of the day. Thus children were turned into witch-hunters and in the process were being taught the lucrative value of being a traitor to one's immediate community.

The attitude to English was the exact opposite: any achievement in spoken or written English was highly rewarded; prizes, prestige, applause; the ticket to higher realms. English became the measure of intelligence and ability in the arts, the sciences, and all the other branches of learning. English became *the* main determinant of a child's progress up the ladder of formal education.

As you may know, the colonial system of education in addition to its apartheid racial demarcation had the structure of a pyramid: a broad primary base, a narrowing secondary middle, and an even narrower university apex. Selections from primary into secondary were through an examination, in my time called Kenya African Preliminary Examination, in which one had to pass six subjects ranging from Maths to Nature Study and Kiswahili.[4] All the papers were written in English. Nobody could pass the exam who failed the English language paper no matter how brilliantly he had done in the other subjects. I remember one boy in my class of 1954 who had distinctions in all subjects except English, which he had failed. He was made to fail the entire exam. He went on to become a turn boy[5] in a bus company. I who had only passes but a credit in English got a place at the Alliance High School, one of the most elitist institutions for Africans in colonial Kenya. The requirements for a place at the University, Makerere University College,[6] were broadly the same: nobody could go on to wear the undergraduate red gown, no matter how brilliantly they had performed in all the other subjects unless they had a credit—not even a simple pass!—in English. Thus the most coveted place in the pyramid and in the system was only available to the holder of an English language credit card. English was the official vehicle and the magic formula to colonial elitedom.

Literary education was now determined by the dominant language while also reinforcing that dominance. Orature (oral literature) in Kenyan languages stopped. In primary school I now read simplified Dickens and Stevenson alongside Rider Haggard. Jim Hawkins, Oliver Twist, Tom Brown—not Hare,

---

3. The Mau Mau, militant African nationalists, led a revolt in 1952 that resulted in four years of British military operations and the deaths of more than eleven thousand insurgents.
4. Swahili, a Bantu language that is the most widely understood language in Africa.
5. I.e., the person who operates a turnstile.
6. University in Kampala, Uganda, that was connected with the University of London in the 1950s and 1960s.

Leopard and Lion—were now my daily companions in the world of imagination.[7] In secondary school, Scott and G. B. Shaw vied with more Rider Haggard, John Buchan, Alan Paton, Captain W. E. Johns.[8] At Makerere I read English: from Chaucer to T. S. Eliot with a touch of Graham Greene.[9]

Thus language and literature were taking us further and further from ourselves to other selves, from our world to other worlds.

* * *

IV

* * *

* * * Language carries culture, and culture carries, particularly through orature and literature, the entire body of values by which we come to perceive ourselves and our place in the world. How people perceive themselves affects how they look at their culture, at their politics and at the social production of wealth, at their entire relationship to nature and to other beings. Language is thus inseparable from ourselves as a community of human beings with a specific form and character, a specific history, a specific relationship to the world.

V

So what was the colonialist imposition of a foreign language doing to us children?

The real aim of colonialism was to control the people's wealth: what they produced, how they produced it, and how it was distributed; to control, in other words, the entire realm of the language of real life. Colonialism imposed its control of the social production of wealth through military conquest and subsequent political dictatorship. But its most important area of domination was the mental universe of the colonised, the control, through culture, of how people perceived themselves and their relationship to the world. Economic and political control can never be complete or effective without mental control. To control a people's culture is to control their tools of self-definition in relationship to others.

For colonialism this involved two aspects of the same process: the destruction or the deliberate undervaluing of a people's culture, their art, dances, religions, history, geography, education, orature and literature, and the conscious elevation of the language of the coloniser. The domination of a people's language by the languages of the colonising nations was crucial to the domination of the mental universe of the colonised.

* * *

7. The English novelist Charles Dickens (1812–1870) wrote *Oliver Twist*. Jim Hawkins is the hero of *Treasure Island*, by the Scottish fiction writer and essayist Robert Louis Stevenson (1850–1894). The English novelist Rider Haggard (1856–1925) wrote African adventure stories. *Tom Brown's Schooldays* is by the English novelist Thomas Hughes (1822–1896).
8. Sir Walter Scott (1771–1832), Scottish novelist. George Bernard Shaw (1856–1950), Anglo-

Irish dramatist. John Buchan (1875–1940), Scottish author of adventure stories. Alan Paton (1903–1988), South African novelist. William Earl Johns (1893–1968), English author of children's fiction.
9. Geoffrey Chaucer (ca. 1343–1400), English poet. T. S. Eliot (1888–1965), Anglo-American poet. Graham Greene (1904–1991), English novelist. "Read": here "majored in."

IX

I started writing in Gĩkũyũ language in 1977 after seventeen years of involvement in Afro-European literature, in my case Afro-English literature.* * * Wherever I have gone, particularly in Europe, I have been confronted with the question: why are you now writing in Gĩkũyũ? Why do you now write in an African language? In some academic quarters I have been confronted with the rebuke, 'Why have you abandoned us?' It was almost as if, in choosing to write in Gĩkũyũ, I was doing something abnormal. But Gĩkũyũ is my mother tongue! The very fact that what common sense dictates in the literary practice of other cultures is being questioned in an African writer is a measure of how far imperialism has distorted the view of African realities. It has turned reality upside down: the abnormal is viewed as normal and the normal is viewed as abnormal. Africa actually enriches Europe: but Africa is made to believe that it needs Europe to rescue it from poverty. Africa's natural and human resources continue to develop Europe and America: but Africa is made to feel grateful for aid from the same quarters that still sit on the back of the continent. Africa even produces intellectuals who now rationalise this upside-down way of looking at Africa.

I believe that my writing in Gĩkũyũ language, a Kenyan language, an African language, is part and parcel of the anti-imperialist struggles of Kenyan and African peoples. In schools and universities our Kenyan languages—that is the languages of the many nationalities which make up Kenya—were associated with negative qualities of backwardness, underdevelopment, humiliation and punishment. We who went through that school system were meant to graduate with a hatred of the people and the culture and the values of the language of our daily humiliation and punishment. I do not want to see Kenyan children growing up in that imperialist-imposed tradition of contempt for the tools of communication developed by their communities and their history. I want them to transcend colonial alienation.

* * *

We African writers are bound by our calling to do for our languages what Spenser, Milton and Shakespeare did for English; what Pushkin and Tolstoy[1] did for Russian; indeed what all writers in world history have done for their languages by meeting the challenge of creating a literature in them, which process later opens the languages for philosophy, science, technology and all the other areas of human creative endeavours.

1986

1. Aleksandr Pushkin (1799–1837), Russian poet, and Leo Tolstoy (1828–1910), Russian novelist.

SALMAN RUSHDIE

In these excerpts from his essay " 'Commonwealth Literature' Does Not Exist,' " fiction writer Salman Rushdie (b. 1947; see the headnote to him and see his story "The Prophet's Hair," later in this volume) counters the nativist view of English as an imperial yoke that must be thrown off. Recounting the spread of English as a world language and describing its indigenization by the non-English, Rushdie claims it as a vital and expressive South Asian literary language, with its own history and tradition.

[English Is an Indian Literary Language]

I'll begin from an obvious starting place. English is by now the world language. It achieved this status partly as a result of the physical colonization of a quarter of the globe by the British, and it remains ambiguous but central to the affairs of just about all the countries to whom it was given, along with mission schools, trunk roads[1] and the rules of cricket, as a gift of the British colonizers.

But its present-day pre-eminence is not solely—perhaps not even primarily—the result of the British legacy. It is also the effect of the primacy of the United States of America in the affairs of the world. This second impetus towards English could be termed a kind of linguistic neo-colonialism, or just plain pragmatism on the part of many of the world's governments and educationists, according to your point of view.

As for myself, I don't think it is always necessary to take up the anti-colonial—or is it post-colonial?—cudgels against English. What seems to me to be happening is that those peoples who were once colonized by the language are now rapidly remaking it, domesticating it, becoming more and more relaxed about the way they use it—assisted by the English language's enormous flexibility and size, they are carving out large territories for themselves within its frontiers.

To take the case of India, only because it's the one with which I'm most familiar. The debate about the appropriateness of English in post-British India has been raging ever since 1947;[2] but today, I find, it is a debate which has meaning only for the older generation. The children of independent India seem not to think of English as being irredeemably tainted by its colonial provenance. They use it as an Indian language, as one of the tools they have to hand.

(I am simplifying, of course, but the point is broadly true.)

There is also an interesting North–South divide in Indian attitudes to English. In the North, in the so-called 'Hindi belt', where the capital, Delhi, is located, it is possible to think of Hindi as a future national language; but in South India, which is at present suffering from the attempts of central government to *impose* this national language on it, the resentment of Hindi is far greater than of English. After spending quite some time in South India, I've become convinced that English is an essential language in India, not only because of its technical vocabularies and the international communication which it makes possible, but also simply to permit two Indians to talk to each other in a tongue which neither party hates.

Incidentally, in West Bengal, where there is a State-led move against English, the following graffito, a sharp dig at the State's Marxist chief minister, Jyoti Basu, appeared on a wall, in English: it said, 'My son won't learn English; your son won't learn English; but Jyoti Basu will send his son abroad to learn English.'

---

1. Main roads, such as the Grand Trunk Road, the immense highway between Calcutta and Amritsar constructed during the British Raj.
2. When the British relinquished control of India.

One of the points I want to make is that what I've said indicates, I hope, that Indian society and Indian literature have a complex and developing relationship with the English language. * * *

English literature has its Indian branch. By this I mean the literature of the English language. This literature is also Indian literature. There is no incompatibility here. If history creates complexities, let us not try to simplify them.

So: English is an Indian literary language, and by now, thanks to writers like Tagore, Desani, Chaudhuri, Mulk Raj Anand, Raja Rao, Anita Desai[3] and others, it has quite a pedigree. * * *

* * *

In my own case, I have constantly been asked whether I am British, or Indian. The formulation 'Indian-born British writer' has been invented to explain me. But, as I said last night, my new book deals with Pakistan. So what now? 'British-resident Indo-Pakistani writer'? You see the folly of trying to contain writers inside passports.

One of the most absurd aspects of this quest for national authenticity is that—as far as India is concerned, anyway—it is completely fallacious to suppose that there is such a thing as a pure, unalloyed tradition from which to draw. The only people who seriously believe this are religious extremists. The rest of us understand that the very essence of Indian culture is that we possess a mixed tradition, a *mélange* of elements as disparate as ancient Mughal[4] and contemporary Coca-Cola American. To say nothing of Muslim, Buddhist, Jain,[5] Christian, Jewish, British, French, Portuguese, Marxist, Maoist, Trotskyist, Vietnamese, capitalist, and of course Hindu elements. Eclecticism, the ability to take from the world what seems fitting and to leave the rest, has always been a hallmark of the Indian tradition, and today it is at the centre of the best work being done both in the visual arts and in literature. * * *

* * *

* * * As far as Eng. Lit. itself is concerned, I think that if *all* English literatures could be studied together, a shape would emerge which would truly reflect the new shape of the language in the world, and we could see that Eng. Lit. has never been in better shape, because the world language now also possesses a world literature, which is proliferating in every conceivable direction.

The English language ceased to be the sole possession of the English some time ago. * * *

1983

---

3. Rabindranath Tagore (1861–1941), Bengali poet; G. V. Desani (1909–2000), Nirad C. Chaudhuri (1897–1999), Mulk Raj Anand (1905–2004), Raja Rao (b. 1909), Anita Desai (b. 1937):
Indian fiction and nonfiction writers.
4. Dynasty of Muslim emperors who reigned in India, 1526–1858.
5. Jainism is one of India's oldest religions.

JOHN AGARD
b. 1949

John Agard was born and raised in British Guiana (now Guyana) and attended a Roman Catholic high school there, before immigrating to England in 1977. Along with his own collections of poetry, steeped in Caribbean wordplay, rhythms, and idioms that are vivified especially in oral performance, he has also published verse collections, plays, and stories for children. In "Listen Mr Oxford don" he represents his use of West Indian Creole as political and poetic rebellion, while playfully acknowledging, for all his defiance, the complexity of his relation to the Queen's English.

Listen Mr Oxford don

Me not no Oxford don°   *tutor*
me a simple immigrant
from Clapham Common[1]
I didn't graduate
5   I immigrate

But listen Mr Oxford don
I'm a man on de run
and a man on de run
is a dangerous one

10   I ent° have no gun   *don't*
I ent have no knife
but mugging de Queen's English[2]
is the story of my life

I dont need no axe
15   to split/   up yu syntax
I dont need no hammer
to mash/   up yu grammar

I warning you Mr Oxford don
I'm a wanted man
20   and a wanted man
is a dangerous one

Dem accuse me of assault
on de Oxford dictionary/
imagine a concise peaceful man like me/
25   dem want me serve time
for inciting rhyme to riot
but I tekking it quiet
down here in Clapham Common

---

1. In Brixton, a part of London settled by Afro-Caribbean immigrants.

2. English regarded as under the queen's guardianship; hence correct.

I'm not a violent man Mr Oxford don
30   I only armed wit mih human breath
but human breath
is a dangerous weapon

So mek dem send one big word after me
I ent° serving no jail sentence   *am not*
35   I slashing suffix in self-defence
I bashing future wit present tense
and if necessary

I making de Queen's English accessory/to my offence

1985

DORIS LESSING
b. 1919

Born in Persia (now Iran) to British parents, Doris Lessing (née Tayler) lived in southern Rhodesia (now Zimbabwe) from 1924 to 1949, before settling in England. Her five-novel sequence with the general title *Children of Violence* (beginning with *Martha Quest*, 1952) combines psychological autobiography with powerful explorations of the relationship between blacks and whites in southern Africa. Her combination of psychological introspection, political analysis, social documentary, and feminism gives a characteristic tone to her novels and short stories. These elements are effectively combined in her novel *The Golden Notebook* (1962), which explores with unexhibitionist frankness the sexual problems of an independent woman while at the same time probing the political conscience of an ex-communist and the needs and dilemmas of a creative writer. In the early 1970s, influenced by the writings of the renegade psychologist R. D. Laing and by the principles of Sufism (the mystical, ecstatic aspects of Islam), Lessing's realistic investigations of social issues took a different turn. In *Briefing for a Descent into Hell* (1971) and *The Memoirs of a Survivor* (1974), she explores myth and fantasy, restrained within a broadly realist context. In a series of novels with the general title *Canopus in Argos: Archives* (written between 1979 and 1983), she draws on her reading of the Old and New Testaments, the Apocrypha, and the Koran and borrows conventions from science fiction to describe the efforts of a superhuman, extraterrestrial race to guide human history. The novels convey the scope of human suffering in the twentieth century with a rare imaginative power. On completion of this novel sequence, Lessing took the unusual step of publishing two pseudonymous novels (now known jointly as *The Diaries of Jane Somers*, 1983–84), in which she reverted to the realist mode with which she is most widely associated. *The Good Terrorist* (1985) is also written in the style of documentary realism, but *The Fifth Child* (1988) combines elements of realism and fantasy, exploring the effect on a happy family of the birth of a genetically abnormal, nonhuman child. Her work since the early 1990s has included two candid volumes of autobiography, *Under My Skin* (1994) and *Walking in the Shade* (1997), the four short novels that comprise *The Grandmothers* (2004), several other novels, and a series of short stories. Some of these stories—which deal with racial and social dilemmas as well as with loneliness, the claims of politics, the problems of aging (especially for women), the conflict between the generations, and a whole spectrum of problems of alienation and isolation—have a special pungency and force. Lessing is very much a writer of her time, deeply involved with the changing patterns of thought, feeling, and culture during the last fifty years. She has consistently explored and tested the boundaries of realist technique, without resort to formal experimentalism. Published just on the cusp of second-wave feminism, the story reprinted here, "To Room Nineteen," is a psychologically penetrating study of a woman who finds ultimate fulfillment in neither her marriage nor her children and, feeling trapped by traditional gender roles, seeks solitude in—to echo the title of Virginia Woolf's feminist classic about gender, space, and identity—a room of her own.

To Room Nineteen

This is a story, I suppose, about a failure in intelligence: the Rawlings' marriage was grounded in intelligence.

They were older when they married than most of their married friends: in their well-seasoned late twenties. Both had had a number of affairs, sweet rather than bitter; and when they fell in love—for they did fall in love—had known each other for some time. They joked that they had saved each other "for the real thing." That they had waited so long (but not too long) for this real thing was to them a proof of their sensible discrimination. A good many of their friends had married young, and now (they felt) probably regretted lost opportunities; while others, still unmarried, seemed to them arid, self-doubting, and likely to make desperate or romantic marriages.

Not only they, but others, felt they were well matched: their friends' delight was an additional proof of their happiness. They had played the same roles, male and female, in this group or set, if such a wide, loosely connected, constantly changing constellation of people could be called a set. They had both become, by virtue of their moderation, their humour, and their abstinence from painful experience people to whom others came for advice. They could be, and were, relied on. It was one of those cases of a man and a woman linking themselves whom no one else had ever thought of linking, probably because of their similarities. But then everyone exclaimed: Of course! How right! How was it we never thought of it before!

And so they married amid general rejoicing, and because of their foresight and their sense for what was probable, nothing was a surprise to them.

Both had well-paid jobs. Matthew was a subeditor on a large London newspaper, and Susan worked in an advertising firm. He was not the stuff of which editors or publicised journalists are made, but he was much more than "a subeditor," being one of the essential background people who in fact steady, inspire and make possible the people in the limelight. He was content with this position. Susan had a talent for commercial drawing. She was humorous about the advertisements she was responsible for, but she did not feel strongly about them one way or the other.

Both, before they married, had had pleasant flats, but they felt it unwise to base a marriage on either flat, because it might seem like a submission of personality on the part of the one whose flat it was not. They moved into a new flat in South Kensington on the clear understanding that when their marriage had settled down (a process they knew would not take long, and was in fact more a humorous concession to popular wisdom than what was due to themselves) they would buy a house and start a family.

And this is what happened. They lived in their charming flat for two years, giving parties and going to them, being a popular young married couple, and then Susan became pregnant, she gave up her job, and they bought a house in Richmond. It was typical of this couple that they had a son first, then a daughter, then twins, son and daughter. Everything right, appropriate, and what everyone would wish for, if they could choose. But people did feel these two had chosen; this balanced and sensible family was no more than what was due to them because of their infallible sense for *choosing* right.

And so they lived with their four children in their gardened house in Richmond and were happy. They had everything they had wanted and had planned for.

And yet . . .

Well, even this was expected, that there must be a certain flatness. . . .

Yes, yes, of course, it was natural they sometimes felt like this. Like what?

Their life seemed to be like a snake biting its tail. Matthew's job for the sake of Susan, children, house, and garden—which caravanserai[1] needed a well-paid job to maintain it. And Susan's practical intelligence for the sake of Matthew, the children, the house and the garden—which unit would have collapsed in a week without her.

But there was no point about which either could say: "For the sake of *this* is all the rest." Children? But children can't be a centre of life and a reason for being. They can be a thousand things that are delightful, interesting, satisfying, but they can't be a wellspring to live from. Or they shouldn't be. Susan and Matthew knew that well enough.

Matthew's job? Ridiculous. It was an interesting job, but scarcely a reason for living. Matthew took pride in doing it well; but he could hardly be expected to be proud of the newspaper: the newspaper he read, *his* newspaper, was not the one he worked for.

Their love for each other? Well, that was nearest it. If this wasn't a centre, what was? Yes, it was around this point, their love, that the whole extraordinary structure revolved. For extraordinary it certainly was. Both Susan and Matthew had moments of thinking so, of looking in secret disbelief at this thing they had created: marriage, four children, big house, garden, charwomen,[2] friends, cars . . . and this *thing*, this entity, all of it had come into existence, been blown into being out of nowhere, because Susan loved Matthew and Matthew loved Susan. Extraordinary. So that was the central point, the wellspring.

And if one felt that it simply was not strong enough, important enough, to support it all, well whose fault was that? Certainly neither Susan's nor Matthew's. It was in the nature of things. And they sensibly blamed neither themselves nor each other.

On the contrary, they used their intelligence to preserve what they had created from a painful and explosive world: they looked around them, and took lessons. All around them, marriages collapsing, or breaking, or rubbing along (even worse, they felt). They must not make the same mistakes, they must not.

They had avoided the pitfall so many of their friends had fallen into—of buying a house in the country *for the sake of the children;* so that the husband became a weekend husband, a weekend father, and the wife always careful not to ask what went on in the town flat which they called (in joke) a bachelor flat. No, Matthew was a full-time husband, a full-time father, and at nights,

---

1. Inn with large courtyard, in West Asia.   2. Household workers.

in the big married bed in the big married bedroom (which had an attractive view of the river) they lay beside each other talking and he told her about his day, and what he had done, and whom he had met; and she told him about her day (not as interesting, but that was not her fault) for both knew of the hidden resentments and deprivations of the woman who has lived her own life—and above all, has earned her own living—and is now dependent on a husband for outside interests and money.

Nor did Susan make the mistake of taking a job for the sake of her independence, which she might very well have done, since her old firm, missing her qualities of humour, balance, and sense, invited her often to go back. Children needed their mother to a certain age, that both parents knew and agreed on; and when these four healthy wisely brought-up children were of the right age, Susan would work again, because she knew, and so did he, what happened to women of fifty at the height of their energy and ability, with grown-up children who no longer needed their full devotion.

So here was this couple, testing their marriage, looking after it, treating it like a small boat full of helpless people in a very stormy sea. Well, of course, so it was. . . . The storms of the world were bad, but not too close—which is not to say they were selfishly felt: Susan and Matthew were both well-informed and responsible people. And the inner storms and quicksands were understood and charted. So everything was all right. Everything was in order. Yes, things were under control.

So what did it matter if they felt dry, flat? People like themselves, fed on a hundred books (psychological, anthropological, sociological) could scarcely be unprepared for the dry, controlled wistfulness which is the distinguishing mark of the intelligent marriage. Two people, endowed with education, with discrimination, with judgement, linked together voluntarily from their will to be happy together and to be of use to others—one sees them everywhere, one knows them, one even is that thing oneself: sadness because so much is after all so little. These two, unsurprised, turned towards each other with even more courtesy and gentle love: this was life, that two people, no matter how carefully chosen, could not be everything to each other. In fact, even to say so, to think in such a way, was banal, they were ashamed to do it.

It was banal, too, when one night Matthew came home late and confessed he had been to a party, taken a girl home and slept with her. Susan forgave him, of course. Except that forgiveness is hardly the word. Understanding, yes. But if you understand something, you don't forgive it, you are the thing itself: forgiveness is for what you *don't* understand. Nor had he *confessed*—what sort of word is that?

The whole thing was not important. After all, years ago they had joked: Of course I'm not going to be faithful to you, no one can be faithful to one other person for a whole lifetime. (And there was the word *faithful*—stupid, all these words, stupid, belonging to a savage old world.) But the incident left both of them irritable. Strange, but they were both bad-tempered, annoyed. There was something unassimilable about it.

Making love splendidly after he had come home that night, both had felt that the idea that Myra Jenkins, a pretty girl met at a party, could be even relevant was ridiculous. They had loved each other for over a decade, would love each other for years more. Who, then, was Myra Jenkins?

Except, thought Susan, unaccountably bad-tempered, she was (is?) the first. In ten years. So either the ten years' fidelity was not important, or she isn't.

(No, no, there is something wrong with this way of thinking, there must be.) But if she isn't important, presumably it wasn't important either when Matthew and I first went to bed with each other that afternoon whose delight even now (like a very long shadow at sundown) lays a long, wand-like finger over us. (Why did I say sundown?) Well, if what we felt that afternoon was not important, nothing is important, because if it hadn't been for what we felt, we wouldn't be Mr and Mrs Rawlings with four children, etc., etc. The whole thing is *absurd*—for him to have come home and told me was absurd. For him not to have told me was absurd. For me to care, or for that matter not to care, is absurd . . . and who is Myra Jenkins? Why, no one at all.

There was only one thing to do, and of course these sensible people did it: they put the thing behind them, and consciously, knowing what they were doing, moved forward into a different phase of their marriage, giving thanks for past good fortune as they did so.

For it was inevitable that the handsome, blond, attractive, manly man, Matthew Rawlings, should be at times tempted (oh, what a word!) by the attractive girls at parties she could not attend because of the four children; and that sometimes he would succumb (a word even more repulsive, if possible) and that she, a good-looking woman in the big well-tended garden at Richmond, would sometimes be pierced as by an arrow from the sky with bitterness. Except that bitterness was not in order, it was out of court. Did the casual girls touch the marriage? They did not. Rather it was they who knew defeat because of the handsome Matthew Rawlings' marriage body and soul to Susan Rawlings.

In that case why did Susan feel (though luckily not for longer than a few seconds at a time) as if life had become a desert, and that nothing mattered, and that her children were not her own?

Meanwhile her intelligence continued to assert that all was well. What if her Matthew did have an occasional sweet afternoon, the odd affair? For she knew quite well, except in her moments of aridity, that they were very happy, that the affairs were not important.

Perhaps that was the trouble? It was in the nature of things that the adventures and delights could no longer be hers, because of the four children and the big house that needed so much attention. But perhaps she was secretly wishing, and even knowing that she did, that the wildness and the beauty could be his. But he was married to her. She was married to him. They were married inextricably. And therefore the gods could not strike him with the real magic, not really. Well, was it Susan's fault that after he came home from an adventure he looked harassed rather than fulfilled? (In fact, that was how she knew he had been *unfaithful*, because of his sullen air, and his glances at her, similar to hers at him: What is it that I share with this person that shields all delight from me?) But none of it by anybody's fault. (But what did they feel ought to be somebody's fault?) Nobody's fault, nothing to be at fault, no one to blame, no one to offer or to take it . . . and nothing wrong, either, except that Matthew never was really struck, as he wanted to be, by joy; and that Susan was more and more often threatened by emptiness. (It was usually in the garden that she was invaded by this feeling: she was coming to avoid the garden, unless the children or Matthew were with her.) There was no need to use the dramatic words, unfaithful, forgive, and the rest: intelligence forbade them. Intelligence barred, too, quarrelling, sulking, anger, silences of withdrawal, accusations and tears. Above all, intelligence forbids tears.

A high price has to be paid for the happy marriage with the four healthy children in the large white gardened house.

And they were paying it, willingly, knowing what they were doing. When they lay side by side or breast to breast in the big civilised bedroom overlooking the wild sullied river, they laughed, often, for no particular reason; but they knew it was really because of these two small people, Susan and Matthew, supporting such an edifice on their intelligent love. The laugh comforted them; it saved them both, though from what, they did not know.

They were now both fortyish. The older children, boy and girl were ten and eight, at school. The twins, six, were still at home. Susan did not have nurses or girls to help her: childhood is short; and she did not regret the hard work. Often enough she was bored, since small children can be boring; she was often very tired; but she regretted nothing. In another decade, she would turn herself back into being a woman with a life of her own.

Soon the twins would go to school, and they would be away from home from nine until four. These hours, so Susan saw it, would be the preparation for her own slow emancipation away from the role of hub-of-the-family into woman-with-her-own-life. She was already planning for the hours of freedom when all the children would be "off her hands." That was the phrase used by Matthew and by Susan and by their friends, for the moment when the youngest child went off to school. "They'll be off your hands, darling Susan, and you'll have time to yourself." So said Matthew, the intelligent husband, who had often enough commended and consoled Susan, standing by her in spirit during the years when her soul was not her own, as she said, but her children's.

What it amounted to was that Susan saw herself as she had been at twenty-eight, unmarried; and then again somewhere about fifty, blossoming from the root of what she had been twenty years before. As if the essential Susan were in abeyance, as if she were in cold storage. Matthew said something like this to Susan one night: and she agreed that it was true—she did feel something like that. What, then, was this essential Susan? She did not know. Put like that it sounded ridiculous, and she did not really feel it. Anyway, they had a long discussion about the whole thing before going off to sleep in each other's arms.

So the twins went off to their school, two bright affectionate children who had no problems about it, since their older brother and sister had trodden this path so successfully before them. And now Susan was going to be alone in the big house, every day of the school term, except for the daily woman who came in to clean.

It was now, for the first time in this marriage, that something happened which neither of them had foreseen.

This is what happened. She returned, at nine-thirty, from taking the twins to the school by car, looking forward to seven blissful hours of freedom. On the first morning she was simply restless, worrying about the twins "naturally enough" since this was their first day away at school. She was hardly able to contain herself until they came back. Which they did happily, excited by the world of school, looking forward to the next day. And the next day Susan took them, dropped them, came back, and found herself reluctant to enter her big and beautiful home because it was as if something was waiting for her there that she did not wish to confront. Sensibly, however, she parked the car in the garage, entered the house, spoke to Mrs Parkes the daily woman about her duties, and went up to her bedroom. She was possessed by a fever which drove her out again, downstairs, into the kitchen, where Mrs Parkes was making cake and did not need her, and into the garden. There she sat on a bench and tried to calm herself, looking at trees, at a brown glimpse of the river. But she was filled with tension, like a panic: as if an enemy was in the garden with her. She spoke to herself severely, thus: All this is quite natural. First, I spent twelve years of my adult life working, *living my own life*. Then I married, and from the moment I became pregnant for the first time I signed myself over, so to speak, to other people. To the children. Not for one moment in twelve years have I been alone, had time to myself. So now I have to learn to be myself again. That's all.

And she went indoors to help Mrs Parkes cook and clean, and found some sewing to do for the children. She kept herself occupied every day. At the end of the first term she understood she felt two contrary emotions. First: secret astonishment and dismay that during those weeks when the house was empty of children she had in fact been more occupied (had been careful to keep herself occupied) than ever she had been when the children were around her needing her continual attention. Second: that now she knew the house would be full of them, and for five weeks, she resented the fact she would never be alone. She was already looking back at those hours of sewing, cooking (but by herself), as at a lost freedom which would not be hers for five long weeks. And the two months of term which would succeed the five weeks stretched alluringly open to her—freedom. But what freedom—when in fact she had been so careful *not* to be free of small duties during the last weeks? She looked at herself, Susan Rawlings, sitting in a big chair by the window in the bedroom, sewing shirts or dresses, which she might just as well have bought. She saw herself making cakes for hours at a time in the big family kitchen: yet usually she bought cakes. What she saw was a woman alone, that was true, but she had not felt alone. For instance, Mrs Parkes was always somewhere in the house. And she did not like being in the garden at all, because of the closeness there of the enemy—irritation, restlessness, emptiness, whatever it was, which keeping her hands occupied made less dangerous for some reason.

Susan did not tell Matthew of these thoughts. They were not sensible. She did not recognize herself in them. What should she say to her dear friend and husband Matthew? "When I go into the garden, that is, if the children are not there, I feel as if there is an enemy there waiting to invade me." "What enemy, Susan darling?" "Well I don't know, really. . . ." "Perhaps you should see a doctor?"

No, clearly this conversation should not take place. The holidays began and Susan welcomed them. Four children, lively, energetic, intelligent, demanding: she was never, not for a moment of her day, alone. If she was in a room, they would be in the next room, or waiting for her to do something for them; or it would soon be time for lunch or tea, or to take one of them to the dentist. Something to do: five weeks of it, thank goodness.

On the fourth day of these so welcome holidays, she found she was storming with anger at the twins, two shrinking beautiful children who (and this is what checked her) stood hand in hand looking at her with sheer dismayed disbelief. This was their calm mother, shouting at them. And for what? They had come to her with some game, some bit of nonsense. They looked at each other, moved closer for support, and went off hand in hand, leaving Susan holding on to the windowsill of the living room, breathing deep, feeling sick. She went to lie down, telling the older children she had a headache. She heard the boy

Harry telling the little ones: "It's all right, Mother's got a headache." She heard that *It's all right* with pain.

That night she said to her husband: "Today I shouted at the twins, quite unfairly." She sounded miserable, and he said gently: "Well, what of it?"

"It's more of an adjustment than I thought, their going to school."

"But Susie, Susie darling. . . ." For she was crouched weeping on the bed. He comforted her: "Susan, what is all this about? You shouted at them? What of it? If you shouted at them fifty times a day it wouldn't be more than the little devils deserve." But she wouldn't laugh. She wept. Soon he comforted her with his body. She became calm. Calm, she wondered what was wrong with her, and why she should mind so much that she might, just once, have behaved unjustly with the children. What did it matter? They had forgotten it all long ago: Mother had a headache and everything was all right.

It was a long time later that Susan understood that that night, when she had wept and Matthew had driven the misery out of her with his big solid body, was the last time, ever in their married life, that they had been—to use their mutual language—with each other. And even that was a lie, because she had not told him of her real fears at all.

The five weeks passed, and Susan was in control of herself, and good and kind, and she looked forward to the end of the holidays with a mixture of fear and longing. She did not know what to expect. She took the twins off to school (the elder children took themselves to school) and she returned to the house determined to face the enemy wherever he was, in the house, or the garden or—where?

She was again restless, she was possessed by restlessness. She cooked and sewed and worked as before, day after day, while Mrs Parkes remonstrated: "Mrs Rawlings, what's the need for it? I can do that, it's what you pay me for."

And it was so irrational that she checked herself. She would put the car into the garage, go up to her bedroom, and sit, hands in her lap, forcing herself to be quiet. She listened to Mrs Parkes moving around the house. She looked out into the garden and saw the branches shake the trees. She sat defeating the enemy, restlessness. Emptiness. She ought to be thinking about her life, about herself. But she did not. Or perhaps she could not. As soon as she forced her mind to think about Susan (for what else did she want to be alone for?) it skipped off to thoughts of butter or school clothes. Or it thought of Mrs Parkes. She realised that she sat listening for the movements of the cleaning woman, following her every turn, bend, thought. She followed her in her mind from kitchen to bathroom, from table to oven, and it was as if the duster, the cleaning cloth, the saucepan, were in her own hand. She would hear herself saying: No, not like that, don't put that there. . . . Yet she did not give a damn what Mrs Parkes did, or if she did it at all. Yet she could not prevent herself from being conscious of her, every minute. Yes, this was what was wrong with her: she needed, when she was alone, to be really alone, with no one near. She could not endure the knowledge that in ten minutes or in half an hour Mrs Parkes would call up the stairs: "Mrs Rawlings, there's no silver polish. Madam, we're out of flour."

So she left the house and went to sit in the garden where she was screened from the house by trees. She waited for the demon to appear and claim her, but he did not.

She was keeping him off, because she had not, after all, come to an end of arranging herself.

She was planning how to be somewhere where Mrs Parkes would not come after her with a cup of tea, or a demand to be allowed to telephone (always irritating since Susan did not care who she telephoned or how often), or just a nice talk about something. Yes, she needed a place, or a state of affairs, where it would not be necessary to keep reminding herself: In ten minutes I must telephone Matthew about . . . and at half past three I must leave early for the children because the car needs cleaning. And at ten o'clock tomorrow I must remember. . . . She was possessed with resentment that the seven hours of freedom in every day (during weekdays in the school term) were not free, that never, not for one second, ever, was she free from the pressure of time, from having to remember this or that. She could never forget herself; never really let herself go into forgetfulness.

Resentment. It was poisoning her. (She looked at this emotion and thought it was absurd. Yet she felt it.) She was a prisoner. (She looked at this thought too, and it was no good telling herself it was a ridiculous one.) She must tell Matthew—but what? She was filled with emotions that were utterly ridiculous, that she despised, yet that nevertheless she was feeling so strongly she could not shake them off.

The school holidays came round, and this time they were for nearly two months, and she behaved with a conscious controlled decency that nearly drove her crazy. She would lock herself in the bathroom, and sit on the edge of the bath, breathing deep, trying to let go into some kind of calm. Or she went up into the spare room, usually empty, where no one would expect her to be. She heard the children calling "Mother, Mother," and kept silent, feeling guilty. Or she went to the very end of the garden, by herself, and looked at the slow-moving brown river; she looked at the river and closed her eyes and breathed slow and deep, taking it into her being, into her veins.

Then she returned to the family, wife and mother, smiling and responsible, feeling as if the pressure of these people—four lively children and her husband—were a painful pressure on the surface of her skin, a hand pressing on her brain. She did not once break down into irritation during these holidays, but it was like living out a prison sentence, and when the children went back to school, she sat on a white stone seat near the flowing river, and she thought: It is not even a year since the twins went to school, since *they were off my hands* (What on earth did I think I meant when I used that stupid phrase?) and yet I'm a different person. I'm simply not myself. I don't understand it.

Yet she had to understand it. For she knew that this structure—big white house, on which the mortgage still cost four hundred a year, a husband, so good and kind and insightful, four children, all doing so nicely, and the garden where she sat, and Mrs Parkes the cleaning woman—all this depended on her, and yet she could not understand why, or even what it was she contributed to it.

She said to Matthew in their bedroom: "I think there must be something wrong with me."

And he said: "Surely not, Susan? You look marvelous—you're as lovely as ever."

She looked at the handsome blond man, with his clear, intelligent, blue-eyed face, and thought: Why is it I can't tell him? Why not? And she said: "I need to be alone more than I am."

At which he swung his slow blue gaze at her, and she saw what she had been dreading: Incredulity. Disbelief. And fear. An incredulous blue stare from a stranger who was her husband, as close to her as her own breath.

He said: "But the children are at school and off your hands."

She said to herself: I've got to force myself to say: Yes, but do you realise that I never feel free? There's never a moment I can say to myself: There's nothing I have to remind myself about, nothing I have to do in half an hour, or an hour, or two hours. . . .

But she said: "I don't feel well."

He said: "Perhaps you need a holiday."

She said, appalled: "But not without you, surely?" For she could not imagine herself going off without him. Yet that was what he meant. Seeing her face, he laughed, and opened his arms, and she went into them, thinking: Yes, yes, but why can't I say it? And what is it I have to say?

She tried to tell him, about never being free. And he listened and said: "But Susan, what sort of freedom can you possibly want—short of being dead! Am I ever free? I go to the office, and I have to be there at ten—all right, half past ten, sometimes. And I have to do this or that, don't I? Then I've got to come home at a certain time—I don't mean it, you know I don't—but if I'm not going to be back home at six I telephone you. When can I ever say to myself: I have nothing to be responsible for in the next six hours?"

Susan, hearing this, was remorseful. Because it was true. The good marriage, the house, the children, depended just as much on his voluntary bondage as it did on hers. But why did he not feel bound? Why didn't he chafe and become restless? No, there was something really wrong with her and this proved it.

And that word *bondage*—why had she used it? She had never felt marriage, or the children, as bondage. Neither had he, or surely they wouldn't be together lying in each other's arms content after twelve years of marriage.

No, her state (whatever it was) was irrelevant, nothing to do with her real good life with her family. She had to accept the fact that after all, she was an irrational person and to live with it. Some people had to live with crippled arms, or stammers, or being deaf. She would have to live knowing she was subject to a state of mind she could not own.

Nevertheless, as a result of this conversation with her husband, there was a new regime next holidays.

The spare room at the top of the house now had a cardboard sign saying: PRIVATE! DO NOT DISTURB! on it. (This sign had been drawn in coloured chalks by the children, after a discussion between the parents in which it was decided this was psychologically the right thing.) The family and Mrs Parkes knew this was "Mother's Room" and that she was entitled to her privacy. Many serious conversations took place between Matthew and the children about not taking Mother for granted. Susan overheard the first, between father and Harry, the older boy, and was surprised at her irritation over it. Surely she could have a room somewhere in that big house and retire into it without such a fuss being made? Without it being so solemnly discussed? Why couldn't she simply have announced: "I'm going to fit out the little top room for myself, and when I'm in it I'm not to be disturbed for anything short of fire"? Just that, and finished; instead of long earnest discussions. When she heard Harry and Matthew explaining it to the twins with Mrs Parkes coming in—"Yes, well, a family sometimes gets on top of a woman"—she had to go right away to the bottom of the garden until the devils of exasperation had finished their dance in her blood.

But now there was a room, and she could go there when she liked, she used it seldom: she felt even more caged there than in her bedroom. One day she had gone up there after a lunch for ten children she had cooked and served because Mrs Parkes was not there, and had sat alone for a while looking into the garden. She saw the children stream out from the kitchen and stand looking up at the window where she sat behind the curtains. They were all—her children and their friends—discussing Mother's Room. A few minutes later, the chase of children in some game came pounding up the stairs, but ended as abruptly as if they had fallen over a ravine, so sudden was the silence. They had remembered she was there, and had gone silent in a great gale of "Hush! Shhhhh! Quiet, you'll disturb her. . . ." And they went tiptoeing downstairs like criminal conspirators. When she came down to make tea for them, they all apologised. The twins put their arms around her, from front and back, making a human cage of loving limbs, and promised it would never occur again. "We forgot, Mummy, we forgot all about it!"

What it amounted to was that Mother's Room, and her need for privacy, had become a valuable lesson in respect for other people's rights. Quite soon Susan was going up to the room only because it was a lesson it was a pity to drop. Then she took sewing up there, and the children and Mrs Parkes came in and out: it had become another family room.

She sighed, and smiled, and resigned herself—she made jokes at her own expense with Matthew over the room. That is, she did from the self she liked, she respected. But at the same time, something inside her howled with impatience, with rage. . . . And she was frightened. One day she found herself kneeling by her bed and praying: "Dear God, keep it away from me, keep him away from me." She meant the devil, for she now thought of it, not caring if she were irrational, as some sort of demon. She imagined him, or it, as a youngish man, or perhaps a middle-aged man pretending to be young. Or a man young-looking from immaturity? At any rate, she saw the young-looking face which, when she drew closer, had dry lines about mouth and eyes. He was thinnish, meagre in build. And he had a reddish complexion, and ginger hair. That was he—a gingery, energetic man, and he wore a reddish hairy jacket, unpleasant to the touch.

Well, one day she saw him. She was standing at the bottom of the garden, watching the river ebb past, when she raised her eyes and saw this person, or being, sitting on the white stone bench. He was looking at her, and grinning. In his hand was a long crooked stick, which he had picked off the ground, or broken off the tree above him. He was absent-mindedly, out of an absent-minded or freakish impulse of spite, using the stick to stir around in the coils of a blindworm or a grass snake (or some kind of snakelike creature: it was whitish and unhealthy to look at, unpleasant). The snake was twisting about, flinging its coils from side to side in a kind of dance of protest against the teasing prodding stick.

Susan looked at him thinking: Who is the stranger? What is he doing in our garden? Then she recognised the man around whom her terrors had crystallised. As she did so, he vanished. She made herself walk over to the bench. A shadow from a branch lay across thin emerald grass, moving jerkily over its roughness, and she could see why she had taken it for a snake, lashing and twisting. She went back to the house thinking: Right, then, so I've seen him with my own eyes, so I'm not crazy after all—there *is* a danger because I've seen him. He is lurking in the garden and sometimes even in the house, and he wants *to get into me and to take me over.*

She dreamed of having a room or a place, anywhere, where she could go and sit, by herself, no one knowing where she was.

Once, near Victoria, she found herself outside a news agent that had Rooms to Let advertised. She decided to rent a room, telling no one. Sometimes she could take the train in to Richmond and sit alone in it for an hour or two. Yet how could she? A room would cost three or four pounds a week, and she earned no money, and how could she explain to Matthew that she needed such a sum? What for? It did not occur to her that she was taking it for granted she wasn't going to tell him about the room.

Well, it was out of the question, having a room; yet she knew she must.

One day, when a school term was well established, and none of the children had measles or other ailments, and everything seemed in order, she did the shopping early, explained to Mrs Parkes she was meeting an old school friend, took the train to Victoria, searched until she found a small quiet hotel, and asked for a room for the day. They did not let rooms by the day, the manageress said, looking doubtful, since Susan so obviously was not the kind of woman who needed a room for unrespectable reasons. Susan made a long explanation about not being well, being unable to shop without frequent rests for lying down. At last she was allowed to rent the room provided she paid a full night's price for it. She was taken up by the manageress and a maid, both concerned over the state of her health . . . which must be pretty bad if, living at Richmond (she had signed her name and address in the register), she needed a shelter at Victoria.

The room was ordinary and anonymous, and was just what Susan needed. She put a shilling in the gas fire, and sat, eyes shut, in a dingy armchair with her back to a dingy window. She was alone. She was alone. She was alone. She could feel pressures lifting off her. First the sounds of traffic came very loud; then they seemed to vanish; she might even have slept a little. A knock on the door: it was Miss Townsend the manageress, bringing her a cup of tea with her own hands, so concerned was she over Susan's long silence and possible illness.

Miss Townsend was a lonely woman of fifty, running this hotel with all the rectitude expected of her, and she sensed in Susan the possibility of under-standing companionship. She stayed to talk. Susan found herself in the middle of a fantastic story about her illness, which got more and more improbable as she tried to make it tally with the large house at Richmond, well-off husband, and four children. Suppose she said instead: Miss Townsend, I'm here in your hotel because I need to be alone for a few hours, above all *alone and with no one knowing where I am*. She said it mentally, and saw, mentally, the look that would inevitably come on Miss Townsend's elderly maiden's face. "Miss Town-send, my four children and my husband are driving me insane, do you under-stand that? Yes, I can see from the gleam of hysteria in your eyes that comes from loneliness controlled but only just contained that I've got everything in the world you've ever longed for. Well, Miss Townsend, I don't want any of it. You can have it, Miss Townsend. I wish I was absolutely alone in the world, like you. Miss Townsend, I'm besieged by seven devils, Miss Townsend, Miss Townsend, let me stay here in your hotel where the devils can't get me. . . ." Instead of saying all this, she described her anaemia, agreed to try Miss Town-send's remedy for it, which was raw liver, minced, between whole-meal bread, and said yes, perhaps it would be better if she stayed at home and let a friend do shopping for her. She paid her bill and left the hotel, defeated.

At home Mrs Parkes said she didn't really like it, no, not really, when Mrs Rawlings was away from nine in the morning until five. The teacher had telephoned from school to say Joan's teeth were paining her, and she hadn't known what to say; and what was she to make for the children's tea, Mrs Rawlings hadn't said.

All this was nonsense, of course. Mrs Parkes's complaint was that Susan had withdrawn herself spiritually, leaving the burden of the big house on her.

Susan looked back at her day of "freedom" which had resulted in her becoming a friend to the lonely Miss Townsend, and in Mrs Parkes's remonstrances. Yet she remembered the short blissful hour of being alone, really alone. She was determined to arrange her life, no matter what it cost, so that she could have that solitude more often. An absolute solitude, where no one knew her or cared about her.

But how? She thought of saying to her old employer: I want you to back me up in a story with Matthew that I am doing part-time work for you. The truth is that . . . but she would have to tell him a lie too, and which lie? She could not say: I want to sit by myself three or four times a week in a rented room. And besides, he knew Matthew, and she could not really ask him to tell lies on her behalf, apart from his being bound to think it meant a lover.

Suppose she really took a part-time job, which she could get through fast and efficiently, leaving time for herself. What job? Addressing envelopes? Canvassing?

And there was Mrs Parkes, working widow, who knew exactly what she was prepared to give to the house, who knew by instinct when her mistress withdrew in spirit from her responsibilities. Mrs Parkes was one of the servers of this world, but she needed someone to serve. She had to have Mrs Rawlings, her madam, at the top of the house or in the garden, so that she could come and get support from her: "Yes, the bread's not what it was when I was a girl. . . . Yes, Harry's got a wonderful appetite, I wonder where he puts it all. . . . Yes, it's lucky the twins are so much of a size, they can wear each other's shoes, that's a saving in these hard times. . . . Yes, the cherry jam from Switzerland is not a patch on the jam from Poland, and three times the price. . . ." And so on. That sort of talk Mrs Parkes must have, every day, or she would leave, not knowing herself why she left.

Susan Rawlings, thinking these thoughts, found that she was prowling through the great thicketed garden like a wild cat: she was walking up the stairs, down the stairs, through the rooms, into the garden, along the brown running river, back, up through the house, down again. . . . It was a wonder Mrs Parkes did not think it strange. But on the contrary, Mrs Rawlings could do what she liked, she could stand on her head if she wanted, provided she was *there*. Susan Rawlings prowled and muttered through her house, hating Mrs Parkes, hating poor Miss Townsend, dreaming of her hour of solitude in the dingy respectability of Miss Townsend's hotel bedroom, and she knew quite well she was mad. Yes, she was mad.

She said to Matthew that she must have a holiday. Matthew agreed with her. This was not as things had been once—how they had talked in each other's arms in the marriage bed. He had, she knew, diagnosed her finally as *unreasonable*. She had become someone outside himself that he had to manage. They were living side by side in this house like two tolerably friendly strangers.

Having told Mrs Parkes, or rather, asked for her permission, she went off on a walking holiday in Wales. She chose the remotest place she knew of. Every morning the children telephoned her before they went off to school, to encourage and support her, just as they had over Mother's Room. Every evening she telephoned them, spoke to each child in turn, and then to Matthew. Mrs Parkes, given permission to telephone for instructions or advice, did so every day at lunchtime. When, as happened three times, Mrs Rawlings was out on the mountainside, Mrs Parkes asked that she should ring back at such and such a time, for she would not be happy in what she was doing without Mrs Rawlings' blessing.

Susan prowled over wild country with the telephone wire holding her to her duty like a leash. The next time she must telephone, or wait to be telephoned, nailed her to her cross. The mountains themselves seemed trammelled by her unfreedom. Everywhere on the mountains, where she met no one at all, from breakfast time to dusk, excepting sheep, or a shepherd, she came face to face with her own craziness which might attack her in the broadest valleys, so that they seemed too small; or on a mountaintop from which she could see a hundred other mountains and valleys, so that they seemed too low, too small, with the sky pressing down too close. She would stand gazing at a hillside brilliant with ferns and bracken, jewelled with running water, and see nothing but her devil, who lifted inhuman eyes at her from where he leaned negligently on a rock, switching at his ugly yellow boots with a leafy twig.

She returned to her home and family, with the Welsh emptiness at the back of her mind like a promise of freedom.

She told her husband she wanted to have an *au pair* girl.[3]

They were in their bedroom, it was late at night, the children slept. He sat, shirted and slippered, in a chair by the window, looking out. She sat brushing her hair and watching him in the mirror. A time-hallowed scene in the connubial bedroom. He said nothing, while she heard the arguments coming into his mind, only to be rejected because every one was *reasonable*.

"It seems strange to get one now, after all, the children are in school most of the day. Surely the time for you to have help was when you were stuck with them day and night. Why don't you ask Mrs Parkes to cook for you? She's even offered to—I can understand if you are tired of cooking for six people. But you know that an *au pair* girl means all kinds of problems, it's not like having an ordinary char[4] in during the day. . . ."

Finally he said carefully: "Are you thinking of going back to work?"

"No," she said, "no, not really," She made herself sound vague, rather stupid. She went on brushing her black hair and peering at herself so as to be oblivious of the short uneasy glances her Matthew kept giving her. "Do you think we can't afford it?" she went on vaguely, not at all the old efficient Susan who knew exactly what they could afford.

"It's not that," he said, looking out of the window at dark trees, so as not to look at her. Meanwhile she examined a round, candid, pleasant face with clear dark brows and clear grey eyes. A sensible face. She brushed thick healthy black hair and thought: Yet that's the reflection of a madwoman. How very strange! Much more to the point if what looked back at me was the gingery green-eyed demon with his dry meagre smile. . . . Why wasn't Matthew agreeing? After all, what else could he do? She was breaking her part of the bargain

3. Live-in foreigner who serves a family in exchange for learning its language.   4. Charwoman.

and there was no way of forcing her to keep it: that her spirit, her soul, should live in this house, so that the people in it could grow like plants in water, and Mrs Parkes remain content in their service. In return for this, he would be a good loving husband, and responsible towards the children. Well, nothing like this had been true of either of them for a long time. He did his duty, perfunctorily; she did not even pretend to do hers. And he had become like other husbands, with his real life in his work and the people he met there, and very likely a serious affair. All this was her fault.

At last he drew heavy curtains, blotting out the trees, and turned to force her attention: "Susan, are you really sure we need a girl?" But she would not meet his appeal at all: She was running the brush over her hair again and again, lifting fine black clouds in a small hiss of electricity. She was peering in and smiling as if she were amused at the clinging hissing hair that followed the brush.

"Yes, I think it would be a good idea on the whole," she said, with the cunning of a madwoman evading the real point.

In the mirror she could see her Matthew lying on his back, his hands behind his head, staring upwards, his face sad and hard. She felt her heart (the old heart of Susan Rawlings) soften and call out to him. But she set it to be indifferent.

He said: "Susan, the children?" It was an appeal that *almost* reached her. He opened his arms, lifting them from where they had lain by his sides, palms up, empty. She had only to run across and fling herself into them, onto his hard, warm chest, and melt into herself, into Susan. But she could not. She would not see his lifted arms. She said vaguely: "Well, surely it'll be even better for them? We'll get a French or a German girl and they'll learn the language."

In the dark she lay beside him, feeling frozen, a stranger. She felt as if Susan had been spirited away. She disliked very much this woman who lay here, cold and indifferent beside a suffering man, but she could not change her.

Next morning she set about getting a girl, and very soon came Sophie Traub from Hamburg, a girl of twenty, laughing, healthy, blue-eyed, intending to learn English. Indeed, she already spoke a good deal. In return for a room— "Mother's Room"—and her food, she undertook to do some light cooking, and to be with the children when Mrs Rawlings asked. She was an intelligent girl and understood perfectly what was needed. Susan said: "I go off sometimes, for the morning or for the day—well, sometimes the children run home from school, or they ring up, or a teacher rings up. I should be here, really. And there's the daily woman. . . ." And Sophie laughed her deep fruity *Fräulein's* laugh, showed her fine white teeth and her dimples, and said: "You want some person to play mistress of the house sometimes, not so?"

"Yes, that is just so," said Susan, a bit dry, despite herself, thinking in secret fear how easy it was, how much nearer to the end she was than she thought. Healthy Fräulein Traub's instant understanding of their position proved this to be true.

The *au pair* girl, because of her own common sense, or (as Susan said to herself with her new inward shudder) because she had been *chosen* so well by Susan, was a success with everyone, the children liking her, Mrs Parkes forgetting almost at once that she was German, and Matthew finding her "nice to have around the house." For he was now taking things as they came, from the surface of life, withdrawn both as a husband and a father from the household.

One day Susan saw how Sophie and Mrs Parkes were talking and laughing in the kitchen, and she announced that she would be away until teatime. She knew exactly where to go and what she must look for. She took the District Line to South Kensington, changed to the Circle, got off at Paddington, and walked around looking at the smaller hotels until she was satisfied with one which had FRED'S HOTEL painted on windowpanes that needed cleaning. The façade was a faded shiny yellow, like unhealthy skin. A door at the end of a passage said she must knock; she did, and Fred appeared. He was not at all attractive, not in any way, being fattish, and run-down, and wearing a tasteless striped suit. He had small sharp eyes in a white creased face, and was quite prepared to let Mrs Jones (she chose the farcical name deliberately, staring him out) have a room three days a week from ten until six. Provided of course that she paid in advance each time she came? Susan produced fifteen shillings (no price had been set by him) and held it out, still fixing him with a bold unblinking challenge she had not known until then she could use at will. Looking at her still, he took up a ten-shilling note from her palm between thumb and forefinger, fingered it; then shuffled up two half crowns, held out his own palm with these bits of money displayed thereon, and let his gaze lower broodingly at them. They were standing in the passage, a red-shaded light above, bare boards beneath, and a strong smell of floor polish rising about them. He shot his gaze up at her over the still-extended palm, and smiled as if to say: What do you take me for? "I shan't," said Susan, "be using this room for the purposes of making money." He still waited. She added another five shillings, at which he nodded and said: "You pay, and I ask no questions." "Good," said Susan. He now went past her to the stairs, and there waited a moment: the light from the street door being in her eyes, she lost sight of him momentarily. Then she saw a sober-suited, white-faced, white-balding little man trotting up the stairs like a waiter, and she went after him. They proceeded in utter silence up the stairs of this house where no questions were asked— Fred's Hotel, which could afford the freedom for its visitors that poor Miss Townsend's hotel could not. The room was hideous. It had a single window, with thin green brocade curtains, a three-quarter bed that had a cheap green satin bedspread on it, a fireplace with a gas fire and a shilling meter by it, a chest of drawers, and a green wicker armchair.

"Thank you," said Susan, knowing that Fred (if this was Fred, and not George, or Herbert or Charlie) was looking at her not so much with curiosity, an emotion he would not own to, for professional reasons, but with a philosophical sense of what was appropriate. Having taken her money and shown her up and agreed to everything, he was clearly disapproving of her for coming here. She did not belong here at all, so his look said. (But she knew, already, how very much she did belong: the room had been waiting for her to join it.) "Would you have me called at five o'clock, please?" and he nodded and went downstairs.

It was twelve in the morning. She was free. She sat in the armchair, she simply sat, she closed her eyes and sat and let herself be alone. She was alone and no one knew where she was. When a knock came on the door she was annoyed, and prepared to show it: but it was Fred himself, it was five o'clock and he was calling her as ordered. He flicked his sharp little eyes over the room—bed, first. It was undisturbed. She might never have been in the room at all. She thanked him, said she would be returning the day after tomorrow, and left. She was back home in time to cook supper, to put the children to bed, to cook a second supper for her husband and herself later. And to welcome Sophie back from the pictures where she had gone with a friend. All these things she did cheerfully, willingly. But she was thinking all the time of the hotel room, she was longing for it with her whole being.

Three times a week. She arrived promptly at ten, looked Fred in the eyes, gave him twenty shillings, followed him up the stairs, went into the room, and shut the door on him with gentle firmness. For Fred, disapproving of her being here at all, was quite ready to let friendship, or at least acquaintanceship, follow his disapproval, if only she would let him. But he was content to go off on her dismissing nod, with the twenty shillings in his hand.

She sat in the armchair and shut her eyes.

What did she *do* in the room? Why, nothing at all. From the chair, when it had rested her, she went to the window, stretching her arms, smiling, treasuring her anonymity, to look out. She was no longer Susan Rawlings, mother of four, wife of Matthew, employer of Mrs Parkes and of Sophie Traub, with these and those relations with friends, schoolteachers, tradesmen. She no longer was mistress of the big white house and garden, owning clothes suitable for this and that activity or occasion. She was Mrs Jones, and she was alone, and she had no past and no future. Here I am, she thought, after all these years of being married and having children and playing those roles of responsibility—and I'm just the same. Yet there have been times I thought that nothing existed of me except the roles that went with being Mrs Matthew Rawlings. Yes, here I am, and if I never saw any of my family again, here I would still be . . . how very strange that is! And she leaned on the sill, and looked into the street, loving the men and women who passed, because she did not know them. She looked at the downtrodden buildings over the street, and at the sky, wet and dingy, or sometimes blue, and she felt she had never seen buildings or sky before. And then she went back to the chair, empty, her mind a blank. Sometimes she talked aloud, saying nothing—an exclamation, meaningless, followed by a comment about the floral pattern on the thin rug, or a stain on the green satin coverlet. For the most part, she wool-gathered—what word is there for it?—brooded, wandered, simply went dark, feeling emptiness run deliciously through her veins like the movement of her blood.

This room had become more her own than the house she lived in. One morning she found Fred taking her a flight higher than usual. She stopped, refusing to go up, and demanded her usual room, Number 19. "Well, you'll have to wait half an hour then," he said. Willingly she descended to the dark disinfectant-smelling hall, and sat waiting until the two, man and woman, came down the stairs, giving her swift indifferent glances before they hurried out into the street, separating at the door. She went up to the room, *her* room, which they had just vacated. It was no less hers, though the windows were set wide open, and a maid was straightening the bed as she came in.

After these days of solitude, it was both easy to play her part as mother and wife, and difficult—because it was so easy: she felt an impostor. She felt as if her shell moved here, with her family, answering to Mummy, Mother, Susan, Mrs Rawlings. She was surprised no one saw through her, that she wasn't turned out of doors, as a fake. On the contrary, it seemed the children loved her more; Matthew and she "got on" pleasantly, and Mrs Parkes was happy in her work under (for the most part, it must be confessed) Sophie Traub. At night she lay beside her husband, and they made love again, apparently just as they used to, when they were really married. But she, Susan, or the being who answered so readily and improbably to the name of Susan, was not there: she was in Fred's Hotel, in Paddington, waiting for the easing hours of solitude to begin.

Soon she made a new arrangement with Fred and with Sophie. It was for five days a week. As for the money, five pounds, she simply asked Matthew for it. She saw that she was not even frightened he might ask what for: he would give it to her, she knew that, and yet it was terrifying it could be so, for this close couple, these partners, had once known the destination of every shilling they must spend. He agreed to give her five pounds a week. She asked for just so much, not a penny more. He sounded indifferent about it. It was as if he were paying her, she thought: *paying her off*—yes, that was it. Terror came back for a moment, when she understood this, but she stilled it: things had gone too far for that. Now, every week, on Sunday nights, he gave her five pounds, turning away from her before their eyes could meet on the transaction. As for Sophie Traub, she was to be somewhere in or near the house until six at night, after which she was free. She was not to cook, or to clean, she was simply to be there. So she gardened or sewed, and asked friends in, being a person who was bound to have a lot of friends. If the children were sick, she nursed them. If teachers telephoned, she answered them sensibly. For the five daytimes in the school week, she was altogether the mistress of the house.

One night in the bedroom, Matthew asked: "Susan, I don't want to interfere—don't think that, please—but are you sure you are well?"

She was brushing her hair at the mirror. She made two more strokes on either side of her head, before she replied: "Yes, dear, I am sure I am well."

He was again lying on his back, his big blond head on his hands, his elbows angled up and part-concealing his face. He said: "Then Susan, I have to ask you this question, though you must understand, I'm not putting any sort of pressure on you." (Susan heard the word pressure with dismay, because this was inevitable, of course she could not go on like this.) "Are things going to go on like this?"

"Well," she said, going vague and bright and idiotic again, so as to escape: "Well, I don't see why not."

He was jerking his elbows up and down, in annoyance or in pain, and, looking at him, she saw he had got thin, even gaunt; and restless angry movements were not what she remembered of him. He said: "Do you want a divorce, is that it?"

At this, Susan only with the greatest difficulty stopped herself from laughing: she could hear the bright bubbling laughter she *would* have emitted, had she let herself. He could only mean one thing: she had a lover, and that was why she spent her days in London, as lost to him as if she had vanished to another continent.

Then the small panic set in again: she understood that he hoped she did have a lover, he was begging her to say so, because otherwise it would be too terrifying.

She thought this out, as she brushed her hair, watching the fine black stuff fly up to make its little clouds of electricity, hiss, hiss, hiss. Behind her head, across the room, was a blue wall. She realised she was absorbed in watching the black hair making shapes against the blue. She should be answering him. "Do *you* want a divorce, Matthew?"

He said: "That surely isn't the point, is it?"

"You brought it up, I didn't," she said, brightly, suppressing meaningless tinkling laughter.

Next day she asked Fred: "Have enquiries been made for me?"

He hesitated, and she said: "I've been coming here a year now. I've made no trouble, and you've been paid every day. I have a right to be told."

"As a matter of fact, Mrs Jones, a man did come asking."

"A man from a detective agency?"

"Well, he could have been, couldn't he?"

"I was asking you . . . well, what did you tell him?"

"I told him a Mrs Jones came every weekday from ten until five or six and stayed in Number Nineteen by herself."

"Describing me?"

"Well Mrs Jones, I had no alternative. Put yourself in my place."

"By rights I should deduct what that man gave you for the information."

He raised shocked eyes: she was not the sort of person to make jokes like this! Then he chose to laugh: a pinkish wet slit appeared across his white crinkled face: his eyes positively begged her to laugh, otherwise he might lose some money. She remained grave, looking at him.

He stopped laughing and said: "You want to go up now?"—returning to the familiarity, the comradeship, of the country where no questions are asked, on which (and he knew it) she depended completely.

She went up to sit in her wicker chair. But it was not the same. Her husband had searched her out. (The world had searched her out.) The pressures were on her. She was here with his connivance. He might walk in at any moment, here, into Room 19. She imagined the report from the detective agency: "A woman calling herself Mrs Jones, fitting the description of your wife (etc., etc., etc.), stays alone all day in room No. 19. She insists on this room, waits for it if it is engaged. As far as the proprietor knows she receives no visitors there, male or female." A report something on these lines, Matthew must have received.

Well of course he was right: things couldn't go on like this. He had put an end to it all simply by sending the detective after her.

She tried to shrink herself back into the shelter of the room, a snail pecked out of its shell and trying to squirm back. But the peace of the room had gone. She was trying consciously to revive it, trying to let go into the dark creative trance (or whatever it was) that she had found there. It was no use, yet she craved for it, she was as ill as a suddenly deprived addict.

Several times she returned to the room, to look for herself there, but instead she found the unnamed spirit of restlessness, a prickling fevered hunger for movement, an irritable self-consciousness that made her brain feel as if it had coloured lights going on and off inside it. Instead of the soft dark that had been the room's air, were now waiting for her demons that made her dash blindly about, muttering words of hate; she was impelling herself from point to point like a moth dashing itself against a windowpane, sliding to the bottom, fluttering off on broken wings, then crashing into the invisible barrier again. And again and again. Soon she was exhausted, and she told Fred that for a while she would not be needing the room, she was going on holiday. Home she went, to the big white house by the river. The middle of a weekday, and she felt guilty at returning to her own home when not expected. She stood unseen, looking in at the kitchen window. Mrs Parkes, wearing a discarded floral overall of Susan's, was stooping to slide something into the oven. Sophie, arms folded, was leaning her back against a cupboard and laughing at some joke made by a girl not seen before by Susan—a dark foreign girl, Sophie's visitor. In an armchair Molly, one of the twins, lay curled, sucking her thumb and watching the grownups. She must have some sickness, to be kept from school. The child's listless face, the dark circles under her eyes, hurt Susan: Molly was looking at the three grownups working and talking in exactly the same way Susan looked at the four through the kitchen window: she was remote, shut off from them.

But then, just as Susan imagined herself going in, picking up the little girl, and sitting in an armchair with her, stroking her probably heated forehead, Sophie did just that: she had been standing on one leg, the other knee flexed, its foot set against the wall. Now she let her foot in its ribbon-tied red shoe slide down the wall, and stood solid on two feet, clapping her hands before and behind her, and sang a couple of lines in German, so that the child lifted her heavy eyes at her and began to smile. Then she walked, or rather skipped, over to the child, swung her up, and let her fall into her lap at the same moment she sat herself. She said "Hopla! Hopla! Molly . . ." and began stroking the dark untidy young head that Molly laid on her shoulder for comfort.

Well. . . . Susan blinked the tears of farewell out of her eyes, and went quietly up the house to her bedroom. There she sat looking at the river through the trees. She felt at peace, but in a way that was new to her. She had no desire to move, to talk, to do anything at all. The devils that had haunted the house, the garden, were not there; but she knew it was because her soul was in Room 19 in Fred's Hotel; she was not really here at all. It was a sensation that should have been frightening: to sit at her own bedroom window, listening to Sophie's rich young voice sing German nursery songs to her child, listening to Mrs Parkes clatter and move below, and to know that all this had nothing to do with her: she was already out of it.

Later, she made herself go down and say she was home: it was unfair to be here unannounced. She took lunch with Mrs Parkes, Sophie, Sophie's Italian friend Maria, and her daughter Molly, and felt like a visitor.

A few days later, at bedtime, Matthew said: "Here's your five pounds," and pushed them over at her. Yet he must have known she had not been leaving the house at all.

She shook her head, gave it back to him, and said, in explanation, not in accusation: "As soon as you knew where I was, there was no point."

He nodded, not looking at her. He was turned away from her: thinking, she knew, how best to handle this wife who terrified him.

He said: "I wasn't trying to . . . it's just that I was worried."

"Yes, I know."

"I must confess that I was beginning to wonder . . ."

"You thought that I had a lover?"

"Yes, I am afraid I did."

She knew that he wished she had. She sat wondering how to say: "For a year now I've been spending all my days in a very sordid hotel room. It's the place where I'm happy. In fact, without it I don't exist." She heard herself saying this, and understood how terrified he was that she might. So instead she said: "Well, perhaps you're not far wrong."

Probably Matthew would think the hotel proprietor lied: he would want to think so.

"Well," he said, and she could hear his voice spring up, so to speak, with relief: "in that case I must confess I've got a bit of an affair on myself."

She said, detached and interested: "Really? Who is she?" and saw Matthew's startled look because of this reaction.

"It's Phil. Phil Hunt."

She had known Phil Hunt well in the old unmarried days. She was thinking: No, she won't do, she's too neurotic and difficult. She's never been happy yet. Sophie's much better: Well Matthew will see that himself, as sensible as he is.

This line of thought went on in silence, while she said aloud: "It's no point in telling you about mine, because you don't know him."

Quick, quick, invent, she thought. Remember how you invented all that nonsense for Miss Townsend.

She began slowly, careful not to contradict herself: "His name is Michael"—(*Michael What?*)—"Michael Plant." (What a silly name!) "He's rather like you—in looks, I mean." And indeed, she could imagine herself being touched by no one but Matthew himself. "He's a publisher." (Really? Why?) "He's got a wife already and two children."

She brought out this fantasy, proud of herself.

Matthew said: "Are you two thinking of marrying?"

She said, before she could stop herself: "Good God, *no!*"

She realised, if Matthew wanted to marry Phil Hunt, that this was too emphatic, but apparently it was all right, for his voice sounded relieved as he said: "It is a bit impossible to imagine oneself married to anyone else, isn't it?" With which he pulled her to him, so that her head lay on his shoulder. She turned her face into the dark of his flesh, and listened to the blood pounding through her ears saying: I am alone, I am alone, I am alone.

In the morning Susan lay in bed while he dressed.

He had been thinking things out in the night, because now he said: "Susan, why don't we make a foursome?"

Of course, she said to herself, of course he would be bound to say that. If one is sensible, if one is reasonable, if one never allows oneself a base thought or an envious emotion, naturally one says: Let's make a foursome!

"Why not?" she said.

"We could all meet for lunch. I mean, it's ridiculous, you sneaking off to filthy hotels, and me staying late at the office, and all the lies everyone has to tell."

What on earth did I say his name was?—she panicked, then said: "I think it's a good idea, but Michael is away at the moment. When he comes back though—and I'm sure you two would like each other."

"He's away, is he? So that's why you've been . . ." Her husband put his hand to the knot of his tie in a gesture of male coquetry she would not before have associated with him; and he bent to kiss her cheek with the expression that goes with the words: Oh you naughty little puss! And she felt its answering look, naughty and coy, come onto her face.

Inside she was dissolving in horror at them both, at how far they had both sunk from honesty of emotion.

So now she was saddled with a lover, and he had a mistress! How ordinary, how reassuring, how jolly! And now they would make a foursome of it, and go about to theatres and restaurants. After all, the Rawlings could well afford that sort of thing, and presumably the publisher Michael Plant could afford to do himself and his mistress quite well. No, there was nothing to stop the four of them developing the most intricate relationship of civilised tolerance, all enveloped in a charming afterglow of autumnal passion. Perhaps they would all go off on holidays together? She had known people who did. Or perhaps Matthew would draw the line there? Why should he, though, if he was capable of talking about "foursomes" at all?

She lay in the empty bedroom, listening to the car drive off with Matthew in it, off to work. Then she heard the children clattering off to school to the accompaniment of Sophie's cheerfully ringing voice. She slid down into the hollow of the bed, for shelter against her own irrelevance. And she stretched out her hand to the hollow where her husband's body had lain, but found no comfort there: he was not her husband. She curled herself up in a small tight ball under the clothes: she could stay here all day, all week, indeed, all her life.

But in a few days she must produce Michael Plant, and—but how? She must presumably find some agreeable man prepared to impersonate a publisher called Michael Plant. And in return for which she would—what? Well, for one thing they would make love. The idea made her want to cry with sheer exhaustion. Oh no, she had finished with all that—the proof of it was that the words "make love," or even imagining it, trying hard to revive no more than the pleasures of sensuality, let alone affection, or love, made her want to run away and hide from the sheer effort of the thing. . . . Good Lord, why make love at all? Why make love with anyone? Or if you are going to make love, what does it matter who with? Why shouldn't she simply walk into the street, pick up a man and have a roaring sexual affair with him? Why not? Or even with Fred? What difference did it make?

But she had let herself in for it—an interminable stretch of time with a lover, called Michael, as part of a gallant civilised foursome. Well, she could not, and she would not.

She got up, dressed, went down to find Mrs Parkes, and asked her for the loan of a pound, since Matthew, she said, had forgotten to leave her money. She exchanged with Mrs Parkes variations on the theme that husbands are all the same, they don't think, and without saying a word to Sophie, whose voice could be heard upstairs from the telephone, walked to the underground, travelled to South Kensington, changed to the Inner Circle, got out at Paddington, and walked to Fred's Hotel. There she told Fred that she wasn't going on holiday after all, she needed the room. She would have to wait an hour, Fred said. She went to a busy tearoom-cum-restaurant around the corner, and sat watching the people flow in and out the door that kept swinging open and shut, watched them mingle and merge and separate, felt her being flow into them, into their movement. When the hour was up she left a half crown for her pot of tea, and left the place without looking back at it, just as she had left her house, the big, beautiful white house, without another look, but silently dedicating it to Sophie. She returned to Fred, received the key of No. 19, now free, and ascended the grimy stairs slowly, letting floor after floor fall away below her, keeping her eyes lifted, so that floor after floor descended jerkily to her level of vision, and fell away out of sight.

No. 19 was the same. She saw everything with an acute, narrow, checking glance: the cheap shine of the satin spread, which had been replaced carelessly after the two bodies had finished their convulsions under it; a trace of powder on the glass that topped the chest of drawers; an intense green shade in a fold of the curtain. She stood at the window, looking down, watching people pass and pass and pass until her mind went dark from the constant movement. Then she sat in the wicker chair, letting herself go slack. But she had to be careful, because she did not want, today, to be surprised by Fred's knock at five o'clock.

The demons were not here. They had gone forever, because she was buying her freedom from them. She was slipping already into the dark fructifying dream that seemed to caress her inwardly, like the movement of her blood . . . but she had to think about Matthew first. Should she write a letter for the coroner? But what should she say? She would like to leave him with the look on his face she had seen this morning—banal, admittedly, but at least confidently healthy. Well, that was impossible, one did not look like that with a wife dead from suicide. But how to leave him believing she was dying because of a man— because of the fascinating publisher Michael Plant? Oh, how ridiculous! How absurd! How humiliating! But she decided not to trouble about it, simply not to think about the living. If he wanted to believe she had a lover, he would believe it. And he *did* want to believe it. Even when he had found out that there was no publisher in London called Michael Plant, he would think: Oh poor Susan, she was afraid to give me his real name.

And what did it matter whether he married Phil Hunt or Sophie? Though it ought to be Sophie, who was already the mother of those children . . . and what hypocrisy to sit here worrying about the children, when she was going to leave them because she had not got the energy to stay.

She had about four hours. She spent them delightfully, darkly, sweetly, letting herself slide gently, gently, to the edge of the river. Then, with hardly a break in her consciousness, she got up, pushed the thin rug against the door, made sure the windows were tight shut, put two shillings in the meter, and turned on the gas. For the first time since she had been in the room she lay on the hard bed that smelled stale, that smelled of sweat and sex.

She lay on her back on the green satin cover, but her legs were chilly. She got up, found a blanket folded in the bottom of the chest of drawers, and carefully covered her legs with it. She was quite content lying there, listening to the faint soft hiss of the gas that poured into the room, into her lungs, into her brain, as she drifted off into the dark river.

1963

PHILIP LARKIN
1922–1985

Philip Larkin was born in Coventry; was educated at its King Henry VIII School and at St. John's College, Oxford; and was for many years librarian of the Hull University Library. He wrote the poems of his first book, *The North Ship* (1945), under W. B. Yeats's strong enchantment. Although this influence persisted in the English poet's formal skill and subdued visionary longings, Larkin began to read Thomas Hardy seriously after World War II, and Hardy's rugged language, local settings, and ironic tone helped counter Yeats's influence. "After that," Larkin said, "Yeats came to seem so artificial—all that crap about masks and Crazy Jane and all the rest. It all rang so completely unreal." Also rejecting the international modernism of Eliot and Pound because of its mythical allusions, polyglot discourse, and fragmentary syntax, Larkin reclaimed a more direct, personal, formally regular model of poetry, supposedly rooted in a native English tradition of Wordsworth, Hardy, A. E. Housman, Wilfred Owen, and W. H. Auden. Even so, his poetry is not so thoroughly antimodernist as are his declarations: witness his imagist precision and alienated personae, his blending of revulsion and attraction toward modernity.

Larkin was the dominant figure in what came to be known as "the Movement," a group of university poets that included Kingsley Amis, Donald Davie, and Thom Gunn, gathered together in Robert Conquest's landmark anthology of 1956, *New Lines*. Their work was seen as counteracting not only the extravagances of modernism but also the influence of Dylan Thomas's high-flown, apocalyptic rhetoric: like Larkin, these poets preferred a civil grammar and rational syntax over prophecy, suburban realities over mythmaking.

No other poet presents the welfare-state world of postimperial Britain so vividly, so unsparingly, and so tenderly. "Poetry is an affair of sanity, of seeing things as they are," Larkin said; "I don't want to transcend the commonplace, I love the commonplace life. Everyday things are lovely to me." Eschewing the grandiose, he writes poetry that, in its everyday diction and melancholy wryness, worldly subjects and regular meters, affirms rather than contravenes the restrictions of ordinary life. Love's failure, the erosion of religious and national abutments, the loneliness of age and death—Larkin does not avert his poetic gaze from these bleak realities. As indicated by the title of his 1955 collection *The Less Deceived*, disillusionment, drabness, and resignation color these poems. Yet Larkin's drearily mundane world often gives way to muted promise, his speakers' alienation to possible communion, his skepticism to encounters even with the sublime. At the end of "High Windows," the characteristically ironic and self-deprecating speaker glimpses both radiant presence and total absence in the sunlit glass: "And beyond it, the deep blue air, that shows / Nothing, and is nowhere, and is endless."

Like Hardy, Larkin wrote novels—*Jill* (1946) and *A Girl in Winter* (1947)—and his poems have a novelist's sense of place and skill in the handling of direct speech. He also edited a controversial anthology, *The Oxford Book of Twentieth-Century English Verse* (1973), which attempted to construct a modern native tradition in England. But his most significant legacy was his poetry, although his output was limited to four volumes. Out of "the commonplace life" he fashioned uncommon poems—some of the most emotionally complex, rhythmically polished, and intricately rhymed poems of the second half of the twentieth century.

Church Going

Once I am sure there's nothing going on
I step inside, letting the door thud shut.
Another church: matting, seats, and stone,
And little books; sprawlings of flowers, cut
For Sunday, brownish now; some brass and stuff   5
Up at the holy end; the small neat organ;
And a tense, musty, unignorable silence,
Brewed God knows how long. Hatless, I take off
My cycle-clips in awkward reverence,

Move forward, run my hand around the font.   10
From where I stand, the roof looks almost new—
Cleaned, or restored? Someone would know: I don't.
Mounting the lectern, I peruse a few

Hectoring large-scale verses,[1] and pronounce
15 "Here endeth" much more loudly than I'd meant.
The echoes snigger briefly. Back at the door
I sign the book, donate an Irish sixpence,[2]
Reflect the place was not worth stopping for.

Yet stop I did: in fact I often do,
20 And always end much at a loss like this,
Wondering what to look for; wondering, too,
When churches fall completely out of use
What we shall turn them into, if we shall keep
A few cathedrals chronically on show,
25 Their parchment, plate and pyx[3] in locked cases,
And let the rest rent-free to rain and sheep.
Shall we avoid them as unlucky places?

Or, after dark, will dubious women come
To make their children touch a particular stone;
30 Pick simples° for a cancer; or on some   *medicinal herbs*
Advised night see walking a dead one?
Power of some sort or other will go on
In games, in riddles, seemingly at random;
But superstition, like belief, must die,
35 And what remains when disbelief has gone?
Grass, weedy pavement, brambles, buttress, sky,

A shape less recognisable each week,
A purpose more obscure. I wonder who
Will be the last, the very last, to seek
40 This place for what it was; one of the crew
That tap and jot and know what rood-lofts[4] were?
Some ruin-bibber, randy for antique,
Or Christmas-addict, counting on a whiff
Of gown-and-bands and organ-pipes and myrrh?[5]
45 Or will he be my representative,

Bored, uninformed, knowing the ghostly silt
Dispersed, yet tending to this cross of ground[6]
Through suburb scrub because it held unspilt
So long and equably what since is found
50 Only in separation—marriage, and birth,
And death, and thoughts of these—for which was built
This special shell? For, though I've no idea
What this accoutred frowsty barn is worth,
It pleases me to stand in silence here;

---

1. I.e., Bible verses printed in large type for reading aloud.
2. An Irish sixpence has no value in England.
3. Box in which communion wafers are kept.
4. Galleries on top of carved screens separating the nave of a church from the choir.

5. Gum resin used in the making of incense; one of three presents given by the Three Wise Men to the infant Jesus. "Gown-and-bands": gown and decorative collar worn by clergypeople.
6. Most churches were built in the shape of a cross.

55 A serious house on serious earth it is,
In whose blent air all our compulsions meet,
Are recognised, and robed as destinies.
And that much never can be obsolete,
Since someone will forever be surprising
60 A hunger in himself to be more serious,
And gravitating with it to this ground,
Which, he once heard, was proper to grow wise in,
If only that so many dead lie round.

1954   1955

MCMXIV[1]

Those long uneven lines
Standing as patiently
As if they were stretched outside
The Oval or Villa Park,[2]
5   The crowns of hats, the sun
On moustached archaic faces
Grinning as if it were all
An August bank Holiday lark;

And the shut shops, the bleached,
10   Established names on the sunblinds,
The farthings and sovereigns,[3]
And dark-clothed children at play
Called after kings and queens,
The tin advertisements
15   For cocoa and twist,° and the pubs   tobacco
Wide open all day;

And the countryside not caring:
The place-names all hazed over
With flowering grasses, and fields
20   Shadowing Domesday lines[4]
Under wheat's restless silence;
The differently-dressed servants
With tiny rooms in huge houses,
The dust behind limousines;

25   Never such innocence,
Never before or since,
As changed itself to past
Without a word—the men
Leaving the gardens tidy,

---

1. 1914, in Roman numerals, as incised on stone memorials to the dead of World War I.
2. London cricket ground and Birmingham football ground.
3. At that time the least valuable and the most valuable British coins, respectively.
4. The still-visible boundaries of medieval farmers' long and narrow plots, ownership of which is recorded in William the Conqueror's *Domesday Book* (1085–86).

30 The thousands of marriages
    Lasting a little while longer:
    Never such innocence again.

1960   1964

Talking in Bed

Talking in bed ought to be easiest,
Lying together there goes back so far,
An emblem of two people being honest.

Yet more and more time passes silently.
5   Outside, the wind's incomplete unrest
Builds and disperses clouds about the sky,

And dark towns heap up on the horizon.
None of this cares for us. Nothing shows why
At this unique distance from isolation

10 It becomes still more difficult to find
Words at once true and kind,
Or not untrue and not unkind.

1960   1964

Ambulances

Closed like confessionals,[1] they thread
Loud noons of cities, giving back
None of the glances they absorb.
Light glossy grey, arms on a plaque,
5   They come to rest at any kerb:
All streets in time are visited.

Then children strewn on steps or road,
Or women coming from the shops
Past smells of different dinners, see
10 A wild white face that overtops
Red stretcher-blankets momently
As it is carried in and stowed,

And sense the solving emptiness
That lies just under all we do,
15 And for a second get it whole,
So permanent and blank and true.
The fastened doors recede. *Poor soul,*
They whisper at their own distress;

1. Enclosed stalls in Roman Catholic churches in which priests hear confession.

For borne away in deadened air
20   May go the sudden shut of loss
Round something nearly at an end,
And what cohered in it across
The years, the unique random blend
Of families and fashions, there

25   At last begin to loosen. Far
From the exchange of love to lie
Unreachable inside a room
The traffic parts to let go by
Brings closer what is left to come,
30   And dulls to distance all we are.

1961   1964

High Windows

When I see a couple of kids
And guess he's fucking her and she's
Taking pills or wearing a diaphragm,
I know this is paradise

5   Everyone old has dreamed of all their lives—
Bonds and gestures pushed to one side
Like an outdated combine harvester,[1]
And everyone young going down the long slide

To happiness, endlessly. I wonder if
10   Anyone looked at me, forty years back,
And thought, *That'll be the life;*
No God any more, or sweating in the dark

About hell and that, or having to hide
What you think of the priest. He
15   *And his lot will all go down the long slide*
Like free bloody birds. And immediately

Rather than words comes the thought of high windows:
The sun-comprehending glass,
And beyond it, the deep blue air, that shows
20   Nothing, and is nowhere, and is endless.

1967   1974

---

1. Farm machine for harvesting grain.

Sad Steps[1]

Groping back to bed after a piss
I part thick curtains, and am startled by
The rapid clouds, the moon's cleanliness.

Four o'clock: wedge-shadowed gardens lie
5   Under a cavernous, a wind-picked sky.
There's something laughable about this,

The way the moon dashes through clouds that blow
Loosely as cannon-smoke to stand apart
(Stone-coloured light sharpening the roofs below)

10 High and preposterous and separate—
Lozenge° of love! Medallion of art!   *diamondlike shape*
O wolves of memory! Immensements! No,

One shivers slightly, looking up there.
The hardness and the brightness and the plain
15 Far-reaching singleness of that wide stare

Is a reminder of the strength and pain
Of being young; that it can't come again,
But is for others undiminished somewhere.

1968   1974

Homage to a Government

Next year we are to bring the soldiers home
For lack of money, and it is all right.
Places they guarded, or kept orderly,
Must guard themselves, and keep themselves orderly.
5 We want the money for ourselves at home
Instead of working. And this is all right.

It's hard to say who wanted it to happen,
But now it's been decided nobody minds.
The places are a long way off, not here,
10 Which is all right, and from what we hear
The soldiers there only made trouble happen.
Next year we shall be easier in our minds.

Next year we shall be living in a country
That brought its soldiers home for lack of money.
15 The statues will be standing in the same
Tree-muffled squares, and look nearly the same.

1. Cf. Sir Philip Sidney's *Astrophil and Stella* 31: "With how sad steps, O Moon, thou climb'st the skies."

Our children will not know it's a different country.
All we can hope to leave them now is money.

Jan. 10, 1969   1974

The Explosion

On the day of the explosion
Shadows pointed towards the pithead:°   mine entrance
In the sun the slagheap° slept.   pile of scrap, refuse

Down the lane came men in pitboots
5   Coughing oath-edged talk and pipe-smoke,
Shouldering off the freshened silence.

One chased after rabbits; lost them;
Came back with a nest of lark's eggs;
Showed them; lodged them in the grasses.

10   So they passed in beards and moleskins,[1]
Fathers, brothers, nicknames, laughter,
Through the tall gates standing open.

At noon, there came a tremor; cows
Stopped chewing for a second; sun,
15   Scarfed as in a heat-haze, dimmed.

The dead go on before us, they
Are sitting in God's house in comfort,
We shall see them face to face—

Plain as lettering in the chapels
20   It was said, and for a second
Wives saw men of the explosion

Larger than in life they managed—
Gold as on a coin, or walking
Somehow from the sun towards them,

25   One showing the eggs unbroken.

1970   1974

This Be The Verse[1]

They fuck you up, your mum and dad.
They may not mean to, but they do.

---

1. Clothes of heavy fabric.
1. Cf. the elegy "Requiem," by Robert Louis Stevenson (1850–1894), of which the final verse reads, "This be the verse you grave for me: / Here *he lies where he longed to be, / Home is the sailor, home from sea, / And the hunter home from the hill."*

They fill you with the faults they had
And add some extra, just for you.

5   But they were fucked up in their turn
By fools in old-style hats and coats,
Who half the time were soppy-stern
And half at one another's throats.

Man hands on misery to man.
10   It deepens like a coastal shelf.[2]
Get out as early as you can,
And don't have any kids yourself.

Apr. ? 1971   1974

Aubade[1]

I work all day, and get half-drunk at night.
Waking at four to soundless dark, I stare.
In time the curtain-edges will grow light.
Till then I see what's really always there:
5   Unresting death, a whole day nearer now,
Making all thought impossible but how
And where and when I shall myself die.
Arid interrogation: yet the dread
Of dying, and being dead,
10   Flashes afresh to hold and horrify.

The mind blanks at the glare. Not in remorse
—The good not done, the love not given, time
Torn off unused—nor wretchedly because
An only life can take so long to climb
15   Clear of its wrong beginnings, and may never;
But at the total emptiness for ever,
The sure extinction that we travel to
And shall be lost in always. Not to be here,
Not to be anywhere,
20   And soon; nothing more terrible, nothing more true.

This is a special way of being afraid
No trick dispels. Religion used to try,
That vast moth-eaten musical brocade
Created to pretend we never die,
25   And specious stuff that says No rational being
Can fear a thing it will not feel, not seeing
That this is what we fear—no sight, no sound,
No touch or taste or smell, nothing to think with,
Nothing to love or link with,
30   The anaesthetic from which none come round.

2. Underwater land off a coast   1. Music or poem announcing dawn.

And so it stays just on the edge of vision,
A small unfocused blur, a standing chill
That slows each impulse down to indecision.
Most things may never happen: this one will,
35 And realisation of it rages out
In furnace-fear when we are caught without
People or drink. Courage is no good:
It means not scaring others. Being brave
Lets no one off the grave.
40 Death is no different whined at than withstood.

Slowly light strengthens, and the room takes shape.
It stands plain as a wardrobe, what we know,
Have always known, know that we can't escape,
Yet can't accept. One side will have to go.
45 Meanwhile telephones crouch, getting ready to ring
In locked-up offices, and all the uncaring
Intricate rented world begins to rouse.
The sky is white as clay, with no sun.
Work has to be done.
50 Postmen like doctors go from house to house.

1977   1977

NADINE GORDIMER
b. 1923

Nadine Gordimer's fiction has given imaginative and moral shape to the recent history of South Africa. Since the publication of her first book, *The Lying Days* (1953), she has charted the changing patterns of response and resistance to apartheid by exploring the place of the European in Africa, selecting representative themes and governing motifs for novels and short stories, and shifting her ideological focus from a liberal to a more radical position. In recognition of this achievement, of having borne untiring and lucid narrative witness, Gordimer was awarded the 1991 Nobel Prize in Literature.

Born to Jewish immigrant parents in the South African mining town of Springs, Gordimer began writing early, from the beginning taking as her subject the pathologies and everyday realities of a racially divided society. Her decision to remain in Johannesburg through the years of political repression reflected her commitment to her subject and to her vision of a postapartheid future. In the years since apartheid was dismantled in 1994, Gordimer has continued to live and write in South Africa, and her recent novels, such as *The House Gun* (1998) and *The Pickup* (2001), retain an uncompromising focus on the inhabitants of a racially fractured culture.

In her nonfiction Gordimer self-consciously places her writing within a tradition of European realism, most notably that defined by the Hungarian philosopher and critic Georg Lukács (1885–1971). Her aim—as shown in her incisive and highly acclaimed novels of the 1970s, *The Conservationist* (1974) and *Burger's Daughter* (1979)—is to evoke by way of the personal and of the precisely observed particular a broader political and historical totality. This method gives her characters, and the stories in which they reside, their representativeness. As Gordimer has famously said, "politics is character in South Africa." Yet throughout the long years of political polar-ization in that country and the banning of three of her own books, Gordimer has distanced herself from polemics and retained a firm humanist belief in what she variously describes as the objectivity and the inwardness of the writer. Although she has referred to an engagement with political reality as imperative and explores per-mutations of the question of engagement in novels such as *Burger's Daughter* and *July's People* (1981), she nevertheless asserts the autonomy of the writer's perspective, "the last true judgment." Narrative for Gordimer helps define and clarify historical experience. Her keen sense of history as formation, and as demanding a continual rewriting, has ensured that her novels can be read as at once contemporary in their reference and symbolic of broader social and historical patterns, as in the paranoia surrounding the case of the buried black body on a white farm in *The Conservationist*, or in the psychosocial portrait of Rosa Burger in *Burger's Daughter*.

Gordimer has drawn criticism both for her apparent lack of attention to feminism in favor of race issues and for the wholeness and unfashionable completeness of her novels—their plottedness, meticulous scene paintings, fully realized characters. How-ever, the searching symbolism and complexity of her narratives generally work against such judgments. As the following short story shows, a prominent feature of her writing is to give a number of different perspectives on a situation, in some cases most poign-antly those of apartheid's supporters, and in this way to represent the broader anatomy of a diseased politics and, more generally, of the human being in history.

The Moment before the Gun Went Off

Marais Van der Vyver shot one of his farm labourers, dead. An accident, there are accidents with guns every day of the week—children playing a fatal game with a father's revolver in the cities where guns are domestic objects, nowadays, hunting mishaps like this one, in the country—but these won't be reported all over the world. Van der Vyver knows his will be. He knows that the story of the Afrikaner farmer—regional Party leader and Commandant of the local security commando—shooting a black man who worked for him will fit exactly *their* version of South Africa, it's made for them. They'll be able to use it in their boycott and divestment campaigns, it'll be another piece of evidence in their truth about the country. The papers at home will quote the story as it has appeared in the overseas press, and in the back-and-forth he and the black man will become those crudely-drawn figures on anti-apartheid banners, units in statistics of white brutality against the blacks quoted at the United Nations—he, whom they will gleefully be able to call "a leading mem-ber" of the ruling Party.

People in the farming community understand how he must feel. Bad enough to have killed a man, without helping the Party's, the government's, the coun-try's enemies, as well. They see the truth of that. They know, reading the Sunday papers, that when Van der Vyver is quoted saying he is "terribly shocked," he will "look after the wife and children," none of those Americans and English, and none of those people at home who want to destroy the white man's power will believe him. And how they will sneer when he even says of the farm boy (according to one paper, if you can trust any of those reporters), "He was my friend, I always took him hunting with me." Those city and over-seas people don't know it's true: farmers usually have one particular black boy they like to take along with them in the lands; you could call it a kind of friend, yes, friends are not only your own white people, like yourself, you take into your house, pray with in church and work with on the Party committee. But how can those others know that? They don't want to know it. They think all blacks are like the big-mouth agitators in town. And Van der Vyver's face, in the photographs, strangely opened by distress—everyone in the district remembers Marais Van der Vyver as a little boy who would go away and hide himself if he caught you smiling at him, and everyone knows him now as a man who hides any change of expression round his mouth behind a thick, soft moustache, and in his eyes by always looking at some object in hand, leaf of a crop fingered, pen or stone picked up, while concentrating on what he is saying, or while listening to you. It just goes to show what shock can do; when you look at the newspaper photographs you feel like apologising, as if you had stared in on some room where you should not be.

There will be an inquiry; there had better be, to stop the assumption of yet another case of brutality against farm workers, although there's nothing in doubt—an accident, and all the facts fully admitted by Van der Vyver. He made a statement when he arrived at the police station with the dead man in his bakkie.[1] Captain Beetge knows him well, of course; he gave him brandy. He was shaking, this big, calm, clever son of Willem Van der Vyver, who inherited the old man's best farm. The black was stone dead, nothing to be done for him. Beetge will not tell anyone that after the brandy Van der Vyver wept. He sobbed, snot running onto his hands, like a dirty kid. The Captain was ashamed, for him, and walked out to give him a chance to recover himself.

Marais Van der Vyver left his house at three in the afternoon to cull a buck from the family of kudu[2] he protects in the bush areas of his farm. He is interested in wildlife and sees it as the farmers' sacred duty to raise game as well as cattle. As usual, he called at his shed workshop to pick up Lucas, a twenty-year-old farmhand who had shown mechanical aptitude and whom Van der Vyver himself had taught to maintain tractors and other farm machinery. He hooted, and Lucas followed the familiar routine, jumping onto the back of the truck. He liked to travel standing up there, spotting game before his employer did. He would lean forward, braced against the cab below him.

Van der Vyver had a rifle and .300 ammunition beside him in the cab. The rifle was one of his father's, because his own was at the gunsmith's in town. Since his father died (Beetge's sergeant wrote "passed on") no one had used the rifle and so when he took it from a cupboard he was sure it was not loaded. His father had never allowed a loaded gun in the house; he himself had been taught since childhood never to ride with a loaded weapon in a vehicle. But this gun was loaded. On a dirt track, Lucas thumped his fist on the cab roof three times to signal: look left. Having seen the white-ripple-marked flank of a kudu, and its fine horns raking through disguising bush, Van der Vyver drove rather fast over a pot-hole. The jolt fired the rifle. Upright, it was pointing straight through the cab roof at the head of Lucas. The bullet pierced the roof and entered Lucas's brain by way of his throat.

That is the statement of what happened. Although a man of such standing in the district, Van der Vyver had to go through the ritual of swearing that it was the truth. It has gone on record, and will be there in the archive of the local police station as long as Van der Vyver lives, and beyond that, through

1. Pickup truck.
2. Large African antelope. The males have long, spirally twisted horns.

the lives of his children, Magnus, Helena and Karel—unless things in the country get worse, the example of black mobs in the towns spreads to the rural areas and the place is burned down as many urban police stations have been. Because nothing the government can do will appease the agitators and the whites who encourage them. Nothing satisfies them, in the cities: blacks can sit and drink in white hotels, now, the Immorality Act[3] has gone, blacks can sleep with whites. . . . It's not even a crime any more.

Van der Vyver has a high barbed security fence round his farmhouse and garden which his wife, Alida, thinks spoils completely the effect of her artificial stream with its tree-ferns beneath the jacarandas.[4] There is an aerial soaring like a flag-pole in the back yard. All his vehicles, including the truck in which the black man died, have aerials that swing their whips when the driver hits a pot-hole: they are part of the security system the farmers in the district maintain, each farm in touch with every other by radio, twenty-four hours out of twenty-four. It has already happened that infiltrators from over the border have mined remote farm roads, killing white farmers and their families out on their own property for a Sunday picnic. The pot-hole could have set off a land-mine, and Van der Vyver might have died with his farm boy. When neighbours use the communications system to call up and say they are sorry about "that business" with one of Van der Vyver's boys, there goes unsaid: it could have been worse.

It is obvious from the quality and fittings of the coffin that the farmer has provided money for the funeral. And an elaborate funeral means a great deal to blacks; look how they will deprive themselves of the little they have, in their lifetime, keeping up payments to a burial society so they won't go in boxwood to an unmarked grave. The young wife is pregnant (of course) and another little one, wearing red shoes several sizes too large, leans under her jutting belly. He is too young to understand what has happened, what he is witnessing that day, but neither whines nor plays about; he is solemn without knowing why. Blacks expose small children to everything, they don't protect them from the sight of fear and pain the way whites do theirs. It is the young wife who rolls her head and cries like a child, sobbing on the breast of this relative and that.

All present work for Van der Vyver or are the families of those who work; and in the weeding and harvest seasons, the women and children work for him, too, carried—wrapped in their blankets, on a truck, singing—at sunrise to the fields. The dead man's mother is a woman who can't be more than in her late thirties (they start bearing children at puberty) but she is heavily mature in a black dress between her own parents, who were already working for old Van der Vyver when Marais, like their daughter, was a child. The parents hold her as if she were a prisoner or a crazy woman to be restrained. But she says nothing, does nothing. She does not look up; she does not look at Van der Vyver, whose gun went off in the truck, she stares at the grave. Nothing will make her look up; there need be no fear that she will look up; at him. His wife, Alida, is beside him. To show the proper respect, as for any white funeral, she is wearing the navy-blue-and-cream hat she wears to church this summer. She is always supportive, although he doesn't seem to notice it; this coldness and reserve—his mother says he didn't mix well as a child—she accepts for herself but regrets that it has prevented him from being nominated, as he should be, to stand as the Party's parliamentary candidate for the district. He does not let her clothing, or that of anyone else gathered closely, make contact with him. He, too, stares at the grave. The dead man's mother and he stare at the grave in communication like that between the black man outside and the white man inside the cab the moment before the gun went off.

The moment before the gun went off was a moment of high excitement shared through the roof of the cab, as the bullet was to pass, between the young black man outside and the white farmer inside the vehicle. There were such moments, without explanation, between them, although often around the farm the farmer would pass the young man without returning a greeting, as if he did not recognize him. When the bullet went off what Van der Vyver saw was the kudu stumble in fright at the report and gallop away. Then he heard the thud behind him, and past the window saw the young man fall out of the vehicle. He was sure he had leapt up and toppled—in fright, like the buck. The farmer was almost laughing with relief, ready to tease, as he opened his door, it did not seem possible that a bullet passing through the roof could have done harm.

The young man did not laugh with him at his own fright. The farmer carried him in his arms, to the truck. He was sure, sure he could not be dead. But the young black man's blood was all over the farmer's clothes, soaking against his flesh as he drove.

How will they ever know, when they file newspaper clippings, evidence, proof, when they look at the photographs and see his face—guilty! guilty! they are right!—how will they know, when the police stations burn with all the evidence of what has happened now, and what the law made a crime in the past. How could they know that *they do not know.* Anything. The young black callously shot through the negligence of the white man was not the farmer's boy; he was his son.

1991

A. K. RAMANUJAN
1929–1993

Born in Mysore, India, Attipat Krishnaswami Ramanujan grew up amid the different languages that later informed his life's work as poet, translator, and linguist: he spoke Kannada in the streets, Tamil with his mother, and English with his father, a mathematics professor at Mysore University. Educated there and at Deccan College, he traveled for graduate studies to Indiana University, staying on in the U.S. to teach at the University of Chicago from 1961. He was the recipient of a MacArthur Fellowship, and in 1976 the Indian government honored him with the Padma Shri for distinguished service to the nation.

Ramanujan affirmed that "cultural traditions in India are indissolubly plural and often conflicting," and his poetry—in its texture and subject matter—embodies this complex intercultural mingling within India and across much of the contemporary world. His poems reflect the influence of modern English-language poets, such as W. B. Yeats, Ezra Pound, William Carlos Williams, and Wallace Stevens, while also drawing on the vivid and structural use of metaphor, the flowing imagery and syntax, the spare diction and paradoxes of ancient and medieval poetry of south India. A poem such as the wittily entitled "Elements of Composition" recalls a traditional Indian vision of identity as embedded in endlessly fluid, concentrically arranged contexts at the same time that it suggests a postmodern vision of the self as decentered, composite, and provisional. "India does not have one past," Ramanujan emphasized, "but many pasts," and the same is true of the self whose multiple pasts he composes and decomposes in his poetry.

Self-Portrait

I resemble everyone
but myself, and sometimes see
in shop-windows,
    despite the well-known laws
5   of optics,
the portrait of a stranger,
date unknown,
often signed in a corner
by my father.

1966

Elements of Composition

Composed as I am, like others,
    of elements on certain well-known lists,
father's seed and mother's egg

gathering earth, air, fire, mostly
5   water, into a mulberry mass,
moulding calcium,

carbon, even gold, magnesium and such,
    into a chattering self tangled
in love and work,

10   scary dreams, capable of eyes that can see,
    only by moving constantly,
the constancy of things

like Stonehenge or cherry trees;

add uncle's eleven fingers
15   making shadow-plays of rajas°   *Indian kings or princes*
and cats, hissing,

becoming fingers again, the look
    of panic on sister's face
an hour before

20   her wedding, a dated newspaper map
of a place one has never seen, maybe
no longer there

after the riots, downtown Nairobi,°   *capital of Kenya*
that a friend carried in his passport
25   as others would

a woman's picture in their wallets;

add the lepers of Madurai,°   *city in south India*
male, female, married,
with children,

30   lion faces, crabs for claws,
clotted on their shadows
under the stone-eyed

goddesses of dance, mere pillars,
moving as nothing on earth
35   can move—

I pass through them
as they pass through me
taking and leaving

affections, seeds, skeletons,

40   millennia of fossil records
of insects that do not last
a day,

body-prints of mayflies,
a legend half-heard
45   in a train

of the half-man searching
for an ever-fleeing
other half[1]

through Muharram tigers,[2]
50   hyacinths in crocodile waters,
and the sweet

twisted lives of epileptic saints,

---

1. In an essay Ramanujan compares the Hindu
myth of the god that "splits himself into male and
female" to "the androgynous figure in Plato's *Symposium*, halved into male and female segments
which forever seek each other and crave union."

2. During the first month of the Islamic calendar,
Muharram processions, often including dancers in
tiger masks, commemorate the martyrdom of
Muhammad's grandson, Husein.

and even as I add,
    I lose, decompose
55 into my elements,

    into other names and forms,
      past, and passing, tenses
    without time,

    caterpillar on a leaf, eating,
60   being eaten.[3]

1986

Foundlings in the Yukon

In the Yukon[1] the other day
miners found the skeleton
of a lemming
curled around some seeds
5 in a burrow:
sealed off by a landslide
in Pleistocene times.°   *the Great Ice Age*

Six grains were whole,
unbroken: picked and planted
10 ten thousand
years after their time,
they took root
within forty-eight hours
and sprouted
15 a candelabra of eight small leaves.

A modern Alaskan lupine,°   *a wildflower*
I'm told, waits three years to come
to flower, but these
upstarts drank up sun
20 and unfurled early
with the crocuses of March
as if long deep
burial had made them hasty

for birth and season, for names,
25 genes, for passing on:
like the kick
and shift of an intra-uterine
memory, like

3. According to a poem in the ancient Sanskrit *Taittiriya Upanishad*, "What eats is eaten, / and what's eaten, eats / in turn" (Ramanujan's translation, in his essay "Some Thoughts on 'Non-Western' Classics").
1. Mountainous territory in northwestern Canada.

this morning's dream of being
30　born in an eagle's
nest with speckled eggs and the screech

of nestlings, like a pent-up
centenarian's sudden burst
of lust, or maybe
35　just elegies in Duino[2] unbound
from the dark,
these new aborigines biding
their time
for the miner's night-light

40　to bring them their dawn,
these infants compact with age,
older than the oldest
things alive, having skipped
a million falls
45　and the registry of tree-rings,
suddenly younger
by an accident of flowering

than all their timely descendants.

1995

2. The Austro-German poet Rainer Maria Rilke (1875–1926) overcame thirteen years of writer's block in Duino Castle (near Trieste), where he wrote a famous series of elegies.

THOM GUNN
1929–2004

The son of a London journalist, Thomson Gunn was educated at University College School, London, then Trinity College, Cambridge, and Stanford University, where he studied under the antimodernist, classically inclined poet Yvor Winters. In a poem addressed to Winters, he wrote: "You keep both Rule and Energy in view, / Much power in each, most in the balanced two." The poems of Gunn's *Fighting Terms* (1954) and *The Sense of Movement* (1957) aimed for the same balance. They were influenced by the seventeenth-century English poet John Donne and the twentieth-century French philosopher Jean-Paul Sartre and introduced a modern Metaphysical poet able to give powerfully concrete expression to abstract ideas. Along with Philip Larkin, he was seen as a member of "the Movement"—English poets who preferred inherited verse forms to either modernist avant-gardism or high-flown Romanticism. In the second half of *My Sad Captains* (1961), he began to move away from the will-driven heroes and the tight-fitting stanzas of his early work into more tentative explorations of experience and more supple syllabic or open verse forms. "Most of my poems are ambivalent," he said. Moving from England to San Francisco, he experimented with LSD and moved also from poems presumably addressed to women to poems frankly homosexual. *The Man with Night Sweats* (1992) ends with a sequence of poems remarkable for their unflinching directness, compassion, and grace about the deaths of friends from AIDS. Gunn was a poet of rare intelligence and power in all his protean changes.

Black Jackets

In the silence that prolongs the span
Rawly of music when the record ends,
   The red-haired boy who drove a van
In weekday overalls but, like his friends,

5   Wore cycle boots and jacket here
To suit the Sunday hangout he was in,
   Heard, as he stretched back from his beer,
Leather creak softly round his neck and chin.

Before him, on a coal-black sleeve
10   Remote exertion had lined, scratched, and burned
   Insignia that could not revive
The heroic fall or climb where they were earned.

On the other drinkers bent together,
Concocting selves for their impervious kit,
15   He saw it as no more than leather
Which, taut across the shoulders grown to it,

   Sent through the dimness of a bar
As sudden and anonymous hints of light
   As those that shipping give, that are
20   Now flickers in the Bay, now lost in night.

He stretched out like a cat, and rolled
The bitterish taste of beer upon his tongue,
   And listened to a joke being told:
The present was the things he stayed among.

25   If it was only loss he wore,
He wore it to assert, with fierce devotion,
   Complicity and nothing more.
He recollected his initiation,

   And one especially of the rites.
30   For on his shoulders they had put tattoos:
   The group's name on the left, The Knights,
And on the right the slogan Born To Lose.

1961

My Sad Captains

One by one they appear in
   the darkness: a few friends, and

a few with historical
names. How late they start to shine!
5   but before they fade they stand
perfectly embodied, all

the past lapping them like a
cloak of chaos. They were men
who, I thought, lived only to
10   renew the wasteful force they
spent with each hot convulsion.
They remind me, distant now.

True, they are not at rest yet,
but now that they are indeed
15   apart, winnowed from failures,
they withdraw to an orbit
and turn with disinterested
hard energy, like the stars.

1961

From the Wave

It mounts at sea, a concave wall
Down-ribbed with shine,
And pushes forward, building tall
Its steep incline.

5   Then from their hiding rise to sight
Black shapes on boards
Bearing before the fringe of white
It mottles towards.

Their pale feet curl, they poise their weight
10   With a learn'd skill.
It is the wave they imitate
Keeps them so still.

The marbling bodies have become
Half wave, half men,
15   Grafted it seems by feet of foam
Some seconds, then,

Late as they can, they slice the face
In timed procession:
Balance is triumph in this place,
20   Triumph possession.

The mindless heave of which they rode
A fluid shelf
Breaks as they leave it, falls and, slowed,
Loses itself.

25 Clear, the sheathed bodies slick as seals
    Loosen and tingle;
And by the board the bare foot feels
    The suck of shingle.

They paddle in the shallows still;
30   Two splash each other;
Then all swim out to wait until
    The right waves gather.

1971

Still Life

I shall not soon forget
The greyish-yellow skin
To which the face had set:
Lids tight: nothing of his,
5 No tremor from within,
Played on the surfaces.

He still found breath, and yet
It was an obscure knack.
I shall not soon forget
10 The angle of his head,
Arrested and reared back
On the crisp field of bed,

Back from what he could neither
Accept, as one opposed,
15 Nor, as a life-long breather,
Consentingly let go,
The tube his mouth enclosed
In an astonished O.

1992

The Missing

Now as I watch the progress of the plague,°   *AIDS*
The friends surrounding me fall sick, grow thin,
And drop away. Bared, is my shape less vague
—Sharply exposed and with a sculpted skin?

5 I do not like the statue's chill contour,
Not nowadays. The warmth investing me
Led outward through mind, limb, feeling, and more
In an involved increasing family.

Contact of friend led to another friend,
10 Supple entwinement through the living mass

Which for all that I knew might have no end,
Image of an unlimited embrace.

I did not just feel ease, though comfortable:
Aggressive as in some ideal of sport,
15 With ceaseless movement thrilling through the whole,
Their push kept me as firm as their support.

But death—Their deaths have left me less defined:
It was their pulsing presence made me clear.
I borrowed from it, I was unconfined,
20 Who tonight balance unsupported here,

Eyes glaring from raw marble, in a pose
Languorously part-buried in the block,
Shins perfect and no calves, as if I froze
Between potential and a finished work.

25 —Abandoned incomplete, shape of a shape,
In which exact detail shows the more strange,
Trapped in unwholeness, I find no escape
Back to the play of constant give and change.

Aug. 1987   1992

DEREK WALCOTT
b. 1930

Derek Walcott was born on the island of Saint Lucia in the British West Indies, where he had a Methodist upbringing in a largely Roman Catholic society. He was educated at St. Mary's College in Saint Lucia and the University of the West Indies in Jamaica. He then moved to Trinidad, where he worked as a book reviewer, art critic, playwright, and artistic director of a theater workshop. Since the early 1980s he has also taught at a number of American colleges and universities, especially Boston University; in 1992 he received the Nobel Prize in Literature.

As a black poet writing from within both the English literary tradition and the history of a colonized people, Walcott has self-mockingly referred to his split allegiances to his Afro-Caribbean and his European inheritances as those of a "schizophrenic," a "mongrel," a "mulatto of style." His background is indeed racially and culturally mixed: his grandmothers were of African descent; his grandfathers were white, a Dutchman and an Englishman. Schooled in the Standard English that is the official language of Saint Lucia, Walcott also grew up speaking the predominantly French Creole (or patois) that is the primary language of everyday life (the island had traded hands fourteen times in colonial wars between the British and the French). In his poetry this cross-cultural inheritance is sometimes the source of pain and ambivalence, as when in "A Far Cry from Africa" he refers to himself as being "poisoned with the blood of both." At other times it fuels a celebratory integration of multiple forms, visions, and energies, as in parts of his long poem *Omeros*, which transposes elements of Homeric epic from the Aegean to the Caribbean.

Even as a schoolboy Walcott knew he was not alone in his effort to sort through his vexed postcolonial affiliations. From a young age he felt a special affinity with Irish writers such as W. B. Yeats, James Joyce, and J. M. Synge, whom he saw as fellow colonials—"They were the niggers of Britain"—with the same paradoxical hatred for the British Empire and worship of the English language. He has repeatedly asked how the postcolonial poet can both grieve the agonizing harm of British colonialism and appreciate the empire's literary gift. Walcott has also acknowledged other English and American writers—T. S. Eliot, Ezra Pound, Hart Crane, W. H. Auden, and Robert Lowell—as enabling influences.

Over the course of his prolific career, Walcott has adapted various European literary archetypes (e.g., the Greek character Philoctetes) and forms (epic, quatrains, terza rima, English meters). He has ascribed his rigorous concern with craft to his youthful Protestantism. At once disciplined and flamboyant as a poet, he insists on the specifically Caribbean opulence of his art: "I come from a place that likes grandeur; it likes large gestures; it is not inhibited by flourish; it is a rhetorical society; it is a society of physical performance; it is a society of style." Although much of his poetry is in a rhetorically elevated Standard English, Walcott adapts the calypso rhythms of a lightly creolized English in "The Schooner *Flight*," and he braids together West Indian English, Standard English, and French patois in *Omeros*. He has a great passion for metaphor, by which he deftly weaves imaginative connections across cultural and racial boundaries. His plays, written in an accurate and energetic language, are similarly infused with the spirit of syncretism, vividly conjoining Caribbean and European motifs, images, and idioms.

A Far Cry from Africa

    A wind is ruffling the tawny pelt
    Of Africa. Kikuyu,[1] quick as flies,
    Batten upon the bloodstreams of the veldt.[2]
    Corpses are scattered through a paradise.
5   Only the worm, colonel of carrion, cries:
    "Waste no compassion on these separate dead!"
    Statistics justify and scholars seize
    The salients of colonial policy.
    What is that to the white child hacked in bed?
10   To savages, expendable as Jews?

    Threshed out by beaters,[3] the long rushes break
    In a white dust of ibises whose cries
    Have wheeled since civilization's dawn
    From the parched river or beast-teeming plain.
15   The violence of beast on beast is read
    As natural law, but upright man
    Seeks his divinity by inflicting pain.
    Delirious as these worried beasts, his wars
    Dance to the tightened carcass of a drum,
20   While he calls courage still that native dread
    Of the white peace contracted by the dead.

1. An east African ethnic group whose members, as Mau Mau fighters, conducted an eight-year campaign of violent resistance against British colonial settlers in Kenya in the 1950s.
2. Open country, neither cultivated nor forest (Afrikaans).
3. In big-game hunting, natives are hired to beat the brush, driving birds—such as ibises—and other animals into the open.

Again brutish necessity wipes its hands
Upon the napkin of a dirty cause, again
A waste of our compassion, as with Spain,[4]
25 The gorilla wrestles with the superman.
I who am poisoned with the blood of both,
Where shall I turn, divided to the vein?
I who have cursed
The drunken officer of British rule, how choose
30 Between this Africa and the English tongue I love?
Betray them both, or give back what they give?
How can I face such slaughter and be cool?
How can I turn from Africa and live?

1956, 1962

From The Schooner *Flight*

1 Adios, Carenage[1]

In idle August, while the sea soft,
and leaves of brown islands stick to the rim
of this Caribbean, I blow out the light
by the dreamless face of Maria Concepcion
5 to ship as a seaman on the schooner *Flight*.
Out in the yard turning grey in the dawn,
I stood like a stone and nothing else move
but the cold sea rippling like galvanize
and the nail holes of stars in the sky roof,
10 till a wind start to interfere with the trees.
I pass me dry neighbour sweeping she yard
as I went downhill, and I nearly said:
"Sweep soft, you witch, 'cause she don't sleep hard,"
but the bitch look through me like I was dead.
15 A route taxi pull up, park-lights still on.
The driver size up my bags with a grin:
"This time, Shabine, like you really gone!"
I ain't answer the ass, I simply pile in
the back seat and watch the sky burn
20 above Laventille[2] pink as the gown
in which the woman I left was sleeping,
and I look in the rearview and see a man
exactly like me, and the man was weeping
for the houses, the streets, the whole fucking island.

25 Christ have mercy on all sleeping things!
From that dog rotting down Wrightson Road
to when I was a dog on these streets;
if loving these islands must be my load,

---

4. The Spanish Civil War (1936–39).
1. Waterfront where schooners are cleaned and

repaired. "Adios": goodbye (Spanish).
2. Hillside slum outside Port of Spain, Trinidad.

out of corruption my soul takes wings,
30 But they had started to poison my soul
with their big house, big car, big-time bohbohl,[3]
coolie, nigger, Syrian, and French Creole,
so I leave it for them and their carnival—
I taking a sea-bath, I gone down the road.
35 I know these islands from Monos to Nassau,[4]
a rusty head sailor with sea-green eyes
that they nickname Shabine, the patois° for   *spoken dialect*
any red nigger, and I, Shabine, saw
when these slums of empire was paradise.
40 I'm just a red nigger who love the sea,
I had a sound colonial education,
I have Dutch, nigger, and English in me,
and either I'm nobody, or I'm a nation.

But Maria Concepcion was all my thought
45 watching the sea heaving up and down
as the port side of dories, schooners, and yachts
was painted afresh by the strokes of the sun
signing her name with every reflection;
I knew when dark-haired evening put on
50 her bright silk at sunset, and, folding the sea,
sidled under the sheet with her starry laugh,
that there'd be no rest, there'd be no forgetting.
Is like telling mourners round the graveside
about resurrection, they want the dead back,
55 so I smile to myself as the bow rope untied
and the *Flight* swing seaward: "Is no use repeating
that the sea have more fish. I ain't want her
dressed in the sexless light of a seraph,°   *angel*
I want those round brown eyes like a marmoset,[5] and
60 till the day when I can lean back and laugh,
those claws that tickled my back on sweating
Sunday afternoons, like a crab on wet sand."
As I worked, watching the rotting waves come
past the bow that scissor the sea like silk,
65 I swear to you all, by my mother's milk,
by the stars that shall fly from tonight's furnace,
that I loved them, my children, my wife, my home;
I loved them as poets love the poetry
that kills them, as drowned sailors the sea.

70 You ever look up from some lonely beach
and see a far schooner? Well, when I write
this poem, each phrase go be soaked in salt;
I go draw and knot every line as tight
as ropes in this rigging; in simple speech

---

3. Or *bobol*: corrupt practices or fraud, organized by people in positions of power (Eastern Caribbean English).

4. Capital of the Bahamas. "Monos": island off the northwest coast of Trinidad.
5. South American monkey.

75 my common language go be the wind,
    my pages the sails of the schooner *Flight*.

1979

The Season of Phantasmal Peace

Then all the nations of birds lifted together
the huge net of the shadows of this earth
in multitudinous dialects, twittering tongues,
stitching and crossing it. They lifted up
5   the shadows of long pines down trackless slopes,
the shadows of glass-faced towers down evening streets,
the shadow of a frail plant on a city sill—
the net rising soundless as night, the birds' cries soundless, until
there was no longer dusk, or season, decline, or weather,
10 only this passage of phantasmal light
that not the narrowest shadow dared to sever.

And men could not see, looking up, what the wild geese drew,
what the ospreys trailed behind them in silvery ropes
that flashed in the icy sunlight; they could not hear
15 battalions of starlings waging peaceful cries,
bearing the net higher, covering this world
like the vines of an orchard, or a mother drawing
the trembling gauze over the trembling eyes
of a child fluttering to sleep;
                                        it was the light
20 that you will see at evening on the side of a hill
in yellow October, and no one hearing knew
what change had brought into the raven's cawing,
the killdeer's screech, the ember-circling chough°   bird in crow family
such an immense, soundless, and high concern
25 for the fields and cities where the birds belong,
except it was their seasonal passing, Love,
made seasonless, or, from the high privilege of their birth,
something brighter than pity for the wingless ones
below them who shared dark holes in windows and in houses,
30 and higher they lifted the net with soundless voices
above all change, betrayals of falling suns,
and this season lasted one moment, like the pause
between dusk and darkness, between fury and peace,
but, for such as our earth is now, it lasted long.

1981

FROM OMEROS[1]

Book One

Chapter III

III

"Mais qui ça qui rivait-'ous, Philoctete?"[2]
                                    "Moin blessé."[3]
"But what is wrong wif you, Philoctete?"
                                    "I am blest
wif this wound, Ma Kilman,[4] *qui pas ka guérir pièce.*

Which will never heal."
                    "Well, you must take it easy.
5   Go home and lie down, give the foot a lickle°   little (West Indian English)
        rest."
Philoctete, his trouser-legs rolled, stares out to sea

from the worn rumshop window. The itch in the sore
tingles like the tendrils of the anemone,
and the puffed blister of Portuguese man-o'-war.°   *jellyfish*

10   He believed the swelling came from the chained ankles
of his grandfathers. Or else why was there no cure?
That the cross he carried was not only the anchor's

but that of his race, for a village black and poor
as the pigs that rooted in its burning garbage,
15   then were hooked on the anchors of the abattoir.°   *slaughterhouse*

Ma Kilman was sewing. She looked up and saw his face
squinting from the white of the street. He was waiting
to pass out on the table. This went on for days.

The ice turned to warm water near the self-hating
20   gesture of clenching his head tight in both hands. She
heard the boys in blue uniforms, going to school,

screaming at his elbow: "Pheeloh! Pheelosophee!"
A mummy embalmed in Vaseline and alcohol.
In the Egyptian silence she muttered softly:

---

1. Modern Greek version of the name Homer. Homer's *Iliad* and *Odyssey* are, along with Dante's *Divine Comedy*, from which Walcott adapts the terza rima stanza, and James Joyce's *Ulysses* (1922), major influences on this Caribbean epic, which moves across centuries and geographies, from Saint Lucia to Africa to Ireland.
2. Pronounced *fee-lock-TET*; a name shared with Philoctetes, who, in the *Iliad* and Sophocles' eponymous play, is abandoned on an island on the way to the Trojan War after receiving a snakebite. The

wound never heals and continually torments Philoctetes, who moans uncontrollably. Later the gods decide that the war cannot be won without him, and the Greek soldiers have to go back to the island and beg him to return with them to battle.
3. French patois, punningly mistranslated below, since *blessé* actually means "wounded."
4. The owner of the No Pain Café, Ma Kilman serves in the poem as a sibyl (female prophet) and an obeah woman (one practicing a kind of West Indian sorcery).

25　"It have a flower somewhere, a medicine, and ways
　　my grandmother would boil it. I used to watch ants
　　climbing her white flower-pot. But, God, in which place?"

　　Where was this root? What senna,° what tepid　　　　　*medicinal herb*
　　　　tisanes,°　　　　　　　　　　　　　　　　*medicinal beverages*
　　could clean the branched river of his corrupted blood,
30　whose sap was a wounded cedar's? What did it mean,

　　this name that felt like a fever? Well, one good heft
　　of his garden-cutlass would slice the damned name clean
　　from its rotting yam. He said, "*Merci.*"° Then he left.　　*Thank you (French)*

Book Six

Chapter XLIX

I

　　She bathed him in the brew of the root.[1] The basin
　　was one of those cauldrons from the old sugar-mill,
　　with its charred pillars, rock pasture, and one grazing

　　horse, looking like helmets that have tumbled downhill
5　from an infantry charge. Children rang them with stones.
　　Wildflowers sprung in them when the dirt found a seam.

　　She had one in her back yard, close to the crotons,°　　*tree or shrub*
　　agape in its crusted, agonized O: the scream
　　of centuries. She scraped its rusted scabs, she scoured

10　the mouth of the cauldron, then fed a crackling pyre
　　with palms and banana-trash. In the scream she poured
　　tin after kerosene tin, its base black from fire,

　　of seawater and sulphur. Into this she then fed
　　the bubbling root and leaves. She led Philoctete
15　to the gurgling lava. Trembling, he entered

　　his bath like a boy. The lime leaves leeched to his wet
　　knuckled spine like islands that cling to the basin
　　of the rusted Caribbean. An icy sweat

　　glazed his scalp, but he could feel the putrescent shin
20　drain in the seethe like sucked marrow, he felt it drag
　　the slime from his shame. She rammed him back to his place

　　as he tried climbing out with: "*Not yet!*" With a rag
　　sogged in a basin of ice she rubbed his squeezed face
　　the way boys enjoy their mother's ritual rage,

---

1. Ma Kilman is bathing Philoctete to heal his wound.

25 and as he surrendered to her, the foul flower
on his shin whitened and puckered, the corolla
closed its thorns like the sea-egg. What else did it cure?

II

The bow leapt back to the palm of the warrior.
The yoke of the wrong name lifted from his shoulders.
30 His muscles loosened like those of a brown river

that was dammed with silt, and then silkens its boulders
with refreshing strength. His ribs thudded like a horse
cantering on a beach that bursts into full gallop

while a boy yanks at its rein with terrified "Whoas!"
35 The white foam unlocked his coffles, his ribbed shallop
broke from its anchor, and the water, which he swirled

like a child, steered his brow into the right current,
as calm as *In God We Troust*[2] to that other world,
and his flexed palm enclosed an oar with the identi-

40 ical closure of a mouth around its own name,
the way a sea-anemone closes slyly
into a secrecy many mistake for shame.

Centuries weigh down the head of the swamp-lily,
its tribal burden arches the sea-almond's° spine,   *a tree*
45 in barracoon[3] back yards the soul-smoke still passes,

but the wound has found her own cure. The soft days spin
the spittle of the spider in webbed glasses,
as she drenches the burning trash to its last flame,

and the embers steam and hiss to the schoolboys' cries
50 when he'd weep in the window for their tribal shame.
A shame for the loss of words, and a language tired

of accepting that loss, and then all accepted.
That was why the sea stank from the frothing urine
of surf, and fish-guts reeked from the government shed,

55 and why God pissed on the village for months of rain.
But now, quite clearly the tears trickled down his face
like rainwater down a cracked carafe from Choiseul,[4]

as he stood like a boy in his bath with the first clay's
innocent prick! So she threw Adam a towel.
60 And the yard was Eden. And its light the first day's.

1990

2. Near the poem's beginning, the character
Achille chisels this misspelled phrase into his
canoe and then decides, "Leave it! Is God' spelling
and mine" (1.1.2).
3. Barracks for housing convicts or slaves.
4. A village in Saint Lucia.

TED HUGHES
1930–1998

Ted Hughes was born in Yorkshire, the son of one of seventeen men from a regiment of several hundred to return from Gallipoli in World War I, a tragedy that imprinted the imagination of the poet. He was educated at Mexborough Grammar School and Pembroke College, Cambridge, where in his last year he changed his course of study from English to archaeology and anthropology, pursuing his interest in the mythic structures that were later to inform his poetry. In 1956 he married the American-born poet Sylvia Plath, who committed suicide in 1963. As poets they explored the world of raw feeling and sensation, a world that Hughes's poems tended to view through the eye of the predator, Plath's through the eye of the victim.

In contrast to the rational lucidity and buttoned-up forms of Philip Larkin and other English poets of "the Movement," Hughes fashions a mythical consciousness in his poems, embodied in violent metaphors, blunt syntax, harsh alliterative clusters, bunched stresses, incantatory repetitions, insistent assonances, and a dark brooding tone. His early books, *The Hawk in the Rain* (1957) and *Lupercal* (1960), show the influence of D. H. Lawrence's *Birds, Beasts and Flowers* (1923), and Hughes's electrifying descriptions of jaguars, thrushes, and pike similarly generate metaphors that relate such creatures to forces underlying all animal and human experience. With *Crow* (1970) and *Gaudete* (1977) he abandoned at once the semblance of realism and the traditional metrical patterning of his early work, in the belief that "the very sound of metre calls up the ghosts of the past and it is difficult to sing one's own tune against that choir. It is easier to speak a language that raises no ghosts." Returning from the wilder shores of myth, Hughes showed in *Moortown* (1979), *Remains of Elmet* (1979), *River* (1983), and *Flowers and Insects* (1989) that he could render the natural world with a delicacy and tenderness as arresting as his earlier ferocity. In *Tales from Ovid* (1997) he brilliantly re-created—rather than translated—twenty-four passages from the Roman poet Ovid's *Metamorphoses*. In the poems of his last volume, *Birthday Letters* (1998), all but two of which are addressed to Plath, Hughes broke a silence of thirty-five years to lift the curtain on the tragic drama of their marriage. That same year he was appointed a member of the Order of Merit, having served as poet laureate of the United Kingdom since 1984. His *Collected Poems* was published in 2003.

Wind

This house has been far out at sea all night,
The woods crashing through darkness, the booming hills,
Winds stampeding the fields under the window
Floundering black astride and blinding wet

5   Till day rose; then under an orange sky
The hills had new places, and wind wielded
Blade-light, luminous and emerald,
Flexing like the lens of a mad eye.

At noon I scaled along the house-side as far as
10   The coal-house door. I dared once to look up—
Through the brunt wind that dented the balls of my eyes
The tent of the hills drummed and strained its guyrope,

The fields quivering, the skyline a grimace,
At any second to bang and vanish with a flap:
15   The wind flung a magpie away and a black-
Back gull bent like an iron bar slowly. The house

Rang like some fine green goblet in the note
That any second would shatter it. Now deep
In chairs, in front of the great fire, we grip
20   Our hearts and cannot entertain book, thought,

Or each other. We watch the fire blazing,
And feel the roots of the house move, but sit on,
Seeing the window tremble to come in,
Hearing the stones cry out under the horizons.

1957

Relic

I found this jawbone at the sea's edge:
There, crabs, dogfish, broken by the breakers or tossed
To flap for half an hour and turn to a crust
Continue the beginning. The deeps are cold:
5   In that darkness camaraderie does not hold:

Nothing touches but, clutching, devours. And the jaws,
Before they are satisfied or their stretched purpose
Slacken, go down jaws; go gnawn bare. Jaws
Eat and are finished and the jawbone comes to the beach:
10   This is the sea's achievement; with shells,
Vertebrae, claws, carapaces, skulls.

Time in the sea eats its tail, thrives, casts these
Indigestibles, the spars of purposes
That failed far from the surface. None grow rich
15   In the sea. This curved jawbone did not laugh
But gripped, gripped and is now a cenotaph.[1]

1960

Pike

Pike, three inches long, perfect
Pike in all parts, green tigering the gold.
Killers from the egg: the malevolent aged grin.
They dance on the surface among the flies.

1. Monument to the dead.

5   Or move, stunned by their own grandeur,
   Over a bed of emerald, silhouette
   Of submarine delicacy and horror.
   A hundred feet long in their world.

   In ponds, under the heat-struck lily pads—
10   Gloom of their stillness:
   Logged on last year's black leaves, watching upwards.
   Or hung in an amber cavern of weeds

   The jaws' hooked clamp and fangs
   Not to be changed at this date;
15   A life subdued to its instrument;
   The gills kneading quietly, and the pectorals.

   Three we kept behind glass,
   Jungled in weed: three inches, four,
   And four and a half: fed fry° to them—   *young fish*
20   Suddenly there were two. Finally one

   With a sag belly and the grin it was born with.
   And indeed they spare nobody.
   Two, six pounds each, over two feet long,
   High and dry and dead in the willow-herb—

25   One jammed past its gills down the other's gullet:
   The outside eye stared: as a vice locks—
   The same iron in this eye
   Though its film shrank in death.

   A pond I fished, fifty yards across,
30   Whose lilies and muscular tench[1]
   Had outlasted every visible stone
   Of the monastery that planted them—

   Stilled legendary depth:
   It was as deep as England. It held
35   Pike too immense to stir, so immense and old
   That past nightfall I dared not cast

   But silently cast and fished
   With the hair frozen on my head
   For what might move, for what eye might move.
40   The still splashes on the dark pond,

   Owls hushing the floating woods
   Frail on my ear against the dream
   Darkness beneath night's darkness had freed,
   That rose slowly towards me, watching.

1959, 1960

1. Variety of freshwater fish.

Out

1 *The Dream Time*

My father sat in his chair recovering
From the four-year mastication° by gunfire and mud,   *grinding; chewing*
Body buffeted wordless, estranged by long soaking
In the colors of mutilation.
               His outer perforations
5   Were valiantly healed, but he and the hearth-fire, its blood-flicker
On biscuit-bowl and piano and table leg,
Moved into strong and stronger possession
Of minute after minute, as the clock's tiny cog
Labored and on the thread of his listening
10 Dragged him bodily from under
The mortised° four-year strata of dead Englishmen   *firmly fixed*
He belonged with. He felt his limbs clearing
With every slight, gingerish movement. While I, small and four,
Lay on the carpet as his luckless double,
15 His memory's buried, immovable anchor,
Among jawbones and blown-off boots, tree-stumps, shell-cases and craters,
Under rain that goes on drumming its rods and thickening
Its kingdom, which the sun has abandoned, and where nobody
Can ever again move from shelter.

2

20 The dead man in his cave beginning to sweat;
The melting bronze visor of flesh
Of the mother in the baby-furnace—

Nobody believes, it
Could be nothing, all
25 Undergo smiling at
The lulling of blood in
Their ears, their ears, their ears, their eyes
Are only drops of water and even the dead man suddenly
Sits up and sneezes—Atishoo!
30 Then the nurse wraps him up, smiling,
And, though faintly, the mother is smiling,
And it's just another baby.

As after being blasted to bits
The reassembled infantryman
35 Tentatively totters out, gazing around with the eyes
Of an exhausted clerk.

3 Remembrance Day[1]

The poppy is a wound, the poppy is the mouth
Of the grave, maybe of the womb searching—

A canvas-beauty puppet on a wire
40   Today whoring everywhere. It is years since I wore one.

It is more years
The shrapnel that shattered my father's paybook

Gripped me, and all his dead
Gripped him to a time

45   He no more than they could outgrow, but, cast into one, like iron,
Hung deeper than refreshing of ploughs

In the woe-dark under my mother's eye—
One anchor

Holding my juvenile neck bowed to the dunkings of the Atlantic.
50   So goodbye to that bloody-minded flower.

You dead bury your dead.
Goodbye to the cenotaphs° on my mother's breasts.   *empty tombs*

Goodbye to all the remaindered charms of my father's survival.
Let England close. Let the green sea-anemone close.

            1967

Theology

No, the serpent did not
Seduce Eve to the apple.
All that's simply
Corruption of the facts.

5   Adam ate the apple.
Eve ate Adam.
The serpent ate Eve.
This is the dark intestine.

The serpent, meanwhile,
10   Sleeps his meal off in Paradise—
Smiling to hear
God's querulous calling.

            1967

---

1. Holiday (November 11) commemorating soldiers who lost their lives in battle. The practice of
wearing red poppies in honor of lost soldiers recalls
John McCrae's poem "In Flanders Fields" (1915),
which depicts the flowers growing between the
graves on a battlefield.

Crow's Last Stand

Burning
> burning
>> burning[1]
>>> there was finally something
5 The sun could not burn, that it had rendered
Everything down to—a final obstacle
Against which it raged and charred

And rages and chars

Limpid° among the glaring furnace clinkers°   *clear / coal remains*
10 The pulsing blue tongues and the red and the yellow
The green lickings of the conflagration

Limpid and black—

Crow's eye-pupil, in the tower of its scorched fort.

    1970

Daffodils

Remember how we[1] picked the daffodils?
Nobody else remembers, but I remember.
Your daughter came with her armfuls, eager and happy,
Helping the harvest. She has forgotten.
5 She cannot even remember you. And we sold them.
It sounds like sacrilege, but we sold them.
Were we so poor? Old Stoneman, the grocer,
Boss-eyed, his blood-pressure purpling to beetroot
(It was his last chance,
10 He would die in the same great freeze as you),
He persuaded us. Every Spring
He always bought them, sevenpence a dozen,
'A custom of the house'.

Besides, we still weren't sure we wanted to own
15 Anything. Mainly we were hungry
To convert everything to profit.
Still nomads—still strangers
To our whole possession. The daffodils
Were incidental gilding of the deeds,[2]
20 Treasure trove. They simply came,
And they kept on coming.
As if not from the sod but falling from heaven.

---

1. Cf. "Burning burning burning burning," line
308 of T. S. Eliot's *Waste Land*, where it is quoted
from the Buddha's Fire Sermon.
1. Hughes is addressing his first wife, the American poet Sylvia Plath (1932–1963).
2. Document establishing legal possession of a
house.

Our lives were still a raid on our own good luck.
We knew we'd live for ever. We had not learned
25 What a fleeting glance of the everlasting
Daffodils are. Never identified
The nuptial flight of the rarest ephemera[3]—
Our own days!
                    We thought they were a windfall.
Never guessed they were a last blessing.
30 So we sold them. We worked at selling them
As if employed on somebody else's
Flower-farm. You bent at it
In the rain of that April—your last April.
We bent there together, among the soft shrieks
35 Of their jostled stems, the wet shocks shaken
Of their girlish dance-frocks—
Fresh-opened dragonflies, wet and flimsy,
Opened too early.

We piled their frailty lights on a carpenter's bench,
40 Distributed leaves among the dozens—
Buckling blade-leaves, limber, groping for air, zinc-silvered—
Propped their raw butts in bucket water,
Their oval, meaty butts,
And sold them, sevenpence a bunch—

45 Wind-wounds, spasms from the dark earth,
With their odourless metals,
A flamy purification of the deep grave's stony cold
As if ice had a breath—

We sold them, to wither.
50 The crop thickened faster than we could thin it.
Finally, we were overwhelmed
And we lost our wedding-present scissors.

Every March since they have lifted again
Out of the same bulbs, the same
55 Baby-cries from the thaw,
Ballerinas too early for music, shiverers
In the draughty wings of the year.
On that same groundswell of memory, fluttering
They return to forget you stooping there
60 Behind the rainy curtains of a dark April,
Snipping their stems.

But somewhere your scissors remember. Wherever they are.
Here somewhere, blades wide open,
April by April
65 Sinking deeper
Through the sod—an anchor, a cross of rust.

1998

3. Insect that lives only a few days.

HAROLD PINTER
b. 1930

Harold Pinter is one of the most original and challenging of the many important playwrights who have emerged in Britain in the last half-century. He was born and educated in East London, studied briefly at the Academy of Dramatic Art, and from the age of nineteen to the age of twenty-seven acted in a repertory company. His first play (in one act), *The Room*, was written and produced in 1957 and was followed immediately by *The Dumb Waiter* and *The Birthday Party*, his first real success. In addition to his prize-winning work for theater and television, he has written a number of screenplays based on novels such as Marcel Proust's *A la Recherche du Temps Perdu* (*In Search of Lost Time*), John Fowles's *The French Lieutenant's Woman*, and Margaret Atwood's *The Handmaid's Tale*; his screenplays were collected and published in three volumes in 2000.

Pinter's early work shows the influence of Samuel Beckett and of absurdist drama, notably that of the French playwright Eugène Ionesco, but his vision rapidly established itself as more naturalistic (though no less alarming) than theirs. His territory is typically a room (refuge, prison cell, trap) symbolic of its occupants' world. Into this, and into their ritualized relationship with its rules and taboos, comes a stranger on to whom—as on to a screen—the occupants project their deepest desires, guilts, neuroses. The breakdown that follows is mirrored in the breakdown of language. Pinter, who has a poet's ear for the rhythms of spoken English, is a master of the pauses, double entendres, and silences that communicate a secondary level of meaning often opposed to the first. He has said of language:

> The speech we hear is an indication of that which we don't hear. It is a necessary avoidance, a violent, sly, and anguished or mocking smoke screen which keeps the other in its true place. When true silence falls we are left with echo but are nearer nakedness. One way of looking at speech is to say that it is a constant stratagem to cover nakedness.

The critic Lois Gordon has well said that "one way of looking at Pinter's plays is to say that they are dramatic stratagems that uncover nakedness."

The Dumb Waiter

SCENE: *A basement room. Two beds, flat against the back wall. A serving hatch, closed, between the beds. A door to the kitchen and lavatory, left. A door to a passage, right.*

BEN *is lying on a bed, left, reading a paper.* GUS *is sitting on a bed, right, tying his shoelaces, with difficulty. Both are dressed in shirts, trousers and braces.*
Silence.
GUS *ties his laces, rises, yawns and begins to walk slowly to the door, left. He stops, looks down, and shakes his foot.*
BEN *lowers his paper and watches him.* GUS *kneels and unties his shoelace and slowly takes off the shoe. He looks inside it and brings out a flattened matchbox. He shakes it and examines it. Their eyes meet.* BEN *rattles his paper and reads.* GUS *puts the matchbox in his pocket and bends down to put on his shoe. He ties his lace, with difficulty.* BEN *lowers his paper and watches him.* GUS *walks to the door, left, stops, and shakes the other foot. He kneels, unties his shoelace, and slowly takes off the shoe. He looks inside it and brings out a flattened cigarette*

packet. He shakes it and examines it. Their eyes meet. BEN *rattles his paper and reads.* GUS *puts the packet in his pocket, bends down, puts on his shoe and ties the lace.*

He wanders off, left.

BEN *slams the paper down on the bed and glares after him. He picks up the paper and lies on his back, reading.*

Silence.

A lavatory chain is pulled twice off left, but the lavatory does not flush.

Silence.

GUS *re-enters, left, and halts at the door, scratching his head.*

BEN *slams down the paper.*

BEN Kaw!

[*He picks up the paper.*]

What about this? Listen to this!

[*He refers to the paper.*]

A man of eighty-seven wanted to cross the road. But there was a lot of traffic, see? He couldn't see how he was going to squeeze through. So he crawled under a lorry.[1]

GUS He what?

BEN He crawled under a lorry. A stationary lorry.

GUS No?

BEN The lorry started and ran over him.

GUS Go on!

BEN That's what it says here.

GUS Get away.

BEN It's enough to make you want to puke, isn't it?

GUS Who advised him to do a thing like that?

BEN A man of eighty-seven crawling under a lorry!

GUS It's unbelievable.

BEN It's down here in black and white.

GUS Incredible.

[*Silence.*

GUS *shakes his head and exits.* BEN *lies back and reads.*

The lavatory chain is pulled once off left, but the lavatory does not flush.

BEN *whistles at an item in the paper.*

GUS *re-enters.*]

I want to ask you something.

BEN What are you doing out there?

GUS Well, I was just—

BEN What about the tea?

GUS I'm just going to make it.

BEN Well, go on, make it.

GUS Yes, I will. [*He sits in a chair. Ruminatively.*] He's laid on some very nice crockery this time, I'll say that. It's sort of striped. There's a white stripe.

[BEN *reads.*]

It's very nice. I'll say that.

[BEN *turns the page.*]

1. Truck.

You know, sort of round the cup. Round the rim. All the rest of it's black, you see. Then the saucer's black, except for right in the middle, where the cup goes, where it's white.

[BEN *reads.*]

Then the plates are the same, you see. Only they've got a black stripe—the plates—right across the middle. Yes, I'm quite taken with the crockery.

BEN   [*Still reading.*] What do you want plates for? You're not going to eat.

GUS   I've brought a few biscuits.

BEN   Well, you'd better eat them quick.

GUS   I always bring a few biscuits. Or a pie. You know I can't drink tea without anything to eat.

BEN   Well, make the tea then, will you? Time's getting on.

[GUS *brings out the flattened cigarette packet and examines it.*]

GUS   You got any cigarettes? I think I've run out.

[*He throws the packet high up and leans forward to catch it.*]

I hope it won't be a long job, this one.

[*Aiming carefully, he flips the packet under his bed.*]

Oh, I wanted to ask you something.

BEN   [*Slamming his paper down.*] Kaw!

GUS   What's that?

BEN   A child of eight killed a cat!

GUS   Get away.

BEN   It's a fact. What about that, eh? A child of eight killing a cat!

GUS   How did he do it?

BEN   It was a girl.

GUS   How did she do it?

BEN   She—

[*He picks up the paper and studies it.*]

It doesn't say.

GUS   Why not?

BEN   Wait a minute. It just says—Her brother, aged eleven, viewed the incident from the toolshed.

GUS   Go on!

BEN   That's bloody ridiculous.

[*Pause.*]

GUS   I bet he did it.

BEN   Who?

GUS   The brother.

BEN   I think you're right.

[*Pause.*]

[*Slamming down the paper.*] What about that, eh? A kid of eleven killing a cat and blaming it on his little sister of eight! It's enough to—

[*He breaks off in disgust and seizes the paper.* GUS *rises.*]

GUS   What time is he getting in touch?

[BEN *reads.*]

What time is he getting in touch?

BEN   What's the matter with you? It could be any time. Any time.

GUS   [*Moves to the foot of* BEN's *bed.*] Well, I was going to ask you something.

BEN   What?

GUS   Have you noticed the time that tank takes to fill?

BEN   What tank?

GUS   In the lavatory.

BEN   No. Does it?

GUS   Terrible.

BEN   Well, what about it?

GUS   What do you think's the matter with it?

BEN   Nothing.

GUS   Nothing?

BEN   It's got a deficient ballcock, that's all.

GUS   A deficient what?

BEN   Ballcock.

GUS   No? Really?

BEN   That's what I should say.

GUS   Go on! That didn't occur to me.

　　　　[GUS *wanders to his bed and presses the mattress.*]

I didn't have a very restful sleep today, did you? It's not much of a bed. I could have done with another blanket too. [*He catches sight of a picture on the wall.*] Hello, what's this? [*Peering at it.*] "The First Eleven."[2] Cricketers. You seen this, Ben?

BEN   [*Reading.*] What?

GUS   The first eleven.

BEN   What?

GUS   There's a photo here of the first eleven.

BEN   What first eleven?

GUS   [*Studying the photo.*] It doesn't say.

BEN   What about that tea?

GUS   They all look a bit old to me.

　　　　[GUS *wanders downstage, looks out front, then all about the room.*]

I wouldn't like to live in this dump. I wouldn't mind if you had a window, you could see what it looked like outside.

BEN   What do you want a window for?

GUS   Well, I like to have a bit of a view, Ben. It whiles away the time.

　　　　[*He walks about the room.*]

I mean, you come into a place when it's still dark, you come into a room you've never seen before, you sleep all day, you do your job, and then you go away in the night again.

　　　　[*Pause.*]

I like to get a look at the scenery. You never get the chance in this job.

BEN   You get your holidays, don't you?

GUS   Only a fortnight.

BEN   [*Lowering the paper.*] You kill me. Anyone would think you're working every day. How often do we do a job? Once a week? What are you complaining about?

GUS   Yes, but we've got to be on tap though, haven't we? You can't move out of the house in case a call comes.

BEN   You know what your trouble is?

GUS   What?

BEN   You haven't got any interests.

GUS   I've got interests.

BEN   What? Tell me one of your interests.

---

2. A school's top team of cricketers.

[*Pause.*]

GUS   I've got interests.

BEN   Look at me. What have I got?

GUS   I don't know. What?

BEN   I've got my woodwork. I've got my model boats. Have you ever seen me
idle? I'm never idle. I know how to occupy my time, to its best advantage.
Then when a call comes, I'm ready.

GUS   Don't you ever get a bit fed up?

BEN   Fed up? What with?

    [*Silence.*

        BEN *reads.* GUS *feels in the pocket of his jacket, which hangs on the
        bed.*]

GUS   You got any cigarettes? I've run out.

        [*The lavatory flushes off left.*]

There she goes.

        [GUS *sits on his bed.*]

No, I mean, I say the crockery's good. It is. It's very nice. But that's about
all I can say for this place. It's worse than the last one. Remember that last
place we were in? Last time, where was it? At least there was a wireless
there. No, honest. He doesn't seem to bother much about our comfort these
days.

BEN   When are you going to stop jabbering?

GUS   You'd get rheumatism in a place like this, if you stay long.

BEN   We're not staying long. Make the tea, will you? We'll be on the job in a
minute.

        [GUS *picks up a small bag by his bed and brings out a packet of tea. He
        examines it and looks up.*]

GUS   Eh, I've been meaning to ask you.

BEN   What the hell is it now?

GUS   Why did you stop the car this morning, in the middle of that road?

BEN   [*Lowering the paper.*] I thought you were asleep.

GUS   I was, but I woke up when you stopped. You did stop, didn't you?

        [*Pause.*]

In the middle of that road. It was still dark, don't you remember? I looked
out. It was all misty. I thought perhaps you wanted to kip,[3] but you were
sitting up dead straight, like you were waiting for something.

BEN   I wasn't waiting for anything.

GUS   I must have fallen asleep again. What was all that about then? Why did
you stop?

BEN   [*Picking up the paper.*] We were too early.

GUS   Early? [*He rises.*] What do you mean? We got the call, didn't we, saying
we were to start right away. We did. We shoved out on the dot. So how
could we be too early?

BEN   [*Quietly.*] Who took the call, me or you?

GUS   You.

BEN   We were too early.

GUS   Too early for what?

        [*Pause.*]

You mean someone had to get out before we got in?

3. Nap.

[*He examines the bedclothes.*]
I thought these sheets didn't look too bright. I thought they ponged[4] a bit.
I was too tired to notice when I got in this morning. Eh, that's taking a bit
of a liberty, isn't it? I don't want to share my bed-sheets. I told you things
were going down the drain. I mean, we've always had clean sheets laid on
up till now. I've noticed it.

BEN   How do you know those sheets weren't clean?

GUS   What do you mean?

BEN   How do you know they weren't clean? You've spent the whole day in
them, haven't you?

GUS   What, you mean it might be my pong? [*He sniffs sheets.*] Yes. [*He sits
slowly on bed.*] It could be my pong, I suppose. It's difficult to tell. I don't
really know what I pong like, that's the trouble.

BEN   [*Referring to the paper.*] Kaw!

GUS   Eh, Ben.

BEN   Kaw!

GUS   Ben.

BEN   What?

GUS   What town are we in? I've forgotten.

BEN   I've told you. Birmingham.

GUS   Go on!
[*He looks with interest about the room.*]
That's in the Midlands. The second biggest city in Great Britain. I'd never
have guessed.
[*He snaps his fingers.*]
Eh, it's Friday today, isn't it? It'll be Saturday tomorrow.

BEN   What about it?

GUS   [*Excited.*] We could go and watch the Villa.[5]

BEN   They're playing away.

GUS   No, are they? Caarr! What a pity.

BEN   Anyway, there's no time. We've got to get straight back.

GUS   Well, we have done in the past, haven't we? Stayed over and watched a
game, haven't we? For a bit of relaxation.

BEN   Things have tightened up, mate. They're tightened up.
[*GUS chuckles to himself.*]

GUS   I saw the Villa get beat in a cup tie once. Who was it against now? White
shirts. It was one-all at half time. I'll never forget it. Their opponents won
by a penalty. Talk about drama. Yes, it was a disputed penalty. Disputed.
They got beat two—one, anyway, because of it. You were there yourself.

BEN   Not me.

GUS   Yes, you were there. Don't you remember that disputed penalty?

BEN   No.

GUS   He went down just inside the area. Then they said he was just acting. I
didn't think the other bloke touched him myself. But the referee had the
ball on the spot.

BEN   Didn't touch him! What are you talking about? He laid him out flat!

GUS   Not the Villa. The Villa don't play that sort of game.

BEN   Get out of it.

4. Smelled.
5. Aston Villa, popularly known as "the Villa," Birmingham's soccer team.

[*Pause.*]

GUS Eh, that must have been here, in Birmingham.

BEN What must?

GUS The Villa. That must have been here.

BEN They were playing away.

GUS Because you know who the other team was? It was the Spurs. It was Tottenham Hotspur.[6]

BEN Well, what about it?

GUS We've never done a job in Tottenham.

BEN How do you know?

GUS I'd remember Tottenham.

     [BEN *turns on his bed to look at him.*]

BEN Don't make me laugh, will you?

     [BEN *turns back and reads.* GUS *yawns and speaks through his yawn.*]

GUS When's he going to get in touch?

     [*Pause.*]

Yes, I'd like to see another football match. I've always been an ardent football fan. Here, what about coming to see the Spurs tomorrow?

BEN [*Tonelessly.*] They're playing away.

GUS Who are?

BEN The Spurs.

GUS Then they might be playing here.

BEN Don't be silly.

GUS If they're playing away they might be playing here. They might be playing the Villa.

BEN [*Tonelessly.*] But the Villa are playing away.

     [*Pause. An envelope slides under the door, right.* GUS *sees it. He stands, looking at it.*]

GUS Ben.

BEN Away. They're all playing away.

GUS Ben, look here.

BEN What?

GUS Look.

     [BEN *turns his head and sees the envelope. He stands.*]

BEN What's that?

GUS I don't know.

BEN Where did it come from?

GUS Under the door.

BEN Well, what is it?

GUS I don't know.

     [*They stare at it.*]

BEN Pick it up.

GUS What do you mean?

BEN Pick it up!

     [GUS *slowly moves towards it, bends and picks it up.*]

What is it?

GUS An envelope.

BEN Is there anything on it?

GUS No.

---

6. A soccer team; Tottenham is in north London.

BEN   Is it sealed?
GUS   Yes.
BEN   Open it.
GUS   What?
BEN   Open it!
           [GUS *opens it and looks inside.*]
   What's in it?
           [GUS *empties twelve matches into his hand.*]
GUS   Matches.
BEN   Matches?
GUS   Yes.
BEN   Show it to me.
           [GUS *passes the envelope.* BEN *examines it.*]
   Nothing on it. Not a word.
GUS   That's funny, isn't it?
BEN   It came under the door?
GUS   Must have done.
BEN   Well, go on.
GUS   Go on where?
BEN   Open the door and see if you catch anyone outside.
GUS   Who, me?
BEN   Go on!
           [GUS *stares at him, puts the matches in his pocket, goes to his bed and
           brings a revolver from under the pillow. He goes to the door, opens it,
           looks out and shuts it.*]
GUS   No one.
           [*He replaces the revolver.*]
BEN   What did you see?
GUS   Nothing.
BEN   They must have been pretty quick.
           [GUS *takes the matches from pocket and looks at them.*]
GUS   Well, they'll come in handy.
BEN   Yes.
GUS   Won't they?
BEN   Yes, you're always running out, aren't you?
GUS   All the time.
BEN   Well, they'll come in handy then.
GUS   Yes.
BEN   Won't they?
GUS   Yes, I could do with them. I could do with them too.
BEN   You could, eh?
GUS   Yes.
BEN   Why?
GUS   We haven't any.
BEN   Well, you've got some now, haven't you?
GUS   I can light the kettle now.
BEN   Yes, you're always cadging matches. How many have you got there?
GUS   About a dozen.
BEN   Well, don't lose them. Red too. You don't even need a box.
           [GUS *probes his ear with a match.*]
   [*Slapping his hand.*] Don't waste them! Go on, go and light it.

GUS   Eh?

BEN   Go and light it.

GUS   Light what?

BEN   The kettle.

GUS   You mean the gas.

BEN   Who does?

GUS   You do.

BEN   [*His eyes narrowing.*] What do you mean, I mean the gas?

GUS   Well, that's what you mean, don't you? The gas.

BEN   [*Powerfully.*] If I say go and light the kettle I mean go and light the kettle.

GUS   How can you light a kettle?

BEN   It's a figure of speech! Light the kettle. It's a figure of speech!

GUS   I've never heard it.

BEN   Light the kettle! It's common usage!

GUS   I think you've got it wrong.

BEN   [*Menacing.*] What do you mean?

GUS   They say put on the kettle.

BEN   [*Taut.*] Who says?

[*They stare at each other, breathing hard.*]

[*Deliberately.*] I have never in all my life heard anyone say put on the kettle.

GUS   I bet my mother used to say it.

BEN   Your mother? When did you last see your mother?

GUS   I don't know, about—

BEN   Well, what are you talking about your mother for?

[*They stare.*]

Gus, I'm not trying to be unreasonable. I'm just trying to point out something to you.

GUS   Yes, but—

BEN   Who's the senior partner here, me or you?

GUS   You.

BEN   I'm only looking after your interests, Gus. You've got to learn, mate.

GUS   Yes, but I've never heard—

BEN   [*Vehemently.*] Nobody says light the gas! What does the gas light?

GUS   What does the gas—?

BEN   [*Grabbing him with two hands by the throat, at arm's length.*] THE KETTLE, YOU FOOL!

[GUS *takes the hands from his throat.*]

GUS   All right, all right.

[*Pause.*]

BEN   Well, what are you waiting for?

GUS   I want to see if they light.

BEN   What?

GUS   The matches.

[*He takes out the flattened box and tries to strike.*]

No.

[*He throws the box under the bed.*
BEN *stares at him.*
GUS *raises his foot.*]

Shall I try it on here?

[BEN *stares.* GUS *strikes a match on his shoe. It lights.*]

Here we are.

BEN   [*Wearily.*] Put on the bloody kettle, for Christ's sake.

> [BEN *goes to his bed, but, realizing what he has said, stops and half turns. They look at each other.* GUS *slowly exits, left.* BEN *slams his paper down on the bed and sits on it, head in hands.*]

GUS   [*Entering.*] It's going.

BEN   What?

GUS   The stove.

> [GUS *goes to his bed and sits.*]

I wonder who it'll be tonight.

> [*Silence.*]

Eh, I've been wanting to ask you something.

BEN   [*Putting his legs on the bed.*] Oh, for Christ's sake.

GUS   No. I was going to ask you something.

> [*He rises and sits on* BEN's *bed.*]

BEN   What are you sitting on my bed for?

> [GUS *sits.*]

What's the matter with you? You're always asking me questions. What's the matter with you?

GUS   Nothing.

BEN   You never used to ask me so many damn questions. What's come over you?

GUS   No, I was just wondering.

BEN   Stop wondering. You've got a job to do. Why don't you just do it and shut up?

GUS   That's what I was wondering about.

BEN   What?

GUS   The job.

BEN   What job?

GUS   [*Tentatively.*] I thought perhaps you might know something.

> [BEN *looks at him.*]

I thought perhaps you—I mean—have you got any idea—who it's going to be tonight?

BEN   Who what's going to be?

> [*They look at each other.*]

GUS   [*At length.*] Who it's going to be.

> [*Silence.*]

BEN   Are you feeling all right?

GUS   Sure.

BEN   Go and make the tea.

GUS   Yes, sure.

> [GUS *exits, left,* BEN *looks after him. He then takes his revolver from under the pillow and checks it for ammunition.* GUS *re-enters.*]

The gas has gone out.

BEN   Well, what about it?

GUS   There's a meter.[7]

BEN   I haven't got any money.

GUS   Nor have I.

BEN   You'll have to wait.

---

7. One that controls the supply of gas and must be fed with shilling coins.

GUS   What for?

BEN   For Wilson.

GUS   He might not come. He might just send a message. He doesn't always
come.

BEN   Well, you'll have to do without it, won't you?

GUS   Blimey.

BEN   You'll have a cup of tea afterwards. What's the matter with you?

GUS   I like to have one before.

[BEN *holds the revolver up to the light and polishes it.*]

BEN   You'd better get ready anyway.

GUS   Well, I don't know, that's a bit much, you know, for my money.

[*He picks up a packet of tea from the bed and throws it into the bag.*]
I hope he's got a shilling, anyway, if he comes. He's entitled to have. After
all, it's his place, he could have seen there was enough gas for a cup of tea.

BEN   What do you mean, it's his place?

GUS   Well, isn't it?

BEN   He's probably only rented it. It doesn't have to be his place.

GUS   I know it's his place. I bet the whole house is. He's not even laying on
any gas now either.

[GUS *sits on his bed.*]
It's his place all right. Look at all the other places. You go to this address,
there's a key there, there's a teapot, there's never a soul in sight—[*He
pauses.*] Eh, nobody ever hears a thing, have you ever thought of that? We
never get any complaints, do we, too much noise or anything like that? You
never see a soul, do you?—except the bloke who comes. You ever noticed
that? I wonder if the walls are soundproof. [*He touches the wall above his
bed.*] Can't tell. All you do is wait, eh? Half the time he doesn't even bother
to put in an appearance, Wilson.

BEN   Why should he? He's a busy man.

GUS   [*Thoughtfully.*] I find him hard to talk to, Wilson. Do you know that,
Ben?

BEN   Scrub round it, will you?

[*Pause.*]

GUS   There are a number of things I want to ask him. But I can never get
round to it, when I see him.

[*Pause.*]
I've been thinking about the last one.

BEN   What last one?

GUS   That girl.

[BEN *grabs the paper, which he reads.*]
[*Rising, looking down at* BEN.] How many times have you read that paper?

[BEN *slams the paper down and rises.*]

BEN   [*Angrily.*] What do you mean?

GUS   I was just wondering how many times you'd—

BEN   What are you doing, criticizing me?

GUS   No, I was just—

BEN   You'll get a swipe round your earhole if you don't watch your step.

GUS   Now look here, Ben—

BEN   I'm not looking anywhere! [*He addresses the room.*] How many times
have I—! A bloody liberty!

GUS   I didn't mean that.

BEN   You just get on with it, mate. Get on with it, that's all.
       [BEN *gets back on the bed.*]
GUS   I was just thinking about that girl, that's all.
       [GUS *sits on his bed.*]
   She wasn't much to look at, I know, but still. It was a mess though, wasn't
   it? What a mess. Honest, I can't remember a mess like that one. They don't
   seem to hold together like men, women. A looser texture, like. Didn't she
   spread, eh? She didn't half spread. Kaw! But I've been meaning to ask you.
       [BEN *sits up and clenches his eyes.*]
   Who clears up after we've gone? I'm curious about that. Who does the
   clearing up? Maybe they don't clear up. Maybe they just leave them there,
   eh? What do you think? How many jobs have we done? Blimey, I can't count
   them. What if they never clear anything up after we've gone.
BEN   [*Pityingly.*] You mutt. Do you think we're the only branch of this organization? Have a bit of common. They got departments for everything.
GUS   What, cleaners and all?
BEN   You birk!
GUS   No, it was that girl made me start to think—
       [*There is a loud clatter and racket in the bulge of wall between the beds,
       of something descending. They grab their revolvers, jump up and face
       the wall. The noise comes to a stop. Silence. They look at each other.
       BEN gestures sharply towards the wall. GUS approaches the wall slowly.
       He bangs it with his revolver. It is hollow. BEN moves to the head of his
       bed, his revolver cocked. GUS puts his revolver on his bed and pats along
       the bottom of the centre panel. He finds a rim. He lifts the panel. Dis-
       closed is a serving-hatch, a "dumb waiter." A wide box is held by pulleys.
       GUS peers into the box. He brings out a piece of paper.*]
BEN   What is it?
GUS   You have a look at it.
BEN   Read it.
GUS   [*Reading.*] Two braised steak and chips. Two sago puddings. Two teas
   without sugar.
BEN   Let me see that. [*He takes the paper.*]
GUS   [*To himself.*] Two teas without sugar.
BEN   Mmnn.
GUS   What do you think of that?
BEN   Well—
       [*The box goes up, BEN levels his revolver.*]
GUS   Give us a chance! They're in a hurry, aren't they?
       [*BEN rereads the note. GUS looks over his shoulder.*]
   That's a bit—that's a bit funny, isn't it?
BEN   [*Quickly.*] No, it's not funny. It probably used to be a café here, that's
   all. Upstairs. These places change hands very quickly.
GUS   A café?
BEN   Yes.
GUS   What, do you mean this was the kitchen, down here?
BEN   Yes, they change hands overnight, these places. Go into liquidation. The
   people who run it, you know, they don't find it a going concern, they move
   out.
GUS   You mean the people who ran this place didn't find it a going concern
   and moved out?

BEN   Sure.

GUS   WELL, WHO'S GOT IT NOW?

      [*Silence.*]

BEN   What do you mean, who's got it now?

GUS   Who's got it now? If they moved out, who moved in?

BEN   Well, that all depends—

      [*The box descends with a clatter and bang.* BEN *levels his revolver.* GUS *goes to the box and brings out a piece of paper.*]

GUS   [*Reading.*] Soup of the day. Liver and onions. Jam tart.

      [*A pause.* GUS *looks at* BEN. BEN *takes the note and reads it. He walks slowly to the hatch.* GUS *follows.* BEN *looks into the hatch but not up it.* GUS *puts his hand on* BEN's *shoulder.* BEN *throws it off.* GUS *puts his finger to his mouth. He leans on the hatch and swiftly looks up it.* BEN *flings him away in alarm.* BEN *looks at the note. He throws his revolver on the bed and speaks with decision.*]

BEN   We'd better send something up.

GUS   Eh?

BEN   We'd better send something up.

GUS   Oh! Yes. Yes. Maybe you're right.

      [*They are both relieved at the decision.*]

BEN   [*Purposefully.*] Quick! What have you got in that bag?

GUS   Not much.

      [GUS *goes to the hatch and shouts up it.*]

  Wait a minute!

BEN   Don't do that!

      [GUS *examines the contents of the bag and brings them out, one by one.*]

GUS   Biscuits. A bar of chocolate. Half a pint of milk.

BEN   That all?

GUS   Packet of tea.

BEN   Good.

GUS   We can't send the tea. That's all the tea we've got.

BEN   Well, there's no gas. You can't do anything with it, can you?

GUS   Maybe they can send us down a bob.[8]

BEN   What else is there?

GUS   [*Reaching into bag.*] One Eccles cake.[9]

BEN   One Eccles cake?

GUS   Yes.

BEN   You never told me you had an Eccles cake.

GUS   Didn't I?

BEN   Why only one? Didn't you bring one for me?

GUS   I didn't think you'd be keen.

BEN   Well, you can't send up one Eccles cake, anyway.

GUS   Why not?

BEN   Fetch one of those plates.

GUS   All right.

      [GUS *goes towards the door, left, and stops.*]

  Do you mean I can keep the Eccles cake then?

BEN   Keep it?

---

8. A shilling (i.e., to insert in the gas meter).
9. A small cake originally made in the Lancashire town of Eccles.

GUS Well, they don't know we've got it, do they?

BEN That's not the point.

GUS Can't I keep it?

BEN No, you can't. Get the plate.

[GUS *exits, left.* BEN *looks in the bag. He brings out a packet of crisps.*[1]
Enter GUS *with a plate.*]

[*Accusingly, holding up the crisps.*] Where did these come from?

GUS What?

BEN Where did these crisps come from?

GUS Where did you find them?

BEN [*Hitting him on the shoulder.*] You're playing a dirty game, my lad!

GUS I only eat those with beer!

BEN Well, where were you going to get the beer?

GUS I was saving them till I did.

BEN I'll remember this. Put everything on the plate.

[*They pile everything on to the plate. The box goes up without the plate.*]

Wait a minute!

[*They stand.*]

GUS It's gone up.

BEN It's all your stupid fault, playing about!

GUS What do we do now?

BEN We'll have to wait till it comes down.

[BEN *puts the plate on the bed, puts on his shoulder holster, and starts
to put on his tie.*]

You'd better get ready.

[GUS *goes to his bed, puts on his tie, and starts to fix his holster.*]

GUS Hey, Ben.

BEN What?

GUS What's going on here?

[*Pause.*]

BEN What do you mean?

GUS How can this be a café?

BEN It used to be a café.

GUS Have you seen the gas stove?

BEN What about it?

GUS It's only got three rings.

BEN So what?

GUS Well, you couldn't cook much on three rings, not for a busy place like
this.

BEN [*Irritably.*] That's why the service is slow!

[BEN *puts on his waistcoat.*]

GUS Yes, but what happens when we're not here? What do they do then? All
these menus coming down and nothing going up. It might have been going
on like this for years.

[BEN *brushes his jacket.*]

What happens when we go?

[BEN *puts on his jacket.*]

They can't do much business.

[*The box descends. They turn about.* GUS *goes to the hatch and brings
out a note.*]

---

1. Potato chips.

GUS   [*Reading.*] Macaroni Pastitsio. Ormitha Macarounada.

BEN   What was that?

GUS   Macaroni Pastitsio. Ormitha Macarounada.

BEN   Greek dishes.

GUS   No.

BEN   That's right.

GUS   That's pretty high class.

BEN   Quick before it goes up.

      [GUS *puts the plate in the box.*]

GUS   [*Calling up the hatch.*] Three McVitie and Price! One Lyons Red Label!
One Smith's Crisps!² One Eccles cake! One Fruit and Nut!

BEN   Cadbury's.³

GUS   [*Up the hatch.*] Cadbury's!

BEN   [*Handing the milk.*] One bottle of milk.

GUS   [*Up the hatch.*] One bottle of milk! Half a pint! [*He looks at the label.*]
Express Dairy! [*He puts the bottle in the box.*]

      [*The box goes up.*]

Just did it.

BEN   You shouldn't shout like that.

GUS   Why not?

BEN   It isn't done.

      [BEN *goes to his bed.*]

Well, that should be all right, anyway, for the time being.

GUS   You think so, eh?

BEN   Get dressed, will you? It'll be any minute now.

      [GUS *puts on his waistcoat.* BEN *lies down and looks up at the ceiling.*]

GUS   This is some place. No tea and no biscuits.

BEN   Eating makes you lazy, mate. You're getting lazy, you know that? You
don't want to get slack on your job.

GUS   Who me?

BEN   Slack, mate, slack.

GUS   Who me? Slack?

BEN   Have you checked your gun? You haven't even checked your gun. It
looks disgraceful, anyway. Why don't you ever polish it?

      [GUS *rubs his revolver on the sheet.* BEN *takes out a pocket mirror and
straightens his tie.*]

GUS   I wonder where the cook is. They must have had a few, to cope with
that. Maybe they had a few more gas stoves. Eh! Maybe there's another
kitchen along the passage.

BEN   Of course there is! Do you know what it takes to make an Ormitha
Macarounada?

GUS   No, what?

BEN   An Ormitha—! Buck your ideas up, will you?

GUS   Takes a few cooks, eh?

      [GUS *puts his revolver in its holster.*]

The sooner we're out of this place the better.

      [*He puts on his jacket.*]

Why doesn't he get in touch? I feel like I've been here years. [*He takes his
revolver out of its holster to check the ammunition.*] We've never let him

---

2. Brands, respectively, of cookies, tea, and potato   3. A brand of chocolate bar.
chips.

down though, have we? We've never let him down. I was thinking only the other day, Ben. We're reliable, aren't we?

[*He puts his revolver back in its holster.*]

Still, I'll be glad when it's over tonight.

[*He brushes his jacket.*]

I hope the bloke's not going to get excited tonight, or anything. I'm feeling a bit off. I've got a splitting headache.

> [*Silence.*
>
> The box descends. BEN *jumps up.*
>
> GUS *collects the note.*]

[*Reading.*] One Bamboo Shoots, Water Chestnuts, and Chicken. One Char Siu and Beansprouts.

BEN   Beansprouts?

GUS   Yes.

BEN   Blimey.

GUS   I wouldn't know where to begin.

> [*He looks back at the box. The packet of tea is inside it. He picks it up.*]

They've sent back the tea.

BEN   [*Anxious.*] What'd they do that for?

GUS   Maybe it isn't teatime.

> [*The box goes up. Silence.*]

BEN   [*Throwing the tea on the bed, and speaking urgently.*] Look here. We'd better tell them.

GUS   Tell them what?

BEN   That we can't do it, we haven't got it.

GUS   All right then.

BEN   Lend us your pencil. We'll write a note.

> [GUS, *turning for a pencil, suddenly discovers the speaking tube, which hangs on the right wall of the hatch facing his bed.*]

GUS   What's this?

BEN   What?

GUS   This.

BEN   [*Examining it.*] This? It's a speaking tube.

GUS   How long has that been there?

BEN   Just the job. We should have used it before, instead of shouting up there.

GUS   Funny I never noticed it before.

BEN   Well, come on.

GUS   What do you do?

BEN   See that? That's a whistle.

GUS   What, this?

BEN   Yes, take it out. Pull it out.

> [GUS *does so.*]

That's it.

GUS   What do we do now?

BEN   Blow into it.

GUS   Blow?

BEN   It whistles up there if you blow. Then they know you want to speak. Blow.

> [GUS *blows. Silence.*]

GUS   [*Tube at mouth.*] I can't hear a thing.

BEN   Now you speak! Speak into it!

[GUS *looks at* BEN, *then speaks into the tube.*]
GUS The larder's bare!
BEN Give me that!

> [*He grabs the tube and puts it to his mouth.*]

[*Speaking with great deference.*] Good evening. I'm sorry to—bother you, but we just thought we'd better let you know that we haven't got anything left. We sent up all we had. There's no more food down here.

> [*He brings the tube slowly to his ear.*]

What?

> [*To mouth.*]

What?

> [*To ear. He listens. To mouth.*]

No, all we had we sent up.

> [*To ear. He listens. To mouth.*]

Oh, I'm very sorry to hear that.

> [*To ear. He listens. To* GUS.]

The Eccles cake was stale.

> [*He listens. To* GUS.]

The chocolate was melted.

> [*He listens. To* GUS.]

The milk was sour.
GUS What about the crisps?
BEN [*Listening.*] The biscuits were mouldy.

> [*He glares at* GUS. *Tube to mouth.*]

Well, we're sorry about that.

> [*Tube to ear.*]

What?

> [*To mouth.*]

What?

> [*To ear.*]

Yes. Yes.

> [*To mouth.*]

Yes certainly. Right away.

> [*To ear. The voice has ceased. He hangs up the tube.*]

[*Excitedly.*] Did you hear that?
GUS What?
BEN You know what he said? Light the kettle! Not put on the kettle! Not light the gas! But light the kettle!
GUS How can we light the kettle?
BEN What do you mean?
GUS There's no gas.
BEN [*Clapping hand to head.*] Now what do we do?
GUS What did he want us to light the kettle for?
BEN For tea. He wanted a cup of tea.
GUS *He* wanted a cup of tea! What about me? I've been wanting a cup of tea all night!
BEN [*Despairingly.*] What do we do now?
GUS What are we supposed to drink?

> [BEN *sits on his bed, staring.*]

What about us?

> [BEN *sits.*]

I'm thirsty too. I'm starving. And he wants a cup of tea. That beats the band, that does.

[BEN *lets his head sink on his chest.*]

I could do with a bit of sustenance myself. What about you? You look as if you could do with something too.

[GUS *sits on his bed.*]

We send him up all we've got and he's not satisfied. No, honest, it's enough to make the cat laugh. Why did you send him up all that stuff? [*Thoughtfully.*] Why did I send it up?

[*Pause.*]

Who knows what he's got upstairs? He's probably got a salad bowl. They must have something up there. They won't get much from down here. You notice they didn't ask for any salads? They've probably got a salad bowl up there. Cold meat, radishes, cucumbers. Watercress. Roll mops.

[*Pause.*]

Hardboiled eggs.

[*Pause.*]

The lot. They've probably got a crate of beer too. Probably eating my crisps with a pint of beer now. Didn't have anything to say about those crisps, did he? They do all right, don't worry about that. You don't think they're just going to sit there and wait for stuff to come up from down here, do you? That'll get them nowhere.

[*Pause.*]

They do all right.

[*Pause.*]

And he wants a cup of tea.

[*Pause.*]

That's past a joke, in my opinion.

[*He looks over at* BEN, *rises, and goes to him.*]

What's the matter with you? You don't look too bright. I feel like an Alka-Seltzer myself.

[BEN *sits up.*]

BEN   [*In a low voice.*] Time's getting on.

GUS   I know. I don't like doing a job on an empty stomach.

BEN   [*Wearily.*] Be quiet a minute. Let me give you your instructions.

GUS   What for? We always do it the same way, don't we?

BEN   Let me give you your instructions.

      [GUS *sighs and sits next to* BEN *on the bed. The instructions are stated and repeated automatically.*]

When we get the call, you go over and stand behind the door.

GUS   Stand behind the door.

BEN   If there's a knock on the door you don't answer it.

GUS   If there's a knock on the door I don't answer it.

BEN   But there won't be a knock on the door.

GUS   So I won't answer it.

BEN   When the bloke comes in—

GUS   When the bloke comes in—

BEN   Shut the door behind him.

GUS   Shut the door behind him.

BEN   Without divulging your presence.

GUS   Without divulging my presence.

BEN He'll see me and come towards me.

GUS He'll see you and come towards you.

BEN He won't see you.

GUS [*Absently.*] Eh?

BEN He won't see you.

GUS He won't see me.

BEN But he'll see me.

GUS He'll see you.

BEN He won't know you're there.

GUS He won't know you're there.

BEN He won't know *you're* there.

GUS He won't know I'm there.

BEN I take out my gun.

GUS You take out your gun.

BEN He stops in his tracks.

GUS He stops in his tracks.

BEN If he turns round—

GUS If he turns round—

BEN You're there.

GUS I'm here.

[BEN *frowns and presses his forehead.*]

You've missed something out.

BEN I know. What?

GUS I haven't taken my gun out, according to you.

BEN You take your gun out—

GUS After I've closed the door.

BEN After you've closed the door.

GUS You've never missed that out before, you know that?

BEN When he sees you behind him—

GUS Me behind him—

BEN And me in front of him—

GUS And you in front of him—

BEN He'll feel uncertain—

GUS Uneasy.

BEN He won't know what to do.

GUS So what will he do?

BEN He'll look at me and he'll look at you.

GUS We won't say a word.

BEN We'll look at him.

GUS He won't say a word.

BEN He'll look at us.

GUS And we'll look at him.

BEN Exactly.

[*Pause.*]

GUS What do we do if it's a girl?

BEN We do the same.

GUS Exactly the same?

BEN Exactly.

[*Pause.*]

GUS We don't do anything different?

BEN We do exactly the same.

GUS Oh.

[GUS *rises, and shivers.*]

Excuse me.

[*He exits through the door on the left.* BEN *remains sitting on the bed, still.*

The lavatory chain is pulled once off left, but the lavatory does not flush.

Silence.

GUS *re-enters and stops inside the door, deep in thought. He looks at* BEN, *then walks slowly across to his own bed. He is troubled. He stands, thinking. He turns and looks at* BEN. *He moves a few paces towards him.*]

[*Slowly in a low, tense voice.*] Why did he send us matches if he knew there was no gas?

[*Silence.*

BEN *stares in front of him.* GUS *crosses to the left side of* BEN, *to the foot of his bed, to get to his other ear.*]

Ben. Why did he send us matches if he knew there was no gas?

[BEN *looks up.*]

Why did he do that?

BEN Who?

GUS Who sent us those matches?

BEN What are you talking about?

[GUS *stares down at him.*]

GUS [*Thickly.*] Who is it upstairs?

BEN [*Nervously.*] What's one thing to do with another?

GUS Who is it, though?

BEN What's one thing to do with another?

[BEN *fumbles for his paper on the bed.*]

GUS I asked you a question.

BEN Enough!

GUS [*With growing agitation.*] I asked you before. Who moved in? I asked you. You said the people who had it before moved out. Well, who moved in?

BEN [*Hunched.*] Shut up.

GUS I told you, didn't I?

BEN [*Standing.*] Shut up!

GUS [*Feverishly.*] I told you before who owned this place, didn't I? I told you.

[BEN *hits him viciously on the shoulder.*]

I told you who ran this place, didn't I?

[BEN *hits him viciously on the shoulder.*]

[*Violently.*] Well, what's he playing all these games for? That's what I want to know. What's he doing it for?

BEN What games?

GUS [*Passionately, advancing.*] What's he doing it for? We've been through our tests, haven't we? We got right through our tests, years ago, didn't we? We took them together, don't you remember, didn't we? We've proved our-selves before now, haven't we? We've always done our job. What's he doing all this for? What's the idea? What's he playing these games for?

[*The box in the shaft comes down behind them. The noise is this time accompanied by a shrill whistle, as it falls.* GUS *rushes to the hatch and seizes the note.*]

[*Reading.*] Scampi!

    [*He crumples the note, picks up the tube, takes out the whistle, blows and speaks.*]

We've got nothing left! Nothing! Do you understand?

    [BEN *seizes the tube and flings* GUS *away. He follows* GUS *and slaps him hard, back-handed, across the chest.*]

BEN   Stop it! You maniac!

GUS   But you heard!

BEN   [*Savagely.*] That's enough! I'm warning you!

    [*Silence.*

        BEN *hangs the tube. He goes to his bed and lies down. He picks up his paper and reads.*

        Silence.

        The box goes up.

        They turn quickly, their eyes meet. BEN *turns to his paper.*

        Slowly GUS *goes back to his bed, and sits.*

        Silence.

        The hatch falls back into place.

        They turn quickly, their eyes meet. BEN *turns back to his paper.*

        Silence.

        BEN *throws his paper down.*]

BEN   Kaw!

    [*He picks up the paper and looks at it.*]

Listen to this!

    [*Pause.*]

What about that, eh?

    [*Pause.*]

Kaw!

    [*Pause.*]

Have you ever heard such a thing?

GUS   [*Dully.*] Go on!

BEN   It's true.

GUS   Get away.

BEN   It's down here in black and white.

GUS   [*Very low.*] Is that a fact?

BEN   Can you imagine it.

GUS   It's unbelievable.

BEN   It's enough to make you want to puke, isn't it?

GUS   [*Almost inaudible.*] Incredible.

    [BEN *shakes his head. He puts the paper down and rises. He fixes the revolver in his holster.*

        GUS *stands up. He goes towards the door on the left.*]

BEN   Where are you going?

GUS   I'm going to have a glass of water.

    [*He exits.* BEN *brushes dust off his clothes and shoes. The whistle in the speaking tube blows. He goes to it, takes the whistle out and puts the tube to his ear. He listens. He puts it to his mouth.*]

BEN   Yes.

    [*To ear. He listens. To mouth.*]

Straight away. Right.

    [*To ear. He listens. To mouth.*]

Sure we're ready.

[*To ear. He listens. To mouth.*]
Understood. Repeat. He has arrived and will be coming in straight away.
The normal method to be employed. Understood.
　　　　[*To ear. He listens. To mouth.*]
Sure we're ready.
　　　　[*To ear. He listens. To mouth.*]
Right.
　　　　[*He hangs the tube up.*]
Gus!
　　　　[*He takes out a comb and combs his hair, adjusts his jacket to diminish
　　　　the bulge of the revolver. The lavatory flushes off left.* BEN *goes quickly
　　　　to the door, left.*]
Gus!
　　　　[*The door right opens sharply.* BEN *turns, his revolver leveled at the door.*
　　　　GUS *stumbles in.*
　　　　He is stripped of his jacket, waistcoat, tie, holster, and revolver.
　　　　He stops, body stooping, his arms at his sides.
　　　　He raises his head and looks at* BEN.
　　　　A long silence.
　　　　They stare at each other.]

CURTAIN

1960

CHINUA ACHEBE
b. 1930

The most celebrated African novelist is Chinua Achebe, whose *Things Fall Apart*
(1958) permanently transformed the landscape of African fiction, both in his own
continent and in the Western imagination. His novels, while steadfastly refusing to
sentimentalize their Nigerian subjects, effectively challenged many of the West's
entrenched impressions of African life and culture, replacing simplistic stereotypes
with portrayals of a complex society still suffering from a legacy of Western colonial
oppression.

Achebe was born in Ogidi, an Igbo-speaking town in eastern Nigeria, and educated—in English—at church schools and University College, Ibadan, where he subsequently taught (briefly) before joining the Nigerian Broadcasting Corporation in
Lagos. He was director of external broadcasting from 1961 to 1966, and then
launched a publishing company with Christopher Okigbo, a poet soon to die in the
Nigerian civil war (1967–70). After the war Achebe taught in the United States,
before returning for a time to the University of Nigeria at Nsukka. Since 1990 Achebe
has been Charles P. Stevenson Jr. Professor of Languages and Literature at Bard
College.

A volume of Achebe's poems was joint winner of the Commonwealth Poetry Prize
in 1972. He also has written short stories and essays, including an attack on corruption in Nigerian politics, *The Trouble with Nigeria* (1983). A more famous attack of
another kind, his essay "An Image of Africa: Racism in Conrad's *Heart of Darkness*,"
is a vigorous polemic that accuses Conrad of racism, while perhaps deflecting attention from Achebe's debt to his Polish-born precursor. Achebe is best-known for his

novels, however: *Things Fall Apart* (1958), *No Longer at Ease* (1960), *Arrow of God* (1964), *A Man of the People* (1966), and *Anthills of the Savannah* (1987). The first of these is a response to Joyce Cary's *Mr. Johnson* (1939), a novel famous in its day for its depiction of Nigerian tribal society. Cary had been a British district officer in Nigeria, and his account of the life and tragic death of a young African clerk, although well meaning, was written from an outsider's patronizing perspective. By contrast, Achebe's *Things Fall Apart*, written with an insider's understanding of the African world and its history, depicts the destruction of an individual, a family, and a culture at the moment of colonial incursion. This novel's hero, Okonkwo, is dignified and courageous, a noble figure, whereas Cary's Mr. Johnson is charming but undignified. Like other tragic heroes, however, Okonkwo is flawed and falls through lack of the balance everywhere celebrated in Achebe's writings.

Taking his title from W. B. Yeats's poem "The Second Coming," Achebe shows how "the blood-dimmed tide is loosed" in a Nigerian village by European colonizers, drowning the ceremonies of the indigenous society. The novel is set in the fictional village of Umuofia during the late nineteenth century, before the arrival of Europeans, and in the ensuing period of British imperial "pacification" of southeast Nigeria from 1900 to 1920, including the Ahiara massacre of 1905 (fictionalized in chapter 15 as the Abame incident) and the destruction of Igbo opposition groups by the Bende-Onitsha Hinterland Expedition. The British asserted colonial authority over the Igbo through a combination of economic trade, missionary religion, and political control, and Achebe represents this process of colonization from the vantage point of villagers who are puzzled, intrigued, co-opted, enraged, divided against themselves, or killed. The imperial incursion seems all the more bewildering and violent because the novel has immersed the reader in this village society's finely calibrated cultural practices in religion and government, athletics and storytelling, agriculture and the family. Helping to rebut Western preconceptions about African primitivism, this rich portrait of a culture also advances Achebe's ambition to help his "society regain belief in itself and put away the complexes of the years of denigration and self-abasement" produced by the distortions of colonialism. He has said he wants his novels to teach his African "readers that their past—with all its imperfections—was not one long night of savagery from which the first Europeans acting on God's behalf delivered them." But while *Things Fall Apart* lays considerable blame for the destruction of Igbo village society at the door of the whites, Achebe carefully avoids rosily idealizing the precolonial Igbo world, and he has frankly acknowledged that "internal problems" also made this African society vulnerable. *Things Fall Apart* is at once Okonkwo's tragedy and that of a complex tribal society, whose members speak a resonantly proverbial language that operates in the book as an image of all the beautiful and traditional structures transformed irrevocably by colonialism.

PRONOUNCING GLOSSARY

The following list uses common English syllables and stress accents to provide rough equivalents of selected words. Most of the names in *Things Fall Apart* are pronounced basically as they would be in English (for example, Okonkwo as *oh-kon'-kwo*), except that Igbo (like other African languages and Chinese) is a tonal language and therefore uses high or low tones for individual syllables.

Chielo: *chee'-ay-loh*	Ikemefuna: *ee-kay-may'-foo-na*
egwugu: *eg-woog'-woo*	mbari: *mbah'-ree*
Erulu: *air-oo'-loo*	Ndulue: *in'-doo-loo'-eh*
Ezeani: *ez-ah'-nee*	Nwakibie: *nwa'-kee-ee'-bee-yay*
Ezeugo: *e'-zoo-goh*	Nwayieke: *nwah'-ee-eh'-kay*
Idemili: *ee-day-mee'-lee*	Umuofia: *oo'-moo-off'-yah*
Igbo: *ee'-boh*	

Things Fall Apart

Turning and turning in the widening gyre
The falcon cannot hear the falconer;
Things fall apart; the centre cannot hold;
Mere anarchy is loosed upon the world.
    W. B. Yeats: 'The Second Coming'

Part One

CHAPTER ONE

Okonkwo[1] was well known throughout the nine villages and even beyond. His fame rested on solid personal achievements. As a young man of eighteen he had brought honour to his village by throwing Amalinze the Cat. Amalinze was the great wrestler who for seven years was unbeaten, from Umuofia to Mbaino.[2] He was called the Cat because his back would never touch the earth. It was this man that Okonkwo threw in a fight which the old men agreed was one of the fiercest since the founder of their town engaged a spirit of the wild for seven days and seven nights.

The drums beat and the flutes sang and the spectators held their breath. Amalinze was a wily craftsman, but Okonkwo was as slippery as a fish in water. Every nerve and every muscle stood out on their arms, on their backs and their thighs, and one almost heard them stretching to breaking point. In the end Okonkwo threw the Cat.

That was many years ago, twenty years or more, and during this time Okonkwo's fame had grown like a bush-fire in the harmattan.[3] He was tall and huge, and his bushy eyebrows and wide nose gave him a very severe look. He breathed heavily, and it was said that, when he slept, his wives and children in their out-houses could hear him breathe. When he walked, his heels hardly touched the ground and he seemed to walk on springs, as if he was going to pounce on somebody. And he did pounce on people quite often. He had a slight stammer and whenever he was angry and could not get his words out quickly enough, he would use his fists. He had no patience with unsuccessful men. He had had no patience with his father.

Unoka,[4] for that was his father's name, had died ten years ago. In his day he was lazy and improvident and was quite incapable of thinking about tomorrow. If any money came his way, and it seldom did, he immediately bought gourds of palm-wine, called round his neighbours and made merry. He always said that whenever he saw a dead man's mouth he saw the folly of not eating what one had in one's lifetime. Unoka was, of course, a debtor, and he owed every neighbour some money, from a few cowries[5] to quite substantial amounts.

He was tall but very thin and had a slight stoop. He wore a haggard and mournful look except when he was drinking or playing on his flute. He was

---

1. Man [*oko*] born on Nkwo Day; the name also suggests stubborn male pride.
2. Four settlements. Umuofia means "children of the forest" (literal trans.); but *ofia* ("forest") also means "bush," or land untouched by European influence.
3. A dusty wind from the Sahara.

4. Home is supreme.
5. Glossy half-inch-long tan-and-white shells, collected in strings and used as money. A bag of twenty-four thousand cowries weighed about sixty pounds and, at the time of the story, was worth approximately £1 British.

very good on his flute, and his happiest moments were the two or three moons after the harvest when the village musicians brought down their instruments, hung above the fireplace. Unoka would play with them, his face beaming with blessedness and peace. Sometimes another village would ask Unoka's band and their dancing *egwugwu*[6] to come and stay with them and teach them their tunes. They would go to such hosts for as long as three or four markets,[7] making music and feasting. Unoka loved the good fare and the good fellowship, and he loved this season of the year, when the rains had stopped and the sun rose every morning with dazzling beauty. And it was not too hot either, because the cold and dry harmattan wind was blowing down from the north. Some years the harmattan was very severe and a dense haze hung on the atmosphere. Old men and children would then sit round log fires, warming their bodies. Unoka loved it all, and he loved the first kites[8] that returned with the dry season, and the children who sang songs of welcome to them. He would remember his own childhood, how he had often wandered around looking for a kite sailing leisurely against the blue sky. As soon as he found one he would sing with his whole being, welcoming it back from its long, long journey, and asking it if it had brought home any lengths of cloth.

That was years ago, when he was young. Unoka, the grown-up, was a failure. He was poor and his wife and children had barely enough to eat. People laughed at him because he was a loafer, and they swore never to lend him any more money because he never paid back. But Unoka was such a man that he always succeeded in borrowing more, and piling up his debts.

One day a neighbour called Okoye[9] came in to see him. He was reclining on a mud bed in his hut playing on the flute. He immediately rose and shook hands with Okoye, who then unrolled the goatskin which he carried under his arm, and sat down. Unoka went into an inner room and soon returned with a small wooden disc containing a kola nut, some alligator pepper and a lump of white chalk.[1]

"I have kola," he announced when he sat down, and passed the disc over to his guest.

"Thank you. He who brings kola brings life. But I think you ought to break it," replied Okoye passing back the disc.

"No, it is for you, I think," and they argued like this for a few moments before Unoka accepted the honour of breaking the kola. Okoye, meanwhile, took the lump of chalk, drew some lines on the floor, and then painted his big toe.[2]

As he broke the kola, Unoka prayed to their ancestors for life and health, and for protection against their enemies. When they had eaten they talked about many things: about the heavy rains which were drowning the yams, about the next ancestral feast and about the impending war with the village of Mbaino. Unoka was never happy when it came to wars. He was in fact a coward and could not bear the sight of blood. And so he changed the subject

---

6. Here masked performers as part of musical entertainment.

7. Counting one important market day a week, roughly two English weeks. The Igbo week has four days: Eke, Oye, Afo, and Nkwo. Eke is a rest day and the main market day; Afo, a half day on the farm; Oye and Nkwo, full workdays.

8. A kind of hawk.

9. Man born on Oye Day; a generic "Everyman" name.

1. Signifies coolness and peace and is offered in rituals of hospitality so that the guest may draw his personal emblem on the floor. "Kola nut": a bitter, caffeine-rich nut that is broken and eaten ceremonially; it indicates life or vitality. "Alligator pepper": black pepper, known as the "pepper for kola" to distinguish it from cooking pepper, or chilies.

2. If the guest has taken the first title, he marks his big toe. Higher titles require different facial markings.

and talked about music, and his face beamed. He could hear in his mind's ear the blood-stirring and intricate rhythms of the *ekwe* and the *udu* and the *ogene*,[3] and he could hear his own flute weaving in and out of them, decorating them with a colourful and plaintive tune. The total effect was gay and brisk, but if one picked out the flute as it went up and down and then broke up into short snatches, one saw that there was sorrow and grief there.

Okoye was also a musician. He played on the *ogene*. But he was not a failure like Unoka. He had a large barn full of yams and he had three wives. And now he was going to take the Idemili title,[4] the third highest in the land. It was a very expensive ceremony and he was gathering all his resources together. That was in fact the reason why he had come to see Unoka. He cleared his throat and began:

"Thank you for the kola. You may have heard of the title I intend to take shortly."

Having spoken plainly so far, Okoye said the next half a dozen sentences in proverbs. Among the Ibo the art of conversation is regarded very highly, and proverbs are the palm-oil with which words are eaten. Okoye was a great talker and he spoke for a long time, skirting round the subject and then hitting it finally. In short, he was asking Unoka to return the two hundred cowries he had borrowed from him more than two years before. As soon as Unoka understood what his friend was driving at, he burst out laughing. He laughed loud and long and his voice rang out clear as the *ogene*, and tears stood in his eyes. His visitor was amazed, and sat speechless. At the end, Unoka was able to give an answer between fresh outbursts of mirth.

"Look at that wall," he said, pointing at the far wall of his hut, which was rubbed with red earth so that it shone. "Look at those lines of chalk;" and Okoye saw groups of short perpendicular lines drawn in chalk. There were five groups, and the smallest group had ten lines. Unoka had a sense of the dramatic and so he allowed a pause, in which he took a pinch of snuff and sneezed noisily, and then he continued: "Each group there represents a debt to someone, and each stroke is one hundred cowries. You see, I owe that man a thousand cowries. But he has not come to wake me up in the morning for it. I shall pay you, but not today. Our elders say that the sun will shine on those who stand before it shines on those who kneel under them. I shall pay my big debts first." And he took another pinch of snuff, as if that was paying the big debts first. Okoye rolled his goatskin and departed.

When Unoka died he had taken no title at all and he was heavily in debt. Any wonder then that his son Okonkwo was ashamed of him? Fortunately, among these people a man was judged according to his worth and not according to the worth of his father. Okonkwo was clearly cut out for great things. He was still young but he had won fame as the greatest wrestler in the nine villages. He was a wealthy farmer and had two barns full of yams, and had just married his third wife. To crown it all he had taken two titles and had shown incredible prowess in two inter-tribal wars. And so although Okonkwo was still young, he was already one of the greatest men of his time. Age was respected

---

3. A bell-shaped gong made from two pieces of sheet iron. "Ekwe": a wooden drum, about three feet long, that produces high and low tones (as does the Igbo language). "Udu": a clay pot with a hole to one side of the neck opening; various resonant tones are produced when the hole is struck with one hand while the other hand covers or uncovers the top.

4. A title of honor named after the river god Idemili, to whom the python is sacred. "Barn": not a building but a walled enclosure for the yam stacks (frames on which individual yams are tied, shaded with palm leaves, and exposed to circulating air).

among his people, but achievement was revered. As the elders said, if a child washed his hands he could eat with kings. Okonkwo had clearly washed his hands and so he ate with kings and elders. And that was how he came to look after the doomed lad who was sacrificed to the village of Umuofia by their neighbours to avoid war and bloodshed. The ill-fated lad was called Ikemefuna.[5]

CHAPTER TWO

Okonkwo had just blown out the palm-oil lamp and stretched himself on his bamboo bed when he heard the *ogene* of the town-crier piercing the still night air. *Gome, gome, gome, gome,* boomed the hollow metal. Then the crier gave his message, and at the end of it beat his instrument again. And this was the message. Every man of Umuofia was asked to gather at the market-place tomorrow morning. Okonkwo wondered what was amiss, for he knew certainly that something was amiss. He had discerned a clear overtone of tragedy in the crier's voice, and even now he could still hear it as it grew dimmer and dimmer in the distance.

The night was very quiet. It was always quiet except on moonlight nights. Darkness held a vague terror for these people, even the bravest among them. Children were warned not to whistle at night for fear of evil spirits. Dangerous animals became even more sinister and uncanny in the dark. A snake was never called by its name at night, because it would hear. It was called a string. And so on this particular night as the crier's voice was gradually swallowed up in the distance, silence returned to the world, a vibrant silence made more intense by the universal trill of a million million forest insects.

On a moonlight night it would be different. The happy voices of children playing in open fields would then be heard. And perhaps those not so young would be playing in pairs in less open places, and old men and women would remember their youth. As the Ibo say: "When the moon is shining the cripple becomes hungry for a walk."

But this particular night was dark and silent. And in all the nine villages of Umuofia a town-crier with his *ogene* asked every man to be present tomorrow morning. Okonkwo on his bamboo bed tried to figure out the nature of the emergency—war with a neighbouring clan? That seemed the most likely reason, and he was not afraid of war. He was a man of action, a man of war. Unlike his father he could stand the look of blood. In Umuofia's latest war he was the first to bring home a human head. That was his fifth head; and he was not an old man yet. On great occasions such as the funeral of a village celebrity he drank his palm-wine from his first human head.

In the morning the market-place was full. There must have been about ten thousand men there, all talking in low voices. At last Ogbuefi Ezeugo stood up in the midst of them and bellowed four times, "*Umuofia kwenu,*"[6] and on each occasion he faced a different direction and seemed to push the air with a clenched fist. And ten thousand men answered "*Yaa!*" each time. Then there was perfect silence. Ogbuefi Ezeugo was a powerful orator and was always chosen to speak on such occasions. He moved his hand over his white head

---

5. My strength should not be dissipated.
6. United Umuofia! An orator's call on the audience to respond as a group. "Ogbuefi": cow killer (literal trans.); indicates someone who has taken a

high title (e.g., the Idemili title) for which the celebration ceremony requires the slaughter of a cow. "Ezeugo": a name denoting a priest or high initiate, someone who wears the eagle feather.

and stroked his white beard. He then adjusted his cloth, which was passed under his right arm-pit and tied above his left shoulder.

"*Umuofia kwenu,*" he bellowed a fifth time, and the crowd yelled in answer. And then suddenly like one possessed he shot out his left hand and pointed in the direction of Mbaino, and said through gleaming white teeth firmly clenched: "Those sons of wild animals have dared to murder a daughter of Umuofia." He threw his head down and gnashed his teeth, and allowed a murmur of suppressed anger to sweep the crowd. When he began again, the anger on his face was gone and in its place a sort of smile hovered, more terrible and more sinister than the anger. And in a clear unemotional voice he told Umuofia how their daughter had gone to market at Mbaino and had been killed. That woman, said Ezeugo, was the wife of Ogbuefi Udo,[7] and he pointed to a man who sat near him with a bowed head. The crowd then shouted with anger and thirst for blood.

Many others spoke, and at the end it was decided to follow the normal course of action. An ultimatum was immediately dispatched to Mbaino asking them to choose between war on the one hand, and on the other the offer of a young man and a virgin as compensation.

Umuofia was feared by all its neighbours. It was powerful in war and in magic, and its priests and medicine-men were feared in all the surrounding country. Its most potent war-medicine was as old as the clan itself. Nobody knew how old. But on one point there was general agreement—the active principle in that medicine had been an old woman with one leg. In fact, the medicine itself was called *agadi-nwayi,* or old woman. It had its shrine in the centre of Umuofia, in a cleared spot. And if anybody was so foolhardy as to pass by the shrine after dusk he was sure to see the old woman hopping about.

And so the neighbouring clans who naturally knew of these things feared Umuofia, and would not go to war against it without first trying a peaceful settlement. And in fairness to Umuofia it should be recorded that it never went to war unless its case was clear and just and was accepted as such by its Oracle—the Oracle of the Hills and the Caves. And there were indeed occasions when the Oracle had forbidden Umuofia to wage a war. If the clan had disobeyed the Oracle they would surely have been beaten, because their dreaded *agadi-nwayi* would never fight what the Ibo call *a fight of blame.*

But the war that now threatened was a just war. Even the enemy clan knew that. And so when Okonkwo of Umuofia arrived at Mbaino as the proud and imperious emissary of war, he was treated with great honour and respect, and two days later he returned home with a lad of fifteen and a young virgin. The lad's name was Ikemefuna, whose sad story is still told in Umuofia unto this day.

The elders, or *ndichie*, met to hear a report of Okonkwo's mission. At the end they decided, as everybody knew they would, that the girl should go to Ogbuefi Udo to replace his murdered wife. As for the boy, he belonged to the clan as a whole, and there was no hurry to decide his fate. Okonkwo was, therefore, asked on behalf of the clan to look after him in the interim. And so for three years Ikemefuna lived in Okonkwo's household.

Okonkwo ruled his household with a heavy hand. His wives, especially the youngest, lived in perpetual fear of his fiery temper, and so did his little chil-

7. Peace.

dren. Perhaps down in his heart Okonkwo was not a cruel man. But his whole life was dominated by fear, the fear of failure and of weakness. It was deeper and more intimate than the fear of evil and capricious gods and of magic, the fear of the forest, and of the forces of nature, malevolent, red in tooth and claw. Okonkwo's fear was greater than these. It was not external but lay deep within himself. It was the fear of himself, lest he should be found to resemble his father. Even as a little boy he had resented his father's failure and weakness, and even now he still remembered how he had suffered when a playmate had told him that his father was *agbala*. That was how Okonkwo first came to know that *agbala* was not only another name for a woman, it could also mean a man who had taken no title. And so Okonkwo was ruled by one passion— to hate everything that his father Unoka had loved. One of those things was gentleness and another was idleness.

During the planting season Okonkwo worked daily on his farms from cockcrow until the chickens went to roost. He was a very strong man and rarely felt fatigue. But his wives and young children were not as strong, and so they suffered. But they dared not complain openly. Okonkwo's first son, Nwoye,[8] was then twelve years old but was already causing his father great anxiety for his incipient laziness. At any rate, that was how it looked to his father, and he sought to correct him by constant nagging and beating. And so Nwoye was developing into a sad-faced youth.

Okonkwo's prosperity was visible in his household. He had a large compound enclosed by a thick wall of red earth. His own hut, or *obi*, stood immediately behind the only gate in the red walls. Each of his three wives had her own hut, which together formed a half moon behind the *obi*. The barn was built against one end of the red walls, and long stacks of yam stood out prosperously in it. At the opposite end of the compound was a shed for the goats, and each wife built a small attachment to her hut for the hens. Near the barn was a small house, the 'medicine house' or shrine where Okonkwo kept the wooden symbols of his personal god and of his ancestral spirits. He worshipped them with sacrifices of kola nut, food and palm-wine, and offered prayers to them on behalf of himself, his three wives and eight children.

So when the daughter of Umuofia was killed in Mbaino, Ikemefuna came into Okonkwo's household. When Okonkwo brought him home that day he called his most senior wife and handed him over to her.

"He belongs to the clan," he told her. "So look after him."

"Is he staying long with us?" she asked.

"Do what you are told, woman," Okonkwo thundered, and stammered. "When did you become one of the *ndichie* of Umuofia?"

And so Nwoye's mother took Ikemefuna to her hut and asked no more questions.

As for the boy himself, he was terribly afraid. He could not understand what was happening to him or what he had done. How could he know that his father had taken a hand in killing a daughter of Umuofia? All he knew was that a few men had arrived at their house, conversing with his father in low tones, and at the end he had been taken out and handed over to a stranger. His mother had wept bitterly, but he had been too surprised to weep. And so the stranger had brought him, and a girl, a long, long way from home, through

8. Child born on Oye Day.

lonely forest paths. He did not know who the girl was, and he never saw her again.

CHAPTER THREE

Okonkwo did not have the start in life which many young men usually had. He did not inherit a barn from his father. There was no barn to inherit. The story was told in Umuofia of how his father, Unoka, had gone to consult the Oracle of the Hills and the Caves to find out why he always had a miserable harvest.

The Oracle was called Agbala,[9] and people came from far and near to consult it. They came when misfortune dogged their steps or when they had a dispute with their neighbours. They came to discover what the future held for them or to consult the spirits of their departed fathers.

The way into the shrine was a round hole at the side of a hill, just a little bigger than the round opening into a hen-house. Worshippers and those who came to seek knowledge from the god crawled on their belly through the hole and found themselves in a dark, endless space in the presence of Agbala. No one had ever beheld Agbala, except his priestess. But no one who had ever crawled into his awful shrine had come out without the fear of his power. His priestess stood by the sacred fire which she built in the heart of the cave and proclaimed the will of the god. The fire did not burn with a flame. The glowing logs only served to light up vaguely the dark figure of the priestess.

Sometimes a man came to consult the spirit of his dead father or relative. It was said that when such a spirit appeared, the man saw it vaguely in the darkness, but never heard its voice. Some people even said that they had heard the spirits flying and flapping their wings against the roof of the cave.

Many years ago when Okonkwo was still a boy his father, Unoka, had gone to consult Agbala. The priestess in those days was a woman called Chika.[1] She was full of the power of her god, and she was greatly feared. Unoka stood before her and began his story.

"Every year," he said sadly, "before I put any crop in the earth, I sacrifice a cock to Ani, the owner of all land. It is the law of our fathers. I also kill a cock at the shrine of Ifejioku, the god of yams. I clear the bush and set fire to it when it is dry. I sow the yams when the first rain has fallen, and stake them when the young tendrils appear. I weed——"

"Hold your peace!" screamed the priestess, her voice terrible as it echoed through the dark void. "You have offended neither the gods nor your fathers. And when a man is at peace with his gods and his ancestors, his harvest will be good or bad according to the strength of his arm. You, Unoka, are known in all the clan for the weakness of your matchet[2] and your hoe. When your neighbours go out with their axe to cut down virgin forests, you sow your yams on exhausted farms that take no labour to clear. They cross seven rivers to make their farms; you stay at home and offer sacrifices to a reluctant soil. Go home and work like a man."

Unoka was an ill-fated man. He had a bad *chi* or personal god, and evil fortune followed him to the grave, or rather to his death, for he had no grave. He died of the swelling which was an abomination to the earth goddess. When a man was afflicted with swelling in the stomach and the limbs he was not

---

9. The Oracle is masculine, but his priestess, or Voice, is feminine.

1. Sky is supreme.
2. Machete.

allowed to die in the house. He was carried to the Evil Forest and left there to die. There was the story of a very stubborn man who staggered back to his house and had to be carried again to the forest and tied to a tree. The sickness was an abomination to the earth, and so the victim could not be buried in her bowels. He died and rotted away above the earth, and was not given the first or the second burial. Such was Unoka's fate. When they carried him away, he took with him his flute.

With a father like Unoka, Okonkwo did not have the start in life which many young men had. He neither inherited a barn nor a title, nor even a young wife. But in spite of these disadvantages, he had begun even in his father's lifetime to lay the foundations of a prosperous future. It was slow and painful. But he threw himself into it like one possessed. And indeed he was possessed by the fear of his father's contemptible life and shameful death.

There was a wealthy man in Okonkwo's village who had three huge barns, nine wives and thirty children. His name was Nwakibie[3] and he had taken the highest but one title which a man could take in the clan. It was for this man that Okonkwo worked to earn his first seed yams.

He took a pot of palm-wine and a cock to Nwakibie. Two elderly neighbours were sent for, and Nwakibie's two grown-up sons were also present in his *obi*. He presented a kola nut and an alligator pepper, which was passed round for all to see and then returned to him. He broke it, saying: "We shall all live. We pray for life, children, a good harvest and happiness. You will have what is good for you and I will have what is good for me. Let the kite perch and let the egret perch too. If one says no to the other, let his wing break."

After the kola nut had been eaten Okonkwo brought his palm-wine from the corner of the hut where it had been placed and stood it in the centre of the group. He addressed Nwakibie, calling him 'Our father'.

"*Nna ayi,*" he said. "I have brought you this little kola. As our people say, a man who pays respect to the great paves the way for his own greatness. I have come to pay you my respects and also to ask a favour. But let us drink the wine first."

Everybody thanked Okonkwo and the neighbours brought out their drinking horns from the goatskin bags they carried. Nwakibie brought down his own horn, which was fastened to the rafters. The younger of his sons, who was also the youngest man in the group, moved to the centre, raised the pot on his left knee and began to pour out the wine. The first cup went to Okonkwo, who must taste his wine before anyone else.[4] Then the group drank, beginning with the eldest man. When everyone had drunk two or three horns, Nwakibie sent for his wives. Some of them were not at home and only four came in.

"Is Anasi not in?" he asked them. They said she was coming. Anasi was the first[5] wife and the others could not drink before her, and so they stood waiting.

Anasi was a middle-aged woman, tall and strongly built. There was authority in her bearing and she looked every inch the ruler of the womenfolk in a large and prosperous family. She wore the anklet of her husband's titles, which the first wife alone could wear.

She walked up to her husband and accepted the horn from him. She then went down on one knee, drank a little and handed back the horn. She rose,

---

3. The child surpasses his neighbors.
4. A ceremonial gesture; one who gives wine tastes
it first to show that it is not poisoned.
5. First or favorite wife—not always the same.

called him by his name and went back to her hut. The other wives drank in the same way, in their proper order, and went away.

The men then continued their drinking and talking. Ogbuefi Idigo was talking about the palm-wine tapper, Obiako, who suddenly gave up his trade.

"There must be something behind it," he said, wiping the foam of wine from his moustache with the back of his left hand. "There must be a reason for it. A toad does not run in the daytime for nothing."

"Some people say the Oracle warned him that he would fall off a palm tree and kill himself," said Akukalia.

"Obiako has always been a strange one," said Nwakibie. "I have heard that many years ago, when his father had not been dead very long, he had gone to consult the Oracle. The Oracle said to him, 'Your dead father wants you to sacrifice a goat to him.' Do you know what he told the Oracle? He said, 'Ask my dead father if he ever had a fowl when he was alive.'" Everybody laughed heartily except Okonkwo, who laughed uneasily because, as the saying goes, an old woman is always uneasy when dry bones are mentioned in a proverb. Okonkwo remembered his own father.

At last the young man who was pouring out the wine held up half a horn of the thick, white dregs and said, "What we are eating is finished." "We have seen it," the others replied. "Who will drink the dregs?" he asked. "Whoever has a job in hand," said Idigo, looking at Nwakibie's elder son Igwelo with a malicious twinkle in his eye.

Everybody agreed that Igwelo should drink the dregs. He accepted the half-full horn from his brother and drank it. As Idigo had said, Igwelo had a job in hand because he had married his first wife a month or two before. The thick dregs of palm-wine were supposed to be good for men who were going in to their wives.

After the wine had been drunk Okonkwo laid his difficulties before Nwakibie.

"I have come to you for help," he said. "Perhaps you can already guess what it is. I have cleared a farm but have no yams to sow. I know what it is to ask a man to trust another with his yams, especially these days when young men are afraid of hard work. I am not afraid of work. The lizard that jumped from the high iroko tree to the ground said he would praise himself if no one else did. I began to fend for myself at an age when most people still suck at their mothers' breasts. If you give me some yam seeds I shall not fail you."

Nwakibie cleared his throat. "It pleases me to see a young man like you these days when our youth have gone so soft. Many young men have come to me to ask for yams but I have refused because I knew they would just dump them in the earth and leave them to be choked by weeds. When I say no to them they think I am hard-hearted. But it is not so. Eneke the bird[6] says that since men have learnt to shoot without missing, he has learnt to fly without perching. I have learnt to be stingy with my yams. But I can trust you. I know it as I look at you. As our fathers said, you can tell a ripe corn by its look. I shall give you twice four hundred yams. Go ahead and prepare your farm."

Okonkwo thanked him again and again and went home feeling happy. He knew that Nwakibie would not refuse him, but he had not expected he would be so generous. He had not hoped to get more than four hundred seeds. He would now have to make a bigger farm. He hoped to get another four hundred yams from one of his father's friends at Isiuzo.[7]

---

6. Proverbial.

7. Head of the road; a small town.

Share-cropping was a very slow way of building up a barn of one's own. After all the toil one only got a third of the harvest. But for a young man whose father had no yams, there was no other way. And what made it worse in Okonkwo's case was that he had to support his mother and two sisters from his meagre harvest. And supporting his mother also meant supporting his father. She could not be expected to cook and eat while her husband starved. And so at a very early age when he was striving desperately to build a barn through share-cropping Okonkwo was also fending for his father's house. It was like pouring grains of corn into a bag full of holes. His mother and sisters worked hard enough, but they grew women's crops, like coco-yams, beans and cassava. Yam, the king of crops, was a man's crop.[8]

The year that Okonkwo took eight hundred seed-yams from Nwakibie was the worst year in living memory. Nothing happened at its proper time; it was either too early or too late. It seemed as if the world had gone mad. The first rains were late, and, when they came, lasted only a brief moment. The blazing sun returned, more fierce than it had ever been known, and scorched all the green that had appeared with the rains. The earth burned like hot coals and roasted all the yams that had been sown. Like all good farmers, Okonkwo had begun to sow with the first rains. He had sown four hundred seeds when the rains dried up and the heat returned. He watched the sky all day for signs of rain-clouds and lay awake all night. In the morning he went back to his farm and saw the withering tendrils. He had tried to protect them from the smouldering earth by making rings of thick sisal leaves around them. But by the end of the day the sisal rings were burnt dry and grey. He changed them every day, and prayed that the rain might fall in the night. But the drought continued for eight market weeks and the yams were killed.

Some farmers had not planted their yams yet. They were the lazy easy-going ones who always put off clearing their farms as long as they could. This year they were the wise ones. They sympathised with their neighbours with much shaking of the head, but inwardly they were happy for what they took to be their own foresight.

Okonkwo planted what was left of his seed-yams when the rains finally returned. He had one consolation. The yams he had sown before the drought were his own, the harvest of the previous year. He still had the eight hundred from Nwakibie and the four hundred from his father's friend. So he would make a fresh start.

But the year had gone mad. Rain fell as it had never fallen before. For days and nights together it poured down in violent torrents, and washed away the yam heaps. Trees were uprooted and deep gorges appeared everywhere. Then the rain became less violent. But it went on from day to day without a pause. The spell of sunshine which always came in the middle of the wet season did not appear. The yams put on luxuriant green leaves, but every farmer knew that without sunshine the tubers would not grow.

That year the harvest was sad, like a funeral, and many farmers wept as they dug up the miserable and rotting yams. One man tied his cloth to a tree branch and hanged himself.

Okonkwo remembered that tragic year with a cold shiver throughout the

---

8. Yams, a staple food in Western Africa, were a sacred crop generally cultivated only by men and eaten either roasted or boiled. "Coco-yams" (a brown root also called taro) and "cassava" (or manioc, which is refined in various ways to remove natural cyanide) were low-status root vegetables, prepared for eating by boiling and pounding.

rest of his life. It always surprised him when he thought of it later that he did not sink under the load of despair. He knew he was a fierce fighter, but that year had been enough to break the heart of a lion.

"Since I survived that year," he always said, "I shall survive anything." He put it down to his inflexible will.

His father, Unoka, who was then an ailing man, had said to him during that terrible harvest month: "Do not despair. I know you will not despair. You have a manly and a proud heart. A proud heart can survive a general failure because such a failure does not prick its pride. It is more difficult and more bitter when a man fails *alone*."

Unoka was like that in his last days. His love of talk had grown with age and sickness. It tried Okonkwo's patience beyond words.

CHAPTER FOUR

"Looking at a king's mouth," said an old man, "one would think he never sucked at his mother's breast." He was talking about Okonkwo, who had risen so suddenly from great poverty and misfortune to be one of the lords of the clan. The old man bore no ill-will towards Okonkwo. Indeed he respected him for his industry and success. But he was struck, as most people were, by Okonkwo's brusqueness in dealing with less successful men. Only a week ago a man had contradicted him at a kindred meeting which they held to discuss the next ancestral feast. Without looking at the man Okonkwo had said: "This meeting is for men." The man who had contradicted him had no titles. That was why he had called him a woman. Okonkwo knew how to kill a man's spirit.

Everybody at the kindred meeting took sides with Osugo[9] when Okonkwo called him a woman. The oldest man present said sternly that those whose palm-kernels were cracked for them by a benevolent spirit should not forget to be humble. Okonkwo said he was sorry for what he had said, and the meeting continued.

But it was really not true that Okonkwo's palm-kernels had been cracked for him by a benevolent spirit. He had cracked them himself. Anyone who knew his grim struggle against poverty and misfortune could not say he had been lucky. If ever a man deserved his success, that man was Okonkwo. At an early age he had achieved fame as the greatest wrestler in all the land. That was not luck. At the most one could say that his *chi* or personal god was good. But the Ibo people have a proverb that when a man says yes his *chi* says yes also. Okonkwo said yes very strongly; so his *chi* agreed. And not only his *chi* but his clan too, because it judged a man by the work of his hands. That was why Okonkwo had been chosen by the nine villages to carry a message of war to their enemies unless they agreed to give up a young man and a virgin to atone for the murder of Udo's wife. And such was the deep fear that their enemies had for Umuofia that they treated Okonkwo like a king and brought him a virgin who was given to Udo as wife, and the lad Ikemefuna.

The elders of the clan had decided that Ikemefuna should be in Okonkwo's care for a while. But no one thought it would be as long as three years. They seemed to forget all about him as soon as they had taken the decision.

At first Ikemefuna was very much afraid. Once or twice he tried to run away,

9. Low-status (*osu*) person.

but he did not know where to begin. He thought of his mother and his three-year-old sister and wept bitterly. Nwoye's mother was very kind to him and treated him as one of her own children. But all he said was: "When shall I go home?" When Okonkwo heard that he would not eat any food he came into the hut with a big stick in his hand and stood over him while he swallowed his yams, trembling. A few moments later he went behind the hut and began to vomit painfully. Nwoye's mother went to him and placed her hands on his chest and on his back. He was ill for three market weeks, and when he recovered he seemed to have overcome his great fear and sadness.

He was by nature a very lively boy and he gradually became popular in Okonkwo's household, especially with the children. Okonkwo's son, Nwoye, who was two years younger, became quite inseparable from him because he seemed to know everything. He could fashion out flutes from bamboo stems and even from the elephant grass. He knew the names of all the birds and could set clever traps for the little bush rodents. And he knew which trees made the strongest bows.

Even Okonkwo himself became very fond of the boy—inwardly of course. Okonkwo never showed any emotion openly, unless it be the emotion of anger. To show affection was a sign of weakness; the only thing worth demonstrating was strength. He therefore treated Ikemefuna as he treated everybody else—with a heavy hand. But there was no doubt that he liked the boy. Sometimes when he went to big village meetings or communal ancestral feasts he allowed Ikemefuna to accompany him, like a son, carrying his stool and his goatskin bag. And, indeed, Ikemefuna called him father.

Ikemefuna came to Umuofia at the end of the carefree season between harvest and planting. In fact he recovered from his illness only a few days before the Week of Peace began. And that was also the year Okonkwo broke the peace, and was punished, as was the custom, by Ezeani, the priest of the earth goddess.

Okonkwo was provoked to justifiable anger by his youngest wife, who went to plait her hair at her friend's house and did not return early enough to cook the afternoon meal. Okonkwo did not know at first that she was not at home. After waiting in vain for her dish he went to her hut to see what she was doing. There was nobody in the hut and the fireplace was cold.

"Where is Ojiugo?" he asked his second wife, who came out of her hut to draw water from a gigantic pot in the shade of a small tree in the middle of the compound.

"She has gone to plait her hair."

Okonkwo bit his lips as anger welled up within him.

"Where are her children? Did she take them?" he asked with unusual coolness and restraint.

"They are here," answered his first wife, Nwoye's mother. Okonkwo bent down and looked into her hut. Ojiugo's children were eating with the children of his first wife.

"Did she ask you to feed them before she went?"

"Yes," lied Nwoye's mother, trying to minimise Ojiugo's thoughtlessness.

Okonkwo knew she was not speaking the truth. He walked back to his *obi* to await Ojiugo's return. And when she returned he beat her very heavily. In his anger he had forgotten that it was the Week of Peace. His first two wives ran out in great alarm pleading with him that it was the sacred week. But

Okonkwo was not the man to stop beating somebody half-way through, not even for fear of a goddess.

Okonkwo's neighbours heard his wife crying and sent their voices over the compound walls to ask what was the matter. Some of them came over to see for themselves. It was unheard-of to beat somebody during the sacred week.

Before it was dusk Ezeani, who was the priest of the earth goddess, Ani, called on Okonkwo in his *obi*. Okonkwo brought out kola nut and placed it before the priest.

"Take away your kola nut. I shall not eat in the house of a man who has no respect for our gods and ancestors."

Okonkwo tried to explain to him what his wife had done, but Ezeani seemed to pay no attention. He held a short staff in his hand which he brought down on the floor to emphasise his points.

"Listen to me," he said when Okonkwo had spoken. "You are not a stranger in Umuofia. You know as well as I do that our forefathers ordained that before we plant any crops in the earth we should observe a week in which a man does not say a harsh word to his neighbour. We live in peace with our fellows to honour our great goddess of the earth without whose blessing our crops will not grow. You have committed a great evil." He brought down his staff heavily on the floor. "Your wife was at fault, but even if you came into your *obi* and found her lover on top of her, you would still have committed a great evil to beat her." His staff came down again. "The evil you have done can ruin the whole clan. The earth goddess whom you have insulted may refuse to give us her increase, and we shall all perish." His tone now changed from anger to command. "You will bring to the shrine of Ani tomorrow one she-goat, one hen, a length of cloth and a hundred cowries." He rose and left the hut.

Okonkwo did as the priest said. He also took with him a pot of palm-wine. Inwardly, he was repentant. But he was not the man to go about telling his neighbours that he was in error. And so people said he had no respect for the gods of the clan. His enemies said his good fortune had gone to his head. They called him the little bird *nza*[1] who so far forgot himself after a heavy meal that he challenged his *chi*.

No work was done during the Week of Peace. People called on their neighbours and drank palm-wine. This year they talked of nothing else but the *nso-ani*[2] which Okonkwo had committed. It was the first time for many years that a man had broken the sacred peace. Even the oldest men could only remember one or two other occasions somewhere in the dim past.

Ogbuefi Ezeudu, who was the oldest man in the village, was telling two other men who came to visit him that the punishment for breaking the Peace of Ani had become very mild in their clan.

"It has not always been so," he said. "My father told me that he had been told that in the past a man who broke the peace was dragged on the ground through the village until he died. But after a while this custom was stopped because it spoilt the peace which it was meant to preserve."

"Somebody told me yesterday," said one of the younger men, "that in some clans it is an abomination for a man to die during the Week of Peace."

---

1. The one that talks back (literal trans.); a small aggressive bird. In the traditional story, it is easily defeated (alternatively, caught by a hawk) when it becomes bold enough to challenge its personal god.

2. Sin, abomination against the Earth goddess Ani.

"It is indeed true," said Ogbuefi Ezeudu. "They have that custom in Obo-doani.[3] If a man dies at this time he is not buried but cast into the Evil Forest. It is a bad custom which these people observe because they lack understanding. They throw away large numbers of men and women without burial. And what is the result? Their clan is full of the evil spirits of these unburied dead, hungry to do harm to the living."

After the Week of Peace every man and his family began to clear the bush to make new farms. The cut bush was left to dry and fire was then set to it. As the smoke rose into the sky kites appeared from different directions and hovered over the burning field in silent valediction. The rainy season was approaching when they would go away until the dry season returned.

Okonkwo spent the next few days preparing his seed-yams. He looked at each yam carefully to see whether it was good for sowing. Sometimes he decided that a yam was too big to be sown as one seed and he split it deftly along its length with his sharp knife. His eldest son, Nwoye, and Ikemefuna helped him by fetching the yams in long baskets from the barn and in counting the prepared seeds in groups of four hundred. Sometimes Okonkwo gave them a few yams each to prepare. But he always found fault with their effort, and he said so with much threatening.

"Do you think you are cutting up yams for cooking?" he asked Nwoye. "If you split another yam of this size, I shall break your jaw. You think you are still a child. I began to own a farm at your age. And you," he said to Ikemefuna, "do you not grow yams where you come from?"

Inwardly Okonkwo knew that the boys were still too young to understand fully the difficult art of preparing seed-yams. But he thought that one could not begin too early. Yam stood for manliness, and he who could feed his family on yams from one harvest to another was a very great man indeed. Okonkwo wanted his son to be a great farmer and a great man. He would stamp out the disquieting signs of laziness which he thought he already saw in him.

"I will not have a son who cannot hold up his head in the gathering of the clan. I would sooner strangle him with my own hands. And if you stand staring at me like that," he swore, "Amadiora[4] will break your head for you!"

Some days later, when the land had been moistened by two or three heavy rains, Okonkwo and his family went to the farm with baskets of seed-yams, their hoes and matchets, and the planting began. They made single mounds of earth in straight lines all over the field and sowed the yams in them.

Yam, the king of crops, was a very exacting king. For three or four moons it demanded hard work and constant attention from cock-crow till the chickens went back to roost. The young tendrils were protected from earth-heat with rings of sisal leaves. As the rains became heavier the women planted maize, melons and beans between the yam mounds. The yams were then staked, first with little sticks and later with tall and big tree branches. The women weeded the farm three times at definite periods in the life of the yams, neither early nor late.

And now the rains had really come, so heavy and persistent that even the village rain-maker no longer claimed to be able to intervene. He could not

---

3. The town of the land (literal trans.); i.e., Any-town, Nigeria.

4. God of thunder and lightning.

stop the rain now, just as he would not attempt to start it in the heart of the dry season, without serious danger to his own health. The personal dynamism required to counter the forces of these extremes of weather would be far too great for the human frame.

And so nature was not interfered with in the middle of the rainy season. Sometimes it poured down in such thick sheets of water that earth and sky seemed merged in one grey wetness. It was then uncertain whether the low rumbling of Amadiora's thunder came from above or below. At such times, in each of the countless thatched huts of Umuofia, children sat around their mother's cooking fire telling stories, or with their father in his *obi* warming themselves from a log fire, roasting and eating maize. It was a brief resting period between the exacting and arduous planting season and the equally exacting but light-hearted month of harvests.

Ikemefuna had begun to feel like a member of Okonkwo's family. He still thought about his mother and his three-year-old sister, and he had moments of sadness and depression. But he and Nwoye had become so deeply attached to each other that such moments became less frequent and less poignant. Ikemefuna had an endless stock of folk tales. Even those which Nwoye knew already were told with a new freshness and the local flavour of a different clan. Nwoye remembered this period very vividly till the end of his life. He even remembered how he had laughed when Ikemefuna told him that the proper name for a corn-cob with only a few scattered grains was *eze-agadi-nwayi*, or the teeth of an old woman. Nwoye's mind had gone immediately to Nwayieke, who lived near the udala tree.[5] She had about three teeth and was always smoking her pipe.

Gradually the rains became lighter and less frequent, and earth and sky once again became separate. The rain fell in thin, slanting showers through sunshine and quiet breeze. Children no longer stayed indoors but ran about singing:

> "The rain is falling, the sun is shining,
> Alone Nnadi[6] is cooking and eating."

Nwoye always wondered who Nnadi was and why he should live all by himself, cooking and eating. In the end he decided that Nnadi must live in that land of Ikemefuna's favourite story where the ant holds his court in splendour and the sands dance forever.

CHAPTER FIVE

The Feast of the New Yam was approaching and Umuofia was in a festival mood. It was an occasion for giving thanks to Ani, the earth goddess and the source of all fertility. Ani played a greater part in the life of the people than any other deity. She was the ultimate judge of morality and conduct. And what was more, she was in close communion with the departed fathers of the clan whose bodies had been committed to earth.

The Feast of the New Yam was held every year before the harvest began, to honour the earth goddess and the ancestral spirits of the clan. New yams could not be eaten until some had first been offered to these powers. Men and

---

5. African star apple tree. "Nwayieke": Woman born on Eke Day.   6. Father is there or Father exists.

women, young and old, looked forward to the New Yam Festival because it began the season of plenty—the new year. On the last night before the festival, yams of the old year were all disposed of by those who still had them. The new year must begin with tasty, fresh yams and not the shrivelled and fibrous crop of the previous year. All cooking-pots, calabashes and wooden bowls were thoroughly washed, especially the wooden mortar in which yam was pounded. Yam foo-foo[7] and vegetable soup was the chief food in the celebration. So much of it was cooked that, no matter how heavily the family ate or how many friends and relations they invited from neighbouring villages, there was always a huge quantity of food left over at the end of the day. The story was always told of a wealthy man who set before his guests a mound of foo-foo so high that those who sat on one side could not see what was happening on the other, and it was not until late in the evening that one of them saw for the first time his in-law who had arrived during the course of the meal and had fallen to on the opposite side. It was only then that they exchanged greetings and shook hands over what was left of the food.

The New Yam Festival was thus an occasion for joy throughout Umuofia. And every man whose arm was strong, as the Ibo people say, was expected to invite large numbers of guests from far and wide. Okonkwo always asked his wives' relations, and since he now had three wives his guests would make a fairly big crowd.

But somehow Okonkwo could never become as enthusiastic over feasts as most people. He was a good eater and he could drink one or two fairly big gourds of palm-wine. But he was always uncomfortable sitting around for days waiting for a feast or getting over it. He would be very much happier working on his farm.

The festival was now only three days away. Okonkwo's wives had scrubbed the walls and the huts with red earth until they reflected light. They had then drawn patterns on them in white, yellow and dark green. They then set about painting themselves with cam wood and drawing beautiful black patterns on their stomachs and on their backs. The children were also decorated, especially their hair, which was shaved in beautiful patterns. The three women talked excitedly about the relations who had been invited, and the children revelled in the thought of being spoilt by these visitors from mother-land. Ikemefuna was equally excited. The New Yam Festival seemed to him to be a much bigger event here than in his own village, a place which was already becoming remote and vague in his imagination.

And then the storm burst. Okonkwo, who had been walking about aimlessly in his compound in suppressed anger, suddenly found an outlet.

"Who killed this banana tree?" he asked.

A hush fell on the compound immediately.

"Who killed this tree? Or are you all deaf and dumb?"

As a matter of fact the tree was very much alive. Okonkwo's second wife had merely cut a few leaves off it to wrap some food, and she said so. Without further argument Okonkwo gave her a sound beating and left her and her only daughter weeping. Neither of the other wives dared to interfere beyond an occasional and tentative, "It is enough, Okonkwo," pleaded from a reasonable distance.

---

7. A mashed edible base that is shaped into balls with the fingers and then indented for cupping and eating soup.

His anger thus satisfied, Okonkwo decided to go out hunting. He had an old rusty gun made by a clever blacksmith who had come to live in Umuofia long ago. But although Okonkwo was a great man whose prowess was universally acknowledged, he was not a hunter. In fact he had not killed a rat with his gun. And so when he called Ikemefuna to fetch his gun, the wife who had just been beaten murmured something about guns that never shot. Unfortunately for her, Okonkwo heard it and ran madly into his room for the loaded gun, ran out again and aimed at her as she clambered over the dwarf wall of the barn. He pressed the trigger and there was a loud report accompanied by the wail of his wives and children. He threw down the gun and jumped into the barn, and there lay the woman, very much shaken and frightened but quite unhurt. He heaved a heavy sigh and went away with the gun.

In spite of this incident the New Yam Festival was celebrated with great joy in Okonkwo's household. Early that morning as he offered a sacrifice of new yam and palm-oil to his ancestors he asked them to protect him, his children and their mothers in the new year.

As the day wore on his in-laws arrived from three surrounding villages, and each party brought with them a huge pot of palm-wine. And there was eating and drinking till night, when Okonkwo's in-laws began to leave for their homes.

The second day of the new year was the day of the great wrestling match between Okonkwo's village and their neighbours. It was difficult to say which the people enjoyed more—the feasting and fellowship of the first day or the wrestling contest of the second. But there was one woman who had no doubt whatever in her mind. She was Okonkwo's second wife, Ekwefi, whom he nearly shot. There was no festival in all the seasons of the year which gave her as much pleasure as the wrestling match. Many years ago when she was the village beauty Okonkwo had won her heart by throwing the Cat in the greatest contest within living memory. She did not marry him then because he was too poor to pay her bride-price. But a few years later she ran away from her husband and came to live with Okonkwo. All this happened many years ago. Now Ekwefi[8] was a woman of forty-five who had suffered a great deal in her time. But her love of wrestling contests was still as strong as it was thirty years ago.

It was not yet noon on the second day of the New Yam Festival. Ekwefi and her only daughter, Ezinma,[9] sat near the fireplace waiting for the water in the pot to boil. The fowl Ekwefi had just killed was in the wooden mortar. The water began to boil, and in one deft movement she lifted the pot from the fire and poured the boiling water on to the fowl. She put back the empty pot on the circular pad in the corner, and looked at her palms, which were black with soot. Ezinma was always surprised that her mother could lift a pot from the fire with her bare hands.

"Ekwefi," she said, "is it true that when people are grown up, fire does not burn them?" Ezinma, unlike most children, called her mother by her name.

"Yes," replied Ekwefi, too busy to argue. Her daughter was only ten years old but she was wiser than her years.

---

8. An abbreviation of "Do you have a cow?"; the cow being a symbol of wealth. Okonkwo would presumably have repaid Ekwefi's bride-price to her first husband.

9. True beauty (literal trans.), or goodness.

"But Nwoye's mother dropped her pot of hot soup the other day and it broke on the floor."

Ekwefi turned the hen over in the mortar and began to pluck the feathers.

"Ekwefi," said Ezinma, who had joined in plucking the feathers, "my eyelid is twitching."

"It means you are going to cry," said her mother.

"No," Ezinma said, "it is this eyelid, the top one."

"That means you will see something."

"What will I see?" she asked.

"How can I know?" Ekwefi wanted her to work it out herself.

"Oho," said Ezinma at last. "I know what it is—the wrestling match."

At last the hen was plucked clean. Ekwefi tried to pull out the horny beak but it was too hard. She turned round on her low stool and put the beak in the fire for a few moments. She pulled again and it came off.

"Ekwefi!" a voice called from one of the other huts. It was Nwoye's mother, Okonkwo's first wife.

"Is that me?" Ekwefi called back. That was the way people answered calls from outside. They never answered yes for fear it might be an evil spirit calling.

"Will you give Ezinma some fire to bring to me?" Her own children and Ikemefuna had gone to the stream.

Ekwefi put a few live coals into a piece of broken pot and Ezinma carried it across the clean-swept compound to Nwoye's mother.

"Thank you, Nma," she said. She was peeling new yams, and in a basket beside her were green vegetables and beans.

"Let me make the fire for you," Ezinma offered.

"Thank you, Ezigbo," she said. She often called her Ezigbo, which means "the good one."

Ezinma went outside and brought some sticks from a huge bundle of firewood. She broke them into little pieces across the sole of her foot and began to build a fire, blowing it with her breath.

"You will blow your eyes out," said Nwoye's mother, looking up from the yams she was peeling. "Use the fan." She stood up and pulled out the fan which was fastened into one of the rafters. As soon as she got up, the troublesome nanny-goat, which had been dutifully eating yam peelings, dug her teeth into the real thing, scooped out two mouthfuls and fled from the hut to chew the cud in the goats' shed. Nwoye's mother swore at her and settled down again to her peeling. Ezinma's fire was now sending up thick clouds of smoke. She went on fanning it until it burst into flames. Nwoye's mother thanked her and she went back to her mother's hut.

Just then the distant beating of drums began to reach them. It came from the direction of the *ilo*, the village playground. Every village had its own *ilo* which was as old as the village itself and where all the great ceremonies and dances took place. The drums beat the unmistakable wrestling dance—quick, light and gay, and it came floating on the wind.

Okonkwo cleared his throat and moved his feet to the beat of the drums. It filled him with fire as it had always done from his youth. He trembled with the desire to conquer and subdue. It was like the desire for woman.

"We shall be late for the wrestling," said Ezinma to her mother.

"They will not begin until the sun goes down."

"But they are beating the drums."

"Yes. The drums begin at noon but the wrestling waits until the sun begins to sink. Go and see if your father has brought out yams for the afternoon."

"He has. Nwoye's mother is already cooking."

"Go and bring our own, then. We must cook quickly or we shall be late for the wrestling."

Ezinma ran in the direction of the barn and brought back two yams from the dwarf wall.

Ekwefi peeled the yams quickly. The troublesome nanny-goat sniffed about, eating the peelings. She cut the yams into small pieces and began to prepare a pottage, using some of the chicken.

At that moment they heard someone crying just outside their compound. It was very much like Obiageli,[1] Nwoye's sister.

"Is that not Obiageli weeping?" Ekwefi called across the yard to Nwoye's mother.

"Yes," she replied. "She must have broken her water-pot."

The weeping was now quite close and soon the children filed in, carrying on their heads various sizes of pots suitable to their years. Ikemefuna came first with the biggest pot, closely followed by Nwoye and his two younger brothers. Obiageli brought up the rear, her face streaming with tears. In her hand was the cloth pad on which the pot should have rested on her head.

"What happened?" her mother asked, and Obiageli told her mournful story. Her mother consoled her and promised to buy her another pot.

Nwoye's younger brothers were about to tell their mother the true story of the accident when Ikemefuna looked at them sternly and they held their peace. The fact was that Obiageli had been making *inyanga*[2] with her pot. She had balanced it on her head, folded her arms in front of her and began to sway her waist like a grown-up young lady. When the pot fell down and broke she burst out laughing. She only began to weep when they got near the iroko tree outside their compound.

The drums were still beating, persistent and unchanging. Their sound was no longer a separate thing from the living village. It was like the pulsation of its heart. It throbbed in the air, in the sunshine, and even in the trees, and filled the village with excitement.

Ekwefi ladled her husband's share of the pottage into a bowl and covered it. Ezinma took it to him in his *obi*.

Okonkwo was sitting on a goatskin already eating his first wife's meal. Obiageli, who had brought it from her mother's hut, sat on the floor waiting for him to finish. Ezinma placed her mother's dish before him and sat with Obiageli.

"Sit like a woman!" Okonkwo shouted at her. Ezinma brought her two legs together and stretched them in front of her.

"Father, will you go to see the wrestling?" Ezinma asked after a suitable interval.

"Yes," he answered. "Will you go?"

"Yes." And after a pause she said: "Can I bring your chair for you?"

"No, that is a boy's job." Okonkwo was specially fond of Ezinma. She looked very much like her mother, who was once the village beauty. But his fondness only showed on very rare occasions.

"Obiageli broke her pot today," Ezinma said.

"Yes, she has told me about it," Okonkwo said between mouthfuls.

1. Born to eat (born into prosperity).   2. Had been showing off.

"Father," said Obiageli, "people should not talk when they are eating or pepper may go down the wrong way."

"That is very true. Do you hear that, Ezinma? You are older than Obiageli but she has more sense."

He uncovered his second wife's dish and began to eat from it. Obiageli took the first dish and returned to her mother's hut. And then Nkechi came in, bringing the third dish. Nkechi was the daughter of Okonkwo's third wife.

In the distance the drums continued to beat.

CHAPTER SIX

The whole village turned out on the *ilo*, men, women and children. They stood round in a huge circle leaving the centre of the playground free. The elders and grandees of the village sat on their own stools brought there by their young sons or slaves. Okonkwo was among them. All others stood except those who came early enough to secure places on the few stands which had been built by placing smooth logs on forked pillars.

The wrestlers were not there yet and the drummers held the field. They too sat just in front of the huge circle of spectators, facing the elders. Behind them was the big and ancient silk-cotton tree which was sacred. Spirits of good children lived in that tree waiting to be born. On ordinary days young women who desired children came to sit under its shade.

There were seven drums and they were arranged according to their sizes in a long wooden basket. Three men beat them with sticks, working feverishly from one drum to another. They were possessed by the spirit of the drums.

The young men who kept order on these occasions dashed about, consulting among themselves and with the leaders of the two wrestling teams, who were still outside the circle, behind the crowd. Once in a while two young men carrying palm fronds ran round the circle and kept the crowd back by beating the ground in front of them or, if they were stubborn, their legs and feet.

At last the two teams danced into the circle and the crowd roared and clapped. The drums rose to a frenzy. The people surged forward. The young men who kept order flew around, waving their palm fronds. Old men nodded to the beat of the drums and remembered the days when they wrestled to its intoxicating rhythm.

The contest began with boys of fifteen or sixteen. There were only three such boys in each team. They were not the real wrestlers; they merely set the scene. Within a short time the first two bouts were over. But the third created a big sensation even among the elders who did not usually show their excitement so openly. It was as quick as the other two, perhaps even quicker. But very few people had ever seen that kind of wrestling before. As soon as the two boys closed in, one of them did something which no one could describe because it had been as quick as a flash. And the other boy was flat on his back. The crowd roared and clapped and for a while drowned the frenzied drums. Okonkwo sprang to his feet and quickly sat down again. Three young men from the victorious boy's team ran forward, carried him shoulder-high and danced through the cheering crowd. Everybody soon knew who the boy was. His name was Maduka, the son of Obierika.[3]

The drummers stopped for a brief rest before the real matches. Their bodies

3. The heart eats [enjoys] more.

shone with sweat, and they took up fans and began to fan themselves. They also drank water from small pots and ate kola nuts. They became ordinary human beings again, talking and laughing among themselves and with others who stood near them. The air, which had been stretched taut with excitement, relaxed again. It was as if water had been poured on the tightened skin of a drum. Many people looked around, perhaps for the first time, and saw those who stood or sat next to them.

"I did not know it was you," Ekwefi said to the woman who had stood shoulder to shoulder with her since the beginning of the matches.

"I do not blame you," said the woman. "I have never seen such a large crowd of people. Is it true that Okonkwo nearly killed you with his gun?"

"It is true indeed, my dear friend. I cannot yet find a mouth with which to tell the story."

"Your *chi* is very much awake, my friend. And how is my daughter, Ezinma?"

"She has been very well for some time now. Perhaps she has come to stay."

"I think she has. How old is she now?"

"She is about ten years old."

"I think she will stay. They usually stay if they do not die before the age of six."

"I pray she stays," said Ekwefi with a heavy sigh.

The woman with whom she talked was called Chielo.[4] She was the priestess of Agbala, the Oracle of the Hills and the Caves. In ordinary life Chielo was a widow with two children. She was very friendly with Ekwefi and they shared a common shed in the market. She was particularly fond of Ekwefi's only daughter, Ezinma, whom she called "my daughter". Quite often she bought bean-cakes and gave Ekwefi some to take home to Ezinma. Anyone seeing Chielo in ordinary life would hardly believe she was the same person who prophesied when the spirit of Agbala was upon her.

The drummers took up their sticks again and the air shivered and grew tense like a tightened bow.

The two teams were ranged facing each other across the clear space. A young man from one team danced across the centre to the other side and pointed at whomever he wanted to fight. They danced back to the centre together and then closed in.

There were twelve men on each side and the challenge went from one side to the other. Two judges walked around the wrestlers and when they thought they were equally matched, stopped them. Five matches ended in this way. But the really exciting moments were when a man was thrown. The huge voice of the crowd then rose to the sky and in every direction. It was even heard in the surrounding villages.

The last match was between the leaders of the teams. They were among the best wrestlers in all the nine villages. The crowd wondered who would throw the other this year. Some said Okafo was the better man; others said he was not the equal of Ikezue.[5] Last year neither of them had thrown the other even though the judges had allowed the contest to go on longer than was the custom. They had the same style and one saw the other's plans beforehand. It might happen again this year.

Dusk was already approaching when their contest began. The drums went

---

4. Chi who plants.

5. Strength is complete (a boastful name).

mad and the crowds also. They surged forward as the two young men danced into the circle. The palm fronds were helpless in keeping them back.

Ikezue held out his right hand. Okafo seized it, and they closed in. It was a fierce contest. Ikezue strove to dig in his right heel behind Okafo so as to pitch him backwards in the clever *ege* style. But the one knew what the other was thinking. The crowd had surrounded and swallowed up the drummers, whose frantic rhythm was no longer a mere disembodied sound but the very heart-beat of the people.

The wrestlers were now almost still in each other's grip. The muscles on their arms and their thighs and on their backs stood out and twitched. It looked like an equal match. The two judges were already moving forward to separate them when Ikezue, now desperate, went down quickly on one knee in an attempt to fling his man backwards over his head. It was a sad miscalculation. Quick as the lightning of Amadiora, Okafo raised his right leg and swung it over his rival's head. The crowd burst into a thunderous roar. Okafo was swept off his feet by his supporters and carried home shoulder-high. They sang his praise and the young women clapped their hands:

> "Who will wrestle for our village?
> Okafo will wrestle for our village.
> Has he thrown a hundred men?
> He has thrown four hundred men.
> Has he thrown a hundred Cats?
> He has thrown four hundred Cats.
> Then send him word to fight for us."

CHAPTER SEVEN

For three years Ikemefuna lived in Okonkwo's household and the elders of Umuofia seemed to have forgotten about him. He grew rapidly like a yam tendril in the rainy season, and was full of the sap of life. He had become wholly absorbed into his new family. He was like an elder brother to Nwoye, and from the very first seemed to have kindled a new fire in the younger boy. He made him feel grown-up; and they no longer spent the evenings in mother's hut while she cooked, but now sat with Okonkwo in his *obi*, or watched him as he tapped his palm tree for the evening wine. Nothing pleased Nwoye now more than to be sent for by his mother or another of his father's wives to do one of those difficult and masculine tasks in the home, like splitting wood, or pounding food. On receiving such a message through a younger brother or sister, Nwoye would feign annoyance and grumble aloud about women and their troubles.

Okonkwo was inwardly pleased at his son's development, and he knew it was due to Ikemefuna. He wanted Nwoye to grow into a tough young man capable of ruling his father's household when he was dead and gone to join the ancestors. He wanted him to be a prosperous man, having enough in his barn to feed the ancestors with regular sacrifices. And so he was always happy when he heard him grumbling about women. That showed that in time he would be able to control his women-folk. No matter how prosperous a man was, if he was unable to rule his women and his children (and especially his women) he was not really a man. He was like the man in the song who had ten and one wives and not enough soup for his foo-foo.

So Okonkwo encouraged the boys to sit with him in his *obi*, and he told them stories of the land—masculine stories of violence and bloodshed. Nwoye knew that it was right to be masculine and to be violent, but somehow he still preferred the stories that his mother used to tell, and which she no doubt still told to her younger children—stories of the tortoise and his wily ways, and of the bird *eneke-nti-oba*[6] who challenged the whole world to a wrestling contest and was finally thrown by the cat. He remembered the story she often told of the quarrel between Earth and Sky long ago, and how Sky withheld rain for seven years, until crops withered and the dead could not be buried because the hoes broke on the stony Earth. At last Vulture was sent to plead with Sky, and to soften his heart with a song of the suffering of the sons of men. Whenever Nwoye's mother sang this song he felt carried away to the distant scene in the sky where Vulture, Earth's emissary, sang for mercy. At last Sky was moved to pity, and he gave to Vulture rain wrapped in leaves of coco-yam. But as he flew home his long talon pierced the leaves and the rain fell as it had never fallen before. And so heavily did it rain on Vulture that he did not return to deliver his message but flew to a distant land, from where he had espied a fire. And when he got there he found it was a man making a sacrifice. He warmed himself in the fire and ate the entrails.

That was the kind of story that Nwoye loved. But he now knew that they were for foolish women and children, and he knew that his father wanted him to be a man. And so he feigned that he no longer cared for women's stories. And when he did this he saw that his father was pleased, and no longer rebuked him or beat him. So Nwoye and Ikemefuna would listen to Okonkwo's stories about tribal wars, or how, years ago, he had stalked his victim, overpowered him and obtained his first human head. And as he told them of the past they sat in darkness or the dim glow of logs, waiting for the women to finish their cooking. When they finished, each brought her bowl of foo-foo and bowl of soup to her husband. An oil lamp was lit and Okonkwo tasted from each bowl, and then passed two shares to Nwoye and Ikemefuna.

In this way the moons and the seasons passed. And then the locusts came. It had not happened for many a long year. The elders said locusts came once in a generation, reappeared every year for seven years and then disappeared for another lifetime. They went back to their caves in a distant land, where they were guarded by a race of stunted men. And then after another lifetime these men opened the caves again and the locusts came to Umuofia.

They came in the cold harmattan season after the harvests had been gathered, and ate up all the wild grass in the fields.

Okonkwo and the two boys were working on the red outer walls of the compound. This was one of the lighter tasks of the after-harvest season. A new cover of thick palm branches and palm leaves was set on the walls to protect them from the next rainy season. Okonkwo worked on the outside of the wall and the boys worked from within. There were little holes from one side to the other in the upper levels of the wall, and through these Okonkwo passed the rope, or *tie-tie*,[7] to the boys and they passed it round the wooden stays and then back to him; and in this way the cover was strengthened on the wall.

The women had gone to the bush to collect firewood, and the little children

6. The swallow with the ear of a crocodile [who is deaf] (literal trans.); a bird who proverbially flies without perching.

7. A creeper used as a rope to lash sections in building (pidgin English from "to tie").

to visit their playmates in the neighbouring compounds. The harmattan was in the air and seemed to distil a hazy feeling of sleep on the world. Okonkwo and the boys worked in complete silence, which was only broken when a new palm frond was lifted on to the wall or when a busy hen moved dry leaves about in her ceaseless search for food.

And then quite suddenly a shadow fell on the world, and the sun seemed hidden behind a thick cloud. Okonkwo looked up from his work and wondered if it was going to rain at such an unlikely time of the year. But almost immediately a shout of joy broke out in all directions, and Umuofia, which had dozed in the noon-day haze, broke into life and activity.

"Locusts are descending," was joyfully chanted everywhere, and men, women and children left their work or their play and ran into the open to see the unfamiliar sight. The locusts had not come for many, many years, and only the old people had seen them before.

At first, a fairly small swarm came. They were the harbingers sent to survey the land. And then appeared on the horizon a slowly-moving mass like a boundless sheet of black cloud drifting towards Umuofia. Soon it covered half the sky, and the solid mass was now broken by tiny eyes of light like shining star-dust. It was a tremendous sight, full of power and beauty.

Everyone was now about, talking excitedly and praying that the locusts should camp in Umuofia for the night. For although locusts had not visited Umuofia for many years, everybody knew by instinct that they were very good to eat. And at last the locusts did descend. They settled on every tree and on every blade of grass; they settled on the roofs and covered the bare ground. Mighty tree branches broke away under them, and the whole country became the brown-earth colour of the vast, hungry swarm.

Many people went out with baskets trying to catch them, but the elders counselled patience till nightfall. And they were right. The locusts settled in the bushes for the night and their wings became wet with dew. Then all Umuofia turned out in spite of the cold harmattan, and everyone filled his bags and pots with locusts. The next morning they were roasted in clay pots and then spread in the sun until they became dry and brittle. And for many days this rare food was eaten with solid palm-oil.

Okonkwo sat in his *obi* crunching happily with Ikemefuna and Nwoye, and drinking palm-wine copiously, when Ogbuefi Ezeudu came in. Ezeudu was the oldest man in this quarter of Umuofia. He had been a great and fearless warrior in his time, and was now accorded great respect in all the clan. He refused to join in the meal, and asked Okonkwo to have a word with him outside. And so they walked out together, the old man supporting himself with his stick. When they were out of ear-shot, he said to Okonkwo:

"That boy calls you father. Do not bear a hand in his death." Okonkwo was surprised, and was about to say something when the old man continued:

"Yes, Umuofia has decided to kill him. The Oracle of the Hills and the Caves has pronounced it. They will take him outside Umuofia as is the custom, and kill him there. But I want you to have nothing to do with it. He calls you his father."

The next day a group of elders from all the nine villages of Umuofia came to Okonkwo's house early in the morning, and before they began to speak in low tones Nwoye and Ikemefuna were sent out. They did not stay very long, but when they went away Okonkwo sat still for a very long time supporting his chin in his palms. Later in the day he called Ikemefuna and told him that he was to be taken home the next day. Nwoye overheard it and burst into tears, whereupon his father beat him heavily. As for Ikemefuna, he was at a loss. His own home had gradually become very faint and distant. He still missed his mother and his sister and would be very glad to see them. But somehow he knew he was not going to see them. He remembered once when men had talked in low tones with his father; and it seemed now as if it was happening all over again.

Later, Nwoye went to his mother's hut and told her that Ikemefuna was going home. She immediately dropped the pestle with which she was grinding pepper, folded her arms across her breast and sighed, "Poor child".

The next day, the men returned with a pot of wine. They were all fully dressed as if they were going to a big clan meeting or to pay a visit to a neighbouring village. They passed their cloths under the right arm-pit, and hung their goatskin bags and sheathed matchets over their left shoulders. Okonkwo got ready quickly and the party set out with Ikemefuna carrying the pot of wine. A deathly silence descended on Okonkwo's compound. Even the very little children seemed to know. Throughout that day Nwoye sat in his mother's hut and tears stood in his eyes.

At the beginning of their journey the men of Umuofia talked and laughed about the locusts, about their women, and about some effeminate men who had refused to come with them. But as they drew near to the outskirts of Umuofia silence fell upon them too.

The sun rose slowly to the centre of the sky, and the dry, sandy footway began to throw up the heat that lay buried in it. Some birds chirruped in the forests around. The men trod dry leaves on the sand. All else was silent. Then from the distance came the faint beating of the *ekwe*. It rose and faded with the wind—a peaceful dance from a distant clan.

"It is an *ozo* dance,"[8] the men said among themselves. But no one was sure where it was coming from. Some said Ezimili, others Abame or Aninta. They argued for a short while and fell into silence again, and the elusive dance rose and fell with the wind. Somewhere a man was taking one of the titles of his clan, with music and dancing and a great feast.

The footway had now become a narrow line in the heart of the forest. The short trees and sparse undergrowth which surrounded the men's village began to give way to giant trees and climbers which perhaps had stood from the beginning of things, untouched by the axe and the bush-fire. The sun breaking through their leaves and branches threw a pattern of light and shade on the sandy footway.

Ikemefuna heard a whisper close behind him and turned round sharply. The man who had whispered now called out aloud, urging the others to hurry up.

"We still have a long way to go," he said. Then he and another man went before Ikemefuna and set a faster pace.

Thus the men of Umuofia pursued their way, armed with sheathed matchets, and Ikemefuna, carrying a pot of palm-wine on his head, walked in their midst. Although he had felt uneasy at first, he was not afraid now. Okonkwo walked behind him. He could hardly imagine that Okonkwo was not his real father. He had never been fond of his real father, and at the end of three years he had become very distant indeed. But his mother and his three-year-old sister . . . of course she would not be three now, but six. Would he recognise

8. Part of the *ozo* rituals, the spiritual ceremonies that accompanied the taking of titles.

her now? She must have grown quite big. How his mother would weep for joy, and thank Okonkwo for having looked after him so well and for bringing him back. She would want to hear everything that had happened to him in all these years. Could he remember them all? He would tell her about Nwoye and his mother, and about the locusts. . . . Then quite suddenly a thought came upon him. His mother might be dead. He tried in vain to force the thought out of his mind. Then he tried to settle the matter the way he used to settle such matters when he was a little boy. He still remembered the song:

> Eze elina, elina!
>   Sala
> Eze ilikwa ya
> Ikwaba akwa oligholi
> Ebe Danda nechi eze
> Ebe Uzuzu nete egwu
>   Sala[9]

He sang it in his mind, and walked to its beat. If the song ended on his right foot, his mother was alive. If it ended on his left, she was dead. No, not dead, but ill. It ended on the right. She was alive and well. He sang the song again, and it ended on the left. But the second time did not count. The first voice gets to Chukwu, or God's house. That was a favourite saying of children. Ikemefuna felt like a child once more. It must be the thought of going home to his mother.

One of the men behind him cleared his throat. Ikemefuna looked back, and the man growled at him to go on and not stand looking back. The way he said it sent cold fear down Ikemefuna's back. His hands trembled vaguely on the black pot he carried. Why had Okonkwo withdrawn to the rear? Ikemefuna felt his legs melting under him. And he was afraid to look back.

As the man who had cleared his throat drew up and raised his matchet, Okonkwo looked away. He heard the blow. The pot fell and broke in the sand. He heard Ikemefuna cry, "My father, they have killed me!" as he ran towards him. Dazed with fear, Okonkwo drew his matchet and cut him down. He was afraid of being thought weak.

As soon as his father walked in, that night, Nwoye knew that Ikemefuna had been killed, and something seemed to give way inside him, like the snapping of a tightened bow. He did not cry. He just hung limp. He had had the same kind of feeling not long ago, during the last harvest season. Every child loved the harvest season. Those who were big enough to carry even a few yams in a tiny basket went with grown-ups to the farm. And if they could not help in digging up the yams, they could gather firewood together for roasting the ones that would be eaten there on the farm. This roasted yam soaked in red palm-oil and eaten in the open farm was sweeter than any meal at home. It was after such a day at the farm during the last harvest that Nwoye had felt for the first time a snapping inside him like the one he now felt. They were returning home with baskets of yams from a distant farm across the stream when they had heard the voice of an infant crying in the thick forest. A sudden

---

9. King don't eat, don't eat / Sala / King if you eat it / You will weep for the abomination / Where Danda installs a king / Where Uzuzu dances / Sala. "Sala": meaningless refrain. "Danda": the ant.

"Uzuzu": sand. Ikemefuna reassures himself by singing his favorite song about the country where the "sands dance forever" (see p. 2632).

hush had fallen on the women, who had been talking, and they had quickened their steps. Nwoye had heard that twins were put in earthenware pots and thrown away in the forest, but he had never yet come across them. A vague chill had descended on him and his head had seemed to swell, like a solitary walker at night who passes an evil spirit on the way. Then something had given way inside him. It descended on him again, this feeling, when his father walked in, that night after killing Ikemefuna.

CHAPTER EIGHT

Okonkwo did not taste any food for two days after the death of Ikemefuna. He drank palm-wine from morning till night, and his eyes were red and fierce like the eyes of a rat when it was caught by the tail and dashed against the floor. He called his son, Nwoye, to sit with him in his *obi*. But the boy was afraid of him and slipped out of the hut as soon as he noticed him dozing.

He did not sleep at night. He tried not to think about Ikemefuna, but the more he tried the more he thought about him. Once he got up from bed and walked about his compound. But he was so weak that his legs could hardly carry him. He felt like a drunken giant walking with the limbs of a mosquito. Now and then a cold shiver descended on his head and spread down his body.

On the third day he asked his second wife, Ekwefi, to roast plantains for him. She prepared it the way he liked—with slices of oil-bean and fish.

"You have not eaten for two days," said his daughter Ezinma when she brought the food to him. "So you must finish this." She sat down and stretched her legs in front of her. Okonkwo ate the food absent-mindedly. 'She should have been a boy,' he thought as he looked at his ten-year-old daughter. He passed her a piece of fish.

"Go and bring me some cold water," he said. Ezinma rushed out of the hut, chewing the fish, and soon returned with a bowl of cool water from the earthen pot in her mother's hut.

Okonkwo took the bowl from her and gulped the water down. He ate a few more pieces of plantain and pushed the dish aside.

"Bring me my bag," he asked, and Ezinma brought his goatskin bag from the far end of the hut. He searched in it for his snuff-bottle. It was a deep bag and took almost the whole length of his arm. It contained other things apart from his snuff-bottle. There was a drinking horn in it, and also a drinking gourd, and they knocked against each other as he searched. When he brought out the snuff-bottle he tapped it a few times against his knee-cap before taking out some snuff on the palm of his left hand. Then he remembered that he had not taken out his snuff-spoon. He searched his bag again and brought out a small, flat, ivory spoon, with which he carried the brown snuff to his nostrils.

Ezinma took the dish in one hand and the empty water bowl in the other and went back to her mother's hut. 'She should have been a boy,' Okonkwo said to himself again. His mind went back to Ikemefuna and he shivered. If only he could find some work to do he would be able to forget. But it was the season of rest between the harvest and the next planting season. The only work that men did at this time was covering the walls of their compound with new palm fronds. And Okonkwo had already done that. He had finished it on the very day the locusts came, when he had worked on one side of the wall and Ikemefuna and Nwoye on the other.

'When did you become a shivering old woman,' Okonkwo asked himself, 'you, who are known in all the nine villages for your valour in war? How can a man who has killed five men in battle fall to pieces because he has added a boy to their number? Okonkwo, you have become a woman indeed.'

He sprang to his feet, hung his goatskin bag on his shoulder and went to visit his friend, Obierika.

Obierika was sitting outside under the shade of an orange tree making thatches from leaves of the raffia-palm. He exchanged greetings with Okonkwo and led the way into his *obi*.

"I was coming over to see you as soon as I finished that thatch," he said, rubbing off the grains of sand that clung to his thighs.

"Is it well?" Okonkwo asked.

"Yes," replied Obierika. "My daughter's suitor is coming today and I hope we will clinch the matter of the bride-price. I want you to be there."

Just then Obierika's son, Maduka, came into the *obi* from outside, greeted Okonkwo and turned towards the compound.

"Come and shake hands with me," Okonkwo said to the lad. "Your wrestling the other day gave me much happiness." The boy smiled, shook hands with Okonkwo and went into the compound.

"He will do great things," Okonkwo said. "If I had a son like him I should be happy. I am worried about Nwoye. A bowl of pounded yams can throw him in a wrestling match. His two younger brothers are more promising. But I can tell you, Obierika, that my children do not resemble me. Where are the young suckers that will grow when the old banana tree dies? If Ezinma had been a boy I would have been happier. She has the right spirit."

"You worry yourself for nothing," said Obierika. "The children are still very young."

"Nwoye is old enough to impregnate a woman. At his age I was already fending for myself. No, my friend, he is not too young. A chick that will grow into a cock can be spotted the very day it hatches. I have done my best to make Nwoye grow into a man, but there is too much of his mother in him."

'Too much of his grandfather,' Obierika thought, but he did not say it. The same thought also came to Okonkwo's mind. But he had long learnt how to lay that ghost. Whenever the thought of his father's weakness and failure troubled him he expelled it by thinking about his own strength and success. And so he did now. His mind went to his latest show of manliness.

"I cannot understand why you refused to come with us to kill that boy," he asked Obierika.

"Because I did not want to," Obierika replied sharply. "I had something better to do."

"You sound as if you question the authority and the decision of the Oracle, who said he should die."

"I do not. Why should I? But the Oracle did not ask me to carry out its decision."

"But someone had to do it. If we were all afraid of blood, it would not be done. And what do you think the Oracle would do then?"

"You know very well, Okonkwo, that I am not afraid of blood; and if anyone tells you that I am, he is telling a lie. And let me tell you one thing, my friend. If I were you I would have stayed at home. What you have done will not please the Earth. It is the kind of action for which the goddess wipes out whole families."

"The Earth cannot punish me for obeying her messenger," Okonkwo said.

"A child's fingers are not scalded by a piece of hot yam which its mother puts into its palm."

"That is true," Obierika agreed. "But if the Oracle said that my son should be killed I would neither dispute it nor be the one to do it."

They would have gone on arguing had Ofoedu[1] not come in just then. It was clear from his twinkling eyes that he had important news. But it would be impolite to rush him. Obierika offered him a lobe of the kola nut he had broken with Okonkwo. Ofoedu ate slowly and talked about the locusts. When he finished his kola nut he said:

"The things that happen these days are very strange."

"What has happened?" asked Okonkwo.

"Do you know Ogbuefi Ndulue?"[2] Ofoedu asked.

"Ogbuefi Ndulue of Ire village," Okonkwo and Obierika said together.

"He died this morning," said Ofoedu.

"That is not strange. He was the oldest man in Ire," said Obierika.

"You are right," Ofoedu agreed. "But you ought to ask why the drum has not been beaten to tell Umuofia of his death."

"Why?" asked Obierika and Okonkwo together.

"That is the strange part of it. You know his first wife who walks with a stick?"

"Yes. She is called Ozoemena."[3]

"That is so," said Ofoedu. "Ozoemena was, as you know, too old to attend Ndulue during his illness. His younger wives did that. When he died this morning, one of these women went to Ozoemena's hut and told her. She rose from her mat, took her stick and walked over to the *obi*. She knelt on her knees and hands at the threshold and called her husband, who was laid on a mat. 'Ogbuefi Ndulue,' she called, three times, and went back to her hut. When the youngest wife went to call her again to be present at the washing of the body, she found her lying on the mat, dead."

"That is very strange indeed," said Okonkwo. "They will put off Ndulue's funeral until his wife has been buried."[4]

"That is why the drum has not been beaten to tell Umuofia."

"It was always said that Ndulue and Ozoemena had one mind," said Obierika. "I remember when I was a young boy there was a song about them. He could not do anything without telling her."

"I did not know that," said Okonkwo. "I thought he was a strong man in his youth."

"He was indeed," said Ofoedu.

Okonkwo shook his head doubtfully.

"He led Umuofia to war in those days," said Obierika.

Okonkwo was beginning to feel like his old self again. All that he required was something to occupy his mind. If he had killed Ikemefuna during the busy planting season or harvesting it would not have been so bad; his mind would have been centred on his work. Okonkwo was not a man of thought but of action. But in the absence of work, talking was the next best.

Soon after Ofoedu left, Okonkwo took up his goatskin bag to go.

"I must go home to tap my palm trees for the afternoon," he said.

1. The ancestors are our guide.
2. Life has arrived.
3. Another bad thing will not happen.
4. A wife dying shortly after her husband was sometimes considered guilty of his death, so the village preserves appearances by burying Ozoemena before announcing Ogbuefi Ndulue's death.

"Who taps your tall trees for you?" asked Obierika.

"Umezulike," replied Okonkwo.

"Sometimes I wish I had not taken the *ozo* title," said Obierika. "It wounds my heart to see these young men killing palm trees in the name of tapping."

"It is so indeed," Okonkwo agreed. "But the law of the land must be obeyed."

"I don't know how we got that law," said Obierika. "In many other clans a man of title is not forbidden to climb the palm tree. Here we say he cannot climb the tall tree but he can tap the short ones standing on the ground. It is like Dimaragana, who would not lend his knife for cutting up dog-meat because the dog was taboo to him, but offered to use his teeth."

"I think it is good that our clan holds the *ozo* title in high esteem," said Okonkwo. "In those other clans you speak of, *ozo* is so low that every beggar takes it."

"I was only speaking in jest," said Obierika. "In Abame and Aninta the title is worth less than two cowries. Every man wears the thread of title on his ankle, and does not lose it even if he steals."

"They have indeed soiled the name of *ozo*," said Okonkwo as he rose to go.

"It will not be very long now before my in-laws come," said Obierika.

"I shall return very soon," said Okonkwo, looking at the position of the sun.

There were seven men in Obierika's hut when Okonkwo returned. The suitor was a young man of about twenty-five, and with him were his father and uncle. On Obierika's side were his two elder brothers and Maduka, his sixteen-year-old son.

"Ask Akueke's mother to send us some kola nuts," said Obierika to his son. Maduka vanished into the compound like lightning. The conversation at once centred on him, and everybody agreed that he was as sharp as a razor.

"I sometimes think he is too sharp," said Obierika, somewhat indulgently. "He hardly ever walks. He is always in a hurry. If you are sending him on an errand he flies away before he has heard half of the message."

"You were very much like that yourself," said his eldest brother. "As our people say, 'When mother-cow is chewing grass its young ones watch its mouth.' Maduka has been watching your mouth."

As he was speaking the boy returned, followed by Akueke,[5] his half-sister, carrying a wooden dish with three kola nuts and alligator pepper. She gave the dish to her father's eldest brother and then shook hands, very shyly, with her suitor and his relatives. She was about sixteen and just ripe for marriage. Her suitor and his relatives surveyed her young body with expert eyes as if to assure themselves that she was beautiful and ripe.

She wore a coiffure which was done up into a crest in the middle of the head. Cam wood was rubbed lightly into her skin, and all over her body were black patterns drawn with *uli*.[6] She wore a black necklace which hung down in three coils just above her full, succulent breasts. On her arms were red and yellow bangles, and on her waist four or five rows of *jigida*, or waist-beads.

When she had shaken hands, or rather held out her hand to be shaken, she returned to her mother's hut to help with the cooking.

"Remove your *jigida* first," her mother warned as she moved near the fire-

---

5. Wealth of Eke (a divinity). Similar names built on *ako* ("wealth") connote riches and are associated with the idea of women as a form of exchangeable material wealth.

6. A liquid made from crushed seeds, which caused the skin to pucker temporarily. It was used to create black tattoolike decorations. "Cam wood": a shrub. The powdered red heartwood of the shrub was used as a cosmetic dye.

place to bring the pestle resting against the wall. "Every day I tell you that *jigida* and fire are not friends. But you will never hear. You grew your ears for decoration, not for hearing. One of these days your *jigida* will catch fire on your waist, and then you will know."

Akueke moved to the other end of the hut and began to remove the waist-beads. It had to be done slowly and carefully, taking each string separately, else it would break and the thousand tiny rings would have to be strung together again. She rubbed each string downwards with her palms until it passed the buttocks and slipped down to the floor around her feet.

The men in the *obi* had already begun to drink the palm-wine which Akueke's suitor had brought. It was a very good wine and powerful, for in spite of the palm fruit hung across the mouth of the pot to restrain the lively liquor, white foam rose and spilled over.

"That wine is the work of a good tapper," said Okonkwo.

The young suitor, whose name was Ibe, smiled broadly and said to his father: "Do you hear that?" He then said to the others: "He will never admit that I am a good tapper."

"He tapped three of my best palm trees to death," said his father, Ukegbu.

"That was about five years ago," said Ibe, who had begun to pour out the wine, "before I learnt how to tap." He filled the first horn and gave to his father. Then he poured out for the others. Okonkwo brought out his big horn from the goatskin bag, blew into it to remove any dust that might be there, and gave it to Ibe to fill.

As the men drank, they talked about everything except the thing for which they had gathered. It was only after the pot had been emptied that the suitor's father cleared his voice and announced the object of their visit.

Obierika then presented to him a small bundle of short broomsticks. Ukegbu counted them.

"They are thirty?" he asked.

Obierika nodded in agreement.

"We are at last getting somewhere," Ukegbu said, and then turning to his brother and his son he said: "Let us go out and whisper together." The three rose and went outside. When they returned Ukegbu handed the bundle of sticks back to Obierika. He counted them; instead of thirty there were now only fifteen. He passed them over to his eldest brother, Machi, who also counted them and said:

"We had not thought to go below thirty. But as the dog said, 'If I fall down for you and you fall down for me, it is play'. Marriage should be a play and not a fight; so we are falling down again." He then added ten sticks to the fifteen and gave the bundle to Ukegbu.

In this way Akueke's bride-price was finally settled at twenty bags of cowries. It was already dusk when the two parties came to this agreement.

"Go and tell Akueke's mother that we have finished," Obierika said to his son, Maduka. Almost immediately the woman came in with a big bowl of foo-foo. Obierika's second wife followed with a pot of soup, and Maduka brought in a pot of palm-wine.

As the men ate and drank palm-wine they talked about the customs of their neighbours.

"It was only this morning," said Obierika, "that Okonkwo and I were talking about Abame and Aninta, where titled men climb trees and pound foo-foo for their wives."

"All their customs are upside-down. They do not decide bride-price as we do, with sticks. They haggle and bargain as if they were buying a goat or a cow in the market."

"That is very bad," said Obierika's eldest brother. "But what is good in one place is bad in another place. In Umunso they do not bargain at all, not even with broomsticks. The suitor just goes on bringing bags of cowries until his in-laws tell him to stop. It is a bad custom because it always leads to a quarrel."

"The world is large," said Okonkwo. "I have even heard that in some tribes a man's children belong to his wife and her family."

"That cannot be," said Machi. "You might as well say that the woman lies on top of the man when they are making the children."

"It is like the story of white men who, they say, are white like this piece of chalk," said Obierika. He held up a piece of chalk, which every man kept in his *obi* and with which his guests drew lines on the floor before they ate kola nuts. "And these white men, they say, have no toes."[7]

"And have you never seen them?" asked Machi.

"Have you?" asked Obierika.

"One of them passes here frequently," said Machi. "His name is Amadi."

Those who knew Amadi laughed. He was a leper, and the polite name for leprosy was 'the white skin'.

CHAPTER NINE

For the first time in three nights, Okonkwo slept. He woke up once in the middle of the night and his mind went back to the past three days without making him feel uneasy. He began to wonder why he had felt uneasy at all. It was like a man wondering in broad daylight why a dream had appeared so terrible to him at night. He stretched himself and scratched his thigh where a mosquito had bitten him as he slept. Another one was wailing near his right ear. He slapped the ear and hoped he had killed it. Why do they always go for one's ears? When he was a child his mother had told him a story about it. But it was as silly as all women's stories. Mosquito, she had said, had asked Ear to marry him, whereupon Ear fell on the floor in uncontrollable laughter. "How much longer do you think you will live?" she asked. "You are already a skeleton." Mosquito went away humiliated, and any time he passed her way he told Ear that he was still alive.

Okonkwo turned on his side and went back to sleep. He was roused in the morning by someone banging on his door.

"Who is that?" he growled. He knew it must be Ekwefi. Of his three wives Ekwefi was the only one who would have the audacity to bang on his door.

"Ezinma is dying," came her voice, and all the tragedy and sorrow of her life were packed in those words.

Okonkwo sprang from his bed, pushed back the bolt on his door and ran into Ekwefi's hut.

Ezinma lay shivering on a mat beside a huge fire that her mother had kept burning all night.

"It is *iba*,"[8] said Okonkwo as he took his matchet and went into the bush to collect the leaves and grasses and barks of trees that went into making the medicine for *iba*.

7. They wear shoes.
8. A fever accompanied by jaundice, probably caused by malaria.

Ekwefi knelt beside the sick child, occasionally feeling with her palm the wet, burning forehead.

Ezinma was an only child and the centre of her mother's world. Very often it was Ezinma who decided what food her mother should prepare. Ekwefi even gave her such delicacies as eggs, which children were rarely allowed to eat because such food tempted them to steal. One day as Ezinma was eating an egg Okonkwo had come in unexpectedly from his hut. He was greatly shocked and swore to beat Ekwefi if she dared to give the child eggs again. But it was impossible to refuse Ezinma anything. After her father's rebuke she developed an even keener appetite for eggs. And she enjoyed above all the secrecy in which she now ate them. Her mother always took her into their bedroom and shut the door.

Ezinma did not call her mother Nne like all children. She called her by her name, Ekwefi, as her father and other grown-up people did. The relationship between them was not only that of mother and child. There was something in it like the companionship of equals, which was strengthened by such little conspiracies as eating eggs in the bedroom.

Ekwefi had suffered a good deal in her life. She had borne ten children and nine of them had died in infancy, usually before the age of three. As she buried one child after another her sorrow gave way to despair and then to grim resignation. The birth of her children, which should be a woman's crowning glory, became for Ekwefi mere physical agony devoid of promise. The naming ceremony after seven market weeks became an empty ritual. Her deepening despair found expression in the names she gave her children. One of them was a pathetic cry, Onwumbiko—'Death, I implore you.' But Death took no notice; Onwumbiko died in his fifteenth month. The next child was a girl, Ozoemena—'May it not happen again.' She died in her eleventh month, and two others after her. Ekwefi then became defiant and called her next child Onwuma—'Death may please himself.' And he did.

After the death of Ekwefi's second child, Okonkwo had gone to a medicine-man, who was also a diviner of the Afa Oracle,[9] to inquire what was amiss. This man told him that the child was an ogbanje, one of those wicked children who, when they died, entered their mothers' wombs to be born again.

"When your wife becomes pregnant again," he said, "let her not sleep in her hut. Let her go and stay with her people. In that way she will elude her wicked tormentor and break its evil cycle of birth and death."

Ekwefi did as she was asked. As soon as she became pregnant she went to live with her old mother in another village. It was there that her third child was born and circumcised on the eighth day. She did not return to Okonkwo's compound until three days before the naming ceremony. The child was called Onwumbiko.

Onwumbiko was not given proper burial when he died. Okonkwo had called in another medicine-man who was famous in the clan for his great knowledge about ogbanje children. His name was Okagbue Uyanwa. Okagbue was a very striking figure, tall, with a full beard and a bald head. He was light in complexion and his eyes were red and fiery. He always gnashed his teeth as he listened to those who came to consult him. He asked Okonkwo a few questions about the dead child. All the neighbours and relations who had come to mourn gathered round them.

---

9. One who communicates with the clients' ancestors by reading patterns made by objects (e.g., seeds, teeth, shells) thrown on a flat surface.

"On what market-day was it born?" he asked.

"*Oye*," replied Okonkwo.

"And it died this morning?"

Okonkwo said yes, and only then realised for the first time that the child had died on the same market-day as it had been born. The neighbours and relations also saw the coincidence and said among themselves that it was very significant.

"Where do you sleep with your wife, in your *obi* or in her own hut?" asked the medicine-man.

"In her hut."

"In future call her into your *obi*."

The medicine-man then ordered that there should be no mourning for the dead child. He brought out a sharp razor from the goatskin bag slung from his left shoulder and began to mutilate the child. Then he took it away to bury in the Evil Forest, holding it by the ankle and dragging it on the ground behind him. After such treatment it would think twice before coming again, unless it was one of the stubborn ones who returned, carrying the stamp of their mutilation—a missing finger or perhaps a dark line where the medicine-man's razor had cut them.

By the time Onwumbiko died Ekwefi had become a very bitter woman. Her husband's first wife had already had three sons, all strong and healthy. When she had borne her third son in succession, Okonkwo had slaughtered a goat for her, as was the custom. Ekwefi had nothing but good wishes for her. But she had grown so bitter about her own *chi* that she could not rejoice with others over their good fortune. And so, on the day that Nwoye's mother celebrated the birth of her three sons with feasting and music, Ekwefi was the only person in the happy company who went about with a cloud on her brow. Her husband's wife took this for malevolence, as husband's wives were wont to. How could she know that Ekwefi's bitterness did not flow outwards to others but inwards into her own soul; that she did not blame others for their good fortune but her own evil *chi* who denied her any?

At last Ezinma was born, and although ailing she seemed determined to live. At first Ekwefi accepted her, as she had accepted others—with listless resignation. But when she lived on to her fourth, fifth and sixth years, love returned once more to her mother, and, with love, anxiety. She determined to nurse her child to health, and she put all her being into it. She was rewarded by occasional spells of health during which Ezinma bubbled with energy like fresh palm-wine. At such times she seemed beyond danger. But all of a sudden she would go down again. Everybody knew she was an *ogbanje*. These sudden bouts of sickness and health were typical of her kind. But she had lived so long that perhaps she had decided to stay. Some of them did become tired of their evil rounds of birth and death, or took pity on their mothers, and stayed. Ekwefi believed deep inside her that Ezinma had come to stay. She believed because it was that faith alone that gave her own life any kind of meaning. And this faith had been strengthened when a year or so ago a medicine-man had dug up Ezinma's *iyi-uwa*.[1] Everyone knew then that she would live because her bond with the world of *ogbanje* had been broken. Ekwefi was reassured. But such was her anxiety for her daughter that she could not rid herself completely of her fear. And although she believed that the *iyi-uwa* which had been

1. Stone that forms the link between an *ogbanje* child and the spirit world. If the *iyi-uwa* is found and destroyed, the cycle is broken and the child will not die.

dug up was genuine, she could not ignore the fact that some really evil children sometimes misled people into digging up a specious one.

But Ezinma's *iyi-uwa* had looked real enough. It was a smooth pebble wrapped in a dirty rag. The man who dug it up was the same Okagbue who was famous in all the clan for his knowledge in these matters. Ezinma had not wanted to co-operate with him at first. But that was only to be expected. No *ogbanje* would yield her secrets easily, and most of them never did because they died too young—before they could be asked questions.

"Where did you bury your *iyi-uwa*?" Okagbue had asked Ezinma. She was nine then and was just recovering from a serious illness.

"What is *iyi-uwa*?" she asked in return.

"You know what it is. You buried it in the ground somewhere so that you can die and return again to torment your mother."

Ezinma looked at her mother, whose eyes, sad and pleading, were fixed on her.

"Answer the question at once," roared Okonkwo, who stood beside her. All the family were there and some of the neighbours too.

"Leave her to me," the medicine-man told Okonkwo in a cool, confident voice. He turned again to Ezinma. "Where did you bury your *iyi-uwa*?"

"Where they bury children," she replied, and the quiet spectators murmured to themselves.

"Come along then and show me the spot," said the medicine-man.

The crowd set out with Ezinma leading the way and Okagbue following closely behind her. Okonkwo came next and Ekwefi followed him. When she came to the main road, Ezinma turned left as if she was going to the stream.

"But you said it was where they bury children?" asked the medicine-man.

"No," said Ezinma, whose feeling of importance was manifest in her sprightly walk. She sometimes broke into a run and stopped again suddenly. The crowd followed her silently. Women and children returning from the stream with pots of water on their heads wondered what was happening until they saw Okagbue and guessed that it must be something to do with *ogbanje*. And they all knew Ekwefi and her daughter very well.

When she got to the big udala tree Ezinma turned left into the bush, and the crowd followed her. Because of her size she made her way through trees and creepers more quickly than her followers. The bush was alive with the tread of feet on dry leaves and sticks and the moving aside of tree branches. Ezinma went deeper and deeper and the crowd went with her. Then she suddenly turned round and began to walk back to the road. Everybody stood to let her pass and then filed after her.

"If you bring us all this way for nothing I shall beat sense into you," Okonkwo threatened.

"I have told you to let her alone. I know how to deal with them," said Okagbue.

Ezinma led the way back to the road, looked left and right and turned right. And so they arrived home again.

"Where did you bury your *iyi-uwa*?" asked Okagbue when Ezinma finally stopped outside her father's *obi*. Okagbue's voice was unchanged. It was quiet and confident.

"It is near that orange tree," Ezinma said.

"And why did you not say so, you wicked daughter of Akalogoli?" Okonkwo swore furiously. The medicine-man ignored him.

"Come and show me the exact spot," he said quietly to Ezinma.

"It is here," she said when they got to the tree.

"Point at the spot with your finger," said Okagbue.

"It is here," said Ezinma touching the ground with her finger. Okonkwo stood by, rumbling like thunder in the rainy season.

"Bring me a hoe," said Okagbue.

When Ekwefi brought the hoe, he had already put aside his goatskin bag and his big cloth and was in his underwear, a long and thin strip of cloth wound round the waist like a belt and then passed between the legs to be fastened to the belt behind. He immediately set to work digging a pit where Ezinma had indicated. The neighbours sat around watching the pit becoming deeper and deeper. The dark top-soil soon gave way to the bright-red earth with which women scrubbed the floor and walls of huts. Okagbue worked tirelessly and in silence, his back shining with perspiration. Okonkwo stood by the pit. He asked Okagbue to come up and rest while he took a hand. But Okagbue said he was not tired yet.

Ekwefi went into her hut to cook yams. Her husband had brought out more yams than usual because the medicine-man had to be fed. Ezinma went with her and helped in preparing the vegetables.

"There is too much green vegetable," she said.

"Don't you see the pot is full of yams?" Ekwefi asked.

"And you know how leaves become smaller after cooking."

"Yes," said Ezinma, "that was why the snake-lizard killed his mother."

"Very true," said Ekwefi.

"He gave his mother seven baskets of vegetables to cook and in the end there were only three. And so he killed her," said Ezinma.

"That is not the end of the story."

"Oho," said Ezinma. "I remember now. He brought another seven baskets and cooked them himself. And there were again only three. So he killed himself too."

Outside the *obi* Okagbue and Okonkwo were digging the pit to find where Ezinma had buried her *iyi-uwa*. Neighbours sat around, watching. The pit was now so deep that they no longer saw the digger. They only saw the red earth he threw up mounting higher and higher. Okonkwo's son, Nwoye, stood near the edge of the pit because he wanted to take in all that happened.

Okagbue had again taken over the digging from Okonkwo. He worked, as usual, in silence. The neighbours and Okonkwo's wives were now talking. The children had lost interest and were playing.

Suddenly Okagbue sprang to the surface with the agility of a leopard.

"It is very near now," he said. "I have felt it."

There was immediate excitement and those who were sitting jumped to their feet.

"Call your wife and child," he said to Okonkwo. But Ekwefi and Ezinma had heard the noise and run out to see what it was.

Okagbue went back into the pit, which was now surrounded by spectators. After a few more hoe-fuls of earth he struck the *iyi-uwa*. He raised it carefully with the hoe and threw it to the surface. Some women ran away in fear when it was thrown. But they soon returned and everyone was gazing at the rag from a reasonable distance. Okagbue emerged and without saying a word or even looking at the spectators he went to his goatskin bag, took out two leaves and began to chew them. When he had swallowed them, he took up the rag with his left hand and began to untie it. And then the smooth, shiny pebble fell out. He picked it up.

"Is this yours?" he asked Ezinma.

"Yes," she replied. All the women shouted with joy because Ekwefi's troubles were at last ended.

All this had happened more than a year ago and Ezinma had not been ill since. And then suddenly she had begun to shiver in the night. Ekwefi brought her to the fireplace, spread her mat on the floor and built a fire. But she had got worse and worse. As she knelt by her, feeling with her palm the wet, burning forehead, she prayed a thousand times. Although her husband's wives were saying that it was nothing more than *iba*, she did not hear them.

Okonkwo returned from the bush carrying on his left shoulder a large bundle of grasses and leaves, roots and barks of medicinal trees and shrubs. He went into Ekwefi's hut, put down his load and sat down.

"Get me a pot," he said, "and leave the child alone."

Ekwefi went to bring the pot and Okonkwo selected the best from his bundle, in their due proportions, and cut them up. He put them in the pot and Ekwefi poured in some water.

"Is that enough?" she asked when she had poured in about half of the water in the bowl.

"A little more . . . I said a *little*. Are you deaf?" Okonkwo roared at her.

She set the pot on the fire and Okonkwo took up his matchet to return to his *obi*.

"You must watch the pot carefully," he said as he went, "and don't allow it to boil over. If it does its power will be gone." He went away to his hut and Ekwefi began to tend the medicine pot almost as if it was itself a sick child. Her eyes went constantly from Ezinma to the boiling pot and back to Ezinma.

Okonkwo returned when he felt the medicine had cooked long enough. He looked it over and said it was done.

"Bring a low stool for Ezinma," he said, "and a thick mat."

He took down the pot from the fire and placed it in front of the stool. He then roused Ezinma and placed her on the stool, astride the steaming pot. The thick mat was thrown over both. Ezinma struggled to escape from the choking and overpowering steam, but she was held down. She started to cry.

When the mat was at last removed she was drenched in perspiration. Ekwefi mopped her with a piece of cloth and she lay down on a dry mat and was soon asleep.

CHAPTER TEN

Large crowds began to gather on the village *ilo* as soon as the edge had worn off the sun's heat and it was no longer painful on the body. Most communal ceremonies took place at that time of the day, so that even when it was said that a ceremony would begin "after the midday meal" everyone understood that it would begin a long time later, when the sun's heat had softened.

It was clear from the way the crowd stood or sat that the ceremony was for men. There were many women, but they looked on from the fringe like outsiders. The titled men and elders sat on their stools waiting for the trials to begin. In front of them was a row of stools on which nobody sat. There were nine of them. Two little groups of people stood at a respectable distance beyond the stools. They faced the elders. There were three men in one group and three men and one woman in the other. The woman was Mgbafo and the three men with her were her brothers. In the other group were her husband, Uzowulu, and his relatives. Mgbafo and her brothers were as still as statues into whose faces the artist has moulded defiance. Uzowulu and his relative, on the other hand, were whispering together. It looked like whispering, but they were really talking at the top of their voices. Everybody in the crowd was talking. It was like the market. From a distance the noise was a deep rumble carried by the wind.

An iron gong sounded, setting up a wave of expectation in the crowd. Everyone looked in the direction of the *egwugwu*[2] house. *Gome, gome, gome, gome* went the gong, and a powerful flute blew a high-pitched blast. Then came the voices of the *egwugwu*, guttural and awesome. The wave struck the women and children and there was a backward stampede. But it was momentary. They were already far enough where they stood and there was room for running away if any of the *egwugwu* should go towards them.

The drum sounded again and the flute blew. The *egwugwu* house was now a pandemonium of quavering voices: *Aru oyim de de de dei!*[3] filled the air as the spirits of the ancestors, just emerged from the earth, greeted themselves in their esoteric language. The *egwugwu* house into which they emerged faced the forest, away from the crowd, who saw only its back with the many-coloured patterns and drawings done by specially chosen women at regular intervals. These women never saw the inside of the hut. No woman ever did. They scrubbed and painted the outside walls under the supervision of men. If they imagined what was inside, they kept their imagination to themselves. No woman ever asked questions about the most powerful and the most secret cult in the clan.

Aru oyim de de de dei! flew around the dark, closed hut like tongues of fire. The ancestral spirits of the clan were abroad. The metal gong beat continuously now and the flute, shrill and powerful, floated on the chaos.

And then the *egwugwu* appeared. The women and children sent up a great shout and took to their heels. It was instinctive. A woman fled as soon as an *egwugwu* came in sight. And when, as on that day, nine of the greatest masked spirits in the clan came out together it was a terrifying spectacle. Even Mgbafo took to her heels and had to be restrained by her brothers.

Each of the nine *egwugwu* represented a village of the clan. Their leader was called Evil Forest. Smoke poured out of his head.

The nine villages of Umuofia had grown out of the nine sons of the first father of the clan. Evil Forest represented the village of Umueru, or the children of Eru, who was the eldest of the nine sons.

"Umuofia kwenu!" shouted the leading *egwugwu*, pushing the air with his raffia arms. The elders of the clan replied, "Yaa!"

"Umuofia kwenu!"

"Yaa!"

"Umuofia kwenu!"

"Yaa!"

Evil Forest then thrust the pointed end of his rattling staff into the earth.

---

2. Here the term refers to the village's highest spiritual and judicial authority, prominent men who, after putting on elaborate ceremonial costumes, embody the village's ancestral spirits.
3. Body of my friend, greetings!

And it began to shake and rattle, like something agitating with a metallic life. He took the first of the empty stools and the eight other *egwugwu* began to sit in order of seniority after him.

Okonkwo's wives, and perhaps other women as well, might have noticed that the second *egwugwu* had the springy walk of Okonkwo. And they might also have noticed that Okonkwo was not among the titled men and elders who sat behind the row of *egwugwu*. But if they thought these things they kept them within themselves. The *egwugwu* with the springy walk was one of the dead fathers of the clan. He looked terrible with the smoked raffia body, a huge wooden face painted white except for the round hollow eyes and the charred teeth that were as big as a man's fingers. On his head were two powerful horns.

When all the *egwugwu* had sat down and the sound of the many tiny bells and rattles on their bodies had subsided, Evil Forest addressed the two groups of people facing them.

"Uzowulu's body, I salute you," he said. Spirits always addressed humans as 'bodies'. Uzowulu bent down and touched the earth with his right hand as a sign of submission.

"Our father, my hand has touched the ground," he said.

"Uzowulu's body, do you know me?" asked the spirit.

"How can I know you, father? You are beyond our knowledge."

Evil Forest then turned to the other group and addressed the eldest of the three brothers.

"The body of Odukwe, I greet you," he said, and Odukwe bent down and touched the earth. The hearing then began.

Uzowulu stepped forward and presented his case.

"That woman standing there is my wife, Mgbafo. I married her with my money and my yams. I do not owe my in-laws anything. I owe them no yams. I owe them no coco-yams. One morning three of them came to my house, beat me up and took my wife and children away. This happened in the rainy season. I have waited in vain for my wife to return. At last I went to my in-laws and said to them, 'You have taken back your sister. I did not send her away. You yourselves took her. The law of the clan is that you should return her bride-price.' But my wife's brothers said they had nothing to tell me. So I have brought the matter to the fathers of the clan. My case is finished. I salute you."

"Your words are good," said the leader of the *egwugwu*. "Let us hear Odukwe. His words may also be good."

Odukwe was short and thick-set. He stepped forward, saluted the spirits and began his story.

"My in-law has told you that we went to his house, beat him up and took our sister and her children away. All that is true. He told you that he came to take back her bride-price and we refused to give it him. That also is true. My in-law, Uzowulu, is a beast. My sister lived with him for nine years. During those years no single day passed in the sky without his beating the woman. We have tried to settle their quarrels time without number and on each occasion Uzowulu was guilty——"

"It is a lie!" Uzowulu shouted.

"Two years ago," continued Odukwe, "when she was pregnant, he beat her until she miscarried."

"It is a lie. She miscarried after she had gone to sleep with her lover."

"Uzowulu's body, I salute you," said Evil Forest, silencing him. "What kind of lover sleeps with a pregnant woman?" There was a loud murmur of approbation from the crowd. Odukwe continued:

"Last year when my sister was recovering from an illness, he beat her again so that if the neighbours had not gone in to save her she would have been killed. We heard of it, and did as you have been told. The law of Umuofia is that if a woman runs away from her husband her bride-price is returned. But in this case she ran away to save her life. Her two children belong to Uzowulu. We do not dispute it, but they are too young to leave their mother. If, on the other hand, Uzowulu should recover from his madness and come in the proper way to beg his wife to return she will do so on the understanding that if he ever beats her again we shall cut off his genitals for him."

The crowd roared with laughter. Evil Forest rose to his feet and order was immediately restored. A steady cloud of smoke rose from his head. He sat down again and called two witnesses. They were both Uzowulu's neighbours, and they agreed about the beating. Evil Forest then stood up, pulled out his staff and thrust it into the earth again. He ran a few steps in the direction of the women; they all fled in terror, only to return to their places almost immediately. The nine egwugwu then went away to consult together in their house. They were silent for a long time. Then the metal gong sounded and the flute was blown. The egwugwu had emerged once again from their underground home. They saluted one another and then reappeared on the ilo.

"Umuofia kwenu!" roared Evil Forest, facing the elders and grandees of the clan.

"Yaa!" replied the thunderous crowd; then silence descended from the sky and swallowed the noise.

Evil Forest began to speak and all the while he spoke everyone was silent. The eight other egwugwu were as still as statues.

"We have heard both sides of the case," said Evil Forest. "Our duty is not to blame this man or to praise that, but to settle the dispute." He turned to Uzowulu's group and allowed a short pause.

"Uzowulu's body, I salute you," he said.

"Our father, my hand has touched the ground," replied Uzowulu, touching the earth.

"Uzowulu's body, do you know me?"

"How can I know you, father? You are beyond our knowledge," Uzowulu replied.

"I am Evil Forest. I kill a man on the day that his life is sweetest to him."

"That is true," replied Uzowulu.

"Go to your in-laws with a pot of wine and beg your wife to return to you. It is not bravery when a man fights with a woman." He turned to Odukwe, and allowed a brief pause.

"Odukwe's body, I greet you," he said.

"My hand is on the ground," replied Odukwe.

"Do you know me?"

"No man can know you," replied Odukwe.

"I am Evil Forest, I am Dry-meat-that-fills-the-mouth, I am Fire-that-burns-without-faggots. If your in-law brings wine to you, let your sister go with him. I salute you." He pulled his staff from the hard earth and thrust it back.

"*Umuofia kwenu!*" he roared, and the crowd answered.

"I don't know why such a trifle should come before the *egwugwu*," said one elder to another.

"Don't you know what kind of man Uzowulu is? He will not listen to any other decision," replied the other.

As they spoke two other groups of people had replaced the first before the *egwugwu*, and a great land case began.

CHAPTER ELEVEN

The night was impenetrably dark. The moon had been rising later and later every night until now it was seen only at dawn. And whenever the moon forsook evening and rose at cock-crow the nights were as black as charcoal.

Ezinma and her mother sat on a mat on the floor after their supper of yam foo-foo and bitter-leaf soup. A palm-oil lamp gave out yellowish light. Without it, it would have been impossible to eat; one could not have known where one's mouth was in the darkness of that night. There was an oil lamp in all the four huts on Okonkwo's compound, and each hut seen from the others looked like a soft eye of yellow half-light set in the solid massiveness of night.

The world was silent except for the shrill cry of insects, which was part of the night, and the sound of wooden mortar and pestle as Nwayieke pounded her foo-foo. Nwayieke lived four compounds away, and she was notorious for her late cooking. Every woman in the neighbourhood knew the sound of Nwayieke's mortar and pestle. It was also part of the night.

Okonkwo had eaten from his wives' dishes and was now reclining with his back against the wall. He searched his bag and brought out his snuff-bottle. He turned it on to his left palm, but nothing came out. He hit the bottle against his knee to shake up the tobacco. That was always the trouble with Okeke's snuff. It very quickly went damp, and there was too much saltpetre in it. Okonkwo had not bought snuff from him for a long time. Idigo was the man who knew how to grind good snuff. But he had recently fallen ill.

Low voices, broken now and again by singing, reached Okonkwo from his wives' huts as each woman and her children told folk stories. Ekwefi and her daughter, Ezinma, sat on a mat on the floor. It was Ekwefi's turn to tell a story.

"Once upon a time," she began, "all the birds were invited to a feast in the sky. They were very happy and began to prepare themselves for the great day. They painted their bodies with red cam wood and drew beautiful patterns on them with *uli*.

"Tortoise saw all these preparations and soon discovered what it all meant. Nothing that happened in the world of the animals ever escaped his notice; he was full of cunning. As soon as he heard of the great feast in the sky his throat began to itch at the very thought. There was a famine in those days and Tortoise had not eaten a good meal for two moons. His body rattled like a piece of dry stick in his empty shell. So he began to plan how he would go to the sky."

"But he had no wings," said Ezinma.

"Be patient," replied her mother. "That is the story. Tortoise had no wings, but he went to the birds and asked to be allowed to go with them.

" 'We know you too well,' said the birds when they had heard him. 'You are full of cunning and you are ungrateful. If we allow you to come with us you will soon begin your mischief.'

" 'You do not know me,' said Tortoise. 'I am a changed man. I have learnt that a man who makes trouble for others is also making it for himself.'

"Tortoise had a sweet tongue, and within a short time all the birds agreed that he was a changed man, and they each gave him a feather, with which he made two wings.

"At last the great day came and Tortoise was the first to arrive at the meeting-place. When all the birds had gathered together, they set off in a body. Tortoise was very happy and voluble as he flew among the birds, and he was soon chosen as the man to speak for the party because he was a great orator.

" 'There is one important thing which we must not forget,' he said as they flew on their way. 'When people are invited to a great feast like this, they take new names for the occasion. Our hosts in the sky will expect us to honour this age-old custom.'

"None of the birds had heard of this custom but they knew that Tortoise, in spite of his failings in other directions, was a widely-travelled man who knew the customs of different peoples. And so they each took a new name. When they had all taken, Tortoise also took one. He was to be called *All of you.*

"At last the party arrived in the sky and their hosts were very happy to see them. Tortoise stood up in his many-coloured plumage and thanked them for their invitation. His speech was so eloquent that all the birds were glad they had brought him, and nodded their heads in approval of all he said. Their hosts took him as the king of the birds, especially as he looked somewhat different from the others.

"After kola nuts had been presented and eaten, the people of the sky set before their guests the most delectable dishes Tortoise had ever seen or dreamt of. The soup was brought out hot from the fire and in the very pot in which it had been cooked. It was full of meat and fish. Tortoise began to sniff aloud. There was pounded yam and also yam pottage cooked with palm-oil and fresh fish. There were also pots of palm-wine. When everything had been set before the guests, one of the people of the sky came forward and tasted a little from each pot. He then invited the birds to eat. But Tortoise jumped to his feet and asked: 'For whom have you prepared this feast?'

" 'For all of you,' replied the man.

"Tortoise turned to the birds and said: 'You remember that my name is *All of you.* The custom here is to serve the spokesman first and the others later. They will serve you when I have eaten.'

"He began to eat and the birds grumbled angrily. The people of the sky thought it must be their custom to leave all the food for their king. And so Tortoise ate the best part of the food and then drank two pots of palm-wine, so that he was full of food and drink and his body filled out in his shell.

"The birds gathered round to eat what was left and to peck at the bones he had thrown all about the floor. Some of them were too angry to eat. They chose to fly home on an empty stomach. But before they left each took back the feather he had lent to Tortoise. And there he stood in his hard shell full of food and wine but without any wings to fly home. He asked the birds to take a message for his wife, but they all refused. In the end Parrot, who had felt more angry than the others, suddenly changed his mind and agreed to take the message.

" 'Tell my wife,' said Tortoise, 'to bring out all the soft things in my house and cover the compound with them so that I can jump down from the sky without very great danger.'

"Parrot promised to deliver the message, and then flew away. But when he reached Tortoise's house he told his wife to bring out all the hard things in the house. And so she brought out her husband's hoes, matchets, spears, guns and even his cannon. Tortoise looked down from the sky and saw his wife bringing things out, but it was too far to see what they were. When all seemed ready he let himself go. He fell and fell and fell until he began to fear that he would never stop falling. And then like the sound of his cannon he crashed on the compound."

"Did he die?" asked Ezinma.

"No," replied Ekwefi. "His shell broke into pieces. But there was a great medicine-man in the neighbourhood. Tortoise's wife sent for him and he gathered all the bits of shell and stuck them together. That is why Tortoise's shell is not smooth."

"There is no song in the story," Ezinma pointed out.

"No," said Ekwefi. "I shall think of another one with a song. But it is your turn now."

"Once upon a time," Ezinma began, "Tortoise and Cat went to wrestle against Yams—no, that is not the beginning. Once upon a time there was a great famine in the land of animals. Everybody was lean except Cat, who was fat and whose body shone as if oil was rubbed on it . . ."

She broke off because at that very moment a loud and high-pitched voice broke the outer silence of the night. It was Chielo, the priestess of Agbala, prophesying. There was nothing new in that. Once in a while Chielo was possessed by the spirit of her god and she began to prophesy. But tonight she was addressing her prophecy and greetings to Okonkwo, and so everyone in his family listened. The folk stories stopped.

"Agbala do-o-o-o! Agbala ekeneo-o-o-o,"[4] came the voice like a sharp knife cutting through the night. "Okonkwo! Agbala ekene gio-o-o-o! Agbala cholu ifu ada ya Ezinmao-o-o-o!"[5]

At the mention of Ezinma's name Ekwefi jerked her head sharply like an animal that had sniffed death in the air. Her heart jumped painfully within her.

The priestess had now reached Okonkwo's compound and was talking with him outside his hut. She was saying again and again that Agbala wanted to see his daughter, Ezinma. Okonkwo pleaded with her to come back in the morning because Ezinma was now asleep. But Chielo ignored what he was trying to say and went on shouting that Agbala wanted to see his daughter. Her voice was as clear as metal, and Okonkwo's women and children heard from their huts all that she said. Okonkwo was still pleading that the girl had been ill of late and was asleep. Ekwefi quickly took her to their bedroom and placed her on their high bamboo bed.

The priestess suddenly screamed. "Beware, Okonkwo!" she warned. "Beware of exchanging words with Agbala. Does a man speak when a god speaks? Beware!"

She walked through Okonkwo's hut into the circular compound and went straight towards Ekwefi's hut. Okonkwo came after her.

---

4. Agbala wants something! Agbala greets.
5. Agbala greets you! Agbala wants to see his daughter Ezinma!

"Ekwefi," she called, "Agbala greets you. Where is my daughter, Ezinma? Agbala wants to see her."

Ekwefi came out from her hut carrying her oil lamp in her left hand. There was a light wind blowing, so she cupped her right hand to shelter the flame. Nwoye's mother, also carrying an oil lamp, emerged from her hut. Her children stood in the darkness outside their hut watching the strange event. Okonkwo's youngest wife also came out and joined the others.

"Where does Agbala want to see her?" Ekwefi asked.

"Where else but in his house in the hills and the caves?" replied the priestess.

"I will come with you, too," Ekwefi said firmly.

"*Tufia-a!*"[6] the priestess cursed, her voice cracking like the angry bark of thunder in the dry season. "How dare you, woman, to go before the mighty Agbala of your own accord? Beware, woman, lest he strike you in his anger. Bring me my daughter."

Ekwefi went into her hut and came out again with Ezinma.

"Come, my daughter," said the priestess. "I shall carry you on my back. A baby on its mother's back does not know that the way is long."

Ezinma began to cry. She was used to Chielo calling her 'my daughter'. But it was a different Chielo she now saw in the yellow half-light.

"Don't cry, my daughter," said the priestess, "lest Agbala be angry with you."

"Don't cry," said Ekwefi, "she will bring you back very soon. I shall give you some fish to eat." She went into the hut again and brought down the smoke-black basket in which she kept her dried fish and other ingredients for cooking soup. She broke a piece in two and gave it to Ezinma, who clung to her.

"Don't be afraid," said Ekwefi, stroking her head, which was shaved in places, leaving a regular pattern of hair. They went outside again. The priestess bent down on one knee and Ezinma climbed on her back, her left palm closed on her fish and her eyes gleaming with tears.

"*Agbala do-o-o-o! Agbala ekeneo-o-o-o,*" Chielo began once again to chant greetings to her god. She turned round sharply and walked through Okonkwo's hut, bending very low at the eaves. Ezinma was crying loudly now, calling on her mother. The two voices disappeared into the thick darkness.

A strange and sudden weakness descended on Ekwefi as she stood gazing in the direction of the voices like a hen whose only chick has been carried away by a kite. Ezinma's voice soon faded away and only Chielo was heard moving farther and farther into the distance.

"Why do you stand there as though she had been kidnapped?" asked Okonkwo as he went back to his hut.

"She will bring her back soon," Nwoye's mother said.

But Ekwefi did not hear these consolations. She stood for a while, and then, all of a sudden, made up her mind. She hurried through Okonkwo's hut and went outside.

"Where are you going?" he asked.

"I am following Chielo," she replied and disappeared in the darkness. Okonkwo cleared his throat, and brought out his snuff-bottle from the goatskin bag by his side.

6. A curse in words meaning "spitting" or "clearing out," often accompanied by spitting.

The priestess's voice was already growing faint in the distance. Ekwefi hurried to the main footpath and turned left in the direction of the voice. Her eyes were useless to her in the darkness. But she picked her way easily on the sandy footpath hedged on either side by branches and damp leaves. She began to run, holding her breasts with her hands to stop them flapping noisily against her body. She hit her left foot against an outcropped root, and terror seized her. It was an ill omen. She ran faster. But Chielo's voice was still a long way away. Had she been running too? How could she go so fast with Ezinma on her back? Although the night was cool, Ekwefi was beginning to feel hot from her running. She continually ran into the luxuriant weeds and creepers that walled in the path. Once she tripped up and fell. Only then did she realise, with a start, that Chielo had stopped her chanting. Her heart beat violently and she stood still. Then Chielo's renewed outburst came from only a few paces ahead. But Ekwefi could not see her. She shut her eyes for a while and opened them again in an effort to see. But it was useless. She could not see beyond her nose.

There were no stars in the sky because there was a rain-cloud. Fireflies went about with their tiny green lamps, which only made the darkness more profound. Between Chielo's outbursts the night was alive with the shrill tremor of forest insects woven into the darkness.

"*Agbala do-o-o-o! . . . . Agbala ekeneo-o-o-o! . . . .*" Ekwefi trudged behind, neither getting too near nor keeping too far back. She thought they must be going towards the sacred cave. Now that she walked slowly she had time to think. What would she do when they got to the cave? She would not dare to enter. She would wait at the mouth, all alone in that fearful place. She thought of all the terrors of the night. She remembered the night, long ago, when she had seen *Ogbu-agali-odu*, one of those evil essences loosed upon the world by the potent 'medicines' which the tribe had made in the distant past against its enemies but had now forgotten how to control. Ekwefi had been returning from the stream with her mother on a dark night like this when they saw its glow as it flew in their direction. They had thrown down their water-pots and lain by the roadside expecting the sinister light to descend on them and kill them. That was the only time Ekwefi ever saw *Ogbu-agali-odu*. But although it had happened so long ago, her blood still ran cold whenever she remembered that night.

The priestess's voice came at longer intervals now, but its vigour was undiminished. The air was cool and damp with dew. Ezinma sneezed. Ekwefi muttered, "Life to you." At the same time the priestess also said, "Life to you, my daughter." Ezinma's voice from the darkness warmed her mother's heart. She trudged slowly along.

And then the priestess screamed. "Somebody is walking behind me!" she said. "Whether you are spirit or man, may Agbala shave your head with a blunt razor! May he twist your neck until you see your heels!"

Ekwefi stood rooted to the spot. One mind said to her: 'Woman, go home before Agbala does you harm.' But she could not. She stood until Chielo had increased the distance between them and she began to follow again. She had already walked so long that she began to feel a slight numbness in the limbs and in the head. Then it occurred to her that they could not have been heading for the cave. They must have by-passed it long ago; they must be going towards Umuachi, the farthest village in the clan. Chielo's voice now came after long intervals.

It seemed to Ekwefi that the night had become a little lighter. The cloud had lifted and a few stars were out. The moon must be preparing to rise, its sullenness over. When the moon rose late in the night, people said it was refusing food, as a sullen husband refuses his wife's food when they have quarrelled.

"*Agbala do-o-o-o! Umuachi! Agbala ekene unuo-o-o!*" It was just as Ekwefi had thought. The priestess was now saluting the village of Umuachi. It was unbelievable, the distance they had covered. As they emerged into the open village from the narrow forest track the darkness was softened and it became possible to see the vague shape of trees. Ekwefi screwed her eyes up in an effort to see her daughter and the priestess, but whenever she thought she saw their shape it immediately dissolved like a melting lump of darkness. She walked numbly along.

Chielo's voice was now rising continuously, as when she first set out. Ekwefi had a feeling of spacious openness, and she guessed they must be on the village *ilo*, or playground. And she realised too with something like a jerk that Chielo was no longer moving forward. She was, in fact, returning. Ekwefi quickly moved away from her line of retreat. Chielo passed by, and they began to go back the way they had come.

It was a long and weary journey and Ekwefi felt like a sleep-walker most of the way. The moon was definitely rising, and although it had not yet appeared on the sky its light had already melted down the darkness. Ekwefi could now discern the figure of the priestess and her burden. She slowed down her pace so as to increase the distance between them. She was afraid of what might happen if Chielo suddenly turned round and saw her.

She had prayed for the moon to rise. But now she found the half-light of the incipient moon more terrifying than darkness. The world was now peopled with vague, fantastic figures that dissolved under her steady gaze and then formed again in new shapes. At one stage Ekwefi was so afraid that she nearly called out to Chielo for companionship and human sympathy. What she had seen was the shape of a man climbing a palm tree, his head pointing to the earth and his legs skywards. But at that very moment Chielo's voice rose again in her possessed chanting, and Ekwefi recoiled, because there was no humanity there. It was not the same Chielo who sat with her in the market and sometimes bought bean-cakes for Ezinma, whom she called her daughter. It was a different woman—the priestess of Agbala, the Oracle of the Hills and Caves. Ekwefi trudged along between two fears. The sound of her benumbed steps seemed to come from some other person walking behind her. Her arms were folded across her bare breasts. Dew fell heavily and the air was cold. She could no longer think, not even about the terrors of night. She just jogged along in a half-sleep, only waking to full life when Chielo sang.

At last they took a turning and began to head for the caves. From then on, Chielo never ceased in her chanting. She greeted her god in a multitude of names—the owner of the future, the messenger of earth, the god who cut a man down when his life was sweetest to him. Ekwefi was also awakened and her benumbed fears revived.

The moon was now up and she could see Chielo and Ezinma clearly. How a woman could carry a child of that size so easily and for so long was a miracle. But Ekwefi was not thinking about that. Chielo was not a woman that night.

"Agbala do-o-o-o! Agbala ekeno-o-o-o! Chi negbu madu ubosi ndu ya nato ya uto daluo-o-o! . . ."[7]

Ekwefi could already see the hills looming in the moonlight. They formed a circular ring with a break at one point through which the foot-track led to the centre of the circle.

As soon as the priestess stepped into this ring of hills her voice was not only doubled in strength but was thrown back on all sides. It was indeed the shrine of a great god. Ekwefi picked her way carefully and quietly. She was already beginning to doubt the wisdom of her coming. Nothing would happen to Ezinma, she thought. And if anything happened to her could she stop it? She would not dare to enter the underground caves. Her coming was quite useless, she thought.

As these things went through her mind she did not realise how close they were to the cave mouth. And so when the priestess with Ezinma on her back disappeared through a hole hardly big enough to pass a hen, Ekwefi broke into a run as though to stop them. As she stood gazing at the circular darkness which had swallowed them, tears gushed from her eyes, and she swore within her that if she heard Ezinma cry she would rush into the cave to defend her against all the gods in the world. She would die with her.

Having sworn that oath, she sat down on a stony ledge and waited. Her fear had vanished. She could hear the priestess's voice, all its metal taken out of it by the vast emptiness of the cave. She buried her face in her lap and waited.

She did not know how long she waited. It must have been a very long time. Her back was turned on the footpath that led out of the hills. She must have heard a noise behind her and turned round sharply. A man stood there with a matchet in his hand. Ekwefi uttered a scream and sprang to her feet.

"Don't be foolish," said Okonkwo's voice. "I thought you were going into the shrine with Chielo," he mocked.

Ekwefi did not answer. Tears of gratitude filled her eyes. She knew her daughter was safe.

"Go home and sleep," said Okonkwo. "I shall wait here."

"I shall wait too. It is almost dawn. The first cock has crowed."

As they stood there together, Ekwefi's mind went back to the days when they were young. She had married Anene because Okonkwo was too poor then to marry. Two years after her marriage to Anene she could bear it no longer and she ran away to Okonkwo. It had been early in the morning. The moon was shining. She was going to the stream to fetch water. Okonkwo's house was on the way to the stream. She went in and knocked at his door and he came out. Even in those days he was not a man of many words. He just carried her into his bed and in the darkness began to feel around her waist for the loose end of her cloth.

CHAPTER TWELVE

On the following morning the entire neighbourhood wore a festive air because Okonkwo's friend, Obierika, was celebrating his daughter's *uri*. It was the day on which her suitor (having already paid the greater part of her bride-price) would bring palm-wine not only to her parents and immediate relatives but to the wide and extensive group of kinsmen called *umunna*. Everybody had been invited—men, women and children. But it was really a

---

7. Agbala wants something! Agbala greets! God who kills a man on the day his life is so pleasant he give thanks! . . .

woman's ceremony and the central figures were the bride and her mother.

As soon as day broke, breakfast was hastily eaten and women and children began to gather at Obierika's compound to help the bride's mother in her difficult but happy task of cooking for a whole village.

Okonkwo's family was astir like any other family in the neighbourhood. Nwoye's mother and Okonkwo's youngest wife were ready to set out for Obierika's compound with all their children. Nwoye's mother carried a basket of coco-yams, a cake of salt and smoked fish which she would present to Obierika's wife. Okonkwo's youngest wife, Ojiugo, also had a basket of plantains and coco-yams and a small pot of palm-oil. Their children carried pots of water.

Ekwefi was tired and sleepy from the exhausting experiences of the previous night. It was not very long since they had returned. The priestess, with Ezinma sleeping on her back, had crawled out of the shrine on her belly like a snake. She had not as much as looked at Okonkwo and Ekwefi or shown any surprise at finding them at the mouth of the cave. She looked straight ahead of her and walked back to the village. Okonkwo and his wife followed at a respectful distance. They thought the priestess might be going to her house, but she went to Okonkwo's compound, passed through his *obi* and into Ekwefi's hut and walked into her bedroom. She placed Ezinma carefully on the bed and went away without saying a word to anybody.

Ezinma was still sleeping when everyone else was astir, and Ekwefi asked Nwoye's mother and Ojiugo to explain to Obierika's wife that she would be late. She had got ready her basket of coco-yams and fish, but she must wait for Ezinma to wake.

"You need some sleep yourself," said Nwoye's mother. "You look very tired."

As they spoke Ezinma emerged from the hut, rubbing her eyes and stretching her spare frame. She saw the other children with their water-pots and remembered that they were going to fetch water for Obierika's wife. She went back to the hut and brought her pot.

"Have you slept enough?" asked her mother.

"Yes," she replied. "Let us go."

"Not before you have had your breakfast," said Ekwefi. And she went into her hut to warm the vegetable soup she had cooked last night.

"We shall be going," said Nwoye's mother. "I will tell Obierika's wife that you are coming later." And so they all went to help Obierika's wife—Nwoye's mother with her four children and Ojiugo with her two.

As they trooped through Okonkwo's *obi* he asked: "Who will prepare my afternoon meal?"

"I shall return to do it," said Ojiugo.

Okonkwo was also feeling tired and sleepy, for although nobody else knew it, he had not slept at all last night. He had felt very anxious but did not show it. When Ekwefi had followed the priestess, he had allowed what he regarded as a reasonable and manly interval to pass and then gone with his matchet to the shrine, where he thought they must be. It was only when he had got there that it had occurred to him that the priestess might have chosen to go round the villages first. Okonkwo had returned home and sat waiting. When he thought he had waited long enough he again returned to the shrine. But the Hills and the Caves were as silent as death. It was only on his fourth trip that he had found Ekwefi, and by then he had become gravely worried.

Obierika's compound was as busy as an ant-hill. Temporary cooking tripods were erected on every available space by bringing together three blocks of sun-dried earth and making a fire in their midst. Cooking pots went up and down the tripods, and foo-foo was pounded in a hundred wooden mortars. Some of the women cooked the yams and the cassava, and others prepared vegetable soup. Young men pounded the foo-foo or split firewood. The children made endless trips to the stream.

Three young men helped Obierika to slaughter the two goats with which the soup was made. They were very fat goats, but the fattest of all was tethered to a peg near the wall of the compound. It was as big as a small cow. Obierika had sent one of his relatives all the way to Umuike to buy that goat. It was the one he would present alive to his in-laws.

"The market of Umuike is a wonderful place," said the young man who had been sent by Obierika to buy the giant goat. "There are so many people on it that if you threw up a grain of sand it would not find a way to fall to earth again."

"It is the result of a great medicine," said Obierika. "The people of Umuike wanted their market to grow and swallow up the markets of their neighbours. So they made a powerful medicine. Every market-day, before the first cock-crow, this medicine stands on the market-ground in the shape of an old woman with a fan. With this magic fan she beckons to the market all the neighbouring clans. She beckons in front of her and behind her, to her right and to her left."

"And so everybody comes," said another man, "honest men and thieves. They can steal your cloth from off your waist in that market."

"Yes," said Obierika. "I warned Nwankwo to keep a sharp eye and a sharp ear. There was once a man who went to sell a goat. He led it on a thick rope which he tied round his wrist. But as he walked through the market he realised that people were pointing at him as they do to a madman. He could not understand it until he looked back and saw that what he led at the end of the tether was not a goat but a heavy log of wood."

"Do you think a thief can do that kind of thing singlehanded?" asked Nwankwo.

"No," said Obierika. "They use medicine."

When they had cut the goats' throats and collected the blood in a bowl, they held them over an open fire to burn off the hair, and the smell of burning hair blended with the smell of cooking. Then they washed them and cut them up for the women who prepared the soup.

All this ant-hill activity was going smoothly when a sudden interruption came. It was a cry in the distance: *Oji odu achu ijiji-o-o!* (*The one that uses its tail to drive flies away!*) Every woman immediately abandoned whatever she was doing and rushed out in the direction of the cry.

"We cannot all rush out like that, leaving what we are cooking to burn in the fire," shouted Chielo, the priestess. "Three or four of us should stay behind."

"It is true," said another woman. "We will allow three or four women to stay behind."

Five women stayed behind to look after the cooking-pots, and all the rest rushed away to see the cow that had been let loose. When they saw it they drove it back to its owner, who at once paid the heavy fine which the village imposed on anyone whose cow was let loose on his neighbours' crops. When the women had exacted the penalty they checked among themselves to see if any woman had failed to come out when the cry had been raised.

"Where is Mgbogo?" asked one of them.

"She is ill in bed," said Mgbogo's next-door neighbour. "She has *iba*."

"The only other person is Udenkwo," said another woman, "and her child is not twenty-eight days yet."

Those women whom Obierika's wife had not asked to help her with the cooking returned to their homes, and the rest went back, in a body, to Obierika's compound.

"Whose cow was it?" asked the women who had been allowed to stay behind.

"It was my husband's," said Ezelagbo. "One of the young children had opened the gate of the cow-shed."

Early in the afternoon the first two pots of palm-wine arrived from Obierika's in-laws. They were duly presented to the women, who drank a cup or two each, to help them in their cooking. Some of it also went to the bride and her attendant maidens, who were putting the last delicate touches of razor to her coiffure and cam wood on her smooth skin.

When the heat of the sun began to soften, Obierika's son, Maduka, took a long broom and swept the ground in front of his father's *obi*. And as if they had been waiting for that, Obierika's relatives and friends began to arrive, every man with his goatskin bag hung on one shoulder and a rolled goatskin mat under his arm. Some of them were accompanied by their sons bearing carved wooden stools. Okonkwo was one of them. They sat in a half circle and began to talk of many things. It would not be long before the suitors came.

Okonkwo brought out his snuff-bottle and offered it to Ogbuefi Ezenwa, who sat next to him. Ezenwa[8] took it, tapped it on his knee-cap, rubbed his left palm on his body to dry it before tipping a little snuff into it. His actions were deliberate, and he spoke as he performed them:

"I hope our in-laws will bring many pots of wine. Although they come from a village that is known for being close-fisted, they ought to know that Akueke is the bride for a king."

"They dare not bring fewer than thirty pots," said Okonkwo. "I shall tell them my mind if they do."

At that moment Obierika's son, Maduka, led out the giant goat from the inner compound, for his father's relatives to see. They all admired it and said that that was the way things should be done. The goat was then led back to the inner compound.

Very soon after, the in-laws began to arrive. Young men and boys in single file, each carrying a pot of wine, came first. Obierika's relatives counted the pots as they came in. Twenty, twenty-five. There was a long break, and the hosts looked at each other as if to say, 'I told you.' Then more pots came. Thirty, thirty-five, forty, forty-five. The hosts nodded in approval and seemed to say, 'Now they are behaving like men.' Altogether there were fifty pots of wine. After the pot-bearers came Ibe, the suitor, and the elders of his family. They sat in a half-moon, thus completing a circle with their hosts. The pots of wine stood in their midst. Then the bride, her mother and half a dozen other women and girls emerged from the inner compound, and went round the circle shaking hands with all. The bride's mother led the way, followed by the bride and the other women. The married women wore their best cloths and the girls wore red and black waist-beads and anklets of brass.

When the women retired, Obierika presented kola nuts to his in-laws. His

8. King from childhood (strong praise).

eldest brother broke the first one. "Life to all of us," he said as he broke it. "And let there be friendship between your family and ours."

The crowd answered: "Ee-e-e!"

"We are giving you our daughter today. She will be a good wife to you. She will bear you nine sons like the mother of our town."

"Ee-e-e!"

The oldest man in the camp of the visitors replied: "It will be good for you and it will be good for us."

"Ee-e-e!"

"This is not the first time my people have come to marry your daughter. My mother was one of you."

"Ee-e-e!"

"And this will not be the last, because you understand us and we understand you. You are a great family."

"Ee-e-e!"

"Prosperous men and great warriors." He looked in the direction of Okonkwo. "Your daughter will bear us sons like you."

"Ee-e-e!"

The kola was eaten and the drinking of palm-wine began. Groups of four or five men sat round with a pot in their midst. As the evening wore on, food was presented to the guests. There were huge bowls of foo-foo and steaming pots of soup. There were also pots of yam pottage. It was a great feast.

As night fell, burning torches were set on wooden tripods and the young men raised a song. The elders sat in a big circle and the singers went round singing each man's praise as they came before him. They had something to say for every man. Some were great farmers, some were orators who spoke for the clan; Okonkwo was the greatest wrestler and warrior alive. When they had gone round the circle they settled down in the centre, and girls came from the inner compound to dance. At first the bride was not among them. But when she finally appeared holding a cock in her right hand, a loud cheer rose from the crowd. All the other dancers made way for her. She presented the cock to the musicians and began to dance. Her brass anklets rattled as she danced and her body gleamed with cam wood in the soft yellow light. The musicians with their wood, clay and metal instruments went from song to song. And they were all gay. They sang the latest song in the village:

> "If I hold her hand
>   She says, 'Don't touch!'
> If I hold her foot
>   She says, 'Don't touch!'
> But when I hold her waist-beads
>   She pretends not to know."

The night was already far spent when the guests rose to go, taking their bride home to spend seven market weeks with her suitor's family. They sang songs as they went, and on their way they paid short courtesy visits to prominent men like Okonkwo, before they finally left for their village. Okonkwo made a present of two cocks to them.

CHAPTER THIRTEEN

Go-di-di-go-go-di-go. Di-go-go-di-go. It was the *ekwe* talking to the clan. One of the things every man learned was the language of the hollowed-out wooden instrument. Diim! Diim! Diim! boomed the cannon at intervals.

The first cock had not crowed, and Umuofia was still swallowed up in sleep and silence when the *ekwe* began to talk, and the cannon shattered the silence. Men stirred on their bamboo beds and listened anxiously. Somebody was dead. The cannon seemed to rend the sky. Di-go-go-di-go-di-di-go-go floated in the message-laden night air. The faint and distant wailing of women settled like a sediment of sorrow on the earth. Now and again a full-chested lamentation rose above the wailing whenever a man came into the place of death. He raised his voice once or twice in manly sorrow and then sat down with the other men listening to the endless wailing of the women and the esoteric language of the *ekwe*. Now and again the cannon boomed. The wailing of the women would not be heard beyond the village, but the *ekwe* carried the news to all the nine villages and even beyond. It began by naming the clan: *Umuofia obodo dike*, 'the land of the brave.' *Umuofia obodo dike! Umuofia obodo dike!* It said this over and over again, and as it dwelt on it, anxiety mounted in every heart that heaved on a bamboo bed that night. Then it went nearer and named the village: *Iguedo⁹ of the yellow grinding-stone!* It was Okonkwo's village. Again and again Iguedo was called and men waited breathlessly in all the nine villages. At last the man was named and people sighed "E-u-u, Ezeudu is dead." A cold shiver ran down Okonkwo's back as he remembered the last time the old man had visited him. "That boy calls you father," he had said. "Bear no hand in his death."

Ezeudu was a great man, and so all the clan was at his funeral. The ancient drums of death beat, guns and cannon were fired, and men dashed about in frenzy, cutting down every tree or animal they saw, jumping over walls and dancing on the roof. It was a warrior's funeral, and from morning till night warriors came and went in their age-groups. They all wore smoked raffia skirts and their bodies were painted with chalk and charcoal. Now and again an ancestral spirit or *egwugwu* appeared from the underworld, speaking in a tremulous, unearthly voice and completely covered in raffia. Some of them were very violent, and there had been a mad rush for shelter earlier in the day when one appeared with a sharp matchet and was only prevented from doing serious harm by two men who restrained him with the help of a strong rope tied round his waist. Sometimes he turned round and chased those men, and they ran for their lives. But they always returned to the long rope he trailed behind. He sang, in a terrifying voice, that Ekwensu, or Evil Spirit, had entered his eye.

But the most dreaded of all was yet to come. He was always alone and was shaped like a coffin. A sickly odour hung in the air wherever he went, and flies went with him. Even the greatest medicine-men took shelter when he was near. Many years ago another *egwugwu* had dared to stand his ground before him and had been transfixed to the spot for two days. This one had only one hand and with it carried a basket full of water.

But some of the *egwugwu* were quite harmless. One of them was so old and infirm that he leaned heavily on a stick. He walked unsteadily to the place where the corpse was laid, gazed at it a while and went away again—to the underworld.

The land of the living was not far removed from the domain of the ancestors. There was coming and going between them, especially at festivals and also when an old man died, because an old man was very close to the ancestors. A

---

9. The yellow grindstone.

man's life from birth to death was a series of transition rites which brought him nearer and nearer to his ancestors.

Ezeudu had been the oldest man in his village, and at his death there were only three men in the whole clan who were older, and four or five others in his own age-group. Whenever one of these ancient men appeared in the crowd to dance unsteadily the funeral steps of the tribe, younger men gave way and the tumult subsided.

It was a great funeral, such as befitted a noble warrior. As the evening drew near, the shouting and the firing of guns, the beating of drums and the brandishing and clanging of matchets increased.

Ezeudu had taken three titles in his life. It was a rare achievement. There were only four titles in the clan, and only one or two men in any generation ever achieved the fourth and highest. When they did, they became the lords of the land. Because he had taken titles, Ezeudu was to be buried after dark with only a glowing brand to light the sacred ceremony.

But before this quiet and final rite, the tumult increased tenfold. Drums beat violently and men leaped up and down in frenzy. Guns were fired on all sides and sparks flew out as matchets clanged together in warriors' salutes. The air was full of dust and the smell of gunpowder. It was then that the one-handed spirit came, carrying a basket full of water. People made way for him on all sides and the noise subsided. Even the smell of gunpowder was swallowed in the sickly smell that now filled the air. He danced a few steps to the funeral drums and then went to see the corpse.

"Ezeudu!" he called in his guttural voice. "If you had been poor in your last life I would have asked you to be rich when you come again. But you were rich. If you had been a coward, I would have asked you to bring courage. But you were a fearless warrior. If you had died young, I would have asked you to get life. But you lived long. So I shall ask you to come again the way you came before. If your death was the death of nature, go in peace. But if a man caused it, do not allow him a moment's rest." He danced a few more steps and went away.

The drums and the dancing began again and reached fever-heat. Darkness was around the corner, and the burial was near. Guns fired the last salute and the cannon rent the sky. And then from the centre of the delirious fury came a cry of agony and shouts of horror. It was as if a spell had been cast. All was silent. In the centre of the crowd a boy lay in a pool of blood. It was the dead man's sixteen-year-old son, who with his brothers and half-brothers had been dancing the traditional farewell to their father. Okonkwo's gun had exploded and a piece of iron had pierced the boy's heart.

The confusion that followed was without parallel in the tradition of Umuofia. Violent deaths were frequent, but nothing like this had ever happened.

The only course open to Okonkwo was to flee from the clan. It was a crime against the earth goddess to kill a clansman, and a man who committed it must flee from the land. The crime was of two kinds, male and female. Okonkwo had committed the female, because it had been inadvertent. He could return to the clan after seven years.

That night he collected his most valuable belongings into head-loads. His wives wept bitterly and their children wept with them without knowing why. Obierika and half a dozen other friends came to help and to console him. They each made nine or ten trips carrying Okonkwo's yams to store in Obierika's barn. And before the cock crowed Okonkwo and his family were fleeing to his motherland. It was a little village called Mbanta,[1] just beyond the borders of Mbaino.

As soon as the day broke, a large crowd of men from Ezeudu's quarter stormed Okonkwo's compound, dressed in garbs of war. They set fire to his houses, demolished his red walls, killed his animals and destroyed his barn. It was the justice of the earth goddess, and they were merely her messengers. They had no hatred in their hearts against Okonkwo. His greatest friend, Obierika, was among them. They were merely cleansing the land which Okonkwo had polluted with the blood of a clansman.

Obierika was a man who thought about things. When the will of the goddess had been done, he sat down in his *obi* and mourned his friend's calamity. Why should a man suffer so grievously for an offence he had committed inadvertently? But although he thought for a long time he found no answer. He was merely led into greater complexities. He remembered his wife's twin children, whom he had thrown away. What crime had they committed? The Earth had decreed that they were an offence on the land and must be destroyed. And *if* the clan did not exact punishment for an offence against the great goddess, her wrath was loosed on all the land and not just on the offender. As the elders said, if one finger brought oil it soiled the others.

Part Two

CHAPTER FOURTEEN

Okonkwo was well received by his mother's kinsmen in Mbanta. The old man who received him was his mother's younger brother, who was now the eldest surviving member of that family. His name was Uchendu,[2] and it was he who had received Okonkwo's mother twenty and ten years before when she had been brought home from Umuofia to be buried with her people. Okonkwo was only a boy then and Uchendu still remembered him crying the traditional farewell: "Mother, mother, mother is going."

That was many years ago. Today Okonkwo was not bringing his mother home to be buried with her people. He was taking his family of three wives and eleven children to seek refuge in his motherland. As soon as Uchendu saw him with his sad and weary company he guessed what had happened, and asked no questions. It was not until the following day that Okonkwo told him the full story. The old man listened silently to the end and then said with some relief: "It is a female *ochu*."[3] And he arranged the requisite rites and sacrifices.

Okonkwo was given a plot of ground on which to build his compound, and two or three pieces of land on which to farm during the coming planting season. With the help of his mother's kinsmen he built himself an *obi* and three huts for his wives. He then installed his personal god and the symbols of his departed fathers. Each of Uchendu's five sons contributed three hundred seed-yams to enable their cousin to plant a farm, for as soon as the first rain came farming would begin.

At last the rain came. It was sudden and tremendous. For two or three moons the sun had been gathering strength till it seemed to breathe a breath of fire on the earth. All the grass had long been scorched brown, and the sands

1. Small town.
2. The thought created by life.

3. Murder, manslaughter.

felt like live coals to the feet. Evergreen trees wore a dusty coat of brown. The birds were silenced in the forests, and the world lay panting under the live, vibrating heat. And then came the clap of thunder. It was an angry, metallic and thirsty clap, unlike the deep and liquid rumbling of the rainy season. A mighty wind arose and filled the air with dust. Palm trees swayed as the wind combed their leaves into flying crests like strange and fantastic coiffure.

When the rain finally came, it was in large, solid drops of frozen water which the people called 'the nuts of the water of heaven'. They were hard and painful on the body as they fell, yet young people ran about happily picking up the cold nuts and throwing them into their mouths to melt.

The earth quickly came to life and the birds in the forests fluttered around and chirped merrily. A vague scent of life and green vegetation was diffused in the air. As the rain began to fall more soberly and in smaller liquid drops, children sought for shelter, and all were happy, refreshed and thankful.

Okonkwo and his family worked very hard to plant a new farm. But it was like beginning life anew without the vigour and enthusiasm of youth, like learning to become left-handed in old age. Work no longer had for him the pleasure it used to have, and when there was no work to do he sat in a silent half-sleep.

His life had been ruled by a great passion—to become one of the lords of the clan. That had been his life-spring. And he had all but achieved it. Then everything had been broken. He had been cast out of his clan like a fish on to a dry, sandy beach, panting. Clearly his personal god or *chi* was not made for great things. A man could not rise beyond the destiny of his *chi*. The saying of the elders was not true—that if a man said yea his *chi* also affirmed. Here was a man whose *chi* said nay despite his own affirmation.

The old man, Uchendu, saw clearly that Okonkwo had yielded to despair and he was greatly troubled. He would speak to him after the *isa-ifi* ceremony.[4]

The youngest of Uchendu's five sons, Amikwu, was marrying a new wife. The bride-price had been paid and all but the last ceremony had been performed. Amikwu and his people had taken palm-wine to the bride's kinsmen about two moons before Okonkwo's arrival in Mbanta. And so it was time for the final ceremony of confession.

The daughters of the family were all there, some of them having come a long way from their homes in distant villages. Uchendu's eldest daughter had come from Obodo, nearly half a day's journey away. The daughters of Uchendu's brothers were also there. It was a full gathering of *umuada*,[5] in the same way as they would meet if a death occurred in the family. There were twenty-two of them.

They sat in a big circle on the ground and the bride sat in the centre with a hen in her right hand. Uchendu sat by her, holding the ancestral staff of the family. All the other men stood outside the circle, watching. Their wives watched also. It was evening and the sun was setting.

Uchendu's eldest daughter, Njide, asked the questions.

"Remember that if you do not answer truthfully you will suffer or even die

---

4. A ceremony to ascertain that a wife (here a promised bride) had been faithful to her husband during a separation.
5. The daughters, who, according to Igbo custom, married outside the clan, perform a special initiation upon returning home for important gatherings.

at child-birth," she began. "How many men have lain with you since my brother first expressed the desire to marry you?"

"None," she replied simply.

"Answer truthfully," urged the other women.

"None?" asked Njide.

"None," she answered.

"Swear on this staff of my fathers," said Uchendu.

"I swear," said the bride.

Uchendu took the hen from her, slit its throat with a sharp knife and allowed some of the blood to fall on his ancestral staff.

From that day Amikwu took the young bride to his hut and she became his wife. The daughters of the family did not return to their homes immediately but spent two or three days with their kinsmen.

On the second day Uchendu called together his sons and daughters and his nephew, Okonkwo. The men brought their goatskin mats, with which they sat on the floor, and the women sat on a sisal mat spread on a raised bank of earth. Uchendu pulled gently at his grey beard and gnashed his teeth. Then he began to speak, quietly and deliberately, picking his words with great care:

"It is Okonkwo that I primarily wish to speak to," he began. "But I want all of you to note what I am going to say. I am an old man and you are all children. I know more about the world than any of you. If there is any one among you who thinks he knows more let him speak up." He paused, but no one spoke.

"Why is Okonkwo with us today? This is not his clan. We are only his mother's kinsmen. He does not belong here. He is an exile, condemned for seven years to live in a strange land. And so he is bowed with grief. But there is just one question I would like to ask him. Can you tell me, Okonkwo, why it is that one of the commonest names we give our children is Nneka, or 'Mother is Supreme'? We all know that a man is the head of the family and his wives do his bidding. A child belongs to its father and his family and not to its mother and her family. A man belongs to his fatherland and not to his motherland. And yet we say Nneka—'Mother is Supreme.' Why is that?"

There was silence. "I want Okonkwo to answer me," said Uchendu.

"I do not know the answer," Okonkwo replied.

"You do not know the answer? So you see that you are a child. You have many wives and many children—more children than I have. You are a great man in your clan. But you are still a child, *my* child. Listen to me and I shall tell you. But there is one more question I shall ask you. Why is it that when a woman dies she is taken home to be buried with her own kinsmen? She is not buried with her husband's kinsmen. Why is that? Your mother was brought home to me and buried with my people. Why was that?"

Okonkwo shook his head.

"He does not know that either," said Uchendu, "and yet he is full of sorrow because he has come to live in his motherland for a few years." He laughed a mirthless laughter, and turned to his sons and daughters. "What about you? Can you answer my question?"

They all shook their heads.

"Then listen to me," he said and cleared his throat. "It's true that a child belongs to its father. But when a father beats his child, it seeks sympathy in its mother's hut. A man belongs to his fatherland when things are good and life is sweet. But when there is sorrow and bitterness he finds refuge in his motherland. Your mother is there to protect you. She is buried there. And that is why we say that mother is supreme. Is it right that you, Okonkwo, should bring to your mother a heavy face and refuse to be comforted? Be careful or you may displease the dead. Your duty is to comfort your wives and children and take them back to your fatherland after seven years. But if you allow sorrow to weigh you down and kill you, they will all die in exile." He paused for a long while. "These are now your kinsmen." He waved at his sons and daughters. "You think you are the greatest sufferer in the world. Do you know that men are sometimes banished for life? Do you know that men sometimes lose all their yams and even their children? I had six wives once. I have none now except that young girl who knows not her right from her left. Do you know how many children I have buried—children I begot in my youth and strength? Twenty-two. I did not hang myself, and I am still alive. If you think you are the greatest sufferer in the world ask my daughter, Akueni, how many twins she has borne and thrown away. Have you not heard the song they sing when a woman dies?

" 'For whom is it well, for whom is it well?
" 'There is no one for whom it is well.'

"I have no more to say to you."

CHAPTER FIFTEEN

It was in the second year of Okonkwo's exile that his friend, Obierika, came to visit him. He brought with him two young men, each of them carrying a heavy bag on his head. Okonkwo helped them put down their loads. It was clear that the bags were full of cowries.

Okonkwo was very happy to receive his friend. His wives and children were very happy too, and so were his cousins and their wives when he sent for them and told them who his guest was.

"You must take him to salute our father," said one of the cousins.

"Yes," replied Okonkwo. "We are going directly." But before they went he whispered something to his first wife. She nodded, and soon the children were chasing one of their cocks.

Uchendu had been told by one of his grandchildren that three strangers had come to Okonkwo's house. He was therefore waiting to receive them. He held out his hands to them when they came into his *obi*, and after they had shaken hands he asked Okonkwo who they were.

"This is Obierika, my great friend. I have already spoken to you about him."

"Yes," said the old man, turning to Obierika. "My son has told me about you, and I am happy you have come to see us. I knew your father, Iweka. He was a great man. He had many friends here and came to see them quite often. Those were good days when a man had friends in distant clans. Your generation does not know that. You stay at home, afraid of your next-door neighbour. Even a man's motherland is strange to him nowadays." He looked at Okonkwo. "I am an old man and I like to talk. That is all I am good for now." He got up painfully, went into an inner room and came back with a kola nut.

"Who are the young men with you?" he asked as he sat down again on his goatskin. Okonkwo told him.

"Ah," he said. "Welcome, my sons." He presented the kola nut to them, and when they had seen it and thanked him, he broke it and they ate.

"Go into that room," he said to Okonkwo, pointing with his finger. "You will find a pot of wine there."

Okonkwo brought the wine and they began to drink. It was a day old, and very strong.

"Yes," said Uchendu after a long silence. "People travelled more in those days. There is not a single clan in these parts that I do not know very well. Aninta, Umuazu, Ikeocha, Elumelu, Abame—I know them all."

"Have you heard," asked Obierika, "that Abame is no more?"

"How is that?" asked Uchendu and Okonkwo together.

"Abame has been wiped out," said Obierika. "It is a strange and terrible story. If I had not seen the few survivors with my own eyes and heard their story with my own ears, I would not have believed. Was it not on an Eke day that they fled into Umuofia?" he asked his two companions, and they nodded their heads.

"Three moons ago," said Obierika, "on an Eke market-day a little band of fugitives came into our town. Most of them were sons of our land whose mothers had been buried with us. But there were some too who came because they had friends in our town, and others who could think of nowhere else open to escape. And so they fled into Umuofia with a woeful story." He drank his palm-wine, and Okonkwo filled his horn again. He continued:

"During the last planting season a white man had appeared in their clan."

"An albino," suggested Okonkwo.

"He was not an albino. He was quite different." He sipped his wine. "And he was riding an iron horse.[6] The first people who saw him ran away, but he stood beckoning to them. In the end the fearless ones went near and even touched him. The elders consulted their Oracle and it told them that the strange man would break their clan and spread destruction among them." Obierika again drank a little of his wine. "And so they killed the white man and tied his iron horse to their sacred tree because it looked as if it would run away to call the man's friends. I forgot to tell you another thing which the Oracle said. It said that other white men were on their way. They were locusts, it said, and that first man was their harbinger sent to explore the terrain. And so they killed him."

"What did the white man say before they killed him?" asked Uchendu.

"He said nothing," answered one of Obierika's companions.

"He said something, only they did not understand him," said Obierika. "He seemed to speak through his nose."

"One of the men told me," said Obierika's other companion, "that he repeated over and over again a word that resembled Mbaino. Perhaps he had been going to Mbaino and had lost his way."

"Anyway," resumed Obierika, "they killed him and tied up his iron horse. This was before the planting season began. For a long time nothing happened. The rains had come and yams had been sown. The iron horse was still tied to the sacred silk-cotton tree. And then one morning three white men led by a band of ordinary men like us came to the clan. They saw the iron horse and went away again. Most of the men and women of Abame had gone to their farms. Only a few of them saw these white men and their followers. For many market weeks nothing else happened. They have a big market in Abame on every other Afo day and, as you know, the whole clan gathers there. That was

6. Bicycle.

the day it happened. The three white men and a very large number of other men surrounded the market. They must have used a powerful medicine to make themselves invisible until the market was full. And they began to shoot. Everybody was killed, except the old and the sick who were at home and a handful of men and women whose *chi* were wide awake and brought them out of that market."[7] He paused.

"Their clan is now completely empty. Even the sacred fish in their mysterious lake have fled and the lake has turned the colour of blood. A great evil has come upon their land as the Oracle had warned."

There was a long silence. Uchendu ground his teeth together audibly. Then he burst out:

"Never kill a man who says nothing. Those men of Abame were fools. What did they know about the man?" He ground his teeth again and told a story to illustrate his point. "Mother Kite once sent her daughter to bring food. She went, and brought back a duckling. 'You have done very well,' said Mother Kite to her daughter, 'but tell me, what did the mother of this duckling say when you swooped and carried its child away?' 'It said nothing,' replied the young kite. 'It just walked away.' 'You must return the duckling,' said Mother Kite. 'There is something ominous behind the silence.' And so Daughter Kite returned the duckling and took a chick instead. 'What did the mother of this chick do?' asked the old kite. 'It cried and raved and cursed me,' said the young kite. 'Then we can eat the chick,' said her mother. 'There is nothing to fear from someone who shouts.' Those men of Abame were fools."

"They were fools," said Okonkwo after a pause. "They had been warned that danger was ahead. They should have armed themselves with their guns and their matchets even when they went to market."

"They have paid for their foolishness," said Obierika. "But I am greatly afraid. We have heard stories about white men who made the powerful guns and the strong drinks and took slaves away across the seas, but no one thought the stories were true."

"There is no story that is not true," said Uchendu. "The world has no end, and what is good among one people is an abomination with others. We have albinos among us. Do you not think that they came to our clan by mistake, that they have strayed from their way to a land where everybody is like them?"

Okonkwo's first wife soon finished her cooking and set before their guests a big meal of pounded yams and bitter-leaf soup. Okonkwo's son, Nwoye, brought in a pot of sweet wine tapped from the raffia palm.

"You are a big man now," Obierika said to Nwoye. "Your friend Anene asked me to greet you."

"Is he well?" asked Nwoye.

"We are all well," said Obierika.

Ezinma brought them a bowl of water with which to wash their hands. After that they began to eat and to drink the wine.

"When did you set out from home?" asked Okonkwo.

"We had meant to set out from my house before cock-crow," said Obierika. "But Nweke did not appear until it was quite light. Never make an early morning appointment with a man who has just married a new wife." They all laughed.

---

7. Achebe bases his account on a similar incident in 1905 when British troops massacred the town of Ahiara in reprisal for the death of a missionary.

"Has Nweke married a wife?" asked Okonkwo.

"He has married Okadigbo's second daughter," said Obierika.

"That is very good," said Okonkwo. "I do not blame you for not hearing the cock crow."

When they had eaten, Obierika pointed at the two heavy bags.

"That is the money from your yams," he said. "I sold the big ones as soon as you left. Later on I sold some of the seed-yams and gave out others to share-croppers. I shall do that every year until you return. But I thought you would need the money now and so I brought it. Who knows what may happen tomorrow? Perhaps green men will come to our clan and shoot us."

"God will not permit it," said Okonkwo. "I do not know how to thank you."

"I can tell you," said Obierika. "Kill one of your sons for me."

"That will not be enough," said Okonkwo.

"Then kill yourself," said Obierika.

"Forgive me," said Okonkwo, smiling. "I shall not talk about thanking you any more."

CHAPTER SIXTEEN

When nearly two years later Obierika paid another visit to his friend in exile the circumstances were less happy. The missionaries had come to Umuofia. They had built their church there, won a handful of converts and were already sending evangelists to the surrounding towns and villages. That was a source of great sorrow to the leaders of the clan; but many of them believed that the strange faith and the white man's god would not last. None of his converts was a man whose word was heeded in the assembly of the people. None of them was a man of title. They were mostly the kind of people that were called *efulefu*, worthless, empty men. The imagery of an *efulefu* in the language of the clan was a man who sold his matchet and wore the sheath to battle. Chielo, the priestess of Agbala, called the converts the excrement of the clan, and the new faith was a mad dog that had come to eat it up.

What moved Obierika to visit Okonkwo was the sudden appearance of the latter's son, Nwoye, among the missionaries in Umuofia.

"What are you doing here?" Obierika had asked when after many difficulties the missionaries had allowed him to speak to the boy.

"I am one of them," replied Nwoye.

"How is your father?" Obierika asked, not knowing what else to say.

"I don't know. He is not my father," said Nwoye, unhappily.

And so Obierika went to Mbanta to see his friend. And he found that Okonkwo did not wish to speak about Nwoye. It was only from Nwoye's mother that he heard scraps of the story.

The arrival of the missionaries had caused a considerable stir in the village of Mbanta. There were six of them and one was a white man. Every man and woman came out to see the white man. Stories about these strange men had grown since one of them had been killed in Abame and his iron horse tied to the sacred silk-cotton tree. And so everybody came to see the white man. It was the time of the year when everybody was at home. The harvest was over.

When they had all gathered, the white man began to speak to them. He spoke through an interpreter who was an Ibo man, though his dialect was different and harsh to the ears of Mbanta. Many people laughed at his dialect and the way he used words strangely. Instead of saying 'myself' he always said 'my buttocks.'[8] But he was a man of commanding presence and the clansmen listened to him. He said he was one of them, as they could see from his colour and his language. The other four black men were also their brothers, although one of them did not speak Ibo. The white man was also their brother because they were all sons of God. And he told them about this new God, the Creator of all the world and all the men and women. He told them that they worshipped false gods, gods of wood and stone. A deep murmur went through the crowd when he said this. He told them that the true God lived on high and that all men when they died went before Him for judgment. Evil men and all the heathen who in their blindness bowed to wood and stone were thrown into a fire that burned like palm-oil. But good men who worshipped the true God lived for ever in His happy kingdom. "We have been sent by this great God to ask you to leave your wicked ways and false gods and turn to Him so that you may be saved when you die," he said.

"Your buttocks understand our language," said someone light-heartedly and the crowd laughed.

"What did he say?" the white man asked his interpreter. But before he could answer, another man asked a question: "Where is the white man's horse?" he asked. The Ibo evangelists consulted among themselves and decided that the man probably meant bicycle. They told the white man and he smiled benevolently.

"Tell them," he said, "that I shall bring many iron horses when we have settled down among them. Some of them will even ride the iron horse themselves." This was interpreted to them but very few of them heard. They were talking excitedly among themselves because the white man had said he was going to live among them. They had not thought about that.

At this point an old man said he had a question. "Which is this god of yours," he asked, "the goddess of the earth, the god of the sky, Amadiora of the thunderbolt, or what?"

The interpreter spoke to the white man and he immediately gave his answer. "All the gods you have named are not gods at all. They are gods of deceit who tell you to kill your fellows and destroy innocent children. There is only one true God and He has the earth, the sky, you and me and all of us."

"If we leave our gods and follow your god," asked another man, "who will protect us from the anger of our neglected gods and ancestors?"

"Your gods are not alive and cannot do you any harm," replied the white man. "They are pieces of wood and stone."

When this was interpreted to the men of Mbanta they broke into derisive laughter. These men must be mad, they said to themselves. How else could they say that Ani and Amadiora were harmless? And Idemili and Ogwugwu too? And some of them began to go away.

Then the missionaries burst into song. It was one of those gay and rollicking tunes of evangelism which had the power of plucking at silent and dusty chords in the heart of an Ibo man. The interpreter explained each verse to the audience, some of whom now stood enthralled. It was a story of brothers who lived in darkness and in fear, ignorant of the love of God. It told of one sheep out on the hills, away from the gates of God and from the tender shepherd's care.

---

8. The Igbo language has high and low tones, so that the same word may have different meanings according to its pronunciation. Here Achebe is probably referring to a famous pair of near-homonyms: *iké* (strength) and *ikè* (buttocks).

After the singing the interpreter spoke about the Son of God whose name was Jesu Kristi. Okonkwo, who only stayed in the hope that it might come to chasing the men out of the village or whipping them, now said:

"You told us with your own mouth that there was only one god. Now you talk about his son. He must have a wife, then." The crowd agreed.

"I did not say He had a wife," said the interpreter, somewhat lamely.

"Your buttocks said he had a son," said the joker. "So he must have a wife and all of them must have buttocks."

The missionary ignored him and went on to talk about the Holy Trinity. At the end of it Okonkwo was fully convinced that the man was mad. He shrugged his shoulders and went away to tap his afternoon palm-wine.

But there was a young lad who had been captivated. His name was Nwoye, Okonkwo's first son. It was not the mad logic of the Trinity that captivated him. He did not understand it. It was the poetry of the new religion, something felt in the marrow. The hymn about brothers who sat in darkness and in fear seemed to answer a vague and persistent question that haunted his young soul—the question of the twins crying in the bush and the question of Ikemefuna who was killed. He felt a relief within as the hymn poured into his parched soul. The words of the hymn were like the drops of frozen rain melting on the dry palate of the panting earth. Nwoye's callow mind was greatly puzzled.

CHAPTER SEVENTEEN

The missionaries spent their first four or five nights in the market-place, and went into the village in the morning to preach the gospel. They asked who the king of the village was, but the villagers told them that there was no king. "We have men of high title and the chief priests and the elders," they said.

It was not very easy getting the men of high title and the elders together after the excitement of the first day. But the missionaries persevered, and in the end they were received by the rulers of Mbanta. They asked for a plot of land to build their church.

Every clan and village had its 'evil forest'. In it were buried all those who died of the really evil diseases, like leprosy and smallpox. It was also the dumping ground for the potent fetishes of great medicine-men when they died. An 'evil forest' was, therefore, alive with sinister forces and powers of darkness. It was such a forest that the rulers of Mbanta gave to the missionaries. They did not really want them in their clan, and so they made them that offer which nobody in his right senses would accept.

"They want a piece of land to build their shrine," said Uchendu to his peers when they consulted among themselves. "We shall give them a piece of land." He paused, and there was a murmur of surprise and disagreement. "Let us give them a portion of the Evil Forest. They boast about victory over death. Let us give them a real battlefield in which to show their victory." They laughed and agreed, and sent for the missionaries, whom they had asked to leave them for a while so that they might 'whisper together'. They offered them as much of the Evil Forest as they cared to take. And to their greatest amazement the missionaries thanked them and burst into song.

"They do not understand," said some of the elders. "But they will understand when they go to their plot of land tomorrow morning." And they dispersed.

The next morning the crazy men actually began to clear a part of the forest and to build their house. The inhabitants of Mbanta expected them all to be dead within four days. The first day passed and the second and third and fourth, and none of them died. Everyone was puzzled. And then it became known that the white man's fetish had unbelievable power. It was said that he wore glasses on his eyes so that he could see and talk to evil spirits. Not long after, he won his first three converts.

Although Nwoye had been attracted to the new faith from the very first day, he kept it secret. He dared not go too near the missionaries for fear of his father. But whenever they came, to preach in the open market-place or the village playground, Nwoye was there. And he was already beginning to know some of the simple stories they told.

"We have now built a church," said Mr Kiaga, the interpreter, who was now in charge of the infant congregation. The white man had gone back to Umuofia, where he built his headquarters and from where he paid regular visits to Mr Kiaga's congregation at Mbanta.

"We have now built a church," said Mr Kiaga, "and we want you all to come in every seventh day to worship the true God."

On the following Sunday, Nwoye passed and re-passed the little red-earth and thatch building without summoning enough courage to enter. He heard the voice of singing and although it came from a handful of men it was loud and confident. Their church stood on a circular clearing that looked like the open mouth of the Evil Forest. Was it waiting to snap its teeth together? After passing and re-passing by the church, Nwoye returned home.

It was well known among the people of Mbanta that their gods and ancestors were sometimes long-suffering and would deliberately allow a man to go on defying them. But even in such cases they set their limit at seven market weeks or twenty-eight days. Beyond that limit no man was suffered to go. And so excitement mounted in the village as the seventh week approached since the impudent missionaries built their church in the Evil Forest. The villagers were so certain about the doom that awaited these men that one or two converts thought it wise to suspend their allegiance to the new faith.

At last the day came by which all the missionaries should have died. But they were still alive, building a new red-earth and thatch house for their teacher, Mr Kiaga. That week they won a handful more converts. And for the first time they had a woman. Her name was Nneka, the wife of Amadi, who was a prosperous farmer. She was very heavy with child.

Nneka had had four previous pregnancies and childbirths. But each time she had borne twins, and they had been immediately thrown away. Her husband and his family were already becoming highly critical of such a woman and were not unduly perturbed when they found she had fled to join the Christians. It was a good riddance.

One morning Okonkwo's cousin, Amikwu, was passing by the church on his way from the neighbouring village, when he saw Nwoye among the Christians. He was greatly surprised, and when he got home he went straight to Okonkwo's hut and told him what he had seen. The women began to talk excitedly, but Okonkwo sat unmoved.

It was late afternoon before Nwoye returned. He went into the *obi* and saluted his father, but he did not answer. Nwoye turned round to walk into the inner compound when his father, suddenly overcome with fury, sprang to his feet and gripped him by the neck.

"Where have you been?" he stammered.

Nwoye struggled to free himself from the choking grip.

"Answer me," roared Okonkwo, "before I kill you!" He seized a heavy stick that lay on the dwarf wall and hit him two or three savage blows.

"Answer me!" he roared again. Nwoye stood looking at him and did not say a word. The women were screaming outside, afraid to go in.

"Leave that boy at once!" said a voice in the outer compound. It was Okonkwo's uncle, Uchendu. "Are you mad?"

Okonkwo did not answer. But he left hold of Nwoye, who walked away and never returned.

He went back to the church and told Mr Kiaga that he had decided to go to Umuofia, where the white missionary had set up a school to teach young Christians to read and write.

Mr Kiaga's joy was very great. "Blessed is he who forsakes his father and his mother for my sake," he intoned. "Those that hear my words are my father and my mother."

Nwoye did not fully understand. But he was happy to leave his father. He would return later to his mother and his brothers and sisters and convert them to the new faith.

As Okonkwo sat in his hut that night, gazing into a log fire, he thought over the matter. A sudden fury rose within him and he felt a strong desire to take up his matchet, go to the church and wipe out the entire vile and miscreant gang. But on further thought he told himself that Nwoye was not worth fighting for. Why, he cried in his heart, should he, Okonkwo, of all people, be cursed with such a son? He saw clearly in it the finger of his personal god or *chi*. For how else could he explain his great misfortune and exile and now his despicable son's behaviour? Now that he had time to think of it, his son's crime stood out in its stark enormity. To abandon the gods of one's father and go about with a lot of effeminate men clucking like old hens was the very depth of abomination. Suppose when he died all his male children decided to follow Nwoye's steps and abandon their ancestors? Okonkwo felt a cold shudder run through him at the terrible prospect, like the prospect of annihilation. He saw himself and his fathers crowding round their ancestral shrine waiting in vain for worship and sacrifice and finding nothing but ashes of bygone days, and his children the while praying to the white man's god. If such a thing were ever to happen, he, Okonkwo, would wipe them off the face of the earth.

Okonkwo was popularly called the "Roaring Flame." As he looked into the log fire he recalled the name. He was a flaming fire. How then could he have begotten a son like Nwoye, degenerate and effeminate? Perhaps he was not his son. No! he could not be. His wife had played him false. He would teach her! But Nwoye resembled his grandfather, Unoka, who was Okonkwo's father. He pushed the thought out of his mind. He, Okonkwo, was called a flaming fire. How could he have begotten a woman for a son? At Nwoye's age Okonkwo had already become famous throughout Umuofia for his wrestling and his fearlessness.

He sighed heavily, and as if in sympathy the smouldering log also sighed. And immediately Okonkwo's eyes were opened and he saw the whole matter clearly. Living fire begets cold, impotent ash. He sighed again, deeply.

CHAPTER EIGHTEEN

The young church in Mbanta had a few crises early in its life. At first the clan had assumed that it would not survive. But it had gone on living and gradually becoming stronger. The clan was worried, but not overmuch. If a gang of *efulefu* decided to live in the Evil Forest it was their own affair. When one came to think of it, the Evil Forest was a fit home for such undesirable people. It was true they were rescuing twins from the bush, but they never brought them into the village. As far as the villagers were concerned, the twins still remained where they had been thrown away. Surely the earth goddess would not visit the sins of the missionaries on the innocent villagers?

But on one occasion the missionaries had tried to overstep the bounds. Three converts had gone into the village and boasted openly that all the gods were dead and impotent and that they were prepared to defy them by burning all their shrines.

"Go and burn your mothers' genitals," said one of the priests. The men were seized and beaten until they streamed with blood. After that nothing happened for a long time between the church and the clan.

But stories were already gaining ground that the white man had not only brought a religion but also a government. It was said that they had built a place of judgment in Umuofia to protect the followers of their religion. It was even said that they had hanged one man who killed a missionary.

Although such stories were now often told they looked like fairy-tales in Mbanta and did not as yet affect the relationship between the new church and the clan. There was no question of killing a missionary here, for Mr Kiaga, despite his madness, was quite harmless. As for his converts, no one could kill them without having to flee from the clan, for in spite of their worthlessness they still belonged to the clan. And so nobody gave serious thought to the stories about the white man's government or the consequences of killing the Christians. If they became more troublesome than they already were they would simply be driven out of the clan.

And the little church was at that moment too deeply absorbed in its own troubles to annoy the clan. It all began over the question of admitting outcasts.

These outcasts, or *osu*, seeing that the new religion welcomed twins and such abominations, thought that it was possible that they would also be received. And so one Sunday two of them went into the church. There was an immediate stir; but so great was the work the new religion had done among the converts that they did not immediately leave the church when the outcasts came in. Those who found themselves nearest to them merely moved to another seat. It was a miracle. But it only lasted till the end of the service. The whole church raised a protest and were about to drive these people out, when Mr Kiaga stopped them and began to explain.

"Before God," he said, "there is no slave or free. We are all children of God and we must receive these our brothers."

"You do not understand," said one of the converts. "What will the heathen say of us when they hear that we receive *osu* into our midst? They will laugh."

"Let them laugh," said Mr Kiaga. "God will laugh at them on the judgment day. Why do the nations rage and the peoples imagine a vain thing? He that sitteth in the heavens shall laugh. The Lord shall have them in derision."

"You do not understand," the convert maintained. "You are our teacher, and you can teach us the things of the new faith. But this is a matter which we know." And he told him what an *osu* was.

He was a person dedicated to a god, a thing set apart—a taboo for ever, and his children after him. He could neither marry nor be married by the free-born. He was in fact an outcast, living in a special area of the village, close to the Great Shrine. Wherever he went he carried with him the mark of his forbidden caste—long, tangled and dirty hair. A razor was taboo to him. An *osu* could not attend an assembly of the free-born, and they, in turn, could not shelter under his roof. He could not take any of the four titles of the clan, and when he died he was buried by his kind in the Evil Forest. How could such a man be a follower of Christ?

"He needs Christ more than you and I," said Mr Kiaga.

"Then I shall go back to the clan," said the convert. And he went. Mr Kiaga stood firm, and it was his firmness that saved the young church. The wavering converts drew inspiration and confidence from his unshakable faith. He ordered the outcasts to shave off their long, tangled hair. At first they were afraid they might die.

"Unless you shave off the mark of your heathen belief I will not admit you into the church," said Mr Kiaga. "You fear that you will die. Why should that be? How are you different from other men who shave their hair? The same God created you and them. But they have cast you out like lepers. It is against the will of God, who has promised everlasting life to all who believe in His holy name. The heathen say you will die if you do this or that, and you are afraid. They also said I would die if I built my church on this ground. Am I dead? They said I would die if I took care of twins. I am still alive. The heathen speak nothing but falsehood. Only the word of our God is true."

The two outcasts shaved off their hair, and soon they were among the strong-est adherents of the new faith. And what was more, nearly all the *osu* in Mbanta followed their example. It was in fact one of them who in his zeal brought the church into serious conflict with the clan a year later by killing the sacred python, the emanation of the god of water.

The royal python was the most revered animal in Mbanta and all the sur-rounding clans. It was addressed as 'Our Father', and was allowed to go wherever it chose, even into people's beds. It ate rats in the house and some-times swallowed hens' eggs. If a clansman killed a royal python accidentally, he made sacrifices of atonement and performed an expensive burial ceremony such as was done for a great man. No punishment was prescribed for a man who killed the python knowingly. Nobody thought that such a thing could ever happen.

Perhaps it never did happen. That was the way the clan at first looked at it. No one had actually seen the man do it. The story had arisen among the Christians themselves.

But, all the same, the rulers and elders of Mbanta assembled to decide on their action. Many of them spoke at great length and in fury. The spirit of war was upon them. Okonkwo, who had begun to play a part in the affairs of his motherland, said that until the abominable gang was chased out of the village with whips there would be no peace.

But there were many others who saw the situation differently, and it was their counsel that prevailed in the end.

"It is not our custom to fight for our gods," said one of them. "Let us not presume to do so now. If a man kills the sacred python in the secrecy of his hut, the matter lies between him and the god. We did not see it. If we put ourselves between the god and his victim we may receive blows intended for the offender. When a man blasphemes, what do we do? Do we go and stop his mouth? No. We put our fingers into our ears to stop us hearing. That is a wise action."

"Let us not reason like cowards," said Okonkwo. "If a man comes into my hut and defæcates on the floor, what do I do? Do I shut my eyes? No! I take a stick and break his head. That is what a man does. These people are daily pouring filth over us, and Okeke says we should pretend not to see." Okonkwo made a sound full of disgust. This was a womanly clan, he thought. Such a thing could never happen in his fatherland, Umuofia.

"Okonkwo has spoken the truth," said another man. "We should do something. But let us ostracise these men. We would then not be held accountable for their abominations."

Everybody in the assembly spoke, and in the end it was decided to ostracise the Christians. Okonkwo ground his teeth in disgust.

That night a bell-man went through the length and breadth of Mbanta proclaiming that the adherents of the new faith were thenceforth excluded from the life and privileges of the clan.

The Christians had grown in number and were now a small community of men, women and children, self-assured and confident. Mr Brown, the white missionary, paid regular visits to them. "When I think that it is only eighteen months since the Seed was first sown among you," he said, "I marvel at what the Lord hath wrought."

It was Wednesday in Holy Week and Mr Kiaga had asked the women to bring red earth and white chalk and water to scrub the church for Easter; and the women had formed themselves into three groups for this purpose. They set out early that morning, some of them with their water-pots to the stream, another group with hoes and baskets to the village red-earth pit, and the others to the chalk quarry.

Mr Kiaga was praying in the church when he heard the women talking excitedly. He rounded off his prayer and went to see what it was all about. The women had come to the church with empty water-pots. They said that some young men had chased them away from the stream with whips. Soon after, the women who had gone for red earth returned with empty baskets. Some of them had been heavily whipped. The chalk women also returned to tell a similar story.

"What does it all mean?" asked Mr Kiaga, who was greatly perplexed.

"The village has outlawed us," said one of the women. "The bell-man announced it last night. But it is not our custom to debar anyone from the stream or the quarry."

Another woman said, "They want to ruin us. They will not allow us into the markets. They have said so."

Mr Kiaga was going to send into the village for his men-converts when he saw them coming on their own. Of course they had all heard the bell-man, but they had never in all their lives heard of women being debarred from the stream.

"Come along," they said to the women. "We will go with you to meet those cowards." Some of them had big sticks and some even matchets.

But Mr Kiaga restrained them. He wanted first to know why they had been outlawed.

"They say that Okoli killed the sacred python," said one man.

"It is false," said another. "Okoli told me himself that it was false."

Okoli was not there to answer. He had fallen ill on the previous night. Before the day was over he was dead. His death showed that the gods were still able to fight their own battles. The clan saw no reason then for molesting the Christians.

CHAPTER NINETEEN

The last big rains of the year were falling. It was the time for treading red earth with which to build walls. It was not done earlier because the rains were too heavy and would have washed away the heap of trodden earth; and it could not be done later because harvesting would soon set in, and after that the dry season.

It was going to be Okonkwo's last harvest in Mbanta. The seven wasted and weary years were at last dragging to a close. Although he had prospered in his motherland Okonkwo knew that he would have prospered even more in Umuofia, in the land of his fathers where men were bold and warlike. In these seven years he would have climbed to the utmost heights. And so he regretted every day of his exile. His mother's kinsmen had been very kind to him, and he was grateful. But that did not alter the facts. He had called the first child born to him in exile Nneka—'Mother is Supreme'—out of politeness to his mother's kinsmen. But two years later when a son was born he called him Nwofia—'Begotten in the Wilderness'.

As soon as he entered his last year in exile Okonkwo sent money to Obierika to build him two huts in his old compound where he and his family would live until he built more huts and the outside wall of his compound. He could not ask another man to build his own *obi* for him, nor the walls of his compound. Those things a man built for himself or inherited from his father.

As the last heavy rains of the year began to fall, Obierika sent word that the two huts had been built and Okonkwo began to prepare for his return, after the rains. He would have liked to return earlier and build his compound that year before the rains stopped, but in doing so he would have taken something from the full penalty of seven years. And that could not be. So he waited impatiently for the dry season to come.

It came slowly. The rain became lighter and lighter until it fell in slanting showers. Sometimes the sun shone through the rain and a light breeze blew. It was a gay and airy kind of rain. The rainbow began to appear, and sometimes two rainbows, like a mother and her daughter, the one young and beautiful, and the other an old and faint shadow. The rainbow was called the python of the sky.

Okonkwo called his three wives and told them to get things together for a great feast. "I must thank my mother's kinsmen before I go," he said.

Ekwefi still had some cassava left on her farm from the previous year. Neither of the other wives had. It was not that they had been lazy, but that they had many children to feed. It was therefore understood that Ekwefi would provide cassava for the feast. Nwoye's mother and Ojiugo would provide the other things like smoked fish, palm-oil and pepper for the soup. Okonkwo would take care of meat and yams.

Ekwefi rose early on the following morning and went to her farm with her daughter, Ezinma, and Ojiugo's daughter, Obiageli, to harvest cassava tubers. Each of them carried a long cane basket, a matchet for cutting down the soft cassava stem, and a little hoe for digging out the tuber. Fortunately, a light rain had fallen during the night and the soil would not be very hard.

"It will not take us long to harvest as much as we like," said Ekwefi.

"But the leaves will be wet," said Ezinma. Her basket was balanced on her head, and her arms folded across her breasts. She felt cold. "I dislike cold water dropping on my back. We should have waited for the sun to rise and dry the leaves."

Obiageli called her "Salt" because she said that she disliked water. "Are you afraid you may dissolve?"

The harvesting was easy, as Ekwefi had said. Ezinma shook every tree violently with a long stick before she bent down to cut the stem and dig out the tuber. Sometimes it was not necessary to dig. They just pulled the stump, and earth rose, roots snapped below, and the tuber was pulled out.

When they had harvested a sizeable heap they carried it down in two trips to the stream, where every woman had a shallow well for fermenting her cassava.

"It should be ready in four days or even three," said Obiageli. "They are young tubers."

"They are not all that young," said Ekwefi. "I planted the farm nearly two years ago. It is a poor soil and that is why the tubers are so small."

Okonkwo never did things by halves. When his wife Ekwefi protested that two goats were sufficient for the feast he told her that it was not her affair.

"I am calling a feast because I have the wherewithal. I cannot live on the bank of a river and wash my hands with spittle. My mother's people have been good to me and I must show my gratitude."

And so three goats were slaughtered and a number of fowls. It was like a wedding feast. There was foo-foo and yam pottage, egusi[9] soup and bitter-leaf soup and pots and pots of palm-wine.

All the *umunna*[1] were invited to the feast, all the descendants of Okolo, who had lived about two hundred years before. The oldest member of this extensive family was Okonkwo's uncle, Uchendu. The kola nut was given to him to break, and he prayed to the ancestors. He asked them for health and children. "We do not ask for wealth because he that has health and children will also have wealth. We do not pray to have more money but to have more kinsmen. We are better than animals because we have kinsmen. An animal rubs its itching flank against a tree, a man asks his kinsman to scratch him." He prayed especially for Okonkwo and his family. He then broke the kola nut and threw one of the lobes on the ground for the ancestors.

As the broken kola nuts were passed round, Okonkwo's wives and children and those who came to help them with the cooking began to bring out the food. His sons brought out the pots of palm-wine. There was so much food and drink that many kinsmen whistled in surprise. When all was laid out, Okonkwo rose to speak.

"I beg you to accept this little kola," he said. "It is not to pay you back for all you did for me in these seven years. A child cannot pay for its mother's

---

9. Melon seed, which is roasted, ground, and cooked in soup.

1. Children of the father (literal trans.); the clan (male).

milk. I have only called you together because it is good for kinsmen to meet."

Yam pottage was served first because it was lighter than foo-foo and because yam always came first. Then the foo-foo was served. Some kinsmen ate it with egusi soup and others with bitter-leaf soup. The meat was then shared so that every member of the *umunna* had a portion. Every man rose in order of years and took a share. Even the few kinsmen who had not been able to come had their shares taken out for them in due turn.

As the palm-wine was drunk one of the oldest members of the *umunna* rose to thank Okonkwo:

"If I say that we did not expect such a big feast I will be suggesting that we did not know how open-handed our son, Okonkwo, is. We all know him, and we expected a big feast. But it turned out to be even bigger than we expected. Thank you. May all you took out return again tenfold. It is good in these days when the younger generation consider themselves wiser than their sires to see a man doing things in the grand, old way. A man who calls his kinsmen to a feast does not do so to save them from starving. They all have food in their own homes. When we gather together in the moonlit village ground it is not because of the moon. Every man can see it in his own compound. We come together because it is good for kinsmen to do so. You may ask why I am saying all this. I say it because I fear for the younger generation, for you people." He waved his arm where most of the young men sat. "As for me, I have only a short while to live, and so have Uchendu and Unachukwu and Emefo. But I fear for you young people because you do not understand how strong is the bond of kinship. You do not know what it is to speak with one voice. And what is the result? An abominable religion has settled among you. A man can now leave his father and his brothers. He can curse the gods of his fathers and his ancestors, like a hunter's dog that suddenly goes mad and turns on his master. I fear for you; I fear for the clan." He turned again to Okonkwo and said, "Thank you for calling us together."

Part Three

CHAPTER TWENTY

Seven years was a long time to be away from one's clan. A man's place was not always there, waiting for him. As soon as he left, someone else rose and filled it. The clan was like a lizard; if it lost its tail it soon grew another.

Okonkwo knew these things. He knew that he had lost his place among the nine masked spirits who administered justice in the clan. He had lost the chance to lead his warlike clan against the new religion, which he was told, had gained ground. He had lost the years in which he might have taken the highest titles in the clan. But some of these losses were not irreparable. He was determined that his return should be marked by his people. He would return with a flourish, and regain the seven wasted years.

Even in his first year in exile he had begun to plan for his return. The first thing he would do would be to rebuild his compound on a more magnificent scale. He would build a bigger barn than he had had before and he would build huts for two new wives. Then he would show his wealth by initiating his sons into the *ozo* society. Only the really great men in the clan were able to do this. Okonkwo saw clearly the high esteem in which he would be held, and he saw himself taking the highest title in the land.

As the years of exile passed one by one it seemed to him that his *chi* might now be making amends for the past disaster. His yams grew abundantly, not only in his motherland but also in Umuofia, where his friend gave them out year by year to share-croppers.

Then the tragedy of his first son had occurred. At first it appeared as if it might prove too great for his spirit. But it was a resilient spirit, and in the end Okonkwo overcame his sorrow. He had five other sons and he would bring them up in the way of the clan.

He sent for the five sons and they came and sat in his *obi*. The youngest of them was four years old.

"You have all seen the great abomination of your brother. Now he is no longer my son or your brother. I will only have a son who is a man, who will hold his head up among my people. If any one of you prefers to be a woman, let him follow Nwoye now while I am alive so that I can curse him. If you turn against me when I am dead I will visit you and break your neck."

Okonkwo was very lucky in his daughters. He never stopped regretting that Ezinma was a girl. Of all his children she alone understood his every mood. A bond of sympathy had grown between them as the years had passed.

Ezinma grew up in her father's exile and became one of the most beautiful girls in Mbanta. She was called Crystal of Beauty, as her mother had been called in her youth. The young ailing girl who had caused her mother so much heartache had been transformed, almost overnight, into a healthy buoyant maiden. She had, it was true, her moments of depression when she would snap at everybody like an angry dog. These moods descended on her suddenly and for no apparent reason. But they were very rare and short-lived. As long as they lasted, she could bear no other person but her father.

Many young men and prosperous middle-aged men of Mbanta came to marry her. But she refused them all, because her father had called her one evening and said to her: "There are many good and prosperous people here, but I shall be happy if you marry in Umuofia when we return home."

That was all he had said. But Ezinma had seen clearly all the thought and hidden meaning behind the few words. And she had agreed.

"Your half-sister, Obiageli, will not understand me," Okonkwo said. "But you can explain to her."

Although they were almost the same age, Ezinma wielded a strong influence over her half-sister. She explained to her why they should not marry yet, and she agreed also. And so the two of them refused every offer of marriage in Mbanta.

"I wish she were a boy," Okonkwo thought within himself. She understood things so perfectly. Who else among his children could have read his thought so well? With two beautiful grown-up daughters his return to Umuofia would attract considerable attention. His future sons-in-law would be men of authority in the clan. The poor and unknown would not dare to come forth.

Umuofia had indeed changed during the seven years Okonkwo had been in exile. The church had come and led many astray. Not only the low-born and the outcast but sometimes a worthy man had joined it. Such a man was Ogbuefi Ugonna,[2] who had taken two titles, and who like a madman had cut the anklet of his titles and cast it away to join the Christians. The white missionary was very proud of him and he was one of the first men in Umuofia to

---

2. Father's honor (with the eagle feather).

receive the sacrament of Holy Communion, or Holy Feast as it was called in Ibo. Ogbuefi Ugonna had thought of the Feast in terms of eating and drinking, only more holy than the village variety. He had therefore put his drinking-horn into his goatskin bag for the occasion.

But apart from the church, the white men had also brought a government. They had built a court where the District Commissioner judged cases in ignorance. He had court messengers who brought men to him for trial. Many of these messengers came from Umuru on the bank of the Great River, where the white men first came many years before and where they had built the centre of their religion and trade and government. These court messengers were greatly hated in Umuofia because they were foreigners and also arrogant and high-handed. They were called *kotma*,[3] and because of their ash-coloured shorts they earned the additional name of Ashy-Buttocks. They guarded the prison, which was full of men who had offended against the white man's law. Some of these prisoners had thrown away their twins and some had molested the Christians. They were beaten in the prison by the *kotma* and made to work every morning clearing the government compound and fetching wood for the white Commissioner and the court messengers. Some of these prisoners were men of title who should be above such mean occupation. They were grieved by the indignity and mourned for their neglected farms. As they cut grass in the morning the younger men sang in time with the strokes of their matchets:

> "Kotma *of the ash buttocks,*
> *He is fit to be a slave.*
> *The white man has no sense,*
> *He is fit to be a slave.*"

The court messengers did not like to be called Ashy-Buttocks, and they beat the men. But the song spread in Umuofia.

Okonkwo's head was bowed in sadness as Obierika told him these things.

"Perhaps I have been away too long," Okonkwo said, almost to himself. "But I cannot understand these things you tell me. What is it that has happened to our people? Why have they lost the power to fight?"

"Have you not heard how the white man wiped out Abame?" asked Obierika.

"I have heard," said Okonkwo. "But I have also heard that Abame people were weak and foolish. Why did they not fight back? Had they no guns and matchets? We would be cowards to compare ourselves with the men of Abame. Their fathers had never dared to stand before our ancestors. We must fight these men and drive them from the land."

"It is already too late," said Obierika sadly. "Our own men and our sons have joined the ranks of the stranger. They have joined his religion and they help to uphold his government. If we should try to drive out the white men in Umuofia we should find it easy. There are only two of them. But what of our own people who are following their way and have been given power? They would go to Umuru and bring the soldiers, and we would be like Abame." He paused for a long time and then said: "I told you on my last visit to Mbanta how they hanged Aneto."

"What has happened to that piece of land in dispute?" asked Okonkwo.

"The white man's court has decided that it should belong to Nnama's family, who had given much money to the white man's messengers and interpreter."

---

3. Court messenger (pidgin English).

"Does the white man understand our custom about land?"

"How can he when he does not even speak our tongue? But he says that our customs are bad; and our own brothers who have taken up his religion also say that our customs are bad. How do you think we can fight when our own brothers have turned against us? The white man is very clever. He came quietly and peaceably with his religion. We were amused at his foolishness and allowed him to stay. Now he has won our brothers, and our clan can no longer act like one. He has put a knife on the things that held us together and we have fallen apart."

"How did they get hold of Aneto to hang him?" asked Okonkwo.

"When he killed Oduche in the fight over the land, he fled to Aninta to escape the wrath of the earth. This was about eight days after the fight, because Oduche had not died immediately from his wounds. It was on the seventh day that he died. But everybody knew that he was going to die and Aneto got his belongings together in readiness to flee. But the Christians had told the white man about the accident, and he sent his *kotma* to catch Aneto. He was imprisoned with all the leaders of his family. In the end Oduche died and Aneto was taken to Umuru and hanged. The other people were released, but even now they have not found the mouth with which to tell of their suffering."

The two men sat in silence for a long while afterwards.

CHAPTER TWENTY-ONE

There were many men and women in Umuofia who did not feel as strongly as Okonkwo about the new dispensation. The white man had indeed brought a lunatic religion, but he had also built a trading store and for the first time palm-oil and kernel[4] became things of great price, and much money flowed into Umuofia.

And even in the matter of religion there was a growing feeling that there might be something in it after all, something vaguely akin to method in the overwhelming madness.

This growing feeling was due to Mr Brown, the white missionary, who was very firm in restraining his flock from provoking the wrath of the clan. One member in particular was very difficult to restrain. His name was Enoch and his father was the priest of the snake cult. The story went around that Enoch had killed and eaten the sacred python, and that his father had cursed him.

Mr Brown preached against such excess of zeal. Everything was possible, he told his energetic flock, but everything was not expedient. And so Mr Brown came to be respected even by the clan, because he trod softly on its faith. He made friends with some of the great men of the clan and on one of his frequent visits to the neighbouring villages he had been presented with a carved elephant tusk, which was a sign of dignity and rank. One of the great men in that village was called Akunna[5] and he had given one of his sons to be taught the white man's knowledge in Mr Brown's school.

Whenever Mr Brown went to that village he spent long hours with Akunna in his *obi* talking through an interpreter about religion. Neither of them succeeded in converting the other but they learnt more about their different beliefs.

---

4. The red fleshy husk of the palm nut is crushed manually to produce cooking oil, leaving a fibrous residue along with hard kernels. The Europeans bought both the red oil and the kernels, from which they could extract a very fine oil by using machines.

5. Father's wealth.

"You say that there is one supreme God who made heaven and earth," said Akunna on one of Mr Brown's visits. "We also believe in Him and call Him Chukwu. He made all the world and the other gods."

"There are no other gods," said Mr Brown. "Chukwu is the only God and all others are false. You carve a piece of wood—like that one" (he pointed at the rafters from which Akunna's carved *Ikenga*[6] hung), "and you call it a god. But it is still a piece of wood."

"Yes," said Akunna. "It is indeed a piece of wood. The tree from which it came was made by Chukwu, as indeed all minor gods were. But He made them for His messengers so that we could approach Him through them. It is like yourself. You are the head of your church."

"No," protested Mr Brown. "The head of my church is God Himself."

"I know," said Akunna, "but there must be a head in this world among men. Somebody like yourself must be the head here."

"The head of my church in that sense is in England."

"That is exactly what I am saying. The head of your church is in your country. He has sent you here as his messenger. And you have also appointed your own messengers and servants. Or let me take another example, the District Commissioner. He is sent by your king."

"They have a queen," said the interpreter on his own account.

"Your queen sends her messenger, the District Commissioner. He finds that he cannot do the work alone and so he appoints *kotma* to help him. It is the same with God, or Chukwu. He appoints the smaller gods to help Him because His work is too great for one person."

"You should not think of him as a person," said Mr Brown. "It is because you do so that you imagine He must need helpers. And the worst thing about it is that you give all the worship to the false gods you have created."

"That is not so. We make sacrifices to the little gods, but when they fail and there is no one else to turn to we go to Chukwu. It is right to do so. We approach a great man through his servants. But when his servants fail to help us, then we go to the last source of hope. We appear to pay greater attention to the little gods but that is not so. We worry them more because we are afraid to worry their Master. Our fathers knew that Chukwu was the Overlord and that is why many of them gave their children the name Chukwuka—'Chukwu is Supreme'."

"You said one interesting thing," said Mr Brown. "You are afraid of Chukwu. In my religion Chukwu is a loving Father and need not be feared by those who do His will."

"But we must fear Him when we are not doing His will," said Akunna. "And who is to tell His will? It is too great to be known."

In this way Mr Brown learnt a good deal about the religion of the clan and he came to the conclusion that a frontal attack on it would not succeed. And so he built a school and a little hospital in Umuofia. He went from family to family begging people to send their children to his school. But at first they only sent their slaves or sometimes their lazy children. Mr Brown begged and argued and prophesied. He said that the leaders of the land in the future would be men and women who had learnt to read and write. If Umuofia failed to send her children to the school, strangers would come from other places to rule them. They could already see that happening in the Native Court, where

---

6. A carved wooden figure with the horns of a ram that symbolized the strength of a man's right hand. Every adult male kept an *Ikenga* in his personal shrine.

the D.C. was surrounded by strangers who spoke his tongue. Most of these strangers came from the distant town of Umuru on the bank of the Great River where the white man first went.

In the end Mr Brown's arguments began to have an effect. More people came to learn in his school, and he encouraged them with gifts of singlets[7] and towels. They were not all young, these people who came to learn. Some of them were thirty years old or more. They worked on their farms in the morning and went to school in the afternoon. And it was not long before the people began to say that the white man's medicine was quick in working. Mr Brown's school produced quick results. A few months in it were enough to make one a court messenger or even a court clerk. Those who stayed longer became teachers; and from Umuofia labourers went forth into the Lord's vineyard. New churches were established in the surrounding villages and a few schools with them. From the very beginning religion and education went hand in hand.

Mr Brown's mission grew from strength to strength, and because of its link with the new administration it earned a new social prestige. But Mr Brown himself was breaking down in health. At first he ignored the warning signs. But in the end he had to leave his flock, sad and broken.

It was in the first rainy season after Okonkwo's return to Umuofia that Mr Brown left for home. As soon as he had learnt of Okonkwo's return five months earlier, the missionary had immediately paid him a visit. He had just sent Okonkwo's son, Nwoye, who was now called Isaac,[8] to the new training college for teachers in Umuru. And he had hoped that Okonkwo would be happy to hear of it. But Okonkwo had driven him away with the threat that if he came into his compound again, he would be carried out of it.

Okonkwo's return to his native land was not as memorable as he had wished. It was true his two beautiful daughters aroused great interest among suitors and marriage negotiations were soon in progress, but, beyond that, Umuofia did not appear to have taken any special notice of the warrior's return. The clan had undergone such profound change during his exile that it was barely recognisable. The new religion and government and the trading stores were very much in the people's eyes and minds. There were still many who saw these new institutions as evil, but even they talked and thought about little else, and certainly not about Okonkwo's return.

And it was the wrong year too. If Okonkwo had immediately initiated his two sons into the *ozo* society as he had planned he would have caused a stir. But the initiation rite was performed once in three years in Umuofia, and he had to wait for nearly two years for the next round of ceremonies.

Okonkwo was deeply grieved. And it was not just a personal grief. He mourned for the clan, which he saw breaking up and falling apart, and he mourned for the warlike men of Umuofia, who had so unaccountably become soft like women.

CHAPTER TWENTY-TWO

Mr Brown's successor was the Reverend James Smith, and he was a different kind of man. He condemned openly Mr Brown's policy of compromise and

---

7. Undershirts, T-shirts.
8. Son of Abraham, offered to God as a sacrifice (Genesis 22).

accommodation. He saw things as black and white. And black was evil. He saw the world as a battlefield in which the children of light were locked in mortal conflict with the sons of darkness. He spoke in his sermons about sheep and goats and about wheat and tares. He believed in slaying the prophets of Baal.

Mr Smith was greatly distressed by the ignorance which many of his flock showed even in such things as the Trinity and the Sacraments. It only showed that they were seeds sown on a rocky soil. Mr Brown had thought of nothing but numbers. He should have known that the kingdom of God did not depend on large crowds. Our Lord Himself stressed the importance of fewness. Narrow is the way and few the number. To fill the Lord's holy temple with an idolatrous crowd clamouring for signs was a folly of everlasting consequence. Our Lord used the whip only once in His life—to drive the crowd away from His church.

Within a few weeks of his arrival in Umuofia Mr Smith suspended a young woman from the church for pouring new wine into old bottles. This woman had allowed her heathen husband to mutilate her dead child. The child had been declared an *ogbanje*, plaguing its mother by dying and entering her womb to be born again. Four times this child had run its evil round. And so it was mutilated to discourage it from returning.

Mr Smith was filled with wrath when he heard of this. He disbelieved the story which even some of the most faithful confirmed, the story of really evil children who were not deterred by mutilation, but came back with all the scars. He replied that such stories were spread in the world by the Devil to lead men astray. Those who believed such stories were unworthy of the Lord's table.

There was a saying in Umuofia that as a man danced so the drums were beaten for him. Mr Smith danced a furious step and so the drums went mad. The over-zealous converts who had smarted under Mr Brown's restraining hand now flourished in full favour. One of them was Enoch, the son of the snake-priest who was believed to have killed and eaten the sacred python. Enoch's devotion to the new faith had seemed so much greater than Mr Brown's that the villagers called him The outsider who wept louder than the bereaved.

Enoch was short and slight of build, and always seemed in great haste. His feet were short and broad, and when he stood or walked his heels came together and his feet opened outwards as if they had quarrelled and meant to go in different directions. Such was the excessive energy bottled up in Enoch's small body that it was always erupting in quarrels and fights. On Sundays he always imagined that the sermon was preached for the benefit of his enemies. And if he happened to sit near one of them he would occasionally turn to give him a meaningful look, as if to say, 'I told you so'. It was Enoch who touched off the great conflict between church and clan in Umuofia which had been gathering since Mr Brown left.

It happened during the annual ceremony which was held in honour of the earth deity. At such times the ancestors of the clan who had been committed to Mother Earth at their death emerged again as *egwugwu* through tiny ant-holes.

One of the greatest crimes a man could commit was to unmask an *egwugwu* in public, or to say or do anything which might reduce its immortal prestige in the eyes of the uninitiated. And this was what Enoch did.

The annual worship of the earth goddess fell on a Sunday, and the masked spirits were abroad. The Christian women who had been to church could not therefore go home. Some of their men had gone out to beg the *egwugwu* to retire for a short while for the women to pass. They agreed and were already retiring, when Enoch boasted aloud that they would not dare to touch a Christian. Whereupon they all came back and one of them gave Enoch a good stroke of the cane, which was always carried. Enoch fell on him and tore off his mask. The other *egwugwu* immediately surrounded their desecrated companion, to shield him from the profane gaze of women and children, and led him away. Enoch had killed an ancestral spirit, and Umuofia was thrown into confusion.

That night the Mother of the Spirits walked the length and breadth of the clan, weeping for her murdered son. It was a terrible night. Not even the oldest man in Umuofia had ever heard such a strange and fearful sound, and it was never to be heard again. It seemed as if the very soul of the tribe wept for a great evil that was coming—its own death.

On the next day all the masked *egwugwu* of Umuofia assembled in the market-place. They came from all the quarters of the clan and even from the neighbouring villages. The dreaded Otakagu came from Imo, and Ekwensu, dangling a white cock, arrived from Uli. It was a terrible gathering. The eerie voices of countless spirits, the bells that clattered behind some of them, and the clash of matchets as they ran forwards and backwards and saluted one another, sent tremors of fear into every heart. For the first time in living memory the sacred bull-roarer was heard in broad daylight.

From the market-place the furious band made for Enoch's compound. Some of the elders of the clan went with them, wearing heavy protections of charms and amulets. These were men whose arms were strong in *ogwu*, or medicine. As for the ordinary men and women, they listened from the safety of their huts.

The leaders of the Christians had met together at Mr Smith's parsonage on the previous night. As they deliberated they could hear the Mother of Spirits wailing for her son. The chilling sound affected Mr Smith, and for the first time he seemed to be afraid.

"What are they planning to do?" he asked. No one knew, because such a thing had never happened before. Mr Smith would have sent for the District Commissioner and his court messengers, but they had gone on tour on the previous day.

"One thing is clear," said Mr Smith. "We cannot offer physical resistance to them. Our strength lies in the Lord." They knelt down together and prayed to God for delivery.

"O Lord save Thy people," cried Mr Smith.

"And bless Thine inheritance," replied the men.

They decided that Enoch should be hidden in the parsonage for a day or two. Enoch himself was greatly disappointed when he heard this, for he had hoped that a holy war was imminent; and there were a few other Christians who thought like him. But wisdom prevailed in the camp of the faithful and many lives were thus saved.

The band of *egwugwu* moved like a furious whirlwind to Enoch's compound and with matchet and fire reduced it to a desolate heap. And from there they made for the church, intoxicated with destruction.

Mr Smith was in his church when he heard the masked spirits coming. He walked quietly to the door which commanded the approach to the church compound, and stood there. But when the first three or four *egwugwu* appeared on the church compound he nearly bolted. He overcame this impulse and instead of running away he went down the two steps that led up to the church and walked towards the approaching spirits.

They surged forward, and a long stretch of the bamboo fence with which the church compound was surrounded gave way before them. Discordant bells clanged, matchets clashed and the air was full of dust and weird sounds. Mr Smith heard a sound of footsteps behind him. He turned round and saw Okeke, his interpreter. Okeke had not been on the best of terms with his master since he had strongly condemned Enoch's behaviour at the meeting of the leaders of the church during the night. Okeke had gone as far as to say that Enoch should not be hidden in the parsonage, because he would only draw the wrath of the clan on the pastor. Mr Smith had rebuked him in very strong language, and had not sought his advice that morning. But now, as he came up and stood by him confronting the angry spirits, Mr Smith looked at him and smiled. It was a wan smile, but there was deep gratitude there.

For a brief moment the onrush of the *egwugwu* was checked by the unexpected composure of the two men. But it was only a momentary check, like the tense silence between blasts of thunder. The second onrush was greater than the first. It swallowed up the two men. Then an unmistakable voice rose above the tumult and there was immediate silence. Space was made around the two men, and Ajofia began to speak.

Ajofia was the leading *egwugwu* of Umuofia. He was the head and spokesman of the nine ancestors who administered justice in the clan. His voice was unmistakable and so he was able to bring immediate peace to the agitated spirits. He then addressed Mr Smith, and as he spoke clouds of smoke rose from his head.

"The body of the white man, I salute you," he said, using the language in which immortals spoke to men.

"The body of the white man, do you know me?" he asked.

Mr Smith looked at his interpreter, but Okeke, who was a native of distant Umuru, was also at a loss.

Ajofia laughed in his guttural voice. It was like the laugh of rusty metal. "They are strangers," he said, "and they are ignorant. But let that pass." He turned round to his comrades and saluted them, calling them the fathers of Umuofia. He dug his rattling spear into the ground and it shook with metallic life. Then he turned once more to the missionary and his interpreter.

"Tell the white man that we will not do him any harm," he said to the interpreter. "Tell him to go back to his house and leave us alone. We liked his brother who was with us before. He was foolish, but we liked him, and for his sake we shall not harm his brother. But this shrine which he built must be destroyed. We shall no longer allow it in our midst. It has bred untold abominations and we have come to put an end to it." He turned to his comrades. "Fathers of Umuofia, I salute you;" and they replied with one guttural voice. He turned again to the missionary. "You can stay with us if you like our ways. You can worship your own god. It is good that a man should worship the gods and the spirits of his fathers. Go back to your house so that you may not be hurt. Our anger is great but we have held it down so that we can talk to you."

Mr Smith said to his interpreter: "Tell them to go away from here. This is the house of God and I will not live to see it desecrated."

Okeke interpreted wisely to the spirits and leaders of Umuofia: "The white man says he is happy you have come to him with your grievances, like friends. He will be happy if you leave the matter in his hands."

"We cannot leave the matter in his hands because he does not understand our customs, just as we do not understand his. We say he is foolish because he does not know our ways, and perhaps he says we are foolish because we do not know his. Let him go away."

Mr Smith stood his ground. But he could not save his church. When the *egwugwu* went away the red-earth church which Mr Brown had built was a pile of earth and ashes. And for the moment the spirit of the clan was pacified.

CHAPTER TWENTY-THREE

For the first time in many years Okonkwo had a feeling that was akin to happiness. The times which had altered so unaccountably during his exile seemed to be coming round again. The clan which had turned false on him appeared to be making amends.

He had spoken violently to his clansmen when they had met in the market-place to decide on their action. And they had listened to him with respect. It was like the good old days again, when a warrior was a warrior. Although they had not agreed to kill the missionary or drive away the Christians, they had agreed to do something substantial. And they had done it. Okonkwo was almost happy again.

For two days after the destruction of the church, nothing happened. Every man in Umuofia went about armed with a gun or a matchet. They would not be caught unawares, like the men of Abame.

Then the District Commissioner returned from his tour. Mr Smith went immediately to him and they had a long discussion. The men of Umuofia did not take any notice of this, and if they did, they thought it was not important. The missionary often went to see his brother white man. There was nothing strange in that.

Three days later the District Commissioner sent his sweet-tongued messenger to the leaders of Umuofia asking them to meet him in his headquarters. That also was not strange. He often asked them to hold such palavers, as he called them. Okonkwo was among the six leaders he invited.

Okonkwo warned the others to be fully armed. "An Umuofia man does not refuse a call," he said. "He may refuse to do what he is asked; he does not refuse to be asked. But the times have changed, and we must be fully prepared."

And so the six men went to see the District Commissioner, armed with their matchets. They did not carry guns, for that would be unseemly. They were led into the court-house where the District Commissioner sat. He received them politely. They unslung their goatskin bags and their sheathed matchets, put them on the floor, and sat down.

"I have asked you to come," began the Commissioner, "because of what happened during my absence. I have been told a few things but I cannot believe them until I have heard your own side. Let us talk about it like friends and find a way of ensuring that it does not happen again."

Ogbuefi Ekwueme[9] rose to his feet and began to tell the story.

9. A person who does what he says (a praise name).

"Wait a minute," said the Commissioner. "I want to bring in my men so that they too can hear your grievances and take warning. Many of them come from distant places and although they speak your tongue they are ignorant of your customs. James! Go and bring in the men." His interpreter left the court-room and soon returned with twelve men. They sat together with the men of Umuofia, and Ogbuefi Ekwueme began again to tell the story of how Enoch murdered an *egwugwu*.

It happened so quickly that the six men did not see it coming. There was only a brief scuffle, too brief even to allow the drawing of a sheathed matchet. The six men were handcuffed and led into the guardroom.

"We shall not do you any harm," said the District Commissioner to them later, "if only you agree to co-operate with us. We have brought a peaceful administration to you and your people so that you may be happy. If any man ill-treats you we shall come to your rescue. But we will not allow you to ill-treat others. We have a court of law where we judge cases and administer justice just as it is done in my own country under a great queen. I have brought you here because you joined together to molest others, to burn people's houses and their place of worship. That must not happen in the dominion of our queen, the most powerful ruler in the world. I have decided that you will pay a fine of two hundred bags of cowries. You will be released as soon as you agree to this and undertake to collect that fine from your people. What do you say to that?"

The six men remained sullen and silent and the Commissioner left them for a while. He told the court messengers, when he left the guardroom, to treat the men with respect because they were the leaders of Umuofia. They said, "Yes, sir," and saluted.

As soon as the District Commissioner left, the head messenger, who was also the prisoners' barber, took down his razor and shaved off all the hair on the men's heads. They were still handcuffed, and they just sat and moped.

"Who is the chief among you?" the court messengers asked in jest. "We see that every pauper wears the anklet of title in Umuofia. Does it cost as much as ten cowries?"

The six men ate nothing throughout that day and the next. They were not even given any water to drink, and they could not go out to urinate or go into the bush when they were pressed. At night the messengers came in to taunt them and to knock their shaven heads together.

Even when the men were left alone they found no words to speak to one another. It was only on the third day, when they could no longer bear the hunger and the insults, that they began to talk about giving in.

"We should have killed the white man if you had listened to me," Okonkwo snarled.

"We could have been in Umuru now waiting to be hanged," someone said to him.

"Who wants to kill the white man?" asked a messenger who had just rushed in. Nobody spoke.

"You are not satisfied with your crime, but you must kill the white man on top of it." He carried a strong stick, and he hit each man a few blows on the head and back. Okonkwo was choked with hate.

As soon as the six men were locked up, court messengers went into Umuofia to tell the people that their leaders would not be released unless they paid a fine of two hundred and fifty bags of cowries.

"Unless you pay the fine immediately," said their headman, "we will take your leaders to Umuru before the big white man, and hang them."

This story spread quickly through the villages, and was added to as it went. Some said that the men had already been taken to Umuru and would be hanged on the following day. Some said that their families would also be hanged. Others said that soldiers were already on their way to shoot the people of Umuofia as they had done in Abame.

It was the time of the full moon. But that night the voice of children was not heard. The village *ilo* where they always gathered for a moon-play was empty. The women of Iguedo did not meet in their secret enclosure to learn a new dance to be displayed later to the village. Young men who were always abroad in the moonlight kept their huts that night. Their manly voices were not heard on the village paths as they went to visit their friends and lovers. Umuofia was like a startled animal with ears erect, sniffing the silent, ominous air and not knowing which way to run.

The silence was broken by the village crier beating his sonorous *ogene*. He called every man in Umuofia, from the Akakanma age-group upwards, to a meeting in the market-place after the morning meal. He went from one end of the village to the other and walked all its breadth. He did not leave out any of the main footpaths.

Okonkwo's compound was like a deserted homestead. It was as if cold water had been poured on it. His family was all there, but everyone spoke in whispers. His daughter Ezinma had broken her twenty-eight-day visit to the family of her future husband, and returned home when she heard that her father had been imprisoned, and was going to be hanged. As soon as she got home she went to Obierika to ask what the men of Umuofia were going to do about it. But Obierika had not been home since morning. His wives thought he had gone to a secret meeting. Ezinma was satisfied that something was being done.

On the morning after the village crier's appeal the men of Umuofia met in the market-place and decided to collect without delay two hundred and fifty bags of cowries to appease the white man. They did not know that fifty bags would go to the court messengers, who had increased the fine for that purpose.

CHAPTER TWENTY-FOUR

Okonkwo and his fellow prisoners were set free as soon as the fine was paid. The District Commissioner spoke to them again about the great queen, and about peace and good government. But the men did not listen. They just sat and looked at him and at his interpreter. In the end they were given back their bags and sheathed matchets and told to go home. They rose and left the court-house. They neither spoke to anyone nor among themselves.

The court-house, like the church, was built a little way outside the village. The footpath that linked them was a very busy one because it also led to the stream, beyond the court. It was open and sandy. Footpaths were open and sandy in the dry season. But when the rains came the bush grew thick on either side and closed in on the path. It was now dry season.

As they made their way to the village the six men met women and children going to the stream with their waterpots. But the men wore such heavy and fearsome looks that the women and children did not say '*nno*' or 'welcome' to them, but edged out of the way to let them pass. In the village little groups of men joined them until they became a sizeable company. They walked silently.

As each of the six men got to his compound, he turned in, taking some of the crowd with him. The village was astir in a silent, suppressed way.

Ezinma had prepared some food for her father as soon as news spread that the six men would be released. She took it to him in his *obi*. He ate absent-mindedly. He had no appetite; he only ate to please her. His male relations and friends had gathered in his *obi*, and Obierika was urging him to eat. Nobody else spoke, but they noticed the long stripes on Okonkwo's back where the warder's whip had cut into his flesh.

The village crier was abroad again in the night. He beat his iron gong and announced that another meeting would be held in the morning. Everyone knew that Umuofia was at last going to speak its mind about the things that were happening.

Okonkwo slept very little that night. The bitterness in his heart was now mixed with a kind of child-like excitement. Before he had gone to bed he had brought down his war dress, which he had not touched since his return from exile. He had shaken out his smoked raffia skirt and examined his tall feather head-gear and his shield. They were all satisfactory, he had thought.

As he lay on his bamboo bed he thought about the treatment he had received in the white man's court, and he swore vengeance. If Umuofia decided on war, all would be well. But if they chose to be cowards he would go out and avenge himself. He thought about wars in the past. The noblest, he thought, was the war against Isike. In those days Okudo[1] was still alive. Okudo sang a war song in a way that no other man could. He was not a fighter, but his voice turned every man into a lion.

'Worthy men are no more,' Okonkwo sighed as he remembered those days. 'Isike will never forget how we slaughtered them in that war. We killed twelve of their men and they killed only two of ours. Before the end of the fourth market week they were suing for peace. Those were days when men were men.'

As he thought of these things he heard the sound of the iron gong in the distance. He listened carefully, and could just hear the crier's voice. But it was very faint. He turned on his bed and his back hurt him. He ground his teeth. The crier was drawing nearer and nearer until he passed by Okonkwo's compound.

'The greatest obstacle in Umuofia,' Okonkwo thought bitterly, 'is that coward, Egonwanne.[2] His sweet tongue can change fire into cold ash. When he speaks he moves our men to impotence. If they had ignored his womanish wisdom five years ago, we would not have come to this.' He ground his teeth. 'Tomorrow he will tell them that our fathers never fought a "war of blame". If they listen to him I shall leave them and plan my own revenge.'

The crier's voice had once more become faint, and the distance had taken the harsh edge off his iron gong. Okonkwo turned from one side to the other and derived a kind of pleasure from the pain his back gave him. 'Let Egon-wanne talk about a "war of blame" tomorrow and I shall show him my back and head.' He ground his teeth.

The market-place began to fill as soon as the sun rose. Obierika was waiting in his *obi* when Okonkwo came along and called him. He hung his goatskin bag and his sheathed matchet on his shoulder and went out to join him. Obi-

---

1. Great eagle feather (a praise name).   2. Wealth of a sibling.

erika's hut was close to the road and he saw every man who passed to the market-place. He had exchanged greetings with many who had already passed that morning.

When Okonkwo and Obierika got to the meeting-place there were already so many people that if one threw up a grain of sand it would not find its way to the earth again. And many more people were coming from every quarter of the nine villages. It warmed Okonkwo's heart to see such strength of numbers. But he was looking for one man in particular, the man whose tongue he dreaded and despised so much.

"Can you see him?" he asked Obierika.

"Who?"

"Egonwanne," he said, his eyes roving from one corner of the huge market-place to the other. Most of the men were seated on goatskins on the ground. A few of them sat on wooden stools they had brought with them.

"No," said Obierika, casting his eyes over the crowd. "Yes, there he is, under the silk-cotton tree. Are you afraid he would convince us not to fight?"

"Afraid? I do not care what he does to *you*. I despise him and those who listen to him. I shall fight alone if I choose."

They spoke at the top of their voices because everybody was talking, and it was like the sound of a great market.

'I shall wait till he has spoken,' Okonkwo thought. 'Then I shall speak.'

"But how do you know he will speak against war?" Obierika asked after a while.

"Because I know he is a coward," said Okonkwo. Obierika did not hear the rest of what he said because at that moment somebody touched his shoulder from behind and he turned round to shake hands and exchange greetings with five or six friends. Okonkwo did not turn round even though he knew the voices. He was in no mood to exchange greetings. But one of the men touched him and asked about the people of his compound.

"They are well," he replied without interest.

The first man to speak to Umuofia that morning was Okika, one of the six who had been imprisoned. Okika was a great man and an orator. But he did not have the booming voice which a first speaker must use to establish silence in the assembly of the clan. Onyeka[3] had such a voice; and so he was asked to salute Umuofia before Okika began to speak.

"*Umuofia kwenu!*" he bellowed, raising his left arm and pushing the air with his open hand.

"*Yaa!*" roared Umuofia.

"*Umuofia kwenu!*" he bellowed again, and again and again, facing a new direction each time. And the crowd answered, "*Yaa!*"

There was immediate silence as though cold water had been poured on a roaring flame.

Okika sprang to his feet and also saluted his clansmen four times. Then he began to speak:

"You all know why we are here, when we ought to be building our barns or mending our huts, when we should be putting our compounds in order. My father used to say to me: 'Whenever you see a toad jumping in broad daylight, then know that something is after its life.' When I saw you all pouring into this meeting from all the quarters of our clan so early in the morning, I knew

---

3. "Who surpasses [God]?" (a rhetorical question).

that something was after our life." He paused for a brief moment and then began again:

"All our gods are weeping. Idemili is weeping, Ogwugwu is weeping, Agbala is weeping, and all the others. Our dead fathers are weeping because of the shameful sacrilege they are suffering and the abomination we have all seen with our eyes." He stopped again to steady his trembling voice.

"This is a great gathering. No clan can boast of greater numbers or greater valour. But are we all here? I ask you: Are all the sons of Umuofia with us here?" A deep murmur swept through the crowd.

"They are not," he said. "They have broken the clan and gone their several ways. We who are here this morning have remained true to our fathers, but our brothers have deserted us and joined a stranger to soil their fatherland. If we fight the stranger we shall hit our brothers and perhaps shed the blood of a clansman. But we must do it. Our fathers never dreamt of such a thing, they never killed their brothers. But a white man never came to them. So we must do what our fathers would never have done. Eneke the bird was asked why he was always on the wing and he replied: 'Men have learnt to shoot without missing their mark and I have learnt to fly without perching on a twig.' We must root out this evil. And if our brothers take the side of evil we must root them out too. And we must do it *now*. We must bale this water now that it is only ankle-deep. . . ."

At this point there was a sudden stir in the crowd and every eye was turned in one direction. There was a sharp bend in the road that led from the market place to the white man's court, and to the stream beyond it. And so no one had seen the approach of the five court messengers until they had come round the bend, a few paces from the edge of the crowd. Okonkwo was sitting at the edge.

He sprang to his feet as soon as he saw who it was. He confronted the head messenger, trembling with hate, unable to utter a word. The man was fearless and stood his ground, his four men lined up behind him.

In that brief moment the world seemed to stand still, waiting. There was utter silence. The men of Umuofia were merged into the mute backcloth of trees and giant creepers, waiting.

The spell was broken by the head messenger. "Let me pass!" he ordered.

"What do you want here?"

"The white man whose power you know too well has ordered this meeting to stop."

In a flash Okonkwo drew his matchet. The messenger crouched to avoid the blow. It was useless. Okonkwo's matchet descended twice and the man's head lay beside his uniformed body.

The waiting backcloth jumped into tumultuous life and the meeting was stopped. Okonkwo stood looking at the dead man. He knew that Umuofia would not go to war. He knew because they had let the other messengers escape. They had broken into tumult instead of action. He discerned fright in that tumult. He heard voices asking: "Why did he do it?"

He wiped his matchet on the sand and went away.

CHAPTER TWENTY-FIVE

When the District Commissioner arrived at Okonkwo's compound at the head of an armed band of soldiers and court messengers he found a small crowd of men sitting wearily in the *obi*. He commanded them to come outside, and they obeyed without a murmur.

"Which among you is called Okonkwo?" he asked through his interpreter.

"He is not here," replied Obierika.

"Where is he?"

"He is not here!"

The Commissioner became angry and red in the face. He warned the men that unless they produced Okonkwo forthwith he would lock them all up. The men murmured among themselves, and Obierika spoke again.

"We can take you where he is, and perhaps your men will help us."

The Commissioner did not understand what Obierika meant when he said, "Perhaps your men will help us." One of the most infuriating habits of these people was their love of superfluous words, he thought.

Obierika with five or six others led the way. The Commissioner and his men followed, their firearms held at the ready. He had warned Obierika that if he and his men played any monkey tricks they would be shot. And so they went.

There was a small bush behind Okonkwo's compound. The only opening into this bush from the compound was a little round hole in the red-earth wall through which fowls went in and out in their endless search for food. The hole would not let a man through. It was to this bush that Obierika led the Commissioner and his men. They skirted round the compound, keeping close to the wall. The only sound they made was with their feet as they crushed dry leaves.

Then they came to the tree from which Okonkwo's body was dangling, and they stopped dead.

"Perhaps your men can help us bring him down and bury him," said Obierika. "We have sent for strangers from another village to do it for us, but they may be a long time coming."

The District Commissioner changed instantaneously. The resolute administrator in him gave way to the student of primitive customs.

"Why can't you take him down yourselves?" he asked.

"It is against our custom," said one of the men. "It is an abomination for a man to take his own life. It is an offence against the Earth, and a man who commits it will not be buried by his clansmen. His body is evil, and only strangers may touch it. That is why we ask your people to bring him down, because you are strangers."

"Will you bury him like any other man?" asked the Commissioner.

"We cannot bury him. Only strangers can. We shall pay your men to do it. When he has been buried we will then do our duty by him. We shall make sacrifices to cleanse the desecrated land."

Obierika, who had been gazing steadily at his friend's dangling body, turned suddenly to the District Commissioner and said ferociously: "That man was one of the greatest men in Umuofia. You drove him to kill himself; and now he will be buried like a dog. . . ." He could not say any more. His voice trembled and choked his words.

"Shut up!" shouted one of the messengers, quite unnecessarily.

"Take down the body," the Commissioner ordered his chief messenger, "and bring it and all these people to the court."

"Yes, sah," the messenger said, saluting.

The Commissioner went away, taking three or four of the soldiers with him. In the many years in which he had toiled to bring civilisation to different parts of Africa he had learnt a number of things. One of them was that a District Commissioner must never attend to such undignified details as cutting down a hanged man from the tree. Such attention would give the natives a poor opinion of him. In the book which he planned to write he would stress that point. As he walked back to the court he thought about that book. Every day brought him some new material. The story of this man who had killed a messenger and hanged himself would make interesting reading. One could almost write a whole chapter on him. Perhaps not a whole chapter but a reasonable paragraph, at any rate. There was so much else to include, and one must be firm in cutting out details. He had already chosen the title of the book, after much thought: *The Pacification of the Primitive Tribes of the Lower Niger.*

1958

From An Image of Africa: Racism in Conrad's Heart of Darkness

Heart of Darkness projects the image of Africa as 'the other world', the antithesis of Europe and therefore of civilization, a place where man's vaunted intelligence and refinement are finally mocked by triumphant bestiality. The book opens on the River Thames, tranquil, resting peacefully 'at the decline of day after ages of good service done to the race that peopled its banks' (1892).[1] But the actual story will take place on the River Congo, the very antithesis of the Thames. The River Congo is quite decidedly not a River Emeritus.[2] It has rendered no service and enjoys no old-age pension. We are told that 'going up that river was like travelling back to the earliest beginning of the world'.

Is Conrad saying then that these two rivers are very different, one good, the other bad? Yes, but that is not the real point. It is not the differentness that worries Conrad but the lurking hint of kinship, of common ancestry. For the Thames too 'has been one of the dark places of the earth'. It conquered its darkness, of course, and is now in daylight and at peace. But if it were to visit its primordial relative, the Congo, it would run the terrible risk of hearing grotesque echoes of its own forgotten darkness, and falling victim to an avenging recrudescence of the mindless frenzy of the first beginnings.

These suggestive echoes comprise Conrad's famed evocation of the African atmosphere in *Heart of Darkness*. In the final consideration his method amounts to no more than a steady, ponderous, fake-ritualistic repetition of two antithetical sentences, one about silence and the other about frenzy. We can inspect samples of this on pages 1914 and 1916: (a) 'It was the stillness of an implacable force brooding over an inscrutable intention' and (b) 'The steamer toiled along slowly on the edge of a black and incomprehensible frenzy.' Of course there is a judicious change of adjective from time to time, so that instead of inscrutable', for example, you might have 'unspeakable', even plain 'mysterious', etc., etc.

The eagle-eyed English critic F. R. Leavis[3] drew attention long ago to

---

1. Page numbers refer to this volume of *The Norton Anthology of English Literature.*
2. Honorably discharged from service.

3. Frank Raymond Leavis (1895–1978), famous English literary critic and Cambridge University academic.

Conrad's 'adjectival insistence upon inexpressible and incomprehensible mystery'. That insistence must not be dismissed lightly, as many Conrad critics have tended to do, as a mere stylistic flaw; for it raises serious questions of artistic good faith. When a writer while pretending to record scenes, incidents and their impact is in reality engaged in inducing hypnotic stupor in his readers through a bombardment of emotive words and other forms of trickery, much more has to be at stake than stylistic felicity. Generally normal readers are well armed to detect and resist such underhand activity. But Conrad chose his subject well—one which was guaranteed not to put him in conflict with the psychological predisposition of his readers or raise the need for him to contend with their resistance. He chose the role of purveyor of comforting myths.

The most interesting and revealing passages in *Heart of Darkness* are, however, about people. I must crave the indulgence of my reader to quote almost a whole page from about the middle of the story when representatives of Europe in a steamer going down the Congo encounter the denizens of Africa:

> We were wanderers on a prehistoric earth, on an earth that wore the aspect of an unknown planet. We could have fancied ourselves the first of men taking possession of an accursed inheritance, to be subdued at the cost of profound anguish and of excessive toil. But suddenly, as we struggled round a bend, there would be a glimpse of rush walls, of peaked grass-roofs, a burst of yells, a whirl of black limbs, a mass of hands clapping, of feet stamping, of bodies swaying, of eyes rolling, under the droop of heavy and motionless foliage. The steamer toiled along slowly on the edge of the black and incomprehensible frenzy. The prehistoric man was cursing us, praying to us, welcoming us—who could tell? We were cut off from the comprehension of our surroundings; we glided past like phantoms, wondering and secretly appalled, as sane men would be before an enthusiastic outbreak in a madhouse. We could not understand because we were too far and could not remember because we were travelling in the night of first ages, of those ages that are gone, leaving hardly a sign— and no memories.
>
> The earth seemed unearthly. We are accustomed to look upon the shackled form of a conquered monster, but there—there you could look at a thing monstrous and free. It was unearthly, and the men were—No, they were not inhuman. Well, you know, that was the worst of it—this suspicion of their not being inhuman. It would come slowly to one. They howled and leaped, and spun, and made horrid faces; but what thrilled you was just the thought of their humanity—like yours—the thought of your remote kinship with this wild and passionate uproar. Ugly. Yes, it was ugly enough; but if you were man enough you would admit to yourself that there was in you just the faintest trace of a response to the terrible frankness of that noise, a dim suspicion of there being a meaning in it which you—you so remote from the night of first ages—could comprehend. (1916)

Herein lies the meaning of *Heart of Darkness* and the fascination it holds over the Western mind: 'What thrilled you was just the thought of their humanity— like yours . . . Ugly.'

Having shown us Africa in the mass, Conrad then zeros in, half a page later, on a specific example, giving us one of his rare descriptions of an African who is not just limbs or rolling eyes:

And between whiles I had to look after the savage who was fireman. He was an improved specimen; he could fire up a vertical boiler. He was there below me, and, upon my word, to look at him was as edifying as seeing a dog in a parody of breeches and a feather hat, walking on his hind legs. A few months of training had done for that really fine chap. He squinted at the steam gauge and at the water gauge with an evident effort of intrepidity—and he had filed his teeth, too, the poor devil, and the wool of his pate shaved into queer patterns, and three ornamental scars on each of his cheeks. He ought to have been clapping his hands and stamping his feet on the bank, instead of which he was hard at work, a thrall to strange witchcraft, full of improving knowledge. (1916–17)

As everybody knows, Conrad is a romantic on the side. He might not exactly admire savages clapping their hands and stamping their feet but they have at least the merit of being in their place, unlike this dog in a parody of breeches. For Conrad things being in their place is of the utmost importance.

'Fine fellows—cannibals—in their place,' he tells us pointedly. Tragedy begins when things leave their accustomed place, like Europe leaving its safe stronghold between the policeman and the baker to take a peep into the heart of darkness.

Before the story takes us into the Congo basin proper we are given this nice little vignette as an example of things in their place:

Now and then a boat from the shore gave one a momentary contact with reality. It was paddled by black fellows. You could see from afar the white of their eyeballs glistening. They shouted, sang; their bodies streamed with perspiration; they had faces like grotesque masks—these chaps; but they had bone, muscle, a wild vitality, an intense energy of movement, that was as natural and true as the surf along their coast. They wanted no excuse for being there. They were a great comfort to look at. (1899)

Towards the end of the story Conrad lavishes a whole page quite unexpectedly on an African woman who has obviously been some kind of mistress to Mr Kurtz and now presides (if I may be permitted a little liberty) like a formidable mystery over the inexorable imminence of his departure:

She was savage and superb, wild-eyed and magnificent . . . She stood looking at us without a stir and like the wilderness itself, with an air of brooding over an inscrutable purpose. (1935)

This Amazon is drawn in considerable detail, albeit of a predictable nature, for two reasons. First, she is in her place and so can win Conrad's special brand of approval; and second, she fulfils a structural requirement of the story: a savage counterpart to the refined, European woman who will step forth to end the story:

She came forward, all in black with a pale head, floating toward me in the dusk. She was in mourning . . . She took both my hands in hers and murmured, 'I had heard you were coming' . . . She had a mature capacity for fidelity, for belief, for suffering. (1945)

The difference in the attitude of the novelist to these two women is conveyed in too many direct and subtle ways to need elaboration. But perhaps the most significant difference is the one implied in the author's bestowal of human expression to the one and the withholding of it from the other. It is clearly not part of Conrad's purpose to confer language on the 'rudimentary souls' of Africa. In place of speech they made 'a violent babble of uncouth sounds'. They 'exchanged short grunting phrases' even among themselves. But most of the time they were too busy with their frenzy. There are two occasions in the book, however, when Conrad departs somewhat from his practice and confers speech, even English speech, on the savages. The first occurs when cannibalism gets the better of them:

> 'Catch 'im,' he snapped, with a bloodshot widening of his eyes and a flash of sharp white teeth—'catch 'im. Give 'im to us.' 'To you, eh?' I asked; 'what would you do with them?' 'Eat 'im!' he said curtly. (1919)

The other occasion was the famous announcement: 'Mistah Kurtz—he dead' (1941).

At first sight these instances might be mistaken for unexpected acts of generosity from Conrad. In reality they constitute some of his best assaults. In the case of the cannibals the incomprehensible grunts that had thus far served them for speech suddenly proved inadequate for Conrad's purpose of letting the European glimpse the unspeakable craving in their hearts. Weighing the necessity for consistency in the portrayal of the dumb brutes against the sensational advantages of securing their conviction by clear, unambiguous evidence issuing out of their own mouth Conrad chose the latter. As for the announcement of Mr Kurtz's death by the 'insolent black head in the doorway', what better or more appropriate *finis* could be written to the horror story of that wayward child of civilization who wilfully had given his soul to the powers of darkness and 'taken a high seat amongst the devils of the land' than the proclamation of his physical death by the forces he had joined?

It might be contended, of course, that the attitude to the African in *Heart of Darkness* is not Conrad's but that of his fictional narrator, Marlow, and that far from endorsing it Conrad might indeed be holding it up to irony and criticism. Certainly Conrad appears to go to considerable pains to set up layers of insulation between himself and the moral universe of his story. He has, for example, a narrator behind a narrator. The primary narrator is Marlow but his account is given to us through the filter of a second, shadowy person. But if Conrad's intention is to draw a cordon sanitaire[4] between himself and the moral and psychological *malaise* of his narrator his care seems to me totally wasted because he neglects to hint, clearly and adequately, at an alternative frame of reference by which we may judge the actions and opinions of his characters. It would not have been beyond Conrad's power to make that provision if he had thought it necessary. Conrad seems to me to approve of Marlow, with only minor reservations—a fact reinforced by the similarities between their two careers.

Marlow comes through to us not only as a witness of truth, but one holding those advanced and humane views appropriate to the English liberal tradition which required all Englishmen of decency to be deeply shocked by atrocities in Bulgaria or the Congo of King Leopold of the Belgians[5] or wherever.

Thus Marlow is able to toss out such bleeding-heart sentiments as these:

---

4. A guarded line between infected and uninfected areas.

5. Leopold II (1835–1909) satisfied a lust for personal wealth by the brutal exploitation of the people of the Belgian Congo.

They were all dying slowly—it was very clear. They were not enemies, they were not criminals, they were nothing earthly now—nothing but black shadows of disease and starvation, lying confusedly in the greenish gloom. Brought from all the recesses of the coast in all the legality of time contracts, lost in uncongenial surroundings, fed on unfamiliar food, they sickened, became inefficient, and were then allowed to crawl away and rest. (1901)

The kind of liberalism espoused here by Marlow/Conrad touched all the best minds of the age in England, Europe and America. It took different forms in the minds of different people but almost always managed to sidestep the ultimate question of equality between white people and black people. That extraordinary missionary, Albert Schweitzer,[6] who sacrificed brilliant careers in music and theology in Europe for a life of service to Africans in much the same area as Conrad writes about, epitomizes the ambivalence. In a comment which has often been quoted Schweitzer says: 'The African is indeed my brother but my junior brother.' And so he proceeded to build a hospital appropriate to the needs of junior brothers with standards of hygiene reminiscent of medical practice in the days before the germ theory of disease came into being. Naturally he became a sensation in Europe and America. Pilgrims flocked, and I believe still flock even after he has passed on, to witness the prodigious miracle in Lamberene, on the edge of the primeval forest.

Conrad's liberalism would not take him quite as far as Schweitzer's, though. He would not use the word 'brother' however qualified; the farthest he would go was 'kinship'. When Marlow's African helmsman falls down with a spear in his heart he gives his white master one final disquieting look:

And the intimate profundity of that look he gave me when he received his hurt remains to this day in my memory—like a claim of distant kinship affirmed in a supreme moment.

It is important to note that Conrad, careful as ever with his words, is concerned not so much about 'distant kinship' as about someone *laying a claim* on it. The black man lays a claim on the white man which is well-nigh intolerable. It is the laying of this claim which frightens and at the same time fascinates Conrad, 'the thought of their humanity—like yours . . . Ugly.'

The point of my observations should be quite clear by now, namely that Joseph Conrad was a thoroughgoing racist. That this simple truth is glossed over in criticisms of his work is due to the fact that white racism against Africa is such a normal way of thinking that its manifestations go completely unremarked. Students of *Heart of Darkness* will often tell you that Conrad is concerned not so much with Africa as with the deterioration of one European mind caused by solitude and sickness. They will point out to you that Conrad is, if anything, less charitable to the Europeans in the story than he is to the natives, that the point of the story is to ridicule Europe's civilizing mission in Africa. A Conrad student informed me in Scotland that Africa is merely a setting for the disintegration of the mind of Mr Kurtz.

Which is partly the point. Africa as setting and backdrop which eliminates the African as human factor. Africa as a metaphysical battlefield devoid of all recognizable humanity, into which the wandering European enters at his peril.

6. Medical missionary (1875–1965), who established a hospital at Lambaréné, Gabon (then in French Equatorial Africa), famous for its treatment of lepers.

Can nobody see the preposterous and perverse arrogance in thus reducing Africa to the role of props for the break-up of one petty European mind? But that is not even the point. The real question is the dehumanization of Africa and Africans which this age-long attitude has fostered and continues to foster in the world. And the question is whether a novel which celebrates this dehumanization, which depersonalizes a portion of the human race, can be called a great work of art. My answer is: No, it cannot.

1975   1977

ALICE MUNRO
b. 1931

Alice Munro has become one of the leading short-story writers of her generation. Her fiction combines spareness and realism—an uncompromising look at a panorama of faltering lives—with magisterial vision and expansiveness. Munro's signature approach to the short story, in which she uses a deceptively simple style to produce complex, layered, and emotionally potent effects, has influenced many of her English-language contemporaries, both within and outside Canada. In addition to one novel, *Lives of Girls and Women* (1972), she has published numerous collections of short stories, including *Dance of the Happy Shades* (1968), *Something I've Been Meaning to Tell You* (1974), *The Moons of Jupiter* (1982), *Friend of My Youth* (1990), *The Love of a Good Woman* (1998), *Hateship, Friendship, Courtship, Loveship, Marriage* (2001), and *Runaway* (2004).

Many of Munro's stories are written in the first person, often from the perspective of women whose voices and experiences suggest the author's history. She was born Alice Anne Laidlaw to a poor family in Wingham, Ontario, and her parents' struggles within a variety of rural occupations continued throughout her childhood. She began writing in her teens and in 1949 enrolled in the University of Western Ontario; she left the university two years later, to marry and raise three daughters. She typically sets her stories in small towns where poverty stamps itself on all facets of life, and where women confront—often in a spirit that combines resignation with stubborn resistance—the triple binds of economic, gender, and cultural confinement. Through a precise and particular emphasis on setting and character, she evokes rural Canadian life in the decades following midcentury, when modernity and the promise of the future are often crowded out by a hardening sense of the past.

In an early writing Munro describes an approach to the outside world that effectively captures her sense of the mystery within the ordinary—the hallmark of her realist style: "It seems as if there are feelings that have to be translated into a next-door language, which might blow them up and burst them altogether; or else they have to be let alone. The truth about them is always suspected, never verified, the light catches but doesn't define them. . . . Yet there is the feeling—I have the feeling—that at some level these things open; fragments, moments, suggestions, open, full of power." This aura of openness and suggestion, conveyed through "next-door language," gives Munro's stories their haunting aspect, their quality of movement, rippling and widening from the small-scale to the magnificent. The story included here, "Walker Brothers Cowboy," exemplifies her ability to imbue "fragments, moments, suggestions" with fullness and power, as we view through a young girl's eyes both the pathos and the degradation of men and women whose lives have fallen into a potentially deadening cycle of promise and decay.

Walker Brothers Cowboy[1]

After supper my father says, "Want to go down and see if the Lake's still there?" We leave my mother sewing under the dining-room light, making clothes for me against[2] the opening of school. She has ripped up for this purpose an old suit and an old plaid wool dress of hers, and she has to cut and match very cleverly and also make me stand and turn for endless fittings, sweaty, itching from the hot wool, ungrateful. We leave my brother in bed in the little screened porch at the end of the front veranda, and sometimes he kneels on his bed and presses his face against the screen and calls mournfully, "Bring me an ice-cream cone!" but I call back, "You will be asleep," and do not even turn my head.

Then my father and I walk gradually down a long, shabby sort of street, with Silverwoods Ice Cream signs standing on the sidewalk, outside tiny, lighted stores. This is in Tuppertown, an old town on Lake Huron,[3] an old grain port. The street is shaded, in some places, by maple trees whose roots have cracked and heaved the sidewalk and spread out like crocodiles into the bare yards. People are sitting out, men in shirtsleeves and undershirts and women in aprons—not people we know but if anybody looks ready to nod and say, "Warm night," my father will nod too and say something the same. Children are still playing. I don't know them either because my mother keeps my brother and me in our own yard, saying he is too young to leave it and I have to mind him. I am not so sad to watch their evening games because the games themselves are ragged, dissolving. Children, of their own will, draw apart, separate into islands of two or one under the heavy trees, occupying themselves in such solitary ways as I do all day, planting pebbles in the dirt or writing in it with a stick.

Presently we leave these yards and houses behind; we pass a factory with boarded-up windows, a lumberyard whose high wooden gates are locked for the night. Then the town falls away in a defeated jumble of sheds and small junkyards, the sidewalk gives up and we are walking on a sandy path with burdocks, plantains, humble nameless weeds all around. We enter a vacant lot, a kind of park really, for it is kept clear of junk and there is one bench with a slat missing on the back, a place to sit and look at the water. Which is generally gray in the evening, under a lightly overcast sky, no sunsets, the horizon dim. A very quiet, washing noise on the stones of the beach. Further along, towards the main part of town, there is a stretch of sand, a water slide, floats bobbing around the safe swimming area, a lifeguard's rickety throne. Also a long dark-green building, like a roofed veranda, called the Pavilion, full of farmers and their wives, in stiff good clothes, on Sundays. That is the part of the town we used to know when we lived at Dungannon and came here three or four times a summer, to the Lake. That, and the docks where we would go and look at the grain boats, ancient, rusty, wallowing, making us wonder how they got past the breakwater let alone to Fort William.

Tramps hang around the docks and occasionally on these evenings wander up the dwindling beach and climb the shifting, precarious path boys have

---

1. Refers to a traveling salesman for a Canadian company, which is probably modeled on the American direct marketer Watkins Products.
2. In time for.

3. One of the Great Lakes, bordering on Ontario and eastern Michigan. Place-names are both real and invented.

made, hanging on to dry bushes, and say something to my father which, being frightened of tramps, I am too alarmed to catch. My father says he is a bit hard up himself. "I'll roll you a cigarette if it's any use to you," he says, and he shakes tobacco out carefully on one of the thin butterfly papers, flicks it with his tongue, seals it and hands it to the tramp, who takes it and walks away. My father also rolls and lights and smokes one cigarette of his own.

He tells me how the Great Lakes came to be. All where Lake Huron is now, he says, used to be flat land, a wide flat plain. Then came the ice, creeping down from the North, pushing deep into the low places. Like *that*—and he shows me his hand with his spread fingers pressing the rock-hard ground where we are sitting. His fingers make hardly any impression at all and he says, "Well, the old ice cap had a lot more power behind it than this hand has." And then the ice went back, shrank back towards the North Pole where it came from, and left its fingers of ice in the deep places it had gouged, and ice turned to lakes and there they were today. They were *new,* as time went. I try to see that plain before me, dinosaurs walking on it, but I am not able even to imagine the shore of the Lake when the Indians were there, before Tuppertown. The tiny share we have of time appalls me, though my father seems to regard it with tranquillity. Even my father, who sometimes seems to me to have been at home in the world as long as it has lasted, has really lived on this earth only a little longer than I have, in terms of all the time there has been to live in. He has not known a time, any more than I, when automobiles and electric lights did not at least exist. He was not alive when this century started. I will be barely alive—old, old—when it ends. I do not like to think of it. I wish the Lake to be always just a lake, with the safe-swimming floats marking it, and the breakwater and the lights of Tuppertown.

My father has a job, selling for Walker Brothers. This is a firm that sells almost entirely in the country, the back country. Sunshine, Boylesbridge, Turnaround—that is all his territory. Not Dungannon where we used to live, Dungannon is too near town and my mother is grateful for that. He sells cough medicine, iron tonic, corn plasters, laxatives, pills for female disorders, mouthwash, shampoo, liniment, salves, lemon and orange and raspberry concentrate for making refreshing drinks, vanilla, food coloring, black and green tea, ginger, cloves, and other spices, rat poison. He has a song about it, with these two lines:

> And have all liniments and oils,
> For everything from corns to boils. . . .

Not a very funny song, in my mother's opinion. A peddler's song, and that is what he is, a peddler knocking at backwoods kitchens. Up until last winter we had our own business, a fox farm. My father raised silver foxes and sold their pelts to the people who make them into capes and coats and muffs. Prices fell, my father hung on hoping they would get better next year, and they fell again, and he hung on one more year and one more and finally it was not possible to hang on anymore, we owed everything to the feed company. I have heard my mother explain this, several times, to Mrs. Oliphant, who is the only neighbor she talks to. (Mrs. Oliphant also has come down in the world, being a schoolteacher who married the janitor.) We poured all we had into it, my mother says, and we came out with nothing. Many people could say the same thing, these days, but my mother has no time for the national calamity, only ours. Fate has flung us onto a street of poor people (it does not matter that we were poor before; that was a different sort of poverty), and the only way to take this, as she sees it, is with dignity, with bitterness, with no reconciliation. No bathroom with a claw-footed tub and a flush toilet is going to comfort her, nor water on tap and sidewalks past the house and milk in bottles, not even the two movie theatres and the Venus Restaurant and Woolworths so marvellous it has live birds singing in its fan-cooled corners and fish as tiny as fingernails, as bright as moons, swimming in its green tanks. My mother does not care.

In the afternoons she often walks to Simon's Grocery and takes me with her to help carry things. She wears a good dress, navy blue with little flowers, sheer, worn over a navy-blue slip. Also a summer hat of white straw, pushed down on the side of the head, and white shoes I have just whitened on a newspaper on the back steps. I have my hair freshly done in long damp curls which the dry air will fortunately soon loosen, a stiff large hair ribbon on top of my head. This is entirely different from going out after supper with my father. We have not walked past two houses before I feel we have become objects of universal ridicule. Even the dirty words chalked on the sidewalk are laughing at us. My mother does not seem to notice. She walks serenely like a lady shopping, like a *lady* shopping, past the housewives in loose beltless dresses torn under the arms. With me her creation, wretched curls and flaunting hair bow, scrubbed knees and white socks—all I do not want to be. I loathe even my name when she says it in public, in a voice so high, proud, and ringing, deliberately different from the voice of any other mother on the street.

My mother will sometimes carry home, for a treat, a brick of ice cream— pale Neapolitan; and because we have no refrigerator in our house we wake my brother and eat it at once in the dining room, always darkened by the wall of the house next door. I spoon it up tenderly, leaving the chocolate till last, hoping to have some still to eat when my brother's dish is empty. My mother tries then to imitate the conversations we used to have at Dungannon, going back to our earliest, most leisurely days before my brother was born, when she would give me a little tea and a lot of milk in a cup like hers and we would sit out on the step facing the pump, the lilac tree, the fox pens beyond. She is not able to keep from mentioning those days. "Do you remember when we put you in your sled and Major pulled you?" (Major our dog, that we had to leave with neighbors when we moved.) "Do you remember your sandbox outside the kitchen window?" I pretend to remember far less than I do, wary of being trapped into sympathy or any unwanted emotion.

My mother has headaches. She often has to lie down. She lies on my brother's narrow bed in the little screened porch, shaded by heavy branches. "I look up at that tree and I think I am at home," she says.

"What you need," my father tells her, "is some fresh air and a drive in the country." He means for her to go with him, on his Walker Brothers route.

That is not my mother's idea of a drive in the country.

"Can I come?"

"Your mother might want you for trying on clothes."

"I'm beyond sewing this afternoon," my mother says.

"I'll take her then. Take both of them, give you a rest."

What is there about us that people need to be given a rest from? Never mind. I am glad enough to find my brother and make him go to the toilet and get us both into the car, our knees unscrubbed, my hair unringleted. My father brings from the house his two heavy brown suitcases, full of bottles, and sets them on the back seat. He wears a white shirt, brilliant in the sunlight, a tie, light trousers belonging to his summer suit (his other suit is black, for funerals, and belonged to my uncle before he died), and a creamy straw hat. His salesman's outfit, with pencils clipped in the shirt pocket. He goes back once again, probably to say goodbye to my mother, to ask her if she is sure she doesn't want to come, and hear her say, "No. No thanks, I'm better just to lie here with my eyes closed." Then we are backing out of the driveway with the rising hope of adventure, just the little hope that takes you over the bump into the street, the hot air starting to move, turning into a breeze, the houses growing less and less familiar as we follow the shortcut my father knows, the quick way out of town. Yet what is there waiting for us all afternoon but hot hours in stricken farmyards, perhaps a stop at a country store and three ice-cream cones or bottles of pop, and my father singing? The one he made up about himself has a title—"The Walker Brothers Cowboy"—and it starts out like this:

> Old Ned Fields, he now is dead,
> So I am ridin' the route instead. . . .

Who is Ned Fields? The man he has replaced, surely, and if so he really is dead; yet my father's voice is mournful-jolly, making his death some kind of nonsense, a comic calamity. "Wisht I was back on the Rio Grande,[4] plungin' through the dusky sand." My father sings most of the time while driving the car. Even now, heading out of town, crossing the bridge and taking the sharp turn onto the highway, he is humming something, mumbling a bit of a song to himself, just tuning up, really, getting ready to improvise, for out along the highway we pass the Baptist Camp, the Vacation Bible Camp, and he lets loose:

> Where are the Baptists, where are the Bapists,
> where are all the Baptists today?
> They're down in the water, in Lake Huron water,
> with their sins all a-gittin' washed away.

My brother takes this for straight truth and gets up on his knees trying to see down to the Lake. "I don't see any Baptists," he says accusingly. "Neither do I, son," says my father. "I told you, they're down in the Lake."

No roads paved when we left the highway. We have to roll up the windows because of dust. The land is flat, scorched, empty. Bush lots at the back of the farms hold shade, black pine-shade like pools nobody can ever get to. We bump up a long lane and at the end of it what could look more unwelcoming, more deserted than the tall unpainted farmhouse with grass growing uncut right up to the front door, green blinds down, and a door upstairs opening on nothing but air? Many houses have this door, and I have never yet been able to find out why. I ask my father and he says they are for walking in your sleep. *What?* Well, if you happen to be walking in your sleep and you want to step outside. I am offended, seeing too late that he is joking, as usual, but my brother says sturdily, "If they did that they would break their necks."

The 1930s. How much this kind of farmhouse, this kind of afternoon seem

---

4. A large river that begins in Colorado and flows south, becoming the border between Mexico and the United States.

to me to belong to that one decade in time, just as my father's hat does, his bright flared tie, our car with its wide running board (an Essex, and long past its prime). Cars somewhat like it, many older, none dustier, sit in the farm-yards. Some are past running and have their doors pulled off, their seats removed for use on porches. No living things to be seen, chickens or cattle. Except dogs. There are dogs lying in any kind of shade they can find, dreaming, their lean sides rising and sinking rapidly. They get up when my father opens the car door, he has to speak to them. "Nice boy, there's a boy, nice old boy." They quiet down, go back to their shade. He should know how to quiet ani-mals, he has held desperate foxes with tongs around their necks. One gentling voice for the dogs and another, rousing, cheerful, for calling at doors. "Hello there, missus, it's the Walker Brothers man and what are you out of today?" A door opens, he disappears. Forbidden to follow, forbidden even to leave the car, we can just wait and wonder what he says. Sometimes trying to make my mother laugh, he pretends to be himself in a farm kitchen, spreading out his sample case. "Now then, missus, are you troubled with parasitic life? Your children's scalps, I mean. All those crawly little things we're too polite to men-tion that show up on the heads of the best of families? Soap alone is useless, kerosene is not too nice a perfume, but I have here—" Or else, "Believe me, sitting and driving all day the way I do I *know* the value of these fine pills. Natural relief. A problem common to old folks too, once their days of activity are over—How about you, Grandma?" He would wave the imaginary box of pills under my mother's nose and she would laugh finally, unwillingly. "He doesn't say that really, does he?" I said, and she said no of course not, he was too much of a gentleman.

One yard after another, then, the old cars, the pumps, dogs, views of gray barns and falling-down sheds and unturning windmills. The men, if they are working in the fields, are not in any fields that we can see. The children are far away, following dry creek beds or looking for blackberries, or else they are hidden in the house, spying at us through cracks in the blinds. The car seat has grown slick with our sweat. I dare my brother to sound the horn, wanting to do it myself but not wanting to get the blame. He knows better. We play I Spy, but it is hard to find many colors. Gray for the barns and sheds and toilets and houses, brown for the yard and fields, black or brown for the dogs. The rusting cars show rainbow patches, in which I strain to pick out purple or green; likewise I peer at doors for shreds of old peeling paint, maroon or yellow. We can't play with letters, which would be better, because my brother is too young to spell. The game disintegrates anyway. He claims my colors are not fair, and wants extra turns.

In one house no door opens, though the car is in the yard. My father knocks and whistles, calls, "Hullo there ! Walker Brothers man!" but there is not a stir of reply anywhere. This house has no porch, just a bare, slanting slab of cement on which my father stands. He turns around, searching the barnyard, the barn whose mow must be empty because you can see the sky through it, and finally he bends to pick up his suitcases. Just then a window is opened upstairs, a white pot appears on the sill, is tilted over and its contents splash down the outside wall. The window is not directly above my father's head, so only a stray splash would catch him. He picks up his suitcases with no partic-ular hurry and walks, no longer whistling, to the car. "Do you know what that was?" I say to my brother. "*Pee.*" He laughs and laughs.

My father rolls and lights a cigarette before he starts the car. The window has been slammed down, the blind drawn, we never did see a hand or face. "Pee, pee," sings my brother ecstatically. "Somebody dumped down pee!" "Just don't tell your mother that," my father says. "She isn't liable to see the joke." "Is it in your song?" my brother wants to know. My father says no but he will see what he can do to work it in.

I notice in a little while that we are not turning in any more lanes, though it does not seem to me that we are headed home. "Is this the way to Sunshine?" I ask my father, and he answers, "No, ma'am, it's not." "Are we still in your territory?" He shakes his head. "We're going *fast*," my brother says approvingly, and in fact we are bouncing along through dry puddle-holes so that all the bottles in the suitcases clink together and gurgle promisingly.

Another lane, a house, also unpainted, dried to silver in the sun.

"I thought we were out of your territory."

"We are."

"Then what are we going in here for?"

"You'll see."

In front of the house a short, sturdy woman is picking up washing, which had been spread on the grass to bleach and dry. When the car stops she stares at it hard for a moment, bends to pick up a couple more towels to add to the bundle under her arm, comes across to us and says in a flat voice, neither welcoming nor unfriendly, "Have you lost your way?"

My father takes his time getting out of the car. "I don't think so," he says. "I'm the Walker Brothers man."

"George Golley is our Walker Brothers man," the woman says, "and he was out here no more than a week ago. Oh, my Lord God," she says harshly, "it's you."

"It was, the last time I looked in the mirror," my father says.

The woman gathers all the towels in front of her and holds on to them tightly, pushing them against her stomach as if it hurt. "Of all the people I never thought to see. And telling me you were the Walker Brothers man."

"I'm sorry if you were looking forward to George Golley," my father says humbly.

"And look at me, I was prepared to clean the henhouse. You'll think that's just an excuse but it's true. I don't go round looking like this every day." She is wearing a farmer's straw hat, through which pricks of sunlight penetrate and float on her face, a loose, dirty print smock, and canvas shoes. "Who are those in the car, Ben? They're not yours?"

"Well, I hope and believe they are," my father says, and tells our names and ages. "Come on, you can get out. This is Nora, Miss Cronin. Nora, you better tell me, is it still Miss, or have you got a husband hiding in the woodshed?"

"If I had a husband that's not where I'd keep him, Ben," she says, and they both laugh, her laugh abrupt and somewhat angry. "You'll think I got no manners, as well as being dressed like a tramp," she says. "Come on in out of the sun. It's cool in the house."

We go across the yard ("Excuse me taking you in this way but I don't think the front door has been opened since Papa's funeral, I'm afraid the hinges might drop off"), up the porch steps, into the kitchen, which really is cool, high-ceilinged, the blinds of course down, a simple, clean, threadbare room with waxed worn linoleum, potted geraniums, drinking-pail and dipper, a round table with scrubbed oilcloth. In spite of the cleanness, the wiped and swept surfaces, there is a faint sour smell—maybe of the dishrag or the tin dipper or the oilcloth, or the old lady, because there is one, sitting in an easy chair under the clock shelf. She turns her head slightly in our direction and says, "Nora? Is that company?"

"Blind," says Nora in a quick explaining voice to my father. Then, "You won't guess who it is, Momma. Hear his voice."

My father goes to the front of her chair and bends and says hopefully, "Afternoon, Mrs. Cronin."

"Ben Jordan," says the old lady with no surprise. "You haven't been to see us in the longest time. Have you been out of the country?"

My father and Nora look at each other.

"He's married, Momma," says Nora cheerfully and aggressively. "Married and got two children and here they are." She pulls us forward, makes each of us touch the old lady's dry, cool hand while she says our names in turn. Blind! This is the first blind person I have ever seen close up. Her eyes are closed, the eyelids sunk away down, showing no shape of the eyeball, just hollows. From one hollow comes a drop of silver liquid, a medicine, or a miraculous tear.

"Let me get into a decent dress," Nora says. "Talk to Momma. It's a treat for her. We hardly ever see company, do we, Momma?"

"Not many makes it out this road," says the old lady placidly. "And the ones that used to be around here, our old neighbors, some of them have pulled out."

"True everywhere," my father says.

"Where's your wife then?"

"Home. She's not too fond of the hot weather, makes her feel poorly."

"Well." This is a habit of country people, old people, to say "well," meaning, "Is that so?" with a little extra politeness and concern.

Nora's dress, when she appears again—stepping heavily on Cuban heels down the stairs in the hall—is flowered more lavishly than anything my mother owns, green and yellow on brown, some sort of floating sheer crêpe, leaving her arms bare. Her arms are heavy, and every bit of her skin you can see is covered with little dark freckles like measles. Her hair is short, black, coarse and curly, her teeth very white and strong. "It's the first time I knew there was such a thing as green poppies," my father says, looking at her dress.

"You would be surprised all the things you never knew," says Nora, sending a smell of cologne far and wide when she moves and displaying a change of voice to go with the dress, something more sociable and youthful. "They're not poppies anyway, they're just flowers. You go and pump me some good cold water and I'll make these children a drink." She gets down from the cupboard a bottle of Walker Brothers Orange syrup.

"You telling me you were the Walker Brothers man!"

"It's the truth, Nora. You go and look at my sample cases in the car if you don't believe me. I got the territory directly south of here."

"Walker Brothers? Is that a fact? You selling for Walker Brothers?"

"Yes, ma'am."

"We always heard you were raising foxes over Dungannon way."

"That's what I was doing, but I kind of run out of luck in that business."

"So where're you living? How long've you been out selling?"

"We moved into Tuppertown. I been at it, oh, two, three months. It keeps the wolf from the door. Keeps him as far away as the back fence."

Nora laughs. "Well, I guess you count yourself lucky to have the work.

Isabel's husband in Brantford, he was out of work the longest time. I thought if he didn't find something soon I was going to have them all land in here to feed, and I tell you I was hardly looking forward to it. It's all I can manage with me and Momma."

"Isabel married," my father says. "Muriel married too?"

"No, she's teaching school out West. She hasn't been home for five years. I guess she finds something better to do with her holidays. I would if I was her." She gets some snapshots out of the table drawer and starts showing him. "That's Isabel's oldest boy, starting school. That's the baby sitting in her carriage. Isabel and her husband. Muriel. That's her roommate with her. That's a fellow she used to go around with, and his car. He was working in a bank out there. That's her school, it has eight rooms. She teaches Grade Five." My father shakes his head. "I can't think of her any way but when she was going to school, so shy I used to pick her up on the road—I'd be on my way to see you—and she would not say one word, not even to agree it was a nice day."

"She's got over that."

"Who are you talking about?" says the old lady.

"Muriel. I said she's got over being shy."

"She was here last summer."

"No, Momma, that was Isabel. Isabel and her family were here last summer. Muriel's out West."

"I meant Isabel."

Shortly after this the old lady falls asleep, her head on the side, her mouth open. "Excuse her manners," Nora says. "It's old age." She fixes an afghan over her mother and says we can all go into the front room where our talking won't disturb her.

"You two," my father says. "Do you want to go outside and amuse yourselves?"

Amuse ourselves how? Anyway, I want to stay. The front room is more interesting than the kitchen, though barer. There is a gramophone and a pump organ and a picture on the wall of Mary, Jesus' mother—I know that much—in shades of bright blue and pink with a spiked band of light around her head. I know that such pictures are found only in the homes of Roman Catholics and so Nora must be one. We have never known any Roman Catholics at all well, never well enough to visit in their houses. I think of what my grandmother and my Aunt Tena, over in Dungannon, used to always say to indicate that somebody was a Catholic. *So-and-so digs with the wrong foot,* they would say. *She digs with the wrong foot.* That was what they would say about Nora.[5]

Nora takes a bottle, half full, out of the top of the organ and pours some of what is in it into the two glasses that she and my father have emptied of the orange drink.

"Keep it in case of sickness?" my father says.

"Not on your life," says Nora. "I'm never sick. I just keep it because I keep it. One bottle does me a fair time, though, because I don't care for drinking alone. Here's luck!" She and my father drink and I know what it is. Whisky. One of the things my mother has told me in our talks together is that my father never drinks whisky. But I see he does. He drinks whisky and he talks of people whose names I have never heard before. But after a while he turns to a familiar

---

5. Relations between Protestants and Catholics within the Irish population in southern Ontario were often strained.

incident. He tells about the chamberpot that was emptied out the window. "Picture me there," he says, "hollering my heartiest. *Oh, lady, it's your Walker Brothers man, anybody home?*" He does himself hollering, grinning absurdly, waiting, looking up in pleased expectation, and then—oh, ducking, covering his head with his arms, looking as if he begged for mercy (when he never did anything like that, I was watching), and Nora laughs, almost as hard as my brother did at the time.

"That isn't true! That's not a word true!"

"Oh, indeed it is, ma'am. We have our heroes in the ranks of Walker Brothers. I'm glad you think it's funny," he says sombrely.

I ask him shyly, "Sing the song."

"What song? Have you turned into a singer on top of everything else?"

Embarrassed, my father says, "Oh, just this song I made up while I was driving around, it gives me something to do, making up rhymes."

But after some urging he does sing it, looking at Nora with a droll, apologetic expression, and she laughs so much that in places he has to stop and wait for her to get over laughing so he can go on, because she makes him laugh too. Then he does various parts of his salesman's spiel. Nora when she laughs squeezes her large bosom under her folded arms. "You're crazy," she says. "That's all you are." She sees my brother peering into the gramophone and she jumps up and goes over to him. "Here's us sitting enjoying ourselves and not giving you a thought, isn't it terrible?" she says. "You want me to put a record on, don't you? You want to hear a nice record? Can you dance? I bet your sister can, can't she?"

I say no. "A big girl like you and so good-looking and can't dance!" says Nora. "It's high time you learned. I bet you'd make a lovely dancer. Here, I'm going to put on a piece I used to dance to and even your daddy did, in his dancing days. You didn't know your daddy was a dancer, did you? Well, he is a talented man, your daddy!"

She puts down the lid and takes hold of me unexpectedly around the waist, picks up my other hand, and starts making me go backwards. "This is the way, now, this is how they dance. Follow me. This foot, see. One and one-two. One and one-two. That's fine, that's lovely, don't look at your feet! Follow me, that's right, see how easy? You're going to be a lovely dancer! One and one-two. One and one-two. Ben, see your daughter dancing!" *Whispering while you cuddle near me, Whispering so no one can hear me . . .*[6]

Round and round the linoleum, me proud, intent, Nora laughing and moving with great buoyancy, wrapping me in her strange gaiety, her smell of whisky, cologne, and sweat. Under the arms her dress is damp, and little drops form along her upper lip, hang in the soft black hairs at the corners of her mouth. She whirls me around in front of my father—causing me to stumble, for I am by no means so swift a pupil as she pretends—and lets me go, breathless.

"Dance with me, Ben."

"I'm the world's worst dancer, Nora, and you know it."

"I certainly never thought so."

"You would now."

She stands in front of him, arms hanging loose and hopeful, her breasts,

---

6. From the popular song "Whispering," whose original 1920 recording was one of the first records to sell a million copies.

which a moment ago embarrassed me with their warmth and bulk, rising and falling under her loose flowered dress, her face shining with the exercise, and delight.

"Ben."

My father drops his head and says quietly, "Not me, Nora."

So she can only go and take the record off. "I can drink alone but I can't dance alone," she says. "Unless I am a whole lot crazier than I think I am."

"Nora," says my father, smiling. "You're not crazy."

"Stay for supper."

"Oh, no. We couldn't put you to the trouble."

"It's no trouble. I'd be glad of it."

"And their mother would worry. She'd think I'd turned us over in a ditch."

"Oh, well. Yes."

"We've taken a lot of your time now."

"Time," says Nora bitterly. "Will you come by ever again?"

"I will if I can," says my father.

"Bring the children. Bring your wife."

"Yes, I will," says my father. "I will if I can."

When she follows us to the car he says, "You come to see us too, Nora. We're right on Grove Street, left-hand side going in, that's north, and two doors this side—east—of Baker Street."

Nora does not repeat these directions. She stands close to the car in her soft, brilliant dress. She touches the fender, making an unintelligible mark in the dust there.

On the way home my father does not buy any ice cream or pop, but he does go into a country store and get a package of licorice, which he shares with us. She digs with the wrong foot, I think, and the words seem sad to me as never before, dark, perverse. My father does not say anything to me about not mentioning things at home, but I know, just from the thoughtfulness, the pause when he passes the licorice, that there are things not to be mentioned. The whisky, maybe the dancing. No worry about my brother, he does not notice enough. At most he might remember the blind lady, the picture of Mary.

"Sing," my brother commands my father, but my father says gravely, "I don't know, I seem to be fresh out of songs. You watch the road and let me know if you see any rabbits."

So my father drives and my brother watches the road for rabbits and I feel my father's life flowing back from our car in the last of the afternoon, darkening and turning strange, like a landscape that has an enchantment on it, making it kindly, ordinary and familiar while you are looking at it, but changing it, once your back is turned, into something you will never know, with all kinds of weathers, and distances you cannot imagine.

When we get closer to Tuppertown the sky becomes gently overcast, as always, nearly always, on summer evenings by the Lake.

1968

GEOFFREY HILL
b. 1932

Geoffrey Hill, born in the Worcestershire village of Bromsgrove, educated at its high school and at Keble College, Oxford, has been a professor of English at Leeds University and a lecturer at Cambridge, and is a professor at Boston University. As a boy he was drawn to the Metaphysical poets' "fusion of intellectual strength with simple, sensuous, and passionate immediacy," and his own poems offer something of the same fusion. What he has said of "Annunciations: 2" might have been said of many of his poems: "But I want the poem to have this dubious end; because I feel dubious; and the whole business is dubious." He is a religious poet but a poet of religious doubt—a skeptic confronting the extremes of human experience, "man's inhumanity to man," on the cross and in the concentration camps—or delight in the abundance of the natural world: pain and pleasure alike rendered with a Keatsian richness and specificity, a modernist allusiveness and syntactic contortion. Distinctively resonant as is the voice of Hill's poems, they are consistently impersonal. Even when the poet's earlier self is conflated with that of Offa, eighth-century king of a large part of Britain, in *Mercian Hymns* (1971), subjectivity is dissolved in the objective projection of a historical imagination of great range and power. That book had been concerned at one level with what medieval historians called "the matter of Britain," but a later collection, *Canaan* (1996), bleakly attempts to diagnose the matter *with* Britain (identifying the U.K. with "Canaan, the land of the Philistines," excoriated in the Bible). Hill is at once one of the most ambitious, most difficult, and most rewarding poets now writing in English.

In Memory of Jane Fraser

When snow like sheep lay in the fold°   *shelter for sheep*
And winds went begging at each door,
And the far hills were blue with cold,
And a cold shroud lay on the moor,

5   She kept the siege. And every day
We watched her brooding over death
Like a strong bird above its prey.
The room filled with the kettle's breath.

Damp curtains glued against the pane
10   Sealed time away. Her body froze
As if to freeze us all, and chain
Creation to a stunned repose.

She died before the world could stir.
In March the ice unloosed the brook
15   And water ruffled the sun's hair.
Dead cones upon the alder shook.

1959

Requiem for the Plantagenet Kings[1]

For whom the possessed sea littered, on both shores,
Ruinous arms; being fired, and for good,
To sound the constitution of just wars,
Men, in their eloquent fashion, understood.

5 Relieved of soul, the dropping-back of dust,
Their usage, pride, admitted within doors;
At home, under caved chantries,[2] set in trust,
With well-dressed alabaster and proved spurs
They lie; they lie; secure in the decay
10 Of blood, blood-marks, crowns hacked and coveted,
Before the scouring fires of trial-day
Alight on men; before sleeked groin, gored head,
Budge through the clay and gravel, and the sea
Across daubed rock evacuates its dead.

1959

September Song[1]

born 19.6.32—deported 24.9.42

Undesirable you may have been, untouchable
you were not. Not forgotten
or passed over at the proper time.

As estimated, you died. Things marched,
5 sufficient, to that end.
Just so much Zyklon and leather, patented
terror, so many routine cries.

(I have made
an elegy for myself it
10 is true)[2]

---

1. Dynastic succession of 12th- to 15th-century English kings, beginning with Henry II, who was followed in turn by Richard I, John, Henry III, Edward I, Edward II, Edward III, and Richard II. They ruled not only over England but also over much of France ("on both shores"). The last Plantagenet king was Richard III, who was killed at the Battle of Bosworth on Aug. 22, 1485.

2. Chapels endowed for priests to sing Masses for the souls of those who founded them. Many chantries have cavelike ceilings of vaulted stone and contain effigies—sometimes in alabaster—of their founders.

1. The poem is about the gassing of Jews in German extermination camps; Zyklon-B was the gas used. Hill's fellow poet Jon Silkin has drawn attention to the kind of wit involved in the subtitle, "where the natural event of birth is placed, simply, beside the human and murderous 'deported' as if the latter were of the same order and inevitability for the victim"; he discusses, too, "the irony of conjuncted meanings between 'undesirable' (touching on both sexual desire and racism) and 'untouchable,' which exploits a similar ambiguity but reverses the emphases" and is "unusually dense *and* simple."

2. As the critic Christopher Ricks pointed out, Hill was born on 18.6.32 (June 18, 1932).

September fattens on vines. Roses
flake from the wall. The smoke
of harmless fires drifts to my eyes.

This is plenty. This is more than enough.

1968

From Mercian Hymns[1]

6

The princes of Mercia were badger and raven. Thrall
to their freedom, I dug and hoarded. Orchards
fruited above clefts. I drank from honeycombs of
chill sandstone.

5   "A boy at odds in the house, lonely among brothers."
But I, who had none, fostered a strangeness; gave
myself to unattainable toys.

Candles of gnarled resin, apple-branches, the tacky
mistletoe. "Look" they said and again "look." But
10   I ran slowly; the landscape flowed away, back to
its source.

In the schoolyard, in the cloakrooms, the children
boasted their scars of dried snot; wrists and
knees garnished with impetigo.

7

Gasholders,[2] russet among fields. Milldams, marlpools[3]
that lay unstirring. Eel-swarms. Coagulations of
frogs: once, with branches and half-bricks, he
battered a ditchful; then sidled away from the
5   stillness and silence.

Ceolred[4] was his friend and remained so, even after
the day of the lost fighter: a biplane, already
obsolete and irreplaceable, two inches of heavy
snub silver. Ceolred let it spin through a hole
10   in the classroom-floorboards, softly, into the rat-
droppings and coins.

---

1. The historical Offa reigned over Mercia (and
the greater part of England south of the Humber)
in the years 757–96 C.E. During early medieval
times he was already becoming a creature of legend. The Offa who figures in this sequence might
perhaps most usefully be regarded as the presiding
genius of the West Midlands, his dominion enduring from the middle of the 8th century until the
middle of the 20th (and possibly beyond). The indication of such a timespan will, I trust, explain and
to some extent justify a number of anachronisms
[Hill's note].
2. Or gasometers, large metal receptacles for gas.
3. Pools in deposits of crumbling clay and chalk.
4. A 9th-century bishop of Leicester, but the
name is here used as a characteristic Anglo-Saxon
Mercian name.

After school he lured Ceolred, who was sniggering
with fright, down to the old quarries, and flayed
him. Then, leaving Ceolred, he journeyed for hours,
15   calm and alone, in his private derelict sandlorry
named *Albion.*[5]

28

Processes of generation; deeds of settlement. The
urge to marry well; wit to invest in the proper
ties of healing-springs. Our children and our
children's children, o my masters.

5   Tracks of ancient occupation. Frail ironworks rusting in the thorn-thicket. Hearthstones; charred
lullabies. A solitary axe-blow that is the echo
of a lost sound.

Tumult recedes as though into the long rain. Groves
10   of legendary holly; silverdark the ridged gleam.

30

And it seemed, while we waited, he began to walk towards us   he vanished

he left behind coins, for his lodging, and traces of
red mud.

1971

From An Apology for the Revival of Christian Architecture in England

the spiritual, Platonic old England . . .
    —STC,[1] *Anima Poetae*

"Your situation," said Coningsby, looking up
the green and silent valley, "is absolutely
poetic."

"I try sometimes to fancy," said Mr Millbank,
with a rather fierce smile, "that I am in the
New World."
    —BENJAMIN DISRAELI,[2] *Coningsby*

9. *The Laurel Axe*

Autumn resumes the land, ruffles the woods
with smoky wings, entangles them. Trees shine

---

5. An old Celtic name for England; also the name
of a famous make of British truck. "Sandlorry":
sand truck.
1. Samuel Taylor Coleridge (1772–1834), English
poet and philosopher. The "old England" here is
an idealized orderly rural one.
2. British novelist and statesman (1804–1881).
The "New World" referred to is that of an idealized
rural America.

out from their leaves, rocks mildew to moss-green;
the avenues are spread with brittle floods.

5 Platonic England, house of solitudes,
rests in its laurels and its injured stone,
replete with complex fortunes that are gone,
beset by dynasties of moods and clouds.

It stands, as though at ease with its own world,
10 the mannerly extortions, languid praise,
all that devotion long since bought and sold,

the rooms of cedar and soft-thudding baize,[3]
tremulous boudoirs where the crystals kissed
in cabinets of amethyst and frost.

1978

3. Billiard rooms in British "stately homes." The "soft-thudding baize" may refer either to the soft green cloth covering billiard tables or to the door traditionally covered with green baize dividing the family side of the home from the servants' quarters.

V. S. NAIPAUL
b. 1932

Widely regarded as the most accomplished novelist from the English-speaking Caribbean, Vidiadhar Surajprasad Naipaul was born to a family of Indian descent in Trinidad and educated at Queen's Royal College, Port of Spain, and at University College, Oxford. After settling in England, he became editor of the *Caribbean Voices* program for the British Broadcasting Corporation (1954–56) and fiction reviewer for the *New Statesman* (1957–61). The recipient of many prestigious prizes and awards, he won the Booker Prize in 1971 for *In a Free State*, was knighted in 1990, and received the Nobel Prize in Literature in 2001. He continues to live and write in England.

Naipaul's first three books, *The Mystic Masseur* (1957), *The Suffrage of Elvira* (1958), and *Miguel Street* (short stories, 1959), are comedies of manners, set in a Trinidad viewed with an exile's acute and ironic eye. These early works present a starkly satiric vision, but a more modulated tone appears in Naipaul's first major novel, partly based on his father's experience, *A House for Mr. Biswas* (1961). Following the declining fortunes of its gentle hero from cradle to grave, this tragicomic novel traces the disintegration of a traditional way of life, on something approaching an epic scale. Subsequent novels, including *The Mimic Men* (1967), *Guerrillas* (1973), *The Enigma of Arrival* (1987), and *Half a Life* (2001), have continued to explore the desperate and destructive conditions facing individuals as they struggle with cultures in complicated states of transition and development. Because of his often bitter, even withering critiques of so-called Third World states and societies, he is controversial among readers of postcolonial fiction.

Naipaul has also produced essays on a variety of themes, including a travel narrative about the southern United States, *A Turn in the South* (1988), and two studies—what he calls "cultural explorations"—of Islam: *Among the Believers: An Islamic Journey* (1981) and *Beyond Belief: Islamic Excursions among the Converted Peoples* (1998). Like his novels, these writings range widely, carrying readers to Africa, England, the Indian subcontinent, the Middle East, South and North America. With the years Naipaul's vision of the human condition has grown darker and more pessimistic, as he brilliantly lays bare the insensitivities and disconnections that bedevil relations among individuals, races, and nations.

Such tremendous disjunctions and dire consequences are revealed in "One Out of Many," the second of three stories that, with two linking diary entries, make up *In a Free State*, a bleakly ironic yet emotionally engaging study of what it means to be enslaved and what it means to be free. The story—its title playing on the American motto *"E pluribus unum"* ("from many, one")—follows the fortunes of Santosh, an Indian immigrant to the U.S., whose sense of self changes dramatically in relation to various liberating and imprisoning spaces, various ethnic, cultural, and sexual others. In contrast to narratives of immigration as empowerment, the story represents the promise of more freedom, more status, more economic opportunity in America as coming at the price of an intensified isolation and alienation. As in the literary journeys of other innocents abroad, Santosh's immersion in America satirically reveals as much about the culture he assumes as about the culture he leaves behind.

One Out of Many

I am now an American citizen and I live in Washington, capital of the world. Many people, both here and in India, will feel that I have done well. But.

I was so happy in Bombay. I was respected, I had a certain position. I worked for an important man. The highest in the land came to our bachelor chambers and enjoyed my food and showered compliments on me. I also had my friends. We met in the evenings on the pavement below the gallery of our chambers. Some of us, like the tailor's bearer[1] and myself, were domestics who lived in the street. The others were people who came to that bit of pavement to sleep. Respectable people; we didn't encourage riff-raff.

In the evenings it was cool. There were few passers-by and, apart from an occasional double-decker bus or taxi, little traffic. The pavement was swept and sprinkled, bedding brought out from daytime hiding-places, little oil-lamps lit. While the folk upstairs chattered and laughed, on the pavement we read newspapers, played cards, told stories and smoked. The clay pipe passed from friend to friend; we became drowsy. Except of course during the monsoon,[2] I preferred to sleep on the pavement with my friends, although in our chambers a whole cupboard below the staircase was reserved for my personal use.

It was good after a healthy night in the open to rise before the sun and before the sweepers came. Sometimes I saw the street lights go off. Bedding was rolled up; no one spoke much; and soon my friends were hurrying in silent competition to secluded lanes and alleys and open lots to relieve themselves. I was spared this competition; in our chambers I had facilities.[3]

Afterwards for half an hour or so I was free simply to stroll. I liked walking beside the Arabian Sea, waiting for the sun to come up. Then the city and the ocean gleamed like gold. Alas for those morning walks, that sudden ocean dazzle, the moist salt breeze on my face, the flap of my shirt, that first cup of hot sweet tea from a stall, the taste of the first leaf-cigarette.

Observe the workings of fate. The respect and security I enjoyed were due to the importance of my employer. It was this very importance which now all at once destroyed the pattern of my life.

My employer was seconded[4] by his firm to Government service and was

1. Servant.
2. Rainy season.
3. I.e., a toilet.
4. Temporarily transferred.

posted to Washington. I was happy for his sake but frightened for mine. He was to be away for some years and there was nobody in Bombay he could second me to. Soon, therefore, I was to be out of a job and out of the chambers. For many years I had considered my life as settled. I had served my apprenticeship, known my hard times. I didn't feel I could start again. I despaired. Was there a job for me in Bombay? I saw myself having to return to my village in the hills, to my wife and children there, not just for a holiday but for good. I saw myself again becoming a porter during the tourist season, racing after the buses as they arrived at the station and shouting with forty or fifty others for luggage. Indian luggage, not this lightweight American stuff! Heavy metal trunks!

I could have cried. It was no longer the sort of life for which I was fitted. I had grown soft in Bombay and I was no longer young. I had acquired possessions, I was used to the privacy of my cupboard. I had become a city man, used to certain comforts.

My employer said, "Washington is not Bombay, Santosh. Washington is expensive. Even if I was able to raise your fare, you wouldn't be able to live over there in anything like your present style."

But to be barefoot in the hills, after Bombay! The shock, the disgrace! I couldn't face my friends. I stopped sleeping on the pavement and spent as much of my free time as possible in my cupboard among my possessions, as among things which were soon to be taken from me.

My employer said, "Santosh, my heart bleeds for you."

I said, "Sahib,[5] if I look a little concerned it is only because I worry about you. You have always been fussy, and I don't see how you will manage in Washington."

"It won't be easy. But it's the principle. Does the representative of a poor country like ours travel about with his cook? Will that create a good impression?"

"You will always do what is right, sahib."

He went silent.

After some days he said, "There's not only the expense, Santosh. There's the question of foreign exchange. Our rupee[6] isn't what it was."

"I understand, sahib. Duty is duty."

A fortnight later, when I had almost given up hope, he said, "Santosh, I have consulted Government. You will accompany me. Government has sanctioned, will arrange accommodation. But no expenses. You will get your passport and your P form. But I want you to think, Santosh. Washington is not Bombay."

I went down to the pavement that night with my bedding.

I said, blowing down my shirt, "Bombay gets hotter and hotter."

"Do you know what you are doing?" the tailor's bearer said. "Will the Americans smoke with you? Will they sit and talk with you in the evenings? Will they hold you by the hand and walk with you beside the ocean?"

It pleased me that he was jealous. My last days in Bombay were very happy.

I packed my employer's two suitcases and bundled up my own belongings in lengths of old cotton. At the airport they made a fuss about my bundles. They said they couldn't accept them as luggage for the hold because they didn't like the responsibility. So when the time came I had to climb up to the aircraft

---

5. Master (Urdu).   6. Indian currency, at this time worth ten cents.

with all my bundles. The girl at the top, who was smiling at everybody else, stopped smiling when she saw me. She made me go right to the back of the plane, far from my employer. Most of the seats there were empty, though, and I was able to spread my bundles around and, well, it was comfortable.

It was bright and hot outside, cool inside. The plane started, rose up in the air, and Bombay and the ocean tilted this way and that. It was very nice. When we settled down I looked around for people like myself, but I could see no one among the Indians or the foreigners who looked like a domestic. Worse, they were all dressed as though they were going to a wedding and, brother, I soon saw it wasn't they who were conspicuous. I was in my ordinary Bombay clothes, the loose long-tailed shirt, the wide-waisted pants held up with a piece of string. Perfectly respectable domestic's wear, neither dirty nor clean, and in Bombay no one would have looked. But now on the plane I felt heads turning whenever I stood up.

I was anxious. I slipped off my shoes, tight even without the laces, and drew my feet up. That made me feel better. I made myself a little betel-nut[7] mixture and that made me feel better still. Half the pleasure of betel, though, is the spitting; and it was only when I had worked up a good mouthful that I saw I had a problem. The airline girl saw too. That girl didn't like me at all. She spoke roughly to me. My mouth was full, my cheeks were bursting, and I couldn't say anything. I could only look at her. She went and called a man in uniform and he came and stood over me. I put my shoes back on and swallowed the betel juice. It made me feel quite ill.

The girl and the man, the two of them, pushed a little trolley of drinks down the aisle. The girl didn't look at me but the man said, "You want a drink, chum?" He wasn't a bad fellow. I pointed at random to a bottle. It was a kind of soda drink, nice and sharp at first but then not so nice. I was worrying about it when the girl said, "Five shillings sterling or sixty cents U.S." That took me by surprise. I had no money, only a few rupees. The girl stamped, and I thought she was going to hit me with her pad when I stood up to show her who my employer was.

Presently my employer came down the aisle. He didn't look very well. He said, without stopping, "Champagne, Santosh? Already we are overdoing?" He went on to the lavatory. When he passed back he said, "Foreign exchange, Santosh! Foreign exchange!" That was all. Poor fellow, he was suffering too.

The journey became miserable for me. Soon, with the wine I had drunk, the betel juice, the movement and the noise of the aeroplane, I was vomiting all over my bundles, and I didn't care what the girl said or did. Later there were more urgent and terrible needs. I felt I would choke in the tiny, hissing room at the back. I had a shock when I saw my face in the mirror. In the fluorescent light it was the colour of a corpse. My eyes were strained, the sharp air hurt my nose and seemed to get into my brain. I climbed up on the lavatory seat and squatted. I lost control of myself. As quickly as I could I ran back out into the comparative openness of the cabin and hoped no one had noticed. The lights were dim now; some people had taken off their jackets and were sleeping. I hoped the plane would crash.

The girl woke me up. She was almost screaming. "It's you, isn't it? Isn't it?"

I thought she was going to tear the shirt off me. I pulled back and leaned

---

7. Evergreen plant, the leaves of which are chewed in the East with areca-nut parings.

hard on the window. She burst into tears and nearly tripped on her sari as she ran up the aisle to get the man in uniform.

Nightmare. And all I knew was that somewhere at the end, after the airports and the crowded lounges where everybody was dressed up, after all those take-offs and touchdowns, was the city of Washington. I wanted the journey to end but I couldn't say I wanted to arrive at Washington. I was already a little scared of that city, to tell the truth. I wanted only to be off the plane and to be in the open again, to stand on the ground and breathe and to try to understand what time of day it was.

At last we arrived. I was in a daze. The burden of those bundles! There were more closed rooms and electric lights. There were questions from officials.

"Is he diplomatic?"[8]

"He's only a domestic," my employer said.

"Is that his luggage? What's in that pocket?"

I was ashamed.

"Santosh," my employer said.

I pulled out the little packets of pepper and salt, the sweets, the envelopes with scented napkins, the toy tubes of mustard. Airline trinkets. I had been collecting them throughout the journey, seizing a handful, whatever my condition, every time I passed the galley.

"He's a cook," my employer said.

"Does he always travel with his condiments?"

"Santosh, Santosh," my employer said in the car afterwards, "in Bombay it didn't matter what you did. Over here you represent your country. I must say I cannot understand why your behaviour has already gone so much out of character."

"I am sorry, sahib."

"Look at it like this, Santosh. Over here you don't only represent your country, you represent me."

For the people of Washington it was late afternoon or early evening, I couldn't say which. The time and the light didn't match, as they did in Bombay. Of that drive I remember green fields, wide roads, many motor cars travelling fast, making a steady hiss, hiss, which wasn't at all like our Bombay traffic noise. I remember big buildings and wide parks; many bazaar areas; then smaller houses without fences and with gardens like bush, with the *hubshi*[9] standing about or sitting down, more usually sitting down, everywhere. Especially I remember the *hubshi*. I had heard about them in stories and had seen one or two in Bombay. But I had never dreamt that this wild race existed in such numbers in Washington and were permitted to roam the streets so freely. O father, what was this place I had come to?

I wanted, I say, to be in the open, to breathe, to come to myself, to reflect. But there was to be no openness for me that evening. From the aeroplane to the airport building to the motor car to the apartment block to the elevator to the corridor to the apartment itself, I was forever enclosed, forever in the hissing, hissing sound of air-conditioners.

I was too dazed to take stock of the apartment. I saw it as only another halting place. My employer went to bed at once, completely exhausted, poor fellow. I looked around for my room. I couldn't find it and gave up. Aching for

8. In the Diplomatic Corps.
9. Derogatory Indian term for African blacks (Hindustani).

the Bombay ways, I spread my bedding in the carpeted corridor just outside our apartment door. The corridor was long: doors, doors. The illuminated ceiling was decorated with stars of different sizes; the colours were grey and blue and gold. Below that imitation sky I felt like a prisoner.

Waking, looking up at the ceiling, I thought just for a second that I had fallen asleep on the pavement below the gallery of our Bombay chambers. Then I realized my loss. I couldn't tell how much time had passed or whether it was night or day. The only clue was that newspapers now lay outside some doors. It disturbed me to think that while I had been sleeping, alone and defenceless, I had been observed by a stranger and perhaps by more than one stranger.

I tried the apartment door and found I had locked myself out. I didn't want to disturb my employer. I thought I would get out into the open, go for a walk. I remembered where the elevator was. I got in and pressed the button. The elevator dropped fast and silently and it was like being in the aeroplane again. When the elevator stopped and the blue metal door slid open I saw plain concrete corridors and blank walls. The noise of machinery was very loud. I knew I was in the basement and the main floor was not far above me. But I no longer wanted to try; I gave up ideas of the open air. I thought I would just go back up to the apartment. But I hadn't noted the number and didn't even know what floor we were on. My courage flowed out of me. I sat on the floor of the elevator and felt the tears come to my eyes. Almost without noise the elevator door closed, and I found I was being taken up silently at great speed.

The elevator stopped and the door opened. It was my employer, his hair uncombed, yesterday's dirty shirt partly unbuttoned. He looked frightened.

"Santosh, where have you been at this hour of morning? Without your shoes."

I could have embraced him. He hurried me back past the newspapers to our apartment and I took the bedding inside. The wide window showed the early morning sky, the big city; we were high up, way above the trees.

I said, "I couldn't find my room."

"Government sanctioned," my employer said. "Are you sure you've looked?"

We looked together. One little corridor led past the bathroom to his bedroom; another, shorter corridor led to the big room and the kitchen. There was nothing else.

"Government sanctioned," my employer said, moving about the kitchen and opening cupboard doors. "Separate entrance, shelving. I have the correspondence." He opened another door and looked inside. "Santosh, do you think it is possible that this is what Government meant?"

The cupboard he had opened was as high as the rest of the apartment and as wide as the kitchen, about six feet. It was about three feet deep. It had two doors. One door opened into the kitchen; another door, directly opposite, opened into the corridor.

"Separate entrance," my employer said. "Shelving, electric light, power point, fitted carpet."

"This must be my room, sahib."

"Santosh, some enemy in Government has done this to me."

"Oh no, sahib. You mustn't say that. Besides, it is very big. I will be able to make myself very comfortable. It is much bigger than my little cubby-hole in the chambers. And it has a nice flat ceiling. I wouldn't hit my head."

"You don't understand, Santosh. Bombay is Bombay. Here if we start living in cupboards we give the wrong impression. They will think we all live in cupboards in Bombay."

"O sahib, but they can just look at me and see I am dirt."

"You are very good, Santosh. But these people are malicious. Still, if you are happy, then I am happy."

"I am very happy, sahib."

And after all the upset, I was. It was nice to crawl in that evening, spread my bedding and feel protected and hidden. I slept very well.

In the morning my employer said, "We must talk about money, Santosh. Your salary is one hundred rupees a month. But Washington isn't Bombay. Everything is a little bit more expensive here, and I am going to give you a Dearness Allowance. As from today you are getting one hundred and fifty rupees."

"Sahib."

"And I'm giving you a fortnight's pay in advance. In foreign exchange. Seventy-five rupees. Ten cents to the rupee, seven hundred and fifty cents. Seven fifty U.S. Here, Santosh. This afternoon you go out and have a little walk and enjoy. But be careful. We are not among friends, remember."

So at last, rested, with money in my pocket, I went out in the open. And of course the city wasn't a quarter as frightening as I had thought. The buildings weren't particularly big, not all the streets were busy, and there were many lovely trees. A lot of the *hubshi* were about, very wild-looking some of them, with dark glasses and their hair frizzed out, but it seemed that if you didn't trouble them they didn't attack you.

I was looking for a café or a tea-stall where perhaps domestics congregated. But I saw no domestics, and I was chased away from the place I did eventually go into. The girl said, after I had been waiting some time, "Can't you read? We don't serve hippies or bare feet here."

O father! I had come out without my shoes. But what a country, I thought, walking briskly away, where people are never allowed to dress normally but must forever wear their very best! Why must they wear out shoes and fine clothes for no purpose? What occasion are they honouring? What waste, what presumption! Who do they think is noticing them all the time?

And even while these thoughts were in my head I found I had come to a roundabout with trees and a fountain where—and it was like a fulfilment in a dream, not easy to believe—there were many people who looked like my own people. I tightened the string around my loose pants, held down my flapping shirt and ran through the traffic to the green circle.

Some of the *hubshi* were there, playing musical instruments and looking quite happy in their way. There were some Americans sitting about on the grass and the fountain and the kerb. Many of them were in rough, friendly-looking clothes; some were without shoes; and I felt I had been over hasty in condemning the entire race. But it wasn't these people who had attracted me to the circle. It was the dancers. The men were bearded, barefooted and in saffron robes, and the girls were in saris and canvas shoes that looked like our own Bata shoes.[1] They were shaking little cymbals and chanting and lifting their heads up and down and going round in a circle, making a lot of dust. It

1. I.e., from the Bata Shoe Company.

was a little bit like a Red Indian dance in a cowboy movie, but they were chanting Sanskrit words in praise of Lord Krishna.[2]

I was very pleased. But then a disturbing thought came to me. It might have been because of the half-caste[3] appearance of the dancers; it might have been their bad Sanskrit pronunciation and their accent. I thought that these people were now strangers, but that perhaps once upon a time they had been like me. Perhaps, as in some story, they had been brought here among the *hubshi* as captives a long time ago and had become a lost people, like our own wandering gipsy folk, and had forgotten who they were. When I thought that, I lost my pleasure in the dancing; and I felt for the dancers the sort of distaste we feel when we are faced with something that should be kin but turns out not to be, turns out to be degraded, like a deformed man, or like a leper, who from a distance looks whole.

I didn't stay. Not far from the circle I saw a café which appeared to be serving bare feet. I went in, had a coffee and a nice piece of cake and bought a pack of cigarettes; matches they gave me free with the cigarettes. It was all right, but then the bare feet began looking at me, and one bearded fellow came and sniffed loudly at me and smiled and spoke some sort of gibberish, and then some others of the bare feet came and sniffed at me. They weren't unfriendly, but I didn't appreciate the behaviour; and it was a little frightening to find, when I left the place, that two or three of them appeared to be following me. They weren't unfriendly, but I didn't want to take any chances. I passed a cinema; I went in. It was something I wanted to do anyway. In Bombay I used to go once a week.

And that was all right. The movie had already started. It was in English, not too easy for me to follow, and it gave me time to think. It was only there, in the darkness, that I thought about the money I had been spending. The prices had seemed to me very reasonable, like Bombay prices. Three for the movie ticket, one fifty in the café, with tip. But I had been thinking in rupees and paying in dollars. In less than an hour I had spent nine days' pay.

I couldn't watch the movie after that. I went out and began to make my way back to the apartment block. Many more of the *hubshi* were about now and I saw that where they congregated the pavement was wet, and dangerous with broken glass and bottles. I couldn't think of cooking when I got back to the apartment. I couldn't bear to look at the view. I spread my bedding in the cupboard, lay down in the darkness and waited for my employer to return.

When he did I said, "Sahib, I want to go home."

"Santosh, I've paid five thousand rupees to bring you here. If I send you back now, you will have to work for six or seven years without salary to pay me back."

I burst into tears.

"My poor Santosh, something has happened. Tell me what has happened."

"Sahib, I've spent more than half the advance you gave me this morning. I went out and had a coffee and cake and then I went to a movie."

His eyes went small and twinkly behind his glasses. He bit the inside of his top lip, scraped at his moustache with his lower teeth, and he said, "You see, you see. I told you it was expensive."

2. Great Hindu deity.
3. Mixed-race, usually in India, descended from or born to an Indian mother and a European father.

I understood I was a prisoner. I accepted this and adjusted. I learned to live within the apartment, and I was even calm.

My employer was a man of taste and he soon had the apartment looking like something in a magazine, with books and Indian paintings and Indian fabrics and pieces of sculpture and bronze statues of our gods. I was careful to take no delight in it. It was of course very pretty, especially with the view. But the view remained foreign and I never felt that the apartment was real, like the shabby old Bombay chambers with the cane chairs, or that it had anything to do with me.

When people came to dinner I did my duty. At the appropriate time I would bid the company goodnight, close off the kitchen behind its folding screen and pretend I was leaving the apartment. Then I would lie down quietly in my cupboard and smoke. I was free to go out; I had my separate entrance. But I didn't like being out of the apartment. I didn't even like going down to the laundry room in the basement.

Once or twice a week I went to the supermarket on our street. I always had to walk past groups of *hubshi* men and children. I tried not to look, but it was hard. They sat on the pavement, on steps and in the bush around their redbrick houses, some of which had boarded-up windows. They appeared to be very much a people of the open air, with little to do; even in the mornings some of the men were drunk.

Scattered among the *hubshi* houses were others just as old but with gas-lamps that burned night and day in the entrance. These were the houses of the Americans. I seldom saw these people; they didn't spend much time on the street. The lighted gas-lamp was the American way of saying that though a house looked old outside it was nice and new inside. I also felt that it was like a warning to the *hubshi* to keep off.

Outside the supermarket there was always a policeman with a gun. Inside, there were always a couple of *hubshi* guards with truncheons, and, behind the cashiers, some old *hubshi* beggar men in rags. There were also many young *hubshi* boys, small but muscular, waiting to carry parcels, as once in the hills I had waited to carry Indian tourists' luggage.

These trips to the supermarket were my only outings, and I was always glad to get back to the apartment. The work there was light. I watched a lot of television and my English improved. I grew to like certain commercials very much. It was in these commercials I saw the Americans whom in real life I so seldom saw and knew only by their gas-lamps. Up there in the apartment, with a view of the white domes and towers and greenery of the famous city, I entered the homes of the Americans and saw them cleaning those homes. I saw them cleaning floors and dishes. I saw them buying clothes and cleaning clothes, buying motor cars and cleaning motor cars. I saw them cleaning, cleaning.

The effect of all this television on me was curious. If by some chance I saw an American on the street I tried to fit him or her into the commercials; and I felt I had caught the person in an interval between his television duties. So to some extent Americans have remained to me, as people not quite real, as people temporarily absent from television.

Sometimes a *hubshi* came on the screen, not to talk of *hubshi* things, but to do a little cleaning of his own. That wasn't the same. He was too different from the *hubshi* I saw on the street and I knew he was an actor. I knew that his television duties were only make-believe and that he would soon have to return to the street.

One day at the supermarket, when the *hubshi* girl took my money, she sniffed and said, "You always smell sweet, baby."

She was friendly, and I was at last able to clear up that mystery, of my smell. It was the poor country weed I smoked. It was a peasant taste of which I was slightly ashamed, to tell the truth; but the cashier was encouraging. As it happened, I had brought a quantity of the weed with me from Bombay in one of my bundles, together with a hundred razor blades, believing both weed and blades to be purely Indian things. I made an offering to the girl. In return she taught me a few words of English. "Me black and beautiful"[4] was the first thing she taught me. Then she pointed to the policeman with the gun outside and taught me: "He pig."

My English lessons were taken a stage further by the *hubshi* maid who worked for someone on our floor in the apartment block. She too was attracted by my smell, but I soon began to feel that she was also attracted by my small-ness and strangeness. She herself was a big woman, broad in the face, with high cheeks and bold eyes and lips that were full but not pendulous. Her largeness disturbed me; I found it better to concentrate on her face. She mis-understood; there were times when she frolicked with me in a violent way. I didn't like it, because I couldn't fight her off as well as I would have liked and because in spite of myself I was fascinated by her appearance. Her smell mixed with the perfumes she used could have made me forget myself.

She was always coming into the apartment. She disturbed me while I was watching the Americans on television. I feared the smell she left behind. Sweat, perfume, my own weed: the smells lay thick in the room, and I prayed to the bronze gods my employer had installed as living-room ornaments that I would not be dishonoured. Dishonoured, I say; and I know that this might seem strange to people over here, who have permitted the *hubshi* to settle among them in such large numbers and must therefore esteem them in certain ways. But in our country we frankly do not care for the *hubshi*. It is written in our books, both holy and not so holy, that it is indecent and wrong for a man of our blood to embrace the *hubshi* woman. To be dishonoured in this life, to be born a cat or a monkey or a *hubshi* in the next!

But I was falling. Was it idleness and solitude? I was found attractive: I wanted to know why. I began to go to the bathroom of the apartment simply to study my face in the mirror. I cannot easily believe it myself now, but in Bombay a week or a month could pass without my looking in the mirror; then it wasn't to consider my looks but to check whether the barber had cut off too much hair or whether a pimple was about to burst. Slowly I made a discovery. My face was handsome. I had never thought of myself in this way. I had thought of myself as unnoticeable, with features that served as identification alone.

The discovery of my good looks brought its strains. I became obsessed with my appearance, with a wish to see myself. It was like an illness. I would be watching television, for instance, and I would be surprised by the thought: are you as handsome as that man? I would have to get up and go to the bathroom and look in the mirror.

I thought back to the time when these matters hadn't interested me, and I saw how ragged I must have looked, on the aeroplane, in the airport, in that café for bare feet, with the rough and dirty clothes I wore, without doubt or

4. Cf. the 1960s slogan "Black is Beautiful."

question, as clothes befitting a servant. I was choked with shame. I saw, too, how good people in Washington had been, to have seen me in rags and yet to have taken me for a man.

I was glad I had a place to hide. I had thought of myself as a prisoner. Now I was glad I had so little of Washington to cope with: the apartment, my cupboard, the television set, my employer, the walk to the supermarket, the *hubshi* woman. And one day I found I no longer knew whether I wanted to go back to Bombay. Up there, in the apartment, I no longer knew what I wanted to do.

I became more careful of my appearance. There wasn't much I could do. I bought laces for my old black shoes, socks, a belt. Then some money came my way. I had understood that the weed I smoked was of value to the *hubshi* and the bare feet; I disposed of what I had, disadvantageously as I now know, through the *hubshi* girl at the supermarket. I got just under two hundred dollars. Then, as anxiously as I had got rid of my weed, I went out and bought some clothes.

I still have the things I bought that morning. A green hat, a green suit. The suit was always too big for me. Ignorance, inexperience; but I also remember the feeling of presumption. The salesman wanted to talk, to do his job. I didn't want to listen. I took the first suit he showed me and went into the cubicle and changed. I couldn't think about size and fit. When I considered all that cloth and all that tailoring I was proposing to adorn my simple body with, that body that needed so little, I felt I was asking to be destroyed. I changed back quickly, went out of the cubicle and said I would take the green suit. The salesman began to talk; I cut him short; I asked for a hat. When I got back to the apartment I felt quite weak and had to lie down for a while in my cupboard.

I never hung the suit up. Even in the shop, even while counting out the precious dollars, I had known it was a mistake. I kept the suit folded in the box with all its pieces of tissue paper. Three or four times I put it on and walked about the apartment and sat down on chairs and lit cigarettes and crossed my legs, practising. But I couldn't bring myself to wear the suit out of doors. Later I wore the pants, but never the jacket. I never bought another suit; I soon began wearing the sort of clothes I wear today, pants with some sort of zippered jacket.

Once I had had no secrets from my employer; it was so much simpler not to have secrets. But some instinct told me now it would be better not to let him know about the green suit or the few dollars I had, just as instinct had already told me I should keep my growing knowledge of English to myself.

Once my employer had been to me only a presence. I used to tell him then that beside him I was as dirt. It was only a way of talking, one of the courtesies of our language, but it had something of truth. I meant that he was the man who adventured in the world for me, that I experienced the world through him, that I was content to be a small part of his presence. I was content, sleeping on the Bombay pavement with my friends, to hear the talk of my employer and his guests upstairs. I was more than content, late at night, to be identified among the sleepers and greeted by some of those guests before they drove away.

Now I found that, without wishing it, I was ceasing to see myself as part of my employer's presence, and beginning at the same time to see him as an outsider might see him, as perhaps the people who came to dinner in the apartment saw him. I saw that he was a man of my own age, around thirty-five; it astonished me that I hadn't noticed this before. I saw that he was plump, in need of exercise, that he moved with short, fussy steps; a man with glasses, thinning hair, and that habit, during conversation, of scraping at his moustache with his teeth and nibbling at the inside of his top lip; a man who was frequently anxious, took pains over his work, was subjected at his own table to unkind remarks by his office colleagues; a man who looked as uneasy in Washington as I felt, who acted as cautiously as I had learned to act.

I remember an American who came to dinner. He looked at the pieces of sculpture in the apartment and said he had himself brought back a whole head from one of our ancient temples; he had got the guide to hack it off.

I could see that my employer was offended. He said, "But that's illegal."

"That's why I had to give the guide two dollars. If I had a bottle of whisky he would have pulled down the whole temple for me."

My employer's face went blank. He continued to do his duties as host but he was unhappy throughout the dinner. I grieved for him.

Afterwards he knocked on my cupboard. I knew he wanted to talk. I was in my underclothes but I didn't feel underdressed, with the American gone. I stood in the door of my cupboard; my employer paced up and down the small kitchen; the apartment felt sad.

"Did you hear that person, Santosh?"

I pretended I hadn't understood, and when he explained I tried to console him. I said, "Sahib, but we know these people are Franks[5] and barbarians."

"They are malicious people, Santosh. They think that because we are a poor country we are all the same. They think an official in Government is just the same as some poor guide scraping together a few rupees to keep body and soul together, poor fellow."

I saw that he had taken the insult only in a personal way, and I was disappointed. I thought he had been thinking of the temple.

A few days later I had my adventure. The *hubshi* woman came in, moving among my employer's ornaments like a bull. I was greatly provoked. The smell was too much; so was the sight of her armpits. I fell. She dragged me down on the couch, on the saffron spread which was one of my employer's nicest pieces of Punjabi folk-weaving. I saw the moment, helplessly, as one of dishonour. I saw her as Kali,[6] goddess of death and destruction, coal-black, with a red tongue and white eyeballs and many powerful arms. I expected her to be wild and fierce; but she added insult to injury by being very playful, as though, because I was small and strange, the act was not real. She laughed all the time. I would have liked to withdraw, but the act took over and completed itself. And then I felt dreadful.

I wanted to be forgiven, I wanted to be cleansed, I wanted her to go. Nothing frightened me more than the way she had ceased to be a visitor in the apartment and behaved as though she possessed it. I looked at the sculpture and the fabrics and thought of my poor employer, suffering in his office somewhere.

I bathed and bathed afterwards. The smell would not leave me. I fancied that the woman's oil was still on that poor part of my poor body. It occurred to me to rub it down with half a lemon. Penance and cleansing; but it didn't hurt as much as I expected, and I extended the penance by rolling about naked on the floor of the bathroom and the sitting-room and howling. At last the tears came, real tears, and I was comforted.

It was cool in the apartment; the air-conditioning always hummed; but I could see that it was hot outside, like one of our own summer days in the hills. The urge came upon me to dress as I might have done in my village on a religious occasion. In one of my bundles I had a dhoti[7]-length of new cotton, a gift from the tailor's bearer that I had never used. I draped this around my waist and between my legs, lit incense sticks, sat down cross-legged on the floor and tried to meditate and become still. Soon I began to feel hungry. That made me happy; I decided to fast.

Unexpectedly my employer came in. I didn't mind being caught in the attitude and garb of prayer; it could have been so much worse. But I wasn't expecting him till late afternoon.

"Santosh, what has happened?"

Pride got the better of me. I said, "Sahib, it is what I do from time to time."

But I didn't find merit in his eyes. He was far too agitated to notice me properly. He took off his lightweight fawn jacket, dropped it on the saffron spread, went to the refrigerator and drank two tumblers of orange juice, one after the other. Then he looked out at the view, scraping at his moustache.

"Oh, my poor Santosh, what are we doing in this place? Why do we have to come here?"

I looked with him. I saw nothing unusual. The wide window showed the colours of the hot day: the pale-blue sky, the white, almost colourless, domes of famous buildings rising out of dead-green foliage; the untidy roofs of apartment blocks where on Saturday and Sunday mornings people sunbathed; and, below, the fronts and backs of houses on the tree-lined street down which I walked to the supermarket.

My employer turned off the air-conditioning and all noise was absent from the room. An instant later I began to hear the noises outside: sirens far and near. When my employer slid the window open the roar of the disturbed city rushed into the room. He closed the window and there was near-silence again. Not far from the supermarket I saw black smoke, uncurling, rising, swiftly turning colourless. This was not the smoke which some of the apartment blocks gave off all day. This was the smoke of a real fire.

"The *hubshi* have gone wild, Santosh. They are burning down Washington."

I didn't mind at all. Indeed, in my mood of prayer and repentance, the news was even welcome. And it was with a feeling of release that I watched and heard the city burn that afternoon and watched it burn that night. I watched it burn again and again on television; and I watched it burn in the morning. It burned like a famous city and I didn't want it to stop burning. I wanted the fire to spread and spread and I wanted everything in the city, even the apartment block, even the apartment, even myself, to be destroyed and consumed. I wanted escape to be impossible; I wanted the very idea of escape to become absurd. At every sign that the burning was going to stop I felt disappointed and let down.

For four days my employer and I stayed in the apartment and watched the city burn. The television continued to show us what we could see and what, whenever we slid the window back, we could hear. Then it was over. The view

7. Loincloth (Hindi).

from our window hadn't changed. The famous buildings stood; the trees remained. But for the first time since I had understood that I was a prisoner I found that I wanted to be out of the apartment and in the streets.

The destruction lay beyond the supermarket. I had never gone into this part of the city before, and it was strange to walk in those long wide streets for the first time, to see trees and houses and shops and advertisements, everything like a real city, and then to see that every signboard on every shop was burnt or stained with smoke, that the shops themselves were black and broken, that flames had burst through some of the upper windows and scorched the red bricks. For mile after mile it was like that. There were *hubshi* groups about, and at first when I passed them I pretended to be busy, minding my own business, not at all interested in the ruins. But they smiled at me and I found I was smiling back. Happiness was on the faces of the *hubshi*. They were like people amazed they could do so much, that so much lay in their power. They were like people on holiday. I shared their exhilaration.

The idea of escape was a simple one, but it hadn't occurred to me before. When I adjusted to my imprisonment I had wanted only to get away from Washington and to return to Bombay. But then I had become confused. I had looked in the mirror and seen myself, and I knew it wasn't possible for me to return to Bombay to the sort of job I had had and the life I had lived. I couldn't easily become part of someone else's presence again. Those evening chats on the pavement, those morning walks: happy times, but they were like the happy times of childhood: I didn't want them to return.

I had taken, after the fire, to going for long walks in the city. And one day, when I wasn't even thinking of escape, when I was just enjoying the sights and my new freedom of movement, I found myself in one of those leafy streets where private houses had been turned into business premises. I saw a fellow countryman superintending the raising of a signboard on his gallery. The signboard told me that the building was a restaurant, and I assumed that the man in charge was the owner. He looked worried and slightly ashamed, and he smiled at me. This was unusual, because the Indians I had seen on the streets of Washington pretended they hadn't seen me; they made me feel that they didn't like the competition of my presence or didn't want me to start asking them difficult questions.

I complimented the worried man on his signboard and wished him good luck in his business. He was a small man of about fifty and he was wearing a double-breasted suit with old-fashioned wide lapels. He had dark hollows below his eyes and he looked as though he had recently lost a little weight. I could see that in our country he had been a man of some standing, not quite the sort of person who would go into the restaurant business. I felt at one with him. He invited me in to look around, asked my name and gave his. It was Priya.

Just past the gallery was the loveliest and richest room I had ever seen. The wallpaper was like velvet; I wanted to pass my hand over it. The brass lamps that hung from the ceiling were in a lovely cut-out pattern and the bulbs were of many colours. Priya looked with me, and the hollows under his eyes grew darker, as though my admiration was increasing his worry at his extravagance. The restaurant hadn't yet opened for customers and on a shelf in one corner I saw Priya's collection of good-luck objects: a brass plate with a heap of uncooked rice, for prosperity; a little copybook and a little diary pencil, for good luck with the accounts; a little clay lamp, for general good luck.

"What do you think, Santosh? You think it will be all right?"

"It is bound to be all right, Priya."

"But I have enemies, you know, Santosh. The Indian restaurant people are not going to appreciate me. All mine, you know, Santosh. Cash paid. No mortgage or anything like that. I don't believe in mortgages. Cash or nothing."

I understood him to mean that he had tried to get a mortgage and failed, and was anxious about money.

"But what are you doing here, Santosh? You used to be in Government or something?"

"You could say that, Priya."

"Like me. They have a saying here. If you can't beat them, join them. I joined them. They are still beating me." He sighed and spread his arms on the top of the red wall-seat. "Ah, Santosh, why do we do it? Why don't we renounce and go and meditate on the riverbank?" He waved about the room. "The yemblems[8] of the world, Santosh. Just yemblems."

I didn't know the English word he used, but I understood its meaning; and for a moment it was like being back in Bombay, exchanging stories and philosophies with the tailor's bearer and others in the evening.

"But I am forgetting, Santosh. You will have some tea or coffee or something?"

I shook my head from side to side to indicate that I was agreeable, and he called out in a strange harsh language to someone behind the kitchen door.

"Yes, Santosh. Yem-*blems*!" And he sighed and slapped the red seat hard.

A man came out from the kitchen with a tray. At first he looked like a fellow countryman, but in a second I could tell he was a stranger.

"You are right," Priya said, when the stranger went back to the kitchen. "He is not of Bharat. He is a Mexican. But what can I do? You get fellow countrymen, you fix up their papers and everything. And then? Then they run away. Run-run-runaway. Crooks this side, crooks that side, I can't tell you. Listen, Santosh. I was in cloth business before. Buy for fifty rupees that side, sell for fifty dollars this side. Easy. But then. Caftan, everybody wants caftan. Caftan-aftan, I say, I will settle your caftan. I buy one thousand, Santosh. Delays India-side,[9] of course. They come one year later. Nobody wants caftan then. We're not organized, Santosh. We don't do enough consumer research. That's what the fellows at the embassy tell me. But if I do consumer research, when will I do my business? The trouble, you know, Santosh, is that this shopkeeping is not in my blood. The damn thing goes *against* my blood. When I was in cloth business I used to hide sometimes for shame when a customer came in. Sometimes I used to pretend I was a shopper myself. Consumer research! These people make us dance, Santosh. You and I, we will renounce. We will go together and walk beside Potomac and meditate."

I loved his talk. I hadn't heard anything so sweet and philosophical since the Bombay days. I said, "Priya, I will cook for you, if you want a cook."

"I feel I've known you a long time, Santosh. I feel you are like a member of my own family. I will give you a place to sleep, a little food to eat and a little pocket money, as much as I can afford."

I said, "Show me the place to sleep."

He led me out of the pretty room and up a carpeted staircase. I was expecting

---

8. Emblems.
9. In India. "Caftan": long loose tunic or shirt (Turkish).

the carpet and the new paint to stop somewhere, but it was nice and new all the way. We entered a room that was like a smaller version of my employer's apartment.

"Built-in cupboards and everything, you see, Santosh."

I went to the cupboard. It had a folding door that opened outward. I said, "Priya, it is too small. There is room on the shelf for my belongings. But I don't see how I can spread my bedding inside here. It is far too narrow."

He giggled nervously. "Santosh, you are a joker. I feel that we are of the same family already."

Then it came to me that I was being offered the whole room. I was stunned.

Priya looked stunned too. He sat down on the edge of the soft bed. The dark hollows under his eyes were almost black and he looked very small in his double-breasted jacket. "This is how they make us dance over here, Santosh. You say staff quarters and they say staff quarters. This is what they mean."

For some seconds we sat silently, I fearful, he gloomy, meditating on the ways of this new world.

Someone called from downstairs, "Priya!"

His gloom gone, smiling in advance, winking at me, Priya called back in an accent of the country, "Hi, Bab!"

I followed him down.

"Priya," the American said, "I've brought over the menus."

He was a tall man in a leather jacket, with jeans that rode up above thick white socks and big rubber-soled shoes. He looked like someone about to run in a race. The menus were enormous; on the cover there was a drawing of a fat man with a moustache and a plumed turban, something like the man in the airline advertisements.

"They look great, Bab."

"I like them myself. But what's that, Priya? What's that shelf doing there?"

Moving like the front part of a horse, Bab walked to the shelf with the rice and the brass plate and the little clay lamp. It was only then that I saw that the shelf was very roughly made.

Priya looked penitent and it was clear he had put the shelf up himself. It was also clear he didn't intend to take it down.

"Well, it's yours," Bab said. "I suppose we had to have a touch of the East somewhere. Now, Priya—"

"Money-money-money, is it?" Priya said, racing the words together as though he was making a joke to amuse a child. "But, Bab, how can *you ask me* for money? Anybody hearing you would believe that this restaurant is mine. But this restaurant isn't mine, Bab. This restaurant is yours."

It was only one of our courtesies, but it puzzled Bab and he allowed himself to be led to other matters.

I saw that, for all his talk of renunciation and business failure, and for all his jumpiness, Priya was able to cope with Washington. I admired this strength in him as much as I admired the richness of his talk. I didn't know how much to believe of his stories, but I liked having to guess about him. I liked having to play with his words in my mind. I liked the mystery of the man. The mystery came from his solidity. I knew where I was with him. After the apartment and the green suit and the *hubshi* woman and the city burning for four days, to be with Priya was to feel safe. For the first time since I had come to Washington I felt safe.

I can't say that I moved in. I simply stayed. I didn't want to go back to the apartment even to collect my belongings. I was afraid that something might happen to keep me a prisoner there. My employer might turn up and demand his five thousand rupees. The *hubshi* woman might claim me for her own; I might be condemned to a life among the *hubshi*. And it wasn't as if I was leaving behind anything of value in the apartment. The green suit I was even happy to forget. But.

Priya paid me forty dollars a week. After what I was getting, three dollars and seventy-five cents, it seemed a lot; and it was more than enough for my needs. I didn't have much temptation to spend, to tell the truth. I knew that my old employer and the *hubshi* woman would be wondering about me in their respective ways and I thought I should keep off the streets for a while. That was no hardship; it was what I was used to in Washington. Besides, my days at the restaurant were pretty full; for the first time in my life I had little leisure.

The restaurant was a success from the start, and Priya was fussy. He was always bursting into the kitchen with one of those big menus in his hand, saying in English, "Prestige job, Santosh, prestige." I didn't mind. I liked to feel I had to do things perfectly; I felt I was earning my freedom. Though I was in hiding, and though I worked every day until midnight, I felt I was much more in charge of myself than I had ever been.

Many of our waiters were Mexicans, but when we put turbans on them they could pass. They came and went, like the Indian staff. I didn't get on with these people. They were frightened and jealous of one another and very treacherous. Their talk amid the biryanis and the pillaus[1] was all of papers and green cards. They were always about to get green cards or they had been cheated out of green cards or they had just got green cards. At first I didn't know what they were talking about. When I understood I was more than depressed.

I understood that because I had escaped from my employer I had made myself illegal in America. At any moment I could be denounced, seized, jailed, deported, disgraced. It was a complication. I had no green card; I didn't know how to set about getting one; and there was no one I could talk to.

I felt burdened by my secrets. Once I had none; now I had so many. I couldn't tell Priya I had no green card. I couldn't tell him I had broken faith with my old employer and dishonoured myself with a *hubshi* woman and lived in fear of retribution. I couldn't tell him that I was afraid to leave the restaurant and that nowadays when I saw an Indian I hid from him as anxiously as the Indian hid from me. I would have felt foolish to confess. With Priya, right from the start, I had pretended to be strong; and I wanted it to remain like that. Instead, when we talked now, and he grew philosophical, I tried to find bigger causes for being sad. My mind fastened on to these causes, and the effect of this was that my sadness became like a sickness of the soul.

It was worse than being in the apartment, because now the responsibility was mine and mine alone. I had decided to be free, to act for myself. It pained me to think of the exhilaration I had felt during the days of the fire; and I felt mocked when I remembered that in the early days of my escape I had thought I was in charge of myself.

The year turned. The snow came and melted. I was more afraid than ever of going out. The sickness was bigger than all the causes. I saw the future as a hole into which I was dropping. Sometimes at night when I awakened my body would burn and I would feel the hot perspiration break all over.

I leaned on Priya. He was my only hope, my only link with what was real.

1. "Biryanis" and "pillaus": Indian dishes.

He went out; he brought back stories. He went out especially to eat in the restaurants of our competitors.

He said, "Santosh, I never believed that running a restaurant was a way to God. But it is true. I eat like a scientist. Every day I eat like a scientist. I feel I have already renounced."

This was Priya. This was how his talk ensnared me and gave me the bigger causes that steadily weakened me. I became more and more detached from the men in the kitchen. When they spoke of their green cards and the jobs they were about to get I felt like asking them: Why? Why?

And every day the mirror told its own tale. Without exercise, with the sickening of my heart and my mind, I was losing my looks. My face had become pudgy and sallow and full of spots; it was becoming ugly. I could have cried for that, discovering my good looks only to lose them. It was like a punishment for my presumption, the punishment I had feared when I bought the green suit.

Priya said, "Santosh, you must get some exercise. You are not looking well. Your eyes are getting like mine. What are you pining for? Are you pining for Bombay or your family in the hills?"

But now, even in my mind, I was a stranger in those places.

Priya said one Sunday morning, "Santosh, I am going to take you to see a Hindi movie today. All the Indians of Washington will be there, domestics and everybody else."

I was very frightened. I didn't want to go and I couldn't tell him why. He insisted. My heart began to beat fast as soon as I got into the car. Soon there were no more houses with gas-lamps in the entrance, just those long wide burnt-out *hubshi* streets, now with fresh leaves on the trees, heaps of rubble on bulldozed, fenced-in lots, boarded-up shop windows, and old smoke-stained signboards announcing what was no longer true. Cars raced along the wide roads; there was life only on the roads. I thought I would vomit with fear.

I said, "Take me back, *sahib*."

I had used the wrong word. Once I had used the word a hundred times a day. But then I had considered myself a small part of my employer's presence, and the word was not servile; it was more like a name, like a reassuring sound, part of my employer's dignity and therefore part of mine. But Priya's dignity could never be mine; that was not our relationship. Priya I had always called Priya; it was his wish, the American way, man to man. With Priya the word was servile. And he responded to the word. He did as I asked; he drove me back to the restaurant. I never called him by his name again.

I was good-looking; I had lost my looks. I was a free man; I had lost my freedom.

One of the Mexican waiters came into the kitchen late one evening and said, "There is a man outside who wants to see the chef."

No one had made this request before, and Priya was at once agitated. "Is he an American? Some enemy has sent him here. Sanitary-anitary, health-ealth, they can inspect my kitchens at any time."

"He is an Indian," the Mexican said.

I was alarmed. I thought it was my old employer; that quiet approach was like him. Priya thought it was a rival. Though Priya regularly ate in the restaurants of his rivals he thought it unfair when they came to eat in his. We both went to the door and peeked through the glass window into the dimly lit dining-room.

"Do you know that person, Santosh?"

"Yes, sahib."

It wasn't my old employer. It was one of his Bombay friends, a big man in Government, whom I had often served in the chambers. He was by himself and seemed to have just arrived in Washington. He had a new Bombay haircut, very close, and a stiff dark suit, Bombay tailoring. His shirt looked blue, but in the dim multi-coloured light of the dining-room everything white looked blue. He didn't look unhappy with what he had eaten. Both his elbows were on the curry-spotted tablecloth and he was picking his teeth, half closing his eyes and hiding his mouth with his cupped left hand.

"I don't like him," Priya said. "Still, big man in Government and so on. You must go to him, Santosh."

But I couldn't go.

"Put on your apron, Santosh. And that chef's cap. Prestige. You must go, Santosh."

Priya went out to the dining-room and I heard him say in English that I was coming.

I ran up to my room, put some oil on my hair, combed my hair, put on my best pants and shirt and my shining shoes. It was so, as a man about town rather than as a cook, I went to the dining-room.

The man from Bombay was as astonished as Priya. We exchanged the old courtesies, and I waited. But, to my relief, there seemed little more to say. No difficult questions were put to me; I was grateful to the man from Bombay for his tact. I avoided talk as much as possible. I smiled. The man from Bombay smiled back. Priya smiled uneasily at both of us. So for a while we were, smiling in the dim blue-red light and waiting.

The man from Bombay said to Priya, "Brother, I just have a few words to say to my old friend Santosh."

Priya didn't like it, but he left us.

I waited for those words. But they were not the words I feared. The man from Bombay didn't speak of my old employer. We continued to exchange courtesies. Yes, I was well and he was well and everybody else we knew was well; and I was doing well and he was doing well. That was all. Then, secretively, the man from Bombay gave me a dollar. A dollar, ten rupees, an enormous tip for Bombay. But, from him, much more than a tip: an act of graciousness, part of the sweetness of the old days. Once it would have meant so much to me. Now it meant so little. I was saddened and embarrassed. And I had been anticipating hostility!

Priya was waiting behind the kitchen door. His little face was tight and serious, and I knew he had seen the money pass. Now, quickly, he read my own face, and without saying anything to me he hurried out into the dining-room.

I heard him say in English to the man from Bombay, "Santosh is a good fellow. He's got his own room with bath and everything. I am giving him a hundred dollars a week from next week. A thousand rupees a week. This is a first-class establishment."

A thousand chips a week! I was staggered. It was much more than any man in Government got, and I was sure the man from Bombay was also staggered, and perhaps regretting his good gesture and that precious dollar of foreign exchange.

"Santosh," Priya said, when the restaurant closed that evening, "that man was an enemy. I knew it from the moment I saw him. And because he was an enemy I did something very bad, Santosh."

"Sahib."

"I lied, Santosh. To protect you. I told him, Santosh, that I was going to give you seventy-five dollars a week after Christmas."

"Sahib."

"And now I have to make that lie true. But, Santosh, you know that is money we can't afford. I don't have to tell you about overheads and things like that. Santosh, I will give you sixty."

I said, "Sahib, I couldn't stay on for less than a hundred and twenty-five."

Priya's eyes went shiny and the hollows below his eyes darkened. He giggled and pressed out his lips. At the end of that week I got a hundred dollars. And Priya, good man that he was, bore me no grudge.

Now here was a victory. It was only after it happened that I realized how badly I had needed such a victory, how far, gaining my freedom, I had begun to accept death not as the end but as the goal. I revived. Or rather, my senses revived. But in this city what was there to feed my senses? There were no walks to be taken, no idle conversations with understanding friends. I could buy new clothes. But then? Would I just look at myself in the mirror? Would I go walking, inviting passers-by to look at me and my clothes? No, the whole business of clothes and dressing up only threw me back into myself.

There was a Swiss or German woman in the cake-shop some doors away, and there was a Filipino woman in the kitchen. They were neither of them attractive, to tell the truth. The Swiss or German could have broken my back with a slap, and the Filipino, though young, was remarkably like one of our older hill women. Still, I felt I owed something to the senses, and I thought I might frolic with these women. But then I was frightened of the responsibility. Goodness, I had learned that a woman is not just a roll and a frolic but a big creature weighing a hundred-and-so-many pounds who is going to be around afterwards.

So the moment of victory passed, without celebration. And it was strange, I thought, that sorrow lasts and can make a man look forward to death, but the mood of victory fills a moment and then is over. When my moment of victory was over I discovered below it, as if waiting for me, all my old sickness and fears: fear of my illegality, my former employer, my presumption, the *hubshi* woman. I saw then that the victory I had had was not something I had worked for, but luck; and that luck was only fate's cheating, giving an illusion of power.

But that illusion lingered, and I became restless. I decided to act, to challenge fate. I decided I would no longer stay in my room and hide. I began to go out walking in the afternoons. I gained courage; every afternoon I walked a little farther. It became my ambition to walk to that green circle with the fountain where, on my first day out in Washington, I had come upon those people in Hindu costumes, like domestics abandoned a long time ago, singing their Sanskrit gibberish and doing their strange Red Indian dance. And one day I got there.

One day I crossed the road to the circle and sat down on a bench. The *hubshi* were there, and the bare feet, and the dancers in saris and the saffron robes. It was mid-afternoon, very hot, and no one was active. I remembered how magical and inexplicable that circle had seemed to me the first time I saw it. Now it seemed so ordinary and tired: the roads, the motor cars, the shops, the trees, the careful policemen: so much part of the waste and futility that was our world. There was no longer a mystery. I felt I knew where everybody had come from and where those cars were going. But I also felt that everybody there felt like me, and that was soothing. I took to going to the circle every day after the lunch rush and sitting until it was time to go back to Priya's for the dinners.

Late one afternoon, among the dancers and the musicians, the *hubshi* and the bare feet, the singers and the police, I saw her. The *hubshi* woman. And again I wondered at her size; my memory had not exaggerated. I decided to stay where I was. She saw me and smiled. Then, as if remembering anger, she gave me a look of great hatred; and again I saw her as Kali, many-armed, goddess of death and destruction. She looked hard at my face; she considered my clothes. I thought: is it for this I bought these clothes? She got up. She was very big and her tight pants made her much more appalling. She moved towards me. I got up and ran. I ran across the road and then, not looking back, hurried by devious ways to the restaurant.

Priya was doing his accounts. He always looked older when he was doing his accounts, not worried, just older, like a man to whom life could bring no further surprises. I envied him.

"Santosh, some friend brought a parcel for you."

It was a big parcel wrapped in brown paper. He handed it to me, and I thought how calm he was, with his bills and pieces of paper, and the pen with which he made his neat figures, and the book in which he would write every day until that book was exhausted and he would begin a new one.

I took the parcel up to my room and opened it. Inside there was a cardboard box; and inside that, still in its tissue paper, was the green suit.

I felt a hole in my stomach. I couldn't think. I was glad I had to go down almost immediately to the kitchen, glad to be busy until midnight. But then I had to go up to my room again, and I was alone. I hadn't escaped; I had never been free. I had been abandoned. I was like nothing; I had made myself nothing. And I couldn't turn back.

In the morning Priya said, "You don't look very well, Santosh."

His concern weakened me further. He was the only man I could talk to and I didn't know what I could say to him. I felt tears coming to my eyes. At that moment I would have liked the whole world to be reduced to tears. I said, "Sahib, I cannot stay with you any longer."

They were just words, part of my mood, part of my wish for tears and relief. But Priya didn't soften. He didn't even look surprised. "Where will you go, Santosh?"

How could I answer his serious question?

"Will it be different where you go?"

He had freed himself of me. I could no longer think of tears. I said, "Sahib, I have enemies."

He giggled. "You are a joker, Santosh. How can a man like yourself have enemies? There would be no profit in it. *I* have enemies. It is part of your happiness and part of the equity of the world that you cannot have enemies. That's why you can run-run-runaway." He smiled and made the running gesture with his extended palm.

So, at last, I told him my story. I told him about my old employer and my escape and the green suit. He made me feel I was telling him nothing he hadn't already known. I told him about the *hubshi* woman. I was hoping for some rebuke. A rebuke would have meant that he was concerned for my honour, that I could lean on him, that rescue was possible.

But he said, "Santosh, you have no problems. Marry the *hubshi*. That will automatically make you a citizen. Then you will be a free man."

It wasn't what I was expecting. He was asking me to be alone forever. I said, "Sahib, I have a wife and children in the hills at home."

"But this is your home, Santosh. Wife and children in the hills, that is very nice and that is always there. But that is over. You have to do what is best for you here. You are alone here. *Hubshi-ubshi*, nobody worries about that here, if that is your choice. This isn't Bombay. Nobody looks at you when you walk down the street. Nobody cares what you do."

He was right. I was a free man; I could do anything I wanted. I could, if it were possible for me to turn back, go to the apartment and beg my old employer for forgiveness. I could, if it were possible for me to become again what I once was, go to the police and say, "I am an illegal immigrant here. Please deport me to Bombay." I could run away, hang myself, surrender, confess, hide. It didn't matter what I did, because I was alone. And I didn't know what I wanted to do. It was like the time when I felt my senses revive and I wanted to go out and enjoy and I found there was nothing to enjoy.

To be empty is not to be sad. To be empty is to be calm. It is to renounce. Priya said no more to me; he was always busy in the mornings. I left him and went up to my room. It was still a bare room, still like a room that in half an hour could be someone else's. I had never thought of it as mine. I was frightened of its spotless painted walls and had been careful to keep them spotless. For just such a moment.

I tried to think of the particular moment in my life, the particular action, that had brought me to that room. Was it the moment with the *hubshi* woman, or was it when the American came to dinner and insulted my employer? Was it the moment of my escape, my sight of Priya in the gallery, or was it when I looked in the mirror and bought the green suit? Or was it much earlier, in that other life, in Bombay, in the hills? I could find no one moment; every moment seemed important. An endless chain of action had brought me to that room. It was frightening; it was burdensome. It was not a time for new decisions. It was time to call a halt.

I lay on the bed watching the ceiling, watching the sky. The door was pushed open. It was Priya.

"My goodness, Santosh! How long have you been here? You have been so quiet I forgot about you."

He looked about the room. He went into the bathroom and came out again. "Are you all right, Santosh?"

He sat on the edge of the bed and the longer he stayed the more I realized how glad I was to see him. There was this: when I tried to think of him rushing into the room I couldn't place it in time; it seemed to have occurred only in my mind. He sat with me. Time became real again. I felt a great love for him. Soon I could have laughed at his agitation. And later, indeed, we laughed together.

I said, "Sahib, you must excuse me this morning. I want to go for a walk. I will come back about tea time."

He looked hard at me, and we both knew I had spoken truly.

"Yes, yes, Santosh. You go for a good long walk. Make yourself hungry with walking. You will feel much better."

Walking, through streets that were now so simple to me, I thought how nice it would be if the people in Hindu costumes in the circle were real. Then I might have joined them. We would have taken to the road; at midday we would have halted in the shade of big trees; in the late afternoon the sinking sun would have turned the dust clouds to gold; and every evening at some village there would have been welcome, water, food, a fire in the night. But that was a dream of another life. I had watched the people in the circle long enough to know that they were of their city; that their television life awaited them; that their renunciation was not like mine. No television life awaited me. It didn't matter. In this city I was alone and it didn't matter what I did.

As magical as the circle with the fountain the apartment block had once been to me. Now I saw that it was plain, not very tall, and faced with small white tiles. A glass door; four tiled steps down; the desk to the right, letters and keys in the pigeonholes; a carpet to the left, upholstered chairs, a low table with paper flowers in the vase; the blue door of the swift, silent elevator. I saw the simplicity of all these things. I knew the floor I wanted. In the corridor, with its illuminated star-decorated ceiling, an imitation sky, the colours were blue, grey and gold. I knew the door I wanted. I knocked.

The *hubshi* woman opened. I saw the apartment where she worked. I had never seen it before and was expecting something like my old employer's apartment, which was on the same floor. Instead, for the first time, I saw something arranged for a television life.

I thought she might have been angry. She looked only puzzled. I was grateful for that.

I said to her in English, "Will you marry me?"

And there, it was done.

"It is for the best, Santosh," Priya said, giving me tea when I got back to the restaurant. "You will be a free man. A citizen. You will have the whole world before you."

I was pleased that he was pleased.

So I am now a citizen, my presence is legal, and I live in Washington. I am still with Priya. We do not talk together as much as we did. The restaurant is one world, the parks and green streets of Washington are another, and every evening some of these streets take me to a third. Burnt-out brick houses, broken fences, overgrown gardens; in a levelled lot between the high brick walls of two houses, a sort of artistic children's playground which the *hubshi* children never use; and then the dark house in which I now live.

Its smells are strange, everything in it is strange. But my strength in this house is that I am a stranger. I have closed my mind and heart to the English language, to newspapers and radio and television, to the pictures of *hubshi* runners and boxers and musicians on the wall. I do not want to understand or learn any more.

I am a simple man who decided to act and see for himself, and it is as though I have had several lives. I do not wish to add to these. Some afternoons I walk to the circle with the fountain. I see the dancers but they are separated from me as by glass. Once, when there were rumours of new burnings, someone scrawled in white paint on the pavement outside my house: *Soul Brother*. I understand the words; but I feel, brother to what or to whom?

I was once part of the flow, never thinking of myself as a presence. Then I looked in the mirror and decided to be free. All that my freedom has brought me is the knowledge that I have a face and have a body, that I must feed this body and clothe this body for a certain number of years. Then it will be over.

1971

TOM STOPPARD
b. 1937

Tom Stoppard was born Tomas Straussler in the former Czechoslovakia. His family emigrated to Singapore in 1939 to escape the Nazis and moved to India in 1941 to escape the Japanese. His father stayed behind and was killed in the invasion of Singapore. Tom and his mother went to England in 1946; on her remarriage he took his stepfather's name of Stoppard. After leaving Pocklington School in Yorkshire at seventeen, he became a journalist, wrote a novel, and in 1962 had two short plays broadcast on the radio. The British theater had been dominated for a decade by realistic "kitchen sink" dramas when Stoppard's *Rosencrantz and Guildenstern Are Dead* (1966) appeared and was hailed as a major theatrical event. Critics recognized a debt to *Waiting for Godot*, but where Samuel Beckett had focused on the hopelessness of his two abandoned characters, Stoppard celebrates the gaiety and perverse vitality that can be generated from despair.

He frequently uses plays by other playwrights as launching pads for his own: Rosencrantz and Guildenstern step out of the shadows of Shakespeare's *Hamlet*; *The Real Inspector Hound* (1968) parodies Agatha Christie's classic country-house murder-mystery play, *The Mousetrap*; and the plot of *Travesties* (1974) is entwined with that of Oscar Wilde's *The Importance of Being Ernest*. Past and present are again entwined, though not intertextually, in his masterpiece, *Arcadia* (1993), which explores the nature of Nature, classical and Romantic theories of landscape gardening, literary history and historians, truth and time. As is appropriate for a play with a double time frame (early nineteenth century spliced with late twentieth century), *Arcadia* has the intricate movement of a grandfather clock, its characters and their concerns interacting with finely geared precision. Appropriately again, the classical mechanism is driven by a Romantic power source: sex—"the attraction which Newton left out."

Newton's classical mechanics posited an order underlying a seemingly disordered world. He saw its "laws" operating via cause-and-effect mechanisms, leading to determinism: given adequate information, one could predict future events. His near-contemporary, however, the wittily named heroine of Stoppard's play, Thomasina [*Tom 'as seen a*] Coverly, has seen another future, one ordered by disorder, what is now known as "chaos theory." (Stoppard found the seed of his play in James Gleick's *Chaos: The Making of a New Science*.) The opposition of order and disorder, past and future (our present), provides the structuring principle of *Arcadia*.

Its action takes place in a large room in a large English country house. Here in 1809 Thomasina, a mathematically and scientifically precocious thirteen-year-old, is being tutored by Septimus, whose friend the poet Lord Byron visits long enough to shoot a hare and, perhaps, another visiting poet, Ezra Chater, in a duel. The opposition of science and poetry is repeated, more than a century and a half later, in the second scene and the same room, when a twentieth-century member of the Coverly family, Valentine, a graduate student "chaotician," tells a visiting literary biographer and theoretician, Hannah Jarvis, about his researches in the new science. The analytically inclined Hannah and a rival, romantically inclined literary critic, Bernard Nightingale, are each embarked on a quest for the truth of Byron's role (if any) in the death of Ezra Chater.

The five principal characters of *Arcadia* are, thus, each engaged in the quest for knowledge. While truth, the whole truth scientific and humanistic, eludes the questers, the interwoven themes of the play reach their resolution in a final scene of astonishing technical virtuosity. After three scenes set in the past and three in the present, the seventh and longest brings past and present—the Romantic age and the postmodern—together. Characters from both periods are on stage simultaneously, all wearing Regency costume (the modern ones for a fancy-dress ball). The scene is at once "chaotic" and supremely ordered, ending—like so many Renaissance and later comedies—with a dance. Here, on the verge of tragedy, humanist and mathematician/ scientist from each period join hands and start to waltz. As the Russian Yevgeny Yevtushenko put it in a war poem called "Weddings," even on the verge of tragedy, "you can't not dance."

Stoppard's most recent plays are *Indian Ink* (1993); *The Invention of Love* (1997), which brings together in one galaxy A. E. Housman, Oscar Wilde, and a sparkling constellation of Victorian worthies; and *The Coast of Utopia* (2002), an epic trilogy that follows the trajectory of romantics and revolutionaries in the twilight of Czarist Russia. He shared an Oscar for the screenplay of *Shakespeare in Love* (1998) and has also written for radio and television, alternating—sometimes in the same work— between a serious handling of political themes and arabesques of exuberant fantasy. As he says: "I never quite know whether I want to be a serious artist or a siren." He has succeeded in being both, often—as in *Arcadia*—at the same time.

Stoppard was knighted in 1997 and three years later was appointed a member of the Order of Merit.

Arcadia[1]

CHARACTERS (IN ORDER OF APPEARANCE)

THOMASINA COVERLY, *aged thirteen, later sixteen*

SEPTIMUS HODGE, *her tutor, aged twenty-two, later twenty-five*

JELLABY, *a butler, middle-aged*

EZRA CHATER, *a poet, aged thirty-one*

RICHARD NOAKES, *a landscape architect, middle-aged*

LADY CROOM, *middle thirties*

CAPT. BRICE, RN,[2] *middle thirties*

HANNAH JARVIS, *an author, late thirties*

CHLOË COVERLY, *aged eighteen*

BERNARD NIGHTINGALE, *a don,[3] late thirties*

VALENTINE COVERLY, *aged twenty-five to thirty*

GUS COVERLY, *aged fifteen*

AUGUSTUS COVERLY, *aged fifteen*

Act One

SCENE ONE

A room on the garden front of a very large country house in Derbyshire in April 1809. Nowadays, the house would be called a stately home. The upstage wall is mainly tall, shapely, uncurtained windows, one or more of which work as doors. Nothing much need be said or seen of the exterior beyond. We come to learn that

1. A mountainous region of central Peloponnese, Greece; scene of idealized and idyllic country life in the pastoral poetry of ancient Greece, notably that of Theocritus, and Italy, notably that of Virgil; its shepherds are called "Arcades."
2. Royal Navy.
3. University teacher of English literature.

the house stands in the typical English park of the time. Perhaps we see an indication of this, perhaps only light and air and sky.

The room looks bare despite the large table which occupies the centre of it. The table, the straight-backed chairs and, the only other item of furniture, the architect's stand or reading stand, would all be collectable pieces now but here, on an uncarpeted wood floor, they have no more pretension than a schoolroom, which is indeed the main use of this room at this time. What elegance there is, is architectural, and nothing is impressive but the scale. There is a door in each of the side walls. These are closed, but one of the french windows[4] is open to a bright but sunless morning.

There are two people, each busy with books and paper and pen and ink, separately occupied. The pupil is THOMASINA COVERLY, *aged 13. The tutor is* SEPTIMUS HODGE, *aged 22. Each has an open book. Hers is a slim mathematics primer.[5] His is a handsome thick quarto,[6] brand new, a vanity production,[7] with little tapes to tie when the book is closed. His loose papers, etc, are kept in a stiff-backed portfolio which also ties up with tapes.*

Septimus has a tortoise which is sleepy enough to serve as a paperweight.

Elsewhere on the table there is an old-fashioned theodolite[8] and also some other books stacked up.

THOMASINA   Septimus, what is carnal embrace?[9]

SEPTIMUS   Carnal embrace is the practice of throwing one's arms around a side of beef.

THOMASINA   Is that all?

SEPTIMUS   No . . . a shoulder of mutton, a haunch of venison well hugged,[1] an embrace of grouse . . . *caro, carnis;*[2] feminine; flesh.

THOMASINA   Is it a sin?

SEPTIMUS   Not necessarily, my lady, but when carnal embrace is sinful it is a sin of the flesh, QED.[3] We had *caro* in our Gallic Wars[4]—'The Britons live on milk and meat'—'*lacte et carne vivunt*'. I am sorry that the seed fell on stony ground.[5]

THOMASINA   That was the sin of Onan,[6] wasn't it, Septimus?

SEPTIMUS   Yes. He was giving his brother's wife a Latin lesson and she was hardly the wiser after it than before. I thought you were finding a proof for Fermat's last theorem.[7]

THOMASINA   It is very difficult, Septimus. You will have to show me how.

SEPTIMUS   If I knew how, there would be no need to ask *you*. Fermat's last theorem has kept people busy for a hundred and fifty years, and I hoped it would keep *you* busy long enough for me to read Mr Chater's poem in praise of love with only the distraction of its own absurdities.

THOMASINA   Our Mr Chater has written a poem?

SEPTIMUS   He believes he has written a poem, yes. I can see that there might be more carnality in your algebra than in Mr Chater's 'Couch of Eros'.[8]

THOMASINA   Oh, it was not my algebra. I heard Jellaby telling cook that Mrs Chater was discovered in carnal embrace in the gazebo.

SEPTIMUS [*Pause*]   Really? With whom, did Jellaby happen to say?

    [THOMASINA *considers this with a puzzled frown.*]

THOMASINA   What do you mean, with whom?

SEPTIMUS   With what? Exactly so. The idea is absurd. Where did this story come from?

THOMASINA   Mr Noakes.

SEPTIMUS   Mr Noakes!

THOMASINA   Papa's landskip[9] architect. He was taking bearings in the garden when he saw—through his spyglass—Mrs Chater in the gazebo in carnal embrace.

SEPTIMUS   And do you mean to tell me that Mr Noakes told the butler?

THOMASINA   No. Mr Noakes told Mr Chater. *Jellaby* was told by the groom, who overheard Mr Noakes telling Mr Chater, in the stable yard.

SEPTIMUS   Mr Chater being engaged in closing the stable door.[1]

THOMASINA   What do you mean, Septimus?

SEPTIMUS   So, thus far, the only people who know about this are Mr Noakes the landskip architect, the groom, the butler, the cook and, of course, Mrs Chater's husband, the poet.

THOMASINA   And Arthur who was cleaning the silver, and the bootboy. And now you.

SEPTIMUS   Of course. What else did he say?

THOMASINA   Mr Noakes?

SEPTIMUS   No, not Mr Noakes. Jellaby. You heard Jellaby telling the cook.

THOMASINA   Cook hushed him almost as soon as he started. Jellaby did not see that I was being allowed to finish yesterday's upstairs[2] rabbit pie before I came to my lesson. I think you have not been candid with me, Septimus. A gazebo is not, after all, a meat larder.

SEPTIMUS   I never said my definition was complete.

THOMASINA   Is carnal embrace kissing?

SEPTIMUS   Yes.

THOMASINA   And throwing one's arms around Mrs Chater?

SEPTIMUS   Yes. Now, Fermat's last theorem—

THOMASINA   I thought as much. I hope you are ashamed.

SEPTIMUS   I, my lady?

THOMASINA   If *you* do not teach me the true meaning of things, who will?

SEPTIMUS   Ah. Yes, I am ashamed. Carnal embrace is sexual congress, which is the insertion of the male genital organ into the female genital organ for purposes of procreation and pleasure. Fermat's last theorem, by contrast, asserts that when x, y and z are whole numbers each raised to power of n, the sum of the first two can never equal the third when n is greater than 2.

    [*Pause.*]

THOMASINA   Eurghhh!

---

8. Greek god of love.
9. Landscape.
1. Proverbial saying that continues "after the horse has bolted."

2. As prepared for Lord and Lady Croom and their guests ("upstairs," as distinct from the servants "below stairs").

SEPTIMUS   Nevertheless, that is the theorem.

THOMASINA   It is disgusting and incomprehensible. Now when I am grown to practise it myself I shall never do so without thinking of you.

SEPTIMUS   Thank you very much, my lady. Was Mrs Chater down this morning?

THOMASINA   No. Tell me more about sexual congress.

SEPTIMUS   There is nothing more to be said about sexual congress.

THOMASINA   Is it the same as love?

SEPTIMUS   Oh no, it is much nicer than that.

[*One of the side doors leads to the music room. It is the other side door which now opens to admit* JELLABY, *the butler.*]

I am teaching, Jellaby.

JELLABY   Beg your pardon, Mr Hodge, Mr Chater said it was urgent you receive his letter.

SEPTIMUS   Oh, very well. [SEPTIMUS *takes the letter.*] Thank you. [*And to dismiss* JELLABY.] Thank you.

JELLABY [*Holding his ground.*]   Mr Chater asked me to bring him your answer.

SEPTIMUS   My answer?

[*He opens the letter. There is no envelope as such, but there is a 'cover' which, folded and sealed, does the same service.*

SEPTIMUS *tosses the cover negligently aside and reads.*]

Well, my answer is that as is my custom and my duty to his lordship I am engaged until a quarter to twelve in the education of his daughter. When I am done, and if Mr Chater is still there, I will be happy to wait upon him in—[*He checks the letter.*]—in the gunroom.

JELLABY   I will tell him so, thank you, sir.

[SEPTIMUS *folds the letter and places it between the pages of 'The Couch of Eros'.*]

THOMASINA   What is for dinner, Jellaby?

JELLABY   Boiled ham and cabbages, my lady, and a rice pudding.

THOMASINA   Oh, goody.

[JELLABY *leaves.*]

SEPTIMUS   Well, so much for Mr Noakes. He puts himself forward as a gentleman, a philosopher of the picturesque,[3] a visionary who can move mountains and cause lakes, but in the scheme of the garden he is as the serpent.[4]

THOMASINA   When you stir your rice pudding, Septimus, the spoonful of jam spreads itself round making red trails like the picture of a meteor in my astronomical atlas. But if you stir backward, the jam will not come together again. Indeed, the pudding does not notice and continues to turn pink just as before. Do you think this is odd?

SEPTIMUS   No.

THOMASINA   Well, I do. You cannot stir things apart.

SEPTIMUS   No more you can, time must needs run backward, and since it will not, we must stir our way onward mixing as we go, disorder out of disorder into disorder until pink is complete, unchanging and unchangeable, and we are done with it for ever.[5] This is known as free will or self-determination.

---

3. Italianate landscape associated with the writers and landscape gardeners of the early-nineteenth-century Romantic movement.
4. Noakes spies on and spoils the happiness of the lovers in the gazebo, as the serpent in the Garden of Eden poisoned the bliss of Adam and Eve (Genesis 3).
5. Evidence offered, with no awareness of its significance, of the then-undiscovered second law of thermodynamics.

[*He picks up the tortoise and moves it a few inches as though it had strayed, on top of some loose papers, and admonishes it.*]

Sit!

THOMASINA Septimus, do you think God is a Newtonian?[6]

SEPTIMUS An Etonian?[7] Almost certainly, I'm afraid. We must ask your brother to make it his first enquiry.

THOMASINA No, Septimus, a Newtonian. Septimus! Am I the first person to have thought of this?

SEPTIMUS No.

THOMASINA I have not said yet.

SEPTIMUS 'If everything from the furthest planet to the smallest atom of our brain acts according to Newton's law of motion, what becomes of free will?'

THOMASINA No.

SEPTIMUS God's will.

THOMASINA No.

SEPTIMUS Sin.

THOMASINA [*Derisively.*] No!

SEPTIMUS Very well.

THOMASINA If you could stop every atom in its position and direction, and if your mind could comprehend all the actions thus suspended, then if you were really, *really* good at algebra you could write the formula for all the future; and although nobody can be so clever to do it, the formula must exist just as if one could.

SEPTIMUS [*Pause.*] Yes. [*Pause.*] Yes, as far as I know, you are the first person to have thought of this. [*Pause. With an effort.*] In the margin of his copy of *Arithmetica*, Fermat wrote that he had discovered a wonderful proof of his theorem but, the margin being too narrow for his purpose, did not have room to write it down. The note was found after his death, and from that day to this—

THOMASINA Oh! I see now! The answer is perfectly obvious.

SEPTIMUS This time you may have overreached yourself.

[*The door is opened, somewhat violently.* CHATER *enters.*] Mr Chater! Perhaps my message miscarried. I will be at liberty at a quarter to twelve, if that is convenient.

CHATER It is not convenient, sir. My business will not wait.

SEPTIMUS Then I suppose you have Lord Croom's opinion that your business is more important than his daughter's lesson.

CHATER I do not, but, if you like, I will ask his lordship to settle the point.

SEPTIMUS [*Pause.*] My lady, take Fermat into the music room. There will be an extra spoonful of jam if you find his proof.

THOMASINA There is no proof, Septimus. The thing that is perfectly obvious is that the note in the margin was a joke to make you all mad.

[THOMASINA *leaves.*]

SEPTIMUS Now, sir, what is this business that cannot wait?

CHATER I think you know it, sir. You have insulted my wife.

SEPTIMUS Insulted her? That would deny my nature, my conduct, and the admiration in which I hold Mrs Chater.

---

6. Believer in the scientific theories of Isaac Newton (1642–1727).

7. Alumnus of the famous English public (i.e., in the U.S., private) school, Eton, which Thomasina's brother Augustus will later attend.

CHATER   I have heard of your admiration, sir! You insulted my wife in the gazebo yesterday evening!

SEPTIMUS   You are mistaken. I made love to your wife in the gazebo. She asked me to meet her there, I have her note somewhere, I dare say I could find it for you, and if someone is putting it about that I did not turn up, by God, sir, it is a slander.

CHATER   You damned lecher! You would drag down a lady's reputation to make a refuge for your cowardice. It will not do! I am calling you out![8]

SEPTIMUS   Chater! Chater, Chater, Chater! My dear friend!

CHATER   You dare to call me that. I demand satisfaction!

SEPTIMUS   Mrs Chater demanded satisfaction and now you are demanding satisfaction. I cannot spend my time day and night satisfying the demands of the Chater family. As for your wife's reputation, it stands where it ever stood.

CHATER   You blackguard!

SEPTIMUS   I assure you. Mrs Chater is charming and spirited, with a pleasing voice and a dainty step, she is the epitome of all the qualities society applauds in her sex—and yet her chief renown is for a readiness that keeps her in a state of tropical humidity as would grow orchids in her drawers in January.

CHATER   Damn you, Hodge, I will not listen to this! Will you fight or not?

SEPTIMUS   [Definitively.]   Not! There are no more than two or three poets of the first rank now living, and I will not shoot one of them dead over a perpendicular poke in a gazebo with a woman whose reputation could not be adequately defended with a platoon of musketry deployed by rota.

CHATER   Ha! You say so! Who are the others? In your opinion?—no—no—!—this goes very ill, Hodge. I will not be flattered out of my course. You say so, do you?

SEPTIMUS   I do. And I would say the same to Milton[9] were he not already dead. Not the part about his wife, of course—

CHATER   But among the living? Mr Southey?[1]

SEPTIMUS   Southey I would have shot on sight.

CHATER   [Shaking his head sadly.]   Yes, he has fallen off. I admired 'Thalaba' quite, but 'Madoc', [He chuckles.] oh dear me!—but we are straying from the business here—you took advantage of Mrs Chater, and if that were not bad enough, it appears every stableboy and scullery maid on the strength—

SEPTIMUS   Damn me! Have you not listened to a word I said?

CHATER   I have heard you, sir, and I will not deny I welcome your regard, God knows one is little appreciated if one stands outside the coterie of hacks and placemen[2] who surround Jeffrey and the Edinburgh—[3]

SEPTIMUS   My dear Chater, they judge a poet by the seating plan of Lord Holland's table![4]

CHATER   By heaven, you are right! And I would very much like to know the name of the scoundrel who slandered my verse drama 'Maid of Turkey' in the Piccadilly Recreation, too!

8. Challenging you to a duel.
9. John Milton (1608–1674), English poet.
1. Robert Southey (1774–1843), English poet, author of the long poems Thalaba and Madoc.
2. Clique of those who write only for money or social advantage.
3. Frances Lord Jeffrey (1773–1850), cofounder and editor of The Edinburgh Review (1802–29), was a stern but generally perceptive literary critic.
4. Henry Richard Vassall Fox, Lord Holland (1773–1840), British politician, exerted considerable influence on literature and politics through the hospitality that Holland House offered the brilliant and distinguished people of his day.

SEPTIMUS   'The Maid of Turkey'! I have it by my bedside! When I cannot sleep
I take up 'The Maid of Turkey' like an old friend!

CHATER [*Gratified.*]   There you are! And the scoundrel wrote he would not
give it to his dog for dinner were it covered in bread sauce and stuffed with
chestnuts. When Mrs Chater read that, she wept, sir, and would not give
herself to me for a fortnight—which recalls me to my purpose—

SEPTIMUS   The new poem, however, will make your name perpetual—

CHATER   Whether it do or not—

SEPTIMUS   It is not a question, sir. No coterie can oppose the acclamation of
the reading public. 'The Couch of Eros' will take the town.

CHATER   Is that your estimation?

SEPTIMUS   It is my intent.

CHATER   Is it, is it? Well, well! I do not understand you.

SEPTIMUS   You see I have an early copy—sent to me for review. I say review,
but I speak of an extensive appreciation of your gifts and your rightful place
in English literature.

CHATER   Well, I must say. That is certainly . . . You have written it?

SEPTIMUS [*Crisply.*]   Not yet.

CHATER   Ah. And how long does . . . ?

SEPTIMUS   To be done right, it first requires a careful re-reading of your book,
of both your books, several readings, together with outlying works[5] for an
exhibition of deference or disdain as the case merits. I make notes, of course,
I order my thoughts, and finally, when all is ready and I am *calm in my
mind* . . .

CHATER [*Shrewdly.*]   Did Mrs Chater know of this before she—before you—

SEPTIMUS   I think she very likely did.

CHATER [*Triumphantly.*]   There is nothing that woman would not do for me!
Now you have an insight to her character. Yes, by God, she is a wife to me,
sir!

SEPTIMUS   For that alone, I would not make her a widow.

CHATER   Captain Brice once made the same observation!

SEPTIMUS   Captain Brice did?

CHATER   Mr Hodge, allow me to inscribe your copy in happy anticipation.
Lady Thomasina's pen will serve us.

SEPTIMUS   Your connection with Lord and Lady Croom you owe to your fighting her ladyship's brother?

CHATER   No! It was all nonsense, sir—a canard![6] But a fortunate mistake, sir.
It brought me the patronage of a captain of His Majesty's Navy and the
brother of a countess. I do not think Mr Walter Scott[7] can say as much, and
here I am, a respected guest at Sidley Park.

SEPTIMUS   Well, sir, you can say you have received satisfaction.

[CHATER *is already inscribing the book, using the pen and ink-pot on
the table.* NOAKES *enters through the door used by* CHATER. *He carries
rolled-up plans.* CHATER, *inscribing, ignores* NOAKES. NOAKES *on seeing
the occupants, panics.*]

NOAKES   Oh!

SEPTIMUS   Ah, Mr Noakes—my muddy-mettled[8] rascal! Where's your
spyglass?

5. Other writers' books.
6. Malicious gossip.
7. Best-selling Scottish poet and, later, novelist

(1771–1832).
8. Dirty-minded.

NOAKES I beg your leave—I thought her ladyship—excuse me—

[*He is beating an embarrassed retreat when he becomes rooted by* CHA-TER'S *voice.* CHATER *reads his inscription in ringing tones.*]

CHATER 'To my friend Septimus Hodge, who stood up[9] and gave his best on behalf of the Author—Ezra Chater, at Sidley Park, Derbyshire, April 10th, 1809.' [*Giving the book to* SEPTIMUS.] There, sir—something to show your grandchildren!

SEPTIMUS This is more than I deserve, this is handsome, what do you say, Noakes?

[*They are interrupted by the appearance, outside the windows, of* LADY CROOM *and* CAPTAIN EDWARD BRICE, RN.[1] *Her first words arrive through the open door.*]

LADY CROOM Oh, no! Not the gazebo!

[*She enters, followed by* BRICE *who carries a leatherbound sketch book.*] Mr Noakes! What is this I hear?

BRICE Not only the gazebo, but the boat-house, the Chinese bridge, the shrubbery—

CHATER By God, sir! Not possible!

BRICE Mr Noakes will have it so.

SEPTIMUS Mr Noakes, this is monstrous!

LADY CROOM I am glad to hear it from *you*, Mr Hodge.

THOMASINA [*Opening the door from the music room.*] May I return now?

SEPTIMUS [*Attempting to close the door.*] Not just yet—

LADY CROOM Yes, let her stay. A lesson in folly is worth two in wisdom.

[BRICE *takes the sketch book to the reading stand, where he lays it open. The sketch book is the work of* MR NOAKES, *who is obviously an admirer of Humphry Repton's 'Red Books'.[2] The pages, drawn in watercolours, show 'before' and 'after' views of the landscape, and the pages are cunningly cut to allow the latter to be superimposed over portions of the former, though Repton did it the other way round.*]

BRICE Is Sidley Park to be an Englishman's garden or the haunt of Corsican brigands?

SEPTIMUS Let us not hyperbolize, sir.

BRICE It is rape, sir!

NOAKES [*Defending himself.*] It is the modern style.

CHATER [*Under the same misapprehension as* SEPTIMUS.] Regrettable, of course, but so it is.

[THOMASINA *has gone to examine the sketch book.*]

LADY CROOM Mr Chater, you show too much submission. Mr Hodge. I appeal to you.

SEPTIMUS Madam, I regret the gazebo, I sincerely regret the gazebo—and the boat-house up to a point—but the Chinese bridge, fantasy!—and the shrubbery I reject with contempt! Mr Chater!—would you take the word of a jumped-up jobbing gardener[3] who sees carnal embrace in every nook and cranny of the landskip!

THOMASINA Septimus, they are not speaking of carnal embrace, are you, Mama?

9. Cf. Septimus's "perpendicular poke in a gazebo" (p. 2758).
1. See p. 2753, n. 2.
2. Repton (1752–1818), a landscape architect, presented his designs in so-called Red Books show-ing "before" and "after" views of his clients' grounds. Noakes is proposing to Gothicize the classical English landscape of Sidley Park.
3. Presumptuously conceited odd-job gardener.

LADY CROOM   Certainly not. What do you know of carnal embrace?

THOMASINA   Everything, thanks to Septimus. In my opinion, Mr Noakes's scheme for the garden is perfect. It is a Salvator![4]

LADY CROOM   What does she mean?

NOAKES [*Answering the wrong question.*]   Salvator Rosa, your ladyship, the painter. He is indeed the very exemplar of the picturesque style.

BRICE   Hodge, what is this?

SEPTIMUS   She speaks from innocence not from experience.

BRICE   You call it innocence? Has he ruined you, child?

[*Pause.*]

SEPTIMUS   Answer your uncle!

THOMASINA [*To* SEPTIMUS.]   How is a ruined child different from a ruined castle?

SEPTIMUS   On such questions I defer to Mr Noakes.

NOAKES [*Out of his depth.*]   A ruined castle is picturesque, certainly.

SEPTIMUS   That is the main difference. [*To* BRICE.]   I teach the classical authors. If I do not elucidate their meaning, who will?

BRICE   As her tutor you have a duty to keep her in ignorance.

LADY CROOM   Do not dabble in paradox, Edward, it puts you in danger of fortuitous wit. Thomasina, wait in your bedroom.

THOMASINA [*Retiring.*]   Yes, mama. I did not intend to get you into trouble, Septimus. I am very sorry for it. It is plain that there are some things a girl is allowed to understand, and these include the whole of algebra, but there are others, such as embracing a side of beef, that must be kept from her until she is old enough to have a carcass of her own.

LADY CROOM   One moment.

BRICE   What is she talking about?

LADY CROOM   Meat.

BRICE   Meat?

LADY CROOM   Thomasina, you had better remain. Your knowledge of the picturesque obviously exceeds anything the rest of us can offer. Mr Hodge, ignorance should be like an empty vessel waiting to be filled at the well of truth—not a cabinet of vulgar curios.[5] Mr Noakes—now at last it is your turn—

NOAKES   Thank you, your ladyship—

LADY CROOM   Your drawing is a very wonderful transformation. I would not have recognized my own garden but for your ingenious book—is it not?—look! Here is the Park as it appears to us now, and here as it might be when Mr Noakes has done with it. Where there is the familiar pastoral refinement of an Englishman's garden, here is an eruption of gloomy forest and towering crag, of ruins where there was never a house, of water dashing against rocks where there was neither spring nor a stone I could not throw the length of a cricket pitch.[6] My hyacinth dell is become a haunt for hobgoblins, my Chinese bridge, which I am assured is superior to the one at Kew,[7] and for all I know at Peking, is usurped by a fallen obelisk overgrown with briars—

NOAKES [*Bleating.*]   Lord Little has one very similar—

4. Salvator Rosa (1615–1673), Italian painter.
5. Strange objects.
6. Area, twenty-two yards long, between cricket-

ers' "wickets."
7. Site of London's Royal Botanical Gardens.

LADY CROOM   I cannot relieve Lord Little's misfortunes by adding to my own.
Pray, what is this rustic hovel that presumes to superpose itself on my
gazebo?

NOAKES   That is the hermitage,[8] madam.

LADY CROOM   I am bewildered.

BRICE   It is all irregular, Mr Noakes.

NOAKES   It is, sir. Irregularity is one of the chiefest principles of the picturesque style—

LADY CROOM   But Sidley Park is already a picture, and a most amiable picture
too. The slopes are green and gentle. The trees are companionably grouped
at intervals that show them to advantage. The rill[9] is a serpentine ribbon
unwound from the lake peaceably contained by meadows on which the right
amount of sheep are tastefully arranged—in short, it is nature as God
intended, and I can say with the painter, '*Et in Arcadia ego!*'[1] 'Here I am in
Arcadia,' Thomasina.

THOMASINA   Yes, mama, if you would have it so.

LADY CROOM   Is she correcting my taste or my translation?

THOMASINA   Neither are beyond correction, mama, but it was your geography
caused the doubt.

LADY CROOM   Something has occurred with the girl since I saw her last, and
surely that was yesterday. How old are you this morning?

THOMASINA   Thirteen years and ten months, mama.

LADY CROOM   Thirteen years and ten months. She is not due to be pert for six
months at the earliest, or to have notions of taste for much longer. Mr
Hodge, I hold you accountable. Mr Noakes, back to you—

NOAKES   Thank you, my—

LADY CROOM   You have been reading too many novels by Mrs Radcliffe, that
is my opinion. This is a garden for *The Castle of Otranto* or *The Mysteries of
Udolpho*—[2]

CHATER   *The Castle of Otranto*, my lady, is by Horace Walpole.

NOAKES   [*Thrilled.*]   Mr Walpole the gardener?!

LADY CROOM   Mr Chater, you are a welcome guest at Sidley Park but while
you are one, *The Castle of Otranto* was written by whomsoever I say it was,
otherwise what is the point of being a guest or having one?
   [*The distant popping of guns heard.*]
Well, the guns have reached the brow[3]—I will speak to his lordship on the
subject, and we will see by and by—[*She stands looking out.*] Ah!—your
friend has got down a pigeon, Mr Hodge. [*Calls out.*] Bravo, sir!

SEPTIMUS   The pigeon, I am sure, fell to your husband or to your son, your
ladyship—my schoolfriend was never a sportsman.

BRICE   [*Looking out.*]   Yes, to Augustus!—bravo, lad!

LADY CROOM   [*Outside.*]   Well, come along! Where are my troops?
   [BRICE, NOAKES *and* CHATER *obediently follow her,* CHATER *making a
   detour to shake* SEPTIMUS's *hand fervently.*]

CHATER   My dear Mr Hodge!
   [CHATER *leaves also. The guns are heard again, a little closer.*]

---

8. Hermit's residence.
9. Stream.
1. Latin phrase, inscribed on a tomb in a painting
by the French artist Nicolas Poussin (1594–1665).
Lady Groom translates it literally, but the speaker
is often taken—as Septimus does below—to be
Death.

2. Ann Radcliffe (1764–1823) wrote Gothic novels, the most famous of which is *The Mysteries of
Udolpho* (1794). Horace Walpole (1717–1797),
author of *The Castle of Otranto* (1764), also pioneered the Gothic style of picturesque landscap-
ing.
3. Top of the hill.

THOMASINA   Pop, pop, pop . . . I have grown up in the sound of guns like the child of a siege. Pigeons and rooks in the close season,[4] grouse on the heights from August, and the pheasants to follow—partridge, snipe, woodcock, and teal—pop—pop—pop, and the culling of the herd. Papa has no need of the recording angel, his life is written in the game book.[5]

SEPTIMUS   A calendar of slaughter. 'Even in Arcadia, there am I!'

THOMASINA   Oh, phooey to Death!

[*She dips a pen and takes it to the reading stand.*]

I will put in a hermit, for what is a hermitage without a hermit? Are you in love with my mother, Septimus?

SEPTIMUS   You must not be cleverer than your elders. It is not polite.

THOMASINA   Am I cleverer?

SEPTIMUS   Yes. Much.

THOMASINA   Well, I am sorry, Septimus. [*She pauses in her drawing and produces a small envelope from her pocket.*] Mrs Chater came to the music room with a note for you. She said it was of scant importance, and that therefore I should carry it to you with the utmost safety, urgency and discretion. Does carnal embrace addle the brain?

SEPTIMUS   [*Taking the letter.*]   Invariably. Thank you. That is enough education for today.

THOMASINA   There. I have made him like the Baptist in the wilderness.[6]

SEPTIMUS   How picturesque.

[LADY CROOM *is heard calling distantly for* THOMASINA *who runs off into the garden, cheerfully, an uncomplicated girl.*

SEPTIMUS *opens Mrs Chater's note. He crumples the envelope and throws it away. He reads the note, folds it and inserts it into the pages of 'The Couch of Eros'.*]

SCENE TWO

The lights come up on the same room, on the same sort of morning, in the present day, as is instantly clear from the appearance of HANNAH JARVIS; *and from nothing else.*

Something needs to be said about this. The action of the play shuttles back and forth between the early nineteenth century and the present day, always in this same room. Both periods must share the state of the room, without the additions and subtractions which would normally be expected. The general appearance of the room should offend neither period. In the case of props—books, paper, flowers, etc., there is no absolute need to remove the evidence of one period to make way for another. However, books, etc., used in both periods should exist in both old and new versions. The landscape outside, we are told, has undergone changes. Again, what we see should neither change nor contradict.

On the above principle, the ink and pens etc., of the first scene can remain. Books and papers associated with Hannah's research, in Scene Two, can have been on the table from the beginning of the play. And so on. During the course of the play the table collects this and that, and where an object from one scene would be an anachronism in another (say a coffee mug) it is simply deemed to have become invisible. By the end of the play the table has collected an inventory of objects.

HANNAH *is leafing through the pages of Mr Noakes's sketch book. Also to hand,*

---

4. Closed to hunters.
5. For recording a sportsman's or sportswoman's kill.

6. Thomasina's hermit looks like John the Baptist (cf. Luke 1.4), who lived many years in the desert.

opened and closed, are a number of small volumes like diaries (these turn out to be Lady Croom's 'garden books'). After a few moments, HANNAH *takes the sketch book to the windows, comparing the view with what has been drawn, and then she replaces the sketch book on the reading stand.*

She wears nothing frivolous. Her shoes are suitable for the garden, which is where she goes now after picking up the theodolite from the table. The room is empty for a few moments.

One of the other doors opens to admit CHLOË *and* BERNARD. *She is the daughter of the house and is dressed casually.* BERNARD, *the visitor, wears a suit and a tie. His tendency is to dress flamboyantly, but he has damped it down for the occasion, slightly. A peacock-coloured display handkerchief boils over in his breast pocket. He carries a capacious leather bag which serves as a briefcase.*

CHLOË   Oh! Well, she *was* here . . .

BERNARD   Ah . . . the french window . . .

CHLOË   Yes. Hang on.

[CHLOË *steps out through the garden door and disappears from view.* BERNARD *hangs on. The second door opens and* VALENTINE *looks in.*]

VALENTINE   Sod.[7]

[VALENTINE *goes out again, closing the door.* CHLOË *returns, carrying a pair of rubber boots. She comes in and sits down and starts exchanging her shoes for the boots, while she talks.*]

CHLOË   The best thing is, you wait here, save you tramping around. She spends a good deal of time in the garden, as you may imagine.

BERNARD   Yes. Why?

CHLOË   Well, she's writing a history of the garden, didn't you know?

BERNARD   No, I knew she was working on the Croom papers but . . .

CHLOË   Well, it's not exactly a history of the garden either. I'll let Hannah explain it. The trench you nearly drove into is all to do with it. I was going to say make yourself comfortable but that's hardly possible, everything's been cleared out, it's en route[8] to the nearest lavatory.

BERNARD   Everything is?

CHLOË   No, this room is. They drew the line at chemical 'Ladies' '.[9]

BERNARD   Yes, I see. Did you say Hannah?

CHLOË   Hannah, yes. Will you be all right?

[*She stands up wearing the boots.*]

I won't be . . . [*But she has lost him.*] Mr Nightingale?

BERNARD   [*Waking up.*]   Yes. Thank you. Miss Jarvis is Hannah Jarvis the author?

CHLOË   Yes. Have you read her book?

BERNARD   Oh, yes. Yes.

CHLOË   I bet she's in the hermitage, can't see from here with the marquee . . .[1]

BERNARD   Are you having a garden party?

CHLOË   A dance for the district, our annual dressing up and general drunkenness. The wrinklies won't have it in the house, there was a teapot we once had to bag back from Christie's[2] in the nick of time, so anything that can be destroyed, stolen or vomited on has been tactfully removed; tactlessly, I should say—

---

7. Angry expletive.
8. On the way to.
9. They would not allow portable toilets for women in the garden.

1. Large tent.
2. Rescue from Christie's, famous London firm of auctioneers.

[*She is about to leave.*]

BERNARD   Um—look—would you tell her—would you mind not mentioning my name just yet?

CHLOË   Oh. All right.

BERNARD [*Smiling.*]   More fun to surprise her. Would you mind?

CHLOË   No. But she's bound to ask . . . Should I give you another name, just for the moment?

BERNARD   Yes, why not?

CHLOË   Perhaps another bird, you're not really a Nightingale.

[*She leaves again.* BERNARD *glances over the books on the table. He puts his briefcase down. There is the distant pop-pop of a shotgun. It takes* BERNARD *vaguely to the window. He looks out. The door he entered by now opens and* GUS *looks into the room.* BERNARD *turns and sees him.*]

BERNARD   Hello.

[GUS *doesn't speak. He never speaks. Perhaps he cannot speak. He has no composure, and faced with a stranger, he caves in and leaves again. A moment later the other door opens again and* VALENTINE *crosses the room, not exactly ignoring* BERNARD *and yet ignoring him.*]

VALENTINE   Sod, sod, sod, sod, sod, sod . . . [*As many times as it takes him to leave by the opposite door, which he closes behind him. Beyond it, he can be heard shouting.* Chlo! Chlo! BERNARD's *discomfort increases. The same door opens and* VALENTINE *returns. He looks at* BERNARD.]

BERNARD   She's in the garden looking for Miss Jarvis.

VALENTINE   Where is everything?

BERNARD   It's been removed for the, er . . .

VALENTINE   The dance is all in the tent, isn't it?

BERNARD   Yes, but this is the way to the nearest toilet.

VALENTINE   I need the commode.[3]

BERNARD   Oh. Can't you use the toilet?

VALENTINE   It's got all the game books in it.

BERNARD   Ah. The toilet has or the commode has?

VALENTINE   Is anyone looking after you?

BERNARD   Yes. Thank you. I'm Bernard Nigh—I've come to see Miss Jarvis. I wrote to Lord Croom but unfortunately I never received a reply, so I—

VALENTINE   Did you type it?

BERNARD   Type it?

VALENTINE   Was your letter typewritten?

BERNARD   Yes.

VALENTINE   My father never replies to typewritten letters.

[*He spots a tortoise which has been half-hidden on the table.*]

Oh! Where have you been hiding, Lightning? [*He picks up the tortoise.*]

BERNARD   So I telephoned yesterday and I think I spoke to you—

VALENTINE   To me? Ah! Yes! Sorry! You're doing a talk about—someone—and you wanted to ask Hannah—something—

BERNARD   Yes. As it turns out. I'm hoping Miss Jarvis will look kindly on me.

VALENTINE   I doubt it.

BERNARD   Ah, you know about research?

VALENTINE   I know Hannah.

BERNARD   Has she been here long?

---

3. Lavatory bowl enclosed in a chair or box with a cover.

VALENTINE   Well in possession,[4] I'm afraid. My mother had read her book, you see. Have you?

BERNARD   No. Yes. Her book. Indeed.

VALENTINE   She's terrifically pleased with herself.

BERNARD   Well, I dare say if I wrote a bestseller—

VALENTINE   No, for reading it. My mother basically reads gardening books.

BERNARD   She must be delighted to have Hannah Jarvis writing a book about her garden.

VALENTINE   Actually it's about hermits.

> [GUS *returns through the same door, and turns to leave again.*]

It's all right, Gus—what do you want?—

> [*But* GUS *has gone again.*]

Well . . . I'll take Lightning for his run.

BERNARD   Actually, we've met before. At Sussex,[5] a couple of years ago, a seminar . . .

VALENTINE   Oh. Was I there?

BERNARD   Yes. One of my colleagues believed he had found an unattributed short story by D. H. Lawrence,[6] and he analysed it on his home computer, most interesting, perhaps you remember the paper?

VALENTINE   Not really. But I often sit with my eyes closed and it doesn't necessarily mean I'm awake.

BERNARD   Well, by comparing sentence structures and so forth, this chap showed that there was a ninety per cent chance that the story had indeed been written by the same person as *Women in Love*. To my inexpressible joy, one of your maths mob was able to show that on the same statistical basis there was a ninety per cent chance that Lawrence also wrote the *Just William* books and much of the previous day's *Brighton and Hove Argus*.[7]

VALENTINE   [*Pause.*]   Oh, Brighton. Yes. I was there. [*And looking out.*] Oh— here she comes, I'll leave you to talk. By the way, is yours the red Mazda?

BERNARD   Yes.

VALENTINE   If you want a tip I'd put it out of sight through the stable arch before my father comes in. He won't have anyone in the house with a Japanese car. Are you queer?

BERNARD   No, actually.

VALENTINE   Well, even so.

> [VALENTINE *leaves, closing the door.* BERNARD *keeps staring at the closed door. Behind him,* HANNAH *comes to the garden door.*]

HANNAH   Mr Peacock?

> [BERNARD *looks round vaguely then checks over his shoulder for the missing Peacock, then recovers himself and turns on the Nightingale bonhomie.*]

BERNARD   Oh . . . hello! Hello. Miss Jarvis, of course. Such a pleasure. I was thrown for a moment—the photograph doesn't do you justice.

HANNAH   Photograph?

> [*Her shoes have got muddy and she is taking them off.*]

BERNARD   On the book. I'm sorry to have brought you indoors, but Lady Chloë kindly insisted she—

---

4. In a position of power.
5. Sussex University at Brighton.
6. English novelist and short-story writer (1885–1930), author of *Women in Love* (1920).

7. A local newspaper. "*Just William* books": series of "schoolboy" novels by the best-selling children's author Richmal Crompton (1890–1969).

HANNAH No matter—you would have muddied your shoes.

BERNARD How thoughtful. And how kind of you to spare me a little of your time.

[*He is overdoing it. She shoots him a glance.*]

HANNAH Are you a journalist?

BERNARD [*Shocked.*] No!

HANNAH [*Resuming.*] I've been in the ha-ha,[8] very squelchy.

BERNARD [*Unexpectedly.*] Ha-*hah*!

HANNAH What?

BERNARD A theory of mine. Ha-*hah*, not ha-ha. If you were strolling down the garden and all of a sudden the ground gave way at your feet, you're not going to go 'ha-ha', you're going to jump back and go 'ha-hah!', or more probably, 'Bloody 'ell!' . . . though personally I think old Murray was up the pole[9] on that one—in France, you know, 'ha-ha' is used to denote a strikingly ugly woman, a much more likely bet for something that keeps the cows off the lawn.

[*This is not going well for* BERNARD *but he seems blithely unaware.*
HANNAH *stares at him for a moment.*]

HANNAH Mr Peacock, what can I do for you?

BERNARD Well, to begin with, you can call me Bernard, which is my name.

HANNAH Thank you.

[*She goes to the garden door to bang her shoes together and scrape off the worst of the mud.*]

BERNARD The book!—the book is a revelation! To see Caroline Lamb[1] through your eyes is really like seeing her for the first time. I'm ashamed to say I never read her fiction, and how right you are, it's extraordinary stuff— Early Nineteenth is my period as much as anything is.

HANNAH You teach?

BERNARD Yes. And write, like you, like we all, though I've never done anything which has sold like *Caro*.[2]

HANNAH I don't teach.

BERNARD No. All the more credit to you. To rehabilitate a forgotten writer, I suppose you could say that's the main reason for an English don.[3]

HANNAH Not to teach?

BERNARD Good God, no, let the brats sort it out for themselves. Anyway, many congratulations. I expect someone will be bringing out Caroline Lamb's oeuvre[4] now?

HANNAH Yes, I expect so.

BERNARD How wonderful! Bravo! Simply as a document shedding reflected light on the character of Lord Byron, it's bound to be—

HANNAH Bernard. You did say Bernard, didn't you?

BERNARD I did.

HANNAH I'm putting my shoes on again.

BERNARD Oh. You're not going to go out?

HANNAH No, I'm going to kick you in the balls.

---

8. Ditch with a wall on its inner side below ground level, forming a boundary to a lawn without interrupting the view from the house.

9. James Murray (1837–1915), editor of the original *Oxford English Dictionary*. Bernard thinks him misguided—"up the [greasy] pole" (slang)—in the pronunciation of "ha-ha" recommended in his *OED*.

1. Novelist (1785–1828), best-known as the mistress of Lord Byron (1788–1824).

2. Title of Hannah's biography. Cf. p. 2754, n. 2.

3. See p. 2753, n. 3.

4. A writer's body of work.

BERNARD   Right. Point taken. Ezra Chater.

HANNAH   Ezra Chater.

BERNARD   Born Twickenham, Middlesex, 1778, author of two verse narratives, 'The Maid of Turkey', 1808, and 'The Couch of Eros', 1809. Nothing known after 1809, disappears from view.

HANNAH   I see. And?

BERNARD   [*Reaching for his bag.*]   There is a Sidley Park connection.
   [*He produces 'The Couch of Eros' from the bag. He reads the inscription.*]
'To my friend Septimus Hodge, who stood up and gave his best on behalf of the Author—Ezra Chater, at Sidley Park, Derbyshire, April 10th 1809.'
   [*He gives her the book.*]
I am in your hands.

HANNAH   'The Couch of Eros'. Is it any good?

BERNARD   Quite surprising.

HANNAH   You think there's a book in him?

BERNARD   No, no—a monograph perhaps for the *Journal of English Studies*. There's almost nothing on Chater, not a word in the *DNB*,[5] of course—by that time he'd been completely forgotten.

HANNAH   Family?

BERNARD   Zilch. There's only one other Chater in the British Library database.

HANNAH   Same period?

BERNARD   Yes, but he wasn't poet like our Ezra, he was a botanist who described a dwarf dahlia in Martinique[6] and died there after being bitten by a monkey.

HANNAH   And Ezra Chater?

BERNARD   He gets two references in the periodical index, one for each book, in both cases a substantial review in the *Piccadilly Recreation*, a thrice weekly folio sheet, but giving no personal details.

HANNAH   And where was this [*the book*]?

BERNARD   Private collection. I've got a talk to give next week, in London, and I think Chater is interesting, so anything on him, or this Septimus Hodge, Sidley Park, any leads at all . . . I'd be most grateful.
   [*Pause.*]

HANNAH   Well! This is a new experience for me. A grovelling academic.

BERNARD   Oh, I say.

HANNAH   Oh, but it is. All the academics who reviewed my book patronized it.

BERNARD   Surely not.

HANNAH   Surely yes. The Byron gang unzipped their flies and patronized all over it. Where is it you don't bother to teach, by the way?

BERNARD   Oh, well, Sussex, actually.

HANNAH   Sussex. [*She thinks a moment.*] Nightingale. Yes; a thousand words in the *Observer*[7] to see me off the premises with a pat on the bottom. You must know him.

BERNARD   As I say, I'm in your hands.

HANNAH   Quite. Say please, then.

---

5. British *Dictionary of National Biography*.
6. One of the Windward Islands of the Caribbean.
7. British Sunday newspaper.

BERNARD   Please.

HANNAH   Sit down, do.

BERNARD   Thank you.

> [*He takes a chair. She remains standing. Possibly she smokes; if so, perhaps now. A short cigarette-holder sounds right, too. Or brown-paper cigarillos.*]

HANNAH   How did you know I was here?

BERNARD   Oh, I didn't. I spoke to the son on the phone but he didn't mention you by name . . . and then he forgot to mention me.

HANNAH   Valentine. He's at Oxford,[8] technically.

BERNARD   Yes, I met him. Brideshead Regurgitated.[9]

HANNAH   My fiancé.

> [*She holds his look.*]

BERNARD [*Pause.*]   I'll take a chance. You're lying.

HANNAH [*Pause*]   Well done, Bernard.

BERNARD   Christ.

HANNAH   He calls me his fiancée.

BERNARD   Why?

HANNAH   It's a joke.

BERNARD   You turned him down?

HANNAH   Don't be silly, do I look like the next Countess of—

BERNARD   No, no—a freebie. The joke that consoles. My tortoise Lightning, my fiancée Hannah.

HANNAH   Oh. Yes. You have a way with you, Bernard. I'm not sure I like it.

BERNARD   What's he doing, Valentine?

HANNAH   He's a postgrad. Biology.

BERNARD   No, he's a mathematician.

HANNAH   Well, he's doing grouse.[1]

BERNARD   Grouse?

HANNAH   Not actual grouse. Computer grouse.

BERNARD   Who's the one who doesn't speak?

HANNAH   Gus.

BERNARD   What's the matter with him?

HANNAH   I didn't ask.

BERNARD   And the father sounds like a lot of fun.

HANNAH   Ah yes.

BERNARD   And the mother is the gardener. What's going on here?

HANNAH   What do you mean?

BERNARD   I nearly took her head off—she was standing in a trench at the time.

HANNAH   Archaeology. The house had a formal Italian garden until about 1740. Lady Croom is interested in garden history. I sent her my book—it contains, as you know if you've read it—which I'm not assuming, by the way—a rather good description of Caroline's garden at Brocket Hall. I'm here now helping Hermione.

BERNARD [*Impressed*]   Hermione.

HANNAH   The records are unusually complete and they have never been worked on.

---

8. University, attended by Sebastian Flyte, anti-hero of Evelyn Waugh's satirical novel of British upper-class life, *Brideshead Revisited* (1945).

9. Vomited up.

1. Valentine is researching into changes in the Sidley Park population of the grouse, a game bird.

BERNARD   I'm beginning to admire you.

HANNAH   Before was bullshit?

BERNARD   Completely. Your photograph does you justice, I'm not sure the book does.

[*She considers him. He waits, confident.*]

HANNAH   Septimus Hodge was the tutor.

BERNARD [*Quietly.*]   Attagirl.

HANNAH   His pupil was the Croom daughter. There was a son at Eton. Septimus lived in the house: the pay book specifies allowances for wine and candles. So, not quite a guest but rather more than a steward.[2] His letter of self-recommendation is preserved among the papers. I'll dig it out for you. As far as I remember he studied mathematics and natural philosophy at Cambridge. A scientist, therefore, as much as anything.

BERNARD   I'm impressed. Thank you. And Chater?

HANNAH   Nothing.

BERNARD   Oh. Nothing at all?

HANNAH   I'm afraid not.

BERNARD   How about the library?

HANNAH   The catalogue was done in the 1880s. I've been through the lot.

BERNARD   Books or catalogue?

HANNAH   Catalogue.

BERNARD   Ah. Pity.

HANNAH   I'm sorry.

BERNARD   What about the letters? No mention?

HANNAH   I'm afraid not. I've been very thorough in your period because, of course, it's my period too.

BERNARD   Is it? Actually, I don't quite know what it is you're . . .

HANNAH   The Sidley hermit.

BERNARD   Ah. Who's he?

HANNAH   He's my peg[3] for the nervous breakdown of the Romantic Imagination. I'm doing landscape and literature 1750 to 1834.

BERNARD   What happened in 1834?

HANNAH   My hermit died.

BERNARD   Of course.

HANNAH   What do you mean, of course?

BERNARD   Nothing.

HANNAH   Yes, you do.

BERNARD   No, no . . . However, Coleridge[4] also died in 1834.

HANNAH   So he did. What a stroke of luck. [*Softening.*] Thank you, Bernard.

[*She goes to the reading stand and opens Noakes's sketch book.*]

Look—there he is.

[BERNARD *goes to look.*]

BERNARD   Mmm.

HANNAH   The only known likeness of the Sidley hermit.

BERNARD   Very biblical.[5]

HANNAH   Drawn in by a later hand, of course. The hermitage didn't yet exist when Noakes did the drawings.

---

2. Chief servant.
3. On which to hang the argument of a book about the Romantic Imagination.

4. Samuel Taylor Coleridge (1722–1834), English Romantic poet.
5. See p. 2763, n. 6.

BERNARD Noakes . . . the painter?

HANNAH Landscape gardener. He'd do these books for his clients, as a sort
of prospectus. [*She demonstrates.*] Before and after, you see. This is how it
all looked until, say, 1810—smooth, undulating, serpentine—open water,
clumps of trees, classical boat-house—

BERNARD Lovely. The real England.

HANNAH You can stop being silly now, Bernard. English landscape was
invented by gardeners imitating foreign painters who were evoking classical
authors. The whole thing was brought home in the luggage from the grand
tour. Here, look—Capability Brown doing Claude, who was doing Virgil.[6]
Arcadia! And here, superimposed by Richard Noakes, untamed nature in
the style of Salvator Rosa. It's the Gothic novel expressed in landscape.
Everything but vampires. There's an account of my hermit in a letter by your
illustrious namesake.

BERNARD Florence?[7]

HANNAH What?

BERNARD No. You go on.

HANNAH Thomas Love Peacock.[8]

BERNARD Ah yes.

HANNAH I found it in an essay on hermits and anchorites[9] published in the
Cornhill Magazine in the 1860s . . . [*She fishes for the magazine itself among
the books on the table, and finds it.*] . . . 1862 . . . Peacock calls him [*She
quotes from memory.*] 'Not one of your village simpletons to frighten the
ladies, but a savant[1] among idiots, a sage of lunacy.'

BERNARD An oxy-moron,[2] so to speak.

HANNAH [*Busy*] Yes. What?

BERNARD Nothing.

HANNAH [*Having found the place.*] Here we are. 'A letter we have seen, written by the author of *Heading Hall* nearly thirty years ago, tells of a visit to
the Earl of Croom's estate, Sidley Park—'

BERNARD Was the letter to Thackeray?[3]

HANNAH [*Brought up short.*] I don't know. Does it matter?

BERNARD No. Sorry.

> [*But the gaps he leaves for her are false promises—and she is not quick
> enough. That's how it goes.*]

Only, Thackeray edited the *Cornhill* until '63 when, as you know, he died.
His father had been with the East India Company where Peacock, of course,
had held the position of Examiner, so it's quite possible that if the essay
were by Thackeray, the *letter* . . . Sorry. Go on.

Of course, the East India Library in Blackfriars has most of Peacock's
letters, so it would be quite easy to . . . Sorry. Can I look?

> [*Silently she hands him the* Cornhill.]

6. Hannah sees Lancelot "Capability" Brown
(1715–1783), England's most celebrated landscape designer, imitating ("doing") Claude Lorrain
(1600–1682), French landscape painter, who was
imitating Virgil's *Georgics*, poems celebrating the
country/pastoral life of an idealized Arcadia.
7. Florence Nightingale (1820–1910), English
nurse considered the founder of modern nursing
(Bernard has temporarily forgotten his alias).
8. English novelist and poet (1785–1866), author
of *Headlong* [not *Heading*] Hall (1816), and one-
time "Examiner" (investigator) with the British
East India Company in India.
9. People who have withdrawn from the world,
usually for religious reasons.
1. Learned man.
2. Phrase that seems to contradict itself ("sage of
lunacy"), here prompting Bernard's pun on
"moron" (meaning "idiot").
3. William Makepeace Thackeray (1811–1863),
English novelist and poet.

Yes, it's been topped and tailed, of course. It might be worth . . . Go on. I'm listening . . .

[*Leafing through the essay, he suddenly chuckles.*] Oh yes, it's Thackeray all right . . .

[*He slaps the book shut.*] Unbearable . . .

[*He hands it back to her.*] What were you saying?

HANNAH Are you always like this?

BERNARD Like what?

HANNAH The point is, the Crooms, of course, had the hermit under their noses for twenty years so hardly thought him worth remarking. As I'm finding out. The Peacock letter is still the main source, unfortunately. When I read this [*the magazine in her hand*], well, it was one of those moments that tell you what your next book is going to be. The hermit of Sidley Park was my . . .

BERNARD Peg.

HANNAH Epiphany.

BERNARD Epiphany, that's it.

HANNAH The hermit was *placed* in the landscape exactly as one might place a pottery gnome. And there he lived out his life as a garden ornament.

BERNARD Did he do anything?

HANNAH Oh, he was very busy. When he died, the cottage was stacked solid with paper. Hundreds of pages. Thousands. Peacock says he was suspected of genius. It turned out, of course, he was off his head. He'd covered every sheet with cabalistic[4] proofs that the world was coming to an end. It's perfect, isn't it? A perfect symbol, I mean.

BERNARD Oh, yes. Of what?

HANNAH The whole Romantic sham, Bernard! It's what happened to the Enlightenment, isn't it? A century of intellectual rigour turned in on itself. A mind in chaos suspected of genius. In a setting of cheap thrills and false emotion. The history of the garden says it all, beautifully. There's an engraving of Sidley Park in 1730 that makes you want to weep. Paradise in the age of reason. By 1760 everything had gone—the topiary, pools and terraces, fountains, an avenue of limes—the whole sublime geometry was ploughed under by Capability Brown. The grass went from the doorstep to the horizon and the best box hedge in Derbyshire was dug up for the ha-ha so that the fools could pretend they were living in God's countryside. And then Richard Noakes came in to bring God up to date. By the time he'd finished it looked like this [*the sketch book*]. The decline from thinking to feeling, you see.

BERNARD [*A judgement.*] That's awfully good.

[HANNAH *looks at him in case of irony but he is professional.*]

No, that'll stand up.

HANNAH Thank you.

BERNARD Personally I like the ha-ha. Do you like hedges?

HANNAH I don't like sentimentality.

BERNARD Yes, I see. Are you sure? You seem quite sentimental over geometry. But the hermit is very very good. The genius[5] of the place.

HANNAH [*Pleased.*] That's my title!

BERNARD Of course.

---

4. Coded.
5. With a pun on the meaning "attendant spirit of a person or a place."

HANNAH [*Less pleased.*] Of course?

BERNARD Of course. Who was he when he wasn't being a symbol?

HANNAH I don't know.

BERNARD Ah.

HANNAH I mean, yet.

BERNARD Absolutely. What did they do with all the paper? Does Peacock say?

HANNAH Made a bonfire.

BERNARD Ah, well.

HANNAH I've still got Lady Croom's garden books to go through.

BERNARD Account books or journals?

HANNAH A bit of both. They're gappy but they span the period.

BERNARD Really? Have you come across Byron at all? As a matter of interest.

HANNAH A first edition of 'Childe Harold' in the library, and *English Bards,* I think.[6]

BERNARD Inscribed?

HANNAH No.

BERNARD And he doesn't pop up in the letters at all?

HANNAH Why should he? The Crooms don't pop up in his.

BERNARD [*Casually.*] That's true, of course. But Newstead[7] isn't so far away. Would you mind terribly if I poked about a bit? Only in the papers you've done with, of course.

    [HANNAH *twigs*[8] *something.*]

HANNAH Are you looking into Byron or Chater?

    [CHLOË *enters in stockinged feet through one of the side doors, laden with an armful of generally similar leather-covered ledgers. She detours to collect her shoes.*]

CHLOË Sorry—just cutting through—there's tea in the pantry if you don't mind mugs—

BERNARD How kind.

CHLOË Hannah will show you.

BERNARD Let me help you.

CHLOË No, it's all right—

    [BERNARD *opens the opposite door for her.*]

Thank you—I've been saving Val's game books. Thanks.

    [BERNARD *closes the door.*]

BERNARD Sweet girl.

HANNAH Mmm.

BERNARD Oh, really?

HANNAH Oh really what?

    [CHLOË's *door opens again and she puts her head round it.*]

CHLOË Meant to say, don't worry if father makes remarks about your car, Mr Nightingale, he's got a thing about—[*and the Nightingale now being out of the bag*] ooh—ah, how was the surprise?—not yet, eh? Oh, well—sorry—tea, anyway—so sorry if I—[*Embarrassed, she leaves again, closing the door. Pause.*]

HANNAH You absolute shit.

    [*She heads off to leave.*]

---

6. Two of Byron's long poems: *English Bards and Scotch Reviewers* (1809) and *Childe Harold's Pilgrimage* (1812).

7. Newstead Abbey, Byron's family home.
8. Perceives.

BERNARD The thing is, there's a Byron connection too.

[HANNAH *stops and faces him.*]

HANNAH I don't care.

BERNARD You should. The Byron gang are going to get their dicks caught in their zip.

HANNAH [*Pause.*] Oh really?

BERNARD If we collaborate.

HANNAH On what?

BERNARD Sit down, I'll tell you.

HANNAH I'll stand for the moment.

BERNARD This copy of 'The Couch of Eros' belonged to Lord Byron.

HANNAH It belonged to Septimus Hodge.

BERNARD Originally, yes. But it was in Byron's library which was sold to pay his debts when he left England for good in 1816. The sales catalogue is in the British Library. 'Eros' was lot 74A and was bought by the bookseller and publisher John Nightingale of Opera Court, Pall Mall . . . whose name survives in the firm of Nightingale and Matlock, the present Nightingale being my cousin.

[*He pauses.* HANNAH *hesitates and then sits down at the table.*]

I'll just give you the headlines. 1939, stock removed to Nightingale country house in Kent. 1945, stock returned to bookshop. Meanwhile, overlooked box of early nineteenth-century books languish in country house cellar until house sold to make way for the Channel Tunnel rail-link.[9] 'Eros' discovered with sales slip from 1816 attached—photocopy available for inspection.

[*He brings this from his bag and gives it to* HANNAH *who inspects it.*]

HANNAH All right. It was in Byron's library.

BERNARD A number of passages have been underlined.

[HANNAH *picks up the book and leafs through it.*]

All of them, and only them—no, no, look at me, not at the book—all the underlined passages, word for word, were used as quotations in the review of 'The Couch of Eros' in the *Piccadilly Recreation* of April 30th 1809. The reviewer begins by drawing attention to his previous notice in the same periodical of 'The Maid of Turkey'.

HANNAH The reviewer is obviously Hodge. 'My friend Septimus Hodge who stood up and gave his best on behalf of the Author.'

BERNARD That's the point. The *Piccadilly* ridiculed both books.

HANNAH [*Pause.*] Do the reviews read like Byron?

BERNARD [*Producing two photocopies from his case.*] They read a damn sight more like Byron than Byron's review of Wordsworth the previous year.

[HANNAH *glances over the photocopies.*]

HANNAH I see. Well, congratulations. Possibly. Two previously unknown book reviews by the young Byron. Is that it?

BERNARD No. Because of the tapes, three documents survived undisturbed in the book.

[*He has been carefully opening a package produced from his bag. He has the originals. He holds them carefully one by one.*]

'Sir—we have a matter to settle. I wait on you in the gun room. E. Chater, Esq.'

---

9. High-speed railway line linking London with the tunnel that crosses the English Channel.

'My husband has sent to town for pistols. Deny what cannot be proven—
for Charity's sake—I keep my room this day.' Unsigned.

'Sidley Park, April 11th 1809. Sir—I call you a liar, a lecher, a slanderer in
the press and a thief of my honour. I wait upon your arrangements for giving
me satisfaction as a man and a poet. E. Chater, Esq.'

[*Pause.*]

HANNAH   Superb. But inconclusive. The book had seven years to find its way
into Byron's possession. It doesn't connect Byron with Chater, or with Sidley
Park. Or with Hodge for that matter. Furthermore, there isn't a hint in
Byron's letters and this kind of scrape is the last thing he would have kept
quiet about.

BERNARD   *Scrape?*

HANNAH   He would have made a comic turn out of it.

BERNARD   Comic turn, fiddlesticks! [*He pauses for effect.*] He killed Chater!

HANNAH [*A raspberry.*]   Oh, really!

BERNARD   Chater was thirty-one years old. The author of two books. Nothing
more is heard from him after 'Eros'. He disappears completely after April
1809. And Byron—Byron had just published his satire, *English Bards
and Scotch Reviewers*, in March. He was just getting a name. Yet he sailed
for Lisbon[1] as soon as he could find a ship, and stayed abroad for two
years. Hannah, *this is fame*. Somewhere in the Croom papers there will be
something—

HANNAH   There isn't, I've looked.

BERNARD   But you were looking for something else! It's not going to jump out
at you like 'Lord Byron remarked wittily at breakfast!'

HANNAH   Nevertheless his presence would be unlikely to have gone unremarked. But there is nothing to suggest that Byron was here, and I don't
believe he ever was.

BERNARD   All right, but let me have a look.

HANNAH   You'll queer my pitch.[2]

BERNARD   Dear girl, I know how to handle myself—

HANNAH   And don't call me dear girl. If I find anything on Byron, or Chater,
or Hodge, I'll pass it on. Nightingale, Sussex.

[*Pause. She stands up.*]

BERNARD   Thank you. I'm sorry about that business with my name.

HANNAH   Don't mention it . . .

BERNARD   What was Hodge's college,[3] by the way?

HANNAH   Trinity.

BERNARD   Trinity?

HANNAH   Yes. [*She hesitates.*] Yes. Byron's old college.

BERNARD   How old was Hodge?

HANNAH   I'd have to look it up but a year or two older than Byron. Twenty-
two . . .

BERNARD   Contemporaries at Trinity?

HANNAH [*Wearily.*]   Yes, Bernard, and no doubt they were both in the cricket
eleven when Harrow played Eton at Lords![4]

1. Capital of Portugal.
2. Spoil my chances.
3. At Cambridge University.
4. Contemporaries also at Harrow School, Byron
and Hodge could have been in the same team (of
eleven players) that played against Eton at Lords
cricket ground in London.

[BERNARD *approaches her and stands close to her.*]

BERNARD [*Evenly.*] Do you mean that Septimus Hodge was at school with Byron?

HANNAH [*Falters slightly.*] Yes . . . he must have been . . . as a matter of fact.

BERNARD Well, you silly cow.

[*With a large gesture of pure happiness,* BERNARD *throws his arms around* HANNAH *and gives her a great smacking kiss on the cheek.* CHLOË *enters to witness the end of this.*]

CHLOË Oh—erm . . . I thought I'd bring it to you.

[*She is carrying a small tray with two mugs on it.*]

BERNARD I have to go and see about my car.

HANNAH Going to hide it?

BERNARD Hide it? I'm going to sell it! Is there a pub I can put up at in the village?

[*He turns back to them as he is about to leave through the garden.*]
Aren't you glad I'm here?

[*He leaves.*]

CHLOË He said he knew you.

HANNAH He couldn't have.

CHLOË No, perhaps not. He said he wanted to be a surprise, but I suppose that's different. I thought there was a lot of sexual energy there, didn't you?

HANNAH What?

CHLOË Bouncy on his feet, you see, a sure sign. Should I invite him for you?

HANNAH To what? No.

CHLOË You can invite him—that's better. He can come as your partner.

HANNAH Stop it. Thank you for the tea.

CHLOË If you don't want him, I'll have him. Is he married?

HANNAH I haven't the slightest idea. Aren't you supposed to have a pony?

CHLOË I'm just trying to fix you up, Hannah.

HANNAH Believe me, it gets less important.

CHLOË I mean for the dancing. He can come as Beau Brummel[5]

HANNAH I don't want to dress up and I don't want a dancing partner, least of all Mr Nightingale. I don't dance.

CHLOË Don't be such a prune. You were kissing him, anyway.

HANNAH He was kissing me, and only out of general enthusiasm.

CHLOË Well, don't say I didn't give you first chance. My genius brother will be much relieved. He's in love with you, I suppose you know.

HANNAH [*Angry.*] That's a joke!

CHLOË It's not a joke to him.

HANNAH Of course it is—not even a joke—how can you be so ridiculous?

[GUS *enters from the garden, in his customary silent awkwardness.*]

CHLOË Hello, Gus, what have you got?

[GUS *has an apple, just picked, with a leaf or two still attached. He offers the apple to* HANNAH.][6]

HANNAH [*Surprised.*] Oh! . . . Thank you!

CHLOË [*Leaving.*] Told you.

---

5. George Bryan Brummel (1778–1840), known as "Beau" because of his elegant clothes.
6. Cf. Genesis 3.1–6, specifically Eve's gift of an apple to Adam in the Garden of Eden; cf. also the golden apple of discord given by Paris to the goddess Aphrodite in Greek legend.

[CHLOË *close the door on herself.*]
HANNAH   Thank you. Oh dear.

SCENE THREE

The schoolroom. The next morning. Present are: THOMASINA, SEPTIMUS, JEL-
LABY. *We have seen this composition before:* THOMASINA *at her place at the table;*
SEPTIMUS *reading a letter which has just arrived;* JELLABY *waiting, having just
delivered the letter.*
   'The Couch of Eros' is in front of SEPTIMUS, *open, together with sheets of paper
on which he has been writing. His portfolio is on the table. Plautus (the tortoise)
is the paperweight. There is also an apple on the table now, the same apple from
all appearances.*

SEPTIMUS [*With his eyes on the letter.*]   Why have you stopped?
   [THOMASINA *is studying a sheet of paper, a 'Latin unseen' lesson.*[7] *She is
      having some difficulty.*]
THOMASINA   *Solio insessa . . . in igne . . .* seated on a throne . . . in the fire . . .
   and also on a ship . . . *sedebat regina . . .* sat the queen . . .
SEPTIMUS   There is no reply, Jellaby. Thank you.
   [*He folds the letter up and places it between the leaves of 'The Couch
      of Eros'.*]
JELLABY   I will say so, sir.
THOMASINA   . . . the wind smelling sweetly . . . *purpureis velis . . .* by, with or
   from purple sails—
SEPTIMUS [*To* JELLABY]   I will have something for the post, if you would be so
   kind.
JELLABY [*Leaving.*]   Yes sir.
THOMASINA   . . . was like as to—something—by, with or from lovers—oh,
   Septimus!—*musica tibiarum imperabat . . .* music of pipes commanded . . .
SEPTIMUS   'Ruled' is better.
THOMASINA   . . . the silver oars—exciting the ocean—as if—as if—amorous—
SEPTIMUS   That is very good.
   [*He picks up the apple. He picks off the twig and leaves, placing these
      on the table. With a pocket knife he cuts a slice of apple, and while he
      eats it, cuts another slice which he offers to Plautus.*]
THOMASINA   *Regina reclinabat . . .* the queen—was reclining—*praeter des-
   criptionem*—indescribably—in a golden tent . . . like Venus and yet more—
SEPTIMUS   Try to put some poetry into it.
THOMASINA   How can I if there is none in the Latin?
SEPTIMUS   Oh, a critic!
THOMASINA   Is it Queen Dido?[8]
SEPTIMUS   No.
THOMASINA   Who is the poet?
SEPTIMUS   Known to you.
THOMASINA   Known to me?
SEPTIMUS   Not a Roman.

---

7. Latin passage that a student is required to
translate: here the Roman historian Plutarch's
description of Cleopatra in her barge, on which
Shakespeare based a famous speech by Enobarbus
(*Antony and Cleopatra* 2.2.196ff.) Below Septimus

pretends Shakespeare's lines are his own translation.
8. Legendary queen of Carthage who, abandoned
by her lover Aeneas, in Virgil's *Aeneid*, commits
suicide.

THOMASINA Mr Chater?

SEPTIMUS Your translation is quite like Chater.

[SEPTIMUS *picks up his pen and continues with his own writing.*]

THOMASINA I know who it is, it is your friend Byron.

SEPTIMUS Lord Byron, if you please.

THOMASINA Mama is in love with Lord Byron.

SEPTIMUS [*Absorbed.*] Yes. Nonsense.

THOMASINA It is not nonsense. I saw them together in the gazebo.

[SEPTIMUS's *pen stops moving, he raises his eyes to her at last.*]

Lord Byron was reading to her from his satire, and mama was laughing, with her head in her best position.

SEPTIMUS She did not understand the satire, and was showing politeness to a guest.

THOMASINA She is vexed with papa for his determination to alter the park, but that alone cannot account for her politeness to a guest. She came downstairs hours before her custom. Lord Byron was amusing at breakfast. He paid you a tribute, Septimus.

SEPTIMUS Did he?

THOMASINA He said you were a witty fellow, and he had almost by heart an article you wrote about—well, I forget what, but it concerned a book called 'The Maid of Turkey' and how you would not give it to your dog for dinner.

SEPTIMUS Ah. Mr Chater was at breakfast, of course.

THOMASINA He was, not like certain lazybones.

SEPTIMUS He does not have Latin to set and mathematics to correct.

[*He takes Thomasina's lesson book from underneath Plautus and tosses it down the table to her.*]

THOMASINA Correct? What was incorrect in it? [*She looks into the book.*] Alpha minus?[9] Pooh! What is the minus for?

SEPTIMUS For doing more than was asked.

THOMASINA You did not like my discovery?

SEPTIMUS A fancy is not a discovery.

THOMASINA A gibe is not a rebuttal.

[SEPTIMUS *finishes what he is writing. He folds the pages into a letter. He has sealing wax and the means to melt it. He seals the letter and writes on the cover. Meanwhile—*]

You are churlish with me because mama is paying attention to your friend. Well, let them elope, they cannot turn back the advancement of knowledge. I think it is an excellent discovery. Each week I plot your equations dot for dot, *x*s against *y*s in all manner of algebraical relation, and every week they draw themselves as commonplace geometry, as if the world of forms were nothing but arcs and angles. God's truth, Septimus, if there is an equation for a curve like a bell, there must be an equation for one like a bluebell, and if a bluebell, why not a rose? Do we believe nature is written in numbers?

SEPTIMUS We do.

THOMASINA Then why do your equations only describe the shapes of manufacture?

SEPTIMUS I do not know.

THOMASINA Armed thus, God could only make a cabinet.

---

9. A grade of A minus.

SEPTIMUS He has mastery of equations which lead into infinities where we cannot follow.

THOMASINA What a faint-heart! We must work outward from the middle of the maze. We will start with something simple. [*She picks up the apple leaf.*] I will plot this leaf and deduce its equation. You will be famous for being my tutor when Lord Byron is dead and forgotten.

    [SEPTIMUS *completes the business with his letter. He puts the letter in his pocket.*]

SEPTIMUS [*Firmly.*] Back to Cleopatra.[1]

THOMASINA Is it Cleopatra?—I hate Cleopatra!

SEPTIMUS You hate her? Why?

THOMASINA Everything is turned to love with her. New love, absent love, lost love—I never knew a heroine that makes such noodles of our sex. It only needs a Roman general to drop anchor outside the window and away goes the empire like a christening mug into a pawn shop. If Queen Elizabeth had been a Ptolemy history would have been quite different—we would be admiring the pyramids of Rome and the great Sphinx of Verona.[2]

SEPTIMUS God save us.

THOMASINA But instead, the Egyptian noodle made carnal embrace with the enemy who burned the great library of Alexandria without so much as a fine for all that is overdue. Oh, Septimus!—can you bear it? All the lost plays of the Athenians! Two hundred at least by Aeschylus, Sophocles, Euripides— thousands of poems—Aristotle's own library brought to Egypt by the noodle's ancestors![3] How can we sleep for grief?

SEPTIMUS By counting our stock. Seven plays from Aeschylus, seven from Sophocles, *nineteen* from Euripides, my lady! You should no more grieve for the rest than for a buckle lost from your first shoe, or for your lesson book which will be lost when you are old. We shed as we pick up, like travellers who must carry everything in their arms, and what we let fall will be picked up by those behind. The procession is very long and life is very short. We die on the march. But there is nothing outside the march so nothing can be lost to it. The missing plays of Sophocles will turn up piece by piece, or be written again in another language. Ancient cures for diseases will reveal themselves once more. Mathematical discoveries glimpsed and lost to view will have their time again. You do not suppose, my lady, that if all of Archimedes[4] had been hiding in the great library of Alexandria, we would be at a loss for a corkscrew? I have no doubt that the improved steam-driven heat-engine which puts Mr Noakes into an ecstasy that he and it and the modern age should all coincide, was described on papyrus. Steam and brass were not invented in Glasgow. Now, where are we? Let me see if I can attempt a free translation for you. At Harrow I was better at this than Lord Byron.

    [*He takes the piece of paper from her and scrutinizes it, testing one or two Latin phrases speculatively before committing himself.*]

    Yes—'The barge she sat in, like a burnished throne . . . burned on the water

---

1. Queen of Egypt (69–30 B.C.E.), mistress of the Roman Marc Antony.
2. In Italy. I.e., if Queen Elizabeth I of England (1533–1603) had been Cleopatra (a member of the Ptolemy family), says Thomasina, Egypt would have overthrown the Roman Empire.
3. The plays of Aeschylus (525–456 B.C.E.), Soph-

ocles (ca. 496–406 B.C.E.), and Euripides (ca. 484–406 B.C.E.) and the library of the philosopher Aristotle (384–322 B.C.E.) had been brought to Egypt from Greece by Cleopatra's forebears.
4. All the writings of the Greek scientist Archimedes (ca. 287–212 B.C.E.), who invented the Archimedean screw to raise water.

. . . the—something—the poop was beaten gold, purple the sails, and—what's this?—oh yes,—so perfumed that—

THOMASINA [*Catching on and furious.*]   Cheat!

SEPTIMUS [*Imperturbably.*]   '—the winds were lovesick with them . . .'

THOMASINA   Cheat!

SEPTIMUS   ' . . . the oars were silver which to the tune of flutes kept stroke . . .'

THOMASINA [*Jumping to her feet.*]   Cheat! Cheat! Cheat!

SEPTIMUS [*As though it were too easy to make the effort worthwhile.*]   ' . . . and made the water which they beat to follow faster, as *amorous* of their strokes. For her own person, it beggared all description—she did lie in her pavilion—'

[THOMASINA, *in tears of rage, is hurrying out through the garden.*]

THOMASINA   I hope you die!

[*She nearly bumps into* BRICE *who is entering. She runs out of sight.* BRICE *enters.*]

BRICE   Good God, man, what have you told her?

SEPTIMUS   Told her? Told her what?

BRICE   Hodge!

[SEPTIMUS *looks outside the door, slightly contrite about* THOMASINA, *and sees that* CHATER *is skulking out of view.*]

SEPTIMUS   Chater! My dear fellow! Don't hang back—come in, sir!

[CHATER *allows himself to be drawn sheepishly into the room, where* BRICE *stands on his dignity.*]

CHATER   Captain Brice does me the honour—I mean to say, sir, whatever you have to say to me, sir, address yourself to Captain Brice.[5]

SEPTIMUS   How unusual. [*To* BRICE.] Your wife did not appear yesterday, sir. I trust she is not sick?

BRICE   My wife? I have no wife. What the devil do you mean, sir?

[SEPTIMUS *makes to reply, but hesitates, puzzled. He turns back to* CHATER.]

SEPTIMUS   I do not understand the scheme, Chater. Whom do I address when I want to speak to Captain Brice?

BRICE   Oh, slippery, Hodge—slippery!

SEPTIMUS [*To* CHATER]   By the way, Chater—[*He interrupts himself and turns back to* BRICE, *and continues as before.*] by the way, Chater, I have amazing news to tell you. Someone has taken to writing wild and whirling letters in your name. I received one not half an hour ago.

BRICE [*Angrily.*]   Mr Hodge! Look to your honour, sir! If you cannot attend to me without this foolery, nominate your second who might settle the business as between gentlemen. No doubt your friend Byron would do you the service.

[SEPTIMUS *gives up the game.*]

SEPTIMUS   Oh yes, he would do me the service. [*His mood changes, he turns to* CHATER.] Sir—I repent your injury. You are an honest fellow with no more malice in you than poetry.

CHATER [*Happily.*]   Ah well!—that is more like the thing! [*Overtaken by doubt.*] Is he apologizing?

BRICE   There is still the injury to his conjugal[6] property, Mrs Chater's—

CHATER   Tush,[7] sir!

---

5. Brice has done Chater "the honour" of agreeing to act as his "second" (supporter) in the duel to which Chater has challenged Septimus. Dueling etiquette required the two seconds to arrange the time, place, and choice of weapons.

6. Marital.

7. Expression of mild irritation, which Brice turns into a vulgar joke.

BRICE   As you will—her tush. Nevertheless—
         [*But they are interrupted by* LADY CROOM, *also entering from the garden.*]
LADY CROOM   Oh—excellently found! Mr Chater, this will please you very much. Lord Byron begs a copy of your new book. He dies to read it and intends to include your name in the second edition of his *English Bards and Scotch Reviewers.*
CHATER   *English Bards and Scotch Reviewers,* your ladyship, is a doggerel aimed at Lord Byron's seniors and betters. If he intends to include me, he intends to insult me.
LADY CROOM   Well, of course he does, Mr Chater. Would you rather be thought not worth insulting? You should be proud to be in the company of Rogers and Moore and Wordsworth—[8] ah! 'The Couch of Eros!' [*For she has spotted Septimus's copy of the book on the table.*]
SEPTIMUS   That is my copy, madam.
LADY CROOM   So much the better—what are a friend's books for if not to be borrowed?
         [*Note: 'The Couch of Eros' now contains the three letters, and it must do so without advertising the fact. This is why the volume has been described as a substantial quarto.*]
         Mr Hodge, you must speak to your friend[9] and put him out of his affectation of pretending to quit us. I will not have it. He says he is determined on the Malta packet sailing out of Falmouth! His head is full of Lisbon and Lesbos, and his portmanteau[1] of pistols, and I have told him it is not to be thought of. The whole of Europe is in a Napoleonic fit,[2] all the best ruins will be closed, the roads entirely occupied with the movement of armies, the lodgings turned to billets[3] and the fashion for godless republicanism not yet arrived at its natural reversion. He says his aim is poetry. One does not aim at poetry with pistols. At poets, perhaps. I charge you to take command of his pistols, Mr Hodge! He is not safe with them. His lameness, he confessed to me, is entirely the result of his habit from boyhood of shooting himself in the foot.[4] What is that *noise?*
         [*The noise is a badly played piano in the next room. It has been going on for some time since* THOMASINA *left.*]
SEPTIMUS   The new Broadwood pianoforte,[5] madam. Our music lessons are at an early stage.
LADY CROOM   Well, restrict your lessons to the *piano* side of the instrument and let her loose on the *forte* when she has learned something.
         [LADY CROOM, *holding the book, sails out back into the garden.*]
BRICE   Now! If that was not God speaking through Lady Croom, he never spoke through anyone!
CHATER   [*Awed.*]   Take command of Lord Byron's pistols!
BRICE   You hear Mr Chater, sir—how will you answer him?
         [SEPTIMUS *has been watching* LADY CROOM'S *progress up the garden. He turns back.*]

---

8. Samuel Rogers (1763–1855), English poet; Thomas Moore (1779–1852), Irish poet, friend and biographer of Byron; William Wordsworth (1770–1850), English poet.
9. Lord Byron.
1. Suitcase. "Packet": mail boat, which also carried passengers. "Lesbos": Greek island.
2. France, under Napoleon, was fighting the Peninsula War (1804–14) against Great Britain, Portugal, and Spanish guerrillas in the Iberian Peninsula.
3. Accommodation for troops.
4. Byron was born with a clubfoot.
5. An early form of the piano, its name combining the Italian words for soft and loud, respectively.

SEPTIMUS   By killing him. I am tired of him.

CHATER [*Startled.*]   Eh?

BRICE [*Pleased.*]   Ah!

SEPTIMUS   Oh, damn your soul, Chater! Ovid[6] would have stayed a lawyer and Virgil a farmer if they had known the bathos[7] to which love would descend in your sportive satyrs and noodle nymphs![8] I am at your service with a half-ounce ball[9] in your brain. May it satisfy you—behind the boat-house at daybreak—shall we say five o'clock? My compliments to Mrs Chater—have no fear for her, she will not want for protection while Captain Brice has a guinea[1] in his pocket, he told her so himself.

BRICE   You lie, sir!

SEPTIMUS   No, sir. Mrs Chater, perhaps.

BRICE   You lie, or you will answer to me!

SEPTIMUS [*Wearily.*]   Oh, very well—I can fit you in at five minutes after five. And then it's off to the Malta packet out of Falmouth. You two will be dead, my penurious[2] schoolfriend will remain to tutor Lady Thomasina, and I trust everybody including Lady Croom will be satisfied!

　　　　[SEPTIMUS *slams the door behind him.*]

BRICE   He is all bluster and bladder. Rest assured, Chater, I will let the air out of him.

　　　　[BRICE *leaves by the other door.* CHATER's *assurance lasts only a moment. When he spots the flaw* . . .[3]]

CHATER   Oh! But . . .

　　　　[*He hurries out after* BRICE.]

SCENE FOUR

HANNAH *and* VALENTINE. *She is reading aloud. He is listening. Lightning, the tortoise, is on the table and is not readily distinguishable from Plautus. In front of* VALENTINE *is Septimus's portfolio, recognizably so but naturally somewhat faded. It is open. Principally associated with the portfolio (although it may contain sheets of blank paper also) are three items: a slim maths primer; a sheet of drawing paper on which there is a scrawled diagram and some mathematical notations, arrow marks, etc.; and Thomasina's mathematics lesson book, i.e. the one she writes in, which* VALENTINE *is leafing through as he listens to* HANNAH *reading from the primer.*

HANNAH   'I, Thomasina Coverly, have found a truly wonderful method whereby all the forms of nature must give up their numerical secrets and draw themselves through number alone. This margin being too mean for my purpose, the reader must look elsewhere for the New Geometry of Irregular Forms discovered by Thomasina Coverly.'

　　　　[*Pause. She hands* VALENTINE *the text book.* VALENTINE *looks at what she has been reading.*

　　　　From the next room, a piano is heard, beginning to play quietly, unintrusively, improvisationally.]

　　　　Does it mean anything?

---

6. Roman poet (43 B.C.E.–17? C.E.)
7. Rhetorical descent from the exalted to the commonplace.
8. Your lustful men and foolish young women.
9. Bullet.

1. British gold coin with a value (in the nineteenth century) of twenty-one shillings.
2. Penniless.
3. Brice, as Chater's "second," could duel with Septimus only if Chater were dead or wounded.

VALENTINE   I don't know. I don't know what it means, except mathematically.

HANNAH   I meant mathematically.

VALENTINE   [*Now with the lesson book again.*]   It's an iterated algorithm.[4]

HANNAH   What's that?

VALENTINE   Well, it's . . . Jesus . . . it's an algorithm that's been . . . iterated. How'm I supposed to . . . ? [*He makes an effort.*] The left-hand pages are graphs of what the numbers are doing on the right-hand pages. But all on different scales. Each graph is a small section of the previous one, blown up. Like you'd blow up a detail of a photograph, and then a detail of the detail, and so on, forever. Or in her case, till she ran out of pages.

HANNAH   Is it difficult?

VALENTINE   The maths isn't difficult. It's what you did at school. You have some x-and-y equation. Any value for x gives you a value for y. So you put a dot where it's right for both x and y. Then you take the next value for x which gives you another value for y, and when you've done that a few times you join up the dots and that's your graph of whatever the equation is.

HANNAH   And is that what she's doing?

VALENTINE   No. Not exactly. Not at all. What she's doing is, every time she works out a value for y, she's using *that* as her next value for x. And so on. Like a feedback. She's feeding the solution back into the equation, and then solving it again. Iteration, you see.

HANNAH   And that's surprising, is it?

VALENTINE   Well, it is a bit. It's the technique I'm using on my grouse numbers, and it hasn't been around for much longer than, well, call it twenty years.

[*Pause.*]

HANNAH   Why would she be doing it?

VALENTINE   I have no idea.

[*Pause.*]

I thought you were doing the hermit.

HANNAH   I am. I still am. But Bernard, damn him . . . Thomasina's tutor turns out to have interesting connections. Bernard is going through the library like a bloodhound. The portfolio was in a cupboard.

VALENTINE   There's a lot of stuff around. Gus loves going through it. No old masters or anything . . .

HANNAH   The maths primer she was using belonged to him—the tutor; he wrote his name in it.

VALENTINE   [*Reading.*] 'Septimus Hodge.'

HANNAH   Why were these things saved, do you think?

VALENTINE   Why should there be a reason?

HANNAH   And the diagram, what's it of?

VALENTINE   How would I know?

HANNAH   Why are you cross?

VALENTINE   I'm not cross. [*Pause.*] When your Thomasina was doing maths it had been the same maths for a couple of thousand years. Classical. And for a century after Thomasina. Then maths left the real world behind, just like modern art really. Nature was classical, maths was suddenly Picassos. But now nature is having the last laugh. The freaky stuff is turning out to be the mathematics of the natural world.

4. Mathematical procedure for computing results through a series of repeated operations.

HANNAH   This feedback thing?

VALENTINE   For example.

HANNAH   Well, could Thomasina have—

VALENTINE   [*Snaps.*]   No, of course she bloody couldn't!

HANNAH   All right, you're not cross. What did you mean you were doing the same thing she was doing? [*Pause.*] What *are* you doing?

VALENTINE   Actually I'm doing it from the other end. She started with an equation and turned it into a graph. I've got a graph—real data—and I'm trying to find the equation which would give you the graph if you used it the way she's used hers. Iterated it.

HANNAH   What for?

VALENTINE   It's how you look at population changes in biology. Goldfish in a pond, say. This year there are *x* goldfish. Next year there'll be *y* goldfish. Some get born, some get eaten by herons, whatever. Nature manipulates the *x* and turns it into *y*. Then *y* goldfish is your starting population for the following year. Just like Thomasina. Your value for *y* becomes your next value for *x*. The question is: what is being done to *x*? What is the manipulation? Whatever it is, it can be written down as mathematics. It's called an algorithm.

HANNAH   It can't be the same every year.

VALENTINE   The details change, you can't keep tabs on everything, it's not nature in a box. But it isn't necessary to know the details. When they are all put together, it turns out the population is obeying a mathematical rule.

HANNAH   The goldfish are?

VALENTINE   Yes. No. The numbers. It's not about the behaviour of fish. It's about the behaviour of numbers. This thing works for any phenomenon which eats its own numbers—measles epidemics, rainfall averages, cotton prices, it's a natural phenomenon in itself. Spooky.

HANNAH   Does it work for grouse?

VALENTINE   I don't know yet. I mean, it does undoubtedly, but it's hard to show. There's more noise with grouse.

HANNAH   Noise?

VALENTINE   Distortions. Interference. Real data is messy. There's a thousand acres of moorland that had grouse on it, always did till about 1930. But nobody counted the grouse. They shot them. So you count the grouse they shot. But burning the heather interferes, it improves the food supply. A good year for foxes interferes the other way, they eat the chicks. And then there's the weather. It's all very, very noisy out there. Very hard to spot the tune. Like a piano in the next room, it's playing your song, but unfortunately it's out of whack, some of the strings are missing, and the pianist is tone deaf and drunk—I mean, the *noise*! Impossible!

HANNAH   What do you do?

VALENTINE   You start guessing what the tune might be. You try to pick it out of the noise. You try this, you try that, you start to get something—it's half-baked but you start putting in notes which are missing or not quite the right notes . . . and bit by bit . . . [*He starts to dumdi-da to the tune of 'Happy Birthday'.*] Dumdi-dum-dum, dear Val-en-tine, dumdi-dum-dum to you— the lost algorithm!

HANNAH   [*Soberly.*]   Yes, I see. And then what?

VALENTINE   I publish.

HANNAH   Of course. Sorry. Jolly good.

VALENTINE That's the theory. Grouse are bastards compared to goldfish.

HANNAH Why did you choose them?

VALENTINE The game books. My true inheritance. Two hundred years of real data on a plate.

HANNAH Somebody wrote down everything that's shot?

VALENTINE Well, that's what a game book is. I'm only using from 1870, when butts and beaters[5] came in.

HANNAH You mean the game books go back to Thomasina's time?

VALENTINE Oh yes. Further. [*And then getting ahead of her thought.*] No— really. I promise you. I *promise* you. Not a schoolgirl living in a country house in Derbyshire in eighteen-something!

HANNAH Well, what was she doing?

VALENTINE She was just playing with the numbers. The truth is, she wasn't doing anything.

HANNAH She must have been doing something.

VALENTINE Doodling. Nothing she understood.

HANNAH A monkey at a typewriter?[6]

VALENTINE Yes. Well, a piano.

[HANNAH *picks up the algebra book and reads from it.*]

HANNAH ' . . . a method whereby all the forms of nature must give up their numerical secrets and draw themselves through number alone.' This feedback, is it a way of making pictures of forms in nature? Just tell me if it is or it isn't.

VALENTINE [*Irritated.*] To *me* it is. Pictures of turbulence—growth—change— creation—it's not a way of drawing an elephant, for God's sake!

HANNAH I'm sorry.

[*She picks up an apple leaf from the table. She is timid about pushing the point.*]

So you couldn't make a picture of this leaf by iterating a whatsit?

VALENTINE [*Off-hand.*] Oh yes, you could do that.

HANNAH [*Furiously.*] Well, tell me! Honestly, I could kill you!

VALENTINE If you knew the algorithm and fed it back say ten thousand times, each time there'd be a dot somewhere on the screen. You'd never know where to expect the next dot. But gradually you'd start to see this shape, because every dot will be inside the shape of this leaf. It wouldn't *be* a leaf, it would be a mathematical object. But yes. The unpredictable and the predetermined unfold together to make everything the way it is. It's how nature creates itself, on every scale, the snowflake and the snowstorm. It makes me so happy. To be at the beginning again, knowing almost nothing. People were talking about the end of physics. Relativity and quantum[7] looked as if they were going to clean out the whole problem between them. A theory of everything. But they only explained the very big and the very small. The universe, the elementary particles. The ordinary-sized stuff which is our lives, the things people write poetry about—clouds—daffodils—waterfalls— and what happens in a cup of coffee when the cream goes in—these things

---

5. "Butts": concealed stands (blinds) for shooting birds. "Beaters": people employed to drive the birds toward the guns.

6. Refers to a once-popular belief that, given sufficient time, a monkey jabbing typewriter keys at random would eventually produce the complete plays of Shakespeare.

7. Twentieth-century advances in physics made by Albert Einstein (1879–1955) and others. Valentine continues with a simplified description of chaos theory.

are full of mystery, as mysterious to us as the heavens were to the Greeks. We're better at predicting events at the edge of the galaxy or inside the nucleus of an atom than whether it'll rain on auntie's garden party three Sundays from now. Because the problem turns out to be different. We can't even predict the next drip from a dripping tap when it gets irregular. Each drip sets up the conditions for the next, the smallest variation blows prediction apart, and the weather is unpredictable the same way, will always be unpredictable. When you push the numbers through the computer you can see it on the screen. The future is disorder. A door like this has cracked open five or six times since we got up on our hind legs. It's the best possible time to be alive, when almost everything you thought you knew is wrong.

    [*Pause.*]

HANNAH   The weather is fairly predictable in the Sahara.

VALENTINE   The scale is different but the graph goes up and down the same way. Six thousand years in the Sahara looks like six months in Manchester, I bet you.

HANNAH   How much?

VALENTINE   Everything you have to lose.

HANNAH [*Pause.*] No.

VALENTINE   Quite right. That's why there was corn in Egypt.[8]

    [*Hiatus. The piano is heard again.*]

HANNAH   What is he playing?

VALENTINE   I don't know. He makes it up.

HANNAH   Chloë called him 'genius'.

VALENTINE   It's what my mother calls him—only *she* means it. Last year some expert had her digging in the wrong place for months to find something or other—the foundations of Capability Brown's boat-house—and Gus put her right first go.

HANNAH   Did he ever speak?

VALENTINE   Oh yes. Until he was five. You've never asked about him. You get high marks here for good breeding.

HANNAH   Yes, I know. I've always been given credit for my unconcern.

    [BERNARD *enters in high excitement and triumph.*]

BERNARD   *English Bards and Scotch Reviewers*. A pencilled superscription.[9] Listen and kiss my cycle-clips!

    [*He is carrying the book. He reads from it.*]

    'O harbinger of Sleep, who missed the press[1]

    And hoped his drone might thus escape redress!

    The wretched Chater, bard of Eros' Couch,

    For his narcotic[2] let my pencil vouch!'

You see, *you have to turn over every page.*

HANNAH   Is it his[3] handwriting?

BERNARD   Oh, come *on.*

HANNAH   Obviously not.

BERNARD   Christ, what do you want?

HANNAH   Proof.

VALENTINE   Quite right. Who are you talking about?

---

8. Cf. Exodus 42.1.
9. Note.
1. O herald . . . who published his poem too late

to be included in the first edition of Byron's work.
2. Sleep-inducing drug.
3. Byron's.

BERNARD   Proof? *Proof?* You'd have to be there, you silly bitch!

VALENTINE [*Mildly.*]   I say, you're speaking of my fiancée.

HANNAH   Especially when I have a present for you. Guess what I found. [*Producing the present for* BERNARD.] Lady Croom writing from London to her husband. Her brother, Captain Brice, married a Mrs Chater. In other words, one might assume, a widow.

   [BERNARD *looks at the letter.*]

BERNARD   I *said* he was dead. What year? 1810! Oh my God, 1810! Well *done,* Hannah! Are you going to tell me it's a different Mrs Chater?

HANNAH   Oh no. It's her all right. Note her Christian name.

BERNARD   Charity. Charity . . . 'Deny what cannot be proven for Charity's sake!'

HANNAH   Don't kiss me!

VALENTINE   She won't let anyone kiss her.

BERNARD   You see! They wrote—they scribbled—they put it on paper. It was their employment. Their diversion. Paper is what they had. And there'll be more. There is always more. We can find it!

HANNAH   Such passion. First Valentine, now you. It's moving.

BERNARD   The aristocratic friend of the tutor—under the same roof as the poor sod whose book he savaged—the first thing he does is seduce Chater's wife. All is discovered. There is a duel. Chater dead, Byron fled! P.S. guess what?, the widow married her ladyship's brother! Do you honestly think no one wrote a word? How could they not! It dropped from sight but we will write it again!

HANNAH   You can, Bernard. I'm not going to take any credit, I haven't done anything.

   [*The same thought has clearly occurred to* BERNARD. *He becomes instantly po-faced.*][4]

BERNARD   Well, that's—very fair—generous—

HANNAH   Prudent. Chater could have died of anything, anywhere.

   [*The po-face is forgotten.*]

BERNARD   But he fought a duel with Byron!

HANNAH   You haven't established it was fought. You haven't established it was Byron. For God's sake, Bernard, you haven't established Byron was even here!

BERNARD   I'll tell you your problem. No guts.

HANNAH   Really?

BERNARD   By which I mean a visceral belief in yourself. Gut instinct. The part of you which doesn't reason. The certainty for which there is no back-reference. Because time is reversed. Tock, tick goes the universe and then recovers itself, but it was enough, you were in there and you bloody *know.*

VALENTINE   Are you talking about Lord Byron, the poet?

BERNARD   No, you fucking idiot, we're talking about Lord Byron the chartered[5] accountant.

VALENTINE [*Unoffended.*]   Oh well, *he* was here all right, the poet.

   [*Silence.*]

HANNAH   How do you know?

VALENTINE   He's in the game book. I think he shot a hare. I read through the whole lot once when I had mumps—some quite interesting people—

---

4. Pompously serious.   5. Certified.

HANNAH   Where's the book?

VALENTINE   It's not one I'm using—too early, of course—

HANNAH   1809.

VALENTINE   They've always been in the commode. Ask Chloë.

> [HANNAH *looks to* BERNARD. BERNARD *has been silent because he has been incapable of speech. He seems to have gone into a trance, in which only his mouth tries to work.* HANNAH *steps over to him and gives him a demure kiss on the cheek. It works.* BERNARD *lurches out into the garden and can be heard croaking for 'Chloë . . . Chloë!']*

VALENTINE   My mother's lent him her bicycle. Lending one's bicycle is a form of safe sex, possibly the safest there is. My mother is in a flutter about Bernard, and he's no fool. He gave her a first edition of Horace Walpole, and now she's lent him her bicycle.

> [*He gathers up the three items [the primer, the lesson book and the diagram] and puts them into the portfolio.*]

Can I keep these for a while?

HANNAH   Yes, of course.

> [*The piano stops.* GUS *enters hesitantly from the music room.*]

VALENTINE   [*To* GUS.]   Yes, finished . . . coming now. [*To* HANNAH.]   I'm trying to work out the diagram.

> [GUS *nods and smiles, at* HANNAH *too, but she is preoccupied.*]

HANNAH   What I don't understand is . . . why nobody did this feedback thing before—it's not like relativity, you don't have to be Einstein.

VALENTINE   You couldn't see to look before. The electronic calculator was what the telescope was for Galileo.[6]

HANNAH   Calculator?

VALENTINE   There wasn't enough time before. There weren't enough *pencils*! [*He flourishes Thomasina's lesson book.*] This took her I don't know how many days and she hasn't scratched the paintwork. Now she'd only have to press a button, the same button over and over. Iteration. A few minutes. And what I've done in a couple of months, with only a *pencil* the calculations would take me the rest of my life to do again—thousands of pages—tens of thousands! And so boring!

HANNAH   Do you mean—?

> [*She stops because* GUS *is plucking* VALENTINE's *sleeve.*]

Do you mean—?

VALENTINE   All right, Gus, I'm coming.

HANNAH   Do you mean that was the only problem? Enough time? And paper? And the boredom?

VALENTINE   We're going to get out the dressing-up box.

HANNAH   [*Driven to raising her voice.*]   Val! Is that what you're saying?

VALENTINE   [*Surprised by her. Mildly.*]   No, I'm saying you'd have to have a reason for doing it.

> [GUS *runs out of the room, upset.*]

[*Apologetically.*] He hates people shouting.

HANNAH   I'm sorry.

> [VALENTINE *starts to follow* GUS.]

But anything else?

VALENTINE   Well, the other thing is, you'd have to be insane.

---

6. Galileo Galilei (1564–1642), Italian astronomer.

[VALENTINE *leaves.*

HANNAH *stays, thoughtful. After a moment, she turns to the table and picks up the* Cornhill Magazine. *She looks into it briefly, then closes it, and leaves the room, taking the magazine with her.*

The empty room.

The light changes to early morning. From a long way off, there is a pistol shot. A moment later there is the cry of dozens of crows disturbed from the unseen trees.]

Act Two

SCENE FIVE

BERNARD *is pacing around, reading aloud from a handful of typed sheets.* VALENTINE *and* CHLOË *are his audience.* VALENTINE *has his tortoise and is eating a sandwich from which he extracts shreds of lettuce to offer the tortoise.*

BERNARD   'Did it happen? Could it happen?

Undoubtedly it could. Only three years earlier the Irish poet Tom Moore appeared on the field of combat to avenge a review by Jeffrey of the *Edinburgh*. These affairs were seldom fatal and sometimes farcical but, potentially, the duellist stood in respect to the law no differently from a murderer. As for the murderee, a minor poet like Ezra Chater could go to his death in a Derbyshire glade as unmissed and unremembered as his contemporary and namesake, the minor botanist who died in the forests of the West Indies, lost to history like the monkey that bit him. On April 16th 1809, a few days after he left Sidley Park, Byron wrote to his solicitor John Hanson: 'If the consequences of my leaving England were ten times as ruinous as you describe, I have no alternative; there are circumstances which render it absolutely indispensable, and quit the country I must immediately.' To which, the editor's note in the Collected Letters reads as follows: 'What Byron's urgent reasons for leaving England were at this time has never been revealed.' The letter was written from the family seat, Newstead Abbey, Nottinghamshire. A long day's ride to the north-west lay Sidley Park, the estate of the Coverlys—a far grander family, raised by Charles II to the Earldom of Croom . . . '

[HANNAH *enters briskly, a piece of paper in her hand.*]
HANNAH   Bernard . . . ! Val . . .
BERNARD   Do you mind?

[HANNAH *puts her piece of paper down in front of* VALENTINE.]
CHLOË   [*Angrily.*]   Hannah!
HANNAH   What?
CHLOË   She's so *rude*!
HANNAH   [*Taken aback.*]   What? Am I?
VALENTINE   Bernard's reading us his lecture.
HANNAH   Yes, I know. [*Then recollecting herself.*] Yes—yes—that *was* rude. I'm sorry, Bernard.
VALENTINE   [*With the piece of paper.*]   What is this?
HANNAH   [*To* BERNARD.]   Spot on—the India Office Library. [*To* VALENTINE.] Peacock's letter in holograph,[7] I got a copy sent—

7. Handwriting.

CHLOË *Hannah!* Shut up!

HANNAH [*Sitting down.*] Yes, sorry.

BERNARD It's all right, I'll read it to myself.

CHLOË *No.*

[HANNAH *reaches for the Peacock letter and takes it back.*]

HANNAH Go on, Bernard. Have I missed anything? Sorry.

[BERNARD *stares at her balefully but then continues to read.*]

BERNARD 'The Byrons of Newstead in 1809 comprised an eccentric widow and her undistinguished son, the "lame brat", who until the age of ten when he came into the title, had been carted about the country from lodging to lodging by his vulgar hectoring monster of a mother—' [HANNAH'*s hand has gone up.*]—overruled—'and who four months past his twenty-first birthday was master of nothing but his debts and his genius. Between the Byrons and the Coverlys there was no social equality and none to be expected. The connection, undisclosed to posterity until now, was with Septimus Hodge, Byron's friend at Harrow and Trinity College—' [HANNAH'*s hand goes up again.*]—sustained—[*He makes an instant correction with a silver pencil.*] 'Byron's contemporary at Harrow and Trinity College, and now tutor in residence to the Croom daughter, Thomasina Coverly. Byron's letters tell us where he was on April 8th and on April 12th. He was at Newstead. But on the 10th he was at Sidley Park, as attested by the game book preserved there: "April 10th 1809—forenoon. High cloud, dry, and sun between times, wind southeasterly. Self—Augustus—Lord Byron. Fourteen pigeon, one hare (Lord B.)." But, as we know now, the drama of life and death at Sidley Park was not about pigeons but about sex and literature.'

VALENTINE Unless you were the pigeon.

BERNARD I don't have to do this. I'm paying you a compliment.

CHLOË Ignore him, Bernard—go on, get to the duel.

BERNARD Hannah's not even paying attention.

HANNAH Yes I am, it's all going in. I often work with the radio on.

BERNARD Oh thanks!

HANNAH Is there much more?

CHLOË *Hannah!*

HANNAH No, it's fascinating. I just wondered how much more there was. I need to ask Valentine about this [*letter.*]—sorry, Bernard, go on, this will keep.

VALENTINE Yes—sorry, Bernard.

CHLOË Please, Bernard!

BERNARD Where was I?

VALENTINE Pigeons.

CHLOË Sex.

HANNAH Literature.

BERNARD Life and death. Right. 'Nothing could be more eloquent of that than the three documents I have quoted: the terse demand to settle a matter in private; the desperate scribble of "my husband has sent for pistols"; and on April 11th, the gauntlet thrown down by the aggrieved and cuckolded author Ezra Chater. The covers[8] have not survived. What is certain is that all three letters were in Byron's possession when his books were sold in

---

8. Envelopelike wrappers of letters. "Cuckolded": whose wife is adulterous.

1816—preserved in the pages of "The Couch of Eros" which seven years
earlier at Sidley Park Byron had borrowed from Septimus Hodge.'

HANNAH Borrowed?

BERNARD I will be taking questions at the end. Constructive comments will
be welcome. Which is indeed my reason for trying out in the provinces
before my London opening[9] under the auspices of the Byron Society prior
to publication. By the way, Valentine, do you want a credit?—'the game
book recently discovered by'?

VALENTINE It was never lost, Bernard.

BERNARD 'As recently pointed out by.' I don't normally like giving credit
where it's due, but with scholarly articles as with divorce, there is a certain
cachet[1] in citing a member of the aristocracy. I'll pop it in ad lib[2] for the
lecture, and give you a mention in the press release. How's that?

VALENTINE Very kind.

HANNAH Press release? What happened to the *Journal of English Studies*?

BERNARD That comes later with the apparatus,[3] and in the recognized tone—
very dry, very modest, absolutely gloat-free, and yet unmistakably 'Eat your
heart out, you dozy bastards'. But first, it's 'Media Don,[4] book early to avoid
disappointment'. Where was I?

VALENTINE Game book.

CHLOË Eros.

HANNAH Borrowed.

BERNARD Right. '—borrowed from Septimus Hodge. Is it conceivable that
the letters were already in the book when Byron borrowed it?'

VALENTINE Yes.

CHLOË Shut up, Val.

VALENTINE Well, it's conceivable.

BERNARD 'Is it *likely* that Hodge would have lent Byron the book without first
removing the three private letters?'

VALENTINE Look, sorry—I only meant, Byron could have borrowed the book
without asking.

HANNAH That's true.

BERNARD Then why wouldn't Hodge get them back?

HANNAH I don't know, I wasn't there.

BERNARD That's right, you bloody weren't.

CHLOË Go on, Bernard.

BERNARD 'It is the third document, the challenge itself, that convinces. Chater "as a man and a poet", points the finger at his "slanderer in the press".
Neither as a man nor a poet did Ezra Chater cut such a figure as to be
habitually slandered or even mentioned in the press. It is surely indisputable
that the slander was the review of "The Maid of Turkey" in the *Piccadilly
Recreation*. Did Septimus Hodge have any connection with the London periodicals? No. Did Byron? Yes! He had reviewed Wordsworth two years earlier,
he was to review Spencer[5] two years later. And do we have any clue as to
Byron's opinion of Chater the poet? Yes! Who but Byron could have written

9. New plays in Britain are frequently first performed outside London in preparation for more-
sophisticated audiences in the capital.
1. Distinction.
2. Short for *ad libitum* (Latin): as an extempora-

neous aside.
3. In the later version with footnotes.
4. Professor in the media spotlight.
5. William Robert Spencer (1769–1834), poet
and wit.

the four lines pencilled into Lady Croom's copy of *English Bards and Scotch Reviewers'*—

HANNAH   Almost anybody.

BERNARD   Darling—

HANNAH   Don't call me darling.

BERNARD   Dickhead, then, is it likely that the man Chater calls his friend Septimus Hodge is the same man who screwed his wife and kicked the shit out of his last book?

HANNAH   Put it like that, almost certain.

CHLOË [*Earnestly.*]   You've been deeply wounded in the past, haven't you, Hannah?

HANNAH   Nothing compared to listening to this. Why is there nothing in Byron's letters about the *Piccadilly* reviews?

BERNARD   Exactly. Because he killed the author.

HANNAH   But the first one, 'The Maid of Turkey', was the year before. Was he clairvoyant?

CHLOË   Letters get lost.

BERNARD   Thank you! Exactly! There is a platonic[6] letter which confirms everything—lost but ineradicable, like radio voices rippling through the universe for all eternity. "My dear Hodge—here I am in Albania and you're the only person in the whole world who knows why. Poor C! I never wished him any harm—except in the *Piccadilly*, of course—it was the woman who bade me eat,[7] dear Hodge!—what a tragic business, but thank God it ended well for poetry. Yours ever, B.—PS. Burn this.'

VALENTINE   How did Chater find out the reviewer was Byron?

BERNARD [*Irritated.*]   I don't know, I wasn't there, was I? [*Pause. To* HANNAH.] You wish to say something?

HANNAH   Moi?[8]

CHLOË   I know. Byron told Mrs Chater in bed. Next day he dumped her so she grassed on him, and pleaded date rape.

BERNARD [*Fastidiously.*]   Date rape? What do you mean, date rape?

HANNAH   April the tenth.

> [BERNARD *cracks. Everything becomes loud and overlapped as* BERNARD *threatens to walk out and is cajoled into continuing.*]

BERNARD   Right!—forget it!

HANNAH   Sorry—

BERNARD   No—I've had nothing but sarcasm and childish interruptions—

VALENTINE   What did I do?

BERNARD   No credit for probably the most sensational literary discovery of the century—

CHLOË   I think you're jolly unfair—they're jealous, Bernard—

HANNAH   I won't say another word—

VALENTINE   Yes, go on, Bernard—we promise.

BERNARD [*Finally.*]   Well, only if you stop *feeding tortoises*!

VALENTINE   Well, it's his lunch time.

BERNARD   And on condition that I am afforded the common courtesy of a scholar among scholars—

HANNAH   Absolutely mum till you're finished—

---

6. Nonexistent ideal.
7. Cf. Genesis 3.12.

8. Me? (French).

BERNARD   After which, any comments are to be couched in terms of accepted academic—

HANNAH   Dignity—you're right, Bernard.

BERNARD   —respect.

HANNAH   Respect. Absolutely. The language of scholars. Count on it.

[*Having made a great show of putting his pages away,* BERNARD *reassembles them and finds his place, glancing suspiciously at the other three for signs of levity.*]

BERNARD   Last paragraph. 'Without question, Ezra Chater issued a challenge to *somebody*. If a duel was fought in the dawn mist of Sidley Park in April 1809, his opponent, on the evidence, was a critic with a gift for ridicule and a taste for seduction. Do we need to look far? Without question, Mrs Chater was a widow by 1810. If we seek the occasion of Ezra Chater's early and unrecorded death, do we need to look far? Without question, Lord Byron, in the very season of his emergence as a literary figure, quit the country in a cloud of panic and mystery, and stayed abroad for two years at a time when Continental travel was unusual and dangerous. If we seek his reason—*do we need to look far?*'

[*No mean performer, he is pleased with the effect of his peroration. There is a significant silence.*]

HANNAH   Bollocks.[9]

CHLOË   Well, I think it's true.

HANNAH   You've left out everything which doesn't fit. Byron had been banging on[1] for months about leaving England—there's a letter in *February*—

BERNARD   But he didn't go, did he?

HANNAH   And then he didn't sail until the beginning of July!

BERNARD   Everything moved more slowly then. Time was different. He was two weeks in Falmouth waiting for wind or something—

HANNAH   Bernard, I don't know why I'm bothering—you're arrogant, greedy and reckless. You've gone from a glint in your eye to a sure thing in a hop, skip and a jump. You deserve what you get and I think you're mad. But I can't help myself, you're like some exasperating child pedalling its tricycle towards the edge of a cliff, and I have to do something. So listen to me. If Byron killed Chater in a duel I'm Marie of Romania.[2] You'll end up with so much *fame* you won't leave the house without a paper bag over your head.

VALENTINE   Actually, Bernard, as a scientist, your theory is incomplete.

BERNARD   But I'm not a scientist.

VALENTINE [*Patiently.*]   No, *as a scientist*—

BERNARD [*Beginning to shout.*]   I have yet to hear a proper argument.

HANNAH   Nobody would kill a man and then pan his book. I mean, not in that order. So he must have borrowed the book, written the review, *posted it,* seduced Mrs Chater, fought a duel and departed, all in the space of two or three days. Who would do that?

BERNARD   Byron.

HANNAH   It's hopeless.

BERNARD   You've never understood him, as you've shown in your novelette.[3]

HANNAH   In my what?

9. Nonsense (slang).
1. Talking (slang).
2. Cf. Dorothy Parker's poem "Comment," lines

3–4: "And love is a thing that can never go wrong; / And I am Marie of Roumania."
3. Sentimental short novel.

BERNARD   Oh, sorry—did you think it was a work of historical revisionism? Byron the spoilt child promoted beyond his gifts by the spirit of the age! And Caroline the closet intellectual shafted by a male society!

VALENTINE   I read that somewhere—

HANNAH   It's his review.

BERNARD   And bloody well said, too!

[*Things are turning a little ugly and* BERNARD *seems in a mood to push them that way.*]

You got them backwards, darling. Caroline was Romantic waffle on wheels with no talent, and Byron was an eighteenth-century Rationalist[4] touched by genius. And he killed Chater.

HANNAH   [*Pause.*]   If it's not too late to change my mind, I'd like you to go ahead.

BERNARD   I intend to. Look to the mote in your own eye![5]—you even had the wrong bloke on the dust-jacket!

HANNAH   Dust-jacket?

VALENTINE   What about my computer model? Aren't you going to mention it?

BERNARD   It's inconclusive.

VALENTINE   [*To* HANNAH.]   The *Piccadilly* reviews aren't a very good fit with Byron's other reviews, you see.

HANNAH   [*To* BERNARD.]   What do you mean, the wrong bloke?

BERNARD   [*Ignoring her.*]   The other reviews aren't a very good fit for each other, are they?

VALENTINE   No, but differently. The parameters—[6]

BERNARD   [*Jeering.*]   Parameters! You can't stick Byron's head in your laptop! Genius isn't like your average grouse.

VALENTINE   [*Casually.*]   Well, it's all trivial anyway.

BERNARD   What is?

VALENTINE   Who wrote what when . . .

BERNARD   Trivial?

VALENTINE   Personalities.

BERNARD   I'm sorry—did you say trivial?

VALENTINE   It's a technical term.[7]

BERNARD   Not where I come from, it isn't.

VALENTINE   The questions you're asking don't matter, you see. It's like arguing who got there first with the calculus. The English say Newton, the Germans say Leibnitz.[8] But it doesn't *matter*. Personalities. What matters is the calculus. Scientific progress. Knowledge.

BERNARD   Really? Why?

VALENTINE   Why what?

BERNARD   Why does scientific progress matter more than personalities?

VALENTINE   Is he serious?

HANNAH   No, he's trivial. Bernard—

VALENTINE   [*Interrupting, to* BERNARD.]   Do yourself a favour, you're on a loser.

BERNARD   Oh, you're going to zap me with penicillin and pesticides. Spare me that and I'll spare you the bomb and aerosols. But don't confuse progress with perfectibility. A great poet is always timely. A great philosopher is an

---

4. Person whose opinions are based on pure reasoning. "Waffle": gossip.
5. Cf. Matthew 7.3.
6. Distinguishing or defining characteristics.

7. From mathematics.
8. Gottfried Wilhelm, Baron von Leibnitz (1646–1716), German philosopher and mathematician.

urgent need. There's no rush for Isaac Newton. We were quite happy with Aristotle's cosmos. Personally, I preferred it. Fifty-five crystal spheres geared to God's crankshaft is my idea of a satisfying universe. I can't think of anything more trivial than the speed of light. Quarks, quasars—big bangs, black holes—who gives a shit? How did you people[9] con us out of all that status? All that money? And why are you so pleased with yourselves?

CHLOË   Are you against penicillin, Bernard?

BERNARD   Don't feed the animals.[1] [*Back to* VALENTINE.] I'd push the lot of you over a cliff myself. Except the one in the wheelchair,[2] I think I'd lose the sympathy vote before people had time to think it through.

HANNAH [*Loudly.*]   What the hell do you mean, the dust-jacket?

BERNARD [*Ignoring her.*]   If knowledge isn't self-knowledge it isn't doing much, mate. Is the universe expanding? Is it contracting? Is it standing on one leg and singing 'When Father Painted the Parlour'? Leave me out. I can expand my universe without you. 'She walks in beauty, like the night of cloudless climes and starry skies, and all that's best of dark and bright meet in her aspect and her eyes.'[3] There you are, he wrote it after coming home from a party. [*With offensive politeness.*] What is it that you're doing with grouse, Valentine, I'd love to know?

>   [VALENTINE *stands up and it is suddenly apparent that he is shaking and close to tears.*]

VALENTINE [*To* CHLOË.]   He's not against penicillin, and he knows I'm not against poetry. [*To* BERNARD.] I've given up on the grouse.

HANNAH   You haven't, Valentine!

VALENTINE [*Leaving.*]   I can't do it.

HANNAH   *Why?*

VALENTINE   Too much noise. There's just too much *bloody noise!*

>   [On which, VALENTINE *leaves the room.* CHLOË, *upset and in tears, jumps up and briefly pummels* BERNARD *ineffectually with her fists.*]

CHLOË   You bastard, Bernard!

>   [*She follows* VALENTINE *out. Pause.*]

HANNAH   Well, I think that's everybody. You can leave now, give Gus a kick on your way out.

BERNARD   Yes, I'm sorry about that. It's no fun when it's not among pros, is it?

HANNAH   No.

BERNARD   Oh, well . . . [*He begins to put his lecture sheets away in his briefcase, and is thus reminded . . .*] do you want to know about your book jacket? 'Lord Byron and Caroline Lamb at the Royal Academy'? Ink study by Henry Fuseli?[4]

HANNAH   What about it?

BERNARD   It's not them.

HANNAH [*She explodes.*]   Who says!?

>   [BERNARD *brings the* Byron Society Journal *from his briefcase.*]

BERNARD   This Fuseli expert in the *Byron Society Journal.* They sent me the latest . . . as a distinguished guest speaker.

HANNAH   But of course it's them! Everyone knows—

---

9. Scientists.
1. Don't encourage them; i.e., don't keep the discussion going.
2. Stephen Hawking (b. 1942), physicist.

3. Lord Byron, "She walks in beauty," lines 1–4.
4. Swiss-born artist (1741–1825) who lived and worked in England.

BERNARD   Popular tradition only. [*He is finding the place in the journal.*] Here we are. 'No earlier than 1820'. He's analysed it. [*Offers it to her.*] Read at your leisure.

HANNAH [*She sounds like* BERNARD *jeering.*]   Analysed it?

BERNARD   Charming sketch, of course, but Byron was in Italy . . .

HANNAH   But, Bernard—I *know* it's them.

BERNARD   How?

HANNAH   How? It just *is*. 'Analysed it', my big toe!

BERNARD   Language!

HANNAH   He's wrong.

BERNARD   Oh, gut instinct, you mean?

HANNAH [*Flatly.*]   He's wrong.

   [BERNARD *snaps shut his briefcase.*]

BERNARD   Well, it's all trivial, isn't it? Why don't you come?

HANNAH   Where?

BERNARD   With me.

HANNAH   To London? What for?

BERNARD   What for.

HANNAH   Oh, your lecture.

BERNARD   No, no, bugger that. Sex.

HANNAH   Oh . . . No. Thanks . . . [*Then, protesting.*] Bernard!

BERNARD   You should try it. It's very underrated.

HANNAH   Nothing against it.

BERNARD   Yes, you have. You should let yourself go a bit. You might have written a better book. Or at any rate the right book.

HANNAH   Sex and literature. Literature and sex. Your conversation, left to itself, doesn't have many places to go. Like two marbles rolling around a pudding basin. One of them is always sex.

BERNARD   Ah well, yes. Men all over.

HANNAH   No doubt. Einstein—relativity and sex. Chippendale—[5] sex and furniture. Galileo—'Did the earth move?' What the hell is it with you people? Chaps sometimes wanted to marry me, and I don't know a worse bargain. Available sex against not being allowed to fart in bed. What do you mean the right book?

BERNARD   It takes a romantic to make a heroine of Caroline Lamb. You were cut out for Byron.

   [*Pause.*]

HANNAH   So, cheerio.

BERNARD   Oh, I'm coming back for the dance, you know. Chloë asked me.

HANNAH   She meant well, but I don't dance.

BERNARD   No, no—I'm going with her.

HANNAH   Oh, I see. I don't, actually.

BERNARD   I'm her date. Sub rosa.[6] Don't tell Mother.

HANNAH   She doesn't want her mother to know?

BERNARD   No—I don't want her mother to know. This is my first experience of the landed aristocracy. I tell you, I'm boggle-eyed.

HANNAH   Bernard!—you haven't seduced that girl?

BERNARD   Seduced her? Every time I turned round she was up a library ladder.

---

5. Thomas Chippendale (1718–1779), famous   6. Secretly (Latin).
English cabinetmaker.

In the end I gave in. That reminds me—I spotted something between her legs that made me think of you.

[*He instantly receives a sharp stinging slap on the face but manages to remain completely unperturbed by it. He is already producing from his pocket a small book. His voice has hardly hesitated.*]

The Peaks Traveller and Gazetteer—James Godolphin 1832—unillustrated, I'm afraid. [*He has opened the book to a marked place.*] Sidley Park in Derbyshire, property of the Earl of Croom . . .'

HANNAH [*Numbly.*] The world is going to hell in a handcart.

BERNARD 'Five hundred acres including forty of lake—the Park by Brown and Noakes has pleasing features in the horrid style—viaduct, grotto,[7] etc— a hermitage occupied by a lunatic since twenty years without discourse or companion save for a pet tortoise, Plautus by name, which he suffers children to touch on request.' [*He holds out the book for her.*] A tortoise. They must be a feature.

[*After a moment* HANNAH *takes the book.*]

HANNAH Thank you.

[VALENTINE *comes to the door.*]

VALENTINE The station taxi is at the front . . .

BERNARD Yes . . . thanks . . . Oh—did Peacock come up trumps?[8]

HANNAH For some.

BERNARD Hermit's name and CV?

[*He picks up and glances at the Peacock letter.*]

'My dear Thackeray . . .' God, I'm good.

[*He puts the letter down.*]

Well, wish me luck— [*Vaguely to* VALENTINE] Sorry about . . . you know . . . [*and to* HANNAH] and about your . . .

VALENTINE Piss off, Bernard.

BERNARD Right.

[BERNARD *goes.*]

HANNAH Don't let Bernard get to you. It's only performance art, you know. Rhetoric, they used to teach it in ancient times, like PT.[9] It's not about being right, they had philosophy for that. Rhetoric was their chat show. Bernard's indignation is a sort of aerobics for when he gets on television.

VALENTINE I don't care to be rubbished by the dustbin man.[1]

[*He has been looking at the letter.*] The what of the lunatic?

[HANNAH *reclaims the letter and reads it for him.*]

HANNAH 'The testament of the lunatic serves as a caution against French fashion . . . for it was Frenchified mathematick that brought him to the melancholy certitude of a world without light or life . . . as a wooden stove that must consume itself until ash and stove are as one, and heat is gone from the earth.'

VALENTINE [*Amused, surprised.*] Huh!

HANNAH 'He died aged two score years and seven, hoary as Job[2] and meagre as a cabbage-stalk, the proof of his prediction even yet unyielding to his labours for the restitution of hope through good English algebra.'

---

7. Artificial cave or cavern. "Horrid": Gothic. "Viaduct": bridgelike structure designed to carry a road over a valley, river, etc.
8. Give you what you wanted.
9. Physical training. "Performance art": nontraditional art form that involves presentation to an audience and sometimes involves acting.
1. Garbage collector.
2. As old as Job, who, according to the Bible, lived to be 140. "Two score years and seven": forty-seven.

VALENTINE That's it?

HANNAH [*Nods.*] Is there anything in it?

VALENTINE In what? We are all doomed? [*Casually.*] Oh yes, sure—it's called the second law of thermodynamics.

HANNAH Was it known about?

VALENTINE By poets and lunatics from time immemorial.

HANNAH Seriously.

VALENTINE No.

HANNAH Is it anything to do with . . . you know, Thomasina's discovery?

VALENTINE She didn't discover anything.

HANNAH Her lesson book.

VALENTINE No.

HANNAH A coincidence, then?

VALENTINE What is?

HANNAH [*Reading.*] 'He died aged two score years and seven.' That was in 1834. So he was born in 1787. So was the tutor. He says so in his letter to Lord Croom when he recommended himself for the job: 'Date of birth— 1787.' The hermit was born in the same year as Septimus Hodge.

VALENTINE [*Pause.*] Did Bernard bite you in the leg?[3]

HANNAH Don't you see? I thought my hermit was a perfect symbol. An idiot in the landscape. But this is better. The Age of Enlightenment banished into the Romantic wilderness! The genius of Sidley Park living on in a hermit's hut!

VALENTINE You don't *know* that.

HANNAH Oh, but I do. I do. Somewhere there will be *something* . . . if only I can find it.

SCENE SIX

The room is empty.

A reprise: early morning—a distant pistol shot—the sound of the crows.

JELLABY *enters the dawn-dark room with a lamp. He goes to the windows and looks out. He sees something. He returns to put the lamp on the table, and then opens one of the french windows and steps outside.*

JELLABY [*Outside.*] Mr Hodge!

  [SEPTIMUS *comes in, followed by* JELLABY, *who closes the garden door.* SEPTIMUS *is wearing a greatcoat.*]

SEPTIMUS Thank you, Jellaby. I was expecting to be locked out. What time is it?

JELLABY Half past five.

SEPTIMUS That is what I have. Well!—what a bracing experience!

  [*He produces two pistols from inside his coat and places them on the table.*]

The dawn, you know. Unexpectedly lively. Fishes, birds, frogs . . . rabbits . . . [*he produces a dead rabbit from inside his coat.*] and very beautiful. If only it did not occur so early in the day. I have brought Lady Thomasina a rabbit. Will you take it?

JELLABY It's dead.

---

3. Like a mad dog, whose bite transmits madness (rabies).

SEPTIMUS   Yes. Lady Thomasina loves a rabbit pie.

[JELLABY *takes the rabbit without enthusiasm. There is a little blood on it.*]

JELLABY   You were missed, Mr Hodge.

SEPTIMUS   I decided to sleep last night in the boat-house. Did I see a carriage leaving the Park?

JELLABY   Captain Brice's carriage, with Mr and Mrs Chater also.

SEPTIMUS   Gone?!

JELLABY   Yes, sir. And Lord Byron's horse was brought round at four o'clock.

SEPTIMUS   Lord Byron too!

JELLABY   Yes, sir. The house has been up and hopping.

SEPTIMUS   But I have his rabbit pistols! What am I to do with his rabbit pistols?

JELLABY   You were looked for in your room.

SEPTIMUS   By whom?

JELLABY   By her ladyship.

SEPTIMUS   In my room?

JELLABY   I will tell her ladyship you are returned.

[*He starts to leave.*]

SEPTIMUS   Jellaby! Did Lord Byron leave a book for me?

JELLABY   A book?

SEPTIMUS   He had the loan of a book from me.

JELLABY   His lordship left nothing in his room, sir, not a coin.[4]

SEPTIMUS   Oh. Well, I'm sure he would have left a coin if he'd had one. Jellaby—here is a half-guinea for you.

JELLABY   Thank you very much, sir.

SEPTIMUS   What has occurred?

JELLABY   The servants are told nothing, sir.

SEPTIMUS   Come, come, does a half-guinea buy nothing any more?

JELLABY   [*Sighs.*]   Her ladyship encountered Mrs Chater during the night.

SEPTIMUS   Where?

JELLABY   On the threshold of Lord Byron's room.

SEPTIMUS   Ah. Which one was leaving and which entering?

JELLABY   Mrs Chater was leaving Lord Byron's room.

SEPTIMUS   And where was Mr Chater?

JELLABY   Mr Chater and Captain Brice were drinking cherry brandy. They had the footman to keep the fire up until three o'clock. There was a loud altercation upstairs, and—

[LADY CROOM *enters the room.*]

LADY CROOM   Well, Mr Hodge.

SEPTIMUS   My lady.

LADY CROOM   All this to shoot a hare?

SEPTIMUS   A rabbit. [*She gives him one of her looks.*] No, indeed, a hare, though very rabbit-like—

[JELLABY *is about to leave.*]

LADY CROOM   My infusion.[5]

JELLABY   Yes, my lady.

---

4. Guests staying in country houses were expected   5. Tea.
to leave tips for the servants.

[*He leaves.* LADY CROOM *is carrying two letters. We have not seen them before. Each has an envelope which has been opened. She flings them on the table.*]

LADY CROOM How dare you!

SEPTIMUS I cannot be called to account for what was written in private and read without regard to propriety.

LADY CROOM Addressed to me!

SEPTIMUS Left in my room, in the event of my death—

LADY CROOM Pah!—what earthly use is a love letter from beyond the grave?

SEPTIMUS As much, surely, as from this side of it. The second letter, however, was not addressed to your ladyship.

LADY CROOM I have a mother's right to open a letter addressed by you to my daughter, whether in the event of your life, your death, or your imbecility. What do you mean by writing to her of rice pudding when she has just suffered the shock of violent death in our midst?

SEPTIMUS Whose death?

LADY CROOM Yours, you wretch!

SEPTIMUS Yes, I see.

LADY CROOM I do not know which is the madder of your ravings. One envelope full of rice pudding, the other of the most insolent familiarities regarding several parts of my body, but have no doubt which is the more intolerable to me.

SEPTIMUS Which?

LADY CROOM Oh, aren't we saucy when our bags are packed! Your friend has gone before you, and I have despatched the harlot Chater and her husband—and also my brother for bringing them here. Such is the sentence, you see, for choosing unwisely in your acquaintance. Banishment. Lord Byron is a rake and a hypocrite, and the sooner he sails for the Levant[6] the sooner he will find society congenial to his character.

SEPTIMUS It has been a night of reckoning.

LADY CROOM Indeed, I wish it had passed uneventfully with you and Mr Chater shooting each other with the decorum due to a civilized house. You have no secrets left, Mr Hodge. They spilled out between shrieks and oaths and tears. It is fortunate that a lifetime's devotion to the sporting gun has halved my husband's hearing to the ear he sleeps on.

SEPTIMUS I'm afraid I have no knowledge of what has occurred.

LADY CROOM Your trollop[7] was discovered in Lord Byron's room.

SEPTIMUS Ah. Discovered by Mr Chater?

LADY CROOM Who else?

SEPTIMUS I am very sorry, madam, for having used your kindness to bring my unworthy friend to your notice. He will have to give an account of himself to me, you may be sure.

[*Before* LADY CROOM *can respond to this threat,* JELLABY *enters the room with her 'infusion'. This is quite an elaborate affair: a pewter tray on small feet on which there is a kettle suspended over a spirit lamp. There is a cup and saucer and the silver 'basket' containing the dry leaves for the tea.* JELLABY *places the tray on the table and is about to offer further assistance with it.*]

---

6. Eastern part of the Mediterranean. "Rake": sexually promiscuous man.

7. Loose woman (Mrs. Chater).

LADY CROOM   I will do it.

JELLABY   Yes, my lady. [*To* SEPTIMUS.] Lord Byron left a letter for you with the valet,[8] sir.

SEPTIMUS   Thank you.

[SEPTIMUS *takes the letter off the tray.* JELLABY *prepares to leave.* LADY CROOM *eyes the letter.*]

LADY CROOM   When did he do so?

JELLABY   As he was leaving, your ladyship.

[JELLABY *leaves.* SEPTIMUS *puts the letter into his pocket.*]

SEPTIMUS   Allow me.

[*Since she does not object, he pours a cup of tea for her. She accepts it.*]

LADY CROOM   I do not know if it is proper for you to receive a letter written in my house from someone not welcome in it.

SEPTIMUS   Very improper, I agree. Lord Byron's want of delicacy is a grief to his friends, among whom I no longer count myself. I will not read his letter until I have followed him through the gates.

[*She considers that for a moment.*]

LADY CROOM   That may excuse the reading but not the writing.

SEPTIMUS   Your ladyship should have lived in the Athens of Pericles![9] The philosophers would have fought the sculptors for your idle hour!

LADY CROOM [*Protesting.*]   Oh, really! . . . [*Protesting less.*] Oh really . . .

[SEPTIMUS *has taken Byron's letter from his pocket and is now setting fire to a corner of it using the little flame from the spirit lamp.*]

Oh . . . really . . .

[*The paper blazes in* SEPTIMUS's *hand and he drops it and lets it burn out on the metal tray.*]

SEPTIMUS   Now there's a thing—a letter from Lord Byron never to be read by a living soul. I will take my leave, madam, at the time of your desiring it.

LADY CROOM   To the Indies?[1]

SEPTIMUS   The Indies! Why?

LADY CROOM   To follow the Chater, of course. She did not tell you?

SEPTIMUS   She did not exchange half-a-dozen words with me.

LADY CROOM   I expect she did not like to waste the time. The Chater sails with Captain Brice.

SEPTIMUS   Ah. As a member of the crew?

LADY CROOM   No, as wife to Mr Chater, plant-gatherer to my brother's expedition.

SEPTIMUS   I knew he was no poet. I did not know it was botany under the false colours.

LADY CROOM   He is no more a botanist. My brother paid fifty pounds to have him published, and he will pay a hundred and fifty to have Mr Chater picking flowers in the Indies for a year while the wife plays mistress of the Captain's quarters. Captain Brice has fixed his passion on Mrs Chater, and to take her on voyage he has not scrupled to deceive the Admiralty, the Linnean Society and Sir Joseph Banks, botanist to His Majesty at Kew.[2]

SEPTIMUS   Her passion is not as fixed as his.

---

8. Manservant.
9. Athenian military commander, statesman, and patron of the arts (ca. 495–429 B.C.E.).
1. West Indies.

2. See p. 2761, n. 7. "Admiralty": headquarters of the British navy. "Linnean Society": Britain's leading botanical association. Sir Joseph Banks (1743–1820), naturalist and patron of the sciences.

LADY CROOM   It is a defect of God's humour that he directs our hearts everywhere but to those who have a right to them.

SEPTIMUS   Indeed, madam. [*Pause.*] But is Mr Chater deceived?

LADY CROOM   He insists on it, and finds the proof of his wife's virtue in his
eagerness to defend it. Captain Brice is *not* deceived but cannot help himself. He would die for her.

SEPTIMUS   I think, my lady, he would have Mr Chater die for her.

LADY CROOM   Indeed, I never knew a woman worth the duel, or the other way
about. Your letter to me goes very ill with your conduct to Mrs Chater, Mr
Hodge. I have had experience of being betrayed before the ink is dry, but
to be betrayed before the pen is even dipped, and with the village notice-
board, what am I to think of such a performance?

SEPTIMUS   My lady, I was alone with my thoughts in the gazebo, when Mrs
Chater ran me to ground, and I being in such a passion, in an agony of
unrelieved desire—

LADY CROOM   Oh . . . !

SEPTIMUS   —I thought in my madness that the Chater with her skirts over
her head would give me the momentary illusion of the happiness to which
I dared not put a face.
[*Pause.*]

LADY CROOM   I do not know when I have received a more unusual compliment, Mr Hodge. I hope I am more than a match for Mrs Chater with her
head in a bucket. Does she wear drawers?

SEPTIMUS   She does.

LADY CROOM   Yes, I have heard that drawers are being worn now. It is unnatural for women to be got up like jockeys. I cannot approve.
[*She turns with a whirl of skirts and moves to leave.*]
I know nothing of Pericles or the Athenian philosophers. I can spare them
an hour, in my sitting room when I have bathed. Seven o'clock. Bring a
book.
[*She goes out.* SEPTIMUS *picks up the two letters, the ones he wrote, and
starts to burn them in the flame of the spirit lamp.*]

SCENE SEVEN

VALENTINE *and* CHLOË *are at the table.* GUS *is in the room.*

CHLOË *is reading from two Saturday newspapers. She is wearing workaday
period clothes, a Regency dress,*[3] *no hat.*

VALENTINE *is pecking at a portable computer. He is wearing unkempt Regency
clothes, too.*

*The clothes have evidently come from a large wicker laundry hamper, from
which* GUS *is producing more clothes to try on himself. He finds a Regency coat
and starts putting it on.*

*The objects on the table now include two geometrical solids, pyramid and cone,
about twenty inches high, of the type used in a drawing lesson; and a pot of dwarf
dahlias (which do not look like modern dahlias).*

CHLOË   'Even in Arcadia—Sex, Literature and Death at Sidley Park'. Picture
of Byron.

---

3. Fashionable in the "Regency" period, 1811–20, when George, Prince of Wales, was regent, ruling
England after his father, George III, had been judged insane.

VALENTINE   Not of Bernard?

CHLOË   'Byron Fought Fatal Duel, Says Don' . . . Valentine, do you think I'm the first person to think of this?

VALENTINE   No.

CHLOË   I haven't said yet. The future is all programmed like a computer—that's a proper theory, isn't it?

VALENTINE   The deterministic[4] universe, yes.

CHLOË   Right. Because everything including us is just a lot of atoms bouncing off each other like billiard balls.

VALENTINE   Yes. There was someone, forget his name, 1820s, who pointed out that from Newton's laws you could predict everything to come—I mean, you'd need a computer as big as the universe but the formula would exist.

CHLOË   But it doesn't work, does it?

VALENTINE   No. It turns out the maths is different.

CHLOË   No, it's all because of sex.

VALENTINE   Really?

CHLOË   That's what I think. The universe is deterministic all right, just like Newton said, I mean it's trying to be, but the only thing going wrong is people fancying people who aren't supposed to be in that part of the plan.

VALENTINE   Ah. The attraction that Newton left out. All the way back to the apple in the garden.[5] Yes.[*Pause.*] Yes, I think you're the first person to think of this.

[HANNAH *enters, carrying a tabloid paper, and a mug of tea.*]

HANNAH   Have you seen this? 'Bonking[6] Byron Shot Poet'.

CHLOË   [*Pleased.*]   Let's see.

[HANNAH *gives her the paper, smiles at* GUS.]

VALENTINE   He's done awfully well, hasn't he? How did they all know?

HANNAH   Don't be ridiculous. [*To* CHLOË] Your father wants it back.

CHLOË   All right.

HANNAH   What a fool.

CHLOË   Jealous. I think it's brilliant. [*She gets up to go. To* GUS.] Yes, that's perfect, but not with trainers. Come on, I'll lend you a pair of flatties,[7] they'll look period on you—

HANNAH   Hello, Gus. You all look so romantic.

[GUS *following* CHLOË *out, hesitates, smiles at her.*]

CHLOË   [*Pointedly.*]   Are you coming?

[*She holds the door for* GUS *and follows him out, leaving a sense of her disapproval behind her.*]

HANNAH   The important thing is not to give two monkeys for what young people think about you.

[*She goes to look at the other newspapers.*]

VALENTINE   [*Anxiously.*]   You don't think she's getting a thing about[8] Bernard, do you?

HANNAH   I wouldn't worry about Chloë, she's old enough to vote on her back. 'Byron Fought Fatal Duel, Says Don'. Or rather—[*Sceptically.*] 'Says Don!'

VALENTINE   It may all prove to be true.

HANNAH   It can't prove to be true, it can only not prove to be false yet.

---

4. Predetermined (see Valentine and Chloë's discussion below).
5. Of Eden; cf. Genesis 3. Also the apple whose fall from the tree alerted Isaac Newton to the law of gravity.
6. Fucking (slang).
7. Flat-soled shoes. "Trainers": sneakers.
8. A crush on.

VALENTINE [*Pleased.*]   Just like science.

HANNAH   If Bernard can stay ahead of getting the rug pulled till he's dead, he'll be a success.

VALENTINE   *Just* like science . . . The ultimate fear is of posterity . . .

HANNAH   Personally I don't think it'll take that long.

VALENTINE   . . . and then there's the afterlife. An afterlife would be a mixed blessing. 'Ah—Bernard Nightingale, I don't believe you know Lord Byron.' It must be heaven up there.

HANNAH   You can't believe in an afterlife, Valentine.

VALENTINE   Oh, you're going to disappoint me at last.

HANNAH   Am I? Why?

VALENTINE   Science and religion.

HANNAH   No, no, been there, done that, boring.

VALENTINE   Oh, Hannah. Fiancée. Have pity. Can't we have a trial marriage and I'll call it off in the morning?

HANNAH [*Amused.*]   I don't know when I've received a more unusual proposal.

VALENTINE [*Interested.*]   Have you had many?

HANNAH   That would be telling.

VALENTINE   Well, why not? Your classical reserve is only a mannerism; and neurotic.

HANNAH   Do you want the room?

VALENTINE   You get nothing if you give nothing.

HANNAH   I ask nothing.

VALENTINE   No, stay.

> [VALENTINE *resumes work at his computer.* HANNAH *establishes herself among her references at 'her' end of the table. She has a stack of pocket-sized volumes,* Lady Croom's 'garden books'.]

HANNAH   What are you doing? Valentine?

VALENTINE   The set of points on a complex plane[9] made by—

HANNAH   Is it the grouse?

VALENTINE   Oh, the grouse. The damned grouse.

HANNAH   You mustn't give up.

VALENTINE   Why? Didn't you agree with Bernard?

HANNAH   Oh, that. It's *all* trivial—your grouse, my hermit, Bernard's Byron. Comparing what we're looking for misses the point. It's wanting to know that makes us matter. Otherwise we're going out the way we came in. That's why you can't believe in the afterlife, Valentine. Believe in the after, by all means, but not the life. Believe in God, the soul, the spirit, the infinite, believe in angels if you like, but not in the great celestial get-together for an exchange of views. If the answers are in the back of the book I can wait, but what a drag. Better to struggle on knowing that failure is final. [*She looks over* VALENTINE's *shoulder at the computer screen. Reacting.*] Oh!, but . . . how beautiful!

VALENTINE   The Coverly set.[1]

HANNAH   The Coverly set! My goodness, Valentine!

VALENTINE   Lend me a finger.

> [He takes her finger and presses one of the computer keys several times.]

---

9. The "complex numbers" of mathematics laid out in a two-dimensional plane.

1. Graphic patterns of changes in Sidley Park's grouse population.

See? In an ocean of ashes, islands of order. Patterns making themselves out of nothing.

　　I can't show you how deep it goes. Each picture is a detail of the previous one, blown up. And so on. For ever. Pretty nice, eh?

HANNAH　Is it important?

VALENTINE　Interesting. Publishable.

HANNAH　Well done!

VALENTINE　Not me. It's Thomasina's. I just pushed her equations through the computer a few million times further than she managed to do with her pencil.

　　[*From the old portfolio he takes Thomasina's lesson book and gives it to* HANNAH. *The piano starts to be heard.*]

You can have it back now.

HANNAH　What does it mean?

VALENTINE　Not what you'd like it to.

HANNAH　Why not?

VALENTINE　Well, for one thing, she'd be famous.

HANNAH　No, she wouldn't. She was dead before she had time to be famous . . .

VALENTINE　She died?

HANNAH　. . . burned to death.

VALENTINE　[*Realizing.*]　Oh . . . the girl who died in the fire!

HANNAH　The night before her seventeenth birthday. You can see where the dormer² doesn't match. That was her bedroom under the roof. There's a memorial in the Park.

VALENTINE　[*Irritated.*]　I know—it's my house.

　　[VALENTINE *turns his attention back to his computer.* HANNAH *goes back to her chair. She looks through the lesson book.*]

HANNAH　Val, Septimus was her tutor—he and Thomasina would have—

VALENTINE　You do yours.

　　[*Pause. Two researchers.*]

　　LORD AUGUSTUS, *fifteen years old, wearing clothes of 1812, bursts in through the non–music room door. He is laughing. He dives under the table. He is chased into the room by* THOMASINA, *aged sixteen and furious. She spots* AUGUSTUS *immediately.*]

THOMASINA　You swore! You crossed your heart!

　　[AUGUSTUS *scampers out from under the table and* THOMASINA *chases him around it.*]

AUGUSTUS　I'll tell mama! I'll tell mama!

THOMASINA　You beast!

　　[*She catches* AUGUSTUS *as* SEPTIMUS *enters from the other door, carrying a book, a decanter³ and a glass, and his portfolio.*]

SEPTIMUS　Hush! What is this? My lord! Order, order!

　　[THOMASINA *and* AUGUSTUS *separate.*]

　　I am obliged.⁴

---

2. Vertical window that projects from a sloping roof.
3. Glass bottle (with a stopper) from which wine is served.
4. Thank you.

[SEPTIMUS *goes to his place at the table. He pours himself a glass of wine.*]

AUGUSTUS Well, good day to you, Mr Hodge!
   [*He is smirking about something.*
      THOMASINA *dutifully picks up a drawing book and settles down to draw the geometrical solids.*
      SEPTIMUS *opens his portfolio.*]

SEPTIMUS Will you join us this morning, Lord Augustus? We have our drawing lesson.

AUGUSTUS I am a master of it at Eton, Mr Hodge, but we only draw naked women.

SEPTIMUS You may work from memory.

THOMASINA Disgusting!

SEPTIMUS We will have silence now, if you please.
   [*From the portfolio* SEPTIMUS *takes Thomasina's lesson book and tosses it to her; returning homework. She snatches it and opens it.*]

THOMASINA No marks?! Did you not like my rabbit equation?

SEPTIMUS I saw no resemblance to a rabbit.

THOMASINA It eats its own progeny.[5]

SEPTIMUS [*Pause.*] I did not see that.
   [*He extends his hand for the lesson book. She returns it to him.*]

THOMASINA I have not room to extend it.
   [SEPTIMUS *and* HANNAH *turn the pages doubled by time.* AUGUSTUS *indolently starts to draw the models.*]

HANNAH Do you mean the world is saved after all?

VALENTINE No, it's still doomed. But if this is how it started, perhaps it's how the next one will come.

HANNAH From good English algebra?

SEPTIMUS It will go to infinity or zero, or nonsense.

THOMASINA No, if you set apart the minus roots they square back to sense.
   [SEPTIMUS *turns the pages.*
      THOMASINA *starts drawing the models.*

   HANNAH *closes the lesson book and turns her attention to her stack of 'garden books'.*]

VALENTINE Listen—you know your tea's getting cold.

HANNAH I like it cold.

VALENTINE [*Ignoring that.*] I'm telling you something. Your tea gets cold by itself, it doesn't get hot by itself. Do you think that's odd?

HANNAH No.

VALENTINE Well, it is odd. Heat goes to cold. It's a one-way street. Your tea will end up at room temperature. What's happening to your tea is happening to everything everywhere. The sun and the stars. It'll take a while but we're all going to end up at room temperature. When your hermit set up shop nobody understood this. But let's say you're right, in 18-whatever nobody knew more about heat than this scribbling nutter[6] living in a hovel in Derbyshire.

---

5. See p. 2783. VALENTINE: "She's feeding the solution back into the equation."   6. Madman.

HANNAH   He was at Cambridge—a scientist.

VALENTINE   Say he was. I'm not arguing. And the girl was his pupil, she had a genius for her tutor.

HANNAH   Or the other way round.

VALENTINE   Anything you like. But not *this*! Whatever he thought he was doing to save the world with good English algebra it wasn't this!

HANNAH   Why? Because they didn't have calculators?

VALENTINE   No. Yes. Because there's an order things can't happen in. You can't open a door till there's a house.

HANNAH   I thought that's what genius was.

VALENTINE   Only for lunatics and poets.

    [*Pause.*]

HANNAH   'I had a dream which was not all a dream.
    The bright sun was extinguished, and the stars
    Did wander darkling in the eternal space,
    Rayless, and pathless, and the icy earth
    Swung blind and blackening in the moonless air . . . '[7]

VALENTINE   Your own?

HANNAH   Byron.

    [*Pause. Two researchers again.*]

THOMASINA   Septimus, do you think that I will marry Lord Byron?

AUGUSTUS   Who is he?

THOMASINA   He is the author of 'Childe Harold's Pilgrimage', the most poetical and pathetic and bravest hero of any book I ever read before, and the most modern and the handsomest, for Harold is Lord Byron himself to those who know him, like myself and Septimus. Well, Septimus?

SEPTIMUS [*Absorbed.*]   No.

    [*Then he puts her lesson book away into the portfolio and picks up his own book to read.*]

THOMASINA   Why not?

SEPTIMUS   For one thing, he is not aware of your existence.

THOMASINA   We exchanged many significant glances when he was at Sidley Park. I do wonder that he has been home almost a year from his adventures and has not written to me once.

SEPTIMUS   It is indeed improbable, my lady.

AUGUSTUS   Lord Byron?!—he claimed my hare, although my shot was the earlier! He said I missed by a hare's breadth. His conversation was very facetious. But I think Lord Byron will not marry you, Thom, for he was only lame and not blind.

SEPTIMUS   Peace! Peace until a quarter to twelve. It is intolerable for a tutor to have his thoughts interrupted by his pupils.

AUGUSTUS   You are not *my* tutor, sir. I am visiting your lesson by my free will.

SEPTIMUS   If you are so determined, my lord.

    [THOMASINA *laughs at that, the joke is for her.* AUGUSTUS, *not included, becomes angry.*]

AUGUSTUS   Your peace is nothing to me, sir. You do not rule over me.

THOMASINA [*Admonishing.*]   Augustus!

SEPTIMUS   I do not rule here, my lord. I inspire by reverence for learning and

7. Byron, "Darkness," lines 1–5.

the exaltation of knowledge whereby man may approach God. There will be a shilling[8] for the best cone and pyramid drawn in silence by a quarter to twelve *at the earliest.*

AUGUSTUS   You will not buy my silence for a shilling, sir. What I know to tell is worth much more than that.

> [*And throwing down his drawing book and pencil, he leaves the room on his dignity, closing the door sharply. Pause.* SEPTIMUS *looks enquiringly at* THOMASINA.]

THOMASINA   I told him you kissed me. But he will not tell.

SEPTIMUS   When did I kiss you?

THOMASINA   What! Yesterday!

SEPTIMUS   Where?

THOMASINA   On the lips!

SEPTIMUS   In which country?

THOMASINA   In the hermitage, Septimus!

SEPTIMUS   On the lips in the hermitage! That? That was not a shilling kiss! I would not give sixpence to have it back. I had almost forgot it already.

THOMASINA   Oh, cruel! Have you forgotten our compact?

SEPTIMUS   God save me! Our compact?

THOMASINA   To teach me to waltz! Sealed with a kiss, and a second kiss due when I can dance like mama!

SEPTIMUS   Ah yes. Indeed. We were all waltzing like mice in London.

THOMASINA   I must waltz, Septimus! I will be despised if I do not waltz! It is the most fashionable and gayest and boldest invention conceivable—started in Germany!

SEPTIMUS   Let them have the waltz, they cannot have the calculus.

THOMASINA   Mama has brought from town a whole book of waltzes for the Broadwood,[9] to play with Count Zelinsky.

SEPTIMUS   I need not be told what I cannot but suffer. Count Zelinsky banging on the Broadwood without relief has me reading in waltz time.

THOMASINA   Oh, stuff! What is your book?

SEPTIMUS   A prize essay of the Scientific Academy in Paris. The author deserves your indulgence, my lady, for you are his prophet.

THOMASINA   I? What does he write about? The waltz?

SEPTIMUS   Yes. He demonstrates the equation of the propagation of heat in a solid body.[1] But in doing so he has discovered heresy—a natural contradiction of Sir Isaac Newton.

THOMASINA   Oh!—he contradicts determinism?

SEPTIMUS   No! . . . Well, perhaps. He shows that the atoms do not go according to Newton.

> [*Her interest has switched in the mercurial way characteristic of her— she has crossed to take the book.*]

THOMASINA   Let me see—oh! In French?

SEPTIMUS   Yes. Paris is the capital of France.

THOMASINA   Show me where to read.

> [*He takes the book back from her and finds the page for her. Meanwhile,*

---

8. British coin (before decimalization) equal to twelve old pennies/pence, or one-twentieth of a pound.
9. Brand of piano.
1. "Paris was the center of such studies: in 1807 Jean-Baptiste Fourier had written about heat flow.

The French scientist most relevant is Sadi Carnot, founder of thermodynamics; but he was only sixteen in 1812. The essay is about the passing of heat from one body to another, which is why Septimus can humourously agree that it is 'about' the 'waltz' " (Jim Hunter, *Tom Stoppard*, 2000).

the piano music from the next room has doubled its notes and its emotion.]

THOMASINA   Four-handed now! Mama is in love with the Count.

SEPTIMUS   He is a Count in Poland. In Derbyshire he is a piano tuner.

[*She has taken the book and is already immersed in it. The piano music becomes rapidly more passionate, and then breaks off suddenly in mid-phrase. There is an expressive silence next door which makes* SEPTIMUS *raise his eyes. It does not register with* THOMASINA. *The silence allows us to hear the distant regular thump of the steam engine which is to be a topic. A few moments later* LADY CROOM *enters from the music room, seeming surprised and slightly flustered to find the schoolroom occupied. She collects herself, closing the door behind her. And remains watching, aimless and discreet, as though not wanting to interrupt the lesson.* SEPTIMUS *has stood, and she nods him back into his chair.*

CHLOË, *in Regency dress, enters from the door opposite the music room. She takes in* VALENTINE *and* HANNAH *but crosses without pausing to the music room door.*]

CHLOË   Oh!—where's Gus?

VALENTINE   Dunno.

[CHLOË *goes into the music room.*]

LADY CROOM   [*Annoyed*]   Oh!—Mr Noakes's engine!

[*She goes to the garden door and steps outside.*

CHLOË *re-enters.*]

CHLOË   Damn.

LADY CROOM   [*Calls out.*]   Mr Noakes!

VALENTINE   He was there not long ago . . .

LADY CROOM   Halloo!

CHLOË   Well, he has to be in the photograph—is he dressed?

HANNAH   Is Bernard back?

CHLOË   No—he's late!

[*The piano is heard again, under the noise of the steam engine.* LADY CROOM *steps back into the room.*

CHLOË *steps outside the garden door. Shouts.*] Gus!

LADY CROOM   I wonder you can teach against such a disturbance and I am sorry for it, Mr Hodge.

[CHLOË *comes back inside.*]

VALENTINE   [*Getting up.*]   Stop ordering everybody about.

LADY CROOM   It is an unendurable noise.

VALENTINE   The photographer will wait.

[*But, grumbling, he follows* CHLOË *out of the door she came in by, and closes the door behind them.* HANNAH *remains absorbed. In the silence, the rhythmic thump can be heard again.*]

LADY CROOM   The ceaseless dull overbearing monotony of it! It will drive me distracted. I may have to return to town to escape it.

SEPTIMUS   Your ladyship could remain in the country and let Count Zelinsky return to town where you would not hear him.

LADY CROOM   I mean Mr Noakes's engine! [*Semi-aside to* SEPTIMUS.] *Would you sulk? I will not have my daughter study sulking.*

THOMASINA [*Not listening.*]   What, mama?

> [THOMASINA *remains lost in her book.* LADY CROOM *returns to close the garden door and the noise of the steam engine subsides.*]

> HANNAH *closes one of the 'garden books', and opens the next. She is making occasional notes.*

> *The piano ceases.*]

LADY CROOM [*To* THOMASINA.]   What are we learning today? [*Pause.*] Well, not manners.

SEPTIMUS   We are drawing today.

> [LADY CROOM *negligently examines what* THOMASINA *had started to draw.*]

LADY CROOM   Geometry. I approve of geometry.

SEPTIMUS   Your ladyship's approval is my constant object.

LADY CROOM   Well, do not despair of it. [*Returning to the window impatiently.*] Where is 'Culpability' Noakes?[2] [*She looks out and is annoyed.*] Oh!—he has gone for his hat so that he may remove it.

> [*She returns to the table and touches the bowl of dahlias.*

> HANNAH *sits back in her chair, caught by what she is reading.*] For the widow's dowry of dahlias I can almost forgive my brother's marriage. We must be thankful the monkey bit the husband. If it had bit the wife the monkey would be dead and we would not be first in the kingdom to show a dahlia. [HANNAH, *still reading the garden book, stands up.*] I sent one potted to Chatsworth.[3] The Duchess was most satisfactorily put out[4] by it when I called at Devonshire House. Your friend was there lording it as a poet.

> [HANNAH *leaves through the door, following* VALENTINE *and* CHLOË.

> *Meanwhile,* THOMASINA *thumps the book down on the table.*]

THOMASINA   Well! Just as I said! Newton's machine which would knock our atoms from cradle to grave by the laws of motion is incomplete! Determinism leaves the road at every corner, as I knew all along, and the cause is very likely hidden in this gentleman's observation.

LADY CROOM   Of what?

THOMASINA   The action of bodies in heat.

LADY CROOM   Is this geometry?

THOMASINA   This? No, I despise geometry!

> [*Touching the dahlias she adds, almost to herself.*] The Chater would overthrow the Newtonian system in a weekend.

SEPTIMUS   Geometry, Hobbes assures us in the *Leviathan*,[5] is the only science God has been pleased to bestow on mankind.

LADY CROOM   And what does he mean by it?

SEPTIMUS   Mr Hobbes or God?

LADY CROOM   I am sure I do not know what either means by it.

---

2. Noakes is called "culpable" (deserving of blame) for ruining the landscape designed by the "capable" Brown (so called because of his habit of saying a landscape had "capabilities," or potential). See p. 2771, n. 6.
3. Derbyshire "stately home" of the duke and duchess of Devonshire, whose London residence is Devonshire House.
4. Jealously annoyed.
5. Philosophic treatise, published in 1651, by Thomas Hobbes (1588–1679).

THOMASINA   Oh, pooh to Hobbes! Mountains are not pyramids and trees are
   not cones. God must love gunnery and architecture if Euclid[6] is his only
   geometry. There is another geometry which I am engaged in discovering by
   trial and error, am I not, Septimus?
SEPTIMUS   Trial and error perfectly describes your enthusiasm, my lady.
LADY CROOM   How old are you today?
THOMASINA   Sixteen years and eleven months, mama, and three weeks.
LADY CROOM   Sixteen years and eleven months. We must have you married
   before you are educated beyond eligibility.[7]
THOMASINA   I am going to marry Lord Byron.
LADY CROOM   Are you? He did not have the manners to mention it.
THOMASINA   You have spoken to him?!
LADY CROOM   Certainly not.
THOMASINA   Where did you see him?
LADY CROOM   [With some bitterness.]   Everywhere.
THOMASINA   Did you, Septimus?
SEPTIMUS   At the Royal Academy where I had the honour to accompany your
   mother and Count Zelinsky.
THOMASINA   What was Lord Byron doing?
LADY CROOM   Posing.
SEPTIMUS   [Tactfully.]   He was being sketched during his visit . . . by the Pro-
   fessor of Painting . . . Mr Fuseli.[8]
LADY CROOM   There was more posing at the pictures than in them. His com-
   panion likewise reversed the custom of the Academy that the ladies viewing
   wear more than the ladies viewed—well, enough! Let him be hanged there
   for a Lamb.[9] I have enough with Mr Noakes, who is to a garden what a bull
   is to a china shop.
   [This as NOAKES enters.]
THOMASINA   The Emperor of Irregularity!
   [She settles down to drawing the diagram which is to be the third item
   in the surviving portfolio.]
LADY CROOM   Mr Noakes!
NOAKES   Your ladyship—
LADY CROOM   What have you done to me!
NOAKES   Everything is satisfactory, I assure you. A little behind, to be sure,
   but my dam will be repaired within the month—
LADY CROOM   [Banging the table.]   Hush!
   [In the silence, the steam engine thumps in the distance.]
   Can you hear, Mr Noakes?
NOAKES   [Pleased and proud.]   The Improved Newcomen steam pump[1]—the
   only one in England!
LADY CROOM   That is what I object to. If everybody had his own I would bear
   my portion of the agony without complaint. But to have been singled out
   by the only Improved Newcomen steam pump in England, this is hard, sir,
   this is not to be borne.
NOAKES   Your lady—

6. Greek mathematician (flourished ca. 300
B.C.E.), famous for his Elements, a presentation of
the geometry and other mathematics known in his
day.
7. Suitability (as a partner in marriage).

8. See p. 2795, n. 4.
9. Cf. the old proverb "One might as well be hung
for a sheep as a lamb."
1. Thomas Newcomen had produced his first, very
inefficient, steam pump in 1712.

LADY CROOM   And for what? My lake is drained to a ditch for no purpose I
can understand, unless it be that snipe and curlew[2] have deserted three
counties so that they may be shot in our swamp. What you painted as forest
is a mean plantation, your greenery is mud, your waterfall is wet mud, and
your mount is an opencast mine for the mud that was lacking in the dell.[3]
[Pointing through the window.] What is that cowshed?

NOAKES   The hermitage, my lady?

LADY CROOM   It is a cowshed.

NOAKES   Madam, it is, I assure you, a very habitable cottage, properly
founded and drained, two rooms and a closet under a slate roof and a stone
chimney—

LADY CROOM   And who is to live in it?

NOAKES   Why, the hermit.

LADY CROOM   Where is he?

NOAKES   Madam?

LADY CROOM   You surely do not supply a hermitage without a hermit?

NOAKES   Indeed, madam—

LADY CROOM   Come, come, Mr Noakes. If I am promised a fountain I expect
it to come with water. What hermits do you have?

NOAKES   I have no hermits, my lady.

LADY CROOM   Not one? I am speechless.

NOAKES   I am sure a hermit can be found. One could advertise.

LADY CROOM   Advertise?

NOAKES   In the newspapers.

LADY CROOM   But surely a hermit who takes a newspaper is not a hermit in
whom one can have complete confidence.

NOAKES   I do not know what to suggest, my lady.

SEPTIMUS   Is there room for a piano?

NOAKES   [Baffled.]   A piano?

LADY CROOM   We are intruding here—this will not do, Mr Hodge. Evidently,
nothing is being learned. [To NOAKES.] Come along, sir!

THOMASINA   Mr Noakes—bad news from Paris!

NOAKES   Is it the Emperor Napoleon?

THOMASINA   No. [She tears the page off her drawing block, with her 'diagram'
on it.] It concerns your heat engine. Improve it as you will, you can never
get out of it what you put in. It repays eleven pence in the shilling at most.
The penny is for this author's thoughts.

[She gives the diagram to SEPTIMUS who looks at it.]

NOAKES   [Baffled again.]   Thank you, my lady.

[NOAKES goes out into the garden.]

LADY CROOM   [To SEPTIMUS.]   Do you understand her?

SEPTIMUS   No.

LADY CROOM   Then this business is over. I was married at seventeen. Ce soir
il faut qu'on parle français, je te demande,[4] Thomasina, as a courtesy to the
Count. Wear your green velvet, please, I will send Briggs to do your hair.
Sixteen and eleven months . . . !

[She follows NOAKES out of view.]

THOMASINA   Lord Byron was with a lady?

---

2. Two species of game bird.
3. Small valley.

4. This evening I must ask you to speak French
(French).

SEPTIMUS   Yes.

THOMASINA   Huh!

> [*Now* SEPTIMUS *retrieves his book from* THOMASINA. *He turns the pages, and also continues to study Thomasina's diagram. He strokes the tortoise absently as he reads.* THOMASINA *takes up pencil and paper and starts to draw* SEPTIMUS *with Plautus.*]

SEPTIMUS   Why does it mean Mr Noakes's engine pays eleven pence in the shilling? Where does he say it?

THOMASINA   Nowhere. I noticed it by the way. I cannot remember now.

SEPTIMUS   Nor is he interested by determinism—

THOMASINA   Oh . . . yes. Newton's equations go forwards and backwards, they do not care which way. But the heat equation cares very much, it goes only one way. That is the reason Mr Noakes's engine cannot give the power to drive Mr Noakes's engine.

SEPTIMUS   Everybody knows that.

THOMASINA   Yes, Septimus, they know it about engines!

SEPTIMUS   [*Pause. He looks at his watch.*]   A quarter to twelve. For your essay this week, explicate[5] your diagram.

THOMASINA   I cannot, I do not know the mathematics.

SEPTIMUS   Without mathematics, then.

> [THOMASINA *has continued to draw. She tears the top page from her drawing pad and gives it to* SEPTIMUS.]

THOMASINA   There. I have made a drawing of you and Plautus.

SEPTIMUS   [*Looking at it.*]   Excellent likeness. Not so good of me.

> [THOMASINA *laughs, and leaves the room.*
>
> AUGUSTUS *appears at the garden door. His manner cautious and diffident.*[6] SEPTIMUS *does not notice him for a moment.*
>
> SEPTIMUS *gathers his papers together.*]

AUGUSTUS   Sir . . .

SEPTIMUS   My lord . . . ?

AUGUSTUS   I gave you offence, sir, and I am sorry for it.

SEPTIMUS   I took none, my lord, but you are kind to mention it.

AUGUSTUS   I would like to ask you a question, Mr Hodge. [*Pause.*] You have an elder brother, I dare say, being a Septimus?[7]

SEPTIMUS   Yes, my lord. He lives in London. He is the editor of a newspaper, the *Piccadilly Recreation.* [*Pause.*] Was that your question?

> [AUGUSTUS, *evidently embarrassed about something, picks up the drawing of Septimus.*]

AUGUSTUS   No. Oh . . . it is you? . . . I would like to keep it. [SEPTIMUS *inclines his head in assent.*] There are things a fellow cannot ask his friends. Carnal things. My sister has told me . . . my sister believes such things as I cannot, I assure you, bring myself to repeat.

SEPTIMUS   You must not repeat them, then. The walk between here and dinner will suffice to put us straight, if we stroll by the garden. It is an easy business. And then I must rely on you to correct your sister's state of ignorance.

> [*A commotion is heard outside—*BERNARD'S *loud voice in a sort of agony.*]

---

5. Explain.
6. Shy.

7. Latin for "seventh."

BERNARD [outside the door.] Oh no—no—no—oh, bloody hell!—

AUGUSTUS Thank you, Mr Hodge, I will.

[Taking the drawing with him, AUGUSTUS allows himself to be shown out through the garden door, and SEPTIMUS follows him.

BERNARD enters the room, through the door HANNAH left by. VALENTINE comes in with him, leaving the door open and they are followed by HANNAH who is holding the 'garden book'.]

BERNARD Oh, no—no—

HANNAH I'm sorry, Bernard.

BERNARD Fucked by a dahlia! Do you think? Is it open and shut? Am I fucked? What does it really amount to? When all's said and done? Am I fucked? What do you think, Valentine? Tell me the truth.

VALENTINE You're fucked.

BERNARD Oh God! Does it mean that?

HANNAH Yes, Bernard, it does.

BERNARD I'm not sure. Show me where it says. I want to see it. No—read it—no, wait . . .

[BERNARD sits at the table. He prepares to listen as though listening were an oriental art.]

Right.

HANNAH [Reading.] 'October 1st, 1810. Today under the direction of Mr Noakes, a parterre[8] was dug on the south lawn and will be a handsome show next year, a consolation for the picturesque catastrophe of the second and third distances. The dahlia having propagated under glass with no ill effect from the sea voyage, is named by Captain Brice 'Charity' for his bride, though the honour properly belongs to the husband who exchanged beds with my dahlia, and an English summer for everlasting night in the Indies.'

[Pause.]

BERNARD Well, it's so round the houses, isn't it? Who's to say what it means?

HANNAH [Patiently.] It means that Ezra Chater of the Sidley Park connection is the same Chater who described a dwarf dahlia in Martinique in 1810 and died there, of a monkey bite.

BERNARD [Wildly.] Ezra wasn't a botanist! He was a poet!

HANNAH He was not much of either, but he was both.

VALENTINE It's not a disaster.

BERNARD Of course it's a disaster! I was on 'The Breakfast Hour'![9]

VALENTINE It doesn't mean Byron didn't fight a duel, it only means Chater wasn't killed in it.

BERNARD Oh, pull yourself together!—do you think I'd have been on 'The Breakfast Hour' if Byron had missed!

HANNAH Calm down, Bernard. Valentine's right.

BERNARD [Grasping at straws.] Do you think so? You mean the Piccadilly reviews? Yes, two completely unknown Byron essays—and my discovery of the lines he added to 'English Bards'. That counts for something.

HANNAH [Tactfully.] Very possible—persuasive, indeed.

BERNARD Oh, bugger persuasive! I've proved Byron was here and as far as I'm concerned he wrote those lines as sure as he shot that hare. If only I

---

8. Level space in a garden occupied by an orna-   9. Popular British TV program.
mental arrangement of flower beds.

hadn't somehow . . . made it all about *killing Chater*. Why didn't you stop me?! It's bound to get out, you know—I mean this—this *gloss*[1] on my discovery—I mean how long do you think it'll be before some botanical pedant[2] blows the whistle on me?

HANNAH The day after tomorrow. A letter in *The Times*.

BERNARD You wouldn't.

HANNAH It's a dirty job but somebody—

BERNARD Darling. Sorry. Hannah—

HANNAH —and, after all, it is my discovery.

BERNARD Hannah.

HANNAH Bernard.

BERNARD Hannah.

HANNAH Oh, shut up. It'll be very short, very dry, absolutely gloat-free. Would you rather it were one of your friends?

BERNARD [*Fervently.*] Oh God, no!

HANNAH And then in *your* letter to *The Times*—

BERNARD Mine?

HANNAH Well, of course. Dignified congratulations to a colleague, in the language of scholars, I trust.

BERNARD Oh, eat shit, you mean?

HANNAH Think of it as a breakthrough in dahlia studies.

 [CHLOË *hurries in from the garden.*]

CHLOË Why aren't you coming?!—Bernard! And you're not dressed! How long have you been back?

 [BERNARD *looks at her and then at* VALENTINE *and realizes for the first time that* VALENTINE *is unusually dressed.*]

BERNARD Why are you wearing those clothes?

CHLOË Do be quick!

 [*She is already digging into the basket and producing odd garments for* BERNARD.]

Just put anything on. We're all being photographed. Except Hannah.

HANNAH I'll come and watch.

 [VALENTINE *and* CHLOË *help* BERNARD *into a decorative coat and fix a lace collar round his neck.*]

CHLOË [*To* HANNAH.] Mummy says have you got the theodolite?

VALENTINE What are you supposed to be, Chlo? Bo-Peep?

CHLOË Jane Austen![3]

VALENTINE Of course.

HANNAH [*To* CHLOË.] Oh—it's in the hermitage! Sorry.

BERNARD I thought it wasn't till this evening. What photograph?

CHLOË The local paper, of course—they always come before we start. We want a good crowd of us—Gus looks gorgeous—

BERNARD [*Aghast.*] The newspaper!

 [*He grabs something like a bishop's mitre*[4] *from the basket and pulls it down completely over his face.*]

[*Muffled.*] I'm ready!

 [*And he staggers out with* VALELNTINE *and* CHLOË, *followed by* HANNAH.

---

1. Explanatory comment.
2. Person excessively concerned with minor details.
3. English novelist (1775–1817). "Bo-Peep": Lit-

tle Bo-Peep, subject of an eighteenth-century nursery rhyme.
4. Bishop's ceremonial headdress.

A light change to evening. The paper lanterns outside begin to glow. Piano music from the next room.

    SEPTIMUS *enters with an oil lamp. He carries Thomasina's algebra primer, and also her essay on loose sheets. He settles down to read at the table. It is nearly dark outside, despite the lanterns.*

    THOMASINA *enters, in a nightgown and barefoot, holding a candlestick. Her manner is secretive and excited.*]

SEPTIMUS My lady! What is it?

THOMASINA Septimus! Shush!

    [*She closes the door quietly.*]

Now is our chance!

SEPTIMUS For what, dear God?

    [*She blows out the candle and puts the candlestick on the table.*]

THOMASINA Do not act the innocent! Tomorrow I will be seventeen!

    [*She kisses* SEPTIMUS *full on the mouth.*]

There!

SEPTIMUS Dear Christ!

THOMASINA Now you must show me, you are paid in advance.

SEPTIMUS [*Understanding.*] Oh!

THOMASINA The Count plays for us, it is God-given! I cannot be seventeen and not waltz.

SEPTIMUS But your mother—

THOMASINA While she swoons, we can dance. The house is all abed. I heard the Broadwood. Oh, Septimus, teach me now!

SEPTIMUS Hush! I cannot now!

THOMASINA Indeed you can, and I am come barefoot so mind my toes.

SEPTIMUS I cannot because it is not a waltz.

THOMASINA It is not?

SEPTIMUS No, it is too quick for waltzing.

THOMASINA Oh! Then we will wait for him to play slow.

SEPTIMUS My lady—

THOMASINA Mr Hodge!

    [*She takes a chair next to him and looks at his work.*]

Are you reading my essay? Why do you work here so late?

SEPTIMUS To save my candles.

THOMASINA You have my old primer.

SEPTIMUS It is mine again. You should not have written in it.

    [*She takes it, looks at the open page.*]

THOMASINA It was a joke.

SEPTIMUS It will make me mad as you promised. Sit over there. You will have us in disgrace.

    [THOMASINA *gets up and goes to the furthest chair.*]

THOMASINA If mama comes I will tell her we only met to kiss, not to waltz.

SEPTIMUS Silence or bed.

THOMASINA Silence!

    [SEPTIMUS *pours himself some more wine. He continues to read her essay.*

    The music changes to party music from the marquee. And there are fireworks—small against the sky, distant flares of light like exploding meteors.

[HANNAH *enters. She has dressed for the party. The difference is not, however, dramatic. She closes the door and crosses to leave by the garden door. But as she gets there,* VALENTINE *is entering. He has a glass of wine in his hand.*]

HANNAH Oh . . .

[*But* VALENTINE *merely brushes past her, intent on something, and half-drunk.*]

VALENTINE [*To her.*] Got it!

[*He goes straight to the table and roots about in what is now a considerable mess of papers, books and objects.* HANNAH *turns back, puzzled by his manner. He finds what he has been looking for—the 'diagram'.*

Meanwhile, SEPTIMUS, *reading Thomasina's essay, also studies the diagram.*

SEPTIMUS *and* VALENTINE *study the diagram doubled by time.*]

VALENTINE It's heat.

HANNAH Are you tight,[5] Val?

VALENTINE It's a diagram of heat exchange.

SEPTIMUS So, we are all doomed!

THOMASINA [*Cheerfully.*] Yes.

VALENTINE Like a steam engine, you see—

[HANNAH *fills Septimus's glass from the same decanter, and sips from it.*]

She didn't have the maths, not remotely. She saw what things meant, way ahead, like seeing a picture.

SEPTIMUS This is not science. This is story-telling.

THOMASINA Is it a waltz now?

SEPTIMUS No.

[*The music is still modern.*]

VALENTINE Like a film.

HANNAH What did she see?

VALENTINE That you can't run the film backwards. Heat was the first thing which didn't work that way. Not like Newton. A film of a pendulum, or a ball falling through the air—backwards, it looks the same.

HANNAH The ball would be going the wrong way.

VALENTINE You'd have to know that. But with heat—friction—a ball breaking a window—

HANNAH Yes.

VALENTINE It won't work backwards.

HANNAH Who thought it did?

VALENTINE She saw why. You can put back the bits of glass but you can't collect up the heat of the smash. It's gone.

SEPTIMUS So the Improved Newtonian Universe must cease and grow cold. Dear me.

VALENTINE The heat goes into the mix.

[*He gestures to indicate the air in the room, in the universe.*]

THOMASINA Yes, we must hurry if we are going to dance.

VALENTINE And everything is mixing the same way, all the time, irreversibly . . .

SEPTIMUS Oh, we have time, I think.

5. Drunk.

VALENTINE   . . . till there's no time left. That's what time means.

SEPTIMUS   When we have found all the mysteries and lost all the meaning,
we will be alone, on an empty shore.

THOMASINA   Then we will dance. Is this a waltz?

SEPTIMUS   It will serve.

[*He stands up.*]

THOMASINA [*Jumping up.*]   Goody!

[SEPTIMUS *takes her in his arms carefully and the waltz lesson, to the
music from the marquee, begins.*

BERNARD *in unconvincing Regency dress, enters carrying a bottle.*]

BERNARD   Don't mind me, I left my jacket . . .

[*He heads for the area of the wicker basket.*]

VALENTINE   Are you leaving?

[BERNARD *is stripping off his period coat. He is wearing his own trousers,
tucked into knee socks and his own shirt.*]

BERNARD   Yes, I'm afraid so.

HANNAH   What's up, Bernard?

BERNARD   Nothing I can go into—

VALENTINE   Should I go?

BERNARD   No, *I'm* going!

[VALENTINE *and* HANNAH *watch* BERNARD *struggling into his jacket and
adjusting his clothes.*

SEPTIMUS, *holding* THOMASINA, *kisses her on the mouth. The waltz lesson
pauses. She looks at him. He kisses her again, in earnest. She puts her
arms round him.*]

THOMASINA   Septimus . . .

[SEPTIMUS *hushes her. They start to dance again, with the slight awkwardness of a lesson.*

CHLOË *bursts in from the garden.*]

CHLOË   I'll kill her! I'll *kill* her!

BERNARD   Oh dear.

VALENTINE   What the hell is it, Chlo?

CHLOË [*Venomously.*]   Mummy!

BERNARD [*To* VALENTINE.]   Your mother caught us in that cottage.

CHLOË   She snooped!

BERNARD   I don't think so. She was rescuing a theodolite.

CHLOË   I'll come with you, Bernard.

BERNARD   No, you bloody won't.

CHLOË   Don't you want me to?

BERNARD   Of course not. What for? [*To* VALENTINE.] I'm sorry.

CHLOË [*In furious tears.*]   What are you saying sorry to *him* for?

BERNARD   Sorry to you too. Sorry one and all. Sorry, Hannah—sorry, Hermione—sorry, Byron—sorry, sorry, sorry, now can I go?

[CHLOË *stands stiffly, tearfully.*]

CHLOË   Well . . .

[THOMASINA *and* SEPTIMUS *dance.*]

HANNAH   What a bastard you are, Bernard.

[CHLOË *rounds on her.*]

CHLOË And you mind your own business! What do you know about anything?

HANNAH Nothing.

CHLOË [*To* BERNARD.] It *was* worth it, though, wasn't it?

BERNARD It was wonderful.

[CHLOË *goes out, through the garden door, towards the party.*]

HANNAH [*An echo.*] Nothing.

VALENTINE Well, you shit. I'd drive you but I'm a bit sloshed.

[VALENTINE *follows* CHLOË *out and can be heard outside calling* 'Chlo! Chlo!']

BERNARD A scrape.

HANNAH Oh . . . [*She gives up.*] Bernard!

BERNARD I look forward to *The Genius of the Place*. I hope you find your hermit. I think out front is the safest.

[*He opens the door cautiously and looks out.*]

HANNAH Actually, I've got a good idea who he was, but I can't prove it.

BERNARD [*With a carefree expansive gesture.*] Publish!

[*He goes out closing the door.*

SEPTIMUS *and* THOMASINA *are now waltzing freely. She is delighted with herself.*]

THOMASINA Am I waltzing?

SEPTIMUS Yes, my lady.

[*He gives her a final twirl, bringing them to the table where he bows to her. He lights her candlestick.*

HANNAH *goes to sit at the table, playing truant from the party. She pours herself more wine. The table contains the geometrical solids, the computer, decanter, glasses, tea mug, Hannah's research books, Septimus's books, the two portfolios, Thomasina's candlestick, the oil lamp, the dahlia, the Sunday papers . . .*

GUS *appears in the doorway. It takes a moment to realize that he is not Lord Augustus; perhaps not until* HANNAH *sees him.*]

SEPTIMUS Take your essay, I have given it an alpha[6] in blind faith. Be careful with the flame.

THOMASINA I will wait for you to come.

SEPTIMUS I cannot.

THOMASINA You may.

SEPTIMUS I may not.

THOMASINA You must.

SEPTIMUS I will not.

[*She puts the candlestick and the essay on the table.*]

THOMASINA Then I will not go. Once more, for my birthday.

[SEPTIMUS *and* THOMASINA *start to waltz together.*

GUS *comes forward, startling* HANNAH.]

HANNAH Oh!—you made me jump.

[GUS *looks resplendent. He is carrying an old and somewhat tattered stiff-backed folio fastened with a tape tied in a bow. He comes to* HANNAH *and thrusts this present at her.*]

6. An A grade.

Oh . . .

[*She lays the folio down on the table and starts to open it. It consists only of two boards hinged, containing Thomasina's drawing.*]

'Septimus with Plautus'. [*To* GUS.] I was looking for that. Thank you.

[GUS *nods several times. Then, rather awkwardly, he bows to her. A Regency bow, an invitation to dance.*]

Oh, dear, I don't really . . .

[*After a moment's hesitation, she gets up and they hold each other, keeping a decorous distance between them, and start to dance, rather awkwardly.*

SEPTIMUS *and* THOMASINA *continue to dance, fluently, to the piano.*]

END

1993

LES MURRAY
b. 1938

Leslie Allan Murray was born at Nabiac on the north coast of New South Wales, Australia, and grew up on a dairy farm at nearby Bunyah. He was educated at Taree High School and the University of Sydney, where he studied modern languages. After military service with the Royal Australian Naval Reserve, he worked as a translator in the Australian National University, Canberra, and as an officer in the prime minister's department. Since 1971 he has been a full-time writer.

Remaining true to his roots in the Australian "outback" (despite the global shuttling expected of a major poet in the late twentieth century), Murray has emerged as a powerful celebrant of the natural world and agricultural work. His substantial *Collected Poems* (1998), dedicated "to the glory of God," bears witness to a staunch and highly individual Roman Catholicism. His celebration of nature includes human nature and reveals a sensibility generously attuned to the hopes and fears, hurts and happinesses of ordinary lives.

Murray seems intent on proving that the provincial farmer living at the margins of the former British Empire can write poetry as learned, authoritative, and technically virtuosic as any from the metropolitan center. The language of his poetry startles and amuses, reveling in the fecundity and elasticity of English. In poems of metaphorical lushness and sonic opulence, he plays on the eddying reflections of homonyms and rhymes, alliterations and consonances, to suggest a profound interconnectedness among things. As Derek Walcott has said of Murray's work: "There is no poetry in the English language so rooted in its sacredness, so broad-leafed in its pleasures, and yet so intimate and conversational."

Morse

Tuckett. Bill Tuckett. Telegraph operator, Hall's Creek,
which is way out back of the Outback, but he stuck it,
quite likely liked it, despite heat, glare, dust and the lack
of diversion or doctors. Come disaster you trusted to luck,
5 ingenuity and pluck. This was back when nice people said pluck,
the sleevelink and green eyeshade epoch.[1]
                    Faced, though, like Bill Tuckett
with a man needing surgery right on the spot, a lot
would have done their dashes. It looked hopeless (dot dot dot)
Lift him up on the table, said Tuckett, running the key hot
10 till Head Office turned up a doctor who coolly instructed
up a thousand miles of wire, as Tuckett advanced slit by slit
with a safety razor blade, pioneering on into the wet,
copper-wiring the rivers off, in the first operation conducted
along dotted lines, with rum drinkers gripping the patient:
d-d-dash it, take care, Tuck!
15   And the vital spark stayed unshorted.
Yallah![2] breathed the camelmen. Tuckett, you did it, you did it!
cried the spattered la-de-dah jodhpur[3]-wearing Inspector of Stock.
We imagine, some weeks later, a properly laconic
convalescent averring Without you, I'd have kicked the bucket . . .

20 From Chungking to Burrenjuck,[4] morse keys have mostly gone silent
and only old men meet now to chit-chat in their electric
bygone dialect. The last letter many will forget
is dit-dit-dit-dah, V for Victory. The coders' hero had speed,
resource and a touch. So ditditdit daah for Bill Tuckett.

                                        1983

On Removing Spiderweb

Like summer silk its denier
but stickily, oh, ickilier,
miffed bunny-blinder, silver tar,
gesticuli-gesticular,
5 crepe when cobbed, crap when rubbed,
stretchily adhere-and-there
and everyway, nap-snarled or sleek,
glibly hubbed with grots to tweak:
ehh weakly bobbined tae yer neb,
10 spit it Phuoc Tuy! filthy web!

                                        1990

1. I.e., the nineteenth century. "Sleevelink": cuff link.
2. God be praised! (Arabic).
3. Long breeches for riding, close-fitting from knee to ankle.
4. I.e., from southwest China to southeast Australia.

Corniche[1]

I work all day and hardly drink at all.[2]
I can reach down and feel if I'm depressed.
I adore the Creator because I made myself
and a few times a week a wire jags in my chest.

5 The first time, I'd been coming apart all year,
weeping, incoherent; cigars had given me up:
any road round a cliff edge I'd whimper along in low gear
then: cardiac horror. Masking my pulse's calm lub-dub.

It was the victim-sickness. Adrenaline howling in my head,
10 the black dog was my brain. Come to drown me in my breath
was energy's black hole, depression, compere° of   *master of ceremonies*
    the predawn show
when, returned from a pee, you stew and welter in your death.

The rogue space rock is on course to snuff your world,
sure. But go acute, and its oncoming fills your day.
15 The brave die but once? I could go a hundred times a week,
clinging to my pulse with the world's edge inches away.

Laugh, who never shrank around wizened genitals there
or killed themselves to stop dying. The blow that never falls
batters you stupid. Only gradually do
20 you notice a slight scorn in you for what appals.

A self inside self, cool as conscience, one to be erased
in your final night, or faxed, still knows beneath
all the mute grand opera and uncaused effect—
that death which can be imagined is not true death.

1996

---

1. Coastal road.
2. Cf. the opening of "Aubade," by the English poet Philip Larkin (1922–1985): "I work all day, and get half drunk at night."

SEAMUS HEANEY
b. 1939

Seamus Heaney was born into a Roman Catholic family in predominantly Protestant North Ireland (or Ulster), and he grew up on a farm in County Derry bordered on one side by a stream that marked the frontier with the largely Catholic Irish Republic (or Eire) to the south. He won scholarships first to St. Columb's College, a Catholic boarding school, and then to Queen's University in Belfast. There he became one of an extraordinary group of Northern Irish poets from both Protestant and Catholic backgrounds, including Michael Longley and Derek Mahon, who read, discussed, and spurred on one another's work. He taught at Queen's University, before moving in 1972 to the Irish Republic, where he became a citizen and full-time writer. He has been Boylston Professor of Rhetoric and Oratory at Harvard and Professor of Poetry at Oxford, and in 1995 won the Nobel Prize in Literature.

With "Digging," placed appropriately as the first poem of his first book, Heaney defined his territory. He dug into his memory, uncovering first his father and then, going deeper, his grandfather. This idea of poetry as an archaeological process of recovery took on a darker cast after the eruption of internecine violence in Northern Ireland in 1969, culminating in the 1972 Bloody Sunday killing of thirteen Catholic civilians by British paratroopers during a civil rights march in Derry. Across several volumes, especially *North* (1975), Heaney wrote a series of grim "bog poems," about well-preserved Iron Age corpses discovered in the peat of Northern Europe and Ireland. In these poems he sees the bog as a "memory bank," or unconscious, that preserves everything thrown into it, including the victims of ritual killings. He views contemporary violence through the lens of ancient myths, sacrifices, and feuds, an oblique approach that gives his poetry about the Troubles an unusual depth and resonance. He had discovered emblems for the violence in Northern Ireland in *The Bog People*, a book by the Danish archaeologist P. V. Glob, published in translation in 1969, "the year the killing started." Heaney wrote of it:

> It was chiefly concerned with preserved bodies of men and women found in the bogs of Jutland, naked, strangled or with their throats cut, disposed under the peat since early Iron Age times. The author . . . argues convincingly that a number of these, and in particular, the Tollund Man, whose head is now preserved near Aarhus in the museum of Silkeburg, were ritual sacrifices to the Mother Goddess, the goddess of the ground who needed new bridegrooms each winter to bed with her in her sacred place, in the spring. Taken in relation to the tradition of Irish political martyrdom for the cause whose icon is Kathleen Ni Houlihan [mythic figure emblematic of Mother Ireland], this is more than an archaic barbarous rite: it is an archetypal pattern. And the unforgettable photographs of these victims blended in my mind with photographs of atrocities, past and present, in the long rites of Irish political and religious struggles. ("Feeling into Words")

In the bog poems Heaney reflects on the poet's responsibilities to write about the dead, yet to do so without prettifying or exploiting them. He probes the vexed relations between lyric song and historical suffering, "beauty and atrocity": the need to be true to his calling as artist, but also to represent the irredeemable carnage of modern political violence—"the actual weight / of each hooded victim / slashed and dumped" ("The Grauballe Man"). The result is a tough-minded witnessing, an ethically scrupulous and self-aware mourning of collective loss and sectarian murder. (For more on the Troubles, see "Imagining Ireland" at Norton Literature Online.)

Since the late 1970s Heaney has continued to elegize victims of the Troubles, such as his acquaintance Louis O'Neill, in "Casualty," as well as more personal losses, such as the natural death of his mother, in "Clearances." He has also written poems about domestic love, such as "The Skunk" and "The Sharping Stone." Heaney is thus both a private poet—skillfully kneading grief, love, and wonder into poems about his family and his humble origins—and a public poet, affirming his affinities with the Catholic civil rights movement, which has struggled against British and Protestant domination. Even in his public poetry he refuses slogans, journalistic reportage, and political pieties, scrutinizing instead the wellsprings of collective identity, the ambivalences of individual response to history.

An Irishman writing in the language of the British Empire, he has translated Gaelic poetry and renewed specifically Irish traditions, such as the *aisling*, or vision poem, but he is also steeped in the English literary canon, drawing on British poetry from *Beowulf* (his prize-winning translation appears in volume 1 of this anthology) to the works of William Wordsworth, Gerard Manley Hopkins, and Ted Hughes. Straddling in his verse a multiplicity of divisions, transubstantiating crisscross feelings into unexpected images and intricate sonorities, Heaney has been embraced by popular audiences for his accessible style and yet also admired by poets and academic critics for his lyric subtlety and rigorous technique.

Formally, his poetry ranges from strenuous free verse—the clipped lines and unrhymed quatrains of the bog poems—to more traditional forms, such as the modified terza rima of "Station Island" and the sonnet sequence "Clearances." His poems are earthy and matter-of-fact, saturated with the physical textures, sights, smells, and sounds of farm life, and they are also visionary, lit up by hope and spirit, enacting penitential pilgrimages and unbridled imaginings. That Heaney's poetry is both earthbound and airborne, free and formed, public and private helps explain why he is seen by many as the most gifted English-language poet of his generation.

Digging

Between my finger and my thumb
The squat pen rests; snug as a gun.

Under my window, a clean rasping sound
When the spade sinks into gravelly ground:
5   My father, digging. I look down

Till his straining rump among the flowerbeds
Bends low, comes up twenty years away
Stooping in rhythm through potato drills[1]
Where he was digging.

10   The coarse boot nestled on the lug, the shaft
Against the inside knee was levered firmly.
He rooted out tall tops, buried the bright edge deep
To scatter new potatoes that we picked
Loving their cool hardness in our hands.

15   By God, the old man could handle a spade.
Just like his old man.

My grandfather cut more turf[2] in a day
Than any other man on Toner's bog.
Once I carried him milk in a bottle
20   Corked sloppily with paper. He straightened up
To drink it, then fell to right away
Nicking and slicing neatly, heaving sods
Over his shoulder, going down and down
For the good turf. Digging.

25   The cold smell of potato mould, the squelch and slap
Of soggy peat, the curt cuts of an edge
Through living roots awaken in my head.
But I've no spade to follow men like them.

---

1. Small furrows in which seeds are sown.
2. Slabs of peat that, when dried, are a common domestic fuel in Ireland.

Between my finger and my thumb
30 The squat pen rests.
I'll dig with it.

1966

The Forge

All I know is a door into the dark.
Outside, old axles and iron hoops rusting;
Inside, the hammered anvil's short-pitched ring,
The unpredictable fantail of sparks
5 Or hiss when a new shoe toughens in water.
The anvil must be somewhere in the centre,
Horned as a unicorn, at one end square,
Set there immoveable: an altar
Where he expends himself in shape and music.
10 Sometimes, leather-aproned, hairs in his nose,
He leans out on the jamb, recalls a clatter
Of hoofs where traffic is flashing in rows;
Then grunts and goes in, with a slam and flick
To beat real iron out, to work the bellows.

1969

The Grauballe Man[1]

As if he had been poured
in tar, he lies
on a pillow of turf
and seems to weep

5 the black river of himself.
The grain of his wrists
is like bog oak,
the ball of his heel

like a basalt egg.
10 His instep has shrunk
cold as a swan's foot
or a wet swamp root.

His hips are the ridge
and purse of a mussel,
15 his spine an eel arrested
under a glisten of mud.

1. A body exhumed from a Danish bog and photographed in P. V. Glob's book *The Bog People*.

The head lifts,
the chin is a visor
raised above the vent
20   of his slashed throat

that has tanned and toughened.
The cured wound
opens inwards to a dark
elderberry place.

25   Who will say 'corpse'
to his vivid cast?
Who will say 'body'
to his opaque repose?

And his rusted hair,
30   a mat unlikely
as a foetus's.
I first saw his twisted face

in a photograph,
a head and shoulder
35   out of the peat,
bruised like a forceps baby,

but now he lies
perfected in my memory,
down to the red horn
40   of his nails,

hung in the scales
with beauty and atrocity:
with the Dying Gaul[2]
too strictly compassed

45   on his shield,
with the actual weight
of each hooded victim,
slashed and dumped.

1969

Punishment[1]

I can feel the tug
of the halter at the nape

2. Roman marble reproduction of a Greek bronze sculpture depicting a wounded soldier of Gaul, whose matted hair identifies him as a Celt, in Rome's Capitoline Museum.
1. In 1951 the peat-stained body of a young girl, who lived in the late 1st century C.E., was recovered from a bog in Windeby, Germany. As P. V. Glob describes her in The Bog People, she "lay naked in the hole in the peat, a bandage over the eyes and a collar round the neck. The band across the eyes was drawn tight and had cut into the neck and the base of the nose. We may feel sure that it had been used to close her eyes to this world. There was no mark of strangulation on the neck, so that it had not been used for that purpose." Her hair "had been shaved off with a razor on the left side

of her neck, the wind
on her naked front.

5   It blows her nipples
to amber beads,
it shakes the frail rigging
of her ribs.

I can see her drowned
10   body in the bog,
the weighing stone,
the floating rods and boughs.

Under which at first
she was a barked sapling
15   that is dug up
oak-bone, brain-firkin:°   small cask

her shaved head
like a stubble of black corn,
her blindfold a soiled bandage,
20   her noose a ring

to store
the memories of love.
Little adultress,
before they punished you

25   you were flaxen-haired,
undernourished, and your
tar-black face was beautiful.
My poor scapegoat,

I almost love you
30   but would have cast, I know,
the stones of silence.
I am the artful voyeur

of your brain's exposed
and darkened combs,°   valleys
35   your muscles' webbing
and all your numbered bones:

I who have stood dumb
when your betraying sisters,
cauled° in tar,   wrapped, enclosed
40   wept by the railings,

---

of the head. . . . When the brain was removed the convolutions and folds of the surface could be clearly seen [Glob reproduces a photograph of her brain]. . . . This girl of only fourteen had had an inadequate winter diet. . . . To keep the young body under, some birch branches and a big stone were laid upon her." According to the Roman historian Tacitus, the Germanic peoples punished adulterous women by shaving off their hair and then scourging them out of the village or killing them. More recently, her "betraying sisters" were sometimes shaved, stripped, tarred, and hand-cuffed by the Irish Republican Army (IRA) to the railings of Belfast in punishment for keeping company with British soldiers.

who would connive
in civilized outrage
yet understand the exact
and tribal, intimate revenge.

1975

Casualty

1

He would drink by himself
And raise a weathered thumb
Towards the high shelf,
Calling another rum
5   And blackcurrant, without
Having to raise his voice,
Or order a quick stout°   *strong dark beer*
By a lifting of the eyes
And a discreet dumb-show
10   Of pulling off the top;
At closing time would go
In waders and peaked cap
Into the showery dark,
A dole-kept[1] breadwinner
15   But a natural for work.
I loved his whole manner,
Sure-footed but too sly,
His deadpan sidling tact,
His fisherman's quick eye
20   And turned observant back.
Incomprehensible
To him, my other life.
Sometimes, on his high stool,
Too busy with his knife
25   At a tobacco plug
And not meeting my eye
In the pause after a slug°   *gulp of liquor*
He mentioned poetry.
We would be on our own
30   And, always politic
And shy of condescension,
I would manage by some trick
To switch the talk to eels
Or lore of the horse and cart
35   Or the Provisionals.[2]

But my tentative art
His turned back watches too:
He was blown to bits
Out drinking in a curfew

---

1. I.e., receiving unemployment benefits.   2. The Provisional branch of the IRA.

40   Others obeyed, three nights
After they shot dead
The thirteen men in Derry.
PARAS THIRTEEN, the walls said,
BOGSIDE NIL.[3] That Wednesday
45   Everybody held
His breath and trembled.

2

It was a day of cold
Raw silence, wind-blown
Surplice and soutane:[4]
50   Rained-on, flower-laden
Coffin after coffin
Seemed to float from the door
Of the packed cathedral
Like blossoms on slow water.
55   The common funeral
Unrolled its swaddling band,[5]
Lapping, tightening
Till we were braced and bound
Like brothers in a ring.

60   But he would not be held
At home by his own crowd
Whatever threats were phoned,
Whatever black flags waved.
I see him as he turned
65   In that bombed offending place,
Remorse fused with terror
In his still knowable face,
His cornered outfaced stare
Blinding in the flash.

70   He had gone miles away
For he drank like a fish
Nightly, naturally
Swimming towards the lure
Of warm lit-up places,
75   The blurred mesh and murmur
Drifting among glasses
In the gregarious smoke.
How culpable was he
That last night when he broke
80   Our tribe's complicity?[6]
'Now you're supposed to be
An educated man,'

---

3. This graffito records—in the form of a soccer match score—that the British Army's Parachute Regiment had killed thirteen people; the Roman Catholic inhabitants of Derry's Bogside district, none. The IRA bombing occurred after the killing of Catholic demonstrators on Bloody Sunday, January 30, 1972.
4. Vestments worn by Roman Catholic priests.
5. Long cloth in which babies were once wrapped to restrain and warm them.
6. The Roman Catholic community's agreement to obey the curfew (of lines 39–40).

I hear him say. 'Puzzle me
The right answer to that one.'

3

85 I missed his funeral,
Those quiet walkers
And sideways talkers
Shoaling out of his lane
To the respectable
90 Purring of the hearse . . .
They move in equal pace
With the habitual
Slow consolation
Of a dawdling engine,
95 The line lifted, hand
Over fist, cold sunshine
On the water, the land
Banked under fog: that morning
I was taken in his boat,
100 The screw° purling, turning   propellor
Indolent fathoms white,
I tasted freedom with him.
To get out early, haul
Steadily off the bottom,
105 Dispraise the catch, and smile
As you find a rhythm
Working you, slow mile by mile,
Into your proper haunt
Somewhere, well out, beyond . . .

110 Dawn-sniffing revenant,[7]
Plodder through midnight rain,
Question me again.

1979

The Skunk

Up, black, striped and damasked like the chasuble[1]
At a funeral mass, the skunk's tail
Paraded the skunk. Night after night
I expected her like a visitor.

5 The refrigerator whinnied into silence.
My desk light softened beyond the verandah.
Small oranges loomed in the orange tree.
I began to be tense as a voyeur.

---

7. One returned from the dead.
1. Sleeveless vestment worn by the priest celebrating Mass, its color regulated by the feast of the
day. "Damasked": woven with elaborate designs.

After eleven years I was composing
10   Love-letters again, broaching the word 'wife'
Like a stored cask, as if its slender vowel
Had mutated into the night earth and air

Of California. The beautiful, useless
Tang of eucalyptus spelt your absence.
15   The aftermath of a mouthful of wine
Was like inhaling you off a cold pillow.

And there she was, the intent and glamorous,
Ordinary, mysterious skunk,
Mythologized, demythologized,
20   Snuffing the boards five feet beyond me.

It all came back to me last night, stirred
By the sootfall of your things at bedtime,
Your head-down, tail-up hunt in a bottom drawer
For the black plunge-line nightdress.

                                                                1979

From Station Island[1]

12

Like a convalescent, I took the hand
stretched down from the jetty, sensed again
an alien comfort as I stepped on ground

to find the helping hand still gripping mine,
5   fish-cold and bony, but whether to guide
or to be guided I could not be certain

for the tall man in step at my side
seemed blind, though he walked straight as a rush
upon his ash plant,[2] his eyes fixed straight ahead.

10   Then I knew him in the flesh
out there on the tarmac° among the cars,   *blacktop surface*
wintered hard and sharp as a blackthorn bush.

---

1. *Station Island* is a sequence of dream encounters with familiar ghosts, set on Station Island on Lough Derg in Co. Donegal. The island is also known as St. Patrick's Purgatory because of a tradition that Patrick was the first to establish the penitential vigil of fasting and praying which still constitutes the basis of the three-day pilgrimage. Each unit of the contemporary pilgrim's exercises is called a 'station,' and a large part of each station involves walking barefoot and praying round the 'beds,' stone circles which are said to be the remains of early medieval monastic cells [Heaney's note]. In this last section of the poem, the familiar ghost is that of Heaney's countryman James Joyce. Cf. the stanza form and encounter with a ghost in T. S. Eliot's "Little Gidding."
2. Walking stick made of ash, like the one carried by Stephen Dedalus in Joyce's *Ulysses*. (See the opening paragraphs of "Proteus," p. 2200.) Joyce was almost blind.

His voice eddying with the vowels of all rivers[3]
came back to me, though he did not speak yet,
15   a voice like a prosecutor's or a singer's,

cunning,[4] narcotic, mimic, definite
as a steel nib's downstroke, quick and clean,
and suddenly he hit a litter basket

with his stick, saying, "Your obligation
20   is not discharged by any common rite.
What you must do must be done on your own

so get back in harness. The main thing is to write
for the joy of it. Cultivate a work-lust
that imagines its haven like your hands at night

25   dreaming the sun in the sunspot of a breast.
You are fasted now, light-headed, dangerous.
Take off from here. And don't be so earnest,

let others wear the sackcloth and the ashes.[5]
Let go, let fly, forget.
30   You've listened long enough. Now strike your note."

It was as if I had stepped free into space
alone with nothing that I had not known
already. Raindrops blew in my face

as I came to. "Old father, mother's son,
35   there is a moment in Stephen's diary
for April the thirteenth, a revelation

set among my stars—that one entry
has been a sort of password in my ears,
the collect of a new epiphany,[6]

40   the Feast of the Holy Tundish."[7] "Who cares,"
he jeered, "any more? The English language
belongs to us. You are raking at dead fires,

a waste of time for somebody your age.
That subject° people stuff is a cod's° game,   *colonized / fool's*
45   infantile, like your peasant pilgrimage.

---

3. The Anna Livia Plurabelle episode of *Finnegans Wake* (p. 2239) resounds with the names of many rivers.
4. "The only arms I allow myself to use—silence, exile, and cunning" (Joyce, *A Portrait of the Artist as a Young Man*).
5. As worn by penitents in biblical times and later.
6. Manifestation of a superhuman being, as of the infant Jesus to the Magi (Matthew 2). In the Christian calendar, the Feast of the Epiphany is January 6. "Epiphany" was also Joyce's term for the

"sudden revelation of the whatness of a thing." "Collect": short prayer assigned to a particular day.
7. See the end of James Joyce's *Portrait of the Artist as a Young Man* [Heaney's note]: "*13 April:* That tundish [funnel] has been on my mind for a long time. I looked it up and find it English and good old blunt English too. Damn the dean of studies and his funnel! What did he come here for to teach us his own language or to learn it from us? Damn him one way or the other!"

You lose more of yourself than you redeem
doing the decent thing. Keep at a tangent.
When they make the circle wide, it's time to swim

out on your own and fill the element
50   with signatures on your own frequency,
echo soundings, searches, probes, allurements,

elver-gleams[8] in the dark of the whole sea."
The shower broke in a cloudburst, the tarmac
fumed and sizzled. As he moved off quickly

55   the downpour loosed its screens round his straight walk.

                                  1984

Clearances

in memoriam M.K.H.,[1] 1911–1984

She taught me what her uncle once taught her:
How easily the biggest coal block split
If you got the grain and hammer angled right.

The sound of that relaxed alluring blow,
5   *Its co-opted and obliterated echo,*
Taught me to hit, taught me to loosen,

Taught me between the hammer and the block
To face the music. Teach me now to listen,
To strike it rich behind the linear black.

1

10   A cobble thrown a hundred years ago
Keeps coming at me, the first stone
Aimed at a great-grandmother's turncoat brow.[2]
The pony jerks and the riot's on.
She's crouched low in the trap
15   Running the gauntlet that first Sunday
Down the brae° to Mass at a panicked gallop.   *steep slope*
He whips on through the town to cries of 'Lundy!'[3]

Call her 'The Convert'. 'The Exogamous[4] Bride'.
Anyhow, it is a genre piece
20   Inherited on my mother's side

8. Gleams as of young eels.
1. Margaret Kathleen Heaney, the poet's mother.
2. Heaney's Protestant great-grandmother married a Catholic.
3. I.e., traitor. In 1688 the Irish colonel Robert

Lundy knew that Derry (or Londonderry) would be invaded by the English, but failed to prepare adequate defenses.
4. Married outside the group.

And mine to dispose with now she's gone.
Instead of silver and Victorian lace,
The exonerating, exonerated stone.

2

Polished linoleum shone there. Brass taps shone.
25 The china cups were very white and big—
An unchipped set with sugar bowl and jug.
The kettle whistled. Sandwich and teascone
Were present and correct. In case it run,
The butter must be kept out of the sun.
30 And don't be dropping crumbs. Don't tilt your chair.
Don't reach. Don't point. Don't make noise when you stir.

It is Number 5, New Row, Land of the Dead,
Where grandfather is rising from his place
With spectacles pushed back on a clean bald head
35 To welcome a bewildered homing daughter
Before she even knocks. 'What's this? What's this?'
And they sit down in the shining room together.

3

When all the others were away at Mass
I was all hers as we peeled potatoes.
40 They broke the silence, let fall one by one
Like solder weeping off the soldering iron:
Cold comforts set between us, things to share
Gleaming in a bucket of clean water.
And again let fall. Little pleasant splashes
45 From each other's work would bring us to our senses.

So while the parish priest at her bedside
Went hammer and tongs at the prayers for the dying
And some were responding and some crying
I remembered her head bent towards my head,
50 Her breath in mine, our fluent dipping knives—
Never closer the whole rest of our lives.

4

Fear of affectation made her affect
Inadequacy whenever it came to
Pronouncing words 'beyond her'. *Bertold Brek.*[5]
55 She'd manage something hampered and askew
Every time, as if she might betray
The hampered and inadequate by too
Well-adjusted a vocabulary.
With more challenge than pride, she'd tell me, 'You

5. Bertolt Brecht (1898–1956), German playwright.

60 Know all them things.' So I governed my tongue
In front of her, a genuinely well-
adjusted adequate betrayal
Of what I knew better. I'd *naw* and *aye*
And decently relapse into the wrong
65 Grammar which kept us allied and at bay.

5

The cool that came off sheets just off the line
Made me think the damp must still be in them
But when I took my corners of the linen
And pulled against her, first straight down the hem
70 And then diagonally, then flapped and shook
The fabric like a sail in a cross-wind,
They made a dried-out undulating thwack.
So we'd stretch and fold and end up hand to hand
For a split second as if nothing had happened
75 For nothing had that had not always happened
Beforehand, day by day, just touch and go,
Coming close again by holding back
In moves where I was x and she was o
Inscribed in sheets she'd sewn from ripped-out flour sacks.

6

80 In the first flush of the Easter holidays
The ceremonies during Holy Week
Were highpoints of our *Sons and Lovers*[6] phase.
The midnight fire. The paschal candlestick.[7]
Elbow to elbow, glad to be kneeling next
85 To each other up there near the front
Of the packed church, we would follow the text
And rubrics° for the blessing of the font.[8]   rules
As the hind longs for the streams, so my soul . . .[9]
Dippings. Towellings. The water breathed on.
90 The water mixed with chrism[1] and with oil.
Cruet[2] tinkle. Formal incensation
And the psalmist's outcry taken up with pride:
Day and night my tears have been my bread.[3]

7

In the last minutes he said more to her
95 Almost than in all their life together.
'You'll be in New Row on Monday night
And I'll come up for you and you'll be glad
When I walk in the door . . . Isn't that right?'

---

6. Novel (1913) by the English writer D. H.
Lawrence (1885–1930) that largely centers on the
oedipal relationship between a mother and son.
7. Large candle lit during a ceremony on Holy Saturday, which precedes Easter.

8. Receptacle for holy water.
9. Psalms 42.1.
1. Mixture of olive oil and balsam.
2. Small vessel for wine or water.
3. Psalms 42.3.

His head was bent down to her propped-up head.
100 She could not hear but we were overjoyed.
He called her good and girl. Then she was dead,
The searching for a pulsebeat was abandoned
And we all knew one thing by being there.
The space we stood around had been emptied
105 Into us to keep, it penetrated
Clearances that suddenly stood open.
High cries were felled and a pure change happened.

8

I thought of walking round and round a space
Utterly empty, utterly a source
110 Where the decked chestnut tree had lost its place
In our front hedge above the wallflowers.
The white chips jumped and jumped and skited[4] high.
I heard the hatchet's differentiated
Accurate cut, the crack, the sigh
115 And collapse of what luxuriated
Through the shocked tips and wreckage of it all.
Deep planted and long gone, my coeval[5]
Chestnut from a jam jar in a hole,
Its heft and hush become a bright nowhere,
120 A soul ramifying and forever
Silent, beyond silence listened for.

1987

The Sharping Stone[1]

In an apothecary's° chest of drawers,   *pharmacist's*
Sweet cedar that we'd purchased second hand,
In one of its weighty deep-sliding recesses
I found the sharping stone that was to be
5 Our gift to him. Still in its wrapping paper.
Like a baton of black light I'd failed to pass.

•

Airless cinder-depths. But all the same,
The way it lay there, it wakened something too . . .
I thought of us that evening on the logs,
10 Flat on our backs, the pair of us, parallel,
Supported head to heel, arms straight, eyes front,
Listening to the rain drip off the trees
And saying nothing, braced to the damp bark.
What possessed us? The bare, lopped loveliness
15 Of those two winter trunks, the way they seemed

---

4. Shot off obliquely.
5. Of the same age.

1. Whetstone for sharpening metal blades.

Prepared for launching, at right angles across
A causeway of short fence-posts set like rollers.
Neither of us spoke. The puddles waited.
The workers had gone home, saws fallen silent.
20 And next thing down we lay, babes in the wood,
Gazing up at the flood-face of the sky
Until it seemed a flood was carrying us
Out of the forest park, feet first, eyes front,
Out of November, out of middle age,
25 Together, out, across the Sea of Moyle.[2]

•

Sarcophage des époux.[3] In terra cotta.
Etruscan couple shown side by side,
Recumbent on left elbows, husband pointing
With his right arm and watching where he points,
30 Wife in front, her earrings in, her braids
Down to her waist, taking her sexual ease.
He is all eyes, she is all brow and dream,
Her right forearm and hand held out as if
Some bird she sees in her deep inward gaze
35 Might be about to roost there. Domestic
Love, the artist thought, warm tones and property,
The frangibility of terra cotta . . .
Which is how they figured on the colour postcard
(*Louvre, Département des Antiquités*)[4]
40 That we'd sent him once, then found among his things.

•

He loved inspired mistakes: his Spanish grandson's
English transliteration, thanking him
For a boat trip: 'That was a marvellous
Walk on the water, granddad.' And indeed
45 He walked on air himself, never more so
Than when he had been widowed and the youth
In him, the athlete who had wooed her—
Breasting tapes and clearing the high bars—
Grew lightsome once again. Going at eighty
50 On the bendiest roads, going for broke
At every point-to-point[5] and poker-school,
'He commenced his wild career' a second time
And not a bother on him. Smoked like a train
And took the power mower in his stride.
55 Flirted and vaunted. Set fire to his bed.
Fell from a ladder. Learned to microwave.

•

So set the drawer on freshets° of thaw water   surges
And place the unused sharping stone inside it:

2. Channel between the northwestern coast of
County Antrim in Ireland and the southwestern
coast of Scotland.
3. Coffin for a married couple.

4. Department of Antiquities, Louvre Museum,
Paris, in which this Etruscan funerary statue,
known as *The Cerveteri Couple*, is to be found.
5. Horse race over jumps.

To be found next summer on a riverbank
60   Where scythes once hung all night in alder trees
And mowers played dawn scherzos[6] on the blades,
Their arms like harpists' arms, one drawing towards,
One sweeping the bright rim of the extreme.

1996

6. Vigorous light and playful musical compositions.

J. M. COETZEE
b. 1940

John Michael Coetzee was born in Cape Town, South Africa. His mother was a schoolteacher; his father, a lawyer who became a sheepherder after losing his job. When Coetzee was eight, his family left the provinces, and he chronicles this and other parts of his childhood in third-person memoirs, *Boyhood: Scenes from a Provincial Life* (1997) and *Youth: Scenes from a Provincial Life II* (2002). Coetzee was educated in Cape Town and then lived in London for a few years, working as a computer programmer, before earning his Ph.D. from the University of Texas at Austin, where he wrote a dissertation on the fiction of Samuel Beckett—a major influence along with Kafka and Dostoyevsky, on Coetzee's fiction. He was appointed, first, assistant professor and, subsequently, Butler Professor of English at the State University of New York at Buffalo. In 1984 he returned to South Africa as professor of general literature at the University of Cape Town, and since 2002 he has lived in Australia. Coetzee is the first novelist to win the prestigious Booker Prize twice, and in 2003 he was awarded the Nobel Prize in Literature.

The central concern of Coetzee's fiction—the oppressive nature of colonialism—made its appearance with his first book, *Dusklands* (1974). This consists of two novellas, one set in the U.S. State Department during the Vietnam War, the other in southern Africa two hundred years earlier. The protagonists of these seemingly different stories—Eugene Dawn, an expert in psychological warfare, and Jacobus Coetzee, an explorer and pioneer—are engaged in similar projects, each leading to oppression and murder. Coetzee's subsequent novels include *In the Heart of the Country* (1977), a feminist anticolonial fable in the voice of a mad South African farmwoman; *Life and Times of Michael K* (1983), about a homeless man trying to survive in war-torn Africa; *Foe* (1986), a retelling of Daniel Defoe's *Robinson Crusoe* from the perspective of a female castaway; *The Master of Petersburg* (1994), a fictionalized account of Dostoyevsky's life; *Disgrace* (1999), about sexual harassment, rape, and race relations; and *Elizabeth Costello: Eight Lessons* (2003), which blends essay and fiction. His many essays and works of criticism have concerned censorship, the rights of animals, South African history, and other themes.

Coetzee is at once a passionate political novelist and an intensely literary one, both qualities emerging in his most compelling indictment of colonialism, *Waiting for the Barbarians* (1980). This novel takes its title and theme from a well-known poem by the Greek poet Constantine Cavafy (1863–1933), which ends (in Rae Dalven's translation):

> . . . night is here but the barbarians have not come.
> Some people arrived from the frontiers,
> And they said that there are no longer any barbarians.

And now what shall become of us without any barbarians?
Those people were a kind of solution.

In Coetzee's novel the rulers of the unnamed empire claim it is threatened by barbarians, but the barbarian threat is, at least in part, a fantasy concocted by the empire to hold itself together. The narrator is a magistrate in charge of a frontier post, poised uneasily between the harmless inhabitants of the region and the empire's ruthless officials, and unable to protect either the natives or himself from his brutal colleague, Colonel Joll. Imprisoned and stripped of his duties, the magistrate becomes increasingly skeptical of the empire's motives. When the imperial army arrives to subdue supposed insurgents, its vicious treatment of prisoners calls into question the relation of "civilization" to "barbarism" and demonstrates, in harrowing scenes of abuse and torture, the ethical dangers of one people's dominance over another. In this medley of realist particularism and allegorical parable, Coetzee leaves the landscape and time of the novel hauntingly unspecified, suggesting that colonialism's degradation and coercion, violence and moral corruption can occur anywhere, at any time.

From Waiting for the Barbarians

First there is the sound of muskets far away, as diminutive as popguns.[1] Then from nearer by, from the ramparts themselves, come volleys of answering shots. There is a stampede of footsteps across the barracks yard. "The barbarians!" someone shouts; but I think he is wrong. Above all the clamour the great bell begins to peal.

Kneeling with an ear to the crack of the door I try to make out what is going on.

The noise from the square mounts from a hubbub to a steady roar in which no single voice can be distinguished. The whole town must be pouring out in welcome, thousands of ecstatic souls. Volleys of musket-shots keep cracking. Then the tenor of the roar changes, rises in pitch and excitement. Faintly above it come the brassy tones of bugles.

The temptation is too great. What have I to lose? I unlock the door. In glare so blinding that I must squint and shade my eyes, I cross the yard, pass through the gate, and join the rear of the crowd. The volleys and the roar of applause continue. The old woman in black beside me takes my arm to steady herself and stands on her toes. "Can you see?" she says. "Yes, I can see men on horseback," I reply; but she is not listening.

I can see a long file of horsemen who, amid flying banners, pass through the gateway and make their way to the centre of the square where they dismount. There is a cloud of dust over the whole square, but I see that they are smiling and laughing: one of them rides with his hands raised high in triumph, another waves a garland of flowers. They progress slowly, for the crowd presses around them, trying to touch them, throwing flowers, clapping their hands above their heads in joy, spinning round and round in private ecstasies. Children dive past me, scrambling through the legs of the grownups to be nearer to their heroes. Fusillade after fusillade comes from the ramparts, which are lined with cheering people.

One part of the cavalcade does not dismount. Headed by a stern-faced young corporal bearing the green and gold banner of the battalion, it passes through

1. The magistrate, narrator of the novel, listens from the prison in which the empire has incarcerated him.

the press of bodies to the far end of the square and then begins a circuit of the perimeter, the crowd surging slowly in its wake. The word runs like fire from neighbour to neighbour: *"Barbarians!"*

The standard-bearer's horse is led by a man who brandishes a heavy stick to clear his way. Behind him comes another trooper trailing a rope; and at the end of the rope, tied neck to neck, comes a file of men, barbarians, stark naked, holding their hands up to their faces in an odd way as though one and all are suffering from toothache. For a moment I am puzzled by the posture, by the tiptoeing eagerness with which they follow their leader, till I catch a glint of metal and at once comprehend. A simple loop of wire runs through the flesh of each man's hands and through holes pierced in his cheeks. "It makes them meek as lambs," I remember being told by a soldier who had once seen the trick: "they think of nothing but how to keep very still." My heart grows sick. I know now that I should not have left my cell.

I have to turn my back smartly to avoid being seen by the two who, with their mounted escort, bring up the rear of the procession: the bareheaded young captain whose first triumph this is, and at his shoulder, leaner and darker after his months of campaigning, Colonel of Police Joll.

The circuit is made, everyone has a chance to see the twelve miserable captives, to prove to his children that the barbarians are real. Now the crowd, myself reluctantly in its wake, flows towards the great gate, where a half-moon of soldiers blocks its way until, compressed at front and rear, it cannot budge.

"What is going on?" I ask my neighbour.

"I don't know," he says, "but help me to lift him." I help him to lift the child he carries on his arm on to his shoulders. "Can you see?" he asks the child.

"Yes."

"What are they doing?"

"They are making those barbarians kneel. What are they going to do to them?"

"I don't know. Let's wait and see."

Slowly, titanically, with all my might, I turn and begin to squeeze my body out, "Excuse me . . . excuse me . . ." I say: "the heat—I'm going to be sick." For the first time I see heads turn, fingers point.

I ought to go back to my cell. As a gesture it will have no effect, it will not even be noticed. Nevertheless, for my own sake, as a gesture to myself alone, I ought to return to the cool dark and lock the door and bend the key and stop my ears to the noise of patriotic bloodlust and close my lips and never speak again. Who knows, perhaps I do my fellow-townsmen an injustice, perhaps at this very minute the shoemaker is at home tapping on his last, humming to himself to drown the shouting, perhaps there are housewives shelling peas in their kitchens, telling stories to occupy their restless children, perhaps there are farmers still going calmly about the repair of the ditches. If comrades like these exist, what a pity I do not know them! For me, at this moment, striding away from the crowd, what has become important above all is that I should neither be contaminated by the atrocity that is about to be committed nor poison myself with impotent hatred of its perpetrators. I cannot save the prisoners, therefore let me save myself. Let it at the very least be said, if it ever comes to be said, if there is ever anyone in some remote future interested to know the way we lived, that in this farthest outpost of the Empire of light there existed one man who in his heart was not a barbarian.

I pass through the barracks gate into my prison yard. At the trough in the middle of the yard I pick up an empty bucket and fill it. With the bucket held up before me, slopping water over its sides, I approach the rear of the crowd again. "Excuse me," I say, and push. People curse me, give way, the bucket tilts and splashes, I forge forward till in a minute I am suddenly clear in the frontmost rank of the crowd behind the backs of the soldiers who, holding staves between them, keep an arena clear for the exemplary spectacle.

Four of the prisoners kneel on the ground. The other eight, still roped together, squat in the shade of the wall watching, their hands to their cheeks.

The kneeling prisoners bend side by side over a long heavy pole. A cord runs from the loop of wire through the first man's mouth, under the pole, up to the second man's loop, back under the pole, up to the third loop, under the pole, through the fourth loop. As I watch a soldier slowly pulls the cord tighter and the prisoners bend further till finally they are kneeling with their faces touching the pole. One of them writhes his shoulders in pain and moans. The others are silent, their thoughts wholly concentrated on moving smoothly with the cord, not giving the wire a chance to tear their flesh.

Directing the soldier with little gestures of the hand is Colonel Joll. Though I am only one in a crowd of thousands, though his eyes are shaded as ever, I stare at him so hard with a face so luminous with query that I know at once he sees me.

Behind me I distinctly hear the word *magistrate*. Do I imagine it or are my neighbours inching away from me?

The Colonel steps forward. Stooping over each prisoner in turn he rubs a handful of dust into his naked back and writes a word with a stick of charcoal. I read the words upside down: *ENEMY . . . ENEMY . . . ENEMY . . . ENEMY.* He steps back and folds his hands. At a distance of no more than twenty paces he and I contemplate each other.

Then the beating begins. The soldiers use the stout green cane staves, bringing them down with the heavy slapping sounds of washing-paddles, raising red welts on the prisoners' backs and buttocks. With slow care the prisoners extend their legs until they lie flat on their bellies, all except the one who had been moaning and who now gasps with each blow.

The black charcoal and ochre dust begin to run with sweat and blood. The game, I see, is to beat them till their backs are washed clean.

I watch the face of a little girl who stands in the front rank of the crowd gripping her mother's clothes. Her eyes are round, her thumb is in her mouth: silent, terrified, curious, she drinks in the sight of these big naked men being beaten. On every face around me, even those that are smiling, I see the same expression: not hatred, not bloodlust, but a curiosity so intense that their bodies are drained by it and only their eyes live, organs of a new and ravening appetite.

The soldiers doing the beating grow tired. One stands with his hands on his hips panting, smiling, gesturing to the crowd. There is a word from the Colonel: all four of them cease their labour and come forward offering their canes to the spectators.

A girl, giggling and hiding her face, is pushed forward by her friends. "Go on, don't be afraid!" they urge her. A soldier puts a cane in her hand and leads her to the place. She stands confused, embarrassed, one hand still over her face. Shouts, jokes, obscene advice are hurled at her. She lifts the cane, brings it down smartly on the prisoner's buttocks, drops it, and scuttles to safety to a roar of applause.

There is a scramble for the canes, the soldiers can barely keep order, I lose sight of the prisoners on the ground as people press forward to take a turn or simply watch the beating from nearer. I stand forgotten with my bucket between my feet.

Then the flogging is over, the soldiers reassert themselves, the crowd scrambles back, the arena is reconstituted, though narrower than before.

Over his head, exhibiting it to the crowd, Colonel Joll holds a hammer, an ordinary four-pound hammer used for knocking in tent-pegs. Again his gaze meets mine. The babble subsides.

"No!" I hear the first word from my throat, rusty, not loud enough. Then again: "No!" This time the word rings like a bell from my chest. The soldier who blocks my way stumbles aside. I am in the arena holding up my hands to still the crowd: "No! No! No!"

When I turn to Colonel Joll he is standing not five paces from me, his arms folded. I point a finger at him. "You!" I shout. Let it all be said. Let him be the one on whom the anger breaks. "You are depraving these people!"

He does not flinch, he does not reply.

"You!" My arm points at him like a gun. My voice fills the square. There is utter silence; or perhaps I am too intoxicated to hear.

Something crashes into me from behind. I sprawl in the dust, gasp, feel the sear of old pain in my back. A stick thuds down on me. Reaching out to ward it off, I take a withering blow on my hand.

It becomes important to stand up, however difficult the pain makes it. I come to my feet and see who it is that is hitting me. It is the stocky man with the sergeant's stripes who helped with the beatings. Crouched at the knees, his nostrils flaring, he stands with his stick raised for the next blow. "Wait!" I gasp, holding out my limp hand. "I think you have broken it!" He strikes, and I take the blow on the forearm. I hide my arm, lower my head, and try to grope towards him and grapple. Blows fall on my head and shoulders. Never mind: all I want is a few moments to finish what I am saying now that I have begun. I grip his tunic and hug him to me. Though he wrestles, he cannot use his stick; over his shoulder I shout again.

"Not with that!" I shout. The hammer lies cradled in the Colonel's folded arms. "You would not use a hammer on a beast, not on a beast!" In a terrible surge of rage I turn on the sergeant and hurl him from me. Godlike strength is mine. In a minute it will pass: let me use it well while it lasts! "Look!" I shout. I point to the four prisoners who lie docilely on the earth, their lips to the pole, their hands clasped to their faces like monkeys' paws, oblivious of the hammer, ignorant of what is going on behind them, relieved that the offending mark has been beaten from their backs, hoping that the punishment is at an end. I raise my broken hand to the sky. "Look!" I shout. "We are the great miracle of creation! But from some blows this miraculous body cannot repair itself! How—!" Words fail me. "Look at these men!" I recommence. "Men!" Those in the crowd who can crane to look at the prisoners, even at the flies that begin to settle on their bleeding welts.

I hear the blow coming and turn to meet it. It catches me full across the face. "I am blind!" I think, staggering back into the blackness that instantly falls. I swallow blood; something blooms across my face, starting as a rosy warmth, turning to fiery agony. I hide my face in my hands and stamp around in a circle trying not to shout, trying not to fall.

What I wanted to say next I cannot remember. A miracle of creation—I pursue the thought but it eludes me like a wisp of smoke. It occurs to me that we crush insects beneath our feet, miracles of creation too, beetles, worms, cockroaches, ants, in their various ways.

I take my fingers from my eyes and a grey world re-emerges swimming in tears. I am so profoundly grateful that I cease to feel pain. As I am hustled, a man at each elbow, back through the murmuring crowd to my cell, I even find myself smiling.

That smile, that flush of joy, leave behind a disturbing residue. I know that they commit an error in treating me so summarily. For I am no orator. What would I have said if they had let me go on? That it is worse to beat a man's feet to pulp than to kill him in combat? That it brings shame on everyone when a girl is permitted to flog a man? That spectacles of cruelty corrupt the hearts of the innocent? The words they stopped me from uttering may have been very paltry indeed, hardly words to rouse the rabble. What, after all, do I stand for besides an archaic code of gentlemanly behaviour towards captured foes, and what do I stand against except the new science of degradation that kills people on their knees, confused and disgraced in their own eyes? Would I have dared to face the crowd to demand justice for these ridiculous barbarian prisoners with their backsides in the air? *Justice:* once that word is uttered, where will it all end? Easier to shout *No!* Easier to be beaten and made a martyr. Easier to lay my head on a block than to defend the cause of justice for the barbarians: for where can that argument lead but to laying down our arms and opening the gates of the town to the people whose land we have raped? The old magistrate, defender of the rule of law, enemy in his own way of the State, assaulted and imprisoned, impregnably virtuous, is not without his own twinges of doubt.

My nose is broken, I know, and perhaps also the cheekbone where the flesh was laid open by the blow of the stick. My left eye is swelling shut.

As the numbness wears off the pain begins to come in spasms a minute or two apart so intense that I can no longer lie still. At the height of the spasm I trot around the room holding my face, whining like a dog; in the blessed valleys between the peaks I breathe deeply, trying to keep control of myself, trying not to make too disgraceful an outcry. I seem to hear surges and lulls in the noise from the mob on the square but cannot be sure that the roar is not simply in my eardrums.

They bring me my evening meal as usual but I cannot eat. I cannot keep still, I have to walk back and forth or rock on my haunches to keep myself from screaming, tearing my clothes, clawing my flesh, doing whatever people do when the limit of their endurance is reached. I weep, and feel the tears stinging the open flesh. I hum the old song about the rider and the juniper bush over and over again, clinging to the remembered words even after they have ceased to make any sense. One, two, three, four . . . I count. It will be a famous victory, I tell myself, if you can last the night.

In the early hours of the morning, when I am so giddy with exhaustion that I reel on my feet, I finally give way and sob from the heart like a child: I sit in a corner against the wall and weep, the tears running from my eyes without stop. I weep and weep while the throbbing comes and goes according to its own cycles. In this position sleep bursts upon me like a thunderbolt. I am amazed to come to myself in the thin grey light of day, slumped in a corner, with not the faintest sense that time has passed. Though the throbbing is still there I find I can endure it if I remain still. Indeed, it has lost its strangeness. Soon, perhaps, it will be as much part of me as breathing.

So I lie quietly against the wall, folding my sore hand under my armpit for comfort, and fall into a second sleep, into a confusion of images among which I search out one in particular, brushing aside the others that fly at me like leaves. It is of the girl. She is kneeling with her back to me before the snow-castle or sandcastle she has built. She wears a dark blue robe. As I approach I see that she is digging away in the bowels of the castle.

She becomes aware of me and turns. I am mistaken, it is not a castle she has built but a clay oven. Smoke curls up from the vent at the back. She holds out her hands to me offering me something, a shapeless lump which I peer at unwillingly through a mist. Though I shake my head my vision will not clear.

She is wearing a round cap embroidered in gold. Her hair is braided in a heavy plait which lies over her shoulder: there is gold thread worked into the braid. "Why are you dressed in your best?" I want to say: "I have never seen you looking so lovely." She smiles at me: what beautiful teeth she has, what clear jet-black eyes! Also now I can see that what she is holding out to me is a loaf of bread, still hot, with a coarse steaming broken crust. A surge of gratitude sweeps through me. "Where did a child like you learn to bake so well in the desert?" I want to say. I open my arms to embrace her, and come to myself with tears stinging the wound on my cheek. Though I scrabble back at once into the burrow of sleep I cannot re-enter the dream or taste the bread that has made my saliva run.

· ·

Colonel Joll sits behind the desk in my office. There are no books or files; the room is starkly empty save for a vase of fresh flowers.

The handsome warrant officer whose name I do not know lifts the cedar-wood chest on to the desk and steps back.

Looking down to refer to his papers, the Colonel speaks. "Among the items found in your apartment was this wooden chest. I would like you to consider it. Its contents are unusual. It contains approximately three hundred slips of white poplar-wood, each about eight inches by two inches, many of them wound about with lengths of string.[2] The wood is dry and brittle. Some of the string is new, some so old that it has perished.

"If one loosens the string one finds that the slip splits open revealing two flat inner surfaces. These surfaces are written on in an unfamiliar script.

"I think you will concur with this description."

I stare into the black lenses. He goes on.

"A reasonable inference is that the wooden slips contain messages passed between yourself and other parties, we do not know when. It remains for you to explain what the messages say and who the other parties were."

He takes a slip from the chest and flicks it across the polished surface of the desk towards me.

I look at the lines of characters written by a stranger long since dead. I do not even know whether to read from right to left or from left to right. In the long evenings I spent poring over my collection I isolated over four hundred different characters in the script, perhaps as many as four hundred and fifty. I have no idea what they stand for. Does each stand for a single thing, a circle for the sun, a triangle for a woman, a wave for a lake; or does a circle merely stand for "circle", a triangle for "triangle", a wave for "wave"? Does each sign

---

2. Over the years the magistrate has conducted archaeological digs outside the city, unearthing these poplar slips and other artifacts.

represent a different state of the tongue, the lips, the throat, the lungs, as they combine in the uttering of some multifarious unimaginable extinct barbarian language? Or are my four hundred characters nothing but scribal embellishments of an underlying repertory of twenty or thirty whose primitive forms I am too stupid to see?

"He sends greetings to his daughter," I say. I hear with surprise the thick nasal voice that is now mine. My finger runs along the line of characters from right to left. "Whom he says he has not seen for a long time. He hopes she is happy and thriving. He hopes the lambing season has been good. He has a gift for her, he says, which he will keep till he sees her again. He sends his love. It is not easy to read his signature. It could be simply 'Your father' or it could be something else, a name."

I reach over into the chest and pick out a second slip. The warrant officer, who sits behind Joll with a little notebook open on his knee, stares hard at me, his pencil poised above the paper.

"This one reads as follows," I say: " 'I am sorry I must send bad news. The soldiers came and took your brother away. I have been to the fort every day to plead for his return. I sit in the dust with my head bare. Yesterday for the first time they sent a man to speak to me. He says your brother is no longer here. He says he has been sent away. "Where?" I asked, but he would not say. Do not tell your mother, but join me in praying for his safety.'

"And now let us see what this next one says." The pencil is still poised, he has not written anything, he has not stirred. " 'We went to fetch your brother yesterday. They showed us into a room where he lay on a table sewn up in a sheet.' " Slowly Joll leans back in his chair. The warrant officer closes his notebook and half-rises; but with a gesture Joll restrains him. " 'They wanted me to take him away like that, but I insisted on looking first. "What if it is the wrong body you are giving me?" I said—"You have so many bodies here, bodies of brave young men." So I opened the sheet and saw that it was indeed he. Through each eyelid, I saw that there was a stitch, "Why have you done that?" I said. "It is our custom," he said. I tore the sheet wide open and saw bruises all over his body, and saw that his feet were swollen and broken. "What happened to him?" I said. "I do not know," said the man, "it is not on the paper; if you have questions you must go to the sergeant, but he is very busy." We have had to bury your brother here, outside their fort, because he was beginning to stink. Please tell your mother and try to console her.'

"Now let us see what the next one says. See, there is only a single character. It is the barbarian character *war*, but it has other senses too. It can stand for *vengeance*, and, if you turn it upside down like this, it can be made to read *justice*. There is no knowing which sense is intended. That is part of barbarian cunning.

"It is the same with the rest of these slips." I plunge my good hand into the chest and stir. "They form an allegory. They can be read in many orders. Further, each single slip can be read in many ways. Together they can be read as a domestic journal, or they can be read as a plan of war, or they can be turned on their sides and read as a history of the last years of the Empire— the old Empire, I mean. There is no agreement among scholars about how to interpret these relics of the ancient barbarians. Allegorical sets like this one can be found buried all over the desert. I found this one not three miles from here in the ruins of a public building. Graveyards are another good place to look in, though it is not always easy to tell where barbarian burial sites lie. It is recommended that you simply dig at random: perhaps at the very spot where you stand you will come upon scraps, shards, reminders of the dead. Also the air: the air is full of sighs and cries. These are never lost: if you listen carefully, with a sympathetic ear, you can hear them echoing forever within the second sphere. The night is best: sometimes when you have difficulty in falling asleep it is because your ears have been reached by the cries of the dead which, like their writings, are open to many interpretations.

"Thank you. I have finished translating."

I have not failed to keep an eye on Joll through all this. He has not stirred again, save to lay a hand on his subordinate's sleeve at the moment when I referred to the Empire and he rose, ready to strike me.

If he comes near me I will hit him with all the strength in my body. I will not disappear into the earth without leaving my mark on them.

The Colonel speaks. "You have no idea how tiresome your behaviour is. You are the one and only official we have had to work with on the frontier who has not given us his fullest co-operation. Candidly, I must tell you I am not interested in these sticks." He waves a hand at the slips scattered on the desk. "They are very likely gambling-sticks. I know that other tribes on the border gamble with sticks.

"I ask you to consider soberly: what kind of future do you have here? You cannot be allowed to remain in your post. You have utterly disgraced yourself. Even if you are not eventually prosecuted—"

"I am waiting for you to prosecute me!" I shout. "When are you going to do it? When are you going to bring me to trial? When am I going to have a chance to defend myself?" I am in a fury. None of the speechlessness I felt in front of the crowd afflicts me. If I were to confront these men now, in public, in a fair trial, I would find the words to shame them. It is a matter of health and strength: I feel my hot words swell in my breast. But they will never bring a man to trial while he is healthy and strong enough to confound them. They will shut me away in the dark till I am a muttering idiot, a ghost of myself; then they will haul me before a closed court and in five minutes dispose of the legalities they find so tiresome.

"For the duration of the emergency, as you know," says the Colonel, "the administration of justice is out of the hands of civilians and in the hands of the Bureau." He sighs. "Magistrate, you seem to believe that we do not dare to bring you to trial because we fear you are too popular a figure in this town. I do not think you are aware of how much you forfeited by neglecting your duties, shunning your friends, keeping company with low people. There is no one I have spoken to who has not at some time felt insulted by your behaviour."

"My private life is none of their business!"

"Nevertheless, I may tell you that our decision to relieve you of your duties has been welcomed in most quarters. Personally I have nothing against you. When I arrived back a few days ago, I had decided that all I wanted from you was a clear answer to a simple question, after which you could have returned to your concubines a free man."

It strikes me suddenly that the insult may not be gratuitous, that perhaps for different reasons these two men might welcome it if I lost my temper. Burning with outrage, tense in every muscle, I guard my silence.

"However, you seem to have a new ambition," he goes on. "You seem to want to make a name for yourself as the One Just Man, the man who is prepared to sacrifice his freedom to his principles.

"But let me ask you: do you believe that that is how your fellow-citizens see you after the ridiculous spectacle you created on the square the other day? Believe me, to people in this town you are not the One Just Man, you are simply a clown, a madman. You are dirty, you stink, they can smell you a mile away. You look like an old beggar-man, a refuse-scavenger. They do not want you back in any capacity. You have no future here.

"You want to go down in history as a martyr, I suspect. But who is going to put you in the history books? These border troubles are of no significance. In a while they will pass and the frontier will go to sleep for another twenty years. People are not interested in the history of the back of beyond."

"There were no border troubles before you came," I say.

"That is nonsense," he says. "You are simply ignorant of the facts. You are living in a world of the past. You think we are dealing with small groups of peaceful nomads. In fact we are dealing with a well organized enemy. If you had travelled with the expeditionary force you would have seen that for yourself."

"Those pitiable prisoners you brought in—are *they* the enemy I must fear? Is that what you say? *You* are the enemy, Colonel!" I can restrain myself no longer. I pound the desk with my fist. "*You* are the enemy, *you* have made the war, and *you* have given them all the martyrs they need—starting not now but a year ago when you committed your first filthy barbarities here! History will bear me out!"

"Nonsense. There will be no history, the affair is too trivial." He seems impassive, but I am sure I have shaken him.

"You are an obscene torturer! You deserve to hang!"

"Thus speaks the judge, the One Just Man," he murmurs.

We stare into each other's eyes.

"Now," he says, squaring the papers before him: "I would like a statement on everything that passed between you and the barbarians on your recent and unauthorized visit to them."

"I refuse."

"Very well. Our interview is over." He turns to his subordinate. "He is your responsibility." He stands up, walks out. I face the warrant officer.

⁕

The wound on my cheek, never washed or dressed, is swollen and inflamed. A crust like a fat caterpillar has formed on it. My left eye is a mere slit, my nose a shapeless throbbing lump. I must breathe through my mouth.

I lie in the reek of old vomit obsessed with the thought of water. I have had nothing to drink for two days.

In my suffering there is nothing ennobling. Little of what I call suffering is even pain. What I am made to undergo is subjection to the most rudimentary needs of my body: to drink, to relieve itself, to find the posture in which it is least sore. When Warrant Officer Mandel and his man first brought me back here and lit the lamp and closed the door, I wondered how much pain a plump comfortable old man would be able to endure in the name of his eccentric notions of how the Empire should conduct itself. But my torturers were not interested in degrees of pain. They were interested only in demonstrating to me what it meant to live in a body, as a body, a body which can entertain notions of justice only as long as it is whole and well, which very soon forgets them when its head is gripped and a pipe is pushed down its gullet and pints of salt water are poured into it till it coughs and retches and flails and voids itself. They did not come to force the story out of me of what I had said to the barbarians and what the barbarians had said to me. So I had no chance to throw the high-sounding words I had ready in their faces. They came to my cell to show me the meaning of humanity, and in the space of an hour they showed me a great deal.

1980

EAVAN BOLAND
b. 1944

Eavan Boland was born in Dublin, the youngest daughter of an Irish diplomat and a painter, but as recalled in "Fond Memory" and other poems, she was displaced as a six-year-old from Ireland to London, where her father was Irish ambassador, and then to New York, where he was his country's representative at the United Nations, before finally returning to Ireland in adolescence. She attended convent schools in these various locations. In Ireland she studied—and then taught—English at Trinity College, Dublin, and since then she has taught at University College, the University of Iowa, and Stanford University.

Boland said in a 1994 lecture, "I am an Irish poet. A woman poet. In the first category I enter the tradition of the English language at an angle. In the second, I enter my own tradition at an even more steep angle." The great puzzle of Boland's career has been how to embrace Irish identity while rejecting certain male-centered assumptions that have long dominated Irish literary culture. For Boland as a young woman writer, the frozen, mythical images of the Irish nation as an idealized woman— Mother Ireland, Dark Rosaleen, Cathleen Ni Houlihan—were inhibiting and insufficient. To bring into Irish verse a national narrative, a "herstory" that interweaves private life and public life, Boland seized on an alternative tradition to that of Irish male poets—namely, the example of American women poets such as Sylvia Plath and Adrienne Rich. Her eye for symbolic detail, her ear for musical structure, her use of form to mirror content have served her well in her effort to recover and vivify Irish women's historical experiences, including domestic labor, motherhood, famine, prostitution, and emigration.

Fond Memory

It was a school where all the children wore darned worsted;°   *woolen fabric*
where they cried—or almost all—when the Reverend Mother
announced at lunch-time that the King[1] had died

peacefully in his sleep. I dressed in wool as well,
5 ate rationed food, played English games and learned
how wise the Magna Carta was, how hard the Hanoverians[2]

---

1. King George VI of the United Kingdom died in 1952. Boland's father was a diplomat, and she spent much of her childhood in London.

2. Family of English monarchs who reigned from 1714 to 1901. "Magna Carta": charter of English liberties granted by King John in 1215.

had tried, the measure and complexity of verse,
the hum and score of the whole orchestra.
At three-o-clock I caught two buses home

10 where sometimes in the late afternoon
at a piano pushed into a corner of the playroom
my father would sit down and play the slow

lilts of Tom Moore[3] while I stood there trying
not to weep at the cigarette smoke stinging up
15 from between his fingers and—as much as I could think—

I thought this is my country, was, will be again,
this upward-straining song made to be
our safe inventory of pain. And I was wrong.

1987

That the Science of Cartography[1] Is Limited

—and not simply by the fact that this shading of
forest cannot show the fragrance of balsam,
the gloom of cypresses
is what I wish to prove.

5 When you and I were first in love we drove
to the borders of Connacht[2]
and entered a wood there.

Look down you said: this was once a famine road.

I looked down at ivy and the scutch grass
10 rough-cast stone had
disappeared into as you told me
in the second winter of their ordeal, in

1847, when the crop[3] had failed twice,
Relief Committees gave
15 the starving Irish such roads to build.

Where they died, there the road ended

and ends still and when I take down
the map of this island, it is never so
I can say here is
20 the masterful, the apt rendering of

the spherical as flat, nor
an ingenious design which persuades a curve

---

3. Irish poet and singer (1779–1852).
1. Mapmaking.
2. Western province of Ireland.

3. Of potatoes, staple diet of Irish peasants in the
19th century. Over a million people died in the
Irish Famine of 1845–49.

into a plane,
but to tell myself again that

25 the line which says woodland and cries hunger
and gives out among sweet pine and cypress,
and finds no horizon

will not be there.

1994

The Dolls Museum in Dublin

The wounds are terrible. The paint is old.
The cracks along the lips and on the cheeks
cannot be fixed. The cotton lawn[1] is soiled.
The arms are ivory dissolved to wax.

5   Recall the Quadrille.[2] Hum the waltz.
Promenade on the yacht-club terraces.
Put back the lamps in their copper holders,
the carriage wheels on the cobbled quays.

And recreate Easter in Dublin.[3]
10 Booted officers. Their mistresses.
Sunlight criss-crossing College Green.
Steam hissing from the flanks of horses.

Here they are. Cradled and cleaned,
held close in the arms of their owners.
15 Their cold hands clasped by warm hands,
their faces memorized like perfect manners.

The altars are mannerly with linen.
The lilies are whiter than surplices.[4]
The candles are burning and warning:
20 Rejoice, they whisper. After sacrifice.

Horse-chestnuts hold up their candles.
The Green is vivid with parasols.
Sunlight is pastel and windless.
The bar of the Shelbourne[5] is full.

25 Laughter and gossip on the terraces.
Rumour and alarm at the barracks.
The Empire is summoning its officers.
The carriages are turning: they are turning back.

---

1. Usually fine linen, but also, as here, fine cotton.
2. A square dance and the music for it.
3. What became known as the "Easter Rising" began on Easter Monday, 1916, when over sixteen hundred Irish Nationalists seized key points in Dublin and an Irish Republic was proclaimed from the General Post Office. See W. B. Yeats's "Easter, 1916" (p. 2031).
4. White linen vestments worn over cassocks.
5. Large Dublin hotel.

Past children walking with governesses,
30   Looking down, cossetting their dolls,
then looking up as the carriage passes,
the shadow chilling them. Twilight falls.

It is twilight in the dolls' museum. Shadows
remain on the parchment-coloured waists,
35   are bruises on the stitched cotton clothes,
are hidden in the dimples on the wrists.

The eyes are wide. They cannot address
the helplessness which has lingered in
the airless peace of each glass case:
40   to have survived. To have been stronger than

a moment. To be the hostages ignorance
takes from time and ornament from destiny. Both.
To be the present of the past. To infer the difference
with a terrible stare. But not feel it. And not know it.

1994

The Lost Land

I have two daughters.

They are all I ever wanted from the earth.

Or almost all.

I also wanted one piece of ground:

5   One city trapped by hills. One urban river.
An island in its element.

So I could say *mine*. *My own.*
And mean it.

Now they are grown up and far away

10   and memory itself
has become an emigrant,
wandering in a place
where love dissembles itself as landscape:

Where the hills
15   are the colours of a child's eyes,
where my children are distances, horizons:

At night,
on the edge of sleep,

I can see the shore of Dublin Bay.
20   Its rocky sweep and its granite pier.

Is this, I say
how they must have seen it,
backing out on the mailboat at twilight,

shadows falling
25   on everything they had to leave?
And would love forever?
And then

I imagine myself
at the landward rail of that boat
30   searching for the last sight of a hand.

I see myself
on the underworld side of that water,
the darkness coming in fast, saying
all the names I know for a lost land:

35   *Ireland. Absence. Daughter.*

1998

SALMAN RUSHDIE
b. 1947

The most influential novelist to have come from South Asia in the last fifty years is Ahmed Salman Rushdie, whose dynamic narratives—stories of magic, suffering, and the vitality of human beings in the grip of history—have helped generate the literary renaissance flowering in India today. "I come from Bombay," Rushdie has said, "and from a Muslim family, too. 'My' India has always been based on ideas of multiplicity, pluralism, hybridity: ideas to which the ideologies of the communalists are diametrically opposed. To my mind, the defining image of India is the crowd, and a crowd is by its very nature superabundant, heterogeneous, many things at once." Rushdie was educated at Cathedral School, Bombay (now Mumbai), and from the age of thirteen, at Rugby School, Warwickshire, and King's College, Cambridge. After living briefly in Pakistan, where his prosperous family had moved, Rushdie eventually settled in England, working as an actor and as a freelance advertising copywriter (1970–80).

His first novel, *Grimus* (1979), passed unnoticed, but his second, *Midnight's Children* (1981), announced the arrival of a major writer. Taking its title from those who were born—two months later than its author—around midnight on August 15, 1947, when the independent state of India was born, *Midnight's Children* is a work of prodigious prodigality, a cornucopia as richly fertile in character, incident, and language as the subcontinent that is its setting. The book's triumphant progress across the world culminated in its being judged "the Booker of Bookers," the best novel to have won Britain's premier fiction prize in its first twenty-five years. Rushdie has said that "we're all radio-active with history," and the books that have followed *Midnight's Children* have again shown a form of "magical realism"—learned from Latin American writers such as Jorge Luis Borges and Gabriel García Márquez—deployed in the service of a powerful political-historical imagination.

In 1988 Rushdie found himself at the perilous center of a real, rather than a magical realist, political-historical storm. His novel *The Satanic Verses* provoked riots in India, Pakistan, and South Africa, and was judged by senior religious figures in Iran to have blasphemed the Prophet Muhammad (called by the offensive name "Mahound" in the novel), founder of the Muslim faith, and a fatwa, or legal decree, calling for his death was pronounced. He was obliged to go into hiding, and for almost a decade lived under round-the-clock protection from British Secret Service agents, while governments argued for and against the lifting of the fatwa, and the author himself became symbolic of the vulnerability of the intellectual in the face of fundamentalism. The lifting of the fatwa in 1998 allowed Rushdie to reappear in public, but it is seen as irrevocable by some religious groups, and so his life remains under constant threat. He has defended his book in the essay "In Good Faith" (1990), while defining the irreverently pluralistic vision behind his "mongrel" aesthetic—a vision that has repeatedly resulted in the burning or banning of his books by political nationalists and religious purists in South Asia and other parts of the world:

> If *The Satanic Verses* is anything, it is a migrant's-eye view of the world. It is written from the very experience of uprooting, disjuncture and metamorphosis (slow or rapid, painful or pleasurable) that is the migrant condition, and from which, I believe, can be derived a metaphor for all humanity.
>
> Standing at the centre of the novel is a group of characters most of whom are British Muslims, or not particularly religious persons of Muslim background, struggling with just the sort of great problems of hybridization and ghettoization, of reconciling the old and the new. Those who oppose the novel most vociferously today are of the opinion that intermingling with a different culture will inevitably weaken and ruin their own. I am of the opposite opinion. *The Satanic Verses* celebrates hybridity, impurity, intermingling, the transformation that comes of new and unexpected combinations of human beings, cultures, ideas, politics, movies, songs. It rejoices in mongrelization and fears the absolutism of the Pure. *Mélange*, hotchpotch, a bit of this and a bit of that is *how newness enters the world*. It is the great possibility that mass migration gives the world, and I have tried to embrace it. *The Satanic Verses* is for change-by-fusion, change-by-conjoining. It is a love-song to our mongrel selves.

An earlier story, published the same year as his groundbreaking *Midnight's Children*, had invoked the Prophet uncontroversially. Like *Midnight's Children*, the story "The Prophet's Hair" buoyantly fuses Standard English with an exuberantly Indianized English, peppered with words of Hindi, Persian, Sanskrit, and Arabic origin—among the many languages that have been used in the extraordinarily polyglot Indian subcontinent. Like *The Satanic Verses*, "The Prophet's Hair" risks playfulness, satire, caricature, and whimsy in its treatment of the religion of his youth (though Rushdie has indicated he was brought up not as a believer but within a relaxed Muslim climate, almost secularized by the variety of other religions surrounding it). The story is at once a moral fable in the tradition of *The Thousand and One Nights* and a magical realist extravaganza, packed with incident, poetic detail ("water to which the cold of the night had given the cloudy consistency of wild honey"), and humor, all brilliantly interwoven at breakneck speed.

The Prophet's[1] Hair

Early in the year 19—, when Srinagar[2] was under the spell of a winter so fierce it could crack men's bones as if they were glass, a young man upon whose cold-pinked skin there lay, like a frost, the unmistakable sheen of wealth was to be seen entering the most wretched and disreputable part of the city, where the houses of wood and corrugated iron seemed perpetually on the verge of losing their balance, and asking in low, grave tones where he might go to engage the services of a dependably professional burglar. The young man's name was Atta, and the rogues in that part of town directed him gleefully into ever darker and less public alleys, until in a yard wet with the blood of a slaughtered chicken he was set upon by two men whose faces he never saw, robbed of the substantial bank-roll which he had insanely brought on his solitary excursion, and beaten within an inch of his life.

Night fell. His body was carried by anonymous hands to the edge of the lake, whence it was transported by shikara[3] across the water and deposited, torn and bleeding, on the deserted embankment of the canal which led to the gardens of Shalimar. At dawn the next morning a flower-vendor was rowing his boat through water to which the cold of the night had given the cloudy consistency of wild honey when he saw the prone form of young Atta, who was just beginning to stir and moan, and on whose now deathly pale skin the sheen of wealth could still be made out dimly beneath an actual layer of frost.

The flower-vendor moored his craft and by stooping over the mouth of the injured man was able to learn the poor fellow's address, which was mumbled through lips that could scarcely move; whereupon, hoping for a large tip, the hawker rowed Atta home to a large house on the shores of the lake, where a beautiful but inexplicably bruised young woman and her distraught, but equally handsome mother, neither of whom, it was clear from their eyes, had slept a wink from worrying, screamed at the sight of their Atta—who was the elder brother of the beautiful young woman—lying motionless amidst the funereally stunted winter blooms of the hopeful florist.

The flower-vendor was indeed paid off handsomely, not least to ensure his silence, and plays no further part in our story. Atta himself, suffering terribly from exposure as well as a broken skull, entered a coma which caused the city's finest doctors to shrug helplessly. It was therefore all the more remarkable that on the very next evening the most wretched and disreputable part of the city received a second unexpected visitor. This was Huma, the sister of the unfortunate young man, and her question was the same as her brother's, and asked in the same low, grave tones:

'Where may I hire a thief?'

The story of the rich idiot who had come looking for a burglar was already common knowledge in those insalubrious[4] gullies, but this time the young woman added: 'I should say that I am carrying no money, nor am I wearing any jewellery items. My father has disowned me and will pay no ransom if I am kidnapped; and a letter has been lodged with the Deputy Commissioner

---

1. The Prophet Muhammad, founder of the Muslim religion, was born in Mecca about 570 and died in 632.

2. Capital of the state of Kashmir.
3. Long swift Kashmiri boat.
4. Unhealthy.

of Police, my uncle, to be opened in the event of my not being safe at home by morning. In that letter he will find full details of my journey here, and he will move Heaven and Earth to punish my assailants.'

Her exceptional beauty, which was visible even through the enormous welts and bruises disfiguring her arms and forehead, coupled with the oddity of her inquiries, had attracted a sizable group of curious onlookers, and because her little speech seemed to them to cover just about everything, no one attempted to injure her in any way, although there were some raucous comments to the effect that it was pretty peculiar for someone who was trying to hire a crook to invoke the protection of a high-up policeman uncle.

She was directed into ever darker and less public alleys until finally in a gully as dark as ink an old woman with eyes which stared so piercingly that Huma instantly understood she was blind motioned her through a doorway from which darkness seemed to be pouring like smoke. Clenching her fists, angrily ordering her heart to behave normally, Huma followed the old woman into the gloom-wrapped house.

The faintest conceivable rivulet of candlelight trickled through the darkness; following this unreliable yellow thread (because she could no longer see the old lady), Huma received a sudden sharp blow to the shins and cried out involuntarily, after which she at once bit her lip, angry at having revealed her mounting terror to whoever or whatever waited before her, shrouded in blackness.

She had, in fact, collided with a low table on which a single candle burned and beyond which a mountainous figure could be made out, sitting cross-legged on the floor. 'Sit, sit,' said a man's calm, deep voice, and her legs, needing no more flowery invitation, buckled beneath her at the terse command. Clutching her left hand in her right, she forced her voice to respond evenly:

'And you, sir, will be the thief I have been requesting?'

Shifting its weight very slightly, the shadow-mountain informed Huma that all criminal activity originating in this zone was well organised and also centrally controlled, so that all requests for what might be termed freelance work had to be channelled through this room.

He demanded comprehensive details of the crime to be committed, including a precise inventory of items to be acquired, also a clear statement of all financial inducements being offered with no gratuities excluded, plus, for filing purposes only, a summary of the motives for the application.

At this, Huma, as though remembering something, stiffened both in body and resolve and replied loudly that her motives were entirely a matter for herself; that she would discuss details with no one but the thief himself; but that the rewards she proposed could only be described as 'lavish'.

'All I am willing to disclose to you, sir, since it appears that I am on the premises of some sort of employment agency, is that in return for such lavish rewards I must have the most desperate criminal at your disposal, a man for whom life holds no terrors, not even the fear of God.

'The worst of fellows, I tell you—nothing less will do!'

At this a paraffin storm-lantern was lighted, and Huma saw facing her a grey-haired giant down whose left cheek ran the most sinister of scars, a cicatrice in the shape of the letter *sín* in the Nastaliq[5] script. She was gripped by the insupportably nostalgic notion that the bogeyman of her childhood nursery had risen up to confront her, because her ayah[6] had always forestalled any incipient acts of disobedience by threatening Huma and Atta: 'You don't watch out and I'll send that one to steal you away—that Sheikh[7] Sín, the Thief of Thieves!'

Here, grey-haired but unquestionably scarred, was the notorious criminal himself—and was she out of her mind, were her ears playing tricks, or had he truly just announced that, given the stated circumstances, he himself was the only man for the job?

Struggling hard against the newborn goblins of nostalgia, Huma warned the fearsome volunteer that only a matter of extreme urgency and peril would have brought her unescorted into these ferocious streets.

'Because we can afford no last-minute backings-out,' she continued, 'I am determined to tell you everything, keeping back no secrets whatsoever. If, after hearing me out, you are still prepared to proceed, then we shall do everything in our power to assist you, and to make you rich.'

The old thief shrugged, nodded, spat. Huma began her story.

Six days ago, everything in the household of her father, the wealthy money-lender Hashim, had been as it always was. At breakfast her mother had spooned khichri[8] lovingly on to the moneylender's plate; the conversation had been filled with those expressions of courtesy and solicitude on which the family prided itself.

Hashim was fond of pointing out that while he was not a godly man he set great store by 'living honourably in the world'. In that spacious lakeside residence, all outsiders were greeted with the same formality and respect, even those unfortunates who came to negotiate for small fragments of Hashim's large fortune, and of whom he naturally asked an interest rate of over seventy per cent, partly, as he told his khichri-spooning wife, 'to teach these people the value of money; let them only learn that, and they will be cured of this fever of borrowing borrowing all the time—so you see that if my plans succeed, I shall put myself out of business!'

In their children, Atta and Huma, the moneylender and his wife had successfully sought to inculcate the virtues of thrift, plain dealing and a healthy independence of spirit. On this, too, Hashim was fond of congratulating himself.

Breakfast ended; the family members wished one another a fulfilling day. Within a few hours, however, the glassy contentment of that household, of that life of porcelain delicacy and alabaster sensibilities, was to be shattered beyond all hope of repair.

The moneylender summoned his personal shikara and was on the point of stepping into it when, attracted by a glint of silver, he noticed a small vial floating between the boat and his private quay. On an impulse, he scooped it out of the glutinous water.

---

5. A Persian cursive script, characterized by rounded forms and elongated horizontal strokes. "Cicatrice": scar of a healed wound.

6. Child's nurse (Anglo-Indian, from Portuguese).
7. Chief (Arabic).
8. Rice and lentils cooked together (Hindi).

It was a cylinder of tinted glass cased in exquisitely wrought silver, and Hashim saw within its walls a silver pendant bearing a single strand of human hair.

Closing his fist around this unique discovery, he muttered to the boatman that he'd changed his plans, and hurried to his sanctum,[9] where, behind closed doors, he feasted his eyes on his find.

There can be no doubt that Hashim the moneylender knew from the first that he was in possession of the famous relic of the Prophet Muhammad, that revered hair whose theft from its shrine at Hazratbal mosque the previous morning had created an unprecedented hue and cry in the valley.

The thieves—no doubt alarmed by the pandemonium, by the procession through the streets of endless ululating[1] crocodiles of lamentation, by the riots, the political ramifications and by the massive police search which was commanded and carried out by men whose entire careers now hung upon the finding of this lost hair—had evidently panicked and hurled the vial into the gelatine bosom of the lake.

Having found it by a stroke of great good fortune, Hashim's duty as a citizen was clear: the hair must be restored to its shrine, and the state to equanimity and peace.

But the moneylender had a different notion.

All around him in his study was the evidence of his collector's mania. There were enormous glass cases full of impaled butterflies from Gulmarg, three dozen scale models in various metals of the legendary cannon Zamzama, innumerable swords, a Naga spear, ninety-four terracotta camels of the sort sold on railway station platforms, many samovars,[2] and a whole zoology of tiny sandalwood animals, which had originally been carved to serve as children's bathtime toys.

'And after all,' Hashim told himself, 'the Prophet would have disapproved mightily of this relic-worship. He abhorred the idea of being deified! So, by keeping this hair from its distracted devotees, I perform—do I not?—a finer service than I would by returning it! Naturally, I don't want it for its religious value . . . I'm a man of the world, of this world. I see it purely as a secular object of great rarity and blinding beauty. In short, it's the silver vial I desire, more than the hair.

'They say there are American millionaires who purchase stolen art masterpieces and hide them away—they would know how I feel. I must, must have it!'

Every collector must share his treasures with one other human being, and Hashim summoned—and told—his only son Atta, who was deeply perturbed but, having been sworn to secrecy, only spilled the beans when the troubles became too terrible to bear.

The youth excused himself and left his father alone in the crowded solitude of his collections. Hashim was sitting erect in a hard, straight-backed chair, gazing intently at the beautiful vial.

9. Private room.
1. Howling.

2. Apparatuses for making tea (Russian for self-boilers).

It was well known that the moneylender never ate lunch, so it was not until evening that a servant entered the sanctum to summon his master to the dining-table. He found Hashim as Atta had left him. The same, and not the same—for now the moneylender looked swollen, distended. His eyes bulged even more than they always had, they were red-rimmed, and his knuckles were white.

He seemed to be on the point of bursting! As though, under the influence of the misappropriated relic, he had filled up with some spectral fluid which might at any moment ooze uncontrollably from his every bodily opening.

He had to be helped to the table, and then the explosion did indeed take place.

Seemingly careless of the effect of his words on the carefully constructed and fragile constitution of the family's life, Hashim began to gush, to spume long streams of awful truths. In horrified silence, his children heard their father turn upon his wife, and reveal to her that for many years their marriage had been the worst of his afflictions. 'An end to politeness!' he thundered. 'An end to hypocrisy!'

Next, and in the same spirit, he revealed to his family the existence of a mistress; he informed them also of his regular visits to paid women. He told his wife that, far from being the principal beneficiary of his will, she would receive no more than the eighth portion which was her due under Islamic law. Then he turned upon his children, screaming at Atta for his lack of academic ability—'A dope! I have been cursed with a dope!'—and accusing his daughter of lasciviousness, because she went around the city barefaced, which was unseemly for any good Muslim girl to do. She should, he commanded, enter purdah[3] forthwith.

Hashim left the table without having eaten and fell into the deep sleep of a man who has got many things off his chest, leaving his children stunned, in tears, and the dinner going cold on the sideboard under the gaze of an anticipatory bearer.[4]

At five o'clock the next morning the moneylender forced his family to rise, wash and say their prayers. From then on, he began to pray five times daily for the first time in his life, and his wife and children were obliged to do likewise.

Before breakfast, Huma saw the servants, under her father's direction, constructing a great heap of books in the garden and setting fire to it. The only volume left untouched was the Qur'an,[5] which Hashim wrapped in a silken cloth and placed on a table in the hall. He ordered each member of his family to read passages from this book for at least two hours per day. Visits to the cinema were forbidden. And if Atta invited male friends to the house, Huma was to retire to her room.

By now, the family had entered a state of shock and dismay; but there was worse to come.

That afternoon, a trembling debtor arrived at the house to confess his inability to pay the latest instalment of interest owed, and made the mistake of

3. Area of certain traditional Indian houses in which Hindu or Muslim women live secluded from the sight of men outside their family circle.

4. Servant.
5. Muslims' sacred book: collection of the Prophet Muhammad's oral revelations.

reminding Hashim, in somewhat blustering fashion, of the Qur'an's strictures against usury. The moneylender flew into a rage and attacked the fellow with one of his large collection of bullwhips.

By mischance, later the same day a second defaulter came to plead for time, and was seen fleeing Hashim's study with a great gash in his arm, because Huma's father had called him a thief of other men's money and had tried to cut off the wretch's right hand with one of the thirty-eight kukri knives[6] hanging on the study walls.

These breaches of the family's unwritten laws of decorum alarmed Atta and Huma, and when, that evening, their mother attempted to calm Hashim down, he struck her on the face with an open hand. Atta leapt to his mother's defence and he, too, was sent flying.

'From now on,' Hashim bellowed, 'there's going to be some discipline around here!'

The moneylender's wife began a fit of hysterics which continued throughout that night and the following day, and which so provoked her husband that he threatened her with divorce, at which she fled to her room, locked the door and subsided into a raga[7] of sniffling. Huma now lost her composure, challenged her father openly, and announced (with that same independence of spirit which he had encouraged in her) that she would wear no cloth over her face; apart from anything else, it was bad for the eyes.

On hearing this, her father disowned her on the spot and gave her one week in which to pack her bags and go.

By the fourth day, the fear in the air of the house had become so thick that it was difficult to walk around. Atta told his shock-numbed sister: 'We are descending to gutter-level—but I know what must be done.'

That afternoon, Hashim left home accompanied by two hired thugs to extract the unpaid dues from his two insolvent clients. Atta went immediately to his father's study. Being the son and heir, he possessed his own key to the moneylender's safe. This he now used, and removing the little vial from its hiding-place, he slipped it into his trouser pocket and re-locked the safe door.

Now he told Huma the secret of what his father had fished out of Lake Dal, and exclaimed: 'Maybe I'm crazy—maybe the awful things that are happening have made me cracked—but I am convinced there will be no peace in our house until this hair is out of it.'

His sister at once agreed that the hair must be returned, and Atta set off in a hired shikara to Hazratbal mosque. Only when the boat had delivered him into the throng of the distraught faithful which was swirling around the desecrated shrine did Atta discover that the relic was no longer in his pocket. There was only a hole, which his mother, usually so attentive to household matters, must have overlooked under the stress of recent events.

Atta's initial surge of chagrin was quickly replaced by a feeling of profound relief.

'Suppose', he imagined, 'that I had already announced to the mullahs[8] that

---

6. Curved knives broadening toward the point (Hindi).
7. Musical improvisation (Sanskrit).

8. Muslims learned in Islamic theology and sacred law.

the hair was on my person! They would never have believed me now—and this mob would have lynched me! At any rate, it has gone, and that's a load off my mind.' Feeling more contented than he had for days, the young man returned home.

Here he found his sister bruised and weeping in the hall; upstairs, in her bedroom, his mother wailed like a brand-new widow. He begged Huma to tell him what had happened, and when she replied that their father, returning from his brutal business trip, had once again noticed a glint of silver between boat and quay, had once again scooped up the errant relic, and was consequently in a rage to end all rages, having beaten the truth out of her—then Atta buried his face in his hands and sobbed out his opinion, which was that the hair was persecuting them, and had come back to finish the job.

It was Huma's turn to think of a way out of their troubles.

While her arms turned black and blue and great stains spread across her forehead, she hugged her brother and whispered to him that she was determined to get rid of the hair *at all costs*—she repeated this last phrase several times.

'The hair', she then declared, 'was stolen from the mosque; so it can be stolen from this house. But it must be a genuine robbery, carried out by a bona-fide thief, not by one of us who are under the hair's thrall—by a thief so desperate that he fears neither capture nor curses.'

Unfortunately, she added, the theft would be ten times harder to pull off now that their father, knowing that there had already been one attempt on the relic, was certainly on his guard.

'Can you do it?'

Huma, in a room lit by candle and storm-lantern, ended her account with one further question: 'What assurances can you give that the job holds no terrors for you still?'

The criminal, spitting, stated that he was not in the habit of providing references, as a cook might, or a gardener, but he was not alarmed so easily, certainly not by any children's djinni[9] of a curse. Huma had to be content with this boast, and proceeded to describe the details of the proposed burglary.

'Since my brother's failure to return the hair to the mosque, my father has taken to sleeping with his precious treasure under his pillow. However, he sleeps alone, and very energetically; only enter his room without waking him, and he will certainly have tossed and turned quite enough to make the theft a simple matter. When you have the vial, come to my room,' and here she handed Sheikh Sín a plan of her home, 'and I will hand over all the jewellery owned by my mother and myself. You will find . . . it is worth . . . that is, you will be able to get a fortune for it . . . '

It was evident that her self-control was weakening and that she was on the point of physical collapse.

'Tonight,' she burst out finally. 'You must come tonight!'

No sooner had she left the room than the old criminal's body was convulsed by a fit of coughing: he spat blood into an old vanaspati[1] can. The great Sheikh,

---

9. In Muslim demonology a spirit (genie) with supernatural powers.

1. Vegetable fat used as butter in India.

the 'Thief of Thieves', had become a sick man, and every day the time drew nearer when some young pretender to his power would stick a dagger in his stomach. A lifelong addiction to gambling had left him almost as poor as he had been when, decades ago, he had started out in this line of work as a mere pickpocket's apprentice; so in the extraordinary commission he had accepted from the moneylender's daughter he saw his opportunity of amassing enough wealth at a stroke to leave the valley for ever, and acquire the luxury of a respectable death which would leave his stomach intact.

As for the Prophet's hair, well, neither he nor his blind wife had ever had much to say for prophets—that was one thing they had in common with the moneylender's thunderstruck clan.

It would not do, however, to reveal the nature of this, his last crime, to his four sons. To his consternation, they had all grown up to be hopelessly devout men, who even spoke of making the pilgrimage to Mecca some day. 'Absurd!' their father would laugh at them. 'Just tell me how you will go?' For, with a parent's absolutist love, he had made sure they were all provided with a lifelong source of high income by crippling them at birth, so that, as they dragged themselves around the city, they earned excellent money in the begging business.

The children, then, could look after themselves.

He and his wife would be off soon with the jewel-boxes of the moneylender's women. It was a timely chance indeed that had brought the beautiful bruised girl into his corner of the town.

That night, the large house on the shore of the lake lay blindly waiting, with silence lapping at its walls. A burglar's night: clouds in the sky and mists on the winter water. Hashim the moneylender was asleep, the only member of his family to whom sleep had come that night. In another room, his son Atta lay deep in the coils of his coma with a blood-clot forming on his brain, watched over by a mother who had let down her long greying hair to show her grief, a mother who placed warm compresses on his head with gestures redolent of impotence. In a third bedroom Huma waited, fully dressed, amidst the jewel-heavy caskets of her desperation.

At last a bulbul[2] sang softly from the garden below her window and, creeping downstairs, she opened a door to the bird, on whose face there was a scar in the shape of the Nastaliq letter *sín*.

Noiselessly, the bird flew up the stairs behind her. At the head of the staircase they parted, moving in opposite directions along the corridor of their conspiracy without a glance at one another.

Entering the moneylender's room with professional ease, the burglar, Sín, discovered that Huma's predictions had been wholly accurate. Hashim lay sprawled diagonally across his bed, the pillow untenanted by his head, the prize easily accessible. Step by padded step, Sín moved towards the goal.

It was at this point that, in the bedroom next door, young Atta sat bolt upright in his bed, giving his mother a great fright, and without any warning— prompted by goodness knows what pressure of the blood-clot upon his brain— began screaming at the top of his voice:

'Thief! Thief! Thief!'

2. Asian song thrush.

It seems probable that his poor mind had been dwelling, in these last moments, upon his own father; but it is impossible to be certain, because having uttered these three emphatic words the young man fell back upon his pillow and died.

At once his mother set up a screeching and a wailing and a keening and a howling so earsplittingly intense that they completed the work which Atta's cry had begun—that is, her laments penetrated the walls of her husband's bedroom and brought Hashim wide awake.

Sheikh Sín was just deciding whether to dive beneath the bed or brain the moneylender good and proper when Hashim grabbed the tiger-striped swords-tick which always stood propped up in a corner beside his bed, and rushed from the room without so much as noticing the burglar who stood on the opposite side of the bed in the darkness. Sín stooped quickly and removed the vial containing the Prophet's hair from its hiding-place.

Meanwhile Hashim had erupted into the corridor, having unsheathed the sword inside his cane. In his right hand he held the weapon and was waving it about dementedly. His left hand was shaking the stick. A shadow came rushing towards him through the midnight darkness of the passageway and, in his somnolent anger, the moneylender thrust his sword fatally through its heart. Turning up the light, he found that he had murdered his daughter, and under the dire influence of this accident he was so overwhelmed by remorse that he turned the sword upon himself, fell upon it and so extinguished his life. His wife, the sole surviving member of the family, was driven mad by the general carnage and had to be committed to an asylum for the insane by her brother, the city's Deputy Commissioner of Police.

Sheikh Sín had quickly understood that the plan had gone awry.

Abandoning the dream of the jewel-boxes when he was but a few yards from its fulfilment, he climbed out of Hashim's window and made his escape during the appalling events described above. Reaching home before dawn, he woke his wife and confessed his failure. It would be necessary, he whispered, for him to vanish for a while. Her blind eyes never opened until he had gone.

The noise in the Hashim household had roused their servants and even man-aged to awaken the night-watchman, who had been fast asleep as usual on his charpoy[3] by the street-gate. They alerted the police, and the Deputy Commis-sioner himself was informed. When he heard of Huma's death, the mournful officer opened and read the sealed letter which his niece had given him, and instantly led a large detachment of armed men into the light-repellent gullies of the most wretched and disreputable part of the city.

The tongue of a malicious cat-burglar named Huma's fellow-conspirator; the finger of an ambitious bank-robber pointed at the house in which he lay concealed; and although Sín managed to crawl through a hatch in the attic and attempt a roof-top escape, a bullet from the Deputy Commissioner's own rifle penetrated his stomach and brought him crashing messily to the ground at the feet of Huma's enraged uncle.

From the dead thief's pocket rolled a vial of tinted glass, cased in filigree silver.

3. Light Indian bedstead.

The recovery of the Prophet's hair was announced at once on All-India Radio. One month later, the valley's holiest men assembled at the Hazratbal mosque and formally authenticated the relic. It sits to this day in a closely guarded vault by the shores of the loveliest of lakes in the heart of the valley which was once closer than any other place on earth to Paradise.

But before our story can properly be concluded, it is necessary to record that when the four sons of the dead Sheikh awoke on the morning of his death, having unwittingly spent a few minutes under the same roof as the famous hair, they found that a miracle had occurred, that they were all sound of limb and strong of wind, as whole as they might have been if their father had not thought to smash their legs in the first hours of their lives. They were, all four of them, very properly furious, because the miracle had reduced their earning powers by 75 per cent, at the most conservative estimate; so they were ruined men.

Only the Sheikh's widow had some reason for feeling grateful, because although her husband was dead she had regained her sight, so that it was possible for her to spend her last days gazing once more upon the beauties of the valley of Kashmir.

1981

ANNE CARSON
b. 1950

Anne Carson was born in Toronto, Canada, and grew up in Ontario, and she received both her B.A. and her Ph.D. in classics from the University of Toronto. The recipient of a MacArthur Fellowship, she has taught classics at McGill University and the University of Michigan, among other schools. Along with poetry, she has published books of criticism on classical literature; translations from Greek; and a novel-in-verse, *Autobiography of Red* (1998).

In her poetry Carson braids together the ruminative texture of the essay, the narrative propulsion of the novel, the self-analysis of autobiography, and the lapidary compression of lyric. In "The Glass Essay," a long poem that reflects on the dislocations of identity through time, love, and madness, she vividly narrates the end of a love affair, a visit with a difficult mother, and the degeneration of a father with Alzheimer's in a nursing home. Into this semiautobiographical tale she weaves commentary on the writings of Charlotte and Emily Brontë, whose works function—like the classical texts she often incorporates into her poetry—as oblique and remote points of comparison for the poet's experience. Both personal and impersonal, Carson's poetry bridges the gap between private narrative and philosophical speculation, between self-excavation and literary-critical analysis. Tightly wound with crisp diction, studded with striking metaphors, etched with epigrams and ironies, her poems are lucid in feeling and intense in thought. They are as intellectually crystalline as they are emotionally volcanic.

From The Glass Essay

Hero

I can tell by the way my mother chews her toast
whether she had a good night
and is about to say a happy thing
or not.

5 Not.
She puts her toast down on the side of her plate.
You know you can pull the drapes in that room, she begins.

This is a coded reference to one of our oldest arguments,
from what I call The Rules Of Life series.
10 My mother always closes her bedroom drapes tight before going to bed at
    night.

I open mine as wide as possible.
I like to see everything, I say.
What's there to see?

Moon. Air. Sunrise.
15 All that light on your face in the morning. Wakes you up.
I like to wake up.

At this point the drapes argument has reached a delta
and may advance along one of three channels.
There is the What You Need Is A Good Night's Sleep channel,

20 the Stubborn As Your Father channel
and random channel.
More toast? I interpose strongly, pushing back my chair.

Those women! says my mother with an exasperated rasp.
Mother has chosen random channel.
25 Women?

Complaining about rape all the time—
I see she is tapping one furious finger on yesterday's newspaper
lying beside the grape jam.

The front page has a small feature
30 about a rally for International Women's Day—
have you had a look at the Sears Summer Catalogue?

Nope.
Why, it's a disgrace! Those bathing suits—
cut way up to here! (she points) No wonder!

35 You're saying women deserve to get raped
because Sears bathing suit ads
have high-cut legs? Ma, are you serious?

Well someone has to be responsible.
Why should women be responsible for male desire? My voice is high.
40 Oh I see you're one of Them.

One of Whom? My voice is very high. Mother vaults it.
And whatever did you do with that little tank suit you had last year the
  green one?
It looked so smart on you.

The frail fact drops on me from a great height
45 that my mother is afraid.
She will be eighty years old this summer.

Her tiny sharp shoulders hunched in the blue bathrobe
make me think of Emily Brontë's little merlin hawk Hero
that she fed bits of bacon at the kitchen table when Charlotte[1] wasn't
  around.

50 So Ma, we'll go—I pop up the toaster
and toss a hot slice of pumpernickel lightly across onto her plate—
visit Dad today? She eyes the kitchen clock with hostility.

Leave at eleven, home again by four? I continue.
She is buttering her toast with jagged strokes.
55 Silence is assent in our code. I go into the next room to phone the taxi.

My father lives in a hospital for patients who need chronic care
about 50 miles from here.
He suffers from a kind of dementia

characterized by two sorts of pathological change
60 first recorded in 1907 by Alois Alzheimer.[2]
First, the presence in cerebral tissue

of a spherical formation known as neuritic plaque,
consisting mainly of degenerating brain cells.
Second, neurofibrillary snarlings

65 in the cerebral cortex and in the hippocampus.[3]
There is no known cause or cure.
Mother visits him by taxi once a week

for the last five years.
Marriage is for better or for worse, she says,
70 this is the worse.

So about an hour later we are in the taxi
shooting along empty country roads towards town.
The April light is clear as an alarm.

---

1. Charlotte Brontë (1816–1855), English novelist, author of *Jane Eyre*, and sister of Emily (1818–
1848), author of *Wuthering Heights*. Throughout
"The Glass Essay," the poet compares her own life
with Emily Brontë's.
2. German neurologist (1864–1915).
3. Parts of the brain. Neurofibrils are nerve fibers.

As we pass them it gives a sudden sense of every object
75 existing in space on its own shadow.
I wish I could carry this clarity with me

into the hospital where distinctions tend to flatten and coalesce.
I wish I had been nicer to him before he got crazy.
These are my two wishes.

80 It is hard to find the beginning of dementia.
I remember a night about ten years ago
when I was talking to him on the telephone.

It was a Sunday night in winter.
I heard his sentences filling up with fear.
85 He would start a sentence—about weather, lose his way, start another.
It made me furious to hear him floundering—

my tall proud father, former World War II navigator!
It made me merciless.
I stood on the edge of the conversation,

90 watching him thrash about for cues,
offering none,
and it came to me like a slow avalanche

that he had no idea who he was talking to.
Much colder today I guess. . . .
95 his voice pressed into the silence and broke off,

snow falling on it.
There was a long pause while snow covered us both.
Well I won't keep you,

he said with sudden desperate cheer as if sighting land.
100 I'll say goodnight now,
I won't run up your bill. Goodbye.

Goodbye.
Goodbye. Who are you?
I said into the dial tone.

105 At the hospital we pass down long pink halls
through a door with a big window
and a combination lock (5–25–3)

to the west wing, for chronic care patients.
Each wing has a name.
110 The chronic wing is Our Golden Mile

although mother prefers to call it The Last Lap.
Father sits strapped in a chair which is tied to the wall
in a room of other tied people tilting at various angles.

My father tilts least, I am proud of him.
115   Hi Dad how y'doing?
His face cracks open it could be a grin or rage

and looking past me he issues a stream of vehemence at the air.
My mother lays her hand on his.
Hello love, she says. He jerks his hand away. We sit.

120   Sunlight flocks through the room.
Mother begins to unpack from her handbag the things she has brought for
     him,
grapes, arrowroot biscuits, humbugs.°   *hard candies*

He is addressing strenuous remarks to someone in the air between us.
He uses a language known only to himself,
125   made of snarls and syllables and sudden wild appeals.

Once in a while some old formula floats up through the wash—
You don't say! or Happy birthday to you!—
but no real sentence

for more than three years now.
130   I notice his front teeth are getting black.
I wonder how you clean the teeth of mad people.

He always took good care of his teeth. My mother looks up.
She and I often think two halves of one thought.
Do you remember that gold-plated toothpick

135   you sent him from Harrod's⁴ the summer you were in London? she asks.
Yes I wonder what happened to it.
Must be in the bathroom somewhere.

She is giving him grapes one by one.
They keep rolling out of his huge stiff fingers.
140   He used to be a big man, over six feet tall and strong,

but since he came to hospital his body has shrunk to the merest bone
     house—
except the hands. The hands keep growing.
Each one now as big as a boot in Van Gogh,⁵

they go lumbering after the grapes in his lap.
145   But now he turns to me with a rush of urgent syllables
that break off on a high note—he waits,

staring into my face. That quizzical look.
One eyebrow at an angle.
I have a photograph taped to my fridge at home.

4. Department store.
5. Vincent van Gogh (1853–1890), Dutch postimpressionist, painted *A Pair of Boots* (1887).

150 It shows his World War II air crew posing in front of the plane.
Hands firmly behind backs, legs wide apart,
chins forward.

Dressed in the puffed flying suits
with a wide leather strap pulled tight through the crotch.
155 They squint into the brilliant winter sun of 1942.

It is dawn.
They are leaving Dover[6] for France.
My father on the far left is the tallest airman,

with his collar up,
160 one eyebrow at an angle.
The shadowless light makes him look immortal,

for all the world like someone who will not weep again.
He is still staring into my face.
Flaps down! I cry.
165 His black grin flares once and goes out like a match.

1995

Epitaph: Zion[1]

Murderous little world once our objects had gazes. Our lives
Were fragile, the wind
Could dash them away. Here lies the refugee breather
Who drank a bowl of elsewhere.

2000

6. Port on the English Channel.
1. In the Hebrew Bible the eastern hill of Jerusalem. In Judaism it came to symbolize a promised

homeland; in Christianity, a heavenly or ideal city
of faith.

PAUL MULDOON
b. 1951

Paul Muldoon was born in Portadown, County Armagh, Northern Ireland. His
mother was a schoolteacher; his father, a farm laborer and mushroom grower. He
grew up in, as he put it, "a little enclave of Roman Catholics living within the predominantly Protestant parish of Loughgall, the village where the Orange Order was
founded in 1795." Despite inheriting strong Republican sympathies, he depicts the
Catholic Church unsympathetically, even going so far as to state that there is "a very
fine line between organized religion and organized crime." He was educated at the
primary school in Collegelands (where his mother taught); St. Patrick's College,
Armagh; and Queen's University, Belfast, where he was tutored by Seamus Heaney
and came to know other poets of the "Belfast Group," such as Derek Mahon and

Michael Longley. He worked as a radio and television producer for the British Broadcasting Corporation in Belfast until, in the mid-1980s, he became a freelance writer and moved to the United States, where he teaches at Princeton University.

Muldoon's first published poems were written in Irish, and although he soon switched to English, Irish words and phrases continued to appear in his work. As with many other Irish poets, America soon loomed large in his imagination. Excited by American films, he adapted cinematic techniques in hectic, hallucinatory long poems. Other poems, such as "Meeting the British," parallel the plight of American Indians with that of Northern Irish Catholics. Still others, such as "The Grand Conversation," turn his marriage to the American Jewish writer Jean Korelitz into a densely specific yet allegorical poem about identity and intercultural experience. His earliest literary influence was, he said, Robert Frost's "strong, classic, lyric line. But the most important thing . . . was his mischievous, shy, multi-layered quality under the surface." It would be hard to improve on that last sentence as a description of Muldoon's own mature style, the expression of an omnivorous imagination that—in "Milkweed and Monarch," for example—mixes his parents' Collegelands grave with other geographically scattered memories into a kaleidoscopic pattern that is at once moving, musically satisfying, and a brilliant postmodern variation on the ancient poetic form of villanelle (with the repetition of its first and third lines).

Meeting the British

We met the British in the dead of winter.
The sky was lavender

and the snow lavender-blue.
I could hear, far below,

5   the sound of two streams coming together
(both were frozen over)

and, no less strange,
myself calling out in French

across that forest-
10   clearing. Neither General Jeffrey Amherst[1]

nor Colonel Henry Bouquet
could stomach our willow-tobacco.

As for the unusual
scent when the Colonel shook out his hand-

1. Commander-in-chief of British forces in the French and Indian War (1754–63); fought against France and its Native American allies. During Pontiac's Rebellion (1763–64), led by Ottawa chief Pontiac in the Great Lakes region, Amherst wrote to the British officer Colonel Bouquet, "Could it not be contrived to Send the *Small Pox* among those Disaffected Tribes of Indians?" Bouquet replied, "I will try to inoculate the Indians by means of Blankets that may fall in their hands, taking care however not to get the disease myself," to which Amherst responded, "You will Do well to try to Innoculate the Indians by means of Blanketts, as well as to try Every other method that can serve to Extirpate this Execreble Race." Apparently as a result of this and similar plans of other British officers, many Native Americans in the area, never having been exposed to smallpox, were killed by the disease in 1763–64. Pontiac concluded a peace treaty with the British in July 1766.

15   kerchief: *C'est la lavande,*
      une fleur mauve comme le ciel.[2]

They gave us six fishhooks
and two blankets embroidered with smallpox.

1987

Gathering Mushrooms

The rain comes flapping through the yard
like a tablecloth that she hand-embroidered.
My mother has left it on the line.
It is sodden with rain.
5   The mushroom shed is windowless, wide,
its high-stacked wooden trays
hosed down with formaldehyde.[1]
And my father has opened the Gates of Troy[2]
to that first load of horse manure.
10   Barley straw. Gypsum.[3] Dried blood. Ammonia.
Wagon after wagon
blusters in, a self-renewing gold-black dragon
we push to the back of the mind.
We have taken our pitchforks to the wind.

15   All brought back to me that September evening
fifteen years on. The pair of us
tripping through Barnett's fair demesne°   domain
like girls in long dresses
after a hail-storm.
20   We might have been thinking of the fire-bomb
that sent Malone House[4] sky-high
and its priceless collection of linen
sky-high.
We might have wept with Elizabeth McCrum.
25   We were thinking only of psilocybin.[5]
You sang of the maid you met on the dewy grass—
And she stooped so low gave me to know
it was mushrooms she was gathering O.

He'll be wearing that same old donkey-jacket[6]
30   and the sawn-off waders.
He carries a knife, two punnets,[7] a bucket.
He reaches far into his own shadow.
We'll have taken him unawares
and stand behind him, slightly to one side.

2. It is lavender, a flower purple as the sky
(French).
1. Formic-acid disinfectant.
2. City besieged by the Greeks in Homer's *Iliad*.
Its walls could not be destroyed from without, and
it was finally captured only by a trick.
3. Hydrated calcium sulfate, used for making plas-

ter of Paris.
4. A mansion in Barnett Demesne, Belfast,
bombed in 1976.
5. Hallucinogenic drug made from mushrooms.
6. Strong jacket with leather shoulder patches.
7. Small shallow baskets for fruit or vegetables.

35 He is one of those ancient warriors
before the rising tide.
He'll glance back from under his peaked cap
without breaking rhythm:
his coaxing a mushroom—a flat or a cup—
40 the nick against his right thumb;
the bucket then, the punnet to left or right,
and so on and so forth till kingdom come.

We followed the overgrown tow-path by the Lagan.[8]
The sunset would deepen through cinnamon
45 to aubergine,
the wood-pigeon's concerto for oboe and strings,
allegro, blowing your mind.
And you were suddenly out of my ken, hurtling
towards the ever-receding ground,
50 into the maw
of a shimmering green-gold dragon.
You discovered yourself in some outbuilding
with your long-lost companion, me,
though my head had grown into the head of a horse
55 that shook its dirty-fair mane
and spoke this verse:

Come back to us. However cold and raw, your feet
were always meant
to negotiate terms with bare cement.
60 *Beyond this concrete wall is a wall of concrete*
and barbed wire. Your only hope
is to come back. If sing you must, let your song
tell of treading your own dung,
let straw and dung give a spring to your step.
65 *If we never live to see the day we leap*
into our true domain,
lie down with us now and wrap
yourself in the soiled grey blanket of Irish rain
that will, one day, bleach itself white.
70 *Lie down with us and wait.*

1983

Milkweed and Monarch

As he knelt by the grave of his mother and father
the taste of dill, or tarragon—
he could barely tell one from the other—

filled his mouth. It seemed as if he might smother.
5 Why should he be stricken
with grief, not for his mother and father,

but a woman slinking from the fur of a sea-otter
in Portland, Maine, or, yes, Portland, Oregon—
he could barely tell one from the other—

10   and why should he now savour
the tang of her, her little pickled gherkin,
as he knelt by the grave of his mother and father?

•

He looked about. He remembered her palaver
on how both earth and sky would darken—
15   "You could barely tell one from the other"—

while the Monarch butterflies passed over
in their milkweed-hunger: "A wing-beat, some reckon,
may trigger off the mother and father

of all storms, striking your Irish Cliffs of Moher
20   with the force of a hurricane."
Then: "Milkweed and Monarch 'invented' each other."

•

He looked about. Cow's-parsley in a samovar.[1]
He'd mistaken his mother's name, "Regan", for "Anger":
as he knelt by the grave of his mother and father
25   he could barely tell one from the other.

1994

The Grand Conversation

She. My people came from Korelitz[1]
where they grew yellow cucumbers
and studied the Talmud.[2]
He. Mine pored over the mud
5   of mangold-° and potato-pits   *a beet*
or flicked through kale plants from Comber[3]
as bibliomancers of old
went a-flicking through deckle-mold.[4]

She. Mine would lie low in the shtetl[5]
10   when they heard the distant thunder
stolen by the Cossacks.[6]
He. It was potato sacks
lumped together on a settle°   *long wooden bed or bench*

1. Russian tea urn.
1. Town, now in Belarus, once famous for its cucumbers. During World War II the Nazis largely massacred its population.
2. Collection of writings that constitutes the Jewish civil and religious law.
3. Village in Northern Ireland.
4. Rough edges of pages before they are trimmed.

"Bibliomancers": people who predicted the future from the text in a book opened at random.
5. Former Jewish village-communities of Eastern Europe.
6. A Polish people known for their horsemanship, they massacred perhaps a hundred thousand Polish Jews in 1648–49.

mine found themselves lying under,
15   the Peep O'Day Boys from Loughgall[7]
    making Defenders[7] of us all.

She. Mine once controlled the sugar trade
from the islets of Langerhans[8]
and were granted the deed
20   to Charlottesville.[9] *He*. Indeed?   *city in Virginia*
My people called a spade a spade
and were admitted to the hanse[9]   *merchant guild*
of pike- and pickax-men, shovels
leaning to their lean-to hovels.

25   *She*. Mine were trained to make a suture
after the bomb and the bombast
have done their very worst.
He. Between *fearsad* and *verst*[9]
we may yet construct our future
30   as we've reconstructed our past
and cry out, my love, each to each
from his or her own quicken-queach.[1]

She. Each from his stand of mountain ash
will cry out over valley farms
35   spotlit with pear blossom.
He. There some young Absalom[2]
picks his way through cache after cache
of ammunition and small arms
hidden in grain wells, while his nag
40   tugs at a rein caught on a snag.

2002

---

7. Eighteenth-century Catholic group in Ireland that fought Protestants who called themselves the Peep O'Day Boys. "Loughgall": village where Protestants formed a larger coalition, the Orange Order, at the beginning of the nineteenth century.
8. The groups of cells in the pancreas that produce the hormone insulin, which regulates the sugar level in the bloodstream.
9. Russian land measure, roughly two-thirds of a mile. "Fearsad": sandbank (Irish).
1. "Queach": dense growth of bushes. Cf. T. S. Eliot's "Love Song of J. Alfred Prufrock": "Do I dare to eat a peach? / . . . I have heard the mermaids singing, each to each."
2. King David's son, killed leading a rebellion against his father (2 Samuel). Riding his mule, he was accidentally hung up on a low branch and was thus made vulnerable to enemy spears.

CAROL ANN DUFFY
b. 1955

Carol Ann Duffy was born in Glasgow, Scotland, to an Irish mother and a Scottish father in a working-class Catholic family. After moving as a child to Stafford, England, she was educated there at St. Joseph's Convent and at Stafford Girls' High School, before studying philosophy at the University of Liverpool. She worked in television, edited a poetry magazine, and taught creative writing in London's schools, and since 1996 she has lectured at Manchester Metropolitan University.

A playwright as well as poet, Duffy is especially skillful in her use of dramatic monologue, fashioning and assuming the voices of mythological, historical, and fictive characters, such as Medusa or Lazarus's imaginary wife. Such poetic ventriloquism is well suited to her feminist revisions of myth and history: it enables her to dramatize a silenced or marginalized female perspective, wittily playing on the ironic contrast between the traditional version of a narrative and her own. The biblical story of Lazarus's resurrection, for example, looks different from the perspective of his wife, who upon his miraculous return from the dead scoffs: "I breathed / his stench."

The author of love poetry and political satire as well as dramatic monologues, Duffy has a sharp eye for detail and uses it deftly in poems characterized by their sensuality, economy, and exuberance. Working in well-constructed stanzas, carefully pacing her rhythms, playing on half-rhymes, effectively conjuring the senses of touch, smell, and sight, she mobilizes the resources of traditional lyric and turns them to contemporary ends—the remaking of master narratives, the celebration of lesbian desire.

Warming Her Pearls

for Judith Radstone[1]

Next to my own skin, her pearls. My mistress
bids me wear them, warm then, until evening
when I'll brush her hair. At six, I place them
round her cool, white throat. All day I think of her,

5 resting in the Yellow Room, contemplating silk
or taffeta, which gown tonight? She fans herself
whilst I work willingly, my slow heat entering
each pearl. Slack on my neck, her rope.

She's beautiful. I dream about her
10 in my attic bed; picture her dancing
with tall men, puzzled by my faint, persistent scent
beneath her French perfume, her milky stones.

I dust her shoulders with a rabbit's foot,
watch the soft blush seep through her skin
15 like an indolent sigh. In her looking-glass
my red lips part as though I want to speak.

Full moon. Her carriage brings her home. I see
her every movement in my head . . . Undressing,
taking off her jewels, her slim hand reaching
20 for the case, slipping naked into bed, the way

she always does . . . And I lie here awake,
knowing the pearls are cooling even now
in the room where my mistress sleeps. All night
I feel their absence and I burn.

1987

1. British political activist and bookseller (1925–2001). According to Radstone's obituary in *The Guardian*, the poem was inspired by a conversation with Radstone about the practice of ladies' maids increasing the luster of their mistresses' pearls by wearing them beneath their clothes.

Medusa[1]

A suspicion, a doubt, a jealousy
grew in my mind,
which turned the hairs on my head to filthy snakes,
as though my thoughts
5 hissed and spat on my scalp.

My bride's breath soured, stank
in the grey bags of my lungs.
I'm foul mouthed now, foul tongued,
yellow fanged.
10 There are bullet tears in my eyes.
Are you terrified?

Be terrified.
It's you I love,
perfect man, Greek God, my own;
15 but I know you'll go, betray me, stray
from home.
So better by far for me if you were stone.

I glanced at a buzzing bee,
a dull grey pebble fell
20 to the ground.
I glanced at a singing bird,
a handful of dusty gravel
spattered down.

I looked at a ginger cat,
25 a housebrick
shattered a bowl of milk.
I looked at a snuffling pig,
a boulder rolled
in a heap of shit.

30 I stared in the mirror.
Love gone bad
showed me a Gorgon.
I stared at a dragon.
Fire spewed
35 from the mouth of a mountain.

And here you come
with a shield for a heart
and a sword for a tongue
and your girls, your girls.

---

1. In Greek mythology the mortal, snake-haired
gorgon with the power to turn anyone who gazed
upon her into stone. Looking at her reflection in a
shield given him by Athena, Perseus cut off
Medusa's head as she slept.

40   Wasn't I beautiful?
      Wasn't I fragrant and young?

      Look at me now.

1999

Mrs Lazarus[1]

I had grieved. I had wept for a night and a day
over my loss, ripped the cloth I was married in
from my breasts, howled, shrieked, clawed
at the burial stones till my hands bled, retched
5   his name over and over again, dead, dead.

Gone home. Gutted the place. Slept in a single cot,
widow, one empty glove, white femur
in the dust, half. Stuffed dark suits
into black bags, shuffled in a dead man's shoes,
10   noosed the double knot of a tie round my bare neck,

gaunt nun in the mirror, touching herself. I learnt
the Stations of Bereavement,[2] the icon of my face
in each bleak frame; but all those months
he was going away from me, dwindling
15   to the shrunk size of a snapshot, going,

going. Till his name was no longer a certain spell
for his face. The last hair on his head
floated out from a book. His scent went from the house.
The will was read. See, he was vanishing
20   to the small zero held by the gold of my ring.

Then he was gone. Then he was legend, language;
my arm on the arm of the schoolteacher—the shock
of a man's strength under the sleeve of his coat—
along the hedgerows. But I was faithful
25   for as long as it took. Until he was memory.

So I could stand that evening in the field
in a shawl of fine air, healed, able
to watch the edge of the moon occur to the sky
and a hare thump from a hedge; then notice
30   the village men running towards me, shouting,

---

1. Lazarus was the man raised from the dead by
Jesus (John 11).
2. Allusion to the Stations of the Cross, a series of
fourteen icons (pictures or carvings) corresponding to the stages of Jesus' crucifixion and over each
of which a prayer is said.

behind them the women and children, barking dogs,
and I knew. I knew by the sly light
on the blacksmith's face, the shrill eyes
of the barmaid, the sudden hands bearing me
35   into the hot tang of the crowd parting before me.

He lived. I saw the horror on his face.
I heard his mother's crazy song. I breathed
his stench; my bridegroom in his rotting shroud,
moist and dishevelled from the grave's slack chew,
40   croaking his cuckold name, disinherited, out of his time.

1999

Poems in Process

Poets have often claimed that their poems were not willed but were inspired, whether by a muse or by divine visitation, or that they emerged full-blown from the poet's unconscious mind. But poets' often untidy manuscripts tell another story, suggesting that, however involuntary the origin of a poem, vision has usually been followed by revision.

Writers have described the second thoughts recorded in their working manuscripts in a number of ways. Revision may be viewed as a work of refinement and clarification, a process revealing or bringing out more vividly a meaning the author always had in mind. In this account, revision involves the perfection of an original, singular intention. But this understanding of revision has not satisfied authors who reject a notion of identity as something given and unchanging and who might be inclined to see revision as a process that makes something new. As W. B. Yeats, a compulsive reviser, wrote in 1908: "The friends that have it I do wrong / Whenever I remake a song, / Should know what issue is at stake: / It is myself that I remake." And people besides the poet can have a hand in the process of revision. As the "Publishing History, Censorship" section of our literary terms appendix outlines, many individuals participate in the labor that takes texts from the forms in which authors produce them to the forms in which they are presented to readers; in a similar if more limited way, revision, too, involves a range of collaborators, both institutional and personal, witting and unwitting. A revised text might, for instance, incorporate changes introduced by the amanuensis who recopies the draft so as to prepare a fair copy for the printer (a role women such as Dorothy Wordsworth and Mary Shelley often played in the nineteenth century—on occasion, Mary Shelley seems to have had primary responsibility for Lord Byron's punctuation). The second thoughts at stake in a revision might reflect the input of trusted advisors and editors, the poet's attempt to anticipate the response of hostile critics or readers, or (as was often the case with the revisions in which William Wordsworth and Yeats engaged) the poet's efforts to bring the political and aesthetic values of the poem into line with the changing times.

Although some earlier manuscripts have survived, it was not until the nineteenth century, when a relatively new conception of authorship as a career gained widespread acceptance, that poets' working drafts began to be preserved with any regularity. The examples from major poets that are transcribed here represent various stages in the composition of a poem, and a variety of procedures by individual poets. The selections from William Blake, Byron, Percy Shelley, John Keats, and Elizabeth Barrett Browning are drafts that were written, emended, crossed out, and rewritten in the heat of first invention; while poems by William Wordsworth, Gerard Manley Hopkins, and Yeats are shown in successive stages of revision over an extended period of time. Shelley's "O World, O Life, O Time" originated in a few key nouns, together with an abstract rhythmic pattern that was only later fleshed out with words. Still other poems—Alfred, Lord Tennyson's "The Lady of Shalott"; Yeats's "The Sorrow of Love"—were subjected to radical revision long after the initial versions had been committed to print. In these examples we look on as poets (no matter how rapidly they achieve a result they are willing to let stand) carry on their inevitably tentative efforts to meet the multiple requirements of meaning, syntax, meter, sound pattern, and the constraints imposed by a chosen stanza.

Our transcriptions from the poets' drafts attempt to reproduce, as accurately as the change from script to print will allow, the appearance of the original manuscript page.

A1

A poet's first attempt at a line or phrase is reproduced in larger type, the emendations in smaller type. The line numbers in the headings that identify an excerpt are those of the final form of the complete poem, as reprinted in this anthology, above.

SELECTED BIBLIOGRAPHY

Autograph Poetry in the English Language, 2 vols., 1973, compiled by P. J. Croft, reproduces and transcribes one or more pages of manuscript in the poet's own hand, from the fourteenth century to the late twentieth century. Volume 1 includes William Blake and Robert Burns; volume 2 includes many of the other poets represented in this volume of *The Norton Anthology of English Literature*, from William Wordsworth to Dylan Thomas. Books that discuss the process of composition and revision, with examples from the manuscripts and printed versions of poems, are Charles D. Abbott, ed., *Poets at Work*, 1948; Phyllis Bartlett, *Poems in Process*, 1951; A. F. Scott, *The Poet's Craft*, 1957; George Bornstein, *Poetic Remaking: The Art of Browning, Yeats, and Pound*, 1988; and Robert Brinkley and Keith Hanley, eds., *Romantic Revisions*, 1992. In *Word for Word: A Study of Authors' Alterations*, 1965, Wallace Hildick analyzes the composition of prose fiction as well as poems. Byron's "Don Juan," ed. T. G. Steffan and W. W. Pratt, 4 vols., 1957, transcribes the manuscript drafts; the Cornell Wordsworth, in process, reproduces and discusses various versions of Wordsworth's poems from the first manuscript drafts to the final publication in his lifetime, and the Cornell Yeats, also in process, does the same for Yeats. The *Bodleian Shelley Manuscripts,* under the general editorship of Donald Reiman, reproduces facsimiles of Percy Shelley's manuscripts. For facsimiles and transcripts of Keats's poems, see *John Keats: Poetry Manuscripts at Harvard*, ed. Jack Stillinger, 1990. Jon Stallworthy, *Between the Lines: Yeats's Poetry in the Making*, 1963, reproduces and analyzes the sequential drafts of a number of Yeats's major poems. Valerie Eliot has edited T. S. Eliot's *The Waste Land: A Facsimile and Transcript of the Original Drafts Including the Annotations of Ezra Pound*, 1971, while Dame Helen Gardner has transcribed and analyzed the manuscript drafts of Eliot's *Four Quartets* in *The Composition of Four Quartets*, 1978.

WILLIAM BLAKE
The Tyger[1]

[*First Draft*]

The Tyger

1
Tyger Tyger burning bright
In the forests of the night
What immortal hand or eye
~~Dare~~ ~~Could frame~~ thy fearful symmetry

2
Burnt in
~~In what distant~~ deeps or skies
~~The cruel Burnt the~~ fire of thine eyes
On what wings dare he aspire
What the hand dare sieze the fire

3
And what shoulder & what art
Could twist the sinews of thy heart
And when thy heart began to beat
What dread hand & what dread feet

---

1. These drafts have been taken from a notebook used by William Blake, called the Rossetti MS because it was once owned by Dante Gabriel Rossetti, the Victorian poet and painter; David V. Erdman's edition of *The Notebook of William Blake* (1973) contains a photographic facsimile. The stanza and line numbers were written by Blake in the manuscript.

~~Could fetch it from the furnace deep~~
~~And in thy horrid ribs dare steep~~
~~In the well of sanguine woe~~
~~In what clay & what mould~~
~~Were thy eyes of fury rolld~~

4   ~~Where~~
    ~~What~~ the hammer ~~where~~ the chain
    In what furnace was thy brain

                    dread grasp
    What the anvil what ~~the arm arm grasp Clasp~~
 Dare ~~Could~~ its deadly terrors ~~clasp grasp~~ clasp

6   Tyger Tyger burning bright
    In the forests of the night
    What immortal hand & eye
       frame
    Dare ~~form~~ thy fearful symmetry

[Trial Stanzas]

Burnt in distant deeps or skies
The cruel fire of thine eye,
Could heart descend or wings aspire
What the hand dare sieze the fire

           dare he ~~smile laugh~~
5 ~~3~~ And ~~did he laugh~~ his work to see
         ankle
  ~~What the shoulder what the knee~~
  Dare
4 ~~Did~~ he who made the lamb make thee
1 When the stars threw down their spears
2 And waterd heaven with their tears

[Second Full Draft]

Tyger Tyger burning bright
In the forests of the night
What Immortal hand & eye
Dare frame thy fearful symmetry

And what shoulder & what art
Could twist the sinews of thy heart
And when thy heart began to beat
What dread hand & what dread feet

When the stars threw down their spears
And waterd heaven with their tears
Did he smile his work to see
Did he who made the lamb make thee

Tyger Tyger burning bright
In the forests of the night
What immortal hand & eye
Dare frame thy fearful symmetry

[Final Version, 1794]²

The Tyger

Tyger Tyger, burning bright,
In the forests of the night;
What immortal hand or eye,
Could frame thy fearful symmetry?

In what distant deeps or skies
Burnt the fire of thine eyes!
On what wings dare he aspire?
What the hand, dare sieze the fire?

And what shoulder, & what art,
Could twist the sinews of thy heart?
And when thy heart began to beat,
What dread hand? & what dread feet?

What the hammer? what the chain,
In what furnace was thy brain?
What the anvil? what dread grasp,
Dare its deadly terrors clasp?

When the stars threw down their spears
And water'd heaven with their tears:
Did he smile his work to see?
Did he who made the Lamb make thee?

Tyger, Tyger burning bright,
In the forests of the night:
What immortal hand or eye,
Dare frame thy fearful symmetry?

WILLIAM WORDSWORTH
She dwelt among the untrodden ways

[Version in a Letter to Coleridge,
December 1798 or January 1799]¹

My hope was one, from cities far
    Nursed on a lonesome heath:
Her lips were red as roses are,
    Her hair a woodbine wreath.

2. As published in *Songs of Experience*.
1. Printed in Ernest de Selincourt's *Early Letters of William and Dorothy Wordsworth* (1935). By deleting two stanzas, and making a few verbal changes, Wordsworth achieved the terse published form of his great dirge.

She lived among the untrodden ways
    Beside the springs of Dove,
A maid whom there were none to praise,
    And very few to love;

A violet by a mossy stone
    Half-hidden from the eye!
Fair as a star when only one
    Is shining in the sky!

And she was graceful as the broom
    That flowers by Carron's side;[2]
But slow distemper checked her bloom,
    And on the Heath she died.

Long time before her head lay low
    Dead to the world was she:
But now she's in her grave, and Oh!
    The difference to me!

[*Final Version, 1800*][3]

Song

She dwelt among th' untrodden ways
    Beside the springs of Dove,
A Maid whom there were none to praise
    And very few to love.

A Violet by a mossy stone
    Half-hidden from the Eye!
—Fair, as a star when only one
    Is shining in the sky!

She *liv'd* unknown, and few could know
    When Lucy ceas'd to be;
But she is in her Grave, and Oh!
    The difference to me.

LORD BYRON
From Don Juan[1]

[*First Draft: Canto 3, Stanza 9*]

~~Life is a play and men.~~
All tragedies are finished by a death,
All Comedies are ended by a marriage,

---

2. The Carron is a river in northwestern Scotland. "Broom" (preceding line) is a shrub with long slender branches and yellow flowers.
3. As published in the second edition of *Lyrical Ballads*.

1. Reproduced from transcripts made of Byron's manuscripts in T. G. Steffan and W. W. Pratt, *Byron's "Don Juan"* (1957). The stanzas were published by Byron in their emended form.

~~For Life can go no further~~
~~These two form the last gasp of Passion's breath~~
~~All further is a blank—I won't disparage~~
~~That holy state—but certainly beneath~~
~~The Sun—of human things—~~
~~These two are levellers, and human breath~~
~~So~~ ~~These point the epigram of human breath,~~
~~Or any~~ The future states of both are left to faith,
~~Though Life and love I like not to disparage~~
~~The~~ For authors ~~think~~ description might disparage

fear
~~Tis strange that poets never try to wreathe~~ [sic?]
~~With oith~~ ~~Tis strange that poets of the Catholic faith~~
~~Neer go beyond—and—but seem to dread miscarriage~~
~~So dramas close with death or settlement for life~~
~~Veiling~~ ~~Leaving the future states of Love and Life~~
~~The paradise beyond like that of life—~~
~~And neer describing either—~~
~~To more conjecture of a devil and or wife~~
~~And don't say much of paradise or wife~~

The worlds to come of both—~~&~~ or fall beneath,
And ~~all~~ ~~both the worlds would blame them for miscarriage~~
And then both worlds would punish their miscarriage—
~~So leaving both with priest & prayerbook ready~~
So leaving ~~Clerg both~~ each their Priest and prayerbook ready,
They say no more of death or of the Lady.

[*First Draft: Canto 14, Stanza 95*]

quote   seldom
Alas! ~~I speak by~~ Experience—~~never~~ yet
~~I had a paramour—and I've had many—~~
               ~~some small—~~
~~To whom I did not cause a deep~~ regret—
~~Whom I had not some reason to~~ regret
~~For Whom—I did not feel myself~~ a Zany—
Alas! by all experience, seldom yet
(I merely quote what I have heard from many)
Had lovers not some reason to regret
The passion which made Solomon a Zany.
~~I also had a wife—~~not to forget—
I've also seen some wives—not to forget—
The marriage state—the best or worst of any—
       were   paragons
Who ~~was~~ the very ~~paragon~~ of wives,
Yet made the misery of ~~both our~~ lives.
              ~~many—~~
              ~~several—~~
            ~~of~~ at least two

PERCY BYSSHE SHELLEY

The three stages of this poem labeled "First Draft" are scattered through one of Shelley's notebooks, now in the Huntington Library, San Marino, California; these drafts have been transcribed and analyzed by Bennett Weaver, "Shelley Works Out the Rhythm of *A Lament*," *PMLA* 47 (1932): 570–76. They show Shelley working with fragmentary words and phrases, and simultaneously with a wordless pattern of pulses that marked out the meter of the single lines and the shape of the lyric stanzas. Shelley left this draft unfinished.

Apparently at some later time, Shelley returned to the poem and wrote what is here called the "Second Draft"; from this he then made, on a second page, a revised fair copy that provided the text that Mary Shelley published in 1824, after the poet's death. These two manuscript pages are now in the Bodleian Library, Oxford; the first page is photographically reproduced and discussed by John Carter and John Sparrow, "Shelley, Swinburne, and Housman," *Times Literary Supplement*, November 21, 1968, pp. 1318–19.

O World, O Life, O Time

[*First Draft, Stage 1*]

Ah time, oh night, oh day
~~Ni nal ni na, na ni~~
~~Ni na ni na, ni na~~
Oh life O death, O time
   Time a di
~~Never Time~~
Ah time, a time O-time
  ~~Time!~~

[*First Draft, Stage 2*]

Oh time, oh night oh day
~~O day oh night, alas~~
  ~~O~~ Death time night ~~oh~~
Oh, Time
Oh time o night oh day

[*First Draft, Stage 3*]

Na na, na na ná na
Nă nă na na na—nă nă
  Nă nă nă nă nă nā
Na na nă nă nâ ă na

Na na na—nă nă—na na
  Na na na na—na na na na na
Na na na na na.
  Na na
Na na na na na

Na na
Na na na na na ˇ na!

Oh time, oh night, o day
       alas
O day ~~serenest~~, o day
O day alas the day
That thou shouldst sleep when we awake to say

O time time—o death—o day
      for
O day, o death life is far from thee
O thou wert never free
For death is now with thee
~~And life is far from~~
O death, o day for life is far from thee

[*Second Draft*]¹   *I am despair*

Out of the day & night
A joy has taken flight
Fresh spring & summer   & winter hoar
Fill my faint heart with grief, but with
                delight
No more—o never more!

~~Wo~~
   O World, o life, o time
  ~~Will ye~~ On whose last steps I climb
Trembling at those which I have trod² before
When will return the glory of yr prime
    No more   Oh never more

Out of the day & night
A joy has taken flight—
        autumn
~~From~~ Green spring, & ~~summer gra~~³ & winter hoar

[FAIR COPY]

O World o Life o Time
On whose last steps I climb
Trembling at that where I had stood before
When will return the glory of yr prime?
    No more, o never more

1. Shelley apparently wrote the first stanza of this draft low down on the page, and ran out of space after crowding in the third line of the second stanza; he then, in a lighter ink, wrote a revised form of the whole of the second stanza at the top of the page. In this revision he left a space after "summer" in line 3, indicating that he planned an insertion that would fill out the four-foot meter of this line, and so make it match the five feet in the corresponding line of the first stanza.

In the upper right-hand corner of this manuscript page, Shelley wrote "I am despair"—seemingly to express his bleak mood at the time he wrote the poem.

For this draft and information, and for the transcript of the fair copy that follows, the editors are indebted to Donald H. Reiman.

2. Shelley at first wrote "trod," then overwrote that with "stood." In the following line, Shelley at first wrote "yr," then overwrote "thy."

3. Not clearly legible; it is either "gra" or "gre." A difference in the ink from the rest of the line indicates that Shelley, having left a blank space, later started to fill it in, but thought better of it and crossed out the fragmentary insertion.

2
Out of the day & night
A joy has taken flight
Fresh spring & summer   ⁴ & winter hoar
Move my faint heart with grief but with delight
No more, o, never more

JOHN KEATS
From The Eve of St. Agnes[1]

[*Stanza 26*]

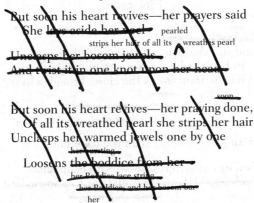

But soon his heart revives—her prayers said
She lays aside her veil   pearled
            strips her hair of all its   wreathes pearl
Unclasps her bosom jewels
And twist it in one knot upon her head

But soon his heart revives—her praying done,   soon
Of all its wreathed pearl she strips her hair
Unclasps her warmed jewels one by one
            her hunting
Loosens the boddice from her
            her Boddice lace string
            her Boddice and her bosom bar
            her

[HERE KEATS BEGINS A NEW SHEET]

Loosens her fragrant boddice and doth bare
Her

26

Anon
But soon his heart revives—her praying done,
            frees:
Of all its wreathe'd pearl her hair she strips
Unclasps her warmed jewels one by one
            by degrees

---

4. This fair copy of the second draft retains, and even enlarges, the blank space, indicating that Shelley still hasn't made up his mind what to insert after the word "summer." We may speculate, by reference to the fragmentary version of this stanza in the second draft, that he had in mind as possibilities either an adjective, "gray" or "green," or else the noun "autumn." Mary Shelley closed up this space when she published the poem in 1824, with the result that editors, following her version, have until very recently printed this line as though Shelley had intended it to be one metric foot shorter than the corresponding line of stanza 1.

1. Transcribed from Keats's first draft of all but the first seven stanzas of *The Eve of St. Agnes*; the manuscript is now in the Houghton Library, Harvard University. Keats's published version of the poem contains additional changes in wording. That published version also incorporates revisions introduced by other hands. Because Keats's friend Richard Woodhouse and his publisher, John Taylor, took alarm at the suggestion, made more explicit in one of the stanzas Keats added to his original draft, that the pleasure of which Madeline would dream would include sexual pleasure particularly, they worked over Woodhouse's transcripts of the poem and produced a less risqué text that combined Keats's draft and his revised fair copy along with, as Jack Stillinger has conjectured, their own suggestions.

For a photographic reproduction of the page of the holograph manuscript of *The Eve of St. Agnes* containing the poem's stanza 30, see the color insert.

Loosens her fragrant boddice: ~~and down slips~~ *to her knees*
Her sweet attire ~~falls light creeps down by~~
          creeps rusteling to her knees
          Mermaid   *in sea weed*
Half hidden like ~~a Syren of the Sea~~
~~And more melodious~~
                    dreaming
She stands awhile in ∧ thought; and sees
                              on
In fancy fair Saint Agnes ~~in~~ her bed
But dares not look behind or all the charm is ~~ȿ~~ dead

[*Stanza 30*]

But
~~And still she slept~~:
And still she slept an azure-lidded sleep
  In blanched linen, smooth and lavender'd
  While he from frorth the closet brough a heap
          ~~fruits~~
  Of candied ~~sweets sweets, with~~
          apple Quince and plumb and gourd
                              creamed
  With jellies soother than the ~~dairy~~ curd
              tinct
  And lucent syrups ~~smooth~~ with ciannamon
~~And sugar'd dates from that oer Euphrates ford~~
          ~~in Brigantine transferd~~
  Manna and daites in ~~Bragtine transferd~~
              ~~and manna wild transferd~~
~~And Manna wild and Bragantine~~
                    sugar'd dates transferred
~~In Brigantine from Fez~~
  From fez—and spiced danties every one
      ~~glutted~~
  From ~~wealthy~~ Samarchand to cedard lebanon
      silken

argosy

To Autumn[2]

Season of Mists and mellow fruitfulness
  Close bosom friend of the naturring sun;
Conspiring with him how to load and bless
  The Vines with fruit that round the thatch eves run
  To bend with apples the moss'd Cottage trees
    And fill all furuits with sweeness to the core
      To swell the gourd, and plump the hazle shells
  With a white kernel; to set budding more
  And still more later flowers for the bees
    Until they think wam days with never cease
      For Summer has o'erbrimm'd their clammy cells—

2. From an untitled manuscript—apparently Keats's first draft of the poem—in the Houghton Library, Harvard University. The many pen-slips and errors in spelling indicate that Keats wrote rapidly, in a state of creative excitement. Keats made a few further changes before publishing the poem in the form included in the selections above.

oft amid thy stores?
Who hath not seen thee? ~~for thy haunts are many~~

abroad
Sometimes whoever seeks ~~for thee~~ may find
Thee sitting careless on a granary floorr
Thy hair soft lifted by the winnowing wind

~~While bright the Sun slants through the~~ barn;—
~~or on a half reap'd furrow sound asleep~~
~~Of sound asleep in a half reaped field~~
Dos'd with ~~ead~~ poppies; while thy reaping hook
~~Spares form some slumbrous~~
~~minutes while warm slumpers creep.~~

Or on a half reap'd furrow sound asleep
Dos'd with the fume of poppies, while thy hook
Spares the next swath and all its twined flowers
~~Spares for some slumbrous minutes the next swath,~~
And sometimes like a gleans thost dost keep
Steady thy laden head across the brook;
Or by a Cyder-press with patent look
Thou watchest the last oozing hours by hours

Where are the songs of Sping? Aye where are they?
Think not of them thou hast thy music too—

barred   bloom
While ~~a gold~~ clouds ~~gilds~~ the soft-dying day
And   with
~~And~~ Touching ~~the~~ the stibble plains ^ rosy hue—
Then in a waiful quire the small gnats mourn
Among the river sallows, ~~on the~~ borne afots
Or sinking as the light wind lives and dies;
And full grown Lambs loud bleat from hilly bourn,
Hedge crickets sing, and now again full soft
The Redbreast whistles from a garden croft:
~~And now flock still~~
And Gather'd Swallows twiter in the Skies—

ALFRED, LORD TENNYSON

From The Lady of Shalott[1]

[*Version of 1832*]

PART THE FIRST.

On either side the river lie
Long fields of barley and of rye,
That clothe the wold, and meet the sky.
And thro' the field the road runs by

1. First published in Tennyson's *Poems* of 1832 (dated 1833 on the title page). The volume was severely criticized by some reviewers; partly in response to this criticism, Tennyson radically revised a number of the poems, including "The Lady of Shalott," before reprinting them in his *Poems* (1842).

Parts 1 and 4 are reproduced here in the version of 1832. The final form of the poem reprinted in the selections from Tennyson, above, differs from the revised version that Tennyson published in 1842 only in line 157, which in 1842 read "A corse between the houses high"; Tennyson changed the line to "Dead-pale between the houses high" in 1855.

To manytowered Camelot.

The yellowleavèd waterlily,
The greensheathèd daffodilly,
Tremble in the water chilly,
Round about Shallot.

Willows whiten, aspens shiver,
The sunbeam-showers break and quiver
In the stream that runneth ever
By the island in the river,
Flowing down to Camelot.
Four gray walls and four gray towers
Overlook a space of flowers,
And the silent isle imbowers
The Lady of Shallot.

Underneath the bearded barley,
The reaper, reaping late and early,
Hears her ever chanting cheerly,
Like an angel, singing clearly,
O'er the stream of Camelot.
Piling the sheaves in furrows airy,
Beneath the moon, the reaper weary
Listening whispers, " 'tis the fairy
Lady of Shalott."

The little isle is all inrailed
With a rose-fence, and overtrailed
With roses: by the marge unhailed
The shallop flitteth silkensailed,
Skimming down to Camelot.
A pearlgarland winds her head:
She leaneth on a velvet bed,
Full royally apparellèd,
The Lady of Shalott.

*   *   *

PART THE FOURTH.

In the stormy eastwind straining
The pale-yellow woods were waning,
The broad stream in his banks complaining,
Heavily the low sky raining
Over towered Camelot:
Outside the isle a shallow boat
Beneath a willow lay afloat,
Below the carven stern she wrote,
THE LADY OF SHALOTT.

A cloudwhite crown of pearl she dight.
All raimented in snowy white
That loosely flew, (her zone in sight,
Clasped with one blinding diamond bright,)

Her wide eyes fixed on Camelot,
Though the squally eastwind keenly
Blew, with folded arms serenely
By the water stood the queenly
     Lady of Shalott.

With a steady, stony glance—
Like some bold seer in a trance,
Beholding all his own mischance,
Mute, with a glassy countenance—
     She looked down to Camelot.
It was the closing of the day,
She loosed the chain, and down she lay,
The broad stream bore her far away,
     The Lady of Shalott.

As when to sailors while they roam,
By creeks and outfalls far from home,
Rising and dropping with the foam,
From dying swans wild warblings come,
     Blown shoreward; so to Camelot
Still as the boathead wound along
The willowy hills and fields among,
They heard her chanting her deathsong,
     The Lady of Shalott.

A longdrawn carol, mournful, holy,
She chanted loudly, chanted lowly,
Till her eyes were darkened wholly,
And her smooth face sharpened slowly
     Turned to towered Camelot:
For ere she reached upon the tide
The first house by the waterside,
Singing in her song she died,
     The Lady of Shalott.

Under tower and balcony,
By gardenwall and gallery,
A pale, pale corpse she floated by,
Deadcold, between the houses high.
     Dead into towered Camelot.
Knight and burgher, lord and dame,
To the plankèd wharfage came:
Below the stern they read her name,
     "The Lady of Shalott."

They crossed themselves, their stars they blest,
Knight, ministrel, abbot, squire and guest.
There lay a parchment on her breast,
That puzzled more than all the rest,
     The wellfed wits at Camelot.
"The web was woven curiously

> *The charm is broken utterly,*
> *Draw near and fear not—this is I,*
> *The Lady of Shalott."*

From Tithonus[2]

[Lines 1–10]

[TRINITY COLLEGE MANUSCRIPT]

Ay me! Ay me! the woods decay & fall

~~The stars blaze out & never rise again.~~

                    the

The vapours weep their substance to ground

Man comes & tills the earth & lies beneath

And after many summers dies the ~~rose~~ swan

Me only fatal immortality

Consumes: I wither slowly in thine arms:

Here at the quiet limit of the world

           e yet

A white-haired shadow roaming like a dream

The ever-silent spaces of the East

Far-folded mists & gleaming halls of morn.

[HEATH MANUSCRIPT]

Tithon

Ay me! ay me! the woods decay and fall,
The vapours weep their substance to the ground,
Man comes and tills the earth and lies beneath,
And after many summers dies the rose.
Me only fatal immortality
Consumes: I wither slowly in thine arms,
Here at the quiet limit of the world,
A white-haired shadow roaming like a dream
The ever-silent spaces of the East,
Far-folded mists, and gleaming halls of morn.

[AS PRINTED IN 1864]

Tithonus

The woods decay, the woods decay and fall,
The vapours weep their burthen to the ground,
Man comes and tills the field and lies beneath,
And after many a summer dies the swan.

2. Three manuscript drafts of "Tithonus" are extant. Two are in Tennyson's Notebooks Nos. 20 and 21, at Trinity College, Cambridge; a third one, written 1833, is in the Commonplace Book compiled by Tennyson's friend J. M. Heath, which is in the Fitzwilliam Museum at Cambridge University. According to Tennyson's editor, Christopher Ricks, the Heath version is later than those in the Trinity Manuscripts. The transcriptions here of Tennyson's opening lines are from the first draft (Trinity College manuscript, Notebook 20), and from the Heath manuscript, where the poem is titled "Tithon." These are followed by the final version of "Tithonus" Tennyson published in 1864. As late as in the edition of 1860, the opening words had remained "Ay me! ay me!" and "field" (line 3) had remained "earth."

Me only cruel immortality
Consumes: I wither slowly in thine arms,
Here at the quiet limit of the world,
A white-haired shadow roaming like a dream
The ever-silent spaces of the East,
Far-folded mists, and gleaming halls of morn.

ELIZABETH BARRETT BROWNING

From The Runaway Slave at Pilgrim's Point[1]

[*From the British Library manuscript, 1846*]

     Why
~~And~~ in that single glance I had
Of my child's face . . I tell you all . .
I saw a look that made me mad—!
The master's look, that used to fall
On my soul like his lash . . or worse:
And so, to save it from my curse
I twisted it round in my shawl.   Does this <u>sound</u> like a slave's article of clothing?[2]

              trembled
And he moaned and ~~struggled~~ from foot to head—
  shivered
He ~~trembled~~ from head to foot—
Till after a time he lay instead
Too suddenly still and mute . .
And I felt, beside, a creeping cold—
I dared to lift up just a fold,
As in lifting a leaf of the mango-fruit.

But <u>my</u> fruit . . . ha, ha—there, had been . .
(I laugh to think on't at this hour . .)
Your fine white angels, (who have seen
God's secrets nearest to His power)
And plucked my fruit to make them wine,
And sucked the soul of that child of mine,
             the soul of
As the hummingbird sucks ∧ the flower.

Ha, ha, for the trick of the angels white!
They freed the white child's spirit so,
I said not a word, but day and night

1. One part of Barrett Browning's manuscript draft of her abolitionist poem is in the British Library in London; another, fittingly, given the poem's initial publication by a Boston abolitionist society, is on the other side of the Atlantic, in the Baylor University's Armstrong Library; a third is in the hands of a private collector. We give six stanzas from the British Library manuscript, along with, first, their counterparts in the initial printed version of the poem in *The Liberty Bell for 1848* (published in December 1847 for the National Anti-Slavery Bazaar), and, then, their counterparts in Barrett Browning's *Poems* of 1850. Barrett Browning added a stanza to the poem after 1847 (the seventh stanza of the 1850 version); stanza 20 in the *Liberty Bell* version corresponds accordingly to stanza 21 in *Poems* and so forth. For discussion of Barrett Browning's revision of the *Liberty Bell* version, see Andrew M. Stauffer, "Elizabeth Barrett Browning's (Re)Vision of Slavery," in *English Language Notes* 34 (1997): 29–48.
2. Written sideways in the right-hand margin of the manuscript, in Robert Browning's handwriting.

I carried the body to and fro—
And it lay on my heart like a stone . . as chill.
The sun may shine out as much as he will.

I am cold, though it happened a ~~year~~ ^{month} ago.

From the white man's house, and the black man's hut
I carried the little body on—

The forest ~~trees~~ ^{'s arms} did around us shut

And silence through the leaves did run— ^{trees}
They asked no questions as I went:

~~The trees were~~ ^{They stood} too high, for astonishment;
They could see God rise on His throne.

My little body, kerchiefed fast,
I bore it on through the forest . . on:
And, when I felt it tired at last,
I scooped a hole beneath the moon—
Through the forest-tops the angels far
With a white fine finger from every star,

Did point ∧ at what was done. ^{and mock}

[*First printed version, from* The Liberty Bell *for* 1848]

XX.

Even in that single glance I had
   Of my child's face,—I tell you all,—
I saw a look that made me mad,—
   The master's look, that used to fall
On my soul like this lash, or worse,—
Therefore, to save it from my curse,
   I twisted it round in my shawl.

XXI.

And he moaned and trembled from foot to head,—
   He shivered from head to foot,—
Till, after a time, he lay, instead,
   Too suddenly still and mute;
And I felt, beside, a creeping cold,—
I dared to lift up just a fold,
   As in lifting a leaf of the mango fruit.

XXII.

But MY fruit! ha, ha!—there had been
   (I laugh to think on 't at this hour!)
Your fine white angels,—who have seen
   God's secret nearest to His power,—
And gathered my fruit to make them wine,

And sucked the soul of that child of mine,
    As the humming-bird sucks the soul of the flower.

XXIII.

Ha, ha! for the trick of the angels white!
    They freed the white child's spirit so;
I said not a word, but day and night
    I carried the body to and fro;
And it lay on my heart like a stone—as chill;
The sun may shine out as much as he will,—
    I am cold, though it happened a month ago.

XXIV.

From the white man's house and the black man's hut
    I carried the little body on;
The forest's arms did around us shut,
    And silence through the trees did run!
They asked no questions as I went,—
They stood too high for astonishment,—
    They could see God rise on his throne.

XXV.

My little body, kerchiefed fast,
    I bore it on through the forest—on—
And when I felt it was tired at last,
    I scooped a hole beneath the moon.
Through the forest-tops the angels far,
With a white fine finger in every star
    Did point and mock at what was done.

[From Poems, 1850]

XXI.

Why, in that single glance I had
    Of my child's face, . . . I tell you all,
I saw a look that made me mad!
    The *master's* look, that used to fall
On my soul like his lash . . . or worse!
And so, to save it from my curse,
    I twisted it round in my shawl.

XXII.

And he moaned and trembled from foot to head,
    He shivered from head to foot;
Till after a time, he lay instead
    Too suddenly still and mute.
I felt, beside, a stiffening cold:
I dared to lift up just a fold,
    As in lifting a leaf of the mango-fruit.

XXIII.

But *my* fruit . . . ha, ha!—there, had been
   (I laugh to think on't at this hour!)
Your fine white angels (who have seen
   Nearest the secret of God's power)
And plucked my fruit to make them wine,
And sucked the soul of that child of mine
   As the humming-bird sucks the soul of the flower.

XXIV.

Ha, ha, the trick of the angels white!
   They freed the white child's spirit so.
I said not a word, but day and night
   I carried the body to and fro,
And it lay on my heart like a stone, as chill.
—The sun may shine out as much as he will:
   I am cold, though it happened a month ago.

XXV.

From the white man's house, and the black man's hut,
   I carried the little body on;
The forest's arms did round us shut,
   And silence through the trees did run:
They asked no question as I went,
They stood too high for astonishment,
   They could see God sit on His throne.

XXVI.

My little body, kerchiefed fast,
   I bore it on through the forest, on;
And when I felt it was tired at last,
   I scooped a hole beneath the moon:
Through the forest-tops the angels far,
With a white sharp finger from every star,
   Did point and mock at what was done.

GERARD MANLEY HOPKINS
Thou art indeed just, Lord[1]

*Justus quidem tu es, Domine, si disputem tecum; verumtamen
justa loquar ad te: quare via impiorum prosperatur?* etc.
—Jer. xii 1.

1. From a manuscript in the Bodleian Library, Oxford University; it is a clean copy, made after earlier drafts, which Hopkins goes on to revise further. Differences in the ink show that the emendation "lacèd they are" (line 10) was made during the first writing, but that the other verbal changes were made later. The interlinear markings are Hopkins's metrical indicators; he explains their sig-

nificance in the "Author's Preface," included in *Poems of Gerard Manley Hopkins* (1970), ed. W. H. Gardner and N. H. MacKenzie.
   The epigraph is from the Vulgate translation of Jeremiah 12.1; a literal translation of the Latin is "Thou art indeed just, Lord, [even] if I plead with Thee; nevertheless I will speak what is just to Thee: Why does the way of the wicked prosper? etc."

March 17 1889

Lord, if I
Thou art indeed just, ~~were I to~~ contend
       sir,   plead
With thee; but, ~~Lord~~, so what I ~~speak~~ is just.

Why do sinners' ways prosper? and why must

Disappointment all I endeavour end?
Wert thou my enemy, O thou my friend,
How wouldst thou worse, I wonder, than thou dost
            O the sots and   of
Defeat, thwart me? ~~Ah! sots, revellers,~~ thralls to lust
Do in   that
~~In~~ spare hours ~~do~~ more thrive than I ~~who~~ spend,
        great   See,
Sir, ~~my~~ life on thy cause. ~~Look,~~ banks and brakes
Now, leavèd   lacèd they are
~~Leavèd~~ how thick! ~~broidered all~~ again
           look
With fretty chervil, ~~now,~~ and fresh winds shakes
Them; birds build—but not I build; no, but strain,
Time's eunuch, and not breed one work that wakes.
Mine, O   send my
~~Then send,~~ thou lord of life, ~~these~~ roots ~~their~~ rain.

WILLIAM BUTLER YEATS

Yeats usually composed very slowly and with painful effort. He tells us in his autobiography that "five or six lines in two or three laborious hours were a day's work, and I longed for somebody to interrupt me." His manuscripts show the slow evolution of his best poems, which sometimes began with a prose sketch, were then versified, and underwent numerous revisions. In many instances, even after the poems had been published, Yeats continued to revise them, sometimes drastically, in later printings.

The Sorrow of Love[1]

[*Manuscript, 1891*][2]

The quarrel of the sparrows in the eaves,
The full round moon and the star-laden sky,
The song of the ever-singing leaves,
Had hushed away earth's old and weary cry.

---

1. Originally composed in Yeats's Pre-Raphaelite mode of the early 1890s, "The Sorrow of Love" was one of his most popular poems. Nonetheless, some thirty years after publication, Yeats rewrote the lyric in accordance with modernism's emphasis on precision and colloquial vigor.

2. Manuscript version composed in October 1891, as transcribed by Jon Stallworthy, *Between the Lines: Yeats's Poetry in the Making* (Oxford University Press, 1963), pp. 47–48.

And then you came with those red mournful lips,
And with you came the whole of the world's tears,
And all the sorrows of her labouring ships,
And all the burden of her million years.

And now the angry sparrows in the eaves,
The withered moon, the white stars in the sky,
The wearisome loud chanting of the leaves,
Are shaken with earth's old and weary cry.

[First Printed Version, 1892][3]

The quarrel of the sparrows in the eaves,
    The full round moon and the star-laden sky,
And the loud song of the ever-singing leaves
    Had hid away earth's old and weary cry.

And then you came with those red mournful lips,
    And with you came the whole of the world's tears,
And all the sorrows of her labouring ships,
    And all burden of her myriad years.

And now the sparrows warring in the eaves,
    The crumbling moon, the white stars in the sky,
And the loud chanting of the unquiet leaves,
    Are shaken with earth's old and weary cry.

[Final Printed Version, 1925][4]

The brawling of a sparrow in the eaves,
    The brilliant moon and all the milky sky,
And all that famous harmony of leaves,
    Had blotted out man's image and his cry.

A girl arose that had red mournful lips
And seemed the greatness of the world in tears,
Doomed like Odysseus and the labouring ships
And proud as Priam murdered with his peers;

---

3. From Yeats's *The Countess Kathleen and Various Legends and Lyrics* (1892). In a corrected page proof for this printing, now in the Garvan Collection of the Yale University Library, lines 7–8 originally read "And all the sorrows of his labouring ships, / And all the burden of his married years." Also, in lines 4 and 12, the adjective was "bitter" instead of "weary." In his *Poems* (1895), Yeats inserted the missing "the" in line 8 and changed "sorrows" (line 7) to "trouble"; "burden" (line 8) to "trouble"; and "crumbling moon" (line 10) to "curd-pale moon."
4. From *Early Poems and Stories* (1925). Yeats wrote in his *Autobiographies* (New York, 1999),

p. 321, that "in later years" he had "learnt that occasional prosaic words gave the impression of an active man speaking," so that "certain words must be dull and numb. Here and there in correcting my early poems I have introduced such numbness and dullness, turned, for instance, 'the curd-pale moon' into the 'brilliant moon', that all might seem, as it were, remembered with indifference, except some one vivid image." Yeats, however, did not recall his emendations accurately. He had in 1925 altered "the full round moon" (line 2) to "the brilliant moon," and "the curd-pale moon" (line 10, version of 1895) to "a climbing moon."

Arose, and on the instant clamorous eaves,
A climbing moon upon an empty sky,
And all that lamentation of the leaves,
Could but compose man's image and his cry.

Leda and the Swan[5]

[First Version]

Annunciation

Now can the swooping Godhead have his will
Yet hovers, though her helpless thighs are pressed
By the webbed toes; and that all powerful bill
Has suddenly bowed her face upon his breast.
How can those terrified vague fingers push
The feathered glory from her loosening thighs?
All the stretched body's laid on that white rush

         strange
And feels the ~~strong~~ heart beating where it lies
A shudder in the loins engenders there
The broken wall, the burning roof and tower
And Agamemnon dead. . . .
               Being so caught up
Did nothing pass before her in the air?
Did she put on his knowledge with his power
Before the indifferent beak could let her drop
           Sept 18 1923

      swooping
The ~~trembl~~ godhead is half hovering still,
    climbs
Yet ~~climbs~~ upon her trembling body pressed
    webbed
By the toes; & ~~through~~ that all powerful bill
       ~~through~~ bowed
Has suddenly ~~bowed~~ her face upon his breast.
How can those terrified vague fingers push
The feathered glory from her loosening thighs
            laid
All the stretched body leans on ~~that~~ white rush
      or
Her ~~falling body thrown on the white white ru~~sh

5. From Yeats's manuscript *Journal*, Sections 248 and 250. This *Journal*, including facsimiles and transcriptions of the drafts of "Leda and the Swan," has been published in W. B. Yeats, *Memoirs*, ed. Denis Donoghue (London, 1972).

The first version, entitled "Annunciation," seems to be a clean copy of earlier drafts; Yeats went on to revise it further, especially the opening octave. Neither of the other two complete drafts, each of which Yeats labeled "Final Version," was in fact final. Yeats crossed out the first draft. The second, although Yeats published it in 1924, was subjected to further revision before he published the poem in *The Tower* (1928), in the final form reprinted in the selections from Yeats, above.

Yeats's handwriting is hasty and very difficult to decipher. The readings of some words in the manuscript are uncertain.

Can feel etc
or Her body can but lean on the white rush

But mounts until her trembling thighs are pressed[6]
B
By the webbed toes; & that all powerful bill
Has suddenly bowed her head on his breast

Final Version

Annunciation

Can hold

The swooping godhead is half hovering still
But mounts, until her trembling thighs are pressed
By the webbed toes, & that all powerful bill
Has hung her helpless body
Has suddenly bowed her head upon his breast.
How can those terrified vague fingers push
The feathered glory from her loosening thighs?
How   now its body leans on
With her body laid on the white rush
       all the stretched body laid on the white rush
and Can feel the strange heart beating where it lies?
A shudder in the loins engenders there
The broken wall, the burning roof & tower
And Agamemnon dead . . .
                            Being mastered so
                  Being so caught up
        So
And mastered by the brute blood of the air
                       Being mastered so
Did nothing pass before her in the air
Did she put on his knowledge with his power
Before the indifferent beak could let her drop.
                            WBY Sept 18 1923
    swoop
A rush upon great wings & hovering still
He sinks until
He has sunk on her down, & her hair
The great bird sinks, till
The bird descends, & her frail thigh thighs are pressed
By the webbed toes, & that all

     that
Now all her body's laid on that white rush[7]
All the stretched body laid on that white rush
Now that whole

6. This passage is written across the blank page opposite the first version; Yeats drew a line indicating that it was to replace the revised lines 2–4, which he had written below the first version.

7. Written on the blank page across from the complete version, with an arrow indicating that it was a revision of the seventh line.

Now t~~...~~rush
Can see

Final Version

Leda & the Swan

A rush, a sudden wheel and

~~A swoop upon great wings &~~ hovering still

    sinks down   ~~bare frail~~

stet The bird ~~descends~~ & her ~~frail~~ thighs are pressed

By the toes webbed toes, & that all powerful bill

    laid

Has ~~driven~~ her helpless face upon his breast.

How can those terrified vague fingers push

The feathered glory from her loosening thighs?

    s laid

All the stretched body ~~laid~~ on that white rush

And ~~feel~~ feels the strange heart beating where it lies.

A shudder in the loins engenders there

The broken wall, the burning roof & tower

And Agamemnon dead.

                  Being so caught up

So mastered by the ~~br~~ brute blood of the air

Did she put on his knowledge with his power

Before the indifferent beak could let her drop.

D. H. LAWRENCE

The Piano[1]

Somewhere beneath that piano's superb sleek black

Must hide my mother's piano, little and brown, with
        the back

    stood close to

That ~~was against~~ the wall, and the front's faded silk, both torn

And the keys with little hollows, that my mother's fingers
        had worn.

Softly, in the shadows, a woman is singing to me

Quietly, through the years I have crept back to see

A child sitting under the piano, in the boom of the

    shaking ~~tingling~~ strings.

---

1. Transcribed from a notebook in which Lawrence at first entered various academic assignments while he was a student at the University College of Nottingham, 1906–8, but then used to write drafts of some of his early poems. These were probably composed in the period from 1906 to 1910. The text reproduced here was revised and published with the title "Piano" in Lawrence's *New Poems*, 1918. A comparison of this draft with "Piano," reprinted above, will show that Lawrence eliminated the first and fourth stanzas (as well as the last two lines of the third stanza); revised the remaining three stanzas, sometimes radically; and most surprisingly, reversed his original conclusion. As Lawrence explained, some of his early poems "had to be altered, where sometimes the hand of commonplace youth had been laid on the mouth of the demon. It is not for technique that these poems are altered: it is to say the real say."

For transcriptions and discussions of this and other poems in Lawrence's early notebook, see Vivian de Sola Pinto, "D. H. Lawrence: Letter-Writer and Craftsman in Verse," in *Renaissance and Modern Studies* 1 (1957): 5–34.

Pressing the little poised feet of the mother who smiles
        as she sings

The full throated woman has chosen a winning, living[2]
        song
And surely the heart that is in me must belong
To the old Sunday evenings, when darkness wandered
        outside
And hymns gleamed on our warm lips, as we watched
        mother's fingers glide
          is
Or is this my sister at home in the old front room
Singing love's first surprised gladness, alone in
        the gloom.
She will start when she sees me, and blushing,
        spread out her hands
To cover my mouth's raillery, till I'm bound in
          heart-spun
      her shame's ~~pleading~~ hands.

A woman is singing me a wild Hungarian
        air
And her arms, and her bosom and the whole
        of her soul is bare
And the great black piano is clamouring as my
        mother's never could clamour
        my mother's [   ]³ tunes are
And ~~the tunes of the past is~~ devoured of this music's
        ravaging glamour.

2. A conjectural reading; the word is not clearly legible.

3. An undecipherable word is crossed out here.

Selected Bibliographies

The Selected Bibliographies consist of a list of Suggested General Readings on English literature, followed by bibliographies for each of the literary periods in this volume. For ease of reference, the authors within each period are arranged in alphabetical order. Entries for certain classes of writings (e.g., "Light Verse") are included, in alphabetical order, within the listings for individual authors.

SUGGESTED GENERAL READINGS

Histories of England and of English Literature

New research and new perspectives have made even the most distinguished of the comprehensive general histories written in past generations seem outmoded. Innovative research in social, cultural, and political history has made it difficult to write a single coherent account of England from the Middle Ages to the present, let alone to accommodate in a unified narrative the complex histories of Scotland, Ireland, Wales, and the other nations where writing in English has flourished. Readers who wish to explore the historical matrix out of which the works of literature collected in this anthology emerged are advised to consult the studies of particular periods listed in the appropriate sections of this bibliography. The multivolume *Oxford History of England* and *New Oxford History of England* are useful, as are the three-volume *Peoples of the British Isles: A New History*, ed. Stanford Lehmberg, 1992, the nine-volume *Cambridge Cultural History of Britain*, ed. Boris Ford, 1992, and the multivolume *Penguin History of Britain*, gen. ed. David Cannadine, 1996–. Given the cultural centrality of London, readers may find *The London Encyclopaedia*, ed. Ben Weinreb and Christopher Hibbert, 1986, and Roy Porter's *London: A Social History*, 1994, valuable.

Similar observations may be made about literary history. In the light of such initiatives as women's studies, new historicism, and postcolonialism, the range of authors deemed most significant has expanded in recent years, along with the geographical and conceptual boundaries of literature in English. Attempts to capture in a unified account the great sweep of literature from *Beowulf* to late last night have largely given way to studies of individual genres, carefully delimited time periods, and specific authors. For these more focused accounts, see the listings by

period. Among the large-scale literary surveys, *The Cambridge Guide to Literature in English*, 1993, is useful, as is the seven-volume *Penguin History of Literature*, 1993–94. *The Feminist Companion to Literature in English*, ed. Virginia Blain, Isobel Grundy, and Patricia Clements, 1990, is an important resource, and the editorial materials in *The Norton Anthology of Literature by Women*, 2nd ed., 1996, ed. Sandra M. Gilbert and Susan Gubar, constitute a concise history and set of biographies of women authors since the Middle Ages. *Annals of English Literature, 1475–1950*, rev. 1961, lists important publications year by year, together with the significant literary events for each year. Four volumes have been published in the *Oxford English Literary History*, gen. ed. Jonathan Bate, 2002–: James Simpson, *Reform and Cultural Revolution, 1350–1547*; Philip Davis, *The Victorians, 1830–1880*; Randall Stevenson, *The Last of England? 1960–2000*; and Bruce King, *The Internationalization of English Literature, 1948–2000*. See also *The Cambridge History of Medieval English Literature*, ed. David Wallace, 1999, and *The Cambridge History of Early Modern English Literature*, ed. David Loewenstein and Janel Mueller, 2002.

Helpful treatments and surveys of English meter, rhyme, and stanza forms are Paul Fussell Jr., *Poetic Meter and Poetic Form*, rev. 1979; Donald Wesling, *The Chances of Rhyme: Device and Modernity*, 1980; Derek Attridge, *The Rhythms of English Poetry*, 1982; Charles O. Hartman, *Free Verse: An Essay in Prosody*, 1983; John Hollander, *Vision and Resonance: Two Senses of Poetic Form*, rev. 1985; and Robert Pinsky, *The Sounds of Poetry: A Brief Guide*, 1998.

On the development of the novel as a form, see Ian Watt, *The Rise of the Novel*, 1957; *The Columbia History of the British Novel*, ed. John Richetti, 1994; Margaret Doody, *The True Story of the Novel*, 1996; *Theory of the Novel: A Historical Approach*, ed. Michael McKeon, 2000; and McKeon, *The Origins of the English Novel, 1600–1740*, 15th anniversary ed., 2002. On women novelists and readers, see Nancy Armstrong, *Desire and Domestic Fiction: A Political History of the Novel*, 1987; and Catherine Gallagher, *Nobody's Story: The Vanishing Acts of Women Writers in the Marketplace, 1670–1820*, 1994.

On the history of playhouse design, see Richard Leacroft, *The Development of the English Playhouse: An Illustrated Survey of Theatre Building in England from Medieval to Modern Times*, 1988. For a survey of the plays that have appeared on these and other stages, see Allardyce Nicoll, *British Drama*, rev. 1962, the eight-volume *Revels History of Drama in English*, gen. eds. Clifford Leech and T. W. Craik, 1975–83; and Alfred Harbage, *Annals of English Drama, 975–1700*, 3rd ed., 1989, rev. S. Schoenbaum and Sylvia Wagonheim.

On some of the key intellectual currents that are at once reflected in and shaped by literature, Arthur O. Lovejoy's classic studies *The Great Chain of Being*, 1936, and *Essays in the History of Ideas*, 1948, remain valuable, along with such works as Lovejoy and George Boas, *Primitivism and Related Ideas in Antiquity*, 1935; Ernst Kantorowicz, *The King's Two Bodies: A Study in Medieval Political Theology*, 1957, new ed. 1997; Richard Popkin, *The History of Skepticism from Erasmus to Descartes*, 1960; M. H. Abrams, *Natural Supernaturalism: Tradition and Revolution in Romantic Literature*, 1971; Michel Foucault, *Madness and Civilization: A History of Insanity in the Age of Reason*, Eng. trans. 1965, *The Order of Things: An Archaeology of the Human Sciences*, Eng. trans. 1970; Mikhail Bakhtin, *Rabelais and his World*, Eng. trans. 1968, and *The Dialogic Imagination*, Eng. trans. 1981; Roland Barthes, *The Pleasure of the Text*, Eng. trans. 1975; Jacques Derrida, *Of Grammatology*, Eng. trans. 1976, and *Dissemination*, Eng. trans. 1981; Raymond Williams, *Keywords: A Vocabulary of Culture and Society*, rev. 1983; Pierre Bourdieu, *Distinction: A Social Critique of the Judgment of Taste*, Eng. trans. 1984; Michel de Certeau, *The Practice of Everyday Life*, Eng. trans. 1984; and Sigmund Freud, *Writings on Art and Literature*, ed. Neil Hertz, 1997.

Reference Works

The single most important tool for the study of literature in English is the *Oxford English Dictionary*, 2nd ed., 1989, also available on CD-ROM, and online to subscribers. The *OED* is written on historical principles: that is, it attempts not only to describe current word use but also to record the history and development of the language from its origins before the Norman conquest to the present. It thus provides, for familiar as well as archaic and obscure words, the widest possible range of meanings and uses, organized chronologically and illustrated with quotations. Beyond the *OED* there are many other valuable dictionaries, such as *The American Heritage Dictionary*, *The Oxford Dictionary of Etymology*, and an array of reference works from *The Cambridge Encyclopedia of the English Language*, ed. David Crystal, 1995, to guides to specialized vocabularies, slang, regional dialects, and the like.

There is a steady flow of new editions of most major and many minor writers in English, along with a ceaseless outpouring of critical appraisals and scholarship. The *MLA International Bibliography* (also online) is the best way to keep abreast of the most recent work and to conduct bibliographic searches. The *New Cambridge Bibliography of English Literature*, ed. George Watson, 1969–77, updated shorter ed. 1981, is a valuable guide to the huge body of earlier literary criticism and scholarship. *A Guide to English and American Literature*, ed. F. W. Bateson and Harrison Meserole, rev. 1976, is a selected list of editions, as well as scholarly and critical treatments. Further bibliographical aids are described in Arthur G. Kennedy, *A Concise Bibliography for Students of English*, rev. 1972; Richard D. Altick and Andrew Wright, *Selective Bibliography for the Study of English and American Literature*, rev. 1979, and James L. Harner, *Literary Research Guide*, rev. 1998.

For compact biographies of English authors, see the multivolume *Oxford Dictionary of National Biography*, ed. H. C. G. Matthew and Brian Harrison, 2004; condensed biographies will be found in the *Concise Dictionary of National Biography*, 2 parts (1920, 1988). Handy reference books of authors, works, and various literary terms and allusions are *The Oxford Companion to the Theatre*, Phyllis Hartnoll, rev. 1990; *Princeton Encyclopedia of Poetry and Poetics*, ed. Alex Preminger and others, rev. 1993; and *The Oxford Companion to English Literature*, ed. Margaret Drabble, rev. 1998. Handbooks that define and illustrate literary concepts and terms are *The Penguin Dictionary of Literary Terms and Literary Theory*, ed. J. A. Cuddon, 1991; W. F. Thrall and Addison Hibbard, *A Handbook to Literature*, ed. C. Hugh Holman, rev. 1992; *Critical Terms for Literary Study*, ed. Frank Lentricchia and Thomas McLaughlin, rev. 1995; and M. H. Abrams, *A Glossary of Literary Terms*, rev. 1992. Also useful are Richard Lanham, *A Handlist of Rhetorical Terms*, 2nd ed., 1991; Arthur Quinn, *Figures of Speech: 60 Ways to Turn a Phrase*, 1993; and the *Barnhart Concise Dictionary of Etymology*, ed. Robert K. Barnhart, 1995. On the Greek and Roman background, see G. M. Kirkwood, *A Short Guide to Classical Mythology*, 1959; *The Oxford Classical Dictionary*, rev. 1996; and *The Oxford Companion to Classical Literature*, ed.

M. C. Howatson and Ian Chilvers, rev. 1993. Useful online resources include Early English Books Online; University of Pennsylvania's SCETI Furness Shakespeare Library; Michael Best's Internet Shakespeare Editions; and the University of Toronto Early Modern English Dictionaries Database, ed. Ian Lancashire.

Literary Criticism and Theory

Seven volumes of the *Cambridge History of Literary Criticism* have been published, 1989– : *Classical Criticism*, ed. George A. Kennedy; *The Renaissance*, ed. Glyn P. Norton; *The Eighteenth Century*, ed. H. B. Nisbet and Claude Rawson; *Romanticism*, ed. Marshall Brown; *Modernism and the New Criticism*, ed. A. Walton Litz, Louis Menand, and Lawrence Rainey; *From Formalism to Poststructuralism*, ed. Raman Selden; and *Twentieth-Century Historical, Philosophical, and Psychological Perspectives*, ed. Christa Knellwolf and Christopher Norris. See also M. H. Abrams, *The Mirror and the Lamp: Romantic Theory and the Critical Tradition*, 1953; William K. Wimsatt and Cleanth Brooks, *Literary Criticism: A Short History*, 1957; René Wellek, *A History of Modern Criticism: 1750–1950*, 9 vols., 1955–93; Frank Lentricchia, *After the New Criticism*, 1980; *Redrawing the Boundaries: The Transformation of English and American Literary Studies*, ed. Stephen Greenblatt and Giles Gunn, 1992; and J. Hillis Miller, *On Literature*, 2002. Raman Selden, Peter Widdowson, and Peter Brooker have written *A Reader's Guide to Contemporary Literary Theory*, 1997. Other useful resources include *The Johns Hopkins Guide to Literary Theory and Criticism*, ed. Michael Groden and Martin Kreiswirth, 1994 (also online); *Literary Theory, an Anthology*, ed. Julie Rivkin and Michael Ryan, 1998; and *The Norton Anthology of Theory and Criticism*, gen. ed. Vincent Leitch, 2001.

The following is a selection of books in literary criticism that have been notably influential in shaping modern approaches to English literature and literary forms: Lionel Trilling, *The Liberal Imagination*, 1950; T. S. Eliot, *Selected Essays*, 3rd ed. 1951, and *On Poetry and Poets*, 1957; Erich Auerbach, *Mimesis: The Representation of Reality in Western Literature*, 1953; William Empson, *Some Versions of Pastoral*, 1935, rpt. 1986, and *Seven Types of Ambiguity*, 3rd ed. 1953; William K. Wimsatt, *The Verbal Icon*, 1954; Northrop Frye, *Anatomy of Criticism*, 1957; Wayne C. Booth, *The Rhetoric of Fiction*, 1961, rev. ed. 1983; W. J. Bate, *The Burden of the Past and the English Poet*, 1970; Harold Bloom, *The Anxiety of Influence*, 1973; Paul de Man, *Allegories of Reading*, 1979; and Stanley Fish, *Is There a Text in This Class?: The Authority of Interpretive Communities*, 1980.

René Wellek and Austin Warren, *Theory of Literature*, rev. 1970, is a useful introduction to the variety of scholarly and critical approaches to literature up to the time of its publication. Jonathan Culler's *Literary Theory: A Very Short Introduction*, 1997, discusses recurrent issues and debates. See also Terry Eagleton, *After Theory*, 2003. Modern feminist literary criticism was fashioned by such works as Patricia Meyer Spacks, *The Female Imagination*, 1975; Ellen Moers, *Literary Women*, 1976; Elaine Showalter, *A Literature of Their Own*, 1977; and Sandra Gilbert and Susan Gubar, *The Madwoman in the Attic*, 1979. More recent studies include Jane Gallop, *The Daughter's Seduction: Feminism and Psychoanalysis*, 1982; Gayatri Chakravorty Spivak, *In Other Worlds: Essays in Cultural Politics*, 1987; Sandra Gilbert and Susan Gubar, *No Man's Land: The Place of the Woman Writer in the Twentieth Century*, 2 vols., 1988–89; Barbara Johnson, *A World of Difference*, 1989; Judith Butler, *Gender Trouble*, 1990; and the critical views sampled in Elaine Showalter, *The New Feminist Criticism*, 1985; *Feminist Literary Theory: A Reader*, ed. Mary Eagleton, 2nd ed., 1995; and *Feminisms: An Anthology of Literary Theory and Criticism*, ed. Robyn R. Warhol and Diane Price Herndl, 2nd ed. 1997. Gay and lesbian studies and criticism are represented in *The Lesbian and Gay Studies Reader*, ed. Henry Abelove, Michele Barale, and David Halperin, 1993, and by such books as Eve Sedgwick, *Between Men: English Literature and Male Homosocial Desire*, 1985, and *Epistemology of the Closet*, 1990; Diana Fuss, *Essentially Speaking: Feminism, Nature, and Difference*, 1989; Gregory Woods, *A History of Gay Literature: The Male Tradition*, 1998; and David Halperin, *How to Do the History of Homosexuality*, 2002.

Convenient introductions to structuralist literary criticism include Robert Scholes, *Structuralism in Literature: An Introduction*, 1974, and Jonathan Culler, *Structuralist Poetics*, 1975. The poststructuralist challenges to this approach are discussed in Jonathan Culler, *On Deconstruction*, 1982; Fredric Jameson, *Poststructuralism; or the Cultural Logic of Late Capitalism*, 1991; John McGowan, *Postmodernism and Its Critics*, 1991; and *Beyond Structuralism*, ed. Wendell Harris, 1996. For Marxism, see *Selections from the Prison Notebooks of Antonio Gramsci*, ed. and trans. Quintin Hoare and Geoffrey Smith, 1971; Raymond Williams, *Marxism and Literature*, 1977; Fredric Jameson, *The Political Unconscious: Narrative as a Socially Symbolic Act*, 1981; and Terry Eagleton, *Literary Theory: An Introduction*, 1983. New historicism is represented in Stephen Greenblatt, *Learning to Curse*, 1990; in the essays collected in *The New Historicism*, ed. Harold Veeser, 1989, and *New Historical Literary Study: Essays on Reproducing Texts, Representing History*, ed. Jeffrey N. Cox and Larry J. Reynolds, 1993; and in Catherine Gallagher and Stephen Greenblatt, *Practicing New Histori-*

cism, 2000. The related social and historical dimension of texts is discussed in Jerome McGann, *Critique of Modern Textual Criticism*, 1983; D. F. McKenzie, *Bibliography and Sociology of Texts*, 1986; Roger Chartier, *The Order of Books*, 1994; and *Scholarly Editing: A Guide to Research*, ed. D. C. Greetham, 1995. Characteristic of new historicism is an expansion of the field of literary interpretation extended still further in cultural studies; for a broad sampling of the range of interests, see *The Cultural Studies Reader*, ed. Simon During, 1993, and *A Cultural Studies Reader: History, Theory, Practice*, ed. Jessica Munns and Gita Rajan, 1997. This expansion of the field is similarly reflected in postcolonial studies: see *The Post-Colonial Studies Reader*, ed. Bill Ashcroft, Gareth Griffiths, and Helen Tiffin, 1995, and such influential books as Ranajit Guha and Gayatri Chakravorty Spivak, *Selected Subaltern Studies*, 1988; Edward Said, *Culture and Imperialism*, 1993; Homi Bhabha, *The Location of Culture*, 1994; Anne McClintock, *Imperial Leather: Race, Gender, and Sexuality in the Colonial Contest*, 1995; and Jonathan Goldberg, *Tempest in the Caribbean*, 2004.

Anthologies representing a range of recent approaches include *Modern Criticism and Theory*, ed. David Lodge, 1988, and *Contemporary Literary Criticism*, ed. Robert Con Davis and Ronald Schlieffer, rev. 1998.

THE TWENTIETH CENTURY AND AFTER

The Twentieth Century and After
Martin Gilbert, *A History of the Twentieth Century*, 3 vols., 1997–99, offers a richly informative account of the first half-century, while Peter Conrad, *Modern Times, Modern Places*, 1999, skillfully interweaves the history of the period with its artistic and intellectual movements.

The social and political background is well covered in Robert Graves and Alan Hodge's *The Long Week End: A Social History of Great Britain, 1918–1939*, 1940; *The Baldwin Age*, ed. John Raymond, 1960; Julian Symons's *The Thirties: A Dream Revolved*, 1960, rev. ed. 1975; Hugh Thomas's *The Spanish Civil War*, 1961, 3rd ed. 1986; Malcolm Bradbury's *The Social Context of Modern English Literature*, 1971; *The Twentieth-Century Mind: History, Ideas, and Literature in Britain*, 3 vols., ed. C. B. Cox and A. E. Dyson, 1972; Paul Fussell's *The Great War and Modern Memory*, 1975, and *Wartime: Understanding and Behavior in the Second World War*, 1989; Samuel Hynes's *The Auden Generation: Literature and Politics in England in the 1930s*, 1976, and *A War Imagined: The First World War and English Culture*, 1991; Valentine Cunningham's *British Writers of the Thirties*, 1988; Alan Sinfield's *Literature, Politics, and Culture in Postwar Britain*, 1989; all of which include useful bibliographies.

The following critical works deal with general aspects of modern English literature: Stephen Spender's *The Struggle of the Modern*, 1963; C. K. Stead's *The New Poetic: Yeats to Eliot*, 1964, rev. ed. 1987, and *Pound, Yeats, Eliot, and the Modernist Movement*, 1986; *The Modern Tradition: Backgrounds of Modern Literature*, ed. Richard Ellmann and Charles Feidelson, 1965; Irving Howe's *The Idea of the Modern in Literature and the Arts*, 1967; Hugh Kenner's *The Pound Era*, 1971; *Modernism 1890–1930*, ed. Malcolm Bradbury and James McFarlane, 1976; David Perkins's *A History of Modern Poetry*, 2 vols., 1976–87; Robert Hughes's *The Shock of the New*, 1981, rev. ed. 1991; Michael Levenson's *A Genealogy of Modernism*, 1984; Carol T. Christ's *Victorian and Modern Poetics*, 1984; Sanford Schwartz's *The Matrix of Modernism: Pound, Eliot and Early Twentieth-Century Thought*, 1985; Maud Ellmann's *The Poetics of Impersonality: T. S. Eliot and Ezra Pound*, 1987; Perry Meisel's *The Myth of the Modern: A Study in British Literature and Criticism after 1850*, 1987; James Longenbach's *Stone Cottage: Pound, Yeats, and Modernism*, 1988; John Bayley's *The Short Story: Henry James to Elizabeth Bowen*, 1988; Sandra M. Gilbert and Susan Gubar's *No Man's Land: The Place of the Woman Writer in the Twentieth Century*, 3 vols., 1988–94; George Watson's *British Literature since 1945*, 1991; Daniel Albright's *Quantum Poetics: Yeats, Pound, Eliot, and the Science of Modernism*, 1997; Lawrence Rainey's *Institutions of Modernism*, 1998; *The Cambridge Companion to Modernism*, ed. Michael Levenson, 1999; Jed Esty's *A Shrinking Island: Modernism and National Culture in England*, 2004; and vols. 11, 12, and 13 of the *Oxford English Literary History*: Chris Baldick's *The Modern Movement*, 2004, which covers 1910–40, Randall Stevenson's *The Last of England?*, 2004, which covers 1960–2000, and Bruce King's *The Internationalization of English Literature*, 2004, which surveys black and Asian British literature from 1948 to 2000.

Useful reference books include John L. Somer and Barbara Eck Cooper's *American and British Literature 1945–1975: An Annotated Bibliography of Contemporary Scholarship*, 1980; Alistair Davies's *An Annotated Critical Bibliography of Modernism*, 1982; *Contemporary Novelists*, ed. D. L. Kirkpatrick and James Vinson, 4th ed. 1986; *Contemporary Dramatists*, ed. K. A. Berney, 5th ed. 1993; *The Oxford Companion to Twentieth-Century Poetry*, ed. Ian

Hamilton, 1994; *The Oxford Companion to Irish Literature*, ed. Robert Welch and Bruce Stewart, 1996; *Contemporary Poets*, ed. Thomas Riggs, 7th ed. 2001; Neil Roberts's *A Companion to Twentieth-Century Poetry*, 2001; and entries in the many volumes of the *Dictionary of Literary Biography* (also available online). The British Council/Book Trust Web site (www .contemporarywriters.com) is a useful source of information about contemporary British authors.

See also entries for **Voices from World War I, Modernist Manifestos, Voices from World War II,** and **Nation and Language.**

Chinua Achebe
Achebe's first novel, *Things Fall Apart*, 1958, was the first of three known collectively as *The African Trilogy*; the other two novels, *No Longer at Ease* and *Arrow of God*, were published in 1960 and 1964, respectively. *A Man of the People* was published in 1966; *Anthills of the Savannah*, in 1987. Collections of Achebe's short stories include *The Sacrificial Egg and Other Stories*, 1962, and *Girls at War and Other Stories*, 1972, and he has written other books for children. A collection of poems, *Beware, Soul-Brother, and Other Poems*, was published in 1971 and revised and enlarged the following year. Achebe's nonfiction includes *Morning Yet on Creation Day: Essays*, 1975; *The Trouble with Nigeria*, 1983; *Hopes and Impediments: Selected Essays 1965–1987*, 1988; *The University and the Leadership Factor in Nigerian Politics*, 1988; *Beyond Hunger in Africa: Conventional Wisdom and a Vision of Africa in 2057*, 1990; *Home and Exile*, 2000; and *The Short Century: Independence and Liberation in Africa, 1945–1994*, cowritten with Okwui Enwezor, 2001. He is editor of *The Heinemann Book of Contemporary African Short Stories*, 1992, and coeditor of *The Insider: Stories of War and Peace from Nigeria*, 1971, and *African Short Stories*, 1985. For his life, see *Chinua Achebe: A Biography*, ed. Ezenwa Ohaeto, 1997; Tijan M. Sallah and Ngozi Okonjo-Iweala, *Chinua Achebe, Teacher of Light: A Biography*, 2003. Bibliographies include B. M. Okpu, *Chinua Achebe: A Bio-Bibliography*, 1984, and *Chinua Achebe: A Bio-Bibliography*, compiled by the staff of Nnamdi Azikiwe Library, University of Nigeria, Nsukka, 1990.

Studies of Achebe's work include Arthur Ravenscroft's *Chinua Achebe*, 1977; C. L. Innes's *Chinua Achebe*, 1990; David Carroll's *Chinua Achebe: Novelist, Poet, Critic*, 2nd ed. 1990; Simon Gikandi's *Reading Chinua Achebe: Language and Ideology in Fiction*, 1991; Chinwe Okechukwu's *Achebe the Orator: The Art of Persuasion in Chinua Achebe's Novels*, 2001; and Ode Ogede's *Achebe and the Politics of Representation: Form against Itself, From Colonial Conquest and Occupation to Post-Independence Disillusionment*, 2001. Useful contextual information is provided by Robert M. Wren's *Achebe's World: The Historical and Cultural Context of the Novels of Chinua Achebe*, 1980; Emmanuel Meziemadu Okoye's *The Traditional Religion and Its Encounter with Christianity in Achebe's Novels*, 1987; Olawale Awosika's *Form and Technique in the African Novel*, 1997; Bernth Lindfors's *Conversations with Chinua Achebe*, Literary Conversations Series, 1997; and M. Keith Booker's *The Chinua Achebe Encyclopedia*, 2003. A collection of essays celebrating Achebe's achievement, *Chinua Achebe: A Celebration*, ed. Kirsten Holst Petersen and Anna Rutherford, was published in 1991.

Studies of *Things Fall Apart* include Kate Turkington's *Chinua Achebe, Things Fall Apart*, 1977; Christopher Heywood's *Chinua Achebe, Things Fall Apart: A Critical View*, ed. Yolande Cantú, 1985; Solomon Ogbede Iyasere's *Understanding Things Fall Apart: Selected Essays and Criticism*, 1998; Emmanuel Edame Egar's *The Rhetorical Implications of Chinua Achebe's Things Fall Apart*, 2000; *Chinua Achebe's Things Fall Apart*, ed. Harold Bloom, 2002; and Isidore Okpweho's *Chinua Achebe's Things Fall Apart: A Casebook*, 2003.

John Agard
Agard's poetry includes the volumes *Shoot Me with Flowers*, 1974; *Man to Pan: A Cycle of Poems to Be Performed with Drums and Steelpans*, 1982; *Mangoes & Bullets: Selected and New Poems, 1972–1984*, 1985; *Lovelines for a Goat-Born Lady*, 1990; *Laughter Is an Egg*, 1990; *Get Back, Pimple!*, 1996; *From the Devil's Pulpit*, 1997; and *Weblines*, 2000. He has written prolifically for children, both fiction and poetry. With Grace Nichols he has edited *A Caribbean Dozen: Poems from Caribbean Poets*, 1994; *No Hickory No Dickory No Dock: Caribbean Nursery Rhymes*, 1995; and *Under the Moon & Over the Sea: A Collection of Caribbean Poems*, 2002. He has also compiled a collection of poetry for teenagers, *Life Doesn't Frighten Me at All*, 1989.

W. H. Auden
Auden's *Selected Poems*, ed. Edward Mendelson, 1979, rev. ed. 1989, reprints many of Auden's poems as they first appeared in his volumes of poetry. *The English Auden: Poems, Essays and Dramatic Writings, 1927–1939*, ed. Mendelson, 1977, also reprints Auden's poems in their original versions—all those published in book form in the 1930s—as well as many previously unpublished and uncollected poems and early prose writings. *W. H. Auden: Collected Poems*, ed. Mendelson, 1976, rev. ed. 1991, contains the poems Auden wished to preserve in their final revised form.

The definitive collected editions of Auden's works proceed under Mendelson's editorship: *Plays and Other Dramatic Writings by W. H.*

Auden, 1928–1938, 1989; W. H. Auden and Chester Kallman: Libretti and Other Dramatic Writings by W. H. Auden, 1939–1973, 1993; Prose and Travel Books in Prose and Verse, Volume I, 1926–1938, 1996; and Prose: Volume II, 1939–1948, 2002. Juvenilia 1922–1928, ed. Katherine Bucknell, 1994, contains Auden's earliest work and appeared in an expanded edition in 2003. "The Dyer's Hand" and Other Essays, 1968, is an essential collection of Auden's lectures and essays. Other such collections include Forewords and Afterwards, 1973, and two posthumous editions, "In Solitude, for Company": W. H. Auden after 1940, ed. Bucknell and Nicholas Jenkins, 1995, and Lectures on Shakespeare, ed. Arthur C. Kirsch, 2000. Auden edited a number of anthologies, including The Poet's Tongue, with John Garrett, 1935; The Oxford Book of Light Verse, 1938; Poets of the English Language, with Norman Holmes Pearson, 1950; An Elizabethan Songbook, with Noah Greenberg and Chester Kallman, 1955; and The Elder Edda: A Selection, 1969. For Auden's life see Humphrey Carpenter's W. H. Auden: A Biography, 1981; The Map of All My Youth: Early Works, Friends, and Influences, ed. Bucknell and Jenkins, 1990; R. P. T. Davenport-Hines's Auden, 1995; Thekla Clark's Wystan and Chester: A Personal Memoir of W. H. Auden and Chester Kallman, 1995, rev. ed 1996; and David Garrett Izzo's W. H. Auden Encyclopedia, 2002, rev. ed. 2004. The standard bibliography is B. C. Bloomfield and Mendelson's W. H. Auden: A Bibliography 1924–1969, 1972, and is updated in Auden Studies, ed. Bucknell and Jenkins, 1990–95.

W. H. Auden: The Critical Heritage, ed. John Haffenden, 1983, traces Auden's critical reception and provides contemporary criticism. For helpful glosses on individual poems, see John Fuller's W. H. Auden: A Commentary, 1998. Useful studies include Monroe K. Spears's The Poetry of W. H. Auden, 1963; Justin Replogle's Auden's Poetry, 1969; Samuel Hynes's The Auden Generation, 1976, rev. ed. 1992; Edward Mendelson's Early Auden, 1981; Edward Callan's Auden: A Carnival of Intellect, 1983; Stan Smith's W. H. Auden, 1985; Lucy McDiarmid's Auden's Apologies for Poetry, 1990; John R. Boly's Reading Auden: The Returns of Caliban, 1991; Anthony Hecht's The Hidden Law, 1993; Marsha Bryant's Auden and Documentary in the 1930s, 1997; Mendelson's Later Auden, 1999; Rainer Emig's W. H. Auden: Towards a Postmodern Poetics, 2000; Richard R. Bozorth's Auden's Games of Knowledge: Poetry and the Meanings of Homosexuality, 2001; Peter Edgerly Firchow's W. H. Auden: Contexts for Poetry, 2002; and Susannah Young-ah Gottlieb, Regions of Sorrow: Anxiety and Messianism in Hannah Arendt and W. H. Auden, 2003. Useful essays are collected in Auden: A Collection of Critical Essays, ed. Monroe K. Spears, 1964, and Critical Essays on W. H. Auden, ed. George W. Bahlke, 1991.

Samuel Beckett

Beckett's dramatic works include Waiting for Godot: Tragicomedy in 2 Acts, 1954, ed. Dougald McMillan and James Knowlson in the revised edition published in 1994; Endgame, 1958, ed. S. E. Gontarski, rev. ed. 1992; Krapp's Last Tape and Other Dramatic Pieces, 1960, ed. Knowlson, rev. ed. 1992; Happy Days: A Play in Two Acts, 1961; and The Shorter Plays: With Revised Texts for Footfalls, Come and Go, and What Where, ed. Gontarski, 2000. Beckett's novels include Murphy, 1938; Molloy, 1951; Watt, 1953; Malone Dies, 1956; The Unnamable, 1958; Four Novellas, 1977; and Nohow On: Three Novels, 1980. Short prose fiction can be found in More Pricks than Kicks, 1930, rev. ed. 1970; As the Story Was Told: Uncollected and Late Prose, 1990; The Complete Short Prose, 1929–1989, ed. Gontarski, 1995; and I Can't Go On, I'll Go On: A Selection from Samuel Beckett's Work, ed. Richard W. Seaver, 1976. Beckett's poetry can be found in Poems in English, 1961, and Collected Poems in English and French, 1977. Beckett also edited Our Examination Round His Factification for Incamination of Work in Progress, a symposium on James Joyce's Finnegans Wake, 1929, 2nd ed. 1962. The standard biography is Knowlson's Damned to Fame: The Life of Samuel Beckett, 1996. Anthony Cronin's Samuel Beckett: The Last Modernist, 1996; Conversations with and about Beckett, ed. Mel Gussow, 1996; and Anne Atik's How It Was: A Memoir of Samuel Beckett, 2001, are also useful. For biographical background for Beckett's early work, see John Pilling's Beckett before Godot, 1997. Bibliographic reference sources include Raymond Federman and John Fletcher's Samuel Beckett: His Works and His Critics: An Essay in Bibliography, 1970; P. J. Murphy's Critique of Beckett Criticism: A Guide to Research in English, French, and German, 1994; and Ruby Cohn's A Beckett Canon, 2001.

Alvarez's Samuel Beckett, 1973; Hugh Kenner's A Reader's Guide to Samuel Beckett, 1973; and C. J. Ackerly's The Grove Companion to Samuel Beckett: A Reader's Guide to His Work, Life, and Thought, 2004, are good introductions to Beckett's work. Criticism of the plays includes Cohn's Just Play: Beckett's Theatre, 1980; Beryl Fletcher and John Fletcher's A Student's Guide to the Plays of Samuel Beckett, 1985; Gontarksi's The Intent of Undoing in Samuel Beckett's Dramatic Texts, 1985; and, specifically on the later drama, Rosemary Pountney's Theatre of Shadows: Samuel Beckett's Drama 1956–76: From All That Fall to Footfalls with Commentaries on the Late Plays, 1988.

On Endgame see Twentieth Century Interpretations of Endgame, ed. B. G. Chevigny, 1969, and Arthur N. Athanason's Endgame: The Ashbin Play, 1993. On the later work in general, see Steven Connor's Samuel Beckett: Repetition Theory and Text, 1986, and Enoch Brater's Beyond Minimalism: Beckett's Late Style in the Theatre, 1987, and The Drama in the Text: Beckett's Late Fiction, 1994.

Among many good general studies are Vivian Mercier's Beckett/Beckett, 1977; Samuel Beckett–Humanistic Perspectives, ed. Morris Beja, 1983; Christopher Ricks's Beckett's Dying Words, 1993; and The Cambridge Companion to Beckett, ed. John Pilling, 1994. Also very useful is Samuel Beckett: The Critical Heritage, ed. Lawrence Graver and Ray Federman, 1979, and David Pattie's The Complete Critical Guide to Samuel Beckett, 2000. The Beckett Archive is housed at the University of Reading, and the twice-yearly Journal of Beckett Studies began publication in 1976; Gontarski is editor of The Beckett Studies Reader, published in 1993.

Louise Bennett
Bennett's Selected Poems, 1982, corr. ed. 1983, was edited by Mervyn Morris and contains his excellent introduction and notes; an earlier selection, also important, is Jamaica Labrish, ed. by Rex Nettleford, 1966. Other volumes of poetry, folktales, and stories include Jamaica Dialect Verses, comp. George R. Bowen, 1942; Anancy Stories and Poems in Dialect, 1944; Jamaican Dialect Poems, 1949; Anancy Stories and Dialect Verse, with others, 1950, 1957; Laugh with Louise: A Pot-Pourri of Jamaican Folklore, Stories, Songs, Verses, with Lois Kelle-Barrow, 1961; and Anancy and Miss Lou, 1979. Aunty Roachy Seh, ed. Mervyn Morris, 1993, is a collection of monologues from Bennett's popular radio broadcasts; her funny and vivid performances of her poetry can be heard on recordings such as Yes M'Dear: Miss Lou Live!, 1983.

Discussions of Bennett's works can be found in Rex Nettleford's introduction to Bennett's Jamaica Labrish, 1966; Lloyd W. Brown's West Indian Poetry, 1978; Edward Kamau Brathwaite's History of the Voice: The Development of Nation Language in Anglophone Caribbean Poetry, 1984; Carolyn Cooper's Noises in the Blood: Orality, Gender and the "Vulgar" Body of Jamaican Popular Culture, 1993; Mervyn Morris's "Is English We Speaking" and Other Essays, 1999; and Jahan Ramazani's The Hybrid Muse, 2001.

Eavan Boland
An Origin Like Water: Collected Poems, 1967–1987 appeared in 1996; it includes selections from New Territory, 1967; The War Horse, 1975; In Her Own Image, 1980; Night Feed, 1982; and The Journey, 1987. Subsequent volumes include Outside History: Selected Poems 1980–1990, 1990; In a Time of Violence, 1994; The Lost Land, 1998; Against Love Poetry, 2001; and

Code, 2001. Boland's nonfiction includes A Kind of Scar: The Woman Poet in a National Tradition, 1989, and Object Lessons: The Life of the Woman and the Poet in Our Time, 1995, both of which provide essential insight into her work. She is coeditor, with Mark Strand, of The Making of a Poem: A Norton Anthology of Poetic Forms, 2000, and edited Three Irish Poets: An Anthology, 2003.

For her life see Patricia L. Hagen and Thomas W. Zelman's biography Eavan Boland and the History of the Ordinary, 2004. Critical studies of Boland's poetry may be found in Patricia Boyle Haberstroh's Women Creating Women: Contemporary Irish Women Poets, 1996; Susan Shaw Sailer's Representing Ireland: Gender, Class, Nationality, 1997; and William H. Gass and Lorin Cuoco's The Writer and Religion, 2000. Irish University Review, Spring/Summer 1993, and Colby Quarterly 35.4, 1999 are special issues dedicated to Boland.

Kamau Brathwaite
Brathwaite's volumes of poetry are The Arrivants: A New World Trilogy, 1973, which includes Rights of Passage, 1967, Masks, 1968, and Islands, 1969; Days and Nights, 1975; Other Exiles, 1975; Black + Blues, 1976; Mother Poem, 1977; Soweto, 1979; Word Making Man: A Poem for Nicólas Guillèn, 1979; Sun Poem, 1982; Third World Poems, 1983; Jah Music, 1986; X/Self, 1987; Sappho Sakyi's Meditations, 1989; Middle Passages, 1992; Shar/Hurricane Poem, 1992; Trench Town Rock, 1994; Words Need Love Too, 2000; and Ancestors: A Reinvention of Mother Poem, Sun Poem, and X/Self, 2001. Brathwaite has also written plays, including Four Plays for Primary Schools, 1964, and Odale's Voice, 1967. A revised edition of his Roots: Essays in Caribbean Literature, 1986, appeared in 1993, incorporating his influential lecture, first published separately, History of the Voice: The Development of Nation Language in Anglophone Caribbean Poetry, 1984. His historical studies of Caribbean culture include The Development of Creole Society in Jamaica, 1770–1820, 1971. Brathwaite has also edited collections of literature, including Iouanaloa: Recent Writing from St. Lucia, 1963, and New Poets from Jamaica, 1979, and he contributed an interview to Talk Yuh Talk: Interviews with Anglophone Caribbean Poets, ed. Kwame Dawes, 2001. Doris Monica Brathwaite's A Descriptive and Chronological Bibliography (1950–1982) of the Work of Edward Kamau Brathwaite was published in 1988.

Studies of Brathwaite's work include Gordon Rohlehr's Pathfinder: Black Awakening in The Arrivants of Edward Kamau Brathwaite, 1981; June D. Bobb's Beating a Restless Drum: The Poetics of Kamau Brathwaite and Derek Walcott, 1998; and Paul Naylor's Poetic Investigations: Singing the Holes in History, 1999. Collections of essays concerned with Brathwaite's work include *The Art of Kamau Brathwaite*, ed. Stewart Brown, 1995; *For the Geography of a Soul: Emerging Perspectives on Kamau Brathwaite*, ed. Timothy J. Reiss, 2001; and *Questioning Creole: Creolisation Discourses in Caribbean Literature*, ed. Verene A. Shepherd and Glen L. Richards, 2002. *World Literature Today* 68.4, 1994, is a special issue dedicated to Brathwaite.

Rupert Brooke
The Poetical Works, 2nd ed. 1970, and *The Letters*, 1968, are both edited by Geoffrey Keynes. *The Prose*, 1956, is edited by Christopher Hassall, who wrote the standard biography, *Rupert Brooke: A Biography*, 1964; Nigel Jones's *Rupert Brooke: Life, Death and Myth* was published in 1999. Volumes of Brooke's correspondence include *Song of Love: The Letters of Rupert Brooke and Noel Olivier, 1909–1915*, ed. Pippa Harris, 1991, and *Friends and Apostles: The Correspondence of Rupert Brooke and James Strachey, 1905–1914*, ed. Keith Hale, 1998. Paul Delany's *The Neo-Pagans: Rupert Brooke and the Ordeal of Youth*, 1987, provides a group portrait, and useful context and criticism appear in Kenneth Millard's *Edwardian Poetry*, 1991.

Studies of Brooke's work include Walter de la Mare's "Rupert Brooke and the Intellectual Imagination," in his *Pleasures and Speculations*, 1940; John H. Johnston's *English Poetry of the First World War*, 1964; Bernard Bergonzi's *Heroes' Twilight: A Study of the Literature of the Great War*, 1966, 2nd ed. 1980; *Rupert Brooke: A Reappraisal and Selection from His Writings, Some Hitherto Unpublished*, ed. Timothy Rogers, 1971; Jon Silkin's *Out of Battle: The Poetry of the Great War*, 1972, 2nd ed. 1998; John Lehmann's *The Strange Destiny of Rupert Brooke*, 1980; Adrian Caesar's *Taking It like a Man: Suffering, Sexuality, and the War Poets: Brooke, Sassoon, Owen, Graves*, 1993; Jonathan Rutherford's *Forever England: Reflections on Race, Masculinity, and Empire*, 1997; and *Poets of World War I: Rupert Brooke & Siegfried Sassoon*, ed. Harold Bloom, 2003.

May Wedderburn Cannan
Cannan's collections of poems include *In War Time*, 1917; *The Splendid Days*, 1919; and *The House of Hope*, 1923. She is also author of the novel *The Lonely Generation*, 1934. Her unfinished autobiography, *Grey Ghosts and Voices*, appeared posthumously in 1976. *The Tears of War: The Love Story of a Young Poet and a War Hero*, ed. Charlotte Fyfe, 2000, combines her poetry with personal narratives.

Anne Carson
Poetry and prose are often combined in Carson's books, which include *Short Talks*, 1992; *Plainwater: Essays and Poetry*, 1995; *Glass, Irony, and God*, 1995; *Autobiography of Red: A Novel in Verse*, 1998; *Men in the Off Hours*, 2000; *The*

Beauty of the Husband: A Fictional Essay in 29 Tangos, 2001; and *If Not, Winter: Fragments of Sappho*, 2002. Other works include her classical study *Eros the Bittersweet: An Essay*, 1986, and *Economy of the Unlost: Reading Simonides of Keos with Paul Celan*, 1999. Criticism of her work can be found in *American and Canadian Women Poets, 1930–Present*, ed. Harold Bloom, 2002.

Charles Causley
Causley's many publications include his *Collected Poems, 1951–2000*, rev. ed. 2000, as well as plays, short stories, and anthologies. Critical discussions of his poetry can be found in Elizabeth Jennings, *Poetry Today 1957–60*, 1961; Vernon Scannell, *Not Without Glory: Poets of the Second World War*, 1976; Edward Levy, "The Poetry of Charles Causley," in *PN Review* 5.2, 1978; Michael Schmidt, *An Introduction to 50 Modern British Poets*, 1979; *Causley at Seventy*, ed. Harry Chambers, 1987; Anthony Thwaite, *Poetry Today: A Critical Guide to British Poetry, 1960–95*, 1996; and Dana Gioia, *Barrier of a Common Language*, 2003.

See also entries for **Voices from World War II.**

J. M. Coetzee
Dusklands, 1974, consists of two linked novellas. It was followed by the novels *In the Heart of the Country*, 1977; *Waiting for the Barbarians*, 1980; *Life & Times of Michael K.*, 1983; *Foe*, 1986; *Age of Iron*, 1990; *The Master of Petersburg*, 1994; *Disgrace*, 1999; and *Elizabeth Costello*, 2003. Coetzee's nonfiction includes *White Writing: On the Culture of Letters in South Africa*, 1988; *Doubling the Point: Essays and Interviews*, 1992; *Giving Offense: Essays on Censorship*, 1996; the fictionalized lecture *The Lives of Animals*, 1999; and *Stranger Shores: Literary Essays, 1986–1999*, 2001. He coedited, with André Philippus Brink, *A Land Apart: A Contemporary South African Reader*, 1986. He edited and translated *Landscape with Rowers: Poetry from the Netherlands*, 2004, a facing-page collection of six twentieth-century Dutch poets. Kevin Goddard, John Read, and Teresa Dovey's *J. M. Coetzee: A Bibliography*, 1990, is comprehensive of his work to 1990. For Coetzee's life see his fictionalized memoirs *Boyhood: Scenes from Provincial Life*, 1997, and *Youth: Scenes from Provincial Life II*, 2002.

An inclusive overview of Coetzee's fiction is Dominic Head's *J. M. Coetzee*, 1997. Allen Penner's *Countries of the Mind: The Fiction of J. M. Coetzee*, 1989, illuminates work up to and including *Foe*. For a range of criticism see Graham Huggan and Stephen Watson's *Critical Perspectives on J. M. Coetzee*, 1996. Coetzee is examined as a specifically South African postcolonial writer in Susan Gallagher's *A Story of South Africa: J. M. Coetzee's Fiction in Context*, 1991; David Attwell's *J. M. Coetzee: South*

Africa and the Politics of Writing, 1993; Sue Kossew's Critical Essays on J. M. Coetzee, 1998; and Derek Attridge's J. M. Coetzee & the Ethics of Reading, 2004. A special issue of South Atlantic Quarterly, 93.1, ed. Michael Valdez Moses, 1994, is devoted to Coetzee's work.

Joseph Conrad
The standard edition of Conrad's works is The Uniform Edition of the Works of Joseph Conrad, 22 vols., 1923–38, reprinted 1946–55 as the Collected Edition of the Works of Joseph Conrad. Useful essays and notes to the novels are provided by the Norton Critical Editions of Lord Jim, ed. Thomas C. Moser, 2nd ed. 1996; The Nigger of the "Narcissus," ed. Robert Kimbrough, 1979; and Heart of Darkness, ed. Robert Kimbrough, 3rd ed. 1988. The Modern Library edition of Nostromo, 1951, also contains an illuminating introductory essay by Robert Penn Warren. Conrad's letters have been published as The Collected Letters of Joseph Conrad, 6 vols., ed. Frederick R. Karl and Laurence Davies, 1983–2002, and the selection Letters from Joseph Conrad, 1895–1924, 1 vol., ed. Edward Garnett, 1928; these are supplemented by material in Joseph Conrad's Letters to R. B. Cunninghame Graham, ed. C. T. Watts, 1969; the collection A Portrait in Letters: Correspondence to and about Conrad, ed. J. H. Stape and Owen Knowles, 1996, is also helpful. Biographies include Zdzislaw Najder's Joseph Conrad: A Chronicle, 1983; Cedric Watts's Joseph Conrad: A Literary Life, 1989; Jeffrey Meyers's Joseph Conrad: A Biography, 1991; and John Batchelor's The Life of Joseph Conrad: A Critical Biography, 1994. Memoirs of Conrad include Jessie Conrad's Joseph Conrad as I Knew Him, 1926, and Joseph Conrad and His Circle, 1935; and Ford Madox Ford's Joseph Conrad: A Personal Remembrance, 1965. See also material collected in Joseph Conrad: Interviews and Recollections, ed. Martin Ray, 1990. The standard bibliography is Joseph Conrad: An Annotated Bibliography, ed. Bruce Teets, 1990.

Ian Watt's Conrad in the Nineteenth Century, 1979; Fredric Jameson's The Political Unconscious: Narrative as a Socially Symbolic Act, 1981; Jakob Lothe's Conrad's Narrative Method, 1989; Vincent P. Pecora's Self and Form in Modern Narrative, 1989, and Michael Greaney's Conrad, Language, and Narrative, 2002, examine Conrad's narrative strategies. Heliéna Krenn's Conrad's Lingard Trilogy: Empire, Race and Women in the Malay Novels, 1990, and Ruth Nadelhaft's Joseph Conrad, 1991, offer feminist perspectives, and gender-theoretical criticism includes Andrew Michael Roberts's Conrad and Gender, 1993, and Conrad and Masculinity, 2000. Christopher GoGwilt's The Invention of the West: Joseph Conrad and the Double-Mapping of Europe and Empire, 1995, presents a postcolonial perspective. Peter J.

Glassman's Language and Being: Joseph Conrad and the Literature of Personality, 1976, offers a psychological analysis. Conrad on Film, ed. Gene M. Moore, 1997, is also helpful.

A guide to Conrad's work is The Cambridge Companion to Joseph Conrad, ed. J. H. Stape, 1996. In addition to the essays in the Norton Critical Editions, criticism on both Heart of Darkness and The Nigger of the "Narcissus" can be found in Conrad: The Critical Heritage, ed. Norman Sherry, 1973; Joseph Conrad, ed. Harold Bloom, 1986; Joseph Conrad: Critical Assessments, 4 vols., ed. Keith Carabine, 1992; A Joseph Conrad Companion, ed. Leonard Orr and Theodore Billy, 1999; and Essays on Conrad, ed. Ian Watt, 2000.

For further reading on The Nigger of the "Narcissus," see Conrad's Manifesto: Preface to a Career: The History of the Preface to The Nigger of the "Narcissus," with Facsimiles of the Manuscripts, ed. David R. Smith and Leonard Baskin, 1966; James W. Parins and Todd K. Bender's A Concordance to Conrad's The Nigger of the "Narcissus," 1981; and chapters in Michael Levenson's A Genealogy of Modernism, 1984, and in Michael North's The Dialect of Modernism, 1994.

For works concerning Heart of Darkness, see Gary Adelman's Heart of Darkness: Search for the Unconscious, 1987; Joseph Conrad's Heart of Darkness, ed. Harold Bloom, 1987; Heart of Darkness: A Case Study in Contemporary Criticism, ed. Ross C. Murfin, 1989; Marlow, ed. Harold Bloom, 1992; Nicolas Tredell's Joseph Conrad: Heart of Darkness, 1999; Peter Edgerley Firchow's Envisioning Africa: Racism and Imperialism in Conrad's Heart of Darkness, 2000; an essay in J. Hillis Miller's Others, 2001, and another by Richard J. Ruppel in Imperial Desire: Dissident Sexualities and Colonial Literature, ed. Philip Holden and Richard J. Ruppel, 2003.

Keith Douglas
Alamein to Zem Zem, ed. John Waller, 1966, a memoir of Douglas's World War II experience in North Africa; A Prose Miscellany, 1985; The Complete Poems, 3rd ed. 1998; and The Letters, 2000, are all edited by Desmond Graham, author of Keith Douglas, 1920–1944: A Biography, 1974. Further critical discussion of Douglas's poems can be found in Vernon Scannell's Not without Glory: Poets of the Second World War, 1976; Penny Pittman Merliss's In Another Country: Three Poets of the Second World War, 1987; and William Scammell's Keith Douglas: A Study, 1988.

Carol Ann Duffy
Duffy's volumes of poetry include "Fleshweathercock" and Other Poems, 1973; Fifth Last Song, 1982; Standing Female Nude, 1985; Thrown Voices, 1986; Selling Manhattan, 1987; The Other Country, 1990; Mean Time, 1993;

Selected Poems, 1994; The Pamphlet, 1998; The World's Wife: Poems, 1999; The Salmon Carol Ann Duffy: Poems Selected and New 1985–1999, 2000; and Feminine Gospels: Poems, 2003. Along with many books for younger readers, she has also written plays, including Take My Husband, 1982; Cavern of Dreams, 1984; Little Women, Big Boys, 1986; and the radio play Loss, 1986. Collections edited by Duffy include I Wouldn't Thank You for a Valentine: Poems for Young Feminists, 1992, and Stopping for Death: Poems of Death and Loss, 1996, both illustrated by Trisha Rafferty. In 1999, when she appeared to be a leading candidate for British poet laureate, a number of profiles and interviews appeared in The Guardian, The Independent, and other British newspapers.

A book-length study of Duffy's work is Deryn Rees-Jones's Carol Ann Duffy, 1999. Other discussions include Four Women Poets, ed. Judith Baxter, 1995, and The Poetry of Carol Ann Duffy: "Choosing Tough Words," ed. Angelica Michelis and Antony Rowland, 2003.

T. S. Eliot

The Complete Poems and Plays of T. S. Eliot was published in 1969. Inventions of the March Hare: Poems, 1909–1917, ed. Christopher Ricks, brought early unpublished work to light in 1996. The fascinating manuscripts of The Waste Land are available as The Waste Land: A Facsimile and Transcript of the Original Drafts Including the Annotations of Ezra Pound, ed. Valerie Eliot, 1971. Also immensely useful is the Norton Critical Edition of The Waste Land, ed. Michael North, 2001, which contains contextual documents and criticism in addition to the poem. Eliot's most important critical essays are to be found in The Sacred Wood: Essays on Poetry and Criticism, 1920; The Use of Poetry and the Use of Criticism: Studies in the Relation of Criticism to Poetry in England, 1933; The Idea of a Christian Society, 1939; Notes towards the Definition of Culture, 1948; On Poetry and Poets, 1957; To Criticize the Critic and Other Writings, 1965; and The Varieties of Metaphysical Poetry, ed. Ronald Schuchard, 1994. Important biographies include Peter Ackroyd's T. S. Eliot: A Life, 1984, and Lyndall Gordon's T. S. Eliot: An Imperfect Life, 1999. Also helpful is The Letters of T. S. Eliot, Vol. I: 1898–1922, ed. Valerie Eliot, 1988.

Studies of Eliot's work include F. O. Matthiessen's The Achievement of T. S. Eliot, 3rd ed. 1958; Northrop Frye's T. S. Eliot, 1963; Bernard Bergonzi's T. S. Eliot, 1972; Stephen Spender's T. S. Eliot, 1976; Ronald Bush's T. S. Eliot: A Study in Character and Style, 1983; Robert Crawford's The Savage and the City in the Work of T. S. Eliot, 1987; Louis Menand's Discovering Modernism, 1987; Richard Shusterman's T. S. Eliot and the Philosophy of Criticism, 1988; Christopher Ricks's T. S. Eliot and Prejudice, 1988; Eric Sigg's The American T. S. Eliot: A Study of the Early Writings, 1989; Michael North's The Political Aesthetic of Yeats, Eliot, and Pound, 1991; Jewel Spears Brooker's Mastery and Escape: T. S. Eliot and the Dialectic of Modernism, 1994; Anthony Julius's T. S. Eliot, Anti-Semitism and Literary Form, 1995; T. S. Eliot, ed. Harriet Davidson, 1999; Ronald Schuchard's Eliot's Dark Angel: Intersections of Life and Art, 1999; and Donald J. Childs's From Philosophy to Poetry: T. S. Eliot's Study of Knowledge and Experience, 2001.

Valuable collections of essays include T. S. Eliot: A Collection of Critical Essays, ed. Hugh Kenner, 1962; T. S. Eliot: A Collection of Criticism, ed. Linda Wagner-Martin, 1974; T. S. Eliot: The Critical Heritage, ed. Michael Grant, 1982; T. S. Eliot: Modern Critical Views, ed. Harold Bloom, 1985; T. S. Eliot, A Voice Descanting: Centenary Essays, ed. Shyamal Bagchee, 1990; T. S. Eliot: The Modernist in History, ed. Ronald Bush, 1991; T. S. Eliot, ed. Harold Bloom, 1999; and T. S. Eliot and Our Turning World, ed. Jewel Spears Brooker, 2001. Donald C. Gallup's T. S. Eliot: A Bibliography, rev. ed. 1969, is also useful.

Helpful guides to the poetry and plays are Grover Smith's T. S. Eliot's Poetry and Plays: A Study in Sources and Meanings, 1956; Carol H. Smith's T. S. Eliot's Dramatic Theory and Practice, from Sweeney Agonistes to The Elder Statesman, 1963; The Cambridge Companion to T. S. Eliot, ed. A. David Moody, 1994; and A Concordance to the Complete Poems and Plays of T. S. Eliot, ed. J. L. Dawson et al., 1995.

For further reading on Eliot's poetry, see Elizabeth Drew's T. S. Eliot, The Design of His Poetry, 1949; Helen Gardner's The Art of T. S. Eliot, 1950; Hugh Kenner's The Invisible Poet, 1959; David Moody's Thomas Stearns Eliot, Poet, 1979; Maud Ellmann's The Poetics of Impersonality: T. S. Eliot and Ezra Pound, 1987; Lee Oser's T. S. Eliot and American Poetry, 1998; and Denis Donoghue's Words Alone: The Poet, T. S. Eliot, 2000. On Four Quartets see Helen Gardner's The Composition of Four Quartets, 1978.

For further reading on The Waste Land, see Eliot in His Time: Essays on the Occasion of the Fiftieth Anniversary of The Waste Land, ed. A. Walton Litz, 1973; Harriet Davidson's T. S. Eliot and Hermeneutics: Absence and Interpretation in The Waste Land, 1985; Calvin Bedient's He Do the Police in Different Voices: The Waste Land and Its Protagonists, 1986; T. S. Eliot's The Waste Land, ed. Harold Bloom, 1986; Nancy K. Gish's The Waste Land: A Poem of Memory and Desire, 1988; and Jewel Spears Brooker and Joseph Bentley's Reading The Waste Land: Modernism and the Limits of Interpretation, 1990.

E. M. Forster

Forster's major novels are *Where Angels Fear to Tread*, 1905; *The Longest Journey*, 1907; *A Room with a View*, 1908; *Howards End*, 1910; and *A Passage to India*, 1924. A sixth novel, *Maurice*, was finished in 1914 but published posthumously in 1971. *The Collected Tales of E. M. Forster* appeared in 1947, and *The Life to Come and Other Stories* was published posthumously in 1972. Philip Gardner edited Forster's *Commonplace Book* in 1985. *Abinger Harvest*, a collection of some eighty essays, was published in 1936, and *Two Cheers for Democracy*, a second collection, was published in 1951. Forster's provocative study of fictional technique, *Aspects of the Novel*, appeared in 1927. His biography of his aunt, *Marianne Thornton: A Domestic Biography, 1797–1887*, 1956, is a contribution to Victorian social history. For his life see *E. M. Forster: A Life*, 1978, by P. N. Furbank, who, with Mary Lago, edited Forster's *Selected Letters*, 2 vols., 1983, 1985; Nicola Beauman's *E. M. Forster: A Biography*, 1994, is also useful. See also P. J. Kirkpatrick's *A Bibliography of E. M. Forster*, 2nd ed. 1985.

Studies of Forster's work include Frederick Crews's *E. M. Forster: The Perils of Humanism*, 1962; Lionel Trilling's *E. M. Forster*, 2nd ed. 1965; Wilfred Stone's *The Cave and the Mountain: A Study of E. M. Forster*, 1966; G. K. Das's *E. M. Forster's India*, 1977; Robin Jared Lewis's *E. M. Forster's Passages to India*, 1979; Barbara Rosecrance's *Forster's Narrative Vision*, 1982; Claude J. Summers's *E. M. Forster*, 1983; David Medalie's *E. M. Forster's Modernism*, 2002; *Narrative Dynamics: Essays on Time, Plot, Closure, and Frames*, ed. Brian Richardson, 2002; James J. Miracky's *Regenerating the Novel: Gender and Genre in Woolf, Forster, Sinclair, and Lawrence*, 2003; and Muhammad Shahin's *E. M. Forster and the Politics of Imperialism*, 2004. Valuable collections of essays are *E. M. Forster: The Critical Heritage*, ed. Philip Gardner, 1973; *Critical Essays on E. M. Forster*, ed. Alan Wilde, 1985; and *E. M. Forster*, ed. Harold Bloom, 1987.

Brian Friel

Plays One, 1984, 1996, and *Plays Two*, 1999, draw from Friel's dramatic works, including *The Saucer of Larks*, 1962; *Philadelphia, Here I Come!*, 1965; *The Gold in the Sea*, 1966; *The Loves of Cass McGuire*, 1967; *Lovers*, 1968; *Crystal and Fox*, 1970; *The Mundy Scheme*, 1970; *The Gentle Island*, 1973; *The Freedom of the City*, 1974; *The Enemy Within*, 1975; *Living Quarters*, 1978; *Volunteers*, 1979; *Aristocrats*, 1980; *Faith Healer*, 1980; *Anton Chekhov's Three Sisters: A Translation*, 1981; *Translations*, 1981; *The Communication Cord*, 1983; *Fathers and Sons: After the Novel by Ivan Turgenev*, 1987; *Making History*, 1989; *Dancing at Lughnasa*, 1990; *The London Vertigo, Based on a Play*

The True Born Irishman, or, The Irish Fine Lady, by Charles Macklin, 1990; *A Month in the Country: After Turgenev*, 1992; *Wonderful Tennessee*, 1993; *Molly Sweeney*, 1994; *Give Me Your Answer, Do!*, 1997; *Uncle Vanya: A Version of the Play by Anton Chekhov*, 1998; *The Yalta Game: After Chekhov*, 2001; *Three Plays After*, 2002. Friel's fiction can be found in *Selected Stories*, 1979, and *The Diviner: The Best Stories of Brian Friel*, 1982. Friel is also editor of Charles McGlinchey's *The Last of the Name*, 1986, 1999.

For biographical information and criticism see *Brian Friel: Essays, Diaries, Interviews, 1964–1999*, ed. Christopher Murray, 1999, and *Brian Friel in Conversation*, ed. Paul Delaney, 2000. *Ten Modern Irish Playwrights: A Comprehensive Annotated Bibliography*, ed. Kimball King, 1979, is a helpful resource.

Brian Friel: A Reference Guide, 1962–1992, ed. George O'Brien, 1995, provides a useful guide to most of Friel's work. For criticism of Friel's work see D. E. S. Maxwell's *Brian Friel*, 1973; Seamus Deane's *Essays in Modern Irish Literature: 1880–1980*, 1985; Ulf Dantanus's *Brian Friel: The Growth of an Irish Dramatist*, 1985, and *Brian Friel: A Study*, 1988; *Critical Approaches to Anglo-Irish Literature*, ed. Michael Allen and Angela Wilcox, 1989; George O'Brien's *Brian Friel*, 1990; Elmer Kennedy-Andrews's *The Art of Brian Friel: Neither Reality nor Dreams*, 1995; *Brian Friel: A Casebook*, ed. William Kerwin, 1997; Nicholas Grene's *The Politics of Irish Drama: Plays in Context from Boucicault to Friel*, 1999; Richard Pine's *The Diviner: The Art of Brian Friel*, 2nd ed. 1999; F. C. McGrath's *Brian Friel's (Post)Colonial Drama: Language, Illusion, and Politics*, 1999; and Tony Corbett's *Brian Friel: Decoding the Language of the Tribe*, 2002. The Norton Critical Edition *Modern Irish Drama*, ed. John P. Harrington, 1991, includes backgrounds and criticism for *Translations*. For criticism of Friel's drama and short stories, see *A Companion to Brian Friel*, ed. Richard Harp and Robert C. Evans, 2002.

Nadine Gordimer

Gordimer's novels include *The Lying Days*, 1953; *A World of Strangers*, 1958; *Occasion for Loving*, 1963; *The Late Bourgeois World*, 1966; *A Guest of Honour*, 1970; *The Conservationist*, 1974; *Burger's Daughter*, 1979; *July's People*, 1981; *A Sport of Nature*, 1987; *My Son's Story*, 1990; *None to Accompany Me*, 1994; *The House Gun*, 1998; and *The Pickup*, 2001. Gordimer's short-story collections include *Face to Face*, 1949; *The Soft Voice of the Serpent*, 1952; *Six Feet of the Country*, 1956; *Friday's Footprints*, 1960; *Not for Publication*, 1965; *Livingstone's Companions*, 1971; *Some Monday for Sure*, 1976; *A Soldier's Embrace*, 1980; *Something*

Out There, 1984; Jump, 1991; and Loot, and Other Stories, 2003. Collected editions of her stories include Why Haven't You Written?: Selected Stories, 1950–1972, 1992, and Selected Stories, 2000. Gordimer's essays are collected in The Essential Gesture: Writing, Politics and Places, ed. Stephen Clingman, 1988; Writing and Being, 1995; and Living in Hope and History: Notes from Our Century, 1999.

A celebration of Gordimer's work, A Writing Life: Celebrating Nadine Gordimer, ed. Andries Walter Oliphant, was published in 1998. For her life see Conversations with Nadine Gordimer, ed. Nancy Topping Bazin and Marilyn Dallman Seymour, 1990. For a bibliography see Nadine Gordimer: A Bibliography of Primary and Secondary Sources, 1937–1992, ed. Dorothy Driver, 1994.

The following critical accounts include postcolonial, feminist, and political perspectives on Gordimer's work: Abdul R. JanMohamed's Manichean Aesthetics: The Politics of Literature in Colonial Africa, 1983; Stephen Clingman's The Novels of Nadine Gordimer: History from the Inside, 1986; Judie Newman's Nadine Gordimer, 1988; Critical Essays on Nadine Gordimer, ed. Rowland Smith, 1990; The Later Fiction of Nadine Gordimer, ed. Bruce King, 1993; Andrew V. Ettin's Betrayals of the Body Politic: The Literary Commitments of Nadine Gordimer, 1993; Dominic Head's Nadine Gordimer, 1994; Kathrin M. Wagner's Rereading Nadine Gordimer, 1994; Barbara Temple-Thurston's Nadine Gordimer Revisited, 1999; Martine Watson Brownley's Deferrals of Domain: Contemporary Women Novelists and the State, 2000; Joya F. Uraizee's This Is No Place for a Woman: Nadine Gordimer, Buchi Emecheta, and Nayantara Saghal and the Politics of Gender, 2000; and Brighton J. Uledi Kamanga's Cracks in the Wall: Nadine Gordimer's Fiction and the Irony of Apartheid, 2002.

Robert Graves

Graves's Complete Poems, ed. Beryl Graves and Dunstan Ward, was published in three volumes in 1995, 1997, and 1999. His Complete Short Stories, ed. Lucia Graves, was published in 1996. A selection of Graves's criticism is Collected Writings on Poetry, ed. Paul O'Prey, 1995. Other important prose works include On English Poetry, 1922; The Meaning of Dreams, 1924; A Survey of Modernist Poetry, with Laura Riding, 1927; The Long Week End: A Social History of England 1919–1939, with Alan Hodge, 1940; The White Goddess, 1948, enl. ed., 1966; The Common Asphodel: Collected Essays on Poetry, 1922–1949, 1949; and On Poetry: Collected Talks and Essays, 1969. Graves also published many historical novels, including I, Claudius, 1934; Claudius the God, 1935; Count Belisarius, 1938; Sergeant Lamb's America, 1940; Wife to Mr. Milton, 1943; and Homer's

Daughter, 1955. Interviews are collected in Conversations with Robert Graves, ed. Frank L. Kersnowski, 1989. Selected letters appear in In Broken Images: Selected Letters of Robert Graves, 1914–1946, ed. O'Prey, 1982; Between Moon and Moon: Selected Letters of Robert Graves, 1946–1972, ed. O'Prey, 1984; and Dear Robert, Dear Spike: The Graves–Milligan Correspondence, ed. Pauline Scudamore, 1991. Graves's autobiography, Good-Bye to All That, was first published in 1929 and then in several revised editions. Biographies include Martin Seymour-Smith's Robert Graves: His Life and Work, 1983; Miranda Seymour's Robert Graves: Life on the Edge, 1995; and Richard Perceval Graves's Robert Graves, 3 vols., 1987–95. An updated version of Fred H. Higginson and William Proctor Williams's A Bibliography of the Writings of Robert Graves was published in 1987.

Studies of Graves's work include Seymour-Smith's Robert Graves, 1956; J. M. Cohen's Robert Graves, 1960; Douglas Day's Swifter than Reason: The Poetry and Criticism of Robert Graves, 1963; George Stade's Robert Graves, 1967; Michael Kirkham's The Poetry of Robert Graves, 1969; John B. Vickery's Robert Graves and the White Goddess, 1972; Paul Fussell's The Great War and Modern Memory, 1975; James S. Mehoke's Robert Graves: Peace-Weaver, 1975; Katherine Snipes's Robert Graves, 1979; Patrick J. Keane's A Wild Civility: Interactions in the Poetry and Thought of Robert Graves, 1980; D. N. G. Carter's Robert Graves: The Lasting Poetic Achievement, 1989; Patrick J. Quinn's The Great War and the Missing Muse: The Early Writings of Robert Graves and Siegfried Sassoon, 1994; and Kersnowski's The Early Poetry of Robert Graves: The Goddess Beckons, 2002. Collections of essays include Robert Graves, ed. Harold Bloom, 1987, and New Perspectives on Robert Graves, ed. Quinn, 1999.

Thom Gunn

Thom Gunn's Collected Poems appeared in 1994; Boss Cupid, in 2000. The Occasions of Poetry: Essays in Criticism and Autobiography, ed. Clive Wilmer, 1982, and Shelf Life: Essays, Memoirs, and an Interview, 1993, are collections of essays and autobiographical writings. For his life see the interview Gunn contributed to Viewpoints: Poets in Conversation with John Haffenden, 1981, and Thom Gunn in Conversation with James Campbell, 2000. Jack W. C. Hagstrom and George Bixby's Thom Gunn: A Bibliography 1940–1978, 1979, lists interviews as well as poems and articles.

Studies of Gunn's work include Alan Norman Bold's Thom Gunn and Ted Hughes, 1976; Three Contemporary Poets: Thom Gunn, Ted Hughes, and R. S. Thomas: A Casebook, ed. A. E. Dyson, 1990. Discussions of Gunn's work can be found in John Press's Rule and Energy: Trends in British Poetry since the Second World

War, 1963; *British Poetry since 1960: A Critical Survey*, ed. Michael Schmidt and Grevel Lindop, 1972; and *Contemporary British Poetry: Essays in Theory and Criticism*, ed. James Acheson and Romana Huk, 1996. *PN Review 70*, 1989, is devoted chiefly to Gunn and contains useful discussions of his work. For further reading on Gunn and "The Movement," see Jerry Bradley's *The Movement: British Poets of the 1950s*, 1993.

Ivor Gurney

During his lifetime Gurney published two volumes: *Severn and Somme*, 1917, and *War's Embers*, 1919, but at his death some seven hundred poems remained unpublished. *Collected Poems of Ivor Gurney*, ed. P. J. Kavanagh, 1982, includes many of the works Gurney left unpublished at his death. Gurney was also a musical composer; of special note are his song accompaniments to *Severn and Somme*. Gurney's letters have been published as *War Letters: A Selection*, 1983, and *Collected Letters*, 1991, both edited by R. K. R. Thornton. For his life see Michael Hurd's *The Ordeal of Ivor Gurney*, 1978, and John Lucas's *Ivor Gurney*, 2001. Thornton and George Walter's *Ivor Gurney: Towards a Bibliography* was published in 1996.

Discussions of Gurney's work can be found in Jon Silkin's *Out of Battle: The Poetry of the Great War*, 1972, 2nd ed. 1998; Paul Fussell's *The Great War and Modern Memory*, 1975; Piers Gray's *Marginal Men: Edward Thomas, Ivor Gurney, J. R. Ackerley*, 1991; Jon Stallworthy's *Great Poets of World War I: Poetry from the Great War*, 2002. The Ivor Gurney Society publishes its journal annually.

Thomas Hardy

Hardy published over a dozen volumes of poetry in his lifetime. His complete poems can be found in *Thomas Hardy: The Complete Poems*, ed. James Gibson, 1978, or *The Complete Poetical Works of Thomas Hardy*, 3 vols., ed. Samuel Lynn Hynes, 1982–95. There are several collected editions of Hardy's complete works, notably the Wessex Edition, 21 vols., 1912–14, and the Mellstock Edition, 37 vols., 1919–20. Useful essays and notes to Hardy's novels are provided by the Norton Critical Editions of *The Return of the Native*, ed. James Gindin, 1969; *Far from the Madding Crowd*, ed. Robert C. Schweik, 1986; *Tess of the D'Urbervilles*, ed. Scott Elledge, 3rd ed. 1991; *Jude the Obscure*, ed. Norman Page, 2nd ed. 1999; and *The Mayor of Casterbridge*, 2nd ed., ed. Phillip Mallett, 2001. Michael Millgate and Richard Little Purdy have edited *The Collected Letters of Thomas Hardy*, 7 vols., 1978–88. Millgate has also edited *Selected Letters*, 1990, and *Thomas Hardy's Public Voice: The Essays, Speeches, and Miscellaneous Prose*, 2001. Harold Orel has edited *Thomas Hardy's Personal Writings: Prefaces, Literary Opinions, Reminiscences*, 1990.

For Hardy's life see Robert Gittings's *Young Thomas Hardy*, 1975, and *Thomas Hardy's Later Years*, 1978; Millgate's *Thomas Hardy: A Biography*, 1982; F. B. Pinion's *Thomas Hardy: His Life and Friends*, 1992; Gibson's *Thomas Hardy: A Literary Life*, 1996; and Paul Turner's *The Life of Thomas Hardy: A Critical Biography*, 1998. *Thomas Hardy: Interviews and Recollections*, ed. Gibson, 1999, is also worth consulting.

The Cambridge Companion to Thomas Hardy, ed. Dale Kramer, 1999, and *The Oxford Reader's Companion to Hardy*, ed. Page, 2000, are good guides to Hardy's work. Pinion's *A Hardy Companion: A Guide to the Works of Thomas Hardy and Their Background*, 1968, continues to be useful. Helpful reference works include Sarah Bird Wright's *Thomas Hardy A to Z: The Essential Reference to His Life and Work*, 2002, and Geoffrey Harvey's *The Complete Critical Guide to Thomas Hardy*, 2003.

For criticism on Hardy's prose and poetry, see *Hardy: A Collection of Critical Essays*, ed. Albert Guérard, 1963; J. Hillis Miller's *Thomas Hardy: Distance and Desire*, 1970; Jean R. Brooks's *Thomas Hardy: The Poetic Structure*, 1971; John Bayley's *An Essay on Hardy*, 1978; *Thomas Hardy: The Writer and His Background*, ed. Page, 1980; *Thomas Hardy*, ed. Harold Bloom, 1982, 2003; and *Thomas Hardy*, ed. Patricia Ingham, 1990, 2003.

For criticism concerning Hardy's poetry, see Hynes's *The Pattern of Hardy's Poetry*, 1956; Donald Davie's *Thomas Hardy and British Poetry*, 1972; Tom Paulin's *Thomas Hardy: The Poetry of Perception*, 1975; *The Poetry of Thomas Hardy*, ed. Patricia Clements and Juliet Grindle, 1980; William Earl Buckler's *The Poetry of Thomas Hardy: A Study in Art and Ideas*, 1983; and James Persoon's *Hardy's Early Poetry: Romanticism through a "Dark Bilberry Eye,"* 2000. For criticism of individual poems J. O. Bailey's *The Poetry of Thomas Hardy: A Handbook and Commentary*, 1970, and Pinion's *A Commentary on the Poems of Thomas Hardy*, 1976, are useful.

For criticism concerning Hardy's fiction see Shirley A. Stave's *The Decline of the Goddess: Nature, Culture, and Women in Thomas Hardy's Fiction*, 1995; Shanta Dutta's *Ambivalence in Hardy: A Study of His Attitude to Women*, 2000; Rosemary Sumner's *A Route to Modernism: Hardy, Lawrence, Woolf*, 2000; and Joanna Devereux's *Patriarchy and Its Discontents: Sexual Politics in Selected Novels and Stories of Thomas Hardy*, 2003.

The Hardy Centennial Number of *The Southern Review*, 1940, was influential in shaping Hardy's critical reputation; the special Hardy issues of *Agenda*, 1970, and *Victorian Poetry*, 1979, are also notable.

Tony Harrison

Harrison's volumes of poetry include *Earthworks*, 1964; *Newcastle Is Peru*, 1969; *The*

Loiners, 1970; *From "The School of Eloquence" and Other Poems*, 1978; *Continuous: Fifty Sonnets from "The School of Eloquence,"* 1981; *A Kumquat for John Keats*, 1981; *U. S. Martial*, 1981; *Selected Poems*, 1984, 1987; *"V." and Other Poems*, 1990; *A Cold Coming*, 1991; *The Gaze of the Gorgon*, 1992; and *Permanently Bard: Selected Poetry*, 1995. Among his collections of dramatic verse are *Theatre Works: 1973–1985*, 1986; *Plays Three*, 1996; *Plays One*, 2001; *Plays Two*, 2002; and *Plays Four*, 2002. Harrison's television and screen credits include *Black Daisies for the Bride*, 1993; *Prometheus*, 1998; and *"The Shadow of Hiroshima" and Other Film/Poems*, 1995. For his life see Joe Kelleher's *Tony Harrison*, 1996. John R. Kaiser's *Tony Harrison: A Bibliography, 1957–1987* was published in 1989.

Collections of essays focusing on Harrison's work include *Tony Harrison*, ed. Neil Astley, 1991, and *Tony Harrison: Loiner*, ed. Sandie Byrne, 1997. Other criticism of his work includes Luke Spencer's *The Poetry of Tony Harrison*, 1994; Byrne's *H, v. & O: The Poetry of Tony Harrison*, 1998; and Antony Rowland's *Tony Harrison and the Holocaust*, 2001.

Seamus Heaney

Heaney's volumes of poetry include *Death of a Naturalist*, 1966; *Door into the Dark*, 1969; *Wintering Out*, 1972; *North*, 1975; *Field Work*, 1979; *Sweeney Astray: A Version from the Irish*, 1983; *Station Island*, 1984; *The Haw Lantern*, 1987; *Seeing Things*, 1991; *Sweeney's Flight*, 1992; *The Spirit Level*, 1996; *Opened Ground: Selected Poems, 1966–1996*, 1998; and *Electric Light*, 2001. He is translator of *The Cure at Troy: A Version of Sophocles's Philoctetes*, 1990, and of *The Midnight Verdict*, based on Ovid's *Metamorphoses* and Brian Merriman's *Cúirt an Mheán Oíche*, 1993; he is cotranslator, with Stanislaw Baranczak, of Jan Kochanowski's *Laments*, 1995. His translation of Ozef Kalda's poems set into a song cycle by Leoš Janáček, *Diary of One Who Vanished: A Song Cycle*, was published in 2000; his translation of *Beowulf* was published in 1999 and released in a Norton Critical Edition edited by Daniel Donoghue in 2002. Heaney is also editor of *The Essential Wordsworth*, 1988. Heaney's essays are collected in *Preoccupations: Selected Prose, 1968–1978*, 1980; *The Government of the Tongue: Selected Prose, 1978–1987*, 1988; *The Redress of Poetry: Oxford Lectures*, 1995; and *Finders Keepers: Selected Prose, 1971–2001*, 2002. For his life see Blake Morrison's *Seamus Heaney*, 1982, and Michael Parker's *Seamus Heaney: The Making of the Poet*, 1993. Bibliographical information can be found in Michael J. Durkan and Rand Brandes's *Seamus Heaney: A Reference Guide*, 1996.

For guides to Heaney's poetry see Neil Corcoran's *Seamus Heaney*, 1986, and *Seamus Heaney: Comprehensive Research and Study Guide*, ed. Harold Bloom, 2003. Studies of Heaney's work include Elmer Andrews's *The Poetry of Seamus Heaney: All the Realms of Whisper*, 1988; Thomas C. Foster's *Seamus Heaney*, 1989; Henry Hart's *Seamus Heaney: Poet of Contrary Progressions*, 1992; Bernard O'Donoghue's *Seamus Heaney and the Language of Poetry*, 1994; John Wilson Foster's *The Achievement of Seamus Heaney*, 1995; Helen Vendler's *Seamus Heaney*, 1998; Eugene O'Brien's *Seamus Heaney and the Place of Writing* and *Seamus Heaney: Creating Irelands of the Mind*, 2002; and Floyd Collins's *Seamus Heaney: The Crisis of Identity*, 2003. Collections of essays focusing on Heaney's work include *Seamus Heaney*, ed. Harold Bloom, 1986; *Seamus Heaney: A Collection of Critical Essays*, ed. Andrews, 1992; *The Art of Seamus Heaney*, ed. Tony Curtis, 3rd ed. 1993; and *Critical Essays on Seamus Heaney*, ed. Robert F. Garratt, 1995.

Geoffrey Hill

Hill's *New and Collected Poems, 1952–1992* was published in 1994. Subsequent works include *Canaan*, 1996; *The Triumph of Love*, 1998; *Speech! Speech!*, 2000; and *The Orchards of Syon*, 2002. His prose works include *The Lords of Limit: Essays on Literature and Ideas*, 1984; *Illuminating Shadows: The Mythic Power of Film*, 1992; and *Style and Faith*, 2003. An interview appears in *Viewpoints: Poets in Conversation with John Haffenden*, 1981.

For an overview of Hill's work, see W. S. Milne's *An Introduction to Geoffrey Hill*, 1998. Collections of criticism include *Geoffrey Hill: Essays on His Work*, ed. Peter Robinson, 1985, and *Geoffrey Hill*, ed. Harold Bloom, 1986. Studies of Hill's work include Henry Hart's *The Poetry of Geoffrey Hill*, 1986; Vincent Sherry's *The Uncommon Tongue: The Poetry and Criticism of Geoffrey Hill*, 1987; E. M. Knottenbelt's *Passionate Intelligence: The Poetry of Geoffrey Hill*, 1990; Eleanor J. McNees's *Eucharistic Poetry: The Search for Presence in the Writings of John Donne, Gerard Manley Hopkins, Dylan Thomas, and Geoffrey Hill*, 1992; and Andrew Michael Roberts's *Geoffrey Hill*, 2003. Critical discussions can also be found in John Silkin's chapter in *British Poetry since 1960*, ed. Michael Schmidt and Grevel Lindop, 1972; Christopher Ricks's *The Force of Poetry*, 1984; John Hollander's *The Work of Poetry*, 1997; William Logan's *Reputations of the Tongue: On Poets and Poetry*, 1999; and Peter McDonald's *Serious Poetry: Form and Authority from Yeats to Hill*, 2002. *Agenda* 17.1, 1979, and *Agenda* 23, 1985–86, are special issues dedicated to Hill.

A. E. Housman

The Poems of A. E. Housman, ed. Archie Burnett, was published in 1997. *Collected Poems and Selected Prose*, ed. Christopher Ricks, 1988, is also valuable. Much of Housman's work as a classicist is available in *The Classical Papers of A. E. Housman*, 3 vols., ed. J. Diggle and F. R. D. Goodyear, 1972. Other essays are published in *Selected Prose*, ed. John Carter, 1961. Henry Maas edited *The Letters of A. E. Housman*, 1971. For Housman's life see Laurence Housman's *My Brother, A. E. Housman*, 1938, and Norman Page's *A. E. Housman: A Critical Biography*, 1983. Important reference materials include John Carter, John Sparrow, and William White's *A. E. Housman: A Bibliography*, 2nd ed. 1982, and Clyde Kenneth Hyder's *A Concordance to the Poems of A. E. Housman*, 1966.

Book-length studies of Housman's work include B. J. Leggett's *The Poetic Art of A. E. Housman: Theory and Practice*, 1978; Richard Perceval Graves's *A. E. Housman, The Scholar-Poet*, 1979; John Bayley's *Housman's Poems*, 1992; Keith Jebb's *A. E. Housman*, 1992; Terence Allan Hoagwood's *A. E. Housman Revisited*, 1995; and Carol Efrati's *The Road of Danger, Guilt, and Shame: The Lonely Way of A. E. Housman*, 2002. Collections of essays about Housman's work include *A. E. Housman: A Collection of Critical Essays*, ed. Ricks, 1968; *A. E. Housman: The Critical Heritage*, ed. Philip Gardner, 1992; and *A. E. Housman: A Reassessment*, ed. Alan W. Holden and J. Roy Birch, 2000. The Housman Society also publishes a journal.

Ted Hughes

Ted Hughes: Collected Poems, ed. Paul Keegan, was published in 2003 and includes poetry from *The Hawk in the Rain*, 1957; *Lupercal*, 1960; *Wodwo*, 1967; *Crow*, 1970; *Season Songs*, 1975; *Gaudete*, 1977; *Cave Birds: An Alchemical Cave Drama*, 1978; *Moortown*, 1979; *Remains of Elmet*, 1979; *River*, 1983; *Flowers and Insects: Some Birds and a Pair of Spiders*, 1986; *Wolfwatching*, 1989; *Capriccio*, 1990; *"Rain-Charm for the Duchy" and Other Laureate Poems*, 1992; *New Selected Poems, 1957–1994*, 1995; *Difficulties of a Bridegroom*, 1995; *Tales from Ovid*, 1997; and *Birthday Letters*, 1998. Hughes's prose works include *Poetry in the Making*, 1967; *Shakespeare and the Goddess of Complete Being*, 1992; and *Winter Pollen: Occasional Prose*, 1994. His translations include Seneca's *Oedipus*, 1969, and Jean Racine's *Phèdre*, 1998. He has also published much literature for children and has edited collections of Shakespeare, Coleridge, Dickinson, Keith Douglas, and Sylvia Plath. For his life see Elaine Feinstein's *Ted Hughes: The Life of a Poet*, 2001, and Diane Middlebrook's *Her Husband: Hughes and Plath—A Marriage*, 2003. Keith Sagar's *The Art of Ted Hughes*, 2nd ed. 1978, offers a detailed critical account of his work as well as a comprehensive bibliography of writings by and about him; Sagar and Stephen Tabor's *Ted Hughes: A Bibliography, 1946–1995*, 1998, is also useful.

Book-length studies of Hughes's work include Sagar's *The Art of Ted Hughes*, 1978; Terry Gifford and Neil Roberts's *Ted Hughes: A Critical Study*, 1981; Thomas West's *Ted Hughes*, 1985; Dennis Walder's *Ted Hughes*, 1987; Craig Robinson's *Ted Hughes as Shepherd of Being*, 1989; Nick Bishop's *Re-Making Poetry: Ted Hughes and a New Critical Psychology*, 1991; Ann Skea's *Ted Hughes: The Poetic Quest*, 1994; Paul Bentley's *The Poetry of Ted Hughes: Language, Illusion, and Beyond*, 1998; and Sagar's *The Laughter of Foxes: A Study of Ted Hughes*, 2000. Collections of essays include *The Achievement of Ted Hughes*, ed. Sagar, 1983; *Critical Essays on Ted Hughes*, ed. Leonard M. Scigaj, 1992; and *The Epic Poise: A Celebration of Ted Hughes*, ed. Nick Gammage, 1999.

David Jones

Jones's major works are the two long poems, *In Parenthesis*, 1937, and *The Anathémata*, 1952. Posthumous volumes of poetry were published as *"The Sleeping Lord" and Other Fragments*, 1974, and *The Roman Quarry and Other Sequences*, ed. Harman Grisewood and René Hague, 1981. A useful selection of Jones's work appears in *Introducing David Jones*, ed. John Matthias, 1980, with a preface by Stephen Spender. Important prose works can be found in *Epoch and Artist: Selected Writings*, 1959, and *"The Dying Gaul" and Other Writings*, 1978, both edited by Grisewood. Jones was also a gifted artist; books he illustrated include Harold Monro's *The Winter Solstice*, 1928, and Roy Fisher's *The Ship's Orchestra*, 1966, as well as his own *In Parenthesis*. Letters are available in *David Jones: Letters to Vernon Watkins*, ed. Ruth Pryor, 1976; *Dai Greatcoat: A Self-Portrait of David Jones in His Letters*, ed. Hague, 1980; *Letters to a Friend*, ed. Aneirin Talfan Davies, 1980; and *Inner Necessities: The Letters of David Jones to Desmond Chute*, ed. Thomas Dilworth, 1984. Samuel Rees's *David Jones: An Annotated Bibliography and Guide to Research* was published in 1977.

For an introduction to Jones see Jon Stallworthy's *Great Poets of World War I: Poetry from the Great War*, 2002. Studies of Jones's poetry include David Blamires's *David Jones: Artist and Writer*, 1972; Jeremy Hooker's *David Jones: An Exploratory Study of the Writings*, 1975; Elizabeth Ward's *David Jones: Mythmaker*, 1983; Dilworth's *The Shape of Meaning in the Poetry of David Jones*, 1988; Kathleen Henderson Staudt's *At the Turn of a Civilization: David Jones and Modern Poetics*, 1994; and Jonathan Miles and Derek Shiel's *David Jones: The Maker Unmade*, 1995. Numerous helpful essays are collected in *David Jones: Artist and Poet*, ed. Paul Hills, 1997. For further reading on *In Parenthesis*, see discussions in John H. Johnston's *English Poetry of the First World War*, 1964; Bernard Bergonzi's *Heroes' Twilight: A Study of the Literature of the Great War*, 1966,

2nd ed. 1980; Jon Silkin's *Out of Battle: The Poetry of the Great War*, 1972, 2nd ed. 1998; and Paul Fussell's *The Great War and Modern Memory*, 1975.

James Joyce
The most reliable edition of *Ulysses*, 1922, is *Ulysses: A Critical and Synoptic Edition*, 3 vols., ed. Hans Walter Gabler with Wolfhard Steppe and Claus Melchoir, 1984, rev. ed. 1986. Annotated editions of *Dubliners*, 1914, and *A Portrait of the Artist as a Young Man*, 1916, are available from Viking, Penguin, and Oxford World's Classics; the Oxford World's Classics edition of *Ulysses*, ed. Jeri Johnson, 1993, uses the 1922 text and has extensive notes and supportive critical material. *Stephen Hero*, ed. John J. Slocum and Herbert Cahoon, 1963, is the novel that provided the basis for *Portrait*. Faber, Minerva, Palladin, and Penguin have all produced good editions of *Finnegans Wake*, which was originally published in 1939. *The Portable James Joyce*, ed. Harry Levin, rev. ed. 1966, conveniently contains selections from *Ulysses* and *Finnegans Wake*, the entire *Portrait*, selections from *Dubliners*, and Joyce's poetry. For Joyce's critical writing see *Critical Writings of James Joyce*, ed. Richard Ellmann and Ellsworth Mason, 1989, and for his poems and shorter pieces see *James Joyce: Poems and Shorter Writings*, ed. Richard Ellmann, A. Walton Litz, and John Whittier-Ferguson, 1991. *The Letters of James Joyce*, 3 vols., was edited by Stuart Gilbert with Ellmann and James F. Spoerri, 1957–66; *Selected Letters of James Joyce*, ed. Ellmann, 1975, is also available. The standard biography of Joyce is Ellmann's *James Joyce*, 3rd ed. 1982. Also useful are Sylvia Beach's *Shakespeare and Company*, 1959; Stanislaus Joyce's *My Brother's Keeper: James Joyce's Early Years*, ed. Ellmann, 1958, and *The Complete Dublin Diary of Stanislaus Joyce*, 1971; Arthur Power's *Conversations with James Joyce*, 1975; *Portraits of the Artist in Exile: Recollections of James Joyce by Europeans*, ed. Willard Potts, 1979; Brenda Maddox's *Nora: A Biography of Nora Joyce*, 1988; and E. H. Mikhail's *James Joyce: Interviews and Recollections*, 1990. The standard bibliography of Joyce's work is *A Bibliography of James Joyce*, ed. Slocum and Cahoon, 2nd ed. 1971. Thomas Jackson Rice's *James Joyce: A Guide to Research*, 1982, and Thomas F. Staley's *An Annotated Critical Bibliography of James Joyce*, 1989, are helpful bibliographies of the secondary literature.

Good general accounts of Joyce's work can be found in Hugh Kenner's *Dublin's Joyce*, 1956, and *Joyce's Voices*, 1978; *James Joyce: The Critical Heritage*, 2 vols., ed. Robert H. Deming, 1970; C. H. Peake's *James Joyce: The Citizen and the Artist*, 1976; Ellmann's *The Consciousness of Joyce*, 1977; Colin MacCabe's *James Joyce and the Revolution of the Word*, 1979; *James Joyce: New Perspectives*, ed. MacCabe,

1982; *A Companion to Joyce Studies*, ed. Zack Bowen and James F. Carens, 1984; Patrick Parrinder's *James Joyce*, 1984; Vicki Mahaffey's *Reauthorizing Joyce*, 1988; *The Cambridge Companion to James Joyce*, ed. Derek Attridge, 1990, 2nd ed. 2004, and Jean-Michel Rabaté's *James Joyce: Authorized Reader*, 1991.

More-specialized studies include Dominic Manganiello's *Joyce's Politics*, 1980; *Women in Joyce*, ed. Suzette A. Henke and Elaine Unkeless, 1982; Fritz Senn's *Joyce's Dislocutions: Essays on Reading as Translation*, 1984; *Post-Structuralist Joyce: Essays from the French*, ed. Attridge and Daniel Ferrer, 1984; Richard Brown's *James Joyce and Sexuality*, 1985; Patrick McGee's *Paperspace: Style as Ideology in Joyce's* Ulysses, 1988; Henke's *James Joyce and the Politics of Desire*, 1990; Margot Norris's *Joyce's Web: The Social Unraveling of Modernism*, 1992; Robert Spoo's *James Joyce and the Language of History: Dedalus's Nightmare*, 1994; Kevin J. H. Dettmar's *The Illicit Joyce of Postmodernism: Reading against the Grain*, 1996; *Semicolonial Joyce*, ed. Attridge and Marjorie Howes, 2000; *Joyce and the City: The Significance of Place*, ed. Michael Begnal, 2002; David Spurr's *Joyce and the Scene of Modernity*, 2002; *Joyce and the Joyceans*, ed. Morton Levitt, 2002; and *James Joyce and the Difference of Language*, ed. Laurent Milesi, 2003.

Don Gifford's *Joyce Annotated: Notes for* Dubliners *and* A Portrait of the Artist as a Young Man, 2nd ed. 1982, is a useful guide for both works. Studies of *Dubliners* include *Twentieth-Century Interpretations of* Dubliners: A Collection of Critical Essays, ed. Peter K. Garrett, 1968; *James Joyce's* Dubliners: Critical Essays, ed. Clive Hart, 1969. *Concordance to James Joyce's* Dubliners: With a Reverse Index, a Frequency List, and a Conversion Tab, ed. Wilhelm Füger, 1980, provides a unique reference source. Critical studies of *A Portrait of the Artist as a Young Man* include Maud Ellmann's essay in *Untying the Text: A Post-Structuralist Reader*, ed. Robert Young, 1981; *James Joyce's* A Portrait of the Artist as a Young Man, ed. Harold Bloom, 1999; *Readings on* A Portrait of the Artist as a Young Man, ed. Clarice Swisher, 2000; *James Joyce's* A Portrait of the Artist as Young Man: A Casebook, ed. Mark A. Wollaeger, 2003. *A Portrait of the Artist as a Young Man: Complete, Authoritative Text with Biographical and Historical Contexts, Critical History, and Essays from Five Contemporary Critical Perspectives*, ed. R. B. Kershner, 1993, is a helpful compendium.

Critical studies of *Ulysses* include Frank Budgen's *James Joyce and the Making of* Ulysses, 1934, rpt. 1960; Stuart Gilbert's *James Joyce's* Ulysses: A Study, 2nd. ed. 1952; William Schutte's *Joyce and Shakespeare: A Study in the Meaning of* Ulysses, 1957; Richard Ellmann's Ulysses *on the Liffey*, 1972; Weldon Thornton's

Allusions in Ulysses: *An Annotated List,* 1973; Ulysses: *Fifty Years,* ed. Staley, 1974; *James Joyce's* Ulysses: *Critical Essays,* ed. Hart and David Hayman, 1974; Michael Seidel's *Epic Geography: James Joyce's* Ulysses, 1976; Marilyn French's *The Book as World: James Joyce's* Ulysses, 1976; Michael Groden's Ulysses *in Progress,* 1977; James H. Maddox's *Joyce's* Ulysses *and the Assault upon Character,* 1978; Karen Lawrence's *The Odyssey of Style in* Ulysses, 1981; Hayman's Ulysses: *The Mechanics of Meaning,* rev. ed. 1982; Hugh Kenner's *Ulysses,* rev. ed. 1987; Gifford and Robert J. Seidman's Ulysses *Annotated: Notes for Joyce's* Ulysses, 2nd. ed. 1988; Enda Duffy's *The Subaltern* Ulysses, 1994; *A Companion to James Joyce's* Ulysses: *Biographical and Historical Contexts, Critical History, and Essays from Five Contemporary Critical Perspectives,* ed. Norris, 1998; *Joycean Cultures, Culturing Joyces,* ed. Vincent J. Cheng, Kimberly J. Devlin, and Norris, 1998; Marilyn Reizbaum's *James Joyce's Judaic Other,* 1999; Paul Schwaber's *The Cast of Characters: A Reading of* Ulysses, 1999; and Andrew Gibson's *Joyce's Revenge: History, Politics, and Aesthetics in* Ulysses, 2002. Collections of essays include *James Joyce's* Ulysses: *A Casebook,* ed. Attridge, 2004; *Leopold Bloom,* ed. Harold Bloom, 2004; and *James Joyce's* Ulysses, ed. Bloom, 2004. David Pierce's *James Joyce's Ireland,* 1992, provides other useful background material. Phillip F. Herring has edited notes and drafts for the novel and compiled them in *Joyce's* Ulysses *Notesheets in the British Museum,* 1972, and *Joyce's Notes and Early Drafts for* Ulysses: *Selections from the Buffalo Collection,* 1977.

Studies of *Finnegans Wake* include Samuel Beckett et al., *Our Examination Round His Factification for Incamination of Work in Progress,* 2nd ed. 1962; Hart's *Structure and Motif in Finnegans Wake,* 1962; James S. Atherton's *The Books at the Wake: A Study of Literary Allusions in James Joyce's* Finnegans Wake, 2nd ed. 1974; Hart's *A Concordance to Finnegans Wake,* rev. ed. 1974; Adaline Glasheen's *A Third Census of* Finnegans Wake: *An Index of the Characters and Their Roles,* 1977; Roland McHugh's *Annotations to* Finnegans Wake, 1980; John Bishop's *Joyce's Book of the Dark:* Finnegans Wake, 1986; Kimberly J. Devlin's *Wandering and Return in* Finnegans Wake: *An Integrative Approach to Joyce's Fictions,* 1991; Thomas C. Hofheinz's *Joyce and the Invention of Irish History:* Finnegans Wake *in Context,* 1995.

Philip Larkin
Larkin's *Collected Poems,* ed. Anthony Thwaite, 2nd ed. 2004, contains a number of hitherto unpublished poems in addition to the contents of his four collections: *The North Ship,* 1945; *The Less Deceived,* 1955; *The Whitsun Weddings,* 1964; and *High Windows,* 1974. *Philip Larkin: The Whitsun Weddings and Selected*

Poems, ed. David Punter, was published in 2003. Thwaite edited *Selected Letters of Philip Larkin, 1940–1985,* 1993, and *Further Requirements: Interviews, Broadcasts, Statements, and Book Reviews, 1952–1985,* 2001. Larkin's other works include his novels, *Jill,* 1946, and *A Girl in Winter,* 1947; a collection of music reviews, *All What Jazz: A Record Diary, 1961–1971,* 1985; and *The Oxford Book of Twentieth-Century English Verse,* 1973, which Larkin edited. Previously unpublished material has recently been published in two posthumous collections: *Larkin's Jazz: Essays and Reviews, 1940–84,* ed. Richard Palmer and John White, 2001, and *"Trouble at Willow Gables" and Other Fictions,* ed. James Booth, 2002. *Required Writing: Miscellaneous Pieces, 1955–1982,* 1983, contains much of Larkin's important prose, including recollections, interviews, and essays on literature and jazz. (For further reading on Larkin and jazz, see B. J. Leggett's *Larkin's Blues: Jazz, Popular Music, and Poetry,* 1999.) The standard biography is Andrew Motion's *Philip Larkin: A Writer's Life,* 1993. B. C. Bloomfield's *Philip Larkin: A Bibliography, 1933–1994,* was first published in 1979 and revised and enlarged in 2002.

Studies of Larkin's work include David Timms's *Philip Larkin,* 1973; Bruce K. Martin's *Philip Larkin,* 1978; Motion's *Philip Larkin,* 1982; Terrence Whalen's *Philip Larkin and English Poetry,* 1986; Salem K. Hassan's *Philip Larkin and His Contemporaries: An Air of Authenticity,* 1988; Janice Rossen's *Philip Larkin: His Life's Work,* 1989; Stephen Regan's *Philip Larkin,* 1992; Booth's *Philip Larkin: Writer,* 1992; Andrew Swarbrick's *Out of Reach: The Poetry of Philip Larkin,* 1995; and A. T. Tolley's *Larkin at Work: A Study of Larkin's Mode of Composition as Seen in His Workbooks,* 1997. Collections of essays include *Larkin at Sixty,* ed. Thwaite, 1982; *Critical Essays on Philip Larkin: The Poems,* ed. Linda Cookson and Bryan Loughrey, 1989; *Philip Larkin: The Man and His Work,* ed. Dale Salwak, 1989; *Philip Larkin,* ed. Regan, 1997; and *New Larkins for Old: Critical Essays,* ed. Booth, 2000.

D. H. Lawrence
The Cambridge Edition of Lawrence's works is nearing completion and will prove definitive. Penguin's paperback editions of Lawrence's novels and short fiction are based on the Cambridge Edition; Oxford World's Classics also offers paperbacks of *The White Peacock, Sons and Lovers, The Rainbow,* and *Women in Love,* among others. *The Portable D. H. Lawrence,* ed. Diana Trilling, 1947, offers selections from *The Rainbow* and *Women in Love* as well as from Lawrence's poems, short stories, criticism, and letters. The eight volumes of Lawrence's *Letters,* ed. James T. Boulton et al., were issued by Cambridge between 1979 and 2000. The best edition

of Lawrence's poetry remains the third edition of *The Complete Poems*, ed. Vivian de Sola Pinto and Warren Roberts, 1977. For Lawrence's life see the Cambridge triptych: John Worthen's *D. H. Lawrence: The Early Years, 1885–1912*, 1991; Mark Kinkead-Weekes's *D. H. Lawrence: Triumph to Exile, 1912–1922*, 1996; and David Ellis's *D. H. Lawrence: Dying Game, 1922–1930*, 1998.

Recent bibliographies of secondary sources include Paul Poplawski and Worthen's *D. H. Lawrence: A Reference Companion*, 1996, and Warren Roberts and Poplawski's *A Bibliography of D. H. Lawrence*, 3rd ed. 2001.

Pioneering studies include F. R. Leavis's *D. H. Lawrence: Novelist*, 1956; Graham Hough's *The Dark Sun*, 1957; H. M. Daleski's *The Forked Flame*, 1965; George Ford's *Double Measure: A Study of the Novels and Stories of D. H. Lawrence*, 1965; and Colin Clarke's *River of Dissolution: D. H. Lawrence and English Romanticism*, 1969. More recent studies include *D. H. Lawrence: The Critical Heritage*, ed. Ronald P. Draper, 1970; Emile Delavenay's *D. H. Lawrence: The Man and His Work: The Formative Years, 1885–1919*, trans. Katherine M. Delavenay, 1972; Frank Kermode's *D. H. Lawrence*, 1973; *D. H. Lawrence: Novelist, Poet, Prophet*, ed. Stephen Spender, 1973; Paul Delaney's *D. H. Lawrence's Nightmare: The Writer and His Circle in the Years of the Great War*, 1978; *D. H. Lawrence*, ed. Harold Bloom, 1986; Christopher Heywood's *D. H. Lawrence: New Studies*, 1987; *The Challenge of D. H. Lawrence*, ed. Michael Squires and Keith Cushman, 1990; Tony Pinkney's *D. H. Lawrence and Modernism*, 1990; *Rethinking Lawrence*, ed. Keith Brown, 1990; *D. H. Lawrence*, ed. Peter Widdowson, 1992; *The Cambridge Companion to D. H. Lawrence*, ed. Anne Fernihough, 2001; *The Complete Critical Guide to D. H. Lawrence*, ed. Fiona Becket, 2002; *D. H. Lawrence: New Worlds*, ed. Cushman and Earl G. Ingersoll, 2003.

For studies of Lawrence and gender, see *Lawrence and Women*, ed. Anne Smith, 1978; Hilary Simpson's *D. H. Lawrence and Feminism*, 1982; Sheila Macleod's *Lawrence's Men and Women*, 1985; Cornelia Nixon's *Lawrence's Leadership Politics and the Turn Against Women*, 1986; James C. Cowan's *D. H. Lawrence: Self and Sexuality*, 2002; and James J. Miracky's *Regenerating the Novel: Gender and Genre in Woolf, Forster, Sinclair, and Lawrence*, 2003. For studies of Lawrence's poetry, see M. J. Lockwood's *A Study of the Poems of D. H. Lawrence: Thinking in Poetry*, 1987; Holly A. Laird's *Self and Sequence: The Poetry of D. H. Lawrence*, 1988; Sandra Gilbert's *Acts of Attention: The Poems of D. H. Lawrence*, 2nd ed. 1990; and Amit Chaudhuri, *D. H. Lawrence and 'Difference': Postcoloniality and the Poetry of the Present*, 2003.

For further reading on Lawrence and philosophy, see Aidan Burns's *Nature and Culture in D. H. Lawrence*, 1980; Colin Milton's *Lawrence and Nietzsche: A Study in Influence*, 1987; Michael H. Black's *D. H. Lawrence: The Early Philosophical Works: A Commentary*, 1992; Michael Bell's *D. H. Lawrence: Language and Being*, 1992; and Robert E. Montgomery's *The Visionary D. H. Lawrence: Beyond Philosophy and Art*, 1994. For Lawrence's aesthetics and politics, see Graham Holderness's *D. H. Lawrence: History, Ideology and Fiction*, 1982, and Fernihough's *D. H. Lawrence: Aesthetics and Ideology*, 1993. For Lawrence's theories of the novel, see Scott R. Sanders's *D. H. Lawrence: The World of the Five Major Novels*, 1974; Alastair Niven's *D. H. Lawrence: The Novels*, 1978; Worthen's *D. H. Lawrence and the Idea of the Novel*, 1979; Charles L. Ross's *Women in Love: A Novel of Mythic Realism*, 1991; and *D. H. Lawrence*, ed. Bloom, 2002.

Doris Lessing

Lessing's first novel, *The Grass Is Singing*, 1950, was followed two years later by the first of the quintet *Children of Violence*, the remaining volumes of which appeared between 1954 and 1969. Lessing published one of her best-known works, *The Golden Notebook*, in 1962. Her other fiction includes *Briefing for a Descent into Hell*, 1971; *The Summer before the Dark*, 1973; *Memoirs of a Survivor*, 1974; the monumental sequence *Canopus in Argus: Archives*, 1979–83; *Diaries of Jane Somers*, 1983; *The Good Terrorist*, 1985; *The Fifth Child*, 1988; *Love, Again*, 1995; *Mara and Dann*, 1999; and *The Grandmothers*, 2004. Lessing's *Collected Stories*, 2 vols., was published in 1978. In 1967 she published a biography of female English novelists and cat owners, *Particularly Cats*; the latest revision appeared in 2000. For Lessing's life see *Under My Skin: The First Volume of My Autobiography, to 1949*, 1994, and *Walking in the Shade: Volume Two of My Autobiography, 1949 to 1962*, 1997. Carole Klein's *Doris Lessing: A Biography*, 2000, and *Doris Lessing: Conversations*, ed. Earl G. Ingersoll, 1994, supplement Lessing's autobiography with helpful second-person and third-person perspectives. *The Doris Lessing Reader*, 1988, contains selections from Lessing's fiction and memoirs; *A Small Personal Voice: Essays, Reviews, Interviews*, ed. Paul Schlueter, 1974, contains a selection of her essays. Useful reference works include Selma R. Burkom's *Doris Lessing: A Checklist of Primary and Secondary Sources*, 1973, and Dee Seligman's *Doris Lessing: An Annotated Bibliography of Criticism*, 1981.

Studies of Lessing's work include Schlueter's *The Novels of Doris Lessing*, 1973; *Doris Lessing: Critical Studies*, ed. Annis Pratt and L. S. Dembo, 1974; Mary Ann Singleton's *The City and the Veld: The Fiction of Doris Lessing*, 1977;

Roberta Rubenstein's *The Novelistic Vision of Doris Lessing: Breaking the Forms of Consciousness*, 1979; *Notebooks, Memoirs, Archives: Reading and Rereading Doris Lessing*, ed. Jenny Taylor, 1982; Lorna Sage's *Doris Lessing*, 1983; Betsy Draine's *Substance under Pressure: Artistic Coherence and Evolving Form*, 1983; Mona Knapp's *Doris Lessing*, 1984; Katherine Fishburn's *The Unexpected Universe of Doris Lessing: A Study in Narrative Technique*, 1985; *Doris Lessing*, ed. Harold Bloom, 1986, 2003; *Critical Essays on Doris Lessing*, ed. Claire Sprague and Virginia Tiger, 1986; *Doris Lessing: The Alchemy of Survival*, ed. Carey Kaplan and Ellen Cronan Rose, 1988; Jean Pickering's *Understanding Doris Lessing*, 1990; Gayle Greene's *Doris Lessing: The Poetics of Change*, 1994; Louise Yelin's *From the Margins of Empire: Christina Stead, Doris Lessing, Nadine Gordimer*, 1998; Yuan-Jung Cheng's *Heralds of the Postmodern: Madness and Fiction in Conrad, Woolf, and Lessing*, 1999; and Deborah Martinson's *In the Presence of Audience: The Self in Diaries and Fiction*, 2003. For theoretical criticisms of Lessing's work, see Jeannette King's *Doris Lessing*, 1989, and Sprague's *Rereading Doris Lessing: Narrative Patterns of Doubling and Repetition*, 1987. Michael Thorpe's *Doris Lessing's Africa*, 1978, examines Lessing's work through the lens of her home continent.

Hugh MacDiarmid
Hugh MacDiarmid: The Complete Poems, 1920–1976, 2 vols., 1978, rev. ed. 1994, was edited by Michael Grieve and W. R. Aitken. *Selected Poetry*, ed. Grieve and Alan Riach, and *Selected Prose*, ed. Riach, were both published in 1992 and are part of Carcanet Press's projected sixteen-volume *Collected Works of Hugh Mac-Diarmid*. MacDiarmid is editor of *The Golden Treasury of Scottish Poetry*, 1940. His correspondence is available in *The Letters of Hugh MacDiarmid*, ed. Alan Bold, 1984; *The Hugh MacDiarmid–George Ogilvie Letters*, ed. Catherine Kerrigan, 1988; and *New Selected Letters*, ed. Dorian Grieve, Owen Dudley Edwards, and Riach, 2001. An autobiography, *Lucky Poet*, was published in 1943, and Gordon Wright's *Mac-Diarmid: An Illustrated Biography*, 1977, covers eighty-five years of the poet's life in photographs, caricatures, poems, press cuttings, and other documents. Bold's *MacDiarmid: Christopher Murray Grieve, A Critical Biography*, 1988, is also very informative. *Hugh MacDiarmid: A Critical Survey*, ed. Duncan Glen, 1972, contains critical essays as well as a comprehensive bibliography.

For a helpful study of MacDiarmid's themes and perspective, see Bold's *MacDiarmid: The Terrible Crystal*, 1983. Kerrigan's *Whaur Extremes Meet: The Poetry of Hugh MacDiarmid 1920–1934*, 1983, and Harvey Oxenhorn's *Elemental Things: The Poetry of Hugh MacDiarmid*,

1984, also provide perceptive critical discussions of his early and middle poetry. A valuable general account of MacDiarmid and his poetry is Kenneth Buthlay's *Hugh MacDiarmid*, 1981. On the Scottish cultural background and Mac-Diarmid's part in Scottish literary movements, see Glen's *Hugh MacDiarmid and the Scottish Renaissance*, 1964. *Hugh MacDiarmid, A Festschrift*, ed. Kugan Dalby Duval and Sydney Goodsir Smith, 1982, is the most important single critical book on MacDiarmid. Other useful studies include Edwin Morgan's *Hugh Mac-Diarmid*, 1976; John Baglow's *Hugh MacDiar-mid: The Poetry of Self*, 1987; Peter McCarey's *Hugh MacDiarmid and the Russians*, 1987; Riach's *Hugh MacDiarmid's Epic Poetry*, 1991; Ruth McQuillan's *Hugh MacDiarmid: The Patrimony*, 1992; and W. N. Herbert's *To Circumjack MacDiarmid*, 1992. Collections of critical essays include *The Age of MacDiarmid*, ed. P. H. Scott and A. C. Davis, 1980, and *Hugh Mac-Diarmid: Man and Poet*, ed. Nancy Gish, 1992. The chapter "A Torchlight Procession of One: On Hugh MacDiarmid," in Seamus Heaney's *The Redress of Poetry*, 1995, is also helpful. *Akros* 23, August 1977, and *Scottish Literary Journal* 5, December 1978, are special Mac-Diarmid issues.

Louis MacNeice
The Collected Poems, 1966, and MacNeice's posthumously published unfinished autobiography, *The Strings Are False*, 1965, were both edited by E. R. Dodds. MacNeice made verse translations of Aeschylus's *Agamemnon*, 1936, and, with E. L. Stahl, of Goethe's *Faust* (an abridged version of parts one and two), 1951. MacNeice and Stephen Spender edited the anthology *Oxford Poetry 1929*, 1929. His Clark Lectures at Cambridge were published as *Varieties of Parable*, 1965. Alan Heuser has edited *Selected Literary Criticism of Louis MacNeice*, 1987; *Selected Prose of Louis MacNeice*, 1990; and, with Peter McDonald, *Selected Plays of Louis MacNeice*, 1993. A collection of Mac-Neice's BBC radio plays is *"The Dark Tower" and Other Radio Scripts*, 1947; Barbara Coulton's *Louis MacNeice in the BBC*, 1980, is a biographical and critical study of his work for radio. *A Bibliography of the Works of Louis MacNeice*, ed. C. M. Armitage and Neil Clark, 1973, lists most of his many other publications. A fine biography is Jon Stallworthy's *Louis MacNeice*, 1995.

Studies of MacNeice's work include Elton Edward Smith's *Louis MacNeice*, 1970; William T. McKinnon's *Apollo's Blended Dream: A Study of the Poetry of Louis MacNeice*, 1971; D. B. Moore's *The Poetry of Louis MacNeice*, 1972; Terence Brown's *Louis MacNeice: Sceptical Vision*, 1975; Robyn Marsack, *The Cave of Making: The Poetry of Louis MacNeice*, 1982; Edna Longley's *Louis MacNeice: A Study*, 1988; and

Peter McDonald's *Louis MacNeice: The Poet in His Contexts*, 1991. Numerous useful essays are collected in *Time Was Away: The World of Louis MacNeice*, ed. Brown and Alec Reid, 1974, and *Louis MacNeice and His Influence*, ed. Kathleen Devine and Alan J. Peacock, 1998.

MacNeice is also often discussed in connection with the group of poets identified with Auden in the 1930s; for more information on this group of poets, see Derek Stanford's *Stephen Spender, Louis MacNeice, Cecil Day Lewis: A Critical Survey*, 1969; Smith, *The Angry Young Men of the Thirties*, 1975; Samuel Hynes's *The Auden Generation: Literature and Politics in the 1930s*, 1976; Michael O'Neill's and Gareth Reeves's *Auden, MacNeice, Spender: The Thirties Poetry*, 1992; and John Whitehead's *A Commentary on the Poetry of W. H. Auden, C. Day Lewis, Louis MacNeice, and Stephen Spender*, 1992.

Katherine Mansfield
The Short Stories of Katherine Mansfield, 1937, contains all of Mansfield's stories, and her poetry is contained in *Poems of Katherine Mansfield*, ed. Vincent O'Sullivan, 1988. *The Critical Writings of Katherine Mansfield*, ed. Clare Hanson, was published in 1987. *Journal of Katherine Mansfield*, ed. John Middleton Murry, 1927; *The Collected Letters of Katherine Mansfield*, 4 vols., ed. O'Sullivan and Margaret Scott, 1984–96; and *The Katherine Mansfield Notebooks*, ed. Scott, 1997, 2002, provide autobiographical resources useful in studying Mansfield's work in depth, and Alexandra Johnson's *The Hidden Writer: Diaries and the Creative Life*, 1997, is a supplement to the volumes of Mansfield's lifewriting. For biographical accounts of her life, see Antony Alpers's *The Life of Katherine Mansfield*, 1980; Claire Tomalin's *Katherine Mansfield: A Secret Life*, 1988; and Angela Smith's *Katherine Mansfield: A Literary Life*, 2000.

Critical studies of Mansfield's work include Marvin Magalener's *The Fiction of Katherine Mansfield*, 1971; Ian A. Gordon's *Undiscovered Country: The New Zealand Stories of Katherine Mansfield*, 1974; Clare Hanson and Andrew Gurr's *Katherine Mansfield*, 1981; C. A. Hankin's *Katherine Mansfield and Her Confessional Stories*, 1983; Kate Fullbrook's *Katherine Mansfield*, 1986; *Critical Essays on Katherine Mansfield*, ed. Rhoda B. Nathan, 1993; *The Critical Response to Katherine Mansfield*, ed. Jan Pilditch, 1996; Patricia Moran's *Word of Mouth: Body Language in Katherine Mansfield and Virginia Woolf*, 1996; Pamela Dunbar's *Radical Mansfield: Double Discourse in Katherine Mansfield's Short Stories*, 1997; Smith's *Katherine Mansfield and Virginia Woolf: A Public of Two*, 1999; and Deborah Martinson's *In the Presence of Audience: The Self in Diaries and Fiction*, 2003.

Claude McKay
Complete Poems, ed. William J. Maxwell, was published in 2004. McKay's volumes of poetry include *Constab Ballads*, 1912; *Songs of Jamaica*, 1912; *"Spring in New Hampshire" and Other Poems*, 1920; and *Harlem Shadows*, 1922. Collections published posthumously include *Selected Poems*, 1953; *The Dialect Poetry*, 1972; and *The Passion of Claude McKay: Selected Poetry and Prose, 1912–1948*, ed. Wayne F. Cooper, 1973. McKay also published the collection of short stories *Gingertown*, 1932, and three novels: *Home to Harlem*, 1928; *Banjo*, 1929; and *Banana Bottom*, 1933. Posthumously published collections of stories are *Trial by Lynching: Stories about Negro Life in America*, ed. A. L. MacLeod, 1977, and *My Green Hills of Jamaica*, ed. Mervyn Morris, 1979. Essay collections include *Harlem: Negro Metropolis*, 1940, and *The Negroes in America*, 1979. McKay's autobiography, *A Long Way from Home*, was published in 1937. Biographies include James R. Giles's *Claude McKay*, 1976; Cooper's *Claude McKay: Rebel Sojourner in the Harlem Renaissance*, 1987; and Tyrone Tillery's *Claude McKay: A Black Poet's Struggle for Identity*, 1992.

Studies of McKay's work include Harold Cruse's *The Crisis of the Negro Intellectual*, 1967; Addison Gayle's *Claude McKay: The Black Poet at War*, 1972; Houston A. Baker's *Modernism and the Harlem Renaissance*, 1987; Michael North's *The Dialect of Modernism*, 1994; George Hutchinson's *The Harlem Renaissance in Black and White*, 1995; Laurence A. Breiner's *An Introduction to West Indian Poetry*, 1998; Heather Hathaway's *Caribbean Waves: Relocating Claude McKay and Paule Marshall*, 1999; Maxwell's *New Negro, Old Left*, 1999; and Winston James's *A Fierce Hatred of Injustice: Claude McKay's Jamaica and his Poetry of Rebellion*, 2001. Numerous useful essays are collected in *Claude McKay: Centennial Studies*, ed. McLeod, 1992, and useful essays appear in A. B. Christa Schwartz's *Gay Voices of the Harlem Renaissance*, 2003, and (by Maxwell) in *Left of the Color Line: Race, Radicalism, and Twentieth Century Literature of the United States*, ed. Bill V. Mullen and James Smethurst, 2003.

Modernist Manifestos
Janet Lyon's *Manifestoes: Provocations of the Modern*, 1999, provides a study of the manifesto as a genre uniquely suited to modernist politics. Helpful literary-historical introductions include Hugh Kenner's *The Pound Era*, 1971, and Michael H. Levenson's *A Genealogy of Modernism: A Study of English Literary Doctrine, 1908–1922*, 1984. Marjorie Perloff's *The Futurist Moment: Avant-garde, Avant Guerre, and the Language of Rupture*, 1986, and Peter Nicholls's *Modernisms: A Literary Guide*, 1995, offer

needed context by examining imagism and vorticism alongside surrealism, Dada, and futurism. *On Modern Poetry: Essays Presented to Donald Davie*, ed. Vereen M. Bell and Laurence Lerner, 1988, includes discussions of Loy, H. D., and Pound.

Helpful studies of imagism include Glenn Hughes's *Imagism and the Imagists: A Study in Modern Poetry*, 1931; Stanley K. Coffman's *Imagism: A Chapter for the History of Modern Poetry*, 1951; *The Imagist Poem: Modern Poetry in Miniature*, ed. William Pratt, 1963, rev. ed. 2001; *Imagist Poetry*, ed. Peter Jones, 1972; J. B. Harmer's *Victory in Limbo: Imagism, 1908–1917*, 1975; John T. Gage's *In the Arresting Eye: The Rhetoric of Imagism*, 1981; and *Homage to Imagism*, ed. Pratt and Robert Richardson, 1992.

For more on vorticism, see William Wees's *Vorticism and the English Avant-Garde*, 1972; Richard Cork's *Vorticism and Abstract Art in the First Machine Age*, 1976; Timothy Materer's *Vortex: Pound, Eliot, and Lewis*, 1979; *Blast: Vorticism 1914–1918*, ed. Paul Edwards, 2000; Paul Peppis's *Literature, Politics, and the English Avant-Garde: Nation and Empire, 1901–1918*, 2000; and Jonathan Black's *Blasting the Future!: Vorticism in Britain 1910–1920*, 2004.

Paul Muldoon

Muldoon's collected *Poems, 1968–1998* appeared in 2001; he published *Moy Sand and Gravel* in 2002. He has also published translations, including one of Nuala Ní Dhomhnaill's *The Astrakhan Cloak*, 1993, and one of Aristophanes's *The Birds*, with Richard Martin, 1999. Muldoon is editor of *The Scrake of Dawn: Poems by Young People from Northern Ireland*, 1979; *The Faber Book of Contemporary Irish Poetry*, 1986; *The Essential Byron*, 1989; and *The Faber Book of Beasts*, 1997. His lectures on Irish literature were published as *To Ireland, I*, 2000. He has also written the libretti for Daron Hagen's operas *Shining Brow*, 1993, and *Bandanna*, 1999; his play, *Six Honest Serving Men*, was published in 1995.

For an introduction to Muldoon's poetry, see Tim Kendall's *Paul Muldoon*, 1996. Studies of Muldoon's work include Clair Wills's *Improprieties: Politics and Sexuality in Northern Irish Poetry*, 1993, and *Reading Paul Muldoon*, 1998. Wills's essay in *The Chosen Ground: Essays on the Contemporary Poetry of Northern Ireland*, ed. Neil Corcoran, 1992, and a chapter in Ian Gregson's *The Male Image: Representations of Masculinity in Postwar Poetry*, 1999, are also useful.

Alice Munro

Munro's works include *"Dance of the Happy Shades" and Other Stories*, 1968; *Lives of Girls and Women: A Novel*, 1971; *Something I've Been Meaning to Tell You: Thirteen Stories*, 1974; *Who Do You Think You Are?: Stories*, 1978; *The Beggar Maid: Stories of Flo and Rose*, 1979; *The Moons of Jupiter*, 1983; *The Progress of Love*, 1986; *Friend of My Youth: Stories*, 1990; *Open Secrets: Stories*, 1994; *The Love of a Good Woman: Stories*, 1998; and *Hateship, Friendship, Courtship, Loveship, Marriage: Stories*, 2001. For Munro's life see Catherine Sheldrick Ross's *Alice Munro: A Double Life*, 1992.

Studies of Munro's work include *Probable Fictions: Alice Munro's Narrative Acts*, ed. Louis K. MacKendrick, 1983; W. R. Martin's *Alice Munro: Paradox and Parallel*, 1987; E. D. Blodgett's *Alice Munro*, 1988; Beverly Jean Rasporich's *Dance of the Sexes: Art and Gender in the Fiction of Alice Munro*, 1990; Magdalene Redekop's *Mothers and Other Clowns: The Stories of Alice Munro*, 1992; Karen E. Smythe's *Figuring Grief: Gallant, Munro, and the Poetics of Elegy*, 1992; James Carscallen's *The Other Country: Patterns in the Writing of Alice Munro*, 1993; Ajay Heble's *The Tumble of Reason: Alice Munro's Discourse of Absence*, 1994; Coral Ann Howells's *Alice Munro*, 1998; and *The Rest of the Story: Critical Essays on Alice Munro*, ed. Robert Thacker, 1999. For archival material accompanying criticism see JoAnn McCaig's *Reading In: Alice Munro's Archives*, 2002.

Les Murray

Murray's volumes of poetry include *The Ilex Tree*, with Geoffrey Lehmann, 1965; *The Weatherboard Cathedral*, 1969; *Poems against Economics*, 1972; *Lunch & Counter Lunch*, 1974; *Selected Poems: The Vernacular Republic*, 1976, rev. ed. 1982; *Ethnic Radio*, 1977; *The People's Otherworld*, 1983; *The Daylight Moon*, 1987; *Dog Fox Field*, 1990; *The Rabbiter's Bounty: Collected Poems*, 1991; *Translations from the Natural World*, 1992; *Subhuman Redneck Poems*, 1996; *Collected Poems*, 1998, rev. ed. 2002; *Conscious and Verbal*, 1999; *Learning Human: Selected Poems*, 2000; and *Poems the Size of Photographs*, 2002. Murray has also composed two verse novels, *The Boys who Stole the Funeral: a Novel Sequence*, 1980, and *Fredy Neptune: A Novel in Verse*, 1999. Murray's essays and reviews are collected in *The Peasant Mandarin: Prose Pieces*, 1978; *Persistence in Folly: Selected Prose Writings*, 1984; *Blocks and Tackles: Articles and Essays 1982–1990*, 1990; and *The Paperbark Tree: Selected Prose*, 1992. Murray is editor of *The New Oxford Book of Australian Verse*, 1986, exp. ed. 1991; *The Anthology of Australian Religious Poetry*, 1986; and *Fivefathers: Five Australian Poets of the Pre-academic Era*, 1994. Peter F. Alexander's biography, *Les Murray: A Life in Progress*, appeared in 2000.

For an introduction to Murray's work, see Lawrence Bourke's *A Vivid Steady State: Les Murray and Australian Poetry*, 1992. Collections of essays on Murray's work include *Counter-*

balancing Light: Essays on Les Murray, ed. Carmel Gaffney, 1997; *The Poetry of Les Murray: Critical Essays*, ed. Laurie Hergenhan and Bruce Clunies Ross, 2001; Steven Matthews's *Les Murray*, 2001; and *Les Murray and Australian Poetry*, ed. Angela Smith, 2002. The chapter "Crocodile Dandy: Les Murray," in Derek Walcott's *What the Twilight Says: Essays*, 1998, is also helpful. *Australian Literary Studies* 20.2, 2001, is a special issue dedicated to Murray and contains Carol Hetherington's bibliographical "Les Murray: A Selective Checklist."

V. S. Naipaul

Naipaul's novels include *The Mystic Masseur*, 1957; *The Suffrage of Elvira*, 1958; *Miguel Street*, 1959; *A House for Mr. Biswas*, 1961; *Mr. Stone and the Knights Companion*, 1963; *The Mimic Men*, 1967; *A Flag on the Island*, 1967; *In a Free State*, 1971; *Guerrillas*, 1975; *A Bend in the River*, 1979; *The Enigma of Arrival*, 1987; *A Way in the World*, 1994; and *Half a Life*, 2001. His literary essays include *Reading and Writing: A Personal Account*, 2000; *The Writer and the World: Essays*, 2002; and *Literary Occasions: Essays*, ed. Pankaj Mishra, 2003. Naipaul's journalism and travel writings include *The Middle Passage: Impressions of Five Societies, British, French and Dutch, in the West Indies and South America*, 1962; *An Area of Darkness*, 1964; *"The Return of Eva Perón," with "The Killings in Trinidad,"* 1966; *The Loss of El Dorado: A Colonial History*, 1969; *The Overcrowded Barracoon and Other Articles*, 1972; *India: A Wounded Civilization*, 1977; *Among the Believers: An Islamic Journey*, 1981; *A Turn in the South*, 1989; *India: A Million Mutinies Now*, 1990; and *Beyond Belief: Islamic Excursions among the Converted Peoples*, 1998. For his life see *Finding the Center: Two Narratives*, 1984, and *Between Father and Son: Family Letters*, ed. Gillon Aitken, 1999; Richard Michael Kelly's biography, *V. S. Naipaul*, 1989, is also useful. For a guide to secondary sources, see Kelvin Jarvis's *V. S. Naipaul: A Selective Bibliography with Annotations, 1957–1987*, 1989.

Introductions to Naipaul can be found in Paul Theroux's *V. S. Naipaul: An Introduction to His Work*, 1972, and Landeg White's *V. S. Naipaul: A Critical Introduction*, 1975. Studies of Naipaul's work include Robert D. Hamner's *V. S. Naipaul*, 1973; Peggy Nightingale's *Journey through Darkness: The Writing of V. S. Naipaul*, 1987; Peter Hughes's *V. S. Naipaul*, 1988; Rob Nixon's *London Calling: V. S. Naipaul, Postcolonial Mandarin*, 1992; Timothy Weiss's *On the Margins: The Art of Exile in V. S. Naipaul*, 1992; Bruce King's *V. S. Naipaul*, 1993; Judith Levy's *V. S. Naipaul: Displacement and Autobiography*, 1995; Helen Hayward's *The Enigma of V. S. Naipaul: Sources and Contexts*, 2002; and John Ball's *Satire and the Postcolonial Novel: V. S. Naipaul, Chinua Achebe, and Salman*

Rushdie, 2003. Useful book chapters include Derek Walcott's "The Garden Path: V. S. Naipaul," in *What the Twilight Says: Essays*, 1998; Edward Said's "Among the Believers: On V. S. Naipaul," in *Reflections on Exile and Other Essays*, 2000; and "V. S. Naipaul, Modernity, and Postcolonial Excrement," in Subramanian Shankar's *Textual Traffic: Colonialism, Modernity, and the Economy of the Text*, 2001.

Nation and Language

Useful introductory collections of essays on world English include *English Literature: Opening up the Canon*, ed. Leslie A. Fiedler and Houston A. Baker, 1981, and *The Language, Ethnicity and Race Reader*, ed. Roxy Harris and Ben Rampton, 2003. I. A. Richard's *So Much Nearer: Essays toward a World English*, 1968; Richard W. Bailey's *Images of English: A Cultural History of the Language*, 1991; David Crystal's *English as a Global Language*, 1997; *The Oxford Guide to World English*, ed. Tom McArthur, 2002; and Janina Brutt-Griffler, *World English: A Study of Its Development*, 2003, provide linguistic contexts.

A book exploring the varieties of English worldwide is Braj B. Kachru's *The Other Tongue: English across Cultures*, 1982, 2nd ed. 1992, along with his *The Indianization of English: The English Language in India*, 1983. Bill Ashcroft, Gareth Griffiths, and Helen Tiffin's *The Empire Writes Back*, 2nd ed. 2002, examines the role of language in postcolonial literatures. Kwame Anthony Appiah probes the connections between language and nation in "Topologies of Nativism," reprinted in his *In My Father's House: Africa in the Philosophy of Culture*, 1992. Charles Bernstein's essay "Poetics of the Americas," reprinted in his book *My Way: Speeches and Poems*, 1999, offers an account of literary resistances to Standard English. Jed Esty's *A Shrinking Island: Modernism and National Culture in England*, 2004, explores the effects of the explosion of world literature on postimperial England.

See also **Chinua Achebe, John Agard, Louise Bennett, Kamau Brathwaite, Brian Friel, Tony Harrison, Hugh MacDiarmid, Claude McKay, Salman Rushdie,** and **Wole Soyinka.**

Ngũgĩ Wa Thiong'o

Ngũgĩ's novels in English include *Weep Not, Child*, 1964; *The River Between*, 1965; *A Grain of Wheat*, 1967; and *Petals of Blood*, 1977. *Devil on the Cross*, 1982, and *Matigari*, 1989, were written first in Gĩkũyũ. *Secret Lives*, a collection of short fiction, was published in 1975. Ngũgĩ's published plays include *The Black Hermit*, 1968; *This Time Tomorrow*, 1970; *The Trial of Dedan Kimathi*, with Micere Mugo, 1976; and *I Will Marry When I Want*, with Ngũgĩ wa Mĩrĩĩ, 1982. Ngũgĩ is a prolific essayist whose collections include *Homecoming: Essays on African and Caribbean Literature, Culture and Politics,*

1972; *Writers in Politics*, 1981, rev. ed. 1997; *Barrel of a Pen: Resistance to Oppression in Neo-Colonial Kenya*, 1983; *Decolonising the Mind: The Politics of Language in African Literature*, 1986; *Mother, Sing for Me: People's Theatre in Kenya*, with Ingrid Björkman, 1989; *Moving the Centre: The Struggle for Cultural Freedoms*, 1992; and *Penpoints, Gunpoints, and Dreams: Toward a Critical Theory of the Arts and the State in Africa*, 1998. Ngũgĩ's autobiographical writings include *Detained: A Writer's Prison Diary*, 1981, and a chapter in Wendy Lesser's *The Genius of Language: Fifteen Writers Reflect on their Mother Tongues*, 2004. *The World of Ngũgĩ wa Thiong'o*, ed. Charles Cantalupo, 1995, contains interviews with the author. See also Carol Sicherman's *Ngugi wa Thiong'o: A Bibliography of Primary and Secondary Sources, 1957–1987*, 1989.

For guides to Ngũgĩ, see *An Introduction to the Writings of Ngugi*, 1980, by G. D. Killam, who also edited *Critical Perspectives on Ngugi's wa Thiong'o*, 1984. Other studies of Ngũgĩ's works include Clifford B. Robson, *Ngugi wa Thiong'o*, 1979; David Cook, *Ngũgĩ wa Thiong'o: An Exploration of his Writings*, 1983, 2nd. ed. 1997; *Ngũgĩ wa Thiong'o: Texts and Contexts*, ed. Cantalupo, 1995; Patrick Williams, *Ngugi wa Thiong'o*, 1998; Simon Gikandi, *Ngugi wa Thiong'o*, 2000; Oliver Lovesey, *Ngũgĩ wa Thiong'o*, 2000; and *Critical Essays on Ngũgĩ wa Thiong'o*, ed. Peter Nazareth, 2000.

George Orwell

The standard edition of Orwell's work is *The Complete Works of George Orwell*, 20 vols., ed. Peter Davison with Ian Angus and Sheila Davison, 1998. Orwell is best-known for two works of fiction: *Animal Farm*, 1945, and *Nineteen Eighty-four*, 1949. Orwell's other fiction includes the autobiographical novels *Down and Out in Paris and London: A Novel*, 1933, and *Burmese Days: A Novel*, 1934, as well as *A Clergyman's Daughter*, 1935; *Keep the Aspidistra Flying*, 1936; and *Coming Up for Air*, 1939. Other nonfiction works also based on his experiences include *The Road to Wigan Pier*, 1937, and *Homage to Catalonia*, 1938. Orwell's collections of essays include *Inside the Whale and Other Essays*, 1940; *The Lion and the Unicorn: Socialism and the English Genius*, 1941; *Shooting an Elephant*, 1950; *England Your England*, 1953; and *Such, Such Were the Joys*, 1953. *Collected Essays, Journalism and Letters*, 4 vols., ed. Angus and Sonia Orwell, was first published in 1968. For his life see Bernard Crick's *George Orwell: A Life*, 1980; Michael Shelden's *Orwell: The Authorised Biography*, 1991; Peter Davison's *Orwell: A Literary Life*, 1996; and Gordon Bowker's *Inside George Orwell*, 2003. Gillian Fenwick's *George Orwell: A Bibliography*, 1998, is also quite useful for secondary sources.

Studies of Orwell's work include George Woodcock's *The Crystal Spirit: A Study of George Orwell*, 1966; *The World of George Orwell*, ed. Miriam Gross, 1971; *George Orwell: A Collection of Critical Essays*, ed. Raymond Williams, 1974; *George Orwell: The Critical Heritage*, ed. Jeffrey Meyers, 1975; *Critical Essays on George Orwell*, ed. Bernard Oldsey and Joseph Browne, 1986; Patrick Reilly's *George Orwell: The Age's Adversary*, 1986; *George Orwell*, ed. Harold Bloom, 1987; Alok Rai's *Orwell and the Politics of Despair: A Critical Study of the Writings of George Orwell*, 1988; *George Orwell*, ed. Graham Holderness, Bryan Loughrey, and Nahem Yousaf, 1998; John Newsinger's *Orwell's Politics*, 1999; Christopher Hitchens's *Why Orwell Matters*, 2002; Anthony Stewart's *George Orwell, Doubleness, and the Value of Decency*, 2003; and James M. Decker's *Ideology*, 2004. Edward Said's chapter "Tourism among the Dogs: On George Orwell," in *Reflections on Exile and Other Essays*, 2000, is also useful.

Many of the aforementioned works contain material on *Animal Farm*, but for further reading on this piece, see Richard I. Smyer's *Animal Farm: Pastoralism and Politics*, 1988; *George Orwell's Animal Farm*, ed. Harold Bloom, 1998; and *Readings on Animal Farm*, ed. Terry O'Neill, 1998. For further reading on *Nineteen Eighty-four* see *Twentieth Century Interpretations of 1984: A Collection of Critical Essays*, ed. Samuel Hynes, 1971; William Steinhoff's *The Origins of 1984*, 1975; *1984 Revisited: Totalitarianism in Our Century*, ed. Irving Howe, 1983; *George Orwell's 1984*, ed. Harold Bloom, 1987; Peter Buitenhuis and Ira B. Nadel's *George Orwell: A Reassessment*, 1988; *The Orwellian Moment: Hindsight and Foresight in a Post-1984 World*, ed. Robert L. Savage, James Combs, and Dan Nimmo, 1989; and Reilly's *Nineteen Eighty-Four: Past, Present, and Future*, 1989.

Wilfred Owen

The Complete Poems and Fragments of Wilfred Owen, 2 vols., 1984, and *The Poems of Wilfred Owen*, 1985, both edited by Jon Stallworthy, are the standard scholarly edition and the standard reader's edition, respectively. *The Collected Letters*, ed. Harold Owen and John Bell, was published in 1967; Bell also edited *Selected Letters*, 1985. For his life see Stallworthy's *Wilfred Owen*, 1974; Harold Owen's *Journey from Obscurity: Memoirs of the Owen Family*, 3 vols., 1963–65; and Dominic Hibberd's *Wilfred Owen: A New Biography*, 2002. William White's *Wilfred Owen (1893–1918): A Bibliography* was published in 1967.

For an introduction to Owen see Stallworthy's *Great Poets of World War I: Poetry from the Great War*, 2002. Studies of Owen's work include Gertrude M. White's *Wilfred Owen*, 1969; Arthur E. Lane's *An Adequate Response: The War Poetry of Wilfred Owen and Siegfried*

Sassoon, 1972; Dennis Welland's *Wilfred Owen: A Critical Study*, rev. ed. 1978; Sven Bäckman's *Tradition Transformed: Studies in the Poetry of Wilfred Owen*, 1979; Desmond Graham's *The Truth of War: Owen, Blunden and Rosenberg*, 1984; Hibberd's *Owen the Poet*, 1986; Adrian Caesar's *Taking It like a Man: Suffering, Sexuality, and the War Poets: Brooke, Sassoon, Owen, Graves*, 1993; Douglas Kerr's *Wilfred Owen's Voices: Language and Community*, 1993; John Purkis's *A Preface to Wilfred Owen*, 1999; and *Poets of WWI: Wilfred Owen and Isaac Rosenberg*, ed. Harold Bloom, 2002. Discussions of Owen's work can also be found in Jon Silkin's *Out of Battle: The Poetry of the Great War*, 1972, 2nd ed. 1998; Jahan Ramazani's *Poetry of Mourning: The Modern Elegy from Hardy to Heaney*, 1994; Patrick J. Quinn's *Recharting the Thirties*, 1996; and *The Literature of the Great War Reconsidered: Beyond Modern Memory*, ed. Quinn and Steven Trout, 2001.

Harold Pinter
Pinter's plays, poetry, and selected prose have been published in paperback as *Complete Works*, 4 vols., 1976–81; and in *Collected Poems and Prose*, 1986. *Collected Screenplays*, 2000, includes *The Proust Screenplay: À la recherche du temps perdu*, written with Joseph Losey and Barbara Bray, 1977, and *The French Lieutenant's Woman and Other Screenplays*, 1982. Pinter's dramatic works include *The Caretaker* and *The Dumb Waiter: Two Plays*, 1960; *The Birthday Party* and *The Room: Two Plays*, 1961; *Three Plays: A Slight Ache, The Collection, The Dwarfs*, 1962; *The Homecoming*, 1966; *The Lover, Tea Party, The Basement: Two Plays and a Film Script*, 1967; *A Night Out: Night School, Revue Sketches: Early Plays*, 1967; *Landscape and Silence*, 1970; *Old Times*, 1971; *Five Screenplays*, 1973; *No Man's Land*, 1975; *Betrayal*, 1978; *The Hothouse: A Play*, 1980; *Other Places: Three Plays*, 1983; *Mountain Language*, 1988; *The Heat of the Day*, 1989; *The Dwarfs: A Novel*, 1990; *Party Time*, 1991; *Moonlight*, 1993; *Ashes to Ashes*, 1996. His nonfiction includes *Various Voices: Prose, Poetry, and Politics*, 1998. For Pinter's life see *Conversations with Pinter*, ed. Mel Gussow, 1994, or Michael Billington's *The Life and Work of Harold Pinter*, 1996. Steven H. Gale published *Harold Pinter: An Annotated Bibliography* in 1978.

The Cambridge Companion to Harold Pinter, ed. Peter Raby, 2001, is a good introduction to Pinter's work. Critical studies include Walter Kerr's *Harold Pinter*, 1967; Lois G. Gordon's *Stratagems to Uncover Nakedness: The Dramas of Harold Pinter*, 1969; Martin Esslin's *The Peopled Wound: The Work of Harold Pinter*, 1970; James R. Hollis's *Harold Pinter: The Poetics of Silence*, 1970; *Pinter: A Collection of Critical Essays*, ed. Arthur Ganz, 1972; Ronald Hayman's *Harold Pinter*, 1973; Simon Trussler's

The Plays of Harold Pinter: An Assessment, 1973; William Baker and Stephen Ely Tabachnick's *Harold Pinter*, 1973; Austin E. Quigley's *The Pinter Problem*, 1975; Esslin's *Pinter: A Study of His Plays*, exp. 2nd ed. 1976; Bernard F. Dukore's *Where Laughter Stops: Pinter's Tragicomedy*, 1976; Gale's *Butter's Going Up: A Critical Analysis of Harold Pinter's Work*, 1977; Guido Almansi and Simon Henderson's *Harold Pinter*, 1983; *Harold Pinter: Critical Approaches*, 1986, and *Critical Essays on Harold Pinter*, 1990, both edited by Gale; *Harold Pinter: A Casebook*, ed. Gordon, 1990; Victor L. Cahn's *Gender and Power in the Plays of Harold Pinter*, 1993; Marc Silverstein's *Harold Pinter and the Language of Cultural Power*, 1993; *Pinter at Sixty*, ed. Katherine H. Burkman and John L. Kundert-Gibbs, 1993; Penelope Prentice's *The Pinter Ethic: The Erotic Aesthetic*, 1994; Stephen Watt's *Postmodern/drama: Reading the Contemporary Stage*, 1998; Raymond Armstrong's *Kafka and Pinter: Shadow-Boxing: The Struggle between Father and Son*, 1999; *Pinter at 70: A Casebook*, ed. Gordon, 2001; and Gale's *Sharp Cut: Harold Pinter's Screenplays and the Artistic Process*, 2002.

A. K. Ramanujan
The Collected Poems of A. K. Ramanujan was published in 1995; *The Collected Essays of A. K. Ramanujan*, ed. Vinay Dharwadker and Stuart H. Blackburn, in 1999. *Uncollected Poems and Prose*, ed. Molly Daniels-Ramanujan and Keith Harrison, was published in 2001. *A Flowering Tree and Other Oral Tales from India*, ed. Blackburn and Alan Dundes, was published in 1997. Ramanujan published many important translations from Tamil and Kannada, including *The Interior Landscape: Love Poems from a Classical Tamil Anthology*, 1967; *Speaking of Siva*, 1973; *Hymns for the Drowning: Poems for Visnu*, 1981; and *Poems of Love and War: From the Eight Anthologies and the Ten Long Poems of Classical Tamil*, 1985. He is coeditor, with Blackburn, of *Another Harmony: New Essays on the Folklore of India*, 1986; editor of *Folktales from India: A Selection of Oral Tales from Twenty-Two Languages*, 1991; coeditor and cotranslator, with Velcheru Narayana Rao and David Dean Shulman, of *When God Is a Customer: Telugu Courtesan Songs*, 1994; and coeditor, with Dharwadker, of *The Oxford Anthology of Modern Indian Poetry*, 1994.

A. N. Dwivedi has published two studies of Ramanujan's work: *A. K. Ramanujan and His Poetry*, 1983, and *The Poetic Art of A. K. Ramanujan*, 1995. Other studies of Ramanujan's poetry include Emmanuel Narendra Lall's *The Poetry of Encounter: Three Indo-Anglian Poets: Dom Moraes, A. K. Ramanujan, and Nissim Ezekiel*, 1983; Bruce King's *Modern Poetry in English*, 1987, rev. ed. 2001, and his *Three Indian Poets: Nissim Ezekiel, A. K. Ramanujan*,

Dom Moraes, 1991; Dharwadker's introduction to Collected Poems; Shirish Chindhade's Five Indian Poets: Nissim Ezekiel, A. K. Ramanujan, Arun Kolatkar, Dilip Chitre, R. Parthasarathy, 1996; and Jahan Ramazani's The Hybrid Muse: Postcolonial Poetry in English, 2001.

Henry Reed
Reed's Collected Poems, edited with a biographical and critical introduction by Jon Stallworthy, 1991, contains not only the contents of his one published volume of poetry, A Map of Verona, 1946, but also many uncollected and unpublished poems. The best of his radio plays are to be found in The Streets of Pompeii and Other Plays for Radio, 1971, and Hilda Tablet and Others: Four Pieces for Radio, 1971. Studies of Reed's poetry include James S. Beggs's The Poetic Character of Henry Reed, 1999, and the chapter "Henry Reed and Others," in Vernon Scannell's Not without Glory: Poets of the Second World War, 1976.

Jean Rhys
Rhys's first collection of short stories is The Left Bank and Other Stories, with an introduction by Ford Madox Ford, 1927. Her second collection, Postures, 1928, is best-known as the novel Quartet, under which title it was republished in 1957. Rhys's other works include After Leaving Mr. Mackenzie, 1931; Voyage in the Dark, 1934; Good Morning, Midnight, 1938; and Wide Sargasso Sea, 1966, which appeared with notes, essays, and contextual documents in Judith Raiskin's Norton Critical Edition in 1999. The Collected Short Stories was published in 1987 and includes stories from Tigers Are Better-Looking, 1968; My Day: Three Pieces, 1974; and Sleep It Off, Lady, 1976. Smile Please: An Unfinished Autobiography was published posthumously in 1979. A selection of her letters, The Letters of Jean Rhys, ed. Francis Wyndham and Diana Melly, was published in 1984. For her life see Carole Angier's Jean Rhys: Life and Work, 1990, and Elaine Savory's Jean Rhys, 1998. Elgin W. Mellown's Jean Rhys: A Descriptive and Annotated Bibliography, 1984, is a useful reference source.
Studies of Rhys's work include Thomas F. Staley's Jean Rhys: A Critical Study, 1979; Peter Wolfe's Jean Rhys, 1980; Judith Kegan Gardiner's Rhys, Stead, Lessing and the Politics of Empathy, 1989; Coral Ann Howells's Jean Rhys, 1991; George B. Handley's Postslavery Literatures in the Americas: Family Portraits in Black and White, 2000; and Delia Caparoso Konzett's Ethnic Modernisms: Anzia Yezierska, Zora Neale Hurston, Jean Rhys, and the Aesthetics of Dislocation, 2002. For readings of Rhys as a specifically Caribbean writer, see Louis James's Jean Rhys, 1978; Margaret Paul Joseph's Caliban in Exile: The Outsider in Caribbean Fiction, 1992; and Mervyn Morris's "Is English We Speaking" and Other Essays, 1999. Helen Nebeker's Jean

Rhys, Woman in Passage: A Critical Study of the Novels of Jean Rhys, 1981; Nancy R. Harrison's Jean Rhys and the Novel as Women's Text, 1988; and Deborah Kelly Kloepfer's The Unspeakable Mother: Forbidden Discourse in Jean Rhys and H. D, 1989, offer feminist perspectives on Rhys's work. For analysis of the shorter fiction, see Cheryl Alexander Malcolm and David Malcolm's Jean Rhys: A Study of the Short Fiction, 1996. For further reading concerning Wide Sargasso Sea, see Selma James's The Ladies and the Mammies: Jane Austen and Jean Rhys, 1983, and Veronica Marie Gregg's Jean Rhys's Historical Imagination: Reading and Writing the Creole, 1995.

Isaac Rosenberg
The Collected Works of Isaac Rosenberg: Poetry, Prose, Letters, Paintings and Drawings, ed. Ian Parsons, 1979, with a foreword by Siegfried Sassoon, is the standard edition of Rosenberg's work. Isaac Rosenberg: Selected Poems and Letters, ed. Jean Liddiard, was published in 2003. Rosenberg's play, Moses, was published in 1916. Biographies include Liddiard's Isaac Rosenberg: The Half Used Life, 1975; Jean Moorcroft Wilson's Isaac Rosenberg, Poet and Painter: A Biography, 1975; Joseph Cohen's Journey to the Trenches: The Life of Isaac Rosenberg, 1890–1918, 1975; and Deborah Maccoby's God Made Blind: Isaac Rosenberg, His Life and Poetry, 1999.
For studies of Rosenberg's work see D. W. Harding's Experience into Words: Essays on Poetry, 1963; John H. Johnston's English Poetry of the First World War: A Study in the Evolution of Lyric and Narrative Form, 1964; Jon Silkin's Out of Battle: The Poetry of the Great War, 1972, 2nd ed. 1998; Desmond Graham's The Truth of War: Owen, Rosenberg and Blunden, 1984; Frank Field's British and French Writers of the First World War: Comparative Studies in Cultural History, 1991; British Poets of the Great War: Brooke, Rosenberg, Thomas: A Documentary Volume, ed. Patrick Quinn, 2000; Jon Stallworthy's Great Poets of World War I: Poetry from the Great War, 2002; and Poets of WWI: Wilfred Owen & Isaac Rosenberg, ed. Harold Bloom, 2002. Diana Collecott's essay "Isaac Rosenberg (1890–1913): A Cross-Cultural Study," in The Jewish East End, 1840–1939, ed. Aubrey Newman, 1981, is also useful.

Salman Rushdie
Rushdie's first full-length work of fiction, Grimus, 1975, was followed by Midnight's Children, 1980; Shame, 1983; The Satanic Verses, 1988; The Moor's Last Sigh, 1995; The Ground beneath Her Feet, 1999; and Fury, 2001. He also has written the children's novel Haroun and the Sea of Stories, 1990, and the volume of short fiction East, West: Stories, 1994. Rushdie's nonfiction includes The Jaguar Smile: A Nicaraguan Journey, 1987; In Good Faith, 1990; The Wizard of

Oz, 1992; and the collections *Imaginary Homelands: Essays and Criticism, 1981–1991*, 1991, and *Step across This Line: Collected Nonfiction 1992–2002*, 2002. With Elizabeth West, Rushdie is coeditor of *Mirrorwork: Fifty Years of Indian Writing, 1947–1997*, 1997. For biographical material and the author's perspective on his work, see *Conversations with Salman Rushdie*, ed. Michael Reder, 2000, and *Salman Rushdie Interviews: A Sourcebook of His Ideas*, ed. Pradyumna S. Chauhan, 2001. Joel Kuortti's *The Salman Rushdie Bibliography: A Bibliography of Salman Rushdie's Work and Rushdie Criticism*, 1997, is a helpful guide to primary and secondary sources.

Studies of Rushdie's works include Timothy Brennan's *Salman Rushdie and the Third World*, 1989; *The Rushdie File*, ed. Lisa Appignanesi and Sara Maitland, 1989; Malise Ruthven's *A Satanic Affair: Salman Rushdie and the Rage of Islam*, 1990; James Harrison's *Salman Rushdie*, 1992; Catherine Cundy's *Salman Rushdie*, 1996; D. C. R. A. Goonetilleke's *Salman Rushdie*, 1998; *Critical Essays on Salman Rushdie*, ed. M. Keith Booker, 1999; and Sabrina Hassumani's *Salman Rushdie: A Postmodern Reading of His Major Works*, 2002. Criticism of Rushdie's work from a postcolonial perspective includes Fawzia Afzal-Khan's *Cultural Imperialism and the Indo-English Novel: Genre and Ideology in R. K. Narayan, Anita Desai, Kamala Markandaya, and Salman Rushdie*, 1993; Michael Gorra's *After Empire: Scott, Naipaul, Rushdie*, 1997; Anuradha Dingwaney Needham's *Using the Master's Tools: Resistance and the Literature of the African and South-Asian Diasporas*, 2000; Jaina C. Sanga's *Salman Rushdie's Postcolonial Metaphors: Migration, Translation, Hybridity, Blasphemy, and Globalization*, 2001; Deepika Bahri's *Native Intelligence: Aesthetics, Politics, and Postcolonial Literature*, 2003; John Clement Ball's *Satire and the Postcolonial Novel: V. S. Naipaul, Chinua Achebe, Salman Rushdie*, 2003; and Alexandra W. Schultheis's *Regenerative Fictions: Postcolonialism, Psychoanalysis, and the Nation as Family*, 2004.

Siegfried Sassoon
Sassoon's *Collected Poems, 1908–1956* was published in 1961 and reprinted in 1984; the selection *The War Poems of Siegfried Sassoon*, ed. Rupert Hart-Davis, was published in 1983. Sassoon is also author of six volumes of autobiographical prose; the first three semifictional volumes, *Memoirs of a Fox-Hunting Man*, 1928; *Memoirs of an Infantry Officer*, 1930; and *Sherston's Progress*, 1936, were collectively published in 1937 as *The Memoirs of George Sherston*; Sassoon followed these with *The Old Century and Seven More Years*, 1938; *In the Weald of Youth*, 1942; and *Siegfried's Journey*, 1945. Hart-Davis edited Sassoon's *Diaries, 1920–1922*, 1981;

Diaries, 1915–1918, 1983; and *Diaries, 1923–1925*, 1985, as well as Sassoon's letters in *Siegfried Sassoon: Letters to Max Beerbohm: With a Few Answers*, 1986. Michael Thorpe edited *Letters to a Critic*, 1976. The first volume of Jean Moorcroft Wilson's biography, *Siegfried Sassoon: The Making of a War Poet: A Biography (1886–1918)*, was published in 1998, and her *Siegfried Sassoon: The Journey from the Trenches: A Biography (1918–1967)*, appeared in 2003. Geoffrey Keynes's *A Bibliography of Siegfried Sassoon* was published in 1962.

For studies of Sassoon's poetry see Bernard Bergonzi's *Heroes' Twilight: A Study of the Literature of the Great War*, 1966; John H. Johnston's *English Poetry of the First World War: A Study in the Evolution of Lyric and Narrative Form*, 1964; Arthur E. Lane's *An Adequate Response: The War Poetry of Wilfred Owen and Siegfried Sassoon*, 1972; Jon Silkin's *Out of Battle: The Poetry of the Great War*, 1972, 2nd ed. 1998; John Lehmann's *The English Poets of the First World War*, 1981; Adrian Caesar's *Taking It like a Man: Suffering, Sexuality, and the War Poets: Brooke, Sassoon, Owen, Graves*, 1993; Patrick J. Quinn's *The Great War and the Missing Muse: The Early Writings of Robert Graves and Siegfried Sassoon*, 1994; Paul Moeyes's *Siegfried Sassoon, Scorched Glory: A Critical Study*, 1997; Patrick Campbell's *Siegfried Sassoon: A Study of the War Poetry*, 1999; Jon Stallworthy's *Great Poets of World War I: Poetry from the Great War*, 2002; and *Poets of World War I: Rupert Brooke & Siegfried Sassoon*, ed. Harold Bloom, 2003. For further discussions of Sassoon's diaries and prose works, see Thorpe's *Siegfried Sassoon: A Critical Study*, 1966, and Paul Fussell's *The Great War and Modern Memory*, 1975.

Edith Sitwell
Sitwell's more than thirty volumes of poetry were assembled as *Collected Poems* first in 1954 and then again in 1967; *The Early Unpublished Poems*, ed. Gerald W. Morton and Karen P. Helgeson, was published in 1994. A volume of *Selected Poems*, with an introduction by John Lehmann, was published in 1965. Important works of criticism include *Alexander Pope*, 1930; *The English Eccentrics*, 1933, rev. ed. 1957; *Aspects of Modern Poetry*, 1934; and *A Poet's Notebook*, 1943. Richard Greene edited *Selected Letters of Edith Sitwell*, 1997. For her life see Sitwell's *Taken Care Of: An Autobiography*, 1965; biographies include Geoffrey Elborn's *Edith Sitwell: A Biography*, 1981, and Victoria Glendinning's *Edith Sitwell: A Unicorn among Lions*, 1981. Portraits of the Sitwell family can be found in Elizabeth Salter's *The Last Years of a Rebel: A Memoir of Edith Sitwell*, 1967; other biographies of the Sitwell family include Lehmann's *A Nest of Tigers: The Sitwells in Their Times*, 1968; John Pearson's *Façades:*

Edith, Osbert, and Sacheverell Sitwell, 1978; and G. A. Cevasco's *The Sitwells: Edith, Osbert, and Sacheverell*, 1987. Bibliographic information is available in Richard Fifoot's *A Bibliography of Edith, Osbert, and Sacheverell Sitwell*, 1971.

Studies of Sitwell's work includes Lehmann's *Edith Sitwell*, 1952; Geoffrey Singleton's *Edith Sitwell: The Hymn to Life*, 1960; Ralph J. Mills's *Edith Sitwell: A Critical Essay*, 1966; J. D. Brophy's *Edith Sitwell: The Symbolist Order*, 1968; and John Press's *A Map of Modern English Verse*, 1969. Useful essays include Kenneth Rexroth's "Poets Old and New: Edith Sitwell," in *Assays*, 1961, and two chapters dedicated to Sitwell in Susan Kavaler-Adler's *The Compulsion to Create: A Psychoanalytic Study of Women Artists*, 1993.

Stevie Smith

The Collected Poems of Stevie Smith, ed. James MacGibbon, was published in 1975 and contains many of Smith's drawings. Other works are available in *Me Again: Uncollected Writings*, ed. Jack Barbera and William McBrien, 1981. Smith also published three novels: *Novel on Yellow Paper*, 1936; *Over the Frontier*, 1938; and *The Holiday*, 1949. Short prose is collected in *A Very Pleasant Evening with Stevie Smith: Selected Short Prose*, 1995, and drawings in *Some Are More Human than Others: A Sketchbook*, 1958. For her life see Barbera and McBrien's *Stevie: A Biography of Stevie Smith*, 1985, and Frances Spalding's *Stevie Smith*, 1989. Interviews appear in *The Poet Speaks: Interviews with Contemporary Poets Conducted by Hilary Morrish, Peter Orr, John Press and Ian Scott-Kilvert*, ed. Peter Orr, 1966, and Kay Dick's *Ivy and Stevie: Ivy Compton-Burnett and Stevie Smith: Conversations and Reflections*, 1971. Barbera, McBrien, and Helen Bajan compiled *Stevie Smith: A Bibliography* in 1987.

Studies of Smith's work include Arthur C. Rankin's *The Poetry of Stevie Smith, "Little Girl Lost,"* 1985; Sanford Sternlicht's *Stevie Smith*, 1990, and *In Search of Stevie Smith*, 1991; Catherine A. Civello's *Patterns of Ambivalence: The Fiction and Poetry of Stevie Smith*, 1997; and Laura Severin's *Stevie Smith's Resistant Antics*, 1997. Other discussions of her work can be found in chapters of Calvin Bedient's *Eight Contemporary Poets: Charles Tomlinson, Donald Davie, R. S. Thomas, Philip Larkin, Ted Hughes, Thomas Kinsella, Stevie Smith, W. S. Graham*, 1974; Seamus Heaney's *Preoccupations: Selected Prose, 1968–1978*, 1980; Philip Larkin's *Required Writing: Miscellaneous Pieces, 1955–1982*, 1983; Christopher Ricks's *The Force of Poetry*, 1984; Gill Plain's *Women's Fiction of the Second World War: Gender, Power, and Resistance*, 1996; Jacqueline Rose's essay on Smith and Virginia Woolf in *Between "Race" and Culture: Representations of "the Jew" in English*

and American Literature, ed. Bryan Cheyette, 1996; and Laura Severin's *Poetry Off the Page: Twentieth-Century British Women Poets in Performance*, 2004.

Wole Soyinka

Soyinka's volumes of poetry include *"Idanre" and Other Poems*, 1967; *Poems from Prison*, 1969, expanded as *A Shuttle in the Crypt*, 1972; *Ogun Abibiman*, 1976; and *"Mandela's Earth" and Other Poems*, 1988. Oxford published a selection of Soyinka's plays, *Collected Plays*, 2 vols., 1973–74, which includes *The Lion and the Jewel*, 1959; *The Swamp Dwellers*, 1959; *A Dance of the Forests*, 1960; *The Strong Breed*, 1963; *The Trials of Brother Jero*, 1963; *The Road*, 1965; *Kongi's Harvest*, 1966; *Madmen and Specialists*, 1970; *The Bacchae of Euripides: A Communion Rite*, 1973; and *Jero's Metamorphosis*, 1973. Other major plays include *Camwood on the Leaves*, 1960; *Death and the King's Horseman*, 1975, also available in a Norton Critical Edition, ed. Simon Gikandi, 2003; *Opera Wonyosi*, 1981; *A Play of Giants*, 1984; *From Zia, with Love*, 1992; and *The Beatification of Area Boy: A Lagosian Kaleidoscope*, 1995. Soyinka is also the author of two novels—*The Interpreters*, 1965, and *Season of Anomy*, 1973—and he has written scripts for radio, television, and film. Works dealing with the politics of Nigeria include his prison diary, *The Man Died: Prison Notes*, 1972, and his lectures in *The Open Sore of a Continent: A Personal Narrative of the Nigerian Crisis*, 1996. Other prose works include *Myth, Literature, and the African World*, 1976; the autobiographical *Aké: The Years of Childhood*, 1981; *The Critic and Society: Barthes, Leftocracy and Other Mythologies*, 1982; *Art, Dialogue and Outrage: Essays on Literature and Culture*, 1988; his 1986 Nobel lecture, *This Past Must Address Its Present*, 1988; *Isara, A Voyage Around Essay*, 1989; *Ibadan: The Penkelemes Years: A Memoir: 1946–1965*, 1994; and *The Burden of Memory, The Muse of Forgiveness*, 1999. Soyinka has also edited the anthology *Poems of Black Africa*, 1975. Biodun Jeyifo edited a book of interviews, *Conversations with Wole Soyinka*, in 2001. B. M. Okpu's *Wole Soyinka: A Bibliography* was published in 1984; James Gibbs, Ketu H. Katrak, and Henry Louis Gates Jr.'s *Wole Soyinka: A Bibliography of Primary and Secondary Sources* appeared in 1986.

For guides to Soyinka see K. L. Goodwin's *Understanding African Poetry: A Study of Ten Poets*, 1982; Obi Maduakor's *Wole Soyinka: An Introduction to His Writing*, 1986; and Aderemi Bamikunle's *Introduction to Soyinka's Poetry: Analysis of* A Shuttle in the Crypt, 1991. Studies of Soyinka's work include Gerald Moore's *Wole Soyinka* 1971, 2nd ed. 1978; Gibbs's *Wole Soyinka*, 1986; Eldred D. Jones's *The Writing of Wole Soyinka*, 3rd ed. 1988; Akomaye Oko's *The Tragic Paradox: A Study of Wole Soyinka and His*

Works, 1992; Derek Wright's Wole Soyinka Revisited, 1993; Tanure Ojaide's The Poetry of Wole Soyinka, 1994; and Tunde Adeniran's The Politics of Wole Soyinka, 1994. Collections of essays dedicated to Soyinka include Critical Perspectives on Wole Soyinka, ed. Gibbs, 1980; Before Our Very Eyes: Tribute to Wole Soyinka, ed. Dapo Adelugba, 1987; Research on Wole Soyinka, ed. Bernth Lindfors and Gibbs, 1993; Soyinka: A Collection of Critical Essays, ed. Oyin Ogunba, 1994; and Jeyifo's Perspectives on Wole Soyinka: Freedom and Complexity, 2001. Other useful discussions of Soyinka's work include Nyong J. Udoeyop's Three Nigerian Poets: A Critical Study of the Poetry of Soyinka, Clark, and Okigbo, 1973; Kole Omotoso's Achebe or Soyinka?: A Study in Contrasts, 1996; Chii P. Akporji's Figures in a Dance: The Theater of Yeats and Soyinka, 2003; and Olakunle George's Relocating Agency: Modernity and African Letters, 2003.

Tom Stoppard

Stoppard's published plays include Rosencrantz and Guildenstern Are Dead, 1967; The Real Inspector Hound, 1968; Enter a Free Man, 1968; Albert's Bridge, 1969; If You're Glad I'll Be Frank, 1969; A Separate Peace, 1969; After Magritte, 1971; Jumpers, 1972; Artist Descending a Staircase, 1973; Where Are They Now?, 1973; Travesties, 1974; Dirty Linen, 1976; New-Found-Land, 1976; The Fifteen Minute Hamlet, 1976; Every Good Boy Deserves Favour, 1978; Professional Foul, 1978; Night and Day, 1978; On the Razzle, 1981; The Real Thing, 1982; Rough Crossing, 1985; Dalliance, 1986; Hapgood, 1988; Arcadia, 1993; Indian Ink, 1995; The Seagull, 1997; The Invention of Love, 1997; and The Coast of Utopia, 2002. He has also published screenplays, radio and television plays, opera libretti, a novel, and short stories. Ira Nadel's Tom Stoppard: A Life, 2002, is the standard biography. Interviews can be found in Paul Delaney, Tom Stoppard in Conversation, 1994, and Mel Gussow, Conversations with Stoppard, 1995.

Critical studies of his works include C. W. E. Bigsby, Tom Stoppard, 1976; Ronald Hayman, Tom Stoppard, 1977; Victor L. Cahn, Beyond Absurdity: The Plays of Tom Stoppard, 1979; Felicia Hardison Londré, Tom Stoppard, 1981; David Bratt, Tom Stoppard: A Reference Guide, 1982; Susan Rusinko, Tom Stoppard, 1986; Anthony Jenkins, The Theatre of Tom Stoppard, 1987, 2nd ed. 1989; Jim Hunter, Tom Stoppard, 2000; and Tom Stoppard, ed. Harold Bloom, 2003. For Studies of Arcadia, see Jeffrey and Prapassaree Kramer's article "Stoppard's Arcadia: Research, Time, Loss" in Modern Drama 40.1, 1997; Paul Edwards's chapter "Science in Hapgood and Arcadia" in The Cambridge Companion to Tom Stoppard, ed. Katherine E. Kelly, 2001; and Shaun McCarthy's Arcadia, 2001.

Dylan Thomas

Collected Poems, ed. Walford Davies and Ralph Maud, 1988, is the standard edition of Thomas's poetry. Dylan Thomas Selected Poems, 1934–1952 was published in 2003. Thomas also wrote the autobiographical prose work Portrait of the Artist as a Young Dog, 1940; a radio play, Under Milk Wood: A Play for Voices, 1954; Quite Early One Morning, 1954, a collection of stories, essays, and minor pieces broadcast over BBC; and the short-fiction collection Adventures in the Skin Trade and Other Stories, 1955. Maud edited The Notebooks of Dylan Thomas, 1967; Paul Ferris edited The Collected Letters of Dylan Thomas, 1985; and Peter Lynch edited The Love-Letters of Dylan Thomas, 2001. For his life see Constantine FitzGibbon's The Life of Dylan Thomas, 1965; Ferris's Dylan Thomas: The Biography, 1977, 2nd ed. 1999; and Andrew Sinclair's Dylan the Bard: A Life of Dylan Thomas, 1999. Bill Read's The Days of Dylan Thomas, 1964, supplements a straightforward narrative with many photographs.

For introductions to Thomas see William York Tindall's A Reader's Guide to Dylan Thomas, 1962, 3rd ed. 1996; Maud's Entrances to Dylan Thomas' Poetry, 1963, and Where Have All the Old Words Got Me?: Explications of Dylan Thomas's Collected Poems, 2003; William T. Moynahan's The Craft and Art of Dylan Thomas, 1966; and John Ackerman's A Dylan Thomas Companion, 1991. For criticism of Thomas's work see C. B. Cox's Dylan Thomas: A Collection of Critical Essays, 1966; R. B. Kershner's Dylan Thomas, 1976; Critical Essays on Dylan Thomas, ed. Georg Gaston, 1989; Barbara Hardy's Dylan Thomas: An Original Language, 2000; and Dylan Thomas, ed. John Goodby and Chris Wigginton, 2001.

Edward Thomas

The Collected Poems of Edward Thomas, ed. R. George Thomas, was published in 1978. Thomas's prose can be found in A Language Not to Be Betrayed: Selected Prose of Edward Thomas, ed. Edna Longley, 1981. R. George Thomas edited Selected Letters, 1995, and Letters from Edward Thomas to Gordon Bottomley, 1968. The Diary of Edward Thomas: 1 January–8 April 1917, with an introduction by Roland Gant, was published in 1977. Thomas's accounts of his travels around England include Oxford, illustrated by John Fulleylove, 1903; The South Country, 1909; and A Literary Pilgrim in England, 1917. For his life see As It Was, 1927, and World without End, 1956, both by his wife, Helen Thomas. The first book of Eleanor Farjeon's Memoirs, Edward Thomas: The Last Four Years, 1958; R. George Thomas's Edward Thomas: A Portrait, 1985; and William Cooke's Edward Thomas: A Critical Biography 1878–1917, 1970, are all quite helpful. An autobiographical fragment, The Childhood of Edward

Thomas, was published in 1983 with a preface by Roland Gant. Bibliographic information is available in Robert P. Eckert's *Edward Thomas: A Biography and Bibliography*, 1937.

For introductions to Thomas see *British Poets of the Great War*, ed. Patrick Quinn, 2000, and Jon Stallworthy's *Great Poets of World War I: Poetry from the Great War*, 2002. For discussions of Thomas's life and work, see H. Coombes's *Edward Thomas*, 1956; Jon Silkin's *Out of Battle: The Poetry of the Great War*, 1972, 2nd ed. 1998; Jan Marsh's *Edward Thomas: A Poet for His Country*, 1978; Andrew Motion's *The Poetry of Edward Thomas*, 1980; Stan Smith's *Edward Thomas*, 1986; Edna Longley's *Poetry in the Wars*, 1987; Piers Gray's *Marginal Men: Edward Thomas, Ivor Gurney, J. R. Ackerley*, 1991; Jeremy Hooker's *Writers in a Landscape*, 1996; and Rennie Parker's *The Georgian Poets*, 1999. Numerous helpful essays are collected in *The Imagination of Edward Thomas*, ed. Michael Kirkham, 1986, and *The Art of Edward Thomas*, ed. Jonathan Barker, 1987.

Voices from World War I
The best anthologies are *Up the Line to Death: The War Poets, 1914–1918*, ed. Brian Gardner, 1964; *Men Who March Away: Poems of the First World War*, ed. I. M. Parsons, 1965; *The Penguin Book of First World War Poetry*, ed. Jon Silkin, 2nd ed. 1981, rev. ed. 1996; and *The Penguin Book of First World War Prose*, ed. Jon Glover and Jon Silkin, 1989. Jon Stallworthy's *Great Poets of World War I: Poetry from the Great War*, 2002, complements an anthology of twelve war poets with critical and biographical introductions for each. The literature is set in much-needed new perspectives by Samuel Hynes's *A War Imagined: The First World War and English Culture*, 1991, and *The Cambridge Companion to the Literature of the First World War*, ed. Vincent Sherry, 2005. Bernard Bergonzi's *Heroes' Twilight: A Study of the Literature of the Great War*, 1966, 2nd ed. 1980, is a balanced introduction to both the poetry and the literary prose of the period, while one of the many strengths of Paul Fussell's *The Great War and Modern Memory*, 1975, is a range of references that includes nonliterary as well as literary writing. Other noteworthy critical studies include John H. Johnston's *English Poetry of the First World War: A Study in the Evolution of Lyric and Narrative Form*, 1964; Desmond Graham's *The Truth of War: Owen, Rosenberg and Blunden*, 1984; Hugh Cecil's *The Flower of Battle: British Fiction Writers of the First World War*, 1995; Allyson Booth's *Postcards from the Trenches: Negotiating the Space between Modernism and the First World War*, 1996; Jon Silkin's *Out of Battle: The Poetry of the Great War*, 1972, 2nd ed. 1998; and Vincent Sherry's *The Great War and the Language of Modernism*, 2003. The British experience is usefully set in

an international context by Patrick Bridgwater's *The German Poets of the First World War*, 1985; *The Lost Voices of World War I: An International Anthology of Writers, Poets & Playwrights*, ed. Tim Cross, 1989; and Frank Field's *British and French Writers of the First World War*, 1991. *Modernism/Modernity* 9.1, 2002, is a special issue devoted to "Men, Women, and World War I."

See also entries under **Rupert Brooke, May Wedderburn Cannan, Robert Graves, Ivor Gurney, David Jones, Wilfred Owen, Isaac Rosenberg, Siegfried Sassoon,** and **Edward Thomas.**

Voices from World War II
The best anthologies are *The Poetry of War, 1939–45*, ed. Ian Hamilton, 1965, and *The Terrible Rain: The War Poets, 1939–45*, ed. Brian Gardner, 1966; and the fullest critical accounts of this poetry are Vernon Scannell's *Not without Glory: Poets of the Second World War*, 1976, and Linda M. Shires's *British Poetry of the Second World War*, 1985. *The Second World War in Fiction*, ed. Holger Michael Klein, J. E. Flower, and Eric Homberger, 1984; Paul Fussell's *Wartime: Understanding and Behavior in the Second World War*, 1989; Sebastian D. G. Knowles's *A Purgatorial Flame: Seven British Writers in the Second World War*, 1990; Bernard Bergonzi's *Wartime and Aftermath: English Literature and Its Background, 1939–60*, 1993; and Mark Rawlinson's *British Writing of the Second World War*, 2000, are useful contextual studies. For studies of the home front in England during the war, see Robert Hewison's *Under Siege: Literary Life in London, 1939–1945*, 1977, and Jed Esty's *A Shrinking Island: Modernism and National Culture in England*, 2004.

See also entries under **Charles Causley, Keith Douglas, Henry Reed,** and **Edith Sitwell.**

Derek Walcott
Walcott's *Collected Poems, 1948–1984*, 1986, included selections from *In a Green Night: Poems 1948–60*, 1960; *The Castaway and Other Poems*, 1965; *The Gulf and Other Poems*, 1969; *Another Life*, 1973; *Sea Grapes*, 1976; *The Fortunate Traveler*, 1981; and *Midsummer*, 1984. Subsequent volumes include *The Arkansas Testament*, 1987; *Omeros*, 1990; *The Bounty*, 1997; *Tiepolo's Hound*, 2000; and *The Prodigal*, 2004. His many plays include *Ti-Jean and His Brothers*, 1958; *Dream on Monkey Mountain*, 1967; *The Joker of Seville*, 1978; *O Babylon!*, 1978; *Three Plays: The Last Carnival; Beef, No Chicken; A Branch of the Blue Nile*, 1986; and *The Odyssey*, 1993. *What the Twilight Says: Essays*, 1998, offers a selection of Walcott's essays, and *Conversations with Derek Walcott*, ed. William Baer, 1996, is a collection of interviews. Walcott's autobiography, *Another Life:*

Fully Annotated, ed. Edward Baugh and Colbert I. Nepaulsingh, was published in 2004. A fine biography is Bruce King's *Derek Walcott: A Caribbean Life*, 2000. The standard bibliography is Irma E. Goldstraw's *Derek Walcott: An Annotated Bibliography of His Works*, 1984.

Studies of Walcott's work include Edward Baugh's *Derek Walcott: Memory as Vision*, 1978; Ned Thomas's *Derek Walcott: Poet of the Islands*, 1980; *The Art of Derek Walcott*, ed. Stewart Brown, 1991; Rei Terada's *Walcott's Poetry: American Mimicry*, 1992; Robert D. Hamner's *Derek Walcott*, 1981, 2nd ed. 1993; *Postcolonial Literatures: Achebe, Ngugi, Desai, Walcott*, ed. Michael Parker and Roger Starkey, 1995; June D. Bobb's *Beating a Restless Drum: The Poetics of Kamau Brathwaite and Derek Walcott*, 1998; John Thieme's *Derek Walcott*, 1999; Paula Burnett's *Derek Walcott: Politics and Poetics*, 2000; Paul Breslin's *Nobody's Nation: Reading Derek Walcott*, 2001; *Approaches to the Poetics of Derek Walcott*, ed. José Luis Martínez-Dueñas Espejo and José María Pérez Fernández, 2001; Patricia Ismond's *Abandoning Dead Metaphors: The Caribbean Phase of Derek Walcott's Poetry*, 2001; and *Derek Walcott*, ed. Harold Bloom, 2003. An essential collection of primary and secondary materials is *Critical Perspectives on Derek Walcott*, ed. Hamner, 1993. *Verse* 11.2, 1994, *South Atlantic Quarterly* 96.2, 1997, and *Callaloo* 28.1, 2005, are special issues dedicated to Walcott.

For further discussion of *Omeros* see Hamner's *Epic of the Dispossessed: Derek Walcott's Omeros*, 1997; Jahan Ramazani's *The Hybrid Muse*, 2001; and Lance Callahan's *In the Shadows of Divine Perfection: Derek Walcott's Omeros*, 2003.

Virginia Woolf

Woolf's ten novels are *The Voyage Out*, 1915; *Night and Day*, 1919; *Jacob's Room*, 1922; *Mrs. Dalloway*, 1925; *To the Lighthouse*, 1927; *Orlando: A Biography*, 1928; *The Waves*, 1931; *Flush: A Biography*, 1933; *The Years*, 1937; and the posthumously published *Between the Acts*, 1941. *Roger Fry: A Biography*, 1940, is an actual biography. *Mrs. Dalloway's Party: A Short Story Sequence*, 1973, and *Freshwater: A Comedy*, 1976, were both published posthumously; Woolf's short stories have been compiled in *The Complete Shorter Fiction*, ed. Susan Dick, 1985.

Woolf was a prolific essayist, and *A Room of One's Own*, 1929, and *Three Guineas*, 1938, are major works of sociopolitical and literary criticism; *The Common Reader*, 1925, and *The Second Common Reader*, 1932, provide selections of her literary criticism; and *The Essays of Virginia Woolf*, 3 vols., ed. Andrew McNeillie, 1986–88, contains much of her prose. Woolf's complete diaries are available in *The Diary of Virginia Woolf*, 5 vols., ed. Anne Olivier Bell and McNeillie, 1977–84; the selection *A Writer's Diary:*

Being Extracts from the Diary of Virginia Woolf, ed. Leonard Woolf, 1954, describes the composition of *The Years* and *Three Guineas*. Woolf's prolific correspondence is collected in *The Letters of Virginia Woolf*, 6 vols., ed. Nigel Nicolson and Joanne Trautmann Banks, 1975–80. For Woolf's early development see *A Passionate Apprentice: The Early Journals, 1897–1909*, ed. Mitchell A. Leaska, 1990. *Moments of Being: Unpublished Autobiographical Writings*, ed. Jeanne Schulkind, 1976, 2nd ed. 1985, contains her autobiographical writings. Quentin Bell's *Virginia Woolf*, 1972, is the standard biography, but Lyndall Gordon's *Virginia Woolf: A Writer's Life*, 1984, and Hermione Lee's *Virginia Woolf*, 1997, are both useful. Phyllis Rose, *Woman of Letters: A Life of Virginia Woolf*, 1978, focuses on her feminism, and Louise A. DeSalvo's *Virginia Woolf: The Impact of Childhood Sexual Abuse on Her Life and Work*, 1989, offers a revised picture of Woolf's childhood and its effect on her writing. For a guide to secondary sources, see B. J. Kirkpatrick and Stuart N. Clarke's *A Bibliography of Virginia Woolf*, 4th ed. 1997.

Perceptive critical studies of Woolf's work include David Daiches's *Virginia Woolf*, 1942, rev. ed. 1963; Joan Bennett, *Virginia Woolf: Her Art as a Novelist*, 2nd ed. 1964; Avrom Fleishman's *Virginia Woolf: A Critical Reading*, 1975; Lee's *The Novels of Virginia Woolf*, 1977; *New Feminist Essays on Virginia Woolf*, ed. Jane Marcus, 1981; *Virginia Woolf: New Critical Essays*, ed. Patricia Clements and Isobel Grundy, 1983; Alex Zwerdling's *Virginia Woolf and the Real World*, 1986; Elizabeth Abel's *Virginia Woolf and the Fictions of Psychoanalysis*, 1989; *Virginia Woolf and War: Fiction, Reality, and Myth*, ed. Mark Hussey, 1991; Michael Tratner's *Modernism and Mass Politics: Joyce, Woolf, Eliot, Yeats*, 1995; Gillian Beer's *Virginia Woolf: The Common Ground*, 1996; *Ambiguous Discourse: Feminist Narratology and British Women Writers*, ed. Kathy Mezei, 1996; Juliet Dusinberre's *Virginia Woolf's Renaissance: Woman Reader or Common Reader?*, 1997; and James J. Miracky's *Regenerating the Novel: Gender and Genre in Woolf, Forster, Sinclair, and Lawrence*, 2003. Since she was a central member of the "Bloomsbury Group," studies of Woolf may also be aided by *Bloomsbury Group: A Collection of Memoirs, Commentary, and Criticism*, ed. S. P. Rosenbaum, 1975, and Mary Ann Caws and Sarah Bird Wright's *Bloomsbury and France: Art and Friends*, 2000.

For further reading on Woolf and feminism, especially regarding *A Room of One's Own*, see Elaine Showalter's *A Literature of Their Own: British Women Novelists from Brontë to Lessing*, 1977, 2nd ed. 1999; Ellen Bayuk Rosenman's *A Room of One's Own: Women Writers and the Politics of Creativity*, 1995; and Rachel Bowlby's *Virginia Woolf: Feminist Destinations*, 1988, rev. ed. 1997.

William Butler Yeats

In addition to poems and plays, Yeats was author to a number of memoirs, works of short fiction, and essays; with Edwin Ellis he was editor of the first complete works of William Blake, 1893, and in 1936 he selected and introduced the poems for *The Oxford Book of Modern Verse*. An authoritative edition of Yeats's poetry is available in the revised edition of *The Poems*, ed. Richard J. Finneran, the first volume of *The Collected Works of W. B. Yeats*, gen. ed. Finneran and George Mills Harper, 1989. Other published texts in this series include, in order by volume number, *The Plays*, ed. David R. Clark and Rosalind E. Clark, 2001; *Autobiographies*, ed. William H. O'Donnell and Douglas N. Archibald, 1999; *Later Essays*, ed. O'Donnell with Elizabeth Bergmann Loizeaux, 1994; *Prefaces and Introductions*, ed. O'Donnell, 1989; *Letters to the New Island*, ed. George Bornstein and Hugh Witemeyer, 1989; *The Irish Dramatic Movement*, ed. Mary FitzGerald and Finneran, 2003; *Early Articles and Reviews*, ed. John P. Frayne and Madeleine Marchaterre, 2004; *Later Articles and Reviews*, ed. Colton Johnson, 2000; and the two short pseudonymous novels, *John Sherman and Dhoya*, ed. Finneran, 1991. Important scholarly editions include *The Variorum Edition of the Poems*, ed. Peter Allt and Russell K. Alspach, 1957; and *The Variorum Edition of the Plays*, ed. Alspach and Catherine C. Alspach, 1966. An excellent paperback selection is the Norton Critical Edition of *Yeats's Poetry, Drama, and Prose*, ed. James Pethica, 2000, which contains secondary criticism in addition to Yeats's work and reprints the poems in their earlier published versions. Also of note are *Mythologies*, 1959, which contains much of Yeats's prose fiction; *Essays and Introductions*, 1961; and the miscellaneous prose in *Explorations*, 1962; and *Memoirs*, ed. Denis Donoghue, 1973, which contains journals and the first published version of the *Autobiographies*. Yeats's mythological system is available in *A Vision*, first published in 1925, substantially revised and reissued in 1937. John Kelly, Eric Domville, and Ronald Schuchard have to date published three volumes of *The Collected Letters of W. B. Yeats*, 1986, 1994, 1997.

R. F. Foster has published the standard biography, *W. B. Yeats: A Life*, 2 vols., 1997, 2003. Also useful is A. N. Jeffares's *W. B. Yeats: A New Biography*, 1989. Bibliographic information is available in Wade's *A Bibliography of the Writings of W. B. Yeats*, 1958, revised by Alspach 1968.

W. B. Yeats: The Critical Heritage, ed. Jeffares, 1977, provides a reception history and contemporary reviews. Jeffares's *A New Commentary on the Poems of W. B. Yeats*, rev. ed. 1984, and *A Commentary on the Plays of W. B. Yeats*, 1975, are indispensable references. Also valuable are Sam McCready's *A William Butler Yeats Encyclopedia*, 1997, and Lester I. Conner's *A Yeats Dictionary*, 1998.

In the vast body of Yeats criticism, some important studies are Richard Ellmann's *Yeats: The Man and the Masks*, 1948, and *The Identity of Yeats*, 2nd ed. 1964; Thomas Parkinson's *W. B. Yeats, Self-Critic: A Study of his Early Verse*, 1951, rpt. 1971 with *The Later Poetry* and a new foreword; Frank Kermode's *Romantic Image*, 1957; Jon Stallworthy's *Between the Lines: W. B. Yeats's Poetry in the Making*, 1963; Helen Vendler's *Yeats's Vision and Later Plays*, 1963; Thomas R. Whitaker's *Swan and Shadow: Yeats's Dialogue with History*, 1964; Harold Bloom's *Yeats*, 1970; Bornstein's *Yeats and Shelley*, 1970; Donoghue's *William Butler Yeats*, 1971; Mary Helen Thuente's *W. B. Yeats and Irish Folklore*, 1981; Elizabeth Butler Cullingford's *Yeats, Ireland and Fascism*, 1981; Loizeaux's *Yeats and the Visual Arts*, 1986; Paul Scott Stanfield's *Yeats and Politics in the 1930s*, 1988; Finneran's *Editing Yeats's Poems*, 1990; Stan Smith's *W. B. Yeats: A Critical Introduction*, 1990; Jahan Ramazani's *Yeats and the Poetry of Death: Elegy, Self-Elegy, and the Sublime*, 1990; Hazard Adams's *The Book of Yeats's Poems*, 1991; Michael North's *The Political Aesthetic of Yeats, Eliot, and Pound*, 1991; Cullingford's *Gender and History in Yeats's Love Poetry*, 1993; M. L. Rosenthal's *Running to Paradise: Yeats's Poetic Art*, 1994; Marjorie Howes's *Yeats's Nations: Gender, Class, and Irishness*, 1996; Michael J. Sidnell's *Yeats's Poetry and Poetics*, 1996; Vicki Mahaffey's *States of Desire: Wilde, Yeats, Joyce, and the Irish Experiment*, 1998; Bornstein's *Material Modernism: The Politics of the Page*, 2001; Gregory Castle's *Modernism and the Celtic Revival*, 2001; and Richard Greaves's *Transition, Reception, and Modernism in W. B. Yeats*, 2002. Collections of essays include *William Butler Yeats*, ed. Bloom, 1986; *Yeats's Political Identities*, ed. Jonathan Allison, 1996; and *W. B. Yeats: Critical Assessments*, ed. David Pierce, 2000. Many essays have appeared annually in the journals *Yeats* and *Yeats Annual*.

Literary Terminology[*]

Using simple technical terms can sharpen our understanding and streamline our discussion of literary works. Some terms, such as the ones in Sections A, B, and C of this appendix, help us address the internal style, form, and structure of works. Other terms, such as those in Section D, provide insight into the material forms in which literary works have been produced.

In analyzing what they called "rhetoric," ancient Greek and Roman writers determined the elements of what we call "style" and "structure." Our literary terms are derived, via medieval and Renaissance intermediaries, from the Greek and Latin sources. In the definitions that follow, the etymology, or root, of the word is given when it helps illuminate the word's current usage.

Most of the examples are drawn from texts in this anthology.

Words **boldfaced** within definitions are themselves defined in this appendix. Some terms are defined within definitions; such words are *italicized*.

A. Style

In literary works the manner in which something is expressed contributes substantially to its meaning. The manner of a literary work is its "style," the effect of which is its "tone." We often can intuit the tone of a text; the following terms offer a set of concepts by which we can analyze the stylistic features that produce the tone. The groups within this section move from the micro to the macro level internal to works.

(i) Diction

"Diction," or "lexis" (from, respectively, Latin "dictio" and Greek "lexis," each meaning "word"), designates the actual words used in any utterance—speech, writing, and, for our purposes here, literary works. The choice of words contributes significantly to the style of a given work.

Connotation: To understand connotation, we need to understand **denotation.** While many words can denote the same concept—that is, have the same basic meaning—those words can evoke different associations, or connotations. Contrast, for example, the clinical-sounding term "depression" and the more colorful, musical, even poetic phrase "the blues."

Denotation: A word has a basic, "prosaic" (factual) meaning prior to the associations it connotes (see **connotation**). The word "steed," for example, might call to mind a horse fitted with battle gear, to be ridden by a warrior, but its denotation is simply "horse."

[*] This appendix was devised and compiled by James Simpson with the collaboration of all the editors.

Lexical set: Words that habitually recur together (e.g., January, February, March, etc.; or red, white, and blue) form a lexical set.

Register: The register of a word is its stylistic level, which can be distinguished by degree of technicality but also by degree of formality. We choose our words from different registers according to context, that is, audience and/ or environment. Thus a chemist in a laboratory will say "sodium chloride," a cook in a kitchen "salt." A formal register designates the kind of language used in polite society (e.g., "Mr. President"), while an informal or colloquial register is used in less formal or more relaxed social situations (e.g., "the boss"). In **classical** and medieval rhetoric, these registers of formality were called *high style* and *low style*. A *middle style* was defined as the style fit for narrative, not drawing attention to itself.

(ii) Rhetorical Figures: Figures of Speech

Literary language often employs patterns perceptible to the eye and/or to the ear. Such patterns are called "figures of speech"; in **classical** *rhetoric they were called* **"schemes"** *(from Greek "schema," meaning "form, figure").*

Alliteration (from Latin "litera," alphabetic letter): the repetition of an initial consonant sound or consonant cluster in consecutive or closely positioned words. This pattern is often an inseparable part of the meter in Germanic languages, where the tonic, or accented **syllable,** is usually the first syllable. Thus all Old English poetry and some varieties of Middle English poetry use alliteration as part of their basic metrical practice. *Sir Gawain and the Green Knight,* line 1: "Sithen the sege and the assaut was sesed at Troye" (see vol. 1, p. 161). Otherwise used for local effects; Stevie Smith, "Pretty," lines 4–5: "And in the pretty pool the pike stalks / He stalks his prey . . ." (see vol. 2, p. 2377).

Anaphora (Greek "carrying back"): the repetition of words or groups of words at the beginning of consecutive sentences, clauses, or phrases. Blake, "London," lines 5–8: "In every cry of every Man, / In every Infant's cry of fear, / In every voice, in every ban . . ." (see vol. 2, p. 94); Louise Bennett, "Jamaica Oman," lines 17–20: "Some backa man a push, some side-a / Man a hole him han, / Some a lick sense eena him head, / Some a guide him pon him plan!" (see vol. 2, p. 2473).

Assonance (Latin "sounding to"): the repetition of identical or near identical stressed vowel sounds in words whose final consonants differ, producing half-rhyme. Tennyson, "The Lady of Shalott," line 100: "His broad clear brow in sunlight glowed" (see vol. 2, p. 1116).

Chiasmus (Greek "crosswise"): the inversion of an already established sequence. This can involve verbal echoes: Pope, "Eloisa to Abelard," line 104, "The crime was common, common be the pain" (see vol. 1, p. 2535); or it can be purely a matter of syntactic inversion: Pope, *Epistle to Dr. Arbuthnot*, line 8: "They pierce my thickets, through my grot they glide" (see vol. 1, p. 2549).

Consonance (Latin "sounding with"): the repetition of final consonants in words or stressed syllables whose vowel sounds are different. Herbert, "Easter," line 13: "Consort, both heart and lute . . ." (see vol. 1, p. 1608).

Homophone (Greek "same sound"): a word that sounds identical to another word but has a different meaning ("bear" / "bare").

Onomatopoeia (Greek "name making"): verbal sounds that imitate and evoke the sounds they denote. Hopkins, "Binsey Poplars," lines 10–12 (about some felled trees): "O if we but knew what we do / When we delve [dig] or hew— / Hack and rack the growing green!" (see vol. 2, p. 1519).

Rhyme: the repetition of identical vowel sounds in stressed syllables whose initial consonants differ ("dead" / "head"). In poetry, rhyme often links the end of one line with another. *Masculine rhyme:* full rhyme on the final syllable of the line ("decays" / "days"). *Feminine rhyme:* full rhyme on syllables that are followed by unaccented syllables ("fountains" / "mountains"). *Internal rhyme:* full rhyme within a single line; Coleridge, *The Rime of the Ancient Mariner*, line 7: "The guests are met, the feast is set" (see vol. 2, p. 430). *Rhyme riche:* rhyming on **homophones**; Chaucer, *General Prologue*, lines 17/18: "seeke" / "seke." *Off rhyme* (also known as *half rhyme, near rhyme,* or *slant rhyme*): differs from perfect rhyme in changing the vowel sound and/or the concluding consonants expected of perfect rhyme; Byron, "They say that Hope is Happiness," lines 5–7: "most" / "lost" (see vol. 2, p. 613). *Pararhyme:* stressed vowel sounds differ but are flanked by identical or similar consonants; Owen, "Miners," lines 9–11: "simmer" / "summer" (see vol. 2, p. 1973).

(iii) Rhetorical Figures: Figures of Thought

Language can also be patterned conceptually, even outside the rules that normally govern it. Literary language in particular exploits this licensed linguistic irregularity. Synonyms for figures of thought are "trope" (Greek "twisting," referring to the irregularity of use) and "conceit" (Latin "concept," referring to the fact that these figures are perceptible only to the mind). Be careful not to confuse "trope" with "topos" (a common error).

Allegory (Greek "saying otherwise"): saying one thing (the "vehicle" of the allegory) and meaning another (the allegory's "tenor"). Allegories may be momentary aspects of a work, as in **metaphor** ("John is a lion"), or, through extended metaphor, may constitute the basis of narrative, as in Bunyan's *Pilgrim's Progress;* this second meaning is the dominant one. See also **symbol** and **type**.

Antithesis (Greek "placing against"): juxtaposition of opposed terms in clauses or sentences that are next to or near each other; Milton, *Paradise Lost* 1.777–80: "They but now who seemed / In bigness to surpass Earth's giant sons / Now less than smallest dwarfs, in narrow room / Throng numberless" (see vol. 1, p. 1849).

Bathos (Greek "depth"): a sudden and sometimes ridiculous descent of tone; Pope, *The Rape of the Lock* 3.157–58: "Not louder shrieks to pitying heaven are cast, / When husbands, or when lapdogs breathe their last" (see vol. 1, p. 2524).

Emblem (Greek "an insertion"): a picture allegorically expressing a moral, or a verbal picture open to such interpretation. Donne, "A Hymn to Christ," lines 1–2: "In what torn ship soever I embark, / That ship shall be my emblem of thy ark" (see vol. 1, p. 1300).

Euphemism (Greek "sweet saying"): the figure by which something distasteful is described in alternative, less repugnant terms (e.g., "he passed away").

Hyperbole (Greek "throwing over"): overstatement, exaggeration; Marvell, "To His Coy Mistress," lines 11–12: "My vegetable love would grow / Vaster than empires, and more slow" (see vol. 1, p. 1703); Auden, "As I Walked Out One Evening," lines 9–12: " 'I'll love you, dear, I'll love you / Till China and Africa meet / And the river jumps over the mountain / And the salmon sing in the street" (see vol. 2, p. 2427).

Irony (Greek "dissimulation"): strictly, a subset of allegory: whereas allegory says one thing and means another, irony says one thing and means its opposite; Byron, *Don Juan* 1.1–2: "I want a hero: an uncommon want, / When every year and month sends forth a new one" (see vol. 2, p. 670). For an extended example of irony, see Swift's "Modest Proposal."

Litotes (from Greek "smooth"): strictly, understatement by denying the contrary; More, *Utopia*: "differences of no slight import" (see vol. 1, p. 524). More loosely, understatement; Swift, "A Tale of a Tub": "Last week I saw a woman flayed, and you will hardly believe how much it altered her person for the worse" (see vol. 1, p. 2320). Stevie Smith, "Sunt Leones," lines 11–12: "And if the Christians felt a little blue— / Well people being eaten often do" (see vol. 2, p. 2373).

Metaphor (Greek "carrying across," etymologically parallel to Latin "translation"): the identification or implicit identification of one thing with another with which it is not literally identifiable. Blake, "London," lines 11–12: "And the hapless Soldier's sigh / Runs in blood down Palace walls" (see vol. 2, p. 94).

Metonymy (Greek "change of name"): using a word to **denote** another concept or other concepts, by virtue of habitual association. Thus "The Press," designating printed news media. Fictional names often work by associations of this kind. A figure closely related to **synecdoche.**

Occupatio (Latin "taking possession"): denying that one will discuss a subject while actually discussing it; also known as "praeteritio" (Latin "passing by"). See Chaucer, *Nun's Priest's Tale*, lines 414–32 (see vol. 1, p. 308).

Oxymoron (Greek "sharp blunt"): conjunction of normally incompatible terms; Milton, *Paradise Lost* 1.63: "darkness visible" (see vol. 1, p. 1833). Ramanujan, "Foundlings in the Yukon," line 41: "these infants compact with age" (see vol. 2, p. 2582).

Paradox (Greek "contrary to received opinion"): an apparent contradiction that requires thought to reveal an inner consistency. Chaucer, "Troilus's Song," line 12: "O sweete harm so quainte" (see vol. 1, p. 316).

Periphrasis (Greek "declaring around"): circumlocution; the use of many words to express what could be expressed in few or one; Sidney, *Astrophil and Stella* 39.1–4 (vol. 1, p. 982).

Personification, or prosopopoeia (Greek "person making"): the attribution of human qualities to nonhuman forces or objects; Shakespeare, *King Lear* 3.2.1: "Blow winds and crack your cheeks, rage! Blow!" (see vol. 1, p. 1182).

Pun: a sometimes irresolvable doubleness of meaning in a single word or expression; Shakespeare, Sonnet 135, line 1: "Whoever hath her wish, thou hast thy *Will*" (see vol. 1, p. 1075).

Sarcasm (Greek "flesh tearing"): a wounding remark, often expressed ironically; Boswell, *Life of Johnson*: Johnson [asked if any man of the modern age could have written the **epic** poem *Fingal*] replied, "Yes, Sir, many men, many women, and many children" (see vol. 1, p. 2792).

Simile (Latin "like"): comparison, usually using the word "like" or "as," of one thing with another so as to produce sometimes surprising analogies. Donne, "The Storm," lines 29–30: "Sooner than you read this line did the gale, / Like shot, not feared till felt, our sails assail." Frequently used, in extended form, in **epic** poetry; Milton, *Paradise Lost* 1.338–46 (see vol. 1, p. 1839).

Symbol (Greek "token"): something that stands for something else, and yet seems necessarily to evoke that other thing. Blake, "The Sick Rose," lines 1–8: "O Rose, thou art sick. / The invisible worm / That flies in the night / In the howling storm / Has found out thy bed / Of crimson joy, And his dark secret love / Does thy life destroy" (see vol. 2, p. 91). In Neoplatonic, and therefore Romantic, theory, to be distinguished from **allegory** thus: whereas allegory involves connections between vehicle and tenor agreed by convention or made explicit, the meanings of a symbol are supposedly inherent to it. For discussion, see Coleridge, "On Symbol and Allegory" (vol. 2, p. 488).

Synecdoche (Greek "to take with something else"): using a part to express the whole, or vice versa; "Donne, "A Hymn to Christ," lines 1–2: "In what torn ship soever I embark / That ship shall be my emblem of thy ark" (see vol. 1, p. 1300).

Type (Greek "impression, figure"): In Christian allegorical interpretation of the Old Testament, pre-Christian figures were regarded as "types," or fore-shadowings, of Christ or the Christian dispensation. *Typology* has been the source of much visual and literary art in which the parallelisms between old and new are extended to nonbiblical figures; thus the virtuous plowman in *Piers Plowman* becomes a type of Christ.

Zeugma (Greek "a yoking"): a syntactic pun whereby the one word is revealed to have more than one sense in the sentence as a whole; Pope, *Rape of the Lock* 3.7–8, in which the word "take" is used in two senses: "Here thou, great Anna! whom three realms obey, / Dost sometimes counsel take—and sometimes tea" (see vol. 1, p. 2521).

(iv) Meter, Rhythm

Verse (from Latin "versus," turned) is distinguished from prose (from Latin "prorsus," straightforward) as a more compressed form of expression, shaped by metrical norms. **Meter** *(Greek "measure") refers to the regularly recurring sound pattern of verse lines. The means of producing sound patterns across lines differ in different poetic traditions. Verse may be* **quantitative,** *or determined by the quantities of syllables (set patterns of long and short syllables), as in Latin and Greek poetry. It may be* **syllabic,** *determined by fixed numbers of syllables in the line, as in the verse of Romance languages (e.g., French and Italian). It may be* **accentual,** *determined by the number of accents, or stresses in the line, with variable numbers of syllables, as in Old English and some varieties of Middle English alliterative verse. Or it may be* **accentual-syllabic,** *determined by the numbers of accents, but possessing a regular pattern of stressed and unstressed syllables, so as to produce regular numbers of syllables per line. Since Chaucer, English verse has worked primarily within the many possibilities of accentual-syllabic meter. The unit of meter is the* **foot.** *In English verse the number of feet per line corresponds to the number of accents in a line. For the types and examples of different meters, see* **monometer, dimeter, trimeter, tetrameter, pentameter,** *and* **hexameter.** *In the definitions below, "u" designates one unstressed syllable, and "/" one stressed syllable.*

*Rhythm is not absolutely distinguishable from meter. One way of making a clear distinction between these terms is to say that rhythm (from the Greek "to flow") denotes the patterns of sound within the feet of verse lines and the combination of those feet. Very often a particular meter will raise expectations that a given rhythm will be used regularly through a whole line or a whole poem. Thus in English verse the pentameter regularly uses an iambic rhythm. Rhythm, however, is much more fluid than meter, and many lines within the same poem using a single meter will frequently exploit different rhythmic possibilities. For examples of different rhythms, see **iamb, trochee, anapest, spondee,** and **dactyl.***

Accent (synonym "stress"): the special force devoted to the voicing of one syllable in a word over others. In the noun "accent," for example, the stress is on the first syllable.

Alexandrine: in French verse a line of twelve syllables, and, by analogy, in English verse a line of six stresses. See **hexameter.**

Anapest: a three-syllable foot following the rhythmic pattern, in English verse, of two unstressed (uu) syllables followed by one stressed (/). Thus, for example, "Illinois."

Caesura (Latin "cut"): a pause or breathing space within a line of verse, generally occurring between syntactic units; Louise Bennett, "Colonization in Reverse," lines 5–8: "By de hundred, by de tousan, / From country an from town, / By de ship-load, by de plane-load, / Jamaica is Englan boun" (see vol. 2, p. 2472).

Dactyl (Greek "finger," because of the finger's three joints): a three-syllable foot following the rhythmic pattern, in English verse, of one stressed (/) followed by two unstressed (uu) syllables. Thus, for example, "Oregon."

Dimeter (Greek "two measure"): a two-stress line, rarely used as the meter of whole poems, though used with great frequency in single poems by Skelton, e.g., "The Tunning of Elinour Rumming" (see vol. 1, p. 516). Otherwise used for single lines, as in Herbert, "Discipline," line 3: "O my God" (see vol. 1, p. 1623).

End-stopping: the placement of a complete syntactic unit within a complete metrical pattern; Auden, "In Memory of W. B. Yeats," line 42: "Earth, receive an honoured guest" (see vol. 2, p. 2430). Compare **enjambment.**

Enjambment (French "striding," encroaching): The opposite of **end-stopping,** enjambment occurs when the syntactic unit does not end with the metrical pattern, i.e., when the sense of the line overflows its meter and, therefore, the line break; Auden, "In Memory of W. B. Yeats," lines 44–45: "Let the Irish vessel lie / Emptied of its poetry" (see vol. 2, p. 2430).

Hexameter (Greek "six measure"): The hexameter line (a six-stress line) is the meter of **classical** Latin **epic;** while not imitated in that form for epic verse in English, some instances of the hexameter exist. See, for example, the last line of a Spenserian stanza, *Faerie Queene* 1.1.2: "O help thou my weake wit, and sharpen my dull tong" (vol. 1, p. 720), or Yeats, "The Lake Isle of Innisfree," line 1: "I will arise and go now, and go to Innisfree" (vol. 2, p. 2025).

Hypermetrical (adj.; Greek "over measured"): describes a breaking of the expected metrical pattern by at least one extra syllable.

Iamb: the basic foot of English verse; two syllables following the rhythmic pattern of unstressed (u) followed by stressed (/) and producing a rising effect. Thus, for example, "Vermont."

Monometer (Greek "one measure"): an entire line with just one stress; *Sir*

Gawain and the Green Knight, line 15, "wyth (u) wynne (/)" (see vol. 1, p. 162).

Pentameter (Greek "five measure"): in English verse, a five-stress line. Between the late fourteenth and the nineteenth centuries, this meter, frequently employing an iambic rhythm, was the basic line of English verse. Chaucer, Shakespeare, Milton, and Wordsworth each, for example, deployed this very flexible line as their primary resource; Milton, *Paradise Lost* 1.128: "O Prince, O Chief of many thronèd Powers" (see vol. 1, p. 1835).

Spondee: a two-syllable foot following the rhythmic pattern, in English verse, of two stressed (//) syllables. Thus, for example, "Utah."

Syllable: the smallest unit of sound in a pronounced word. The syllable that receives the greatest stress is called the *tonic* syllable.

Tetrameter (Greek "four measure"): a line with four stresses. Coleridge, *Christabel*, line 31: "She stole along, she nothing spoke" (see vol. 2, p. 450).

Trimeter (Greek "three measure"): a line with three stresses. Herbert, "Discipline," line 1: "Throw away thy rod" (see vol. 1, p. 1623).

Trochee: a two-syllable foot following the pattern, in English verse, of stressed (/) followed by unstressed (u) syllable, producing a falling effect. Thus, for example, "Texas."

(vi) Verse Forms

The terms related to meter and rhythm describe the shape of individual lines. Lines of verse are combined to produce larger groupings, called verse forms. These larger groupings are in the first instance stanzas (Italian "rooms"): groupings of two or more lines, though "stanza" is usually reserved for groupings of at least four lines. Stanzas are often joined by rhyme, often in sequence, where each group shares the same metrical pattern and, when rhymed, rhyme scheme. Stanzas can themselves be arranged into larger groupings. Poets often invent new verse forms, or they may work within established forms, a list of which follows.

Ballad stanza: usually a **quatrain** in alternating **iambic tetrameter** and **iambic trimeter** lines, rhyming abcb. See "Sir Patrick Spens" (vol. 1, p. 2902); Louise Bennett's poems (vol. 2, pp. 2469–74); Eliot, "Sweeney among the Nightingales" (vol. 2, p. 2293); Larkin, "This Be The Verse" (vol. 2, p. 2572).

Ballade: a form consisting usually of three stanzas followed by a four-line envoi (French, "send off"). The last line of the first stanza establishes a **refrain**, which is repeated, or subtly varied, as the last line of each stanza. The form was derived from French medieval poetry; English poets, from the fourteenth to the sixteenth centuries especially, used it with varying stanza forms. Chaucer, "Complaint to His Purse" (see vol. 1, p. 318).

Blank verse: unrhymed **iambic pentameter** lines. Blank verse has no stanzas, but is broken up into uneven units (verse paragraphs) determined by sense rather than form. First devised in English by Henry Howard, Earl of Surrey, in his translation of two books of Virgil's *Aeneid* (see vol. 1, p. 614), this very flexible verse type became the standard form for dramatic poetry in the seventeenth century, as in most of Shakespeare's plays. Milton and Wordsworth, among many others, also used it to create an English equivalent to **classical epic**.

Couplet: in English verse two consecutive, rhyming lines usually containing the same number of stresses. Chaucer first introduced the **iambic pentameter** couplet into English (*Canterbury Tales*); the form was later used in many types of writing, including drama; imitations and translations of **classical epic** (thus *heroic couplet*); essays; and **satire** (see Dryden and Pope). The *distich* (Greek "two lines") is a couplet usually making complete sense; Aemilia Lanyer, *Salve Deus Rex Judaeorum*, lines 5–6: "Read it fair queen, though it defective be, / Your excellence can grace both it and me" (see vol. 1, p. 1315).

Ottava rima: an eight-line stanza form, rhyming abababcc, using **iambic pentameter;** Yeats, "Sailing to Byzantium" (see vol. 2, p. 2040). Derived from the Italian poet Boccaccio, an eight-line stanza was used by fifteenth-century English poets for inset passages (e.g., Christ's speech from the Cross in Lydgate's *Testament*, lines 754–897). The form in this rhyme scheme was used in English poetry for long narrative by, for example, Byron (*Don Juan;* see vol. 2, p. 669).

Quatrain: a stanza of four lines, usually rhyming abcb, abab, or abba. Of many possible examples, see Crashaw, "On the Wounds of Our Crucified Lord" (see vol. 1, p. 1644).

Refrain: usually a single line repeated as the last line of consecutive stanzas, sometimes with subtly different wording and ideally with subtly different meaning as the poem progresses. See, for example, Wyatt, "Blame not my lute" (vol. 1, p. 602).

Rhyme royal: a stanza form of seven **iambic pentameter** lines, rhyming ababbcc; first introduced by Chaucer and called "royal" because the form was used by James I of Scotland for his *Kingis Quair* in the early fifteenth century. Chaucer, "Troilus's Song" (see vol. 1, p. 316).

Sonnet: a form combining a variable number of units of rhymed lines to produce a fourteen-line poem, usually in rhyming **iambic pentameter** lines. In English there are two principal varieties: the Petrarchan sonnet, formed by an octave (an eight-line stanza, often broken into two **quatrains** having the same rhyme scheme, typically abba abba) and a sestet (a six-line stanza, typically cdecde or cdcdcd); and the Shakespearean sonnet, formed by three quatrains (abab cdcd efef) and a **couplet** (gg). The declaration of a sonnet can take a sharp turn, or "volta," often at the decisive formal shift from octave to sestet in the Petrarchan sonnet, or in the final couplet of a Shakespearean sonnet, introducing a trenchant counterstatement. Derived from Italian poetry, and especially from the poetry of Petrarch, the sonnet was first introduced to English poetry by Wyatt, and initially used principally for the expression of unrequited erotic love, though later poets used the form for many other purposes. See Wyatt, "Whoso list to hunt" (vol. 1, p. 595); Sidney, *Astrophil and Stella* (vol. 1, p. 975); Shakespeare, *Sonnets* (vol. 1, p. 1060); Wordsworth, "London, 1802" (vol. 2, p. 319); McKay, "If We Must Die" (vol. 2, p. 2464); Heaney, "Clearances" (vol. 2, p. 2833).

Spenserian stanza: the stanza developed by Spenser for *The Faerie Queene*; nine **iambic** lines, the first eight of which are **pentameters,** followed by one **hexameter,** rhyming ababbcbcc. See also, for example, Shelley, *Adonais* (vol. 2, p. 822), and Keats, *The Eve of St. Agnes* (vol. 2, p. 888).

Tercet: a stanza or group of three lines, used in larger forms such as **terza rima,** the **Petrarchan sonnet,** and the **villanelle.**

Terza rima: a sequence of rhymed **tercets** linked by rhyme thus: aba bcb cdc, etc. First used extensively by Dante in *The Divine Comedy*, the form was adapted in English **iambic pentameters** by Wyatt and revived in the nineteenth century. See Wyatt, "Mine own John Poins" (vol. 1, p. 604); Shelley, "Ode to the West Wind" (vol. 2, p. 772); and Morris, "The Death of Guinevere" (vol. 2, p. 1483). For modern adaptations see Eliot, lines 78–149 (though unrhymed) of "Little Gidding" (vol. 2, pp. 2315–16); Heaney, "Station Island" (vol. 2, p. 2831); Walcott, *Omeros* (vol. 2, p. 2591).

Triplet: a **tercet** rhyming on the same sound. Pope inserts triplets among heroic **couplets** to emphasize a particular thought; see *Essay on Criticism*, 315–17 (vol. 1, p. 2504).

Villanelle: a fixed form of usually five **tercets** and a **quatrain** employing only two rhyme sounds altogether, rhyming aba for the tercets and abaa for the quatrain, with a complex pattern of two **refrains.** Derived from a French fixed form. Thomas, "Do Not Go Gentle into That Good Night" (see vol. 2, p. 2450).

(v) Syntax

Syntax (Greek "ordering with") designates the rules by which sentences are constructed in a given language. Discussion of meter is impossible without some reference to syntax, since the overall effect of a poem is, in part, always the product of a subtle balance of meter and sentence construction. Syntax is also essential to the understanding of prose style, since prose writers, deprived of the full shaping possibilities of meter, rely all the more heavily on syntactic resources. A working command of syntactical practice requires an understanding of the parts of speech (nouns, verbs, adjectives, adverbs, conjunctions, pronouns, prepositions, and interjections), since writers exploit syntactic possibilities by using particular combinations and concentrations of the parts of speech. The list below offers some useful terms for the description of syntactic features of a work.

Apposition: the repetition of elements serving an identical grammatical function in one sentence. The effect of this repetition is to arrest the flow of the sentence, but in doing so to add extra semantic nuance to repeated elements. This is an especially important feature of Old English poetic style. See, for example, Caedmon's Hymn (vol. 1, p. 24), where the phrases "heaven kingdom's guardian," "the Measurer's might," "his mind-plans," and "the work of the Glory-Father" each serve an identical syntactic function as the direct objects of "praise."

Hyperbaton (Greek "overstepping"): the rearrangement, or inversion, of the expected word order in a sentence or clause. Gray, "Elegy Written in a Country Churchyard," line 38: "If Memory o'er their tomb no trophies raise" (vol. 1, p. 2867). Poets can suspend the expected syntax over many lines, as in the first sentences of the *Canterbury Tales* (vol. 1, p. 218) and of *Paradise Lost* (vol. 1, p. 1832).

Hypotaxis, or subordination (respectively Greek and Latin "ordering under"): the subordination, by the use of subordinate clauses, of different elements of a sentence to a single main verb. Milton, *Paradise Lost* 9.513–15: "As when a ship by skillful steersman wrought / Nigh river's mouth or foreland, where the wind / Veers oft, as oft so steers, and shifts her sail; So varied he" (vol. 1, p. 1984). The contrary principle to **parataxis.**

Parataxis, or coordination (respectively Greek and Latin "ordering beside"):

the coordination, by the use of coordinating conjunctions, of different main clauses in a single sentence. Malory, "Morte Darthur": "So Sir Lancelot departed and took his sword under his arm, and so he walked in his mantel, that noble knight, and put himself in great jeopardy" (see vol. 1, p. 442). The opposite principle to **hypotaxis.**

(vii) Point of View

*All of the many kinds of writing (see "B. Genre and Mode," below) involve a point of view from which a text is, or seems to be, generated. The presence of such a point of view may be powerful and explicit, as in many novels, or deliberately invisible, as in much drama. In some genres, such as the **novel,** the narrator does not necessarily tell the story from a position we can predict; that is, the needs of a particular story, not the **conventions** of the genre, determine the narrator's position. In other genres, the narrator's position is fixed by convention; in certain kinds of love poetry, for example, the narrating voice is always that of a suffering lover. Not only does the point of view significantly inform the style of a work, but it also informs the structure of that work. Most of the terms below are especially relevant to narrative in either verse or prose, but many also apply to other modes of writing.*

Deixis (Greek "pointing"): Every work has, implicitly or explicitly, a "here" and a "now" from which it is narrated. Words that refer to or imply this point from which the voice of the work is projected (such as "here," "there," "this," "that," "now," "then") are examples of deixis, or "deictics." This technique is especially important in drama, where it is used to create a sense of the events happening as the spectator witnesses them.

First-person narration: a narrative in which the voice narrating refers to itself with forms of the first-person pronoun ("I," "me," "my," etc., or possibly "we," "us," "our"), and in which the narrative is determined by the limitations of that voice. Thus Mary Wollstonecraft Shelley, *Frankenstein*.

Frame narrative: Some narratives, particularly collections of narratives, involve a frame narrative that explains the genesis of, and/or gives a perspective on, the main narrative or narratives to follow. Thus Chaucer, *Canterbury Tales*; Mary Wollstonecraft Shelley, *Frankenstein*; or Conrad, *Heart of Darkness*.

Free indirect style: a narratorial voice that manages, without explicit reference, to imply, and often implicitly to comment on, the voice of a **character** in the narrative itself. Virginia Woolf, "A Sketch of the Past," where the voice, although strictly that of the adult narrator, manages to convey the child's manner of perception: "—I begin: the first memory. This was of red and purple flowers on a black background—my mother's dress" (see vol. 2, p. 2155).

Omniscient narrator (Latin "all-knowing narrator"): a narrator who, in the fiction of the narrative, has complete access to both the deeds and the thoughts of all **characters** in the narrative. Thus Thomas Hardy, "On the Western Circuit" (see vol. 2, p. 1852).

Order: A story may be told in different orders. A narrator might use the sequence of events as they happened, and thereby follow what **classical** rhetoricians called the *natural order*; alternatively, the narrator might reorder the sequence of events, beginning the narration either in the middle or at the end of the sequence of events, thereby following an *artificial order*. If a narrator begins in the middle of events, he or she is said to begin *in medias res* (Latin "in the middle of the matter"). For a brief discussion of these concepts, see Spenser, *Faerie Queene*, "A Letter of the Authors" (vol. 1, p. 716). Modern narratology makes a related distinction, between *histoire* (French "story") for the natural order that readers mentally reconstruct, and *discours* (French, here "narration") for the narrative as presented.

Plot: the sequence of events in a story as narrated.

Stream of consciousness: usually a **first-person** narrative that seems to give the reader access to the narrator's mind as it perceives or reflects on events, prior to organizing those perceptions into a coherent narrative. Thus (though generated from a **third-person** narrative) Joyce, *Ulysses*, "Lestrygonians" (see vol. 2, p. 2213).

Third-person narration: a narration in which the narrator recounts a narrative of **characters** referred to explicitly or implicitly by third-person pronouns ("he," she," etc.), without the limitation of a **first-person narration**. Thus Johnson, *The History of Rasselas*.

Unities: According to a theory supposedly derived from Aristotle's *Poetics*, the events represented in a play should have unity of time, place, and action: that the play take up no more time than the time of the play, or at most a day; that the space of action should be within a single city; and that there should be no subplot. See Johnson, *The Preface to Shakespeare* (vol. 1, p. 2756).

B. Genre and Mode

*The style, structure, and, often, length of a work, when coupled with a certain subject matter, raise expectations that a literary work conforms to a certain **genre** (French "kind"). Good writers might upset these expectations, but they remain aware of the expectations and thwart them purposefully. Works in different genres may nevertheless participate in the same **mode**, a broader category designating the fundamental perspectives governing various genres of writing. For mode, see **tragic, comic, satiric**, and **didactic modes**. All the other terms in this list refer to more or less specific literary genres. Genres are fluid, sometimes very fluid (e.g., the **novel**); the word "usually" should be added to almost every statement!*

Animal fable: a short narrative of speaking animals, followed by moralizing comment, written in a low style and gathered into a collection. Robert Henryson, "The Cock and the Fox" (see vol. 1, p. 457).

Aubade (originally from Spanish "alba," dawn): a lover's dawn song or lyric bewailing the arrival of the day and the necessary separation of the lovers; Donne, "The Sun Rising" (see vol. 1, p. 1266). Larkin recasts the genre in "Aubade" (see vol. 2, p. 2573).

Autobiography (Greek "self-life writing"): a narrative of a life written by the subject; Wordsworth, *The Prelude* (see vol. 2, p. 322). There are subgenres, such as the spiritual autobiography, narrating the author's path to conversion and subsequent spiritual trials, as in Bunyan's *Grace Abounding*.

Beast epic: a continuous, unmoralized narrative, in prose or verse, relating the victories of the wholly unscrupulous but brilliant strategist Reynard the

Fox over all adversaries. Chaucer arouses, only to deflate, expectations of the genre in *The Nun's Priest's Tale* (see vol. 1, p. 298).

Biography (Greek "life-writing"): a life as the subject of an extended narrative. Thus Izaak Walton, *The Life of Dr. Donne* (see vol. 1, p. 1309).

Comedy: a term primarily applied to drama, and derived from ancient drama, in opposition to **tragedy.** Comedy deals with humorously confusing, sometimes ridiculous situations in which the ending is, nevertheless, happy. Shakespeare, *Twelfth Night* (see vol. 1, p. 1079).

Comic mode: many genres (e.g., **romance, fabliau, comedy**) involve a happy ending in which justice is done, the ravages of time are arrested, and that which is lost is found. Such genres participate in a comic mode.

Dialogue (Greek "conversation"): Dialogue is a feature of many genres, especially in both the **novel** and drama. As a genre itself, dialogue is used in philosophical traditions especially (most famously in Plato's *Dialogues*), as the representation of a conversation in which a philosophical question is pursued among various speakers.

Didactic mode (Greek "teaching mode"): genres in a didactic mode are designed to instruct or teach, sometimes explicitly (e.g., sermons, philosophical **discourses, georgic**), and sometimes through the medium of fiction (e.g., **animal fable, parable**).

Discourse (Latin "running to and fro"): broadly, any nonfictional speech or writing; as a more specific genre, a philosophical meditation on a set theme. Thus Newman, *The Idea of a University* (see vol. 2, p. 1035).

Dramatic monologue (Greek "single speaking"): a poem in which the voice of a historical or fictional **character** speaks, unmediated by any narrator, to an implied though silent audience. See Tennyson, "Ulysses" (vol. 2, p. 1123); Browning, "The Bishop Orders His Tomb" (vol. 2, p. 1259); Eliot, "The Love Song of J. Alfred Prufrock" (vol. 2, p. 2289); Carol Ann Duffy, "Medusa" and "Mrs Lazarus" (vol. 2, pp. 2875–76).

Elegy: In **classical** literature elegy was a form written in elegiac **couplets** (a **hexameter** followed by a **pentameter**) devoted to many possible topics. In Ovidian elegy a lover meditates on the trials of erotic desire (e.g., Ovid's *Amores*). The **sonnet** sequences of both Sidney and Shakespeare exploit this genre, and, while it was still practiced in classical tradition by Donne ("On His Mistress" [see vol. 1, p. 1281]), by the later seventeenth century the term came to denote the poetry of loss, especially through the death of a loved person. See Tennyson, *In Memoriam* (vol. 2, p. 1138); Yeats, "In Memory of Major Robert Gregory" (vol. 2, p. 2034); Auden, "In Memory of W. B. Yeats" (see vol. 2, p. 2429); Heaney, "Clearances" (vol. 2, p. 2833).

Epic (synonym, *heroic poetry*): an extended narrative poem celebrating martial heroes, invoking divine inspiration, beginning in medias res (see **order**), written in a high style (including the deployment of **epic similes**; on high style, see **register**), and divided into long narrative sequences. Homer's *Iliad* and Virgil's *Aeneid* were the prime models for English writers of epic verse. Thus Milton, *Paradise Lost* (see vol. 1, p. 1829); Wordsworth, *The Prelude* (see vol. 2, p. 322); and Walcott, *Omeros* (see vol. 2, p. 2591). With its precise repertoire of stylistic resources, epic lent itself easily to **parodic** and **burlesque** forms, known as **mock epic;** thus Pope, *The Rape of the Lock* (see vol. 1, p. 2513).

Epigram: a short, pithy poem wittily expressed, often with wounding intent. See Jonson, *Epigrams* (see vol. 1, p. 1427).

Epigraph (Greek "inscription"): any formal statement inscribed on stone; also the brief formulation on a book's title page, or a quotation at the beginning of a poem, introducing the work's themes in the most compressed form possible.

Epistle (Latin "letter"): the letter can be shaped as a literary form, involving an intimate address often between equals. The *Epistles* of Horace provided a model for English writers from the sixteenth century. Thus Wyatt, "Mine own John Poins" (see vol. 1, p. 604), or Pope, "Epistle to a Lady" (vol. 1, p. 2598). Letters can be shaped to form the matter of an extended fiction, as the eighteenth-century epistolary **novel** (e.g., Samuel Richardson's *Pamela*).

Epitaph: a pithy formulation to be inscribed on a funeral monument. Thus Ralegh, "The Author's Epitaph, Made by Himself" (see vol. 1, p. 923).

Epithalamion (Greek "concerning the bridal chamber"): a wedding poem, celebrating the marriage and wishing the couple good fortune. Thus Spenser, *Epithalamion* (see vol. 1, p. 907).

Essay (French "trial, attempt"): an informal philosophical meditation, usually in prose and sometimes in verse. The journalistic periodical essay was developed in the early eighteenth century. Thus Addison and Steele, periodical essays (see vol. 1, p. 2470); Pope, *An Essay on Criticism* (see vol. 1, p. 2496).

Fabliau (French "little story," plural *fabliaux*): a short, funny, often bawdy narrative in low style (see **register**) imitated and developed from French models most subtly by Chaucer; see *The Miller's Prologue and Tale* (vol. 1, p. 239).

Farce: a play designed to provoke laughter through the often humiliating antics of stock **characters**. Congreve's *The Way of the World* (see vol. 1, p. 2228) draws on this tradition.

Georgic (Greek "farming"): Virgil's *Georgics* treat agricultural and occasionally scientific subjects, giving instructions on the proper management of farms. Unlike **pastoral**, which treats the countryside as a place of recreational idleness among shepherds, the georgic treats it as a place of productive labor. For an English poem that critiques both genres, see Crabbe, "The Village" (vol. 1, p. 2887).

Heroic poetry: see **epic**.

Homily (Greek "discourse"): a sermon, to be preached in church; *Book of Homilies* (see vol. 1, p. 635). Writers of literary fiction sometimes exploit the homily, or sermon, as in Chaucer, *The Pardoner's Tale* (see vol. 1, p. 284).

Journal (French "daily"): a diary, or daily record of ephemeral experience, whose perspectives are concentrated on, and limited by, the experiences of single days. Thus Pepys, *Diary* (see vol. 1, p. 2134).

Lai: a short narrative, often characterized by images of great intensity; a French term, and a form practiced by Marie de France (see vol. 1, p. 141).

Legend (Latin "requiring to be read"): a narrative of a celebrated, possibly historical, but mortal **protagonist**. To be distinguished from **myth**. Thus the "Arthurian legend" but the "myth of Proserpine."

Lullaby: a bedtime, sleep-inducing song for children, in simple and regular meter. Adapted by Auden, "Lullaby" (see vol. 2, p. 2423).

Lyric (from Greek "lyre"): Initially meaning a song, "lyric" refers to a short poetic form, without restriction of meter, in which the expression of personal emotion, often by a voice in the first person, is given primacy over narrative sequence. Thus "The Wife's Lament" (see vol. 1, p. 113); Yeats, "The Wild Swans at Coole" (see vol. 2, p. 2033).

Masque: costly entertainments of the Stuart court, involving dance, song, speech, and elaborate stage effects, in which courtiers themselves participated. See Jonson, *The Masque of Blackness* (see vol. 1, p. 1327).

Myth: the narrative of **protagonists** with, or subject to, superhuman powers. A myth expresses some profound foundational truth, often by accounting for the origin of natural phenomena. To be distinguished from **legend.** Thus the "Arthurian legend" but the "myth of Proserpine."

Novel: an extremely flexible genre in both form and subject matter. Usually in prose, giving high priority to narration of events, with a certain expectation of length, novels are preponderantly rooted in a specific, and often complex, social world; sensitive to the realities of material life; and often focused on one **character** or a small circle of central characters. By contrast with chivalric **romance** (the main European narrative genre prior to the novel), novels tend to eschew the marvelous in favor of a recognizable social world and credible action. The novel's openness allows it to participate in all modes, and to be co-opted for a huge variety of subgenres. In English literature the novel dates from the late seventeenth century and has been astonishingly successful in appealing to a huge readership, particularly in the nineteenth and twentieth centuries. The English and Irish tradition of the novel includes, for example, Fielding, Austen, the Brontë sisters, Dickens, George Eliot, Conrad, Woolf, Lawrence, Joyce, to name but a few very great exponents of the genre.

Novella: a short **novel,** often characterized by imagistic intensity. Conrad, *Heart of Darkness* (see vol. 2, p. 1890).

Ode (Greek "song"): a **lyric** poem in elevated, or high style (see **register**), often addressed to a natural force, a person, or an abstract quality. The Pindaric ode in English is made up of **stanzas** of unequal length, while the Horatian ode has stanzas of equal length. For examples of both types, see, respectively, Wordsworth, "Ode: Intimations of Immortality" (vol. 2, p. 306); and Marvell, "An Horatian Ode" (vol. 1, p. 1712), or Keats, "Ode on Melancholy" (vol. 2, p. 906). For a fuller discussion, see the headnote to Jonson's "Ode on Cary and Morison" (vol. 1, p. 1439).

Panegyric: Demonstrative, or epideictic (Greek "showing"), rhetoric was a branch of **classical** rhetoric. Its own two main branches were the rhetoric of praise on the one hand and of vituperation on the other. Panegyric, or eulogy (Greek "sweet speaking"), or encomium (plural *encomia*), is the term used to describe the speeches or writings of praise.

Parable: a simple story designed to provoke, and often accompanied by, **allegorical** interpretation, most famously by Christ as reported in the Gospels.

Pastoral (from Latin "pastor," shepherd): Pastoral is set among shepherds, making often refined **allusion** to other apparently unconnected subjects (sometimes politics) from the potentially idyllic world of highly literary if illiterate shepherds. Pastoral is distinguished from **georgic** by representing recreational rural idleness, whereas the georgic offers instruction on how to manage rural labor. English writers had classical models in the *Idylls* of Theocritus in Greek and Virgil's *Eclogues* in Latin. Pastoral is also called bucolic (from the Greek word for "herdsman"). Thus Spenser, *Shepheardes Calender* (see vol. 1, p. 708).

Romance: From the twelfth to the sixteenth century, the main form of European narrative, in either verse or prose, was that of chivalric romance. Romance, like the later **novel,** is a very fluid genre, but romances are often characterized by (i) a tripartite structure of social integration, followed by disintegration, involving moral tests and often marvelous events, itself the prelude to reintegration in a happy ending, frequently of marriage; (ii) **high-style** diction; (iii) aristocratic social mileux. Thus *Sir Gawain and the Green Knight* (see vol. 1, p. 160); Spenser's (unfinished) *Faerie Queene* (vol. 1, p. 713). The immensely popular, fertile genre was absorbed, in both domesticated and undomesticated form, by the novel. For an adaptation of romance, see Chaucer, *Wife of Bath's Tale* (vol. 1, p. 256).

Satire: In Roman literature (e.g., Juvenal), the communication, in the form of a letter between equals, complaining of the ills of contemporary society. The genre in this form is characterized by a first-person narrator exasperated by social ills; the letter form; a high frequency of contemporary reference; and the use of invective in **low-style** language. Pope practices the genre thus in the *Epistle to Dr. Arbuthnot* (see vol. 1, p. 2548). Wyatt's "Mine own John Poins" (see vol. 1, p. 604) draws ultimately on a gentler, Horatian model of the genre.

Satiric mode: Works in a very large variety of genres are devoted to the more or less savage attack on social ills. Thus Swift's travel narrative *Gulliver's Travels* (see vol. 1, p. 2323), his **essay** "A Modest Proposal" (vol. 1, p. 2462), Pope's mock-**epic** *The Dunciad* (vol. 1, p. 2559), and Gay's *Beggar's Opera* (vol. 1, p. 2613), to look no further than the eighteenth century, are all within a satiric mode.

Short story: generically similar to, though shorter and more concentrated than, the **novel;** often published as part of a collection. Thus Mansfield, "The Daughters of the Late Colonel" (see vol. 2, p. 2333).

Topographical poem (Greek "place writing"): a poem devoted to the meditative description of particular places. Thus Gray, "Ode on a Distant Prospect of Eton College" (see vol. 1, p. 2863).

Tragedy: a dramatic representation of the fall of kings or nobles, beginning in happiness and ending in catastrophe. Later transferred to other social mileux. The opposite of **comedy.** Shakespeare, *King Lear* (see vol. 1, p. 1139).

Tragic mode: Many genres (**epic** poetry, **legend**ary chronicles, **tragedy,** the **novel**) either do or can participate in a tragic mode, by representing the fall of noble **protagonists** and the irreparable ravages of human society and history.

Tragicomedy: a play in which potentially tragic events turn out to have a happy, or **comic,** ending. Thus Shakespeare, *Measure for Measure.*

C. Miscellaneous

Act: the major subdivision of a play, usually divided into **scenes.**

Aesthetics (from Greek, "to feel, apprehend by the senses"): the philosophy of artistic meaning as a distinct mode of apprehending untranslatable truth, defined as an alternative to rational enquiry, which is purely abstract. Developed in the late eighteenth century by the German philosopher Immanuel Kant especially.

Allusion: Literary allusion is a passing but illuminating reference within a literary text to another, well-known text (often biblical or **classical**). Topical allusions are also, of course, common in certain modes, especially **satire**.

Anagnorisis (Greek "recognition"): the moment of **protagonists'** recognition in a narrative, which is also often the moment of moral understanding.

Apostrophe (from Greek "turning away"): an address, often to an absent person, a force, or a quality. For example, a poet makes an apostrophe to a Muse when invoking her for inspiration.

Blazon: strictly, a heraldic shield; in rhetorical usage, a **topos** whereby the individual elements of a beloved's face and body are singled out for **hyperbolic** admiration. Spenser, *Epithalamion*, lines 167–84 (see vol. 1, p. 907). For an inversion of the **topos**, see Shakespeare, Sonnet 130 (vol. 1, p. 1074).

Burlesque (French and Italian "mocking"): a work that adopts the **conventions** of a genre with the aim less of comically mocking the genre than of satirically mocking the society so represented (see **satire**). Thus Pope's *Rape of the Lock* (see vol. 1, p. 2513) does not mock **classical epic** so much as contemporary mores.

Canon (Greek "rule"): the group of texts regarded as worthy of special respect or attention by a given institution. Also, the group of texts regarded as definitely having been written by a certain author.

Catastrophe (Greek "overturning"): the decisive turn in **tragedy** by which the plot is resolved and, usually, the **protagonist** dies.

Catharsis (Greek "cleansing"): According to Aristotle, the effect of **tragedy** on its audience, through their experience of pity and terror, was a kind of spiritual cleansing, or catharsis.

Character (Greek "stamp, impression"): a person, personified animal, or other figure represented in a literary work, especially in narrative and drama. The more a character seems to generate the action of a narrative, and the less he or she seems merely to serve a preordained narrative pattern, the "fuller," or more "rounded," a character is said to be. A "stock" character, common particularly in many comic genres, will perform a predictable function in different works of a given genre.

Classical, Classicism, Classic: Each term can be widely applied, but in English literary discourse, "classical" primarily describes the works of either Greek or Roman antiquity. "Classicism" denotes the practice of art forms inspired by classical antiquity, in particular the observance of rhetorical norms of **decorum** and balance, as opposed to following the dictates of untutored inspiration, as in Romanticism. "Classic" denotes an especially famous work within a given **canon**.

Climax (Greek "ladder"): a moment of great intensity and structural change, especially in drama. Also a figure of speech whereby a sequence of verbally linked clauses is made, in which each successive clause is of greater consequence than its predecessor. Bacon, *Of Studies*: "Studies serve for pastimes, for ornaments, and for abilities. Their chief use for pastimes is in privateness and retiring; for ornament, is in discourse; and for ability, is in judgement" (see vol. 1, p. 1561).

Convention: a repeatedly recurring feature (in either form or content) of works, occurring in combination with other recurring formal features, constitutes a convention of a particular genre.

Decorum (Latin "that which is fitting"): a rhetorical principle whereby each formal aspect of a work should be in keeping with its subject matter and/ or audience.

Denouement (French "unknotting"): the point at which a narrative can be resolved and so ended.

Dramatic irony: a feature of narrative and drama, whereby the audience knows that the outcome of an action will be the opposite of that intended by a **character.**

Ecphrasis (Greek "speaking out"): a **topos** whereby a work of visual art is represented in a literary work. Auden, "Musée des Beaux Arts" (see vol. 2, p. 2428).

Exegesis (Greek "leading out"): interpretation, traditionally of the biblical text, but, by transference, of any text.

Exemplum (Latin "example"): an example inserted into a usually nonfictional writing (e.g., sermon or **essay**) to give extra force to an abstract thesis. Thus Johnson's example of "Sober" in his essay "On Idleness" (see vol. 1, p. 2678).

Hermeneutics (from the Greek god Hermes, messenger between the gods and humankind): the science of interpretation, first formulated as such by the German philosophical theologian Friedrich Schleiermacher in the early nineteenth century.

Imitation: the practice whereby writers strive ideally to reproduce and yet renew the **conventions** of an older form, often derived from **classical** civilization. Such a practice will be praised in periods of classicism (e.g., the eighteenth century) and repudiated in periods dominated by a model of inspiration (e.g., Romanticism).

Parody: a work that uses the **conventions** of a particular genre with the aim of comically mocking a **topos,** a genre, or a particular exponent of a genre. Shakespeare parodies the topos of **blazon** in Sonnet 130 (see vol. 1, p. 1074).

Pathetic fallacy: the attribution of sentiment to natural phenomena, as if they were in sympathy with human feelings. Thus Milton, *Lycidas*, lines 146– 47: "With cowslips wan that hang the pensive head, / And every flower that sad embroidery wears" (see vol. 1, p. 1810). For critique of the practice, see Ruskin (who coined the term), "Of the Pathetic Fallacy" (vol. 2, p. 1322).

Peripeteia (Greek "turning about"): the sudden reversal of fortune (in both directions) in a dramatic work.

Persona (Latin "sound through"): originally the mask worn in the Roman theater to magnify an actor's voice; in literary discourse persona (plural *personae*) refers to the narrator or speaker of a text, by whose voice the author may mask him- or herself. Eliot, "The Love Song of J. Alfred Prufrock" (see vol. 2, p. 2289).

Protagonist (Greek "first actor"): the hero or heroine of a drama or narrative.

Rhetoric: the art of verbal persuasion. **Classical** rhetoricians distinguished three areas of rhetoric: the forensic, to be used in law courts; the deliberative, to be used in political or philosophical deliberations; and the demonstrative, or epideictic, to be used for the purposes of public praise or blame. Rhetorical manuals covered all the skills required of a speaker, from the management of style and structure to delivery. These manuals powerfully influenced the theory of poetics as a separate branch of verbal practice, particularly in the matter of style.

Scene: a subdivision of an **act,** itself a subdivision of a dramatic performance and/or text. The action of a scene usually occurs in one place.

Sensibility (from Latin, "capable of being perceived by the senses"): as a literary term, an eighteenth-century concept derived from moral philosophy that stressed the social importance of fellow feeling and particularly of sympathy in social relations. The concept generated a literature of "sensibility," such as the sentimental **novel** (the most famous of which was Goethe's *Sorrows of the Young Werther* [1774]), or sentimental poetry, such as Cowper's passage on the stricken deer in *The Task* (see vol. 1, p. 2893).

Soliloquy (Latin "single speaking"): a **topos** of drama, in which a **character,** alone or thinking to be alone on stage, speaks so as to give the audience access to his or her private thoughts. Thus Viola's soliloquy in Shakespeare, *Twelfth Night* 2.2.17–41 (vol. 1, p. 1095).

Sublime: As a concept generating a literary movement, the sublime refers to the realm of experience beyond the measurable, and so beyond the rational, produced especially by the terrors and grandeur of natural phenomena. Derived especially from the first-century Greek treatise *On the Sublime,* sometimes attributed to Longinus, the notion of the sublime was in the later eighteenth century a spur to Romanticism.

Taste (from Italian "touch"): Although medieval monastic traditions used eating and tasting as a metaphor for reading, the concept of taste as a personal ideal to be cultivated by, and applied to, the appreciation and judgment of works of art in general was developed in the eighteenth century.

Topos (Greek "place," plural *topoi*): a commonplace in the content of a given kind of literature. Originally, in **classical** rhetoric, the topoi were tried-and-tested stimuli to literary invention: lists of standard headings under which a subject might be investigated. In medieval narrative poems, for example, it was commonplace to begin with a description of spring. Writers did, of course, render the commonplace uncommon, as in Chaucer's spring scene at the opening of *The Canterbury Tales* (see vol. 1, p. 218).

Tradition (from Latin "passing on"): A literary tradition is whatever is passed on or revived from the past in a single literary culture, or drawn from others to enrich a writer's culture. "Tradition" is fluid in reference, ranging from small to large referents: thus it may refer to a relatively small aspect of texts (e.g., the tradition of **iambic pentameter**), or it may, at the other extreme, refer to the body of texts that constitute a **canon.**

Translation (Latin "carrying across"): the rendering of a text written in one language into another.

Vernacular (from Latin "verna," servant): the language of the people, as distinguished from learned and arcane languages. From the later Middle Ages especially, the "vernacular" languages and literatures of Europe distinguished themselves from the learned languages and literatures of Latin, Greek, and Hebrew.

Wit: Originally a synonym for "reason" in Old and Middle English, "wit" became a literary ideal in the Renaissance as brilliant play of the full range of mental resources. For eighteenth-century writers, the notion necessarily involved pleasing expression, as in Pope's definition of true wit as "Nature to advantage dressed, / What oft was thought, but ne'er so well expressed" (*Essay on Criticism,* lines 297–98; see vol. 1, p. 2503). See also Johnson, *Lives of the Poets,* "Cowley," on "metaphysical wit" (see vol. 1, p. 2766). Romantic theory of the imagination deprived wit of its full range of apprehension, whence the word came to be restricted to its modern sense, as the clever play of mind that produces laughter.

D. Publishing History, Censorship

By the time we read texts in published books, they have already been treated— that is, changed by authors, editors, and printers—in many ways. Although there are differences across history, in each period literary works are subject to pressures of many kinds, which apply before, while, and after an author writes. The pressures might be financial, as in the relations of author and patron; commercial, as in the marketing of books; and legal, as in, during some periods, the negotiation through official and unofficial censorship. In addition, texts in all periods undergo technological processes, as they move from the material forms in which an author produced them to the forms in which they are presented to readers. Some of the terms below designate important material forms in which books were produced, disseminated, and surveyed across the historical span of this anthology. Others designate the skills developed to understand these processes. The anthology's introductions to individual periods discuss the particular forms these phenomena took in different eras.

Bookseller: In England, and particularly in London, commercial bookmaking and -selling enterprises came into being in the early fourteenth century. These were loose organizations of artisans who usually lived in the same neighborhoods (around St. Paul's Cathedral in London). A bookseller or dealer would coordinate the production of hand-copied books for wealthy patrons (see **patronage**), who would order books to be custom-made. After the introduction of **printing** in the late fifteenth century, authors generally sold the rights to their work to booksellers, without any further **royalties.** Booksellers, who often had their own shops, belonged to the **Stationers' Company.** This system lasted into the eighteenth century. In 1710, however, authors were for the first time granted **copyright,** which tipped the commercial balance in their favor, against booksellers.

Censorship: The term applies to any mechanism for restricting what can be published. Historically, the reasons for imposing censorship are heresy, sedition, blasphemy, libel, or obscenity. External censorship is imposed by institutions having legislative sanctions at their disposal. Thus the pre-Reformation Church imposed the Constitutions of Archbishop Arundel of 1409, aimed at repressing the Lollard "heresy." After the Reformation, some key events in the history of censorship are as follows: 1547, when anti-Lollard legislation and legislation made by Henry VIII concerning treason by writing (1534) were abolished; the Licensing Order of 1643, which legislated that works be licensed, through the Stationers' Company, prior to publication; and 1695, when the last such Act stipulating prepublication licensing lapsed. Postpublication censorship continued in different periods for different reasons. Thus, for example, British publication of D. H. Lawrence's *Lady Chatterley's Lover* (1928) was obstructed (though unsuccessfully) in 1960, under the Obscene Publications Act of 1959. Censorship can also be international: although not published in Iran, Salman Rushdie's *Satanic Verses* (1988) was censored in that country, where the leader, Ayatollah Ruhollah Khomeini, proclaimed a fatwa (religious decree) promising the author's execution. Very often censorship is not imposed externally, however: authors or publishers can censor work in anticipation of what will incur the wrath of readers or the penalties of the law. Victorian and Edwardian publishers of **novels,** for example, urged authors to remove potentially offensive material, especially for serial publication in popular magazines.

Codex (Latin "book"): having the format of a book (usually applied to manuscript books), as distinguished originally from the scroll, which was the standard form of written document in ancient Rome.

Copyright: the legal protection afforded to authors for control of their work's publication, in an attempt to ensure due financial reward. Some key dates in the history of copyright in the United Kingdom are as follows: 1710, when a statute gave authors the exclusive right to publish their work for fourteen years, and fourteen years more if the author were still alive when the first term had expired; 1842, when the period of authorial control was extended to forty-two years; and 1911, when the term was extended yet further, to fifty years after the author's death. In 1995 the period of protection was harmonized with the laws in other European countries to be the life of the author plus seventy years. In the United States no works first published before 1923 are in copyright. Works published since 1978 are, as in the United Kingdom, protected for the life of the author plus seventy years.

Copy text: the particular text of a work used by a textual editor as the basis of an edition of that work.

Folio: Books come in different shapes, depending originally on the number of times a standard sheet of paper is folded. One fold produces a large volume, a *folio* book; two folds produce a *quarto,* four an *octavo,* and six a very small *duodecimo.* Generally speaking, the larger the book, the grander and more expensive. Shakespeare's plays were, for example, first printed in quartos, but were gathered into a folio edition in 1623.

Foul papers: versions of a work before an author has produced, if she or he has, a final copy (a "fair copy") with all corrections removed.

Manuscript (Latin, "written by hand"): Any text written physically by hand is a manuscript. Before the introduction of **printing** with moveable type in 1476, all texts in England were produced and reproduced by hand, in manuscript. This is an extremely labor-intensive task, using expensive materials (e.g., animal skins); the cost of books produced thereby was, accordingly, very high. Even after the introduction of printing, many texts continued to be produced in manuscript. This is obviously true of letters, for example, but until the eighteenth century, poetry written within aristocratic circles was often transmitted in manuscript copies.

Paleography (Greek "ancient writing"): the art of deciphering, describing, and dating forms of handwriting.

Patronage (Latin "protector"): Many technological, legal, and commercial supports were necessary before professional authorship became possible. Although some playwrights (e.g., Shakespeare) made a living by writing for the theater, other authors needed, principally, the large-scale reproductive capacities of **printing** and the security of **copyright** to make a living from writing. Before these conditions obtained, many authors had another main occupation, and most authors had to rely on patronage. In different periods, institutions or individuals offered material support, or patronage, to authors. Thus in Anglo-Saxon England, monasteries afforded the conditions of writing to monastic authors. Between the twelfth and the seventeenth centuries, the main source of patronage was the royal court. Authors offered patrons prestige and ideological support in return for financial support. Even as the conditions of professional authorship came into being at the beginning of the eighteenth century, older forms of direct patronage were not altogether displaced until the middle of the century.

Periodical: Whereas journalism, strictly, applies to daily writing (from French "jour," day), periodical writing appears at larger, but still frequent, intervals, characteristically in the form of the **essay.** Periodicals were developed especially in the eighteenth century.

Printing: Printing, or the mechanical reproduction of books using moveable type, was invented in Germany in the mid-fifteenth century by Johannes Gutenberg; it quickly spread throughout Europe. William Caxton brought printing into England from the Low Countries in 1476. Much greater powers of reproduction at much lower prices transformed every aspect of literary culture.

Publisher: the person or company responsible for the commissioning and publicizing of printed matter. In the early period of **printing,** publisher, printer, and bookseller were often the same person. This trend continued in the ascendancy of the **Stationers' Company,** between the middle of the sixteenth and the end of the seventeenth centuries. Toward the end of the seventeenth century, these three functions began to separate, leading to their modern distinctions.

Royalties: an agreed-upon proportion of the price of each copy of a work sold, paid by the publisher to the author, or an agreed-upon fee paid to the playwright for each performance of a play.

Scribe: in **manuscript** culture, the scribe is the copyist who reproduces a text by hand.

Stationers' Company: The Stationers' Company was an English guild incorporating various tradesmen, including printers, publishers, and booksellers, skilled in the production and selling of books. It was formed in 1403, received its royal charter in 1557, and served as a means both of producing and of regulating books. Authors would sell the manuscripts of their books to individual stationers, who incurred the risks and took the profits of producing and selling the books. The stationers entered their rights over given books in the Stationers' Register. They also regulated the book trade and held their monopoly by licensing books and by being empowered to seize unauthorized books and imprison resisters. This system of licensing broke down in the social unrest of the Civil War and Interregnum (1640–60), and it ended in 1695. Even after the end of licensing, the Stationers' Company continued to be an intrinsic part of the **copyright** process, since the 1710 copyright statute directed that copyright had to be registered at Stationers' Hall.

Subscription: An eighteenth-century system of bookselling somewhere between direct **patronage** and impersonal sales. A subscriber paid half the cost of a book before publication and half on delivery. The author received these payments directly. The subscriber's name appeared in the prefatory pages.

Textual criticism: works in all periods often exist in many subtly or not so subtly different forms. This is especially true with regard to manuscript textual reproduction, but it also applies to printed texts. Textual criticism is the art, developed from the fifteenth century in Italy but raised to new levels of sophistication from the eighteenth century, of deciphering different historical states of texts. This art involves the analysis of textual variants, often with the aim of distinguishing authorial from scribal forms.

Geographic Nomenclature

The **British Isles** refers to the prominent group of islands off the northwest coast of Europe, especially to the two largest, **Great Britain** and **Ireland**. At present these comprise two sovereign states: **the Republic of Ireland**, or **Éire**, and **the United Kingdom of Great Britain and Northern Ireland**—known for short as the **United Kingdom** or the **U.K.** Most of the smaller islands are part of the **U.K.** but a few, like the **Isle of Man** and the tiny **Channel Islands**, are largely independent. The **U.K.** is often loosely referred to as "Britain" or "Great Britain" and is sometimes called simply, if inaccurately, "England." For obvious reasons, the latter usage is rarely heard among the inhabitants of the other countries of the **U.K.**—**Scotland, Wales,** and **Northern Ireland** (sometimes called **Ulster**). England is by far the most populous part of the kingdom, as well as the seat of its capital, London.

From the first to the fifth century C.E. most of what is now **England** and **Wales** was a province of the Roman Empire called **Britain** (in Latin, **Britannia**). After the fall of Rome, much of the island was invaded and settled by peoples from northern Germany and Denmark speaking what we now call Old English. These peoples are collectively known as the Anglo-Saxons, and the word **England** is related to the first element of their name. By the time of the Norman Conquest (1066) most of the kingdoms founded by the Anglo-Saxons and subsequent Viking invaders had coalesced into the kingdom of **England,** which, in the latter Middle Ages, conquered and largely absorbed the neighboring Celtic kingdom of **Wales**. In 1603 James VI of **Scotland** inherited the island's other throne as James I of **England,** and for the next hundred years—except for the brief period of Puritan rule—**Scotland** (both its English-speaking **Lowlands** and its Gaelic-speaking **Highlands**) and **England** (with **Wales**) were two kingdoms under a single king. In 1707 the Act of Union welded them together as **the United Kingdom of Great Britain. Ireland,** where English rule had begun in the twelfth century and been tightened in the sixteenth, was incorporated by the 1800–1801 Act of Union into **the United Kingdom of Great Britain and Ireland**. With the division of Ireland and the establishment of **the Irish Free State** after World War I, this name was modified to its present form, and in 1949 **the Irish Free State** became **the Republic of Ireland**. In 1999 **Scotland** elected a separate parliament it had relinquished in 1707, and **Wales** elected an assembly it lost in 1409; neither Scotland nor Wales ceased to be part of the **United Kingdom**.

The **British Isles** are further divided into counties, which in **Great Britain** are also known as shires. This word, with its vowel shortened in pronunciation, forms the suffix in the names of many counties, such as **Yorkshire, Wiltshire, Somersetshire**.

The Latin names **Britannia (Britain), Caledonia (Scotland),** and **Hibernia (Ireland)** are sometimes used in poetic diction; so too is **Britain's** ancient Celtic name, **Albion**. Because of its accidental resemblance to *albus* (Latin for "white"), **Albion** is especially associated with the chalk cliffs that seem to gird much of the English coast like defensive walls.

The **British Empire** took its name from **the British Isles** because it was created not only by the **English** but also by the **Irish, Scots,** and **Welsh,** as well as by civilians and servicemen from other constituent countries of the empire. Some of the empire's **overseas colonies**, or **crown colonies**, were populated largely by settlers of European origin and their descendants. These predominantly white **settler colonies**, such as **Canada, Australia,** and **New Zealand,** were allowed significant self-government in the nineteenth century and recognized as **dominions** in the early twentieth century.

The **white dominions** became members of **the Commonwealth of Nations**, also called **the Commonwealth, the British Commonwealth**, and "**the Old Common-wealth**" at different times, an association of sovereign states under the symbolic leadership of the British monarch.

Other **overseas colonies** of the empire had mostly indigenous populations (or, in the Caribbean, the descendants of imported slaves, indentured servants, and others). These **colonies** were granted political independence after World War II, later than the **dominions**, and have often been referred to since as **postcolonial** nations. In South and Southeast Asia, **India** and **Pakistan** gained independence in 1947, followed by other countries including **Sri Lanka** (formerly **Ceylon**), **Burma** (now **Myanmar**), **Malaya** (now **Malaysia**), and **Singapore**. In West and East Africa, the **Gold Coast** was decolonized as **Ghana** in 1957, **Nigeria** in 1960, **Sierra Leone** in 1961, **Uganda** in 1962, **Kenya** in 1963, and so forth, while in southern Africa, the white minority government of **South Africa** was already independent in 1931, though majority rule did not come until 1994. In the Caribbean, **Jamaica** and **Trinidad and Tobago** won independence in 1962, followed by **Barbados** in 1966, and other islands of the British West Indies in the 1970s and '80s. Other regions with nations emerging out of British colonial rule included Central America (**British Honduras**, now **Belize**), South America (**British Guiana**, now **Guyana**), the Pacific islands (**Fiji**), and Europe (**Cyprus, Malta**). After decolonization, many of these nations chose to remain within a newly conceived **Commonwealth** and are sometimes referred to as "**New Commonwealth**" countries. Some nations, such as **Ireland, Pakistan**, and **South Africa**, withdrew from the **Commonwealth**, though **South Africa** and **Pakistan** eventually rejoined, and others, such as **Burma** (**Myanmar**), gained independence outside the **Commonwealth**. Britain's last major overseas colony, **Hong Kong**, was returned to Chinese sovereignty in 1997, but while Britain retains only a handful of dependent territories, such as **Bermuda** and **Montserrat**, the scope of the **Commonwealth** remains vast, with 30 percent of the world's population.

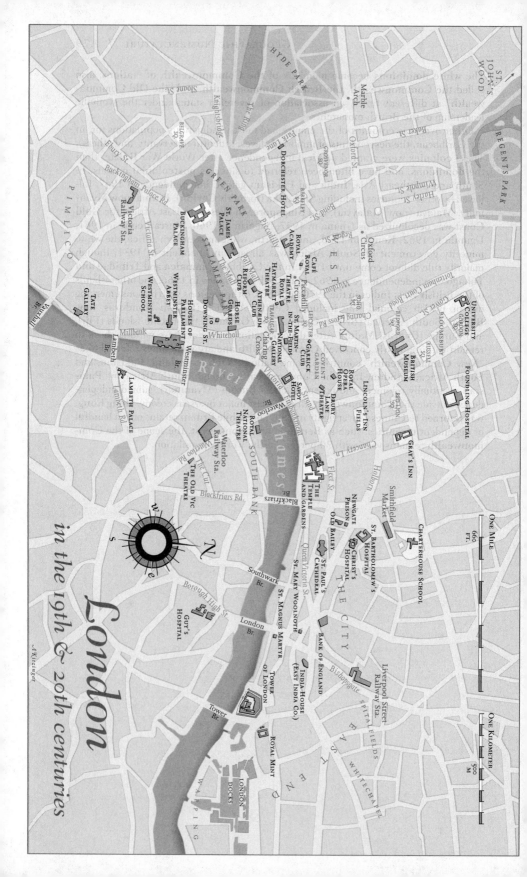

London in the 19th & 20th centuries

ONE MILE

660 FT.

ONE KILOMETER

500 M

HYDE PARK

REGENTS PARK

ST. JOHN'S WOOD

GREEN PARK

ST. JAMES'S PARK

HYDE PARK

Marble Arch

Oxford Circus

Piccadilly Circus

Leicester Square

DORCHESTER HOTEL

ROYAL ACADEMY

ST. JAMES' PALACE

BUCKINGHAM PALACE

Café Royal

HAYMARKET THEATRE

THEATRE ROYAL

REFORM CLUB

ATHENAEUM CLUB

HORSE GUARDS

ST. MARTIN'S-IN-THE-FIELDS

GARRICK CLUB

NATIONAL GALLERY

Charing Cross

COVENT GARDEN

ROYAL OPERA HOUSE

DRURY LANE THEATRE

UNIVERSITY COLLEGE

BRITISH MUSEUM

FOUNDLING HOSPITAL

GRAY'S INN

LINCOLN'S INN FIELDS

TATE GALLERY

WESTMINSTER SCHOOL

WESTMINSTER ABBEY

HOUSES OF PARLIAMENT

Downing St.

Whitehall

Millbank

SAVOY HOTEL

LAMBETH PALACE

WATERLOO NATIONAL THEATRE

ROYAL NATIONAL THEATRE

Waterloo Railway Sta.

THE OLD VIC THEATRE

THE CUT

SOUTH BANK

THE TEMPLE AND GARDENS

NEWGATE PRISON

OLD BAILEY

ST. BARTHOLOMEW'S HOSPITAL

Smithfield Market

CHRIST'S HOSPITAL

ST. PAUL'S CATHEDRAL

CHATTERHOUSE SCHOOL

Victoria Railway Sta.

Victoria St.

PIMLICO

BELGRAVIA

River Thames

Lambeth Br.

Vauxhall Br.

Westminster Br.

Lambeth Rd.

Blackfriars Rd.

Southwark Br.

London Br.

Borough High St.

GUY'S HOSPITAL

ST. MAGNUS MARTYR

TOWER OF LONDON

Tower Br.

ROYAL MINT

LONDON DOCKS

WAPPING

ST. MARY WOOLNOTH

BANK OF ENGLAND

INDIA HOUSE (EAST INDIA CO.)

Liverpool Street Railway Sta.

Bishopsgate

SPITALFIELDS

WHITECHAPEL

THE CITY

Queen Victoria St.

Fleet St.

Holborn

Chancery Ln.

Charing Cross Rd.

Tottenham Court Road

Gower St.

BLOOMSBURY

Bedford Sq.

Russell Sq.

Bedford Sq.

Harley St.

Wimpole St.

Baker St.

Oxford St.

Park Lane

Grosvenor Sq.

Berkeley Sq.

Bond St.

Regent St.

Piccadilly

Pall Mall

The Mall

Buckingham Palace Rd.

Ebury St.

Sloane St.

Knightsbridge

The Ring

N

A. Kitzinger

British Money

One of the most dramatic changes to the system of British money came in 1971. In the system previously in place, the pound consisted of 20 shillings, each containing 12 pence, making 240 pence to the pound. Since 1971, British money has been calculated on the decimal system, with 100 pence to the pound. Britons' experience of paper money did not change very drastically: as before, 5- and 10-pound notes constitute the majority of bills passing through their hands (in addition, 20- and 50-pound notes have been added). But the shift necessitated a whole new way of thinking about and exchanging coins and marked the demise of the shilling, one of the fundamental units of British monetary history. Many other coins, still frequently encountered in literature, had already passed. These include the groat, worth 4 pence (the word "groat" is often used to signify a trifling sum); the angel (which depicted the archangel Michael triumphing over a dragon), valued at 10 shillings; the mark, worth in its day two-thirds of a pound or 13 shillings 4 pence; and the sovereign, a gold coin initially worth 22 shillings 6 pence, later valued at 1 pound, last circulated in 1932. One prominent older coin, the guinea, was worth a pound and a shilling; though it has not been minted since 1813, a very few quality items or prestige awards (like the purse in a horse race) may still be quoted in guineas. (The table below includes some other well-known, obsolete coins.) Colloquially, a pound was (and is) called a quid; a shilling a bob; sixpence, a tanner; a copper could refer to a penny, a half-penny, or a farthing (¼ penny).

Old Currency	New Currency
1 pound note	1 pound coin (or note in Scotland)
10 shilling (half-pound note)	50 pence
5 shilling (crown)	
2½ shilling (half crown)	20 pence
2 shilling (florin)	10 pence
1 shilling	5 pence
6 pence	
2½ pence	1 penny
2 pence	
1 penny	
½ penny	
¼ penny (farthing)	

In recent years, the British government and people have been contemplating and debating a change even greater than the shift to the decimal system. Britain, a member of the European Union, may adopt the EU's common currency, the Euro, and eventually see the pound itself become obsolete. More than many other EU-member countries, Britain has resisted this change: many people strongly identify their country with its rich commercial history and tend to view their currency patriotically as a national symbol.

Even more challenging than sorting out the values of obsolete coins is calculating for any given period the purchasing power of money, which fluctuates over time by its very nature. At the beginning of the twentieth century, 1 pound was worth about 5 American dollars, though those bought three to four times what they now do. Now, the pound buys anywhere from $1.50 to $1.90. As difficult as it is to generalize, it is clear that money used to be worth much more than it is currently. In Anglo-Saxon times, the most valuable circulating coin was the silver penny: four would buy a sheep. Beyond long-term inflationary trends, prices varied from times of plenty to those marked by poor harvests; from peacetime to wartime; from the country to the metropolis (life in London has always been very expensive); and wages varied according to the availability of labor (wages rose sharply, for instance, during the devastating Black Death in the fourteenth century). The chart below provides a glimpse of some actual prices of given periods and their changes across time, though all the variables mentioned above prevent them from being definitive. Even from one year to the next, an added tax on gin or tea could drastically raise prices, and a lottery ticket could cost much more the night before the drawing than just a month earlier. Still, the prices quoted below do indicate important trends, such as the disparity of incomes in British society and the costs of basic commodities. In the chart below, the symbol £ is used for pound, s. for shilling, d. for a penny (from Latin *denarius*); a sum would normally be written £2.19.3, i.e., 2 pounds, 19 shillings, 3 pence. (This is Leopold Bloom's budget for the day depicted in Joyce's novel *Ulysses* [1922]; in the new currency, it would be about £2.96.)

circa	1390	1590	1650	1750	1815	1875	1950
food and drink	gallon (8 pints) of ale, 1.5d.	tankard of beer, .5d.	coffee, 1d. a dish	"drunk for a penny, dead drunk for twopence" (gin shop sign in Hogarth print)	ounce of laudanum, 3d.	pint of beer, 3d.	pint of Guinness stout, 11d.
	gallon (8 pints) of wine, 3 to 4d.	pound of beef, 2s. 5d.	chicken, 1s. 4d.	dinner at a steakhouse, 1s.	ham and potato dinner for two, 7s.	dinner in a good hotel, 5s.	pound of beef, 2s. 2d.
	pound of cinnamon, 1 to 3s.	pound of cinnamon, 10s. 6d.	pound of tea, £3 10s.	pound of tea, 16s.	Prince Regent's dinner party for 2000, £12.000	pound of tea, 2s.	dinner on railway car, 7s. 6d.
entertainment	no cost to watch a cycle play	admission to public theater, 1 to 3d.	falcon, £11 5s.	theater tickets, 1 to 5s.	admission to Covent Garden theater, 1 to 7s.	theater tickets, 6d. to 7s.	admission to Old Vic theater, 1s. 6d. to 10s. 6d.
	contributory admission to professional troupe theater	cheap seat in private theater, 6d.	billiard table, £25	admission to Vauxhall Gardens, 1s.	annual subscription to Almack's (exclusive club), 10 guineas	admission to Madam Tussaud's waxworks, 1s.	admission to Odeon cinema, Manchester, 1s. 3d.
	maintenance for royal hounds at Windsor, .75d. a day	"to see a dead Indian" (qtd. in *The Tempest*), 1.25d. (ten "doits")	three-quarter-length portrait painting, £31	lottery ticket, £20 (shares were sold)	Jane Austen's piano, 30 guineas	annual fees at a gentleman's club, 7–10 guineas	tropical fish tank, £4 4s.
reading	cheap romance, 1s.	play quarto, 6d.	pamphlet, 1 to 6d.	issue of *The Gentleman's Magazine*, 6d.	issue of *Edinburgh Review*, 6s.	copy of *The Times*, 3d.	copy of *The Times*, 3d.

circa	1390	1590	1650	1750	1815	1875	1950
	a Latin Bible, 2 to £4	Shakespeare's *First Folio* (1623), £1	student Bible, 6s.	cheap edition of Milton, 2s.	membership in circulating library (3rd class), £1 4s. a year	illustrated edition of *Through the Looking-glass*, 6s.	issue of *Eagle* comics, 4.5d.
	payment for illuminating a liturgical book, £22 9s.	Foxe's *Acts and Monuments*, 24s.	Hobbes's *Leviathan*, 8s.	Johnson's *Dictionary*, folio, 2 vols., £4 10s.	1st edition of Austen's *Pride and Prejudice*, 18s.	1st edition of Trollope's *The Way We Live Now*, 2 vols., £1 1s.	Orwell's *Nineteen Eighty-Four*, paperback, 3s. 6d.
transportation	night's supply of hay for horse, 2d.	wherry (whole boat) across Thames, 1d.	day's journey, coach, 10s.	boat across Thames, 4d.	coach ride, outside, 2 to 3d. a mile; inside, 4 to 5d. a mile	15-minute journey in a London cab, 1s. 6d.	London tube fare, about 2d. a mile
	coach, £8	hiring a horse for a day, 12d.	coach horse, £30	coach fare, London to Edinburgh, £4 10s.	palanquin transport in Madras, 5s. a day	railway, 3rd class, London to Plymouth, 18s. 8d. (about 1d. a mile)	petrol, 3s. a gallon
	quality horse, £10	hiring a coach for a day, 10s.	fancy carriage, £170	transport to America, £5	passage, Liverpool to New York, £10	passage to India, 1st class, £50	midsize Austin sedan, £449 plus £188 4s. 2d. tax
clothes	clothing allowance for peasant, 3s. a year	shoes with buckles, 8d.	footman's frieze coat, 15s.	working woman's gown, 6s. 6d.	checked muslin, 7s. per yard	flannel for a cheap petticoat, 1s. 3d. a yard	woman's sun frock, £3 13s. 10d.

circa	1390	1590	1650	1750	1815	1875	1950
labor/incomes	shoes for gentry wearer, 4d.	woman's gloves, £1 5s.	falconer's hat, 10s.	gentleman's suit, £8	hiring a dressmaker for a pelisse, 8s.	overcoat for an Eton schoolboy, £1 1s.	tweed sports jacket, £3 16s. 6d.
	hat for gentry wearer, 10d.	fine cloak, £16	black cloth for mourning household of an earl, £100	very fine wig, £30	ladies silk stockings, 12s.	set of false teeth, £2 10s.	"Teddy boy" drape suit, £20
	hiring a skilled building worker, 4d. a day	actor's daily wage during playing season, 1s.	agricultural laborer, 6s. 5d. a week	price of boy slave, £32	lowest-paid sailor on Royal Navy ship, 10s. 9d. a month	seasonal agricultural laborer, 14s. a week	minimum wage, agricultural laborer, £4 14s. per 47-hour week
	wage for professional scribe, £2 3s. 4d. a year + food, clothing, cloak	household servant 2 to £5 a year + food, clothing	tutor to nobleman's children, £30 a year	housemaid's wage, £6 to £8 a year	contributor to *Quarterly Review,* 10 guineas per sheet	housemaid's wage, £10 to £25 a year	shorthand typist, £367 a year
	minimum income to be called gentleman, £10 a year; for knighthood, 40 to £400	minimum income for eligibility for knighthood, £30 a year	Milton's salary as Secretary of Foreign Tongues, £288 a year	Boswell's allowance, £200 a year	minimum income for a "genteel" family, £100 a year	income of the "comfortable" classes, £800 and up a year	middle manager's salary, £1,480 a year
	income from land of richest magnates, £3,500 a year	income from land of average earl, £4000 a year	Earl of Bedford's income, £8,000 a year	Duke of Newcastle's income, £40,000 a year	Mr. Darcy's income, *Pride and Prejudice,* £10,000	Trollope's income, £4,000 a year	barrister's salary, £2,032 a year

The British Baronage

The English monarchy is in principle hereditary, though at times during the Middle Ages the rules were subject to dispute. In general, authority passes from father to eldest surviving son, from daughters in order of seniority if there is no son, to a brother if there are no children, and in default of direct descendants to collateral lines (cousins, nephews, nieces) in order of closeness. There have been breaks in the order of succession (1066, 1399, 1688), but so far as possible the usurpers have always sought to paper over the break with a legitimate, i.e., hereditary, claim. When a queen succeeds to the throne and takes a husband, he does not become king unless he is in the line of blood succession; rather, he is named prince consort, as Albert was to Victoria. He may father kings, but is not one himself.

The original Saxon nobles were the king's thanes, ealdormen, or earls, who provided the king with military service and counsel in return for booty, gifts, or landed estates. William the Conqueror, arriving from France, where feudalism was fully developed, considerably expanded this group. In addition, as the king distributed the lands of his new kingdom, he also distributed dignities to men who became known collectively as "the baronage." "Baron" in its root meaning signifies simply "man," and barons were the king's men. As the title was common, a distinction was early made between greater and lesser barons, the former gradually assuming loftier and more impressive titles. The first English "duke" was created in 1337; the title of "marquess," or "marquis" (pronounced "markwis"), followed in 1385, and "viscount" ("vyekount") in 1440. Though "earl" is the oldest title of all, an earl now comes between a marquess and a viscount in order of dignity and precedence, and the old term "baron" now designates a rank just below viscount. "Baronets" were created in 1611 as a means of raising revenue for the crown (the title could be purchased for about £1000); they are marginal nobility and have never sat in the House of Lords.

Kings and queens are addressed as "Your Majesty," princes and princesses as "Your Highness," the other hereditary nobility as "My Lord" or "Your Lordship." Peers receive their titles either by inheritance (like Lord Byron, the sixth baron of that line) or from the monarch (like Alfred Lord Tennyson, created first Baron Tennyson by Victoria). The children, even of a duke, are commoners unless they are specifically granted some other title or inherit their father's title from him. A peerage can be forfeited by act of attainder, as for example when a lord is convicted of treason; and, when forfeited, or lapsed for lack of a successor, can be bestowed on another family. Thus in 1605 Robert Cecil was made first earl of Salisbury in the third creation, the first creation dating from 1149, the second from 1337, the title having been in abeyance since 1539. Titles descend by right of succession and do not depend on tenure of land; thus, a title does not always indicate where a lord dwells or holds power. Indeed, noble titles do not always refer to a real place at all. At Prince Edward's marriage in 1999, the queen created him earl of Wessex, although the old kingdom of Wessex has had no political existence since the Anglo-Saxon period, and the name was all but forgotten until it was resurrected by Thomas Hardy as the setting of his novels. (This is perhaps but one of many ways in which the world of the aristocracy increasingly resembles the realm of literature.)

The king and queen	(These are all of the royal line.)
Prince and princess	
Duke and duchess	(These may or may not be of the royal line, but are
Marquess and marchioness	ordinarily remote from the succession.)
Earl and countess	
Viscount and viscountess	
Baron and baroness	
Baronet and lady	

Scottish peers sat in the parliament of Scotland, as English peers did in the parliament of England, till at the Act of Union (1707) Scottish peers were granted sixteen seats in the English House of Lords, to be filled by election. (In 1963, all Scottish lords were allowed to sit.) Similarly, Irish peers, when the Irish parliament was abolished in 1801, were granted the right to elect twenty-eight of their number to the House of Lords in Westminster. (Now that the Republic of Ireland is a separate nation, this no longer applies.) Women members (peeresses) were first allowed to sit in the House as nonhereditary Life Peers in 1958 (when that status was created for members of both genders); women first sat by their own hereditary right in 1963. Today the House of Lords still retains some power to influence or delay legislation, but its future is uncertain. In 1999, the hereditary peers (then amounting to 750) were reduced to 92 temporary members elected by their fellow peers. Holders of Life Peerages remain, as do senior bishops of the Church of England and high-court judges (the "Law Lords").

Below the peerage the chief title of honor is "knight." Knighthood, which is not hereditary, is generally a reward for services rendered. A knight (Sir John Black) is addressed, using his first name, as "Sir John"; his wife, using the last name, is "Lady Black"—unless she is the daughter of an earl or nobleman of higher rank, in which case she will be "Lady Arabella." The female equivalent of a knight bears the title of "Dame." Though the word itself comes from the Anglo-Saxon *cniht*, there is some doubt as to whether knighthood amounted to much before the arrival of the Normans. The feudal system required military service as a condition of land tenure, and a man who came to serve his king at the head of an army of tenants required a title of authority and badges of identity—hence the title of knighthood and the coat of arms. During the Crusades, when men were far removed from their land (or even sold it in order to go on crusade), more elaborate forms of fealty sprang up that soon expanded into orders of knighthood. The Templars, Hospitallers, Knights of the Teutonic Order, Knights of Malta, and Knights of the Golden Fleece were but a few of these companionships; not all of them were available at all times in England.

Gradually, with the rise of centralized government and the decline of feudal tenures, military knighthood became obsolete, and the rank largely honorific; sometimes, as under James I, it degenerated into a scheme of the royal government for making money. For hundreds of years after its establishment in the fourteenth century, the Order of the Garter was the only English order of knighthood, an exclusive courtly companionship. Then, during the late seventeenth, the eighteenth, and the nineteenth centuries, a number of additional orders were created, with names such as the Thistle, Saint Patrick, the Bath, Saint Michael and Saint George, plus a number of special Victorian and Indian orders. They retain the terminology, ceremony, and dignity of knighthood, but the military implications are vestigial.

Although the British Empire now belongs to history, appointments to the Order of the British Empire continue to be conferred for services to that empire at home or abroad. Such honors (commonly referred to as "gongs") are granted by the monarch in her New Year's and Birthday lists, but the decisions are now made by the government in power. In recent years there have been efforts to popularize and democratize the dispensation of honors, with recipients including rock stars and actors. But this does not prevent large sectors of British society from regarding both knighthood and the peerage as largely irrelevant to modern life.

The Royal Lines of England and Great Britain

England

SAXONS AND DANES

Egbert, king of Wessex	802–839
Ethelwulf, son of Egbert	839–858
Ethelbald, second son of Ethelwulf	858–860
Ethelbert, third son of Ethelwulf	860–866
Ethelred I, fourth son of Ethelwulf	866–871
Alfred the Great, fifth son of Ethelwulf	871–899
Edward the Elder, son of Alfred	899–924
Athelstan the Glorious, son of Edward	924–940
Edmund I, third son of Edward	940–946
Edred, fourth son of Edward	946–955
Edwy the Fair, son of Edmund	955–959
Edgar the Peaceful, second son of Edmund	959–975
Edward the Martyr, son of Edgar	975–978 (murdered)
Ethelred II, the Unready, second son of Edgar	978–1016
Edmund II, Ironside, son of Ethelred II	1016–1016
Canute the Dane	1016–1035
Harold I, Harefoot, natural son of Canute	1035–1040
Hardecanute, son of Canute	1040–1042
Edward the Confessor, son of Ethelred II	1042–1066
Harold II, brother-in-law of Edward	1066–1066 (died in battle)

HOUSE OF NORMANDY

William I the Conqueror	1066–1087
William II, Rufus, third son of William I	1087–1100 (shot from ambush)
Henry I, Beauclerc, youngest son of William I	1100–1135

HOUSE OF BLOIS

Stephen, son of Adela, daughter of William I	1135–1154

HOUSE OF PLANTAGENET

Henry II, son of Geoffrey Plantagenet by Matilda, daughter of Henry I	1154–1189
Richard I, Coeur de Lion, son of Henry II	1189–1199
John Lackland, son of Henry II	1199–1216
Henry III, son of John	1216–1272
Edward I, Longshanks, son of Henry III	1272–1307
Edward II, son of Edward I	1307–1327 (deposed)
Edward III of Windsor, son of Edward II	1327–1377
Richard II, grandson of Edward III	1377–1399 (deposed)

HOUSE OF LANCASTER

Henry IV, son of John of Gaunt, son of Edward III	1399–1413
Henry V, Prince Hal, son of Henry IV	1413–1422
Henry VI, son of Henry V	1422–1461 (deposed), 1470–1471 (deposed)

HOUSE OF YORK

Edward IV, great-great-grandson of Edward III	1461–1470 (deposed), 1471–1483
Edward V, son of Edward IV	1483–1483 (murdered)
Richard III, Crookback	1483–1485 (died in battle)

HOUSE OF TUDOR

Henry VII, married daughter of Edward IV	1485–1509
Henry VIII, son of Henry VII	1509–1547
Edward VI, son of Henry VIII	1547–1553
Mary I, "Bloody," daughter of Henry VIII	1553–1558
Elizabeth I, daughter of Henry VIII	1558–1603

HOUSE OF STUART

James I (James VI of Scotland)	1603–1625
Charles I, son of James I	1625–1649 (executed)

COMMONWEALTH & PROTECTORATE

Council of State	1649–1653
Oliver Cromwell, Lord Protector	1653–1658
Richard Cromwell, son of Oliver	1658–1660 (resigned)

HOUSE OF STUART (RESTORED)

Charles II, son of Charles I	1660–1685
James II, second son of Charles I	1685–1688

(INTERREGNUM, 11 DECEMBER 1688 TO 13 FEBRUARY 1689)

William III of Orange, by Mary,
    daughter of Charles I   1689–1701
    and Mary II, daughter of James II   –1694
Anne, second daughter of James II   1702–1714

Great Britain

HOUSE OF HANOVER

George I, son of Elector of Hanover and
    Sophia, granddaughter of James I   1714–1727
George II, son of George I   1727–1760
George III, grandson of George II   1760–1820
George IV, son of George III   1820–1830
William IV, third son of George III   1830–1837
Victoria, daughter of Edward, fourth son
    of George III   1837–1901

HOUSE OF SAXE-COBURG AND GOTHA

Edward VII, son of Victoria   1901–1910

HOUSE OF WINDSOR (NAME ADOPTED 17 JULY 1917)

George V, second son of Edward VII   1910–1936
Edward VIII, eldest son of George V   1936–1936 (abdicated)
George VI, second son of George V   1936–1952
Elizabeth II, daughter of George VI   1952–

Religions in England

In the sixth century C.E., missionaries from Ireland and the Continent introduced Christianity to the Anglo-Saxons—actually, reintroduced it, since it had briefly flourished in the southern parts of the British Isles during the Roman occupation, and even after the Roman withdrawal had persisted in the Celtic regions of Scotland and Wales. By the time the earliest poems included in the *Norton Anthology* were composed, therefore, the English people had been Christians for hundreds of years; such Anglo-Saxon poems as "The Dream of the Rood" bear witness to their faith. Our knowledge of the religion of pre-Christian Britain is sketchy, but it is likely that vestiges of paganism assimilated into, or coexisted with, the practice of Christianity: fertility rites were incorporated into the celebration of Easter resurrection, rituals commemorating the dead into All-Hallows Eve and All Saints Day, and elements of winter solstice festivals into the celebration of Christmas. In English literature such "folkloric" elements often elicit romantic nostalgia. Geoffrey Chaucer's Wife of Bath looks back to a magical time before the arrival of Christianity in which the land was "fulfilled of fairye." Hundreds of years later, the seventeenth-century writer Robert Herrick honors the amalgamation of Christian and pagan elements in agrarian British culture in such poems as "Corinna's Gone A-Maying" and "The Hock Cart."

Medieval Christianity was fairly uniform across Western Europe—hence called "catholic," or universally shared—and its rituals and expectations, common to the whole community, permeated everyday life. The Catholic Church was also an international power structure. In its hierarchy of pope, cardinals, archbishops, and bishops, it resembled the feudal state, but the church power structure coexisted alongside a separate hierarchy of lay authorities with a theoretically different sphere of social responsibilities. The sharing out of lay and ecclesiastical authority in medieval England was sometimes a source of conflict. Chaucer's pilgrims are on their way to visit the memorial shrine to one victim of such struggle: Thomas a Becket, Archbishop of Canterbury, who opposed the policies of King Henry III, was assassinated on the king's orders in 1120 and later made a saint. As an international organization, the church conducted its business in the universal language of Latin, and thus although statistically in the period the largest segment of literate persons were monks and priests, the clerical contribution to great writing in English was relatively modest. Yet the lay writers of the period reflect the importance of the church as an institution and the pervasiveness of religion in everyday life.

Beginning in 1517 the German monk Martin Luther, in Wittenberg, Germany, openly challenged many aspects of Catholic practice and by 1520 had completely repudiated the authority of the Pope, setting in train the Protestant Reformation. Luther argued that the Roman Catholic Church had strayed far from the pattern of Christianity laid out in scripture. He rejected Catholic doctrines for which no biblical authority was to be found, such as the belief in Purgatory, and translated the Bible into German, on the grounds that the importance of scripture for all Christians made its translation into the vernacular tongue essential. Luther was not the first to advance such views—followers of the Englishman John Wycliffe had translated the Bible in the fourteenth century. But Luther, protected by powerful German rulers, was able to speak out with impunity and convert others to his views, rather than suffer the persecution usually meted out to heretics. Soon other reformers were following in Luther's footsteps: of these, the Swiss Ulrich Zwingli and the French Jean Calvin would be especially influential for English religious thought.

At first England remained staunchly Catholic. Its king, Henry VIII, was so severe to heretics that the Pope awarded him the title "Defender of the Faith," which British monarchs have retained to this day. In 1534, however, Henry rejected the authority of the Pope to prevent his divorce from his queen, Catherine of Aragon, and his marriage to his mistress, Ann Boleyn. In doing so, Henry appropriated to himself ecclesiastical as well as secular authority. Thomas More, author of *Utopia*, was executed for refusing to endorse Henry's right to govern the English church. Over the following six years, Henry consolidated his grip on the ecclesiastical establishment by dissolving the powerful, populous Catholic monasteries and redistributing their massive landholdings to his own lay followers. Yet Henry's church largely retained Catholic doctrine and liturgy. When Henry died and his young son, Edward, came to the throne in 1547, the English church embarked on a more Protestant path, a direction abruptly reversed when Edward died and his older sister Mary, the daughter of Catherine of Aragon, took the throne in 1553 and attempted to reintroduce Roman Catholicism. Mary's reign was also short, however, and her successor, Elizabeth I, the daughter of Ann Boleyn, was a Protestant. Elizabeth attempted to establish a "middle way" Christianity, compromising between Roman Catholic practices and beliefs and reformed ones.

The Church of England, though it laid claim to a national rather than pan-European authority, aspired like its predecessor to be the universal church of all English subjects. It retained the Catholic structure of parishes and dioceses and the Catholic hierarchy of bishops, though the ecclesiastical authority was now the Archbishop of Canterbury and the Church's "Supreme Governor" was the monarch. Yet disagreement and controversy persisted. Some members of the Church of England wanted to retain many of the ritual and liturgical elements of Catholicism. Others, the Puritans, advocated a more thoroughgoing reformation. Most Puritans remained within the Church of England, but a minority, the "Separatists" or "Congregationalists," split from the established church altogether. These dissenters no longer thought of the ideal church as an organization to which everybody belonged; instead, they conceived it as a more exclusive group of likeminded people, one not necessarily attached to a larger body of believers.

In the seventeenth century, the succession of the Scottish king James to the English throne produced another problem. England and Scotland were separate nations, and in the sixteenth century Scotland had developed its own national Presbyterian church, or "kirk," under the leadership of the reformer John Knox. The kirk retained fewer Catholic liturgical elements than did the Church of England, and its authorities, or "presbyters," were elected by assemblies of their fellow clerics, rather than appointed by the king. James I and his son Charles I, especially the latter, wanted to bring the Scottish kirk into conformity with Church of England practices. The Scots violently resisted these efforts, with the collaboration of many English Puritans, in a conflict that eventually developed into the English Civil War in the mid-seventeenth century. The effect of these disputes is visible in the poetry of such writers as John Milton, Robert Herrick, Henry Vaughan, and Thomas Traherne, and in the prose of Thomas Browne, Lucy Hutchinson, and Dorothy Waugh. Just as in the mid-sixteenth century, when a succession of monarchs with different religious commitments destabilized the church, so the seventeenth century endured spiritual whiplash. King Charles I's highly ritualistic Church of England was violently overturned by the Puritan victors in the Civil War—until 1660, after the death of the Puritan leader, Oliver Cromwell, when the Church of England was restored along with the monarchy.

The religious and political upheavals of the seventeenth century produced Christian sects that de-emphasized the ceremony of the established church and rejected as well its top-down authority structure. Some of these groups were ephemeral, but the Baptists (founded in 1608 in Amsterdam by the English expatriate John Smyth) and Quakers, or Society of Friends (founded by George Fox in the 1640s), flourished outside the established church, sometimes despite cruel persecution. John Bunyan, a Baptist, wrote the Christian allegory *Pilgrim's Progress* while in prison. Some dissenters, like the Baptists, shared the reformed reverence for the absolute authority of scripture but interpreted the scriptural texts differently from their fellow Protestants. Others, like the Quakers, favored, even over the authority of the Bible, the "inner light" or voice of individual conscience, which they took to be the working of the Holy Spirit in the lives of individuals.

The Protestant dissenters were not England's only religious minorities. Despite crushing fines and the threat of imprisonment, a minority of Catholics under Elizabeth and James openly refused to give their allegiance to the new church, and others remained secret adherents to the old ways. John Donne was brought up in an ardently Catholic family, and several other writers converted to Catholicism as adults—Ben Jonson for a considerable part of his career, Elizabeth Carey and Richard Crashaw permanently, and at profound personal cost. In the eighteenth century, Catholics remained objects of suspicion as possible agents of sedition, especially after the "Glorious Revolution" in 1688 deposed the Catholic James II in favor of the Protestant William and Mary. Anti-Catholic prejudice affected John Dryden, a Catholic convert, as well as the lifelong Catholic Alexander Pope. By contrast, the English colony of Ireland remained overwhelmingly Roman Catholic, the fervor of its religious commitment at least partly inspired by resistance to English occupation. Starting in the reign of Elizabeth, England shored up its own authority in Ireland by encouraging Protestant immigrants from Scotland to settle in northern Ireland, producing a virulent religious divide the effects of which are still playing out today.

A small community of Jews had moved from France to London after 1066, when the Norman William the Conqueror came to the English throne. Although despised and persecuted by many Christians, they were allowed to remain as moneylenders to the Crown, until the thirteenth century, when the king developed alternative sources of credit. At this point, in 1290, the Jews were expelled from England. In 1655 Oliver Cromwell permitted a few to return, and in the late seventeenth and early eighteenth centuries the Jewish population slowly increased, mainly by immigration from Germany. In the mid-eighteenth century some prominent Jews had their children brought up as Christians so as to facilitate their full integration into English society: thus the nineteenth-century writer and politician Benjamin Disraeli, although he and his father were members of the Church of England, was widely considered a Jew insofar as his ancestry was Jewish.

In the late seventeenth century, as the Church of England reasserted itself, Catholics, Jews, and dissenting Protestants found themselves subject to significant legal restrictions. The Corporation Act, passed in 1661, and the Test Act, passed in 1673, excluded all who refused to take communion in the Church of England from voting, attending university, or working in government or in the professions. Members of religious minorities, as well as Church of England communicants, paid mandatory taxes in support of Church of England ministers and buildings. In 1689 the dissenters gained the right to worship in public, but Jews and Catholics were not permitted to do so.

During the eighteenth century, political, intellectual, and religious history remained closely intertwined. The Church of England came to accommodate a good deal of variety. "Low church" services resembled those of the dissenting Protestant churches, minimizing ritual and emphasizing the sermon; the "high church" retained more elaborate ritual elements, yet its prestige was under attack on several fronts. Many Enlightenment thinkers subjected the Bible to rational critique and found it wanting: the philosopher David Hume, for instance, argued that the "miracles" described therein were more probably lies or errors than real breaches of the laws of nature. Within the Church of England, the "broad church" Latitudinarians welcomed this rationalism, advocating theological openness and an emphasis on ethics rather than dogma. More radically, the Unitarian movement rejected the divinity of Christ while professing to accept his ethical teachings. Taking a different tack, the preacher John Wesley, founder of Methodism, responded to the rationalists' challenge with a newly fervent call to evangelism and personal discipline; his movement was particularly successful in Wales. Revolutions in America and France at the end of the century generated considerable millenarian excitement and fostered more new religious ideas, often in conjunction with a radical social agenda. Many important writers of the Romantic period were indebted to traditions of protestant dissent: Unitarian and rationalist protestant ideas influenced William Hazlitt, Anna Barbauld, Mary Wollstonecraft, and the young Samuel Taylor Coleridge. William Blake created a highly idiosyncratic poetic mythology loosely indebted to radical strains of Christian mysticism. Others were even more heterodox: Lord Byron and Robert Burns, brought up as Scots Presbyterians, rebelled fiercely, and Percy Shelley's writing of an atheistic pamphlet resulted in his expulsion from Oxford.

Great Britain never erected an American-style "wall of separation" between church and state, but in practice religion and secular affairs grew more and more distinct during the nineteenth century. In consequence, members of religious minorities no longer seemed to pose a threat to the commonweal. A movement to repeal the Test Act failed in the 1790s, but a renewed effort resulted in the extension of the franchise to dissenting Protestants in 1828 and to Catholics in 1829. The numbers of Roman Catholics in England were swelled by immigration from Ireland, but there were also some prominent English adherents. Among writers, the converts John Newman and Gerard Manley Hopkins are especially important. The political participation and social integration of Jews presented a thornier challenge. Lionel de Rothschild, repeatedly elected to represent London in Parliament during the 1840s and 1850s, was not permitted to take his seat there because he refused to take his oath of office "on the true faith of a Christian"; finally, in 1858, the Jewish Disabilities Act allowed him to omit these words. Only in 1871, however, were Oxford and Cambridge opened to non-Anglicans.

Meanwhile geological discoveries and Charles Darwin's evolutionary theories increasingly cast doubt on the literal truth of the Creation story, and close philological analysis of the biblical text suggested that its origins were human rather than divine. By the end of the nineteenth century, many writers were bearing witness to a world in which Christianity no longer seemed fundamentally plausible. In his poetry and prose, Thomas Hardy depicts a world devoid of benevolent providence. Matthew Arnold's poem "Dover Beach" is in part an elegy to lost spiritual assurance, as the "Sea of Faith" goes out like the tide: "But now I only hear / Its melancholy, long, withdrawing roar / Retreating." For Arnold, literature must replace religion as a source of spiritual truth, and intimacy between individuals substitute for the lost communal solidarity of the universal church.

The work of many twentieth-century writers shows the influence of a religious upbringing or a religious conversion in adulthood. T. S. Eliot and W. S. Auden embrace Anglicanism, William Butler Yeats spiritualism. James Joyce repudiates Irish Catholicism but remains obsessed with it. Yet religion, or lack of it, is a matter of individual choice and conscience, not social or legal mandate. In the past fifty years, church attendance has plummeted in Great Britain. Although 71 percent of the population still identified itself as "Christian" on the 2000 census, only about 7 percent of these regularly attend religious services of any denomination. Meanwhile, immigration from former British colonies has swelled the ranks of religions once alien to the British Isles—Muslim, Sikh, Hindu, Buddhist—though the numbers of adherents remain small relative to the total population.

PERMISSIONS ACKNOWLEDGMENTS

Chinua Achebe: THINGS FALL APART. Copyright © 1958 by Chinua Achebe. First published by William Heinemann Ltd., 1958. Reprinted by permission of Harcourt Education Limited. Excerpt from "An Image of Africa: Racism in Conrad's HEART OF DARKNESS" from HOPES AND IMPEDIMENTS: SELECTED ESSAYS. Copyright © by Chinua Achebe. Reprinted by permission of the author.

John Agard: "Listen Mr Oxford Don" from MANGOES & BULLETS: SELECTED AND NEW POEMS. Serpent's Tail: London, 1990. Reprinted with permission.

W. H. Auden: Introduction to THE POET'S TONGUE [Poetry as a Memorable Speech] by W. H. Auden. Copyright © 1935 by W. H. Auden. Reprinted by permission of Curtis Brown, Ltd. "Petition" ("Sir, no man's enemy") and "Spain 1937" from THE ENGLISH AUDEN by W. H. Auden, edited by Edward Mendelson. Copyright © 1934, 1940 and renewed 1962, 1968 by W. H. Auden. Reprinted by permission of Random House, Inc., and Faber & Faber Ltd. "On This Island," "Musée des Beaux Arts," "Lullaby," "In Memory of W. B. Yeats," "In Praise of Limestone," "The Shield of Achilles," "The Unknown Citizen," and "September 1, 1939" all from W. H. AUDEN: COLLECTED POEMS by W. H. Auden, edited by Edward Mendelson. Copyright © 1937, 1940, 1951, 1952 and renewed 1965, 1968 by W. H. Auden. Reprinted by permission of Random House, Inc., and Faber & Faber Ltd. "As I Walked Out One Evening" copyright © 1940 & renewed 1968 by W. H. Auden, from COLLECTED POEMS by W. H. Auden. Used by permission of Random House, Inc.

Samuel Beckett: *Endgame.* Copyright © 1958 by Samuel Beckett; copyright renewed © 1986 by Samuel Beckett. Used by permission of Grove/Atlantic, Inc., and Faber & Faber Ltd.

Louise Bennett: "Jamaica Language" from AUNTY ROACHY SEH. "Dry-Foot Bwoy," "Jamaica Oman," "Colonization in Reverse" from SELECTED POEMS OF LOUISE BENNETT. Reprinted by permission of Sangster Books.

Eavan Boland: "Fond Memory" and "The Lost Land" from THE LOST LAND. "That the Science of Cartography Is Limited" and "The Dolls Museum in Dublin" from IN A TIME OF VIOLENCE by Eavan Boland. Copyright © 1994 by Eavan Boland. Reprinted by permission of W. W. Norton & Company, Inc., and Carcanet Press Ltd.

Kamau Brathwaite: Extract from HISTORY OF THE VOICE by Kamau Brathwaite, published by New Beacon Books in 1994. Reprinted with the permission of the publisher. "Calypso" from THE ARRIVANTS, copyright © 1981. Reprinted by permission of Oxford University Press.

May Cannan: Excerpt from GRAY GHOSTS AND VOICES and "Rouen" from IN WAR TIME, POEMS. Reprinted by permission of James Cannan Slater.

Anne Carson: "Hero" by Anne Carson, from GLASS IRONY AND GOD, copyright © 1995 by Anne Carson. Reprinted by permission of New Directions Publishing Corp. "Epitaph: Zion" from MEN IN THE OFF HOURS by Anne Carson, copyright © 2000 by Anne Carson. Used by permission of Alfred A. Knopf, a division of Random House, Inc.

Charles Causley: "At the British Cemetery, Bayeux" and "Armistice Day" from UNION STREET. Reprinted by permission of David Higham Associates.

J. M. Coetzee: Excerpt from WAITING FOR THE BARBARIANS by J. M. Coetzee. Copyright © 1980 by J. M. Coetzee. Used by permission of Viking Penguin, a division of Penguin Putnam, Inc., and Secker and Warburg. Used by permission of The Random House Group Limited.

Keith Douglas: "Gallantry," "Vergissmeinnicht," and "Aristocrats" from THE COMPLETE POEMS OF KEITH DOUGLAS, edited by Desmond Graham (1978). Copyright © Marie J. Douglas, 1978. Reprinted by permission of Faber & Faber Ltd.

Carol Ann Duffy: "Warming Her Pearls" is taken from SELLING MANHATTAN by Carol Ann Duffy, published by Anvil Press Poetry in 1987. "Medusa" and "Mrs. Lazarus" from THE WORLD'S WIFE by Carol Ann Duffy. Reprinted by permission of Macmillan Publishers Ltd.

T. S. Eliot: "The Love Song of J. Alfred Prufrock," "Sweeney among the Nightingales," and *The Waste Land* from COLLECTED POEMS 1909–1962 by T. S. Eliot. Reprinted by permission of Faber & Faber Ltd. "The Hollow Men" and "Journey of the Magi" from COLLECTED POEMS 1909–1962 by T. S. Eliot, copyright © 1964, 1963 by T. S. Eliot, reprinted by permission of the publishers, Harcourt, Inc., and Faber & Faber Ltd. "Little Gidding" from FOUR QUARTETS, copyright © 1942 by T. S. Eliot and renewed 1970 by Esme Valerie Eliot. Reprinted by permission of Harcourt, Inc., and Faber & Faber Ltd. "Metaphysical Poets" from SELECTED ESSAYS by T. S. Eliot, copyright © 1950 by Harcourt, Inc., and renewed 1978 by Esme Valerie Eliot. Reprinted by permission of the publishers, Harcourt, Inc., and Faber & Faber Ltd. "Tradition and the Individual Talent" from SELECTED ESSAYS by T. S. Eliot. Reprinted by permission of Faber & Faber Ltd.

E. M. Forster: "The Other Boat" from THE LIFE TO COME AND OTHER STORIES by E. M. Forster. Copyright © 1972 by the Provost and Scholars of King's College, Cambridge, and the Society of Author as the Literary Representatives of the Estate of E. M. Forster. Used by permission of W. W. Norton & Company, Inc.

Brian Friel: TRANSLATIONS by Brian Friel. Copyright © 1981 by Brian Friel. Reprinted by permission of Faber and Faber, Inc., an affiliate of Farrar, Straus and Giroux, LLC.

Nadine Gordimer: "The Moment before the Gun Went Off" from JUMP AND OTHER STORIES by Nadine Gordimer, published by Bloomsbury Publishing PLC in 1991. Copyright © 1991 by Felix Licensing, B.V. Reprinted by permission of Farrar, Straus & Giroux, Inc., Penguin Books Canada Limited, and Bloomsbury Publishing PLC.

Robert Graves: From GOODBYE TO ALL THAT. Reprinted by permission of Carcanet Press Ltd. "Recalling War" from COMPLETE POEMS VOL II. Reprinted by permission Carcanet Press Ltd. "The Dead Fox Hunter" from COMPLETE POEMS. All poems reprinted from COMPLETE POEMS by Robert Graves. Reprinted by permission of Carcanet Press Ltd.

Thom Gunn: "Black Jackets," "My Sad Captains," "From the Wave," and "Still Life" from COLLECTED POEMS by Thom Gunn. Copyright © 1994 by Thom Gunn. Reprinted by permission of Farrar, Straus & Giroux, Inc., and Faber & Faber Ltd. "The Missing" from THE MAN WITH NIGHT SWEATS. Reprinted by permission of Faber & Faber.

Ivor Gurney: "To His Love" and "The Silent One" from COLLECTED POEMS OF IVOR GURNEY. Reprinted by permission of Carcanet Press Ltd.

Thomas Hardy: "He Never Expected Much" reprinted with the permission of Simon & Schuster from THE COMPLETE POEMS OF THOMAS HARDY, edited by James Gibson. Copyright © 1976 by Macmillan London Ltd.

Tony Harrison: All poems from SELECTED POEMS by Tony Harrison. Reprinted by permission of Gordon Dickerson.

Seamus Heaney: "Digging," "The Forge," "Punishment," "Station Island XII," "Clearances," and "The Grauballe Man" from SELECTED POEMS 1966–1987 by Seamus Heaney. Copyright © 1998 by Seamus Heaney. "The Sharpening Stone" from THE SPIRIT LEVEL by Seamus Heaney. Copyright © 1996 by Seamus Heaney. "Skunk" and "Casualty" from FIELD WORK. All reprinted by permission of Farrar, Straus & Giroux, LLC, and Faber & Faber Ltd.

Geoffrey Hill: "In Memory of Jane Fraser" and "Requiem for the Plantagenet Kings" from NEW AND COLLECTED POEMS 1952–1992. Copyright © 1994 by Geoffrey Hill. Previously published in FOR THE UNFALLEN (1959). "September Song" from NEW AND COLLECTED POEMS 1952–1992. Copyright © 1994 by Geoffrey Hill. Previously published in KING LOG (1968). Four hymns from NEW AND COLLECTED POEMS 1952–1992. Copyright © 1994 by Geoffrey Hill. Previously published in MERCIAN HYMNS (1971). "The Laurel Axe" from "An Apology for the Revival of Christian Architecture in England," in NEW AND COLLECTED POEMS 1952–1992. Copyright © 1994 by Geoffrey Hill. Previously published in TENEBRAE (1978). All reprinted by permission of Houghton Mifflin Co. All rights reserved. Two poems from GEOFFREY HILL: COLLECTED POEMS (Penguin Books, 1985, first published in FOR THE UNFALLEN, 1959), copyright © Geoffrey Hill, 1959, 1985: "In Memory of Jane Fraser" (p. 22, 16 lines) and "Requiem for the Plantagenet Kings" (p. 29, 14 lines). "September Song" (p. 67, 14 lines) from GEOFFREY HILL: COLLECTED POEMS (Penguin Books, 1985, first published in KING LOG, 1968), copyright © Geoffrey Hill, 1968, 1985. "VI" (p. 110, 14 lines), "VII" (p. 111, 16 lines), "XXVIII" (p. 132, 10 lines), "XXX" (p. 134, 4 lines) from GEOFFREY HILL: COLLECTED POEMS (Penguin Books, 1985, first published in MERCIAN HYMNS, 1971), copyright © Geoffrey Hill, 1971, 1985. "9. The Laurel Axe" (p. 160, 14 lines) from "An Apology for the Revival of Christian Architecture in England," in GEOFFREY HILL: COLLECTED POEMS (Penguin Books, 1985, first published in TENEBRAE, 1978), copyright © Geoffrey Hill, 1978, 1985. All reproduced by permission of Penguin Books Ltd.

A. E. Housman: "Loveliest of Trees," "When I Was One-and-Twenty," "To an Athlete Dying Young," and "Terence, This Is Stupid Stuff" from THE COLLECTED POEMS OF A. E. HOUSMAN. Reprinted by permission of the Society of Authors as the literary representative of the Estate of A. E. Housman. "The Chestnut Casts His Flambeaux" and "Epitaph on an Army of Mercenaries" from THE COLLECTED POEMS OF A. E. HOUSMAN, by A. E. Housman. Copyright © 1922, 1939, 1940, © 1965 by Holt, Rinehart & Winston. Copyright © 1950 by Barclay's Bank. Copyright © 1967, 1968 by Robert E. Symons. Reprinted by permission of Henry Holt & Company, LLC, and the Society of Authors as the literary representative of the Estate of A. E. Housman.

Ted Hughes: "Wind" from THE HAWK IN THE RAIN by Ted Hughes. Copyright © 1956 by Ted Hughes. Reprinted by permission of HarperCollins and Faber & Faber Ltd. "Relic" and "Pike" from LUPERCAL by Ted Hughes. Reprinted by permission of Faber & Faber Ltd. "Out" and all lines from "Theology" from WODWO by Ted Hughes. Copyright © 1961 by Ted Hughes. Copyright renewed. Reprinted by permission of HarperCollins Publishers, Inc., and Faber & Faber Ltd. "Daffodils" from BIRTHDAY LETTERS. Copyright © 1998 by Ted Hughes. Reprinted by permission of Farrar, Straus and Giroux, LLC, and Faber & Faber Ltd. "Crow's Last Stand" from CROW. Reprinted by permission of Faber & Faber.

T. E. Hulme: From THE COLLECTED WRITING OF T. E. HULME, edited by Karen Csengeri. Copyright © 1994. Reprinted by permission of Oxford University Press.

David Jones: Excerpts from IN PARENTHESIS by David Jones. Reprinted by permission of Faber & Faber Ltd.

James Joyce: "Araby" and "The Dead" from DUBLINERS by James Joyce. Copyright © 1916 by B. W. Heubsch. Definitive text copyright © 1967 by the Estate of James Joyce. Used by permission of Viking Penguin, a division of Penguin Putnam, Inc. From FINNEGANS WAKE by James Joyce. Copyright © 1939 by James Joyce, copyright renewed © 1967 by Giorgio Joyce and Lucia Joyce. Used by permission of Viking Penguin, a division of Penguin Putnam, Inc. From ULYSSES by James Joyce. Copyright © 1934 and renewed 1962 by Lucia & George Joyce. Reprinted by permission of Random House, Inc. Reproduced with the permission of the Estate of James Joyce, copyright © Estate of James Joyce.

Philip Larkin: "Church Going" by Philip Larkin is reprinted from THE LESS DECEIVED by permission of The Marvell Press, England and Australia. "MCMXIV," "Talking in Bed," "Ambulances," "High Windows," "Sad Steps," "Explosion," "Homage to a Government," "This Be The Verse," and "Aubade" from PHILIP LARKIN: COLLECTED POEMS, edited by Anthony Thwaite. Copyright © 1988, 2003 by the Estate of Philip Larkin. All reprinted by permission of Farrar, Straus & Giroux, LLC, and Faber & Faber Ltd.

D. H. Lawrence: "Odour of Chrysanthemums" copyright © 1933 by the Estate of D. H. Lawrence, renewed © 1961 by Angelo Ravagli and C. M. Weekley, Executors of the Estate of Frieda Lawrence, from COMPLETE SHORT STORIES OF D. H. LAWRENCE. Used by permission of Viking Penguin, a division of Penguin Putnam, Inc., and Laurence Pollinger Ltd. "The Horse Dealer's Daughter," also from THE COMPLETE SHORT STORIES OF D. H. LAWRENCE. Reprinted by permission of the Estate of Frieda Lawrence Ravagli and Laurence Pollinger Ltd. "Why the Novel Matters" from PHOENIX: THE POSTHUMOUS PAPERS OF D. H. LAWRENCE, edited by Edward McDonald. Copyright © 1936 by Frieda Lawrence, renewed © 1964 by the Estate of the late Frieda Lawrence Ravagli. Used by permission of

Index

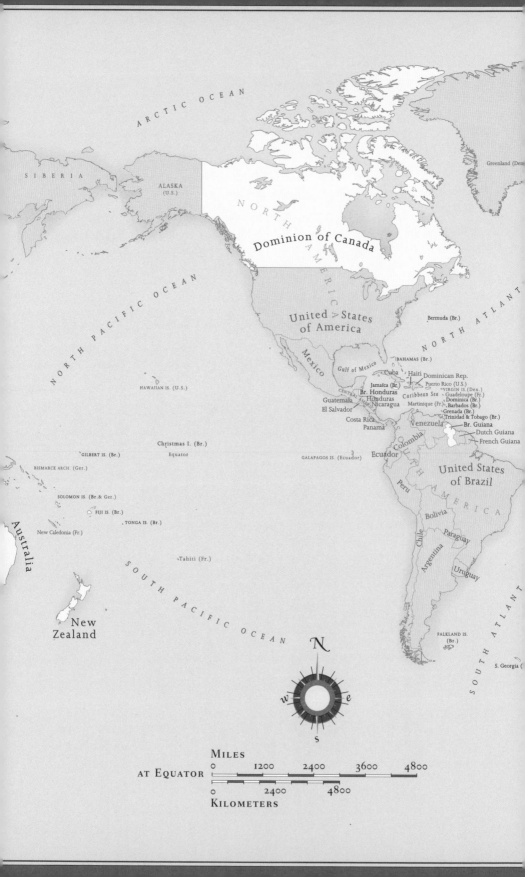

ARCTIC OCEAN

SIBERIA

ALASKA
(U.S.)

NORTH AMERICA

Greenland (Den.)

Dominion of Canada

United States
of America

Bermuda (Br.)

NORTH PACIFIC OCEAN

Mexico

Gulf of Mexico

NORTH ATLANTIC

HAWAIIAN IS. (U.S.)

BAHAMAS (Br.)

Cuba   Haiti Dominican Rep.
Jamaica (Br.)   Puerto Rico (U.S.)
Caribbean Sea   VIRGIN IS. (Den.)
CENTRAL   Br. Honduras   · Guadeloupe (Fr.)
Guatemala   Honduras   Dominica (Br.)
El Salvador   Nicaragua   Martinique (Fr.)   Barbados (Br.)
Costa Rica   Grenada (Br.)
Panama   Trinidad & Tobago (Br.)
Venezuela   Br. Guiana
Dutch Guiana
Colombia   French Guiana

Christmas I. (Br.)
Equator

GILBERT IS. (Br.)

GALAPAGOS IS. (Ecuador)   Ecuador

BISMARCK ARCH. (Ger.)

SOLOMON IS. (Br.& Ger.)

FIJI IS. (Br.)

TONGA IS. (Br.)

New Caledonia (Fr.)

Australia

Tahiti (Fr.)

SOUTH PACIFIC OCEAN

Peru

SOUTH AMERICA

United States
of Brazil

Bolivia

Chile   Paraguay

Argentina   Uruguay

New
Zealand

N

W   E

S

FALKLAND IS.
(Br.)

SOUTH ATLANTIC

S. Georgia (Br.)

MILES
AT EQUATOR
0   1200   2400   3600   4800

0   2400   4800

KILOMETERS

The
British Empire
ca. 1913